PENGUIN CLASSICS

WAR AND PEACE

LEO TOLSTOY was born in central Russia in 1828. He studied Oriental languages and law (though failed to earn a degree in the latter) at the University of Kazan, and after a dissolute youth eventually joined an artillery regiment in the Caucasus in 1852. He took part in the Crimean War, and the *Sebastopol Sketches* that emerged from it established his reputation. After living for some time in St Petersburg and abroad, he married Sofya Behrs in 1862 and they had thirteen children. The happiness this brought gave him the creative impulse for his two greatest novels, *War and Peace* (1869) and *Anna Karenina* (1877). Later in life his views became increasingly radical as he gave up his possessions in order to live a simple peasant life. After a quarrel with his wife he fled home secretly one night to seek refuge in a monastery. He became ill during this dramatic flight and died at the small railway station of Astapovo in 1910.

ANTHONY BRIGGS has written, translated or edited twenty books in the field of Russian and English Literature, including volumes on Tolstoy and Pushkin. He has edited five volumes of English poetry and translated three books by the former Russian dissident Roy Medvedev.

ORLANDO FIGES is the author of the acclaimed *A People's Tragedy* and *Natasha's Dance: A Cultural History of Russia.*

LEO TOLSTOY

War and Peace

Translation by Anthony Briggs
With an Afterword by Orlando Figes

PENGUIN BOOKS

PENGUIN CLASSICS

Published by the Penguin Group
Penguin Books Ltd, 80 Strand, London WC2R ORL, England
Penguin Group (USA) Inc., 375 Hudson Street, New York, New York 10014, USA
Penguin Group (Canada), 90 Eglinton Avenue East, Suite 700, Toronto, Ontario, Canada M4P 2Y3
(a division of Pearson Penguin Canada Inc.)
·Penguin Ireland, 25 St Stephen's Green, Dublin 2, Ireland
(a division of Penguin Books Ltd)
Penguin Group (Australia), 250 Camberwell Road, Camberwell, Victoria 3124, Australia
(a division of Pearson Australia Group Pty Ltd)
Penguin Books India Pvt Ltd, 11 Community Centre, Panchsheel Park, New Delhi – 110 017, India
Penguin Group (NZ), 67 Apollo Drive, Rosedale, North Shore 0632, New Zealand
(a division of Pearson New Zealand Ltd)
Penguin Books (South Africa) (Pty) Ltd, 24 Sturdee Avenue, Rosebank, Johannesburg 2196, South Africa

Penguin Books Ltd, Registered Offices: 80 Strand, London WC2R ORL, England

www.penguin.com

First published 1868–9
This translation published as a Penguin hardback Classic 2005
Published in Penguin Classics 2007

035

Translation and editorial material copyright © Anthony Briggs, 2005
Afterword copyright © Orlando Figes, 2005
All rights reserved

The moral right of the translator and author of the Afterword has been asserted

Typeset by Rowland Phototypesetting Ltd, Bury St Edmunds, Suffolk
Printed in Great Britain by Clays Ltd, Elcograf S.p.A.

978-0-140-44793-4

www.greenpenguin.co.uk

Contents

Chronology

1724 Pyotr Tolstoy (great-great-great grandfather) given hereditary title of Count by Tsar Peter the Great

1821 Death of Prince Nikolay Volkonsky, Tolstoy's grandfather, at Yasnaya Polyana, Tula Province, 130 miles south-west of Moscow

1822 Marriage of Count Nikolay Tolstoy and Princess Marya Volkonskaya

1828 28 August (Old Style) Birth of fourth son, Leo Nikolayevich Tolstoy, at Yasnaya Polyana

1830 Death of mother

1832 The eldest, Nikolay, informs his brothers that the secret of earthly happiness is inscribed on a green stick, buried at Yasnaya Polyana (Tolstoy later buried there)

1836 Nikolay Gogol's *Government Inspector*

1837 Death of Alexander Pushkin in duel
Death of father

1840 Mikhail Lermontov's *A Hero of Our Time*

1841 Death of Lermontov in duel
Death of first guardian Alexandra Osten-Saken, an aunt. The Tolstoy children move to Kazan to live with another aunt, Pelageya Yushkova

1842 Gogol's *Dead Souls*

1844 Enters Kazan University, reads Oriental languages

1845 Transfers to Law after failing examinations. Dissolute lifestyle: drinking, visits to prostitutes

1846 Fyodor Dostoyevsky's 'Poor Folk'

1847 Inherits estate of Yasnaya Polyana. Recovering from gonorrhoea, compiles scheme for self-perfection. Leaves university without completing studies, 'on grounds of ill health and domestic circumstances'

1848–50 In Moscow and St Petersburg, debauchery and gambling, large debts. Studies music

1850 Ivan Turgenev's *A Month in the Country*

1851 Travels to the Caucasus with Nikolay, who is serving in the army there. Reads Laurence Sterne: starts translating his *Sentimental Journey* (not completed). Writes 'A History of Yesterday' (unfinished, first evidence of his powers of psychological analysis). Begins writing *Childhood*

1852 Enters the army as a cadet (junker); based mainly in the Cossack station of Staroglad Kovskaya. Sees action against the Chechens, and narrowly escapes capture

Death of Gogol. Turgenev's *Sketches from a Hunter's Album* *Childhood*

1853 Turkey declares war on Russia
'The Raid'

1854 France and England declare war on Russia. Crimean War starts Commissioned, serves on Danube front. November: transferred at own request to Sevastopol, then under siege by allied forces *Boyhood*

1855 Death of Nicholas I; accession of Alexander II
In action until the fall of Sevastopol in August. Gains celebrity with 'Sevastopol in December' and the following sketches 'Sevastopol in May', 'Sevastopol in August' (1856), 'Memoirs of a Billiard Marker', 'The Woodfelling'

1856 Peace signed between Russia, Turkey, France and England Turgenev's *Rudin*
In St Petersburg, moves in literary circles; associates with Turgenev, Ivan Goncharov, Nikolay Nekrasov, Afanasy Fet and others. Leaves army due to illness. Death of brother Dmitry
'The Snowstorm', 'Two Hussars', 'A Landowner's Morning'

1857 February–August First trip abroad, to Paris (lasting impression of witnessing an execution by guillotine), Geneva and Baden-Baden *Youth*, 'Lucerne'

1858 Long-term relationship with peasant woman on estate, Aksinya Bazykina, begins
'Albert'

1859 Goncharov's *Oblomov*; Turgenev's *Home of the Gentry*
Founds primary school at Yasanaya Polyana
'Three Deaths', *Family Happiness*

1860 Death of Nikolay from tuberculosis at Hyeres (France)
Dostoyevsky's *Notes from the House of the Dead* (1860–61) Turgenev's *On the Eve*

1860–61 Emancipation of serfs (1861). Formation of revolutionary Land and Liberty movement. Commencement of intensive industrialization; spread of railways. Elective District Councils (*zemstvos*) set up; judicial reform

Serves as Arbiter of the Peace, dealing with post-Emancipation land settlements. Quarrels with Turgenev and challenges him (no duel). Travels in France, Germany, Italy and England. Loses great deal of money through gambling. Meets Proudhon in Brussels

1862 Turgenev's *Fathers and Sons*

Starts a magazine at Yasnaya Polyana on education for the peasants; abandoned after less than a year. Police raid on Yasnaya Polyana. Considers emigrating to England and writes protest to the Tsar. Marries Sofya Andreyevna Behrs (b. 1844)

1863 Polish rebellion

Birth of first child, Sergey (Tolstoy and his wife were to have thirteen children – nine boys and four girls – of whom five died in childhood). Begins work on a novel 'The Decembrists', which was later abandoned, but developed into *War and Peace*

'Polikushka', *The Cossacks*

1865 Nikolay Leskov's 'Lady Macbeth of the Mtsensk District'

First part of *War and Peace* (titled *1805*)

1866 Attempted assassination of Tsar Alexander II

Dostoyevsky's *Crime and Punishment*

1867 Turgenev's *Smoke*

Visits Borodino in search of material for battle scene in *War and Peace*

1868 Dostoyevsky's *The Idiot*

1869 Publication of *War and Peace* completed

1870–71 Franco–Prussian War. Municipal Government reform

Dostoyevsky's *Devils*

Studies ancient Greek. Illness; convalesces in Samara (Bashkiriya). Begins work on primer for children. First mention of *Anna Karenina*. Reads Arthur Schopenhauer and other philosophers. Starts work on novel about Peter the Great (later abandoned)

1872 'God Sees the Truth But Waits', 'A Prisoner of the Caucasus'

1873 Begins *Anna Karenina*. Raises funds during famine in Bashkiriya, where he has bought an estate. Growing obsession with problems of death and religion; temptation to commit suicide

1874 Much occupied with educational theory

1875 Beginning of active revolutionary movement

1875–7 Instalments of *Anna Karenina* published (in book form in 1878)

1877 Turgenev's *Virgin Soil*

Journal publication of *Anna Karenina* completed

1877–8 Russo–Turkish War

1878 Reconciliation with Turgenev, who visits him at Yasnaya

Polyana. Works on 'The Decembrists' and again abandons it. Works on *Confession* (completed 1882, but banned by the religious censor and published in Geneva in 1884)

1879 Dostoyevsky's *Brothers Karamazov*

1880 Works on *Critique of Dogmatic Theology*

1881 Assassination of Tsar Alexander II. With ascension of Alexander III, the government returns to reactionary policies

Death of Dostoyevsky

Writes to Tsar Alexander III asking him to pardon his father's assassins

1882 Student riots in St Petersburg and Kazan universities. Jewish pogroms and repressive measures against minorities

Religious works, including new translation of the Gospels. Begins 'Death of Ivan Ilyich' and *What Then Must We Do?*. Studies Hebrew

1883 Deathbed letter from Turgenev urging Tolstoy not to abandon his art

1884 Family relations strained, first attempt to leave home. 'What I Believe' banned

Collected works published by his wife

1885 Tension with his wife over new beliefs. Works closely with Vladimir Chertkov, with whom (and others) he founds a publishing house, The Intermediary, to produce edifying literature for the common folk. Many popular stories written 1885–6, including 'What Men Live By', 'Where Love Is, God Is', 'Strider'

1886 Walks from Moscow to Yasnaya Polyana in five days. Works on land during the summer. Denounced as a heretic by Archbishop of Kherson

Death of Ivan Ilyich, 'How Much Land Does a Man Need?', *What Then Must We Do?*

1887 Meets Leskov

'On Life'

1888 Chekhov's *The Steppe*

Renounces meat, alcohol and tobacco. Growing friction between his wife and Chertkov. *The Power of Darkness*, banned in 1886, performed in Paris

1889 Finishes 'Kreutzer Sonata'. Begins *Resurrection* (works on it for ten years)

1890 'Kreutzer Sonata' banned, though on appeal by his wife to the Tsar publication was permitted in Collected Works

1891 Convinced that personal profits from writing are immoral, renounces copyright on all works published after 1881 and all future works. His family thus suffers financially, though his wife retains copyright in all the earlier works. Helps to organize famine relief in Ryazan province. Attacks smoking and alcohol in 'Why Do Men Stupefy Themselves?'

1892 Organizes famine relief. *Fruits of Enlightenment* (published 1891) produced in Maly Theatre, Moscow

1893 Finishes 'Kingdom of God Is Within You'

1894 Accession of Tsar Nicholas II. Strikes in St Petersburg
   Writes preface to Maupassant collection of stories. Criticizes *Crime and Punishment*

1895 Meets Chekhov. *Power of Darkness* produced in Maly Theatre, Moscow
   'Master and Man'

1896 Chekhov's *The Seagull*
   Sees production of *Hamlet* and *King Lear* at Hermitage Theatre, severely critical of Shakespeare

1897 Appeals to authorities on behalf of Dukhobors, a pacifist religious sect, to whom permission is granted to emigrate to Canada
   What is Art?

1898 Formation of Social Democratic Party. Dreyfus Affair
   Works for famine relief

1899 Widespread student riots
   Serial publication of *Resurrection* (in book form in 1900)

1900 Meets Maxim Gorky, whom he calls a 'real man of the people'

1901 Foundation of Socialist Revolutionary Party
   Excommunicated from Orthodox Church for writing works 'repugnant to Christ and the Church'. Seriously ill, convalesces in Crimea; visitors include Chekhov and Gorky

1902 Finishes 'What is Religion?'. Writes to Tsar Nicholas II on evils of autocracy and ownership of property

1903 Protests against Jewish pogroms in Kishinev
   'After the Ball'

1904 Russian fleet destroyed in Tsushima Straits. Assassination of V. K. Plehve, Minister of the Interior
   Death of Chekhov
   Death of second-eldest brother Sergey. Pamphlet on Russo–Japanese war published in England
   'Shakespeare and the Drama'

1905 Attempted revolution in Russia (attacks all sides involved). *Potemkin* mutiny. S.Y. Witte becomes Prime Minister
   Anarchical publicist pamphlets
   Introduction to Chekhov's 'Darling'

1908 Tolstoy's secretary N. N. Gusev exiled
    'I Cannot Be Silent', a protest against capital punishment
1909 Increased animosity between his wife and Chertkov, she threatens
    suicide
1910 Corresponds with Mahatma Gandhi concerning latter's doctrine
    of non-violent resistance to evil. His wife threatens suicide; demands
    all Tolstoy's diaries for past ten years, but Tolstoy puts them in
    bank vault. Final breakdown of relationship with her. 28 October:
    leaves home. 7 November: dies at Astapovo railway station. Buried
    at Yasnaya Polyana
1911 'The Devil', 'Father Sergius', 'Hadji Murat', 'The Forged Coupon'

Introduction

PEACE AND WAR

Although *War and Peace* has often been described as the greatest novel ever written, Tolstoy once claimed it wasn't a novel at all. Henry James, giving the title as *Peace and War*, called it a fluid pudding and included it in a list of 'large, loose baggy monsters'.[1] By contrast, it has also been compared to *The Iliad* in scope and technique, and Prince Dmitri Mirsky, the distinguished émigré historian of Russian literature, called it 'the most important work in the whole of Russian realistic fiction'.[2]

Tolstoy's protestation that it wasn't a novel had a particular purpose. He wanted his readers to expect something broader and deeper than the romances they were used to finding in fiction. There would be no single hero and heroine, no straightforward system of exposition, crisis and resolution, no orthodox ending. It was a book in which Tolstoy made up new rules as it expanded: a society novel that turned into a family story, only to grow into a historical chronicle and a mighty epic that was underwritten by a deep interest in individual destinies and intimate human detail. It was a fifteen-year tranche of human experience (1805–20), fictional and real, located in Russian society in an age of critical importance for Europe as a whole, and Tolstoy made an unprecedented attempt to bring together the widest possible range of interests – personal, social, psychological and historical. But most important is his instinctive skill as a teller of stories and creator of characters. The lasting quality of *War and Peace* lies in its compelling narrative and fascinating people, imagined and historical. Perhaps *Peace and War* might have been a more appropriate title, because only about a third of the action takes place on or near the battlefield. Anyone coming to this novel for the first time can be assured of one thing: you are going to enjoy some very good stories.

But first we need to sketch in some background. Tolstoy begins his novel by throwing an evening party to welcome his characters and his readers. The year is 1805 and Napoleon's aggressive actions, especially the recent seizure of Genoa and Lucca, seem likely to threaten Russia's western borders. The huge and bumbling Pierre Bezukhov and the neat, self-assured Prince Andrey Bolkonsky are guests, and their maturation and misadventures will form the main interest of the novel. At first the two young men have everything going for them. Pierre inherits a huge fortune and marries well. The efficient Andrey will find success in all that he does as a landowner and soldier. But both of these gifted and fortunate men will make many mistakes, feel constantly unhappy with the course of their lives, take appallingly bad decisions and have to live with the consequences. The same applies to the leading female character, Natasha, whose progress from childhood to full maturity is so convincingly depicted that she has been described as 'certainly the most wonderfully made character in any novel'.[3] The strength of *War and Peace* is in the weakness of its characters. The novel is a detailed casebook of human inadequacy and imperfection; so many avoidable errors are made that it will be a long time before contentment and equilibrium start to emerge, and for some of the characters new insight comes too late.

Oscar Wilde said that what made Russian writers' books 'so great is the pity they put in them'.[4] They have seen life, tackled it and tried their best, and they know a truth that rarely declares itself, especially in stories that are meant for entertainment. It is this: virtually everyone – even people in advantageous or privileged circumstances – finds the living of life a worrying and difficult business most of the time. The novel takes us in rich detail through all the seven ages of man from childhood to old age, and explores their difficulties, all of which are played out under the gathering shadow of death, the one certainty. As another Russian writer, Boris Pasternak, concluded in the novel *Dr Zhivago*: 'Living life is not just a walk across a field.'[5]

But there is more. Only a few of the 500 characters in the novel pause to think about the complex and difficult process by which human lives evolve, but Pierre and Andrey are never happier than when unhappily gnawing at the meanings, difficult choices and hidden possibilities that may or may not underlie human existence and searching for clues to make life better and easier. A series of vital questions is waiting for them and for the reader: What and where is happiness? How do you distinguish it from fun? How is it possible to live on in the sure and certain knowledge of death? Is the concept of God any help? What are the roles of fate and luck in human experience? How can a person find complete freedom? Are there any ultimate philosophical truths that we can rely on? What should you *do* with a human life?

LIFE AND LOVE

But Tolstoy knows that you cannot spend all your time philosophizing. The sheer thrill of being alive, the excitement of surrendering to the moment and revelling in pleasure, are infectiously represented in a series of set pieces. Sometimes the occasion is exquisite enough to be the high point in an individual's life. It is hard to imagine Count Ilya Rostov ever being any happier than when he dances the 'Daniel Cooper' at home (Volume I, Part I, Chapter 17), unless it is when he proposes a toast to General Bagration at a lavish dinner that he has put on at the English Club with money he cannot afford to spend (II, I, 3). For senior soldiers there is the glorious opportunity to be noticed by an emperor; hence the obsequious behaviour of an elderly general before Tsar Alexander I (I, II, 3), and the suicidal rush into the River Viliya by a Polish general anxious to please Napoleon, which costs the lives of forty men but wins him a medal (III, I, 2). Even young Petya Rostov is borne away with mindless rapture at the mere sight of the Tsar (III, I, 21). By contrast, almost all of the younger characters find sublime happiness in falling in love, and at one point the entire Rostov household seems to be dizzy from it:

> Love was in the air at the Rostovs' at this time, as it always is when there are very young and very charming girls around. Any young man arriving at their house and seeing those young girls' faces, so sensitive and always smiling (probably at their own good fortune) amid all the chasing and scurrying, and hearing all their frivolous girlish chatter, so good-natured, open to everything, brimming with hope, and their equally frivolous singing and music-making, enjoyed the same sensations of love-sickness and impending bliss that the young Rostovs were themselves enjoying. (II, I, 10)

There are many occasions for tears of joy. Dancing is one such: for example, Natasha's instinctive Russian dancing after the hunt (II, IV, 7) is a reminder of her father's happy evening with the Daniel Cooper, her own unspeakable delight at her first ball, whirling around with Prince Andrey (II, III, 16) and Denisov's amazing mazurka at Iogel's (II, I, 12). It is useful to emphasize such bliss not least because Russian literature has a reputation for gloomy introspection which is only partly deserved. It gives the novel its most unusual quality, Tolstoy's ability to lead us through disappointment, frustration and tragedy without bitterness or cynicism. He declares, against all odds, the goodness of living. This is the spirit of the whole novel; you will see it at its best in Volume II, Part IV – all thirteen chapters.

LIFE AND DEATH

War and Peace was written during one of the few periods in Leo Tolstoy's life when he had a sense of tranquillity and purpose. Superlatives are needed to describe him: a big, strong man with a formidable intellect, powerful emotions, and extraordinary qualities and defects that ran to extremes. He lived a long life, and left behind work that fills ninety large printed volumes, the biggest and richest individual contribution to the treasure-house of nineteenth-century Russian culture.

Leo Nikolayevich Tolstoy was born in 1828 into the Russian aristocracy, at Yasnaya Polyana, 130 miles south-west of Moscow. His parents died when he was young, but he and his siblings grew up happily, cocooned by female relatives. At the age of sixteen, he entered the university at Kazan but failed his courses and returned to Yasnaya, which he had just inherited. By then, aged nineteen, he had contracted his first dose of venereal disease, a continuing risk during the following years of debauchery and gambling in Moscow and St Petersburg.

Tolstoy's largely autobiographical *Childhood* was accepted by the *Contemporary* in 1852, the first writing he had submitted for publication. Despite its modest aims and rather dry realism, it was popular and was followed by *Boyhood* (1854) and *Youth* (1857). Even greater success attended the three-part *Sevastopol in December, May* and *August* (1855–6) – which presented his experiences and observations as an artillery officer while leading men under fire during the Crimean war (1854–6), and undermined the false glamour of warfare. He soon became well known in St Petersburg literary circles, though he found celebrity uncongenial and hurried back to Yasnaya.

Tolstoy was occupied with *War and Peace* throughout the 1860s. The serious writing began in 1863, just as his first son was born. His wife Sonya (short form of Sofya Andreyevna) was only eighteen, and she bore him another twelve children. He devoted the 1870s to *Anna Karenina*, and despite his artistic and commercial success, he became obsessed by thoughts of his own mortality and tormented by a religious yearning that could not be reconciled with the activities of the Church, and he thought constantly about suicide; this spiritual crisis is minutely described in *A Confession* (1878–9).

Eventually he came through it, but his life was radically changed.

He now avoided society, living and working at Yasnaya Polyana, wearing a peasant's shirt and doing much manual work, he renounced writing, violence, stimulants of all kinds, including meat-eating, and he required impeccable moral standards of all. This was his new religion: the best of Jesus, without his church. His moral stance – especially his pacifism – attracted interest from all over the world, and Tolstoyan communities were formed in several countries by disciples. But he was impossible to live with. His lack of love and charity towards those closest to him, especially his wife, remains as a blot on his reputation. He did continue to write, including *The Death of Ivan Ilyich* (1886), *Resurrection* (1899) and *Hadji Murat* (1911), and a moving five-act tragedy of gruesome subject matter, *The Power of Darkness* (1890).

But at the age of eighty-two Tolstoy, estranged from all his family except for one daughter, Alexandra, fled with her, for a monastery. He fell ill at a (now famous) railway junction, where he died. His body was interred at the top of a small ravine at Yasnaya, where as a small boy he had searched for a little green stick on which was supposedly inscribed a secret formula guaranteeing permanent happiness and brotherly love.

LIFE AND LITERATURE

However, when newly married and fully occupied in his mid thirties, Tolstoy had looked for the rewards of family happiness (the title of a story written in 1859), and for a few years he found them. Sonya devoted herself to him and to their children, ran the home and the business side of the estate, and found time to help him with his work. A woman of striking intelligence, she had a good education at home and at university, where she had obtained a teaching diploma. She had also tried writing, and a short novel which she destroyed was said by her sister to have contained the germ of the relationship between Natasha Rostov and her mother.[6] Now Sonya would transcribe what Tolstoy had written during the day, and once claimed to have written out much of *War and Peace* no fewer than seven times. She discussed the story with her husband, decoded his difficult handwriting and corrected minor errors of spelling and grammar. Her hand in the shaping of his work was strong and decisive; it may have been more influential than has ever been fully acknowledged.

The novel grew and grew. In 1856 Tolstoy had drafted several chapters about a man who had returned from exile in Siberia, for his involvement in the abortive Decembrist uprising of 1825. Then Tolstoy pushed back in history to 1812, and finally to 1805: he would start when Napoleon, a self-appointed emperor, moved against the Austrian–Russian coalition. Tolstoy planned that events in 1825 and 1856 would form later volumes of a trilogy. But his main interest was in writing about the joys and misfortunes of aristocratic family life. Plans and drafts were adopted, revised, abandoned and replaced in profusion.[7] In 1865 thirty-eight chapters were published in the *Russian Messenger*, and came out in book form the following year, under the title *1805*; still at this stage only a relatively short work was envisaged. Later Tolstoy decided on a new title, *All's Well That Ends Well*, but as the historical and military interest developed this was reflected in the final title, adopted in March 1867. Sonya insisted on abandoning serial publication, for good financial reasons – there was more money to be made from publishing (and republishing) in book form than from a journal – and the novel came out in six volumes in 1868 and 1869.

Tolstoy drew heavily on real-life sources. For military scenes, his extensive research, including memoirs, and his own first-hand experience guaranteed the sureness of his grip on the details of battle. For characters, his family contributed: his maternal grandfather, Nikolay Volkonsky, monster that he must have been, provided a prototype for Andrey's father; his own father for Nikolay Rostov; and his wife's sister, the impish Tanya, for Natasha. The dualism in Tolstoy's own personality is reflected in Andrey and Pierre – intellect versus spirit, discipline versus laxity, stiff pride versus spontaneity and generosity. As the Russian novelist and critic Dmitri Merezhovsky said: 'The artistic work of Leo Tolstoy is at bottom nothing less than one tremendous diary, kept for fifty years, one endless, explicit confession.'[8]

There had been much discussion of the novel in Russia as it had emerged, and not all of it was complimentary. But by 1870 the first edition had sold out, and the author was basking in national acclaim – and we know from her diaries that his wife was well satisfied with her supportive role. Both were pleased with the money that rolled in from royalties, though Tolstoy soon came to regard such earnings as immoral.

HISTORY AND PHILOSOPHY

The inclusion of Tolstoy's reflections on the workings of history and the methods used by historians has always been controversial. But the common accusation that these musings bog down the novel, making it a struggle to get through, is quite false. At an early stage he realized the danger of this, and swept them all out of the main story into an appendix (Epilogue, Part II). The few that are left are discreetly deployed. A short reflective passage is sometimes used to punctuate events – for example to introduce new sections in a measured and thoughtful manner. (See the opening chapters of all three parts of Volume III.) The epilogue itself may seem too long or repetitive, but it certainly adds to the scope of the novel, and should not be ignored. Tolstoy's ideas on warfare, history and historians are still relevant to the modern world. Consider, for instance the following quotation from Sir Winston Churchill: 'Never, never, never believe that any war will be smooth and easy ... The Statesman who yields to war fever must realise that, once the signal is given, he is no longer the master of policy but the slave of unforeseeable and uncontrollable events.'[9] This is a sharp summary of one concept developed by Tolstoy in the epilogue.

Another example can be seen in the popular political view that when the British Prime Minister retired from office in 2007 he did so having secured peace in Ireland after generations of bloody conflict, and that this was perhaps the most important part of his 'legacy'. Mr Blair pulled the levers: peace resulted. Do you believe it? Tolstoy tells us that this is an unsophisticated view of how history works. It is probably truer to say that Mr Blair happened to be in the right place (and thus eligible for credit) at a time when all the multitudinous circumstances leading up to the final peace settlement (war-weariness among them) came together to end the conflict for good. It could have been the previous prime minister, or the next one, or somebody else; it happened to be Tony Blair.

These are the kind of ideas that Tolstoy advances in his epilogue. His general purpose is to debunk. Most of all, he wants to cut Napoleon down to size, not only because he was a hated enemy of Russia, but because he was also a ludicrous figure of overweening, pompous pride. At the same time Tolstoy is keen to take issue with the traditional writers of history, who distort the truth by their narrow-minded attitudes and over-simplification. As Henry Gifford wrote: '*War and Peace* has its pages of pamphleteering. But they cannot be torn out, because the argument is continuous. On every page lies the imprint of the same evolving experience.'[10]

The 1860s were a golden decade in Russian literature. In 1862 Ivan Turgenev published *Fathers and Children,* and Fyodor Dostoyevsky was at his most prolific, issuing *Notes from Underground* in 1864, *Crime and Punishment* in 1866, *The Idiot* in 1867–8, and starting work on *Devils* in 1869. A measure of the achievement of *War and Peace* is that it transcends even these masterpieces. Virginia Woolf made the point succinctly: 'There remains the greatest of all novelists – for what else can we call the author of *War and Peace?*'[11]

NOTES

1. Preface to *The Tragic Muse* (1907–9), and letter to Hugh Walpole, 19 May 1912; see Henry Gifford (ed.), *Leo Tolstoy: A Critical Anthology* (Harmondsworth, Penguin, 1971), pp. 104–5.
2. D. S. Mirsky, *A History of Russian Literature* (New York, Alfred A. Knopf, 1960), p. 258.
3. Op. cit., p. 260.
4. Alvin Redman (ed.), *The Epigrams of Oscar Wilde* (London, Bracken Books, 1995), p. 86.
5. Boris Pasternak, *Dr Zhivago,* translated by Max Hayward and Manya Harari (London, Collins and Harvill Press, 1958).
6. See Aylmer Maude, *The Life of Tolstoy: First Fifty Years* (Oxford, Oxford University Press, n.d.), Vol. I, p. 286.
7. A short 'early version' of *War and Peace* was published in Moscow (2000) based on published material, odd pages and extracts from notebooks up to 1866. This was immediately rejected and transcended; it is now of interest only to a few scholars. The recent English translation of this abandoned draft, which omits valuable material from the novel and radically alters the ending, should be ignored.
8. From D. Merezhovsky, *Tolstoy as Man and Artist (L. Tolstoy and Dostoyevsky)* (London, Constable, 1902), cited in Gifford, *Leo Tolstoy: A Critical Anthology,* p. 113.
9. Winston Churchill, *My Early Years*; cited in a reader's letter to *The Times,* 5 February 2007.
10. Henry Gifford, *Tolstoy* (Oxford, Oxford University Press, 1982), pp. 30–31.
11. From Virginia Woolf, 'The Russian Point of View', cited in Gifford, *Leo Tolstoy: A Critical Anthology,* p. 188.

Translator's Note

This novel has been well served by its several translators into English. Only the very first attempt suffers from serious shortcomings, but it was a brave undertaking by Clara Bell, less than twenty years after publication (1885–6). She worked from a French text created by a woman identified only as 'Une Russe', and her version is surprisingly effective, though much of the original has been omitted and what survives is nearer to paraphrase than translation. The early translations by N. H. Dole (1889) and Leo Wiener (1904) were more accurate, though they still contain plenty of small slips, and their American phrasing now has an archaic ring. Constance Garnett, the admirable early doyenne of Russian literature in English translation, produced a sensitive version in 1904; she had a delicate feel for language, though there are some errors. Then, in 1923, came the masters, Louise and Aylmer Maude, who lived in Russia and had the advantage of being able to consult Tolstoy himself. He gave their work his personal endorsement, even claiming that 'better translators . . . could not be invented'.[1] Their version of *War and Peace,* now fast approaching its centenary, is still read as a classic in its own right, and the errors that it contains are so few as to be negligible. It has been succeeded by Rosemary Edmonds's equally reliable (at times derivative) translation (1957), which Penguin has used for nearly half a century, (updated in 1978); and then by a sound American version, by Ann Dunnigan, in 1968.

So why do we need another translation?

It is not unusual for the great classics to be retranslated every couple of generations. Language changes and, without worshipping modernity for its own sake, publishers recognize the need to accommodate new readers by using phrasing more closely attuned to their way of speaking. Infelicities will be edited out, such as 'Andrey spent the evening with a few gay friends', 'Natasha went about the house flushing', 'he exposed himself on the parade ground' or 'he ejaculated with a grimace'; we cannot read phrases like these without raising an inappropriate smile.

On the other hand, it is most important not to over-modernize. Tempting though it may be, I cannot use popularized phrases like 'buzzword', 'oddball' or 'hooliganism'.

Secondly, a translator hopes to squeeze out one or two errors or ambiguities that still linger. Previous translators have missed the fact that that an object referred to in a famous Tolstoyan metaphor about things colliding and recoiling is not a ball in flight but a billiard ball on the table; and they all translated the phrase 'smotret' ispodlob'ya' as 'to look at from under the brows' when it means to look sullenly or furtively.

But these reasons are hardly enough on their own to justify a new translation. There is one way in which all the existing versions fall short: from Constance Garnett onwards they have been produced by women of a particular social and cultural background (Louise having contributed more than Aylmer to the Maudes' version), with some resulting flatness and implausibility in the dialogue, especially that between soldiers, peasants and all the lower orders. A specialist critic puts it well, speaking of the Maudes, who are the most highly regarded translators: 'Their work can always be counted on for . . . negative virtues: sobriety, explicitness, a firm hold on the argument. However, their resources are limited in range of tone. They have little sense of colloquial idiom . . .'[2]

To take a specific example: Pierre, watching as a cannonball crashes down into the Rayevsky redoubt and takes a man's leg off, hears another soldier call out in response: 'Ekh! Neskladnaya!' (III, II, 31). The English versions of this are: 'Ekh! You beastly thing!' (Dole); 'Oh, awkward one!' (Weiner); 'Hey, awkward hussy!' (Garnett); 'Awkward baggage!' (Maude); 'Oh you hussy!' (Edmonds); 'Ah, you're a bungler!' (Dunnigan). Curiously enough the best in terms of natural speech is Clara Bell's: 'Ah, you brute!' The original, with connotations of both awkwardness and femininity, is rather difficult to translate, but one thing is certain: no soldier in the heat of battle ever said anything like most of the phrases we have been offered so far.

The previous translations also have an excess of niceness and exactitude that can sound jarring to today's readers. Natasha looks in the mirror and says: 'Can this be I?' Lavrushka is sent off 'in quest of fowls'. More than once we hear that 'Pierre fell to musing'. Elsewhere someone says: 'Ay, listen what folks are prating of'. Similarly, there must be better ways of saying: 'The crushing weight of his arm fell impotent as though spellbound', or 'the resolutive moment of battle had come'. Non-existent English exclamations like 'Ay!', 'Ey!', 'Ekh!'

or the misused 'Eh!' still abound. In such old-fashioned phrasing I have tried to make improvements.

This is not to denigrate the translations that have been enjoyed by millions; it is merely to indicate that this version follows a translation strategy that is slightly different from what has gone before.

In the introduction to his *Don Quixote*, John Rutherford divides translators into cavaliers and puritans. The cavalier takes some liberties; the puritan is a stickler for exactitude. Rutherford's intention was to combine the virtues of both and avoid their vices, a sensible if difficult plan. The previous translations of *War and Peace* have erred slightly too much on the puritan side, literal fidelity being set at a higher premium than writing naturally in English. It is now time to move somewhat in the other direction.

Let me give a couple of small examples. If a Russian asks, 'Did you study in Kiev?', another Russian will respond by saying, 'In Kiev'. The puritan will use that repetition, while the cavalier would give the normal English speaker's response, 'Yes', or 'Yes, I did.' Similarly, when a Russian mother says to her child, 'Ne nado!', the puritan will be tempted to render this literally as 'That's not necessary!', whereas the cavalier will go for 'Don't!'

The reason for this puritanism is not far to seek. It lies in what Rutherford refers to as a 'mistaken attitude of reverence for the original artist beside whom it's all too easy to feel like humble artisans who can only ever aspire to produce a pale shadow of the original. . .a self-fulfilling prediction. . .Literary translators must conquer these fears.'[3] This is good advice. Without ever drifting too far away from the original, it does seem reasonable to aim for the kind of English that would have occurred naturally in its context and now sounds appropriate.

Another way to look at this is to imagine how the average Russian reads *War and Peace* and to try to recapture something similar in the translated text. Tolstoy's literary style has its faults – such as undue repetition, grammatical inaccuracy and some sentences of excessive length[4] – and many of them have to be faithfully reproduced in order to avoid falsification, but by and large he is an easy read for a Russian (and comparatively easy to translate). Stylistic angularities, shocks and surprises are infrequent, and the dialogue in particular is individualized but always natural. It seems most important to ensure in any translation the same kind of smooth reading, and varied but realistic-sounding dialogue. In rendering colloquial speech, of course, a translator has to choose a particular regional dialect and its idioms, and I have used a

British English form of speech, without, I hope, making the text unnatural for non-British readers.

The first edition (1868–9) of the novel had long passages in French. But Tolstoy had second thoughts and removed most of them during a drastic revision in 1873. Previous translators cut these further and provided translations in footnotes. But few readers today have a sound knowledge of French, so I have decided to translate all of it.

Does this change matter? Sometimes it does, but it is possible to indicate that a speaker is using another language. It is not unusual for Tolstoy himself to say (in Russian) for example, 'Since Pierre was speaking French at the time he . . .' I have used this kind of formula on those few occasions when a linguistic choice or shift has real significance, e.g. in the second paragraph on the opening page. It remains true that certain characters – Bilibin, for example – lose some of their finesse because of this treatment, but there seems to be an overall gain in following the lead established by Tolstoy (and the Maudes with his blessing) by making the text more directly accessible.

A NOTE ON THE TEXT

For almost a century several editions of *War and Peace* vied for acceptance. The first book version appeared in six volumes (four in 1868 and two in 1869), but was riddled with errors, nearly 2,000 of them. Then, in 1873 Tolstoy published his revised edition. In the 1930s Russian scholars preparing the *Jubilee Edition of the Complete Works of L. N. Tolstoy* decided to use the fifth edition of 1886, even though Tolstoy had not been involved in its publication, but they did incorporate some of the 1873 emendations (a second edition was based on the 1873 text). When it was discovered later that numerous changes in the 1873 edition had been introduced by N. N. Strakhov, most of them without Tolstoy's approval, a team of scholars led by E. Zaydenshnur set about the formidable task of collating and comparing all versions, including the manuscripts, copies (mainly in Sonya Tolstoy's hand), annotated editions and corrected or half-corrected proofs, with the goal of eliminating any alterations introduced by outsiders. Their work bore fruit in the early 1960s, when a truly definitive text emerged, from which all subsequent editions derive.

The present translation is based on the text of *War and Peace* prepared by E. Zaydenshnur in the 1960–65 twenty-volume *Collected Works of L. N. Tolstoy*, published by Goslitizdat (State Publishing

House for Literature), edited by N. N. Akopova, N. K. Gudzy, N. N. Gusev and M. B. Khrapchenko.

NOTES

1. *War and Peace,* translated by Louise and Aylmer Maude (Oxford, Oxford University Press, n.d.), vol. I, p. 442.
2. Henry Gifford, 'On Translating Tolstoy', in Malcolm Jones, ed, *New Essays on Tolstoy*, Cambridge University Press, 1978, p. 22.
3. Cervantes, *Don Quixote*, translated by John Rutherford (London, Penguin, 2000), pp. xv and xvi.
4. For further details see R. F. Christian, *Tolstoy's 'War and Peace': A Study* (Oxford, Clarendon Press, 1962), pp. 148–66.

War and Peace

VOLUME I

PART I

'Well, Prince, Genoa and Lucca are now nothing more than estates taken over by the Buonaparte family.[1] No, I give you fair warning. If you won't say this means war, if you will allow yourself to condone all the ghastly atrocities perpetrated by that Antichrist – yes, that's what I think he is – I shall disown you. You're no friend of mine – not the "faithful slave" you claim to be . . . But how *are* you? How are you keeping? I can see I'm intimidating you. Do sit down and talk to me.'

These words were spoken (in French) one evening in July 1805 by the well-known Anna Pavlovna Scherer, maid of honour and confidante of the Empress Maria Fyodorovna, as she welcomed the first person to arrive at her soirée, Prince Vasily Kuragin, a man of high rank and influence. Anna Pavlovna had had a cough for the last few days and she called it *la grippe* – *grippe* being a new word not yet in common currency. A footman of hers in scarlet livery had gone around that morning delivering notes written in French, each saying precisely the same thing:

> If you have nothing better to do, Count (or Prince), and if the prospect of spending an evening with a poor sick lady is not too unnerving, I shall be delighted to see you at my residence between seven and ten. ANNETTE SCHERER

'My goodness, what a violent attack!' replied the prince, who had only just come in and was not in the least put out by this welcome. Dressed in his embroidered court uniform with knee-breeches, shoes and stars across his chest, he looked at her with a flat face of undisturbed serenity. His French was the elegant tongue of our grandparents, who used it for thought as well as speech, and it carried the soft tones of condescension that come naturally to an eminent personage grown old in high society and at court. He came up to Anna Pavlovna and kissed her hand, presenting to her a perfumed and glistening bald pate, and then seated himself calmly on the sofa.

'First things first,' he said. 'How are you, my dear friend? Put my mind at rest.' His voice remained steady, and his tone, for all its courtesy and sympathy, implied indifference and even gentle mockery.

'How can one feel well when one is ... suffering in a moral sense? Can any sensitive person find peace of mind nowadays?' said Anna Pavlovna. 'I do hope you're staying all evening.'

'Well, there is that reception at the English Ambassador's. It's Wednesday. I must show my face,' said the prince. 'My daughter is coming to take me there.'

'I thought tonight's festivities had been cancelled. I must say all these celebrations and fireworks are becoming rather tedious.'

'If they had known you wanted the celebration cancelled, it would have been,' said the prince with the predictability of a wound-up clock. Sheer habit made him say things he didn't even mean.

'Stop teasing me. Come on, tell me what's been decided about Novosiltsev's dispatch?[2] You know everything.'

'What is there to tell?' replied the prince in a cold, bored tone. 'What's been decided? They've decided that Bonaparte has burnt his boats, and I rather think we're getting ready to burn ours.'

Prince Vasily always spoke languidly, like an actor declaiming a part from an old play. Anna Pavlovna Scherer was just the opposite – all verve and excitement, despite her forty years. To be an enthusiast had become her special role in society, and she would sometimes wax enthusiastic when she didn't feel like it, so as not to frustrate the expectations of those who knew her. The discreet smile that never left her face, though it clashed with her faded looks, gave her the appearance of a spoilt child with a charming defect that she was well aware of, though she neither wished nor felt able to correct it, nor even thought it necessary to do so.

Then suddenly in the middle of this political discussion Anna Pavlovna launched forth in great excitement. 'Oh, don't talk to me about Austria![3] Perhaps it's all beyond me, but Austria has never wanted war and she still doesn't want war. She's betraying us. Russia alone must be Europe's saviour. Our benefactor is aware of his exalted calling and he'll live up to it. That's the one thing I do believe in. The noblest role on earth awaits our good and wonderful sovereign, and he is so full of decency and virtue that God will not forsake him. He will do what has to be done and scotch the hydra of revolution, which has become more dreadful than ever in the person of this murdering villain.[4] We alone must avenge the blood of the righteous. And whom can we trust, I ask you? England, with that commercial spirit of hers, cannot understand the lofty soul of our Emperor Alexander, and never will. She has refused to evacuate Malta.[5] She keeps on looking for an ulterior motive behind our actions. What did they say to Novosiltsev? Nothing. They didn't understand, they're not capable of understanding, how altruistic our Emperor is – he wants nothing for himself but everything for the good of mankind. And what have they promised? Nothing. And what little they have promised, they won't carry out. Prussia has already declared that Bonaparte is invincible and that the whole of Europe is powerless to oppose him . . . I for one don't believe a single word from Hardenberg or Haugwitz. That much-vaunted Prussian neutrality is just a trap. I put my faith in God and the noble calling of our beloved Emperor. He'll be the saviour of Europe!'

She stopped suddenly, amused at her own passionate outburst.

'I think if they had sent you instead of our dear Wintzengerode,'[6] said the prince with a similar smile, 'an onslaught like that from you would have got the King of Prussia to agree. You are so eloquent. May I have some tea?'

'Yes, of course. By the way,' she added, calming down, 'there are two very interesting men coming here tonight – the Vicomte de Mortemart, a Montmorency through the Rohan line, one of the best French families. He's the right kind of émigré, one of the genuine ones. And the Abbé Morio – such a profound thinker. Do you know him? He's been received by the Emperor. Have you heard?'

'Oh, it will be a pleasure to meet them,' said the prince. 'But tell me,' he added, with studied nonchalance, as if an idea had just occurred to him, though this question was the main reason for his visit, 'is it true that the Dowager Empress wants Baron Funke to become First Secretary in Vienna? They do say he's a miserable creature, that baron.'

Prince Vasily wanted this post for his son, but other people were working through the Empress Maria Fyodorovna to get it for the baron. Anna Pavlovna half-closed her eyes to indicate that neither she nor anyone else could pass judgement on what the Empress might feel like doing or want to do. 'Baron Funke has been recommended to the Dowager Empress by her sister,' was all she said, in a dry, lugubrious tone. As she pronounced the name of the Empress, Anna Pavlovna's face took on an expression of profound and sincere devotion mixed with respect and tinged with sadness, which invariably came upon her when she had occasion to mention her exalted patroness. She said that her Majesty had been gracious enough to show Baron Funke great respect, at which her face once again dissolved into sadness.

The prince said nothing and showed no feeling. Anna Pavlovna, with all the sensitivity and quick thinking of both a courtier and a woman, decided to rebuke the prince for daring to refer in such a way to a person recommended to the Empress, and at the same time to console him. 'But, on the subject of your family,' she said, 'do you realize how much your daughter has delighted everyone in society since she came out? They say she's as beautiful as the day is long.'

The prince bowed as a mark of his gratitude and respect.

'I often think,' Anna Pavlovna resumed after a short pause, edging closer to the prince and smiling sweetly to indicate that the political and social conversation was now at an end, and personal conversation was in order, 'I often think that good fortune in life is sometimes distributed most unfairly. Why has fate given you two such splendid children? I don't include Anatole, your youngest – I don't like him,' she commented in a peremptory tone and with raised eyebrows. 'Such charming children. And I must say you seem to appreciate them less than anyone. You really don't deserve them.'

And she smiled her exuberant smile.

'What can I do? Lavater would have said that I have no paternity bump,'[7] said the prince.

'Oh, do stop joking. I wanted a serious talk with you. Listen, I'm not pleased with your younger son. Just between ourselves,' her face went all gloomy again, 'his name has been mentioned in her Majesty's presence, and people are feeling sorry for you . . .'

The prince said nothing, while she gave him a knowing look, waiting in silence for his reply. Prince Vasily frowned.

'What *can* I do?' he said at last. 'You know I've done everything a father could do to bring them up well, and they have both turned out to be idiots. At least Hippolyte's a fool on the quiet – Anatole's the rowdy one. That's the only difference between them,' he said, with an unusually awkward and forced smile, which gave a sharp twist to the lines round his mouth, making it surprisingly ugly and coarse.

'Why do men like you have children? If you weren't a father, I could find no fault with you,' said Anna Pavlovna, looking up pensively.

'I'm your faithful slave. I wouldn't admit it to anyone else, but my children are the bane of my life. They're the cross I have to bear. That's how I explain it to myself. What would *you* . . . ?' He broke off with a gesture that signalled his resignation to a cruel fate. Anna Pavlovna thought things over.

'That prodigal son of yours, Anatole, haven't you thought of marrying him off? They do say,' she went on, 'that old maids have a mania for matchmaking. So far I've never been conscious of this failing in myself, but I do have a certain little person in my mind, someone who is very unhappy with her father – a relative of ours, the young Princess Bolkonsky.'

Prince Vasily made no reply, but being quick on the uptake and good at remembering things – qualities that came naturally to the denizens of high society – he gave a slight nod to show that he had noted her comment and was considering it.

'No, listen, do you realize that boy's costing me forty thousand roubles a year?' he said, obviously unable to check the dismal drift of his thinking. He paused. 'What will it be like in five years' time if he carries on like this? You see what the benefits of fatherhood are . . . This princess of yours, is she rich?'

'Her father's a very rich man and a miser. He lives out in the country. You know, Prince Bolkonsky. He's very well known. He retired under the late Emperor. They used to call him "the King of Prussia". He's a very clever man, but he's a crank, not easy to get on with. Poor little thing, she's as miserable as any girl could be. It was her brother who married Liza Meinen not too long ago. He's one of Kutuzov's adjutants. He's coming here tonight.'

'Listen, my dear Annette,' said the prince, suddenly taking his companion's hand and pressing it downwards for reasons best known to himself. 'You set this up for me, and I'll serve you like a faithful slave for ever. (Or *slafe*, with an 'f', as my village elder puts it when he writes to me.) She's a girl from a good family, and she's rich. That's all I need.'

And with the freedom, familiarity and sheer style that were his hallmark, he took hold of the maid of honour's hand, kissed it and gave it a little shake, easing back into his armchair and looking away from her.

'Wait a minute,' said Anna Pavlovna, thinking things over. 'I'll have a little talk with Lise, young Bolkonsky's wife, this very evening. Perhaps something can be arranged. I'll use your family to start learning the old maid's trade.'

CHAPTER 2

Anna Pavlovna's drawing-room was steadily filling up. All the important people in St Petersburg society were there, varying enormously in age and character for all their shared social background. Prince Vasily's daughter, the beautiful Hélène, had just arrived to take him on to the Ambassador's reception; she was wearing a ballgown enhanced by a maid of honour's monogram. The young Princess Bolkonsky, a slip of a girl known as the most seductive woman in Petersburg, was there too; married the previous winter, she no longer appeared at large occasions because she was pregnant, but she did still attend small soirées. Prince Vasily's son, Prince Hippolyte, arrived with Mortemart, and introduced him. Also present were the Abbé Morio and many other people.

Anna Pavlovna was welcoming her guests as they arrived with a 'Have you met my aunt?' or 'I don't think you know my aunt' before steering them with great solemnity towards a little old lady with big bows in her hair, who had come sailing in from the next room as soon as the guests had begun to arrive. Anna Pavlovna would announce them by name, slowly transferring her gaze from guest to aunt, and then move on. All the guests went through the motions of greeting this aunt, who was unknown, uninteresting and unneeded by anyone. Anna Pavlovna observed their greetings with sadness and solemn sympathy, a picture of silent approval. The lady known as 'my aunt' spoke in the same way to every new arrival, commenting on their health, her own health and the health of her Majesty, who was by now, thank God, feeling better. All those who approached were polite enough to refrain from showing undue haste, but once this onerous duty had been fulfilled they walked away from the old lady with a sense of relief, and never went near her again all evening.

Young Princess Bolkonsky had brought some work with her in a gold-embroidered velvet bag. Her pretty little upper lip, slightly shadowed with down, barely covered her teeth, but that made it all the prettier when it rose up and lovelier still when it curled down to meet the lower lip. As tends to happen with the best-looking women, a defect – in this case a short lip and a half-open mouth – came out as a distinctive and beautiful feature. Everyone enjoyed the sight of this pretty little mother-to-be, brimming with health and vitality and making light of her condition. After a few minutes in her company and the exchange of a word or two, old men and bored, morose young men felt as if they themselves were becoming like her. Anyone who talked to her, watching her as every word she spoke revealed that bright little smile and the constant gleam of those dazzling white teeth, walked away feeling full of bonhomie. Everybody did.

The little princess waddled slightly as she tripped rapidly round the table, holding her tiny workbag, then she cheerfully smoothed down her dress and sat on a sofa near the silver samovar. Everything she did seemed like a treat for herself and everyone around her.

'I've brought my work,' she said in French, opening her reticule and addressing all the company. 'But listen, Annette, you must stop playing tricks on me,' she said, turning to the hostess. 'You wrote and said it was only a little party. Just look what I've got on.' And she spread her arms wide to display an elegant grey dress, decorated with lace and set off by a broad sash just below the bosom.

'Don't worry, Lise, you'll always be the prettiest,' answered Anna Pavlovna.

'Did you know my husband is deserting me?' she said to a general, continuing to speak French and using just the same tone. 'He's going off to get himself killed. Do tell me what this awful war is all about,' she asked of Prince Vasily, but before he could answer she had moved on to his daughter, the beautiful Hélène.

'Isn't she a gorgeous creature, this little princess?' said Prince Vasily to Anna Pavlovna.

Shortly after the little princess's arrival, in walked a big, generously proportioned young man with close-cropped hair and spectacles, wearing the last word in light-coloured breeches and a tan coat with a jabot. This stout young man was the illegitimate son of a celebrated grandee from Catherine's age, old Count Bezukhov, who was now on his deathbed in Moscow. He had not yet entered any branch of the service, having only just returned from abroad, where he had been completing his education. This was his first appearance in society. Anna Pavlovna welcomed him with the kind of bow she reserved for the lowest persons in the hierarchy of her drawing-room. But even as she bestowed her meanest welcome on this new arrival Anna Pavlovna's face was transformed; she looked ill at ease and full of alarm, like someone who had come across some gross object, oversized and out of place. By a small margin Pierre was indeed the largest man in the room, but her look of dismay must surely have derived from this man's special look – intelligent, rather diffident, but also piercing and spontaneous – that made him a distinctive figure in the drawing-room.

'It is most kind of you, Monsieur Pierre, to come to see a poor sick woman,' said Anna Pavlovna, looking anxiously across at her aunt as she steered him in her direction. Pierre mumbled something unintelligible, and continued to stare around the room, looking for something. He beamed with pleasure, bowed to the little princess as if she was a close friend of his, and then went over to the aunt. Anna Pavlovna's worst fears were confirmed when Pierre walked off without hearing the full story of her Majesty's health. Rattled, Anna Pavlovna detained him with a question.

'You don't know the Abbé Morio, do you? Such an interesting man . . .'

'Yes, I've heard about him and his scheme for everlasting peace. All very interesting, but not really feasible.'

'Don't you think so?' asked Anna Pavlovna for the sake of saying something before getting back to her duties as hostess, but Pierre now committed the opposite kind of *faux pas*. Fresh from walking away without listening properly to a lady who was speaking to him, he now talked on and detained a lady who needed to get away from him. With his head lowered and his great legs thrust wide apart, he set about explaining to Anna Pavlovna why he thought the abbé's scheme was a silly fancy.

'Could we talk about this later on?' smiled Anna Pavlovna.

Detaching herself from this young man who had no idea how to conduct himself, she resumed her duties as hostess, watching and listening carefully, ready to render assistance at any point where the conversation was beginning to flag. Just as the foreman of a spinning-mill settles the workers down and then strolls about the place on the lookout for a breakdown or any funny noise from a spindle, the slightest squeak or knock that would bring him rushing over to ease the machinery or make an adjustment, so Anna Pavlovna patrolled her drawing-room, walking over to any group where the talk was too little or too loud, and easing the machinery of conversation back into its proper, steady hum with a single word here or a tiny manoeuvre there. But busy as she was with all these preoccupations, she was still clearly worried about Pierre. She watched him anxiously as he went over to hear what was being said in Mortemart's circle, and then set off for a different group where the abbé was holding forth.

Pierre had been educated abroad, and this evening party at Anna Pavlovna's was his first such occasion in Russia. Knowing that all the intelligentsia of Petersburg was gathered here, he was like a child in a toyshop, his eyes darting about everywhere. He was afraid of missing any intellectual talk that might have been his to hear. As he gazed at the assembled company, their faces pictures of refinement and self-confidence, he was expecting to hear something very clever at any moment. Eventually he came over to Morio. The conversation struck him as interesting, so he stood there waiting for a chance to launch forth with his own ideas, as young people are wont to do.

CHAPTER 3

Anna Pavlovna's soirée was now in full swing. On all sides the spindles were humming away non-stop. Apart from the aunt, and her sole companion, an elderly lady with a thin, careworn face, who seemed rather out of place in this brilliant society, the company had split into three groups. The one with most men in it centred around the abbé; another group, of younger people, was dominated by the beautiful Princess Hélène, Prince Vasily's daughter, and the pretty little Princess Bolkonsky, with her blushing features and a figure too full for her young age. Mortemart and Anna Pavlovna formed part of the third group.

The viscount was a pleasant-looking young man with gentle features and manners, obviously full of his own importance, but modest enough, because of his good breeding, to indulge any company that he might find himself in. Anna Pavlovna was clearly showing him off to her guests. Just as a skilful head waiter can pass off as a supreme delicacy a cut of beef that would be inedible if you'd seen it in the filthy kitchen, Anna Pavlovna served up to her guests that evening first the viscount and then the abbé as if they were supreme delicacies. In Mortemart's group the conversation had turned to the execution of the Duke of Enghien.[8] The viscount held that the duke had perished through his own magnanimity, and there were special reasons behind Bonaparte's animosity towards him.

'Oh, I say! Do tell us all about it, Viscount,' said Anna Pavlovna, delighted to feel she had insinuated a touch of Louis XV[9] in the old-fashioned French phrase she had used. The viscount gave a polite bow and a willing smile. Anna Pavlovna brought them into a circle around him and beckoned everyone over to hear his story.

'The viscount was a personal friend of the duke,' she whispered to one of them, and murmured to someone else, 'The viscount is such a good raconteur.' To a third person she said, 'You see – what a man of quality!', and the viscount was presented in the most refined and advantageous light, served up like a joint of beef garnished with salad on a hot platter.

The viscount was preparing to launch forth; his smile was subtle.

'My dear Hélène, do come over here,' said Anna Pavlovna to the gorgeous princess sitting in the very centre of the other group a little way off.

Princess Hélène rose with a smile, the same unchanging beautiful woman's smile with which she had entered the room. With a gentle rustle of her white ballgown trimmed with ivy and moss, with her glistening white shoulders, glossy hair and sparkling diamonds, she moved between the men as they stepped aside to make way for her. Without looking anyone in the face, but beaming at the company in general and apparently bestowing permission for everyone to admire her wonderful figure, her full shoulders and her fashionably exposed bosom and back, she glided up to Anna Pavlovna, and the brilliance of the ballroom seemed to come with her. Hélène was so exquisite that she not only avoided the slightest hint of flirtatiousness, she even seemed to be embarrassed by the all-too-evident, truly devastating beauty that was hers. It was as if she wanted to tone down the effect of her beauty, but couldn't do so.

'What a beautiful woman!' said everyone who saw her. The viscount shrugged and looked down, as if transfixed by a mysterious force, as she arranged herself to sit before him, not sparing him that ever-dazzling smile.

'Madame, I doubt my abilities in front of such an audience,' he said, bowing with a smile.

The princess rested her round, bare arm on a little table and found it unnecessary to say anything. She smiled, and she waited. Sitting up straight throughout the viscount's story, she glanced down occasionally either at her beautiful, round arm so casually draped across the table, or at her still lovelier bosom and the diamond necklace above it that kept needing adjustment. Several times she also adjusted the folds of her gown, and whenever the narrative made a strong impact on the audience she would glance across at Anna Pavlovna in order to imitate whatever expression she could see written on the maid of honour's face before resuming her radiant smile.

The little Princess Bolkonsky had also moved away from the tea table, following Hélène. 'Wait a minute, I must have my work,' she said. 'Come along, what are you thinking about?' she demanded of Prince Hippolyte. 'Please fetch my bag.'

With a smile and a word for everyone, the little princess got the whole group to rearrange itself, and then sat down and settled her skirts.

'Now I'm all right,' she insisted, and took up her work, inviting the viscount to begin. Prince Hippolyte brought her little bag, walked round behind her, moved up a chair and sat down beside her.

The 'charming' Hippolyte bore a close resemblance to his beautiful sister; it was even more remarkable that in spite of the similarity he was a very ugly man. His features were like his sister's, but whereas she glowed with *joie de vivre*, classical beauty and the smiling self-assurance of youth, her brother's face was just the opposite – dim with imbecility, truculent and peevish – and his body was thin and feeble. His eyes, nose and mouth – all his features seemed to twist themselves into in a vague kind of obtuse snarl, while his arms and legs were always in an awkward tangle.

'It's not a ghost story, is it?' he asked, settling down next to the princess and jerking his lorgnette up to his eyes, as if he needed this instrument before he could say anything.

'Why no, my dear fellow,' said the astonished viscount with a shrug.

'It's just that I can't abide ghost stories,' said Prince Hippolyte, his tone implying that he had blurted all this out before realizing what it meant. Because of the self-confidence with which he had spoken, no one could tell whether what he had said was very clever or very stupid. He was dressed in a dark green frock-coat, stockings, light shoes and knee-breeches of a colour he referred to as 'the thigh of a startled nymph'.

The viscount then gave a nice rendition of a story that was doing the rounds. Apparently the Duke of Enghien had driven to Paris for a secret assignation with a young woman, Mlle George, only to run into Bonaparte, who was also enjoying the favours of the same famous actress. On meeting the duke, Napoleon had fallen into one of his fainting fits and had been completely at the duke's mercy. The duke had not taken advantage of this, but Bonaparte had later rewarded his magnanimity by having him put to death.

This was a very charming and interesting story, especially the bit when the rivals suddenly recognized each other, and it seemed to excite the ladies. 'Delightful!' said Anna Pavlovna, with an inquiring glance at the little princess. 'Delightful!' whispered the little princess, stabbing her needle into her sewing to show that the interest and charm of the story were getting in the way of her work. With a grateful smile of appreciation at this silent tribute, the viscount resumed his narrative, but Anna Pavlovna, who never took her eyes off the dreadful young man who was worrying her so much, could hear him holding forth with the abbé too forcefully and too heatedly, so she sped across into the danger zone on a rescue mission. Sure enough, Pierre had managed to get into a political conversation with the abbé about the balance of power, and the abbé, evidently taken by young man's naive passion, was expounding to him his cherished idea. Both men were listening too earnestly and talking too bluntly, and Anna Pavlovna didn't like it.

'You do it by means of the balance of power in Europe and the rights of the people,' the abbé was saying. 'If one powerful state like Russia – despite its reputation for barbarity – were to take a disinterested stand as the head of an alliance aimed at guaranteeing the balance of power in Europe, it would save the world!'

'But how are you going to get such a balance of power?' Pierre was gathering himself to say, but at that moment Anna Pavlovna came across, glowered at Pierre and asked the Italian how he was surviving the local climate. His face changed instantly and assumed the sickly sweet, patronizing air which he obviously reserved for conversations with women. 'I am so enchanted by the delightful wit and culture of the society people – especially the ladies – by whom I have had the good fortune to be received, that I have not yet had time to think about the climate,' he said. Determined not to let go of the abbé and Pierre, Anna Pavlovna steered them into the larger group, where it would be easier to keep an eye on them.

At this point in walked another guest, the young Prince Andrey Bolkonsky, husband of the little princess. He was quite short, but a very handsome young man, with sharp, clear-cut features. Everything about him, from his languid, bored expression to his slow and steady stride, stood in stark contrast to his vivacious little wife. He made it obvious that he knew everybody in the room, and was so fed up with the whole lot that just looking at them and listening to them drove him to distraction. And of all the wearisome faces it was the face of his own pretty wife that seemed to bore him most. With a snarl distorting his handsome face he turned away from her. He kissed Anna Pavlovna's hand, screwed up his eyes and scanned the whole company.

'Are you enlisting for the war, Prince?' said Anna Pavlovna.

'General Kutuzov has been kind enough to want me as an aide,' said Bolkonsky, saying 'Kutuzóv', like a Frenchman, rather than 'Kutúzov'.

'And what about Lise, your wife?'

'She's going into the country.'

'Shame on you, depriving us of your charming wife!'

'*André!*' said his wife, addressing her husband in the flirtatious tone that she normally reserved for other men. 'The viscount has just told us a wonderful story about Mlle George and Bonaparte!'

Prince Andrey scowled and turned away. Pierre had been looking at this man with a joyful, affectionate gaze since the moment he walked in, and now he went over and took him by the arm. Before looking round, Prince Andrey gave a pained look of irritation as he felt the touch, but the moment he saw Pierre's smiling face he smiled back in an unusually sweet and pleasant way.

'It's you! . . . Out in society!' he said to Pierre.

'I knew you'd be here,' answered Pierre. 'I'm coming to dine with you,' he added in a low voice, so as not to interrupt the viscount, who was going on with his story. 'Is that all right?'

'Of course it isn't!' laughed Prince Andrey, but his handshake told Pierre he had no need to ask. He was about to go on, but at that moment Prince Vasily and his daughter stood up and the two young men rose to let them go by.

'Do excuse me, my dear Viscount,' said Prince Vasily to the Frenchman, gently tugging down on his sleeve to persuade him not to get up. 'This confounded reception at the Ambassador's deprives me of a pleasure and interrupts you. I'm so sorry to leave your delightful party,' he said to Anna Pavlovna.

Delicately holding on to the folds of her gown, his daughter, Princess Hélène, moved off between the chairs, and the smile on her gorgeous face was more radiant than ever. Pierre watched this vision of beauty go past, his eyes brimming with rapture and something not far from terror.

'Isn't she lovely?' said Prince Andrey.

'Yes, she is,' said Pierre.

As he went past, Prince Vasily took Pierre by the arm and turned to Anna Pavlovna.

'Can you please train this bear for me?' he said. 'He's been staying with me for a month and this is the first time I've seen him out in society. There's nothing more important for a young man than the company of intelligent women.'

CHAPTER 4

Anna Pavlovna gave a smile and promised to look after Pierre, knowing he was related to Prince Vasily on his father's side. The elderly lady, who earlier on had been sitting by the aunt, got up hurriedly and overtook Prince Vasily in the hall. Her look of pretended interest had vanished, and her kindly, careworn face showed nothing but anxiety and alarm.

'Prince, what can you tell me about my Boris?' she asked, catching up with him in the hall. (She put a peculiar stress on the 'o' in Boris.) 'I can't stay on in Petersburg. Tell me please, what news may I take to my poor boy?'

Although Prince Vasily's reluctance to deal with the elderly lady verged on impoliteness, even impatience, she gave him a sweetly ingratiating smile, and stopped him from going by clutching at his arm.

'It will cost you very little to put in a good word with the Emperor, and he'll be transferred straight into the guards,' she implored.

'Believe me, Princess, I'll do anything I can,' answered Prince Vasily; 'but it's not easy for me to petition the Emperor. I would advise you to see Rumyantsev, through Prince Golitsyn. That would be the more sensible thing to do.'

The elderly lady, Princess Drubetskoy, came from one of Russia's best families, but she was impoverished, she had been too long out of society and by this time she had lost all her old contacts. She had come now to make representations and get her only son into the guards. For this reason alone – to see Prince Vasily – she had invited herself to Anna Pavlovna's party, turned up and sat through the viscount's story. She was shaken by the prince's words; her face with its faded beauty flashed with resentment, but only for a moment. She smiled again and tightened her grip on Prince Vasily's arm.

'Please listen, Prince,' she said. 'I've never asked you to do me a favour, and I never shall do so again. I've never reminded you how close my father was to you. But now, in God's name I beseech you, just do this for my son, and I shall always think of you as a benefactor.' Then, hurriedly, she added, 'Please don't be angry, but do promise. I've already asked Golitsyn, and he said no. Please be the nice gentleman you always used to be.' She did her best to smile, though there were tears in her eyes.

'Papa, we're going to be late,' said Princess Hélène from the doorway, her exquisite head looking back over statuesque shoulders.

But influence in society is capital, which must be carefully conserved so it doesn't run out. Prince Vasily was aware of this, and, realizing that, if he were to petition for everybody who petitioned him, all too soon he would be unable to petition for himself, he rarely made use of his influence. In Princess Drubetskoy's case, however, her new appeal had given him something akin to a qualm of conscience. She had reminded him of the truth: his earliest progress in the service had been due to her father. Beyond that, he could see from her actions that she was one of those women – especially mothers – who, once they get their teeth into something, are not going to let go until they get their own way, and if they don't get their own way they are going to go on pestering every minute of every day, and they might even make a scene. This last consideration gave him pause.

'My dear Anna Mikhaylovna,' he said, as always unceremoniously and with boredom in his voice, 'it is virtually impossible for me to do what you want, but to demonstrate my affection for you, and to honour your late father's memory, I shall achieve the impossible. Your son will be transferred to the guards. Here is my hand on it. Does that satisfy you?'

'My dear Prince, you are our benefactor! I expected nothing less. I knew you were a good man.' He tried to get away. 'Wait a moment. Just one more thing. When he's in the guards . . .' She hesitated. 'You are on good terms with General Kutuzov. Please recommend Boris as one of his aides. Then I can relax, then I . . .'

Prince Vasily smiled. 'That's something I can't promise. You know how besieged Kutuzov has been since he became commander-in-chief. He told me himself that all the ladies in Moscow have got together to offer their children as aides.'

'No, you must promise. I won't take no for an answer. You are such a good, kind benefactor . . .'

'Papa,' said the beautiful Hélène, exactly as before, 'we're going to be late.'

'Well, I must be off. I bid you goodbye. You see how things are.'

'Tomorrow, then, you will speak to the Emperor?'

'Yes indeed, but I can't promise anything about Kutuzov.'

'Oh, *Basile*, you must,' Anna Mikhaylovna called after him, smiling like a young flirt, which might have suited her in days gone by, but now ill became her scrawny face. She had obviously forgotten her age, and habit had told her to let go with all her ancient womanly wiles. But the moment he had gone her face resumed its former cold, affected expression. She went back to the group where the viscount was still holding forth, and again pretended to listen, but now that she had done what she had come to do she was only waiting for a suitable moment to go home.

'And what about this latest farce of a coronation in Milan?' said Anna Pavlovna. 'And that other farce in Genoa and Lucca with the people coming forward and presenting their petitions to Monsieur Buonaparte. Monsieur Buonaparte sits on a throne and grants nations their petitions! How very charming! Oh, it's enough to drive me mad! The whole world seems to have gone off its head.'

Prince Andrey smiled and looked Anna Pavlovna straight in the face.

'This crown is God-given. Woe betide the man who touches it,' he said (Bonaparte's words when the crown was placed on his head). 'They say he looked superb as he spoke those words,' he added, and he repeated the same words in Italian: '*Dio mi la dona, guai a qui la tocca.*'

'I only hope,' Anna Pavlovna went on, 'that at long last this is the straw that breaks the camel's back. Really, the European sovereigns cannot continue to put up with this man. He is a threat to everything.'

'The sovereigns! I am not talking about Russia,' said the viscount, respectful but despairing . . . 'But Madame, the sovereigns! What did they do for Louis XVI, the Queen, Madame Elisabeth? Nothing,' he went on, gathering confidence. 'And believe me, they're being punished now for their betrayal of the Bourbon cause. The European sovereigns! They are sending ambassadors to congratulate the usurper.'

And he gave a scornful sigh as he shifted position. Then, at these words, Prince Hippolyte, who had been studying the viscount through his lorgnette, suddenly turned right round to face the little princess, borrowed a needle from her and used it to scratch an outline of the Condé family coat-of-arms on the tabletop. He began to explain it in some detail as if this was something she had asked for. 'Staff, gules, engrailed with azure gules – the House of Condé,' he said. The princess smiled as she listened.

'If Bonaparte stays on the throne of France for another year,' said the viscount, taking up the thread of the conversation with the air of an informed person pursuing his own train of thought and ignoring everybody else, 'things will have gone too far. After all the plotting and violence, the exiles and executions, society – I mean good, French society – will have been destroyed for ever, and then . . .'

He gave a shrug, and spread his hands. Pierre was about to say something – the conversation fascinated him – but the ever-vigilant Anna Pavlovna intervened.

'Emperor Alexander,' she said with that doleful manner that she always adopted when referring to the royal family, 'has announced that he will leave it to the French people to choose their own form of government. I myself have no doubt the entire nation, once it is delivered from the usurper, will rush to embrace its lawful king,' said Anna Pavlovna, trying to be nice to a royalist émigré.

'That's doubtful,' said Prince Andrey. 'The viscount is right when he says things have gone too far. I think it will be difficult to turn the clock back.'

'From what I hear,' said Pierre, reddening as he got back into the conversation, 'almost all the aristocrats have gone over to Bonaparte.'

'That's what the Bonapartists say,' said the viscount without looking at Pierre. 'It's not easy nowadays to find out what public opinion is in France.'

'That's what Bonaparte said,' observed Prince Andrey with a grin. It was obvious that he didn't like the viscount, and he was directing his remarks at him without looking his way.

' "I have shown them the path to glory, but they wouldn't take it," ' he said after a brief pause, once more quoting Napoleon. '"I have opened my antechambers to them, and the crowds rushed in . . ." I don't know what justification he had for saying that.'

'None at all!' retorted the viscount. 'Since the duke's murder, even his strongest supporters have ceased to regard him as a hero. There may be some people who made a hero of him,' said the viscount, turning to Anna Pavlovna, 'but since the duke's assassination there has been one more martyr in heaven, and one hero less on earth.'

Anna Pavlovna and the others had barely had time to smile in appreciation of the viscount's words when Pierre broke into the conversation again, and although Anna Pavlovna knew in advance he was going to put his foot in it, this time she couldn't stop him.

'The execution of the Duke of Enghien,' said Pierre, 'was a political necessity, and in my opinion it was a measure of Napoleon's true greatness that he didn't baulk at assuming total responsibility for it.'

'Merciful heaven!' Anna Pavlovna intoned in a horrified whisper.

'So Monsieur Pierre! You think murder is the measure of true greatness,' said the little princess, smiling and drawing in her work.

Ohs and ahs came from all sides.

'Capital!' said Prince Hippolyte, using the English word, and he began slapping his knee. The viscount merely shrugged.

Pierre looked solemnly over his spectacles at his audience.

'The reason I say this,' he carried on in some despair, 'is that the Bourbons were running away from the Revolution, leaving the people to anarchy, and Napoleon was the only one capable of understanding the Revolution, and transcending it, and that was why, for the public good, he couldn't baulk at the taking of one man's life.'

'Would you like to come over to this other table?' asked Anna Pavlovna. But Pierre didn't answer; he was in full flow.

'Oh no,' he said, warming to his task, 'Napoleon is great because he towered above the Revolution, he stopped its excesses and he preserved all its benefits – equality, free speech, a free press. That was his only reason for assuming supreme power.'

'Yes, if only he had transferred it to the lawful king once he had obtained power, instead of using it to commit murder,' said the viscount, 'then I might have called him a great man.'

'He couldn't have done that. The people had given him power to get rid of the Bourbons, that was all, and also because they thought he was a great man. The Revolution was a splendid achievement,' Monsieur Pierre insisted, his desperate and challenging pronouncement betraying extreme youth and a desire to blurt everything out at once.

'Revolution and regicide are splendid achievements? ... Well, what-ever next? ... Are you sure you wouldn't like to come over to this table?' repeated Anna Pavlovna.

'Ah, the Social Contract,'[10] said the viscount with a pinched smile. 'I'm not talking about regicide. I'm talking about ideas.'

'Yes, ideas. Robbery, murder, regicide!' an ironical voice put in.

'These were the extremes, of course, but they weren't the meaning of the whole Revolution. That was in human rights, freedom from prejudice, equality ... Those were the strong ideas that Napoleon stood up for.'

'Liberty and equality,' said the viscount contemptuously. He seemed at last to have made up his mind to take this young man seriously and demonstrate how silly his outpourings had been. 'Nothing but loud slogans, long compromised. Which of us does not love liberty and equality? Our Saviour himself preached liberty and equality. Have the people been any happier since the Revolution? Quite the reverse. We wanted liberty, but Bonaparte has destroyed it.'

Prince Andrey smiled at them all, Pierre, viscount and hostess.

Just for a moment following Pierre's outburst Anna Pavlovna had been taken aback, for all her social skills, but when she saw that the viscount was not greatly put out by Pierre's sacrilegious way of speaking, and realized there was no stopping it, she rallied, came in on the viscount's side and attacked the other speaker.

'But my dear Monsieur Pierre,' she said, 'how do you account for a great man being capable of executing a duke, a human being after all, who was innocent and untried?'

'What I should like to ask,' said the viscount, 'is how Monsieur accounts for the 18th Brumaire?[11] That was very underhand, wasn't it? It was a sneaky piece of work, nothing like a great man's way of doing things.'

'And what about all those prisoners that he killed in Africa?'[12] said the little princess. 'That was horrible!' And she gave a shrug.

'He's an upstart, whatever you say,' said Prince Hippolyte.

Not knowing which one to answer, Monsieur Pierre surveyed them all with a smile. His smile was not like theirs – theirs were not real smiles. Whenever he smiled a sudden and immediate change came over his serious, perhaps rather gloomy face, and a very different face appeared, childish, good-natured, a bit on the silly side, half-apologetic. Noticing him for the first time, the viscount realized that this Jacobin[13] was much less formidable than the words he uttered.

For a while no one spoke.

'Is he supposed to answer everybody at once?' asked Prince Andrey.

'Anyway, in the actions of a statesman, you do have to distinguish between how he acts as a private person and what he does as a general or an emperor. That's how it seems to me.'

'Yes, yes, of course,' put in Pierre, delighted that someone had come in on his side.

'You have to admit,' pursued Prince Andrey, 'that Napoleon on the bridge at Arcola was a great man, and also in the hospital at Jaffa when he shook hands with the plague-victims,[14] but . . . well, there are other actions it would be hard to justify.'

Prince Andrey, clearly intent on relieving Pierre's embarrassment, now got up to go, signalling to his wife.

All of a sudden Prince Hippolyte got to his feet and gestured for them all to stop and sit down again. Then he spoke. 'Er, I heard a really good Moscow story today. I must tell you. Begging your pardon, Viscount, it will have to be in Russian, or you won't get the point.' And Prince Hippolyte began speaking in Russian, imitating the kind of speech that Frenchmen achieve after a year or so in Russia. Everyone stopped and paid attention, the prince having insisted so urgently that they should listen to his story.

'Well there was this lady, *une dame*, in Moscow. Very stingy. She had to have two footmen behind her carriage. Very tall footmen. That was her taste. And she had a lady's maid, also very tall. She said . . .' He hesitated, obviously having trouble getting his story together.

'She said . . . Yes, that's it, she said, "You, girl," (to the lady's maid) "put your livery on and get up behind the carriage. We're going out visiting."'

At this point Prince Hippolyte snorted and laughed out loud, running well ahead of his listeners, which created a really bad impression of him as a storyteller. Still, there were plenty of people, including the elderly lady and Anna Pavlovna, who did manage a smile.

'She drove off. Suddenly a strong wind blew up. The girl lost her hat, and her long hair was scattered about all over the place . . .'

Then, unable to contain himself any longer, he burst out laughing, and just managed to say through all the laughter, 'And everybody got to know about it . . .'

And that's all there was to the story. Nobody could understand why he had told it, or why he had insisted on telling it in Russian, and yet Anna Pavlovna and several other people appreciated the genteel diplomacy of Prince Hippolyte in so nicely putting an end to Monsieur Pierre's unpleasant and intemperate outburst. After this story the conversation broke down into chitchat about the last ball and the next one, the theatre, and where and when who would meet whom.

CHAPTER 5

Thanking Anna Pavlovna for a delightful evening, the guests began to go home.

Pierre was ungainly, stout, quite tall and possessed of huge red hands. It was said of him that he had no idea how to enter a drawing-room and was worse still at withdrawing from one, or saying something nice as he left. He was also absent-minded. He stood up now, picked up a general's nicely plumed three-cornered hat instead of his own, and held on to it, pulling at the feathers, until the general asked for it back. But all his absent-mindedness and his inability to enter a drawing-room or talk properly once inside it were redeemed by his expression of good-natured simplicity and modesty. Anna Pavlovna turned to him, forgiving his outburst with Christian humility, nodded and said, 'I hope we shall see you again, but I also hope you will change your ideas, my dear Monsieur Pierre.'

She spoke, but he didn't answer. All he did was bow and show everyone another of his smiles, a smile that simply said, 'Never mind ideas, look what a nice, good-hearted fellow I am.' And everyone, including Anna Pavlovna, couldn't help but agree. Prince Andrey had gone out into the hall, and as he offered his shoulders to the servant ready with his cloak, he listened indifferently to his wife as she chattered with Prince Hippolyte, who had come along with her. Hippolyte stood close to the pregnant little princess who looked so pretty, and stared at her through his lorgnette.

'Go back inside, Annette, you'll catch cold,' said the little princess, taking leave of Anna Pavlovna. 'It is settled, then,' she added quietly.

Anna Pavlovna had managed to have a few words with Liza about the match she was setting up between Anatole and the little princess's sister-in-law.

'I'm relying on you, my dear,' said Anna Pavlovna, no less quietly. 'Write to her and let me know how her father sees things. *Au revoir!*' And she left the hall.

Prince Hippolyte moved in on the little princess and, bending down with his face close to hers, started speaking to her in a half-whisper.

Two servants, one the princess's, the other his own, stood by with shawl and coat waiting for them to finish talking. The French was incomprehensible to them, but the servants' faces suggested for all the world that they did understand what was being said, though they would never show it. The princess, as always, smiled as she talked and laughed when she listened.

'I'm so glad I didn't go to the Ambassador's,' Prince Hippolyte was saying. 'Such a bore . . . This has been a delightful evening, hasn't it? Delightful.'

'They say it will be a very fine ball,' answered the little princess, drawing up her downy little lip. 'All our pretty women will be there.'

'Not all of them. You won't be there,' said Prince Hippolyte, with a happy laugh. He then snatched the shawl from the servant, shoving him out of the way, and began draping it around the little princess. Either from awkwardness or deliberately – no one could have said which – he kept his arms round her for some time after the shawl had been put on, seeming to clasp the young woman in his embrace.

With good grace and still smiling, she wriggled free, turned and glanced at her husband. Prince Andrey's eyes were closed: he seemed to be weary and drowsy.

'Are you ready?' he asked his wife, looking over her head.

Prince Hippolyte hurried into his long coat. It was the last word in fashion, going right down to his heels, and he caught his foot in it as he ran out on to the steps after the princess. A servant was assisting her into the carriage. '*Au revoir*, Princess!' he yelled, his tongue tripping over things just like his legs.

The princess picked up her gown, and took her seat, settling back into the darkness of the carriage while her husband was arranging his sword. Prince Hippolyte pretended to help, but all he did was get in the way.

'If you don't mind, sir,' said Prince Andrey, curtly and pointedly in Russian, to Prince Hippolyte, who was standing in his way.

'I'll see you soon, Pierre,' said the same voice in warm and friendly tones.

The coachman jerked forward, and the carriage rattled off. Prince Hippolyte honked with laughter, as he stood on the steps waiting for the viscount, having promised to drop him off at home.

'Well, my dear fellow, your little princess is very nice, very nice,' said the viscount, as he got into the carriage with Hippolyte. 'Very nice indeed.' He kissed his fingertips. 'And very French.' Hippolyte snorted and laughed.

'And, you know, you are awful with that innocent little way of yours,' went on the viscount. 'I pity the poor husband, that baby officer who fancies himself a prince regent.' Hippolyte honked again, and said through his laughter, 'And you told me that Russian ladies weren't as good as French ladies. You just have to know how to get things going.'

Pierre arrived ahead of the others. Like one of the family he walked straight into Prince Andrey's study, lay down on the sofa as he usually did, and took up the first book that came to hand (Caesar's *Commentaries*).[15] Propped up on one elbow, he opened it in the middle and started to read.

'What have you done to Mademoiselle Scherer? She'll have the vapours,' said Prince Andrey, as he came into the study rubbing his small white hands.

Pierre rolled his massive body so that the sofa creaked, looked at Prince Andrey with an eager smile, and gave an airy wave.

'No, that abbé was very interesting, only he's got things wrong ... The way I see it, eternal peace is possible, but ... oh, I don't know how to put it ... Well, not through the balance of power, anyway ...'

Prince Andrey was obviously not interested in abstract talk like this.

'My dear fellow, you can't always come straight out with what you're thinking. Come on, then. Have you made your mind up? Are you going to be a cavalryman or a diplomat?' asked Prince Andrey, after a short pause.

Pierre sat up on the sofa with his legs tucked under him. 'You won't find it hard to believe I still don't know. I don't fancy either of those jobs.'

'But you'll have to decide, won't you? Your father's waiting.'

At the age of ten Pierre had been sent abroad with an abbé as his tutor, and there he had stayed till he was twenty. When he returned to Moscow, his father had dismissed the tutor and said to the young man, 'Off you go to Petersburg, have a good look round, and decide for yourself. I'll agree to anything. Here is a letter to Prince Vasily and here's some money. Write and tell me everything. I'll give you every assistance.' Pierre had spent the last three months choosing a career and had done nothing. This was the decision that Prince Andrey was talking about. Pierre rubbed his forehead.

'I'm sure he must be a freemason,'[16] he said, thinking of the abbé he had seen at the party.

'That's all nonsense,' said Prince Andrey, stopping him in his tracks. 'Let's get down to business. Have you been to the horse guards?'

'No, I haven't, but listen – I've had one idea I'd like to talk to you about. We're at war with Napoleon. If we were fighting for freedom, I'd understand it, I'd be the first to enlist, but helping England and Austria against the greatest man in the world – that's not right.'

Prince Andrey gave a shrug; it was all he could do in the face of such childish words from Pierre. His manner suggested there was no answer to such absurdities. And indeed it would have been hard to find any answer to this naive question other than the one he gave now. 'If everybody fought for nothing but his own convictions, there wouldn't be any wars,' he said.

'And a good thing too,' said Pierre.

Prince Andrey grinned at him. 'Yes it probably would be a good thing, but it won't ever happen . . .'

'Well, why are you going to war?' asked Pierre.

'Why? I don't know. Because I have to. I'm just going.' He paused. 'I'm going because the life I'm leading here, this life is . . . not to my taste!'

CHAPTER 6

From the next room came the rustling of a woman's dress. Prince Andrey jumped, as if he had just woken up, and his face resumed the expression it had worn in Anna Pavlovna's drawing-room. Pierre lowered his legs from the sofa. In came the princess. She had changed into an informal dress every bit as fresh and elegant as the earlier one. Prince Andrey got to his feet and courteously pushed an easy-chair towards her.

'I often wonder why it is,' she began, as always in French, speedily and fussily settling herself into the chair, 'that Annette never married? You must be very foolish, all you men, not to have married her. Forgive me for saying so, but you really don't know the first thing about women. And Monsieur Pierre, you really are a man for an argument!'

'I've just been arguing with your husband. I can't imagine why he wants to go off to war,' said Pierre to the princess without any of the inhibitions which so often affect the attitude of a young man to a young woman.

The princess reacted sharply – Pierre's words had clearly touched a raw nerve.

'That's what I keep on saying,' she said. 'I can't understand it, I simply can't understand why men can't get by without war. Why is it we women don't want anything to do with it, don't need it? You can be the judge of this. I keep saying to him: here he is, one of uncle's adjutants, a brilliant position to be in. Everybody knows him, everybody admires him. Only the other day at the Apraksins' I heard one lady say, "Is that the famous Prince Andrey?" I swear it's true!' She laughed. 'He gets invited everywhere. He could easily end up in the royal entourage. You know the Emperor has spoken very graciously to him. Annette and I were just saying how easy it would be to arrange. What do you think?'

One glance at Prince Andrey told Pierre his friend didn't like this subject, so he said nothing.

'When are you off?' he asked.

'Oh, please don't talk to me about his going away, not that. I won't have it spoken about,' said the princess in the same tone, all silly and playful, that she had used with Hippolyte at the party, quite out of place within the family circle – and Pierre was almost one of the family. 'Today, when I suddenly thought of all these dear friendships that will have to be broken off . . . Besides, you know what, Andrey?' She flashed a meaningful look at her husband. 'I'm scared! I am scared!' she whispered, with a sudden shudder. Her husband glanced at her as if he was surprised to find someone else in the room other than himself and Pierre, but he questioned her with icy politeness.

'What is it you're scared of, Liza? I don't understand,' he said.

'See how selfish men are, all of them. Every one of them selfish! Just because he fancies it, heaven knows why, he's leaving me, shutting me away all on my own in the country.'

'With my father and my sister, don't forget,' said Prince Andrey quietly.

'I'll still be on my own. *My* friends won't be there . . . And he tells me not to be scared.' Her tone was plaintive now, and her lip curled into a sneer, which made her look anything but happy, rather like a wild animal, squirrel-like and nasty. She said no more, as if it seemed wrong to talk about her pregnancy while Pierre was there, though that was what this was all about.

'I still don't understand what it is you're scared of,' Prince Andrey said deliberately, without taking his eyes off his wife. The princess blushed, and waved her hands in despair.

'No, André, I tell you this: you've changed. You really have . . .'

'The doctor says you shouldn't be late getting to bed,' said Prince Andrey. 'You ought to get some sleep.'

The princess said nothing, but suddenly her tiny, downy lip began to tremble. Prince Andrey got to his feet, gave a shrug and started pacing up and down.

Pierre glanced over his spectacles from one to the other in naive wonderment, squirming as if he too had meant to get up, but had thought better of it.

'I don't care if Monsieur Pierre is here,' said the little princess suddenly, her pretty face contorted into a tearful grimace. 'I've been wanting to ask you, Andrey – why have you changed so much towards me? What have I done to you? You're going off into the army, and you won't listen. Why not?'

'Liza!' Prince Andrey spoke only a single word, but it contained a request, a threat and – clearest of all – an assurance that she would live to regret these words. Nevertheless, she went on hurriedly to say, 'You treat me like an invalid, or a child. I can see it all. You weren't like this six months ago, were you?'

'Liza, I'm asking you to stop,' said Prince Andrey, more meaningfully still.

Pierre had been growing more and more agitated during this conversation, and now he got to his feet and walked over to the princess. Clearly the sight of her weeping was too much for him, and he was on the point of tears himself.

'Please don't be so upset, Princess. I know how it seems to you . . . honestly, I've been through it myself . . . because . . . er, what I mean is . . . No, sorry, you don't want other people . . . Oh, please don't be so upset . . . I must go.'

Prince Andrey caught him by the arm and stopped him.

'No, wait, Pierre. The princess is very kind. She wouldn't want to deprive me of the pleasure of spending an evening with you.'

'No, he's just thinking about himself,' the princess declared, with no attempt to check her bitter tears.

'Liza,' said Prince Andrey sharply, raising his voice to a level that declared his patience to be at an end.

All at once the princess's lovely little face changed its angry squirrel-like expression into a look of fear that made her seem both beautiful and sympathetic. She frowned and glared, directing her lovely eyes at her husband, but her face wore the timid, apologetic look of a dog wagging its drooping tail quickly but without much confidence.

'Oh, good Lord!' murmured the princess, and with one hand holding her gown she walked over to her husband and gave him a kiss on the forehead.

'Goodnight, Liza,' said Prince Andrey, getting up to kiss her hand, politely, as if she was a stranger to him.

The two friends were silent. Neither wished to start a conversation. Pierre kept looking across at Prince Andrey; Prince Andrey rubbed his forehead with a small hand.

'Let's go and have some supper,' he said with a sigh as he got to his feet and went over to the door.

They went into the elegant, newly decorated and richly appointed dining-room. Everything from the dinner napkins to the silver, the china and the glass, bore the special stamp of newness that exists in the households of recently married couples. Half-way through supper Prince Andrey leant on one elbow, and with the air of a man who has something on his mind and has suddenly decided to talk about it he assumed an expression of nervous irritability the like of which Pierre had never seen in his friend before, and began to speak.

'Never, never get married, my dear fellow, that's my advice to you. Don't get married, not until you can say you've done everything possible, and until you have stopped loving your chosen woman, until you can see her clearly – otherwise you will be making a cruel mistake that cannot be put right. Marry when you're old and good for nothing . . . Otherwise everything good and noble in you will be finished. It will all be frittered away over trifles. Yes, yes, yes! Don't look so surprised. If you're expecting some kind of future for yourself, you'll feel every step of the way that everything is closed to you, blocked off, except the drawing-room, where you'll operate on the same level as the court lackey and the fool. Oh, why bother?' He made a vigorous gesture with his arm.

Pierre took off his spectacles, which transformed his face, making it look even more benevolent, and gazed in amazement at his friend.

'My wife,' Prince Andrey went on, 'is a splendid woman. She is one of those rare women with whom you feel your honour is secure, but, my God!, what wouldn't I give now to be an unmarried man! You're the first and only person I have said this to, because I'm close to you.'

As Prince Andrey said this he seemed less than ever like the earlier Bolkonsky who had sat sprawling in Anna Pavlovna's drawing-room screwing up his eyes and forcing French phrases through his teeth. Now every muscle in his thin face was quivering with nervous excitement; his eyes, in which all the fire of life had seemed to have gone out, now shone with a radiant, vivid gleam. Clearly, the more lifeless he might seem at ordinary times, the more energetic he became when he was roused.

'You don't understand why I'm saying this,' he went on. 'Well, this is life itself. You talk about Bonaparte and his career,' he said, though Pierre had not spoken about Bonaparte; 'you talk about Bonaparte, but Bonaparte, when he was working his way step by step straight towards his goal, he was free, he had nothing but his goal to go for and he got there. But you tie yourself to a woman and you'll lose all your freedom, like a convict in fetters. And all the hope and strength there is in you just drags you down and tortures you with regret. Drawing-rooms, gossip, balls, vanity, vacuous nonsense – that's the vicious circle I'm stuck in. I'm off to the war, the greatest war there's ever been, and I know nothing, I'm useless. I'm a nice fellow and I have a sharp tongue,' he went on, 'and at Anna Pavlovna's people listen when I speak. And all these stupid people without whom my wife can't exist, all these women . . . If you only knew what these fine women are, or let's say women in general! My father's right. Selfish, vain, stupid, totally vacuous – that's what women are when they show themselves in their true colours. You see them out in society, you think there might be something there, but no, there's nothing, nothing. Don't get married, my dear fellow, just don't!'

'It seems odd,' said Pierre, 'that *you*, you consider *yourself* a failure and your life ruined. You've got your whole life in front of you, everything. And you . . .'

He did not say what about *you*, but his tone showed how much he admired his friend, and how much he was expecting from him in the future.

'How can he talk like that?' Pierre thought. He regarded Prince Andrey as a model of all the virtues, because he combined in the highest degree all the qualities he himself lacked – they were best summed up in a single concept: will power. Pierre always admired Prince Andrey's ability to get on easily with all sorts of people, his remarkable memory, his wide reading (he had read everything, he knew everything and he could understand something about everything), and most of all his capacity for hard work and learning. If Pierre was sometimes struck by Andrey's inability to dream dreams and philosophize (activities that Pierre was particularly prone to) he saw this not as a defect but as a positive quality.

Even in the very warmest, friendliest and simplest of relationships you need either flattery or praise in the way that you need grease to keep wheels turning.

'I'm yesterday's man,' said Prince Andrey. 'There's no point in talking about me. Let's talk about you,' he said after a short pause, smiling at his own thoughts of consolation. His smile was instantly reflected on Pierre's face.

'Why, what is there to say about me?' said Pierre, his mouth broadening in an easy-going, happy smile. 'What am I? I am a bastard.' And he suddenly blushed to the roots of his hair. Clearly, it cost him a great effort to say this. 'No name, no fortune . . . And really, when all's said and done . . .' But he didn't say really *what*. 'Anyway, I'm free for the time being and I'm doing all right. It's just that I've no idea what to get going on. I wanted to talk things over with you seriously.'

Prince Andrey looked at him with kindly eyes. But as he looked, for all his friendliness and kindness he knew his own superiority.

'I feel close to you because you're the only living person in our social group. You'll be all right. Choose anything; it won't make any difference. You'll always be all right, but there is one thing – stop knocking about with the Kuragins and leading their kind of life. It doesn't suit you, all that riotous living, debauchery and all that stuff . . .'

'Can't be helped, old man,' said Pierre with a shrug. 'Women, my dear fellow, women.'

'I can't see it,' answered Andrey. 'Decent women are all very well, but Kuragin's women, women and wine . . . No, I just can't see it!' Pierre was staying at Prince Vasily Kuragin's, and sharing in the dissipated lifestyle of his son Anatole, the young man whom they were proposing to marry off to Prince Andrey's sister – in order to reform him.

'You know what?' said Pierre, as though a happy thought had suddenly struck him. 'Seriously, I've been thinking that for quite a while now. With this kind of life I can't make any decisions, or think anything through. I've got a permanent headache and no money in my pocket. He's invited me tonight, but I'm not going.'

'Promise me you won't go.'

'I promise.'

It was past one o'clock when Pierre left his friend. On one of those limpid 'white nights' typical of Petersburg in June[17] Pierre got into a hired cab with every intention of going home. But the nearer he got, the more he realized it would be impossible to get to sleep on a night like this, when it was more like evening or morning. You could see right down the empty streets. On the way Pierre remembered that the old gambling school would be meeting at Anatole Kuragin's that night, and it would usually lead on to a drinking session followed by one of Pierre's favourite pastimes.

'It would be nice to go to Kuragin's,' he thought, but then remembered he had promised Prince Andrey he wouldn't go there again.

But, as so often happens with people who might be described as spineless, he felt such a strong urge for one more shot at the old debauchery that he decided to go. And it suddenly occurred to him that his promise wasn't valid anyway because he had already promised Prince Anatole that he would go before promising Andrey that he wouldn't. Then he began to think that all promises like that were relative, they had no definite meaning, especially if you imagined that tomorrow you might be dead or something so strange might happen that there would be no difference between honesty and dishonesty. Pierre was very prone to this kind of speculation which destroyed all his resolutions and intentions. He went to Kuragin's.

He drove up to the front of a mansion near the horse guards' barracks where Anatole lived, went up the well-lit steps and the staircase, and walked in through an open door. There was no one in the vestibule; empty bottles, cloaks and overshoes were scattered about everywhere. The place reeked of drink, and in the distance he could hear people talking and shouting.

They had finished playing cards and supper was over, but the party had not broken up. Pierre threw off his cloak, and went into the first room, where there were some leftovers from supper, and a servant, thinking that no one could see him, was downing half-empty glasses on the side. From the third room came great roars of laughter, the sound of familiar voices shouting, and a bear growling. Eight or nine young men were jostling each other by an open window. Three others were playing with a bear-cub, one of them yanking at its chain and scaring the others with it.

'A hundred on Stevens!' cried one.

'No holding on to the window!' shouted another.

'My money's on Dolokhov!' shouted a third. 'You're my witness, Kuragin.'

'Forget that bear. There's a bet on here.'

'Down in one, or you've lost!' cried a fourth.

'Yakov. Bring us a bottle, Yakov!' shouted Anatole himself, a tall, handsome man, standing in his shirtsleeves in the middle of the group, his fine shirt-front unbuttoned down to mid-chest. 'Hang on, gentlemen. Look who's come – it's old Pierre! Good man!' He had turned towards Pierre.

From the window a blue-eyed man of average height, conspicuously sober amidst the drunken uproar, called out clearly, 'Come on over here. Sort out your bets!' This was Dolokhov, an officer in the Semyonov regiment, a notorious gambler and swaggering madcap, at present living with Anatole. Pierre beamed at the company.

'I don't get it. What's happening?'

'Hang on, he's not drunk. Get him a bottle!' said Anatole. He took a glass from the table and walked over to Pierre.

'First things first. Have a good drink.'

Pierre proceeded to down glass after glass, looking doubtfully at the drunken revellers, who were crowding round the window again, and listening to what they were saying. Anatole kept his glass topped up and told him that Dolokhov had made a bet with an English sailor by the name of Stevens, who was passing through, that he, Dolokhov, could drink a bottle of rum sitting on the third-floor window-sill with his legs dangling outside.

'Come on, finish that bottle,' said Anatole, giving Pierre the last glass, 'or I'm not letting you go!'

'No, I don't want it,' said Pierre, shoving Anatole away, and he went over to the window.

Dolokhov had a grip on the Englishman's arm and he was meticulously explaining the terms of the bet, looking mainly at Anatole and Pierre.

Dolokhov was a man of average height in his mid-twenties, with curly hair and bright blue eyes. Like all infantry officers he wore no moustache, so that his mouth, the most striking thing about him, was fully revealed. The lines of that mouth were very finely curved. The upper lip closed sharply down in the middle wedge-like over the firm lower one, and at the two corners the mouth always worked itself into something like a double smile. All of this, together with the decisive, brazen, shrewd look in his eyes, was so impressive that no one could fail to notice this face. Dolokhov was a man of few resources and no contacts. And yet somehow, despite the fact that Anatole doled out his money in tens of thousands, Dolokhov lived with him and managed to present himself in such a way that Anatole himself and everybody who knew them admired Dolokhov more than Anatole. Dolokhov gambled on everything, and usually won. However much he drank, he always kept a clear head. Both of them, Kuragin and Dolokhov, were currently infamous figures among the fast-and-loose young men of Petersburg.

The bottle of rum was brought. Two servants, clearly flustered and intimidated by shouts and directions issuing from gentlemen on all sides, were in the process of removing the section of the window-frame that prevented anyone sitting on the outer sill. Anatole swaggered across to the window, eager to smash something. He shoved the servants out of the way and pulled at the frame, but it wouldn't give. He broke one of the panes.

'Come on, Hercules, you have a go,' he said, turning to Pierre. Pierre grabbed hold of the cross-piece and heaved, broke the oak frame with a crash and wrenched it out.

'Get the lot out, or they'll think I'm holding on,' said Dolokhov.

'The Englishman's bragging, isn't he? . . . Is everything all right?' said Anatole.

'Yes,' said Pierre, watching Dolokhov go over to the window, bottle in hand. The light of the sky shone in with the merging of dusk and dawn. Dolokhov jumped up on to the window-sill, still holding his bottle. 'Listen!' he shouted, standing there and facing back into the room. Silence fell.

'I bet you,' (he spoke in French so the Englishman could understand what he was saying, and his French wasn't too good) 'I bet you fifty imperials . . . make it a hundred?' he added, turning to the Englishman.

'No, fifty,' said the Englishman.

'All right, fifty it is – that I can drink a whole bottle of rum without taking it away from my lips. I'll drink it sitting outside the window, there,' (he bent down and pointed to the downward-sloping ledge on the outside) 'without holding on to anything . . . Is that it?'

'Yes,' said the Englishman.

Anatole turned to the sailor, took hold of a button on his coat and looked down at him (he was quite short), and went through the terms of the bet once again in English.

'Hang on a minute!' shouted Dolokhov, calling for attention by banging the bottle on the window-sill. 'Hang on, Kuragin. Listen: if anybody else can do it I'll pay him a hundred imperials. All right?' The sailor nodded with no indication of whether he accepted this new bet or not. Anatole hung on to him, and although the sailor nodded to say he fully understood, Anatole kept on translating Dolokhov's words into English. A skinny young life guardsman, who had lost a lot that evening, climbed up on to the window-sill, stuck his head out and looked down.

'Ugh!' he said, staring down at the pavement.

'Atten-shun!' cried Dolokhov, yanking him back in, so that he tripped over his spurs and came tumbling down awkwardly into the room.

Standing the bottle on the sill to keep it within easy reach, Dolokhov climbed slowly and deliberately out through the window and let his legs dangle down outside. Bracing himself with both hands against the sides of the frame, he settled himself, sat down, let go with his hands, shuffled slightly to the right, then to the left, and reached for the bottle. Anatole brought two candles, and put them on the window-ledge, even though it was quite light. Dolokhov's back with his white shirt and his curly head were lit up from both sides. Everybody swarmed round the window, the English sailor at the front. Pierre smiled, and said nothing. One of the party, a bit older than the rest, suddenly pushed his way through with a scared and angry face, and tried to grab at Dolokhov's shirt.

'Gentlemen, this is crazy. He'll get killed,' said this more sensible man.

Anatole stopped him.

'Don't touch him. You'll put him off, and then he will get killed. Eh? What about that?'

Dolokhov looked round, shifting his position, still supporting himself with both hands.

'If anybody tries to get hold of me again,' he said, forcing out his words one by one through tight thin lips, 'I'll chuck him down there . . . Right then!'

Whereupon he turned round again to face the outside, took his hands away, picked up the bottle and put it to his mouth, bent his head back and held his free hand up in the air to balance himself. One of the servants, who had begun clearing up the broken glass, stood transfixed in a stooping posture, his eyes glued on the window and Dolokhov's back. Anatole stood erect, staring. The Englishman winced as he watched from one side. The man who had tried to stop it all had rushed across into a corner and now lay on the sofa facing the wall. Pierre covered his eyes, a feeble, forgotten smile lingered on his lips, and his face was now full of fear and horror. Nobody spoke. Pierre took his hands away from his eyes; there was Dolokhov still sitting in the same position, only his head was bent so far back that the curls on his neck touched his shirt collar, and the hand with the bottle rose higher and higher, trembling with the effort. The bottle was draining nicely, and went higher as it did so, bending the head further back. 'Why is it taking so long?' thought Pierre. More than half an hour seemed to have passed. Suddenly Dolokhov's spine jerked back, and his arm trembled nervously, enough to shift his whole body as he sat on the sloping ledge. He slipped, and his arm and head shook even more violently as he struggled. One hand rose to clutch at the window-sill, but fell back again. Pierre shut his eyes again, and swore he would never open them. Then suddenly he was aware of things beginning to move round about him. He glanced up. There was Dolokhov standing on the window-ledge, his pale face full of delight.

'All gone!'

He tossed the bottle to the Englishman, who caught it neatly. Dolokhov jumped down from the window stinking of rum.

'Well done! Bravo! That's a real bet! You're a right devil, you are!' came the shouts from all sides.

The Englishman took out his purse and counted out the money. Dolokhov stood there frowning and silent. Pierre leapt up on to the window-sill.

'Gentlemen! Anybody betting? I can do that!' he shouted suddenly.

'I don't even need a bet. No, I don't. Tell them to get me a bottle. I'll do it . . . Just get me a bottle . . .'

'Go on! Let him do it!' said Dolokhov with a grin.

'What, are you mad? No one will let you. You get dizzy walking downstairs,' came the various protests.

'I'll drink it. Give me that bottle of rum,' roared Pierre, thumping the table with a deliberate, drunken gesture, and he climbed up into the well of the window. People snatched at his arms, but he was so strong he sent them flying if they came anywhere near.

'No, you'll never talk him out of it like that,' said Anatole. 'Hang on. I know how to fool him . . . Listen, Pierre, I accept your bet, but for tomorrow night. Right now we're all going on to you know where.'

'Right, let's go!' yelled Pierre. 'Let's go! We can take Bruin with us . . .'

And he grabbed the bear, hugged it, lifted it right off the floor and took it waltzing round the room.

CHAPTER 7

Prince Vasily kept the promise he had made to Princess Drubetskoy at Anna Pavlovna's soirée, when she had asked for his help with her only son, Boris. His case had been presented to the Emperor, and though it was not to be regarded as a precedent, he was transferred to the Semyonovsky guards regiment as an ensign. But Boris did not get the post of aide or attaché in Kutuzov's service despite Anna Mikhaylovna's best efforts and entreaties. Shortly after the evening at Anna Pavlovna's, Anna Mikhaylovna returned to Moscow, and went straight to her rich relatives, the Rostovs, with whom she stayed when she was in Moscow. It was with this family that her dear little Boris, who had only recently entered a regiment of the line and was now transferring to the guards, had been brought up since childhood and had lived for many years. The guards had left Petersburg on the 10th of August, and her son, after staying behind in Moscow to get kitted out, was to catch up with them on the road to Radzivilov.

The Rostovs were enjoying a name-day[18] celebration for both mother and younger daughter, their two Natalyas. Since early morning a constant stream of well-wishers in six-horse carriages had been driving to and from Countess Rostov's mansion on Povarsky Street, which was famous throughout Moscow. The countess was sitting in the drawing-room with her lovely elder daughter receiving the many visitors who kept turning up one after another.

A woman of about forty-five with a narrow, rather oriental face, the countess was clearly exhausted from bearing children – she had had twelve. Her slowness of movement and speech, deriving from physical weakness, lent her an air of importance which inspired respect. Princess Anna Mikhaylovna Drubetskoy, as a family member, sat with them assisting in the business of receiving and entertaining the guests. The youngsters were in the back rooms, not feeling obliged to play any part in receiving visitors. The count welcomed the visitors, saw them out and issued dinner invitations to every last one of them.

'I really am most grateful to you, my dear,' he said to every visitor, making no distinctions for persons of higher or lower social standing, 'both for myself and my two dear name-day ladies. Do please come to dinner, or I shall be offended, my dear. I am inviting you most sincerely on behalf of all the family, my dear lady.' These words, always accompanied by exactly the same expression on his round, cheery, clean-shaven face, and the same firm handshake and repeated short bows, were spoken to all without exception or variation. When he had seen one guest out the count would return to some gentleman or lady who was still in the drawing-room. Moving the chairs up, and adopting the manner of a man who knows about life and enjoys it, he would sit down, spread his legs out like a youngster, put his hands on his knees, and rock to and fro with some dignity as he indulged in a little weather-forecasting or dispensed advice about health, some of this in Russian, some of it in very bad but confident French. Then he would get up again, and with the air of a tired man still zealous in the call of duty, he would escort guests to the door, rearranging the grey strands over his bald patch, and again he would issue invitations to dinner. Sometimes on his way back from the vestibule, he would walk through the conservatory and the butler's room and enter a great marble hall, where a table was being set for eighty guests. There he would inspect the waiters bringing in the silver and the china, setting out tables and unfolding damask linen for them; he would summon Dmitry, the young man of quality who acted as his steward and general assistant, and say to him, 'Now then, Mitenka, make sure everything's all right. Yes, yes, you will make sure, won't you?' Then he would take great pleasure in surveying the immense table opened out to its full extent, and add, 'What matters – is the service ... That's the secret ...' And with a sigh of satisfaction off he went again in the direction of the drawing-room.

'Madame Marya Karagin and her daughter!' boomed the countess's huge footman in his deep bass voice at the drawing-room door. The countess thought for a moment, and took a pinch of snuff from a gold snuff-box bearing her husband's portrait.

'I'm worn out with all these callers,' she said. 'Well, this is the last one I'm seeing. Oh, she's so affected. Show her in,' she said in a voice full of sadness, as though she were saying, 'Go on, then, finish me off!'

Into the drawing-room, with skirts rustling, walked a tall, stout, grandiose lady and her round-faced, smiling daughter.

'My dear Countess, it's been such a long time . . . She's been laid up, poor child . . . It was at the Razumovskys' ball . . . and the Countess Apraksin . . . I was so glad . . .' The women's voices could be heard chattering away, interrupting each other and blending in with the sound of dresses rustling and chairs scraping. It was the kind of conversation calculated to last just long enough for the caller to get up at the first pause, skirts again rustling, murmur, 'I'm so delighted . . . Mamma's health . . . and the Countess Apraksin . . .' and walk out again, still rustling, into the vestibule to don cloak or coat and drive away. The conversation dealt with the latest news in town: the illness of the wealthy old Count Bezukhov, who had cut such a dashing figure in Catherine's time,[19] and his illegitimate son, Pierre, who had behaved so badly at one of Anna Pavlovna's soirées. 'I'm so sorry for the poor count,' said the visitor. 'His health has been so poor, and now this nasty business with his son. It'll be the death of him!'

'What's all this?' asked the countess, as if she had no idea what the lady was saying, though she had heard about the cause of Count Bezukhov's distress at least fifteen times already.

'This is what modern education does for you! When he was abroad,' the visitor continued, 'this young man was given a free rein, and now in Petersburg, so they say, he's been doing such terrible things they've had to send him away under police guard.'

'You don't say so!' said the countess.

'He's in with the wrong set,' put in Princess Anna Mikhaylovna. 'He and Prince Vasily's son, and apparently another young man called Dolokhov, have . . . well, heaven knows what dreadful things they've been up to. And they've both paid the price. Dolokhov has been reduced to the ranks, and Bezukhov's son has been banished to Moscow. Anatole Kuragin's father has managed to hush things up for him. But he's been sent away too.'

'Why, what did they do?' asked the countess.

'They're absolute scoundrels, especially Dolokhov,' said the visitor. 'He's the son of Marya Dolokhov, such a respectable lady, you know, but there you are! Just imagine, the three of them somehow got hold of a bear, they put it in a carriage and went off with it to see some actresses. The police rushed in to stop them. They got a police officer, tied him back to back with the bear and dropped the bear into the Moika. The bear swam about with the policeman on his back.'

'That policeman, my dear, what a picture!' cried the count, helpless with laughter.

'Oh, how shocking! Count, this is no laughing matter.' But the ladies couldn't help laughing too.

'They only just managed to save the wretched man,' the visitor went on. 'And that's the clever sort of trick the son of Count Kirill Bezukhov gets up to!' she added. 'And people said he was so well educated and clever. This is what foreign education has done for us. I hope no one will receive him here, in spite of his wealth. They tried to introduce him to me. I refused point-blank. I have daughters.'

'What makes you say this young man is so wealthy?' asked the countess, turning away from the girls, who at once pretended not to be listening. 'All his children are illegitimate. I believe Pierre is also . . . illegitimate.'

The visitor waved her hand. 'He has a score of them, I believe.'

Princess Anna Mikhaylovna intervened, clearly wanting to demonstrate her contacts and her knowledge of society matters. 'I'll tell you what it's all about,' she said in a meaningful half-whisper. 'Count Kirill's reputation is something we all know. He's lost count of how many children he has, but this Pierre has always been his favourite.'

'What a handsome man he was,' said the countess, 'only a year ago! A better-looking man I've never seen.'

'He's very different now,' said Anna Mikhaylovna. 'But what I wanted to say was this,' she went on. 'On his wife's side the direct heir to the whole estate is Prince Vasily, but the father is very fond of Pierre. He took trouble over his education, and he has written a letter to the Emperor . . . so if he dies (he's in such a bad state that it's expected any moment, and Lorrain has come down from Petersburg), nobody knows whether that huge fortune will go to Pierre or Prince Vasily. Forty thousand serfs and millions of roubles. I know it's true – Prince Vasily has told me himself. And Kirill happens to be a third cousin of mine on my mother's side. And he's Boris's godfather too,' she added, apparently attaching no significance to this circumstance.

'Prince Vasily arrived in Moscow yesterday. Some sort of inspection, I was told,' said the visitor.

'Yes, but just between the two of us,' said the princess, 'that's just an excuse. He's really come to see Count Kirill, knowing he's in such a bad way.'

'Well, really, my dear, that was a splendid bit of fun,' said the count, and noticing that the elder visitor was not listening, he turned to the young ladies. 'That policeman. What a picture! I can just see him.'

And acting out the role of a policeman waving his arms, he boomed out his rich bass laughter, his whole body shaking with mirth, as people do after a good meal, and more so after a good drink. 'Oh, please, you must come to dinner with us,' he said.

CHAPTER 8

For a while nobody spoke. The countess was smiling pleasantly at her lady guest without disguising the fact that she would not be greatly put out if she were to get up and go. The visiting daughter was fidgeting with her gown and looking inquiringly at her mother when suddenly they all heard a racket from the next room as several boys and girls ran to the door, bumping into a chair and knocking it over with a bang, and a girl of thirteen dashed in with something tucked into her short muslin frock. She came to a halt in the middle of the room, evidently having misjudged everything, gone too far and burst in on them. And there behind her in the doorway stood a student with a crimson collar on his coat, a young guards officer, a fifteen-year-old girl and a fat little boy with rosy cheeks, dressed in a child's smock.

The count jumped up, swayed a little from one side to the other, held his arms out wide and put them right round the little girl who had run in.

'Here she is!' he cried, laughing. 'A happy name-day, darling!'

'My dear child, there is a time for everything,' said the countess, pretending to be firm. 'You do spoil that child, Ilya,' she added to her husband.

'Good morning, my dear. Many happy returns,' said the visitor. 'What a delightful child!' she added, turning to the mother.

The dark-eyed young girl was not pretty – her mouth was too big – but she was full of life, and with her childish uncovered shoulders and her bodice slipping down from all that running, her curly black hair tossed back, her slender bare arms and little legs in lace-trimmed drawers and open slippers on her feet, she was at that charming age when the girl is no longer a child, and the child is not yet a young girl. She wriggled free from her father, ran across to her mother, ignoring her rebuke, hid her flushed face in her mother's lace veil and laughed.

She was laughing at nothing and she burbled something about her doll, pulling it out from the folds of her frock.

'See? . . . Dolly . . . Mimi . . . You see?' And Natasha found the whole thing irresistibly amusing. She fell upon her mother, and laughed and laughed, so loudly that everybody joined in, even the starchy visitor – they couldn't help it.

'Come on, off you go, you and your little monster!' said her mother, pushing her daughter away and pretending to be annoyed. 'This is my younger daughter,' she said to the visitor. Natasha, looked out from her mother's lace veil for a minute, peeped up at her through tears of laughter, and buried her face again.

The visiting lady, compelled to admire this domestic scene, felt obliged to take some part in it. She turned to Natasha and said, 'Tell me, my dear – who is Mimi? Is she your baby?' Natasha didn't like this patronizing baby-talk from the visiting lady. She stared at her morosely and said nothing.

By now all the younger generation – Boris, the officer, Anna Mikhaylovna's son; Nikolay, the count's eldest son, a student; Sonya, the count's niece, fifteen years old; and little Petya, his younger son – had spread themselves across the drawing-room, and were all too obviously trying to contain within the bounds of decorum the excitement and glee which still showed in their features. Out there in the back rooms where they had been before they had come rushing in, the conversation had obviously been much more fun than the small-talk in here, nothing but scandal, the weather and Countess Apraksin. Once or twice they glanced at each another and could hardly contain their laughter.

The two young men, student and officer, were the same age and had been friends since childhood. Both were good-looking, but in different ways. Boris was a tall, fair-haired youth with fine regular features, a handsome face and a look of composure. Nikolay was a small young man with a shock of hair and an innocent look. His upper lip showed the beginnings of a black moustache, and his whole face expressed energy and enthusiasm. He had blushed as he came into the room, clearly trying to think of something to say and not being able to do so. Boris, by contrast, was immediately at his ease; he talked fluently and amusingly about Mimi, the doll – he had known her as a young girl before her nose got broken, and my, how she had grown up during the five years he had known her, and by the way she had a great crack right across her skull. He said all this and then looked at Natasha. She turned away, glanced at her younger brother, who had screwed up his face and was shaking with suppressed laughter; no longer able to restrain herself, she leapt up and sprinted out of the room as fast as her little legs could go. Boris did not laugh.

'Mama, weren't you about to go too? Do you want the carriage?' he asked, smiling at his mother.

'Yes, do go and tell them to get it ready,' she said with a smile. Boris followed Natasha slowly out through the door. The fat little boy ran angrily after them, apparently annoyed that his busy life had been so rudely interrupted.

CHAPTER 9

The only youngsters left in the drawing-room – apart from the countess's elder daughter, who was four years older than her sister and had assumed grown-up status, and also the young lady visitor – were Nikolay and Sonya, the niece. Sonya was a slim, petite brunette, with gentle eyes shaded by long lashes, a thick black braid of hair double-coiled round her head, with a sallow hue to her face and more so to her neck, and rather skinny bare arms that were sinewy but nicely shaped. There was a smoothness in the way she moved, a gentle suppleness in her little limbs and a kind of wary aloofness that suggested a pretty half-grown kitten that would one day turn into a lovely cat. She seemed to have thought it necessary to get involved in the general conversation if only by smiling, but now, in spite of herself, she found her eyes under their long thick lashes turning to her cousin, who was going off into the army. Her girlish passion bordering on adoration was so obvious that her smile didn't fool anyone; it was clear that the kitten had crouched down only to pounce faster than ever on her cousin and tease him the moment they could get out of the drawing-room like Boris and Natasha.

'Yes, my dear,' said the old count, addressing the visitor and pointing at Nikolay, 'now that his friend Boris has got his commission, because of their friendship he doesn't want to be left behind, so he's giving up university and his poor old father. He's going into the army, my dear. There was a place waiting for him in the Archives, and all that . . . But that's friendship for you, isn't it?'

'They do say war has been declared,' said the visitor.

'They've been saying that for ages,' said the count. 'They'll say it again lots of times before they stop. But that's friendship for you, my dear!' he repeated. 'He's joining the hussars.'

The visitor shook her head, at a loss for words.

'It's nothing to do with friendship,' Nikolay blustered, exploding as if this was a dreadful insult. 'It's not friendship – I just want to be in the army. It's my vocation.'

He turned to look at his cousin and the young lady visitor; they returned his look with a smile of approval.

'Colonel Schubert's dining with us tonight. He's with the Pavlograd hussars. Been here on leave, and he's taking Nikolay back with him. Can't be helped,' said the count, shrugging his shoulders and making a joke out of something that had obviously caused him a lot of distress.

'Papa, I've told you already,' said his son, 'if you really don't want me to go, I'll stay. But I know I'm useless anywhere except in the army. I'm not a diplomat or a civil servant. I'm no good at hiding my feelings,' he said, keeping the flirtatious eye of a handsome young man on Sonya and the young lady.

The kitten, with her eyes glued on him, seemed likely at any second to pounce like a real cat and start teasing him.

'Very well, then,' said the old count. 'Such passion. It's that man Bonaparte. He's turned all their heads. They keep thinking about him rising from little corporal to Emperor. Well, God bless them . . .' he added, not noticing the visitor's smile of amusement.

While their elders began talking about Bonaparte, Julie, Madame Karagin's daughter, turned to young Rostov, and said, 'I missed you at the Arkharovs on Thursday. It was very dull without you,' she said, giving him a sweet smile. Feeling flattered, he smiled his flirtatious young man's smile and moved closer to her. With the equally smiling Julie he started a private conversation, blissfully unaware that his spontaneous smile had pierced a jealous Sonya to the heart; she was left with a forced smile on her blushing face. In mid-conversation he happened to glance at her. Sonya glared back venomously, got to her feet and left the room, scarcely holding back her tears, and still wearing that forced smile. Nikolay's liveliness evaporated. He waited for the first break in the conversation, and went off to find Sonya, his face a picture of dismay.

'Oh, these young people, they do wear their hearts on their sleeves!' said Anna Mikhaylovna, nodding after Nikolay's retreating figure. 'Cousins, cousins, troubles in dozens,' she added.

'Yes,' said the countess, when the ray of sunshine that had come into the room with the young people had vanished, as if she was answering a question that no one had asked but was always on her mind. 'How many trials and tribulations we have to go through in order to enjoy them as they are now! And even now, I'll swear there's more dread than enjoyment. You're always, always afraid for them.

Especially at this age when there are so many dangers both for girls and boys.'

'It all depends on how they were brought up,' said the visitor.

'You're quite right,' the countess went on. 'Up to now, thank God, I've been a good friend to my children and they trust me completely.' The countess was repeating the delusion of so many parents, who imagine their children have no secrets from them. 'I know my daughters will always turn to me as their first confidante, and I know that if Nikolay, with his impulsive nature, gets up to no good (boys will be boys) it won't be anything like those young gentlemen in Petersburg.'

'Yes, they're splendid children, splendid,' agreed the count, who resolved all his thorny problems by finding everything splendid. 'Just imagine! My son a hussar! Still, whatever you want, my dear.'

'Your younger girl is such a nice creature!' said the visitor. 'What a fireball!'

'She's a fireball, all right,' said the count. 'Takes after me. And what a voice! I know she's my daughter, but I'm telling you she's going to be a singer, another Salomoni.[20] We've engaged an Italian to give her lessons.'

'Isn't she too young? They say it damages the voice to train it at that age.'

'Too young? No, she isn't,' said the count. 'Don't forget – our mothers used to get married at twelve or thirteen.'

'Well, she's certainly in love – with your Boris! How about that?' said the countess, smiling gently and looking at Boris's mother. Once again prompted by an idea that was constantly on her mind, she went on, 'If I was too strict with her, you see, if I was to stop her . . . Heaven knows what they might get up to on the quiet,' (she had in mind kissing) 'whereas now I know every word she speaks. Tonight she'll come to me and tell me everything. Perhaps I do spoil her a bit, but, well, I think it's the best thing to do . . . I was strict with the eldest.'

'Yes. I was brought up quite differently,' said the girl in question, the radiant young Countess Vera, with a smile. But, unusually, it was a smile that did nothing for Vera's face; on the contrary she looked unnatural, and therefore unpleasing. She, the elder daughter, was good-looking, quite intelligent, good at her lessons and well brought up; she had a nice voice and she talked good sense. But, it was odd – everybody there, including the visitor and the countess, looked at her in some surprise when she spoke and they were all embarrassed.

'You're always too clever by half with the first ones, trying to do something different,' said the visitor.

'Our sins will out. My dear countess was a bit too clever with Vera,' said the count. 'Never mind, she's turned out splendid all the same,' he added, with a wink of approval in Vera's direction.

The visitors got up and left, accepting the dinner invitation.

'Dreadful manners. I thought they'd never go,' said the countess as she saw them off.

CHAPTER 10

When Natasha came rushing out of the drawing-room, she ran only as far as the conservatory, where she stopped and listened to them still talking in the drawing-room, and she waited for Boris to come out. She soon began to lose patience, stamping her little foot and almost bursting into tears when he didn't come, but then she suddenly heard someone's footsteps, not too relaxed, not too quick, the measured tread of a young man. Natasha nipped between two tubs of flowers and hid.

Boris came to a halt and stood there in the middle of the room, glanced round, flicked a speck of dirt off the sleeve of his uniform and went over to the mirror to examine his handsome face. Natasha kept quiet and peeped out of her hiding-place, wondering what he was going to do. He stood there for a moment before the glass, smiled at himself and walked towards the opposite door. Natasha was just about to call him when she had second thoughts. 'Let him look for me,' she said to herself.

Boris had only just gone when in through the other door came Sonya, all red in the face and mouthing some angry words through her tears. Natasha stopped herself from running out to meet her, and stayed in hiding, as if she was magically invisible, to watch what was going on in the world. She was enjoying an exquisite new pleasure. Sonya was muttering something and glaring round at the drawing-room door. The door opened and out came Nikolay.

'Sonya! What's wrong with you? How could you?' said Nikolay, running up to her.

'It's nothing. Leave me alone!' Sonya was sobbing.

'No, I know what it is.'

'That's all right then. Go back to her.'

'So-o-onya! Just let me speak! Can you really want to torture me – and yourself – over a silly bit of nonsense?' said Nikolay, taking her hand. Sonya left her hand where it was, and stopped crying.

Natasha, holding her breath, as quiet as a mouse, looked out from her hiding-place with gleaming eyes. 'What's next?' she thought.

'Oh, Sonya! You're more than the whole world to me! You're everything,' said Nikolay. 'I'll prove it to you.'

'I don't like it when you talk like that.'

'Well, I won't then. Please forgive me, Sonya.' He pulled her close and kissed her.

'Oh, how nice!' thought Natasha, and when Sonya and Nikolay had gone out of the room she followed them and called for Boris.

'Boris, please come here,' she said with a sly, meaningful look. 'I've got something to tell you. Here, here,' she said, and she led him into the conservatory, to the place where she had been hiding between the tubs. Boris followed, smiling.

'What *something*?' he inquired. She was embarrassed. She looked round, and when she saw the doll she had dropped on to a tub she picked it up.

'Kiss my doll,' she said. Boris looked at her eager face, closely, tenderly, and said nothing. 'You won't? Well, come here then,' she said, plunging further in among the flowers, and she threw the doll away. 'Closer, closer!' she whispered. She grabbed hold of the young officer's cuffs, and her blushing face was a mixture of triumph and alarm.

'Would you like to kiss me?' Her whisper was barely audible, as she peeped up at him coyly, grinning and almost weeping with emotion.

Boris went red in the face. 'You are a funny girl' he managed to say, bending down towards her, redder than ever, but without actually doing anything. He was waiting for the next move. Suddenly she skipped up on to a tub to make herself taller than Boris, flung her slender, bare arms right round his neck, and flicked her hair back with a toss of the head. Then she kissed him right on the lips.

She slipped away between the plant-pots, went round behind the flowers and stood there with her head bowed.

'Natasha,' he said, 'you know I love you, but . . .'

'Are you really in love with me?' Natasha broke in.

'Yes, of course I am, but, please, we mustn't do that again . . . In four years' time . . . Then I shall ask for your hand.'

Natasha thought things over.

'Thirteen, fourteen, fifteen, sixteen,' she said, counting on her tiny little fingers.

'Good. It's all settled then?' And her excited face radiated delight and relief.

'Yes,' said Boris.

'For ever?' said the little girl. 'Till death us do part?' And, taking his arm, with happiness written all over her face she walked quietly beside him into the next room.

CHAPTER 11

The countess was so tired from receiving visitors that she gave orders not to admit any more, and the porter was told just to issue dinner invitations to anyone else who turned up with name-day congratulations. The countess was looking forward to an intimate chat with her childhood friend, Princess Anna Mikhaylovna, whom she had not seen properly since she had arrived from Petersburg. Anna Mikhaylovna, with her pleasant, careworn face, moved closer to the countess in her easy-chair.

'With you I can speak my mind,' said Anna Mikhaylovna. 'We're old friends, and there aren't many of us left! That's why I value your friendship so much.'

Anna Mikhaylovna looked at Vera and paused. The countess pressed her friend's hand.

'Vera,' said the countess to her elder daughter (clearly not the favourite one), 'you don't seem to understand anything. Can't you see you're not wanted now? Go and see your sisters, or something . . .'

The lovely young countess gave a scornful smile, not at all disconcerted.

'If only you had told me, Mama, I would have gone away ages ago,' she said, and went off to her room. But passing by the sitting-room, she noticed two couples arranged symmetrically in front of two windows. She stopped and gave a contemptuous smile. Sonya was sitting close by Nikolay, who was copying out some poetry for her, the first he had ever written. Boris and Natasha were sitting by another window, and they stopped speaking when Vera came in. Sonya and Natasha looked at Vera with guilty, happy faces.

It was amusing and quite touching to see these lovesick little girls, but the sight of them didn't seem to arouse any pleasant feelings in Vera. 'How many times have I asked you,' she said, 'not to take my things? You have rooms of your own.' She took the inkstand away from Nikolay.

'Wait, wait, wait,' he said, dipping his pen in.

'You have no sense of timing,' said Vera. 'Trust you to come rushing into the drawing-room and embarrass everybody.' Despite her being in the right, or perhaps because of that, nobody answered, and the four of them simply looked at one another. She lingered in the room, holding the inkstand. 'And what secrets can you have at your age, Natasha and Boris? And you two! Stupid nonsense!'

'What's it got to do with you, Vera?' said Natasha in their defence, speaking very softly. Today she seemed to be sweeter and nicer than ever to them all.

'Don't be stupid,' said Vera; 'I'm ashamed of you. What kind of secrets . . .'

'Everybody has secrets. We don't interfere with you and Berg,' said Natasha, getting angry.

'I should think not,' said Vera, 'because there is nothing wrong in anything I do. But I shall tell Mama how you behave with Boris.'

'Natalya behaves perfectly well with me,' said Boris. 'I have no complaint.'

'Oh, shut up, Boris, you're such a diplomat.' ('Diplomat' was a catchword with the children, who had given it their own special meaning.) 'I'm fed up with this,' said Natasha, her voice trembling with resentment, 'why does she always pick on me? You'll never understand,' she said to Vera, 'because you've never been in love, you've no heart, you're just a Madame de Genlis'[21] (this nickname, bestowed on Vera by Nikolay, was intended to be very insulting) 'and nothing gives you more pleasure than being nasty to other people. You can flirt with Berg as much as you like,' she said quickly.

'Well, one thing I won't do is go running after a young man in front of visitors . . .'

'Now she's got what she wanted,' Nikolay put in. 'She's said nasty things to everybody, and upset us all. Let's go to the nursery.'

All four rose like a startled flock of birds and left the room.

'You said nasty things to me. I didn't say anything nasty to anybody,' said Vera.

'Madame de Genlis! Madame de Genlis!' cried their laughing voices through the door.

This beautiful girl who had caused so much offence and unpleasantness to them all smiled, and, evidently quite indifferent to what had been said to her, she went over to the mirror and tidied her scarf and hair. One look at her own lovely face and she seemed to grow colder and more composed than ever.

In the drawing-room they were still talking.

'Alas, my dear,' said the countess, 'my path is not strewn with roses either. Do you think I can't see that, the way things are going, our fortune won't last much longer? With him it's the club and being generous to everyone. When we're in the country do you think we get any rest? Theatricals, hunting parties, heaven knows what else. But let's not talk about me. Come on, tell me how you managed it. Annette, you amaze me, the way you go galloping off in your carriage, on your own, at your age, to Moscow, Petersburg, seeing all those ministers and important people, and you certainly know how to get round them. You amaze me. Well, how did you manage it? All this is beyond me.'

'Oh, my dear!' answered Princess Anna Mikhaylovna. 'God willing, you'll never know what it's like to be left a widow, with no one to support you and a son you love to distraction. You just learn how to get by,' she said with some pride. 'My lawsuit has taught me a good deal. If I want to see one of these bigwigs, I send them a note: "Princess X desires to meet Minister Y," and I go myself in a cab two or three times – maybe four or five – until I get what I want. I don't care what people think about me.'

'Well, come on, whom did you talk to about your little Boris?' asked the countess. 'Your boy's a guards officer now, and my little Nikolay's going in as a cadet. We have no one to put a word in for him. But whom did you ask?'

'Prince Vasily. He was so kind. He agreed to everything straightaway, and then he put it to the Emperor,' said Princess Anna Mikhaylovna with some delight, forgetting all the humiliation she had gone through to get what she wanted.

'And how is he, Prince Vasily? Getting on a bit?' inquired the countess. 'I haven't seen him since our theatricals at the Rumyantsevs'. He must have forgotten me by now. He flirted with me, you know.' She smiled at the memory of it.

'He hasn't changed,' answered Anna Mikhaylovna. 'So approachable, so full of generosity. All those honours haven't gone to his head. "I regret that I can do so little for you, my dear Princess," he said, "but do tell me what you want." Yes, he's a splendid man, and he knows that blood's thicker than water. But Natalie, you know how much I love my son. I don't know what I wouldn't do to make him happy. But now my affairs are in such a bad state,' Anna Mikhaylovna went on, lowering her voice with great sadness in her face. 'I'm in the most dreadful situation. My wretched lawsuit is gobbling up everything I have, and it's not getting anywhere. Can you imagine, I literally haven't got a penny to my name, and I have no idea how to get Boris kitted out.' She took out her handkerchief and began to weep. 'I must have five hundred roubles, and all I have is one twenty-five rouble note. I'm in such a desperate situation . . . My only hope now is Count

Kirill Bezukhov. If he won't agree to support his godson – you did know he was Boris's godfather, didn't you? – and give him a small allowance, all my efforts will have been in vain. I shan't be able to kit him out.'

The countess, who could feel her own eyes filling with tears, thought things over but said nothing.

'I often think . . . perhaps it's sinful to do so,' said the princess, 'but I do often think: here he is, Count Kirill, living all alone . . . that huge fortune . . . and what is he living for? Life is a burden to him, and my Boris is only just beginning his life.'

'I'm sure he'll leave something to Boris,' said the countess.

'Heaven knows, my dear! These wealthy grandees are so selfish. Anyway I'm going to see him at once with Boris, and I shall tell him straight. People can think what they want. I really don't care when my son's fate depends on it.' The princess got to her feet. 'It's two o'clock, and you dine at four. I can just get there and back.'

And so, like a Petersburg businesswoman who knows how to manage her time, Anna Mikhaylovna sent for her son, and went out with him into the hall.

'Goodbye, my dear,' she said to the countess, who was seeing her off. 'Wish me luck,' she whispered so her son couldn't hear.

'You're off to see Count Kirill, my dear?' said the count, coming from the dining-room into the hall. 'If he's feeling better, invite Pierre to dine with us. He's been here lots of times. Used to dance with the children. Make sure you invite him, my dear. We'll see what happens, but I think Taras will surpass himself this time. He says Count Orlov[22] has never had a dinner like the one we're having tonight.'

CHAPTER 12

'Boris, my dear,' said Anna Mikhaylovna as Countess Rostov's carriage took them along the straw-covered street and turned into the wide courtyard of Count Kirill Bezukhov's house. 'Boris, my dear,' said the mother, freeing her hand from her old mantle and laying it on her son's hand with a timid caress, 'be affectionate and be attentive. Count Kirill is your godfather, when all's said and done, and your future depends on him. Remember that, my dear, and do be nice to him. You know you can.'

'If I could be sure that anything would come of this other than humiliation . . .' her son began coldly. 'But I did promise, and I'm doing it for your sake.' Despite the fact someone's carriage was standing at the entrance, the porter, studying the mother and son (who had walked straight in unannounced through the glass vestibule between two rows of statues in niches), and eyeing the old mantle suspiciously, asked who they wanted to see, the princesses or the count. On hearing that they wanted the count, he said that his Excellency was worse today and could not receive any visitors.

'We may as well go,' the son said in French.

'My dear, please,' pleaded his mother, touching her son's hand again, as though the contact might either pacify him or rouse him. Boris made no response, other than looking quizzically at his mother, and he didn't take off his overcoat.

'My good man,' said Anna Mikhaylovna to the porter in her sweetest tone, 'I know Count Kirill is very ill . . . that's why I'm here . . . I'm a relative . . . I shall not disturb him, my good man . . . I need only see Prince Vasily Kuragin, and I know he's staying here. Be so good as to announce us.'

The porter scowled, pulled a cord that rang upstairs and turned away.

'Princess Drubetskoy to see Prince Vasily Kuragin,' he called to a footman in knee-breeches, slippers and a swallowtail coat, who had run across the landing and was looking down.

The mother straightened the folds of her dyed silk gown, checked herself in the full-length Venetian mirror on the wall and then walked jauntily up the carpeted staircase in her shabby shoes.

'You did promise, my dear,' she said, turning again to her son and urging him on with a touch on the arm. Eyes down, the son walked on quietly behind her.

They entered a huge room, from which a door led to the apartments assigned to Prince Vasily.

Just as mother and son reached the middle of the room and were about to ask directions from an old footman who had jumped up when they came in, a bronze handle of one of the doors turned, and out came Prince Vasily, dressed in a velvet house jacket with a star on the breast, accompanied by a handsome man with black hair. This was the celebrated Petersburg physician Dr Lorrain.

'It is positive, then?' the prince was saying.

'Prince, *errare humanum est*,'[23] answered the doctor, lisping the Latin words in a French accent.

'Very well, very well . . .'

When he saw Anna Mikhaylovna and her son, Prince Vasily dismissed the doctor with a bow, and came over to meet them, in silence and with a questioning look. The son watched as his mother's eyes switched on an expression of profound sadness, and he gave a slight smile.

'Yes, we meet again, Prince, but in what sad circumstances . . . And how is our dear invalid?' she said, seeming not to notice the frigid, offensive glance that was levelled at her. Nonplussed, Prince Vasily stared at her, then at Boris, with a look of inquiry. Boris bowed politely. Prince Vasily ignored his bow, turned to Anna Mikhaylovna and responded to her question by shaking his head and pursing his lips, all of which suggested little hope for the patient.

'Can it be true?' cried Anna Mikhaylovna 'Oh, this is terrible! It doesn't bear thinking about . . . This is my son,' she added, indicating Boris. 'He wanted to thank you in person.'

Boris made another polite bow.

'Believe me, Prince, a mother's heart will never forget what you have done for us.'

'I am pleased to have been of service, my dear Anna Mikhaylovna,' said Prince Vasily, straightening the frill on his shirt, and exuding in voice and manner here in Moscow (for the benefit of Anna Mikhaylovna, who was under an obligation to him) even more gravitas than at Anna Pavlovna's soirée in St Petersburg.

'Try to do your duty and be a worthy soldier,' he added, turning severely to him. 'I'm so pleased . . . Are you here on leave?' he asked in his offhand way.

'I am awaiting orders, your Excellency, to embark upon my new assignment,' answered Boris, with no sign of resentment at the prince's abrasive tone, nor any desire to get into conversation, but he spoke with such calmness and courtesy that the prince gave him a close look.

'I suppose you're living with your mother?'

'I'm living at Countess Rostov's,' said Boris, not forgetting to add 'your Excellency'.

'That's Ilya Rostov, who married Natalya Shinshin,' said Anna Mikhaylovna.

'Yes, I'm well aware of that,' said Prince Vasily in his dull monotone. 'I've never been able to understand how Natalie Shinshin came to marry that half-licked cub. A completely stupid and ridiculous person. And a gambler, so they say.'

'But a very kind man, Prince,' observed Anna Mikhaylovna, with a persuasive smile, as though she knew full well that Count Rostov deserved these strictures, but begged him not to be too hard on the poor old man.

'What do the doctors say?' asked the princess, after a brief pause, and the expression of profound sadness reappeared on her careworn face.

'There is little hope,' said the prince.

'And I did so want to thank *our uncle* once more for all his many kindnesses to me and to Boris. He is his godson,' she added rather as if this news ought to please Prince Vasily beyond measure.

Prince Vasily thought for a moment and frowned. Anna Mikhaylovna saw he was afraid she might have a rival claim on Count Bezukhov's will, so she hastened to put his mind at ease. 'If it were not for my genuine love and devotion for *Uncle* . . .' she said, uttering the last word casually and yet with some emphasis, 'I know what he's like, so generous and upright, but with only the princesses about him . . . They are so young . . .' She bent forward and added in a whisper: 'Has he performed his last duty,[24] Prince? Those last moments, they are priceless! Things couldn't be worse, it seems. It is absolutely necessary to prepare him, if he is as bad as all that. We women, Prince,' she smiled tenderly, 'always know how to say these things. I really must see him, however painful it may be. But then, I am used to suffering.'

It seemed to dawn on the prince, as it had done at Anna Pavlovna's, that Anna Mikhaylovna was extremely difficult to get rid of.

'Do you not think that such a meeting might be too much for him, my dear Anna Mikhaylovna?' he asked. 'Let's wait till tonight. The doctors think the crisis is due.'

'There can be no question of waiting, Prince, at a time like this. Don't forget, it is a matter of saving his soul. Ah! One's Christian duty is a terrible thing.'

A door from the inner rooms opened, and one of the princesses, the count's niece, entered with a cold and sorrowful face. Her elongated body was strikingly wrong for her short legs.

Prince Vasily turned to her. 'Well, how is he?'

'Still the same. What do you expect with all this noise?' said the princess, inspecting Anna Mikhaylovna, who was not known to her.

'Oh, I didn't recognize you, my dear,' said Anna Mikhaylovna, beaming at her, and she strolled over to the count's niece. 'I've just arrived, and I am at your service to help with the nursing of *my uncle*. I know what you must have gone through,' she added sympathetically, rolling her eyes.

The princess made no reply, didn't even smile, but walked straight off. Anna Mikhaylovna removed her gloves, and, having won this ground, she ensconced herself in an armchair and invited Prince Vasily to sit down beside her.

'Boris!' she said to her son, and she smiled at him. 'I'm going in to see my uncle, the count. You must go and see Pierre, my dear – oh, and don't forget to give him the Rostovs' invitation. They want him to come to dinner. I don't suppose he'll go?' she said to the prince.

'On the contrary,' said the prince, visibly disconcerted. 'I'd be very pleased if you would take that young man off my hands . . . He won't go out anywhere. The count hasn't once asked for him.'

He shrugged. A footman conducted the young man down one staircase and up another to Pierre's apartment.

CHAPTER 13

Pierre had not managed to decide on a career in Petersburg, and had indeed been banished to Moscow for disorderly conduct. The story told about him at Count Rostov's had been true; he had helped to tie the police officer to the bear. He had arrived in Moscow a few days before and was staying, as always, in his father's house. Though he had assumed the story would already be known in Moscow, and the ladies surrounding his father, all of them against him, would take advantage of his visit to make trouble for him with the count, on the day of his arrival he went over to his father's part of the house. He walked into the drawing-room, the princesses' favourite domain, and greeted the ladies, two of whom were doing embroidery, while one read aloud from a book. The eldest, a neat and prim maiden-lady with a long waist – the one who had come out to see Anna Mikhaylovna – was doing the reading. Both of the younger girls were rosy-cheeked and pretty; the only difference between them was that one had a little mole just above her lip which made her look lovelier still. They were both working at their embroidery frames. Pierre was received like a corpse or a plague-victim. The eldest princess stopped reading and stared at him in silence, with a look of alarm. The younger one without the mole assumed precisely the same attitude. The youngest, the one with the mole, who had a delightful sense of humour, bent over her frame to hide her smile, evidently anticipating a very amusing scene. Scarcely able to suppress her laughter, she pulled the wool down and bent over as though the pattern needed sorting out.

'Good morning, cousin,' said Pierre. 'Don't you recognize me?'

'Oh yes, I do, only too well.'

'How is the count? Can I see him?' Pierre asked, awkwardly as always but without any embarrassment.

'The count is suffering both physically and mentally, and you seem to have done your best to add to his mental suffering.'

'Please can I see him?' repeated Pierre.

'Well . . . if you want to kill him, kill him outright, then you can. Olga, do go and see if Uncle's beef-tea is ready. It will soon be time for it,' she added, to demonstrate for Pierre's benefit that they were busy people, busy tending to his father, whereas he seemed to be busy upsetting him.

Olga went out. Pierre stood there for a moment looking at the sisters, then he bowed and said, 'I shall go to my room, then. When I can see him, please tell me.' He went out and behind him he clearly heard the sister with the mole laughing softly.

The next day Prince Vasily had arrived and taken up residence in the count's house. He sent for Pierre and said to him, 'My dear fellow, if you behave here as you did in Petersburg you'll come to a bad end. That's all I have to say to you. The count is very, very ill. You must not go to see him.'

Since then Pierre had not been disturbed by any of them, and he had spent the whole day alone up in his room.

When Boris walked in to see him, Pierre was stalking around his room, stopping now and then at the corners to make menacing gestures at the wall, as though stabbing some invisible enemy with a sword, then he would glower over his spectacles and stride up and down again, mumbling, shrugging and gesticulating.

'England is done for!' he announced, scowling and pointing as if there was someone there. 'Mr Pitt[25] has betrayed the nation and the rights of man, and is therefore condemned to . . .' He never quite managed to pronounce sentence on Pitt – at that moment he was Napoleon, in whose heroic person he had survived a perilous crossing of the Channel and conquered London – because there before him, entering the room, he saw a handsome young officer of solid proportions. Boris halted. Pierre had last seen him as a boy of fourteen, and hadn't the slightest recollection of him. Nevertheless he took him by the arm with his usual ready warm-heartedness, and beamed at him.

'Do you remember who I am?' asked Boris quietly with a pleasant smile. 'I've come with my mother to see the count, but it seems he's not very well.'

'No, he does seem to be quite poorly. People are always bothering him,' answered Pierre, trying to think who this young man could be.

Boris could see that Pierre didn't recognize him, but felt it wasn't for him to make himself known, so he looked him straight in the face, unperturbed.

'Count Rostov wants to invite you to dinner this evening,' he said, after rather a long silence, an awkward one for Pierre.

'Ah, Count Rostov,' began Pierre, delighted. 'You must be his son Ilya. You won't believe it, but I didn't recognize you for a minute. Do you remember how we used to drive out to the Sparrow Hills with Madame Jacquot . . . all those years ago?'

'You are mistaken,' said Boris, deliberately, with a strong and slightly amused smile. 'I'm Boris, the son of Princess Anna Mikhay-lovna Drubetskoy. Count Rostov senior is called Ilya. His son is Nikolay. And I don't know anybody called Madame Jacquot.'

Pierre shook his head and waved his hands as if he was being attacked by a swarm of midges or bees.

'Oh dear, what can I be thinking about? I've got it all wrong. I have so many relatives in Moscow! You're Boris . . . yes. All right then, we've got things straight. Tell me, what do you think of the Boulogne expedition? The English are finished, you know, if Napoleon gets across the Channel. I think an invasion is very possible. I just hope that Villeneuve[26] doesn't mess things up!'

Boris knew nothing at all about the Boulogne expedition, he didn't read the newspapers and this was the first he had heard of Villeneuve. 'Here in Moscow we are more interested in dinner parties and scandal than politics,' he said calmly and with some amusement. 'I don't know anything about that. I just don't think about it. The main thing in Moscow is the gossip,' he went on. 'And at the moment it's all about you and the count.'

Pierre smiled his warm smile, evidently worried that his companion might say something he would come to regret, but Boris spoke distinctly, clearly and sharply, looking Pierre straight in the eyes. 'There's nothing to do in Moscow but gossip,' he went on. 'Everybody's dying to know who the count will leave his fortune to, though he might well outlive the lot of us, and I sincerely hope he does.'

'Yes, it's awful,' Pierre interposed, 'absolutely awful.' Pierre was still worried that this officer might inadvertently touch on something that could prove embarrassing.

'And it must seem to you,' said Boris, flushing slightly, but not changing his voice or his attitude, 'it must seem to you that everybody's thinking of nothing but getting something from him.'

'That's it exactly,' thought Pierre.

'I'd just like to say – to prevent any misunderstanding – that you're very much mistaken if you include me and my mother with all those people. We're very poor, but I – speaking for myself – even if your father is rich, I don't consider myself a relative of his, and neither

I nor my mother would ever ask him for anything, and we wouldn't take anything from him.'

It took Pierre a little time, but at last he understood, and when he did he leapt up from the sofa, reached down and seized Boris by the arm with his usual hastiness and awkwardness, and blushing far more than Boris, began speaking with a mixture of embarrassment and irritation.

'Well, that's strange, isn't it? You don't suppose I . . . I mean, how could anyone think . . . I do know . . .'

But Boris interrupted again. 'I'm glad I've put my cards on the table. Maybe you don't like it. Please forgive me,' he said, trying to put Pierre at his ease instead of being put at his ease by him, 'and I hope I haven't offended you, but I always call a spade a spade. By the way, what shall I tell the Rostovs? You will come to dinner?' And Boris, with a great weight off his mind, having got himself out an awkward situation and put somebody else into one, became perfectly pleasant again.

'No, listen,' said Pierre, regaining his composure, 'you're someone out of the ordinary. What you have just said was good, it was very good. Of course you don't know me, it's ages since we met . . . not since we were children . . . perhaps you expect me to . . . I understand, I quite understand. I wouldn't have done it, I wouldn't have had the strength, but it's splendid. I'm very pleased to have met you. It's funny,' he added, pausing and smiling, 'what you must have expected from me.' He laughed. 'But well. Let's get to know each other better, shall we?' He shook hands with Boris. 'Do you know I haven't seen the count once . . . He hasn't sent for me . . . I'm sorry for him, man to man . . . But what can I do?'

'Anyway, you do think Napoleon will get his army across?' asked Boris with a smile.

Pierre saw that Boris was trying to change the subject, so he launched into an explanation of the Boulogne campaign with all its good points and bad points.

A servant came in to fetch Boris; the princess was ready to leave. Pierre promised to come to dinner to see more of Boris, and gave him a warm handshake, looking affectionately over his spectacles into Boris's face.

When he had gone, Pierre paced the room again for some time, no longer stabbing at an unseen foe, but smiling at the memory of that pleasant, intelligent and confident young man. As so often happens with very young people, especially if they are leading a solitary existence, he felt a strange warmth towards this young man, and made up his mind to become friends with him.

Prince Vasily went to see the princess out. She was holding a handkerchief to her eyes, and her face was tearful.

'This is dreadful, truly dreadful!' she was saying, 'but never mind
the cost, I shall carry out my duty. I'll come for the night. He can't
be left like this. Every minute is precious. I can't see what his nieces
are waiting for. With God's help I shall find a way to prepare him.
Goodbye, Prince, God keep you . . .'

'Goodbye, my kind friend,' answered Prince Vasily, turning away.

'Oh, he's in such a dreadful state!' said the mother to her son, when
they were back in the carriage. 'He hardly knows anyone.'

'I don't understand his attitude to Pierre, Mamma.'

'His will is going to clear that up, my dear. And our fate depends
upon it too . . .'

'But what makes you think he'll leave us anything?'

'Oh, my dear! He's so rich, and we're so poor.'

'That doesn't seem enough reason, Mamma.'

'Oh dear, oh dear, how poorly he is!' cried his mother.

CHAPTER 14

When Anna Mikhaylovna had driven off with her son to Count Kirill
Bezukhov's, Countess Rostov sat there all alone for quite some time,
pressing a handkerchief to her eyes. At last she rang the bell.

'What do you think you're doing, girl?' she said testily to the maid,
who had kept her waiting a few minutes. 'Don't you want to remain
in my service, eh? I can always find you somewhere else to work.'

The countess, grief-stricken by her friend's demeaning poverty, was
not feeling herself, and that always made her say 'you girl!' or 'you
there!' to the servants.

'I'm sorry, madam,' said the maid.

'Ask the count to come to me.'

The count came waddling in to see his wife, looking very shifty,
as always.

'Listen, my little countess! What a sauté we're going to have, my
dear – woodcocks in Madeira! I've just tried it. Good job I gave a
thousand roubles to get Taras.[27] Worth every penny!'

He sat down by his wife, jauntily splaying his elbows on his knees,
and ruffling his grey hair. 'What is your command, little countess?'

'It's this, my dear . . . What's this stain on you here?' she said,
pointing to his waistcoat. 'Oh, it must be the sauté,' she added, with

a smile. 'It's this, my dear – I need some money.' Her face took on a gloomy aspect.

'Oh, my little countess!' And the count rummaged for his pocketbook.

'I need rather a lot, Count – five hundred roubles.' She took out her cambric handkerchief and rubbed her husband's waistcoat with it.

'It won't take me a minute. Hey, you there!' he shouted, as men do when they know for certain that someone will come running. 'Get Mitenka for me!'

Mitenka, the young man of good birth who had been brought up in the count's house and now ran all his business affairs, stepped softly into the room.

'There you are, my dear boy,' said the count to the respectful young man as he approached. 'Go and get me,' – he thought a moment – 'let's say, seven hundred roubles. Yes. And none of your torn and dirty notes like last time. Get me some nice ones now, for the countess.'

'Yes, Mitenka, do make sure they're nice and clean, please,' said the countess with a gloomy sigh.

'Your Excellency, when do you want them delivered?' said Mitenka. 'Sir, you must realize ... But don't worry, sir,' he added, noticing that the count was beginning to breathe rapidly and deeply – always a sign of approaching anger. 'I was forgetting ... Do you require them immediately?'

'Yes, yes, I do. Just get them and give them to the countess.'

'That Mitenka, he's worth his weight in gold,' smiled the count, when the young man had gone out. 'Never says it can't be done. I can't abide that sort of thing. Anything's possible.'

'Oh, my dear count, money, money, money – how much trouble it causes in this world!' said the countess. 'But I do need it very much.'

'My sweet little countess, everybody knows you're a shocking spendthrift,' said the count, who then kissed his wife's hand and went back to his own room.

When Anna Mikhaylovna returned from the Bezukhovs the countess had the money ready under a handkerchief on her little table, all in crisp new notes. Anna Mikhaylovna could see something was worrying her.

'Well, how did you get on, my dear?' asked the countess.

'Oh, he's in a dreadful state! Unrecognizable. He's so ill, so ill ... I was only there for a minute, and I hardly said a thing.'

'Annette, for heaven's sake, please don't refuse,' the countess blurted out with a blush which looked rather odd on her ageing, thin, aristocratic face as she produced the money from under the cloth. Immediately understanding, Anna Mikhaylovna leant forward, ready to embrace when the moment came.

'This is for Boris, from me, to get him kitted out . . .'

Anna Mikhaylovna's arms were round her. She was weeping, and the countess wept too. They wept for their friendship, their kind-heartedness and the unfortunate need for lifelong friends to soil their hands with anything as sordid as money, and they wept also for their lost youth . . . But the tears of both women were sweet . . .

CHAPTER 15

Countess Rostov was sitting in the drawing-room with her daughters and a large number of guests. The count had taken the gentlemen into his study to show them his special collection of Turkish pipes. Now and then he would venture forth to inquire whether or not 'she' had arrived. They were waiting for Marya Dmitriyevna Akhrosimov, known in society as 'the dreaded dragon' and celebrated not for wealth or rank, but for her sharp wit and plain speaking. She hobnobbed with royalty, and was known throughout Moscow and Petersburg; in both cities people may have marvelled at her, laughed at her coarse behaviour behind her back and told many a story about her, but she was feared and respected by every last one of them.

In the count's smoke-filled room there was talk of the war, which had just been declared in a manifesto, and of recruitment. As yet, no one had read the manifesto, but everybody knew it had been issued. The count was sitting on a pouffe with a guest smoking and talking on either hand. He himself was neither smoking nor talking, but, as he turned his head from side to side, he watched those who were with obvious enjoyment, following the argument between his two neighbours that he had steered them into.

One of them was a civilian with a thin, wrinkled, sallow, clean-shaven face, getting on in years but still dressed like the most fashionable young man. He sat with his feet up on the pouffe, making himself at home, and with an amber mouthpiece thrust deeply into the side of his mouth, he sucked up the smoke intermittently, screwing up his eyes. This was Shinshin, an old bachelor cousin of the countess, famed in the drawing-rooms of Moscow for his acid tongue. He seemed to be patronizing his companion, a fresh-faced, rosy-cheeked guards officer, impeccably washed, groomed and buttoned, who held his pipe in the middle of his mouth, sucked up a little smoke and let it coil out through his pink lips. This was Lieutenant Berg, an officer in the Semyonovsky regiment, which he was about to join with Boris, the person Natasha had teasingly identified as Vera's intended. The count sat between them, all ears. His favourite occupation, apart from playing boston,[28] a game he really loved, was listening to conversations, especially when he could get a good argument going between two talkative guests.

'So, my dear chap, *mon très honorable* Alphonse Karlych,' said Shinshin with a sarcastic smile, indulging his own speciality, which was to combine the raciest Russian with the most elegant French, 'you're expecting to get one income from the state, and another from your company, are you?'

'No, sir, I only want to show that cavalry service brings few advantages when you compare it with the infantry. Take my own situation, for instance, Pyotr Nikolaich.' As a talker Berg was always precise, calm and polite. He had only one topic of conversation – himself. He always maintained an aloof silence when any subject was broached that did not directly concern him. And he could keep quiet like this for hours on end, without the slightest embarrassment to himself or anyone else. But the moment a conversation touched him personally, he would launch forth expansively and with obvious pleasure.

'Take my situation, Pyotr Nikolaich. If I were in the cavalry, I would get two hundred roubles every four months at the most, even at the rank of lieutenant, whereas now I get two hundred and thirty,' he explained with a gleeful, friendly smile, looking at Shinshin and the count as though his personal success would obviously and always be the one thing everyone else would wish to advance. 'And another thing, Pyotr Nikolaich – by transferring to the guards, I shall stand out,' Berg persisted, 'and there are many more vacancies in the foot guards. And just imagine how much better off I'll be on two hundred and thirty roubles. I'll be able to save and send something home to my father.' He released a smoke-ring.

'There is a balance in all things. A German knows how to skin a flint, as the Russian proverb says,' said Shinshin, switching his pipe to the other side of his mouth and winking at the count.

The count roared with laughter. Other guests, seeing that Shinshin was in charge of the conversation, came over to listen. Oblivious to any ridicule or indifference, Berg rambled on about his transfer to the guards and how he was now one step ahead of his old army colleagues, how easily a company commander could get killed in wartime, and he would be next in line and might easily become a commander, and how popular he was with everyone in the regiment, and how pleased his father was with him . . . Berg was revelling in all of this, and it never seemed to occur to him that other people might have their own interests too. But everything he said was so pleasant, he was so old beyond his years and his youthful egoism seemed so open and ingenuous that his listeners were all disarmed.

'Well, my dear chap, infantry or cavalry, you'll always get on. That's my prediction,' said Shinshin, patting him on the shoulder, and taking his feet down from the pouffe. Berg beamed with pleasure. The count and all his guests then trooped out into the drawing-room.

It was that time just before a formal dinner when the assembled guests do not get involved in lengthy conversations, because they are expecting a summons to hors d'œuvres in the dining-room, while at the same time they feel they ought to keep moving about and saying something, to show that they are not over-anxious to get to the table. Host and hostess keep glancing at the doors and occasionally at one another. The visitors try to guess from these glances who or what may be holding things up – some important relative late in arriving, or some dish not yet ready?

Pierre had arrived just in time for dinner, and was sprawling awkwardly in mid-drawing-room in the first chair he had come across, thus blocking everyone's way. The countess tried to get him talking, but he stared round naively through his spectacles as though he were looking for someone, and answered all her questions in monosyllables. He was an embarrassment, and only he was unaware of it. Most of the guests, knowing the bear story, looked curiously at this great big, stout, inoffensive person, at a loss to think how such a bumbling, unassuming young man could ever have played such a prank on a policeman.

'When did you arrive, just recently?' the countess asked him.

'Yes, madame.'

'I don't suppose you've seen my husband.'

'No, madame.' He smiled – just the wrong thing to do.

'I believe you were in Paris until recently? Very interesting, I imagine.'

'Yes.'

The countess exchanged glances with Anna Mikhaylovna, who saw that she was being asked to take the young man under her wing, so she sat down next to him and began talking about his father. Again he responded in monosyllables. The other guests were busy chatting amongst themselves. 'The Razumovskys . . . It was so charming . . . You're too kind . . . Countess Apraksin . . .' – the conversation came from all sides. The countess got up and went into the reception hall. 'Marya Dmitriyevna?' she could be heard asking from there.

'The very same,' a rough woman's voice was heard to reply, and Marya Dmitriyevna walked into the room. All the girls and even the ladies, except the very old ones, got to their feet. Marya Dmitriyevna paused in the doorway and drew herself up to her full height. A plump woman of fifty or so, she held her head high with all its grey curls, contemplated the guests and then carefully arranged the wide sleeves of her gown as though rolling them up for action. Marya Dmitriyevna always used Russian.

'Greetings to the name-day lady and her children,' she boomed in her deep voice that drowned all other sounds. 'Now, you old sinner,' she went on, turning to the count who was kissing her hand, 'I imagine you're tired of Moscow – nowhere to run the dogs? Well, sir, there's not much you can do. These fledglings will soon be grown up . . .' She pointed to the girls. 'Like it or not, you'll have to find husbands for them.'

'Now, my little Cossack,²⁹ what about you?' she said – Marya Dmitriyevna always called Natasha a Cossack – stroking Natasha's arm, as the girl came forward to kiss her hand cheerfully and without a trace of shyness. 'I know you're a little pest, but I like you all the same.'

From her huge reticule she extracted some teardrop amber ear-rings and gave them to Natasha, who grinned at her, flushed with pleasure on the day of her party. Then she turned away abruptly and directed her attention to Pierre.

'Hey you, my friend! Come over here!' she said, lowering and refining her voice with some affectation. 'Come over here, sir!' And, ominously, she rolled her sleeves up even higher.

Pierre approached, looking at her ingenuously over his spectacles.

'Come a bit nearer, sir! I was the only one who told your father the truth when he was in high favour, and it's my Christian duty to do the same for you.' She paused. An expectant hush fell on the room: what would happen next? Surely this was only a prelude. 'A fine young man, and no mistake. A truly fine young man! . . . His father's on his deathbed, and he's off enjoying himself, getting a policeman to ride on a bear! Shame on you, sir, real shame! You should have gone to the war.'

She turned away and gave her hand to the count, who could hardly contain his laughter.

'Well, shall we sit down? I think dinner must be ready,' said Marya Dmitriyevna. The count led the way with her, followed by the countess alongside a colonel of the hussars, a man worth cultivating, since Nikolay was due to travel with him to join his regiment; then came Anna Mikhaylovna with Shinshin. Berg gave his arm to Vera, and a smiling Julie Karagin walked in with Nikolay. After them came a string of other couples, stretching all round the hall, and right at the end the children were tagged on with their tutors and governesses, trooping in one by one. The waiters stirred themselves, chairs scraped, the band struck up in the gallery and the guests took their places. The music provided by the household band soon gave way to the clatter of knives and forks, the buzz of conversation, and the gentle tread of waiters. The countess presided over the lady guests at one end of the table, with Marya Dmitryevna on her right and Anna Mikhaylovna on her left. At the other end sat the count and all the male guests, with the colonel of hussars on his left and Shinshin on his right. Midway down the huge table sat the grown-up youngsters, Vera beside Berg, Pierre beside Boris. Opposite them were the younger children with their tutors and governesses. The count peeped over the glittering glassware, the decanters and fruit-dishes, looking at his wife with her tall cap and its blue ribbons, and generously poured out wine for his neighbours, not forgetting himself. The countess, too, while attending properly to her duties as hostess, cast meaningful glances over the pineapples at her spouse, whose face and bald head, she noticed, stood out with a brighter than normal redness against his grey hair. A steady babble of chatter flowed from the ladies' end, but at the other end of the table the men's voices grew louder and louder, especially that of the colonel of hussars as he reddened so much with all his eating and drinking that the count held him up as an example to the others. Berg was telling Vera with a tender smile that love was not an earthly emotion but a heavenly one. Boris was telling his new friend Pierre the names of the guests at table, all the time exchanging glances with Natasha sitting opposite. Saying very little, Pierre looked round at all the new faces and ate a great deal. Faced with the choice of two soups he went for the turtle, and then straight on to the fish-pasties and the game, without missing a single dish, or any of the wines offered by the butler, who would solemnly thrust a bottle wrapped in a napkin over his neighbour's shoulder, murmuring, 'Dry Madeira', 'Hungarian', or 'Rhine wine'. Pierre would simply lift up a goblet chosen at random from the four crystal glasses engraved with the count's monogram that were set at each place, and he drank with great pleasure, surveying the guests with mounting benevolence. Natasha, sitting opposite, gazed at Boris as girls of thirteen gaze at a boy they have just kissed for the first time, and with whom they are in love.

Sometimes this same gaze found its way to Pierre, and the look on that excited little girl's amused face made him feel like laughing too, though he couldn't have said why.

Nikolay was sitting well away from Sonya, next to Julie Karagin, and he was talking to her with the same spontaneous smile. Sonya too wore a façade of a smile, but she was visibly tormented with jealousy, her face alternating between deathly pallor and bright crimson as she strained every nerve to catch what Nikolay and Julie were saying to each other. The governess kept looking round uneasily, as though preparing to defend the children against any possible offence. The German tutor was trying to memorize all the various courses, desserts, and wines, in order to write a detailed description of them to his people back home in Germany, and he was most annoyed when the butler with the bottle in the napkin missed him out. The German scowled, making out that he hadn't wanted that particular wine, but what really annoyed him was the general failure to understand that he had wanted the wine not because he was thirsty or greedy, but out of blameless curiosity.

CHAPTER 16

At the men's end of the table the conversation was becoming more and more animated. The colonel told them that war had been declared through a manifesto issued in Petersburg and that he had seen with his own eyes a copy sent by courier to the commander-in-chief.

'But why the devil should we fight Bonaparte?' said Shinshin. 'He's already brought Austria down a peg or two. I'm afraid it could be our turn next.'

The colonel was a stout, tall and florid-faced German, evidently a keen officer and good Russian patriot. He resented Shinshin's words.

'Ze reason vy, my goot sir,' he said, in his German accent, 'eez just zat ze Emperor knows zis too. In ze proclamation he says zat he cannot stend beck and vatch ze danger treating Russia, and zat ze security of ze empire, its dignity, and ze sacredness of its *alliances* . . .' He emphasized the word 'alliances', as if this was what really mattered. And with his typically impeccable memory for bureaucratic detail, he was able to quote verbatim from the Introduction to the proclamation:

'. . . and the desire, constituting the sole and immutable aim of the Sovereign, to establish peace in Europe on a firm foundation, has determined him this day to dispatch a section of the army abroad, and to renew every effort towards the achievement of that purpose.'

'Zis is ze reason vy, my dear sir.' He finished his little homily by tossing off a glass of wine and looking to the count for encouragement.

'Do you know the saying, "Stay, Jerome, do not roam, there is work to do at home"?' said Shinshin, smiling through his frown. 'That suits us down to the ground. Look at Suvorov,[30] even he was chopped into little pieces, and where will you find any Suvorovs today? I ask you,' he said, going in and out of Russian and French as he spoke.

'Ve must fight to ze last trop of our ploot,' said the colonel, thumping the table, 'and die for our Emperor, and zen all vill be vell. And sink about sings as leedle as possible,' he concluded, turning again to the count, and drawing out the word 'po-ossible'. 'Zat ees how ve old zoldiers see it, and zat ees all zere ees to see. You are a younk man and a younk zoldier – how do you see it?' he added, addressing Nikolay, who had abandoned his conversation with Julie once the subject of war had cropped up, and was now all eyes and all ears on the colonel.

'I'm in total agreement,' Nikolay spluttered, turning his plate around and shifting his wine glasses with desperate determination, almost as if he was in dire danger at that very moment. 'It is my conviction that the Russians must win, or die in the attempt,' he said. The moment the words were out of his mouth he realized as everyone else did that they had been a little too fervent and bombastic for this occasion, and therefore slightly embarrassing.

'That was a very fine thing, what you've just said,' gushed Julie, sitting beside him. Sonya had trembled all over while Nikolay was speaking and blushed to the roots of her hair, and the colour flooded past her ears and down her neck and shoulders. But Pierre had been listening to the colonel's remarks, and he nodded his approval.

'Yes, splendid,' was his comment.

'You're a true zoldier, younk fellow,' the colonel shouted, thumping the table again.

'Why are you making all that noise?' Marya Dmitriyevna's deep voice rang down the table. 'Why do you keep banging on the table?' she asked the colonel. 'What's all the noise about? You haven't got the French here, you know!'

'I spik ze truce,' came the smiling reply.

'It's war talk,' the count shouted across the table. 'My son's going, Marya Dmitriyevna. He's off soon.'

'I have four sons in the army, but I don't go on about it. We're all in God's hands. One man can die in his bed over the stove while God spares another in battle,' the deep voice boomed back effortlessly from the far end of the table.

'That is true.'

And the conversation split in two again, one at the ladies' end and the other at the men's.

'You're not going to ask, are you?' said her little brother to Natasha. 'Go on, I dare you!'

'Oh yes I am,' answered Natasha. Her face suddenly glowed with a comical sense of desperate determination. She half-rose, her eyes darting across to Pierre sitting opposite, inviting him to listen, and turned to her mother.

'Mama!' she sang out down the table in her girlish contralto.

'What do you want?' the countess asked in some alarm. But when she saw from her daughter's face that she was playing up she waved her hand at her with a forbidding look and an ominous shake of her head.

The conversation died down.

'Mama! What's for dessert?' Natasha's tiny voice rang out more insistently. She would not stop.

The countess couldn't quite manage a frown, but Marya Dmitriyevna shook a fat finger and said threateningly, 'Cossack!'

Most of the guests looked at the parents, wondering what to make of this little outburst.

'Watch what you're saying!' said the countess.

'Mama! What *is* for dessert?' Natasha called out cheerily, with deliberate impertinence, sure that her little frolic wouldn't be taken amiss. Sonya and fat little Petya were doubled up, giggling.

'See, I did,' Natasha whispered to her little brother and to Pierre as she gave him another glance.

'Ices, but you're not having any,' said Marya Dmitriyevna. Natasha could see there was nothing to be afraid of, not even Marya Dmitriyevna.

'Marya Dmitriyevna! What kind of ices? I don't like ice-cream.'

'Carrot ices.'

'No, but what kind, Marya Dmitriyevna, what kind?' she almost shrieked. 'I want to know.' Marya Dmitriyevna and the countess burst out laughing, and so did all the guests. They were not laughing at Marya Dmitriyevna's answer but at the unheard-of cheekiness of a clever little girl, who had the daring and the wit to take on Marya Dmitriyevna.

Natasha gave up only when she had been told it would be pineapple ice-cream. Before that course, more champagne was served. The band struck up again, the count kissed his little countess, and the guests began to get up from the table, thanking the countess and clinking glasses across the table with the count, the children and each other. Once more the waiters scurried around, chairs scraped and the guests filed out in the same order as before but with much redder faces, some to the drawing-room and others to the count's study.

CHAPTER 17

Card-tables were set up and partners arranged for boston and the count's guests proceeded to one of the two drawing-rooms, the sitting-room or the library.

As he fanned out his cards the count found it hard to keep awake – he usually had a nap after dinner – and this made him prone to laugh at anything. The young people, at the countess's instigation, gathered round the clavichord and harp. Julie went first by common request, performing a short theme and variations on the harp. Then she joined the other young ladies in inviting Natasha and Nikolay to sing; they were known for their musical ability. Natasha was being treated by everyone as an adult, which made her feel proud but also rather shy.

'What shall we sing?' she asked.

' "The Spring",'[31] answered Nikolay.

'Come on then, quick! Over here Boris,' said Natasha. 'Where's Sonya gone?' She looked around, saw that her companion was not in the room and ran out to find her.

She raced up to Sonya's room, but her friend wasn't there, so Natasha ran to the nursery – she wasn't there either. Natasha knew she must be out in the corridor sitting on the chest. That chest in the corridor was a place of sorrow for the females of the younger genera-tion of the house of Rostov. Yes, there she was face-down on the chest, squashing her filmy pink party-dress on their old nanny's dirty, striped feather mattress. Her face was buried in her tiny fingers, and her bare little shoulders were convulsed with sobbing. Natasha's face, glowing from the day's excitement, changed at once; her eyes narrowed, her broad neck quivered and her mouth turned down at the corners.

'Sonya! What's wrong? What's happened? Oo-oo-oo!'

And Natasha, with her large mouth gaping, which made her look quite ugly, howled like a baby, for no reason, just because Sonya was crying. Sonya tried to look up, tried to answer, but she couldn't, and she buried her face deeper than ever. Still crying, Natasha sat down on the dark-blue mattress and hugged her friend. With a big effort, Sonya struggled half-way up, wiped tears away and began to talk: 'Nikolay's going away next week, his . . . papers . . . have come . . . he told me himself . . . I ought not to cry . . .' (she showed Natasha the sheet of paper she was holding in her hand – poetry written by Nikolay), 'I know I ought not to cry, but you just can't . . . no one can understand . . . he's got such a lovely . . . soul.'

And she burst into floods of tears again at the thought of how lovely his soul was.

'It's all right for you . . . I'm not jealous . . . I love you and Boris too,' she said, pulling herself together a little. 'He's so nice . . . there's nothing to stop you. But Nikolay's my cousin[32] . . . it would take . . . the Archbishop . . . and they won't . . . So, if anyone tells Mamma,' (Sonya looked on the countess as a mother and called her Mamma) 'she'll just say I'm ruining Nikolay's career, I'm heartless and ungrateful, but really . . . I swear to God' (she made the sign of the cross) 'that I do love her, I love all of you – except Vera . . . What's wrong with her? What have I done to her? I really am grateful to you, I'd sacrifice anything for you, but there's nothing for me to . . .'

Sonya broke down again and buried her head in her hands and the mattress. Natasha was beginning to calm down, and her face showed that she grasped the full significance of her friend's distress.

'Sonya!' she snapped. She seemed to have guessed the real reason for her cousin's misery. 'Has Vera been talking to you since dinner? She has, hasn't she?'

'Yes, it's these poems that Nikolay wrote himself, and I copied out some other poetry, and she found it all on my table, and said she'd show it to Mamma, and she said I was an ungrateful girl, and Mamma would never let him marry me, and he was going to marry Julie. And you've seen him all day with her . . . Oh, Natasha, why?'

And again she burst into tears, more bitter than ever. Natasha pulled her up, gave her a hug and started to comfort her, smiling through her own tears.

'Sonya, you mustn't believe her, darling, you really mustn't. Do you remember us talking together in the sitting-room, the three of us, you, me and Nikolay? You remember – after supper. We worked everything out for the future. I can't quite remember how, but, you remember, everything was going to be all right and nothing would be impossible. Listen, Uncle Shinshin's brother is married to his cousin, and we're only *second* cousins. And Boris said it's definitely possible. You know I told him everything. He's so clever and so good,' said Natasha. 'Don't cry, Sonya, lovely, sweet, darling Sonya,' and she laughed as she kissed her. 'Vera's spiteful. Never mind her! Everything will be all right, and she won't tell Mamma. Nikolay will tell her himself, and he's never even thought about Julie.'

And she kissed her on the top of her head. Sonya half-rose, and the kitten in her revived, its eyes gleaming; it seemed ready to flick its tail, pounce about on its soft paws and start playing with a ball, as good kittens do.

'Do you think so? No, really, do you?' she said rapidly, smoothing dress and hair.

'Yes, I really do,' answered Natasha, tucking some straggling hair back into place on her friend's head, and they laughed together.

'All right, then, let's go and sing "The Spring".'

'Yes, let's.'

'And you know that fat Pierre who sat opposite me, he's so funny!' Natasha said suddenly and she stopped. 'I'm having such a wonderful time!' she shouted, and ran off down the corridor.

Brushing the fluff off her dress, and hiding the poetry in her bodice next to her throat and bony little chest, Sonya ran after Natasha, with flushed face and light, happy steps, down the corridor and into the sitting-room. By popular request the youngsters sang a quartet called 'The Spring', which everyone enjoyed, then Nikolay sang a song he had just learnt by heart.

> There where the evening moonlight shimmers,
> How sweet and lovely to renew
> And trust the happy hope that glimmers,
> *For somewhere, someone thinks of you!*
>
> And she will strain her little fingers
> And they the golden harp will strum.
> With harmony and love that lingers
> She calls to *you*, 'O come, O come!'
>
> Though paradise will one day beckon
> Alas! Your love will not be there . . .

Before he could get to the end, out in the big hall the young people started getting ready for the dancing, and the gallery musicians began stamping their feet and coughing.

Pierre was sitting in the drawing-room, where Shinshin – knowing he was just back from abroad – came over and started up a conversation about politics which Pierre found very boring. Others joined them. When the orchestra struck up, Natasha walked in, went straight up to Pierre, laughing and blushing, and said, 'Mamma told me to ask you to dance.'

'I'm afraid I can never get the figures right,' said Pierre, 'but if you'll be my teacher . . .' and he reached down to offer his big arm to the tiny little girl.

While the couples were taking up their places and the band tuned up, Pierre sat down with his little lady. Natasha's happiness was complete. She was going to dance with *a grown-up* and with someone who had just come home *from abroad*. She sat there for all to see and talked to him like a grown-up lady. In one hand she held a fan, which a lady had given her to hold. Posing, like a real society lady – heaven knows where and when she learnt all this – she spoke to her champion with much fluttering of the fan and many a glance over it.

'What *is* she doing? Just look at her!' said the old countess, striding across the hall and pointing to Natasha. Her daughter blushed a little and gave a laugh.

'Well, Mama? Why are you looking at me like that? What's so surprising?'

Half-way through the third écossaise there was a scraping of chairs in the sitting-room, where the count and Marya Dmitriyevna had been playing cards with the more distinguished and older guests, and most of them stood up to stretch after sitting for so long, before putting away their pocket-books and purses and walking through to the ballroom. Marya Dmitriyevna and the count led the way, both looking very jolly. With flamboyant politeness and mincing like a ballet-dancer, the count crooked his arm and offered it to Marya Dmitriyevna. Then he drew himself up, a dashing figure with a clever smile on his face, and as the écossaise came to an end he clapped his hands to the gallery musicians and called up to the leader, 'Semyon! Can you play a Daniel Cooper?' This had been his favourite dance since the days of his youth, though properly speaking the Daniel Cooper was one movement in the anglaise.[33]

'Watch Papa dance!' Natasha shouted to the whole ballroom, completely forgetting that her partner was a grown-up, and her laughter rang through the room as her curly head went down to her knees. Everyone was indeed enjoying the sight of the jolly old gentleman with his rather taller partner, the majestic Marya Dmitriyevna, as he linked arms with her to the rhythm of the music, put back his shoulders, tapped the floor with his turned-out toes, beaming ever more benevolently at his audience and whetting their appetite for what was to come. By the time the band struck up with the rousing strains of the Daniel Cooper, a merry country dance in all but name, every doorway into the ballroom had become filled with the smiling faces of servants, men on one side and women on the other, as they piled in to watch the master enjoying himself.

In one doorway stood the old nurse applauding the master in the traditional peasant manner, calling him 'Our little father!' and 'Our eagle!'[34]

The count was a good dancer and he knew it, but his lady couldn't dance at all, and didn't want to. Her great big body stood stiffly, and her sturdy arms dangled (she had handed her evening-bag to the countess). The only thing about her that did any dancing was her face, a nice mixture of grimness and beauty. Whereas the count performed with the whole of his rotund form, Marya Dmitriyevna did so with nothing more than a broadening smile and a slight quivering of the nose. The count may have enchanted the audience with his ever-increasing energy, his amazingly nimble and gentle prancing and capering, but Marya Dmitriyevna made no less impact with a mere twitch of the shoulders or the curving of an arm as they turned or halted to mark time, and her contribution was greatly admired, in view of her stout figure and legendary dourness. Their dancing became more and more hectic. The opposite couple couldn't make any impression, nor did they try to. All eyes were on the count and Marya Dmitriyevna. Natasha tugged at every sleeve and gown, urging everyone to watch Papa dancing, though that's what they were already doing. In any brief pauses the count gasped for breath and waved to the band, shouting to them to speed things up. Faster and faster he whirled, faster and nimbler than ever, rising on tiptoes, crashing down on his heels, swirling around his partner and finally swinging her back into her place with one last flourish and a leg kicked up neatly behind him. Now he bowed a perspiring head, beamed at the company and gave a huge sweep of his right arm to thunderous applause and much laughter, especially from Natasha. Both partners stood there, getting their breath back and mopping their faces with fine cambric handkerchiefs.

'That's the way we danced in our day, my dear,' said the count.

'Good for Daniel Cooper!' said Marya Dmitriyevna, taking a long, deep breath and tucking back her sleeves.

CHAPTER 18

At the moment when the sixth anglaise was being danced in the
Rostovs' hall to the badly timed strains of a weary orchestra, and exhausted cooks and waiters were getting supper ready, Count Bezukhov
suffered his sixth stroke. The doctors pronounced no hope of recovery,
the sick man was given silent confession and Holy Communion, and
the last rites were prepared. As always on such occasions, there was
much coming and going in the house and a dreadful air of expectancy.
Outside, hordes of undertakers hid beyond the gates, avoiding any
approaching carriages, but eagerly anticipating a nice fat order for the
count's funeral. The military governor of Moscow, who had sent a
string of aides to inquire after the count's condition, came in person
that evening to take leave of this famous grandee of Catherine's court,
Count Bezukhov.

The magnificent reception-room was full. Everyone stood up
respectfully when the governor emerged from the sick room after half
an hour alone with the sick man. He gave a curt nod and then made
his escape as quickly as possible from the onlooking doctors, church
dignitaries and relatives. Prince Vasily, who had grown thinner and
paler over recent days, escorted the governor out, whispering to him
several times. After seeing him on his way, the prince sat down alone
on a chair in the hall, crossed one leg high over the other, leant an
elbow on his knee and covered his eyes with his hand. He sat like that
for some time and then got to his feet and hurried off faster than usual
down the long corridor, looking around in some alarm, and heading
for the rear of the house and the eldest princess.

Those left behind in the dimly lit room murmured occasionally in
hushed tones, but all paused and watched with intense interest whenever the door to the dying man's room creaked open as someone went
in or out.

'The human span,' said a little old man, some sort of cleric, to a
lady who had come to sit by him and was now listening naively to
everything he said, 'that span is determined and may not be exceeded.'

'I was wondering whether it might be too late for the last rites?'
inquired the lady, using his clerical title, herself apparently devoid of
any opinion on this matter.

'It is all a great mystery, madam,' answered the cleric, stroking his
bald head with its few thin strands of greying hair combed across.

'What? Did I hear you say the governor's been here?' someone asked
at the other end of the room. 'Doesn't look his age, does he?'

'No, he's over sixty! I gather the count can't recognize anyone. Are they still giving him the last rites?'

'I knew a man who had the last rites seven times.'

The second princess emerged from the sick room with tears in her eyes, and sat next to Dr Lorrain, who had arranged himself in a pose under a portrait of Catherine the Great and was leaning against the table.

'It's a very nice day,' said the doctor in reply to a question about the weather, 'a very nice day, Princess, but then being in Moscow is just like being in the country.'

'Is it really?' said the princess with a sigh. 'Now, can we give him anything to drink?' Lorrain paused for reflection.

'Has he had his medicine?'

'Yes.'

The doctor consulted his watch.

'Take a glass of boiled water and add a pinch of cream of tartar.' (His delicate fingers showed her what a pinch meant.)

'Zere 'as neffer bin a case,' said a German doctor to an adjutant in his broken Russian, 'zat anypody liffed on after ze t'ird sdroke.'

'And didn't he look after himself!' said the adjutant. 'And who's going to inherit all this?' he added in a whisper.

'Ze customers vill come,' smiled the German, in reply.

The door creaked, and everyone turned. It was the second princess, who had made up the drink prescribed by the doctor and was now taking it in. The German doctor went over to Lorrain.

'Can he hold out till tomorrow morning?' asked the German, speaking French with a ghastly accent.

Lorrain pursed his lips and wagged a stern finger in front of his nose to say no.

'During the night, at the latest,' he said softly, with a courteous smile of smug confidence in his unique ability to interpret and transmit the precise condition of his patient so clearly. Then he stood up and walked away.

Meanwhile Prince Vasily had opened the door of the princess's room, which was in semi-darkness with only two small lamps burning before the icons. There was a pleasing scent of incense and flowers. The room was filled with small pieces of furniture, tiny knick-knacks, bookcases and tables. White covers on a high feather-bed were just visible behind a screen. A little dog yapped.

'Is that you, Cousin?'

She got up and smoothed her hair, which was always, even now, so extraordinarily smooth that it seemed to have been made out of one piece along with her head and given a coat of gloss.

'Has anything happened?' she asked. 'You startled me.'

'No, nothing has changed. I've just dropped in for a little chat, Katishe, about business,' said the prince, sinking wearily into the low chair from which she had just got up. 'Oh, it's quite warm in here,' he said. 'Come and sit down. Let's talk.'

'I was just wondering whether anything had happened,' said the princess, and with that perpetually stony look on her prim face she sat down opposite the prince, ready to listen. 'I have been trying to get some sleep, Cousin, but I can't.'

'Well now, my dear,' said Prince Vasily, taking the princess's hand, and pressing it downwards as he often did. This little phrase clearly touched on things that both of them knew but neither spoke of.

The princess, with her spare, rigid body, too long for her legs, looked straight at the prince with no sign of emotion in her prominent grey eyes. She shook her head and looked round at the icons with a sigh. This movement might have been interpreted as an expression of sorrow and devotion, or perhaps one of weariness and the hope for a speedy release. Prince Vasily opted for weariness.

'Do you imagine it's any easier for me?' he said. 'I'm as worn out as a post-horse. But I must speak to you, Katishe. It's something serious.'

Prince Vasily broke off, and his cheeks began to twitch nervously, first on one side, then on the other, giving his face an unpleasant look the like of which was never seen when he was in a drawing-room. His eyes, too, were different; they either stared out with a kind of crude humour in them or they darted about furtively.

The princess held her lap dog with her thin, dry hands, staring closely at Prince Vasily, and it was soon obvious that she was not going to break the silence, if she had to sit there till morning.

'Well, it's like this, my dear princess and cousin, Katerina Semyonovna,' said Prince Vasily, clearly struggling to continue. 'At times like this, one must think of everything. We must think about the future – about you. I love all of you as I love my own children. You know that.' The princess looked at him with the same fixed, inscrutable gaze.

'But when all's said and done, we have to think of my family too,' continued Prince Vasily, petulantly shoving away a little table while avoiding her eyes. 'You know, Katishe, that you three Mamontov sisters and my wife are the only direct heirs of the count. I know, I know, it is distressing for you to speak and think about such things. I don't find it any easier. But, my dear, I'm over fifty now and I must be ready for anything. Did you know I had sent for Pierre, and that the count pointed to his portrait and asked to see him?'

Prince Vasily looked inquiringly at the princess, but he couldn't work out whether she was absorbing what he had said, or just looking at him.

'Cousin, I pray constantly for one thing only . . .' she replied, 'that God may have mercy on his noble soul as he departs this . . .'

'Yes, yes,' Prince Vasily went on impatiently, wiping his bald head and angrily pulling back the table he had just shoved away, 'but as things stand . . . er, well, the point is this – I'm sure you know that last winter the count made a will which bypassed his direct heirs including us and left all his estate to Pierre.'

'He must have made lots of wills,' the princess said placidly, 'but he couldn't leave everything to Pierre. Pierre is illegitimate.'

'My dear cousin,' he snapped, clutching the table in his growing excitement and hurrying his words, 'what if a letter had been written by the count to the Emperor asking for permission to adopt Pierre as his legitimate son? You must realize that the count's service would mean that his request would be granted.'

The princess smiled, as people do when they think they know more than the person they are talking to.

'I'll go further,' said Prince Vasily, taking her hand. 'That letter has been written, and although it was never sent, the Emperor knows of its existence. The only question is – has it been destroyed or not? If not, when it's . . . *all over*,' Prince Vasily sighed, giving her a chance to see what he meant by the words 'all over', 'and they go through the count's papers, the will and the letter will be given to the Emperor together, and his request will probably be granted. As the legitimate son, Pierre will get everything.'

'What about our share?' asked the princess with a twisted smile, as if anything could happen, only not that.

'Why, my poor Katishe, it's as clear as daylight. He will then be the sole legal heir to everything, and you won't get a thing. You must surely know, my dear, whether the will and the letter were written, and whether or not they were destroyed. And if by any chance they have been mislaid, then you ought to know where they are and be able to find them, because . . .'

'Now you have gone too far!' the princess interrupted, with a sardonic smile and no change in the expression of her eyes. 'I'm a woman, and you think we're all stupid, but I do know this: an illegitimate son cannot inherit . . . He is a . . . *bastard*,' she added, the last word in French, as if its use would demonstrate the flaw in his thinking.

'Katishe, you really don't seem to understand! If you're that intelligent, why can't you see that if the count has written to the Emperor asking for recognition of Pierre as legitimate, he won't be Pierre any more, he'll be Count Bezukhov, and he'll inherit everything under the will? And if the will and the letter have not been destroyed, then – apart from the consolation of having done your duty and all the rest of it – you are left with nothing. And that's a fact.'

'I do know the will was made, but I also know that it is invalid. You seem to take me for a complete fool, my dear cousin,' said the princess, with the air of a woman who has come out with something clever and scathing.

'My dear princess, Katerina Semyonovna!' Prince Vasily was losing patience. 'I haven't come here just to annoy you. I'm talking to you as a relative, a good, kind, true relative, about your own interests. I am telling you for the umpteenth time that if that letter to the Emperor and the will made out in Pierre's favour are still among the count's papers, neither you, my dear girl, nor your sisters are heiresses. If you don't believe me, you must believe other people who know about these things. I've just been talking to Dmitry Onufrich' (the family solicitor) 'and he says the same thing.'

A sudden and obvious change now came over the princess's train of thought. Her thin lips paled, though her eyes stayed the same, and when she spoke her voice seemed to come out more thunderously than she was expecting.

'That would be a fine thing,' she said. 'I wanted nothing, and I still want nothing.' She pushed the dog down from her lap and smoothed out the folds of her skirt. 'There's gratitude for you. That's what you get for sacrificing everything,' she said. 'Wonderful! Splendid! I have no need of anything, Prince.'

'Yes, but it's not just you. You have two sisters,' answered Prince Vasily. But the princess was not listening.

'Yes, I've always known, but I had forgotten, that in this house I could never expect anything but unfairness, deceit, jealousy and double-dealing – only ingratitude, the blackest ingratitude . . .'

'Do you or do you not know where that will is?' Prince Vasily insisted, his cheeks twitching more than ever.

'Oh yes, I've been stupid. I've kept faith with people, given them my love and sacrificed everything. But you can't succeed nowadays without being mean and horrible. I know who's been double-dealing.'

The princess was about to stand up, but the prince held her back by the arm. She had the air of someone who has suddenly lost faith in the whole human race. She glared at him malevolently.

'There is still time, my dear. Remember, Katishe, this was an accident, something done in a moment of anger, of illness, and then
forgotten. Our duty, my dear, is to correct his mistake, to relieve him
in his last moments by not letting him commit this injustice, not letting
him die with the thought that he has brought unhappiness to . . .'

'People who have sacrificed everything for him,' the princess
responded. She made another effort to get up, but the prince restrained
her, ' – a sacrifice he's never been able to appreciate. No, cousin,' she
added with a sigh, 'I shall remember that there are no rewards in this
world, that in this world there is no honour or justice. In this world
you need to be clever and wicked.'

'Well, we shall see. Don't upset yourself. I know your noble heart.'

'No, I have a wicked heart.'

'I know your heart,' repeated the prince. 'I value your friendship,
and I would like you to think the same of me. So, don't upset yourself
and let's talk sensibly together while there is still time, whether it's a
whole day or just an hour. Tell me everything you know about that
will. The most important thing is – where is it? You must know. We'll
take it to the count and show it to him. He's probably forgotten all
about it, and he'll want it destroyed. Please understand that my sole
desire is to carry out his wishes religiously. That's what I came here
for. I am here only to be of service to him and to you.'

'Oh, I see. Now I know who's doing the double-dealing. Yes, I
know,' said the princess.

'You've got it wrong, my dear.'

'It's that Anna Mikhaylovna, your lovely protégée. I wouldn't have
her as a housemaid – ghastly, horrible woman.'

'Please, we're wasting time.'

'Don't you talk to me! Last winter she wormed her way in here and
told the count so many rotten, terrible things about all of us, especially
Sophie – I can't repeat them – that it made the count ill, and for two
weeks he refused to see us. I'm sure that was when he wrote that
awful, dreadful document, but I thought it didn't matter.'

'There we have it. Why didn't you tell me?'

Instead of replying the princess said, 'It's in that inlaid portfolio
that he keeps under his pillow . . . I can see it all now. If I have
one sin on my conscience, it is a big one – I loathe that vile woman!'
She was a different woman, virtually shrieking. 'And why does she
come crawling in here? I'll give her a piece of my mind . . . My time
will come!'

CHAPTER 19

While these conversations were taking place in the reception-room and in the princess's room, a carriage was bringing Pierre (who had been sent for) and Anna Mikhaylovna (who had found it necessary to come along too) into the courtyard of Count Bezukhov's house. As the carriage wheels crunched softly over the straw laid down beneath the windows, Anna Mikhaylovna turned consolingly to her companion only to find him asleep in his corner of the carriage. She woke him up. Pierre roused himself and followed Anna Mikhaylovna out of the carriage, and only then turned his mind to the impending visit to his dying father. He noticed that they had not come to the main entrance, but had gone round to the back door. As he got down from the carriage, two men dressed like tradesmen scurried away from the doorway into the shadow of the wall. Pausing for a moment, he could just make out several other similar figures standing in the shadows on both sides of the house. But Anna Mikhaylovna, the servant and the coachman, who must have seen these men, simply ignored them, so Pierre decided all was as it should be and followed her in. Anna Mikhaylovna hurried up the badly lit, narrow stone staircase, calling for Pierre not to lag behind. He couldn't see why he had to visit the count at all, still less why they had to use the back stairs, but Anna Mikhaylovna's confident manner and sense of urgency made him think it must be absolutely necessary. Half-way up the steps they were almost knocked off their feet by some men who came clomping down towards them in big boots, carrying buckets, but who squeezed back against the wall to let Pierre and Anna Mikhaylovna pass by, and didn't seem the least bit surprised to see them there.

'Is this the way to the princess's apartments?' Anna Mikhaylovna asked one of them.

'Yes, madam,' answered a footman in a loud, strong voice, as though anything were now permissible, 'the door on the left.'

'Perhaps the count didn't really ask for me,' said Pierre, as he reached the landing. 'I think I ought to go to my own room.'

Anna Mikhaylovna waited for him to catch up. 'Ah, my friend,' she said, touching his arm just as she had touched her son's arm that morning. 'Believe me, I am suffering as much as you, but be a man.'

'Really, hadn't I better go?' Pierre asked, peering amiably at her over his spectacles.

'Ah, my friend, forget the wrongs that may have been done to you:

keep thinking this is your father . . . and perhaps in his death agony,' she sighed. 'I took to you and I've loved you like a son. Trust me, Pierre. I shall not forget your interests.'

Pierre couldn't understand a word of this, but he sensed even more strongly that all was as it should be, so he meekly followed Anna Mikhaylovna, who was already opening a door into the back-stairs vestibule. In one corner sat one of the princess's old manservants knitting a stocking. Pierre had never been in this part of the house, and hadn't even suspected the existence of these rooms. A maid went past carrying a tray with a decanter on it, and Anna Mikhaylovna (calling her 'my dear' and 'good girl') inquired after the princesses' health, and then took Pierre on down the stone-flagged corridor. The first door on the left led through to the princesses' living quarters. The maid with the decanter was in such a hurry (everything in the house seemed to be done in a hurry just then) that she didn't close the door behind her. Pierre and Anna Mikhaylovna, in passing, happened to glance into the room where the eldest princess and Prince Vasily were in close conversation. Seeing them go by, Prince Vasily fell back in his chair with a gesture of irritation, but the princess leapt to her feet and in sheer desperation slammed the door with all her might and put the bolt on. This action was so out of character for the princess, with her perpetual serenity, and the shock on Prince Vasily's face was so out of tune with his dignity, that Pierre stopped in his tracks and gave a bewildered look at his guide over his spectacles. But Anna Mikhaylovna, showing no surprise, gave a thin smile and sighed, as if to indicate that this was just what she had expected.

'Be a man, my friend. I shall be looking after your interests,' she said in response to his glance and quickened her pace down the corridor.

Pierre still couldn't understand what was going on, and he had even less idea of what was meant by 'looking after his interests', but he did gather one thing – everything was as it should be. The corridor brought them into the half-lit hall just off the count's reception-room. This was one of the cold, magnificently furnished rooms that Pierre normally entered from the main staircase. But even here there was an empty bath in the middle of the room, and water had been splashed on the carpet. Tiptoeing in their direction came a servant and a deacon with a censer, who ignored them. They went on into the reception-room, which Pierre knew well, with its two Italian windows and a door into the winter garden, its large bust and full-length portrait of Catherine. The same people were still sitting there in almost the same positions, whispering. Everyone paused and looked round at

Anna Mikhaylovna as she came in with her pale, tear-stained face, and at the large, stout figure of Pierre, who trailed along meekly in her wake, hanging his head.

Anna Mikhaylovna's face betrayed her awareness that the moment of crisis had arrived. With her Petersburg businesswoman's air she strode into the room even more assertively than in the morning, keeping Pierre close by her. Since she was bringing the person the dying man wanted to see, she felt sure of a warm welcome for herself. With a rapid glance she took in the whole room, and particularly the presence of the count's spiritual adviser. Without actually bowing, she seemed somehow to shrink into herself before gliding slowly over to the priest and reverently offering herself for a blessing to the two ecclesiastics one after the other.

'Thank God we are in time,' she said to the priest. 'We are family, and we have been terribly worried. This young man is the count's son,' she added more softly. 'This is a dreadful time.'

This said, she went over to the doctor.

'Dear doctor,' she said to him, 'this young man is the count's son . . . Is there any hope at all?'

Without speaking the doctor gave a quick shrug and rolled his eyes upwards. With precisely the same gesture Anna Mikhaylovna shrugged and looked upwards, almost closing her eyes, then with a sigh she walked away from the doctor and went back to Pierre. She addressed him with particular respect and sad solemnity.

'Have faith in his mercy,' she said to him, and indicating a small sofa for him to sit on and wait, she went soundlessly over to the door that all the eyes were on. It opened almost inaudibly, and she slid through as it closed behind her.

Pierre, having decided to obey his guide in everything, went over towards the sofa she had pointed to. The moment Anna Mikhaylovna disappeared he noticed the eyes of everyone in the room turning towards him with something more than curiosity and sympathy. He noticed they were all talking in whispers, looking across at him with something like a mixture of awe and sycophancy. They showed him the kind of respect he had never seen before. A lady quite unknown to him stopped talking to the priest, got to her feet and offered him a seat; an adjutant picked up a glove that Pierre had dropped and handed it back to him; the doctors fell into a polite silence when he passed by and stood aside for him. Pierre's first desire was to sit somewhere else so as not to disturb the lady, to pick up the glove himself and to go round the doctors, who weren't in his way at all, but suddenly he realized that to do so would be improper. He realized that tonight he had become a special person, obliged to endure some ghastly ceremony because it was expected of him, and this meant he was bound to accept favours from everyone. He took the glove from the adjutant in silence, sat down in the lady's place, spreading out his big hands symmetrically on his knees and posing innocently like some Egyptian statue, and then made up his mind that all was as it should be, and that to avoid losing his head and doing stupid things tonight he must not act on his own initiative but bend wholly to the will of those who were guiding him.

In a couple of minutes Prince Vasily marched into the room, majestic in his coat with the three stars on it, and carrying his head high. He seemed to have grown thinner since the morning. His eyes seemed wider than usual as he glanced round the room and picked out Pierre. He came across and took his hand (something he had never done before), pressing it downwards, as if he wanted to test the strength of its grip.

'Do take courage, my friend. He has asked to see you. That's a good thing . . .'

He made as if to leave, but Pierre felt a need to ask something. 'How is, er . . .' He hesitated, undecided whether it was proper for him to call the dying man 'the count', but embarrassed to call him 'father'.

'He had another stroke half an hour ago. Do take courage, my friend.'

Pierre was in such a confused state of mind that the word 'stroke' made him think of a blow from some heavy body. He looked nonplussed at Prince Vasily, and it was some time before he realized that a stroke is an illness. Prince Vasily said a few words to Lorrain in passing and tiptoed out. He was not very adept at tiptoeing, and his whole body jerked and twitched awkwardly. He was followed by the eldest princess, then by the clergy and the deacons; a few servants also went out. Beyond the door people could be heard moving about, and before long Anna Mikhaylovna ran out, her face still pale but resolute in doing her duty. She touched Pierre on the arm and said, 'God's goodness is inexhaustible. The last rites are beginning. Come with me.'

Pierre went in, and as he trod the soft carpet he noticed that the adjutant and the unknown lady and even one or two servants came trooping in too, as if it was no longer necessary to ask permission to enter that room.

CHAPTER 20

Pierre knew it well, this huge room divided by columns and an arch, the floor covered with Persian carpets. That part of the room beyond the columns, where a high mahogany bedstead with silk hangings stood on one side, and with a huge stand and many icons on the other, was lit up with a bright red light, like a church prepared for evening service. Under the ornamental icon-coverings stood a deep Voltaire armchair,[35] and in it Pierre saw, propped up on snow-white, un-crumpled, freshly changed pillows and covered waist-high with a bright green quilt, a familiar and majestic figure, his father, Count Bezukhov, slumping there with the familiar grey lion's mane over his broad brow, and the typically aristocratic lines deeply etched into a handsome, reddish-yellow face. He lay there immediately under the icons with his big thick arms at rest on the quilt. In his right hand, palm down, a wax candle had been thrust between thumb and forefinger and was being held in place by an old servant bending over him from behind. Around the chair hovered the churchmen with their long hair trailing down over splendid glittering vestments. Holding lighted candles in their hands, they were performing their offices with un-hurried solemnity. Just behind them stood the two younger princesses, clutching handkerchiefs and intermittently dabbing their eyes, and in front of them the eldest, Katishe, a picture of spiteful determination, kept her eyes glued on the icons, as though declaring to all and sundry that she wouldn't answer for the consequences if she were to look away from them. Anna Mikhaylovna, all meekness, sorrowfulness and forgiveness, stood near the door with the unknown lady. Prince Vasily was standing beside the invalid chair on the other side of the door. He had drawn up a carved, velvet chair and was resting his left hand on its back, holding a candle, and using his right hand to cross himself, rolling his eyes upwards every time he put his fingers to his forehead. His face conveyed a gentle piety and resignation to the will of God. 'If you cannot understand feelings like these,' his face seemed to say, 'that's too bad for you.'

Behind him stood the adjutant, the doctors and the men servants; the men and the women had separated as in church. They all made the sign of the cross in silence, and the only sounds came from the holy reading, the subdued, deep bass chanting, and in moments of silence from some sighing and the shuffling of feet. With a meaningful air which showed she knew what she was doing, Anna Mikhaylovna walked across the room to Pierre and handed him a candle. He lit it, but was then so busy watching the people around him that he used the hand holding the candle to cross himself.

The youngest princess, Sophie, the rosy-cheeked one with the mole and the sense of humour, had her eyes on him. She smiled, hid her face in her handkerchief and kept it there for some time, but soon looked at Pierre again, and gave another giggle. She was obviously incapable of looking at him without giggling, but she couldn't resist looking at him, so she removed the temptation by gliding behind a column. In mid-service the voices of the priests suddenly ceased, and they started whispering to one another. The old servant, who was holding the count's hand, straightened up and turned to the ladies. Anna Mikhaylovna stepped forward, bent down over the sick man and beckoned behind her back to Lorrain. The French doctor had been standing there without a candle, leaning against a column, but with the respectful attitude of a foreigner, who, despite differences of religion, fully acknowledges the solemnity of the ceremony and even approves of it. Now, with the noiseless steps of a man in his prime he strode over to his patient, extended delicate, white fingers to raise a hand from the quilt, turned to one side and began feeling the pulse thoughtfully. They gave the sick man something to drink, a few people around him stirred, then they all went back to their places, and the service continued. During this break in the proceedings Pierre watched Prince Vasily leave his chair-back, and with the same air of authority – he knew what he was doing and it was too bad for anyone who couldn't understand him – he walked straight past the sick man and joined the eldest princess. Together they went off to the far end of the room towards the high bedstead with its silk hangings. They went past the bed and out through a rear door, but before the end of the service they came back in one after the other and resumed their places. Pierre paid no more attention to this development than to any other, having made up his mind once and for all that tonight everything unfolding before him was necessary and inevitable.

The sound of chanting stopped and the priest's voice could be heard reverently congratulating the sick man on having received the mystery. The patient lay there, showing no sign of life or movement. Round about him there was a shuffling and a rustling and voices whispering, Anna Mikhaylovna's louder than the rest. Pierre heard her say, 'Yes, he must be moved across to the bed. It's impossible here . . .'

The sick man was now so hemmed in by doctors, princesses and servants that Pierre could no longer see the reddish-yellow face with the grey mane that he had never for a moment lost sight of during the ceremony, even though there had been other faces to watch as well.

From the gingerly manoeuvring of people round the chair he surmised that they were lifting the dying man up and moving him over
to the bed.

'Hold on to my arm or you'll drop him,' he heard one of the servants
whisper in panic. 'Down a bit . . .', 'Somebody else here . . .', said
voices. Laboured breathing, heavy steps and a gathering rush made it
seem as if the weight they were carrying was too much for them.

The bearers struggled past, Anna Mikhaylovna among them, and
the young man caught a glimpse over their backs and necks of the sick
man – the fleshy expanse of his huge chest, the curling grey of his
leonine head and the massive shoulders, all hunched up as people
grasped him under the armpits. That head, with its broad brow and
prominent cheekbones, a handsome, sensual mouth and an aloof expression of high dignity, was not disfigured by the approach of death.
It was the same head that Pierre remembered from three months ago,
when his father had seen him off to Petersburg, but now it flopped
about helplessly to the stumbling steps of the bearers, and the cold,
apathetic eyes were focused on nothing.

After a few minutes' commotion around the high bed, the bearers
went back to their places. Anna Mikhaylovna touched Pierre's arm
and said, 'Come with me.' The two of them approached the bed on
which the sick man had been laid in some style perhaps to accord with
the mystery that had just been enacted. He was lying with his head
propped up on high pillows, his hands symmetrically spread, palms
down, on the green silk quilt. When Pierre came up, the count looked
straight at him, but with a gaze unintelligible to mortal man in its
purpose and significance. Either these eyes said nothing at all, but
simply stared because they had to look at something, or else they said
too much. Pierre stopped, not knowing what he ought to do, and
turned to his guide for help. Anna Mikhaylovna looked at him,
motioning quickly with her eyes towards the sick man's hand and
using her lips to float down a kiss. Pierre got the message, thrusting
his neck forward with a great effort to avoid getting caught in the
quilt, and kissing the solid, broad hand. Nothing stirred, neither the
hand itself, nor any muscle on the count's face. Again Pierre sought
guidance from Anna Mikhaylovna as to what to do next. Her eyes
indicated an armchair beside the bed. Meekly, Pierre made as if to sit
down in it, his eyes still wondering whether he was doing the right
thing. Anna Mikhaylovna nodded approvingly. Pierre resumed his
innocent, symmetrical pose as an Egyptian statue, obviously ruing the
fact that his big clumsy body took up so much space, and doing his
utmost mentally to reduce himself in size. He looked at the count. The

count still gazed ahead at where Pierre's face had been when he had stood before him. Anna Mikhaylovna's attitude acknowledged all the pathos and significance of this last meeting between father and son. It lasted two minutes, but they seemed like an hour to Pierre. Suddenly a tremor passed over the big muscles and deep lines on the count's face. The shudder intensified and the handsome mouth was contorted (it was now that Pierre realized how near death his father was), and from the contorted mouth came a hoarse wheeze. Anna Mikhaylovna looked anxiously into the sick man's eyes, trying to work out what he wanted; she pointed at Pierre, then at a drink, then in a whispered question she mentioned the name of Prince Vasily, then she pointed to the quilt. The sick man's eyes and face registered some impatience. He made a great effort to look round at the servant, immovable at the head of the bed.

'His Excellency wishes to be turned over on to his other side,' whispered the servant, and he got up to turn the count's heavy body towards the wall. Pierre stood up to help.

While the count was being turned over, one of his arms got caught helplessly behind him and he made a vain attempt to drag it back. Whether or not the count noticed the horror with which Pierre stared at that lifeless arm, or whether some other idea flashed through his dying mind at that instant, he looked down at his unresponsive arm, then at the expression of horror on Pierre's face, then back at his arm, and finally his face produced a smile which jarred with his fine features, a pathetically weak smile that seemed to mock his own helplessness. Suddenly, at the sight of that smile, Pierre felt a shudder in his chest and a prickling in his nose, and his eyes clouded over with tears. They finished turning the sick man towards the wall. He gave a sigh.

'He's having a little doze,' said Anna Mikhaylovna, noticing that one of the princesses was coming to take her turn by the bedside. 'Let's go.'

Pierre went out.

CHAPTER 21

By now there was no one in the reception-room except Prince Vasily and the eldest princess, who were sitting under the portrait of Catherine engaged in a lively conversation. They stopped talking the moment they caught sight of Pierre and his guide, and he thought he saw the princess hide something away as she mumbled, 'I can't abide that woman.'

'Katishe has arranged for tea to be served in the little drawing-room,' said Prince Vasily to Anna Mikhaylovna. 'My poor dear, you must go and take a little something or you won't hold out.'

Saying nothing to Pierre, he simply squeezed his upper arm sympathetically. Pierre and Anna Mikhaylovna went into the little drawing-room.

'There is nothing like a cup of this excellent Russian tea after a sleepless night,' said Lorrain with subdued enthusiasm as he sipped from a delicate Chinese cup without a handle, standing in the little round room at a table with tea-things and some cold supper on it. All of those who had foregathered that night in Count Bezukhov's house had come to fortify themselves at this table. Pierre had fond memories of this little round room with its mirrors and tiny tables. When balls were held in the count's house, Pierre, who was no dancer, had enjoyed sitting in that little room of mirrors, watching the ladies in their ballroom finery decked out with diamonds and pearls on their bare necks, as they passed through and admired themselves in the brightly lit mirrors that multiplied their reflections over and over. Now in the middle of the night in that same room dim light came from two candles, and the tea-things and refreshments were scattered about on one of the little tables, while all sorts of people in ordinary clothes sat there whispering together, showing with every gesture, every word, that no one could ignore what was happening at that moment and what was about to happen in the bedroom. Pierre didn't eat anything even though he was feeling very hungry. He turned to consult his guide, and saw her tiptoeing back to the reception-room where Prince Vasily had stayed behind with the eldest princess. Pierre assumed that this also had to be, so after a moment's hesitation he followed. Anna Mikhaylovna was standing beside the princess, and they were talking in emotional whispers both at the same time.

'Allow me, Princess, to know what is necessary and what is not necessary,' Princess Katishe was saying, her highly emotional state no different from when she had slammed the door of her room.

'But, my dear princess,' Anna Mikhaylovna was saying with gentle persuasiveness, barring the way to the bedroom and not letting her pass, 'don't you think that might be rather too taxing for poor Uncle just now, when he needs to rest? At a time like this to talk of worldly affairs when his soul has been prepared . . .'

Prince Vasily was sitting in a low chair in his customary pose, one leg crossed high above the other. Both of his cheeks were twitching furiously, and when they relaxed they made him look heavy-jowled, but his air was that of a man little interested in the two ladies' discussion.

'No, no, my dear Anna Mikhaylovna, let Katishe do what she wants. You know how the count loves her.'

'I don't know what's in this document,' said Princess Katishe to Prince Vasily, pointing to the inlaid portfolio which she held in her hand. 'What I do know is that the real will is in his desk, and this is a paper that has been forgotten . . .'

She tried to get past Anna Mikhaylovna, who skipped across to bar her way again.

'I know, my dear, sweet princess,' said Anna Mikhaylovna, taking hold of the portfolio, so strongly that it was clear she had no intention of letting go again. 'My dear princess, I beg you, I implore you, spare him. I appeal to you.'

The princess said nothing. The only sound was a scuffling over the portfolio. There could be no doubt that if she had said anything it wouldn't have been complimentary to Anna Mikhaylovna. The latter held on grimly, but her voice still managed to retain its unctuous charm and honeyed gentleness.

'Pierre, come over here, my dear. He is not out of place, I think, in any family council. Don't you agree, Prince?'

'Cousin, say something, please!' Princess Katishe screamed suddenly, so loud that her voice was heard in the drawing-room where it caused some alarm. 'Why don't you say something when a nobody comes in here meddling and making a scene outside a dying man's room? You scheming hussy!' she muttered viciously, and heaved at the portfolio with all her strength, but Anna Mikhaylovna took a few steps forward to keep hold of it and get a better grip.

'Oh dear,' said Prince Vasily, amazed and full of reproach. He got up. 'This is ridiculous. Now, come on. Let go, I tell you.' Princess Katishe did so.

'You too.'

Anna Mikhaylovna did not respond.

'Let go, I tell you. I take full responsibility. I shall go and ask him. I . . . Let that be enough for you.'

'But, Prince,' said Anna Mikhaylovna, 'after that solemn sacrament let him have a moment's peace. Pierre, tell us your opinion,' said she, turning to the young man, who had come up to her and was staring in amazement at her face, malicious beyond all decency, and at Prince Vasily with his twitching cheeks.

'Please remember you will have to answer for the consequences,' said Prince Vasily sternly. 'You don't know what you are doing.'

'Foul woman!' screamed Princess Katishe, suddenly pouncing on Anna Mikhaylovna and wrenching the portfolio from her hands. Prince Vasily bowed his head and spread his hands.

At that moment the door, that dreaded door at which Pierre had gazed so long and which usually opened so softly, was suddenly flung open and banged against the wall, and the second of the three sisters rushed out wringing her hands.

'What are you doing?' she said, in despair. 'He is passing away, and you leave me alone.'

Her sister dropped the portfolio. Anna Mikhaylovna swooped down, grabbed the object of contention and ran into the bedroom. The eldest princess and Prince Vasily pulled themselves together and followed. A few minutes later the eldest princess was the first to re-emerge with a pale, dry face, biting her lip. At the sight of Pierre her face crumbled into uncontrolled hatred.

'Oh, it's all right for you,' she said, 'you've got what you wanted.' She buried her face in her handkerchief and ran sobbing out of the room.

Then came Prince Vasily. He staggered as far as the sofa where Pierre was sitting and sank down on it, covering his eyes with one hand. Pierre noticed he was pale, and his jaw was quivering and twitching as if he was having a fit.

'Oh, my dear boy,' he said, taking Pierre by the elbow, his voice ringing with a sincerity and weakness that Pierre had never seen in him before, 'we sin, we cheat, and what's it all for? I'm over fifty, my friend . . . And I too . . . Everything ends in death, everything does. Death is so horrible . . .' And he burst into tears.

Anna Mikhaylovna was the last to emerge. She came over to Pierre with slow and quiet steps. 'Pierre,' she said. Pierre looked inquiringly at her. She kissed the young man on the forehead, wetting him with her tears. She did not speak for a while, but then she said, 'He's gone . . .'

Pierre gazed at her over his spectacles.

'Come on. I'll take you in again. Cry if you can. There is nothing like tears for the easing of pain.' She led him into the dark room, and Pierre was glad that in there no one could see his face. Anna Mikhaylovna left him alone, and when she came back he had put one arm under his head and was fast asleep.

In the morning Anna Mikhaylovna said to Pierre, 'Yes, my dear, it is a great loss for all of us. I cannot speak for you. But the Lord will keep you. You are still young, and now you are, I hope, at the head of an immense fortune. The will has not yet been opened. I know you well enough to be sure you won't let this go to your head, but it does impose certain duties, and you must be a man.'

Pierre said nothing.

'Perhaps, later, I may tell you, my dear, that if I had not been there . . . God knows what might have happened. You know my uncle promised me only the day before yesterday he wouldn't forget Boris. But he didn't have enough time. I do hope, my dear friend, that you will carry out your father's wishes.'

Pierre didn't understand a word she was saying. Blushing shyly, he looked at Anna Mikhaylovna and still said nothing. After her little talk with him, Anna Mikhaylovna drove home to the Rostovs, and went to bed. When she awoke the following morning, she told the Rostovs and all her acquaintances the details of Count Bezukhov's death. She said the count had died exactly as she would wish to die, his end had been more than touching, it had been truly inspiring, the last meeting between father and son had been so moving that she couldn't recall it without weeping, and she couldn't say who had behaved better in those dreadful moments – the father, who had remembered everything and everyone so well at the last and had said such moving things to his son, or Pierre, who made such a heartbreaking sight, so utterly distraught and yet struggling to hide his grief so as not to upset his dying father. 'It is hard to bear, but it does one good. It uplifts the soul to see such men as the old count and his worthy son,' she said. She whispered to them in the strictest confidence, sotto voce, about the machinations of the princess and Prince Vasily, of which she could not approve.

CHAPTER 22

At Bald Hills, the estate of Prince Nikolay Bolkonsky, the arrival of young Prince Andrey and his wife was expected daily, but this expectation did not disrupt the orderly system according to which life in the old prince's household was organized. Prince Nikolay, a former commander-in-chief (nicknamed 'The King of Prussia' in high society), had been exiled to his estate in the reign of Paul,[36] and had remained at Bald Hills ever since with his daughter, Princess Marya, and her companion, Mademoiselle Bourienne. Under the new Tsar, even though he was now allowed to visit the capital cities, he had stayed on resolutely in the country, saying that anyone who needed him could travel the hundred miles from Moscow to Bald Hills, while he himself wanted nobody and needed nothing. He used to claim that there were only two sources of human depravity – idleness and superstition; and only two virtues – hard work and intelligence. He was educating his daughter and in order to inculcate these two cardinal virtues he was still teaching her algebra and geometry when she was nearly twenty, and had organized her whole life around one unending course of study. He himself had many occupations – writing his memoirs, solving mathematical problems, turning snuff-boxes on his lathe, working at his garden or supervising the building work which never stopped on his estate. Since the main prerequisite for hard work is good order, good order dictated his lifestyle to the last degree of exactitude. The details of his appearances at the meal-table were unvarying, timed to the minute rather than the hour. With those around him, from daughter to servant, the prince was brusque and always demanding so that without actually being cruel he inspired the kind of fear and respect that the cruellest of men would have found difficult to achieve. Although he was now retired and without political influence of any kind, every senior figure in the province where he lived felt obliged to call on him, and they were no different from the architect, the gardener or Princess Marya – they had to wait in the lofty antechamber until the precise time set for the prince's arrival. And in that room everyone felt the same kind of deference bordering on dread as the immensely tall door of the study swung open to reveal the small figure of an old man in a powdered wig, with tiny withered hands and bushy grey eyebrows that were prone to gather in a frown and thus hide the gleam in his shrewd, young man's eyes.

On the morning of the day when the young people were expected, Princess Marya went to the antechamber as usual at lesson time to wish her father good morning, crossing herself with dread in her heart and saying a silent prayer. Every day she went in like this to her father, and every day she prayed for a happy outcome to their daily encounter. The powdered old manservant rose smoothly from his seat there and whispered, 'Please go through.'

From the other side of the door came the steady hum of a lathe. The princess eased the door open timidly and stood in the doorway. The prince, busy at the lathe, glanced up once and went on with his work.

It was a vast work-room full of objects evidently in constant use. A huge table with books and plans laid out, tall glass-fronted bookcases with keys in the doors, a high desk for writing standing up, with an open note-book on top, the carpenter's lathe with a scattering of tools and shavings – all of this betokened constant, continually varied and systematic hard work. The motion of the prince's tiny foot in its silver-trimmed Tartar bootee and the firm pressure of his lean and sinewy hand spoke of resolute strength and indefatigable energy taken through to old age. A few more turns of the lathe and he took his foot off the pedal, wiped a chisel, dropped it into a leather pouch attached to the lathe, came to the table and called his daughter over. He was not one to bother with blessings for his children, and he simply offered her a bristly unshaven cheek before looking her over in a manner that somehow managed to mix strictness with care and tenderness. Then he spoke. 'You all right? Very well, sit down!'

He took out a geometry exercise-book with his writing in it, and dragged a chair over with one foot.

'For tomorrow,' he said, turning rapidly to a particular page and using his thick nail to mark out two paragraphs together. The princess bent over the table and the exercise-book. 'Wait, there's a letter for you,' said the old man suddenly, taking an envelope with a woman's handwriting on it from a pouch hanging above the table and tossing it down before her.

The princess coloured up blotchy red at the sight of the letter. She took it hurriedly and bent down to open it.

'From your Héloïse?'[37] asked the prince, with a cold smile, showing teeth that were yellowing but still strong.

'Yes, it's from Julie,' said the princess, with a timid glance and an equally timid smile.

'Two more letters I'll let through, but the third one I shall read,' said the prince severely. 'I'm afraid you must be writing a lot of nonsense. The third one I shall read.'

'Read this one, Father,' answered the princess, redder still, and she offered him the letter.

'The third one, I said the third one,' the prince cried brusquely, thrusting the letter away before leaning his elbows on the table and bringing up the book with the geometrical figures in it.

'Now, madam,' began the old man, poring over the book close to his daughter and placing one arm along the back of the chair she was sitting on, so that the princess felt herself completely swamped by her father and his long-familiar acrid odour of tobacco and old age. 'Come along, madam, these triangles are equal. Be so good as to note that the angle ABC . . .'

The princess glanced in trepidation at her father's gleaming eyes so close beside her. More red blotches spread across her face, and she was obviously taking nothing in. So scared was she that fear itself prevented her from understanding any of the explanations her father went on to give, however clear they might have been. Whoever was to blame, teacher or pupil, every day the selfsame scene repeated itself. The princess's eyes glazed over, she could see and hear nothing, she could feel nothing but the close proximity of her strict father with his desiccated face, stale breath and body odour, and she could think of nothing but how to get away from there as soon as possible and somehow work out the problem in the freedom of her room. The old man would lose patience, scraping his chair backwards and forwards, then struggle to control himself, not to lose his temper, which he almost always did, and then he shouted at her, sometimes flinging the book across the room.

The princess got one of her answers wrong.

'How can you be so stupid?' he roared, pushing the book away, and turning from her sharply. But then he got up, paced up and down, laid a hand on the princess's hair and sat down again. He drew close to the table and went on with his explanations.

'No, no, you can't do that,' he said, as Princess Marya took the exercise-book with the homework in it, closed it and made as if to leave the room. 'Mathematics is a great subject, madam. And you, being like the silly young ladies of today is something I do not want. Persevere and all will come clear.' He patted her on the cheek. 'This will drive the silliness out of your head.' She tried to get away, but he signalled for her to stop and took a new book with uncut pages[38] down from the high desk.

'And here's a book from your Héloïse. Hm . . . *A Key to the Mystery* . . .[39] Something religious. Well, I don't interfere with anybody's religious faith . . . I've had a look at it. Here you are. Go on then, run along.'

He patted her on the shoulder, and went himself to close the door after her.

Princess Marya went back to her room with that gloomy, frightened look that rarely left her, making her sickly, plain face even plainer. She sat down at her desk with its miniature portraits and scattered books and writing paper. The princess was as untidy as her father was tidy. She put down the geometry exercise-book and eagerly tore open the letter. It was from her dearest childhood friend, the very Julie Karagin who had been at the Rostovs' name-day party, and was written in French:

My dear and excellent friend,
What a terrible and awful thing absence is! I tell myself that half of my existence and happiness is in you, that for all the distance that divides us,

our hearts are united by indissoluble bonds, yet my own rebels against destiny, and in spite of the pleasures and distractions that surround me, I cannot overcome a certain secret sadness which I have sensed at the bottom of my heart ever since our separation. Why are we not together as we were last summer in your huge study, on that blue sofa, the 'sofa of secrets'? Why can I not, as I did three months ago, draw new moral strength from those eyes of yours, so gentle, so calm, so penetrating, eyes that I have loved so well and seem to see before me even as I write.

At this point, Princess Marya sighed and looked around at the tall mirror to her right. The glass reflected a feeble, unattractive body and a skinny face. The ever-gloomy eyes looked at themselves more hopelessly than ever. 'She's flattering me,' thought the princess as she turned back to read on. But Julie was not flattering her friend; her eyes were large, deep and radiant (sometimes a warm light seemed to pour out of them), really so winsome that very often, in spite of the plainness of the face as a whole, her eyes held a greater appeal than mere beauty. But the princess had never seen the beautiful expression in her own eyes, an expression they assumed only when she wasn't thinking about herself. Like everyone else's, her face took on a strained, artificial and disagreeable expression the moment she looked at herself in the mirror. She read on.

All Moscow talks only of war. One of my brothers is abroad and the other is in the guards, who are about to march to the frontier. Our dear Emperor has left Petersburg and he now intends, so it is said, to expose his precious person to the hazards of war. God grant that the Corsican monster who is destroying the peace of Europe may be brought down by the angel whom the Almighty in his mercy has given us as sovereign. Apart from my brothers, this war has deprived me of one of those dearest to my heart. I refer to young Nikolay Rostov, who with all his keenness could not endure inaction, and who has left university to enrol in the army. Well, dear Marie, I must admit that, for all his extreme youth, his departure for the army has caused me great pain. This young man, of whom I spoke to you last summer, has so much of that nobility and true youthfulness that is rarely encountered in our age among our men who are old by twenty. Above all, he has so much openness and emotion. He is so pure and poetic that my acquaintance with him, brief though it has been, has been one of the sweetest pleasures of my poor heart, which has already suffered so much. One day I will tell you about our farewells and all that was said between us as we parted. As yet, it is all too fresh in my mind. Ah, dear friend, you are fortunate in knowing none of these joys and these troubles which are so poignant. Fortunate, because the latter are usually the stronger! I know only too well that Count Nikolay is too young ever to become more than a friend to me, but our sweet friendship, our closeness, so poetic and so pure, these have satisfied my heart's need. But enough of this. The great news of the day, the talk of all Moscow, is the death of old Count Bezukhov, and his inheritance. Just imagine, the three princesses have got almost nothing, Prince Vasily nothing at all, and everything has gone to Monsieur Pierre, who – to crown it all – has been acknowledged as a legitimate son and therefore as Count Bezukhov, owner of the finest fortune in Russia. They do say Prince Vasily played a very nasty part in this story and he has returned to Petersburg all down in the mouth.

I confess I understand very little about all these matters – legacies and wills – but I do know that ever since the young man whom we all used to know as plain Monsieur Pierre became Count Bezukhov and owner of one of the largest fortunes in Russia I have been greatly amused to observe certain changes in the tone and manner of mammas burdened with daughters who need to be married, and of the young ladies themselves, towards that person – who, incidentally, has always seemed to me a miserable specimen of manhood. As people have found it amusing to keep marrying me off for the last two years, usually to husbands I don't even know, the Moscow Marriage News is now making a Countess Bezukhov out of me. But I am sure you will appreciate that I have no desire whatsoever to become such. Speaking of marriage, by the way, did you know that Everybody's Auntie, Anna Mikhaylovna, has confided to me, under the seal of the strictest confidence, a marriage scheme for you. It is with none other than Prince Vasily's son, Anatole. They would like him to settle down and marry someone rich and distinguished, and his relatives' choice has fallen on you. I don't know how you will look on this matter, but, well, I considered it my duty to warn you in advance. He is said to be very handsome and very naughty, and that's all I have been able to find out about him.

That's enough gossiping. I'm coming to the end of my second sheet, and mamma has sent for me – we are dining with the Apraksins. Do read the mystical book which I am sending you – it is all the rage here. There are some things in this book which are difficult for our feeble human thinking to grasp, though it is an admirable book, and reading it is relaxing and spiritually uplifting. Goodbye for now. My respects to your father and my compliments to Mlle Bourienne.

I embrace you and continue to love you.

JULIE

P.S. Do send news of your brother and his charming little wife.

Princess Marya paused, pensive and smiling, her radiant eyes lighting up and utterly transforming her face, then she got up quickly and
with her heavy tread went over to the table. She took out some paper
and soon her hand was speeding across it. This is what she wrote, also
in French:

Dear and excellent friend,
Your letter of the 13th was a delight to read. So you do still love me,
my poetic Julie, and absence, which you so roundly denounce, has not
had its usual effect on you. You complain about absence – what would I
say, if I could only *dare* to complain, deprived as I am of all who are dear
to me? Oh, if we had no religion to console us, life would be so very sad.
Why do you imagine I should look askance when you tell me of your
affection for that young man? In these matters I am hard on myself and
no one else. I understand such feelings in other people even if I have never
had them myself, and if I cannot condone them, neither do I condemn
them. Only it seems to me that Christian love, love for one's neighbour,
love for one's enemies, is more deserving, sweeter, more beautiful than
any feelings aroused by a young man's lovely eyes in a romantically
inclined young girl like yourself.
News of Count Bezukhov's death reached us before your letter; my
father was very moved by it. He says the count was the last but one
representative of the Great Century[40] and he'll be the next to go, but he
will do his best to put this off as long as possible. God save us from that
terrible misfortune. I cannot share your opinion of Pierre, whom I knew
as a child. He always seemed to me to have an excellent heart, and this is
the quality I value most in people. As to his inheritance and the part
played in it by Prince Vasily, it is very sad for both of them. Oh, my dear
friend, our divine Saviour's words, that it is easier for a camel to go
through the eye of a needle than for a rich man to enter into the kingdom
of God,[41] are terribly true. I pity Prince Vasily, but I am sorrier still for
Pierre. So young and burdened with this wealth, what temptations will
he have to resist! If anyone asked what I would like most in the world, it
would be to be poorer than the poorest beggar. Many thanks, dear friend,
for the work you have sent me which is all the rage where you are.
However, since you tell me that amid several good things there are others
which our feeble human thinking cannot grasp, it seems to me rather
useless to spend time reading something unintelligible, which in the nature
of things must turn out to be fruitless. I have never been able to understand
the passion that some people have for befogging their thoughts by cleaving
to the study of mystical books which can only awaken doubts in their
minds, while inflaming the imagination and inclining them towards

exaggeration, which goes right against Christian simplicity. Let us read the Apostles and the Gospel. Let us not seek to penetrate what they contain that is mysterious, for how dare we presume, miserable sinners that we are, to admit ourselves into the terrible and holy secrets of Providence while we still wear this mortal flesh that raises an impenetrable veil between us and the Eternal? Let us rather confine ourselves to the study of those sublime principles which our divine Saviour has left for our guidance here below; let us seek to obey and to follow them; let us persuade ourselves that the less scope we give to our feeble human minds the more pleasing this will be to God, who rejects all knowledge that cometh not from him and the less we seek to peruse that which he has been pleased to conceal from us, the sooner will he reveal it to us through his Holy Spirit.

My father has not spoken to me of any suitor; all he has said is that he received a letter and has been expecting a visit from Prince Vasily. In relation to any marriage scheme concerning me, I can tell you, my dear and excellent friend, that I consider marriage to be a divine institution to which we must conform. However painful it may be for me, if the Almighty should ever impose upon me the duties of wife and mother, I shall strive to fulfil them as faithfully as I can, without troubling to consider my feelings towards him whom he may give me for a husband.

I have received a letter from my brother, who announces that he is coming to Bald Hills with his wife. This will be a pleasure of brief duration, since he is leaving us to become part of this unhappy war in which we have become embroiled, God alone knows how and why. It is not only with you, at the centre of business and society, that all the talk is of war. Here too, with the countryman at his labour and nature at peace, which is how city-dwellers usually imagine the countryside, painful rumours of war are heard and felt. My father talks of nothing but marching and counter-marching, of which I have no understanding, and the day before yesterday, while out for my customary walk down the village street, I witnessed a heart-rending scene ... It was a convoy of recruits who had been enrolled here and were being sent off to the army ... You should have seen what a state they were in, the mothers, wives and children of the men who were going, and heard the sobbing on both sides! It seemed as if humanity had forgotten the laws of its divine Saviour, who preached love and forgiveness, and were placing the greatest merit in the art of killing one another.

Goodbye for now, my dear, good friend. May our divine Saviour and his most Holy Mother keep you and guard you in their holiness and strength.

                                                                    MARIE

'Oh, you are sending a letter, Princess. I've already sent mine. I've written to my poor mother,' said a smiling Mademoiselle Bourienne, sharply and brightly in her pleasant, ringing voice with its very throaty *r*s. She had swept into the stiflingly sad and gloomy atmosphere surrounding the princess bringing with her a quite different world of light-hearted and self-sustaining frivolity. 'Princess, I have to warn you,' she added, lowering her voice, 'the prince has had an altercation,' she said, with the *r* throatier than ever, and seeming to enjoy hearing herself speak. 'An altercation with Mikhail Ivanovich. He's in a bad mood, very grumpy. Be warned. Now you know . . .'

'Oh, my dear friend,' answered Princess Marya, 'I have asked you never to tell me in advance about my father's moods. I do not allow myself to pass judgement on him and would not wish others do so.'

The princess glanced at her watch, and saw that she was already five minutes late for clavichord practice. She went into the sitting-room with alarm written all over her face. From twelve to two, as laid down by the timetable for each day, the prince took his rest and the princess played the clavichord.

CHAPTER 23

The grey-haired valet was sitting in the ante-room dozing and listening to the prince snoring away in his immense study. From the far end of the house through all the closed doors came the sound of music, the hard passages of a Dussek sonata[42] being repeated twenty times over.

Two carriages, one large, one small, drove up to the steps. Prince Andrey got out of one, helped his little wife down and let her go on ahead. Grey old Tikhon in his wig slipped out from the ante-room and whispered that the prince was taking his nap, and closed the door quickly after himself. Tikhon knew that no unusual events, not even the arrival of his son, must infringe the timetable for each day. Prince Andrey clearly knew this as well as Tikhon. He consulted his watch as if wondering whether his father's habits might have changed while he had been away, and when he was satisfied that they hadn't he turned to his wife.

'He'll be up in twenty minutes. Let's go and see Princess Marya,' he said.

The little princess had filled out recently, but her eyes and that short upper lip with its touch of down and its bright smile popped up as sweetly and cheerfully as ever when she spoke.

'But it's a palace!' she exclaimed to her husband, staring around and speaking like someone at a ball who wants to praise the host. 'Come on, let's hurry!' She still stared round, smiling at them all, Tikhon, her husband and the servant helping them in.

'Is that Marie practising? Let's go in quietly and surprise her.' Prince Andrey followed politely behind her, looking depressed.

'You've aged a bit, Tikhon,' he said as he walked by the old man, who was kissing his hand.

Just as they reached the room where the clavichord was being played a pretty blonde Frenchwoman skipped out through a side door. Mademoiselle Bourienne seemed beside herself with joy.

'Oh, what a treat for the princess!' she exclaimed. 'At last! I must tell her.'

'No, no, please don't . . .' said the little princess, kissing her. 'You must be Mademoiselle Bourienne. I know about you because you have been such a good friend to my sister-in-law. She's not expecting us!'

They went to the sitting-room door through which came the sounds of the same passage being repeated over and over again. Prince Andrey stopped with a frown, as if something unpleasant was about to happen.

Then the little princess went in. The playing stopped half-way through. He heard an exclamation followed by the heavy footsteps of Princess Marya and kissing noises. When Prince Andrey came in the two princesses, who had met only once before, briefly, at the wedding, were hugging each other and kissing hard wherever they happened to touch. Mademoiselle Bourienne was standing near them, hand on heart, smiling blissfully and not knowing whether to laugh or to cry. Prince Andrey shrugged and scowled like a music-lover frowning at a false note. The two ladies let go, then immediately seized each other's hands as if every second counted, kissed them, tore them away, smothered each other's faces with more kisses and then amazed Prince Andrey by bursting into floods of tears, both of them, before carrying on with yet more kissing. Mademoiselle Bourienne cried too. Prince Andrey was clearly embarrassed, but to the two women crying seemed the most natural thing in the world; it would never have occurred to them that this meeting could have taken place without it.

'Oh, my dear! . . . My dear Marie! . . .' both ladies blurted out together, and then laughed. 'I had a dream last night . . . You really didn't expect us? . . . Oh, Marie, you've lost weight.' 'And you've put some on . . .'

'I recognized the princess straightaway,' put in Mademoiselle Bourienne.

'No, I had no idea! . . .' cried Princess Marya. 'Oh, Andrey, I didn't see you there.'

Prince Andrey and his sister kissed each other's hands, and he told her she was just the same crybaby she always had been. Princess Marya turned to her brother, and through all the tears her wide and radiant eyes, shining for an instant with a rare beauty, lingered with gentle, loving tenderness on Prince Andrey's face. The little princess chattered away. Her short, downy upper lip would flick down momentarily to meet the rosy, lower lip at just the right point, only to flit away in a smile, teeth gleaming and eyes sparkling. She was describing something that had happened to them on Spassky Hill that could have been serious for someone in her condition, and went on to say that she had left all her dresses behind in Petersburg and God knows what she would walk about in here, that Andrey had completely changed, that Kitty Odyntsov had married an old man, and that someone 'quite serious' had turned up as a suitor for Princess Marya, but that was something they could talk about later. Princess Marya was still gazing in silence at her brother, her lovely eyes filled with affection and sadness. She was clearly thinking thoughts of her own, miles away from the young bride's chatter. In the middle of her sister-in-law's description of the last holiday celebration in Petersburg she spoke to her brother.

'So, it's settled, then. You are going to the war, Andrey?' she asked with a sigh. Liza sighed with her.

'Yes, I'm going tomorrow,' answered her brother.

'He's deserting me. God knows why, when he could have been promoted . . .'

Princess Marya stopped listening, followed her own train of thought and then turned to Liza, directing sympathetic eyes to her figure.

'It's true, then?' she asked.

Liza's face changed, and she gave a sigh.

'Yes, it's true,' she said. 'Oh! I'm so scared . . .'

Liza's lip drooped. She brought her face close to her sister-in-law's, and yet again she burst into tears.

'She needs to rest,' said Prince Andrey with a frown. 'Don't you, Liza? Take her to your room, while I go and see Father. How is he – same as always?'

'Yes, just the same. I don't know what you'll make of him,' Princess Marya answered with some delight.

'The same old timetable, walks in the avenues, that lathe?' asked Prince Andrey with a barely noticeable smile which showed that he loved and respected his father but knew about his eccentricities.

'The same timetable, the same lathe, still mathematics – and my geometry lessons,' Princess Marya answered cheerfully, as though geometry lessons were one of the most delightful prospects in her life.

When the old prince's twenty minutes for getting up had come and gone, Tikhon arrived to summon the young man to his father. The old man allowed one infringement of his normal routine in honour of his son's arrival, arranging for him to be admitted to his rooms while he was dressing for dinner. The old prince dressed in the old style – all kaftan and powder. And when Prince Andrey walked into his father's room, not with the moody face and attitude that he assumed for entering fashionable drawing-rooms, but with the eager look he had shown when talking to Pierre, the old man was sitting in a big leather armchair with his head abandoned to the ministrations of Tikhon.

'Aha! The warrior comes! So you want to fight Bonaparte?' said the old man, shaking his powdered head and pigtail as best he could, with Tikhon still working on it. 'And you get after him as soon as you like, or he'll have us down as his subjects sooner than you think. Hello, my boy!'

And he offered a cheek.

The old gentleman was in fine fettle after his nap before dinner. (Sleep after dinner is silver, sleep before dinner is gold, was his motto.) He aimed delighted sideways glances at his son from beneath his thick bushy eyebrows. Prince Andrey walked forward and kissed his father on the appointed spot. He avoided any comment on his father's hobby horse – joking about today's military men and especially Bonaparte.

'Yes, I have come to you, Father, with a wife who is pregnant,' said Prince Andrey, his lively, respectful eyes following every movement of his father's face. 'How are you keeping?'

'It's only fools and libertines that fall ill, my boy, and you know me – busy from dawn to dusk and I don't indulge. Of course I'm well.'

'Thank God for that,' said his son with a smile.

'God doesn't come into it. Come on then, start telling me,' the old man continued, back on his favourite topic, 'what have the Germans taught you about fighting Bonaparte with this new scientific stuff – strategy, or whatever they call it?'

Prince Andrey smiled.

'Give me a minute to recover, Father,' he said, with a smile which showed that his father's foibles did not prevent his respecting and loving him. 'I haven't even been to my room yet.'

'Nonsense, my boy,' cried the old man, shaking his pigtail to make sure it was properly plaited, and taking his son by the hand. 'The house is ready for your wife. Marie will take her around and show her everything, and they'll talk the hind leg off a donkey. That's the way with women. I'm pleased she's come. So, sit down and talk to me. I know about Mikhelson's army, and Tolstoy's[43] . . . simultaneous attacks . . . But what's the Southern Army going to be doing? Then there's Prussia, she's neutral . . . I know about that. What about Austria?' he asked, getting up from his chair and pacing up and down the room, with Tikhon trotting at his heels, handing him various articles of clothing. 'And Sweden? And how will they get through Pomerania?'

After listening to question after question put so insistently by his father, Prince Andrey started to outline the plan of operations of the proposed campaign. Reluctant at first, he soon became more and more enthusiastic, and as he spoke he followed his usual habit of alternating between Russian and French. He told him an army of ninety thousand was to threaten Prussia in order to bring her out of neutrality and into the war, some of these men were to join with the Swedes at Stralsund, two hundred and twenty thousand Austrians would combine with a hundred thousand Russians in Italy and on the Rhine, fifty thousand Russians and fifty thousand English were to land at Naples, and the entire half-a-million-strong army would then attack the French on several different fronts. The old prince showed no sign of interest in what he was saying – he seemed not to be listening – and he carried on getting dressed as he walked up and down, but he did make three sudden interruptions.

Once he stopped and shouted, 'The white one! The white one!', meaning that Tikhon had handed him the wrong waistcoat.

Another time he stopped and asked, 'When is she due?', shaking his head reproachfully: 'Hmm . . . Too bad! Well, get on with it.'

The third time was when Prince Andrey was coming towards the end of his story. Suddenly the old man's wobbly falsetto sang out the French song, 'Marlborough is off to war, God knows when we'll see him . . .'[44] His son merely smiled.

'I don't say it's a plan I approve of,' he said. 'I'm just telling you how things are. Napoleon has his own plan and it's no worse than ours.'

'Well, you've told me nothing new.'

Pensively the old man gabbled to himself, ' "God knows when we'll see him . . ." Go on into dinner.'

CHAPTER 24

Exactly on time, the prince, well powdered and clean-shaven, strode into the dining-room, to be welcomed by his daughter-in-law, Princess Marya, Mademoiselle Bourienne and the prince's architect, who was allowed to dine with them by some strange whim of the master, even though such an unimportant person of no significant status was hardly entitled to such an honour. Normally a stickler for social distinctions, the prince was loath to admit to his table even important local dignitaries, but he had suddenly lighted on the architect Mikhail Ivanovich, who had a habit of going into a corner to blow his nose into a checked handkerchief, as living proof that all men are equal, and had repeatedly impressed on his daughter that Mikhail Ivanovich was by no means an inferior. At meals the prince spent most of his time talking to the architect, who never said anything back.

Like all the other rooms in the house, the dining-room was vast, with a high ceiling. With the prince about to enter, servants and waiters stood there expectantly, one behind each chair. The butler, with a napkin draped over his arm, was checking the table and giving eye-signals to the servants, all the time glancing uneasily from the wall-clock to the doorway through which the prince would soon enter. Prince Andrey was staring at something new – an immense gilt frame containing the Bolkonsky family tree and across from it another frame, just as big, with a badly painted image of a crowned Prince Regent (obviously done by some amateur domestic), supposedly a descendant of Rurik[45] and founder of the Bolkonsky dynasty. Prince Andrey shook his head as he looked at this family tree and laughed as you would at an unintended caricature.

'That's him to a T!' he said to Princess Marya as she came up to him.

Princess Marya looked at her brother in surprise, not seeing anything funny about it. Everything her father did was beyond criticism and inspired reverence.

'Everyone has an Achilles' heel,' Prince Andrey went on. 'All *his* vast intellect, and he sinks to this level of crassness!'

Princess Marya couldn't understand her brother's biting criticism and was just about to protest when the footsteps they were all listening for were heard coming from the study. In strode the prince with a brisk joviality. This was how he always walked, as if consciously contradicting the strict household regime with a bustling manner of his own. On the instant the big clock struck two and another clock in the drawing-room echoed with a thinner chime. The prince stopped and peered out sternly from under his great bushy eyebrows, his sharp eyes glinting as they first surveyed all the diners and then lighted on the little princess. She felt like a courtier at the entrance of the Tsar, such was the feeling of intimidation and profound respect that this old man evoked in everyone about him. He stroked her hair, and then rather awkwardly gave her a pat on the neck.

'Yes, I'm very pleased,' he said, and after staring into her eyes he walked off and sat down in his place. 'Do sit down, everyone. Mikhail Ivanovich, do sit down.'

He motioned for his daughter-in-law to sit beside him, and a footman pulled back a chair for her.

'Oho!' said the old man, looking at her rounded figure. 'You've not wasted any time. Not a good thing!' His laugh was dry, cold and disagreeable; as always he laughed with his mouth, but not with his eyes. 'You must go out walking, plenty of walking, yes, as much as you can,' he said.

The little princess, not hearing him, or perhaps not wanting to, sat there in silence, looking embarrassed. But when the prince asked after her father she began to talk and smile. He also asked about common acquaintances, at which she became more and more animated, and began chattering away, conveying best wishes from various people and telling him the city gossip.

'Countess Apraksin has lost her husband and she cried her eyes out, poor dear,' she said, growing livelier by the moment. As she did so, the prince stared at her more and more severely, and then suddenly, as though he had studied all there was to study about her and formed a clear impression, he turned the other way and spoke to Mikhail Ivanovich.

'Well, Mikhail Ivanovich, our friend Bu . . . onaparte is in for a bad time. Prince Andrey' (he always spoke of his son in the third person) 'has just been telling me what forces are being massed against him! And you and I always thought he was a nobody.'

Mikhail Ivanovich had no knowledge of a time when 'you and I' had said any such thing about Napoleon, but he could see that he was needed so that they could get round to the prince's favourite subject, so he sat there staring at the younger prince, nonplussed and wondering what might now develop.

'He's my master tactician!' said the prince to his son, pointing to the architect, and once again the conversation turned to the war, Napoleon, and the latest generals and politicians. The old prince seemed convinced that all these public men were babes-in-arms without the slightest knowledge of warfare and politics, and Napoleon was a useless French nonentity who had been successful only because there were no more Potyomkins[46] and Suvorovs to stop him. He was even convinced there weren't any political difficulties in Europe, there wasn't any war, only a kind of puppet show with people fooling around, pretending to be doing something serious. Prince Andrey accepted his father's sneering attitude towards the new people quite cheerfully, and egged his father on to say more. He obviously enjoyed listening.

'The past always seems better,' he said, 'but didn't Suvorov fall into a trap he couldn't get out of, set by Moreau?'

'Who told you that? Who said so?' cried the prince. 'Suvorov!' He flung his plate away and Tikhon caught it deftly. 'Suvorov! . . . Think again, Prince Andrey. Here we have two men – Frederick and Suvorov . . . Moreau? Moreau would have been a prisoner if Suvorov's hands hadn't been tied behind his back – by that Hofs-kriegs-wurst-schnapps-rath.[47] That lot would stop the devil himself. Oh, you'll soon find out about these Hofs-kriegs-wurst-schnapps-raths! Suvorov couldn't cope with them, so how can Mikhail Kutuzov? No, my dear fellow,' he went on, 'you and your generals won't get past Napoleon. You'll have to get hold of some Frenchmen – set a thief to catch a thief! That German, Pahlen, has been sent off to New York in America to get that Frenchman, Moreau,' he said, having in mind that Moreau had been invited to enter the Russian service that year. 'It's marvellous, isn't it? All those Potyomkins, Suvorovs and Orlovs, they weren't Germans, were they? No, my boy, either you've all lost your wits, or I've outgrown mine. God help you, but we'll see what happens. So now they've got Napoleon down as a great general, have they? Pah! . . .'

'I'm not saying that all our preparations are perfect,' said Prince Andrey; 'but I can't see how you can judge Napoleon like that. You can laugh all you want, but Napoleon *is* a great general!'

'Mikhail Ivanovich!' the old prince shouted to the architect, who was enjoying his meat and rather hoped they had forgotten about him. 'I told you Bonaparte was a master tactician? Now he says so too.'

'Ah well, your Excellency,' replied the architect.

The prince gave another chilling laugh.

'Napoleon was born with a silver spoon in his mouth. He's got some splendid soldiers – and besides that he picked the Germans to attack first. You'd have to be pretty slow not to beat the Germans. Since time began everybody has beaten the Germans. And they've never beaten anybody – except each other. He made his name fighting them.'

And off went the prince analysing all the blunders he thought Bonaparte had perpetrated in his wars and even in politics. His son made no objection, but it was clear that whatever arguments he might have to face, he was as unlikely to change his mind as the old prince himself. Prince Andrey listened, managing not to object. He couldn't help wondering how this old man, who had spent so many years alone in the countryside, never going anywhere, could keep abreast of all the military and political developments in Europe over recent years and discuss them in such detail and with such accuracy.

'You think I'm an old man and I don't know how things stand, don't you?' he said, drawing things to a close. 'I'm telling you I do! Sometimes I can't sleep for nights on end. Anyway, where is this great general of yours? Where has he proved himself?'

'That would be a long story,' answered his son.

'Go on with you, you and your Napoleon. Mademoiselle Bourienne, here's someone else who admires your country bumpkin of an emperor!' he cried in excellent French.

'You know I am not a Bonapartist, Prince.'

' "God knows when we'll see him . . ." ' the prince hummed tunelessly, and his laugh was even more grating as he rose from the table.

The little princess had sat through the whole argument and the rest of the dinner without saying a word, looking in some alarm from Princess Marya to her father-in-law. When they left the table she took her sister-in-law's arm and led her off into another room.

'What a clever man your father is,' she said. 'Perhaps that's why I'm so scared of him.'

'Oh, he is so kind!' said Princess Marya.

CHAPTER 25

It was the next evening, and Prince Andrey was preparing to leave. The old prince, not one to disrupt his regular routine, had retired to his room after dinner. The little princess was with her sister-in-law. Prince Andrey had put on his civilian travelling coat and spent some time cloistered with his valet, packing. After making a personal inspection of the carriage and the stowing of his trunks he gave orders for the horses to be harnessed. In the room there was nothing left but a few things that Prince Andrey always carried with him: a travelling case, a silver canteen, two Turkish pistols and a sabre, the last a present from his father brought back from Suvorov's siege of Ochakov.[48] All of these travelling essentials were in excellent order; everything was spick and span, covered with cloth and meticulously taped up.

At a time of departure and change thinking people usually find themselves in a serious frame of mind. At such a time you tend to review the past and make plans for the future. Prince Andrey's face was gentle and very thoughtful. He paced briskly up and down the room from one corner to another with his arms behind his back, staring ahead and pensively shaking his head. Whether he was worried about going off to war or sad at leaving his wife – or perhaps a little of both – he evidently didn't want to be caught like that; at the sudden sound of approaching footsteps he quickly unclasped his hands and stood by a table, pretending to be fastening the lid of the case, and he resumed his normally calm and inscrutable expression. He had heard the heavy tread of Princess Marya.

'They told me you were having the horses harnessed,' she said, all out of breath (she must have been running), 'and I did want to have one more little talk with you on our own. Heaven knows how long we shall be apart this time. I hope you're not angry that I've come? Andryusha, you really have changed, you know,' she added, as if that justified her question.

She smiled as she called him 'Andryusha'. She could hardly imagine that this forbiddingly handsome man was the same Andryusha as that wiry, mischievous little boy who had been the companion of her childhood.

'Where's Lise?' he asked, and a smile was his only answer.

'She was so tired she fell asleep on the sofa in my room. Oh, Andrey, what a treasure of a wife you have,' she said, sitting down on the sofa facing her brother. 'She's just a perfect child, such a sweet, happy child. I've really taken to her.' Prince Andrey said nothing, but the princess watched as a look of irony and scorn came over his face.

'But you have to put up with little weaknesses. We all have them, Andrey. Don't forget she's been brought up and educated in high society. And besides, her present position is not all that rosy. We must try to put ourselves in other people's places. When you understand everything you can forgive everything. Just think what it must be like for her, poor girl, after the life she's been used to, to part from her husband and then be left alone in the country, and in her condition too. It's very hard on her.'

Prince Andrey looked at his sister and smiled the kind of smile we reserve for people we think we can see through.

'You live in the country and you don't find it too awful,' he said.

'It's not the same thing. Don't bring me into it. I don't wish for any other kind of life, and I couldn't if I wanted to, because I don't know any other kind of life. But just think, Andrey, what it means for a young woman who is used to living in society to bury herself away in the country for the best years of her life and all on her own – because Papa is always busy, and I . . . well, you know me . . . I'm poor company for a society woman. There's only Mademoiselle Bourienne . . .'

'I don't like her, that Bourienne woman,' said Prince Andrey.

'Oh, you mustn't say that! She's so kind, and so sweet, and – well, you have to be sorry for her too. She has nobody, nobody at all. If you want to know the truth, she's no use to me, in fact I find her oppressive. You know I've always been unsociable, and now I'm worse than ever. I like to be on my own . . . Father's very fond of her. She and Mikhail Ivanovich are the only two people he gets on with and keeps his temper with, because they are both beholden to him. As Laurence Sterne says: "We love people not so much for the good they have done to us as for the good we have done to them." Father picked her up off the streets as an orphan, and she's very good-hearted. And father likes the way she reads. She reads to him in the evenings. She does it very well.'

'But be honest, Marie, I can only think sometimes it must be hard for you living with Father. You know the way he is,' Prince Andrey suggested suddenly. Princess Marya was taken aback, then shocked by this question.

'Me? . . . me? . . . Hard for me!' she said.

'He's always been on the stern side, but now I think he's getting quite difficult,' said Prince Andrey, disparaging their father so easily that he must surely have meant to tease his sister – or test her.

'You're a good man, Andrey, but there is a kind of intellectual pride about you,' said the princess, apparently following her own train of thought rather than the thread of the conversation, 'and this is a great sin. How can we pass judgement on our own father? And even if we could, what feeling but the deepest admiration could a man like Father evoke? I am so pleased and happy to be with him. I just wish all of you were as happy as I am.'

Her brother shook his head in some doubt.

'The only thing that bothers me – honestly, Andrey – is our father's cast of mind in a religious sense. I can't understand how a man of such vast intellect can fail to see what is as clear as daylight, and can get things so wrong. That's the one thing that disturbs me. And even here I think I've seen a glimmer of improvement recently. Lately he has not been so bitter with his mockery, and he has been willing to receive a monk and he talked to him for a very long time.'

'Well, my dear, I'm afraid you and your monk are wasting your powder,' said Prince Andrey in amused but affectionate tones.

'Oh, my dear friend, all I can do is pray to God and hope that he will hear me. Andrey,' she said timidly, after a moment's pause, 'I have a great favour to ask you.'

'What is it, my dear?'

'Promise me you won't refuse. It will cost you almost nothing and it won't involve anything disreputable. Only it will be such a comfort to me. Promise, Andryusha,' she said, thrusting one hand into her handbag and getting hold of something without showing it, as though what she was holding concerned the favour she was asking, but until she had a promise that it would be granted she could not take that *something* out. She looked sheepishly at her brother, imploring him with her eyes.

'Even if it cost me a great deal . . .' answered Prince Andrey, who seemed almost to have guessed what it was all about.

'I don't mind what you think about it. I know you're like father. Think what you want, but do it for my sake, please. Father's own father, our grandfather, wore this whenever he went to war . . .' She still didn't take what she was holding out of her bag. 'You promise?'

'Of course I do. What is it?'

'Andrey, I am going to bless you with a holy icon, and you must promise never to take it off . . . Do you promise?'

'As long as it doesn't weigh a hundredweight and won't break my neck . . . To please you . . .' said Prince Andrey. At this little joke he noticed instantly that a pained expression came over his sister's face, and he regretted it. 'I'm really pleased, my dear, really pleased,' he added.

'Even against your will He will save you and spare you and bring you to himself, because in Him alone are truth and peace,' she said in a voice shaking with emotion, solemnly holding before him with both hands a little antique oval icon depicting the Saviour with a black face, in a silver setting, on a very finely wrought silver chain. She crossed herself, kissed the icon and handed it to Andrey.

'Please, Andrey, do it for me.'

Her great wide eyes shone timidly with loving kindness. They lit up the whole of her thin, sickly face and turned it into a thing of beauty. Her brother reached for the icon, but she stopped him. Andrey understood, crossed himself and kissed the icon. He was moved, and his face showed a mixture of amusement and tenderness.

'Thank you, my dear.' She kissed him on the forehead and sat down again on the sofa.

Neither spoke . . .

'So, as I was saying, Andrey, please be kind and generous as you always used to be. Don't judge Lise too harshly,' she began again. 'She is so sweet and kind, and her present situation is very difficult.'

'Masha, I don't think I've said anything about blaming my wife for anything or being dissatisfied with her. Why do you go on like this?'

Princess Marya went all red and blotchy, and stopped speaking as though she felt guilty.

'I have said nothing to you, but *other people have*. That's what makes me sad.'

The red blotches stood out stronger than ever on her forehead, cheeks and neck. She would have liked to say something, but couldn't get it out. Her brother had guessed the truth: his wife had shed tears after dinner, saying she knew she was in for a difficult birth and was terrified of it, and she had cursed her misfortune, her father-in-law and her husband. Only then had she fallen asleep. Prince Andrey was sorry for his sister.

'I can tell you one thing, Masha, I can't reproach *my wife* for anything, I never have done and never shall do, nor do I reproach myself in relation to her, and that will always be so in any circumstances whatsoever. But if you really want to know . . . well, whether I'm happy, the answer is no. Is she happy? No. Why not? I don't know . . .'

As he said this, he stood up, went over to his sister and bent to kiss her on the forehead. His handsome eyes were shining with an unusual brightness and kindness, but he was looking past his sister's head through the open door into the darkness beyond.

'Let's go to her. I have to say goodbye. Or you go on your own and wake her up, and I'll come in a moment. Petrushka!' he called to his valet. 'Come and take these things out. This goes in the seat and that on the right-hand side.'

Princess Marya got up and moved towards the door. She stopped. 'Andrey, if you had faith, you would have turned to God and asked Him to give you the love that you do not feel, and your prayer would have been answered.'

'Yes, you may be right,' said Prince Andrey. 'Go on, Masha, I'll follow you in a minute.'

On the way to his sister's room, in the gallery connecting the two parts of the house, Prince Andrey came across Mademoiselle Bourienne, who smiled sweetly at him. It was the third time that day that she had happened on him in out-of-the-way passages, always with a nice beaming smile on her face.

'Oh, I thought you were in your room,' she said, blushing for some reason and looking down. Prince Andrey glanced at her sharply, and a look of bitter displeasure came over his face. He glared at her in silence, not at her eyes but at her forehead and hair, with such contempt that she turned bright red and walked off without another word. When he got to his sister's room, the little princess was awake and her cheery little voice could be heard through the open door, chattering away like mad. Her French poured out as if she had been too long restrained and now wanted to make up for lost time.

'No, but just think of old Countess Zubov, with all those false curls and her mouth full of false teeth[49] as though she was trying to turn back the years. Hee-hee-hee, Marie!'

This was the fifth or sixth time that Prince Andrey had heard his wife speak these very words about Countess Zubov, and always with the same laugh. He walked quietly into the room. The little princess was sitting in a chair with some sewing in her hands, all round and rosy, coming out with a stream of Petersburg memories and fashionable phrases. Prince Andrey walked over, stroked her on the head and asked if she had got over her tiredness from the journey. She nodded and went on with her tale.

The carriage with six horses stood at the steps. It was an autumn night, so dark the coachman couldn't see the main shaft of his carriage. Servants with lanterns were running up and down the steps. The vast house stood there with its huge windows blazing. House serfs thronged the entrance, eager to wish their young prince Godspeed. All the members of the household were gathered in the great hall: Mikhail Ivanovich, Mademoiselle Bourienne, Princess Marya and the little princess. Prince Andrey had been summoned to his father's study, so they could be alone to say goodbye, and now everyone was waiting for him to come out again. When Prince Andrey went into the study, the old prince was wearing his old-age spectacles and his white dressing-gown, in which he never saw anyone but his son. He was sitting at the table writing. He looked round.

'You're off then?' And he went on writing.

'I've come to say goodbye.'

'Kiss me here.' He offered his cheek. 'Thank you very much!'

'What are you thanking me for?'

'For not hanging about and not being tied to your wife's apron strings. Duty comes first. Thank you very much indeed!' And he went on writing, with ink splattering from his scratching pen. 'If you want to say something, say it. I can manage two things at once,' he added.

'Well, my wife . . . I'm rather embarrassed to be leaving her in your hands . . .'

'What are you rambling on about? Say what you mean.'

'When her time comes, please send to Moscow for a specialist . . . I want him here.'

The old prince stopped, bemused, and glared harshly at his son.

'I know no one can help if nature doesn't,' said Prince Andrey, much embarrassed. 'I know it's only a chance in a million, but it's her one nightmare – and mine. She has heard things, she's had bad dreams and she's very scared.'

'Hm . . . hm . . .' mumbled the old prince, going on with his writing. 'I'll see to it.' He signed with a flourish, and then turned sharply to his son and laughed.

'Bad business, eh?'

'What is, father?'

'Wife!' said the old prince, curt but emphatic.

'I don't know what you mean,' said Prince Andrey.

'Can't be helped, dear boy,' said the old prince, 'they're all like that, and you can't get unmarried now. Don't worry, I shan't tell anyone, but you know it's true.'

He grasped his son's hand with bony little fingers and shook it, looking him straight in the face with sharp eyes that seemed to see right through him, and gave another chilling laugh.

The son sighed, inadvertently admitting that his father had seen through him. The old man was busy folding and sealing the letters, helter-skelter as always, snatching up wax, seal and paper and throwing them down again. 'Can't be helped. She's a pretty thing. I'll do everything. Not to worry,' he said in his staccato manner as he finished sealing the letters.

Andrey said nothing, feeling both pleased and displeased that his father had seen through him. The old man got up and gave his son the first letter.

'Listen,' he said. 'Don't worry about your wife. What can be done will be done. Now, keep listening. Give this letter to General Kutuzov. I've written to ask him to use you properly and not leave you long as an adjutant – ghastly job! Tell him I remember him with affection. And let me know how he receives you. If he's all right, serve him well. No son of Nikolay Bolkonsky needs to serve out of charity. Now, come here.'

He was gabbling so much that half his words never got finished, but his son was used to understanding him. He took Prince Andrey over to the bureau, opened the top and pulled out a drawer, taking from it a note-book filled from cover to cover with his big, bold, closely written handwriting.

'I'm sure to die before you do. See, these are my notes, to be given to the Emperor after my death. Now see here, this is a State Lottery Bond and there's a letter with it. It's a prize for the first person to write a history of Suvorov's wars. Send it to the Academy. Here are my notes. They're for you to read when I'm gone. Should be of some use to you.'

Andrey didn't tell his father he probably still had many years to live. He knew it went without saying.

'I shall do what you say, Father,' he said.

'Well, goodbye then!' He gave his son his hand to kiss and then embraced him. 'Remember this, Prince Andrey, if you get killed, it will be a great sadness to me in my old age . . .' He broke off sharply, and then bawled at him, 'but if I hear that you have not behaved like the son of Nikolay Bolkonsky, I shall be . . . *ashamed* of you.'

'You needn't have told me that, Father,' said his son with a smile.

The old man now said nothing.

'There's just one more thing I wanted to ask you,' went on Prince Andrey. 'If I do get killed, and if I have a son, don't let them take him away from you. As I said yesterday, let him grow up with you . . . please.'

'Don't give him up to your wife?' said the old man with a laugh.

They stood there in silence facing each other. The old man's sharp eyes were fixed firmly on his son's. A kind of tremor ran over the lower part of the old prince's face.

'We've said goodbye . . . Just go!' he said suddenly. 'Go!' he cried in a loud angry voice, opening the study door.

'What is it? What's wrong?' asked the two princesses when they saw Prince Andrey, and caught a glimpse of the old prince without his wig, wearing his white dressing-gown and his old-age spectacles, and heard him shouting angrily.

Prince Andrey sighed and made no reply.

'Come on, then,' he said, turning to his wife, and his 'Come on, then' sounded like a cold rebuke, as if he had said, 'Let's see you put on your little act.'

'Andrey, it can't be time to go!' cried the little princess, turning pale and looking fearfully at her husband. He embraced her. She gave a little cry and fell in a faint on his shoulder.

He eased her away from his shoulder, looked her in the face and carefully sat her down in a chair.

'Goodbye, Masha,' he said softly to his sister, and they kissed hands. Then he strode briskly out of the room.

The little princess flopped back, sprawling across the armchair, and Mademoiselle Bourienne began to massage her temples, while Princess Marya also offered support, but with her tearful eyes still glued to the door through which Prince Andrey had disappeared.

She made the sign of the cross. From the study came the angry sounds of an old man blowing his nose, like one pistol shot after another. The moment Prince Andrey left the room, his study door was flung open and out peered the forbidding figure of the old man in his white dressing-gown.

'Has he gone? Good thing too!' he said, glaring at the swooning princess. He shook his head in disapproval and slammed the door.

PART II

In October 1805 Russian troops were busy occupying towns and villages in the Archduchy of Austria, with new regiments arriving all the time from Russia and settling near the fortress of Braunau, making life hard for the inhabitants on whom they were billeted. Braunau was the headquarters of the commander-in-chief, General Kutuzov.

On the 11th of October 1805[1] one of the newly arrived infantry regiments had halted half a mile from Braunau, awaiting inspection by the commander-in-chief. The countryside and the general situation may have looked foreign with all those orchards, stone walls, tiled roofs, mountains in the distance and foreign peasants gawking at the Russian soldiers, but the regiment looked just like any Russian regiment getting ready for inspection anywhere in the depths of Russia.

Yesterday evening, on the last stage of the march, an order had been received: the commander-in-chief would inspect the regiment on the march. The wording of the order was not quite clear to the commanding officer, leaving open the question of whether or not the men should be in battle dress or in full dress uniform. It was decided after consultation with the battalion commanders to present the regiment in full dress; as they say, better to bow too low than not low enough. And after marching twenty-five miles the men had been kept up all night mending and cleaning, while the staff officers checked numbers and gave orders. By morning the regiment, a straggling shambles on the eve of the last march, looked like an orderly formation of two thousand men, everyone knowing his place and his duty, buttons firm and straps tight, everything spick and span and gleaming. And not only on the surface; if it should occur to the commander-in-chief to check underneath the uniform he would see that every man was wearing a clean shirt, and in every knapsack he would find the regulation number of articles, the complete soldier's 'soap and sewing kit'. There was only one thing that no one could be happy with – their foot-gear.

More than half the boots had holes in them. This was no fault of the commanding officer; in spite of repeated demands the Austrian authorities had left him under-supplied, and the regiment had now marched over seven hundred miles.

The regimental commander was an ageing ruddy-faced general with grizzled whiskers and eyebrows, rather portly, broader from front to back than from side to side. His uniform was brand new and still nicely creased, with great big golden epaulettes which wouldn't lie down properly on his big shoulders. He had the air of a man who was happily fulfilling one of life's most solemn duties. He paraded up and down the front rank and as he did so his body quivered and his back was arched. Here was a general unmistakably proud of his regiment, happy with it and serving it with all his energy and spirit. Even so, his quivering walk seemed to suggest that his personal interests extended well beyond the military to include good society and the fair sex.

'Well now, my good Mikhail Mitrich,' he said, addressing one of the battalion commanders who had stepped forward with a smile on his face. (They were clearly in good spirits, both of them.) 'Last night kept us on our toes, didn't it? . . . Still, the regiment's not too bad now . . . Must be one or two worse than ours, eh?'

The major understood this ironical banter and he laughed.

'Fit for the best parade ground, even Tsaritsyn Field.'[2]

'What's that?' said the commander.

Two riders had come into view down the road from the town where signalmen had been posted. They were an aide-de-camp with a Cossack riding along behind him. The aide had been sent from staff headquarters to confirm what had not been clearly stated in the previous order, that the commander-in-chief wished to inspect the regiment just as it was on the road – in greatcoats, carrying rucksacks and with no special preparation. A member of the Hofkriegsrath from Vienna had come to Kutuzov the previous day with a proposal, nay a demand, that he proceed as soon as possible to join forces with the army of Archduke Ferdinand and General Mack. Kutuzov considered this inadvisable, and now, as part of his supporting argument, he wanted to demonstrate to the Austrian general the pitiable condition the troops were in after marching all the way from Russia. With this in mind he intended to ride out and meet them on the road: the worse the regiment looked, the more delighted the commander-in-chief would be. The aide was not privy to all the details, but he did communicate the commander-in-chief's categorical insistence that the men be in greatcoats and marching order, and that anything other than that would incur his displeasure.

At these words the commanding officer's head sank down; he gave a shrug, and flung up his arms with some passion.

'Now we've done it!' he said. 'Mikhail Mitrich, I told you "on the march" meant dressed in greatcoats,' he rebuked the major. 'Oh, my God!' he added, but then he stepped forward resolutely. 'Company captains!' he roared in a voice well used to bawling commands. 'Sergeant-majors! . . . When will his Excellency be here?' he asked, turning to the aide with an expression of obsequious deference that was really meant for the person he was referring to.

'In an hour's time, I believe.'

'Have we time to change?'

'I couldn't say, General . . .'

The general went down among the ranks to supervise personally the change back into greatcoats. Captains rushed through their companies, sergeant-majors worried about greatcoats that weren't quite right, and it took only a few moments for the solid and silent rectangles to stir, straggle and buzz with talk. Soldiers ran about everywhere – jerking their shoulders to lift up their rucksacks, pulling the straps over their heads, fishing out their greatcoats and reaching up with their arms to pull down the sleeves.

Half an hour later everything was back to normal, but the rectangles were grey rather than black. The general set off with his quivering walk to parade himself before the regiment, scanning it from some way off.

'What the . . . ? What's all this?' he roared, coming to a halt. 'Captain of the third company!'

'Captain of the third company, report to the general! Company captain to the general! . . . Third company to the captain! . . .' Voices rang out down the ranks, and an aide ran off to find the laggardly officer. When this urgent clamour reached its destination, having mixed up all the orders until eventually they were shouting 'General to report to the third company!', the officer in question emerged from the rear of his company, and, although he was an elderly man and no great runner, he managed a fair trot towards the general, tripping over his own toes as he came. The captain looked like a shifty schoolboy who had been told to run through some homework that he hadn't done. His face, already bright red in colour – he was clearly no abstainer – now turned blotchy and his mouth twitched. The general looked him up and down as he ran forward, gasping and slowing down with every step.

'Do you want your men in women's dresses! What's the meaning of this?' roared the general, setting his jaw and pointing in the ranks of the third division to a soldier wearing a different-coloured greatcoat from everyone else's, the colour of factory cloth. 'And where have you been? The commander-in-chief is expected, and you're not where you should be! Eh? . . . I'll teach you to put your men in fancy dress for an inspection! . . . Eh?'

The captain, never taking his eyes off his superior officer, pressed his two fingers harder and harder against the peak of his cap, as if his only hope of safety lay in saluting as hard as he could.

'Well, why don't you *say something*? Who's that man dressed up like a Hungarian?' The general's joke was a bitter one.

'Your Excellency.'

'What do you mean, "your Excellency?" I'll give you "your Excellency"! You say it, but nobody knows what you mean!'

'Your Excellency, that man is Private Dolokhov. He's been reduced to the ranks,' the captain said softly.

'Are you sure he wasn't reduced to field marshal? If he's a private, he should be dressed like the others, regulation kit.'

'Your Excellency, you gave him permission, on the march.'

'Permission? What permission? There you go, you're all the same, you youngsters,' said the general, cooling down a little. 'Permission? A simple remark, and you take it . . .' He paused. 'Yes, you, er, take it . . . Well, what about it?' he said, newly infuriated. 'Kindly make sure your men are properly turned out . . .'

And the general, looking round at his aide, walked his quivering way back to the regiment, patently delighted with his own show of displeasure and now, as he walked through the ranks, looking for other excuses to blow his top. He tore a strip off one officer for having a dirty badge, and another because his column was out of line; then he came to the third company.

'Call that standing to attention? What's that leg doing? That leg, what's it doing?' the general roared with his long-suffering tone, and he was still five men short of Dolokhov, the man in the blue greatcoat. Dolokhov slowly straightened his leg, and looked brazenly with his clear eyes at the general's face.

'Why are you wearing a blue coat? Get it off! . . . Sergeant-major! Change this man's coat . . . the filthy sw . . .' But he wasn't allowed to complete the word.

'General, I am bound to obey orders, but not to put up with . . .' Dolokhov spoke rapidly.

'No talking in the ranks! . . . No talking there! No talking!'

'. . . not to put up with insults,' Dolokhov persisted in a clear and confident voice. The eyes of general and private met. The general demurred, angrily pulling down on his tight scarf.

'Be so kind as to change your coat,' he said, and walked on.

CHAPTER 2

'He's coming!' came the call from a signalman. The general, red in the face, ran to his horse, grasped the stirrup with trembling hands, swung himself up and across, settled down in the saddle, drew his sword, and with a look of pleasure and determination opened one side of his mouth, ready to shout. The regiment stirred itself like a bird settling its feathers, then all was still and silent.

'Atten-shun!' roared the general in a voice that would shake souls, a voice of personal pleasure, of warning to the regiment and of welcome to the approaching commander-in-chief.

Towards them down the broad, tree-lined country road came a tall, blue Viennese coach drawn by six horses at a smart trot, creaking on its springs. The general's entourage and an escort of Croats followed on behind the coach. At Kutuzov's side sat an Austrian general in a white uniform that looked out of place among the black Russian ones. The coach drew up before the regiment. Kutuzov and the Austrian general were chatting together in low voices, and Kutuzov gave a slight smile as he stepped down ponderously from the carriage step, for all the world as if these two thousand men watching him and the other general with bated breath simply didn't exist.

A command rang out; the regiment jerked into life and presented arms with a ringing clatter. Then through the deathly silence came the reedy voice of the commander-in-chief. The regiment roared its response: 'Long live His Ex – cellency! . . . ency . . . ency!' Then silence again. At first Kutuzov stood rooted to one spot while the regiment changed formation, then he began walking along the ranks, accompanied by the general in white and followed by his entourage.

From the way the regimental commander saluted his commander-in-chief, staring fixedly at him, rigidly to attention and yet somehow cringing, from the way he bent forward eagerly as he followed the generals down the ranks, barely disguising his quivering walk, and jumped nervously at every word and movement of the commander-in-chief, it was evident that he was enjoying his role as a subordinate even more than his role as a commander. Because of his strictness and keenness, the regiment was in fine fettle compared with others that had reached Braunau at the same time. The sick and the stragglers numbered no more than two hundred and seventeen, and everything was in splendid order – except the soldiers' boots.

Kutuzov walked the ranks, stopping occasionally to say a few friendly words to officers he had known in the Turkish war, and sometimes to the other ranks. More than once, looking down at their boots, he shook his head sadly, and pointed them out to the Austrian general, as if to say that, although no one was to blame, he couldn't help noticing how bad things were. Each time this happened the regimental commander sprang forward so as not to miss a single word the commander-in-chief might say about his men. Following on behind Kutuzov, near enough for the slightest whisper to carry, came the twenty-strong entourage. These gentlemen were talking among themselves, and occasionally laughing. Closest of all to the commander-in-chief walked a handsome adjutant. It was Prince Andrey Bolkonsky. Alongside him was his comrade Nesvitsky, a tall and very fat staff-officer with a kind smile, a handsome face and watery eyes. Nesvitsky could hardly help laughing at a dark-skinned hussar near by. This officer, unsmiling and looking ahead doggedly with unblinking eyes, was goggling intently at the commander's back, mimicking his every movement. Each time the commanding officer quivered and bent forward, the hussar officer quivered and bent forward in exactly the same way. Nesvitsky was laughing and nudging the others so they didn't miss him playing the fool.

Kutuzov walked at a slow, leisurely pace past the thousands of eyes almost straining out of their sockets in an effort to see him. When he got to the third company he stopped abruptly. The entourage had not foreseen such a sudden stop and couldn't help pressing up close behind.

'Ah, Timokhin!' said the commander-in-chief, recognizing the red-nosed captain who had been in trouble over the blue greatcoat.

It might have seemed impossible for anyone to stand as erect as Timokhin had done when the regimental commander had rebuked him, but now, finding himself spoken to by the commander-in-chief, the captain stretched himself to attention so rigidly that he seemed unlikely to survive the experience, should the commander-in-chief stay there much longer looking at him. For this reason Kutuzov, seeing how things stood and wishing him nothing but good, turned away sharply. A flicker of a smile passed over Kutuzov's podgy, battle-scarred face.

'Another old comrade from Izmail!' he said. 'A gallant officer! Are you pleased with him?' Kutuzov asked the general in command. And the general, oblivious to the mirror-like mimicry of the hussar behind him, quivered, pressed forward and responded, 'Yes, sir, very pleased indeed.'

'We all have our little weaknesses,' said Kutuzov, smiling as he walked away. 'His was a predilection for Bacchus.'[3]

The commander was worried that this might be his fault, so he said nothing in reply. At that moment the hussar officer noticed the red-nosed captain's face and his pulled-in stomach, and he mimicked them both so closely that Nesvitsky laughed out loud. Kutuzov turned round. The officer seemed able to do anything with his features. Even as Kutuzov turned round he managed to pull another funny face before assuming the gravest expression of innocence and respect.

The third company was the last one, and Kutuzov paused for a moment as if he was trying to remember something. Prince Andrey stepped forward and spoke quietly to him in French. 'Sir, you asked me to remind you about Dolokhov, the officer in this regiment who was reduced to the ranks.'

'Where is Dolokhov?' asked Kutuzov.

Dolokhov, who had by now changed into a grey private soldier's coat, didn't wait to be called. The slim figure of the fair-haired soldier, with his clear blue eyes, stepped out of the front rank, marched up to the commander-in-chief and presented arms.

'Any complaint?' asked Kutuzov with a slight frown.

'This is Dolokhov, sir,' said Prince Andrey.

'Ah!' said Kutuzov. 'Well, let this be a lesson to you. Do your duty as a soldier. The Emperor is merciful. I shan't forget you, if you do well.'

The clear blue eyes looked at the commander-in-chief just as braz-enly as at the regimental commander; they seemed almost to rip away the veil of convention that set the commander-in-chief so far above the common soldier.

'I ask only one favour, your most high Excellency,' he said in his loud, confident voice, not hurrying his words, 'and that is a chance to atone for my offence and prove my devotion to his Majesty the Emperor, and to Russia.'

Kutuzov turned away. His eyes lit up with the same flicker of a smile with which he had turned away from Captain Timokhin. He turned away and frowned, as if to indicate that everything Dolokhov had said to him, and anything that he could say, was old hat, too tedious for words and not at all what was needed. He turned away and walked off towards the coach.

The regiment broke down by companies and the men set off for their appointed quarters at no great distance from Braunau, where they hoped to find new boots and clothes, and have a good rest after so long on the march.

'Don't hold it against me, Prokhor Ignatich, will you?' said the regimental commander, overtaking the third company and riding up to Captain Timokhin, who was leading it. The general's face was beaming with irrepressible delight following such a successful inspection. 'It's all in the Tsar's service . . . you can't, er . . . sometimes you have to be a bit hard . . . I'm the first to apologize. You know me . . . He said how pleased he was.' And he held out a hand to the captain.

'Please, General, as if I would,' answered the captain, his nose redder than ever. He smiled, and his smile showed that his two front teeth were missing – they had been knocked out by a rifle-butt at Izmail.

'Oh, and tell Dolokhov to rest easy – I shan't forget him. By the way, I've been meaning to ask: what is he doing? How's he getting on? . . .'

'He is diligent in the performance of his duty, sir. But he can be temperamental,' said Timokhin.

'What do you mean, "temperamental"?' asked the general.

'Different things on different days, sir,' said the captain. 'Sometimes he's sensible and intelligent and good-natured. Then he can be like a wild animal. When we were in Poland, I should tell you, he all but killed a Jew . . .'

'Yes, yes, I see,' said the general. 'Still you have to go easy on a young fellow when he's in trouble. He is well connected, you know . . . I think you should, er . . .'

'Yes, sir. Yes, sir,' said Timokhin, his smile indicating that he knew what was required of him.

'Very well, then, very well.'

The general went to find Dolokhov in the ranks and reined in his horse. 'Come the first action you could get your epaulettes back,' he said to him. Dolokhov looked round but said nothing. The sardonic smile that played about his mouth stayed the same.

'Well, that's all right then,' the general went on. 'Vodka all round – on me!' he added, loud enough for the soldiers to hear. 'My thanks to you all. God be praised!' He galloped past that company and on to the next one.

'He's a good man, you know. Worth serving with,' said Timokhin to a junior officer at his side.

'"King of Hearts", that's the only word for him,' said the officer with a laugh, that being the general's nickname.

The officers' buoyant mood following the inspection was caught by the soldiers. The company marched along merrily with soldiers' voices chattering away on all sides.

'Who was it said Kutuzov's blind in one eye?'

'Well, he is. Blind as they come.'

'Nay, boys, he's got better eyes than you. Soon spotted our boots and leg-bands,[4] didn't he?'

'Listen, mate, when he looked at my legs . . . I says to myself . . .'

'And what about that Austrian bloke with him – looked like they'd chalked him all over. White as flour. I bet they strips him down and cleans him like we does the guns!'

'Hey, Fedya . . . did he say anything about when it all starts? You were nearer than me. Somebody said Bonaparte's here in Braunau.'

'In Braunau? Rubbish! Come off it! It's the Prussians what's revolting now. The Austrians, they got to put 'em down. When that's done, that's when there's a war with Bonaparte. And your mate says Bonaparte's here now! Must be stupid. You keep your ears open.'

'Blasted quartermasters! Look! Fifth company's turning off into that village. They'll have their porridge cooked, and we're nowhere near!'

'Give us a bit of your biscuit, old man.'

'What? Did you give me any baccy yesterday? See what I mean? Go on, then, you can have a bit.'

'We ought to have a halt here, or we'll have to do another three or four miles with nothing inside us.'

'Wasn't it great when them Germans gave us a lift in their carts! Got a move on then, didn't we?'[5]

'But listen, boys, the folks round here be a weird lot. Up to now it's been all Poles and suchlike, all under the Russian crown, from now on it's all Germans, me boy.'

'Singers to the front!' came the captain's call, and a couple of dozen men went forward from various ranks. The drummer, who was also the leader, turned round to face the choir, waved an arm and struck up a long, meandering soldier's song, beginning: 'As the morning sun was dawning . . .', and ending: 'Therefore, boys, we march to glory, all with Father Kamensky.' This song had been composed in Turkey, and now it was being sung in Austria, except that instead of 'Kamensky' they sang 'Kutuzov'.

Rapping out the last words in military fashion with a downward sweep of his arms as if he was throwing something on the ground, the drummer, a lean, handsome soldier about forty years old, looked grimly at the soldiers' choir and frowned. Then, satisfied that everyone was looking at him, he made as if he was delicately raising some unseen treasure over his head with both hands, held it there for a few seconds ... and then suddenly hurled it down in one furious movement.

'Ah, the bosom of my cottage ...'

And two dozen voices came in with the next line, 'My new cottage ...', and the wooden-spoon player, in spite of all his accoutrements, leapt smartly to the front and walked backwards facing the company, jerking his shoulders and pretending to threaten people with his spoons. The soldiers stepped out to the rhythm of the song, swinging their arms and instinctively coming into step. Suddenly, from behind the company came the sound of wheels, the crunching of springs and the clattering of horses' hooves. Kutuzov and his entourage were returning to the town. The commander-in-chief gave a signal for the soldiers to carry on, and soon he and all his followers were enjoying the singing, the antics of the dancing soldier and the happy men marching on so smartly. There, in the second row from the right flank, which the carriage had to drive past, one figure stood out – the blue-eyed soldier, Dolokhov, marching to the rhythm of the song with a special bounce and panache, and looking at the faces of those who were driving by with apparent pity for anyone who was not marching with them then and there in the ranks. The young hussar officer in Kutuzov's suite, Zherkov, who had been mimicking the general, dropped back from the carriage and rode up to Dolokhov.

Zherkov had at one time belonged to the wild set in Petersburg which had had Dolokhov as its leader. He had come across Dolokhov outside Russia as a common soldier, and had not seen fit to recognize him. But now, following Kutuzov's conversation with the disgraced officer, he addressed him with all the joviality of an old friend.

'My dear fellow, how are you?' he asked through all the singing, while manoeuvring his horse to keep pace with the marching soldiers.

'How am I?' Dolokhov answered coldly. 'Can't you see?'

The lively song gave a particular thrust to Zherkov's free-and-easy cheerfulness as he spoke, and to the deliberate iciness of Dolokhov's responses.

'Well, how do you get on with the officers?'

'Not bad. They're good fellows. How did you manage to worm your way on to the staff?'

'I was seconded. Just for a spell.'

They were silent.

> I took my hawk and let him leave
> From my right arm, from my sleeve ...

The song rang out, automatically arousing feelings of brightness and joy. No doubt they would have had a different kind of conversation if they hadn't been talking against the singing.

'Have the Austrians really been beaten?' asked Dolokhov.

'They keep damn well saying so.'

'I'm glad,' came Dolokhov's clear, snappy reply, as demanded by the song.

'I say, why don't you drop round one evening? We'll have a game of cards,' said Zherkov.

'Have you got plenty of money, then?'

'Well, do come.'

'I can't. I've sworn not to. No drinking or betting till I'm promoted.'

'Oh well, come the first action . . .'

'We'll see what happens.'

Another pause.

'Well, drop by if you need anything. Someone at staff headquarters can always help . . .'

Dolokhov grinned. 'Don't worry. What I want, I'm not going to ask for. I'll get it myself.'

'Yes, well, I only . . .'

'Me too.'

'Goodbye.'

'Keep well.'

> Go fond flier, ever higher,
> To your country far away . . .

Zherkov put spurs to his horse, which reared on its hind legs two or three times in great excitement as if it couldn't decide which foreleg to lead off with, then it galloped past the company, and caught up with the carriage, still moving to the rhythm of the song.

CHAPTER 3

Once back from the review, Kutuzov took the Austrian general into his private room and summoned his aide, asking for certain papers concerning the condition of the newly arrived troops, and some letters received from the Archduke Ferdinand, who was in command of the advance army. Prince Andrey Bolkonsky came into the commander-in-chief's room with the necessary documents. Kutuzov and the Austrian representative of the Hofkriegsrath were sitting over a plan that lay unfolded on the table.

'Oh yes,' said Kutuzov, looking round at Bolkonsky and using the phrase as an invitation for his aide to stay with them. Then he continued his conversation.

'I have only one thing to say, General,' said Kutuzov, using French of such agreeable elegance and persuasive intonation that the listener was obliged to concentrate on each carefully enunciated word. And Kutuzov was clearly not averse to the sound of his own voice. 'All I can say is that if this were a matter of my personal preference, the desire of his Majesty, Emperor Francis, would have been fulfilled long ago. I would have lost no time in joining the Archduke. I give you my word that for me personally to hand over the high command of the army to more knowledgeable and experienced generals – which Austria has in abundance – and to cast off such a heavy responsibility, this for me personally would be a relief. But circumstances are sometimes too much for us, General.' And Kutuzov smiled with an expression that seemed to say, 'You have every right to disbelieve me, and I don't much care whether you do or you don't, but you have no grounds for saying that out loud. And that's it.'

The Austrian general looked unhappy, but he dared not adopt the wrong tone with Kutuzov.

'On the contrary,' he snapped with a petulance that belied the meaning of his unctuous words. 'On the contrary, the participation of your most high Excellency in our joint enterprise is highly appreciated by his Majesty. But we do believe that the present delay is depriving the gallant Russian troops and their commander-in-chief of the laurels they are accustomed to winning in the field,' he concluded a sentence obviously prepared in advance.

Kutuzov bowed, still smiling the same smile.

'But I am equally certain, to judge by the last letter with which his Highness the Archduke Ferdinand has honoured me,' he said, 'and I put it to you indeed that the Austrian troops under the command of so skilful a leader as General Mack have already achieved total victory and have no further need of our assistance.'

The general frowned. Though there had been no definite news of an Austrian defeat, there was too much circumstantial evidence confirming this as an unpleasant possibility, and that made Kutuzov's assertion of an Austrian victory sound rather like a sneer. But Kutuzov's brief smile contained the same suggestion as before – that he had every right to say what he did. As it happened the last letter he had received from the army of General Mack had informed him of victory, and of the army's most favourable strategic position.

'Hand me that letter,' said Kutuzov to Prince Andrey. 'See here.' And Kutuzov, with a sardonic smile playing about the corners of his mouth, read out in German for the benefit of the Austrian general this excerpt from the letter of the Archduke Ferdinand:

'We have a fully concentrated force of nearly seventy thousand men, and therefore stand ready to attack and defeat the enemy in the event of his crossing the Lech. Since we already hold Ulm we are in a position to maintain the advantage of commanding both banks of the Danube, and therefore would be able at a moment's notice, should the enemy decide not to cross the Lech, to cross the Danube ourselves and fall upon their line of communications, recross the river downstream and frustrate the enemy's intentions should he decide to mount a mass attack against our faithful ally. On this account we shall await with confidence the full readiness of the Imperial Russian Army, whereupon we shall easily proceed together in preparing for the enemy that fate which he so richly deserves.'

Kutuzov gave a heavy sigh as he finished reading the extract and he turned sympathetically to the representative of the Hofkriegsrath, eyeing him closely.

'But as you well know, your Excellency, it is always wise to prepare for the worst,' said the Austrian general, clearly eager to stop playing around and get down to business. He glanced with displeasure at the adjutant.

'Excuse me, General,' Kutuzov interrupted him, and he too turned to Prince Andrey. 'My dear fellow, I want you to collect all our intelligence reports from Kozlovsky. Here are two letters from Count Nostitz, here's one from his Highness the Archduke Ferdinand and there's all these others,' he said, handing him several documents. 'Take all this and write me a memorandum, a note in your neatest French clearly presenting all the information we've received about any movements of the Austrian army. Do that, please, and then show it to his Excellency.'

Prince Andrey gave a nod which indicated that he had understood from the outset not only what was said but also what Kutuzov would have liked to say. He gathered up the papers, gave a single bow and padded across the carpeted floor and out into the reception-room.

Although it was not long since Prince Andrey had left Russia, he had changed a great deal during that time. His facial expression and the way he moved and walked showed barely a trace of his former affectation and languid boredom. He had the air of a man too absorbed in enjoyable and fascinating work to think about making an impression on other people. His face showed greater contentment – with himself and those around him. His smile was easier; a warmer charm shone in his eyes.

General Kutuzov, whom he had caught up with in Poland, had received him very graciously and promised not to forget him. He gave him preference over the other adjutants and took him to Vienna, entrusting him with the more important commissions. From Vienna Kutuzov wrote as follows to his old comrade, Prince Andrey's father: 'Your son, with his knowledge, spirit and attention to detail, has the potential to become an outstanding officer. I consider myself lucky to have such an able subordinate.'

On Kutuzov's staff, among his fellow officers and in the army generally, Prince Andrey was what he had been in Petersburg society, a man with two completely different reputations. Some people – the minority – considered him a cut above themselves and everybody else; they expected a lot from him, they listened to him, admired and imitated him, and with these people Prince Andrey was open and agreeable. Others – the majority – didn't like him at all, seeing him as petulant, aloof and thoroughly unpleasant. But Prince Andrey knew enough to ensure that even these people treated him with respect and sometimes a certain awe.

He left Kutuzov's room and walked across the ante-room to his comrade, the duty adjutant, Kozlovsky, who was sitting by the window reading.

'What is it, Prince?' queried Kozlovsky.

'I've been told to write a note saying why we're not going on.'

'Well, why aren't we?'

Prince Andrey shrugged.

'No news from Mack?' asked Kozlovsky.

'No.'

'If he really had been beaten we would have heard by now.'

'Quite likely,' said Prince Andrey, moving towards the door. But he was confronted on the way out by a tall man who walked into the ante-room and slammed the door behind him. The new arrival was an Austrian general in a long coat, with a black cloth around his head and the Order of Maria Theresa around his neck. Prince Andrey stopped short.

'Ze Commander-in-Chief Kutuzoff?' asked the general, speaking quickly with a rough German accent. He looked to both sides and walked straight on to the door of the private room.

'The commander-in-chief is busy,' said Kozlovsky, hurrying over to the unknown general and barring his way to the door. 'Who shall I say has arrived?'

The newcomer looked down on the diminutive Kozlovsky, apparently surprised not to be recognized.

'The commander-in-chief is busy,' Kozlovsky repeated calmly.

The general's face contorted, his lips twitching and trembling. He took out a note-book, jotted something down in pencil, tore the page out and handed it to Kozlovsky, and then strode swiftly to the window, where he threw himself into a small chair and looked around at the others as though wondering why they were watching him. Then he looked up and thrust his neck out as though about to speak, only to start humming with a kind of forced nonchalance, a strange sound which he snapped off almost immediately. The door of the private room opened, and there was Kutuzov in the doorway. As though fleeing from some danger, the general with the bandaged head bent forward and sped towards him on spindly legs.

'You see before you the unfortunate Mack,' he managed to say in French, his voice breaking.

Kutuzov's face, as he stood there in the doorway, remained impassive for a few moments. Then a wrinkle rippled across it like a wave, and left his forehead smooth. He bowed his head respectfully, closed his eyes, ushered Mack in without a word and closed the door behind him.

So, the rumour that had been going round – that the Austrians had been defeated and the whole army had surrendered at Ulm – had turned out to be true. Within half an hour aides had been dispatched in every direction with orders to the effect that the Russian troops which had so far been inactive would soon have to confront the enemy.

Prince Andrey was one of those few staff officers with a genuine interest in the overall progress of the war. On observing Mack and learning the details of his downfall, he saw immediately that the campaign was half lost. He could sense the enormous difficulty which now faced the Russian troops, and imagine what lay ahead of them; he could also foresee the part that he personally would have to play. He couldn't resist a thrill of real pleasure at the thought of the arrogant Austrians suffering such humiliation, and the prospect of, perhaps in less than a week, witnessing, even taking part in, an encounter between the Russians and the French, the first since Suvorov's day. But he was afraid of Bonaparte's genius – this man might turn out to be stronger than all the brave Russian troops put together; and yet at the same time he couldn't bear to think of his hero being disgraced.

Excited and unnerved by these thoughts, Prince Andrey decided to go to his room and write to his father, which he did every day, but in the corridor he met his room-mate Nesvitsky and Zherkov the clown. As usual they had found something to laugh at.

'What are you looking so miserable about?' asked Nesvitsky, notic-ing Prince Andrey's pale face with its gleaming eyes.

'There's nothing to celebrate,' answered Bolkonsky.

Just as Prince Andrey encountered Nesvitsky and Zherkov, down the corridor towards them came the two Austrian generals who had arrived the previous night, Strauch, an attaché charged with pro-visioning the Russian army, and the Hofkriegsrath representative. There was plenty of room in the wide corridor for the generals to pass the three officers with something to spare. Nevertheless Zherkov shoved Nesvitsky to one side and called out breathlessly, 'Mind your backs, please! . . . Make way! . . . Stand aside!'

The generals walked on looking as if they would have liked to avoid any embarrassing display of respect, but Zherkov the clown suddenly smirked with what seemed to be uncontrollable glee.

'Your Excellency,' he said in German, moving forward and address-ing the Austrian general, 'my compliments to you, sir.' He began bowing and scraping, awkwardly, like a child getting his legs mixed up at a dancing lesson. The Hofkriegsrath man looked at him sharply, but, detecting something serious behind the silly smirk, he couldn't refuse him a moment's attention. He frowned with concentration to show that he was listening.

'My compliments indeed, sir, on General Mack's arrival. He seems to be well. Just a bit of trouble up here,' he added, tapping his head with an even broader smile.

The general's frown deepened; he turned away and hurried off.

'Stupid boy!' he said angrily, a few steps further on.

Nesvitsky roared with laughter and threw his arms around Prince Andrey, but Bolkonsky, turning even paler, pushed him away with a furious glare and turned to Zherkov. The nervous tension brought on by the sight of Mack, the news of his defeat and the thought of what the Russian army was in for expressed itself in a furious reaction to Zherkov's tasteless joke.

'Sir, if you insist on acting like a *buffoon*,' he began cuttingly, with a slight trembling of the jaw, 'it is not for me to stop you, but if you *dare* play the fool once more in my presence I'll teach you how to behave.' Nesvitsky and Zherkov were so taken aback by this outburst that they gazed in silence at Bolkonsky with wide-open eyes.

'Huh, I only gave them my compliments,' said Zherkov.

'I'm not joking, sir! Please be silent!' Bolkonsky roared, and taking Nesvitsky by the arm he walked away from Zherkov, leaving him lost for words.

'I say, come on, old fellow,' said Nesvitsky, trying to soothe him.

'Come on?' said Prince Andrey, pausing, still very excited. 'Listen. Either we are officers serving Tsar and country, rejoicing in allied successes and grieving together in defeat, or we're just hired servants who have no interest in our master's business. Forty thousand men massacred and the allied army destroyed, and you think that's funny,' he said, choosing his phrases carefully, in French, to emphasize what he was saying. 'It may be all right for a stupid young idiot like that friend of yours, but it's not all right for you – not for you. *Schoolboys* joke like that,' Prince Andrey added, going into Russian but saying the word with a French accent. He had noticed that Zherkov was still within hearing, and waited for some response from the cornet. But no, he turned away from them and walked out of the corridor.

CHAPTER 4

The Pavlograd hussars were stationed two miles from Braunau. The squadron in which Nikolay Rostov was serving as an ensign was billeted on a German village, Salzeneck. The squadron commander, Captain Denisov, known throughout the cavalry division as Vaska, had been given the best quarters and Ensign Rostov was sharing with him, as he had done ever since he had joined the regiment in Poland.

On the 8th of October, the day when headquarters was shocked out of its complacency by the news of Mack's defeat, life in this squadron had been going smoothly in its old routine.

Denisov had spent all night losing at cards and was still out when Rostov came back early that morning from a foraging expedition. Rostov rode up to the steps in his cadet's uniform, reined in his horse, swung one leg over the saddle with the ease of a fit young man, stood up in the stirrup for a second as though reluctant to let go of the horse, and then leapt down and called for an orderly.

'Ah, Bondarenko, my dear fellow,' he said to the hussar who came rushing up to his horse. 'Give him a walk, there's a good fellow,' he said, with the kind of cheery familiarity which good-hearted young people show to everyone when they are in a happy mood.

'Yes, sir,' answered the Ukrainian boy with a cheerful toss of his head.

'Mind you give him a decent walk!'

Another hussar had rushed up by now, but Bondarenko had already thrown the reins of the snaffle-bit over the horse's head.

The young cadet was obviously a good tipper, well worth working for. Rostov stroked the horse on its neck and flank and then paused for a while on the steps.

'First rate! What a horse he's going to be!' he said to himself with a smile. Holding his sabre up, he ran up the steps with clattering spurs. The German on whom they were billeted, wearing his thick shirt and pointed cap, and holding a fork which he was using for mucking out, glanced out from the cowshed. His face lit up when he saw Rostov. With a cheerful smile and a quick wink he greeted him in German. 'Good morning, a very good morning to you!' He seemed to take pleasure in welcoming the young man.

'You're out working early!' said Rostov, also in German, with the happy, friendly smile that never left his eager face. 'Hurrah for the Austrians! Hurrah for the Russians! Long live the Emperor Alexander!' he said, using phrases that had often been said before by the German, who now came out of his cowshed, laughing, pulled off his cap and waved it above his head, shouting, 'And long live the whole world!'

Rostov did the same with his cap and cried out laughingly, 'Yes, long live the whole world!' There was no reason for either of them to celebrate, the German mucking out, or Rostov coming back from foraging for hay, but these two people beamed at each other in sheer delight and brotherly love, wagging their heads at one another to show mutual affection, and then they went off smiling, the German to his cowshed and Rostov to the rough cottage he was sharing with Denisov.

'Where's your master?' he asked Lavrushka, Denisov's valet, and a well-known rogue.

'He's been out all night. Must have been losing,' answered Lavrushka. 'I know him by now. If he wins he comes home early and tells us all about it – if he's not back by morning, that means that he's lost. He'll be furious when he does come home. Shall I serve some coffee?'

'Yes, please.'

Ten minutes later Lavrushka brought in the coffee.

'He's coming now!' said he. 'There'll be trouble!'

Through the window Rostov could see Denisov returning home, a small figure of a man, red in the face, with sparkling black eyes, wayward black moustaches and tousled hair. His long cloak was unfastened, his baggy breeches hung down in folds and his hussar's cap had slid down the back of his head, all crumpled. A picture of gloom, with downcast eyes, he walked to the steps.

'Lavwushka!' he yelled in a loud angry voice that emphasized his speech impediment, 'Come on, get it off, man!'

'Yes, that's what I am doing,' came Lavrushka's voice in reply.

'Oh, you're up then,' said Denisov, coming into the room.

'Ages ago,' said Rostov. 'I've been out foraging – and I've seen Fräulein Mathilde.'

'Have you? And I've been losing, bwother, all night long, like a son of a bitch,' cried Denisov. 'Wotten luck? You've never seen anything like it! Since the moment you left, no luck at all. Hey you, bwing me some tea!'

Denisov's face wrinkled into something like a smile, which showed off his small, strong teeth, and he began working with the short fingers of both hands to ruffle the dense tangled thicket of his tousled black hair.

'Devil knows why I had to take on that wotten wat,' (one of the officers was nicknamed 'rat') he said, rubbing his forehead and face with both hands. 'Can you believe it? He never dealt me a decent card, not one, not one, not one!' Denisov accepted the lighted pipe that was handed to him, squeezed it in his fist, tapped it on the floor with a shower of sparks, and carried on shouting. 'Lets you win stwaight, and he wins the doubles. Me stwaight, him doubles.'

He scattered more sparks, the pipe broke and he threw it away. Then he paused and turned his gleaming black eyes sharply on Rostov.

'If only there were some women! But here you have a dwink and then there's nothing else to do. What we need is some fighting, and soon . . . Hey, who's that?' he called, turning towards the door, hearing someone stop with a clattering of thick boots and clanking spurs, followed by a polite cough.

'Quartermaster!' called out Lavrushka. Denisov wrinkled his face up more than ever.

'Oh damn!' he said, flinging down a purse with a few gold coins in it. 'Wostov, dear boy, would you count how much is left, and shove the purse under my pillow?' he said, and went out to see the quartermaster. Rostov took the money and began to sort it automatically into two heaps, old coins and new ones, which he then began to count.

'Ah, Telyanin! Good morning to you! Cleaned me wight out last night,' he could hear Denisov saying in the other room.

'Where were you? At Bykov's? At the rat's? . . . I knew it,' said another person's reedy voice, and into the room walked Lieutenant Telyanin, a small fellow officer.

Rostov stuffed the purse under the pillow, and went to shake the damp little hand that was offered. For some reason Telyanin had been transferred from the guards just before the regiment had marched off. He had behaved well enough with them, but no one liked him and

Rostov in particular couldn't abide him or even manage to hide his unreasonable dislike of this officer.

'Well now, my young cavalryman, how are you getting on with my Little Rook?' (Little Rook was his young horse, well broken-in for riding, that Telyanin had sold to Rostov.) The lieutenant never looked anyone in the eye when he was speaking; his own eyes were continually darting from one object to another. 'I saw you out on him today . . .'

'Oh, not bad at all. He's a good ride,' answered Rostov, though the horse for which he had paid seven hundred roubles wasn't really worth half that amount. 'He's limping a bit on the left fore-leg . . .' he added.

'Got a cracked hoof! It's nothing. I'll teach you. I'll show you how to put a rivet in.'

'I'd be glad if you would,' said Rostov.

'I'll show you, I'll show you. Nothing secret about it. But you'll be glad you bought that horse.'

'Good, I'll have him brought round,' said Rostov, anxious to get rid of Telyanin, and he went out to arrange for them to get the horse.

Outside, Denisov was squatting on the threshold with a new pipe, facing the quartermaster, who was reporting to him. Seeing Rostov, Denisov screwed up his face, pointed a thumb over his shoulder towards the room where Telyanin was still sitting, frowned and shuddered with revulsion.

'Ugh! I can't stand that fellow,' he said, ignoring the quartermaster.

Rostov shrugged as if to say, 'Neither can I, but what can you do?' He gave his instructions and went back in to Telyanin, who was sitting as before, in the same languid pose, rubbing his little white hands together.

'Some people are just too awful for words!' thought Rostov as he entered.

'Well, have you ordered them to fetch the horse?' said Telyanin, getting up and looking around casually.

'Yes.'

'Well, you come too. I just dropped in to ask Denisov about yesterday's order. Have you got it, Denisov?'

'No, not yet. Where are you off to?'

'I'm going to show this young man how to shoe a horse,' said Telyanin.

They went out, down the steps and into the stable. The lieutenant showed Rostov how to fix a rivet and then went off to his own quarters.

When Rostov got back, there on the table stood a bottle of vodka and some sausage. Denisov was sitting there, and his pen was scratching across a sheet of paper. He looked glumly into Rostov's face.

'I am witing to her,' he said. He leant his elbows on the table, pen in hand, and was obviously so delighted at the prospect of speaking much faster than he could write that he gave Rostov the benefit of his whole letter. 'You see, my dear fellow,' he said, 'we are asleep until we fall in love . . . we are the childwen of dust and ashes . . . but once you have loved you are a god, as pure as on the first day of cweation . . . Who's *that*? Send him away, dammit! I've no time!' he bawled at Lavrushka, who, nothing daunted, went up to him.

'Who do you expect? *You* invited him. It's the quartermaster, come for his money.'

Denisov scowled and seemed as if he would say something, but didn't.

'Wotten business altogether!' he said to himself. 'How much was there left in that purse?' he asked Rostov.

'Seven new, three old.'

'Well, don't just stand there like a big wag doll! Bwing in the quartermaster!' Denisov shouted to Lavrushka.

'Denisov, please, here's some money. I've got plenty,' said Rostov, reddening.

'I don't like bowwowing from fwiends. I weally don't,' growled Denisov.

'But if you won't accept money from me – a comrade – I'll be offended. I've really got plenty,' repeated Rostov.

'Oh no.' And Denisov went over to the bed to get the purse out from under the pillow.

'Where did you put it, Wostov?'

'Under the bottom pillow.'

'Well it's not there.' Denisov threw both the pillows down on to the floor. No purse. 'Well, I'm blessed!'

'Hang on, you must have dropped it,' said Rostov, picking the pillows up one at a time and shaking them. He pulled the quilt off and shook it out. Still no purse.

'Have I forgotten something? No, I remember thinking you'd be sleeping on a secret treasure,' said Rostov. 'I did put the purse there. Where's it gone?' He turned to Lavrushka.

'I was never in the room. It must be where you put it.'

'Well, it isn't.'

'That's you all over, thwowing things about and forgetting where they are. Look in your pockets.'

'No, if I hadn't thought of it like a secret treasure . . .' said Rostov, 'but I do remember where I put it.'

Lavrushka rummaged through the whole bed, looked underneath it and under the table, rummaged through the entire room and then stood still in the middle of it. Denisov followed Lavrushka's movements in silence, and when Lavrushka spread his hands in amazement to show that it was nowhere to be found, he looked round at Rostov.

'Wostov, is this one of your widiculous schoolboy jokes?'

Rostov could sense Denisov glaring at him; he glanced up and then rapidly down again. All the blood in his body seemed to have been blocked somewhere just below the throat, and it rushed to his face and eyes. He could hardly get his breath.

'And no one's been in the room, nobbut the lieutenant and yourselves. It's got to be here somewhere,' said Lavrushka.

'Wight then, damn you. Move yourself! Find it!' Denisov yelled suddenly, turning purple and rushing at the valet with a menacing gesture. 'Find that purse, or I'll have you flogged! The lot of you!'

Studiously avoiding Denisov's eyes, Rostov began buttoning up his jacket, fastening on his sword and putting on his cap.

'I'm telling you that pocket-book has got to be here!' roared Denisov, shaking the orderly by the shoulders and banging him against the wall.

'Denisov, leave him alone. I know who's taken it,' said Rostov, heading for the door without looking up.

Denisov paused, thought for a moment and seemed to get Rostov's drift. He seized him by the arm.

'Oh, wubbish, Wostov!' he roared, the veins standing out like cords on his neck and forehead. 'I'm telling you, you're cwazy. No, I won't let you . . . That pocket-book is here somewhere. I'll flay this wogue alive, then it'll turn up.'

'I know who has taken it,' repeated Rostov, in a tremulous voice, and went to the door.

'And I'm telling you – don't you dare . . .' cried Denisov, hurtling after the ensign to hold him back. But Rostov freed his arm, looked up straight into his eyes and glared at Denisov with the kind of fury you reserve for your worst enemy.

'Do you know what you're saying?' he said in a quavering voice. 'I'm the only person who's been in that room. So, if it's not there, you think . . .'

Lost for words, he fled from the room.

'Oh, damn you! And all the west of you!' were the last words Rostov heard.

Rostov went over to Telyanin's quarters.

'The master's not in, he's gone over to HQ,' Telyanin's orderly told him. 'Has something happened?' the orderly added, taken aback by the ensign's worried face.

'No, nothing's happened.'

'You've only just missed him,' said the orderly.

The headquarters were nearly two miles from Salzeneck. Rostov took his horse and rode there without calling in at his own quarters. In the village which the staff had taken over there was an inn much frequented by the officers. Rostov went there. Telyanin's horse was at the door.

In the second room the lieutenant was sitting at a table with a dish of sausage and a bottle of wine before him.

'Oh, so you've come here too, young man,' he said, smiling and raising his eyebrows.

'Yes, I have.' Rostov seemed to force the words out with a great effort. He sat down at the next table.

Neither man spoke. There were two Germans and a Russian officer in the room. Silence reigned, the only sounds being the scraping of knives on plates and the lieutenant munching away. When Telyanin had finished his meal, he took out a double-sided purse, parted the rings with the curved tips of his tiny white fingers, took out a gold coin, raised his eyebrows and handed the money to the waiter.

'I'd be glad if you would hurry,' he said.

It was a new gold coin. Rostov got up and went over to Telyanin.

'Please let me look at that purse,' he said, his voice barely audible.

With shifty eyes, and eyebrows still raised, Telyanin handed over the purse.

'Nice little purse, isn't it? Yes, yes,' he said, suddenly turning white. 'Do have a look at it, young man,' he added.

Rostov took hold of the purse and examined it, also checking the money inside, and he stared at Telyanin. The lieutenant let his eyes wander around everywhere, as he always did, and suddenly he seemed remarkably cheerful.

'If we get to Vienna, I suppose I shall leave it all there, but just now there's nothing to buy in these ghastly little places,' he said. 'So, let me have it back, young man, and I'll be on my way.'

Rostov said nothing.

'What are you going to do, then? Are you lunching too? They do a decent meal,' Telyanin went on. 'Please could I have it back?'

He put out his hand and took hold of the purse. Rostov let go of it. Telyanin took the purse and casually began to slide it back into his breeches pocket, with his eyebrows still raised and his mouth half-open, as if to say, 'Yes, yes, I'm putting my purse in my pocket, that's all there is to it, and it's nobody's business but mine.'

'Well, young man?' he said with a sigh, staring out from under those raised eyebrows for once straight into Rostov's eyes. A strange glint surged like a charge of electricity from Telyanin's eyes to Rostov's and back again, to and fro in a split second.

'Come over here,' said Rostov, grabbing Telyanin by the arm and almost dragging him to the window. 'That money is Denisov's. You took it . . .' he whispered in his ear.

'You what? . . . What? . . . How dare you? What do you mean? . . .' said Telyanin. But the words sounded pathetic, almost desperate, a plea for forgiveness. The moment Rostov heard that tone of voice, a great boulder of doubt seemed to fall from him and roll away. He felt a thrill of delight, mixed immediately with some pity for the miserable creature standing before him, but this was something that had to be taken all the way.

'God knows what these people might think,' Telyanin was muttering. He snatched up his cap and went over to a small empty room. 'We need to talk . . .'

'Yes, I know we do. I can prove it,' said Rostov.

'I . . .'

Telyanin's terrified face, drained of all colour, now twitched in every muscle, and his eyes darted about everywhere, but only downwards, never coming to the level of Rostov's face. His sobs were pitiful to hear.

'Count! . . . please don't ruin me . . . I'm only young . . . here's the wretched money, take it! . . .' He threw it down on the table. 'My mother . . . my father's an old man . . .'

Rostov took the money, avoiding Telyanin's eyes, and left the room without a word. But he stopped in the doorway and looked back.

'My God!' he said, with tears in his eyes, 'how could you have done that?'

'Count . . .' said Telyanin, coming nearer.

'Don't you touch me,' said Rostov, backing away. 'If you're so badly off, keep the money.'

He flung the purse at him and ran out of the inn.

CHAPTER 5

That same evening in Denisov's quarters a heated discussion was taking place among some of the squadron officers.

'But I'm telling you, Rostov, that you're going to have to apologize to the colonel.' The words came from a staff captain, a tall man with greying hair, a vast spread of whiskers, bold features and a deeply furrowed face. Rostov was bright red with excitement. Kirsten, the staff captain in question, had been reduced to the ranks twice for affairs of honour, both times regaining his commission.

'I won't let anybody call me a liar!' cried Rostov. 'He said I was lying and I said he was. And that's it. He can put me on extra duty every day of the week, he can put me under arrest but no one's going to make me apologize, because if he thinks that being our colonel means it's beneath his dignity to give me satisfaction, then . . .'

'Hang on, old fellow, you just listen to me,' put in the staff captain in his deep bass voice, calmly smoothing his long whiskers. 'You tell the CO with officers present that another officer has been stealing . . .'

'Well, it's not my fault there were other officers around when I spoke. Maybe I shouldn't have spoken while they were there, but I'm no diplomat. That's why I joined the hussars. I didn't think there would be any hair-splitting here. So when he calls me a liar . . . let him give me satisfaction.'

'That's all very well, but nobody thinks you're a coward. That's not the point. Denisov will tell you whether it's even remotely possible for a cadet to challenge his CO.'

Denisov was biting his moustache and looking rather grim as he listened to the conversation, evidently not wanting to be drawn into it. He shook his head in response to the captain's question.

'So there you are in the presence of other officers sounding off to the CO about this nasty business,' the staff captain persisted. 'Bogdanych' (the colonel) 'brings you into line . . .'

'That's not what he did. He said I wasn't telling the truth.'

'Yes, and you said some stupid things, for which you must now apologize.'

'Not on your life!' shouted Rostov.

'This is something I never expected from you,' said the staff captain, with a grave and stern look about him. 'You won't apologize, but, my good sir, it's not only him, it's the whole regiment, all of us, that you've offended. You're completely in the wrong. Listen. If only you'd stopped and thought for a minute, taken a bit of advice about what to do ... but no, you had to go and blurt it all out before all the officers. So what's the colonel supposed to do next? Charge the officer and disgrace the whole regiment? Shame the whole regiment because of one cad? Go on, should he do that? I'll tell you what we think – no! Bogdanych was a good fellow. He just told you that what you were saying couldn't be true. It's not very nice, but what else could he do? Listen, old man, you brought this on yourself. And now when people are trying to hush things up a bit, you get on your high horse and refuse to apologize – you want the whole story to come out. You see red because you've been given some extra duty. Well, why can't you just go and apologize to an old and honourable officer? Say what you will about Bogdanych, but he is an honourable and gallant old colonel. But oh no, you feel you've been slighted, and you don't mind disgracing the whole regiment!' The staff captain's voice became shaky. 'You, sir, are a new boy in this regiment. You're here today, and tomorrow you'll be a nice little adjutant somewhere else. You couldn't care less if people start saying there is thieving among the Pavlograd officers! But we care! Don't we, Denisov? Don't we care?'

Denisov neither moved nor spoke. Now and then his gleaming black eyes settled on Rostov.

'Your pride means a lot to you, so you won't apologize,' continued the staff captain, 'but we old-timers, we've grown up in this regiment and please God we'll die in it ... and the honour of our regiment means a lot to us, and Bogdanych knows that. I'll say it does! But this is wrong. It's just wrong! I don't want to offend you, but I always speak plain. And this is wrong!'

At this the staff captain got up and turned his back on Rostov.

'Too damn twue!' shouted Denisov, jumping to his feet. 'Come on, Wostov, what about it?'

Rostov, turning red and then white, looked from one to the other.

'No, gentlemen, no ... er, please don't think ... I ... I see what you mean ... you've got me wrong ... for me ... for the honour of the regiment ... I'd ... well listen, I'll show you what ... I can honour our colours ... well, anyway, what you say is true, I am in the wrong!' His eyes had filled with tears. 'I'm completely in the wrong! Well, what more do you want?'

'Now you're talking, Count,' cried the staff captain, turning round and clapping him on the shoulder with a huge hand.

'I tell you,' shouted Denisov, 'he's a weal man.'

'That's better, Count,' repeated the captain, using his title in appreciation of his confession. 'Go and apologize, your Excellency. Yes, sir, that's what you must do.'

'Gentlemen, I'll do anything. You won't hear a peep out of me,' Rostov went on in a voice of supplication, 'but I can't apologize, for God's sake. I just can't, whatever you say! How can I go and apologize, like a little boy asking to go unpunished?'

Denisov laughed.

'It'll be worse if you don't. Bogdanych has a long memory. He'll make you pay for being awkward,' said Kirsten.

'Good God, I'm not being awkward! I can't describe how it feels . . . No, I can't do it!'

'Well, it's your decision,' said the staff captain. 'By the way, where has that swine hidden himself?' he asked Denisov.

'He's weported sick. There's an order for him to be stwuck off tomowwow,' said Denisov.

'Well, he must be ill. There's no other explanation,' said the staff captain.

'Ill or not, he'd better keep out of my way – I'll kill him,' came the bloodthirsty cry from Denisov.

In came Zherkov.

'What are you doing here?' cried the officers, turning to the newcomer.

'We're going into battle, gentlemen. Mack has surrendered – with his whole army.'

'Nonsense!'

'I've seen him with my own eyes.'

'You've what? Seen Mack alive, with all his limbs intact?'

'Into battle! Into battle! Give that man some vodka for bringing news like that! But why have you come?'

'I've been sent back to my regiment because of that devil, Mack. The Austrian general filed a complaint against me. All I did was compliment him on Mack's arrival . . . Hey, what's wrong with you, Rostov? You look as if you've just come out of the bath-house.'

'Oh, we've had a spot of bother for a couple of days, old man.'

Then the regimental adjutant came in and confirmed Zherkov's news. They were under marching orders for the next day.

'Into battle, gentlemen!'

'Well, thank God for that! We've been stuck here long enough!'

CHAPTER 6

Kutuzov pulled back towards Vienna, destroying bridges behind him over the river Inn (in Braunau) and the river Traun (in Linz). On the 23rd of October the Russian troops crossed the river Enns. By midday Russian baggage-wagons, artillery and columns of troops were strung out in long lines throughout the town of Enns on both sides of the bridge. It was a warm but showery autumn day. The broad panorama that unfolded below the Russian batteries guarding the bridge was sometimes closed off by a gossamer curtain of slanting rain, but then would spread itself out again in bright sunlight so that far-off objects could be seen clearly in the distance glinting as if newly varnished. The little town stood out sharply down below with its white houses and their red roofs, its cathedral and its bridge, on which streaming masses of Russian troops crowded together at both ends. At a bend of the Danube they could see ships, an island and a castle in parkland, surrounded by the waters of the Enns flowing into the Danube, and the Danube's own rocky, pine-covered left bank with its mysterious green peaks and bluish gorges receding into the distance. The towers of a convent rose up out of the wild virgin pine forest, and straight ahead across the Enns, on a hill in the far distance, enemy troops could be seen riding on patrol.

Among the field guns at the top of the hill stood two men in a forward position, the general in command of the rearguard and one of his staff officers. They were scanning the countryside through field-glasses. Just behind them, sitting on the trail of a gun carriage, was Nesvitsky, who had been sent to the rearguard by the commander-in-chief. His Cossack orderly had handed him knapsack and flask, and Nesvitsky was now dishing out little pasties and real doppel-kümmel[6] to the other officers. They circled around him, squatting down contentedly, some on their knees, some cross-legged Turkish-fashion.

'That Austrian prince who built a castle here knew what he was doing. It's a magnificent spot. Why aren't you eating, gentlemen?' said Nesvitsky.

'I'm most grateful, Prince,' answered one officer, delighted to be talking to a staff officer of such importance. 'Yes, it is a magnificent spot. We marched in past the park and we saw a couple of deer. And the house is simply wonderful!'

'Look over there, Prince,' said someone else, hungry for another pasty but too embarrassed to take one and thus making a show of studying the countryside. 'Look where our infantry boys have got to. There they are, just past that village, three of them, carrying something across a field. They'll soon smash their way into that palace,' he said, with some relish.

'I'm sure they will,' said Nesvitsky. 'But that's not it. You know what?' he added, his handsome mouth moist from munching a pasty, 'I'd like to see them get in there.' He was pointing to the convent towers on the far hillside. He smiled, with a special glint in his narrowed eyes. 'Be all right, wouldn't it, gentlemen!' The officers laughed.

'Shake those nuns up a bit. Italian girls, they do say, nice young ones. Worth five years of anybody's life!'

'And they must be bored stiff,' laughed one of the cheekier officers.

Meanwhile the officer up front was pointing out something to the general, and he peered through his field-glass.

'Yes, it is, it is,' said the general angrily, lowering the telescope with a shrug, 'you're right, they're going to get fired on, crossing that river. Why are they taking so long?'

On the far side the enemy and their batteries, with milky-white smoke rising from them, were visible to the naked eye. After the smoke came the sound of a distant shot, and our troops could be seen perceptibly speeding up the crossing.

Nesvitsky got up slightly out of breath and went over to the general, smiling.

'Sir, would you like a bite of something?' he asked.

'It's a bad business,' said the general, without answering. 'Our men have taken too long.'

'Shall I ride down there, your Excellency?' said Nesvitsky.

'Yes, please do,' said the general, going on to repeat an order that had already been given in detail, 'and tell the hussars they must cross last and then set fire to the bridge. I've already told them. And they must double-check the kindling materials on the bridge.'

'Very good,' answered Nesvitsky. He beckoned to the Cossack who was holding his horse, told him to clear away the knapsack and flask, and then swung his great bulk easily into the saddle.

'Well, I think I'll just drop in on those nuns,' he said to the amused officers watching him, and rode off down the winding hill path.

'Come on then, Captain, let's see how far we can fire,' said the general, turning to the artillery officer. 'A bit of fun to relieve the boredom.'

'Man the guns!' At this command the gunners instantly left the shelter of their camp fires and came running up, keen to start loading.

'Number one!' came the order. Number one cannon recoiled smartly with a deafening metallic boom. The ball whistled out over the heads of our men down below and flew across, but fell a long way short of the enemy. A puff of rising smoke showed where it had landed and exploded.

The faces of the soldiers and officers lit up at the sound. They all got to their feet and went to watch the movements of our troops down below, looking for all the world like tiny creatures in the palm of your hand, and the movements of the advancing enemy up ahead. At that moment the sun came fully out from behind the clouds and the wonderful bang of that single shot, melting into blazing sunlight, gave them all a feeling of fun and high spirits.

CHAPTER 7

Down on the bridge two enemy cannonballs had whistled over them, and the bridge itself was crammed with people. Half-way across stood Prince Nesvitsky, who had dismounted and was now leaning with his portly figure squashed heavily into the railings. He kept glancing back in amusement at his Cossack, who was standing a few paces behind him holding both horses by their bridles. Every time Nesvitsky tried to walk on, the crush of soldiers and wagons forced him to stop and squeezed him back against the railings. He simply had to smile.

'Hey, you, my boy,' said the Cossack to a driver who was forcing his wagon through the mass of walking soldiers flattened against his wheels and horses, 'what do you think you're doing? You'll have to wait. Look, the general wants to get through.'

But the convoy driver, unimpressed by the mention of a general, just yelled at the soldiers who were blocking his way, 'Come on, boys, get over to the left! Hang on a minute!' But the boys themselves, shoulder to shoulder, bayonets clinking together, were surging across the bridge in one great mass. Looking down over the railing, Prince Nesvitsky could see the splashing low waves of the fast-moving Enns as they rippled and swirled, chasing each other and crashing against the bridge-supports. Then looking back along the bridge he saw the same kind of formless living tidal wave of soldiers, with their covered shakos,[7] knapsacks, bayonets, long muskets, and beneath the shakos the broad faces and sunken cheeks of men reduced to an apathetic weariness, their legs tramping across the boards of the bridge through a thick layer of sticky mud. Sometimes amid the featureless waves of soldiers, like a fleck of white foam on the waves of the Enns, an officer in his cloak would wriggle through, his face looking quite different from those of the soldiers around him. Sometimes, like a splinter of wood borne on the current, an individual would be swirled across the bridge amid the waves of infantrymen – a hussar walking without his horse, an orderly or a civilian. Sometimes a baggage-wagon belonging to a company commander or some other officer would struggle across like a floating log, hemmed in on all sides, piled up high and draped with leather covers.

'It's like a dam-burst!' said the Cossack, stopping helplessly. 'Are there many more after you?'

'Oh, must be a million!' said a soldier in a torn coat, winking cheerfully as he disappeared from sight. Just behind him strode an old soldier.

'If *he*' (the enemy) 'has a go at the bridge now,' said the old soldier gloomily, turning to a comrade, 'you'll forget about scratching yourself.' And he too passed out of sight. Then came another soldier riding on a wagon.

'Where the hell did you put the leg-rags?' said an orderly, scrambling after the wagon and rummaging in the back. He and the wagon passed by.

Next came some high-spirited soldiers who had obviously been at the bottle.

'Yes, up with the butt he went, and give him a smack in the teeth,' said one soldier in a tucked-up greatcoat, gleefully punching upwards with his arm.

'Nice bit of ham,' laughed another one. And on they went. Nesvitsky never did find out who got smashed in the teeth and where the ham came into it.

'Look at 'em running! *He* lets one go, and you'd think they were all getting killed,' said an infuriated NCO, full of scorn.

'It went right over my 'ead, Sarge, that cannonball did,' said a young soldier with a huge mouth, hardly able to stop himself laughing. 'Nearly fainted, didn't I? Put the fear of God in me, that did!' said the soldier, making a kind of boast out of being scared.

He too went on his way. Along came a wagon different from all the previous ones, a German cart pulled by two horses, with what seemed like a houseful of stuff on top. The horses were led by a German, and a splendid brindle cow with an enormous udder was tied at the back. Sitting on feather mattresses were a woman with a tiny baby, an older woman and a young, rather pretty German girl with bright red cheeks. They must have been country people on the move, with a special permit to travel. All the soldiers' eyes turned to the women, and as the wagon trundled by at walking pace the two younger women were the only subject of conversation. Every face smiled virtually the same smile; every man thought his salacious thoughts about one of them.

'Hey, pumpernickel's on the road!'

'Sell us your missus,' said another soldier to the German, who was striding on, alarmed and angry but not looking up.

'Tarted herself up a bit, hasn't she? Trollops!'

'Wouldn't mind being billeted on them, Fedotov!'

'Seen worse, mate.'

'Where are you heading for?' asked the infantry officer, eating an apple and half-smiling as he stared at the pretty girl. The German father shut his eyes as if to say he didn't understand.

'Here you are,' said the officer, offering the apple to the girl. She smiled and took it. Nesvitsky was no different from the rest – he couldn't take his eyes off the women till they had passed by. When they had gone, they were followed by the same soldiers saying the same things, and then suddenly everything stopped. It was the usual thing – the horses in a company wagon had got themselves into a tangle at the end of the bridge, and the whole crowd had to stand and wait.

'Why are we waiting? Who's in charge?' said the soldiers. 'Who do you think you're shoving? Go to hell? Just hang on a minute. Damn sight worse if *he* sets fire to the bridge. Look, there's an officer got stuck too.' The voices came from the standing crowd, as men looked round at one another and everybody pressed forward to get off the bridge.

As he was looking down at the waters of the Enns flowing under the bridge, Nesvitsky suddenly heard a sound he had never heard before ... something hurtling towards him ... something big, and then a great splash in the water.

'They've got our range!' said a grim-faced soldier near by as he looked towards the sound.

'He's just telling us to get a move on,' said another uneasily. The crowd moved on. Nesvitsky realized it was a cannonball.

'Hey, Cossack, give me my horse!' he said. 'You there, stand aside! Stand aside! Get out of the way!'

With a great effort he managed to struggle to his horse. Shouting non-stop, he began to move forward. The soldiers pulled back to let him through, but soon squashed in on him again, crushing his leg, and those nearest him were not to blame, because they were being shoved even harder from behind.

'Nesvitsky! Nesvitsky! You, old wogue!' called a hoarse voice from behind him.

Nesvitsky looked round and there, fifteen paces away, separated by the seething mass of moving infantry, he saw the red-and-black shaggy figure of Vaska Denisov with his cap on the back of his head, and his cloak flung jauntily over one shoulder.

'Tell 'em to make way, the damned devils!' roared Denisov, who seemed to be wildly excited. His gleaming, coal-black eyes were rolling, their whites all bloodshot, and he was brandishing his sheathed sword, clasped in a small bare hand as red as his face.

'Hey! Vaska!' Nesvitsky called back with delight. 'What are you doing here?'

'The squadwon can't get thwough!' roared Vaska Denisov with a snarl that bared his white teeth, putting the spurs to his fine black thoroughbred Bedouin. The horse's ears kept twitching as it brushed up against the bayonets; it was snorting and spattering foam from the bit, its hooves clanging on the boards of the bridge, and it seemed all set to leap over the railings, if only its rider would let it.

'What's all this! A wight lot of sheep! . . . Out of the woad! . . . Let me fwough! . . . Stay where you are! You and your damned wagon! I'll cut you to pieces!' he roared, actually drawing his sword and beginning to brandish it.

The soldiers, looking quite terrified, squeezed closer together, and Denisov joined Nesvitsky.

'How come you aren't drunk today?' said Nesvitsky, as he rode up.

'No time to get dwunk!' answered Vaska Denisov. 'They've been dwagging the wegiment here, there and evwywhere all day. Fighting's all wight, but God knows what this is all about!'

'You're looking very smart today!' said Nesvitsky, looking at the new cloak and saddle cloth.

Denisov smiled, reached into his sabretache[8] and pulled out a handkerchief reeking of scent, which he shoved under Nesvitsky's nose.

'Mustn't get things wong, I'm going into battle! Shaved, cleaned my teeth and put on a bit of scent!'

Nesvitsky's imposing figure, the presence alongside him of his Cossack and Denisov's determination based on much sword-waving and lusty shouting – all of this produced so great an effect that they did manage to get through to the other end of the bridge and halt the infantry. There Nesvitsky found the colonel to whom he was to deliver the command. Mission completed, he set off to ride back.

Having cleared the route, Denisov stopped at the bridge. Casually reining in his mount, which was neighing to the other horses and stamping its hoof, he watched as his squadron came towards him. The hollow clang of hooves on the boards of the bridge sounded like lots of horses galloping, and the squadron rode four abreast, officers leading, across the bridge and on to the far bank.

The halted infantrymen, crowded together in the trampled mud near the bridge, looked on as the clean, smart hussars rode past them so stylishly, with that special feeling of unfriendly rivalry and derision which different branches of the service usually show to each other when they meet.

'Pretty boys, aren't they? Do well in the circus!'

'Useless lot. Showmen and showhorses!' said another voice.

'Infantrymen, no dust please!' joked a hussar, as his horse pranced up and splattered an infantry soldier with mud.

'I'd like to see you marching two days with a pack on your back. Bit of muck on your tassels,' said the infantryman, wiping the mud off his face with his sleeve, 'More like a bird than a man up there!'

'Zikin, we should get you on a horse. What a rider!' joked a corporal to a skinny soldier, stooping under the weight of his pack.

'Put a stick between your legs – that's your kind of horse,' the hussar called back.

CHAPTER 8

The rest of the infantrymen funnelled on to the bridge and hurried across. Eventually all the baggage-wagons were over, there was less of a crush and the last battalion strode on to the bridge. Only the hussars of Denisov's squadron were left on the far side of the river facing the enemy. The enemy, visible at a distance from the opposite hillside, could not yet be seen from the bridge below, because the river valley created a horizon not more than half a mile away at the top of the rising ground. Ahead lay an open space where the only movement came from the odd little group of our patrolling Cossacks. Suddenly along the road on the opposite slope some troops and artillery appeared; the men were wearing blue greatcoats. It was the French. A Cossack patrol trotted back downhill. The officers and men of Denisov's squadron chatted on, trying to ignore all this and look elsewhere, but every last one of them had his mind on what was up there on the hillside and nothing else; they kept glancing at dark patches appearing on the skyline, which they knew to be enemy forces.

The weather had cleared during the afternoon, and the sun shone brightly as it began to go down over the Danube and the dark surrounding hills. It was quiet. Except that now and then the far hillside rang with sounds: a bugle call or the enemy shouting. No one but a few patrolling men stood now between the squadron and the enemy. A mere half-mile of empty space separated the two sides. The enemy held their fire, increasing the sense of that dark, menacing, mysterious and intangible dividing line that exists between two warring armies.

'One step across that dividing line, so like the one between the living and the dead, and you enter an unknown world of suffering and death. What will you find there? Who will be there? There, just beyond that field, that tree, that sunlit roof? No one knows, and yet you want to know. You dread crossing that line, and yet you still want to cross it. You know sooner or later you will have to go across and find out what is there beyond it, just as you must inevitably find out what lies beyond death. Yet here you are, fit and strong, carefree and excited, with men all around you just the same – strong, excited and full of life.' This is what all men think when they get a sight of the enemy, or they feel it if they do not think it, and it is this feeling that gives a special lustre and a delicious edge to the awareness of everything that is now happening.

High on the enemy slope a puff of smoke indicated a shot, and a cannonball whistled over the heads of the hussar squadron. The officers, who had been standing together, scattered to their various posts. The hussars began to ease their horses back into line. The whole squadron was silent. All the men were watching the enemy ahead and waiting for an order from the squadron commander. Another cannonball flew over, then a third. They were definitely firing at the hussars, but the cannonballs soared with their steady whine right over their heads and landed somewhere behind them. The hussars didn't look back, but at the sound of each flying ball, as if responding to an order, the entire squadron, a sea of faces so alike yet so different, rose in the stirrups, each man holding his breath as the ball whizzed by, then sank down again. The soldiers didn't turn their heads, but they angled glances at each other, curious to note the effect on their comrades. Every face from Denisov's down to the bugler's showed about the lips and chin the same suggestion of a struggle between anxiety and excitement. The sergeant surveyed the men with a scowl, as though threatening punishment. Officer-cadet Mironov ducked every time a cannonball flew over. Out on the left flank, Rostov on his Little Rook – a handsome mount despite the weakness in his legs – looked rather like a cheerful schoolboy appearing at a public examination which he knows he is going to pass with flying colours. He looked at them all coolly and closely, as though inviting them to notice how calm he was under fire. But despite his best efforts even his face showed about the mouth that same suggestion of living through something new and dangerous.

'Who's that bobbing up and down? Officer-cadet Miwonov! That's not wight! Watch me!' roared Denisov, unable to settle in one place and galloping up and down in front of the squadron.

Vaska Denisov, with his snub-nosed face, black hair, his small stocky figure and the sinewy hand with its hairy little fingers clasping the hilt of his naked sword, looked exactly his normal self, as he did in the evening with a couple of bottles inside him, only a bit redder still in the face. Tossing back his mane of hair like a bird drinking, he ruthlessly drove the spurs on his little feet into his good horse Bedouin, reared right back in the saddle and galloped across to the far flank of the squadron, where he roared at the men in a hoarse voice, telling them to look to their pistols. Then he rode over to Kirsten. The staff captain on his rather plump, staid old mare jogged towards him at a gentle walking pace. The staff captain's face with its long whiskers was as stern as ever, but his eyes gleamed brighter than usual.

'Well,' he said to Denisov, 'there won't be any fighting. You watch, we shall pull back.'

'It's widiculous! What the hell are we doing?' growled Denisov. 'Ah, Wostov!' he called to the ensign, noticing his beaming face. 'This is it!' And he smiled approval, visibly pleased at the sight of the ensign. Rostov had now achieved perfect happiness. Just then the commanding officer appeared on the bridge. Denisov galloped over to him.

'Sir, let's wide into the attack! I'll wun 'em back!'

'What do you mean, attack?' said the colonel languidly, scowling as if annoyed by a passing fly. 'Why are you hanging about here? You can see the flanks are retreating. Lead the squadron back.'

The squadron crossed the bridge and passed unscathed out of the enemy's range. Number two squadron followed on behind, and the Cossacks brought up the rear, leaving the far bank deserted.

Once over the bridge, the two squadrons of the Pavlograd regiment retired uphill one after the other. Their colonel, Karl Schubert (known to all by his patronymic, Bogdanych), had come over to join Denisov's squadron, and was now riding at walking pace not far from Rostov, ignoring him even though this was the first time they had met since the Telyanin affair. Rostov, conscious of being at the front in the hands of a man that he had wronged, couldn't take his eyes off the colonel's athletic back, fair hair and red neck. One moment, Rostov imagined that Bogdanych was only pretending to ignore him, and that his main purpose was now to test the ensign's courage, so he kept drawing himself up and looking around cheerfully. The next, he fancied that Bogdanych was riding close to him because he wanted to show off his own valour. Then the thought struck him that his adversary was about to launch the squadron into a hopeless attack simply in order to punish him, Rostov. This led to another idea – when the attack was over the colonel would come to him as he lay there wounded and magnanimously extend the hand of reconciliation.

Then the colonel was approached by a familiar figure in the Pavlograd hussars, that of the stiff-shouldered Zherkov, who had recently left the regiment. After his dismissal from the staff of the commander-in-chief, he had not remained with them because, as he put it, he was not fool enough to slog on at the front when he could get more pay for doing nothing on the staff, and he had wangled an appointment as orderly to Prince Bagration. Now he rode over to his old colonel with an order from the rearguard commander.

'Colonel,' he said, with his usual moroseness, addressing Rostov's adversary, and looking round at his former comrades, 'the order is to halt, go back and burn the bridge down.'

'Order? *Who to?*' asked the colonel grimly.

'Well, Colonel, I don't know, *who to*,' answered the cornet gravely. 'All I know is the prince gave me a command. "Ride down," he said, "and tell the colonel the hussars are to double back and burn the bridge down."'

Zherkov was followed by an officer of the commander's entourage, who rode up with exactly the same order. And after him came the stout figure of Nesvitsky on a Cossack horse, which could hardly manage a gallop with him on board.

'Colonel,' he shouted, still galloping, 'I told you to burn the bridge, and someone's messed things up. It's a madhouse over there, everything's all over the place.'

The colonel stopped the regiment, unhurried, and turned to Nesvitsky.

'You haff tell me about ze kindling,' he said, 'but not about ze burning – you never said a word.'

'My good man,' said Nesvitsky, as he came to a halt, removed his cap and passed a podgy hand over his sweaty hair, 'was it really necessary to say "burn the bridge" when you were packing it with kindling materials?'

'Don't you "gut man" me, Mr Staff Officer,' said Schubert, his marked German accent worsening. 'You deed not tell me to set fire to ze brich! I know my serfice, and ees my habit to carry out strictly mine orders. You said ze bridge vill be burnt, but who iss going to burn it I by Holy Spirit couldn't tell.'

'Well, that's always the way,' said Nesvitsky with a wave of his arm. 'What are you doing here?' he added, turning to Zherkov.

'Same as you. Look, you're all wet through. Let me help . . .'

'But Mr Staff Officer, vat you say vas . . .' the colonel was insisting in an aggrieved tone.

'Colonel,' interrupted the first officer, 'we must hurry, or the enemy will have moved up their guns and started using grapeshot.'

The colonel looked dumbly from him to the stout staff officer, then to Zherkov, and he scowled.

'I vill ze brich fire,' he said with great solemnity and the air of a man determined to do his duty, however difficult they made things for him.

Spurring his horse with his long muscular legs, as though it were the guilty party, the colonel rode forward and ordered number two squadron, in which Rostov was serving under Denisov's command, to return to the bridge.

'I was right,' thought Rostov, 'he does want to test me!' His heart missed a beat and the blood rushed to his face. 'I'll show him whether I'm a coward or not!' he thought. That same grave look which had overtaken them under fire returned to every cheerful face in the squadron. Rostov stared closely at his adversary, the colonel, searching his face for confirmation of his suspicions. But the colonel never once glanced at Rostov; as always he was looking ahead sternly and solemnly. The word of command was given.

'Come on, let's get on with it!' said several voices around him.

Sabres snagging in the reins and spurs jingling, the hussars dismounted at speed, without knowing what they were going to do. The soldiers crossed themselves. Rostov had stopped looking at the colonel; there was no time. His one great dread, which he felt with a sinking heart, was of falling behind the hussars. His hand shook as he gave his horse to an orderly, and he could feel his heart pumping blood. Denisov rode past, rearing back and calling out. Rostov could see nothing but hussars all round him, running everywhere with jingling spurs and clanking sabres.

'Stretcher here!' called a voice behind him. It never occurred to Rostov what stretcher meant. He just ran on, trying to keep to the front. But right by the bridge, running along without looking down, he slipped on the well-trodden mud, staggered and fell on his hands. The others ran round him.

'For boss ze zides, Captain,' he heard the shout from the colonel who must have galloped on ahead, and had now reined in his horse by the bridge, watching with triumph and delight written on his face.

Rostov wiped his muddy hands on his riding breeches and looked round at his adversary. He made as if to run on, with the idea that the further he could get the better it would be, but Bogdanych, without recognizing him or even looking at him, gave a shout.

'Who ees mittel of ze brich? On ze right! Ensign, get back!' he shouted furiously, rounding on Denisov, who had ridden with swaggering bravado on to the boards of the bridge.

'Why run the risk, Captain? You should dismount,' said the colonel.

'If the bullet has your number on it . . .' said Vaska Denisov, turning in the saddle.

Meanwhile Nesvitsky, Zherkov and the officer from the commander's entourage were standing together out of range, watching the two groups of men, those in yellow shakos, gold-braided dark-green jackets and blue breeches swarming towards the bridge, and those on the other bank in the blue greatcoats and some with horses, easily recognizable as artillerymen approaching in the distance.

'Will they burn it down or not? Who'll get there first? Will they get through and set fire to it, or will the French get their grapeshot going and mow them down?' These were the questions that each man instinctively asked himself with a sinking heart, in the great mass of troops looking down on the bridge. In the bright evening sunlight they were staring down at the bridge and the hussars, and across at the blue greatcoats on the other side, advancing with guns and bayonets.

'Ugh! The hussars are in for it!' said Nesvitsky. 'They're within range of that grapeshot now.'

'He shouldn't have taken so many men,' said one of the officers of the suite.

'Quite right,' said Nesvitsky. 'Could've sent two brave boys. Wouldn't have made any difference.'

'Oh no, your Excellency,' put in Zherkov, his eyes fixed on the hussars, but still with that innocent manner which made it difficult to tell whether he was serious or not. 'Oh no, sir. The very idea! Send two men? He wouldn't get the Vladimir medal and ribbon for that, would he? As things stand, if we get wiped out he'll still be able to recommend the squadron for honours and go and collect a personal ribbon. Our good friend Bogdanych knows how things get done.'

'Hey!' exclaimed the first officer, 'here comes the grapeshot.'

He pointed to the French guns, which had been taken down from the carriages and were being swiftly trundled into position.

On the French side, smoke rose in puffs from the groups with cannons – one, two, three almost simultaneously, and just as the sound of the first shot reached them a fourth puff rose up. Two more bangs, one right after the other, then the fourth.

'Oh no!' moaned Nesvitsky, clutching at the officer's arm as though in intense pain. 'Look, there's a man down! He's down!'

'Two, I think.'

'If I were the Tsar, I'd never go to war,' said Nesvitsky, recoiling.

The French cannons were swiftly reloaded. The blue-coated infantry were sprinting towards the bridge. More puffs of smoke rose at scattered intervals, and the grapeshot sizzled, rattling down on the bridge. But this time Nesvitsky couldn't see what was happening at the bridge. Dense smoke rose from it. The hussars had done it, they had set fire to the bridge, and the French batteries were firing now not to stop them but just because the guns were there and they had someone to fire at.

The French had managed three rounds of grapeshot before the hussars got back to the men holding their horses. Two were badly directed, and the shot flew over them high and wide, but the last volley fell right in the middle of the group of hussars and three men were felled.

Rostov, preoccupied by his relations with Bogdanych, had stepped on to the bridge without knowing what to do. There was no one to slash at with his sword, which was how he had always imagined a battle would go, and he couldn't contribute to the bridge-burning because, unlike the other soldiers, he had forgotten to bring any straw. He was just standing there looking around when suddenly there was a great rattling sound on the bridge, like a scattering of nuts, and one of the hussars standing right next to him fell with a groan against the railing. Rostov ran to him along with the others. Again a voice called out, 'Stretcher here!' Four men took hold of the hussar and started to lift him. 'Ooooh! ... Jesus Christ, leave me alone!' screamed the wounded man, but they went ahead, lifted him and laid him on a stretcher. Nikolay Rostov turned away and began staring into the distance, at the waters of the Danube, at the sky, at the sun, as if he were looking for something. How lovely that sky looked, how blue and calm and deep! Oh, the brightness and magnificence of that setting sun! The warm glow of the water on the far Danube! Even lovelier were the distant hills that shone so blue beyond the Danube, the convent, the mysterious gorges, the pine woods misted over to their tops . . . everything so calm and happy . . . 'I would ask for nothing, nothing in the world if only I could be there,' thought Rostov. 'In me, only in me and that sunshine, there is so much happiness, and *here* . . . all this groaning and agony, this feeling of dread, all the uncertainty, this rushing about . . . There they are, shouting again, everybody's running back somewhere, and I'm running too, and here is death – hanging over me, all around me . . . One flash, and I'll never see that sunshine, that water, that mountain gorge ever again . . .'

Just then the sun disappeared behind the clouds, and more stretcher-bearers came into view ahead of Rostov. And the dread of death and of the stretchers, and the loss of all sunshine and life, everything fused into a single sensation of sickening horror.

'Dear God, who art in heaven, save, forgive and deliver me,' Rostov whispered to himself.

The hussars ran back to their waiting horses; their voices grew louder and more settled; the stretchers disappeared from sight.

'Well, my boy, you've had a weal sniff of powder!' Vaska Denisov shouted in his ear.

'It's all over, but I'm a coward. I really am,' thought Rostov, and with a heavy sigh he received Little Rook, who was resting one of his legs, from the orderly and prepared to mount.

'What was that – grapeshot?' he asked Denisov.

'Too damn twue!' cried Denisov. 'Hewoes, all of us, but wotten work! A cavalwy charge is fine – chop the dogs down – but for God's sake – that was pwoviding target pwactice!'

And Denisov rode away to join the group that had stopped close to Rostov: the colonel, Nesvitsky, Zherkov and the officer of the suite.

'Anyway, nobody seems to have noticed,' Rostov thought to himself. And nobody had. All of them knew the feeling that this ensign, never before under fire, was now experiencing for the first time.

'This'll look good when they write it up,' said Zherkov. 'I'll get my promotion to second lieutenant before the day's out, eh?'

'Please to inform ze prince I have ze brich burnt,' said the colonel, a picture of bonhomie and triumph.

'And what if he wants to know about losses?'

'Nossing vors mentioning,' boomed the colonel. 'Two hussars vounded, one dead in his tracks,' he said with a delight that was obvious to all. He could not resist a smile of smug contentment as he relished the splendid sound of that phrase, 'dead in his tracks'.

CHAPTER 9

General Kutuzov's Russian army of thirty-five thousand men was retreating along the Danube, pursued by a hundred thousand Frenchmen under Napoleon. They were getting a hostile reception from the local populations, and had lost all confidence in their allies; they were running out of supplies, and were forced to operate in ways that no one could ever have foreseen. They halted whenever they were overtaken by the enemy and defended themselves in rearguard action, but only long enough to secure further retreat without losing their heavy equipment. They had fought at Lambach, Amstetten and Melk, but, for all their courage and tenacity – acknowledged even by the enemy – the only consequence was an even faster retreat by the Russians. The Austrian troops that had escaped capture at Ulm and joined Kutuzov at Braunau had now separated from the Russian army, and all Kutuzov had at his disposal were his own weak and exhausted forces. There could be no question now of defending Vienna. Gone was the elaborate plan of attack handed to Kutuzov in Vienna by the Austrian Hofkriegs-rath, based on the latest scientific laws of field strategy; now Kutuzov's sole aim – and even this was almost impossible – was to survive with his army, unlike Mack at Ulm, and somehow join up with the fresh troops marching from Russia.

On the 28th of October Kutuzov took his troops across to the left bank of the Danube and halted for the first time, with the river separating his army from the bulk of the enemy. On the 30th he attacked Mortier's division, which was still on the left bank, and defeated it. In this action for the first time they captured some trophies – a flag, several cannons and two enemy generals. For the first time in a fortnight of retreating the Russian troops had halted, fought, won the field and driven the French back. The troops were without clothing and exhausted, they had lost a third of their strength wounded, killed or missing; many of the sick and wounded had been abandoned on the other side of the Danube with a letter from Kutuzov commending them to the humanity of the enemy; and they still had casualties beyond the capacity of the local infirmaries and makeshift hospitals – but none of this could prevent a great surge in the troops' morale following the halt at Krems and the victory over Mortier. Wildly optimistic rumours (without any foundation) ran through the whole army and even through headquarters: that the columns from Russia were almost here, that the Austrians had won a battle and that Napoleon was on the run with his tail between his legs.

During this engagement Prince Andrey had been in attendance on the Austrian General Schmidt, who had been killed in the field. His own horse had been wounded, and he had received a slight bullet wound to the arm. As a mark of special favour on the part of the commander-in-chief, he was dispatched with news of this victory to the Austrian court, now at Brno rather than Vienna, which was under French threat. On the night of the battle, still excited but not weary (despite Prince Andrey's apparently slender build he could bear fatigue better than the strongest of men), he had ridden into Krems with a report from Dokhturov to Kutuzov and was then sent straight on with a special dispatch to Brno. This commission, apart from the decoration it would bring, meant an important step towards promotion.

It was a dark but starry night and the road shone black against the white snow that had fallen on the day of the battle. Prince Andrey bowled along in his post-chaise, his mind filled with images of battle, pleasantly anticipating the effect that his news of victory would create, and still enjoying the memory of his commander-in-chief and his comrades sending him on his way. His feelings were those of a man who has found the beginnings of a long-sought happiness. The moment he closed his eyelids, his ears rang with the rattle of muskets and the boom of cannon-fire, sounds that blended with the rumble of the wheels and the sensation of victory. First he began to dream that the Russians were on the run and he had been killed, then he would wake up with a start and realize with great relief that none of this had happened – it was the French who were running away. Once more he savoured the details of their victory, including his own courage and steadiness under fire; then, fully reassured, he began to doze off . . . The dark, starry night was followed by a bright and sunny morning. The snow was thawing in the sunshine, the horses were running well and on either side of the road new and different kinds of forest, fields and trees flew by.

At one posting-station he caught up with a convoy of Russian wounded. The Russian officer in charge of the transport sprawled back in the leading wagon, swearing volubly at a soldier. In each of the long German carts half a dozen pale-faced, bandaged and filthy casualties were being jolted along the stony road. Some of them were talking (he could hear Russian being spoken), others were munching bread, but the worst of the wounded gazed out impassively as the courier's carriage went trotting by, showing no more concern than the feeblest of sick children.

Prince Andrey told the driver to stop, and asked a soldier what battle they had been in when they were wounded.

'Day before yesterday on the Danube,' answered the soldier. Prince Andrey took out his purse and gave the soldier three gold pieces.

'For all of you,' he added, addressing an officer who now came up. 'Let's see you get better, boys,' he said to the soldiers. 'There's a lot more work to be done.'

'Any news, sir?' asked the officer, eager for conversation.

'Yes, good news! . . . Drive on!' he called out, and off they went.

It was quite dark when Prince Andrey drove into Brno, and found himself surrounded by tall mansions, well-lit shops, houses with bright windows, street lamps, fine carriages rattling down the streets and the whole atmosphere of a great living town which is so appealing to a soldier back from camp. Prince Andrey had lost a night's sleep on the hurried journey, but now, as he drove up to the palace, he felt even more alert than he had on the previous evening. His eyes had a feverish glint in them, and all manner of thoughts raced through his mind with remarkable clarity. As he ran over every last detail of the battle, his ideas were not now blurred but sharp and concise, just as he could see himself presenting them to Emperor Francis. He also ran over all the casual questions that might be put to him, and the answers he would provide. He assumed he would be taken straight to the Emperor, but no, at the main entrance to the palace an official ran out to meet him, saw that he was a special messenger and took him round to another entrance.

'Down the corridor on your right you will find the duty adjutant, your Excellency,' said the official. 'He will take you to the minister of war.'

On receiving Prince Andrey, the duty adjutant asked him to wait and went in to see the war minister. Five minutes later he returned, bowing low with great courtesy and, ushering Prince Andrey ahead of him, led him across the corridor and into a private room where the war minister was at work. The adjutant seemed to be using this exaggerated courtesy to protect himself from any attempt at familiarity on the part of the Russian aide. Prince Andrey's joyful enthusiasm was considerably dampened as he walked to the door of the minister's room. He felt humiliated, and the sense of humiliation soon transformed itself imperceptibly into a quite unjustified belief that they were treating him with contempt. His fertile mind immediately hit on the right attitude for him to adopt to be able to treat them, the adjutant and the minister of war, with equal contempt. 'They've never smelled powder. I'm sure they think winning victories is the easiest thing in the world!' he thought. His eyes narrowed with scorn; he walked very slowly into the war minister's room. The feeling was reinforced when the minister of war, sitting at a big table, ignored his visitor for a full two minutes. The minister sat with his bald head, which retained some grey hair at the temples, bowed down between two wax candles; he was reading some papers and making pencilled notes on them. Determined to finish, he did not look up when the door opened and he heard the approaching footsteps.

'Take this and give it to him,' said the minister of war to his adjutant, handing him the papers, and still ignoring the Russian courier.

Prince Andrey felt that either the minister of war was less interested in the activities of Kutuzov's army than in any of his other business, or this was the impression that he wanted to create. 'Well,' he thought, 'why should I care?' The minister squared off the remaining papers and put them to one side. Only then did he look up. He had the distinctive head of an intellectual, but the moment he turned to Prince Andrey, the war minister's shrewd and concentrated look changed into a contrived facial expression that he had all too obviously grown used to assuming. His face was left wearing an inane smile – the forced smile, with no attempt to disguise the effort behind it, of a man who receives endless petitioners one after another.

'From General Field-Marshal Kutuzov?' he asked. 'Good news, I hope? Has there been an encounter with Mortier? A victory? Not before time!'

He took the dispatch, which was addressed to him, and began to read it with a glum expression.

'Oh my God! My God! Schmidt!' he said in German. 'What a disaster! What a disaster!' He skimmed the dispatch, laid it on the table and glanced up at Prince Andrey, greatly preoccupied.

'Oh my God, what a disaster! So, you say the action was decisive?' ('But Mortier wasn't taken,' he thought to himself.) 'Very glad you've brought such good news, though the death of Schmidt is a heavy price to pay. His Majesty is sure to wish to see you, but not today. My thanks to you. Please go and rest. Come to the reception tomorrow morning, after the review. Anyway, I'll be in touch.'

The inane smile, which had disappeared during the conversation, now returned to the war minister's face.

'*Au revoir.* Many thanks indeed. His Majesty the Emperor will probably wish to see you,' he repeated, bowing his head.

Prince Andrey left the palace with the feeling that all the excitement and pleasure that had been his following the victory had now drained away into the uncaring hands of the minister and his unctuous adjutant. His entire cast of mind had changed in an instant. The battle figured in his memory as something far away and long ago.

CHAPTER 10

In Brno Prince Andrey stayed with a Russian diplomat of his acquaintance, Bilibin.

'My dear prince, I couldn't have a more welcome guest,' said Bilibin, advancing to meet Prince Andrey. 'Franz, take the prince's things to my bedroom,' he said to the servant, who was ushering Bolkonsky in. 'So, you're the herald of victory? Splendid. I've been ill, as you can see. Not allowed out.'

After washing and dressing, Prince Andrey came into the diplomat's opulent study and sat down to the dinner prepared for him. Bilibin settled down comfortably by the fireplace.

So long deprived of the niceties of cleanliness and sophistication, not only during his journey but throughout the whole campaign, Prince Andrey now felt a delightful sense of relaxation as he returned to the kind of luxurious surroundings he had been accustomed to since childhood. Besides which, after his Austrian reception, he was glad not so much to speak Russian – they spoke in French – but at least to talk to someone who was Russian, and a man who would presumably share the general Russian antipathy towards the Austrians, now at its sharpest.

Bilibin was a bachelor in his mid-thirties from the same background as Prince Andrey. They had known each other in Petersburg, but had become closer during Prince Andrey's last stay in Vienna with Kutuzov. If Prince Andrey was a young man with a promising military career ahead of him, Bilibin promised even more in the diplomatic field. Still young in years, he was not young in diplomacy. Joining the service at the age of sixteen, he had been posted to Paris and Copenhagen, and now occupied a responsible position in Vienna. Both the chancellor and our ambassador in Vienna knew him and thought highly of him. He was not one of that vast army of diplomats required to display negative qualities, those men who rise to the top by speaking French and not doing certain things. He was a diplomat who liked his work and understood it, and for all his natural indolence he would sometimes spend whole nights at his desk. He was equally adept at every aspect of his work, and more interested in the question how than the question why. He didn't mind what kind of diplomatic assignment came his way; it was always an exquisite pleasure for him to work with subtle conciseness and a touch of elegance in composing any circular, memorandum or report. But apart from his written work, Bilibin was also valued for his easy manner when moving and talking in the highest circles.

Bilibin enjoyed talking as much as working, as long as the conversation was stylish and clever. In society he always hung back, waiting for a chance to say something very striking, and would not enter any conversation unless he could do so. His speech was invariably salted with polished phrases, original, witty but of general application. They were fabricated in some inner laboratory of Bilibin's mind, portable and ready-made for social nonentities to commit to memory and take around the other drawing-rooms. Bilibin's *bons mots*, widely peddled in every Viennese salon, often went on to influence what people thought of as important matters.

His thin, lean, sallow face was covered all over with deep wrinkles, but they always looked as wholesome and scrupulously cleansed as fingertips fresh from a bath. All the variations of his facial expression were played out in the manipulation of these wrinkles. One moment his brow would furrow up in thick folds as his eyebrows rose, the next his eyebrows would plunge, leaving deep lines all down his cheeks. His small, deep-set eyes looked out openly and shone with good humour.

'Well, come on then, tell us about your deeds of valour,' he said.

With exemplary modesty and without any reference to himself, Bolkonsky described the engagement and his subsequent reception by the war minister.

'They welcomed me and my news like a dog in a skittle-alley,' he concluded. Bilibin grinned, relaxing all his wrinkles.

'All the same, my dear fellow,' he said, taking a long view of his fingernails and bunching up the skin over his left eye, 'for all my admiration of Holy Russia's military machine, I must say your victory was not very victorious.'

He carried on speaking French, using Russian only for words which he wanted to invest with particular derision.

'Just think. You and your massed ranks fell on the miserable Mortier with his single division, and Mortier slipped through your fingers! Is that victory?'

'No, but seriously,' answered Prince Andrey, 'at least we can claim without boasting that it's an improvement on Ulm . . .'

'You might have caught us a marshal, just one!'

'Well, things don't always turn out the way you plan them. It's not like being all neat and tidy on the parade ground. As I said, we had expected to attack the enemy in the rear at seven in the morning, but we didn't even get there till five in the afternoon.'

'But *why* didn't you arrive at seven in the morning? You *should have* arrived at seven in the morning,' said Bilibin with a smile. '*You should have arrived at seven in the morning.*'

'Why didn't you manage to persuade Napoleon through diplomatic channels that he had better leave Genoa alone?' said Prince Andrey, adopting the same tone.

'I know what you're thinking,' broke in Bilibin. 'It's not difficult to capture a marshal sitting on a sofa by the fireside. That's fine, but the question remains – why didn't you capture him? You shouldn't be too surprised if the most august Emperor and King Francis, like the war minister, is not too delighted by your victory. I'm not all that jubilant, and I'm just a poor secretary in the Russian embassy . . .'

He looked directly at Prince Andrey and suddenly relaxed the bunched-up folds on his forehead.

'All right, dear boy. Now it's my turn to ask you a few questions,' said Bolkonsky. 'There's something here I don't understand. Maybe there are some diplomatic subtleties beyond my feeble intellect, but I still don't understand. Mack loses a whole army, Archduke Ferdinand and Archduke Karl give no sign of life and make one blunder after another, Kutuzov is the only one to win a proper battle, thus destroying all the mystique of the French – and the minister of war shows not the slightest interest in any of the details!'

'My dear fellow, that's the whole point! Listen. Three cheers for the Tsar, for Russia and the faith! All very nice, but why should *we* – the Austrian court – get excited about *your* victories? Bring us some news of a victory by Archduke Karl or Ferdinand – one archduke's much the same as another, as you well know. I don't care if they've beaten Napoleon's fire brigade – it will be something different, and we'll fire a big-gun salute. Otherwise this can only tantalize us, and it seems almost deliberate. Archduke Karl does nothing, Archduke Ferdinand covers himself with disgrace and you walk out on Vienna. No more defence. You might as well say it straight out: "God's with us, and you and your capital can go to the devil." You take one of our generals, Schmidt, loved by all and sundry, you stick him in the way of a bullet, and then congratulate us on a great victory! . . . You must admit – anything more infuriating than the news you brought would be hard to imagine. You seem to have done it on purpose. That's what it looks like. And setting that aside, if you really were to win a brilliant victory, even if Archduke Karl did, what difference would it make to the general course of events? It's too late now. Vienna has been occupied by the French forces.'

'What do you mean occupied? Vienna hasn't been occupied, has it?'

'Yes, and that's not all. Bonaparte is at Schönbrunn, and the count – our dear Count Vrbna – is going to see him to receive his orders.'

After the tiring demands and all the varied impressions of his journey and then his reception, and even more after the dinner he'd just eaten, Bolkonsky felt unable to take in the full significance of what he had just heard.

'Count Lichtenfels was here this morning,' Bilibin continued, 'and he showed me a letter containing every last detail of a French parade through Vienna. Prince Murat and all the rest of them . . . So you see – your victory is no great cause for rejoicing, and you can hardly expect to be received as a saviour!'

'But honestly, I'm not bothered about that – I really am not!' said Prince Andrey, as it dawned on him that his news about the battle at Krems paled into insignificance in the light of events like the occupation of Austria's capital city. 'How was Vienna taken? What about the bridge and those famous fortifications, and Prince Auersperg? We heard it said that Prince Auersperg was defending Vienna.'

'Prince Auersperg is stationed on this side – our side. He's defending us, not very effectively it seems, but he is defending us. Vienna's across the river. No, the bridge has not been taken, and I hope it won't be, because it's been mined and orders have been given to blow it up. Otherwise, we'd have been up in the mountains of Bohemia ages ago, and you and your army would have had a bad time of it between two fires.'

'That still doesn't mean that the campaign is finished,' said Prince Andrey.

'I think it is. So do all the bigwigs here, though they don't dare admit it. I said when the campaign started that it wouldn't be settled by gunpowder – not by your little squabble at Dürrenstein – but only by those who invented it,' said Bilibin – this was one of his *bons mots* – relaxing the wrinkles on his forehead and pausing for a moment. 'The only question now is what will come out of the meeting between Emperor Alexander and the Prussian king. If Prussia enters the alliance, that will force Austria's hand and there'll be war. If she doesn't, all we have to do is agree on a place where the articles of a new Campo Formio⁹ can be drawn up.'

'What an amazing genius that man is!' Prince Andrey burst out, clenching his small fist and banging it on the table. 'And amazingly lucky too!'

'Who is, Buonaparte?' queried Bilibin, puckering up his forehead – a clear sign that a *bon mot* was on its way. 'Bu-onaparte?' he repeated, stressing the *u*. 'Still, I think we might let him off the "u" now; after all, he is dictating Austria's laws from Schönbrunn. That's it, I've decided once and for all to accept the innovation and just call him Bonaparte.'

'No listen, joking apart,' said Prince Andrey, 'do you really think the campaign is finished?'

'I'll tell you what I think. Austria has been made a fool of, and she is not used to that. She'll be out for vengeance. And why was she made a fool of? First, because her provinces have been pillaged (they say the Holy Russian army is good at looting), her army has been destroyed, her capital has been occupied, and all this to please the pretty eyes of his Sardinian Majesty. So, between you and me, old fellow, instinct tells me we're having the wool pulled over our eyes. Instinct tells me of negotiations with France and plans for a peace treaty, a secret agreement done on the side.'

'That's impossible!' said Prince Andrey. 'That would be too vile for words.'

'Time will tell,' said Bilibin, relaxing the creases on his forehead again, an indication that the subject was now closed.

When Prince Andrey retired to the room they had prepared for him and lay down in clean sheets on the feather bed with his head on the fragrant, nicely warmed pillows, the battle he had come to report on seemed to have receded into the distant past. His mind was full of the Prussian alliance, the treachery of Austria, Bonaparte's latest triumph, tomorrow's parade and reception, and his audience with Emperor Francis. His eyes closed. Instantly his ears rang with cannon-fire, muskets discharging and rumbling wheels; he could see a long line of musketeers running downhill and the French firing back at them; he could feel his heart miss a beat and watch himself galloping to the front with Schmidt, with bullets whistling all around him, and he was once again enjoying that tenfold delight in living that he had not known since childhood.

Then he woke.

'Yes, it really did happen!' he told himself with the happy smile of a young child, before relapsing into a deep, youthful slumber.

CHAPTER 11

Next morning he woke late. Reviewing his recent impressions, he remembered first of all that today he was to be presented to the Emperor Francis, and he also recalled the minister of war, the unctuous adjutant, Bilibin and last night's conversation. He put on his full dress uniform, which he had not worn for a long time, and walked into Bilibin's room with his arm in a sling, looking fresh, eager and handsome. Four gentlemen of the diplomatic corps were already there. Prince Hippolyte Kuragin, a secretary in the embassy, was already known to him; Bilibin introduced the others.

The visitors were a set of fashionable, wealthy and high-spirited young men who made up a special circle, originally in Vienna and now in Brno, a circle which Bilibin, their leader, referred to as 'our people'. They were almost all diplomats, but their interests extended well beyond the war and politics to take in fashionable society, relations with certain women and the official side of the service. These young gentlemen clearly took to Prince Andrey, welcoming him straightaway as 'one of ours' – a rare distinction. Out of politeness and to break the ice they asked him one or two questions about the army and the battle, but soon the conversation slipped back into inconsequential chitchat, jokes and gossip.

'No, but the best bit of all,' said one of them, describing a disaster that had happened to a service colleague, 'yes, the best bit was that the minister had told him that his appointment to London was definitely a promotion and that was how he should see it. Imagine his face! . . .'

'Worse than that, gentlemen – now I'm going to give Kuragin away – a fellow runs into a bit of trouble and this Don Juan takes full advantage! Shocking fellow!'

Prince Hippolyte was sprawling in a Voltaire armchair with his legs over the arm. He laughed and said, 'Tell me more.'

'Don Juan! You reptile!' cried various voices.

'Something you don't know, Bolkonsky,' said Bilibin, turning to Prince Andrey. 'All the atrocities of the, er, French army – I nearly said the Russian army – are nothing compared with this fellow's achievements with women.'

'A woman is . . . a good companion for a man,' declared Prince Hippolyte, peering at his elevated legs through a lorgnette.

Bilibin and the rest of 'our people' roared with laughter, staring at Hippolyte. Prince Andrey could now see that this Hippolyte, who, if he was honest about it, had brought him to the verge of jealousy over his wife, was the butt of this circle.

'No, I must treat you to a bit of Kuragin,' Bilibin whispered to Bolkonsky. 'He's wonderful when you get him going on politics. You must see the depth of his thinking.'

He sat down by Hippolyte, wrinkled up his forehead and started a conversation about politics. Prince Andrey and the others gathered round.

'The Berlin cabinet cannot express any feelings concerning an alliance,' Hippolyte began, with a knowing look, 'without expressing . . . as in its last note . . . you do see, don't you? . . . And besides, if his Majesty the Emperor doesn't go back on the principle of our alliance . . .'

'Wait, I haven't finished,' he said to Prince Andrey, seizing him by the hand. 'I can only imagine that intervention will be stronger than non-intervention. And besides . . .' He paused. 'Non-receipt of our dispatch of November the 28th doesn't count as imputing . . . Anyway, that's how it's all going to end.' And he let go of Bolkonsky's hand to indicate that he had quite finished.

'Demosthenes, I know you by the pebble in your golden mouth!'[10] said Bilibin, his thick thatch of hair rippling with delight.

Everyone laughed, no one louder than Hippolyte. He was almost choking from obvious distress, but he couldn't hold back from frenzied laughter that sent spasms across his usually impassive features.

'Now listen, gentlemen,' said Bilibin, 'Bolkonsky is my guest even here in Brno and I want to entertain him to the best of my ability with all the pleasures of our life in this town. If we were in Vienna it would all be very easy, but here, in this godforsaken Moravian hole it's more difficult, and I am asking all of you to help. He must be given the freedom of Brno. You take the theatre, I'll take society life, and, of course, you, Hippolyte – the women.'

'We must show him Amélie. She's gorgeous!' said one of 'our people', kissing his fingertips.

'To cut a long story short,' said Bilibin, 'we must turn this bloodthirsty warrior more towards love of his fellow creatures.'

'I'm afraid I shan't be able to accept your hospitality, gentlemen. It's time for me to go,' said Bolkonsky, glancing at his watch.

'Where are you off to?'

'The Emperor!'

'Oh! Oh! Oh!'

'Well, *au revoir*, Bolkonsky! *Au revoir*, Prince! Come back for an early dinner,' said various voices. 'We're going to look after you.'

'While you're talking to the Emperor do what you can to praise the procurement and route-mapping,' said Bilibin, seeing Bolkonsky into the hall.

'I'd love to do that, but from what I've seen I shan't be able to,' answered Bolkonsky with a smile.

'Well, try to do all the talking, anyway. He's a great holder of audiences, but he doesn't like talking. In fact, he can't talk at all. You'll see for yourself.'

CHAPTER 12

At the reception Prince Andrey took up his appointed place among the Austrian officers. Emperor Francis merely looked at him closely in the face and nodded his elongated head. But after the reception the adjutant of the previous evening obsequiously communicated to Bolkonsky the Emperor's desire to grant him an audience. Emperor Francis received him standing in the middle of the room. Prince Andrey was surprised to observe that before beginning the conversation, the Emperor seemed embarrassed; he didn't know what to say, and went red in the face.

'Tell me when the battle began,' he blurted out. Prince Andrey answered. The question was followed by others, just as simple: Was Kutuzov well? When did he leave Krems? and so on. The Emperor spoke as though his sole aim was to get through a series of set questions. The answers seemed not to hold the slightest interest for him.

'At what time of day did the battle begin?' asked the Emperor.

'I cannot inform your Majesty at what precise time the battle began at the front, but at Dürrenstein, where I was, the troops began the attack about six in the evening,' said Bolkonsky, warming to his task and beginning to think he would now have a chance to launch into his carefully prepared description of all he knew and had seen. But the Emperor interrupted him with a smile:

'How many miles is it?'

'From where to where, your Majesty?'

'From Dürrenstein to Krems.'

'Three and a half miles, your Majesty.'

'The French abandoned the left bank?'

'According to intelligence, the last of them crossed on rafts during the night.'

'Have you enough provisions at Krems?'

'Well, we were rather short of . . .'

The Emperor interrupted.

'What time was General Schmidt killed?'

'Seven o'clock, I believe.'

'At seven o'clock? Very sad! Very sad!'

The Emperor said he was grateful and bowed. Prince Andrey withdrew and was immediately surrounded on all sides by courtiers. Everywhere he saw warm, friendly eyes looking at him, and heard warm, friendly voices talking to him. Yesterday's adjutant reproached him for not staying in the palace, and offered him his own house. The minister of war came up and congratulated him on the Order of Maria Theresa (Third Class) which the Emperor wished to award him. The Empress's chamberlain invited him to call upon her Majesty. The Archduchess, too, wished to see him. He didn't know which answer should come first, and took a few seconds to gather his senses. The Russian Ambassador took him by the shoulder, led him away to a window and began to talk.

Despite all that Bilibin had said, his news was received with rejoicing. A service of thanksgiving was arranged. Kutuzov was awarded the Grand Cross of Maria Theresa, and further awards went to the whole army. Bolkonsky received invitations from all and sundry, and spent the whole morning paying visits to the top people in the Austrian government. These went on into the afternoon and it was past four o'clock when Prince Andrey was able to make his way back to Bilibin's, mentally composing a letter to his father about the battle and his reception at Brno. On the way he stopped off at a bookshop to stock up on reading material for the campaign, and stayed there for some time. When he finally reached the steps of Bilibin's house, there stood a carriage half-stowed with luggage, and here was Franz, Bilibin's servant, struggling in the doorway with a travelling trunk.

'What's happened?' asked Bolkonsky.

'Oh dear, your Excellency!' said Franz, heaving the trunk on to the carriage. 'We're moving on. That villain's at our heels again!'

'You what?' queried Prince Andrey.

Bilibin came out to meet Bolkonsky. His usually composed face showed some agitation.

'No, no, you'll have to admit there's a nice little story here,' he said. 'It's the Tabor bridge at Vienna – they crossed it without a shot being fired.'

Prince Andrey couldn't follow him.

'Where've you been? You don't seem to know what every coachman in the town has heard by now.'

'I've been with the Archduchess. I heard nothing there.'

'Haven't you seen everybody packing their things?'

'I haven't seen anything . . . What's gone wrong?' Prince Andrey asked impatiently.

'Gone wrong? What's gone wrong is that the French have crossed the bridge that Auersperg was supposed to be defending, and they didn't blow it up, so even as we speak Murat is coming hotfoot down the road to Brno, and they'll be here soon – tomorrow at the latest.'

'What do you mean? Why wasn't the bridge blown up? I thought it had been mined.'

'Why? That's what I'm asking you. Nobody knows why. Even Bonaparte doesn't know why.'

Bolkonsky shrugged.

'But if they're over the bridge, the army's finished. It'll be cut off,' he said.

'Of course it will,' answered Bilibin. 'Listen to this. The French enter Vienna, as I said. Fine. The following day, yesterday, Marshals Murat, Lannes and Beliard jump on their horses and ride down to the bridge. (Please note: all three are Gascons.)[11] "Gentlemen," says one, "you know the Tabor bridge has been mined and countermined. It is protected by formidable defences, oh and fifteen thousand troops with orders to blow it up and stop us getting across. But our Sovereign Emperor Napoleon will be very pleased if we take the bridge. So, let the three of us go and take it." "Yes, let's," say the others, and they set off and they take the bridge, and they march across, and now with their entire army on this side of the Danube they're heading straight for us – and for you and your lines of communication.'

'It's no joke,' said Prince Andrey, saddened and serious. The news grieved Prince Andrey, but it also gave him pleasure. Once he knew the Russian army was in such a hopeless situation, it immediately occurred to him that he might be the very man destined to extricate the Russian army from that situation, and that just as Napoleon rose from obscurity at Toulon[12] this was where he would be raised for ever from the ranks of anonymous officers. This was his first step on the road to glory! Even as he listened to Bilibin he could see himself getting through to the army, presenting to a council of war his version of events, the army's only salvation, and taking personal responsibility for the execution of his plan.

'It's no joke,' he said.

'I'm not joking,' Bilibin went on. 'Nothing could be truer or sadder than this. These three gentlemen advance to the bridge unaccompanied and waving white handkerchiefs. It's a truce, they say, and they, the marshals, have come to parley with Prince Auersperg. The duty officer lets them on to the bridgehead. They spin him a thousand gasconades: the war is over, Emperor Francis has arranged a meeting with Bonaparte, they wish to see Prince Auersperg and so on. The officer sends for Auersperg. These Gascon gentlemen embrace the officers, make a lot of jokes and sit there on the big guns, and meanwhile a French

battalion creeps up quietly on to the bridge, hurls the sacks of incendiary material down into the river, and marches up to the bridgehead.
Eventually the lieutenant-general appears, our dear Prince Auersperg
von Mautern, no less. "Esteemed enemy! Flower of the Austrian yeom-
anry! Hero of the Turkish wars! Hostilities are at end. We can all
shake hands . . . Emperor Napoleon has a burning desire to make the
acquaintance of Prince Auersperg." In a nutshell, these gentlemen –
true Gascons all – bamboozle Auersperg with their clever talk; he is
so flattered by this rapidly developed intimacy with French marshals,
so dazzled by Murat's fine cloak and ostrich feathers, that he is blinded
by their fire and forgets that firing's what he ought to be doing to the
enemy.' (Carried away as he was by the lively telling of his story,
Bilibin did not forget to pause after this *bon mot*, to allow it to sink
in.) 'A French battalion storms the bridgehead, spikes the cannons
and that's it, the bridge is taken. But wait, the best part of the whole
story,' he went on, a skilled raconteur relaxing in mid-narrative, 'is
that the sergeant in charge of the cannon which was due to give the
signal to light the fuses and blow up the bridge, this sergeant, seeing
the French troops running on to the bridge, wanted to open fire, but
Lannes stayed his hand. The sergeant, obviously brighter than his
general, goes up to Auersperg and he says, "Prince, it's a trick. Look,
the French are coming!" Murat sees that all is lost if he lets the sergeant
have his say. With pretended amazement (a true Gascon indeed!)
he addresses Auersperg: "Is this Austrian discipline, famed the world
over?" he asks. "How can you let a man of low rank address you
like that?" This was a stroke of genius. Prince Auersperg preserves
his honour by having the sergeant arrested. Be honest, this Tabor
bridge affair makes a sweet little story, doesn't it? No stupidity, no
cowardice . . .'

'It could be treason,' said Prince Andrey, still vividly imagining grey
overcoats, wounds, gunsmoke and roaring cannons – and the glory
that would be his.

'Oh, it's not that. But it does put the court in an awkward spot,'
pursued Bilibin. 'It's not treason, or cowardice, or stupidity – it's Ulm
all over again.' He seemed to pause for reflection, wondering just how
to put it, 'It's that man Mack . . . We have been *Macked*!' he said,
satisfied that he had coined another *bon mot*, a brand-new one that
was going to get repeated. His wrinkled brow relaxed smartly in
self-congratulation, and with a thin smile he began to inspect his
fingernails.

'Where are you off to?' he asked abruptly, turning to Prince Andrey,
who had got up and was heading for his room.

'I must get going.'

'Where to?'

'Back to the army.'

'I thought you were going to stay on for a couple of days.'

'Not now. I've got to leave at once.'

And Prince Andrey, after making the necessary arrangements for the journey, went to his room.

'You know, my dear fellow,' said Bilibin, following him in, 'I've been thinking about you. Why do you have to go?' As if to prove the sureness of his coming argument, all the wrinkles disappeared from his face.

Prince Andrey looked at him quizzically but said nothing.

'Why do you have to go? I know duty calls – you must gallop off to the army now that the army is in danger. I understand this, my boy. It's called heroism.'

'Absolutely not,' said Prince Andrey.

'But you're a cultivated man, so be one in the fullest sense. Look at things the other way round and you'll see you've got it all wrong. Your duty is to take care of yourself. Leave that sort of thing to other people who are good for nothing better . . . No one has ordered you back, and you haven't been dismissed from here, so you can stay on and go with us wherever misfortune takes us. I've heard it said we're going to Olmütz. Olmütz is a very charming town. And we can travel there together quite pleasantly in my carriage.'

'That's enough of the jokes, Bilibin,' said Bolkonsky.

'No, I speak sincerely as a friend. Think it over. Where are you off to now, and why are you going at all when you can stay on here? There are only two possibilities,' (he wrinkled up the skin of his left temple) 'either peace will be declared before you get back to the army, or it will mean defeat and disgrace along with Kutuzov and the whole army.'

And Bilibin relaxed his brow again, confident that this dilemma was irrefutable.

'This is something I can't argue about,' said Prince Andrey coldly, but he thought to himself, 'I have to go – to save the army.'

'My dear fellow, you're a hero,' said Bilibin.

CHAPTER 13

The same night, after taking leave of the war minister, Bolkonsky was on his way to rejoin the army, not knowing where to find it and worried about being captured by the French on the way to Krems.

At Brno the whole court and everyone attached to it was busy packing, and the heavy baggage was already on the road to Olmütz. Near Etzelsdorf, Prince Andrey came to the road along which the Russian army was moving with maximum speed and in maximum disorder. It was so blocked with wagons that no carriage could possibly get through. Prince Andrey procured a horse and a Cossack from the officer in charge of the Cossacks, and, hungry and weary as he was, he wove in and out between the wagons and rode on in search of the commander-in-chief and his own luggage. The most sinister rumours about the situation of the army reached him along the road, and they were confirmed by the sight of the army fleeing in such disorder.

He recalled the words of Napoleon's address to his army at the beginning of the campaign: 'That Russian army which English gold has brought from the ends of the universe is going to suffer at our hands the same fate – the fate of the army of Ulm.' These words aroused in him simultaneously open-mouthed admiration for the genius of his hero, a feeling of hurt pride and the hope of glory. 'And what if there's nothing left but to die?' he thought. 'Well if I must – I'll do it as well as the next man!'

Prince Andrey turned his scornful gaze on the endless, chaotic mass of detachments, wagons, supply vehicles, artillery and more wagons, wagons, wagons of every size and shape, overtaking one another and blocking the muddy road three and four abreast. On all sides, right up front and way behind, as far as the ear could strain in every direction, you could hear wheels rumbling, carts rattling, wagons creaking, gun-carriages groaning, horses trampling, whips cracking, drivers shouting and everybody swearing, soldiers, orderlies and officers. The roadsides were littered everywhere with fallen horses, flayed and unflayed, broken-down wagons with solitary soldiers sitting by them just waiting, other soldiers separated from their units, heading in little groups for the next village or carrying loot from the last one – chickens, sheep, hay, or sackfuls of something or other. When the road went uphill or downhill the crowds squashed together even closer, and there was an endless hubbub of shouts and groans. Soldiers floundering knee-deep in mud heaved guns and wagons along with their bare hands while the whips cracked, hoofs slithered, traces snapped and the air rang with the most heart-rending cries. The transport officers rode up and down, in and out of the wagons, their voices barely audible amid the general uproar and their faces showing all too clearly that they despaired of ever controlling this chaos.

'And this is our well-loved Holy Russian military machine,' thought Bolkonsky, recalling Bilibin's words.

He rode up to a convoy, intending to ask someone where he could find the commander-in-chief. There in front of him trundled a strange one-horse vehicle obviously knocked up by some soldiers out of any everyday bits and pieces they could lay their hands on, part-wagon, part-carriage, part-cab. A soldier was driving, and under a cover behind the leather hood sat a woman swathed in shawls. Prince Andrey rode up and was just beginning to ask the soldier a question when he was distracted by the desperate cries of the woman sitting in this contraption. The transport officer had lashed out at the soldier in the coachman's seat for trying to overtake, and the whip had cracked against the cover of the vehicle. The woman was screaming. Catching sight of Prince Andrey, she thrust her head out from under the cover, waved at him with her thin little arms sticking out from under the matting shawls, and yelled, 'Adjutant! Sir! . . . For heaven's sake . . . give us some protection . . . What's going to happen to us? . . . I'm a doctor's wife – in the Seventh Chasseurs[13] . . . they won't let us get past. We're miles behind. We've lost our own people.'

'I'll cut you to pieces! Get back!' shouted the exasperated officer to the soldier. 'Get back and take that whore with you!'

'Sir, please protect us. What does he think he's doing?' screamed the doctor's wife.

'Kindly let this carriage through. Can't you see there's a lady in it?' said Prince Andrey, riding up to the officer.

The officer glanced at him, said nothing and turned back to the soldier. 'I'll teach you to shove in . . . Get back!'

'Let it through, I tell you,' repeated Prince Andrey, tightening his lips.

'Who do you think you are?' cried the officer, turning upon him suddenly in a drunken rage. 'Just who are you? Are you in charge here?' he asked with brazen insubordination. 'No, you're not, I'm in charge! You get back!' he repeated, 'or I'll cut you to pieces!' – a phrase which had obviously caught his imagination.

'One in the eye for our little adjutant,' came a voice from the background.

Prince Andrey could see the officer was in one of those drunken senseless rages when people don't remember what they have been saying. He could see that his championing of the doctor's wife in that odd contraption was exposing him to the one thing he most dreaded – becoming a laughing stock – but instinct spoke differently. Hardly were these last words out of the officer's mouth when Prince Andrey rode straight up to him, his face distorted with fury, and raised his riding whip.

'Let – them – through!'

The officer waved at him and galloped off.

'It's their fault, these staff officers, all this chaos,' he grumbled. 'Do what you want now.'

Prince Andrey, without looking up, hurried to get away from the doctor's wife, who was calling him her saviour, and with every last detail of this humiliating scene nauseatingly lodged in his memory, he galloped on towards the village where he had been told he would find the commander-in-chief.

Once in the village, he got off his horse and went up to the very first house with the intention of relaxing for a minute or two, finding a bite to eat and somehow sorting out all the hateful impressions that were tormenting him. 'It's a gang of crooks, not an army,' he thought, and he was just going up to a window when he heard a familiar voice calling his name.

He looked round. There before him was the handsome face of Nesvitsky, sticking out of a little window. Nesvitsky was munching something (as his moist lips showed), waving like mad and calling him in.

'Bolkonsky! Hey, Bolkonsky! Come on in. Quick!' he shouted.

Prince Andrey went in and found Nesvitsky and another adjutant eating. They turned round quickly to ask Bolkonsky whether he had any news. Prince Andrey read alarm and uneasiness on their familiar features, especially Nesvitsky's, which were usually so good-humoured.

'Where's the commander-in-chief?' asked Bolkonsky

'He's here – over there in that house,' answered the adjutant.

'Well, is it true – peace and surrender?' asked Nesvitsky.

'I thought you might know. I don't know anything – beyond the fact that it wasn't easy to get here.'

'Wait till you hear about us, my boy! It's terrible! To think I laughed at Mack. We're worse off than he ever was,' said Nesvitsky. 'But look, sit down and have something to eat.'

'You won't find your baggage or anything else here, Prince, and God knows where your man's gone,' said the other adjutant.

'Where are the headquarters?'

'We're spending the night in Znaim.'

'Well, I managed to pack everything I need on two horses,' said Nesvitsky. 'Very good packs too. They'd see me over the mountains of Bohemia. We're up against it, old fellow. But look at you, you don't look very well. You're shivering.' Nesvitsky had seen Prince Andrey jump as if he'd had an electric shock.

'No, I'm all right,' answered Prince Andrey. He had just recalled the brush between the doctor's wife and the transport officer.

'What is the commander-in-chief doing here?' he asked.

'I haven't the slightest idea,' said Nesvitsky.

'All I know is – it's a disaster, an absolute disaster,' said Prince Andrey, and he went over to the house where the commander-in-chief was said to be.

He walked past Kutuzov's carriage, the weary saddle horses belonging to members of his entourage, and the Cossacks talking loudly together, and approached the entry. He was informed that Kutuzov was in the inner room of the hut with Prince Bagration and Weierother, an Austrian general who had taken Schmidt's place. There in the entry sat little Kozlovsky squatting on his heels in front of a copying-clerk. The latter was sitting on an upturned tub with the cuffs of his uniform rolled up, writing at speed. Kozlovsky looked worn out, someone else who had obviously not slept all night. He glanced up at Prince Andrey, but didn't even nod.

'Line two . . . Have you got that?' he went on, dictating to the clerk. 'The Kiev Grenadiers, the Podolyan . . .'

'You're going too fast, sir,' protested the clerk with a brazen, angry glance at Kozlovsky. At that moment he heard Kutuzov's strong and impatient voice through the door, with another unknown voice interrupting him. The sound of those voices, Kozlovsky's perfunctory glance at him, the rudeness of the harassed clerk, the fact that he and Kozlovsky were sitting around a tub on the floor at so little distance from the commander-in-chief and those Cossack horse-minders laughing so raucously just outside the window – all of this made Prince Andrey feel that some great and ghastly misfortune was about to descend on them.

He turned to Kozlovsky with some urgent questions.

'Prince, you'll have to wait . . .' said Kozlovsky. 'The disposition of Bagration's troops . . .'

'Is it surrender?'

'No, it's not. We're getting ready to take them on!'

Prince Andrey walked over towards the door of the room from which the voices were coming. But just as he was about to open it, the voices inside stopped speaking; the door opened and there in the doorway stood Kutuzov with his familiar aquiline nose and podgy features. Prince Andrey was standing directly opposite Kutuzov, but from the look in the commander-in-chief's one good eye it was clear that he was observing very little, being preoccupied with so many thoughts and anxieties. He looked his adjutant straight in the face and didn't recognize him.

'Well, have you finished?' he inquired of Kozlovsky.

'Very nearly, your Excellency.'

Bagration followed his commander-in-chief out of the room, a short lean man, still relatively young, his semi-oriental features suggesting a phlegmatic man of strong character.

'Beg to report back, sir.' Prince Andrey had to say it twice in rather a loud voice before handing Kutuzov an envelope.

'Oh yes, back from Vienna? Very good! Later, later!' Kutuzov went out to the steps accompanied by Bagration.

'Well, Prince, I bid you farewell,' he said to Bagration. 'Christ be with you! You have my blessing for the great task ahead!' Kutuzov's face suddenly softened; there were tears in his eyes. With his left hand he drew Bagration to him, and with the other, which bore a ring, he made the sign of the cross over him, a gesture which seemed to have become second nature. He offered him a podgy cheek, but Bagration ended up kissing him on the neck. 'Christ be with you!' repeated Kutuzov, walking away towards his carriage. 'Get in with me,' he said to Bolkonsky.

'Your most high Excellency, I would like to be of some use here. Please allow me to remain in Prince Bagration's detachment.'

'Come in,' said Kutuzov, and noticing that Bolkonsky was still hanging back, he added, 'I need some good officers myself. Yes, indeed I do.'

They took their seats in the carriage and for some time neither of them spoke.

'We still have a very great deal ahead of us,' Kutuzov said, seeming to penetrate with the sharp wisdom of a veteran all the spiritual torment that was troubling Bolkonsky. 'If one-tenth of his detachment gets through tomorrow, I shall thank God for it,' added Kutuzov, apparently to himself.

Prince Andrey glanced at this man, only inches away from him, and his eyes were drawn to the sharp outline of the scar on his temple where that bullet had gone through his head at Izmail, and the empty eye-socket. 'Oh yes, he's earned the right to talk so casually about the destruction of all these men,' thought Bolkonsky.

'That's why I'm asking you to send me to that detachment,' he said.

Kutuzov didn't reply. He seemed to have forgotten what he had been saying, and sat deep in thought. But five minutes later, rocking comfortably in the smoothly sprung carriage, Kutuzov looked at Prince Andrey. His face now showed no trace of emotion. With shrewd amusement he questioned Prince Andrey about the details of his interview with the Emperor, and how the court had reacted to the Krems affair and also about certain ladies known to them both.

CHAPTER 14

On the 1st of November Kutuzov received an intelligence report that placed his army in an almost impossible situation. A spy reported that the French, having crossed the bridge at Vienna, were moving in great numbers on Kutuzov's line of communications with the reinforcements marching up from Russia. If Kutuzov were to remain at Krems, Napoleon's army of a hundred and fifty thousand men would cut him off from all communications, and surround his weary army of forty thousand, and he would find himself in the same situation as Mack before Ulm. If he wanted to abandon the road connecting him with the Russian reinforcements, he would have to go off the roads altogether into unknown territory, the mountainous region of Bohemia, pursued by the cream of the enemy's forces, and would give up all hope of joining with Buxhöwden. If he decided to retreat down the road from Krems to Olmütz to join up with the forces coming from Russia he ran the risk of being intercepted by the French who had crossed the Vienna bridge and having to engage them on the march, encumbered with stores and transport – an enemy three times as numerous and hemming him in on two sides. Kutuzov went for this last option.

According to his intelligence the French, once over the river, had set off on a forced march towards Znaim, which was on Kutuzov's route, sixty or seventy miles away. To get to Znaim before the French offered the best hope of saving the army. To let the French get there first would mean exposing the whole army to a disgrace like that of the Austrians at Ulm, or to complete destruction. But to reach Znaim with the whole army before the French got there was impossible. The road for the French from Vienna to Znaim was shorter and better than the road for the Russians from Krems to Znaim.

On the night he received the report Kutuzov dispatched Bagration's advance guard of four thousand men off to the right over the moun-

tains from the Krems–Znaim road to the Vienna–Znaim road.
Bagration was to march without stopping, and take up a position
facing Vienna with his back to Znaim, and if he did manage to get
there before the French, his task was to delay them for as long as
possible. Meanwhile Kutuzov set off for Znaim with all the heavy
transport.

Bagration covered the thirty miles over the mountains at night in
foul weather, with no road and with hungry, badly shod soldiers.
Leaving a third of his men straggling in his wake, Bagration reached
Hollabrünn, on the Vienna–Znaim road, a few hours before the
French, who were marching there from Vienna. Kutuzov still needed
a good twenty-four hours to get to Znaim with his heavy transport
and so, to save the army, Bagration with his four thousand hungry
and exhausted soldiers needed to hold up the entire enemy army
confronting him at Hollabrünn for a day and a night – an obvious
impossibility. But an odd twist of fate made the impossible possible.
The success of the trick that had given the Vienna bridge into the
hands of the French encouraged Murat to try and outwit Kutuzov
too. Encountering Bagration's feeble detachment on the Znaim road,
Murat mistook it for Kutuzov's whole army. With a view to adminis-
tering one final, crushing defeat to this army, he decided to wait for
the troops coming up behind him from Vienna. With this in mind he
proposed a three-day truce on condition that neither army changed
position or made any movement. Murat insisted that peace negotiations were under way and this truce was proposed to avoid unnecessary bloodshed. Count Nostitz, the Austrian general in charge of the
advance posts, trusted Murat's word as conveyed by an emissary
and fell back, leaving Bagration's detachment unprotected. Another
emissary rode along the Russian lines to make the same announcement
about peace negotiations and propose a three-day truce to the Russian
troops. Bagration's response was that he had no authority to accept
or to decline any truce, and he dispatched an adjutant to Kutuzov
with a report of the French proposal.

A truce was Kutuzov's only hope of gaining time in order to give
Bagration's exhausted forces some rest and to get the transport and
heavy convoys (the movement of which was concealed from the
French) one stage further along the road to Znaim. The offer of a
truce gave them out of the blue one last chance to save the army.
Once informed of it, Kutuzov promptly dispatched Adjutant General
Wintzengerode, who was with him, to the enemy's camp. Wintzengerode was instructed not only to accept the truce, but to propose
terms for surrender, and meanwhile Kutuzov sent his adjutants back

to speed up the transport of the baggage and equipment of the whole army along the Krems–Znaim road. Bagration's starving and exhausted detachment was to provide cover single-handedly for the troop and transport convoy by just staying there facing an enemy eight times as strong.

Kutuzov was right in two respects: that the offer of surrender, which did not tie his hands in any way, gave time for at least some of the transport to reach Znaim, and also that Murat's blunder would very soon be discovered. Napoleon was at Schönbrunn, less than twenty miles from Hollabrünn, when he received Murat's dispatch and the proposals for a truce and surrender. He saw through the trick immediately and sent the following letter to Murat by return:

Schönbrunn,
25 Brumaire, 1805 at eight o'clock in the morning.

TO PRINCE MURAT

I can find no words to express to you my displeasure. As a mere advance guard commander you have no right to enter into truces without orders from me. You are losing for me the spoils of a whole campaign. Break the truce immediately and march on the enemy. You must have it declared to them that the general who signed this surrender had no right to do so, and that only the Emperor of Russia has that right. If, however, the Emperor of Russia should ratify the aforesaid convention, I shall do likewise; but this is nothing but a trick. March on and destroy the Russian army . . . You are well placed to seize its baggage and artillery.

The Russian Emperor's aide-de-camp is an impostor. Officers are nothing when they have no power; this one had none . . . The Austrians let themselves be tricked into allowing us across the Vienna bridge; now you are falling for a trick played on you by one of the Emperor's adjutants.

NAPOLEON.

Napoleon's adjutant galloped off at full speed bearing this ominous letter to Murat. Distrusting his generals, Napoleon himself moved to the battlefield with his whole guard, worried that a ready victim might slip through his fingers. Meanwhile the four thousand men of Bagration's detachment cheerfully lit their campfires, dried themselves out and got warm, and cooked porridge for the first time in three days, none of them realizing or even dreaming of what might be in store for them.

CHAPTER 15

It was nearly four o'clock in the afternoon when Prince Andrey, who had finally persuaded Kutuzov to release him, reached Grunth and joined Bagration. Napoleon's adjutant had not yet reached Murat's detachment and the battle had not yet begun. In Bagration's detachment they had no idea how things were going. There was talk of peace, but no one believed it was possible. There was also talk of battle, but no one believed that was about to happen either.

Knowing Bolkonsky to be a popular and trusted adjutant, Bagration gave him his warmest welcome and special indulgence, as a commanding officer. He informed him that action would probably begin that day or the next, and gave him absolute freedom either to remain with him during the battle or to retire to the rearguard and supervise the order of the retreat, also 'a matter of some importance'.

'But I don't think there'll be any fighting today,' said Bagration reassuringly to Prince Andrey.

'If he is one of the run-of-the-mill little staff dandies sent here to win himself a cross,' he was thinking, 'he can do that in the rearguard, but if he really wants to be with me, I may as well let him . . . I can use him, if he's got any guts.' Without replying, Prince Andrey asked leave to ride around the territory and learn the disposition of the forces, so that if he had to deliver any messages he would know where to take them. One of the duty officers, a handsome and elegantly dressed man with a diamond ring on his forefinger, a confident speaker of bad French, was detailed to conduct Prince Andrey.

On all sides they could see rain-soaked officers with dejected faces who seemed to be looking for something, and soldiers carrying doors, planks and fences from somewhere in the village.

'Just look at these men. They're all over the place,' said the staff officer, pointing to them. 'Their officers let them run riot. And look here.' He pointed to a canteen set up under a tent. 'They come in here and just sit around doing nothing. I sent them all out this morning, and look, it's full again. I must just ride over and give them a scare, Prince. One moment.'

'Let's both go, and I'll get myself some bread and cheese,' said Prince Andrey, who had not yet had time to eat.

'Why didn't you say, Prince? I could have offered you something.'

They got off their horses and went in under the tent. Several officers, with flushed and exhausted faces, were sitting at the tables, eating and drinking.

'Now what's all this, gentlemen?' said the staff officer, in the reproachful tone of a man who has said the same thing over and over again. 'You can't keep leaving your posts like this. The prince gave orders that nobody should be in here. What about you, Captain?' he said to a grimy, thin little artillery officer standing there in his stockings having handed his boots to the stallholder to dry them. He stood up when they came in, with a rather forced smile on his face.

'What about you, Captain Tushin? Shame on you,' the staff officer persisted. 'I'd have expected you as an artillery officer to set an example, and here you are in bare feet. If the alarm goes you'll look fine with no boots on.' (The staff officer smiled.) 'Back to your stations, gentlemen, if you don't mind,' he added in a tone of authority.

Prince Andrey couldn't help smiling as he glanced at Captain Tushin. Saying not a word, Tushin was smiling at them, hopping from one bare foot to the other and looking inquiringly with his big, shrewd, kindly eyes from Prince Andrey to the staff officer and back.

'The men say it's easier in your bare feet,' said Captain Tushin, with a shy smile, keen to cover his embarrassment with a joke or two. But before the words were out of his mouth he could see that this one was going wrong; they didn't like it. He was even more embarrassed.

'Please go back to your post,' said the staff officer, struggling to maintain due gravity.

Prince Andrey glanced again at the little figure of the artillery officer. There was something odd about him, something unmilitary, rather comic but very engaging.

The staff officer and Prince Andrey mounted their horses and rode on.

Riding out beyond the village, continually meeting or overtaking soldiers and officers of various divisions, they saw that on their left trenches were being dug, piling up mounds of fresh red clay. Several battalions of soldiers, in shirtsleeves despite the cold wind, were swarming like white ants all over the trench works; spadefuls of red clay came soaring out on to the mounds thrown up by hands unseen. They went over to inspect the work and then rode on further. Just beyond the entrenchment they came across dozens of soldiers continually running over to the latrine, changing places and running off again, and they had to hold their noses and get their horses to trot away from the noxious atmosphere.

'Here we have it – the nice side of camp life,' said the staff officer.

They rode up the hill opposite, from where they could get a good view of the French. Prince Andrey stopped and looked.

'That's our battery up yonder,' said the staff-officer, showing him the highest point, 'commanded by that funny fellow sitting there with no boots on. From there you can see everything. Shall we go up, Prince?'

'I'm most grateful to you, but I can manage now,' said Prince Andrey, anxious to be rid of the staff officer. 'Please don't worry about me.'

The staff officer rode off, and Prince Andrey went on alone.

The further forward and the closer to the enemy he went, the more orderly and cheerful he found the troops. The worst of the disorder and despondency had been seen in the transport column just outside Znaim which Prince Andrey had passed that morning, six or seven miles away from the French. He had also felt some degree of alarm and a vague sense of apprehension at Grunth. But the nearer Prince Andrey got to the actual French lines, the more confident our troops appeared to be. The soldiers stood in orderly ranks wearing their greatcoats while their sergeant-major and the captain were numbering off, poking the last soldier in each section in the chest and telling him to raise his hand. Soldiers were scattered about everywhere, bringing logs and brushwood, knocking up little shacks, chatting together and laughing in high spirits. They sat round the campfires, some dressed and some stripped, drying off their shirts and leg-bands or seeing to their boots and coats. Many of them thronged around the cauldrons and porridge pots. In one company the meal was ready and the soldiers gazed at the steaming pots with ravenous faces, waiting for the quarter-master sergeant to take a bowlful over to an officer sitting on a log outside his shack so that he could sample it.

In another company, luckier than most – they didn't all get vodka – the soldiers crowded around their thick-set, pockmarked sergeant while he tilted a keg of vodka and poured it into the canteen lids offered up in turn. With a heavenly look on their faces the soldiers lifted the lids to their mouths, tossed them back, licked their lips and then, wiping their mouths on their coat sleeves, strolled off looking nice and merry. Every face was calm; it was as if all this were happening not in sight of the enemy and just before a battle in which at least half of them would be left behind on the field, but somewhere back home in Russia, with the prospect of a nice quiet halt for the night. Prince Andrey rode past a chasseur regiment and on to the ranks of the Kiev Grenadiers, splendid men, all engaged in the same peaceful activities. Not far from the colonel's rather superior little hut he came upon a platoon of grenadiers, with a man stripped naked lying on the ground in front of them. Two soldiers held him down while two others were swinging supple birches, lashing them down rhythmically across the man's bare back. The man screamed like nothing on earth. A stout major was walking up and down in front of the platoon, ignoring the screams and saying to the men, 'It's a disgrace for a soldier to steal. A soldier must be honest, honourable and brave. Anyone who steals from a brother must be without honour. He's a swine! Keep it going!'

The measured lashing continued; so did the desperate screaming, though some of it may have been for effect.

'Keep it going!' said the major over and again.

A young officer walked away from the flogging, his face a picture of bewilderment and sorrow, looking quizzically at the adjutant.

Prince Andrey rode out to the front and then along the line. On both flanks the two lines, ours and the enemy's, were quite a long way away from each other, but in the centre, where the emissaries had come over that morning, the lines came so close together that the soldiers of the two armies could see each other's faces and talk to each other. Besides the picket line itself, many onlookers had gathered on both sides, enjoying a good laugh as they scrutinized the enemy, who looked to them like weird and alien beings.

Since early morning, although the line was officially out of bounds, the commanding officers had not been able to keep the curious onlookers away. The soldiers who made up the line were now carrying on like showmen with some novelty to offer. They had stopped looking at the French and were wholly absorbed by the men who had come up to have a look – anything to distract them from boredom as they waited to be relieved. Prince Andrey stopped and took his measure of the French.

'Hey, mate, look at them two,' said one soldier to his pal, pointing to a Russian musketeer who had gone up to the very front with an officer and was repeatedly bellowing something across to a French grenadier. ''E can go on a bit, can't 'e? Old froggy can't get a word in. 'Ow about that, Sidorov?'

''Ang on, let's listen. Dead right, 'e knows 'is stuff,' replied Sidorov, who fancied himself as a bit of a French expert.

The soldier they were pointing to and laughing at was Dolokhov. Prince Andrey recognized him and listened to what he was saying. Dolokhov had come over with his captain from the left flank, where his regiment was stationed.

'Go on, ask him again!' the captain urged, straining forward in an attempt to catch every word, even though he didn't understand them. 'Please keep it going. What's he trying to say?'

Dolokhov didn't answer the captain, having been drawn into a fierce argument with the French grenadier. They were talking, inevitably, about the campaign. The Frenchman had got the Austrians and the Russians mixed up, and he was claiming that the Russians had surrendered and had been on the run all the way from Ulm. Dolokhov was telling him that the Russians had never surrendered – no, they had beaten the French.

'Our orders are to drive you out of here, and that's what we're going to do,' said Dolokhov.

'Make sure you don't get captured, you and your Cossacks,' said the French grenadier to a roar of laughter from everyone watching and listening on the French side.

'Remember Suvorov? He made you dance and we'll have you dancing again!' said Dolokhov.

'What's he on about?' asked a Frenchman.

'Ancient history,' said another, guessing that it had something to do with previous wars. 'Our Emperor will give you a dose of Suvara, same as he did with all the others . . .'

'Bonaparte . . .' Dolokhov began, only to be interrupted by the Frenchman.

'Don't you say Bonaparte. He is the Emperor! His name is sacred!' came the angry shout.

'Damn and sod your Emperor!' And Dolokhov cursed like a soldier in his vilest Russian, before shouldering his gun and walking away.

'Come on, Ivan Lukich,' he said to his captain, 'let's go.'

'Bit of good froggy French there,' said the soldiers down the line. 'Come on, Sidorov, your turn!' Sidorov winked at them, turned to face the French and began to gabble strange words as fast as he could. 'Kari mala tafa safi muter kaska!' he rattled out, trying to embellish his message with the most expressive intonation he could manage.

The Russian soldiers burst into a great roar of happy, hearty laughter, and the French line took it up so spontaneously that you would have thought the only thing to do now was to unload the guns, blow up the ammunition and get back home as soon as possible. But the muskets remained loaded, the marksmen's slits in buildings and earthworks stared out as ominously as ever, and the big guns still stood ready, ranged against each other.

CHAPTER 16

After doubling around the whole front line from right flank to left, Prince Andrey rode uphill to the battery which the staff officer had described as offering a good view of the whole field. Here he dismounted and stood by the farthest cannon in a line of four, prepared for firing. An artilleryman on sentry duty in front of the big guns looked ready to come to attention at the approach of an officer, but at a signal he resumed the steady, tedious pace of his patrol. Behind the cannon stood the front sections of their carriages, and behind them were the tethered horses and campfires of the artillerymen. To the left, not far from the farthest cannon, the sounds of officers' voices in lively conversation emerged from a little, new wattle hut.

And indeed, the battery gave a splendid view of almost the whole spread of the Russian forces, and most of the enemy's too. Straight across from the battery, on the crest of the opposite hill he could see the village of Schöngrabern, to the left and right of which there were three places where masses of French troops could be seen through the campfire smoke, though it was clear that most of them had been kept back in the village itself and over the hill. To the left of the village something resembling a battery lurked in the smoke, indistinct to the naked eye. Our right flank was deployed on a rather steep hillside dominating the French position. Our infantry had been placed there too, and the dragoons were visible behind them on the very top of the ridge. In the centre stood Tushin's battery, from which Prince Andrey was now surveying the landscape; here the ground below fell away very steeply before rising towards the stream that separated us from Schöngrabern. On the left our troops stuck close to the woods, and smoke rose up from campfires where our infantry had been detailed to cut wood. The French line was wider than ours, and it would obviously be an easy task for the French to outflank us on both sides. To our rear there was a precipitous ravine, down which retreat with artillery and cavalry would be difficult.

Prince Andrey leant one elbow on the cannon, took out a note-book and sketched a plan of the disposition of the troops. In two places he jotted down some pencilled notes, meaning to bring them up with Bagration. His first proposal would be to concentrate all the artillery in the centre, and the second would involve pulling the cavalry back and sending them to the other side of the ravine. Prince Andrey was used to standing near the commander-in-chief, watching the movements of masses of men and large-scale manoeuvres, and he had long been a student of military history, so now it was inevitable that he would take a generalized view of the impending operations. He always imagined things on a grand scale. 'If the enemy attacks us on the right flank,' he told himself, for example, 'the Kiev Grenadiers and Podolsky Chasseurs will have to hold their positions until reserves from the centre reach them. In this event the dragoons could counter-attack and drive them back. In case of an attack on the centre, though, we should deploy the central battery on this height, and use its cover to withdraw the left flank and effect a staged retreat as far as the ravine.' This was his way of thinking . . .

As he stood there in the battery next to the cannon, he was aware of officers' voices emanating from the hut, but, as often happens, he wasn't taking in a word of what they were saying. Then suddenly he heard someone speak with such feeling that he couldn't help listening.

'No, my dear fellow,' said a pleasant voice that struck him as vaguely familiar, 'I'm telling you – if we could know what's going to happen after we're dead not one of us would be scared of dying. There you have it, old man.'

A younger voice interrupted him to say, 'Anyway, scared or not, it comes to us all.'

'But you're still scared! You lot with your education,' said a different, mature voice, cutting across the first two. 'You gunners think you know it all, because you can take everything with you. Never short of a drop to drink or a bite to eat.'

This brought a laugh from the owner of the mature voice, apparently an infantry officer.

'But we're still scared,' insisted the first voice, the one that Prince Andrey half-recognized. 'We're scared of the unknown, that's what it's all about. It's all right saying the soul goes up to heaven . . . we know for certain there isn't any heaven – there's only the atmosphere up there.'

Once again the mature voice interrupted. 'Come on, Tushin, give us a drop of your home-made vodka.'

'Oh, it's that captain in the canteen with no boots on,' thought Prince Andrey, delighted to recognize that pleasant voice now so full of philosophy.

'Yes, have a swig,' said Tushin, 'but listen, the idea of a life to come . . .'

He never finished his sentence. At that moment a great whoosh came through the air. Nearer, nearer, faster and louder, louder and faster, and a cannonball – also not quite saying everything it wanted to say – thudded into the ground not far away, blasting the earth with superhuman force. The earth seemed to groan at receiving such a terrible blow. Immediately the diminutive Tushin dashed out of the hut before anyone else, with his short pipe stuck in the corner in his mouth and his kind, bright face looking rather pale. Then came the owner of the mature voice, a dashing infantry officer, who rushed off to get back to his company, buttoning up his jacket as he ran.

CHAPTER 17

Prince Andrey mounted his horse but stayed at the battery for a while, staring at the smoke rising from the cannon that had fired the ball. His eyes swept the wide open spaces. What registered with him was that the previously solid masses of the French were beginning to move, and there really was a battery on the left-hand side, the smoke above it having not yet cleared. Two French horsemen, probably adjutants, were galloping across the hill. A small column of enemy troops was clearly visible, moving downhill, probably to strengthen the line. Before the smoke of the first shot had cleared there came another puff of smoke and another report. The battle was beginning. Prince Andrey turned his horse and galloped back to Grunth to find Prince Bagration. Behind him he could hear the bombardment getting louder and more frequent – a sign that our guns were beginning to respond. Musket-fire rang out down below at the spot where the lines were closest.

Lemarrois had only just delivered Napoleon's ominous letter, and the humiliated Murat, desperate to make up for his mistake, rapidly moved his forces for an attack from the centre and a double flanking manoeuvre, hoping to destroy the puny detachment facing him before evening and before the arrival of the Emperor.

'It's started! This is it!' thought Prince Andrey, feeling the blood surging around his heart. 'But where do I look? How do I find my Toulon?' he wondered.

Riding through companies that only a quarter of an hour earlier had been eating porridge and drinking vodka, he could see the same rapid movement everywhere as soldiers fell in and got their muskets ready, and on every face he could see the same excitement that he felt in his heart. 'It's here! This is it! God, I'm scared, but it's marvellous!' said every face of officer and man. Before he got back to the unfinished earthworks, through the late afternoon gloom of a dull autumn day he saw several men riding towards him. The first of them, wearing a cloak and an astrakhan cap, and riding a white horse, was Prince

Bagration. Prince Andrey stopped and waited for him to come on. Prince Bagration reined in his horse, recognized Prince Andrey and nodded to him. He continued to gaze ahead while Prince Andrey told him what he had seen.

A touch of *It's here! This is it!* was noticeable even on Prince Bagration's strong brown face, with his half-closed, dull-looking eyes that betrayed a lack of sleep. With excited curiosity Prince Andrey kept glancing at that impassive face, wondering whether this man was thinking and feeling anything at this moment, and then *what* he was thinking and feeling. 'Is there anything there behind that straight face?' Prince Andrey asked himself as he watched him. Prince Bagration nodded to acknowledge Andrey's words, and said, 'Carry on,' in a tone which implied that all these events, everything reported to him, were going to plan. Prince Andrey was out of breath from his hard riding, and he spoke rapidly. Prince Bagration had an oriental accent and now pronounced his words with great deliberation, as if to impress upon him that there was no need to hurry. He did, however, spur his horse to a trot before riding towards Tushin's battery. Prince Andrey went after him as part of the entourage. The party consisted of an officer of the suite, Bagration's personal aide, Zherkov, an orderly officer, the duty staff officer on a handsome bobtailed horse and a civil servant, an auditor, who had asked permission to watch the action. The auditor, a podgy man with a podgy face, looked around with a naive smile of amusement, flopping about on his horse, a preposterous figure among the hussars, Cossacks and adjutants with his camel-hair coat and borrowed saddle.

'He wants to see some action,' said Zherkov to Bolkonsky, with a nod towards the auditor, 'but his tummy's playing up already.'

'That's enough of that,' beamed the auditor, with a simple but knowing smile, as if he felt quite flattered to be ridiculed by Zherkov, and wanted to make himself seem stupider than he really was.

'Most amusing, my Mr Prince,' said the duty staff officer, who knew there was a special way of using the Russian title *knyaz* (prince) in French, but kept getting it wrong. By this time they had all ridden up close to Tushin's battery, and a cannonball hit the ground not far ahead of them.

'What was that?' asked the auditor with his naive smile.

'A French pancake,' said Zherkov.

'So that's what they fight with,' observed the auditor. 'That's awful!' But he seemed nevertheless to swell up with pleasure. Hardly were these words out of his mouth when suddenly there came another terrible whoosh ending in a thudding splash into something soft, and with a great squelch a Cossack riding just behind him to the right toppled to the ground from his horse. Zherkov and the staff officer bent over their saddles and turned their horses away. The auditor stopped a short distance from the Cossack and gave him close scrutiny. He was dead, but his horse still struggled.

Prince Bagration looked round squinting, noted what the delay was and casually turned back as if to say, 'I can't be bothered with silly details.' He reined in with the skill of an expert horseman, leant slightly to one side and freed his sword which had snagged in his cloak. It was an old-fashioned sword, no longer worn by anyone. Prince Andrey recalled the story that Suvorov had given his sword to Bagration in Italy, and the memory of it gave him a particular thrill at that moment. By now they had reached the battery from which Prince Andrey had surveyed the battlefield.

'Who's in charge here?' Prince Bagration asked an NCO gunner standing beside the ammunition boxes.

When he asked, 'Who's in charge here?', he seemed to be saying, 'Not gone soft, have you?' and the gunner understood.

'Captain Tushin, sir,' came the breezy response from the red-haired, freckle-faced young man as he came to attention.

'Good, good,' said a deeply preoccupied Bagration and he rode past the gun-carriages towards the end cannon. Just before he got there a shot boomed out from it, deafening him and his suite, and through the smoke that suddenly enveloped the big gun they watched the gunners grab the cannon, strain against it and trundle it back into position. A huge burly soldier, the number one gunner holding the cleaning rod, sprang up to the wheel, his legs widely braced, while number two rammed the charge down the cannon's mouth with a shaking hand. Captain Tushin, short and stooping, tripped over the gun-carriage as he dashed forward, without noticing the general, to stare into the distance, shading his eyes with a tiny hand.

'Two points up. That'll do,' he shouted in a shrill voice, with attempted bravura which didn't quite square with his small figure. 'Fire number two!' he piped. 'Hammer them, Medvedev!'

Bagration called the officer over and Tushin went up to the general, raising three fingers to his cap with a timid and gawky movement, more like a priest blessing someone than a soldier saluting. Tushin's guns had originally been intended to bombard the valley, but he was now lobbing incendiary bombs straight over at Schöngrabern village, where great masses of French soldiers could be seen advancing out and down.

Tushin had not been told what to fire at or what charges to use, so after consulting his sergeant, Zakharchenko, a man he greatly respected, he had decided it would be a good thing to set the village on fire. 'Carry on!' said Bagration when he heard what the officer had to say, and he began scrutinizing the entire battlefield that lay unfolded before him. He seemed to be working things out. The French had advanced furthest on the right side. From the hollow with the stream at the bottom, downhill from the Kiev regiment, came a continuous soul-stirring crackle of musket-fire. Much further away to the right, behind the dragoons, the officer of the suite showed Bagration where we were being outflanked by a French column. To the left the nearby woods rose to the skyline. Prince Bagration gave orders for two battalions from the centre to move to the right to reinforce that flank. The officer of the suite ventured to remark to the prince that the transfer of these battalions would leave the big guns without cover. Prince Bagration turned and stared at him with lacklustre eyes, saying nothing. Prince Andrey thought the officer had a good point, and really nothing could be said against it. But just then an adjutant galloped up with a message from the regimental colonel down in the hollow that the French were coming down on them in huge numbers, and his men were retreating in disorder uphill towards the Kiev Grenadiers. Prince Bagration gave a nod of acknowledgement and approval. He then rode off to the right at walking pace, and dispatched an aide to the dragoons with orders to attack the French. But this man returned half an hour later with the news that the colonel of the dragoons had already retreated beyond the ravine in the face of overwhelming fire to avoid unnecessary further losses, and now had his marksmen dismounted in the wood.

'Carry on!' said Bagration.

Just as he began to ride away from the battery, more shots rang out, this time in the wood on the left. Since it was too far to go himself, Prince Bagration dispatched Zherkov to tell the senior general – the one whose regiment had been inspected by Kutuzov at Braunau – to retreat with all speed beyond the ravine, because the right flank would probably not be able to hold the enemy much longer. Tushin and the battalion that was supposed to cover him were forgotten. Prince Andrey listened carefully to what was said between Prince Bagration and the commanding officers, and to any orders issued, and he was astounded to observe that no orders were really given; Prince Bagration was just trying to pretend that everything they were being forced to do, every accidental development or anything brought about by individual commanders, was happening, if not according to his orders, then at least as part of his plan. Prince Andrey noticed, on the other hand, that even though everything was happening by pure chance and had nothing to do with the commander's volition, the tact shown by Prince Bagration meant that his presence there was of enormous value. Commanding officers who rode up to Bagration looking desperately worried quickly regained their composure; soldiers and officers hailed him with good cheer, they found his presence reinvigorating and he put a swagger and new courage into their steps.

CHAPTER 18

After riding up to the highest point on our right flank, Prince Bagration started off downhill, where a continuous rattle of gunfire rang out and nothing could be seen for the smoke. The further they descended into the hollow the less they could see, but the more sharply they could sense the proximity of actual battle. They began to come across wounded men. Two soldiers were dragging a third along with his arms around their necks. His head was covered with blood; he had lost his cap. He was hawking and spitting blood, a bullet having evidently got him in the mouth or throat. Another man came towards them, walking sturdily on his own with no gun, moaning and groaning, and shaking his wounded arm as pain hit him, while the blood poured down his greatcoat like liquid from a bottle. To judge by his face he seemed more scared than hurt: he had been wounded only a moment before. They crossed the road and started down a steep incline, where they saw several men lying on the sloping ground. Then they were met by a crowd of soldiers, some of them not wounded. These soldiers, gasping for breath as they hurried uphill, took no notice of the general and went on shouting to each other with much waving of their arms. Ahead of them through the smoke they could now see whole ranks of grey coats, and once the commanding officer set eyes on Bagration he ran off after the retreating mass of soldiers, shouting for them to come back. Bagration rode up to the ranks, where noisy sporadic fire drowned all speech including the officers' shouted commands. The air was thick with gunsmoke. The soldiers' faces were all animated and smudged with gunpowder. Ramrods plunged in and out, powder was poured into pans, charges came out of pouches, guns fired. What they were firing at couldn't be seen for the smoke that hung undispersed by the wind. Much of the time the air was full of sweet sounds – the whine and whistle of bullets.

'What's all this?' wondered Prince Andrey, as they rode up to the crowd of soldiers. 'It can't be the front line – they're all bunched up together. It can't be an assault group – nobody's moving. And they're certainly not forming a square.'

A skinny, frail-looking old colonel with a sweet smile and eyelids that drooped down, more than half-covering his weary old eyes, all of which made him look like a gentle sort of person, rode up to meet Prince Bagration and greet him like a host welcoming a favourite guest. He reported that his regiment had been attacked by the French cavalry, and that although the attack had been repulsed, the regiment had lost more than half its men. The colonel said that the attack had been repulsed because that seemed like a suitable military term for what had happened, but he had no real idea of anything that had taken place during that half-hour of skirmishes involving his troops, and couldn't have said with any certainty whether the attack had been repulsed or his regiment had been destroyed by the attack. All he knew was that the action had started with cannonballs and grenades raining down on his regiment and hitting his men, then someone had shouted 'Cavalry!' and our men had opened fire. And they were still at it, firing not now at the cavalry because they had disappeared, but at French infantrymen who had turned up in the hollow and started firing at us. Prince Bagration nodded his head as a sign that this was just what he had wanted and planned for. Turning to an aide, he ordered him to bring down from the hill the two battalions of the Sixth Chasseurs they had ridden past. Prince Andrey was struck at that moment by a change that had come over Prince Bagration's face. It had assumed the concentration and wilful delight of a man who has decided to take a plunge on a hot day and is now on his run-up to a dive. Gone were the lacklustre, dozy eyes and that forced appearance of profound thought. His round, sharp, hawk-like eyes peered ahead with new exhilaration and some disdain without actually seeing anything, though he still moved with the same leisureliness and steady rhythm.

The colonel then urged Prince Bagration to go back since it was too dangerous where they were. 'Sir, I implore you in God's name!' he kept saying, glancing at the officer of the suite for support, but he was looking away.

'See what I mean, your Excellency!' he said, reminding him of the bullets which never stopped whining, singing and hissing all around them. He spoke like a carpenter remonstrating with his master who has just picked up an axe: 'We're hardened to it, sir, but you'll get blisters on your hands.' He talked as if he couldn't be killed by these bullets, and his half-closed eyes gave his words extra conviction. The staff officer added his protests to the colonel's, but Bagration made no reply. All he did was give the order for a ceasefire and re-formation to create space for the two battalions of reinforcements. As he spoke a breeze lifted the pall of smoke covering the hollow like an unseen hand sweeping from right to left, giving them a view of the opposite hillside with all the French soldiers moving across it. Every eye turned instinctively to that French column bearing down on them, weaving in and out and up and down as it came. They could see the soldiers' shaggy caps, the differences between officers and men and their standard flapping on its staff.

'Nice bit of marching,' said someone in Bagration's suite.

The head of the column was well down into the hollow. Any fighting would now take place on this side . . .

The remnants of our regiment that had already been in action fell in as fast as they could and started to move off to the right; meanwhile, behind them the two battalions of the Sixth Chasseurs were marching up in good order, scattering the stragglers. Well before they drew level with Bagration they heard the heavy tramp, tramp, tramp of massed men marching in step. On their left flank, nearest to Bagration, marched the captain, an imposing man with a round face which looked rather silly in its cheerfulness – the infantry officer who had followed Tushin out of the wattle hut. At that moment he was clearly oblivious to everything except the swaggering style of his march past in front of the commanding officer.

With the smugness of an end man on parade, he bounced along on his sinewy legs, effortlessly marching to attention, floating with a lightness of step remarkably different from the heavy tread of the soldiers keeping time with him. Down by his thigh he carried, unsheathed, a thin little sword – it was a small curved sabre, for ceremonial use only – and he looked and turned sideways to the commander and back to the men behind, without straining his big powerful frame or getting out of step. He seemed to strive with every fibre of his soul to march past his commander with maximum style, and his strong sense of doing this well made him a happy man. 'Left . . . left . . . left . . .' he seemed to be mouthing to himself at each alternate step, and that was the rhythm to which the solid wall of military men, weighed down by packs and guns, advanced; each face was different in its stern concentration, and each one of these hundreds of soldiers seemed to mouth his own 'Left . . . left . . . left . . .' at each alternate step. A stout major skipped around a bush on the road, puffing and panting, and losing step. A soldier who had fallen behind trotted along in an effort to catch up with the company, panic at his offence written over his face. And then a cannonball whooshed over the heads of Prince Bagration and his suite – they could feel its pressure through the air – and, exactly in step with the 'Left . . . left . . . left . . .', it crashed into the column.

'Close ranks!' the captain sang out in a chirpy voice well suited to his swaggering step. The soldiers circled around something at the spot where the ball had landed, and an old cavalryman NCO, who had fallen behind near the dead bodies, now caught up with his line, fell into step with the march and strode on, glaring angrily about him. 'Left . . . left . . . left . . .' seemed to echo through the ominous silence and the tedious tramp, tramp, tramp of synchronized feet.

'Well done, men!' said Prince Bagration.

'Thank you, sir . . . sir . . . sir!' echoed down the ranks. One surly-looking soldier marching on the left stared straight at Bagration as he shouted, as if to say, 'We don't need you to tell us!' Another looked rigidly ahead as he marched past, opened his mouth wide and bawled out, as if he daren't risk any lapse of concentration.

Then they were brought to a halt and allowed to take off their packs.

Bagration rode around the ranks of men that had marched past and then dismounted. He gave the reins to a Cossack, took off his cloak and handed that over too, stretched his legs and set his cap straight. And there, suddenly, was the French column, officers in front, coming into sight as they climbed the hill.

'God be with us!' cried Bagration in a clear strong voice. He turned for a moment to the front line, and then marched forward over the rough terrain, swinging his arms a little and lumbering along awkwardly like a man more used to riding. Prince Andrey felt himself drawn forward by an irresistible force, and he had a sensation of supreme happiness.*

The French were getting nearer, and now Prince Andrey, walking beside Bagration, could clearly make out their bandoliers and red epaulettes, even their faces. (He had a clear view of one bandy-legged old French officer wearing gaiters, who had to grab hold of bushes because climbing uphill was so hard for him.) Prince Bagration gave no further orders; he just marched on silently ahead of the ranks. Suddenly the crack of a shot came from the French side, then another,

---

* [Author's note] This was the attack of which Thiers says: 'The Russians behaved valiantly and – a rarity in warfare – two bodies of infantry were observed marching resolutely against each other without either of them giving way until they clashed.' And Napoleon on St Helena said, 'Some Russian battalions showed no fear.'

and a third ... smoke rose and gunfire rang out down the ragged ranks of the enemy. Some of our men fell, one of them the round-faced officer who had been putting so much effort and pleasure into his marching. But when the very first shot rang out, Bagration had looked round and roared, 'Hurrah!' A great sustained 'Hurra ... a ... a ... ah!' went echoing down our lines, and our men raced past Prince Bagration and overtook one another, hurtling chaotically downhill in one inspired and jubilant mob to get at the scattering Frenchmen.

CHAPTER 19

The attack of the Sixth Chasseurs secured the retreat of our right flank. In the centre Tushin's forgotten battery had succeeded in setting fire to Schöngrabern and was thus delaying the advance of the French. They were so busy putting out fires fanned by the breeze that the Russians had plenty of time to retreat. The retreat of the centre across the ravine was carried out at speed amid the din although the different units managed to keep themselves apart. But the Azovsky and Podolsky infantry and the Pavlograd hussars on the left were simultaneously attacked and outflanked by the pick of the French troops under Lannes and torn apart. Bagration dispatched Zherkov to the general in command there with orders for an immediate retreat.

Zherkov responded smartly; still saluting, he spurred his horse and galloped off. But the moment he was out of Bagration's sight his courage failed him. He panicked uncontrollably and could not bring himself to ride into the danger area. Approaching the left-flank troops, instead of riding straight ahead into the gunfire, he veered off to look for the general and his officers in places where they couldn't possibly be. So the order was not passed on.

The left flank was commanded by the senior general of Dolokhov's regiment, the one that Kutuzov had inspected before Braunau. But the extreme left flank was commanded by the colonel of the Pavlograd hussars, Nikolay Rostov's regiment. The two commanders were at cross purposes. There was a feud between them, and while battle was raging on the right flank and the French had already begun to advance, these two officers were still in discussions devoted to mutual abuse. The two regiments, cavalry and infantry, were anything but ready for the action to come. Not a man among them, soldier or general, was expecting a battle. All were going about their peaceful occupations; cavalrymen feeding horses and footsoldiers cutting wood.

'Yes, I know he outrankink me,' said the German colonel of the hussars, growing very red and addressing an adjutant who had just ridden over. 'So let him to do how he likes. Mine hussars I *not* zacrifice. Bugler! Sound ze retreat!'

But things were getting urgent. On the right and in the centre cannon and musket now thundered in concert, and the French greatcoats of Lannes's sharpshooters had crossed the dam by the millpond and were re-forming on this side a couple of musket shots away.

The infantry general walked over to his horse, quivering as always, mounted, sat up very straight and tall, and rode off to see the Pavlograd colonel. The two commanders met with polite bows and secret venom in their hearts.

'Now look here, Colonel,' said the general, 'I cannot leave half my men in the wood. I *beg* you. I *beg* you,' he repeated. '*Get into position*, and prepare to attack.'

'And I am peggink you not meddlink in ozzer pipple's business,' answered the colonel, roused to fury. 'If you voz cavalry officer . . .'

'I am not a cavalry officer, Colonel, but I am a Russian general, and if you are unaware . . .'

'Avare of zis I am. *Sir*.' Suddenly the colonel, purple with rage, put spurs to his horse and yelled at the general, 'Kindly pliss to come to ze front viz me, you vill see zis position no goot! I vill not testroy my regiment chest to pliss you.'

'You forget yourself, Colonel. I am not thinking of my own pleasure, and I cannot allow such a thing to be said.'

The general saw the colonel's proposition as a challenge to his courage, so he squared his chest and rode off with him, scowling, towards the front line, as if the whole argument between them would be settled once and for all when they were there under fire. When they arrived at the front several bullets flew by, and they just halted in silence. There was nothing new to be seen – it was obvious from where they had been standing before that the cavalry couldn't operate here because of bushes and gullies, and also that the French were out-flanking them to the left. The general and the colonel glared at each other with sour determination on both sides, like two cocks strutting around ready for a fight, vainly searching for the slightest sign of cowardice. Both passed the test. There was nothing more to be said, and neither was willing to give the other any grounds for claiming that he had been the first to withdraw from under fire, and they might have stayed there for ever locked in this trial of strength, but for a burst of musket-fire and several voices shouting just behind them in the wood. The French had attacked some of our soldiers collecting wood in the copse. No one could retreat now, neither the hussars nor the infantry. They were cut off from retreat on the left by the French line. Now, never mind the rough terrain, they were going to have to fight their way through.

The hussars of Nikolay Rostov's squadron had scarcely had time to mount their horses when suddenly there they were, confronting the enemy. Once again, as on the Enns bridge, there was no one between the squadron and the enemy, but there was that dreadful dividing line of uncertainty and fear, so similar to the line between the living and the dead. All of them sensed this, and one question worried them all: would they cross it or not, and if yes, *how* they would cross it?

The colonel rode up to the front, gave some testy answers to questions posed by the officers and, like a man desperate to have his own way, rapped out an order. There had been no definite word, but a rumour had swept the squadron that they were going to attack. Now the order to fall in was followed by the slash of sabres coming out of scabbards. Still no one moved. The left-flank infantry and hussars sensed that their commanders had no idea what to do, and their uncertainty was soon transmitted to the soldiers.

'Come on, come on!' thought Rostov, feeling that at long last the moment had come to enjoy the thrill of a charge, which his regimental comrades had so often told him about.

'God be with you, men,' rang out Denisov's voice. 'Fow-ward! Quick-twot!'

In the front line the horses stirred their haunches. Little Rook pulled on the reins and set off on his own.

To his right Rostov could see the leading ranks of his own hussars. Up ahead he could make out a dark strip, not very clear but presumably the enemy. Shots could be heard, but they were some way off.

'Faster now!' came the word of command, and Rostov felt Little Rook's hindquarters dip as he surged into a gallop. Rostov knew the horse's every movement in advance, and he was getting more and more excited. He noticed a solitary tree just ahead. That tree had once been in front of him, right in the middle of the dividing line that had seemed so terrible. But now they had crossed that line and nothing terrible had happened – except that he felt even more elated and excited. 'God how I'll slash him!' thought Rostov, squeezing down on his sabre-hilt.

All voices roared a huge *hurrah!*

'Let 'em all come!' he thought, spurring Little Rook to go even faster, sweeping past the others and moving into a full gallop. Now the enemy could be seen ahead. And then suddenly something happened: it came like a great lash across the whole squadron as if it had been slapped by a big broom. Rostov had his sabre raised, ready to slash with it, but at that moment Nikitenko, who had just galloped past, suddenly disappeared and Rostov felt himself flying through the air at an amazing speed and yet at the same time not moving. Was he dreaming? One of his comrades, Bandarchuk, almost crashed into him and flashed him a furious glare. Bandarchuk's horse veered away and galloped on.

'What's happened? Why can't I move? I'm down. I'm dead.' For a moment Rostov questioned and answered himself. There he was on his own in the middle of a field. Instead of the galloping horses and the hussars' backs, all he could see around him was the earth and stubble, and no movement of any kind. There was warm blood under him.

'No, I'm only wounded. It's my horse that's dead.' Little Rook struggled to get up on to his forelegs, but sank back, pinning his rider's leg. Blood was flowing from the horse's head. He was thrashing about; he couldn't get up. Rostov tried to get up too, and fell back down. His sabretache had snagged in the saddle. Where were our men? Where were the French? He had no idea. There was no one in sight.

He managed to free his leg and stood up. 'Which way now? Where's that dividing line that separated us off so neatly?' he wondered, but this time there was no answer. 'Something's gone terribly wrong. Do things like this really happen? What do you do?' he kept wondering as he got to his feet. Then he suddenly felt there was something dangling on his numb left arm that shouldn't be there. The wrist seemed not to belong to his arm. He stared down at his hand, looking for blood. 'Oh, look, someone's coming,' he thought with great delight, seeing some men running towards him. 'They'll help me!' The first wore a strange shako and a blue coat; he had a swarthy sunburnt face and a hooked nose. He was followed by two others, and there were a lot more just behind him. One of them said something funny, not in Russian. Rostov could see a Russian hussar standing among the same sort of men wearing the same sort of hat. They were pinning him by the arms and holding his horse too, a bit further back.

'It's one of our boys. He's been taken prisoner . . . Yes, he has . . . Are they going to take me? Who are these people?' Rostov was still wondering – he could hardly believe his eyes. 'Is it the French?' He looked at the Frenchmen running towards him, and although only a few seconds before he had been galloping along, dying to get at them and hack them to pieces, now that they were so near everything seemed so ghastly that again he couldn't believe his eyes. 'Who are they? Why are they running? They're not after me! They can't be after me! Why? They can't want to kill me! *Me*. Everybody loves me!' He remembered all the love he had had from his mother, from his family and his friends, and the idea of the enemy wanting to kill him seemed absurd. 'But they might want to!' He had been standing there rigid for more than ten seconds, not taking anything in. The hook-nosed Frenchman was getting near, so near you could see the look on his face. And the sight of this rampaging foreigner's face as he sprinted breathlessly towards him with fixed bayonet suddenly terrified Rostov. He grabbed his pistol, and instead of firing he hurled it at the Frenchman and dashed towards the bushes as fast as his legs would carry him. Gone were the feelings of doubt and conflict that had pursued him across the bridge at Enns – he was running now like a hare chased by dogs. His whole being was reduced to a single sensation – he was terrified and running for his young and happy life. He scorched the ground, flew across fields and soared over hedges like the lively child he had once been, chasing his friends, once or twice turning his kind, pale, youthful face to look back, only to feel a chill of horror run down his spine. 'No, don't look back,' he thought, but when he got to the bushes he did glance round once more. The Frenchmen had given up, and even as he looked round the first man was just slowing down from a gentle trot to a walk, and turning round to yell back to one of his pals. Rostov stopped.

'It can't be right,' he thought. 'They can't have been going to kill me.' Meanwhile his left arm felt heavy, as if a great weight had been hung on it. He could run no further. The Frenchman stopped too and aimed at him. Rostov squeezed his eyes shut and ducked. One bullet sang past his head, then another. He gathered what strength he had left, took his left hand in his right and ran into the bushes. There in the bushes were the Russian marksmen.

CHAPTER 20

The infantry regiments that had been caught napping in the wood were now rushing out with companies mixing together, and all of them retreating in a shambles. It only took one panicky soldier to call out, 'We're cut off!', meaningless words perhaps but terrifying on any battlefield, for them to affect the entire mass of men.

'Surrounded! Cut off! We've had it!' they shouted as they ran.

The moment their general heard musket-fire and shouting from the rear he realized something terrible had happened to his regiment, and the thought that he, an exemplary officer with a long and blameless service career, might now be accused by his superiors of negligence or dereliction of duty struck him so forcibly that he suddenly became oblivious of everything else – the insubordinate cavalry colonel, his own important role as a general and, what mattered most, any sense of danger or thought of self-preservation. Clutching the pommel of his saddle and spurring his horse, he galloped off to the regiment under a hail of bullets that sprayed everywhere but luckily didn't hit him. His sole purpose was to find out what was wrong and put it right if it had been his fault, anything to avoid being censured, now, after twenty-two years of exemplary, unblemished service.

He galloped unscathed through the French forces and emerged from the wood into a field where our men were ignoring orders and running away downhill. This was now one of those decisive moral points which turn a battle. Would this rabble of soldiers respond to their commander's voice, or would they just look at him and keep running? Despite all the desperate shouts from a commander who had once put the fear of God into every last soldier, despite his infuriated, purple face, contorted beyond all recognition, even despite the wild brandishing of his sabre, the soldiers kept running, yelling at each other, firing in the air and ignoring every word of command. That moral turning point on which a battle hinges was unmistakably the way of panic.

Coughing from the shouting and the smoke, the general stopped in despair. All seemed lost, when suddenly the French, who had been advancing on our men, ran back for no apparent reason, and disappeared from the outskirts of the wood. There among the trees were the Russian marksmen. It was Timokhin's company, the only one to have maintained order and discipline in the wood, which had hidden in a gully, ambushed the French and now mounted a swift attack. Timokhin rushed at the French with such a furious yell, assailing them with such wild and drunken zeal with nothing but a sword in his hand, that the French were taken by surprise – they dropped their guns and fled. Dolokhov, running beside Timokhin, killed one French soldier at close quarters, and was the first to grab the collar of an officer who wanted to give himself up. Our men who had been running away returned, the battalions re-formed and the French, who had been on the point of splitting the left-flank forces, were for the moment driven back. Our reserves had time to join the main forces, and everyone stopped running away. The general had halted alongside Major Ekonomov and was seeing the retreating companies over a bridge when a soldier ran up to him, grabbed hold of his stirrup and almost clung to him. He was wearing a bluish coat of fine cloth, he had no pack or shako, his head was bandaged and a French ammunition pouch was slung across his shoulders. He was clutching an officer's sword in both hands. The soldier had a very pale face, and his blue eyes looked defiantly into the general's face; there was a smile on his mouth. The general was busy giving instructions to Major Ekonomov, but he could hardly ignore this man.

'Sir, I have two trophies for you,' said Dolokhov, pointing to the French sword and ammunition pouch. 'I took an officer prisoner. I stopped a company.' Dolokhov was gasping from exhaustion and he spoke haltingly. 'The whole company is my witness. Please remember this, sir!'

'Very good, very good,' said the general, and he turned away to Major Ekonomov. But Dolokhov wouldn't go; he undid his bandage, yanked it off and showed congealed blood on his head.

'A bayonet wound. I stayed there at the front. Please remember this, your Excellency.'

Tushin's battery had been forgotten, and it was only at the very end of the action that Prince Bagration, hearing the bombardment still coming from the centre, sent the duty staff officer and then Prince Andrey to order the battery to retreat with all speed. Any support for Tushin's cannons had been ordered away in mid-battle, but the battery had kept on firing and was not taken by the French simply because the enemy didn't believe that four guns could have the effrontery to go on firing without any protection. Quite the reverse, from the sustained action of this battery the French came to believe that the main Russian forces were concentrated here in the centre, and mounted two attacks on that point; both times they were driven back by grapeshot from the four cannons standing in solitude at the top of the hill.

It was not long after Prince Bagration's departure that Tushin had succeeded in setting fire to Schöngrabern.

'That's got 'em moving! It's on fire! Look at the smoke! Good shot! Well done! Look at the smoke! Look at the smoke!' cried the gunners, taking heart.

In the absence of any instructions the four guns had been pointed towards the conflagration. The soldiers seemed to be urging the cannonballs on their way; every shot was hailed with a roar: 'Good shot! There she goes! Look at that! . . . Nice one!' Fanned by the wind, the fire was spreading quickly. French columns that had marched out of the village came straight back, but evidently in revenge for this nasty turn of events, the enemy positioned ten guns outside the village to the right, and began firing back at Tushin.

In their childlike glee at setting fire to the village, and the excitement of their lucky firing on the French, our gunners failed to spot this battery until two cannonballs and then four more fell among their guns, one killing two horses and another blowing a wagon driver's leg off. Their blood was up, though, and their energies, far from flagging, simply found another outlet. The horses were replaced by others from a stand-by gun-carriage; the wounded were carried away and their four guns were ranged against a ten-strong enemy battery. One of Tushin's fellow officers had been killed at the outset, and after an hour's firing seventeen of the battery's forty gunners were out of action, but the rest were as bright and eager as ever. Twice they had seen the French encroach on them from below; twice they had sprayed them with grapeshot.

The diminutive Tushin with his clumsy little gestures kept asking his orderly to 'refill my pipe for this one', as he put it, and he was forever running about scattering sparks all over and peering across at the French from under his tiny little hand.

'Come on, men, let 'em 'ave it!' he never stopped saying, and he was not averse to heaving at the cannon wheels and working the screws himself. In all the smoke, deafened by the incessant banging of the cannons that made him jump at every shot, Tushin ran from one cannon to the next, his stubby pipe never out of his mouth, taking aim, checking the charges, arranging for killed and wounded horses to be unharnessed and replaced, and shouting to everyone in his unimpressive shrill little voice. His face became more and more animated, although when someone got killed or wounded he would frown, turn away from him and shout angrily at the men who were always dilatory in picking up a wounded soldier or a dead body. Every one of the soldiers, for the most part handsome, strapping boys, head and shoulders taller than their officer and twice as broad in the chest (inevitable in the artillery), looked at their commanding officer as do children in trouble, and whatever expression they found on his face was invariably reflected on their own.

With all the fearful clamour and banging, and the need to concentrate and keep busy, Tushin never felt the slightest nasty touch of fear, and the idea that he might be killed or badly wounded never entered his head. Quite the reverse, he felt more and more buoyant. The moment he had first seen the enemy and fired his first shot now seemed a long, long time ago – yesterday maybe – and that little plot of earth where he now stood was a familiar place and he felt at home in it. He missed nothing, thought of every last detail and did everything as well as the finest officer could have done in his situation, but nevertheless he was always in a state of mind not far from feverish delirium or the abandonment of a drunk.

The devastating sound of his own guns around him, the whoosh and bang of enemy shells, the sight of his gunners, red-faced and sweating as they rushed around the cannons, the sight of blood from men and horses, and the puffs of smoke from the enemy across the hillside, inevitably followed by a cannonball soaring across and hitting the earth, a man, a horse or a gun – all of this created for him a fantastic world of his own, which for the moment gave him immense pleasure. He imagined the enemy guns not as guns but pipes from which an invisible smoker blew puffs of smoke every so often.

'There he goes, puffing away again,' Tushin would murmur to himself as another smoke cloud rose from the hillside to be wafted away by the wind to the left in a single streak. 'Here comes the ball – we've got to hit it back.'

'What was that, sir?' asked a gunner standing near by who had heard him muttering.

'Never mind, it's just a grenade . . .' came the answer. 'Right, Matthew's girl,' he would sometimes say to himself. 'Matthew's girl' was the name his fancy gave to the huge cannon, an old-fashioned casting, that stood at one end. The French swarming around their big guns he saw as ants. Also in his dream-world that handsome soldier who liked a drink or two, his number one gunner on the second cannon, was known as 'Uncle'; Tushin looked at him more than anyone else and revelled in his every movement. The sound of musket-fire at the bottom of the hill dying away and building up again seemed to him like somebody breathing. He listened for the rise and fall of these sounds.

'There she goes, another breath,' he would say to himself. He imagined himself as a great Herculean figure lobbing cannonballs at the French with both hands.

'Come on, Matthew's girl. Come on, old lady, don't let us down!' he was saying, moving away from the cannon, when a strange unknown voice called over his head, 'Captain Tushin! Captain!'

Tushin whipped round in some panic. There stood the same staff officer who had sent him out of the tent at Grunth. Getting his breath back, he shouted to him, 'What's all this? You must be mad. Twice ordered to retreat, and here you are . . .'

'Why are they getting at me?' Tushin wondered, looking in alarm at his superior officer.

'I . . . er . . . can't . . .' he began, raising two fingers to his cap. 'I . . .'

But the staff officer didn't get any more out. A cannonball zoomed over near by and made him duck down on his horse. He paused, and just as he was about to say something else, another cannonball stopped him. He turned his horse and galloped away.

'Retreat, everybody! Retreat!' he shouted from a long way off.

The soldiers laughed at him. Then, a minute later an adjutant arrived with the same order. It was Prince Andrey. The first thing he saw when he got to where Tushin's cannons were stationed was an unharnessed horse with a broken leg, neighing piteously beside the harnessed horses. Blood gushed from its leg like water down a brook. Among the gun carriers lay several dead men. One cannonball after another flew past him as he rode up, and he felt a nervous shudder run down his back. But the very idea that he was afraid was enough to rouse him again. 'I cannot be frightened,' he thought, and he took his time dismounting between the guns. When he had transmitted the order he did not leave the battery. He decided to stay on and watch the guns dismounted and taken away. Stepping over corpses and under terrible fire from the French, he helped Tushin move his big guns.

'One of them staff officers came up just now. Didn't stay long,' said one of the gunners to Prince Andrey. 'Not like you, sir.'

Prince Andrey and Tushin didn't talk. They were both so busy that they hardly seemed to be aware of each other. When they had got the two surviving guns on to their carriages and were moving off downhill (a smashed cannon and a howitzer were left behind), Prince Andrey went up to Tushin.

'Well, goodbye for now,' said Prince Andrey, holding out his hand to Tushin.

'Goodbye, my dear fellow,' said Tushin, 'You're a good soul! Goodbye, my dear fellow,' he said through tears which had filled his eyes for no apparent reason.

CHAPTER 21

The wind had dropped and black clouds loured above the battlefield, melting on the horizon into the pother of gunsmoke. Two fires blazed more and more brightly in the gathering darkness. The cannonade was dying down, but there was a build-up of musket-fire from behind and to the right. As soon as Tushin had manoeuvred his big guns out of firing range, trundling around some wounded men and running over others, he began to descend into the ravine and was met by some senior officers, including the staff officer and Zherkov, who had been sent to Tushin's battery twice and never went there. They were all trying to outshout each other in the issuing of orders, telling people how to proceed and where to go, and showering Captain Tushin with blame and criticism. Tushin came on behind riding his gunner's nag; he had lost all control of his emotions and said nothing to them, afraid to open his mouth because every word brought him inexplicably to the brink of tears. Orders had been given to abandon the wounded, but many of them dragged themselves after the troops and begged for a lift on the gun-carriages. The dashing infantry officer who had rushed out of Tushin's little wattle hut just before the battle had been hoisted, shot through the stomach, up on to the carriage of 'Matthew's girl'. At the bottom of the hill a pale hussar cadet came up to Tushin, holding one arm in his other hand, begging for a lift.

'Captain, for God's sake. I've hurt my arm,' he said timidly. 'For God's sake . . . I can't walk. For God's sake!' This was clearly not the first time the cadet had asked for a lift, and everyone else had refused. He asked in a pitifully diffident voice, 'Please tell them to let me get on, for God's sake!'

'Let him get on, let him on,' said Tushin. 'You, Uncle, spread that coat out.' He turned to his favourite soldier. 'Hey, where's that wounded officer gone?'

'We had to chuck him off. He was dead,' someone answered.

'Well, give him a hand up. Sit yourself down, my dear fellow. There you are. Get that coat under him, Antonov.'

The cadet was Rostov. He was still holding one arm with the other hand. He was pale, his jaw was trembling and he was shivering feverishly. They hoisted him up on to 'Matthew's girl', from where they had just removed the dead officer. There was blood on the coat that was laid under him, and Rostov's breeches and arm were smeared with it.

'So, you're wounded, old fellow?' asked Tushin, going across to the gun-carriage on which Rostov was sitting.

'No, it's only a sprain.'

'What's all this blood on the side plate?' asked Tushin.

'It was that officer, sir. He stained it,' answered a gunner, wiping the blood off with his coat sleeve as if to apologize for the dirty state of the cannon.

With much effort and some assistance from the infantry, they hauled the cannon uphill and stopped when they got to the village of Guntersdorf. By now it was so dark you couldn't see the soldiers' uniforms ten paces away, and the firing was beginning to die down. All of a sudden shouts rang out not far away to the right followed by some shooting. Gunshots flashed through the darkness. It was a last attack by the French, and an immediate response came from our men who had taken refuge in the village houses. They rushed out from the village, but Tushin's big guns couldn't move; the gunners, Tushin and the cadet looked at each other in silence, wondering what might happen to them. But then the firing on both sides began to subside, and some soldiers streamed out of a side street, talking excitedly to one another.

'You all right, Petrov?' inquired one.

'We gave it to 'em hot, men. That'll keep 'em quiet,' another said.

'Couldn't see nothing. They were hitting their own men! Couldn't see nothing for the dark, mates. Anything to drink?'

The French had been driven back for the last time. Once again Tushin's big guns, shielded by the noisy infantry, trundled forward, moving on in pitch darkness.

Through the darkness streamed a kind of invisible black river, always flowing in one direction, abuzz with whispers, words, clopping hooves and rumbling wheels. Amid the dull murmur, only the sounds of wounded men moaning and calling out rang through the dark night with any clarity. Their moans seemed to swell and fill the surrounding darkness. Moaning and darkness melted into one. After a while, a wave of excitement swept through the moving crowd. Someone with an entourage had ridden past on a white horse and said something as he went by.

'What'd he say? Where are we goin' now? Are we goin' to halt? Thanked us, did he?'

Eager voices called out on all sides, and the whole surging mass began to squeeze together – the men at the front must have stopped, and a rumour swept back that the order had been given to halt. Everybody came to a stop on the muddy road, just where they were.

Fires were lit and there was a lot more talking. Captain Tushin gave some instructions to his battery, then sent some soldiers to find a dressing station or a doctor for the cadet and finally sat down by a fire lit by his soldiers at the roadside. Rostov struggled to the fire. His whole body was trembling feverishly from the pain, the cold and the damp. He was utterly weary, but he couldn't get to sleep because of the agonizing pain in his aching, dislocated arm. His eyes would close, and then open again, to stare into the fire, a blazing red blur, or at the feeble, hunched figure of Tushin squatting at his side. Tushin's wide, bright, kindly eyes were fixed on him with sympathy and commiseration. He could see that Tushin wanted to help him with all his heart, but there was nothing he could do.

From all sides they could hear the footsteps and chatter of infantry-men as they walked past, drove by or settled down not far away. The sounds of those voices, and footsteps and horses' hooves squelching through the mud, and firewood crackling near by and far away, blended together into a dull throbbing murmur.

The invisible black river flowing through the darkness had turned into a dismal sea, subsiding but still agitated after a storm. Rostov's uncomprehending eyes and ears followed what was going on in front of and around him. An infantry soldier came to the fire, squatted on his heels, held his hands to the heat and turned towards Tushin.

'Is this all right, sir?' he asked. 'You see, sir, I've lost my company. I've no idea where I am. It's terrible!'

With him an infantry officer with a bandaged cheek came to the fire to ask for the cannon to be shifted over a little so that a wagon could get through. Then two soldiers ran up; they were swearing fearfully, struggling and fighting over a boot.

'Oh no you don't! Picked it up, did you? That's a good 'un!' shouted one in a hoarse voice.

Then a thin, pale soldier with a bloodstained rag bandage on his neck came over, furiously demanding water from the gunners.

'Expect me to die like a dog?' he said.

Tushin told them to give him some water. After that a good-humoured soldier ran up to ask for some burning embers for the infantry.

'A bit of fire and heat for the infantry! Bless you, men. Thanks for the loan. We'll pay it back with interest,' he said, carrying some glowing pieces of wood off into the darkness.

He was followed by four soldiers who walked past carrying some-thing heavy in an overcoat. One of them stumbled.

'Dammit, they've dropped firewood all over the road,' he grumbled.

'He's dead. Not worth carrying him now,' said another voice.

'You shut up!' And they vanished into the darkness with their heavy load.

'Bit painful, eh?' Tushin asked Rostov in a whisper.

'Yes, it is.'

'Sir, the general wants to see you. He's just over there in a hut,' said a gunner, coming up to Tushin.

'Right, my friend.' Tushin got up, buttoned his coat, straightened his clothes and strode away from the fire.

In a hut made ready for him not far away from the gunners' fire,

Prince Bagration was taking dinner with several section commanders who had gathered about him. The little old colonel with the droopy eyes was there, greedily gnawing at a mutton bone, and also the general with twenty-two years of unblemished service, red in the face from a glass of vodka and the food, along with the staff officer wearing the signet ring, and Zherkov, who kept glancing nervously from one person to another, and Prince Andrey, looking pallid with his tense lips and feverishly glittering eyes.

Leaning in the corner of the cottage was the captured French standard, and the naive-looking auditor kept feeling the material, shaking his head and looking puzzled, perhaps because he really was interested in the flag, or perhaps because it was not very nice for a hungry man to watch them all eating when no place had been laid for him. In the next cottage was the French colonel taken prisoner by the dragoons. Our officers were continually flocking in to have a look at him. Prince Bagration was thanking the various commanding officers, and inquiring about the details of the battle and the losses. The general whose regiment had been inspected at Braunau was reporting that as soon as the engagement began he had withdrawn from the wood, picked up the wood-cutting contingent, let the French through, and then gone at them with the bayonets of two battalions and destroyed them.

'Your Excellency, as soon as I saw that the first battalion was in trouble, I stood there in the road and I says to myself, "Why don't I let them through and then open fire on them?" – and that's just what I did.'

This was so much what he wanted to have done, and so much regretted not doing, that he seemed to think it had really happened like that. Well, maybe it had. Who could tell in all that confusion what had happened and what hadn't?

'Oh, by the way, sir, I beg to report,' he went on, remembering Dolokhov's conversation with Kutuzov and his own recent encounter with the disgraced officer, 'that Private Dolokhov, who was reduced to the ranks, took a French officer prisoner before my very eyes and fought with particular distinction.'

'Sir, I watched the attack of the Pavlograd hussars, er . . . here,' put in Zherkov glancing around uneasily. He hadn't seen a single hussar all day, but he had heard something about them from an infantry officer. 'They broke up two squares, sir.'

Several men smiled, as always when Zherkov held forth, expecting a joke. But realizing that his words redounded to the glory of our armed struggle on that momentous day, they all suddenly looked serious, though many of them knew full well that what he was saying was a complete fabrication. Prince Bagration turned to the old colonel.

'Gentlemen, I thank you one and all. Every branch of the service has behaved heroically – infantry, cavalry and artillery. How did two cannons come to be abandoned in the centre?' he inquired, looking for someone to respond. (Prince Bagration didn't even ask about the guns on the left flank; he knew they had all been abandoned at the very outset.) 'Didn't I send you?' he added, addressing the duty staff officer.

'One was put out of action,' answered the staff officer, 'but the other . . . well, I can't explain. I was there all the time myself, fully in control, and I'd just left there . . . Well, yes, it was pretty hot,' he added modestly.

Someone said that Captain Tushin was at hand in the village and had been sent for.

'Oh, but you went there,' said Prince Bagration, turning to Prince Andrey.

'Yes, I did. We must have just missed each other,' said the staff officer, smiling affably at Bolkonsky.

'I didn't have the pleasure of seeing you,' said Prince Andrey, coldly and sharply.

No one spoke. Tushin appeared in the doorway, timidly squeezing through at the back of the generals. Edging around behind them in the crowded hut, embarrassed as always before his superior officers, Tushin failed to see the flagstaff and tripped over it, to laughter from some of the officers.

'How did the cannon come to be abandoned?' asked Bagration, frowning not so much at the captain as at the highly amused officers, among whom Zherkov was laughing loudest of all. Only now, stared at so fiercely by his commander, did Tushin conceive the full horror of his crime and disgrace in losing two cannons and remaining alive. He had been so excited that until this very moment nothing like this had occurred to him. The officers' laughter had confused him even more. He stood there in front of Bagration, his jaw quivering, scarcely able to get his words out.

'Sir . . . I . . . I don't know . . . I . . . er . . . didn't have the men, sir.'

'You could have got men from your cover!'

Tushin didn't say there hadn't been any cover, although that was the truth. He was afraid that saying this might get another officer into trouble, so without uttering a word he gazed with staring eyes straight into Bagration's face, like a schoolboy whose mind has gone blank and can only goggle at the examiner.

The silence went on for some time. Prince Bagration clearly did not wish to be severe but couldn't think of anything to say; nobody ventured to intervene. Prince Andrey was looking askance at Tushin and his fingers were twitching nervously.

'Sir,' Prince Andrey broke the silence with his sharp voice. 'You were kind enough to send me to Captain Tushin's battery. When I got there I found two-thirds of the men and horses dead or wounded, two guns destroyed and no cover whatever.'

Prince Bagration and Tushin looked with equal intentness at Bolkonsky, who was speaking with controlled emotion.

'And if your Excellency will allow me to express an opinion,' he went on, 'we owe today's triumph more to the action of that battery and the heroic determination of Captain Tushin and his men than to anything else,' said Prince Andrey, who then rose and walked away from the table without waiting for a reply.

Prince Bagration glanced at Tushin and, evidently reluctant to express any disbelief in Bolkonsky's rather impudent comment, yet not quite disposed to believe it entirely, he dismissed Tushin with a nod. Prince Andrey followed him out.

'My dear fellow, thank you. Got me out of a mess,' Tushin said to him.

Prince Andrey looked at Tushin, and walked off without a word. He was feeling bitterly disappointed. It was all so strange, so unlike what he had been looking forward to.

'Who are these people? Why are they here? What do they want? When will it all end?' thought Rostov, staring at the shadowy figures dancing before his eyes. The pain in his arm was more and more agonizing. He was heavy with sleep, crimson circles danced before his eyes, and impressions of these voices and these faces together with a feeling of loneliness all merged into a single sensation of pain. There they were, these soldiers, wounded or not wounded, there they were pressing him and crushing him, twisting the sinews and searing the flesh in his damaged arm and shoulder. To get rid of them he closed his eyes.

He dozed off for a moment, but in that brief span of oblivion he dreamt of things without number. He dreamt of his mother and her large, white hand, Sonya with her slender shoulders, Natasha's eyes and laughter, Denisov with his voice and his moustache, Telyanin and all that business with Telyanin and Bogdanych. All that business blurred into one soldier with a harsh voice, and together these things, 'all that business' and the one soldier were crushing, pulling and twisting his arm so agonizingly, relentlessly, on and on in the same direction. He was trying to get away from them, but they wouldn't let go of his shoulder, not for anything, not for a second. He would have been free from pain, everything would have been all right if only they would stop twisting it – but there was no getting rid of them.

He opened his eyes and looked up. Night's black canopy hovered only a couple of feet above the firelight, through which snowflakes were fluttering down. Tushin had not returned; no doctor had come. He was all alone, except for one soldier sitting naked on the other side of the fire, warming his skinny, yellow body.

'Nobody's bothered about me!' thought Rostov. 'There's nobody to help me, nobody to feel sorry for me. And to think I was at home only the other day, all strong, and happy, and with people who loved me,' he sighed, and the sigh turned into an unintended groan.

'Still hurting, eh?' asked the soldier, shaking his shirt out over the fire, and without waiting for an answer he wheezed on, 'Aye, there's a fair number bought it today – it's a bad business!'

Rostov couldn't hear what he was saying. He gazed into the snow-flakes swirling above the fire and thought of Russian winters at home, warm and bright, snug in his cosy fur coat, with a speeding sledge, rude health and his family with all their love and tenderness. And he wondered, 'Why did I ever come here?'

Next day the French decided not to renew the attack, and the remnant of Bagration's detachment joined up with Kutuzov's army.

PART III

Prince Vasily was not given to planning ahead. Still less would he think of doing any harm to other people in order to gain an advantage. He was a man of the world pure and simple, someone who had found success in society and turned success into a habit. Various plans and considerations were always forming in his mind, according to circumstances and individual encounters, but he was never fully conscious of them, even though they were his main interest in life. At any time he had on the go not just one or two such plans and considerations but dozens of them, some just emerging in his mind, some coming to fruition, and others coming to nothing. He never said to himself, for instance, 'Here is a man with power. I must gain his friendship and confidence, and use him to obtain a grant from some special fund,' nor did he say, 'Now that Pierre is a wealthy man, I must hoodwink him into marrying my daughter and lending me the forty thousand I need.' But whenever he came across a man of power he knew instinctively whether this man might be of some use, and Prince Vasily would ingratiate himself and take the first opportunity – again instinctively and without any forethought – to flatter him, get on familiar terms with him and then tell him what he wanted.

With Pierre at hand in Moscow, Prince Vasily secured him an appointment as gentleman of the bedchamber, a position which put him on the same footing as a state councillor,[1] and he insisted that the young man travel with him to Petersburg and stay at his house. Quite inadvertently, it seemed, though with absolute certainty that he was doing the right thing, Prince Vasily did everything to ensure that Pierre would marry his daughter. Had Prince Vasily been given to thinking his plans out in advance, he could never have behaved so naturally or been so direct and familiar in his relations with everyone, whether higher or lower in rank. There was something that always drew him towards men richer or more powerful than himself, and he had the rare gift of knowing precisely when he could and should make use of such persons.

Pierre's unexpected elevation to wealth and the title of Count Bezukhov, coming as it did after a life of solitude and easy-going pleasure, now made him feel so hemmed in and preoccupied that the only time he could be alone with his thoughts was in bed. He had to sign papers, put in official appearances with no clear idea of what he was doing, consult his chief steward, go out to his estate near Moscow and receive a host of people who had never wanted to know of his existence before but would have been hurt and offended now if he had refused to see them. These different people – businessmen, relatives, acquaintances – showed the same friendliness and affection to the young heir; every last one of them, ostentatiously and beyond all doubt, was convinced of Pierre's noble qualities. He kept hearing people say, 'With your remarkably kind disposition . . .' or, 'With a heart as good as yours . . .' or, 'Count, you are so pure-minded . . .' or, 'If only he was as clever as you . . .' and so on, until he came to believe genuinely in his own exceptional kindness and his own exceptional intelligence, especially since at the bottom of his heart he had always thought of himself as both very kind-hearted and very intelligent. Even people who had once been nasty to him and sometimes openly hostile now showed him warmth and affection. The eldest princess, she of the long waist and doll-like plastered-down hair, so bad-tempered before, had gone to see Pierre in his room after the funeral. With eyes downcast and many a blush she told him how greatly she regretted the misunderstandings that had arisen between them; now she felt she had no right to ask for anything except only his permission, following the blow that had befallen her, to stay on for a few weeks in the house she had always been so fond of, and where she had sacrificed so much. At these words she lost control and lapsed into tears. Deeply moved by the change that had come over such a statue-like person, Pierre took the princess by the hand and apologized to her, though he had no idea for what. From that day on the princess began knitting a striped scarf for Pierre, and she adopted a completely different attitude towards him.

'Do this for her sake, dear boy. She had a lot to put up with from the late count,' Prince Vasily said to him, handing him a document to sign for the princess's benefit. Prince Vasily had decided it might be worth throwing the poor princess a bone to chew on (a draft for thirty thousand) so that it wouldn't occur to her to open her mouth about Prince Vasily's part in the business of the inlaid portfolio. Pierre signed, and from then on the princess became even sweeter. Her younger sisters were also very nice to him, especially the youngest, the pretty one with the mole, who often embarrassed Pierre with her smiles and her own embarrassment at the sight of him.

It seemed so natural to Pierre that he should be liked by one and all, and it would have seemed so unnatural if anyone had not liked him, that he couldn't help believing in the sincerity of everyone around him. In any case, he had no time to wonder about their sincerity or insincerity. There was no time for anything; he wandered about in a permanent state of mild and agreeable intoxication. There he was, apparently the central figure in an important social system, a man from whom something was always expected, someone who, if he failed to do this or that, would let people down and disappoint them; whereas if he did do this and that, all would be well – so he did do what was demanded of him, though any happy outcomes belonged to the future.

In these early days it was Prince Vasily more than anyone who took charge of Pierre's affairs, and of Pierre himself. Since the death of old Count Bezukhov he had kept a firm hold on Pierre. Prince Vasily went about with the air of a man weighed down by affairs, careworn and weary, but ultimately too sensitive to abandon this helpless youth, heir to such a huge fortune and the son of a friend to boot, by leaving him to an uncertain destiny and open to exploitation. During those few days spent in Moscow following the death of Count Bezukhov, he had summoned Pierre, or gone to see him, and had prescribed for him everything that had to be done in tones of such weariness and authority that he seemed to be saying by way of a refrain, 'You're aware that I'm a very busy man and my concern for you is based on charity alone, and in any case I'm sure you appreciate that what I am proposing is the only thing to do.'

'Well, my dear boy, tomorrow we're off at last,' he said one day, closing his eyes and gently squeezing Pierre's elbow, seeming to imply that what he was saying had been settled long before, and couldn't have been settled in any other way.

'Yes, we're off tomorrow, and I can give you a place in my coach. I'm very glad. All our important business is settled here. And I really should have been back long ago. Look what I've just received from the chancellor. I applied on your behalf and you've been placed on the diplomatic list and made a gentleman of the bedchamber. Now a career in diplomacy lies open to you.'

His tone of weariness combined with authority was having its usual effect, but Pierre had spent so long worrying about his future career that he now made as if to protest. But Prince Vasily cut across him by cooing away in a deep bass that precluded any possibility of interruption, a device that he had recourse to whenever he needed to be at his most persuasive.

'No, dear boy, I've done this for myself, for my own conscience. Please don't thank me. No one has ever complained of being too much loved. In any case you're quite free; you could give it all up tomorrow. You'll see for yourself in Petersburg. And it's high time you got away from all these painful memories.' Prince Vasily sighed. 'So that's it, my dear boy. By the way, my valet can go in your coach. Oh – I almost forgot,' he added. 'I'm sure you know, dear boy, your father owed me a little something, so I'll take it out of what has come in from the Ryazan estate. It's nothing you need to bother about. We can sort the details out later.'

What had 'come in from the Ryazan estate' were several thousand roubles paid in lieu of service by Pierre's peasants; these Prince Vasily now kept for himself.

Petersburg was just like Moscow; Pierre was enveloped by the same atmosphere of tenderness and affection. He couldn't resign from his post, or rather the title (for he did nothing) that Prince Vasily had obtained for him, and as for his acquaintances, invitations and social obligations, these were so numerous that Pierre felt even more bewildered, rushed off his feet and expectant of some future benefit which was always on the way but never realized.

Not many of his former bachelor acquaintances were left in the city. The guards were away on active service, Dolokhov had been reduced to the ranks, Anatole was also doing army service somewhere in the provinces and Prince Andrey was abroad; so Pierre had no opportunity of nights out like the ones he had loved before, nor could he bare his soul in intimate conversation with a respected older friend. When he was not out at dinners and balls he spent most of his time at Prince Vasily's in the company of his wife, the fat princess, and their beautiful daughter, Hélène.

Anna Pavlovna Scherer was no different from anyone else in showing Pierre how much society's attitude towards him had changed.

Formerly, when Pierre had been with Anna Pavlovna he had always felt that whatever he was saying sounded unseemly, tactless or out of place; phrases that had seemed so clever as he formed them in his mind always came out as something stupid, whereas Hippolyte's silliest remarks were taken as clever and pleasing. Now every word he uttered was deemed delightful. Anna Pavlovna may not have actually said so, but he could see she was longing to, and it was only respect for his modesty that kept her from doing so.

At the beginning of the winter of 1805–6, Pierre received one of

Anna Pavlovna's customary pink invitation-cards, to which had been added: 'Here you will find the lovely Hélène, of whom one can never see enough.'

As he read this Pierre felt for the first time that a kind of bond had formed between him and Hélène, which people were now noticing, and this idea both alarmed him, because it seemed like a growing obligation that he could not fulfil, and yet pleased him as an amusing prospect.

Anna Pavlovna's soirée was just like the previous one, except that the special attraction provided for her guests was not Mortemart, but a diplomat fresh back from Berlin with the latest details of Emperor Alexander's visit to Potsdam,[2] and of the indissoluble alliance sworn between two distinguished friends to uphold the cause of righteousness against an enemy of the human race. Pierre was welcomed by Anna Pavlovna with just a touch of sadness at the recent loss sustained by the young man on the death of old Count Bezukhov. (Everyone seemed to think that Pierre needed constant assurance that he was much distressed by the death of a father he had hardly known.) Her sadness was much like the even more exalted emotion that she always displayed at any reference to her most august Majesty the Empress Maria Fyodorovna. Pierre felt flattered by it. Anna Pavlovna had used all her old skill to set up different circles in her drawing-room. One large group, which included Prince Vasily and some generals, had the benefit of the diplomat. Another group was positioned near the tea table. Pierre made a move to join the first group, but Anna Pavlovna – who was behaving like an exasperated general on the battlefield thinking up thousands of unachievable bright ideas – on seeing Pierre, fingered his coat sleeve and said, 'Wait, I have plans for you for this evening.'

She looked round at Hélène and beamed at her.

'My dear Hélène, please show some charity to my poor aunt, who simply adores you. Go and keep her company just for ten minutes. And so that you don't find it too tiresome, here's our dear count who will surely not refuse to follow you.'

The lovely Hélène moved off towards the old aunt, but Anna Pavlovna kept Pierre back at her side, with the air of somebody who has one last, essential arrangement to put in place.

'She is gorgeous, isn't she?' she said to Pierre, nodding after the majestic beauty as she floated away from them. 'Look how she carries herself! For such a young girl, what sensitivity, what magnificent deportment! It comes from the heart, you know. It will be a happy man who wins her. A man with no social skills would occupy a brilliant place in society beside her, don't you think? I just wanted to know what you think.' And she let him go.

Pierre was speaking sincerely when he gave a positive response to her question about Hélène's perfect deportment. If he ever gave a thought to Hélène it was to recall her beauty and that extraordinary way she had of maintaining an aloof and dignified silence in society.

The old aunt welcomed the two young people into her corner but seemed less eager to express her adoration of Hélène than to demonstrate her fear of Anna Pavlovna. She kept glancing at her niece as if wondering what she was supposed to do with them. Before moving on, Anna Pavlovna again fingered Pierre's sleeve, and said: 'I hope you will never again say that my parties are boring,' and she glanced at Hélène.

Hélène smiled back in a way that suggested she knew it was impossible for her to be looked at without being admired. The old aunt coughed, swallowed and said in French that she was very glad to see Hélène; then she turned to Pierre with the same greeting and the same set facial expression. In the middle of a desultory and tedious conversation Hélène looked round at Pierre and treated him to one of the bright and beautiful smiles which everyone received from her. Pierre was so used to it, this smile that meant so little to him, that he virtually ignored it. The aunt was speaking at that moment about a collection of snuff-boxes which had belonged to old Count Bezukhov, and she showed them her own little box. Princess Hélène asked if she could look at the portrait of the aunt's husband on the snuff-box lid.

'I think it's by Vinesse,' said Pierre, mentioning a celebrated miniaturist as he bent forward over the table to take the snuff-box, though he was actually eavesdropping on the conversation at the other table. He half rose, meaning to go over, but the aunt passed him the snuff-box behind Hélène's back. This caused Hélène to thrust forward to make room, and she looked round with another smile. She was wearing a fashionable evening dress cut very low at the front and back. Her bosom, which had always seemed like marble to Pierre, was so close to his short-sighted eyes that he could hardly miss the vibrant delights of her neck and shoulders, and so near his lips that he was only a few inches away from kissing it all. He could sense the warmth of her body, the aroma of her perfume, and he could hear the slight creaking of her corset as she breathed. What he saw was not marble beauty at one with her gown, what he saw and sensed was the sheer delight of her body, veiled from him only by her clothes. And once he had seen this, he could never again see it otherwise, just as we cannot reconstruct an illusion once it has been explained.

She glanced round, stared him in the face, her dark eyes flashing, and gave him her smile.

'So it's taken you all this time to notice how lovely I am?' Hélène seemed to be saying. 'How could you not see that I'm a woman? Yes, a woman, who might belong to anyone – yes, even to you,' her eyes said. At that moment Pierre suddenly felt that Hélène not only could, but must, become his wife – it had to be so.

He knew it at that moment as surely as he would have done standing beside her under the wedding crown. How it would happen and when, he didn't know. Neither did he know whether or not it would turn out to be a good thing – he had an inkling that it wouldn't – but he did know it was going to happen.

Pierre looked down, and then up again, trying to reinstate her as the remote, inaccessible beauty that he had seen in her every day until then, but it couldn't be done. It couldn't be done any more than a man who has been staring through a fog at a patch of tall steppe grass thinking it was a tree could ever see a tree in it again once he has recognized it as a patch of grass. She was terribly close to him. Now she had him in her power. And now between him and her there were no barriers of any kind, other than those of his own volition.

'Well, I'll leave you in your little corner,' came Anna Pavlovna's voice. 'I can see you like it here.' And Pierre, coming round with a shock and wondering whether he'd done something badly wrong, blushed as he looked around. He seemed to think that everyone knew as well as he what had happened to him.

Shortly afterwards, when he went over to the larger group, Anna Pavlovna said to him, 'They say you're making improvements to your house in Petersburg.' This was true. The architect had told him it had to be done, and Pierre, without knowing why, was having his immense house done up.

'That's a good idea, but don't move away from Prince Vasily's. It is a good thing to have a friend like the prince,' she said, smiling at Prince Vasily. 'I know a thing or two about that, don't I? And you're still very young. You need advice. Now don't get cross with me for taking advantage of an old woman's privileges.'

She paused, as women do, expecting some comment after mentioning their age. 'Now if you were to get married, it would be different.' And she conjoined them in a single glance. Pierre did not look at Hélène, nor she at him. But she was still terribly close.

He mumbled something and blushed.

When Pierre got home it took a long time to get to sleep. He kept going over what had happened to him. What exactly had happened?

Nothing. He had simply become aware that a woman he had known since childhood of whom he used to say quite casually, 'Yes, she is pretty,' when people had told him she was a real beauty – he had become aware that this woman might now be his.

'But she's stupid. I used to say that myself – she is stupid,' he thought. 'This can't be love. No, there's something disgusting about the way she has aroused me – it's forbidden fruit. Somebody told me that her brother, Anatole, was in love with her, and she with him, and there was a bit of a scandal, and that's why Anatole was sent away. Hippolyte's another brother . . . And her father is Prince Vasily . . . It's not good,' he mused. And just as he was thinking this through (the thoughts never came to any conclusion), he caught himself smiling and became conscious of another pattern of thoughts bubbling up through the earlier ones – that he was simultaneously dwelling on her uselessness and dreaming of how she would become his wife, how she might fall in love with him, how she might change into someone quite different, and perhaps everything he had thought and heard about her might be untrue. And again he saw her, not as some daughter born to Prince Vasily – no, he saw her whole body thinly veiled by a grey dress. 'No, but, why did I never think of that before?' And again he told himself that it was impossible for there to be anything disgusting or, as he had thought, unnatural or dishonourable, in this marriage. He remembered her earlier words and glances, and the words and glances from other people who had seen them together. He remembered the words and glances of Anna Pavlovna, when she had spoken about his house, and hundreds of hints like that from Prince Vasily and other people, and he horrified himself by wondering whether one way or another he might already have tied himself into something that was obviously not a good thing to be involved in, something he ought not to do. But the moment he began to find a way of expressing this to himself, from another part of his mind she emerged again, her image floating up in all its feminine loveliness.

CHAPTER 2

In November 1805 Prince Vasily was due to set off on a tour of inspection taking him through four provinces. He had arranged this assignment for two reasons: first, to visit his run-down estates and then to pick up his son, Anatole, from where his regiment was stationed and take him on a visit to old Prince Nikolay Bolkonsky, with a view to marrying him to the rich old man's daughter. But before he could leave and deal with these new matters, Prince Vasily wanted to settle things with Pierre, who for some days now had certainly been hanging about the house (Prince Vasily's house where he was still staying), mooning around stupidly and looking all excited when Hélène was there, as befits a young man in love, but he had still not made a proposal.

'This is fine, but it's got to be settled,' Prince Vasily said to himself one morning, with a sad sigh, feeling that Pierre, who owed him so much ('but let that pass'), was not behaving too well in this matter. 'Ah, the folly of youth . . . still, God bless him,' thought Prince Vasily, much enjoying his own good-heartedness, 'but it's got to be settled. It's little Hélène's name-day the day after tomorrow. I'll invite a few people round, and if he can't see what he's supposed to do, I'll have to do it for him. Yes, it's up to me. I am her father.'

Six weeks after Anna Pavlovna's party and the sleepless night of worry when Pierre had decided that marriage to Hélène would be a disaster and he must avoid her and get away – six weeks later, Pierre had still not left Prince Vasily's and he was horrified to think that with each passing day he was becoming more and more closely associated with Hélène in people's minds, that he could never recover his former attitude towards her, that he couldn't possibly tear himself away from her and that even though it would all work out horribly he would have to unite his life to hers. He might just have been able to extricate himself, but not a day passed without Prince Vasily (who almost never gave receptions) holding an evening party which Pierre had to attend if he was not to spoil people's pleasure and let them all down. On the rare occasions when Prince Vasily was at home he would catch Pierre by the arm as they passed, casually offer him a clean-shaven, wrinkled cheek for a kiss and say, 'I'll see you tomorrow,' or, 'Don't miss dinner, or I shan't see you,' or, 'I'm staying in for your sake,' or something like that. But even though Prince Vasily, when he did stay in 'for Pierre's sake', never spoke two words to him, Pierre hadn't the heart to let him down. Every day he said the same thing to himself over and over again. 'I really must try to understand her and work out who she is. Was I wrong then, or am I wrong now? No, she's not stupid. No, she's a lovely young woman,' he told himself sometimes. 'She never puts a foot wrong. She's never said anything stupid. She doesn't say much at all, but what she does say is always straightforward and clear, so she can't be stupid. She's always self-possessed . . . never loses control. She can't be all that bad!' When he was with her he would often start to develop an idea or think out loud, and she would always respond with a terse but relevant comment that showed she wasn't interested, or else with a silent smile and peculiar look, the most palpable indication of her superiority. She was right to think that any spoken arguments were nonsensical when set against that smile.

She now smiled at him in a special way; it was a cheerful, reassuring smile which meant more than the society smile that was always there adorning her face. Pierre knew that everyone was just waiting for him to say the word, cross the line, and he knew he would cross it sooner or later, but he was inexplicably horrified whenever he thought of taking this dreadful step. During those six weeks, as he felt himself sucked down deeper and deeper into the ghastly abyss, Pierre had said to himself a thousand times, 'What am I doing? I've got to be firm! Surely I can manage that!'

He struggled to make a decision, but was dismayed to realize that in this case he lacked the will power which he had once known in himself and really did possess. Pierre was one of those people who can show strength only when their intentions are absolutely pure. And ever since the evening when he had felt so powerfully aroused as the snuff-box was being passed at Anna Pavlovna's, an unconscious sense of sinfulness in that impulse had paralysed his will power.

On Hélène's name-day Prince Vasily gave a small dinner party for 'a few of their own', as his wife put it – just a handful of relatives and friends. All these relatives and friends were given to believe that this was the day when the young lady's destiny would be decided. They were all now at the table. Princess Kuragin, a huge, imposing woman who had once been beautiful, sat at the head, with guests of honour on either side – an old general and his wife, and Anna Pavlovna Scherer. At the other end of the table sat the less elderly and less important guests, including Pierre and Hélène, who were family, sitting side by side. Prince Vasily did not eat. He wandered up and down the table in jovial mood, sitting down beside one guest and then another. To each he addressed a few pleasant and casual words, except Pierre and Hélène, whose presence he seemed not to notice. Prince Vasily was the life and soul of the party. The wax candles burnt brightly, silver and crystal glistened on the table, as did the ladies' finery and the gold and silver of the men's epaulettes. Servants wove in and out around the table in their red livery. There was a clinking of knives, glasses and plates, and a buzz of lively chatter from several conversations around the table. At one end an ageing chamberlain could be heard assuring an elderly baroness of his ardent love for her, and she was laughing. At the other end someone was describing the misfortune

of a certain Marya Viktorovna. In mid-table Prince Vasily had collected his own little audience. With a playful smile on his lips he was
telling the ladies about last Wednesday's session of the privy council
when Sergey Kuzmich Vyazmitinov, the newly appointed military
governor of St Petersburg, read out a missive – much talked of at the
time – which he had received from Emperor Alexander. Writing from
the army, the Emperor had assured Sergey Kuzmich that from all sides
he was receiving tokens of devotion from his people, he found the one
from St Petersburg particularly gratifying, it was an honour for him
to be at the head of such a nation and he would do his best to live up
to it. The missive began with the words, 'Sergey Kuzmich. From all
sides reports are reaching me . . .'

'Are you saying he never got further than "Sergey Kuzmich"?' one
lady asked.

'No, no, not a syllable,' Prince Vasily answered with a laugh.
' "Sergey Kuzmich . . . From all sides." "From all sides . . . Sergey
Kuzmich . . ." Poor old Vyazmitinov, he just couldn't get any further.
He kept starting again, but as soon as he says "Sergey," . . . he starts
sniffing . . . "Kuz . . . mi . . . ich" . . . then tears . . . and "From all
sides" is smothered in sobs, and he can't go on. Out comes the hand-
kerchief again . . . "Sergey Kuzmich. From all sides" . . . more tears.
We had to get somebody else to read it . . . !'

' "Kuzmich . . . From all sides" . . . and tears . . .' someone repeated,
laughing.

'Don't be so nasty to him,' said Anna Pavlovna from the other end
of the table, wagging a finger at him. 'He's a worthy and excellent
man, our good Vyazmitinov.'

Everyone was laughing heartily. At the head of the table among the
honoured guests everyone seemed to be enjoying the evening; in their
various ways they were all in a good mood and high spirits. Only
Pierre and Hélène sat there in silence towards the bottom of the table.
Both of them managed a broad grin, but it had no connection with
Sergey Kuzmich – it was a smile of embarrassment at what they were
feeling. But for all the happy chatter, the laughter and the joking, for
all their enjoyment of the white wine, the sauté and the ices, for all their
scrupulous avoidance of looking at the young couple, the apparent
indifference and studied lack of interest, it was still somehow felt from
the odd stolen glance that the story about Sergey Kuzmich and all the
laughter and the food were a false front, because everybody there was
really concentrating on nothing but the two of them, Pierre and
Hélène. As he mimicked the sniffs of Sergey Kuzmich, Prince Vasily
carefully avoided any glance in his daughter's direction, but as he

laughed his expression seemed to say, 'Yes, it's going well, it'll be settled today.' Anna Pavlovna may have wagged her finger at him for laughing at 'our good Vyazmitinov', but when her eyes flashed towards Pierre, Prince Vasily read her look as congratulations on gaining a future son-in-law and a daughter's happiness. Old Princess Kuragin, sighing sadly as she offered more wine to the lady next to her, glanced huffily at her daughter, and her sigh to her companion seemed to say, 'No, there's nothing left for you and me now, my dear, nothing but sweet wine – it's time for these infuriating youngsters to flaunt their happiness!' 'What a lot of rubbish I'm spouting – as if I had any interest in it,' the diplomat was thinking as he stole a glance at the lovers' happy faces. 'Now that's what I call happiness!'

The trivialities and affectations shared by all the guests had been invaded by a simple feeling – the mutual attraction between two handsome and healthy young creatures. And this one human feeling dominated everything else and soared above all their affected chatter. Jokes fell flat, news was boring, the jollity was obviously forced. It was not only the guests – even the servants seemed to have the same feeling as they neglected their duties to glance at the lovely Hélène with her radiant look and the broad, red, happy face of the uneasy Pierre. The very candlelight seemed to be concentrated on those two happy faces.

Pierre sensed that he was the centre of everything, a situation that he found both agreeable and embarrassing. He was like a man deeply preoccupied, with no clarity of vision, no proper hearing, no understanding of anything. Only now and then did a few desultory ideas and fleeting impressions of reality flash across his mind.

'It's all over, then!' he was thinking. 'How did it come about? It's been so quick! I can see now *it* is definitely going to happen – not for her sake and not just for mine, but for everybody else's. They're all expecting *it*, they're all so sure it's coming – I can't let them down, I just can't. But how will it work out? I don't know, but there's one thing for sure – it will happen, it will!' thought Pierre, glancing at the dazzling shoulders so close to his eyes.

Then suddenly a vague sense of shame would come over him. He felt embarrassed to be the sole object of attention, such a lucky man in the eyes of everyone else, a man with a plain face acting like Paris possessing his Helen.[3] 'Oh well, I suppose it's always like this. There's no other way,' he would tell himself by way of consolation. 'But what have I done to deserve this? When did it all start? I came up from Moscow with Prince Vasily. Nothing happened. After that why shouldn't I have stayed with him? Then I played cards with her, I picked up her evening bag and we went skating. When did it all start? When did it happen?' And here he was sitting next to her, a virtual fiancé, hearing and seeing, sensing her closeness, her breathing, the movements of her body, her beauty. Then it suddenly seemed to him that *he* was the extraordinarily good-looking one, not Hélène, and that was why they were all looking at him, and there he was, revelling in the general admiration, sitting up straight, tilting his head and rejoicing in his happiness. Then suddenly he heard a voice, a familiar voice, repeating something to him.

Pierre was so absorbed that he couldn't take in what was being said.

'I was asking whether you'd heard from Bolkonsky,' said Prince Vasily for the third time. 'You're getting a bit absent-minded, my boy.' Prince Vasily smiled, and Pierre saw that everyone, everyone was smiling at him and Hélène.

'All right, all right. You all know, don't you?' Pierre was saying to himself. 'So what? Yes, it's all true.' He smiled his gentle, childlike smile, and Hélène smiled too.

'When did you hear from him? Was he in Olmütz?' repeated Prince Vasily, who needed to know in order to settle an argument.

'Why are they talking and thinking such stupid things?' Pierre wondered.

'Er, yes, it was from Olmütz,' he answered with a sigh.

When dinner was over Pierre took his lady into the drawing-room following the others. The guests began to take their leave, several without saying goodbye to Hélène. Apparently not wanting to distract her from the serious business of the evening, some guests went up to her for only a moment and then scuttled away, refusing any offer to be shown out. The diplomat was silent and glum as he left the drawing-room, comparing the futility of his diplomatic career with Pierre's happiness. The old general growled angrily at his wife when she asked how his leg was. 'Stupid old fool,' he thought. 'That Hélène will be just like her when she's fifty.'

'I believe congratulations are in order,' Anna Pavlovna whispered to Princess Kuragin, giving her an affectionate kiss. 'I would stay, but I'm afraid I have a headache.' The princess didn't respond; she was writhing with envy at her daughter's happiness.

While the guests were leaving Pierre found himself left alone with Hélène for some time in the little drawing-room where they had gone to sit down. During the last six weeks he had often been left alone with Hélène, but he had never spoken to her of love. He now sensed that this was inevitable but still couldn't bring himself to take the last step. He still had a feeling of shame; here at Hélène's side he seemed to be occupying some other man's place. 'This happiness is not for you,' an inner voice told him. 'This happiness is for people who don't have what you have.' But something had to be said, so he launched himself by asking whether she had enjoyed the evening. She replied with her usual straightforwardness – this name-day had been one of the nicest she'd ever had.

A few of the closest relatives were still there, lingering on, sitting in the large drawing-room. Prince Vasily walked casually over towards Pierre. Pierre stood up and said it was getting late. Prince Vasily fixed him with a stern, questioning look, as if his words were so strange he must have misheard. But the stern glance soon disappeared and Prince Vasily took Pierre by the arm, drawing him down into a seat and beaming affectionately.

'And how's my little daughter?' he said to her abruptly, using the casual tone of familiar affection that comes naturally to parents who have cuddled their children since childhood, but in his case had been worked out by imitating other parents. Again he turned to Pierre. '"Sergey Kuzmich. From all sides . . ."' he proclaimed, undoing the top button of his waistcoat.

Pierre smiled, but his smile showed that he knew Prince Vasily was not really interested in Sergey Kuzmich, and that Prince Vasily knew that Pierre knew. Then Prince Vasily suddenly mumbled something and walked away. Pierre got the impression that Prince Vasily was quite embarrassed, and he was moved by the sight of embarrassment in this old man of the world. He glanced round at Hélène and she looked embarrassed too. Her eyes seemed to say, 'Well, you did it.'

'I must cross that line, but I can't, I just can't do it . . .' thought Pierre, and he launched into something different, asking about Sergey Kuzmich and the point of the story because he hadn't quite heard it. Hélène smiled and said she didn't know either.

Prince Vasily had gone into the drawing-room, where the princess was talking about Pierre in subdued tones to an elderly lady.

'Yes, of course it's a very brilliant match, but – *happiness*, my dear.'

'Marriages are made in heaven,' retorted the elderly lady.

Prince Vasily walked to the far corner and sat down on a sofa as if he hadn't heard them. He closed his eyes and seemed to nod off. His head began to droop, but then he roused himself.

'Aline,' he said to his wife, 'go and see what they are doing.'

The princess went to the door and, strolling past with an air of studied nonchalance, she managed a glance into the little drawing-room. Pierre and Hélène were sitting there talking just as before.

'Just the same,' she said in answer to her husband.

Prince Vasily frowned, twisting his mouth to one side, and his cheeks began to twitch with that nasty, brutal expression of his. He shook himself, got up, tossed his head back and walked with firm steps past the ladies and into the little drawing-room. He strode in quickly and went straight up to Pierre, full of delight. The prince's face was so outrageously triumphant that Pierre rose in alarm the moment he saw him.

'Thank God!' he said. 'My wife has told me.' He put one arm around Pierre, the other around his daughter. 'My dear boy! Hélène! I am so very pleased.' His voice quavered. 'I was so fond of your father . . . and she will make you a good wife . . . God bless you both!' He embraced his daughter, then Pierre again, and kissed him with his old man's mouth. There were real tears on his cheeks. 'Aline, come here,' he called out.

The princess came in and she wept too. The elderly lady also wiped an eye with her handkerchief. They kissed Pierre, and he kissed the hand of his lovely Hélène several times. Soon they found themselves alone together again.

'All this had to be and couldn't have been otherwise,' thought Pierre, 'so it's no use wondering whether it's a good thing or a bad thing. It has to be a good thing because it's something definite, and there's no more of that agonizing suspense.' Pierre held his fiancée's hand in silence and gazed at the rise and fall of her superb bosom.

'Hélène!' he said out loud, and immediately stopped. 'There's something special that's supposed to be said on these occasions,' he thought, but for the life of him he couldn't remember what was supposed to be said on these occasions. He looked her in the eyes. She leant forward closer to him. Her face glowed red.

'Oh, please . . . take them off,' she asked, pointing to his spectacles.

Pierre took them off, and in his eyes, besides that strange look that people always have when they remove their spectacles, there was a look of alarm and bemusement. He made an attempt to bend down and kiss her hand but after one quick, rough toss of her head she found his lips and brought them to her own. Pierre was struck by the new, unpleasantly distorted expression on her face.

'It's too late now, it's all over and I do love her,' thought Pierre.

'I love you!' he said in formal French, suddenly recalling what was supposed to be said on these occasions. But the words sounded so feeble that he felt sick and ashamed.

Six weeks later he was living as a married man in the enormous, newly refurbished Petersburg mansion of the Counts Bezukhov, the proud owner, as people pointed out, of a beautiful wife and millions of roubles.

CHAPTER 3

In December 1805 old Prince Nikolay Bolkonsky received a letter from Prince Vasily proposing a visit with his son. ('I am going on a tour of inspection, and it will only mean a little detour of seventy miles for me to visit you, my honoured benefactor,' he had written. 'My Anatole is coming with me on his way to the army, and I hope you will allow him to express to you in person the high esteem in which, following his father's example, he holds you.')

'Well, there's obviously no need to wheel Marie out. The suitors are coming here,' the little princess said rather crudely when she heard this. Prince Nikolay frowned and said nothing.

Two weeks after the letter Prince Vasily's servants arrived one evening in advance of him, and the next day he and his son arrived.

Old Bolkonsky had never had a high opinion of Prince Vasily's character, especially in recent years under the new reigns of Paul and Alexander when Prince Vasily had risen high in rank and honour. Now he could see from the letter and the little princess's insinuations what was afoot, and his low opinion of Prince Vasily turned into hostility and contempt. He couldn't mention his name without an indignant snort. On the day when Prince Vasily was due to arrive the old prince was unhappy and in a particularly bad mood. Whether he was in a bad mood because Prince Vasily was coming, or whether his being in a bad mood exacerbated his unhappiness at Prince Vasily's visit, the fact is he was in a bad mood, and early that morning Tikhon had advised the architect against reporting to the prince.

'Listen to him stamping about,' said Tikhon, nodding towards the sound of the prince's footsteps. 'Banging down on his heels . . . we all know what that means . . .'

Nevertheless at nine o'clock the old prince went for his usual walk, wearing his short, velvet coat with the sable collar and a sable cap. Snow had fallen overnight. Prince Nikolay's favourite path down to the conservatories had been cleared; there were broom marks in the swept snow and a spade had been left sticking out of one of the loosely piled snowbanks on either side of the path. The prince strode through the conservatories, the servants' quarters and the outbuildings, scowling and silent.

'Can a sledge get through?' he asked a venerable old steward rather like his master in looks and manner, who was escorting him back to the house.

'The snow is deep, your Excellency. I'm having the avenoo cleared.'

The prince nodded, walking towards the steps.

'Thank heaven for that!' thought the steward. 'The storm has passed! . . . It would have been a hard drive, your Excellency,' he added. 'And I did hear tell, sir, there's a minister coming to visit your Excellency.' The prince turned to the steward and glared at him scowling.

'You what? A minister? What minister? Who told you to do that?' he began in his thin, harsh voice. 'You don't clear the road for the princess my daughter, but you do for a minister! There are no ministers in my house!'

'Your Excellency, I just thought . . .'

'You just thought?' roared the prince, speaking faster and faster, and more and more incoherently. 'You just thought! You're all crooks and villains! . . . I'll give you just thought.' He brandished his stick at Alpatych and was going to hit him, but the steward instinctively dodged away. 'Just thought! . . . You villains!' He was still gabbling. But although Alpatych, shocked at his own temerity in dodging the blow, moved closer to the prince, bowing his bald head submissively (or perhaps it was because of this), the prince kept his stick down and ran off to his room, still yelling, 'Villains! . . . Put that snow back where it came from!'

Princess Marya and Mademoiselle Bourienne stood waiting for the old prince, just before lunch, well aware of his bad mood. Mademoiselle Bourienne's beaming face seemed to say, 'I don't know anything, I'm just the same as ever,' but Princess Marya looked down, pale-faced and terrified. The worst thing for Princess Marya was that she knew that she ought to do what Mademoiselle Bourienne did at times like this, but she simply couldn't. She felt, 'If I pretend not to have noticed anything, he'll think I'm not sympathetic. But if I pretend to be depressed and in a bad mood myself, he'll say' (as he often did) 'that I'm sulking . . .' and so on.

The prince glanced at his daughter's apprehensive face and gave a snort.

'Pfooh!' he muttered, or it may have been, 'Little fool! . . . And she's not here! What have they been saying to her?' he thought, noticing that the little princess was not in the dining-room.

'Where's Princess Liza?' he asked. 'Hiding away?'

'She's not very well,' said Mademoiselle Bourienne with a bright smile. 'She won't be coming down. It's quite natural in her condition.'

'Hm! hm! huh! huh!' growled the prince, sitting down to the table. He thought he'd been given a dirty plate, so he pointed to a stain and flung it away. Tikhon caught it and handed it on to a footman. The little princess was not unwell, but she was so abjectly terrified of the prince that when she heard he was in a bad temper she decided not to come down.

'I'm afraid for my baby,' she told Mademoiselle Bourienne. 'You never know what a scare might do.'

And indeed the little princess's life at Bald Hills was lived in a state of continual dread of the old prince, and a thorough dislike of him, which she wasn't aware of because the overriding terror obscured any other feeling. The prince had the same thorough dislike of her, but on his side it was blotted out by contempt. As the days went by at Bald Hills the little princess made a close friend of Mademoiselle Bourienne. She would spend whole days with her, and sometimes invited her to sleep in her room, and she often talked about her father-in-law, and spoke badly of him.

'We're to have company then, Prince,' said Mademoiselle Bourienne, unfolding her white napkin with pink fingers. 'His Excellency Prince Kuragin and his son, I believe,' she said in a tone of inquiry.

'Hm! . . . *His Excellency* is a nobody. I got his career going,' the old prince said spitefully. 'And I haven't the slightest idea why that son of his is coming. Maybe Princess Lizaveta and Princess Marya can tell us. I don't know what he's bringing his son for. I don't want him.' And he looked at his daughter, who had turned bright red. 'Not well, is she? More likely scared of the "minister", as that stupid Alpatych called him just now.'

'Oh no, father.'

Unabashed by her failed attempt at conversation, Mademoiselle Bourienne carried on chattering away about the conservatories and a beautiful flower that had just opened. By the end of the soup course the prince had subsided.

After dinner he went to see his daughter-in-law. The little princess was sitting at a small table chatting with her maid, Masha. She turned pale at the sight of her father-in-law.

The little princess had changed a great deal and now looked more ugly than pretty. Her cheeks were sunken, her lip was drawn up and there were bags under her eyes. 'Yes, I feel a bit weighed down,' she said in answer to the prince's inquiry after her health.

'Do you need anything?'

'No thank you, Father.'

'Good. Very well then.'

He went out and walked to the servants' room. There stood Alpatych with downcast head.

'Have you put that snow back?'

'Yes, sir, we have. God forgive me, sir, it was a silly mistake.'

The prince cut him short with his weird laugh.

'Oh, very well, then, very well.' He held out a hand for Alpatych to kiss, and then went off to his study.

That evening Prince Vasily arrived. He was met on what the staff called 'the avenoo' by the Bolkonsky coachmen and servants, who with much shouting struggled with the carriages and sledge over a road deliberately re-covered with snow and brought them through to one wing of the house.

Prince Vasily and Anatole were conducted to their separate rooms.

Taking off his coat, Anatole sat beside a table, hands on hips, his beautiful big eyes staring at one corner, with a distracted smile on his face. He looked on life as one long party that someone was bound to arrange for him. It was in that spirit that he now viewed his visit to the irritable old country-gentleman and his rich, ugly heiress of a daughter. As he saw it, he might be in for a very jolly and amusing time. 'Well, why not get married, if she's got all that money? Never comes amiss, does it?' thought Anatole.

He shaved and perfumed himself with the scrupulous elegance that was now second nature to him, and with his natural look of disarming good humour he strolled into his father's room, with his head held high. Two valets were busy dressing Prince Vasily. He glanced around eagerly, and when his son came in nodded cheerfully, as if to say, 'Yes, that's just what I wanted you to look like.'

'Come on, Father, joking apart, is she really as ugly as all that?' Anatole asked in French, as though half-way through a subject much discussed on the way there.

'Don't be silly! The great thing is for you to try and be nice and polite to the old prince.'

'If he gets nasty, I'm off,' said Anatole. 'I can't stand old men like him. Can you?'

'Don't forget, as far as you're concerned everything depends on this.'

Meanwhile, in the maids' room not only the arrival of the minister and his son, but their physical appearance was known and described in detail. Princess Marya was sitting alone in her room struggling to control her emotions.

'Why did they write? Why did Lise tell me about it? It's quite impossible!' she thought, glancing at the mirror. 'How am I to go into the drawing-room? Even if I like him, I could never be my normal self with him now.' The very thought of her father's look reduced her to terror.

The little princess and Mademoiselle Bourienne had by now obtained all the necessary intelligence from the maid, Masha. They knew what a dashing fellow the minister's son was, with his rosy face and black eyebrows. They knew that whereas his father had struggled up the steps he had flown up them three at a time like a young eagle. Furnished with this intelligence, the little princess and Mademoiselle Bourienne, whose eager voices had reached her from the hallway, went into Princess Marya's room.

'They're here, Marie. Didn't you know?' said the little princess, waddling in and sinking heavily into an armchair. She was wearing a different gown, not the one she had had on that morning, but one of her finest dresses. Her hair had been beautifully done, and her face was excited, though it still looked wasted and drawn. Dressed in the fine clothes which she used to wear in Petersburg society, she showed the loss of her good looks all the more noticeably. Mademoiselle Bourienne, too, had added one or two nice finishing touches, which made her sweet fresh face look even prettier. 'So, you're staying like that, are you, Princess? They'll be here in a minute to tell us the gentlemen are in the drawing-room,' she began. 'We'll have to go down, and you haven't done anything to yourself!'

The little princess got up from her chair, rang for the maid, scurrying to work out what Princess Marya should wear, and then eagerly getting it all done. Princess Marya's self-respect had been offended by her own agitation at the arrival of a prospective suitor, and she was even more offended by the fact that her two companions couldn't conceive of anything different. To speak of the embarrassment she felt on her own account and theirs would have been to admit just how agitated she was, and to refuse to be dolled up as they were proposing would have led to no end of ridicule and to further persuasion. She flushed, the light went out of her lovely eyes, her face went blotchy, resuming its all too familiar and unpleasant look of victimization, and she gave herself up to Mademoiselle Bourienne and Liza. Both women strove *with the utmost sincerity* to beautify her. She was so plain that the idea of her being a rival could never have entered their heads, so they were genuinely sincere in their efforts at fixing her up, which they went about with the simple-minded womanly certainty that good toilette can make any face beautiful.

'No, no, dear, that dress won't do,' said Liza, backing off and looking obliquely at Princess Marya. 'Get her to fetch your maroon velvet. I mean it! You do realize this could decide your whole future. No, this one's too light. It won't do at all.'

It wasn't the dress that wouldn't do, but the princess's face and her figure, but this didn't occur to Mademoiselle Bourienne and the little princess. They still imagined that if they just swept her hair up and put a blue ribbon in it, and arranged the blue sash down a little on her maroon dress, and so on, then all would be well. They were forgetting that nothing could change Princess Marya's frightened face and her figure, and however much they tinkered with its setting and adornment, the face itself would still look pathetically unattractive. Princess Marya submitted like a lamb, and after two or three failed attempts her hair was scraped up on top of her head (which changed her completely and ruined her looks), and on went the best maroon velvet dress with the blue sash. The little princess walked around her a couple of times, straightened a fold here and eased the sash down there, and then looked at her, tilting her head first on one side and then the other.

'No, it's still not right,' she said firmly, throwing up her hands. 'No, Marie, it just doesn't suit you. I like you better in your everyday frock, the little grey one. No, please do it for me. Katya,' she said to the maid, 'bring the princess her grey dress, and, Mademoiselle Bourienne, you watch me arrange it,' she said, smiling as she looked forward to an artistic pleasure. But when Katya brought the dress Princess Marya was still sitting stolidly before the mirror, looking at her face, and in the mirror she could see her eyes brimming with tears and her mouth trembling – she was on the verge of breaking down and sobbing.

'Come on, dear Princess,' said Mademoiselle Bourienne, 'just one more little try.'

The little princess took the dress from the maid and went over to Princess Marya. 'Now, we're going to do something nice and straight-forward,' she said. And the three voices, hers, Mademoiselle Bourienne's and the giggling Katya's, blended into a kind of happy babble like birds twittering.

'No, leave me alone,' said the princess, and there was so much urgency and suffering in her voice that the twittering stopped abruptly. They looked at the big beautiful eyes, full of tears and of thoughts, looking back at them imploringly and they saw that resistance would be useless, even cruel.

'Please change your hairstyle,' said the little princess. 'I told you,' she said reproachfully to Mademoiselle Bourienne, 'that Marie has the kind of face that this style doesn't suit. It really doesn't. Change it, please!'

'Just leave me alone, I tell you. None of this makes any difference,' said a voice near to tears.

Mademoiselle Bourienne and the little princess had to admit to themselves that Princess Marya looked awful dolled up like this, far worse than usual, but it was too late. She was looking at them with an expression they knew all too well, one that was thoughtful and sad. The expression wasn't frightening – she was incapable of frightening anyone, but they knew that when that expression came over her face she was going to be mute and immovable in anything she decided.

'You will alter it, won't you?' asked Liza, and when Princess Marya refused to reply Liza went out of the room.

Princess Marya was left alone. She didn't do what Liza had wanted, she didn't rearrange her hair, she didn't even glance at the mirror. With her eyes and hands drooping helplessly, she sat there daydreaming in silence. She dreamed of a husband, a man strong and masterful, an unimaginably attractive creature, come to bear her off into an entirely different world of his own, a world of happiness. She dreamt of a child, *her own baby* – like the one she had seen with her old nurse's daughter only the day before – and saw it at her own breast, the husband standing there, gazing tenderly at her and the child. 'But no, it's impossible. I'm too ugly,' she thought.

'Tea is served. The prince will be going in immediately,' came the maid's voice through the door. She gave a start, horrified at what she had been thinking. And before going downstairs she rose, went to her icons, fixed her eyes on one gently illuminated black countenance, a large image of the Saviour, and stood before it for several minutes with her hands together. Princess Marya's soul was racked with doubt. Could she ever know the joy of love, earthly love for a man? In her thoughts about marriage, Princess Marya dreamt of family happiness, a home with children, but her first, her strongest, her most secret desire was for earthly love. This feeling was at its strongest when she was trying hardest to conceal it from others, and even from herself. 'O Lord God,' she said, 'how am I to subdue in my heart these thoughts that come from the devil? How am I to renounce for ever all evil thinking, so as to live at peace and fulfil thy will?' And the moment she formed this question God's answer came to her in her own heart. 'Desire nothing for thyself, seek for nothing, be not disturbed, envy not. Man's future and thy destiny shall be unknown to thee; but live in readiness for anything. If it be God's will to prove thee in the duties of marriage, be prepared to do his will.' With this soothing thought in mind (though also hoping that her forbidden earthly dream still might come true), Princess Marya crossed herself with a sigh and went downstairs, with no thought for her dress, or how her hair was done, or how she would go in, or what she would find to say. What could all of this signify beside the predestined will of God, without whom not a hair falls from the head of man?

CHAPTER 4

When Princess Marya came into the drawing-room Prince Vasily and his son were already there, talking to the little princess and Mademoiselle Bourienne. She clomped in, heavily on her heels, and the gentlemen and Mademoiselle Bourienne rose, while the little princess gestured towards her for the gentlemen's sake and said, 'This is Marie!' Princess Marya saw them all and saw them in detail. She saw Prince Vasily falter at the sight of her and take on a serious look for a moment, though it soon turned into a smile, and she took in the little princess's face watching the guests to see what they would make of her, Marie. She saw Mademoiselle Bourienne, too, with her ribbon, turning her pretty face towards *him* with a keener look than she had ever shown before. But *him* she could not see, only something big, bright and handsome that had moved towards her as she entered the room. Prince Vasily was the first to approach her, and she kissed his bald pate as he bent to kiss her hand, replying to a question from him – yes, she remembered him very well. Then Anatole came up to her. She still couldn't see him. All she felt was a strong, soft hand taking hers, and she allowed her lips to brush a white forehead beneath beautiful fair hair smelling of pomade. When she did glance at him, she was struck by his handsome looks. Anatole was standing with his right thumb crooked around a button on his uniform, chest out and spine back, swinging one foot with his weight on the other leg, his head gently tilted as he glanced at the princess in breezy silence, obviously not taking her in at all. Anatole was not a quick-witted or eloquent conversationalist, but he did have one attribute that is invaluable in society – composure stemming from total self-confidence. If a man lacking in confidence says nothing when introduced and lets people see that he knows his silence is wrong and he is struggling for something to say, the effect will be bad. But Anatole said nothing as he swung his leg and cheerfully observed the princess's hairstyle. It was clear that he was capable of serenely saying nothing for a very long time. 'Anybody who finds silence embarrassing can always start talking,' he seemed to imply, 'I'm not that way inclined.' Besides that, in his dealings with the fair sex Anatole had mastered the special attitude that most effectively arouses a woman's curiosity, awe and even love – an attitude of disdainful awareness of his own superiority. His manner seemed to say to them, 'I know you, yes I do, but why should I make the effort? That's just what you'd like me to do!' He may not have actually thought this on meeting women (and probably didn't because he was no great thinker at the best of times), but that was the impression created by his manner and attitude. Princess Marya sensed this and, as if to show that she didn't expect to interest him, she turned away to his father. The conversation ranged widely and was very animated largely because of the little princess with her tiny voice and the little downy lip that kept popping up and down over her white teeth. She met Prince Vasily with the bantering tone so often adopted by out-going, chatty people, seemingly based on a long-established fund of amusing stories, mutual jokes and shared memories, some of them private, existing between two conversationalists, whereas there aren't really any shared memories at all, as in the case of Prince Vasily and the little princess. Prince Vasily was only too pleased to fall in with this tone, and the little princess managed to involve Anatole in the non-existent amusing stories from their past, though she scarcely knew him. Mademoiselle Bourienne soon caught on, and even Princess Marya was pleased to feel herself being drawn into the fun of reminiscing.

'Now, we're going to make the most of you, dear Prince,' said the little princess (in French, of course) to Prince Vasily. 'Not like those evenings at Annette's when you were always running away. You do remember our dear Annette?'

'Ah yes, but you won't make me talk politics, like Annette!'

'And our little tea table?'

'Oh yes!'

'Why were you never at Annette's?' the little princess asked Anatole. 'Oh yes, I know,' she said with a wink. 'Your brother, Hippolyte, told me all about you. Oh!' She wagged a tiny finger at him. 'And I know what you got up to in Paris!'

'But there's one thing Hippolyte didn't tell you,' said Prince Vasily to his son, taking the little princess by the arm, as if she was trying to run away from him and he had just managed to catch her. 'He didn't tell you that *he* was eating his heart out for our sweet princess, and she showed him the door.'

'She really is a pearl among women,' he said, turning to Princess Marya.

At the mention of Paris Mademoiselle Bourienne was not going to miss the opportunity of joining them in their shared memories.

She ventured to ask how long Anatole had been away from Paris and whether he liked the city. Anatole, delighted to respond to the French girl, smiled and stared at her as they talked about her homeland. The moment he had set eyes on the pretty Mademoiselle, Anatole had decided that even here at Bald Hills he might be in for a good time. 'Hm, easy on the eye,' he thought as he examined her. 'Quite something to look at, this lady's companion! I do hope Marya will bring her along when we're married,' he mused. 'She's a nice little thing.'

Up in his room the old prince was taking his time dressing, scowling as he wondered what to do. The visitors annoyed him. 'Prince Vasily and his son, they're nothing to me. The old man is a stupid windbag and his son can't be much better,' he growled to himself. What annoyed him was that this visit raised in his mind a secret unanswered question that he was always running away from: could he ever bear to part with his daughter and give her to a husband? The prince always avoided this direct question, because he knew in advance that any answer would involve the truth, and the truth would undermine not just his feelings, but the meaning of his whole life. Little as he appeared to value her, for the old prince life without Princess Marya was unthinkable. 'What would marriage do for her?' he thought. 'Make her unhappy, that's for sure. Look at Liza married to Andrey (and I don't think you'd find a better husband these days) – she's not happy with her situation. And who would marry Marya for love? She's a plain girl and so gauche. They'd want her for her connections and her money. Old maids don't do too badly, do they? I think they're happier!' These were Prince Nikolay's thoughts as he dressed, but the long-deferred question now had to be resolved. It was obvious that Prince Vasily had brought his son to make a proposal, and within a day or two he would ask for a straight answer. The family name and their social standing were immaculate. 'Well, I'm not against it,' the prince kept saying to himself, 'I just hope he's worthy of her. One day we shall see,' he said out loud. 'One day we shall. One day.'

And with his usual briskness he strode into the drawing-room and took in the whole scene at a single rapid glance: the little princess had changed her dress, Mademoiselle Bourienne was wearing a ribbon, Princess Marya's hair looked hideous and the French girl and Anatole were smiling at each other while his daughter was being left out of the conversation. 'She's dolled herself up like a fool!' he thought, glaring furiously at his daughter. 'Has she no shame? And he doesn't want to have anything to do with her!'

He went over to Prince Vasily.

'Well, how d'ye do, how d'ye do, glad to see you.'

'Friendship smiles at a hundred miles,' said Prince Vasily, as always rapid, confident and familiar in his speech. 'This is my younger son. I hope he will win your favour and sympathy.'

Prince Nikolay examined Anatole.

'Yes, a splendid young man!' he said. 'Well, come and give me a kiss,' he added, offering a cheek. Anatole kissed the old man, and watched him with composure and curiosity, waiting for one of the idiosyncrasies his father had told him to expect.

The old prince sat down in his usual place at one end of the sofa, pulled up an armchair for Prince Vasily, pointed to it and began to ask him about political developments and the latest news. He pretended to be listening closely to what Prince Vasily was saying, but his eyes kept turning to Princess Marya.

'So, letters are coming from Potsdam now, are they?' He repeated Prince Vasily's last words, then he suddenly got up and went over to his daughter.

'So you've got yourself all dressed up like this for the visitors, have you?' he said. 'You look very nice, I'm sure. A new hairstyle for the visitors – well, in front of the visitors I'm telling you this – in future don't even change your dress without consulting me.'

'Father, it was my fault . . .' the little princess interceded, blushing.

'*You* may do whatever you want,' said the old prince, with a mocking bow to his daughter-in-law, 'but she has no need to disfigure herself – she's ugly enough as it is.' And he sat down again in his place, ignoring his daughter, who had by now been reduced to tears.

'Oh no, that hairstyle suits the princess very well,' said Prince Vasily.

'Well, sir, this young prince, what's his name?' said the old prince, turning to Anatole. 'Come over here. Let's have a talk and get to know each other.'

'This is where the fun begins,' thought Anatole, and he smiled as he sat down by the old prince.

'Good, there we are. Now, my dear boy, they tell me you were educated abroad. Not like your father and me, taught to read and write by the local deacon. Tell me, are you in the horse guards?' asked the old man, looking closely and insistently at Anatole.

'No, I have transferred into the line,' answered Anatole, finding it hard not to laugh.

'Ah! A splendid thing. So you want to serve your Tsar and your country? These are times of war. A fine young man like you ought to be a serving soldier, yes, a serving soldier. Ordered to the front, eh?'

'No, Prince, our regiment has gone to the front. But I'm attached ... What is it I'm attached to, Papa?' Anatole turned to his father with a laugh.

'He is a credit to the service, indeed. What am I attached to! Ha-ha-ha!' laughed the old prince, and Anatole laughed louder. Suddenly the old prince frowned. 'Off you go then,' he said to Anatole. Smiling broadly, Anatole returned to the ladies.

'So you had them educated abroad, Prince Vasily? Eh?' said the old prince.

'One did what one could. I must say the education there is much better than ours.'

'Yes, it's all different now, new-fangled. A splendid boy! Splendid! Well, let's go to my room.' He took Prince Vasily by the arm and led him away to his study.

Alone with Bolkonsky, Prince Vasily lost no time in making known his hopes and his desires.

'What do you think?' said the old prince angrily. 'I'm hanging on to her? I can't let go of her? The very idea!' he protested furiously. 'I'd do it tomorrow! But I will say this – I want to know my future son-in-law better. You know my golden rule: everything out in the open! Tomorrow I shall ask her in your presence. If she says yes, let him stay on. Let him stay on, and I'll see.' The prince snorted. 'Let her get married. I don't care!' he screamed with the same piercing shriek as when he had said goodbye to his son.

'I'll be quite candid,' said Prince Vasily sounding like a crafty man who sees it's no use being crafty with such a sharp mind. 'I know you can see right through people. Anatole is no genius, but he's a good, honest boy, a fine son and a family man.'

'Yes, yes. We'll see about that.'

As always with lonely women long deprived of male company, the moment Anatole appeared on the scene, all three women in Prince Nikolay's house felt as one that they had not been living a real life until then. Suddenly their thought processes, feelings and powers of observation were ten times sharper. It was as if lives spent in darkness had suddenly been flooded with a bright light full of new meaning.

Princess Marya forgot all about her face and hairstyle. The handsome, open face of the man who might turn out to be her husband absorbed her whole attention. He seemed so kind, brave, strong, manly and noble. She was sure of it. Dreams of a future married life rose in her imagination by the thousand. She drove them away and tried to conceal them.

'But perhaps I'm being too cold with him?' thought Princess Marya. 'I'm trying to control myself because at the bottom of my heart I can feel myself getting too close to him. But still, he doesn't know what I think of him. He might even think I don't like him.'

She tried to be nice to him and didn't know how.

'Poor girl, she is terribly ugly,' Anatole was thinking.

Mademoiselle Bourienne had also been roused by Anatole's arrival into a state of high excitement, but her thoughts were of a different order. Naturally, a beautiful young girl with no fixed position in society, with no friends or relations, not even a country of her own, was not looking forward to a life spent waiting on Prince Nikolay Bolkonsky, reading to him and being a good friend to Princess Marya. Mademoiselle Bourienne had long been looking forward to the day when a Russian prince sensitive enough to see her as superior to all those ugly, dowdy, clumsy Russian princesses would fall in love with her and carry her off. Now he had come. Mademoiselle Bourienne remembered a favourite story of her aunt's which she had adapted and loved to run over in her imagination. It was about a young girl who had been seduced, and her poor mother had appeared to her and reproached her for giving herself to a man without getting married. Mademoiselle was often moved to tears when she imagined herself telling *him*, her would-be seducer, this story. Now *he* was here – a real Russian prince. He would carry her off, then 'my poor mother' would come on the scene, and they would be married. This future history of hers had been unfolding in Mademoiselle Bourienne's mind all the time they were talking about Paris. Mademoiselle Bourienne was not a scheming woman (she certainly never planned ahead), but everything had been prepared within her long before this and it had suddenly focused on Anatole the moment he appeared, after which she longed to please him and tried as hard as she could.

As for the little princess, she was like an old warhorse hearing a trumpet-blast, ready to gallop off into yet another flirtation, instinctively oblivious to her present situation, without a backward glance or the slightest qualm, her fun-loving heart full of nothing but simple gaiety.

In female company Anatole usually adopted the pose of a man weary of being chased by women, but his vanity was pleasantly tickled by the effect he was having on these three women. More than that, he was beginning to feel towards the pretty and seductive Mademoiselle Bourienne the kind of animal passion that sometimes swept over him with amazing speed and urged him to indulge in the most reckless and boorish behaviour.

After tea the party moved into the sitting-room, and Princess Marya was asked to play the clavichord. Anatole leant on one elbow opposite her and close to Mademoiselle Bourienne; his eyes, full of fun and laughter, were fixed on Princess Marya. She was agonized and delighted to feel his eyes upon her. Her favourite sonata bore her away to a world of soulful poetry, and the feeling of his eyes upon her brought even more poetry into that world. But the look in Anatole's eyes which seemed to be directed at her had rather more to do with the writhing of Mademoiselle's little foot, entwined with his under the piano. Mademoiselle Bourienne was also gazing at Princess Marya, and her lovely eyes also shone with a mixture of alarm, joy and longing that was new to the princess.

'Oh, she does love me!' Princess Marya was thinking. 'How happy I am now and shall be in the future with such a friend and such a husband! Dare I say husband?' she thought, not bold enough to glance at his face but still sensing his eyes fixed upon her.

When the party broke up after supper, Anatole kissed Princess Marya's hand. Where she got the strength from she would never know, but as the handsome face came close to her she managed to squint straight at it with her short-sighted eyes. After the princess, he went to kiss the hand of Mademoiselle Bourienne (this was discourteous, but he acted with composure and simplicity), and Mademoiselle Bourienne coloured, glancing in dismay at the princess.

'She's so sensitive!' thought Princess Marya. 'How could Amélie' (Mademoiselle's name) 'possibly imagine I might be jealous of her, and not value her tenderness and devotion to me?' She went over to Mademoiselle Bourienne and gave her a particularly warm kiss. Anatole moved towards the little princess.

'Oh no you don't, sir! When your father writes and tells me that you're being a good boy, then I shall give you my hand to kiss. But not before.' And wagging her tiny finger at him, she left the room smiling.

CHAPTER 5

They went to their rooms, and everyone except Anatole, who dropped off the moment he got into bed, took a long time to get to sleep that night. 'Is he really going to be my husband, that stranger, that good, handsome man. He is good – that's the most important thing,' thought Princess Marya, and she was struck by the kind of terror she had scarcely ever felt before. She was afraid to turn her head – was that someone standing there behind the screen in the corner? It might be the devil – and he might be that man with the white forehead, black eyebrows and red lips.

She rang for her maid and asked her to sleep in her room.

Mademoiselle Bourienne strolled about the winter garden for a long time that evening, waiting in vain for someone, smiling at someone or else weepy at the thought of her 'poor mother' reproaching her for her fall.

The little princess was uncomfortable in bed and complained to her maid. She couldn't lie on her side or on her front. She felt weighed down and awkward in every position. Her big lump got in the way – got in the way more than ever that night, because Anatole's presence had transported her vividly back to another time when she didn't have it and had been light and carefree. She went and sat in a low chair in her dressing jacket and nightcap. Katya, sleepy and with dishevelled hair, turned the heavy feather bed and plumped it up for the third time, grumbling as she did so.

'I told you it was all bumps and hollows,' the little princess insisted. 'I want to get to sleep, so it can't be my fault.' She spoke with a quavering voice like a child on the verge of tears.

The old prince also found sleep difficult. Tikhon, half-asleep, could hear him stamping about and snorting in his anger. The old prince felt as though his daughter had been used to insult him. The insult was all the more hurtful for being levelled not at him but at someone else, his daughter, whom he loved more than himself. He told himself to reconsider the whole business and decide what was right and what must be done, but instead of that all he did was work himself up more and more.

'The first man that happens along she forgets her father and everything else, she runs upstairs and has her hair all scraped up, then goes all coy – she's not the same woman! Only too glad to drop her old father! And she knew I was bound to notice. Grr ... grr ... grr ... They must think I'm blind ... that fool has eyes for no one but that

Bourienne girl . . . must get rid of her. How can she have so little pride that she can't see it? If she can't show any pride for herself, can't she show some for me? I must show her that that young idiot isn't thinking about her, his eyes are on Bourienne. She has no pride, but I'll show her . . .'

But the old prince knew that by telling his daughter she was making a mistake and that Anatole was busy flirting with Mademoiselle Bourienne he would undermine her self-respect, and his cause – to avoid being parted from his daughter – would be lost, so eventually he began to calm down. He summoned Tikhon and began undressing.

'Damn them for coming here!' he thought, as Tikhon slipped a nightshirt over his desiccated old body and his chest covered with grey hair. 'I didn't invite them. They come here and turn my life upside down. And there's not much of it left. Damn them!' he mumbled while his head was hidden in the nightshirt. Tikhon was used to the prince's habit of sometimes thinking aloud, and his face didn't change when he encountered an inquiring angry glare emerging from the nightshirt.

'In bed?' asked the prince.

Like any good valet Tikhon had a flair for following his master's thoughts. He guessed that the question referred to Prince Vasily and his son.

'Their Honours have retired and put out their lights, sir.'

'They had no reason, no reason at all,' the prince gabbled, shuffling his feet into his slippers and his arms into his dressing-gown before going over to the couch where he slept.

Although nothing had been said between Anatole and Mademoiselle Bourienne, they had a perfect understanding over the first part of their affair, up to the 'poor mother' episode. Knowing they had much to say to each other in private, they watched from early morning for the first opportunity of meeting alone. As soon as the princess went in for the usual hour with her father, Mademoiselle Bourienne and Anatole met in the winter garden.

That morning Princess Marya went to the study door even more flustered than usual. She could only imagine that everybody knew her fate would be settled today, and everybody knew what she thought of it all. She read this on Tikhon's face and on the face of Prince Vasily's valet, who met her in the corridor carrying hot water and bowed low to her.

The old prince's attitude to his daughter that morning was extremely affectionate and forbearing. This look of forbearance on her father's face was only too well known to Princess Marya. It was the same look that came over his face when his withered hands were clenched with vexation at her failure to understand some arithmetical problem, after which he would get up and walk away, repeating the same words in a low voice over and over again.

He began talking, rather formally, and came straight to the point. 'A proposal has been made to me on your behalf,' he said with a forced smile. 'I'm sure you must have guessed,' he went on, 'that Prince Vasily has not come here with his ward' (inexplicably this was how the old prince referred to Anatole) 'to look at my beautiful eyes. Yesterday, they made me a proposal on your behalf. You know my principles. I refer the matter to you.'

'I don't think I understand you, Father,' said the princess, turning pale and red in turn.

'There's nothing to understand!' cried her father angrily. 'Prince Vasily finds you to his taste as a daughter-in-law, and is proposing to you on behalf of his ward. That's all there is to it. How can you not understand? . . . Well, come on, I'm waiting.'

'I don't know about you, Father,' the princess whispered.

'Me? Me? What's it got to do with me? Leave me out of it. I'm not the one getting married. What do *you* say? That is what it would be desirable to know.'

The princess could see that her father was bitterly against it, but it suddenly occurred to her that now or never her life's destiny would be decided. She looked down to avoid the gaze which rendered her incapable of thought, incapable of anything but her usual deference. 'My only wish is to do your will,' she said, 'but if I had to express my own desire . . .'

Before she could finish the prince cut her short. 'Well, that's splendid then!' he shouted. 'He'll go off with you and your dowry, and take Mademoiselle Bourienne along too. She'll be his wife, and you . . .' The prince stopped. He could see the effect of these words on his daughter. She had lowered her head and was on the verge of tears.

'Now listen, I was only joking,' he said. 'Remember this, Princess: I stick to the rule that a girl has every right to choose. And I give you complete freedom. Remember this: your happiness in life depends on your decision. No need to worry about me.'

'But I don't know . . . Father.'

'There's nothing to talk about. He'll do what he's told, whether it's marrying you or anybody else, but you are at liberty to choose . . . Now go to your room, think it over, come back in an hour's time and say yes or no in his presence. I know you will pray for guidance. Well, pray if you like. Only you'd be better off thinking. Off you go.'

'Yes or no, yes or no, yes or no!' he kept on shouting long after the princess had tottered out of the room as if she was groping her way through a fog.

Her fate had been decided, and her happiness was now secure. But what had her father said about Mademoiselle Bourienne? That had been a horrible jibe. Of course it wasn't true, but it was still horrible and she couldn't get it out of her mind. She walked straight on through the winter garden seeing and hearing nothing when she was suddenly brought to her senses by a familiar voice whispering – it was Mademoiselle Bourienne. She looked up and not two paces away saw Anatole with his arms round the French girl, whispering to her. Anatole whipped round and looked at Princess Marya with a horrified expression on his handsome face, but he was in no hurry to let go of Mademoiselle Bourienne's waist – who hadn't yet seen her.

'Who's that? What do you want? Wait a minute!' was the message on Anatole's face. Princess Marya gazed blankly at them. She couldn't believe what she was seeing. Then at last Mademoiselle Bourienne gave a cry and fled. Anatole bowed to Princess Marya with a sweet smile, as if inviting her to share his amusement at this strange turn of events, and then with a shrug he went in through the door leading to his room.

Within the hour Tikhon came to summon Princess Marya to the old prince, adding that Prince Vasily was with him. When Tikhon came Princess Marya was sitting on the sofa in her room with her arms around a weeping Mademoiselle Bourienne. Princess Marya was softly stroking her hair. Her lovely eyes shone with the serenity of old as she gazed with warm love and commiseration into Mademoiselle Bourienne's pretty little face.

'Oh, Princess, I have lost your heart for ever,' Mademoiselle Bourienne was saying.

'Why? I love you more than ever,' said Princess Marya, 'and I shall try to do everything in my power to make you happy.'

'But you must despise me. You're so pure. You could never understand a passionate longing like this. Oh, only my poor mother . . .'

'I understand everything,' said Princess Marya with the saddest of smiles. 'Now, you calm down, my dear. I'm going to see Father,' she said and went out.

Prince Vasily was sitting there with one leg crossed high over the other, snuff-box in hand, his face suffused with emotion so extreme that he seemed ruefully embarrassed by his own sensitivity. When she came in he took a hasty pinch of snuff.

'Ah, my dear girl, my dear girl!' he said, rising to take hold of both her hands. He heaved a sigh and went on, 'My son's destiny is in your hands. Make your decision, good, dear, sweet Marie, whom I have always loved like my own daughter.' He stood back. There were real tears in his eyes.

'Hmph!' snorted the old prince. 'On behalf of his ward . . . er, his son . . . the Prince is making a proposal to you. Do you or do you not wish to be the wife of Prince Anatole Kuragin? Yes or no?' he shouted. 'After which I reserve the right to express an opinion of my own. Yes, my own opinion and nobody else's,' – this to Prince Vasily in response to a beseeching look. 'Yes or no! What have you to say?'

'My wish, Father, is never to leave you, never to separate my life from yours. I do not wish to marry,' she said with certainty, turning her lovely eyes on Prince Vasily and her father.

'Nonsense! Fiddlesticks! Stuff and nonsense!' roared the old prince with a great scowl. He took his daughter's hand, pulled her towards him, bent over without kissing her to place his forehead against hers so they were just touching, and squeezed her hand so violently that she winced and cried out. Prince Vasily rose to his feet.

'My dear girl, I must say this is a moment I shall never forget, never, but you are so kind, can you not leave us some small hope of touching such a good and generous heart? Say that perhaps one day . . . The future is so vast . . . Perhaps, one day . . .'

'Prince, I have told you all that is in my heart. You do me honour and I thank you, but I shall never be your son's wife.'

'Well, that's it, my dear fellow. It's been so nice to see you, so nice to see you. Go to your room, Princess, go along now,' said the old prince. 'It's been so nice to see you,' he kept repeating as he embraced Prince Vasily.

'My vocation is different,' Princess Marya was telling herself. 'My happiness will be in other people's happiness, the happiness of love and self-sacrifice. Whatever it costs I must make poor Amélie happy. She is so passionately in love with him. She is so passionately penitent. I shall do all I can to arrange for them to be married. If he's not rich I shall give her some money. I shall ask Father, I shall ask Andrey. I'll be so happy when she is his wife. She is so unhappy now, a stranger, all alone and helpless! Oh Lord, how passionately she must love him to be able to forget herself like that. Who knows, I might have done the same thing! . . .' thought Princess Marya.

CHAPTER 6

It had been some time since the Rostovs had had any news of their little Nikolay. It was mid-winter before one day a letter was handed to Count Rostov with what he recognized as his son's handwriting on the envelope. Letter in hand and dreading the worst, the count tiptoed rapidly off to his room, trying not to be noticed, shut himself in and began to read. Anna Mikhaylovna soon found out about the letter (nothing escaped her in that house) and stole silently in to see the count. She caught him still holding the letter, and simultaneously sobbing and laughing. She still lived with the Rostovs despite the upturn in her fortune.

'My dear friend?' Anna Mikhaylovna inquired gravely, ready to offer any kind of sympathy. This made the count sob more violently.

'Little Nikolay . . . the letter . . . wounded . . . he would . . . he was . . . my dear friend . . . my darling boy . . . wounded . . . my little countess . . . commissioned . . . how can I tell my little countess?'

Anna Mikhaylovna sat down beside him, used her own handkerchief to wipe his eyes and then the tear-stained letter, dried her own tears, read the letter through, reassured the count and decided she would spend the afternoon preparing the countess, and after tea, with God's help, she would tell her everything. Over dinner Anna Mikhaylovna talked about the rumours from the war front and dear little Nikolay. Twice she asked when they had last heard from him, though she knew perfectly well, and then she thought they might well get a letter from him soon, perhaps this very day. Whenever these hints looked as if they were disturbing the countess and she began to direct worried looks first at the count and then Anna Mikhaylovna, Anna adroitly turned the conversation to something trivial. Natasha, who was more sensitive to subtleties of intonation, meaningful glances and facial expressions than anyone else in the family, immediately pricked up her ears and sensed something between her father and Anna Mikhaylovna, something to do with her brother, and she knew that Anna Mikhaylovna was preparing the ground. For all her boldness Natasha knew how touchy her mother was over anything to do with their dear Nikolay, so she decided it was best not to ask any questions over dinner. Not that she could eat anything – she was too excited to eat – she just kept wriggling on her chair, ignoring the protests of her governess. Once dinner was over she hurtled after Anna Mikhaylovna, raced across the sitting-room and flung herself on her neck.

'Auntie, darling, do tell me what's happening!'

'Nothing, my dear.'

'Oh no, you darling, sweet, lovely angel, I won't stop. I know you know something.'

Anna Mikhaylovna shook her head. 'You are a sharp little thing!' she said.

'Is it a letter from dear Nikolay? It is!' cried Natasha, reading an affirmative signal on Anna Mikhaylovna's face.

'Shh, for heaven's sake be careful. You know it could be a real shock for your mother.'

'I will, I will, but tell me about it. You won't? All right, I'll go and tell her now.'

Anna Mikhaylovna told Natasha roughly what was in the letter, on condition that she wouldn't tell anyone.

'On my honour,' said Natasha, crossing herself, 'I won't tell anyone,' and she rushed off to tell Sonya. She broke the news with triumphant delight: 'It's Nikolay . . . wounded . . . a letter . . .'

'Nikolay!' was all Sonya could manage, her face instantly drained of colour. Seeing Sonya so badly affected by the news that her brother had been wounded, Natasha suddenly became aware of the sad side of it all.

She rushed over to Sonya, hugged her and began to cry. 'Lightly wounded, but commissioned as an officer and now he's all right – he says so himself,' she forced out through her tears.

'Oh, I can see you women are all cry-babies,' said Petya, marching boldly up and down the room. 'Me, I'm just glad, very very glad that my brother has distinguished himself. All you can do is blubber about it! You don't understand the first thing about it.'

Natasha smiled through her tears.

'You didn't read the letter, did you?' asked Sonya.

'No, but she said it's all over and he's an officer . . .'

'Thank God for that,' said Sonya, crossing herself. 'But she might not have been telling the truth. Let's go and see Mamma.'

Petya was still marching around the room in silence.

'If I'd been where Nikolay was I'd have killed a lot more Frenchmen,' he said. 'They're a lot of savages! I'd have kept on killing them till they were lying around in heaps,' Petya went on.

'Don't talk like that, Petya, you're being silly!'

'I'm not being silly. Silly people cry when there's nothing to cry about,' said Petya.

'Can you still remember him?' Natasha asked suddenly, after a moment's silence.

Sonya smiled.

'Who, Nikolay?'

'No, Sonya, not just remember him, *really* remember him, everything about him,' said Natasha with an eager gesture, as if wanting to put real strength behind her words. 'I can remember Nikolay, remember him quite well,' she said. 'But I can't remember Boris. I can't remember him at all . . .'

'What do you mean, you can't remember Boris?' Sonya asked in some surprise.

'No, I don't really mean I can't remember him. I know what he's like, but I remember Nikolay much better. I only have to close my eyes and I can see him, but not Boris . . .' (she closed her eyes) 'no, there's nothing there!'

'Oh, Natasha!' said Sonya, looking away, all solemn and serious, as if she thought Natasha was unworthy of what she was now going to say, or as if she was saying it to a different person who was not someone to joke with. 'I have fallen in love with your brother, and whatever happens to him or me I shall never stop loving him for the rest of my life.'

Natasha gazed at Sonya, too surprised and puzzled to speak. She sensed that what Sonya was talking about was true, that such love did exist, only she had never known anything like it. She believed it might happen but she couldn't understand it.

'Are you going to write to him?' she asked. Sonya sank into thought. The question of how she should write to Nikolay, or whether she should write at all, was worrying her. Now that he was an officer and a wounded hero was this the right time for her to remind him that she existed and that he had undertaken certain obligations towards her?

'I really don't know. I suppose if he writes to me I'll write back,' she said, blushing.

'You won't be too embarrassed to write to him?' Sonya smiled.

'No.'

'Oh, I'd be too embarrassed to write to Boris. I'm not going to.'

'Why should you be?'

'I don't know. I just feel awkward and embarrassed.'

'I know why,' said Petya, still stinging from Natasha's earlier comment. 'Because she fell in love with that fat man with the glasses,' (this was what Petya called his namesake, now Count Bezukhov) 'and now she's in love with that there singer,' (meaning Natasha's Italian singing-master) 'that's why she's embarrassed.'

'Petya, you are stupid,' said Natasha.

'No stupider than you, ma'am,' said nine-year-old Petya, for all the world like an elderly brigadier.

The countess had been prepared by Anna Mikhaylovna's hints over dinner. Back in her room she sat down in an armchair to gaze long and hard at the miniature of her son painted on her snuff-box lid, and her eyes were watering. Anna Mikhaylovna now tiptoed over to the countess's room with the letter and stopped at the door.

'Don't you come in,' she said to the old count who was following her. 'You can come in later,' and she closed the door after her. The count put his ear to the keyhole and listened.

At first he could hear them talking about this and that, but then there was only Anna Mikhaylovna's voice speaking and she went on and on until she was interrupted by a little shriek followed by a short silence, and then both voices were talking in tones of delight, then he heard footsteps approaching, and there was Anna Mikhaylovna opening the door. She wore a proud look, like a surgeon who has performed a tricky amputation and now invites the public in to admire his skill.

'It is done,' she announced triumphantly, motioning the count in to see the countess, who with the snuff-box and portrait in one hand and the letter in the other was pressing her lips first to one and then to the other. On seeing the count, she held out both arms to him, embraced his bald head, looked over it at the letter and the portrait, and then pushed the bald head slightly to one side so she could press them to her lips again. Vera, Natasha, Sonya and Petya came into the room, and the reading of the letter began. It contained a brief description of the march, the two battles in which their dear Nikolay had taken part and his promotion, and it said that he kissed the hands of his mamma and papa, asking for their blessing, and sent kisses to Vera, Natasha and Petya. Greetings also to Monsieur Schelling, Madame Schoss and his old nurse, and a special kiss from him to his darling Sonya, whom he still loved and remembered as always. This made Sonya blush till her eyes watered. To get away from the staring eyes, she ran out into the hall, chased about, whirled round and round and then sank to the floor, her skirts ballooning, her face flushed and beaming. The countess was weeping.

'What can you be crying about, Mamma?' asked Vera. 'From what he writes we ought to be celebrating, not crying.'

This was true, of course, but the count and the countess and Natasha all looked at her reproachfully. 'Who does she think she is?' thought the countess.

Nikolay's letter was read out hundreds of times and anyone considered worthy of hearing it had to come in to see the countess, who never let go of it. The tutors went in, the nurses, Mitenka and several acquaintances. Every time the countess read the letter she did so with renewed enjoyment, and every time she discovered new virtues in her dear son, Nikolay. How strange it seemed, how extraordinary and how delightful, to think that her son, the little baby whose tiny limbs had stirred within her twenty years ago, the subject of many a row with the count for spoiling him, that son whose first little words she remembered so well – that son was now far away in a foreign land, in strange surroundings, a war hero, all on his own with no help or guidance, doing a man's job. The age-old experience of people the world over which tells us that babies in their cradles grow up bit by bit into men meant nothing to the countess. Every stage in Nikolay's ascent to manhood had come as a shock to her – it was as if there had never been millions and millions of other men growing up the same way. Twenty years before she couldn't believe that the little creature lying somewhere under her heart would one day cry out and suck her breast and learn to talk, and now she couldn't believe that the same little creature could have turned into such a strong, brave man, an example to all, if his letter was anything to go by.

'Oh, his descriptions! He writes with such *style*!' she said, rereading the descriptive passages. 'And such a dear soul! Not a word about himself . . . not a word! There's a lot about a man called Denisov, though I wouldn't be surprised if he himself was the bravest of them all. He doesn't say anything about his suffering. Such a kind heart! How like him it is! He's thought of everyone! No one forgotten. I've always said it, always, when he was that high I always used to say . . .'

It took them more than a week of hard work on rough drafts and fair copies to compose letters to Nikolay from all the household. Under the eagle eye of the countess and with the count's careful assistance, cash to cover the outfit of a young officer and various necessary items were put together. The pragmatic Anna Mikhaylovna had succeeded in obtaining special patronage for herself and her son while he was in the army, and this even extended to correspondence. Any letters from her could be addressed to the Grand Duke Konstantin, who was in command of the guards. The Rostovs assumed that 'The Russian Guards Serving Abroad' was an adequate address, and if a letter reached the grand duke in command of the guards there was no reason why it shouldn't get through to the Pavlograd regiment, which must surely be serving somewhere not too far away. And so it was decided to send the letters and the money to Boris via the grand duke's special messenger, and it would be up to Boris to have them forwarded to Nikolay. There were letters from the count, the countess, Petya, Vera,

Natasha and Sonya, six thousand roubles for his kitting out and a few other bits and pieces that the count wanted his son to have.

CHAPTER 7

On the 12th of November, Kutuzov's fighting forces were camped near Olmütz, getting ready to be inspected the following day by the two Emperors – of Russia and Austria. The guards, who had only just marched in from Russia, had spent the night ten miles outside Olmütz, and by ten o'clock the next morning they stood ready for inspection in the town square.

That day Nikolay Rostov had received a note from Boris informing him that the Izmailov regiment was bivouacked for the night ten miles outside Olmütz, and he hoped to see him so he could hand over a letter and some money. The money would be particularly welcome just now, with the troops back from the front garrisoned near Olmütz and the camp swarming with well-stocked hawkers and Austrian Jews offering tempting wares of every kind. The Pavlograd hussars had held a string of good dinners celebrating honours received in the field, and not a few trips into Olmütz, where a certain Hungarian lady by the name of Caroline had recently opened a restaurant with girls as waitresses. Rostov was fresh from celebrating his commission as a cornet. He had also bought Denisov's horse, Bedouin, and borrowed extensively from comrades and camp hawkers. On receiving Boris's note, Rostov rode to Olmütz with a friend, had dinner, drank a bottle of wine and then rode on alone to the guards' camp to seek out his childhood friend. Rostov had not yet got his uniform. He was wearing a shabby cadet's jacket with a private's cross, equally shabby riding breeches lined with worn leather, and an officer's sword with the usual ribbon. The Don horse he was riding had been bought from a Cossack during the campaign. He wore a crumpled hussar's cap rakishly shoved back and to one side. As he rode towards the Izmailov camp he was thinking of the fine figure he would cut for Boris and his friends by looking every inch the hussar recently under fire at the front.

The guards had treated their march like a pleasant excursion, flaunting their smartness and discipline. They had come by easy stages, their knapsacks being carried for them in wagons, and at every halt the Austrian government had ensured that the officers dined well. The regiments paraded into and out of every town to the music of a military band, and the guards prided themselves on having followed the grand duke's order to the letter by having the men march in step every inch of the way, with the officers also on foot and properly spaced.

Throughout the march Boris had walked and bivouacked beside Berg, now a captain. Berg, who had been promoted during the march, had ingratiated himself with his superior officers by hard work and a punctilious attitude, and had set up financial arrangements much to his advantage. Boris meanwhile had made a number of useful contacts, and had used a reference from Pierre to make the acquaintance of Prince Andrey Bolkonsky, through whom he aspired to a post on the staff of the commander-in-chief. Well rested from the previous day's march, Berg and Boris were playing chess at a round table in their spotless quarters, nicely turned out in their smart uniforms. Berg had a hookah gripped between his knees. It was Berg's move and without taking his eyes off his opponent's face, Boris was building a neat little pyramid of draughtsmen with his slender white fingers. Totally absorbed in the game, he was as always concentrating on the thing in hand.

'Well, how are you going to get out of that?' he said.

'We'll do what we can,' answered Berg, touching a pawn and immediately taking away his hand.

At that instant the door opened.

'Found you at last!' shouted Rostov. 'And Berg too. Hey you *petizanfan, alley cooshey dormir!*'[4] he cried, mimicking the French of their old nurse – a joke that he had once shared with Boris.

'My, how you've changed!' Boris got up to welcome Rostov, and as he rose, he held on to the board and put back some pieces that had been knocked over. He was about to embrace his friend, but Nikolay drew back. With a young person's dislike of well-trodden ways, the urge to avoid imitation, to express oneself in a personal and original way, not to do the conventional things that older people did, often hypocritically, Nikolay felt like doing something special on meeting his friend. He wanted somehow to pinch his arm or give him a little shove, anything rather than kiss him, which was what people always did on these occasions. Boris was quite the opposite – he embraced Rostov in an easy, friendly manner and gave him the usual three kisses.

They hadn't seen each other for nearly six months. Young as they were, just setting out on life's journey, they now saw immense changes in each other, new reflections of the differing social circumstances in which they had taken their first steps. Both had indeed changed considerably since their last meeting, and both were desperately keen to show just how much they had changed.

'Well, you damned floor-polishers! All neat and tidy as if you've been out for a little stroll,' said Rostov, pointing to his own mud-stained riding breeches. He spoke in a rich baritone and looked a military man, which was new to Boris. The German landlady looked round the door at the sound of Rostov's loud voice.

'Pretty little thing, eh?' said he with a wink.

'You're a bit too loud. It frightens them,' said Boris. 'I didn't expect you today,' he added. 'I only sent the note yesterday – through a friend of mine called Bolkonsky – he's one of Kutuzov's adjutants. I didn't expect him to get it to you so quickly. Well, how are you? You've been under fire, then?' asked Boris.

Instead of answering, Rostov, now the complete soldier, dangled the George Cross hanging from the braid of his uniform, and pointed to his bandaged arm before glancing at Berg with a smile.

'As you see,' he said.

'Yes, indeed,' said Boris, smiling, 'and we have had a splendid march too. You probably know the Tsarevich came along with us all the way, so we did have a few extras and advantages. In Poland – oh, the parties, the dinners, the balls! – I can't begin to tell you. And the Tsarevich was very gracious to all our officers.' And both friends began telling their stories, the one describing the hussars and their high jinks, and then what it was like to be at the front, while the other went on about the pleasures and luxuries of service under people of the highest rank.

'Oh, you guards!' said Rostov. 'Anyway, do send for some wine.' Boris frowned.

'Well, if you really want some,' he said. And he went over to the bed, took a purse out from under the clean pillows and ordered some wine. 'Oh yes, I ought to give you your letter and money,' he added.

Rostov took the letter, threw the money down on the sofa, propped both elbows on the table and started to read. He had only read a line or two when he turned and gave Berg an angry look. Meeting his eyes, Rostov stuck the letter in front of his face.

'I see they sent you a decent lot of money,' said Berg, looking at the heavy purse that sank into the sofa. 'I suppose we just about manage on our pay, Count. Take me, for instance . . .'

'I say, Berg, old fellow,' said Rostov, 'when you get a letter from home and meet somebody close who you want to talk things over with, well, if I'm on the scene I'll clear off straightaway so as not to get in the way. Listen, please go – anywhere, anywhere at all . . . I don't damn well care where you go!' he cried, but then he took Berg by the shoulder, gave him the warmest of looks, obviously keen to soften his rudeness, and added, 'Don't be angry with me, old fellow. I'm just talking straight to someone I've known for a long time.'

'Don't worry, Count, I quite understand,' said Berg, getting to his feet and speaking half to himself in a kind of muffled, throaty growl.

'Go and see the people of the house. You've been invited,' put in Boris.

Berg put on an immaculately clean coat without a mark on it, looked in the mirror to brush his hair up at the temples in the style made fashionable by the Emperor himself, watched Rostov's face until he was sure that his coat had been noticed and left the room with a sweet smile on his face.

'Oh dear, I've behaved like an animal,' said Rostov, turning to the letter.

'What do you mean?'

'Oh, I've been a real swine, not writing, and giving them such a scare. What a swine I am!' he repeated, his face all flushed. 'Anyway, did you send Gavrilo for some wine? Come on, then, let's have a drink!' he said.

The letters from home included a note of recommendation to Prince Bagration, suggested by Anna Mikhaylovna, obtained through various contacts by Countess Rostov and now sent on to her son for him to deliver and make use of.

'Stupid nonsense! A fat lot of good that is,' said Rostov, throwing the letter under the table.

'Why did you throw it away?' asked Boris.

'Oh, it's some sort of reference. What the devil do I need a letter like that for?'

'What the devil do you need it for?' said Boris, picking it up and reading the heading. 'This letter could be very useful to you.'

'I've got everything I need, and I'm not going to be anybody's adjutant.'

'Why not?' asked Boris.

'It's a flunkey's job.'

'Still the great thinker, I see,' said Boris, with a shake of his head.

'And you're still the great diplomat. But that's not the point . . . Anyway, how have you been getting on?' asked Rostov.

'Well, you can see. So far everything's fine, but I don't mind admitting I'd be very glad to make adjutant and not get stuck in the front line.'

'Why?'

'Well, if you go in for a military career you might as well try and make it as brilliant a career as you can.'

'Oh, I see,' said Rostov, obviously miles away. He was staring closely into his friend's eyes, thinking about something else, looking in vain for the solution to some question or other.

Old Gavrila brought in the wine.

'Shall we send for Alphonse now?' said Boris. 'He'll drink with you. I can't.'

'Yes, do. How are you getting on with our Teutonic friend?' asked Rostov, with a disdainful smile.

'He's a very, very nice, decent, pleasant fellow,' said Boris.

Rostov stared again into Boris's face and sighed. Berg came back in, and over a bottle the conversation between the three officers grew animated. The guardsmen told Rostov about their march and how they had been celebrated in Russia, in Poland and abroad. They talked of the sayings and doings of their commander, the grand duke, and told stories about his kind-heartedness and his short temper. Berg held back, as usual, when the subject didn't concern him personally, but when it came to the grand duke's temper he enjoyed telling how he had once fallen foul of the grand duke in Galicia, when his Highness was doing the rounds of the regiments and had got himself worked up over some irregularity in the troop movements. With the same sweet smile on his face he described how the grand duke had ridden up to him in a towering rage, shouting 'Arnauts!' (this insult, normally reserved for Albanians serving in the Turkish army, being the Tsarevich's favourite term of abuse when he lost his temper) . . . and how he had asked for the captain . . . 'Believe it or not, Count, I wasn't terribly bothered because I knew I was in the right. I don't mean to boast, you understand, Count, but I think I can claim to know the regimental rule-book backwards, and the standing orders too. I know them as well as I know the Lord's Prayer. So you see, Count, in my company nothing gets overlooked. And I had nothing on my conscience. So I stepped forward.' (Berg stood up and rehearsed how he had come forward with his hand at the salute. You couldn't have imagined anything more deferential on a man's face – or anything more confident.) 'Well, then he laid into me, on and on for dear life – dear death for me – yelling "Arnauts!", "Damn and blast!", "Siberia!"' said Berg, with a knowing smile. 'I knew I was in the right so I kept quiet – wouldn't you have done, Count? "Have you lost your tongue?" he roared at me. I just kept quiet and – you know what, Count? – next day there wasn't a word about it in the orders of the day. It just shows – all you have to do is keep cool,' said Berg, pulling at his pipe and sending up smoke rings.

'Oh yes, well done,' said Rostov with a smile, but Boris could see that Rostov was preparing to make fun of Berg so he shrewdly changed the subject by asking Rostov to tell them how and where he had been wounded. That pleased Rostov and he launched into his story, getting more and more excited as he told it. His version of the battle at Schöngrabern was the usual version of a man who has been in a battle: he tells it as he would have liked it to have been, or as described by someone else, or in a version that just sounds good, anything but the way it really happened. Rostov was an honest young man who would never tell a deliberate lie. He set out with every intention of describing exactly what had occurred, but imperceptibly, unconsciously and inevitably he drifted into falsehood. If he had told the truth to these two, who had heard as many descriptions of cavalry charges as he had, had their own clear idea of what a charge was like and were expecting something similar, either they wouldn't have believed him, or worse still, they would have assumed it was Rostov's fault for not managing to do what was normally done by narrators of cavalry charges. He couldn't just tell them that they'd been trotting forward together when he fell off his horse, sprained his arm and then ran as hard as he could into a wood to get away from a Frenchman. Besides, to tell everything exactly as it happened would have demanded enough self-control to say only what happened and nothing else. To tell the truth is a very difficult thing, and young people are hardly ever capable of it. His listeners were expecting to hear him describe how he had felt himself burning with excitement, stormed the enemy's square defences, oblivious to everything, hacked his way in, mown men down right, left and centre, tasted blood with his sabre before collapsing from exhaustion, and all the rest. And that's what he did describe.

He was in mid-story and had got to the point where he was saying, 'You can't imagine that feeling of fury during the charge,' when in walked Prince Andrey Bolkonsky, whom Boris had been expecting. Prince Andrey liked to help and encourage younger men and was flattered when they wanted his patronage. He was well disposed to Boris, who had impressed him the day before, and he was now keen to do whatever the young man wanted him to do. Fresh from delivering some documents from Kutuzov to the Tsarevich, he had called in on Boris, hoping to find him alone. When he came into the room and saw the hussar holding forth about his exploits in the field (Prince Andrey couldn't stand the kind of man who liked doing this), he gave Boris a warm smile, but frowned and screwed up his features as he turned to Rostov with a slight bow. He then eased his tired body languidly down on to a sofa, regretting that he had dropped in on such disagreeable company. Rostov saw all this and flared up, but it didn't matter – this man was nothing to him. One glance at Boris told him that he too seemed embarrassed by the battle-scarred hussar. Despite Prince Andrey's offhand, sneering manner, and the contempt in which Rostov, a fighting man who knew what action was, held staff adjutants in general – and the newcomer was clearly one of them – he still felt embarrassed, blushed and stopped talking. Boris inquired what the latest news was at staff headquarters – without being indiscreet surely he could say something about future developments.

'They seem likely to advance,' answered Bolkonsky, clearly reluctant to say more in front of other people. Berg took the opportunity to ask with great deference whether the company captains' forage allowance was to be doubled as he had heard. To this Prince Andrey replied with a smile that he could offer no opinion on such vital matters of state, and Berg laughed with delight.

'Oh, about that little matter of yours,' said Prince Andrey turned back to Boris, 'we'll have a word later,' and he glanced at Rostov. 'Come and see me after the inspection and we'll see what can be done.' Then looking around the room he picked out Rostov, who was in a desperate state of childish pique bordering on truculence which until now he had seen fit to ignore. 'I believe you were talking about Schöngrabern? Were you there?'

'Yes I was,' Rostov said aggressively – an obvious insult to the adjutant. Bolkonsky could see the state he was in, and it seemed to amuse him. There was mockery in his smile.

'Oh yes, they do go on about that engagement, don't they?'

'Yes they do!' said Rostov in a loud voice, glaring at Boris as well as Bolkonsky with sudden fury in his eyes. 'Maybe they do go on a bit, but the ones who are going on about it are men who've been under fire, they have something to go on about, not like nobodies on the staff who pick up honours for doing nothing.'

'A category to which you assume I belong,' said Prince Andrey, with a relaxed manner and a particularly pleasant smile.

Rostov felt moved by a strange feeling of hostility tempered with respect for the tranquil bearing of this person.

'Well, I don't know about you,' he said. 'I don't know you, and frankly I don't want to. I'm talking about staff officers in general.'

'Just let me say this,' Prince Andrey interrupted in a tone of quiet authority. 'You're doing your best to insult me, and I must accept it's not a hard thing to do if you are going to go on showing your own lack of self-respect. But I'm sure you'll agree this is neither the time nor the place for a squabble. In a few days' time we shall be taking part in a real duel much more serious than this, and incidentally, Boris

Drubetskoy tells me he's an old friend of yours – it's not his fault that you don't like the look of my face. Anyway,' he said, getting up, 'you know who I am and where you can find me. And don't forget,' he added, 'I don't consider either of us to have been insulted. My advice to you, as an older man, is to let the matter drop. So – Friday, then, after the inspection, I'll be expecting you, Drubetskoy. Goodbye till then,' Prince Andrey concluded, and he went out, bowing to them both.

By the time Rostov thought of a suitable answer he had gone, and he was all the more livid for not having thought of it in time. He had his horse brought round at once, took leave of Boris coldly and rode off. What should he do – ride over to headquarters tomorrow and challenge that stuck-up adjutant, or really let the matter drop? The question worried him all the way back. One moment he thought vindictively how much pleasure he would take in scaring that over-bearing feeble little shrimp with his pistol, and the next he was surprised to find himself thinking there was no one he would rather have as a friend than that insufferable adjutant.

CHAPTER 8

The day after Rostov's visit to Boris there was to be a general review of the troops, Austrian and Russian, including the reinforcements freshly arrived from Russia and the troops back from campaigning with Kutuzov. The Russian Emperor was accompanied by his heir, the Tsarevich, and the Austrian by the archduke, and together they were to review the allied forces, an army of eighty thousand men. From early morning the troops, all spick and span, had begun moving out on to the plain before the fortress and lining up. Banners flapped in the breeze, legs marched and bayonets moved in thousands, halting at the word of command, turning, forming up and spacing out, blocks of infantry in different uniforms wheeling around each other. The cavalry jingled into position with a steady clip-clop, smartly turned out in blue, red and green braided uniforms and riding black, chestnut and grey horses, the bandsmen in front covered with frills. Between the infantry and the cavalry came the artillery, a long line of buffed and gleaming cannons trembling on their carriages, clanging as they trundled past, linstocks reeking, and rolled into their appointed places. Not only the generals in full dress uniform with scarves and medals, all of them, fat or thin, impossibly squeezed in at the waist, and with red necks squashed into stiff collars; not only the pomaded, dandified officers, but every last well-scrubbed and clean-shaven soldier with his weapons buffed to the last degree of brilliance, every horse groomed till its coat shone like stain, with every hair lying true on its dampened mane – all of them felt they were doing something profound, solemn and serious. Every general and every soldier was aware of his own insignificance, like a tiny grain of sand in an ocean of humanity, yet as a part of that vast whole they sensed a huge collective strength. Since early morning it had been all tension, bustle and hard work, but by ten o'clock everything was in place. Serried ranks of soldiers stood upon the vast plain, an entire army stretched out in three lines: cavalry in front, artillery next, infantry at the rear.

The different branches of service were separated by gaps almost as wide as streets, and the army was sharply divided into three sections: Kutuzov's men (with the Pavlograd hussars front right), the newly arrived line-regiments and guards, and the Austrian troops. But they all stood in a single line, under a single command, and in similar order.

Like a wind rustling the leaves a murmur of excitement swept through the ranks. 'They're here! They're here!' nervous voices called out, and the troops stirred with a flurry of finishing touches.

A group of horsemen came into sight moving towards them from Olmütz, and at that very moment, although there hadn't been any wind before, a faint breeze fluttered over the army, stirring the streamers on the lances and setting the unfurled colours flapping against their staffs. It was as if the army were quivering with joy as the Emperors approached. A single voice called out, 'Atten-shun!' Other voices took up the call like cockerels crowing at dawn. Then silence.

The deathly stillness was broken only by the clip-clop of hooves. It was the Emperors and their suite. As the two monarchs rode up to one flank, the trumpets of the first cavalry regiment struck up a military march. The sound appeared not to come from the buglers but as a spontaneous burst of music from the army itself, delighted at the Emperors' arrival. Through the music only one voice could be heard clearly, the genial, youthful tones of Emperor Alexander. He gave a few words of greeting, and the first regiment roared out, 'Hurrah!' The sound was so deafening, so prolonged and ecstatic that the men themselves felt a great shock, realizing the strength and enormity of their mass.

Rostov was standing in the front ranks of Kutuzov's army, those which the Tsar approached first, and he was seized by the same feeling as every other soldier in that army, a feeling of utter self-forgetfulness, a proud sense of mighty power and a passionate devotion to the man who was the cause of this sensation of solemn triumph.

Feeling as he did that at a single word from this man the entire vast mass of them (including him, no more than a grain of sand) would go through fire and water, commit any crime, face death or fight on to glory, he could not suppress a shivering thrill at the immanency of that word.

'Hurrah! Hurrah! Hurrah!' thundered on all sides, and one regiment after another greeted the Tsar with the strains of the march followed by another 'Hurrah!' . . . then the music again, then more and more hurrahs surging louder and expanding until they merged into one solid, deafening roar.

Waiting for the Tsar, each regiment in its rigid silence seemed like a lifeless body. But once the Tsar reached them each regiment erupted in new life and further clamour, joining in unison with the general roar from all down the line where the Tsar had been. And to the dreadful sound of these shattering cheers, moving in and out among the great rectangles of massed troops standing rigidly to attention as if turned to stone, some hundreds of men rode about casually, freely, defying all symmetry. These were the officers in the royal suite, and ahead of them rode two men, the Emperors, on whom the uncontainable passion of all that mass of men was focused.

It was Emperor Alexander, young and handsome in the uniform of the horse guards with a cocked hat, who attracted most of the attention because of his pleasant face and his soft rich voice.

Rostov was standing near the buglers, and with his keen eyes he spotted the Tsar a long way off and watched him approaching. When the Tsar was only twenty paces away and Nikolay could clearly see every detail of Alexander's handsome, young and happy face, he experienced a surge of emotion and ecstasy such as he had never known before. Everything about the Tsar – every feature, every movement – seemed to him utterly captivating.

Coming to a halt before the Pavlograd regiment, the Tsar said something in French to the Austrian Emperor and smiled. Seeing him smile, Rostov automatically began to smile himself and felt an even stronger spasm of love for his Emperor. He longed for some means of expressing his love for the Tsar. His eyes watered from knowing it was impossible. The Tsar called up the colonel of the regiment and said a few words to him.

'My God! What would I do if the Emperor spoke to me?' thought Rostov. 'I think I'd die of happiness.'

The Tsar addressed the officers, too.

'I thank you all, gentlemen,' he said, every word sounding to Rostov like music from heaven, 'I thank you from the bottom of my heart.'

Rostov would have gladly died there and then for his Emperor.

'You have won the colours of St George and you will be worthy of them.'

'Oh, if only I could die for him, die for him!' thought Rostov.

The Tsar said something else that Rostov couldn't hear, and the men, lungs bursting, roared their hurrah.

Rostov, too, thrusting forward in his saddle, roared with all his might, willing to do himself an injury cheering, as long as he could give full voice to his zeal for the Tsar.

The Tsar stood for a few seconds facing the hussars as if wondering what to do next.

'How could the Emperor wonder what to do next?' Rostov asked himself, but then sure enough, even this hesitation seemed to him majestic and enchanting, like everything the Tsar did.

The Tsar's hesitation lasted only an instant. Then the royal foot in its fashionable narrow-pointed boot touched the belly of his bobtailed chestnut mare. The royal hand in its white glove gathered up the reins, and he moved off, accompanied by a sea of aides bobbing up and down. He moved further and further away, stopping at other regiments, until eventually all that Rostov could see of him through the suite surrounding the Emperors was the white plume of his cocked hat.

Among the gentlemen of the suite, Rostov noticed Bolkonsky, sitting in a slack, indolent pose. Rostov remembered yesterday's quarrel and again wondered whether or not to challenge him. 'Of course not,' Rostov reflected. 'How could anyone even think or talk about such things at a time like this? A time of such love, such bliss, such self-sacrifice, what do our insults and squabbles matter? This is a time when I love everybody and forgive everybody,' thought Rostov.

When the Tsar had inspected almost all the regiments, the troops began their march past, and Rostov, bringing up the rear on Bedouin, so recently bought from Denisov, was the last rider in his squadron, and completely exposed to the Tsar's view.

Still some distance away from him, Rostov, a first-class horseman, twice put his spurs to Bedouin, urging him into the frenzied, eye-catching trot which Bedouin always fell into when he was worked up. Bending his foaming nose down to his chest, arching his tail, virtually floating in mid-air without touching the ground, Bedouin seemed no less conscious of the Tsar's eye upon him as he lifted his legs in a graceful high action, trotting past in superb style.

Rostov himself drew his legs back and sucked his stomach in, very much at one with his horse, and rode past the Tsar with a frowning but ecstatic face, looking a 'wight devil', as Denisov would have said.

'Bravo, Pavlograds!' shouted the Tsar.

'My God! I'd be so happy if he ordered me to go through fire here and now,' thought Rostov.

When the review was over the officers of both groups, the reinforcements and Kutuzov's men, began to break down into little clusters. The talk was of honours won, the Austrians and their uniforms, their front line, Napoleon and the trouble in store for him once Essen's corps arrived and Prussia came in on our side. But the main topic of conversation in every circle was Emperor Alexander, his every word and gesture recalled with huge delight.

They were united in a single desire: under the Emperor's leadership to march on the enemy at the earliest opportunity. With the Emperor himself in command they could not fail to conquer any foe – this was the opinion of Rostov and most of the officers after the review. After the review they all felt more confident of victory than they would have done if they'd had a couple of victories behind them.

CHAPTER 9

The day after the inspection Boris Drubetskoy donned his best uniform and rode into Olmütz, bolstered by his comrade Berg's best wishes, to see Bolkonsky, hoping to take advantage of his good relationship with him to improve his own position by becoming an adjutant to some person of significance, an army post that he saw as particularly attractive.

'It's all right for Rostov with a father who keeps sending him the odd ten thousand to talk about not sucking up to people and not being anybody's flunkey. I'm not like him – I've got to rely on my brains and I have a career to make. I can't afford to miss any opportunities. I've got to take them when they come.'

He didn't find Prince Andrey in Olmütz that day. But the very sight of the town where the staff headquarters and the diplomatic corps were based and where both Emperors were staying with their suites, household and court, only served to reinforce his desire to belong to this elevated world.

He didn't know anybody there, and in spite of his stylish guardsman's uniform, all these exalted persons scurrying up and down the streets in their fine carriages, plumes, ribbons and medals – courtiers and military men – seemed to be so infinitely far above him, a little guards officer, that they were not so much reluctant to recognize his existence as simply unaware of it. At the quarters of the commander-in-chief, Kutuzov, where he asked for Bolkonsky, all the aides and even the orderlies looked at him as though they wished to impress on him that there were always plenty of officers like him hanging around and they were all heartily sick of seeing them. Despite this, or rather because of it, he went back the following day, the 15th, after dinner, walked into the house occupied by Kutuzov and asked for Bolkonsky. Prince Andrey was in, and Boris was shown into a large room probably once used for dancing though now it contained five beds and various other pieces of furniture: a table, some chairs and a clavier. One adjutant was sitting near the door dressed in a Persian dressing gown, writing at a table. Another, the stout, red-faced Nesvitsky, was lying on a bed with his arms under his head, sharing a joke with an officer sitting at his side. A third was playing a Viennese waltz on the clavier, while a fourth leant on the instrument, humming along. Bolkonsky wasn't there. These gentlemen saw Boris come in, but not one of them moved. Boris approached the one who was writing, and he turned round looking irritated and said that Bolkonsky was the duty adjutant, and if he wanted to see him he should go through the door on the left into the reception-room. Boris thanked him, and did as instructed. In the reception-room he found a dozen men, officers and generals.

When Boris entered Prince Andrey was wincing disdainfully (with the air of polite weariness which so clearly says, 'If I was off duty I wouldn't waste a minute of my time talking to you'), as he listened to an old Russian general weighed down with medals, who was standing there rigidly almost on tiptoe, red in the face, expounding something to Prince Andrey and looking as obsequious as any common soldier.

'Very good, if you'll kindly wait for a moment,' he said to the general in Russian but with the French accent that he always adopted when he wanted to speak scornfully, and once he saw Boris, Prince Andrey ignored the general (who came trotting along begging him to listen because he had more to say) and nodded to Boris with a bright smile as he turned towards him. At that moment Boris clearly saw what he had always suspected, that in the army, alongside the ranking and discipline written into the manuals, recognized throughout the regiment and known to him personally, there was a different order of ranking, a more important one, that could force this rigid, red-faced general to stand and wait politely while Prince Andrey – a mere captain – found it pleasant and convenient to have a chat with Lieutenant

Drubetskoy. Boris felt all the more determined that from now on he was going to follow not the written code laid down in the regulations, but the unwritten one. He sensed that just by being recommended to Prince Andrey he was one up on the general, who in another setting, say at the front, could have annihilated him, a mere lieutenant. Prince Andrey came over and shook hands.

'I'm so sorry you didn't find me in yesterday. I was busy all day with the Germans. I went out with Weierother to check the disposition. You know what Germans are like about details – they go on for ever!'

Boris smiled, as if he understood as a matter of common knowledge what Prince Andrey was talking about. But it was the first time he'd heard the name Weierother, and he didn't know what 'disposition' meant in this context.

'Well, my dear fellow, I assume you still want to be an adjutant. I've been thinking about that since we last met.'

'Yes,' said Boris, colouring for some reason, 'I was thinking of asking the commander-in-chief. He's had a letter about me from Prince Kuragin. I wanted to ask because,' he added, apparently by way of an apology, 'I'm afraid the guards won't be in action.'

'Splendid! Splendid! We can talk about this in a minute,' said Prince Andrey. 'Just let me deal with this gentleman and I'm all yours.' While Prince Andrey was away reporting to the commander-in-chief on behalf of the red-faced general, the general himself – he seemed not to share Boris's views on the superiority of the unwritten code – glared so fiercely at the impertinent lieutenant who had stopped him saying his piece that Boris felt embarrassed. He turned away and waited impatiently for Prince Andrey to emerge from the commander-in-chief's room.

'Yes, old fellow, I have been thinking about you – along these lines,' said Prince Andrey, when they had gone into the big room with the clavier in it. 'It's no good going to the commander-in-chief. He'll be very nice to you, and invite you to dinner,' ('which wouldn't come amiss in the service of that unwritten code,' thought Boris) 'but nothing would come of it. Adjutants, staff officers – we'll soon have our own battalion. But I'll tell you what we can do. I have a friend who is an adjutant general, an excellent fellow – Prince Dolgorukov. And you may not know it, but the fact is – Kutuzov, his staff, the whole lot of us don't count for anything now. Everything's concentrated around the Emperor. So let's pay a visit to Dolgorukov. I need to see him, and I've already told him about you. We'll be able to see whether he can find you a job on his staff, or somewhere else closer to the sun.'

Prince Andrey was always invigorated by guiding a young man and helping him on in the world. This propensity for helping other people – the kind of help he would have been too proud ever to accept for himself – kept him in close touch with the circle which had success in its gift, and which he found attractive. Only too pleased to take up Boris's cause, he took him to see Prince Dolgorukov.

It was late evening when they entered the palace in Olmütz which was occupied by the two Emperors, each with his entourage. Earlier that day a council of war had been held, attended by the members of the Hofkriegsrath and the two Emperors. They had decided to ignore the advice of the older generation, Kutuzov and Prince Schwartzenberg, to advance immediately and mount a general offensive against Napoleon. The council of war had just finished when Prince Andrey walked into the palace with Boris to see Prince Dolgorukov. All the staff at headquarters were still under the spell of today's triumph by the younger party at the council. The voices of delay that said wait, do not advance, had been so unanimously shouted down and their arguments refuted by such convincing evidence of the advantages to be gained from an attack that the main business of the council, the coming battle and certain victory, seemed to belong not to the future but to the past. All the advantages were on our side. Our immense forces, undoubtedly superior to Napoleon's, were concentrated in one place, morale had been raised by the presence of the two Emperors and they were straining to go. The commander of the troops, the Austrian general Weierother, knew the overall battle plan in minute detail. As it happened, the Austrian forces had been on manoeuvres last year on the very terrain where they were now proposing to fight the French, and every feature of the locality was known and mapped. Napoleon, meanwhile, was evidently weakened and doing precisely nothing.

Dolgorukov, who had been one of the most passionate advocates of attack, had just come back from the council, weary and exhausted, but excited and proud of his victory. Prince Andrey introduced his protégé, but although Prince Dolgorukov shook hands politely and warmly, he said nothing to Boris, and, obviously unable to contain the thoughts which now obsessed him, he spoke to Prince Andrey in French.

'Well, my dear fellow, what a battle we have won! I pray to God that what happens next will be just as victorious. Anyway, my dear fellow,' he blurted out in his enthusiasm, 'I must admit I owe them an apology, the Austrians, and especially Weierother. The accuracy, the eye for detail, the knowledge of the locality, the anticipation of everything, every development, every last point! No, my dear fellow, better

conditions than these could never have been devised. Austrian planning combined with Russian courage – what more could you want?'

'So we definitely are going to attack?' said Bolkonsky.

'And do you know, old fellow, I'm sure Napoleon doesn't know
what day it is. Did you know the Emperor heard from him today?'
Dolgorukov gave a knowing smile.

'No! What did he say?' asked Bolkonsky.

'What could he say? Tiddly-om-pom-pom or words to that effect –
he's just playing for time. I tell you we've got him, haven't we? Oh,
but you've not heard the funniest bit,' he said with a burst of friendly
laughter. 'They couldn't think what to call him when they wrote back.
Not "Consul", definitely not "Emperor" – I think I'd have said "To
General Bonaparte".'

'But there's a world of difference between refusing to recognize him
as Emperor and calling him General Bonaparte,' said Bolkonsky.

'That's the point,' Dolgorukov burbled on, still laughing. 'You know
Bilibin – such a bright fellow – he suggested addressing it, "To the
Usurper and Enemy of Humanity".' Dolgorukov roared with happy
laughter.

'And that was it?' observed Bolkonsky.

'Well no, Bilibin thought up a proper form of address. He lives by
his wit, and his wits.'

'What was it?'

'"To the Head of the French Government",' said Dolgorukov
with some satisfaction, now speaking seriously. 'That's quite good,
isn't it?'

'Yes, very good. He's bound to hate it,' observed Bolkonsky.

'I'll say he will! My brother knows him, he's had dinner with him
– the Emperor we should call him nowadays – more than once in
Paris, and he used to tell me he'd never seen a sharper and more crafty
diplomat – you know, a combination of French finesse and Italian
showmanship! You know all those stories about Napoleon and Count
Markov? Count Markov was the only man who had the measure of
him. Have you heard the one about the handkerchief? It's a gem!'

Dolgorukov was now in full flood and kept turning from Boris to
Prince Andrey as he told his story: to test our ambassador, Markov,
Napoleon deliberately dropped his handkerchief in front of him and
stood watching, probably expecting Markov to pick it up for him, but
Markov just dropped his own handkerchief beside it and then picked
it up again without touching Bonaparte's.

'Lovely story,' said Bolkonsky. 'But listen, Prince, I've come to ask
a favour for my young friend here. It's like this . . .' But before Prince

Andrey could finish, an adjutant came into the room to summon Prince
Dolgorukov to the Emperor.

'Oh, how infuriating!' said Dolgorukov, getting up hurriedly and
shaking hands with Prince Andrey and Boris. 'Count on me to do
everything I can for both of you, you and this charming young man.'
Once more he shook hands with Boris with a look of genuine good
will, for all his distracted excitement. 'But you see how things are . . .
Some other time!'

Boris was transported by the very thought of being at that moment
so close to the highest authorities. He was suddenly aware that he was
in direct contact with the mainsprings that regulated all those vast
movements of the masses in which he in his regiment felt himself
playing such a tiny, humble, insignificant part. They followed Prince
Dolgorukov out into the corridor where they came across (coming out
of a door to the Tsar's room where Dolgorukov went in) a short man
in civilian clothing with a bright face and a jaw that jutted out, not
spoiling his face but giving him a sharp and rather wily look. This
short man nodded to Dolgorukov as if they were close friends, but
stared icily at Prince Andrey and walked straight towards him, apparently expecting him to bow or give way. Prince Andrey did neither.
There was a nasty look on his face, and it was the short young man
who stepped aside and walked off down one side of the corridor.

'Who was that?' asked Boris.

'He's a very remarkable man – and very unpleasant to me. It's the
Minister of Foreign Affairs, Prince Adam Czartoryski. He's the kind
of man,' added Bolkonsky with an uncontainable sigh as they left the
palace, 'he's the kind of man who decides the fates of nations.'

Next day the troops were on the march, and Boris had no opportunity of seeing Bolkonsky or Dolgorukov again before the battle of
Austerlitz. For the time being he would stay with the Izmailov
regiment.

CHAPTER 10

At dawn on the 16th the squadron in which Nikolay Rostov was
serving under Denisov (part of Prince Bagration's detachment) moved
on after a good night's sleep and was told it was going into action.
After marching the best part of a mile behind other columns they were
halted on the highway, and Rostov watched as many troops went on

past them – the Cossacks, the first and second squadrons of hussars, infantry battalions with artillery, even the two generals, Bagration and Dolgorukov, and their adjutants. All the dread of battle that had been building up in him again, all the inner conflict which had enabled him to overcome that dread, all his dreams of personal glory in this battle as a fighting hussar – all of this now counted for nothing. His squadron was held back in reserve, and Nikolay Rostov spent a tedious and miserable day. It was still not quite nine o'clock in the morning when he heard firing and loud cheers up ahead, then he saw some wounded men being brought back (not many of them) and finally he watched a whole detachment of French cavalry being brought in surrounded by a Cossack unit. It was clear that the action was over, and no less clear that the action had been small-scale but successful. The returning soldiers and officers spoke of a brilliant victory in which the town of Wischau had been seized and a whole French squadron taken prisoner. It was a bright and sunny day following a sharp overnight frost, and the cheery autumn sunshine went well with the news of victory coming from the participants but also visible on the happy faces of soldiers, officers, generals and adjutants riding up and down in front of Nikolay Rostov. It rankled with him all the more that he had fought down his dread of battle only to spend that whole happy day doing nothing.

'Hey, Wostov, come over here! Let's dwink to dwown our sow-wow!' called Denisov from the roadside where he was sitting with a bottle and some food. The officers had gathered around Denisov's hamper for a drink and a bite to eat.

'Here comes another one!' said one of the officers, pointing to a French prisoner, a dragoon, being brought in on foot by two Cossacks. One of them was leading his horse, a big, beautiful French charger.

'Sell us your horse!' Denisov called out to the Cossacks.

'Yes, sir.'

The officers got up and surrounded the Cossacks and the prisoner. The French dragoon was a young boy from Alsace who spoke French with a German accent. Red in the face and breathless with excitement, once he heard the French language he began jabbering at all of the officers, all of them one after another. He said he wouldn't have been caught, it wasn't his fault that he had been, it was the corporal's fault, he'd sent him for some horse-cloths, though he had told him the Russians were there. And all the time he kept on stroking his charger and saying, 'Please don't let them hurt my little horse.' He obviously had no idea where he was. One minute he was apologizing for having been taken prisoner, the next he was trying to prove to imaginary superior officers what a good, keen serving soldier he was. He was wafting over to us in the rearguard the full flavour of the French army, which we found utterly alien.

The Cossacks sold the horse for two gold pieces, and since Rostov was currently the richest officer, having just received money from home, he bought it.

'Please don't hurt my little horse!' the Alsatian said lovingly to Rostov as the horse was handed over.

Rostov reassured the dragoon with a smile and gave him some money.

'Alley! Alley!' said one of the Cossacks, plucking the prisoner by the arm to make him walk on.

'The Tsar's coming! It's him!' came a sudden call among the hussars. There was a frenzied scurrying and Rostov saw several horsemen with white plumes in their hats, riding up the road towards them. Everyone snapped into place and stood waiting.

Rostov had no sense or recollection of rushing to his post and getting on his horse. His disappointment at missing the battle disappeared in a flash, along with his jaded mood among familiar faces. All thought of self had vanished – he was totally absorbed in the blissful feeling brought on by the Emperor's approach, which was more than enough to compensate for a lost day. He was as happy as a lover when at last he meets his beloved. Too scared to glance down the line and without needing to, he thrilled to the sense of *his* approach. And he sensed it not only from the clip-clop of the coming cavalcade, he felt it because as the Tsar came nearer the atmosphere around him brightened with joy, purpose and celebration. Nearer and nearer moved this sun (as Rostov saw him), radiating its gentle, majestic light on every side until he felt himself enfolded in that radiance and heard *that* voice – so caressing, serene, majestic, and yet so simple. A deathly silence fell, which Rostov sensed as right and proper. Through it came the sound of the Tsar's voice.

'Are you the Pavlograd hussars?' came his inquiry.

'The reserve, sire,' replied a voice, so down to earth after the supernatural voice that had uttered the words, 'Are you the Pavlograd hussars?'

The Tsar came alongside Rostov and stopped. Alexander's face was even finer than at the inspection three days before. It glowed with the boyish delight and youthful innocence of a giddy fourteen-year-old, yet it was still the face of a majestic emperor. Glancing casually along the squadron, the Tsar's eyes met Rostov's, and lingered there not more than two seconds. Whether or not the Tsar could tell what was happening in the depths of Rostov's soul (and Rostov was almost sure that he could), he did stare into Rostov's face for two solid seconds, with his blue eyes emitting a soft and gentle radiance. Then with a sudden jerk of his eyebrows he stabbed his left foot sharply back into his horse, galloped off and was gone.

Once he had heard firing from the front the young Emperor couldn't resist the temptation to go and watch the fighting, so at twelve o'clock, ignoring all protests from his courtiers, he had left the escorting third column and ridden towards the vanguard. Before he could catch up with the hussars, however, several adjutants met him with news of the engagement and its successful outcome.

The engagement, such as it was, had resulted in the capture of a French squadron and this had been built up into a brilliant victory over the enemy. With the smoke still hanging over the battlefield the Tsar and the entire army believed that the French had been routed and forced to retreat. A few minutes after the Tsar had gone by, the Pavlograd hussar division was called forward. In Wischau itself, a little German town, Rostov caught another glimpse of the Tsar. In the marketplace, which had seen a sharp exchange of fire just before the Tsar's arrival, lay several dead and wounded soldiers who had not yet been picked up. Surrounded by his officers and courtiers, the Tsar was mounted on another bobtailed chestnut mare, not the one he had ridden to inspect the troops. Bending to one side with a graceful gesture and holding a gold lorgnette to his eyes, he was staring at a soldier lying face-down with blood all over his uncovered head. The wounded man looked so filthy, disgusting and ghastly that Rostov was deeply offended by his closeness to the Emperor. Rostov saw the Tsar's stooping shoulders shudder, as if from an icy tremor, at which his left foot jerked spasmodically, driving its spur into the horse's side, but the well-trained animal just looked around indifferently without moving an inch. Adjutants dismounted and went to lift the soldier under the arms to lay him on a stretcher that had suddenly appeared. The soldier gave a groan.

'Steady, steady! Can't you do it more gently?' said the Tsar, who seemed to be suffering more than the dying soldier, and he rode away.

Rostov had seen tears in the Tsar's eyes and he heard him say to Czartoryski in French as he rode off, 'What a terrible thing war is, what a terrible thing!'

The advance troops were positioned outside Wischau in sight of the enemy line, which had spent the whole day retreating before us at the slightest sign of firing. The Tsar's thanks were conveyed to the vanguard, rewards were promised and a double ration of vodka was issued to the men. The campfires crackled even more merrily than the previous night, and everywhere soldiers were singing. Tonight Denisov was celebrating his promotion to major, and as the party drew on, a less than sober Nikolay Rostov proposed a toast to the Emperor. 'Not just "to our Sovereign the Emperor", as they say at official dinners,' he said, 'but to our Emperor, a good man, a charming man, a great man. Here's to him, and certain defeat for the French!'

'If we fought before,' he said, 'and wouldn't give them an inch, as we did at Schöngrabern, what will happen now with him at our head? We'll die, gladly die for him, every last one of us. What do you say, gentlemen? Perhaps I'm not saying it right – I've drunk quite a bit – but anyway that's how I feel, and so do you. I give you Alexander the First! Hurrah!'

His cheer was echoed by a fervent roar from the officers. And old Captain Kirsten roared as wildly and sincerely as the twenty-year-old Rostov.

When the officers had drunk the toast and smashed their glasses, Kirsten poured out some more, and then went off in his shirt sleeves and riding breeches, stopping at the soldiers' campfires and standing there with his long grey whiskers, glass in hand, waving his arm in a majestic stance, his chest gleaming white in the firelight through his open shirt.

'Here you are, boys, I give you our Sovereign the Emperor and victory over the enemy! Hurrah!' he roared in his old hussar's baritone.

The hussars crowded around, responding warmly with a great roar of their own.

Late that night, when they had all gone off, Denisov clapped his young favourite, Rostov, on the shoulder with his little hand. 'There we have it. No one to fall in love with in the field, so Wostov falls in love with the Tsar,' he said.

'Denisov, don't joke about it,' cried Rostov, 'it's such a noble and wonderful feeling, it's . . .'

'Quite wight, quite wight, my dear fellow, I agwee, I appwove . . .'

'No, you just don't understand!' And Rostov got up and walked off to wander among the campfires, dreaming of how blissful it would be to die – not saving the Emperor's life, which he wouldn't dare to dream of – but just to die, there, before the Emperor's eyes.

He had, of course, fallen in love with the Tsar and Russian military honour and the hope of future glory. And he was not alone in these sentiments during those memorable days in the run up to the battle of Austerlitz. At that moment nine-tenths of all the men in the Russian army were in love, albeit less ecstatically, with their Tsar and Russian military honour.

CHAPTER 11

Next day the Tsar stayed in Wischau. His physician, Villier, was summoned to see him several times. At headquarters and among the troops stationed near by the word went round that the Tsar was ill. Those close to him reported that he had had nothing to eat and had slept badly. The cause of this indisposition was said to be the terrible shock suffered by the Tsar, with his sensitive soul, at the sight of the dead and wounded.

At dawn on the 17th a French officer was escorted into Wischau from our forward positions under a flag of truce for a meeting with the Russian Emperor. This officer was Savary. The Tsar had only just fallen asleep, so Savary had to wait. At midday he was allowed in to see the Emperor, and an hour later he rode back to the French army outposts, taking Prince Dolgorukov with him. Rumour had it that Savary had been sent to propose peace and a meeting between Alexander and Napoleon. A private meeting was refused, much to the pride and delight of the entire army, and instead of the Tsar Prince Dolgorukov, the victorious general at Wischau, was dispatched with Savary for talks with Napoleon to discover whether such exchanges – contrary to all expectations – were genuinely founded on a desire for peace. In the evening Dolgorukov came back, went straight to the Tsar and spent a long time alone with him.

On the 18th and 19th the troops moved forward in two stages, and the enemy outposts, after a brief exchange of fire, fell back. The army's higher echelons were all bustle and excitement from midday on the 19th till the morning of the 20th of November, the day when the famous battle of Austerlitz was fought.

Until midday on the 19th all the activity, urgent discussions, scurrying around and dispatching of adjutants was confined to the Emperors' headquarters; after midday the activity was transferred to Kutuzov's headquarters and the column command staff. Throughout the afternoon this activity was transmitted by adjutants to every last army outpost and unit, and in the early hours of 20th November the eighty-thousand-strong allied army rose from a few hours' sleep and lumbered off, a six-mile heaving mass of men abuzz with chatter.

The intense activity that had begun that morning in the Emperors' headquarters and then stimulated all the ensuing activity was like the first turn of the centre wheel in a great tower clock. One wheel began its slow rotation, another one turned, then another, and round they went faster and faster, wheels and cogs all revolving, chimes playing, figures popping in and out, and the hands measuring time, all because of that first movement.

Military movement is like the movement of a clock: an impetus, once given, leads inexorably to a particular result while the untouched working parts wait in silent stillness for the action to reach them. Wheels creak on their spindles as the cogs bite, the speeding sprockets hum and the next wheel stands and waits patiently, as if resigned to centuries of immobility. But the moment comes when the lever slips into place and the submissive wheel rotates with a creak, blending into the common movement without knowing where it goes or why.

In a clock the complex action of countless different wheels works its way out in the even, leisurely movement of hands measuring time; in a similar way the complex action of humanity in those 160,000 Russians and Frenchmen – all their passions, longings, regrets, humiliation and suffering, their rushes of pride, fear and enthusiasm – only worked its way out in defeat at the battle of Austerlitz, known as the battle of the three Emperors, the slow tick-tock of the age-old hands on the clock face of human history.

Prince Andrey was a duty officer that day, inseparable from the commander-in-chief. Shortly before six o'clock in the evening Kutuzov drove over to the Emperors' headquarters, had a brief meeting with the Tsar and went in to see the grand marshal, Count Tolstoy.

Bolkonsky used this opportunity to call on Dolgorukov in an attempt to find out some details of the coming action. He had sensed that Kutuzov was worried and unhappy about something, and that they were unhappy with him at headquarters, and that all the staff at imperial headquarters were treating him as if only they were in the know – which was why he wanted to talk with Dolgorukov.

'Ah, good evening, my dear fellow,' said Dolgorukov, who was sitting with Bilibin, drinking tea. 'The fun starts tomorrow. How's old Kutuzov? Down in the mouth?'

'I wouldn't say that, but I think he would like to be listened to.'

'But he was listened to at the council of war, and he will be listened to when he starts talking sense. But to sit around waiting for something to happen when the one thing Bonaparte dreads is a combined attack – that's just not possible.'

'You've seen him, haven't you?' said Prince Andrey. 'Well, what did you make of Napoleon? How did he strike you?'

'Yes, I did see him, and I came away convinced there's nothing in the world he dreads more than a combined attack,' repeated Dolgorukov, who evidently set great store by this general conclusion that he had come to during his meeting with Napoleon. 'If he hadn't been too scared to fight why on earth would he have asked for that meeting, and for talks – most of all, why would he retreat when retreat goes against his whole method of fighting a war? Believe me, he's scared, scared of a mass attack. His hour has come. You mark my words.'

'But you haven't said what he's like or what he said,' Prince Andrey insisted.

'He's a man in a grey overcoat who wants to be called "Your Majesty", but I disappointed him. He didn't get any titles out of me. That's the sort of man he is, and that's all there is to him,' answered Dolgorukov, glancing round with a smile at Bilibin.

'I yield to no one in my respect for old Kutuzov,' he continued, 'but we'd look pretty stupid if we dithered long enough to let him get away or do something clever, when here he is virtually in our hands. No, we should never forget Suvorov and his golden rule – attack, don't be attacked. Believe me, when it comes to fighting, young men's energy is often a better guide than all your dilatory old veterans.'

'But where are you going to attack? I've been at the outposts today, and you can't tell where his main forces are concentrated,' said Prince Andrey. He was longing to tell Dolgorukov about his own approach, the plan of attack he had worked out.

'It doesn't make any difference,' was the curt response from Dolgorukov as he got up and spread a map on the table. 'We've thought of everything. Say he concentrates on Brno . . .' And Prince Dolgorukov gave a quick, rather vague account of Weierother's plan of a flanking manoeuvre.

Prince Andrey demurred and began to explain his own plan, which might have been just as good as Weierother's, though it did have one drawback – Weierother's had already been approved. The moment Prince Andrey began to outline that plan's weaknesses and the advantages of his own idea, Prince Dolgorukov stopped listening and stared vacantly not at the map but at Prince Andrey's face.

'Anyway, there's a council of war at Kutuzov's tonight. You can have your say then,' said Dolgorukov.

'I certainly shall,' said Prince Andrey, walking away from the map.

'What *are* you worrying about, gentlemen?' said Bilibin, who thus far had been listening to them with a broad smile on his face but was now unmistakably on the verge of making a joke. 'Whether tomorrow brings victory or defeat, Russian military honour is assured. Except for your man Kutuzov, every single column is commanded by a non-Russian. Look at the commanders: *Herr General* Wimpfen, *le comte de* Langeron, *le prince de* Liechtenstein, *le prince de* Hohenlohe, and then there's Prshprshprsh-all-consonants-and-no-vowels – like all Polish names.'

'That's enough slander,' said Dolgorukov. 'You're wrong anyway, there are two Russians: Miloradovich and Dokhturov, and there would have been another, Count Arakcheyev, but for his bad nerves.'

'Anyway, I think General Kutuzov has just come out,' said Prince Andrey. 'Good luck to you, gentlemen, and every success,' he added, shaking hands with both men before he left.

Driving back with Kutuzov Prince Andrey couldn't help asking the general, who was sitting beside him in complete silence, what he thought about tomorrow's battle. Kutuzov looked sternly at his adjutant, paused for a moment and said, 'I think we shall lose. That's what I said to Count Tolstoy and I asked him to tell the Tsar. And do you know what he said? "My dear General, I like dabbling in cutlets and rice – warfare I leave to you." Yes . . . That was all he said!'

CHAPTER 12

It was after nine o'clock in the evening when Weierother took his plans over to Kutuzov's quarters, where the council of war was to take place. The column commanders had been told to attend, and all except Prince Bagration, who refused to come, arrived at the appointed hour.

Weierother had full responsibility for planning the proposed battle, and he was excited and impatient, in sharp contrast to the grumpy and sleepy Kutuzov, who had reluctantly assumed the role of president and chairman of the council. Weierother clearly saw himself as the head of a movement that had now become unstoppable. He was like a horse in harness hauling a load downhill. He wasn't sure whether he was pulling or it was pushing, but he was hurtling along at top speed with no time to consider where this headlong rush might take him. Weierother had been out twice that evening to make a personal inspection of the enemy's line, and he had reported in detail to two Emperors, one Russian, one Austrian, and then called in at his office to dictate the disposition of the German troops. And now here he was at Kutuzov's, quite exhausted.

He was evidently too preoccupied to be polite to his commander-in-chief. He kept on interrupting, spoke too fast and rambled on without looking at the person he was talking to and ignored all questions put to him. He sat there spattered with mud, looking pathetically weary and bemused and yet also confident and condescending.

Kutuzov had taken over a small castle belonging to a nobleman near Ostralitz. There in the drawing-room, converted into a study for the commander-in-chief, the members of the council of war were assembled, including Kutuzov himself and Weierother. They were drinking tea and waiting only for Prince Bagration to arrive so that the council could get down to business. Then Bagration's orderly officer arrived with a message that the prince would not be able to attend. Prince Andrey came in to inform the commander-in-chief of this, and he remained in the room, acting on Kutuzov's permission earlier for him to be present at the council.

'Well, since Prince Bagration isn't coming, I think we can begin,' said Weierother, jumping to his feet and crossing over to a table on which an enormous map was spread out, showing Brno and the surrounding locality.

Kutuzov sat there in a Voltaire armchair with his uniform unbuttoned, his fat neck bulged out over his collar as if escaping, and his podgy old hands laid out symmetrically along the arms of the chair. He was nearly asleep. At the sound of Weierother's voice he forced his one eye open and said, 'Yes, yes, do that or it'll be too late,' after which he nodded his head, then let it droop and closed his eye again.

If at first the council members had believed that Kutuzov was only pretending to be asleep, the nasal sounds issuing from him during the reading that followed proved beyond doubt that the commander-in-chief was attending to something much more important than the wish to pour scorn on their disposition of troops or anything else; he was attending to an irresistible human need – sleep. He really was asleep. Weierother moved like a man too busy to waste any time, glanced across at Kutuzov to make sure he was asleep, took up a document and started reading out in a loud drone the entire disposition of the troops in the impending battle, not omitting the title: 'Disposition for an assault on the enemy's position behind Kobelnitz and Sokolnitz, 20th November, 1805.'

The disposition was very complicated and hard to understand. Written originally in German, it began as follows:

Whereas the left wing of the enemy reposes against the forested hills and his right wing is extended by way of Kobelnitz and Sokolnitz behind the ponds there situated, while conversely our left wing greatly surpasses their right, it will be advantageous for us to attack the latter aforesaid enemy wing, especially if we occupy the villages of Sokolnitz and Kobelnitz, it then being within our capacity to mount an assault on the enemy

flank and pursue him across the open terrain between Schlapanitz and
the forest of Thuerassa thereby avoiding the defiles of Schlapanitz and
Bellowitz by which the enemy's front is covered. With this in mind it will
be essential . . . The first column marches . . . The second column marches
. . . The third column marches . . .

Weierother went on and on.

The generals seemed less than keen to listen to such a demanding
account of the disposition of the troops. The tall, fair-haired General
Buxhöwden leant against the wall and stared at a burning candle,
apparently not listening and not even wanting people to think that he
was. Directly opposite Weierother, fixing him with gleaming, wide-
open eyes, sat the red-faced Miloradovich, whiskers combed up and
shoulders high, striking a military attitude with his hands on his knees
and his elbows bent outwards. He sat there in grim-faced silence,
staring straight at Weierother and looking away only when the Austrian commander stopped speaking. Then Miloradovich looked round
knowingly at the other generals. But the knowing glance didn't make
it clear whether he agreed or disagreed, was pleased or not pleased
with the troop disposition. Right next to Weierother sat Count Langeron, with a subtle smile that never left his typically southern French
face throughout the reading as he looked down at his delicate fingers
and played with the corners of a golden snuff-box with a portrait on
the lid, twirling it round and round. In the middle of a particularly
turgid paragraph he stopped twirling the snuff box, looked up and
with fulsome courtesy lingering at the corners of his thin-lipped mouth
he broke in and was about to speak. But the Austrian general wouldn't
stop. He flapped his elbows as if to say, 'Later, you can tell me what
you think later, but now be so good as to look at the map and listen.'
Langeron rolled his eyes upwards with a bemused look and glanced
round at Miloradovich as though seeking enlightenment, only to
encounter a knowing look from Miloradovich, who actually knew
nothing, so he looked down again sadly and went back to twirling his
snuff-box.

'A geography lesson,' he mumbled, ostensibly under his breath but
loud enough for all to hear.

Przebyszewski's display of dignified courtesy was more genuine; he
cupped one ear towards Weierother and had every appearance of close
concentration. The diminutive Dokhturov sat across from Weierother,
self-effacing and eager to please, and bent over the outspread map,
conscientiously poring over the disposition of the troops and the
unfamiliar territory. Several times he asked Weierother to repeat cer-

tain words and difficult names of villages that he hadn't quite caught. Weierother obliged and Dokhturov wrote it all down.

The reading went on for more than an hour and when it was over Langeron stopped twirling his box and spoke out, without looking at Weierother or anyone in particular. His point was that such a disposition might be difficult because it assumed knowledge of the enemy's situation, but such knowledge was doubtful with the enemy on the move. For all the substance in these objections it was clear that the main purpose in presenting them was to get at Weierother, who had been so patronizing, as if he was reading his plans to a lot of schoolboys, and make him realize that he wasn't dealing with fools but with men who could teach him a thing or two about military matters.

The moment Weierother's voice stopped droning Kutuzov opened his eye, like a miller waking up at the slightest hiccup in the sleepy rumbling of his mill-wheels, listened to Langeron and then as if to say, 'Huh, still the same old rubbish!' snapped his eye tight shut and allowed his head to slump down even lower.

Langeron, weighing into Weierother with the sharpest sarcasm for his pompous attitude as a military leader and planner, pointed out that Napoleon might well go on the offensive instead of waiting to be attacked, and that would render all this disposition business utterly futile. Weierother countered every misgiving with a confident smile and a sneer, obviously well prepared for objections and for anything that might be said.

'If he'd been able to attack us, he would have done it today,' he said.

'So you think he's helpless, then?' said Langeron.

'I doubt he has more than forty thousand men,' answered Weierother, smiling like a doctor approached by a junior nurse with her own diagnosis.

'In which case he's asking for trouble if he sits there waiting for us to attack,' said Langeron with his subtly sarcastic smile, looking to Miloradovich for support. But Miloradovich's mind was on anything but this row between generals.

'God save us,' he said, 'tomorrow all will become clear on the battlefield.'

Weierother smiled again, and his smile implied that he of all people found it odd and amusing to encounter objections from Russian generals and to have to explain for their benefit something that he knew to be a certainty, and so did the royal Emperors.

'The enemy has put out his fires and a continual noise comes from his camp,' he said. 'What does this mean? Either he is retreating and that's all we have to fear, or else he's changing position.' (He smiled his smile.) 'But even if he set himself up in Thuerassa, that would only save us a good deal of trouble and all our arrangements would stay in place, every last detail.'

'How can that be? . . .' said Prince Andrey, who had long been waiting for a chance to voice his own doubts. Kutuzov woke up, cleared his throat hoarsely and scanned the generals.

'Gentlemen,' he said, 'the disposition for tomorrow, no, for today – it's past midnight – cannot now be changed. You have heard it, and we shall all do our duty. But before a battle there's nothing more important than . . .' (he paused) 'a good night's sleep.'

He made it clear that he was about to rise from his chair. The generals bowed and left. It was past midnight. Prince Andrey went out.

The council of war at which Prince Andrey had not managed to voice his opinion in the way that he had hoped had left him with a feeling of uncertainty and unease. Who was right – Dolgorukov and Weierother on the one hand, or Kutuzov and Langeron and the other men who disapproved of the plan of attack? He didn't know. But couldn't Kutuzov have gone straight to the Tsar with his views? Couldn't it all have been handled differently? Was it really necessary to put tens of thousands of lives at risk, including my life, *mine*, just because of personal vanity and niceties at court? These were his thoughts.

'Yes, I could easily get killed tomorrow,' he mused.

And suddenly, at the thought of death, a whole chain of memories, some distant, some close to his heart, rose up in his imagination. He remembered saying goodbye to his father and his wife; he remembered falling in love with her, thought of her being pregnant, which made him feel sorry for her and for himself; and it was in a state of emotion and nervous anxiety that he walked out of the hut that he was sharing with Nesvitsky and began to stroll about outside. It was a foggy night and the moonlight shimmered mysteriously through the mist. 'Tomorrow, oh yes, tomorrow!' he thought. 'Maybe tomorrow will see the last of me, and there will be no more memories – all these memories will have no more meaning for me. Maybe tomorrow – yes, it must be tomorrow – I can feel it coming – for the first time I shall have to show what I'm made of.' And he imagined the battle, the loss of it, the fighting concentrated at one point and all the commanding officers in terrible confusion. And then he could sense the happy moment – at long last it would be like Toulon for Napoleon. With challenging frankness he voices his opinion before Kutuzov and Weierother and the Emperors. All are struck by the correctness of his approach, but no one is prepared to carry it through, so there he goes, leading a regiment, a division, with the sole proviso that no one is to interfere with his plans, and he leads his division through the crisis and on to a victory that is his alone. 'Yes, but what about death and agony?' says a different voice. Prince Andrey ignores it and goes on with his triumphs. Comes the next battle, and it is for him alone to plan the disposition. He may be described as a lowly aide to Kutuzov, but here he is doing everything on his own. The next battle is won by him. Kutuzov is replaced; he is the replacement . . . 'Yes, but what comes next?' queries the other voice. 'Say you can manage to avoid getting wounded, killed or cheated a dozen times or more? What happens next?' 'Well, er . . .' Prince Andrey answered himself, 'I don't know what happens next, I can't possibly know, I don't wish to know, but if that's what I want, if I want glory, if I want to be famous and loved by everyone, it's not my fault that I want this, that this is all I care for, the only thing I live for. Yes, only this! I won't breathe a word of it to anyone, but, my God!, what can I do, if I care for nothing but glory and the love of men? Death, wounds, the loss of my family – nothing can frighten me. I know many people are dear and precious to me, my father, my sister, my wife – my nearest and dearest, yet, however terrible and unnatural it may seem, I would give them all up for one moment of glory, triumph over men, to be loved by men I don't even know, and never shall know, to be loved by these people there,' he thought, listening to men talking in the courtyard of Kutuzov's castle. They were the voices of the officers' servants doing the packing. Someone, probably one of the drivers, was teasing Kutuzov's old cook, well known to Prince Andrey, about his name – Titus.

'Hey, Tighty Titus!' he said.

'What d'you want?' answered the old man.

'Titus a drum!' said the funny man.

'Garn!' said the cook's voice, but it was swamped by the laughter of valets and servants.

'And to think the only thing I love and treasure is triumphing over all these people. All the magical power and glory hanging over me up there in this mist!'

CHAPTER 13

That same night Nikolay Rostov was out with a platoon of pickets along the outposts ahead of Bagration's detachment. His hussars were paired off down the line and he was patrolling it, struggling against overwhelming drowsiness. Behind him our soldiers' campfires could be seen flickering over a huge area; misty darkness lay ahead. Peer as he may into this misty distance, Rostov could see nothing, as grey blurred into black, and what might have been the flicker of an enemy campfire suddenly seemed more like a trick of the light. His eyes were closing, and he kept imagining he could see first the Emperor, then Denisov, then the Moscow of old, and whenever he opened his eyes again with a start, it was only the head and ears of his horse or maybe the odd black shape of a hussar six yards away, and in the distance still the same misty darkness. 'Why not? It could easily happen,' mused Rostov. 'The Emperor might meet me and give me an order, as if I was any old officer, and he'd say, "Go and find out about that over there." I've heard so many stories about him getting to know an officer just like that and taking him on. Oh, if only he would take me on! Oh, how closely I would guard him, and I'd tell him the truth, I'd expose anybody who tried to deceive him!' And by way of imagining his love and devotion to the Tsar more vividly, Rostov dreamt of some enemy or a treacherous German that he was about to enjoy dispatching and he would slap him across the face right in front of the Tsar. Then suddenly a distant shout brought him to his senses. He opened his eyes with a start.

'Where am I? Oh yes, out on the line. The password's "shaft" and "Olmütz" is the watchword. It's awful to think that our squadron will be held in reserve tomorrow . . .' he thought. 'I'm going to ask if I can go forward. It may be my only chance of seeing the Emperor. It'll soon be the end of my watch. I'll go round once more and when I get back I'll go and ask the general.' He sat up in the saddle and set off to make one last check on his men. It seemed to be getting lighter. To the left he could see a moonlit hillside and a black slope opposite that looked as steep as a wall. On this slope there was a white patch which Rostov couldn't make out at all – was it a clearing in the wood catching the moonlight, some snow that hadn't melted or white houses? He could have sworn there was something moving across the white patch. 'It must be snow, or could it be white ash? . . . Why tash . . . ?' Rostov mused dreamily. 'Not white ash . . . Tash . . . Na – *tasha* . . . sister . . . black eyes. Na – *tasha*. (Imagine her surprise when

I tell her I've seen the Emperor!) Natasha ... tasha ... This is my
sabre – *tache*.'

'A bit to the right, sir. Some bushes here,' a hussar's voice said to
Rostov, who was nodding as he rode by. Rostov's head had flopped
down almost on to his horse's mane; he wrenched it up and reined in
beside the hussar, still unable to shake off the overpowering urge to
sleep like a baby. 'Wait a minute, what was I thinking about? Mustn't
forget. Oh yes, speaking to the Emperor! No, that's not it – that's
tomorrow. I know! Na – *tasha*, mount an at – *tasha*. Hussars and
mous*taches* ... That hussar with a mous*tache dash*ing down the
Tverskaya, I was just thinking about him ... opposite Guryev's ...
Old Guryev ... Ah, Denisov, he's a good fellow! Oh, this is all stupid.
The main thing is – the Emperor's here. He looked at me and he was
dying to say something, but he just didn't dare ... Wait a minute ...
it was me ... I didn't dare. Oh, it's all stupid ... the thing is ... not
to forget ... I was thinking about something important, yes, Natasha,
mount an attasha, yes ... yes ... I've got it now.' And again he
dropped his head down on his horse's neck. Then suddenly – what
was this? – was he being fired at. 'Eh? What? ... Cut them to pieces!
What's that?' Rostov stammered out as he came round. The moment
he opened his eyes, Rostov heard from the enemy territory ahead the
great long roaring of a thousand voices. His own horse and the horse
of the nearby hussar pricked up their ears at all this shouting. Over
there where the shouts were coming from, a light flashed and went
out, then another, and then all along the line of the French troops on
the hillside fires were being lit and the shouts grew louder and louder.
Rostov could hear the sounds of French words but he couldn't work
out what they were. Too many booming voices. All he could hear was
'aaaa!' and the French 'rrrr!'

'What is it? What do you make of that?' Rostov said to the hussar
next to him. 'It's the enemy, isn't it?'

The hussar said nothing.

'Well, can't you hear it?' Rostov asked again, after waiting some
time for a reply.

'Don't know, sir,' the hussar managed reluctantly.

'Coming from there it must be the enemy,' Rostov said again.

'Maybe 'tis, maybe 'tisn't,' mumbled the hussar, ' 'tis too dark. Hey,
steady!' he shouted to his fidgety horse. Rostov's horse was just as
restive, pawing the frozen ground as it listened to the shouts and
looked at the lights. The shouting grew louder still until it became one
great sustained roar that could only have come from an army of
thousands. The lights stretched further and further, probably marking

the line of the French camp. Rostov wasn't sleepy any more – the happy roar of triumph from the enemy's army had shaken him into life. 'Long live the Emperor! The Emperor!' There was no mistaking the words now.

'Not too far away . . . They must be just across the stream,' he said to the hussar near him.

The hussar sighed, but didn't reply. He gave an angry grunt. Then they heard a horse trotting towards them down the line of their men, and suddenly the figure of a sergeant of hussars loomed up out of the dark mist like some enormous elephant.

'Sir, the generals are here!' said the sergeant, riding up to Rostov. Rostov, still looking over towards the lights and shouting, rode with the sergeant to meet several men on horseback coming down the line. One was on a white horse. It was Prince Bagration, who had ridden out with Prince Dolgorukov and some of his adjutants to watch the strange display of lights and listen to the shouting from the enemy ranks. Rostov rode up to Bagration, reported what he had heard and seen and joined the adjutants, listening to what the generals were saying.

'Take my word for it,' Prince Dolgorukov was saying to Bagration, 'this is just a trick. They've retreated and told the rearguard to light fires and make a racket to fool us.'

'I hardly think so,' said Bagration. 'I've been watching them on that rise all evening. If they'd retreated, they'd have gone from there. Officer,' Prince Bagration turned to Rostov, 'are the enemy pickets still there?'

'They were there this evening, but now I can't tell, sir. Shall I take some men and find out?' said Rostov.

Bagration stood still and before answering he tried to make out Rostov's face through the mist.

'Yes, you do that,' he said after a brief pause.

'Sir.'

Spurring his horse, Rostov called out to Sergeant Fedchenko and two other hussars, told them to follow him and trotted off downhill in the direction of the shouting, which showed no signs of dying down. Rostov felt scared and exhilarated to be riding alone with three hussars down into that mysterious and dangerous, misty distance, where no one had ridden before. Bagration had yelled at him from the hillside not to cross the stream, but Rostov had pretended not to hear, and he rode on and on without stopping, continually getting things wrong, mistaking bushes for trees and gullies for men, and continually discovering his mistakes. He trotted downhill and soon lost sight of our men and the enemy's fires, but the shouting of the Frenchmen was louder and clearer. At the bottom he saw just ahead something that looked like a river, but once he rode up to it he saw that it was a well-travelled road. As he got out on the road he reined in his horse and wondered whether to go along it or to cross over and ride uphill through a black field. Riding down the road where it was still misty but brighter would be less dangerous because you'd get a better sight of any figures. 'Follow me,' he said, then crossed the road and galloped off uphill heading for the area where the French pickets had been seen that evening.

'Sir, look!' cried one of the hussars from behind, and before Rostov could see what it was, something black loomed up in the mist, there was a blinding flash, the crack of a shot and the whine of a bullet which flew past and died away. Another gun misfired, but there was a flash in the pan. Rostov turned his horse and galloped back. He heard four more shots at varying intervals, and four more bullets sang their different tunes into the mist. Rostov reined in his horse, which seemed as excited as he was by all this shooting, and brought him to a walk. 'More, more, give me more!' cried an excited inner voice. But there were no more shots. Rostov waited until he was getting near to Bagration before galloping his horse again, and he rode up saluting.

Dolgorukov was still insisting that the French were in retreat, and the fires had been lit in order to fool them. 'What does this prove?' he was saying as Rostov rode up. 'They might have retreated and still left pickets.'

'It's clear they haven't all gone, Prince,' said Bagration. 'We must see what morning brings. In the morning we shall know all there is to know.'

'The picket's still there on the hill, your Excellency, where it was yesterday evening,' Rostov announced, still saluting and quite unable to resist a smile of delight after his sortie and especially the whine of bullets.

'Well done, well done,' said Bagration. 'My thanks to you, officer.'

'Your Excellency,' said Rostov, 'may I ask a favour?'

'What is it?'

'Tomorrow our squadron is held in reserve. Could I possibly be attached to the first squadron?'

'What's your name?'

'Count Rostov.'

'Splendid. You may stay with me as an orderly officer.'

'Ilya Andreich's son?' said Dolgorukov, but Rostov ignored him.

'May I count on it, sir?'

'I will give the order.'

'Tomorrow, it's more than possible – I might get sent to the Tsar with a message,' he thought. 'Glory be!'

All the shouting and lighting of fires in the enemy camp had come about because Napoleon himself had ridden among the bivouacs while his proclamation was being read out to the troops. When they saw him the soldiers set fire to armfuls of straw and ran after him chanting, 'Long live the Emperor!' Napoleon's proclamation ran as follows:

> Soldiers! The Russian army is marching against you in order to avenge the Austrian army, the army of Ulm. These are the same forces that you defeated at Hollabrünn and have been driving relentlessly towards this place. The positions that we occupy are strong ones, and should they march round me to the right, they will expose their flank to me! Soldiers! I shall myself be at the head of your battalions. I shall be out of the firing line as long as you display your habitual courage by carrying disorder and confusion into the ranks of the enemy. But if victory is for a single moment in doubt, you will see your Emperor facing the direct onslaught of the enemy, for there can be no vacillation on the verge of victory, especially on this day, when the honour of the French infantry is at stake, and with it the honour of our nation. Do not break ranks even for the purpose of removing the wounded! May every last man among you be imbued with the need to destroy these hirelings of England, who are inspired by such hatred of our country. With this victory our campaign will be concluded, and we can return to our winter quarters to be joined by new troops at present mobilizing in France. And then the peace which I shall conclude will be worthy of our people, worthy of you and of me.
>
> NAPOLEON

CHAPTER 14

At five in the morning it was still quite dark. There was no movement among the troops in the centre, nor in the reserves, nor on Bagration's right flank. But on the left flank the infantry, cavalry and artillery columns who would be the first to plunge down and attack the French on their right flank, driving them off into the Bohemian mountains – according to Weierother's battle plan – were already up and about. They had been throwing all the leftovers into the campfires, and the smoke now stung the eyes. It was cold and dark. The officers were gulping down tea and snatching breakfast, while the men munched their dry biscuits and stamped their feet against the cold, gathering around the fires for some warmth and throwing all the unwanted bits and pieces into the flames – wood from their temporary huts, chairs, tables, wheels, tubs, anything that couldn't go with them. Austrian column leaders were moving in and out among the Russian troops, their presence heralding imminent advance. As soon as an Austrian officer arrived at a commander's quarters, the regiment stirred itself into action: the soldiers hurried away from the fires, stuffing their pipes down the tops of their boots and their bags into wagons, quick to sort out their muskets and fall in. The officers buttoned up their uniforms, buckled on their sabres and pouches, and paced up and down the ranks shouting. The baggage handlers and officers' orderlies harnessed the horses, packed the wagons and lashed them up. The adjutants and the officers commanding regiments and battalions got on their horses, crossed themselves, issued final orders, exhortations and instructions to the men who were staying behind with the baggage, and then the steady tramp of a thousand feet began. The columns moved off with no idea where they were going, blinded by the surrounding hordes, the smoke and the gathering mist so that they couldn't see what they were leaving behind or what they were marching into.

A soldier on the march is enclosed, boxed in and carried along by his regiment as tightly as any sailor in a ship. However far he goes, however alien, mysterious and perilous the latitudes into which he advances, he always has around him, like the sailor with his deck, masts and rigging, the same comrades, the same marching ranks, the same sergeant Ivan Mitrich, the same regimental dog Zhuchka, the same officers. A soldier rarely wants to know what latitude his ship has ended up in, but come the day of battle – God knows how or where it comes from – the moral consciouness of warriors one and all rings with a new harsh note announcing the approach of something solemn and serious, and raising them to unknown heights of curiosity. Come the days of battle, soldiers strive to look beyond the interests of their regiment; they are all eyes and ears, anxious to know what is going on around them.

The fog had come down so thickly that although it was getting light they couldn't see ten paces ahead. Bushes looked like huge trees, flat stretches looked like soaring cliffs and slopes. At any point and from any direction they might come across an invisible enemy ten paces away. But the columns marched doggedly on through the fog, up hill and down dale, past gardens and fences, over countryside new and unknown, with no sign of the enemy. Quite the reverse, there was a growing consciousness of our own Russian columns up ahead, to the rear and on every side, all of them moving in the same direction. Every last soldier felt buoyed up by knowing that wherever he was going – not that anyone knew where that was – so were all the other Russians in their vast numbers.

'Hey, the Kurskies have gone on,' went the word in the ranks.

'Damn good force we've got together! Did you see them fires burning last night? Went on for ever. Like looking at Moscow!'

Although the column commanders were not riding over to the ranks or talking to the soldiers (the commanding officers, as we saw at the council of war, were not in the mood because they didn't like what they were having to do, so they carried out their orders without any effort to inspire the men), the soldiers still marched on in high spirits, as they always do when they are going into action, especially attacking.

But after marching for an hour or so through the thick fog, most of the troops were brought to a halt, and a nasty sense of confusion and mismanagement spread through the ranks. It is very difficult to tell how this kind of awareness spreads. But spread it does, with amazing accuracy and speed, slowly but surely, like water flooding a valley. Had the Russian army been acting alone, with no allies, it might have taken a lot longer for this awareness of mismanagement to become common knowledge. As things stood, there was much pleasure to be had, naturally enough, from attributing this shambles to the senseless Germans, and soon everybody believed they were in a dangerous mess because of the bungling sausage-makers.

'Why have we stopped? Road blocked ahead? Or have we got to the French?'

'No, can't hear anything. They'd have been firing. Told us to get going quick, and we did, and now look at us, stuck in the middle of a field, God knows why . . . Blasted krauts, mucking things up! Damned idiots!'

'I'd have sent them out first. No fear, crowds of 'em at the back . . . Got to stand here now with nothing to eat.'

'Get a move on!'

'I've heard that the cavalry's blocking the road,' said an officer.

'Damned Germans, don't even know their own country,' said another.

'Which division are you?' shouted an adjutant, riding up.

'Eighteenth.'

'What are you doing here? You should have been up at the front ages ago. You won't get there now until tonight.'

'It's all stupid. They've no idea what they're doing,' said the officer, and he galloped away. Then a general came trotting up and yelled at them furiously in a foreign language.

'Oo, oo, parlyvoo, it's all double Dutch to me,' said a soldier, mimicking the retreating general. 'Shoot the lot of 'em, lousy scum!'

'Supposed to get there by nine, and we're not half-way there yet. Wonderful management!' was repeated on all sides, and the feeling of energy that the troops had started out with began to turn to resentment and anger against the ridiculous arrangements and the Germans.

The muddle stemmed from a redirection of the Austrian cavalry; when they were well under way moving towards the left flank, the top brass had come to the conclusion that our centre was too far away from the right flank, so all the cavalry were ordered to cross over to the right. Thousands of mounted troops had to cross in front of the infantry, and the infantry had to wait for them to pass.

Ahead of the troops a row had broken out between an Austrian column leader and a Russian general. The Russian general shouted for the cavalry to stop. The Austrian tried to explain that it wasn't his fault – the top brass were to blame. Meanwhile the troops stood there, getting more and more bored and dispirited. After an hour's delay they moved on at last, and began to march downhill. The fog that had thinned out on the hilltop lay thicker than ever down below where the troops were going. Ahead in the fog they heard a shot, then another, random firing at first, at irregular intervals; rat-a-tat-tat, then growing more regular and frequent. The battle of Holdbach (only a little stream) had begun.

Not expecting to confront the enemy down there at the stream, stumbling across them unexpectedly in the fog and hearing no word of encouragement from their commanding officers, frustrated to the last man by arriving too late, and with nothing visible ahead of them or on either side in the fog, the Russians loosed off a few desultory shots at the enemy, moved forward a little and then stopped again in the absence of any orders from the officers or adjutants, who were themselves blundering about in the fog on unfamiliar territory not knowing where their own divisions were. This was how the battle began for columns one, two and three, which had marched down together. Column four, with Kutuzov in it, had stayed behind on the Pratzen heights.

Down below where the action had started thick fog still obscured everything. Higher up it was getting clearer, but still nothing could be seen of the action ahead. Whether the full enemy strength was more than five miles away, as we had been assuming, or whether they were here in that patch of fog, no one knew until after eight o'clock.

Nine o'clock came. The low ground was engulfed in a sea of fog, but high up in the village of Schlapanitz, where Napoleon stood surrounded by his marshals, it was now completely clear. The sky overhead was bright blue, and the vast orb of the sun shimmered like a huge, hollow crimson float bobbing on the surface of the milky sea of fog. The French troops with Napoleon himself and all his staff were not on the other side of the streams and gullies near to the villages of Sokolnitz and Schlapanitz, which we had intended to pass before forming up ready for attack, they were on this side, so close to us that Napoleon could tell a cavalryman from a foot-soldier in our army with the naked eye. Napoleon was positioned just ahead of his marshals, mounted on a little grey Arab horse, wearing the same blue overcoat he had worn through the Italian campaign. He was staring in silence at the hills which seemed to stride up out of the sea of mist, watching the Russian troops as they moved across them in the distance, and he was listening to the sound of gunfire in the valley. Not a muscle twitched on his face, which in those days was still rather thin; his eyes glinted as he stared at one spot. His predictions had come true. Part of the Russian army was going down towards the ponds and lakes in the valley; the other part was abandoning the heights of Pratzen, which he had planned to attack, since it was the crucial position. Through the fog he scanned the hollow between two hills near the village of Pratzen and watched as the Russian columns with bayonets gleaming moved as one man down into the valleys and disappeared one by one into the mist. Intelligence received overnight, the sounds of wheels and footsteps heard during the night at the outposts and all the confusion in the marching Russian columns, everything told him that the allies thought he was a long way away, that the columns on the move near Pratzen constituted the centre of the Russian army and that the centre itself was now too weak to mount a successful attack. But still he held back; the battle did not yet begin.

Today was a day of celebration for him – the anniversary of his coronation. He had slept for a few hours before dawn and woken up feeling fresh, in good health and high spirits. Enjoying that happy frame of mind when nothing seems impossible and everything succeeds, he had mounted his horse and ridden out. He sat there now without moving, looking at the heights rising from the fog, and his cold face wore the odd look of well-earned but over-confident pleasure that you might see on the face of a lucky young man in love. Behind him stood the marshals, not daring to distract him. He stared at the heights of Pratzen, and then at the sun floating up out of the mist.

When the sun had completely emerged from the fog, and the fields and the mist were ablaze with its brilliance (as if this was what he had been waiting for to begin the battle), he slid the glove from one of his fine white hands and signalled with it to his marshals, thus ordering battle to commence. The marshals, accompanied by adjutants, galloped off in every direction, and a few minutes later the main force of the French army began to move towards the heights of Pratzen, which were being steadily abandoned by the Russian troops as they moved down left into the valley.

CHAPTER 15

At eight o'clock Kutuzov set off for Pratzen at the head of Miloradovich's fourth column, the one which was to replace the columns of Przebyszewski and Langeron, who had by this time gone down into the valley. He greeted the men of the foremost regiment and gave the order to march, a clear indication that he had every intention of leading that column himself. Just outside the village of Pratzen he halted. Prince Andrey was close behind, one among many in the commander-in-chief's entourage. He was experiencing that mixture of nervous irritation and controlled calm that often besets a man whose long-awaited moment has come, and was totally convinced that today would be the making of him, something like Napoleon's key victories at Toulon or Arcola. He had no idea how things would work out, but he was totally convinced that it was going to happen. He had made himself as familiar with the locality and the position of our troops as anyone in our army could have done. It was now inconceivable that his own strategy could be implemented, so he forgot all about it. Throwing all his weight behind Weierother's plan, Prince Andrey was busy going over every last contingency that might arise, and imagining all sorts of new circumstances which could call for his quick thinking and determination.

Down below in the fog, on the left-hand side, invisible enemies could be heard firing at each other. That's where the action would be, Prince Andrey decided; that's where there would be trouble. 'That's where I'll be sent,' he thought, 'with a brigade or a division, and that's where I'll grab the colours, march forward and smash everything before me.'

Prince Andrey could not look unmoved at the colours of other battalions as they went past. Looking at a flag he kept thinking to himself, 'Perhaps that's the very flag I shall hold when I'm leading my men.' By morning the fog had gone from the heights, leaving behind nothing but hoar-frost rapidly melting into dew, but the valleys still swam in a milky-white sea. Nothing at all could be seen in the valley down to the left where our troops had vanished, now ringing with gunfire. Over the hill-tops the clear sky shone dark blue, and on the right was the vast orb of the sun. On the far-distant shore wooded hills rose from that sea of mist; that was where the enemy's army ought to be, and something could be seen moving about over there. From the right came the sound of hoofbeats, the rumble of wheels and the odd flash of a bayonet, as the guards descended into the realm of mist, and on the left, beyond the village, the same massed cavalry was moving down to be swallowed up in the sea of fog. Ahead of them and to the rear marched the infantry. The commander-in-chief was standing by the road leading out of the village, watching the march-past. Kutuzov seemed exhausted and edgy that morning. Then the men came to a sudden halt, not because they had been ordered to do so, but apparently because of some blockage up ahead.

'Do tell the men to form battalion columns and march around the village!' an angry Kutuzov snapped at a general who had ridden up. 'Isn't it obvious to you, my dear sir, that we can't have them stretched out along a narrow village street when we are marching on the enemy?'

'I was intending to re-form outside the village, sir,' replied the general.

Kutuzov gave a sardonic laugh.

'A nice position to be in, deploying your front right in sight of the enemy – very nice!'

'The enemy's a long way away, sir. According to the disposition . . .'

'The disposition!' Kutuzov roared out venomously. 'Who told you that? . . . Kindly do as you are commanded.'

'Yes, sir.'

'My dear fellow,' Nesvitsky whispered to Prince Andrey, 'the old man's in a foul temper.'

An Austrian officer in a white uniform and with green plumes in his hat galloped up to Kutuzov and asked him in the Emperor's name whether the fourth column had started yet.

Kutuzov turned away without answering and his glance happened to light on Prince Andrey, who was standing near by. Seeing Bolkonsky, Kutuzov relaxed his bitter scowl, as though to acknowledge that his adjutant wasn't to blame for what was being done. Still ignoring the Austrian adjutant, he addressed Bolkonsky.

'My dear fellow, go and see whether the third division has gone past the village. Tell them to stop and wait for my orders.'

Prince Andrey had scarcely started when he was stopped again.

'And ask whether the marksmen have been deployed,' he added. 'What they are doing? What they are doing?' he murmured to himself, still not responding to the Austrian.

Prince Andrey galloped off to carry out the order. Overtaking all the battalions ahead of them, he stopped the third division and soon found out that there really was no line of marksmen in advance of our columns. The commander of the leading regiment was greatly shocked to receive an order from the commander-in-chief to deploy his marksmen. There he stood, sure in the knowledge that there were other troops ahead of him, and the enemy had to be at least six or seven miles away. And in fact there was nothing visible in front of him but an empty downhill slope blanketed with fog. Having passed on the commander-in-chief's order to put things right, Prince Andrey galloped back. Kutuzov was still in the same place, his portly figure slumped in the saddle with the lassitude of age, and he was yawning wearily with his good eye closed. Instead of moving on, the troops had been told to order arms.

'Good, good,' he said to Prince Andrey before turning to the general, who was saying, watch in hand, that it must be time for them to get going because all the columns of the left flank had gone down already.

'There's plenty of time, your Excellency,' Kutuzov got out between yawns. 'Plenty of time!' he repeated.

At that moment from a long way behind Kutuzov came the sound of regiments cheering, and the noise of it began to sweep towards them down the long, strung-out line of advancing Russian columns. Whoever was the cause of it must have been riding quickly. When the soldiers in the regiment near to Kutuzov started cheering he rode off to one side and looked around with a scowl. Towards them down the road from Pratzen galloped what seemed like an entire squadron of multicoloured horsemen. Two of them were riding side by side ahead of the rest at full gallop, one dressed in a black uniform with white plumes, on a bobtailed chestnut thoroughbred, the other dressed in white and riding a black horse. It was the two Emperors and their entourage. With all the panache expected from a veteran of the line, Kutuzov brought the men to attention and rode at the salute towards the Emperors. His whole body and manner had been suddenly transformed. He had adopted the air of an unquestioning subordinate. With an exaggerated display of respect which was clearly not to Alexander's taste he rode up and saluted the Tsar.

A look of displeasure, no more than a wisp of mist in a clear blue sky, flashed across the Emperor's young and happy face and vanished. That day, following his indisposition, he looked rather thinner than at Olmütz, where Bolkonsky had seen him for the first time abroad. But his fine grey eyes shone with the same captivating mixture of majesty and gentleness, and his delicate mouth, with its expressive versatility, showed most of all his noble spirit and young innocence.

If at Olmütz he had been more majestic, here he was brighter and more energetic. Slightly red in the face from a quick two-mile gallop, he reined in his horse, drew a long deep breath and looked round at his entourage, faces as young and eager as his own. Behind the Tsar, chatting and smiling, stood Czartoryski and Novosiltsev, Prince Volkonsky and Stroganov, and all the other high-spirited young men in opulent uniforms astride their splendid horses, which looked well groomed, still fresh and only slightly heated from the gallop. Emperor Francis, a long-faced young man with a ruddy complexion, sat bolt upright on his handsome black stallion and glanced around slowly with a rather worried look. He called one of his white adjutants over and asked him something. 'Probably wants to know what time they started,' thought Prince Andrey, watching his old acquaintance with an irrepressible smile as he recalled his audience with him in Brno. The imperial entourage included a number of elite young orderly officers – Russians and Austrians – from the guards and regiments of the line. Among them were grooms with spare horses, splendid animals from the royal stables, covered with embroidered saddle-cloths.

This glittering cavalcade of young people galloping up with so much youthful energy and assurance acted on Kutuzov's demoralized staff like a breath of fresh country air blowing through an open window into a stuffy room.

'Why aren't you moving forward, Mikhail Larionovich?' Emperor Alexander asked Kutuzov rather abruptly, stealing a respectful glance towards Emperor Francis.

'I am waiting to see, your Majesty,' Kutuzov answered with a polite bow.

The Emperor cupped an ear with a slight frown, as if he hadn't quite heard.

'I'm waiting to see, your Majesty,' repeated Kutuzov. (Prince Andrey noticed that Kutuzov's upper lip had a strange twitch as he announced that he was waiting.) 'Not all the columns are in place yet, your Majesty.' The Tsar heard what he said but didn't seem to like the answer. He shrugged his hunched shoulders and glanced across at

Novosiltsev, who was not far away, with a look that seemed to censure Kutuzov.

'You do realize this is not the Tsaritsyn Parade Ground, Mikhail Larionovich? We can begin without the last regiment,' said the Tsar, glancing round again at the Emperor Francis as though inviting him to listen to what he was saying even if he didn't want to get involved. But Emperor Francis, whose eyes were elsewhere, was not listening.

'That's why I'm holding back, sire,' said Kutuzov, raising his voice as if speaking to someone who might not be able to hear properly, and again his face was twitching. 'I'm holding back, sire, precisely because we are not on parade and this is not the Tsaritsyn Ground,' he spelled out most distinctly.

All the members of the entourage exchanged rapid glances, every face dark with accusation and reproach. 'It doesn't matter how old he is, he ought not to speak like that, ever,' the faces seemed to say.

The Tsar continued to look steadily at Kutuzov, wondering whether he had anything more to say. But all Kutuzov did was to bow his head respectfully, as if he was waiting too. The silence lasted almost a minute.

'However, if that's an order, your Majesty . . .' said Kutuzov, look-ing up again and resuming his earlier way of speaking like an obtuse, unquestioning and thoroughly obedient general. He moved his horse away, beckoned to Miloradovich, the column commander, and ordered him to advance.

The ranks stirred into movement, and two battalions of the Novgo-rod regiment and a battalion of the Apsheron marched past the Tsar.

While the Apsheron battalion was going by, the florid-faced Milora-dovich, without his greatcoat, his uniform covered with medals, and a well-plumed hat turned-up and tilted, rode forward, high-stepping his horse while saluting in the grand manner, and then reined in before the Tsar.

'God be with you, General,' said the Tsar.

'I give you my word, sire, whatever it is in our power to do, we shall do it,' he answered brightly in bad French, much to the amusement of the gentlemen in the Tsar's entourage.

Miloradovich wheeled his horse round sharply and took up a pos-ition just behind the Tsar. The Apsheron infantrymen, much inspired by the presence of the Sovereign, stepped out in grand style as they marched past the Emperors and their suites.

'Listen, men!' shouted Miloradovich in his loud, cheery, confident voice, so worked up by the gunfire, the smell of battle and the sight of Apsheron comrades known to him since Suvorov's day that he seemed to have forgotten the Tsar was there. 'Go on men! You've taken villages before today!' he roared.

'We're ready!' the soldiers roared back. The Tsar's horse was startled by the sudden shout. This horse, who had carried the Tsar at reviews in Russia, now bore her rider on the field of Austerlitz, putting up with thoughtless spurring from the royal left boot, pricking up her ears at real gunfire as she used to do on the Field of Mars parade ground, and making nothing of it all – the gunshots, the proximity of Emperor Francis's black stallion, and all that was being said or experienced by the man on her back, or what was passing through his mind.

The Tsar turned to one member of his entourage, pointed with a smile to the gallant boys of the Apsheron regiment and said something to him.

CHAPTER 16

Kutuzov, accompanied by his adjutants, rode on at walking pace following the carabineers.

After covering half a mile or so at the rear of the column, he stopped at a solitary, deserted house (probably once an inn), by a fork in the road. Two ways led downhill and the troops were marching down both of them.

The fog was beginning to thin, and not much more than a mile away enemy troops could be seen, albeit not too clearly, high on the opposite hillside. Down below on the left the gunfire was getting louder. Kutuzov stood talking to an Austrian general. Watching them all the time from a few feet away, Prince Andrey turned to an adjutant, anxious to borrow his telescope.

'Look! Look!' this adjutant said, looking not at the troops a long way away, but just down the hill. 'It's the French!'

The two generals and the adjutant began fighting over the telescope, grabbing it one after the other. Their faces had fallen, all of them horror-stricken. The French ought to have been more than a mile away, but suddenly here they were right in front of us.

'Is that the enemy? . . . Can't be . . . It is, you know . . . Dead certain . . . What's happened?' voices could be heard saying.

Prince Andrey needed no telescope to see just below them down to the right a dense column of French soldiers climbing the slope towards the Apsheron regiment, no more than five hundred yards from where Kutuzov was standing.

'This is it. It's here, my big moment! This is my chance,' thought Prince Andrey, spurring his horse, and he rode over to Kutuzov.

'Your Excellency,' he shouted, 'we must stop the Apsheron regiment.'

But at that instant everything disappeared in a cloud of smoke, guns went off close by and not two paces from Prince Andrey a voice cried out in pure terror, 'Hey, mates, we've had it!' And this voice was as good as a command – one call, and everyone panicked and ran.

Hordes of men from all over the place, swelling into great crowds, fled back towards the area where five minutes earlier they had been marching past the two Emperors. Not only was it going to be difficult to stop this rush, it was impossible not to be swept back along with the mob. Bolkonsky's main concern was not to lose contact with Kutuzov, and all he could do was stare around in bewilderment, unable to take in what was happening before his eyes. Nesvitsky's blood was up; unrecognizable in all his fury, he kept yelling at Kutuzov that if he didn't get away at once he was sure to be taken prisoner. Rooted to the spot, Kutuzov was busy taking out his handkerchief and he didn't answer. Blood ran down his cheek. Prince Andrey forced his way through to him.

'Are you wounded?' he asked, his jaw quivering uncontrollably.

'Not here – there!' said Kutuzov, pressing the handkerchief to his bleeding cheek and pointing to the fleeing soldiers.

'Somebody stop them!' he roared, and then, probably realizing that nobody could do that, he spurred his horse and rode off to the right. Another wave of panicking humanity engulfed him and swept him back.

The troops were running away in such huge numbers that once you were caught in the middle of the crowd it was no easy matter to get out of it. Someone yelled, 'Go on! Get out of my way!' Another man was lurching around to fire in the air; somebody else was even lashing out at Kutuzov's horse. With one huge thrust Kutuzov managed to extricate himself from the torrent of men, and rode off towards the cannon-fire with his suite cut down by half. Prince Andrey also struggled free, still fighting to keep in touch with Kutuzov, but then he saw something through the smoke on the hillside – a Russian battery still firing and the French running towards it. Just uphill from them there were some Russian infantrymen going nowhere, neither hurrying forward to support the battery nor running back in the same

direction as the runaways. A general on horseback had detached himself
from the infantry and ridden over to Kutuzov. Of Kutuzov's suite only
four men were left. Pale-faced and staring, they said not a word.

'Cowardly swine! Stop them!' said a breathless Kutuzov to the
regimental commander, pointing to the fleeing soldiers. But at that
moment, as if to punish him for saying what he did, a shower of
bullets whistled over the regiment and Kutuzov's suite like a flock of
birds. The French were after the battery, but once they caught sight
of Kutuzov they had turned their fire on him. With this volley the
general clutched at his leg, several soldiers went down and a second
lieutenant holding the flag let it slide from his hands. The flag wobbled
and got caught on the guns of the nearest soldiers as it fell. The soldiers
had begun firing without orders.

'Oh no!' Kutuzov groaned in despair as he looked around everywhere. 'Bolkonsky,' he whispered in a quavering voice which betrayed
his awareness of being too old and too feeble. 'Bolkonsky,' he whispered, pointing towards the shattered battalion and the enemy, 'what's
all this?'

But before he could get the words out, Prince Andrey, choking on
tears of humiliation and fury, was off his horse and racing for the flag.

'Come on, boys! This way!' he shrieked, piping like a boy. 'This is
it!' Prince Andrey thought, seizing the flagstaff, exhilarated by the
scream of bullets clearly meant for him. Several soldiers went down.

'Hurrah!' roared Prince Andrey, finding the heavy flag hard to hold
but rushing forward quite sure that the whole battalion would run
after him. And he wasn't alone for more than a few steps. One soldier
lunged, then another, and then the whole battalion was there, echoing
his 'hurrah!', running on and racing past him. A battalion sergeant
ran up and took the flag, which was too heavy for Prince Andrey and
wobbled in his grip, but he was killed on the spot. Prince Andrey
snatched the flag up again and dragged it by the staff as he ran on
with the battalion. In front of him he could see our gunners, some still
fighting, some running towards him with the cannons abandoned. He
could see French infantrymen, too, taking hold of our artillery horses
and heaving the cannons the other way round. Prince Andrey and the
battalion were less than twenty yards from the big guns. He heard
bullets whining incessantly overhead. Soldiers moaned and dropped
right and left, but he didn't stop to look; his eyes were fixed on what
was happening over there at the battery. He could make out one
figure clearly, a red-haired gunner, with his shako skewed to one side,
heaving on a cleaning-rod while a French soldier heaved against him
the other way. Now he had a clear view of the two men's faces,

distorted with anguish and fury even though they had no real idea of what they were doing.

'What *are* they doing?' wondered Prince Andrey as he watched. 'The red-haired man's got no gun – why doesn't he just run away? Why doesn't the Frenchman bayonet him? He won't get far before the Frenchman remembers his gun and runs him through.' And then, in fact, another Frenchman ran up to the two fighting men with his gun levelled at them, thus probably sealing the fate of the red-haired gunner, who had no inkling of what was in store for him as he wrenched the cleaning-rod away in triumph. But Prince Andrey never saw how it all ended. All he felt was a terrible blow on the head which he was hazily aware of having come from one of the nearby soldiers, who must have set about him with a huge piece of wood. It didn't hurt much – what really annoyed him was that such pain as there was distracted him and stopped him seeing what he was looking at.

'What's happening? . . . I think I'm falling . . . My legs are going,' he thought, collapsing on his back. He opened his eyes, hoping to see how the fight between the French soldiers and our gunner ended. Was the gunner killed or not? Did they get the cannons or were they saved? But he saw none of that. Above him was nothing, nothing but the sky – the lofty sky, not a clear sky, but still infinitely lofty, with grey clouds creeping gently across. 'It's so quiet, peaceful and solemn, not like me rushing about,' thought Prince Andrey, 'not like us, all that yelling and scrapping, not like that Frenchman and our gunner pulling on that cleaning-rod, with their scared and bitter faces, those clouds are different, creeping across that lofty, infinite sky. How can it be that I've never seen that lofty sky before? Oh, how happy I am to have found it at last. Yes! It's all vanity, it's all an illusion, everything except that infinite sky. There is nothing, nothing – that's all there is. But there isn't even that. There's nothing but stillness and peace. Thank God for that!'

CHAPTER 17

Over on the right flank, where Bagration was in command, it was nine o'clock and the battle had still not begun. Looking for an excuse not to accede to Dolgorukov's request for them to get things started, and anxious in fact to offload all responsibility, Prince Bagration proposed to Dolgorukov that they should send a messenger to ask for instructions from the commander-in-chief. Given that the two flanks were well over five miles apart, Bagration knew full well that, even if the courier didn't get himself killed (and he probably would), and if he eventually managed to find the commander-in-chief (a very difficult task), he would hardly be back before evening.

Bagration scanned the members of his entourage, his wide eyes devoid of all expression and still full of sleep, and the first thing that caught his eye was the boyish face of Nikolay Rostov, transfixed with excitement and hope. So he sent him.

'Sir, what if I meet his Majesty before the commander-in-chief?' said Rostov with a long salute.

'You can give the same message to his Majesty,' said Dolgorukov, quick to interrupt Bagration.

Once off duty Rostov had snatched a few hours' sleep before morning and now he felt cheerful, bold and resolute. He moved with a spring in his step and he felt lucky, a frame of mind which made everything seem bright and easily achievable.

All his dreams had come true that morning: there was going to be a full battle and he was due to take part in it. More importantly, he was serving one of the bravest of generals, and, more importantly still, he was now responsible for taking a message to Kutuzov, perhaps even to the Tsar himself. It was a fine morning and he had a good horse under him. His spirits overflowed with joy and happiness. Fully briefed, he gave the horse his head and galloped off down the line. First he rode past Bagration's stationary troops, as yet held back from the action, then he was soon into the territory of Uvarov's cavalry, where at last he could see signs of movement and preparations for battle. Beyond them he began to hear the distinct sound of gunfire and the booming of cannons ahead. The firing got louder and louder.

The sounds were different now in the fresh morning air. Gone were the desultory shots loosed off two or three at a time and accompanied by the occasional bang from a cannon. Now, all down the sloping hillsides before Pratzen he could hear long volleys of gunfire, with intermittent booming from the big guns so sustained that sometimes it sounded not like individual shots but one great roaring cannonade.

He could see puffs of musket smoke chasing each other down the hillsides, while cannon smoke wreathed up in clouds that floated away and melted together. The glint of bayonets through the smoke told him that masses of infantry were on the move down there, and one or two narrow strips indicated artillery with green caissons.

Rostov stopped his horse on a little rise to watch for a moment and see what was happening. But however much he concentrated he couldn't begin to sort out or understand what was going on. Some sort of men seemed to be moving about down there in the smoke, lines of troops were moving up from front and rear – but what for? Who were they? Where were they going? He just couldn't tell. But he found this spectacle and all these sounds far from depressing or discouraging; they only added to his energy and determination.

'Come on, come on, let's have some more!' was his mental response to the sounds he heard. He galloped off again down the line, farther and farther into territory where the troops had gone into action.

'I don't know what it's like down there, but I'm sure it'll be all right!' thought Rostov.

After riding past some Austrian troops, Rostov noticed that the next section (the guards) had gone off to fight.

'Good, that's better! I'll get a close look,' he thought.

He was now riding almost along the front line itself. Several horsemen came galloping towards him – a troop of our Uhlans returning in disorder from an attack. As he passed, Rostov noticed one of them covered in blood, but he galloped on.

'Nothing to do with me!' he thought.

Only a few hundred yards further on he suddenly saw, coming from the left and spread out over the whole battlefield, an immense mass of cavalrymen on black horses, in dazzling white uniforms, cutting across and bearing down on him. Rostov rode flat out to avoid them all, and he would have managed it if they had moved at the same pace, but they kept coming faster and faster until several horses were galloping. Louder and louder came the hoofbeats and the rattling of their weapons; clearer and clearer were the horses, the figures, even the faces. They were our men, horse guards, charging against the advancing French cavalry.

They were now all at the gallop, though the horses were still being restrained. Rostov could see their faces as the commander shouted, 'Charge!' and let his thoroughbred go at full speed. Rostov was now in danger of being run down or swept into the attack against the French, so he galloped his horse flat out across their lines, but to no avail – he still couldn't avoid them.

The last rider, a giant of a man with a pock-marked face, scowled viciously when Rostov suddenly appeared in front of him and a collision seemed inevitable. This man would certainly have brought Rostov and Bedouin down (Rostov felt so tiny and feeble alongside these gigantic men and horses), but he just managed to lash out with his riding-crop across the horse's face. The massive black charger, sixteen hands if he was an inch, flattened his ears and reared back, but the pock-marked rider brought him down with a vicious thrust of his big spurs, and the horse responded by lashing its tail and stretching its neck before hurtling on faster than ever. The horse guards had barely gone past him when Rostov heard them roar their 'Hurrah!' and when he looked closer he saw their leading ranks getting tangled up with some other cavalrymen with red epaulettes, probably French. That was all he saw because at that moment cannons thundered somewhere near by and everything was blotted out in smoke.

As the horse guards rushed past him and vanished in the smoke, Rostov wondered whether to gallop after them or go on with his mission. This was one of those brilliant cavalry charges by our horse guards which even the French were said to admire. Rostov was appalled to learn later that the vast mass of these big, fine men, all those brilliant, rich young officers and cadets who had galloped past him on horses worth thousands, after the charge had been reduced to eighteen survivors.

'I don't need to envy them. My turn will come, and anyway I might see the Emperor!' thought Rostov as he galloped off.

When he reached the foot guards he could tell that cannonballs were whizzing about everywhere not so much from the sound of them as from the soldiers' worried faces and an unusually grave and aggressive look about the officers.

He was riding behind a line of foot guards when he heard someone call his name: 'Rostov!'

'Who's that?' he called back without seeing that it was Boris.

'I say, we've just been in the front line! Our regiment's been attacking!' said Boris, grinning cheerfully like any young man who has just been under fire for the first time.

Rostov stopped.

'You haven't!' he said. 'What was it like?'

'We beat them back!' said Boris, excited and eager to talk. 'Can you imagine? . . .' And Boris began describing how the guards had got into position, seen some troops in front of them and assumed they were Austrians, only to discover from the cannonballs coming at them that they were in the very front line and had to go straight into battle. Rostov couldn't stay for the end of the story – he urged his horse on.

'Where are you off to?' asked Boris.

'Taking a message to his Majesty.'

'But he's here!' said Boris, who had mistaken Rostov's 'his Majesty' for 'his Highness'. Thinking he wanted the grand duke, he pointed him out a hundred yards away, wearing a helmet and a horse guard's jacket, distinctive with his high shoulders and dark scowl and busy shouting at a pale-faced Austrian officer in a white uniform.

'No, that's the grand duke. I need the commander-in-chief or the Emperor,' said Rostov, on the point of galloping away.

'Count! Count!' shouted Berg, running up from the other side, just as excited as Boris. 'I've been wounded in my right hand,' (and he pointed to his bloodstained hand bandaged in a handkerchief) 'but I stayed there at the front, Count, holding my sword in my left hand. All of us, Count, the Von Bergs, we've all been valiant knights.' Berg rambled on, but Rostov rode away without listening to any more.

Leaving the guards behind and crossing some open land, Rostov rode along past the reserves to make sure he didn't end up (like last time with the charging cavalrymen) back in the front line, and he made a big detour to avoid the area where the gunfire and cannonade were at their loudest. Then suddenly, right in front of him and behind our troops, in a place where it would be unthinkable to find the enemy, he heard several muskets going off quite close.

'What can it be?' thought Rostov. 'The enemy at the rear of our troops? It can't be,' he thought as a sense of dread gripped him, fear for himself and for the outcome of the whole battle. 'Oh well, whatever happens,' he said to himself, 'I can't keep on making detours. I must find out whether the commander-in-chief is here, and if it's all over my job is to die with the others.'

The dark forebodings that had descended on Rostov seemed to be more and more justified the farther he advanced into the region beyond the village of Pratzen, which was teeming with troops of every kind.

'What does it mean? What's it all about? Who are they firing at? Who's firing?' Rostov started asking the Austrian and Russian soldiers cutting across him in a confused, scurrying shambles.

'God knows!' 'All of them killed!' 'We've had it!' Answers emerged from the running hordes in Russian, German and Czech, but these people knew no more than he did.

'Kill them Germans!' shouted one voice.

'To hell with 'em – can't trust 'em!'

'To hell with these Russians,' growled someone in German.

There were wounded men walking along the road. Shouts, moans and curses came together in a noisy chorus. The firing had begun to subside, and Rostov was to discover later that the Russian and Austrian soldiers had been firing at each other.

'My God! What's it all about?' thought Rostov. 'To think that any minute now the Emperor could arrive and see them! No, no, there can't be many of these cowardly swine. This will soon be over, it's not the real thing, it can't be,' he thought. 'I just wish they'd get a move on!'

Nikolay Rostov could not get his head around the idea of being defeated and running away. Even though he could see French cannons and French troops deployed on Pratzen hill, the very hill where he had been told to look for the commander-in-chief, he could not and would not believe it.

CHAPTER 18

Rostov had been told to look for Kutuzov and the Emperor somewhere near the village of Pratzen. But they were not there, nor was there a single officer to be found in command, nothing but motley crowds of shambling troops. He urged on his weary horse to get through this rabble as fast as he could, but the further he went the more ragged the crowds became. When he reached the high road he found it teeming with carriages and every kind of vehicle, and all sorts of Austrian and Russian soldiers, some wounded, some not. There was a dull roar of people and traffic swarming along to the sinister sound of the cannon-balls whizzing over from the French batteries now deployed on the heights of Pratzen.

'Where's the Emperor? Where's Kutuzov?' Rostov asked anyone prepared to stop. He got no answers.

At last, grabbing a soldier by the collar, he forced him to respond.

'Listen, mate – that lot went off ages ago!' the soldier said to Rostov, laughing for no good reason as he wrenched himself free. Letting him go – he must surely have been drunk – Rostov stopped the horse of a batman or groom serving someone of rank and started to interrogate him. He informed Rostov that only an hour before the Tsar had been driven down this very road in a carriage going at full speed, and the Tsar was seriously wounded.

'It can't be him,' said Rostov. 'It must be someone else.'

'Saw it with my own eyes,' said the groom with a complacent smirk, 'I'm one as ought to know the Emperor – seen him lots of times in Petersburg. Sat in his carriage white as a sheet. You should've seen them driving those four black horses! Went past like thunder! You'd have to know the Tsar's horses and Ilya Ivanych. Old Ilya, never drives nobody but the Tsar.'

Rostov let go of his horse and was about to move on when a wounded officer who happened to be passing spoke to him. 'Who is it you're looking for?' he asked. 'The commander-in-chief? Oh, he was killed by a cannonball. Got him in the chest right in front of our regiment.'

But another officer corrected him. 'No, he was wounded, not killed.'
'Who? Kutuzov?' asked Rostov.

'No, not Kutuzov, that other one, what's his name? Same difference
– not many left alive. That's the way. Go to that village. They're all
there, the commanding officers,' said the officer, pointing to the village
of Gostieradeck, and he walked away.

Rostov kept his horse at walking pace, not knowing why he should
go on or who to look for. The Tsar was wounded, the battle lost. He
had to believe it now. He was heading where he had been directed,
and in the distance he could see a church with a tower. Why hurry?
What would he say now to the Tsar or Kutuzov, even if they were still
alive and not wounded?

'Go down this road, sir, and you'll get killed!' a soldier shouted to
him. 'You'll get killed down there!'

'Stupid nonsense!' said another. 'There's no other way. That's nearest.' Rostov wondered for a moment but then rode off towards the
place where they had said he would get killed.

'It makes no difference now! If the Emperor's wounded why should
I save my skin?' he thought. He rode into a patch of land where more
men had been killed running away from Pratzen than anywhere else.
The French had yet to take that ground, though the Russians – those
who were unscathed or only lightly wounded – had long abandoned
it. The dead and wounded lay about everywhere like heaps of manure
on good plough-land, half a dozen bodies to an acre. The wounded
crawled together in little groups of two or three with pitiful shouts
and groans, though some of them struck Rostov as rather forced. He
put his horse to a trot to avoid seeing all those suffering people, and
now he felt scared, scared that he might lose not his life but the courage
that he needed so much, and he knew it would not survive the sight
of those wretched creatures.

The French had stopped firing at this field strewn with dead and
wounded, because there was no one left to fire at, but once they spotted
an adjutant trotting across they aimed a cannon at him and loosed off
a few cannonballs. The impression made on him by these terrible
whizzing noises and the dead bodies all round him blurred into a
single sensation – he felt horrified and sorry for himself. He thought
of his mother's last letter. 'What would she think,' he wondered, 'if
she could see me now on this field with cannons aiming at me?'

In the village of Gostieradeck there were some Russian troops,
disorientated but still in some sort of order, walking away from the
battlefield. Here they were out of range of the French cannons and the
sounds of gunfire seemed a long way away. Here it was clear to

everyone that the battle had been lost, and defeat was on everyone's lips. Rostov asked around, but no one could tell him where the Tsar, or Kutuzov, might be found. Some said that the rumour about the Tsar being wounded was true. Others said it wasn't, and the false report that had spread like wildfire could be easily explained – it was the Grand Marshal Tolstoy, a member of the Emperor's entourage out with the others on the battlefield, who had been seen rushing back in the Tsar's carriage all pale and terrified. One officer mentioned to Rostov that over to the left outside the village he had seen a senior officer from headquarters, and Rostov rode off in that direction, no longer hoping to find anyone, but just to keep his conscience clear. He had ridden for a couple of miles, passing the last of the Russian troops, when he came to a kitchen-garden enclosed by a ditch; two men on horseback stood facing the ditch. One of them had a white plume in his hat and Rostov fancied he had seen him before. The other man was a stranger on a fine chestnut (in his case it was the horse that looked familiar). He rode up to the ditch, gave his horse a touch of the spurs, loosened the reins and jumped easily across into the garden, disturbing nothing but a little earth that crumbled down from the bank under his horse's hind hooves. Turning the horse sharply, he jumped back over the ditch and made a respectful approach to the horseman with the white plume, as if inviting him to do the same. Rostov was suddenly fascinated by the rider whose general appearance had struck him as familiar, and when this man made a gesture of refusal with his head and his hand Rostov instantly recognized his idolized and much-lamented sovereign.

'No, it can't be. Not him on his own in the middle of this empty field,' thought Rostov. At that moment Alexander turned his head and Rostov caught sight of the beloved features so sharply etched into his memory. The Tsar was pale, his cheeks looked haggard and his eyes hollow, but this made his features look even more charming and gentle. Rostov was delighted to discover that the rumour about the Emperor being wounded was untrue. He was delighted to see him. Now was his chance – indeed it was his duty – to go straight up to him and deliver the message entrusted to him by Dolgorukov.

But, just as a lovelorn youth dithers and freezes, too scared to force out the words he has dreamt about for nights on end, panics and looks around for help or any chance of delay and escape now that the longed-for moment is here and he and she are alone together, so Rostov, suddenly presented with what he wanted most in all the world, had no idea how to approach the Emperor, and his mind was assailed by thousands of reasons why it would be wrong, inconvenient and impossible to do so.

'No! It would be like taking advantage of him when he's alone and despondent. It might be unpleasant and painful for him to see an unfamiliar face when he's suffering like that. Anyway, what could I say to him now, when one look at him makes my heart leap and my mouth go all dry?' In his imagination he had composed innumerable speeches addressed to the Tsar, but not one of them came to mind now. They had been intended for other occasions; they were meant to be spoken mainly at moments of victory and triumph, and predominantly on his deathbed, when the Emperor thanked him for his heroism and he with his dying breath gave voice to the love that he had just proved in action.

'Then again, how can I ask the Emperor for instructions about the right flank when it's nearly four o'clock in the afternoon and we've lost the battle? No, I mustn't go up to him. I mustn't interrupt him while he's thinking. Better die a thousand deaths than get one angry glance from him, one sign of his disapproval,' Rostov decided, and with a heavy heart he rode away in some despair, constantly turning to look back at the Tsar, still standing there, a picture of indecision.

While Rostov was thinking things over and riding sadly away, a certain Captain Von Toll happened to ride up to the same spot, saw the Emperor and went straight up to him, offering his services and helping him to walk across the ditch. Feeling unwell and in need of rest, the Tsar sat down under an apple-tree, and Von Toll remained at his side. Rostov looked back down the long road and watched with envy and regret as Von Toll stayed with the Emperor for some time, talking eagerly, and the Emperor, clearly in tears, put a hand over his eyes and shook hands with Von Toll.

'And it could have been me not him!' Rostov thought, and hardly able to hold back his tears of sympathy for the Tsar, he rode away in the depths of despair, not knowing where to go or why. Worst of all, he knew that his despair was all his own fault – his weakness had caused all this misery. He could have gone up to the Emperor . . . he should have done. This had been his one chance to demonstrate his devotion to the Emperor. And he had missed it . . . 'What have I done?' he thought. He turned his horse and galloped back to the place where he had seen the Emperor, but there was no one there across the ditch. Nothing but wagons and carriages going by. He learnt from one of the drivers that Kutuzov's staff were not far away; they were in the village where the wagons were going. Rostov followed them.

In front of him Kutuzov's groom was leading horses covered with their cloths. A wagon followed the groom, and after the wagon came a bow-legged old servant, hobbling along in cap and jacket.

'Hey, Titus!' said the groom.

'What?' answered the old man absent-mindedly.

'Titus a drum!'

'Stupid idiot!' said the old man, spitting angrily. For a few minutes they all moved on in silence, and then the same silly joke was repeated.

It was coming up to five o'clock and the battle had been lost at every point. More than a hundred cannons were in French hands. Przebyszewski and his corps had surrendered. The other columns, having lost half their men, were retreating in complete disarray. The surviving forces of Langeron and Dokhturov mingled together in crowds on the banks of dams and ponds near the village of Augest.

By six o'clock the Augest dam was the only place where heavy gunfire could still be heard, and it came only from the French side, where several batteries newly deployed on the hillside outside Pratzen continued to fire down on our troops as they retreated.

In the rearguard Dokhturov and the others had re-formed their battalions and were firing back at the pursuing French cavalry. It was now getting dark. On the bank of the narrow Augest dam, where year after year the old miller in his cap had sat fishing while his grandson rolled up his sleeves and ran his fingers through the silvery fish thrashing about in the bucket; on the same dam where year after year the Moravians in their shaggy caps and blue jackets had peacefully driven their two-horse wagons of wheat up to the mill, and trundled back, dusty with flour that whitened their carts – on this narrow dam hideous men with hideous expressions running for their lives now scrambled together, jostling with wagons and cannons, falling under horses' hooves and carriage-wheels, all squashed up close, falling down dead, stepping over dying men and killing each other, only to stagger a few steps and get killed in the same way.

Every ten seconds a cannonball would blast the air and come whizzing down, or a grenade would burst in the thick of the crowd, dealing out death and splashing the bystanders with blood. The newly promoted Dolokhov, who had been wounded in the hand, walked along with a dozen soldiers of his company and his general on horseback, the sole survivors from an entire regiment. Borne along by the crowd, they all squeezed together in the approach to the dam and stood there, squashed in from every side because a horse pulling a cannon had fallen down and the crowd were dragging it away. A cannonball killed somebody behind them, another one crashed down just ahead and

Dolokhov was spattered with blood. The crowd surged forward desperately, squeezed up, moved on a step or two and stopped again. Everyone had the same thought: 'If I can just get through the next hundred yards I'm sure I'll be all right. Two minutes here and I'm a dead man.'

Dolokhov scrambled through from the centre of the crowd to the edge of the dam, shoved two soldiers aside and ran down on to the slippery ice that covered the millpond.

'Come on down here!' he shouted, bounding over the ice as it cracked under him. 'Come on down here!' he kept shouting to the cannon crew. 'The ice is good! . . .'

The ice was good, but it sank and cracked, and it was obviously going to give way under his weight alone, never mind a cannon or a crowd of people. They all stared down at him and flooded to the brink, too scared to venture out on to the ice. His regimental commander, waiting on horseback at the end of the dam, raised one hand and opened his mouth wide to speak to Dolokhov. Suddenly a stray cannonball whizzed across so low over the heads of the crowd that everybody ducked. There was a terrible splashing sound and the general fell from his horse in a pool of blood. No one even looked at him, let alone thought of picking him up.

'On to the ice! Get on the ice! Come down here! This way! Can't you hear? Come on!' Voices rang out on all sides after the ball had hit the general, though nobody knew what he was shouting or why.

One of the rear cannons that had been manhandled up on to the dam was trundled down on to the ice. Crowds of soldiers began running down on to the frozen surface. The ice cracked under one of the leading soldiers, and one leg slipped into the water. He tried to drag himself out but he was in waist-deep. The nearest soldiers tried to stop, the cannon driver reined in his horse, but still the shouts came from behind: 'Get down on the ice. Don't stop! Go on! Go on!' Screams of horror came from the crowd. The soldiers near to the cannon waved furiously at the horses, and lashed at them to make them turn round and go back. But the horses moved on and stepped over the edge. The ice that had been strong enough to hold walking people cracked across in one huge piece and three dozen men standing on it lunged forwards and backwards, shoving one another down into the water.

Meanwhile cannonballs continued to zoom across and crash down everywhere, on the ice, in the water, and more often than not straight into the crowd that had engulfed the dam, the nearby ponds and the bank.

CHAPTER 19

Up on the Pratzen heights Prince Andrey Bolkonsky was lying where he had fallen with the flagstaff in his hands, bleeding from a head-wound and moaning pitifully, without being aware of it, in a soft voice like that of a child. By late afternoon he had stopped moaning and lay there perfectly still. He had no idea how long he had been unconscious, but now suddenly he felt alive again, not least from the burning, lacerating pain in his head.

'Where's it gone, that lofty sky that I had never known before until I saw it today?' was his first thought. 'And I've never known pain like this before either,' he thought. 'No, up to now I have known nothing, absolutely nothing. But where am I?'

He listened, and there was the sound of approaching hooves and French-speaking voices. He opened his eyes wide. There was the same lofty sky above him, with clouds floating higher than ever and through them glimpses of a blue infinity. He didn't turn his head and couldn't see the men who, if the voices and the hooves were anything to go by, had ridden up near by and stopped.

It was Napoleon himself with two of his adjutants. Bonaparte was going round everywhere, issuing final instructions for reinforcing the batteries firing down at the Augest dam, and inspecting the dead and wounded on the battlefield.

'Fine men!' said Napoleon, looking down at a dead Russian grenadier lying on his belly with his face rammed into the soil. The back of his head had gone black and one of his arms, flung out wide, was already stiffening.

'The field-guns are out of ammunition, your Majesty,' said an adjutant, arriving that moment from the batteries that were firing at Augest.

'Bring some more up from the reserves,' said Napoleon before riding on a few steps and then coming to a halt right above Prince Andrey, who was lying on his back with the flagstaff still where he had dropped it, though the flag itself had been taken by the French as a trophy.

'A fine death this one!' said Napoleon, looking down at Bolkonsky. Prince Andrey knew they were talking about him, and Napoleon was doing the talking – he had heard the speaker addressed as 'your Majesty'. But the words sounded like buzzing flies. They were of no interest to him, he didn't take them in and he immediately forgot them. He had a burning headache, he could feel himself losing blood, and there above him was the lofty, far-distant, unending sky. He knew it was Napoleon – his hero – but at that moment Napoleon seemed to him such a tiny, inconsequential creature compared with everything that was now transpiring between his spirit and that lofty, sky-blue infinity with its busy clouds. At that moment he could not have cared less who was standing over him, or what they were saying about him. He was just glad that someone had stopped and was standing over him, and his only desire was for these people to help him and bring him back to life, because life was good and he saw it all differently now. He made a huge effort to move and make some kind of noise. He stirred one leg faintly, and produced a feeble, sickly moan that he himself found moving.

'Oh, he's alive,' said Napoleon. 'Pick him up, this young man and have him taken to a dressing-station!'

This said, Napoleon rode on to meet Marshal Lannes, who had removed his hat and was now advancing, all smiles, to meet his Emperor and congratulate him on his victory.

Prince Andrey remembered nothing more. He had lost consciousness from the terrible pain that shot through him as they laid him on the stretcher and continued with every jolt as they carried him over to the dressing-station and began to explore the extent of his wound. When at last he came round it was late evening and he was being taken to the field-hospital along with some other wounded and captured Russian officers. During the transfer he felt a little stronger and could look around, even speak.

The first words he heard on coming round came from a French convoy officer who was gabbling, 'We must stop here. The Emperor's coming soon. He'll enjoy seeing these gentlemen prisoners.'

'Too many prisoners today, nearly the whole Russian army – he's probably had enough of them,' said another officer.

'Yes, but look. They say this one is the chief commander of Alexander's guards,' said the first speaker, pointing to a wounded Russian officer in the white uniform of the horse guards. Bolkonsky recognized him as Prince Repnin, having met him in Petersburg society. Next to him stood another wounded horse guards officer, a boy of nineteen.

Napoleon arrived at a gallop and came to a halt.

'Which one is the senior officer?' he said, seeing the prisoners.

They named the colonel, Prince Repnin.

'Are you the commander of Emperor Alexander's horse guards regiment?' asked Napoleon.

'I was in command of a squadron,' replied Repnin.

'Your regiment did its duty honourably,' said Napoleon.

'Praise from a great general is a soldier's highest reward,' said Repnin.

'I bestow it upon you with pleasure,' said Napoleon. 'Who is this young man at your side?'

Prince Repnin named him as Lieutenant Sukhtelen.

Napoleon looked at him and said with a smile, 'He's a bit young to be meddling with us.'

'Being young doesn't stop you being brave,' said Sukhtelen with a tremor in his voice.

'A splendid answer,' said Napoleon. 'Young man, you will go far.'

Prince Andrey, who had been pushed forward under the Emperor's nose as a prize capture, could hardly have failed to attract his attention. Napoleon seemed to remember seeing him on the field, and in speaking to him he used the same epithet, 'young man', which his first sight of Bolkonsky had deposited in his memory.

'What about you, young man,' he said to him. 'How are you feeling, my dear fellow?'

Even though five minutes earlier Prince Andrey had been able to say a few words to the soldiers who were carrying him, now, with his eyes glued on Napoleon, he said nothing . . . All the things that Napoleon stood for seemed so trivial at that moment, his hero seemed so petty in his squalid vanity and triumphalism, compared with that lofty, righteous and kindly sky which he had seen and understood, that he couldn't reply. Everything in the world seemed pointless and trivial beside the solemn and serious line of thinking induced in him by weakness from loss of blood, great pain and a brush with death. Looking Napoleon straight in the eye, Prince Andrey mused on the insignificance of greatness, on the insignificance of human life, the meaning of which no one could understand, and most of all the insignificance of death, which no living person could make sense of or explain.

The Emperor, after pausing for a reply that never came, turned to go and before riding away he spoke to one the officers in command. 'I want these gentlemen well looked after and taken to my camp. Let my surgeon, Dr Larrey, see to their wounds. *Au revoir*, Prince Repnin,' he said and galloped away. His face was a picture of smug self-satisfaction.

The soldiers carrying Prince Andrey had come across the gold icon that Princess Marya had hung around her brother's neck and removed it, but once they had seen the Emperor's benevolent attitude to the prisoners they soon put it back again.

Prince Andrey didn't see anyone put it back, or how it was done, but suddenly there it was again on his chest outside his uniform, his icon on its delicate gold chain.

'Wouldn't it be nice,' thought Prince Andrey, as he glanced down at the little icon which his sister had hung round his neck with such feeling and reverence, 'wouldn't it be nice if everything was as clear-cut and straightforward as it seems to Marie? Wouldn't it be nice if we knew where to turn to for help in this life and what to expect when it's over, beyond the grave?'

'What happiness and peace of mind would be mine if I only could say now, "Lord have mercy upon me! . . ." But who would I be talking to? Either some indeterminate, inaccessible power, which I cannot have any contact with and cannot even put into words, the great All or Nothing,' he said to himself, 'or else that God sewn up in a little bag like Marie's icon? No, nothing is certain, nothing but the nothingness of all that we can understand, and the splendour of something we can't understand, but we know to be infinitely important!'

The stretcher was on the move again. At every jolt he was racked with unbearable pain. His temperature rose and soon he was delirious. Images of his father, his wife, his sister and his unborn son, the tenderness he had felt on the eve of battle, the petty little figure of Napoleon, and above all the lofty sky – these were the essential ideas in his raving mind. He dreamt of a quiet life and peaceful family happiness at Bald Hills. He was settling down to enjoy this happiness when suddenly that little man Napoleon turned up with his callous, shrivelled look of someone revelling in the misery of others, and then came doubts and more agony, with only the sky promising peace. By morning all his dreams had merged and melted away into the chaos and darkness of unconsciousness and oblivion, with death, according to Napoleon's surgeon, Dr Larrey, a much more likely prospect than recovery.

'He's a bad patient, all nerves and bile,' said Larrey. 'He's not going to recover.'

Prince Andrey, with all the other hopeless cases, was left behind in the care of the local inhabitants.

VOLUME II

PART I

It was 1806, early in the year, and Nikolay Rostov was going home on leave. So was Denisov, and since he lived in Voronezh Rostov persuaded him to call in at Moscow, break his journey and stay with them. Denisov met his comrade at the last posting station but one, and drank three bottles of wine with him, after which not even the potholes on the Moscow road could keep him awake, slumped as he was at the bottom of the sledge beside Rostov, who was getting more and more impatient the nearer they came to Moscow.

'Oh, how much further is it? How much further? Oh, these awful streets, shops, bakers' signs, street lamps, sledges!' thought Rostov, when they had signed in at the city gates and entered the outskirts of Moscow.

'Denisov, we're here! Still asleep!' he kept saying, urging his body forward as though that might make the sledge go faster. Denisov made no response.

'This is the crossroads corner where Zakhar used to wait with his sledge. There he is – that's Zakhar! Still the same horse. Oh, we used to buy cakes at that little shop. Oh, do get a move on! Please!'

'Which house is it?' asked the driver.

'That one at the end, the big one. Are you blind? That's our house,' Rostov kept saying. 'Oh yes, that's our house.'

'Denisov! Denisov! We're nearly there!'

Denisov glanced up, cleared his throat and said nothing.

'Dmitry,' said Rostov to his valet on the box, 'the lights are still on at home, aren't they?'

'They certainly are. There's even a light in your papa's study.'

'They haven't gone to bed yet, have they?'

'Make sure you get my new tunic out straightaway,' he added, fingering his newly grown moustache. 'Will you get a move on!' he yelled at the driver. 'Come on, do wake up, Vaska,' he said to Denisov, whose head had drooped again. 'Oh, do get a move on! I'll give you a tip, three roubles, if you'll only *move*!' shouted Rostov when they were only three houses away. The horses seemed to be standing still. At long last the sledge turned right through the entry and there it all was – the familiar chipped cornice up on high, with the steps and the stone kerb down below. The sledge was still moving when he jumped out and ran up into the entrance hall. The house stood there, stolidly unwelcoming as if it hadn't the slightest interest in whoever might have arrived. There was no one there. 'Oh God! Is everything all right?' Rostov wondered, stopping for a moment with a sinking heart, and then running on through the hall and up the familiar winding stairs. Still the same door handle, the bane of his mother's life when it got dirty, and still loose. In the hall there was a single tallow candle burning.

Old Mikhaylo was lying on his wooden chest fast asleep, but the footman, Prokofy, a man strong enough to lift the back of a carriage right off the ground, was sitting there busily making peasant shoes out of strips of selvage. He glanced towards the door as it was flung open and his expression of dozy indifference changed instantly to a mixture of joy and alarm.

'Merciful heavens! If it's not the young master!' he cried, recognizing the young count. 'It can't be! My dear, dear boy!' And Prokofy, shaking with emotion, leapt for the drawing-room door, probably wanting to announce him, but then thought better of it, came back and fell on his young master's shoulder.

'Is everyone well?' asked Rostov, withdrawing his arm.

'Yes, thank God! They're all well, thank God! Just finished supper! Oh, let me have a good look at you, your Excellency!'

'Is everything all right?'

'Oh yes, thank God. Thank God!'

Forgetting all about Denisov and not wanting them to have any warning of his arrival, Rostov flung off his fur coat and tiptoed quickly into the big, dark reception-hall. Nothing had changed – the same card tables, the same chandelier with its cover on . . . but someone had seen him, and before he could get to the drawing-room something hurtled out of a side door and overwhelmed him with a deluge of hugging and kissing. A second figure, then a third dashed in through two other doors; more hugs, more kisses, more shouts and tears of joy. Papa, Natasha, Petya . . . he couldn't tell who was who or who was where. Everybody was shouting and talking and kissing him, all at the same time. Only his mother was missing – as he suddenly noticed.

'I just didn't know . . . Nicky . . . My darling boy!'

'Here he is . . . our boy . . . my darling Kolya . . . Hasn't he changed!'

'Get some candles! Let's have some tea!'

'Oh, give me a kiss!'

'My dear darling . . . me too.'

Sonya, Natasha, Petya, Anna Mikhaylovna, Vera and the old count were all hugging him, and then the servants and the maids flocked into the room, filling it with their chatter and all their oohs and ahs.

Petya swung from his legs yelling, 'Me too!'

Natasha, who had grabbed him to herself and smothered his face with kisses, now hopped away, seized the hem of his jacket and skipped up and down on one spot like a goat, splitting their ears with her shrieks.

On every side were loving eyes, glittering tears of joy and lips hungry for kisses.

Sonya too, as red as a beetroot, clung to his arm and positively beamed at him, gazing blissfully into those eyes of his which she had missed so much. Sonya had just turned sixteen and she looked very pretty, especially at this moment of eager, rapturous excitement. She gazed at him, unable to take her eyes off him, grinning and breathless. He glanced at her thankfully, but still he was looking and waiting for someone else – the old countess still hadn't appeared.

Footsteps were heard suddenly outside the door. They were so rapid that they could hardly be his mother's – but they were. In she came wearing a new dress that he hadn't seen before, obviously made while he had been away. Everybody let go of him, and he ran across to her. When they came together, she sank down on his chest, sobbing. Quite incapable of looking up, she could do nothing but press her face into the cold braiding of his hussar's jacket. Denisov, who had stolen in unnoticed, stood there looking at them and rubbing his eyes.

'Vasily Denisov, fwiend of your son,' he said, introducing himself to the count, who had turned to him with a quizzical look.

'You're most welcome. I've heard all about you,' said the count, kissing and embracing Denisov. 'Nikolay wrote to us . . . Natasha, Vera, look who's here – Denisov.'

The same blissfully happy faces turned to the tousled figure of Denisov with his black moustache and swarmed round him.

'Darling Denisov,' squealed Natasha, beside herself with delight, and she lost no time in dashing over to hug him and kiss him. Everyone was embarrassed by Natasha's behaviour. Denisov reddened too, but with a smile he took Natasha's hand and kissed it.

Denisov was conducted to the room prepared for him, while the

Rostovs all gathered about their little Nikolay in the sitting-room. The old countess sat beside him, clasping him by the hand; not a minute passed without her bestowing a kiss on it. The others crowded round, drinking in every movement, every glance, every word he uttered; they couldn't take their eager and adoring eyes off him. His brother and sisters squabbled over him, struggling for the seat nearest to him and fighting for the privilege of bringing him tea, a handkerchief, a pipe.

Rostov was very happy with all the love showered upon him. But that first moment of their meeting had been sheer bliss and now his happiness seemed somehow reduced, as if more could be expected, more and more again.

Next morning, following their long drive, the new arrivals slept through until ten o'clock.

The adjoining room was one big mess – swords, bags, sabretaches, open trunks and dirty boots everywhere. Two pairs of nice clean boots with spurs had recently been put by the wall. The servants brought in wash-basins, hot shaving water and their clothes, neatly brushed. The room reeked of tobacco and young men.

'Hey, Gwishka, bwing me a pipe!' shouted Vaska Denisov in a husky voice. 'Wostov, time to get up!'

Rostov, rubbing the sleep out of his eyes, lifted his head from the hot pillow, his hair all over the place.

'Why? What time is it?'

'You're late. It's nearly ten o'clock,' answered Natasha's voice, and from the next room came the rustling of starched skirts, the sound of whispering and girlish laughter. The door was open half an inch and through it came a flash of something blue, a play of ribbons, black hair and merry faces. Natasha had come along with Sonya and Petya to see if he was up yet.

'Come on Nikolay, it's time to get up!' Natasha's voice rang out through the door.

'I'm coming!'

Meanwhile in the outer room Petya had spotted the swords and seized them with the rapture small boys feel at the sight of an elder brother who is in the army. Forgetting that it was not proper for his sisters to see young men in a state of undress, he opened the bedroom door.

'Is this your sabre?' he shouted.

The girls skipped away. Denisov hid his hairy legs under the bed-clothes, grimacing and appealing to his friend for help. The door admitted Petya and closed again after him. Giggling could be heard from outside.

'Nikolay, put on your dressing-gown,' cried Natasha's voice.

'Is this your sabre?' asked Petya. 'Or is it yours?' He turned with enormous respect to the black-moustached Denisov.

Rostov pulled on his shoes and stockings at great speed, put on his dressing-gown and went out. Natasha had put on one of his spurred boots and was getting into the other. Sonya had been twirling round and as he came in her skirt ballooned out and she sank down. The girls were dressed alike in new frocks of cornflower blue; they looked fresh, rosy and high-spirited. Sonya ran away, but Natasha took her brother by the arm, led him away into the sitting-room and began to talk to him. There wasn't enough time in the world for them to ask and answer questions about the thousand little details that only they would have wanted to know about. Natasha laughed at every word he said and at every word she said, not because what they said was funny but because she was so exuberant she couldn't contain her joy and it kept overflowing into laughter.

'Oh, it's wonderful! Isn't it marvellous?' she said to everything. For the first time in a year and a half, basking in the warmth of all this love radiating from Natasha, Rostov could feel his spirit and his features expanding into a childish smile, the like of which he had not smiled since he left home.

'Oh, listen,' she said, 'you're a real man now, aren't you? I'm awfully glad you're my brother.' She touched his moustache. 'I do want to know what you're like, you men. Are you like us?'

'No. Why did Sonya run away?' asked Rostov.

'Oh, that's a long story! How are you going to speak to Sonya? Will you call her "*tu*" or "*vous*"?'[1]

'I'll see what happens,' said Rostov.

'Call her "*vous*", please. I'll tell you why later.'

'No, but why?'

'Oh, all right, I'll tell you now. You know Sonya's my friend. She's such a close friend that I'd burn my arm for her. Look.' She rolled up her muslin sleeve and showed him a red scar on her long, thin, soft little arm well above the elbow near the shoulder (on a part which is always covered even in a ballgown).

'I did that to prove my love for her. I just heated a ruler in the fire and pressed it there.'

Sitting in his old school-room on the sofa with little cushions on both arms, and looking into Natasha's desperately eager eyes, Rostov was transported back into that world of family life and childhood which meant nothing to anyone else but gave him some of the sweetest pleasures in his life, where burning your arm with a ruler as a token

of love didn't seem a silly thing to do – he understood it and it came
as no surprise.

'Well, what about it?' he asked.

'Well, that's us, really close friends! I know the ruler and all that is
stupid, but we are friends for ever. If she loves anybody, it'll be for
ever. I can't understand that. I forget things so easily.'

'Well, what about it?'

'Well, you see, she loves me and you.' Natasha suddenly blushed.
'Well, you remember what happened before you went away . . . She
wants you to forget all about it . . . She said I'll always love him, but
let him be free. Isn't that wonderful? I think it's a noble thing to do.
She's being really noble. Isn't she?' Natasha was being serious and
emotional – it was clear that what she was saying now she had gone
through before in tears. Rostov considered.

'I never go back on my word,' he said. 'Anyway, Sonya's so lovely
– who'd be stupid enough to throw away his own happiness?'

'No, no, no,' cried Natasha. 'We've talked about that already. We
knew you'd say that. But it won't do. Oh, look, if you say that – if
you think you can't go back on your word – it makes it seem as if she
said it all on purpose. It makes it seem as if you're being forced into
marrying her, and it's all gone wrong.'

Rostov could see that it had all been well thought through by the
pair of them. Sonya had struck him as really beautiful yesterday;
today, even though he had only caught a glimpse of her, she had
looked even prettier. She was a charming sixteen-year-old, obviously
passionately in love with him – he didn't doubt this for a minute.
'Why shouldn't he love her and even get married to her one day? But
not now,' mused Rostov. 'Just now there is so much else to do and
enjoy!'

'Yes, they have thought it through,' he thought; 'I must keep my
freedom.'

'Well, that's all right, then,' he said, 'we can talk about this later
on. Oh, I'm so glad to be back with you!' he added. 'Now, you tell
me, you've not been unfaithful to Boris, have you?'

'Don't be silly!' cried Natasha, laughing. 'I never think about him
or anybody else. I'm not interested.'

'And what exactly do you mean by that?'

'What do I mean?' Natasha queried, and her face lit up with a happy
smile. 'Have you seen Duport?'[2]

'No.'

'You haven't? Duport, the famous ballet-dancer? Oh, you won't
understand then. This is me now . . .' Forming her arms into a circle,

Natasha held out her skirt like a ballerina, tripped a few steps away, twirled round in a pirouette and then did a little entrechat, tapping her toes together in mid-air, coming down on the very tips of them and tripping forward a few steps.

'Look, I'm on points. Can't you see?' she said, but she couldn't stay up on her toes. 'That's me from now on! I'm never going to get married. I'm going to be a ballet-dancer. But don't tell anybody.'

Rostov roared with laughter so merrily that Denisov in his room felt a pang of jealousy, and Natasha couldn't help laughing too.

'No, but that's good, isn't it?' she kept asking.

'Of course it is. So you're not going to marry Boris?'

Natasha flared up.

'I'm not going to marry anybody! I'll tell him myself when I see him.'

'All right then,' said Rostov.

'But this is all stupid,' Natasha burbled on. 'Tell me about Denisov. Is he nice?' she asked.

'Yes, he is.'

'Well, off you go then. Go and get dressed . . . I'm scared of Denisov.'

'What do you mean scared?' asked Nikolay. 'No, Vaska's a good man.'

'Is that what you call him – Vaska? . . . Doesn't it sound funny! Is he very nice, then?'

'Yes, he is.'

'Get ready quickly and come and have some tea. We'll all be there together.'

And Natasha rose on to her points and tiptoed out of the room like a ballerina, but she was smiling the smile of a happy fifteen-year-old girl. In the drawing-room Rostov blushed when he came across Sonya, not knowing how to approach her. Yesterday they had kissed in that first joyful moment of meeting, but today he felt he couldn't do that. He could sense quizzical eyes upon him, his mother's and his sisters' – they were all wondering how he would behave with her. He kissed her hand and called her *vous* and *Sonya*. But their eyes when they met were on *tu* terms and they shared a tender kiss. Her eyes apologized for having dared to use Natasha as an emissary and remind him of his promise, and they thanked him for his love. His eyes thanked her for offering him his freedom, and told her that whatever happened he would never stop loving her, because it was impossible not to love her.

'It's odd, though – isn't it?' said Vera, choosing her moment when everyone was silent, 'odd that Sonya and Nikolay have gone all formal, like strangers.'

Vera's remark was true, like all her remarks, but like most of them it made everybody feel rather embarrassed – they all reddened, not just Sonya, Nikolay and Natasha, but even the countess, who was wary of her son's love for Sonya because it might threaten his prospects of a brilliant marriage, even she blushed like a little girl. Much to Rostov's surprise, when Denisov came into the drawing-room dressed in his new uniform, with his hair slicked down and nicely perfumed, he cut the same dashing figure as he had done on the battlefield, and behaved with the kind of sophistication and courtesy towards the ladies that Rostov had never expected to see in him.

CHAPTER 2

On his return to Moscow from the army Nikolay Rostov was received by his family as a hero and idol, the best of sons; by his relatives as a pleasant, charming and courteous young man; and by his acquaintances as a handsome lieutenant of hussars, a good dancer and one of the most eligible bachelors in town.

All Moscow knew the Rostovs. The old count was not without money that year after remortgaging all of his estates, and this made it possible for dear little Nikolay, who kept his own racehorse and wore the very latest riding breeches – a new style as yet unseen in Moscow – and the most fashionable boots with very pointed toes and tiny silver spurs, to enjoy himself. It didn't take long for Rostov, once back, to resume the old ways and feel good. He now considered himself grown up, a real man. The despair he had once felt when he had failed a Divinity examination, the times he had borrowed money from Gavrilo to pay his sledge-drivers, those stolen kisses with Sonya – he looked back on it all as childish nonsense belonging to the infinitely distant past. Now look at him – a lieutenant of hussars with silver braid on his jacket and a St George's Cross, owner of a horse in training for a race and on familiar terms with well-known men of the track, elderly and respected persons. He had also taken up with a certain lady living on the boulevard whom he visited of an evening. He had led the mazurka at the Arkharovs' ball,[3] discussed the war with Field-Marshal Kamensky, become a regular at the English Club and was on intimate terms with a forty-year-old colonel whom he had met through Denisov.

His passion for the Tsar had cooled a little in Moscow as time went by and he never saw him. But he never stopped talking about the

Emperor and his love for him, always with an implication that he was holding something back, that his own feeling for the Emperor had something about it that was beyond most people, though he joined wholeheartedly in the general feeling of adoration for Emperor Alexander, who had been dubbed 'the angel incarnate' by Moscow society of the day.

During this brief interlude in Moscow before returning to the army, far from growing closer to Sonya, he broke with her. She was very pretty and charming, and it was obvious that she was passionately in love with him. But he was at that stage of a young man's life when he thinks he is too busy for that sort of thing and he is reluctant to tie himself down because freedom is so precious and necessary when there is so much to be done. Whenever he thought about Sonya during this stay in Moscow, he said to himself, 'Oh dear, there are plenty more fish in the sea, so many girls like her waiting somewhere for me to meet them. There's plenty of time for me to think about falling in love when I feel like it, but I'm too busy just now.' He also began to consider that female company somehow undermined his masculinity. Whenever he went to a ball, knowing he was going to be with the ladies, he did so with a great show of reluctance. The races, the English Club, nights out with Denisov and *visits to a certain place* – that was all different, that was just what a dashing young hussar was meant to do.

At the beginning of March old Count Ilya Rostov set himself the demanding task of arranging a dinner at the English Club in honour of Prince Bagration.

The count would parade up and down the big hall in his dressing-gown, giving instructions to the chief bursar and to Feoktist, the renowned head chef, concerning the asparagus, fresh cucumbers, strawberries, veal and fish on the menu for Prince Bagration's dinner. The count was both founder-member and doyen of the club. He had been entrusted with the organization of the Bagration banquet because it would have been difficult to find anyone more capable of organizing a dinner on such a grand and lavish scale, let alone anyone more able and willing to put in some money of his own, should the organization require it. The chef and the bursar listened to the count's orders with humorous indulgence written all over their faces, because they knew that he was the best man around for throwing a dinner costing thousands from which good money could be made on the side.

'Oh yes, croutons, we must have croutons in the turtle soup.'

'How many cold dishes – three, I suppose? . . .' queried the chef.

The count thought this over.

'Yes, there'll have to be three ... Number one – mayonnaise,' he said, counting on a crooked finger.

'And did you decide on the large sturgeon?' asked the bursar.

'Yes, it can't be helped. We'll have to have them even if they won't bring the prices down. Good gracious, I nearly forgot. We must have another entrée. My godfathers!' He clutched at his head. 'Who's going to get the flowers for me? Mitenka! Where's Mitenka! Oh, there you are. What I want you to do,' he said to the steward, who was quick to respond to his call, 'is get down to my country place as fast as you can,' (it was just outside the city) 'and tell Maksimka the gardener to organize some serf labour. Tell him to empty the conservatories and send everything here, packed in felt. Two hundred pots, and I want them here by Friday.'

After handing out various instructions right, left and centre, he was just about to go home to the countess for a rest when suddenly something else occurred to him, so he came back, summoning the chef and the bursar yet again and issuing further orders. Then in the doorway they heard the light tread and jingling spurs of a young man approaching, and in came Nikolay, looking all rosy and handsome, with his darkening moustache, visibly relaxed and healthier after his easy life in Moscow.

'Hello, my boy! My head's going round,' said the old gentleman, with a chagrined smile at his son. 'Come on, I need your help! We must get hold of some singers. We've got the band, but shouldn't we have some gypsy singers too? You military men love that sort of thing.'

'If you want my opinion, Papa, I think Prince Bagration made less fuss getting ready for Schöngrabern than you're doing now,' said his son with a smile.

The old count pretended to be angry.

'It's easy to talk like that! You try!' The count turned to the chef, and he eyed the pair of them closely and affectionately with a shrewd but respectful look on his face.

'Ah, Feoktist, I don't know about young people today,' he said. 'They like laughing at us old fogeys!'

'I know, sir. They're very good at eating a nice dinner, but arranging it all and serving it up, they don't want to know about that!'

'True, true!' cried the count, and cheerfully grabbing his son by both hands, he shouted, 'I've got you now! Take the sledge and pair this minute and get over to Bezukhov. Tell him Count Ilya Rostov has sent for some of his strawberries and fresh pineapples. You won't find them anywhere else. If he's not in, go and see the princesses and give them the same message. Then go on to the Gaiety – the coachman, Ipatka, he knows the way – and get hold of Ilyushka, that gypsy who danced at Count Orlov's, you remember, in a white Cossack coat, and bring him here.'

'And a few gypsy girls too?' asked Nikolay, laughing.

'Now, now! . . .'

At this moment Anna Mikhaylovna padded into the room with that air of busy practicality allied to Christian meekness that never left her face. Although Anna Mikhaylovna ran across the count in his dressing-gown every day of the week, he was always embarrassed when she did and invariably apologized for his attire. He did so now.

'My dear count, don't mention it,' she said with a demure closing of the eyes. 'I'll go and see Bezukhov,' she said. 'Young Bezukhov has just come back, Count, and we're sure to get everything we need from his conservatories. I had to see him anyway. He has forwarded a letter from Boris. Thank God, Boris is now a staff-officer.'

The count was only too pleased to let Anna Mikhaylovna take over one of his responsibilities and he ordered the light carriage for her.

'Tell Bezukhov he must come. I'll put his name down. Is his wife with him?' he asked.

Anna Mikhaylovna rolled her eyes up, and her face was suffused with profound sorrow.

'Oh, my dear, he's not a happy man,' she said. 'If it's true what people say things are awful. Little did we think it would turn out like this when we were celebrating his good fortune! And he has such a noble, angelic nature, young Bezukhov! Yes, my heart goes out to him, and I shall do what I can to comfort him.'

'Why, what's it all about?' asked both the Rostovs, young and old together.

Anna Mikhaylovna heaved a deep sigh.

'It's Dolokhov, Marya Ivanovna's son,' she said in a confiding whisper. 'They say he has quite compromised her. The count looked after him, invited him into his house in Petersburg, and now it's come to this! . . . She came down here, and that madcap has followed her,' said Anna Mikhaylovna. Anxious to sympathize with Pierre, she unwittingly allowed her tone of voice and the ghost of a smile to imply equal sympathy for the man she was describing as a madcap. 'They do say Pierre is desperately unhappy.'

'Well, tell him to come to the club, anyway. It will all blow over. This is going to be some banquet!'

Just before two o'clock the next day, the 3rd of March, the two hundred and fifty members of the English Club and fifty of their guests were awaiting the arrival of their guest of honour, Prince Bagration, hero of the Austrian campaign.

When news came through of defeat at Austerlitz all Moscow was nonplussed. This was a time when the Russians had become so used to victories that news of a defeat was rejected as unbelievable by some people, while others said there must be some special reason behind such a strange event. At the English Club, a forum for anyone of substance, anyone in the know, anyone who carried any weight, during December, when the news began to filter through, there was virtually a conspiracy of silence – not a word was spoken about the war and the latest defeat. The men who dominated club conversation, such as Count Rostopchin, Prince Yury Dolgoruky, Valuyev, Count Markov and Prince Vyazemsky, kept away from the building but continued to meet in private circles in their various houses.

Those people in Moscow who couldn't think for themselves (and that included Count Rostov) were stuck for some time without anyone to lead them and without any clear views on how the war was going. Moscow society sensed that things were going wrong, but bad news was painful to dwell on, so they kept quiet. But it wasn't long before the bigwigs re-emerged like jurymen from a jury room to voice an opinion in the club, and a clear-cut stance was adopted. Causes had been discovered to account for such an incredible, unprecedented impossibility as defeat for the Russians; suddenly all was clear and the same version of events swept Moscow from one end to the other. The causes were as follows: Austrian treachery; poor logistical support; two treacherous foreigners, the Pole Przebyszewski and the Frenchman Langeron; Kutuzov's incompetence (mentioned only in whispers); the youth and inexperience of the Emperor, who had put his trust in stupid nonentities. But the army, the Russian army, everyone agreed, had been extraordinary, performing miracles of valour. The soldiers, officers and generals – they were heroes to a man. And the hero of heroes was Prince Bagration, who had distinguished himself at Schöngrabern and during the retreat from Austerlitz, where he alone had kept his column in good order and had spent a whole day fighting off an enemy twice as strong. Bagration's rise to heroic status in Moscow had much to do with his being a non-Muscovite with no connections in the city. In his person they were paying tribute to the common Russian soldier who knew nothing about influence or intrigue and was still nostalgically associated with General Suvorov and the Italian campaign. Besides which, the honours bestowed on him were the most effective demonstration of their dislike and disapproval of Kutuzov.

'If there had been no Bagration, they would have had to invent him,' said one wit, Shinshin, parodying the words of Voltaire.

Kutuzov's name was never mentioned except to disparage him in malicious whispers by calling him a courtier who blew with the wind, or an old goat.

All Moscow was repeating Prince Dolgorukov's saying, 'If you keep playing with fire you're sure to get burnt' – his way of finding consolation for defeat in the memory of former victories. Equally popular was Rostopchin's assertion that Frenchmen have to be inspired to fight by fine phrases, Germans need to see a logical argument that it's more dangerous to run away than go forward, whereas all you have to do with a Russian soldier is tell him to hold back and say, 'Steady!' More and more stories emerged on every side, of individual acts of courage performed by our officers and men at Austerlitz. One man had saved a flag, another had killed five Frenchmen, another had done all the loading for five cannons. There was even a story told about Berg – by people who didn't know him – that when wounded in his right hand he had held his sword in his left hand and battled on. There were no stories about Bolkonsky. Only those close to him said how sorry they were that he had died so young, leaving a pregnant wife in the hands of his eccentric old father.

CHAPTER 3

On the 3rd of March every room in the English Club was abuzz with conversation and the members and guests, resplendent in uniforms or morning dress, some of them even with powdered hair and wearing Russian kaftans, were like busy bees in springtime, coming and going, sitting and standing, settling together and flying apart. Powdered and liveried footmen wearing stockings and buckled shoes stood at every doorway, anxiously watching for the slightest gesture from a guest or member so they could offer their services. Most of those present were old and distinguished people with beaming, confident faces, podgy fingers, powerful gestures and strong voices. Guests and members at this level of society sat in their own habitual places and came together in their own special little groups. A few of those present were occasional guests – young men for the most part, including Denisov, Rostov and Dolokhov, who had by now been re-commissioned in the Semyonovsky regiment. The younger men's faces, especially those of the officers, carried a look of ironic deference towards their elders which seemed to say to the members of that generation, 'We don't mind offering you respect and deference, but don't forget – the future belongs to us.'

Nesvitsky was there too, as a member of long standing. Pierre Bezukhov, who had obeyed instructions from his wife to let his hair grow long and abandon his spectacles, was wandering from room to room dressed *comme il faut* but looking depressed and gloomy. He was surrounded, as always, by an atmosphere of people kowtowing to his wealth, and he treated them with a kind of offhand and contemptuous sense of superiority that had now become second nature to him.

Although he belonged in years to the younger generation, his wealth and connections conferred membership of the older circles, which was why he was strolling from one group to another. The groups revolved around the most distinguished of their elder members, and even strangers would sometimes approach these circles, with due deference, in order to hear famous people holding forth. The largest groups had formed round Count Rostopchin, Valuyev and Naryshkin. Rostopchin was describing how the Russians had been overwhelmed by fleeing Austrians and had had to fix bayonets in order to force their way through. Valuyev was informing his circle in strict confidence that Uvarov had been sent down from St Petersburg to gauge opinion in Moscow in regard to Austerlitz.

In the third group Naryshkin was retelling an old story about a meeting of the Austrian council of war at which Suvorov responded to the obtuseness of the Austrian generals by crowing like a cock. Shinshin, standing near by, tried to make a joke out of this by saying that Kutuzov had apparently not even managed to learn from Suvorov the not too demanding art of crowing like a cock, but the elder club members looked askance at him with a clear indication that this kind of joke, even at Kutuzov's expense, was not the done thing on a day like this.

Count Ilya Rostov scurried about anxiously, sidling in and out of the dining-room and drawing-room in his soft boots, saying a quick hello to everyone indiscriminately, the worthy and the not so worthy, all of whom he knew personally. More than once his eyes sought out the graceful figure of his hero son, lingering on him with great delight and giving him the odd wink. Young Rostov was standing by the window talking to Dolokhov, whose acquaintance he had recently made and greatly prized. The old count went over to them and shook hands with Dolokhov.

'You must come and see us ... any friend of my fine boy ... out

there together, doing all those heroic things . . . Ah! Vassily Ignatych
. . . my dear fellow, I do hope you're well . . .' He had turned to greet
an old gentleman who was passing by, but before he could finish there
was a general commotion and a distressed footman ran in with an
announcement: 'Our visitor is here!'

Bells rang, the stewards rushed forward and guests who had
been scattered about in different rooms scraped themselves together like shovelled rye and stood waiting at the door of the grand
drawing-room.

There in the doorway of the ante-room stood the figure of Bagration,
without hat or sword, which had been deposited with the hall porter
in accordance with club practice. The astrakhan cap and the whip
over his shoulder that Rostov had seen him with on the night before
the battle of Austerlitz had gone; he now wore a tight new uniform
decorated with Russian and foreign medals and the Star of St George
on his left breast. He had just had his hair cut and side-whiskers
trimmed, obviously with the banquet in mind, but this did nothing
for his appearance. He seemed to be in a kind of silly holiday mood
which hardly squared with his strong, manly features and made his
face look rather ridiculous. Bekleshov and Fyodor Uvarov, who had
come with him, stood still in the doorway so that he could go in first
as the guest of honour, but an embarrassed Bagration seemed not to
want such courtesy. There was a hold-up in the doorway, but eventually Bagration did come in first. He shambled timidly across the parquet floor of the reception-room, not knowing what do with his hands.
He would have been more relaxed and more at home walking through
a hail of bullets across a ploughed field, as he had done recently at the
head of the Kursk regiment at Schöngrabern. The senior members
welcomed him at the first door, saying how delightful it was to see
such an honoured guest, and before he had time to respond they all
but overwhelmed him, encircling him and conducting him towards
the drawing-room. The entry then became impossible – no one could
get in or out for the crowds of members and guests crushing each
other and straining for a look over each other's shoulders at Bagration,
as if he were some rare species of animal. Count Rostov laughed
louder than anyone as he called out, 'Make way for him, dear boy,
make way, make way!' He shoved his way through the crowd, led the
guests in and invited them to be seated on a sofa in the middle of
the drawing-room. The bigwigs of the club, the most distinguished
members, swarmed round the newly arrived guests. Count Rostov
elbowed his way back out through the crowd only to reappear a
minute later with another senior member bearing a massive silver

salver which he then offered to Prince Bagration. On the salver lay a
poem, specially composed and printed in honour of the hero. Bagration took one look at the salver and glanced round in alarm, as if
appealing for help. But every eye was on him, willing him to submit.
In his impotence Bagration seized the dish with both hands, looking
daggers at the count who had brought it. Someone helpfully relieved
Bagration of the salver for fear that he might hold on to it till bed-time
or take it with him to the table, and drew his attention to the poem.
'Yes, well, I suppose I ought to read it,' Bagration seemed to say, and
with weary eyes glued to the text he started reading with some gravity
and close concentration. The author of the poem took it from him
and began to read it out loud. Prince Bagration bowed his head and
listened.

> Sing hymns to Alexander's age!
> Long live upon his throne our Russian Titus!
> Our fearsome leader be, and be a righteous sage,
> A host at home, afield – a Caesar to incite us!
>   And then the glad Napoleón
> Shall rue the day he crossed swords with Bagratión
> And he shall shake with fear and come no more to fight us . . .[4]

But before he could finish, the major-domo boomed out, 'Dinner is
served!' and the door opened to the thunderous strains of a polonaise
issuing from the dining-room:

> Hail the victor! Loud the anthem!
> Valiant Russians, sing your joy . . .

Count Rostov glared at the author, who was still reading his poem,
and bowed low to Bagration. All the company rose, dinner holding
greater appeal than poetry, and went in to dine; once again Bagration
led the way. He was placed at the head of the table between two
Alexanders, Bekleshov and Naryshkin, a calculated allusion to the
name of the Tsar, and three hundred diners took up their places
according to rank and importance, with the very important people
nearest the distinguished guest, as naturally as water flowing down to
find its own level.

Just before dinner Count Rostov had presented his son to the prince.
Bagration recognized him and said a few words to him, as bumbling
and incoherent as all the other words spoken by him that day. The

older count looked around at everyone with pride and joy while
Bagration was speaking to his son.

Nikolay Rostov sat down, alongside Denisov and his new acquaintance Dolokhov, almost in the middle of the table. Opposite them sat
Pierre with Prince Nesvitsky. The old Count Rostov was sitting with
other senior members across from Bagration, a picture of Moscow
bonhomie lavishing hospitality on the prince.

His efforts had not been in vain. For everyone there, observers of
Lent or otherwise, the banquet was magnificent, but he would not be
able to relax until it was all over. He winked messages to the carver,
whispered instructions to the waiters and awaited the serving of each
familiar dish with trepidation. Everything went splendidly. During
the second course, which involved the colossal sturgeon (the sight of
which brought a blush of self-conscious delight to his face), the footman began popping corks and pouring champagne. After the somewhat sensational fish, Rostov exchanged glances with the other senior
members. 'There'll be a lot of toasts. It's time to begin!' he whispered,
and rose, glass in hand. Silence fell. What would he say?

'I give you our Sovereign, the Emperor!' he shouted, his kindly eyes
watering with tears of sheer delight. At that instant the band struck
up with, 'Hail the victor! Loud the anthem!' and they all got to their
feet and roared 'Hurrah!' And Bagration shouted 'Hurrah!' just as he
had done on the field at Schöngrabern. The eager voice of the young
Rostov rang out above three hundred others. He was on the verge of
tears. 'Our Sovereign, the Emperor,' he roared. 'Hurrah!' Downing
his drink in one, he hurled the glass to the floor. Many followed his
example. And the raucous cheering seemed as if it would never end.
When the uproar subsided, the footmen cleared away the broken glass,
and the diners resumed their places, amused at the racket they had
made, and the talking began again. Count Rostov soon rose to his feet
once more with a quick glance at a note beside his plate, and proposed
a toast to the hero of our last campaign, Prince Pyotr Ivanovich
Bagration, and again his blue eyes were watering with tears. 'Hurrah!'
rang out again from three hundred throats, and this time instead of
the band playing, a small choir launched into a setting of some verses
written by Pavel Ivanovich Golenishchev-Kutuzov:[5]

> Onward Russians, never yield!
> Be ye brave and win the prize!
> Give Bagratión the field,
> See the foeman as he dies . . .

The choir stopped singing, more and more toasts followed, Count Rostov senior became more and more emotional, more glass was shattered and a lot more noise was made. They toasted Bekleshov, Naryshkin, Uvarov, Dolgorukov, Apraksin, Valuyev, the senior members, the club committee, all the members and their guests, and then finally a special toast was drunk to the organizer of the banquet, Count Ilya Andreyevich Rostov. This toast was too much for the count, who took out his handkerchief, buried his face in it and broke into floods of tears.

CHAPTER 4

Pierre was sitting opposite Dolokhov and Nikolay Rostov. As always, he ate greedily and drank a lot. But those close to him could see that a great change had come over him that day. He sat through dinner without saying a word to anyone, glancing around with a scowl and a frown or staring vaguely into empty air while he rubbed the bridge of his nose with one finger. He looked thoroughly depressed and gloomy and seemed to see or hear nothing of what was going on around him. Something was worrying him, something serious that he would have to attend to.

What worried him was a series of hints dropped by the princess in Moscow about Dolokhov being rather too close to his wife, and also an anonymous letter which he had received that morning. Written in that despicable tone of forced humour common to all anonymous letters, it had said that he couldn't see the nose in front of his face even with his glasses on and that his wife's liaison with Dolokhov was an open secret for everybody except him. Pierre refused categorically to believe either the princess's hints or the anonymous letter, but he was now scared to look at Dolokhov, who was sitting opposite. Every time his glance happened to encounter Dolokhov's handsome and challenging eyes Pierre could feel something terrible and disgusting rising up in his soul, and he was quick to look away. He couldn't help running over his wife's past history and her attitude to Dolokhov, and he could see that what was said in the letter might have been true, or might seem to be true, if only it had related to someone else, *not his wife*. Pierre remembered how Dolokhov had returned to Petersburg fully reinstated as an officer following the campaign, and come to see him. Taking advantage of a friendship with Pierre which went back to their days of riotous living, Dolokhov simply moved in, and Pierre had set him up and lent him money. Pierre recalled Hélène's smile as she complained about Dolokhov living with them, and Dolokhov's cynical look as he had praised his wife's beauty to him. Since that time he had never left their side, and that included coming down to Moscow.

'Yes, he is good-looking,' thought Pierre, 'and I know him. He would be only too delighted to drag my name through the mud and laugh at me, just because I've looked after him, supported him and helped him out. Yes, I can see it. I know how he would relish any betrayal of me – if it was true. Yes, if it was true, but I don't believe it. I have no right to, and I just can't.' He recalled the expression on Dolokhov's face when he was being cruel – when he had tied the policeman to the bear and dropped them in the water, when he had challenged a man to a duel for no good reason or shot a sledge-driver's horse with his pistol. The same expression often came over Dolokhov's face when he was looking at him. 'Yes, he's a cruel brute,' thought Pierre. 'He wouldn't think twice about killing a man, and he must think everyone's afraid of him. I think he likes that. He must think I'm afraid of him . . . And I am,' Pierre mused, and as he did so he felt the thing again, something dreadful and disgusting rising up in his soul. Dolokhov, Denisov and Rostov were sitting across from Pierre and they seemed to be having a wonderful time. Rostov was chatting away animatedly with his two friends, one of them a dashing hussar, the other a holy terror and notorious philanderer, only now and then directing a sardonic glance at Pierre, who stood out in that company because of his great bulk and his vacant, worried look. Rostov had little time for Pierre. For one thing, he, the smart young hussar, saw Pierre as a rich civilian who may have married a great beauty but was still an old woman. And for another, Pierre had been too obsessed and dreamy-eyed to recognize Rostov – he hadn't even returned his bow. When they all stood up to toast the Tsar, Pierre sat there deep in thought and didn't even reach for his glass.

'What's wrong with you?' Rostov yelled across, his triumph tinged with exasperation. 'Aren't you listening? We're toasting the Emperor!'

Pierre rose obediently with a sigh, drained his glass, waited for them all to be seated again and then turned to Rostov with his usual kindly smile. 'I'm sorry, I didn't recognize you,' he said. But Rostov was miles away, bellowing his 'Hurrah!'

'Aren't you going to renew your acquaintance?' said Dolokhov to Rostov.

'I can't be bothered with him. He's an idiot,' said Rostov.

'Oh, you should always be nice to the husbands of pretty women,' said Denisov. Pierre couldn't hear what they were saying, but he knew they were talking about him. He reddened and looked away. 'So, I propose a toast to pretty women,' said Dolokhov, looking very serious but allowing a smile to play at the corners of his mouth as he turned to Pierre.

'Here's to pretty women, my dear little Pierre,' he said. 'And to their lovers.'

Pierre was looking down, sipping from his glass and avoiding Dolokhov's eyes. He didn't respond. A footman came round distributing Kutuzov's cantata and laid a copy down by Pierre, one of the more important guests. Pierre was on the point of picking it up when Dolokhov leant across, snatched the paper out of his hand and started to read it. Pierre glanced up at Dolokhov and then down again. That terrible and disgusting feeling that had been tormenting him all through dinner surged up and overwhelmed him. He leant across the table with all the weight of his big body.

'How dare you?' he yelled.

Hearing the shout and seeing who he was shouting at, Nesvitsky and Pierre's neighbour on the other side turned quickly towards Bezukhov in some alarm.

'Sh! What do you think you're doing?' whispered panic-stricken voices. Dolokhov directed his clear, mocking, cruel eyes straight at Pierre, still with the same smile, as if to say, 'I'll do what I like.'

'I've got it,' he spelt out.

Pale, lips quivering, Pierre snatched the copy.

'You . . . you . . . swine! . . . I challenge you,' he said, moving his chair back and rising from the table. And as Pierre did this and pronounced these words he suddenly realized that the question of his wife's guilt that had been tormenting him for twenty-four hours had been settled once and for all – in the affirmative. He hated her now. They were finished – for ever. Despite Denisov's protestations that he ought not to get involved, Rostov agreed to be Dolokhov's second, and when dinner was over he discussed the terms of the duel with Nesvitsky, Bezukhov's second. Pierre went home, but Rostov, along with Dolokhov and Denisov, stayed on at the club until late at night listening to the gypsies and the singers.

'Good night then. I'll see you tomorrow at Sokolniki,' said Dolokhov as he parted from Rostov on the steps of the club.

'How are you feeling?' asked Rostov.

Dolokhov stopped.

'Well, I'll put it like this. Here's the whole secret of duelling. If you get ready for a duel by making a will and writing long tender letters to your parents thinking that you might get killed, you're a fool – you're as good as done for. But if you go out with every intention of killing your man stone dead in short order, everything will be all right. As our bear-hunter from Kostroma used to say to me, "A bear," he'd say, "who's not afraid of a bear? But once you've actually seen one the fear's all gone and your only thought is to stop him getting away!" So that's what I feel like. I'll see you tomorrow, old fellow.'

At eight o'clock next morning Pierre and Nesvitsky reached the woods at Sokolniki and found Dolokhov, Denisov and Rostov already there. Pierre had the air of a man distracted by matters not connected with the business in hand. After a sleepless night he looked haggard and sallow-faced. He peered around vaguely, squinting as if the sun were in his eyes. Two considerations excluded all others: his wife's guilt, which a sleepless night had confirmed for him beyond a shadow of doubt, and the innocence of Dolokhov, who had no reason to defend the honour of a person who meant nothing to him. 'Perhaps I'd have done the same thing if I'd been him,' thought Pierre. 'In fact I know I would. So what's this duel all about, this murder? Either I shall kill him, or he will shoot me in the head, in the elbow or the knee. If only I could escape, run away and bury myself somewhere,' came the persistent thought. But whenever such ideas arose in his mind he would assume a kind of tranquillity and detachment that commanded respect in the onlookers, and simply ask, 'When is it to be?' or 'Is everything ready?'

And when everything was ready sabres were stuck in the snow to show where the barrier was, and the pistols were loaded. Then Nesvitsky went up to Pierre.

'I should be failing in my duty, Count,' he ventured timidly, 'and not worthy of your confidence or the honour you have done me in choosing me for your second, if at this grave moment, this very grave moment, I failed to speak the whole truth to you. I submit to you that this matter is without proper foundation and is not worth shedding blood over . . . You were in the wrong. You got a bit excited . . .'

'You're quite right. It was desperately stupid,' said Pierre.

'Then allow me to say you are sorry, and I'm sure that our opponents will agree to accept your apology,' said Nesvitsky, who was like the other participants and everyone else at times like this in refusing to believe that the quarrel would really end in an duel. 'You know, Count, it is far nobler to acknowledge a mistake than to push things beyond redemption. There was no insult on either side. Why don't I have a word with . . . ?'

'No! There's nothing more to be said,' Pierre insisted. 'I don't care any more . . . Are we ready to proceed?' he added. 'Just tell me where to go and what to shoot at,' he said, forcing a gentle smile. He picked up one of the pistols and asked how to fire it, never having held one before, though he preferred not to admit it. 'Yes, that's it. I do know. I just forgot for a moment,' he said.

'No apology. Definitely not,' Dolokhov was reporting to Denisov, who had made his own attempt at reconciliation on the other side, and he too walked forward to the appointed spot.

The duelling ground was situated about eighty paces from the road where the sledges had been left, in a small clearing in a pine-wood, covered with snow that had been thawing in the warmer weather of recent days. The antagonists stood about forty paces apart, one at each edge of the clearing. Measuring out the paces, the seconds left tracks in the deep, wet snow from the spot where they had been standing to the sabres borrowed from Nesvitsky and Denisov, which were stuck in the ground ten paces apart to mark the barrier. The thaw and mist persisted. At forty paces you could hardly see your opponent. All had been ready for a good three minutes, but now they seemed reluctant to start. Nobody spoke.

CHAPTER 5

'Well, shall we begin?' said Dolokhov.

'Why not?' said Pierre, smiling the same smile.

Fear was building up. It was now obvious to all that the affair that had begun so lightly could not now be averted, it had its own momentum nothing to do with anyone's will, and it would have to run its course. Denisov was the first to come forward to the barrier and once there he made his announcement: 'Since the adversawies wefuse all weconciliation we may as well pwoceed. Take your pistols, and at the word "fwee" you may begin to advance . . . O-ne! Tw-o! Fwee! . . .' Denisov roared furiously, and then strode away. The two contestants walked forward over the tracks trodden down for them, coming closer and closer, picking each other out through the mist. They had the right to fire at any point as they approached the barrier. Dolokhov was walking slowly, not raising his pistol, and looking his antagonist straight in the face with his clear, shining blue eyes. His mouth wore its usual hint of a smile.

After the count of three Pierre walked forward quickly, stumbled off the beaten track and had to go on through untrodden snow. He was holding his pistol at arm's length in his right hand, obviously scared of shooting himself with his own weapon. His left arm was deliberately thrust back behind him, because he was tempted to use it to support his right arm, and he knew that this was against the rules. After advancing half-a-dozen paces off the track and into the snow, Pierre glanced down at his feet, looked up at Dolokhov again very quickly, then crooked his finger as he had been told, and fired. Shocked by the loudness of the bang, Pierre jumped at his own shot and came to a halt, grinning at all that was happening to him. The smoke was thicker than it might have been because of the fog and for a moment he could see nothing. The anticipated return shot did not come. All he heard were some rapid footsteps, Dolokhov's, as the figure of his opponent emerged from the smoke, with one hand clutching at his left side and his lowered pistol gripped in the other. His face had gone pale. Rostov ran up and said something to him.

'No-o!' Dolokhov muttered through clenched teeth. 'No, it's not over . . .' He struggled forward a few steps, stumbling and staggering as far as the sabre, where he flopped down in the snow. He rubbed his bloodstained left hand on his coat and propped himself up on it. There was a dark frown on his trembling pale face.

'P-p-p . . .' Dolokhov began, hardly able to speak, but then with a great effort he managed one word: 'Please . . .'

Pierre could hardly restrain his sobs as he ran towards Dolokhov, and he would have crossed the space between the barriers if Dolokhov had not cried out, 'Your barrier!' Realizing what was required of him, Pierre stopped right next to his sabre. They were only ten paces apart. Dolokhov dropped his head down into the snow and had a good bite at it, looked up again, struggled up into a sitting position, wobbling as he searched for a good centre of gravity. He swallowed, sucking down the cold snow, while his trembling lips were still smiling and his hate-filled eyes glinted from the effort as his strength ebbed away. He raised his pistol and took aim.

'Sideways on! Use the pistol for cover!' said Nesvitsky.

'Covah!' yelled Denisov instinctively even though he was supposed to be on Dolokhov's side.

Full of sympathy and remorse, Pierre stood gently smiling, with legs and arms helplessly outstretched and his broad chest fully open to Dolokhov. He looked down at him in great sadness. Denisov, Rostov and Nesvitsky all winced. At that instant they heard a bang followed by an angry shout from Dolokhov.

'Missed!' Dolokhov cried, flopping down helplessly face-down in the snow. Pierre clutched at his head, turning aside, and stumbled off into the wood, away from the path into deep snow, muttering incoherently.

'Stupid . . . stupid! Death . . . all lies . . .' he kept repeating, scowling. Nesvitsky stopped him and took him home.

Rostov and Denisov drove away with the wounded Dolokhov.

Dolokhov lay still in the sledge with his eyes closed and in complete silence, refusing to utter a word in response to any questions put to him. But as they were driving into Moscow, he suddenly recovered, made an effort to raise his head and took hold of Rostov's hand. Rostov, sitting next to him, was struck by the complete change that had come over Dolokhov's face, which had suddenly melted into a kind of rapturous gentleness.

'Well? How do you feel?' asked Rostov.

'Terrible! But that doesn't matter. Listen, my friend,' said Dolokhov, in a shaky voice. 'Where are we? . . . I know we're in Moscow . . . I'm not important, but this will kill her, *her* . . . She'll never get over it . . . She won't survive . . .'

'Who?' asked Rostov.

'My mother. My mother. She's an angel, an angel, and I adore her, my mother.' Dolokhov squeezed Rostov's hand and burst into tears. He took a few moments to compose himself and then explained to Rostov that he lived with his mother, and if she suddenly saw him half-dead she would never get over the shock. He begged Rostov to go on ahead and prepare her.

Rostov went on ahead to do as he was bidden. To his utter astonishment he found out that the rough, tough Dolokhov, Dolokhov the swaggering bully, lived in Moscow with his old mother and a hunchback sister. He was a loving son and brother.

CHAPTER 6

In recent days Pierre had rarely been alone with his wife. In Petersburg and in Moscow the house had been constantly full of guests. The night after the duel he avoided the bedroom, as he often did, and spent the night in his vast study, formerly his father's room, the room in which old Count Bezukhov had died. The night before had been sleepless, an agony of inner turmoil; this one would be even more agonizing.

He lay down on the sofa and tried to go to sleep in an effort to forget everything that had happened, but he couldn't manage it. His mind was clouded with such a storm of ideas, emotions and memories that sleep was out of the question. Unable to remain in one place, he was forced to jump to his feet and stride boldly up and down the room. First he conjured up a vision of his wife as she had been in the first days of their marriage, with those naked shoulders and those eyes, languid pools of passion, then suddenly at her side was a handsome, insolent, hard and jeering face – Dolokhov at the banquet – and then a different Dolokhov, pale and trembling, in terrible pain, the man who had spun around and slumped down on to the snow.

'What have I done?' he asked himself. 'I have killed *her lover* ... I've killed my wife's lover. I really have. Why? How did I get into all this?'

By marrying her, came an inner voice.

'It's not my fault, is it?' he asked himself.

Yes it is. You weren't in love with her when you got married and you pulled the wool over your own eyes and hers.

All too vividly he recalled the moment after supper at Prince Vasily's when he had found the words 'I love you' so difficult to say. 'That's when it all started. I knew it even then,' he thought. 'Even then I knew it was wrong and I had no right to do it. And that's how it's turned out.' He recalled the honeymoon and blushed at the memory of it. One particularly vivid, humiliating and embarrassing memory haunted him: one morning, not long after the wedding, he had emerged from his bedroom into the study at nearly mid-day still in his silk dressing-gown, and there was his head steward bowing and scraping and looking at Pierre's face and then at his dressing-gown, smiling a little as if to communicate respectful acknowledgement of his master's happiness.

'And I used to be so proud of her, with that majestic beauty and that poise,' he thought, 'so proud of my house when she was entertaining all Petersburg, proud of her aloofness and her beauty. So much for pride! I used to think then that I didn't understand her. Time after time I've thought about her personality and told myself it was my fault for not understanding her, not understanding that perpetual composure and complacency, the lack of any yearning or desire, and it all comes down to one dreadful word – immorality; she's a dissolute woman. Say the word and it all becomes clear.

'Anatole used to come borrowing money from her, and he used to kiss her on her bare shoulders. She didn't give him any money, but she didn't mind being kissed. Her father used to tease her, trying to make her jealous; she would just smile serenely and say she wasn't fool enough to be jealous. Let him do what he wants, she used to say about me. I asked her once if she had noticed any signs of pregnancy. She laughed contemptuously and said she wasn't stupid enough to want children, and she would *never have a child by me.*'

Then he thought of the sheer coarseness of her thinking and her vulgar way of speaking, even though she had been brought up in the highest aristocratic circles. She would say things like, 'I ain't nobody's fool . . . just you try it . . . get away with you . . .' Often, observing the impact she made on young and old, men and women, Pierre was at a loss to understand why he couldn't love her. 'No, I never loved her,' Pierre told himself. 'I knew she was a dissolute woman,' he repeated to himself, 'but I didn't dare admit it.

'And now Dolokhov sits there in the snow and forces himself to smile and dies with some clever quip on his lips – and that's how he treats my remorse.'

Pierre was one of those characters who seem on the outside to be weak but who do not share their troubles with other people. He worked through his troubles on his own.

'It's her fault,' he said to himself, 'it's all her fault. But what difference does that make? Why did I tie myself to her? Why did I tell her I loved her when it was a lie, worse than a lie?' he asked himself. 'It's my fault. I ought to suffer . . . What? Disgrace and misery? What a load of rubbish,' he thought. 'Disgrace, honour, everything's relative; nothing depends on me.'

'Louis XVI was executed because *they* said he was a dishonourable criminal,' (the idea suddenly occurred to Pierre) 'and from their point of view they were right. But so were the others who died an excruciating death acknowledging him as a saint. Robespierre was executed for tyranny. Who's right and who's wrong? No one is. Just live for the day . . . tomorrow you die . . . I could have died an hour ago. And why worry when you've only got a second to live on the scale of eternity?' But the moment he began to draw some comfort from this kind of thinking he suddenly had another vision of *her*, and him too at his most passionate, falsely declaring his love to her, and this brought a rush of blood to his heart, and he felt a need to leap up and walk about smashing and tearing anything that came to hand. 'Oh, why did I say "I love you"?' he asked himself over and over again. At the tenth time of asking a quotation from Molière occurred to him: 'How the devil was he going to get himself out of a mess like that?'[6] and he laughed at himself.

During the night he woke up his valet and told him to pack for Petersburg. He could no longer live under the same roof with her. He couldn't imagine even talking to her now. He would go away in the morning, he decided, and leave a letter telling her they were separating for ever.

When morning came and the valet brought his coffee, Pierre was lying on a low sofa, fast asleep with an open book in his hands.

He woke up and stared around for a long time in some alarm, with no idea where he was.

'The countess has asked me to inquire whether your Excellency is at home,' said the valet.

But before Pierre had time to think of a reply, in walked the countess herself, calmly and majestically, clad in a white satin dressing-gown embroidered with silver, and her hair done up in two huge plaits coiled round her exquisite head like a coronet. Her only disfiguring feature was a tiny line on her rather prominent marble brow, indicating anger. Disciplined and unruffled as always, she kept her counsel while the valet was still in the room. She knew about the duel and had come to discuss it. She waited for the valet to set for coffee and go out. Pierre looked at her diffidently over his spectacles. His attempt to go on reading made him seem like a hare surrounded by the pack, lying there in full view of the enemy with its ears laid back. Sensing that this was absurd and impossible, he launched another diffident glance in her direction. She remained standing and looked down at him with a scornful smile, waiting for the valet to disappear.

'Now what's all this? What have you been up to? Answer me,' she said sternly.

'Me? What do you mean?' said Pierre.

'So you want to be a hero now! What's all this about a duel? What are you trying to prove? Well say something! I asked you a question.' Pierre turned over ponderously on the sofa and opened his mouth, but nothing came out.

'If you're not prepared to answer, I'll do the talking . . .' Hélène went on. 'You'll believe anything. They told you . . .' Hélène laughed, 'that Dolokhov was my lover,' she said in French, with her usual bluntness, pronouncing the word *amant* like any other word, 'and you believed them! So what does this prove? What have you proved by fighting this duel? That you're a fool, an idiot – but this is common knowledge. Where does it get us? I'm a laughing-stock all over Moscow, everyone's saying you got drunk, didn't know what you were doing and needlessly challenged a man you were jealous of.' Hélène's voice was getting louder and louder as she became more and more passionate. 'A better man than you in every way . . .'

'Hm . . . hm . . .' Pierre growled, scowling, looking away from her and not moving a muscle.

'And what made you think he is my lover? ... Eh? Because I like his company? If you were brighter and a bit nicer to me, I should prefer yours.'

'Please ... Don't talk to me like that ...' Pierre muttered huskily.

'Why not? I'll say what I want, and I'm telling you there's not many wives with husbands like you who wouldn't take lots of lovers, but I haven't!' she said. Pierre tried to say something, glanced at her with strange eyes, whose meaning she did not comprehend, and lay down again. He was in physical agony at that moment; he felt a weight on his chest and he couldn't breathe. He knew he must do something to put an end to this agony but what he wanted to do was too horrible for words.

'We ... er ... we'd better ... separate,' he stammered out.

'Yes, let's! As long as you look after me financially,' said Hélène. 'Separation! Some threat!'

Pierre sprang up from the sofa and ran at her, staggering.

'I'll kill you!' he yelled, and wrenching the marble top off a table with unprecedented strength he lurched towards her brandishing it.

Horror-stricken, Hélène screamed and jumped aside. Pierre was now his father's son, on the rampage, out of control, and enjoying it. He hurled the marble slab away, shattering it to pieces, and went for Hélène with outstretched arms, yelling 'Get out!' in a voice so terrible it sent shock-waves through the house. Heaven knows what he might have done to her at that moment if Hélène hadn't rushed out of the room.

Within a week Pierre had made over to his wife the title to all his estates in Great Russia, which constituted the larger part of his property, and had gone back to Petersburg alone.

CHAPTER 7

Two months had passed since news of the defeat at Austerlitz and Prince Andrey's disappearance had reached Bald Hills. Despite any number of inquiries and letters through the Russian embassy his body had not been found, nor was he listed as a prisoner-of-war. What made it worse for his family was the lingering hope that he might have been picked up on the battlefield by local people and could even now be on a sick-bed somewhere, alone among strangers, recovering or dying, unable to send word. The old prince had first heard of the defeat at Austerlitz from the newspapers, but as always they had given only brief and vague accounts of how the Russians, after a series of brilliant victories, had been forced into a retreat which had been conducted in perfect order. The old prince read between the lines of this official account and knew our army had been defeated. The newspaper containing news of the defeat was followed a week later by a letter from Kutuzov, who described for the old prince's benefit what had happened to his son.

'I saw your son with my own eyes,' wrote Kutuzov, 'bearing the standard and leading his regiment, and he fell like a hero, a credit to his father and his country. To my own regret and that of the whole army it is still not known whether he is alive or not. I console myself and you with the hope that your son is still alive, since if he were not he would have been listed among the officers found on the battlefield whose names have been given to me under flag of truce.'

The old prince received the news late one evening alone in his study and said not a word to anyone. Next morning he went out for his usual walk, but he remained tight-lipped with the bailiff, the gardener and the architect, glaring at them but saying nothing. When Princess Marya went in to see him at the normal time he was working on the lathe and as usual he didn't look round. 'Ah, Princess Marya!' he snapped in a strained voice, and put down his chisel. (The wheel continued to rotate under its own momentum and Princess Marya would long remember its fading whine for ever associated with what now followed.)

She went up to him, took one look at his face and felt something snap inside her. Her eyes misted over. It wasn't that her father's face seemed sad or crestfallen, but it looked vicious and extraordinarily agitated, and it told her she was about to be swamped by some terrible calamity that was hanging over them, the worst of all calamities, one that she had never known before, a calamity that would prove to be irrevocable and beyond all understanding – the death of a loved one.

'What is it, father? Is it Andrey? . . .' The gawky, graceless princess spoke with a selfless sorrow of such ineffable beauty that it proved too much for her father, who turned away sobbing.

'I have some news . . . Not among the prisoners, not reported dead . . . It's from Kutuzov,' he shrieked at her as if hoping this would drive her away. 'He's dead!'

The princess did not collapse or faint away with sickness. When she heard these words her face, already pallid, was transformed, and a special glow came to her lovely luminous eyes. A kind of joy, a heavenly joy transcending all the joys and sorrows of the world, had drowned the sorrow within her. Forgetting any dread of her father, she went over and took him by the hand, drawing him into an embrace with one arm round his scraggy, sinewy neck.

'Father,' she said, 'please don't turn away from me. Let us weep for him together.'

'Blackguards, scoundrels!' screamed the old man, wrenching his face away. 'Army destroyed, men destroyed! What for? . . . Go on, go and tell Liza.'

Princess Marya sank down helplessly into an armchair beside her father and burst into tears. She could see her brother just as he had been at the moment of parting from her and Liza, with that look on his face, a mixture of affection and aloofness. She could see him amused and affectionate as he put on the icon. 'Was he a believer? Had he repented of his unbelief? Was he up there now? There in the realm of eternal peace and happiness?' she wondered.

'Father, tell me what happened,' she said through her tears.

'Go away, go away – killed in battle, the best men of Russia and the glory of Russia led to defeat and destruction. Go away, Princess Marya. Go and tell Liza. I'll come along soon.'

When Princess Marya came back from seeing her father the little princess was sitting at her work, and she glanced up with that pregnant woman's special look of inner peace and contentment. Her eyes were obviously not seeing Princess Marya; she was looking in at herself, at some sweet mystery building up within her.

'Marie,' she said, easing away from the embroidery frame and leaning back heavily, 'feel here.' She took the princess's hand and placed it on her belly. Her eyes smiled invitingly as her little downy lip rose and stayed up in childlike rapture. Princess Marya knelt down in front of her and buried her face in the folds of the young girl's dress.

'There it is. There. Can you feel it? It's a funny feeling. Oh, Marie, I'm going to love him so much!' said Liza, looking at her sister-in-law with a radiant happiness in her eyes. Princess Marya could not bring herself to look up; she was crying.

'What's wrong, Marie?'

'Nothing's wrong . . . I just felt sad . . . about Andrey,' she said, brushing away the tears on the folds of her sister-in-law's dress. Several times in the course of that morning Princess Marya made a move towards preparing her sister-in-law for the bad news, but every time she did so she broke down in tears. The little princess, although generally unobservant, was upset by all this weeping, which she couldn't understand. She didn't say anything, but she kept glancing round the room uneasily as if she was looking for something. Before dinner the old prince came into her room. She was always scared of him and this time he seemed unusually edgy and angry, though he walked out without saying a word. She glanced at Princess Marya with the same inwardly directed look of a pregnant woman, and suddenly burst into tears.

'You haven't heard from Andrey, have you?' she asked.

'No. You know we couldn't have heard anything yet, but father is a bit restless and it makes me feel frightened.'

'You really haven't?'

'No,' said Princess Marya, with a resolute look in her luminous eyes. She had decided not to tell her, and had persuaded her father to hide the terrible news from her until after the birth, which could be expected any day now. Princess Marya and the old prince managed in different ways to bear their grief and hide it. The old prince abandoned all hope, convinced in his own mind that Prince Andrey was dead, and although he dispatched an official to Austria to look for any signs of his son, he sent an order to Moscow for a monument in his memory which he could put up in the garden, and he went around telling everyone his son was dead. He tried to go on exactly as before, but his strength was failing. He took fewer walks, ate less, slept less and grew weaker with each passing day. But Princess Marya went on hoping. She prayed for her brother as if he was still alive and fully expected him to return at any moment.

CHAPTER 8

'Marie, my dear,' said the little princess shortly after breakfast on the morning of the 19th of March. Her little downy upper lip rose as always, but because of the sorrow that had pervaded everything in that house since the terrible news had come – every smile, every word spoken or step taken – and because the little princess was a prey to the general mood without knowing the reason behind it, her smile did little more than serve as a reminder of the general sorrow.

'Marie, my dear, I'm afraid this morning's breakfast, what the cook calls *frustik*,[7] might have disagreed with me.'

'What is it, my darling? You do look pale. Very pale,' said Princess Marya in alarm, hurrying softly across the room to her sister-in-law with her heavy tread.

'Do you think we should fetch Marya Bogdanovna, your Excellency?' asked one of the maids who happened to be there. (Marya

Bogdanovna was a midwife from a nearby town who had been living at Bald Hills for the last two weeks.)

'I think we should,' Princess Marya agreed. 'You could be right. I'll go and get her. Be brave, my angel.' She kissed Liza and turned to walk out of the room.

'Oh no, don't!' The little princess's face, already pallid, shone with a child's dread of inevitable physical pain.

'No, it's just indigestion, tell me it's indigestion, tell me, Marie, please!' And the little princess began to cry, wringing her little hands in girlish misery like a rather spoilt child and not without a touch of theatricality. Princess Marya ran out to fetch Marya Bogdanovna.

'Oh dear! Oh dear!' she heard behind her. But there was the midwife, already on her way, rubbing her small, plump white hands and wearing a knowing look of calm self-control.

'Marya Bogdanovna! I think she's started,' said Princess Marya, wide-eyed and frightened.

'God be praised,' said Marya Bogdanovna, refusing to be hurried. 'Now, you young ladies don't need to be involved in this.'

'But why is the doctor taking so long to get here from Moscow?' said the princess. (In accordance with the wishes of Liza and Prince Andrey they had sent for a Moscow doctor and he was expected at any moment.)

'It doesn't matter, Princess. You mustn't worry,' said Marya Bogdanovna. 'We can manage without a doctor.'

Five minutes later, from inside her room the princess heard something heavy being carried past. She peeped out. For some reason the footmen were moving a leather sofa from Prince Andrey's study into the bedroom. The men looked all solemn and subdued.

Princess Marya sat alone in her room, listening to the sounds of the house, opening the door from time to time if someone went past and watching any action in the corridor. Some of the female staff that kept padding to and fro would glance across at the princess and quickly turn away. Afraid to ask any questions, she would go back into her room closing the door behind her and sit down in an armchair, or pick up her prayer-book, or kneel down at the icon-stand. She was unpleasantly surprised to discover that prayer did nothing to calm her nerves. Suddenly her door opened softly and there in the doorway stood her old nurse, Praskovya Savishna, with a scarf over her head. The old prince was so strict that the old woman almost never entered her room.

'It's only me, little Masha,' said the nurse. 'I've come to sit with you for a few minutes and look, I've brought the prince's wedding candles to light before his saint, my angel,' she said with a deep sigh.

'Oh, nurse, I'm so pleased to see you!'

'God is merciful, my darling.' The nurse lit the gilt candles, placed them before the icon-stand and sat down near the door with her knitting. Princess Marya picked up a book and started reading. Only when they heard footsteps or voices did they look up at each other, the princess anxiously wondering, the nurse full of reassurance. The emotions that Princess Marya was feeling as she sat in her room had spread through the whole house and taken possession of everyone in it. Acting on the old superstition that the fewer the people who know about the sufferings of a woman in labour, the less she suffers, everyone pretended to know nothing about it. Nobody said anything, but the usual steadiness and respectful sense of propriety that was always to be expected from servants in the prince's household had been overtaken by a general feeling of anxiety, a melting of hearts and an awareness that at this time they were in the presence of some great, unfathomable mystery. No laughter came from the large parlour assigned to the maids. In their hall the men sat in silence, ready to turn their hands to anything. Torches and candles were still burning in the serfs' quarters, and no one slept. The old prince paced up and down his study, banging down on his heels, and sent Tikhon to Marya Bogdanovna to ask for any news.

'Just say the prince has sent you to ask for any news, and come back and tell me what she says.'

'You may inform the prince that the princess has gone into labour,' said Marya Bogdanovna, with a knowing look at the messenger. Tikhon came back with the report.

'That's good,' said the prince, closing the door behind him, and from then on Tikhon heard not the slightest sound from the study. After a short interval Tikhon went in again on the pretext of checking the candles and saw the prince lying on the sofa. Tikhon looked at him, shook his head at the sight of the prince's worried face, went silently over and kissed him on the shoulder, and then left the room without touching the candles or saying why he had come. The world's most solemn mystery was now being slowly enacted. Evening passed, night came on, and the feeling of suspense and the melting of hearts before the great unknown, far from fading away, grew stronger and stronger. No one slept.

It was one of those March nights when winter, desperate for one last fling, hurls down its snows and slings its squalls with a special fury. A relay of horses had been sent out to the main road to meet the German doctor, who was expected at any moment, and several men had ridden out with lanterns to wait at the turn-off and guide him in past the deep ruts and watery hollows hidden by the snow.

Princess Marya, her book long since abandoned, sat in silence staring with her luminous eyes at the wrinkled face of her old nurse, which she knew in its every last detail, at the lock of grey hair that had dropped down from the headscarf and the baggy folds of skin under her chin.

Nurse Savishna held on to her knitting and rambled on in a soft voice without hearing her own words or following their meaning. For the hundredth time she described how the late princess had given birth to Princess Marya at Kishinyov with only a Moldavian peasant woman to assist instead of a midwife.

'God will provide. Don't need no doctors,' she said.

Suddenly a gust of wind buffeted one of the window-frames (the prince had decreed that one outer panel should be taken down in every room as soon as the larks returned), tore open a loose window catch, swirling the brocade curtain and whistling through with a cold, snowy draught that blew out the candle. Princess Marya shuddered. The nurse put down her knitting and went over to the window, where she put her head out and tried to get hold of the open frame. The cold wind flapped at the corners of her headscarf, and locks of grey hair slipped out and tumbled down.

'Princess, my love, someone be drivin' down the avenoo!' she said, holding on to the window-frame without closing it. 'Be lanterns there. 'Tis the doctor . . .'

'Oh, thank God! Thanks be to God!' said Princess Marya. 'I must go and meet him. He doesn't speak Russian.'

Princess Marya flung a shawl over her shoulders and rushed off to meet the men who were riding up to the house. Hurrying across the top landing, she looked down through a window and saw a carriage with lanterns standing at the entrance. She went to the head of the stairs. On a banister-post stood a tallow candle guttering in the draught. Half-way down, the footman Filipp, a picture of alarm, was standing on the first landing holding another candle. Right at the bottom, around the turn of the stairs, someone could be heard coming up in thick boots. And then a voice spoke, and Princess Marya thought she knew whose it was.

'Thank God for that!' said the voice. 'And what about father?'

'He has retired for the night,' came the voice of the butler, Demyan, already downstairs.

Then the first voice spoke again, and Demyan's reply was followed by the sound of those thick boots coming up the unseen part of the staircase faster and faster.

'It's Andrey!' thought Princess Marya. 'No, it can't be, that would be too much.' And as she stood there thinking about it, down on the landing where the footman stood with his candle, the face and figure of Prince Andrey suddenly appeared. He was still wearing his fur coat, its collar covered in snow. Yes, it was him, but he had changed; he looked pale and thin, in a strange way gentler, and very worried. He came up the stairs to embrace his sister.

'Didn't you get my letter?' he asked, and without waiting for an answer which was never going to come from the speechless princess, he turned back to fetch the doctor who had arrived with him (they had met at the last posting station), and then flew back up the stairs and again embraced his sister.

'How strange fate is!' he said. 'Dear Masha!' Slipping out of his coat and boots, he set off for the little princess's apartment.

CHAPTER 9

The little princess in her white night-cap was lying propped up with pillows. A wave of pain had just passed. Her black hair curled in thick strands around her feverish, perspiring cheeks; her pretty pink mouth, with its downy lip, was open, and she was smiling with joy. Prince Andrey came in and stood facing her at the foot of the couch where she lay. Her eyes shone like a child's, full of fear and anxiety, and when they rested on him they didn't change. 'I love all of you. I've never done anybody any harm. Why should I suffer like this? Help me,' was the message in them. She saw her husband but couldn't take in the meaning of his sudden appearance. Prince Andrey walked around the couch and kissed her on the forehead.

'My little darling,' he said, never having called her that before, 'God is merciful . . .'

Her little girl's eyes looked at him wondering, full of reproach, as if trying to say to him, 'I turned to you for help and you did nothing. Even you did nothing!' It wasn't that she was surprised to see him; she just didn't realize he had come. His arrival had nothing to do with her labour pains or any relief from them. Another wave was coming, and Marya Bogdanovna advised Prince Andrey to leave the room.

The doctor came in as he went out. There was Princess Marya, and they went back to her room together. When they spoke it was in whispers, and the conversation kept breaking down. They waited and they listened.

'Go and see her, my dear,' said Princess Marya. Prince Andrey went back to see his wife and sat down in the next room waiting to be summoned. A woman ran out of the bedroom looking very frightened, and she was most disconcerted to see Prince Andrey. He buried his face in his hands and sat like that for several minutes. The most pitiful, helpless, animal cries could be heard from inside the room. Prince Andrey stood up, went across to the door and tried to open it. Someone was holding it shut.

'Go away! You can't come in!' said a frightened voice on the other side. He paced up and down the room. The screams died down, and a few seconds passed. Then suddenly the most fearful scream – it couldn't be hers, she couldn't have screamed like that – came from inside the room. Prince Andrey ran to the door. The screaming stopped and he heard a different sound, the wail of a baby.

'Why have they taken a baby in there?' Prince Andrey wondered for a split-second. 'A baby? Whose baby is it? . . . What's a baby doing in there? Has it been born?'

When the delightful meaning of the baby's wail dawned on him he choked with tears, leant on the window-sill with both elbows and cried like a child sobbing his heart out. The door opened. The doctor came out of the room with no coat on and his shirt-sleeves rolled up; he looked pale and his jaw was trembling. Prince Andrey turned to speak to him, but the doctor walked past with a far-away look in his eye and said nothing. A woman came running out and stopped in the doorway, hesitating, when she saw Prince Andrey. He went into his wife's room. She was dead, still lying in the same position he had seen her in five minutes earlier, and despite the staring eyes and the white cheeks the same expression still haunted that lovely, shy little girl's face with its tiny upper lip covered with fine dark hair. 'I loved all of you, I never hurt anybody, and look what you have done to me, just look what you have done to me,' was the message on her dead face in all its pitiful beauty. In one corner of the room something small and red lay mewling and snuffling in the trembling white hands of Marya Bogdanovna.

Two hours later Prince Andrey walked quietly in to see his father. The old man knew what had happened. He was standing near the door, and the moment it opened he put his rough old arms round his son's neck in a vice-like grip, and without a word sobbed like a child.

*

Three days later at the little princess's funeral, Prince Andrey climbed the steps of the bier to say a last goodbye to her. Even in the coffin her face was the same, though the eyes were closed. 'Look what you have done to me,' was still the message for Prince Andrey and something seemed to rend his soul; he felt guilty of a crime that he could neither expiate nor ever forget. He was incapable of tears. The old man came in too and kissed the little waxen hand that lay so peacefully and prominently crossed over the other one, and to him too her face said, 'Look what you have done to me. Why did you do it?' And the old man turned away angrily when he saw the look on her face.

Another five days passed and the young prince, Nikolay Andreyevich, was christened. The wet-nurse bunched up his swaddling-clothes under her chin while the priest took a goose feather and anointed the baby's red and wrinkled little palms and soles.

His grandfather, who was his godfather, all shaky and afraid of dropping the baby, carried him around the battered tin font and handed him over with great care to his godmother, Princess Marya. Prince Andrey sat in the next room waiting for the ceremony to end, beside himself with fear that they might drown the baby. He looked at his son with great delight when the nurse brought him out, and nodded approvingly as she informed him that when they had dropped some of the baby's hair in a piece of wax into the font, it hadn't sunk but had floated on the surface of the water.[8]

CHAPTER 10

Rostov's involvement in the duel between Dolokhov and Bezukhov had been hushed up by the old count, and instead of being reduced to the ranks as expected he had been appointed adjutant to the governor-general of Moscow. As a result he was unable to go to the country with the rest of the family, and spent the whole summer in Moscow busy with his new duties. Dolokhov recovered, and Rostov became close to him during his convalescence, when Dolokhov lay ill in the house of his passionately doting mother, Marya Ivanovna. She took to Rostov because of his friendship with her Fedya and often talked about her son.

'Yes, Count, he is too noble, too pure in heart,' she would often say, 'for today's corrupt world. Nobody admires virtue nowadays. You get it thrown back in your face. Tell me this, Count – was

Bezukhov righteous and honourable in what he did? Fedya has always been noble-hearted and he loved him, and even now he won't have a word said against him. There was that silly business with the policeman in Petersburg – they did play a few tricks on people up there – but weren't they all in it together? Oh yes, but Bezukhov gets off scot-free and my Fedya shoulders all the blame. The things he's had to put up with! I know he's been reinstated, but how could he not have been? I don't imagine there were all that many patriotic sons out there as brave as he was! And now – this duel! Is there nobody with any feeling, any sense of honour nowadays? Challenging him like that – he knew he was an only son – and then aiming straight at him! I thank God for his mercy on us. And what was it all about? I ask you, who doesn't have affairs nowadays? I mean, if he was all that jealous – which I fully understand – he could have let people know a lot earlier, instead of letting it run on for a year. I know why he challenged him – he was counting on Fedya refusing to fight because he owed him money. It's obscene! Depraved! I know you understand Fedya, my dear count. That's why I'm so fond of you, believe me. Not many people do. He has the kind of soul that is too exalted, too angelic!'

And during his convalescence Dolokhov himself began to speak to Rostov in a way that no one would have expected of him.

'I know they all think I'm a nasty piece of work,' he would say. 'Let them think what they want. The only people I want to know are the ones I love. But those that I do love, I would lay down my life for them, and I'll crush anybody else who gets in my way. There's my mother – I adore her, she's a treasure – and one or two friends, including you. Apart from them I ignore everybody unless they are useful or dangerous. And most of them are dangerous, especially the women. Oh yes, dear boy,' he went on, 'I've met one or two men who were loving, noble and high-minded. But I've yet to meet a woman who wasn't for sale – countesses, cooks, they're all the same. I'm looking for a woman with the purity of a saint and complete devotion – and I've yet to meet one. If I could find a woman like that, I'd lay down my life for her! But this lot! . . .' He made a gesture of contempt. 'Believe me, if I value my life, I value it because I'm still hoping I might meet a heavenly creature like that who would restore me and purify me and lift me to a higher level. I don't suppose you understand.'

'Oh yes I do,' answered Rostov, very much under the influence of his new friend.

In the autumn the Rostov family returned to Moscow. At the beginning of the winter Denisov also came back and stayed with the Rostovs.

For Nikolay Rostov and all his family the early days of the 1806 winter in Moscow were the happiest and merriest of times. Nikolay brought a lot of young men back home with him into his parents' house. Vera was by now a beautiful young woman of twenty, Sonya, a sixteen-year-old girl with all the charm of an unfolding flower, while Natasha, half-adult, half-child, could be an amusing little girl one minute and an enchanting young woman the next.

Love was in the air at the Rostovs' at this time, as it always is when there are very young and very charming girls around. Any young man arriving at their house and seeing those young girls' faces, so sensitive and always smiling (probably at their own good fortune) amid all the chasing and scurrying, and hearing all their frivolous girlish chatter, so good-natured, open to everything, brimming with hope, and their equally frivolous singing and music-making, enjoyed the same sensations of love-sickness and impending bliss that the young Rostovs were themselves enjoying.

One of the first young men brought home by Nikolay was Dolokhov, who won over everyone in the house except Natasha. She almost came to blows with her brother over Dolokhov. She insisted that he was a bad lot, that in the duel with Bezukhov, Pierre had been in the right and Dolokhov in the wrong, and that he was a horrible monster.

'I understand the whole thing,' Natasha would cry with resolute self-certainty. 'He's a wicked man and he has no heart. Now take your Denisov – I like him. I know he's a rogue, and all that . . . but still I like him, so I do understand. I don't know how to put it – with Dolokhov everything's done deliberately, and I don't like that. Now Denisov . . .'

'Oh, Denisov's different,' answered Nikolay, implying that Denisov didn't even begin to compare with Dolokhov. 'You have to get through to Dolokhov and understand his soul. You should see him with his mother. What a tender heart!'

'I don't know about that. I just don't feel comfortable with him. You do realize he's fallen in love with Sonya, don't you?'

'Don't be stupid!'

'He has, you know. You'll see.'

Natasha was proved right. Dolokhov, who was no great lover of the ladies, became a regular visitor to the house and the question of whom he was coming to see (which no one actually asked) was soon settled: it was Sonya. And though Sonya would never have dared to admit it, she knew, and she turned beetroot-red every time Dolokhov put in an appearance.

Dolokhov often dined at the Rostovs', never missed any cultural performance that they were going to see, and went to all the balls 'for the under-twenties' at Iogel's, where the Rostovs were regular attenders. He paid a lot of attention to Sonya, and looked at her with such longing in his eyes that Sonya was not the only one who reddened under his gaze – even the old countess and Natasha blushed when they saw him looking at her like that.

It became obvious that this strange, strong man was irresistibly attracted to the dark and elegant young girl who loved someone else.

Rostov sensed something different between Dolokhov and Sonya, but he couldn't put his finger on what was new about their relationship. 'Oh, they're all in love with somebody,' he said, thinking of Sonya and Natasha. But he no longer felt at ease with Sonya and Dolokhov, and before long he was less frequently at home.

That autumn once again the talk was of war with Napoleon, and there was more enthusiasm for it than last year.[9] Enforced recruitment began: from every thousand of the population ten men were sent into the army and another nine to the militia. Napoleon's name was cursed right, left and centre, and the coming war was the only topic of conversation in Moscow. As far as the Rostov family was concerned the only thing that mattered in all these preparations for war was their dear Nikolay's categorical refusal to stay behind in Moscow. He was only waiting for the end of Denisov's leave at the end of the holiday season for the pair of them to rejoin their regiment. His impending departure, far from being an obstacle to his enjoyment, spurred him on to enjoy life even more. He spent most of his time out of the house, at dinners, parties and balls.

CHAPTER 11

On the third day after Christmas Nikolay dined at home – a rare occurrence in recent days. The occasion was a grand farewell dinner; Nikolay was due to rejoin his regiment with Denisov after Epiphany. There were a couple of dozen dinner-guests including Dolokhov and Denisov.

Love was still in the air at the Rostovs'; never had the atmosphere of the house been so palpably full of love-sickness as it was during those Christmas holidays. 'Seize the moment of bliss! Love and be loved! This is the only real thing in the whole world. Nothing else makes sense. Here and now this is all we are interested in' – the atmosphere was full of thoughts like these.

After exhausting two pairs of horses as usual – and he still never managed to go everywhere and see everyone – Nikolay arrived home just in time for dinner. The moment he entered the house he could sense the same atmosphere of love-sickness, but something else as well: he became aware of a curious kind of embarrassment between some of the company. The worst affected were Sonya, Dolokhov, the old countess and to some extent Natasha. Nikolay realized something must have happened between Sonya and Dolokhov before dinner, and during the meal he used his customary sensitivity to tread warily and be nice to the pair of them. That same evening there was to be one of the dances put on for his pupils during the holidays by Iogel, the dancing-master.

'Nikolay, are you coming to Iogel's? Please say yes,' said Natasha. 'He asked about you specially, and Denisov's coming.'

'I will go anywhere the countess wequires!' said Denisov, who had joked his way into the role of Natasha's champion knight within the household. 'I stand weady for the shawl dance.'

'If I can fit it in! I did promise to go to the Arkharovs – they're throwing a party,' said Nikolay.

'What about you?' he said, turning to Dolokhov. And the moment he had asked the question, he realized he shouldn't have done.

'Yes, well possibly . . .' Dolokhov's response was frigid and furious, as he glanced first at Sonya and then at Nikolay, treating him to exactly the same scowl he had launched at Pierre over dinner at the English Club.

'Something wrong here,' thought Nikolay, and his suspicions were confirmed when Dolokhov left immediately after dinner. He called Natasha over and asked what was going on.

'Oh, I've been looking for you,' said Natasha, skipping over to him. 'I told you, didn't I? You wouldn't believe me,' she said triumphantly. 'He's proposed to Sonya.'

Sonya had not been much in Nikolay's mind of late, but he still felt a great wrench inside him when he heard this. Dolokhov was a good match for an orphan girl like Sonya, who had no dowry – in some ways a brilliant match. From the point of view of the countess and in the eyes of society there could be no question of a refusal. And so Nikolay's immediate reaction was to feel annoyed with Sonya. He worked himself up to say, 'Oh splendid. Of course she'll have to forget all those childish promises and accept,' but before he could get the words out Natasha went on to say, 'But can you imagine? She turned him down! Just like that! . . . She told him she's in love with somebody else,' she added after a brief pause.

'Yes, my Sonya couldn't have done anything else!' thought Nikolay.

'Mamma went on and on at her not to, but she turned him down, and I know she's not going to change her mind, not if she said . . .'

'Mamma begged her not to?' Nikolay said reproachfully.

'Yes,' said Natasha. 'Listen, darling Nikolay – don't get angry with me – I know you'll never marry her. Don't ask me how I know – I just know for certain you'll never marry her.'

'You can't possibly know that,' said Nikolay, 'but I must have a word with her. Oh, Sonya, she is lovely!' he added with a smile.

'Yes, she is! I'll send her in.' And Natasha gave her brother a kiss and ran off.

A minute later in came Sonya, looking scared, upset and guilty. Nikolay went over and kissed her hand. It was the first time since his return that they had been alone together and talked about love.

'Sophie,' he said to her, timidly at first but getting braver by the minute, 'if you want to turn down a brilliant match, very much to your advantage . . . well, he's a splendid fellow, thoroughly noble . . . he's my friend . . .' Sonya interrupted him.

'I have turned him down,' she blurted out.

'If you are turning him down because of me, I'm afraid I . . .'

Again Sonya cut him short. She looked at him, anxious and imploring.

'Please, Nikolay, don't say that,' she said.

'No, I have to. Perhaps I'm being a bit conceited, but it's better to have the whole thing out. If you're turning him down because of me, I have to be honest with you. I do love you. I think I love you more than anyone in the world . . .'

'That's enough for me,' said Sonya, beetroot-red.

'No, but listen – I've been in love thousands of times, and I shall be again and again, though I could never feel the same kind of warmth and trust and love that I do towards you. Besides, I'm still a young man. And Mamma doesn't want me to. Well . . . that's it . . . I can't promise you anything . . . Please think carefully about Dolokhov's proposal,' he said, not finding it easy to say the name of his friend.

'Oh, don't say that. I don't want anything. I love you as a brother, and I always will, and I don't need anything else.'

'You're an angel. I don't deserve you. I'm just scared . . . I don't want to deceive you.' And Nikolay kissed her hand again.

CHAPTER 12

The balls put on by Iogel were the best in Moscow. This is what all the mothers said as they watched their young daughters performing the dances they had been recently learning. So did the boys and girls themselves as they danced till they were ready to drop; so did the grown-up young men and women, who came along thinking these dances were rather beneath them and ended up enjoying every minute. That year two matches had been made at these dances. Two pretty young princesses, the Gorchakov sisters, had both found suitors here and married them, which made the dances more popular than ever. There was one special feature about these dances – they had no host and hostess, only good old Iogel himself, who put his own art to good service with much mincing and bowing as he flitted around his guests like a feather and collected their tickets. Another feature was that these dances were attended only by those who really wanted to dance and enjoy themselves, in the way that girls of thirteen or fourteen do when they are wearing long dresses for the first time. With one or two exceptions they were pretty girls, or they managed to look pretty, with their smiling faces and sparkling eyes. Sometimes the best pupils were allowed to perform the difficult shawl dance, and that included Natasha, who danced more gracefully than anyone else. But at this latest ball they only danced the schottische, the anglaise and the mazurka, which was becoming all the rage. Iogel had taken a ballroom in Bezukhov's house, and everyone pronounced the evening a great success. There were many pretty girls there, and the Rostov girls were among the prettiest. They both felt particularly happy and high-spirited that evening. Sonya was feeling so proud to have received a proposal from Dolokhov and turned him down and then had things out with Nikolay that, before they had even left for the ball, she had gone twirling around the room, not giving her maid a chance to finish doing her hair, and now she positively glowed with energy and joy.

Natasha was just as proud and even happier – this was her first real ball in a long dress. Both girls wore white muslin dresses with pink ribbons.

Natasha made sure she fell in love the moment she stepped into the ballroom, not with anyone in particular, in love with everyone. Every time she looked at someone she fell in love, and the love lasted no longer than the look. She kept running up to Sonya and saying, 'Oh, isn't it marvellous?'

Nikolay and Denisov strolled from room to room, watching the dancers with a kind of protective benevolence.

'She's so sweet. She'll be a weal beauty,' said Denisov.

'Who will?'

'Countess Natasha,' answered Denisov.

After a short pause he said again, 'Look at her dancing. So gwaceful!'

'Who are you talking about?'

'Oh, weally, I'm talking about your sister!' cried Denisov angrily.

Rostov laughed.

'My dear count, you were one of my best pupils – you must dance,' said little Iogel, coming up to Nikolay. 'Look at all these pretty young ladies!' He turned with the same request to Denisov, also an ex-pupil.

'No, my dear fellow, I'm a wotten dancer but a good wallflower,' said Denisov. 'Don't you wemember how little cwedit I did to your instwuction?'

'Oh no!' said Iogel, quick to reassure him. 'You didn't concentrate, but you had talent, plenty of talent.'

The band struck up with a mazurka, the latest thing. Nikolay felt he couldn't refuse Iogel, so he asked Sonya to dance. Denisov sat down by some elderly ladies and leant towards them with one elbow on his sabre. Tapping his foot in time to the music, he managed to keep them amused while keeping an eye on the young people dancing. Iogel was dancing the first couple with Natasha, his star pupil, his pride and joy. Light as thistledown in his tiny slippers, Iogel led the way, swooping across the room with a diffident Natasha studiously concentrating on her steps. Denisov couldn't take his eyes off her. He tapped out the rhythm with his sabre, which was meant to imply that if he wasn't dancing it was because he chose not to, not because he couldn't dance. While the dancers were in the middle of a figure he saw Rostov walking past and beckoned him over.

'It's not wight, you know,' he said. 'Is this weckoned to be a Polish mazurka? . . . But she's such a good dancer.'

Knowing that even in Poland Denisov had been famous for dancing the Polish mazurka, Nikolay ran over to Natasha.

'Go and invite Denisov. He can dance, you know. He's marvellous at it!' he said.

When Natasha's turn came round again, she got up and tripped rather timidly across the room in her tiny dancing-shoes with their pretty bows to the corner where Denisov was sitting. She could feel everyone's eyes on her as people waited to see what might happen. Nikolay watched as a little amiable argument took place between

Denisov and Natasha, with Denisov saying no to something, but with a broad smile on his face. He ran across.

'Oh, please, Vasily Dmitrich,' Natasha was saying. 'Do come and dance.'

'Oh, Countess, weally and twuly, I . . .' Denisov was saying.

'Come off it, Vaska,' said Nikolay.

'They're stwoking me like a kitten,' said Denisov with great good humour.

'I'll sing for you – all night!' said Natasha.

'Little sorsowess, she's got me wapped awound her little finger!' said Denisov, unbuckling his sabre. He came out from behind the chairs, took his partner firmly by the hand, tilted his head back and put one foot forward, waiting for the beat. Denisov's short stature went unnoticed only when he was on horseback or dancing the mazurka; then he looked every inch the dashing hero he always felt himself to be. When the beat came round he gave a smile of triumph, took a sideways glance at his partner, suddenly stamped his foot and leapt off the floor like a rubber ball, soaring away and whirling his partner round with him. He swooped silently half-way across the room on one foot, heading straight for some chairs which he didn't seem to have seen, only to stop dead suddenly, spurs jingling, legs apart, down on his heels, holding it there for a second, then off again, stamping both feet, jangling his spurs, spinning round dizzily, clicking his heels, swooping off into another turn. Instinctively aware of what he was going to do next, Natasha abandoned herself and followed his lead quite unconsciously. He whirled her round on his right arm, then on his left, dropped down on one knee and guided her round, then leapt up again and galloped away madly as if he intended sweeping through every room in the palace without stopping for breath. But then – a sudden stop, a pause, and off again into some new and adventurous steps. With a final swirling flourish he swung his partner back into her place, halted smartly with jingling spurs and bowed to her, but Natasha didn't even curtsey in return. She was staring at him quizzically with a smile on her puzzled face, as if she didn't know him.

'What was that all about?' she said.

Although Iogel refused to accept this kind of dancing as a proper mazurka, everyone was delighted with Denisov's performance, and he was in great demand as a partner. Meanwhile old gentlemen smiled the time away, going on about Poland and the good old days, and as for Denisov, red in the face from his exertions in the mazurka and mopping his brow with a handkerchief, he sat down next to Natasha and never left her side for the rest of the evening.

CHAPTER 13

For the next two days Rostov did not see Dolokhov at his own home, nor did he catch him in when he called. On the third day he received a note from him.

> Since I have no intention of visiting your house again for reasons which are well known to you, and I am going back to join the regiment soon, I am giving a farewell supper tonight for my friends. Come to the English Hotel.

Shortly before ten o'clock that evening Rostov went on to the English Hotel from the theatre where he had been with his family and Denisov. He was taken straight to the best room in the hotel, which Dolokhov had hired for the night.

A couple of dozen young men were gathered around a table where Dolokhov was sitting between two candles. There were gold coins and banknotes on the table, and Dolokhov was keeping the bank. Nikolay had not seen him since his proposal and Sonya's refusal, and he felt some embarrassment at the thought of meeting him again.

Dolokhov's clear, cold eyes met Rostov even as he came in through the door, as if he had long been waiting for him.

'We haven't met for some time,' he said. 'Thanks for coming. Just let me finish dealing – and Ilyushka will soon be here with his singers.'

'I called on you several times,' said Rostov, reddening.

Dolokhov didn't respond.

'You can place your bet now,' he said.

Rostov instantly recalled a curious conversation he had once had with Dolokhov, who had said to him, 'Relying on luck's a fool's game.'

'Unless you're too scared to bet against me?' Dolokhov said now, as if he could guess what was going through Rostov's mind, and he smiled. Rostov could see lurking behind that smile the same mood that had settled on him at the club dinner, and on other occasions when Dolokhov had seemed to be tired of life with its dull routine and desperate to escape from it by doing something reckless and usually cruel.

Rostov felt uneasy. He racked his brains for some flippant response to Dolokhov's words, but couldn't think of anything. And while he was gathering his thoughts Dolokhov looked him straight in the face and said with slow deliberation for all to hear, 'Remember what we used to say about relying on luck? . . . It's a fool's game. You should play safe, and I'd like to have a go.'

'What at – relying on luck or playing safe?' wondered Rostov. 'No, you'd better stay out of it,' Dolokhov added. Snapping down a newly opened pack, he said, 'Gentlemen, the bank!'

Pushing some money forward, Dolokhov started to deal.

Rostov sat down next to him. At first he held back. Dolokhov kept glancing at him.

'Not playing, then?' he asked. And Nikolay felt a strangely irrepressible urge to take a card, stake a small sum on it and get into the game.

'I have no money on me,' said Rostov.

'I'll trust you!'

Rostov staked five roubles on a card and lost, staked again and lost again. Dolokhov 'made a killing' by winning ten times in succession. He had now been dealing for quite some time. 'Gentlemen,' he said, 'will you please put your money on your cards, or I might get the sums wrong.'

One of the players said he hoped he could be trusted.

'Yes, you can, but I don't want to get anything wrong. Please put your money on your cards,' answered Dolokhov. 'Don't worry, you and I can settle up later,' he added to Rostov.

The gambling continued. A footman brought round an endless supply of champagne.

Every one of Rostov's cards lost, and eight hundred roubles were written up against him. He made as if to stake the whole eight hundred roubles on a single card, but while champagne was being poured out for him he thought again and changed back to his normal stake of twenty roubles.

'Leave it there,' said Dolokhov, though he seemed to be looking away from Rostov. 'You'll win it back faster. I keep losing to everyone else. From you I win. Or are you afraid of me?' he asked again.

Rostov complied, let the eight-hundred stake go ahead, and laid down the seven of hearts, a card with a torn corner which he had picked up from the floor. He would long remember that card. He laid it down, the seven of hearts, took a small piece of chalk and wrote 800 on it in big round figures. He then drank the proffered glass of warm champagne, smiled at Dolokhov's words, and waited with a sinking heart for another seven to turn up, watching the pack in Dolokhov's hands. Winning or losing on that card meant a lot to Rostov. Only the previous Sunday his father, Count Ilya, had given his son two thousand roubles, and although he never liked talking about money he told him this was the last he would get till May and he begged him to be a bit more careful with it. Nikolay said that this was too much anyway, and, word of honour, he wouldn't come back for any for more until the spring. Yet already he was down to his last twelve hundred. So if he were to lose on that seven of hearts it would mean not only having to find sixteen hundred roubles, but also going back on his word. So it was with a sinking heart that he watched Dolokhov's hands, and thought, 'Come on, quick, deal me that card, and I'll get my cap and go home to supper with Denisov, Natasha and Sonya, and this time I know I'll never touch the cards again.' At that moment his family life – joking with Petya, chatting to Sonya, singing duets with Natasha, playing piquet[10] with his father, even his comfortable bed in the house on Povarskaya Street – rose up in his imagination so clear, so bright, so lovely that it seemed like something from the distant past, something lost and gone that he had never properly appreciated. He couldn't imagine that blind chance, by arranging for the seven to appear on the right, not the left, might rob him of the happiness that he now saw in such a new light, and plunge him into an abyss of unknown and uncertain misery. Surely it could never happen, but he still watched with dread in his heart as Dolokhov's hands began to move. Those broad, reddish-coloured hands, with hairs curling out from the shirt cuffs, laid down the pack of cards and took up the glass and pipe that were offered to him.

'So you're not too scared to bet against me?' repeated Dolokhov. Putting the cards down, he rocked back in his chair as though he were about to launch into a funny story, and began to speak, grinning and refusing to be hurried.

'So, gentlemen, in this city the word is – so they say – that I'm rather sharp with the cards. I do advise you to watch your step when you're playing with me.'

'Deal, will you!' said Rostov.

'Ugh, the gossip in Moscow!' said Dolokhov, and he took up the cards with a smile.

'Aagh!' Rostov almost screamed, raising both hands to cover his hair. The seven that he needed was lying face-up on top of the pack. He had lost more than he could pay.

'You mustn't go ruining yourself, though,' said Dolokhov, flashing a quick glance at Rostov as he went on dealing.

CHAPTER 14

An hour and a half went past, by which time most of the gamblers had lost all serious interest in their own play. All eyes were on Rostov. Instead of a mere sixteen hundred roubles he now had written up against him a long column of figures, which he would have put at something coming up to ten thousand, though a vague impression was dawning on him that it might have risen to fifteen thousand. In fact the total had already gone past twenty thousand roubles. Dolokhov was no longer listening to stories or telling them, he was following every movement of Rostov's hands, with the odd passing glance at the total against him. He had decided to keep the game going until the total reached forty-three thousand. He had lighted on this figure because forty-three represented his age and Sonya's added together. The table was a mess of wine stains, cards and chalk-marks, and Rostov sat there with his head in both hands. One impression tormented him relentlessly – those broad, reddish-coloured hands with the hairs curling out from the shirt-cuffs, those hands, loved and loathed, which held him in their power.

'Six hundred roubles, ace, corner there,[11] nine . . . No chance of winning it back! . . . How nice it would have been at home . . . Jack, no, it can't be! . . . Why is he doing this to me? . . .' Rostov wondered, thinking back. Now and then he went for a high stake, but Dolokhov would always decline and fix the stake himself. Nikolay always complied. One minute he was praying as he had done under fire on the bridge over the Enns; the next he was speculating that he might save himself by picking up the first card that came to hand in the crumpled pile under the table; then he counted the cords on his jacket and tried staking all his losses on a card with that number; then he looked round helplessly at the other gamblers, or stared into Dolokhov's coldly impassive face and tried to work out what was going on inside him.

'He knows full well what this loss means to me,' he told himself. 'Does he want to ruin me? He was my friend. I loved him . . . But it's not really his fault – he can't help it if he has a run of luck. It's not my fault either,' he kept saying to himself. 'I haven't done anything wrong. I haven't murdered anybody or offended anybody. I don't wish anybody any harm. Where did this disaster come from? When did it start? It all happened so quickly – I just sat down at this table thinking I might win a hundred roubles and buy Mamma that little casket for her name-day, and then go home. I was happy and free and in such a good mood. I didn't realize how happy I was. When did that end, and when did this ghastly business begin? What signalled the change? I just stayed here in my place at this table picking out cards and pushing them forward, and watching those broad hands doing their tricks. What's happened to me, and when did it happen? I'm fit and well, still the same, still in the same place. It's just not possible. Surely it's all going to come to nothing.'

He was red and sweating even though the room was not hot. His face looked terrible, a pathetic sight, all the worse for his useless efforts to look calm.

His total reached the fateful number – forty-three thousand. Rostov had just bent the corner of a new card to double up on the last three thousand put down to him when Dolokhov slammed the cards down on the table, pushed them to one side, took a piece of chalk and began totting up Rostov's losses rapidly in his clear, bold hand. The chalk snapped as he did so.

'Supper! Supper is served! And the gypsies are here.' And indeed, some swarthy men and women were coming in from the cold, saying something in a gypsy accent. Nikolay knew it was all over, but he managed to say off-handedly, 'Oh, aren't we going on then? I had such a nice little card ready,' as if the only thing that mattered to him was the fun of playing.

'That's it. I'm finished,' he thought. 'A bullet through my head – it's the only way out,' but his voice spoke breezily: 'Come on, just one more card.'

'All right,' answered Dolokhov, finishing his adding up. 'All right. Twenty-one roubles it is,' he said, pointing to the figure twenty-one, the amount by which his total exceeded forty-three thousand. He took a new pack and sat there ready to deal. Rostov bent the corner of his card, but instead of the intended six thousand he complied with Dolokhov and carefully wrote down twenty-one.

'I don't mind one way or the other,' he said. 'I'd just like to know whether you'll win or lose on that ten.'

Dolokhov had a grave look about him as he dealt. Oh, how Rostov loathed those reddish-coloured hands, with their stubby fingers and the hairs curling out from the shirt sleeves, those hands that had him in their power . . . The ten came up.

'Forty-three thousand against you, Count,' said Dolokhov, stretching as he rose from the table. 'All this sitting down makes you feel tired,' he said.

'Yes, I'm tired too,' said Rostov.

Dolokhov cut him short as if to remind Rostov that this was no laughing matter.

'When shall I have the money, Count?'

Rostov blushed as he drew Dolokhov aside into the next room.

'I can't pay it all just like that. Will you take an IOU?'

'Listen, Rostov,' said Dolokhov with a sunny smile, looking Nikolay straight in the eye, 'you know what they say, "Lucky in love, unlucky at cards." Your cousin's in love with you. I know that.'

'Oh! How horrible to be like this – in this man's power,' thought Rostov. He knew what a shock the news of this loss would be to his father and mother – oh, if only he could be rid of it all! – and he sensed that Dolokhov now wanted to play cat and mouse with him, in the full knowledge that only he could free him from all the shame and grief.

'Your cousin . . .' Dolokhov started to say, but Nikolay cut him short.

'My cousin has nothing to do with this! Keep her out of it!' he cried with fury.

'When do I get it, then?' asked Dolokhov.

'Tomorrow,' said Rostov, and left the room.

CHAPTER 15

To utter the word 'tomorrow' with a semblance of politeness was not too difficult, but to arrive home alone, to see sisters and brother, mother and father, to confess and ask for money which he had no right to after giving his word of honour, was ghastly.

They were still up. The younger members of the family had come back from the theatre to a good supper, and were now gathered round the clavichord. The moment Nikolay set foot in the hall he felt himself absorbed into the poetic atmosphere of love which had ruled their household that winter and seemed to have intensified around Sonya and Natasha ever since Dolokhov's proposal and Iogel's ball, like pressure building up before a storm. Sonya and Natasha, still wearing the light-blue dresses they had worn for the theatre, stood by the clavichord, pretty girls and conscious of it, happy and smiling. Vera was playing chess with Shinshin in the drawing-room. The old countess, waiting for her son and her husband to come home, was playing patience with an elderly gentlewoman who lived in with them. Denisov, with his gleaming eyes and unkempt hair, was sitting at the clavichord with one leg pushed back behind him, playing chords with his stubby little fingers and rolling his eyes as he applied his thin, reedy but tuneful voice to a poem of his own composition, 'The Sorceress', which he was trying to set to music.

> O sorcewess, what is this power that lingers,
> Weturning me to my forsaken lyre?
> What wapture this that floods into my fingers?
> Why did you fill my waging heart with fire?

He was singing with great passion, his black, agate eyes gleaming at the frightened but delighted Natasha.

'Oh, that's splendid! Perfect!' Natasha cried. 'Another verse please,' she said, not noticing Nikolay.

'Nothing's changed here,' thought Nikolay, glancing into the drawing-room, where he could see Vera and his mother and the old lady sitting with her.

'Oh, here he is! Nikolay!' Natasha ran over to him.

'Is Papa back yet?' he asked.

'Oh, I'm so pleased you've come,' said Natasha, ignoring his question. 'We're having such a marvellous time. Vasily Dmitrich is staying on another day just for me. Did you know?'

'No, Papa is still out,' answered Sonya.

'Darling Nikolay, is that you? Come here, my dear,' came the old countess's voice from the drawing-room. Nikolay went in to see his mother, kissed her hand, sat down by her table and started to watch her hands in silence as they placed the cards. From the hall came the sounds of laughter and happy voices urging Natasha to sing.

'All wight! All wight!' Denisov cried. 'No excuses now, it's your turn to sing the barcawolle – at my wequest!'

The countess glanced at her silent son.

'Is something wrong?' she asked him.

'No, no,' he said, as if he'd heard this question many times before and was getting fed up with it. 'Will Papa be long?'

'No, I shouldn't think so.'

'Nothing's changed here. They don't know a thing about it. What can I do with myself?' thought Nikolay, and he went back into the hall where they were playing the clavichord.

Sonya was at the keyboard, playing the prelude to Denisov's favourite barcarolle. Natasha was getting ready to sing. Denisov was watching her, enraptured. Nikolay began pacing up and down the room.

'Why do they want to get her singing? What can she sing? There's nothing to be happy about,' thought Nikolay.

Sonya played the opening chord of the prelude.

'My God, I'm ruined. My honour's gone. Bullet through the head, that's my only way out, not singing,' he thought. 'Shall I run away? Where to? Oh, it makes no difference – let them get on with the singing.' Still pacing, Nikolay glanced darkly at Denisov and the girls, avoiding their eyes.

'Nikolay, what's wrong?' asked Sonya's staring eyes. She had known immediately that something must have happened to him.

Nikolay turned away. Natasha, too, with her usual acuteness, had instantly sensed her brother's state of mind. She did notice him, but she was in such high spirits at that moment, so remote from sorrow, gloom and censure, that she deliberately indulged in a little self-delusion, as young people often do. 'No, I'm too happy at this moment to spoil my happiness by sympathizing with someone else's sorrow,' was what she felt, though she said to herself, 'No, I've probably got it all wrong. He must be as happy as I am.'

'Come on, Sonya,' she said, walking out into the middle of the room, where she thought the acoustics were best. Tilting her head, and letting her arms dangle lifelessly like a ballet-dancer, Natasha performed a strong heel-and-toe figure in the middle of the room and then stood still.

'Here I am! Look at me!' she seemed to be saying in response to Denisov's enraptured gaze, which never left her.

'What is she so pleased about?' Nikolay wondered, looking at his sister. 'Why doesn't she get fed up with all this? Has she no shame?' As Natasha sang the first note her throat swelled, her chest rose and her eyes became serious. Oblivious for the moment of everyone and everything, she spread her mouth into a broad smile and out came the sounds of her voice, sounds that might have left you cold if you had heard them a thousand times identically pitched and held, but then suddenly, the thousand and first time, you would be reduced to tears and trembling.

That winter Natasha had begun to take her singing seriously for the first time, especially since Denisov had been so complimentary about her voice. She no longer sang like a child. She had got rid of the childish straining for effect that had made her singing rather amusing until recently. But she was not yet a good singer, according to the musical experts who heard her. 'No polish. A nice voice, but it needs polishing,' they all said. But this was usually said a long time after her voice had stopped. While that unpolished voice was actually singing, for all its wrong breathing and moments of strain, even the experts kept quiet, enjoying the voice, however unpolished, and longing to hear more of it. It had a virginal purity, intuitive power and an easy velvety smoothness, so closely bound up with its own artistic imperfections that it seemed untouchable – as if nothing could be done to that voice without spoiling it.

'How can she?' thought Nikolay with staring eyes when he heard her sing. 'What's got into her? How can she sing at a time like this?' he thought. But then suddenly his whole world was concentrated on waiting for the next note, the next cadence, and everything in the world had a three-beat rhythm: *Oh, mio crudele affetto* . . . One, two, three . . . One, two, three . . . One . . . *Oh, mio crudele affetto* . . . One, two, three . . .

'Oh, the stupidity of human life!' thought Nikolay. 'All these things – this disaster, money, Dolokhov, evil, honour – it's all rubbish . . . *This* is what matters . . . Go on, Natasha! Go on, darling! Go on, my lovely girl! . . . Can she get that top B? Yes! Well done!' and, unaware that he was singing too, he accompanied her a third below to strengthen her top note. 'My God, how marvellous! Did I get that high? Wonderful feeling!' he thought.

Oh, the beauty of their singing in thirds, Oh, the lovely tremolo! Rostov felt a thrill of something nobler in his soul. And that something was detached from everything in the world, and higher than anything in the world. Gambling debts? Dolokhovs? Honour? What were they compared with this? Rubbish! You can murder and steal and still be happy . . .

CHAPTER 16

It was a long time since Rostov had felt such enjoyment in music as he did that day. But as soon as Natasha had finished her barcarolle he was brought back down to reality. He walked out without saying anything and went down to his room. A quarter of an hour later, the old count came in from his club, jolly and contented. Nikolay, hearing him drive up, went to see him.

'Had a good time, then?' asked the old count, a proud and delighted man, smiling cheerfully at his son. Nikolay tried to say yes, but he couldn't; he was choking with sobs. The count was busy lighting his pipe and did not notice the state his son was in.

'Oh well, it's got to be done!' thought Nikolay, once and for all. And out it came: feeling ashamed for doing so, he said to his father quite off-handedly, as if he was asking to use the carriage for a trip down town, 'Oh, Papa, there's a bit of business we ought to discuss. I nearly forgot. I need some money.'

'Dear me,' said his father, who happened to be in a very good mood. 'I said you wouldn't have enough. How much?'

'A lot,' said Nikolay, blushing and smiling a crass, casual smile for which he would never be able to forgive himself. 'I've lost a bit at cards, well rather a lot really, an awful lot – forty-three thousand.'

'What? Who to? ... You must be joking!' cried the count, an apoplectic red spreading over his neck and the back of his neck, as it does with old people.

'I promised to pay up tomorrow,' said Nikolay.

'Oh no!' exclaimed the count, throwing his arms in the air as he flopped down helplessly on to a sofa.

'Can't be helped! Everybody does it!' said his son, outwardly brazen and breezy but feeling in his heart of hearts that he was an unspeakable cad and his crime could never be redeemed in a lifetime. He felt like kissing his father's hands, going down on his knees and begging for forgiveness, and here he was casually, even rather rudely, telling him this sort of thing happened to everybody.

Count Ilya lowered his eyes at these words from his son, and began fidgeting as if he was looking for something.

'Yes, yes ...' he managed to say. 'It will be difficult, I'm afraid, difficult to raise ... but it happens to everybody! Yes, it happens to everybody ...' The old count flashed a look at his son, straight in the face, and walked out of the room ... Nikolay had been preparing himself for a refusal, but this he had not expected.

'Papa! Pa-pa!' he cried out, sobbing, after the retreating figure. 'Please, forgive me!' Seizing his father's hand, he pressed it to his lips and burst into tears.

While father and son were having this discussion, another one, hardly less important, was taking place between mother and daughter. Natasha had rushed in wildly excited and run over to her mother.

'Mamma! ... Mamma! ... he's done it ... he's ...'

'Done what?'

'He's ... He's proposed to me! Mamma! Mamma!' she cried.

The countess couldn't believe her ears. Denisov proposing? Who to? ... Her tiny little Natasha, who had only just grown out of playing with dolls and was still in the school-room.

'Natasha, that's enough. Don't be so silly!' she said, hoping it might be a joke.

'I'm not being silly! I'm telling you what's happened,' said Natasha angrily. 'I've come to ask you what to do, and you say I'm being silly!'

The countess shrugged.

'If it is true that *Monsieur* Denisov has made a proposal, it may be amusing but you must go and tell him he is a fool. That's all there is to it.'

'But he's not a fool,' said Natasha, serious and resentful.

'Well, what do you want, then? You all seem to be in love nowadays. Oh well, if you're in love perhaps you'd better marry him,' said the countess with an angry smile. 'Good luck to you.'

'No, Mamma, I'm not in love with him. I don't think I am.'

'Well, go and tell him.'

'Mamma, are you angry with me? Don't be angry, dearest Mamma. It's not my fault, is it?'

'No, of course I'm not, darling. If you like, I'll go and tell him,' said the countess with another smile.

'No, I can do it, only tell me what to say. It's all so easy for you,' she added, warming to her smile. 'Oh, if only you could have seen him saying it! I know he didn't mean to. He just blurted it out.'

'Well, anyway, you've got to go and refuse him.'

'No, I can't. I feel sorry for him! He's so nice.'

'Well, you'd better accept then. Yes, it's about time you got married,' said her mother with pointed irony.

'No, Mamma, but I am sorry for him. I don't know what to say.'

'Well, you don't have to say anything. I'll speak to him myself,' said the countess, indignant at the very idea of someone treating her little Natasha like an adult.

'No, no, you mustn't! I'll do it. You come and listen at the door.'

And Natasha ran across the drawing-room into the hall where Denisov was still sitting at the clavichord in the same chair, with his face buried in his hands. He leapt to his feet at the sound of her little footsteps.

'Natalie,' he said, hurrying towards her, 'decide my fate. It is in your hands!'

'Vasily Dmitrich, I'm sorry! . . . You are so nice . . . but we can't . . . you know . . . but I'll always love you as I do now.'

Denisov bent over her hand and she heard some strange, incomprehensible sounds. She kissed him on his unkempt curly black head. At that moment they heard the hurried rustling of the old countess's skirts as she bore down on them.

'Vasily Dmitrich, I thank you for the honour you do us,' said the countess in an embarrassed tone which Denisov took as a harsh one, 'but my daughter is so young, and I would have thought that as a friend of my son you would have approached me first. If you had, you would not have put me in the position of having to make this refusal.'

'Countess . . .' began Denisov with downcast eyes and a guilty face. He wanted to say more but he had dried up. Natasha could not look calmly on such a pathetic sight. She broke down in a series of loud sobs.

'Countess, I do wegwet this,' he stammered out, 'but I weally do adore your daughter and all your family and I'd sacwifice more than one life . . .' He looked at the countess and took in her stern face. 'Wight then, I weally must say goodbye, Countess,' he said, kissing her hand, and without a glance at Natasha he strode quickly out of the room with an air of great determination.

The following day Rostov went to Denisov, who wasn't prepared to spend another day in Moscow, to see him on his way. All his Moscow friends gave him a grand send-off at the Gypsies', and he had no memory of being stowed in his sledge or of travelling the first three stations.

With Denisov gone Rostov hung on for another two weeks in Moscow waiting for his money, which the count needed some time to get together. He never went out, and he spent most of his time in the young girls' room.

Sonya was more attentive and affectionate than ever. She seemed anxious to show him that his loss at cards was a splendid achievement that made her love him more than ever. But Nikolay now felt unworthy of her.

He filled the girls' albums with poetry and music, and then at last, having sent off the entire sum of forty-three thousand roubles to Dolokhov and got his receipt, he left Moscow at the end of November without saying goodbye to any of his acquaintances, to rejoin his regiment, which was already in Poland.

PART II

After having things out with his wife, Pierre left for Petersburg. At Torzhok, either there were no horses, or the station-master would not release any. Pierre had to wait. Without removing his overcoat, he lay down on a leather sofa in front of a round table, put his big feet up on it, still wearing his thick boots, and sank into thought.

'Shall I fetch the bags in? Should I make up a bed for you? Would you like some tea?' his valet kept asking.

No reply came from Pierre, who was hearing and saying nothing. He had been deep in thought since the last station and was still thinking about something so important that he had no idea of anything that was going on around him. He was quite unconcerned about arriving in Petersburg sooner rather than later, or whether there would or would not be somewhere for him to rest at this station. Compared with all that was going through his mind at the moment, it was a matter of complete indifference to him whether he spent a few hours or the rest of his life here.

The station-master and his wife, his valet and a peasant woman selling Torzhok embroidery kept coming in and out offering their services. Without shifting his raised feet, Pierre stared at them over his spectacles, wondering what they could possibly want and how they could go on living without answering the questions that were worrying him. They were the same questions that had worried him ever since the day he had returned from the duel at Sokolniki and had spent that first agonizing, sleepless night, but now, all alone and on the road, he had become obsessed by them. Whatever the direction of his thoughts he kept coming back to the same unanswerable but inescapable questions. It was as if the working of his head had stripped the main screw that held his life together. The screw wouldn't go in or come out; it just turned without biting on anything, always in the same hole, and he couldn't stop it turning.

The station-master came in and asked his Excellency obsequiously whether he would mind waiting just a while, only an hour or two, by which time – come what might – he would let his Excellency have the special post-horses. He was lying, of course, in the hope of squeezing more money out of the traveller.

'Is this a good thing or a bad thing?' Pierre wondered. 'Good for me, but bad for the next traveller, and anyway he can't help it – he has to eat. He told me an officer thrashed him for that. But the officer thrashed him because he was in a hurry. And I shot Dolokhov because I considered myself insulted. Louis XVI was executed because he was considered a criminal, and within a year the men who executed him were killed as well for doing something or other. What's bad and what's good? What should we love and what should we hate? What is life for, and what am I? What is life? What is death? What kind of force is it that directs everything?' he kept asking himself. And there were no answers to any of these questions, except one illogical response that didn't answer any of them. And that response was: 'You're going to die, and it will be over and done with. You're going to die and you'll either come to know everything or stop asking.' But dying was horrible too.

The Torzhok pedlar woman was whining away, offering her wares, especially some goatskin slippers. 'I've got hundreds of roubles, money I don't know what to do with, and she stands there in her tatty coat hardly daring to look at me,' thought Pierre. 'And what does she want money for? As if it could give her a hair's breadth of extra happiness or put her soul at rest. Is there anything in the world that can make her and me any less subject to evil and death? Death, the end of everything, and it must come today or tomorrow – either way it's a split second on the scale of eternity.' And again he twisted the screw that wouldn't bite, and the screw went on turning in the same hole.

His servant handed him a half-cut volume – it was a novel in letters by Madame de Souza.[1] He started reading about the trials and struggle for virtue of someone called Amélie de Mansfeld. 'Why did she resist her seducer,' he thought, 'when she loved him? God couldn't have filled her heart with any desires that went against his will. My ex-wife didn't, and maybe she was right. Nothing has been discovered,' Pierre said to himself again, 'and nothing has been invented. The only thing we can know is that we don't know anything. And that is the summit of human wisdom.'

Everything within and around him struck him as confused, senseless and disgusting. And yet in his very disgust at everything around him Pierre found a source of nagging enjoyment.

'If I could just ask your Excellency to squeeze up a little and make room for this gentleman,' said the station-master, bringing in another traveller delayed by the lack of horses. This traveller was a stocky, large-boned old man, yellow, wrinkled and with grey bushy eyebrows and eyes that gleamed with a greyish colour.

Pierre took his feet down from the table, stood up and went to lie on the bed that had been got ready for him, glancing across now and again at the gloomy and weary newcomer, who did not look back at him as he struggled out of his top-coat assisted by his servant. Keeping on his shabby nankeen-covered sheepskin coat and with felt boots on his thin bony legs, the traveller sat down on the sofa, leaned back his close-cropped head, which was unusually large and broad at the temples, and looked at Bezukhov. He had a shrewd, austere and sharp look that impressed Pierre, who felt like striking up a conversation, but just as he was about to ask him about the roads, the traveller closed his eyes and folded his wrinkled old hands, one finger displaying a large iron ring with a death's head seal on it. He sat there quite still, either relaxing or, as seemed more likely to Pierre, in a state of profound and tranquil meditation. The newcomer's servant was also old, yellow and wrinkled. He had no beard or moustache, not because he had shaved them off, but because he had clearly never been able to grow any. The old retainer fussed about, unpacking a hamper and setting up a little tea table, and then went to fetch a boiling samovar. When it was all ready, the traveller opened his eyes, moved over to the table and poured out one glass of tea for himself and another which he handed to the beardless old man. Pierre began to feel restless, as if it was necessary, even inevitable, for him to get into conversation with the traveller.

The servant came back with his empty glass inverted and a half-nibbled piece of sugar beside it, and asked if anything more was required.

'No. Give me my book,' said the traveller. The servant passed him a book which Pierre took to be a devotional work, and the traveller became engrossed in it. Pierre watched him. Suddenly the stranger marked his place in the book, closed it and put it down. He then shut his eyes, leant back on the sofa and resumed his earlier position. Pierre was still watching him, too late to look away, when the old man opened his austere, resolute eyes and fastened them on Pierre. Pierre felt embarrassed and tried to avoid that look, but the gleaming old eyes kept a magnetic hold on him.

CHAPTER 2

'I have the pleasure of addressing Count Bezukhov, if I'm not mistaken,' said the stranger in a loud, unhurried voice. Pierre said nothing but looked quizzically over his spectacles at the speaker. 'I have heard of you,' continued the stranger, 'and I have also heard about what has happened to you, sir. Your misfortune.' He seemed to emphasize the last word as if to say, *Oh yes, misfortune. Call it what you will, but I know that what happened to you in Moscow was a misfortune.*

'You have my deepest sympathy, sir.'

Pierre reddened and hurriedly put his legs down from the bed, leaning forward towards the old man with a shy and awkward smile.

'I mention this, sir, not from mere curiosity, but for more serious reasons.' He paused, still fixing Pierre with his eyes, and moved aside on the sofa – an invitation for Pierre to come and sit next to him. Pierre felt reluctant to enter into conversation with this old man, but he complied automatically, came over and sat down beside him.

'You are unhappy, sir,' he went on. 'You are young and I am old. I should like to help you, as far as I am able.'

'Oh yes,' said Pierre with another awkward smile. 'I'm most grateful to you . . . Have you come far?' The stranger's face showed no warmth; it was rather frigid and forbidding, but for all that the words and features of this new acquaintance fascinated Pierre beyond resistance.

'But if for any reason you find conversation with me uncongenial,' said the old man, 'please say so, my dear sir.' And his face suddenly lit up with an unexpected smile of fatherly indulgence.

'No, no, quite the reverse. I'm very pleased to meet you,' said Pierre, glancing down again at the stranger's hands and looking more closely at the ring. There was the death's head, the symbol of freemasonry.[2]

'May I ask you something?' he said. 'Are you a mason?'

'Yes, I do belong to the brotherhood of freemasons,' said the stranger, plumbing the depths of Pierre's eyes more and more deeply. 'In my own name and in theirs I extend a brotherly hand to you.'

'I'm afraid,' said Pierre with a smile, vacillating between confidence inspired by the personality of this mason and his usual habit of laughing at masonic beliefs, 'I'm afraid I'm a long way from understanding – how can I put it? – I'm afraid that my way of thinking about the whole of creation is so opposed to yours that we are not going to understand each other.'

'I am aware of your way of thinking,' said the mason, 'but the way of thinking that you speak of, and which you see as emerging from your own thought processes, is the way of thinking of most men, and invariably the fruit of pride, indolence and ignorance. Forgive me for saying it, my dear sir, but if I had not been aware of it, I should not have spoken to you. Your way of thinking is a sad delusion.'

'Yes, but I may equally claim that you are deluded,' said Pierre with a trace of a smile.

'I would never dare to claim that I know the truth,' said the mason, whose manner of speaking, with its firmness and preciseness, impressed Pierre more and more. 'No one person can attain truth. It is only stone by stone, with everyone's involvement, over millions of generations from our forefather Adam down to our own day, that a temple arises to be a dwelling-place worthy of Almighty God,' said the freemason, and he closed his eyes.

'I ought to tell you that I don't believe, don't . . . believe in God.' said Pierre ruefully, feeling himself obliged to make every effort to tell the whole truth.

The mason looked closely at Pierre and smiled the smile of a rich man with millions in his hands beaming at some poor wretch who might have said to him that all he needed as a poor man was five roubles to make him happy.

'But you do not know Him, sir,' said the freemason. 'You cannot know Him. You know Him not, and that is why you are unhappy.'

'Yes, I am unhappy,' Pierre agreed, 'but what can I do about it?'

'You know Him not, sir, and that's why you are very unhappy. You know Him not, but He is here, He is within me, He is in my words, He is in thee, and even in those blasphemous words that thou hast uttered,' said the mason, his sharp voice quavering.

He paused and sighed in an obvious effort to collect himself.

'If He did not exist,' he said softly, 'we should not be speaking of Him, sir. Of what, of whom have we been speaking? Whom hast thou denied?' he blurted out, with impassioned solemnity and authority in his voice. 'Who has invented Him, if He does not exist? How was there born in thee any conception that such an ineffable Being could exist? How did it happen that thou and all the world together have postulated the existence of such an inconceivable Being, a Being omnipotent, eternal and infinite in all His qualities? . . .' He stopped and said nothing more for some time.

Pierre could not and would not interrupt this silence.

'He exists, but He is not easy to comprehend,' the mason went on, looking straight ahead, not at Pierre, his old man's hands fidgeting with inner emotion as he turned the pages of his book. 'If it were the existence of a man that thou hadst doubted, I could have brought the man before thee, taken him by the hand and shown him to thee. But how can I, a mere mortal, display the omnipotence, the eternity, the blessedness of Him to one who is blind, or to one who closes his eyes so as not to see, not to understand Him, and not to see or understand his own vileness and sinfulness.'

Again he paused. 'Who art thou? What art thou? Thou seest thyself as a wise man because thou wast able to pronounce such words of blasphemy,' he said with a dark, sardonic smile, 'whereas thou art more foolish and artless than a small child who plays with the parts of an ingeniously constructed watch and dares to say that because he does not know what the watch is for, he will not believe in the creator who made it. He is not easy to know. Down the ages, from our forefather Adam to our day we have been working towards this knowledge, and are still infinitely distant from the attainment of our goal, but in our lack of understanding we see only our own weakness and His greatness . . .'

Pierre's heart thrilled to these words as he gazed with shining eyes into the mason's face. He listened without interrupting or asking any questions, and with all his soul he believed what this stranger was saying to him. Whether he was believing rational arguments coming from the mason, or trusting more like a child in the persuasive intonation, the sense of authority, the sincerity of the words spoken, the quavering voice that sometimes seemed on the verge of breaking down, or the gleaming aged eyes grown old in that conviction, or the tranquillity, the certainty and true sense of vocation radiating from the old man's whole being and striking Pierre very forcibly, given the state of his own debasement and despair – whatever was happening to him, he longed to believe with all his soul, and he did believe and he felt a joyful sense of calm, renewal and return to life.

'He is attained not through reason, but through living,' said the mason.

'I don't understand,' said Pierre, dismayed at the doubts surging up inside him. Put off by the vagueness and weakness of the freemason's arguments, he felt the dread of unbelief. 'I don't understand,' he said, 'why human reason cannot attain the knowledge you speak of.'

The freemason smiled his gentle, fatherly smile.

'The highest wisdom and truth is like unto the purest liquid which we try to absorb into ourselves,' he said. 'Can I receive that pure liquid into an impure vessel and judge of its purity? Only through the inner purification of myself can I bring the liquid received within me to some degree of purity.'

'Yes, yes. That's it!' said Pierre joyfully.

'The highest wisdom is founded not on reason alone, not on the worldly sciences – physics, history, chemistry and the like – into which intellectual knowledge is divided. The highest wisdom is one. The highest wisdom knows only a single science – the science of the whole, the science that explains the whole of creation and the place of mankind within it. In order to assimilate this science it is necessary to purify and renew the inner self, and so, before we can know, we must have faith and be made perfect. And for the attainment of these aims we have had implanted into our souls the light of God, which is called conscience.'

'Yes, yes,' Pierre assented.

'Look with a spiritual eye into thine inner being, and ask thyself whether thou art content with thyself. What hast thou achieved relying on intellect alone? What art thou? My dear sir, you are a young man, you are wealthy and well educated. What have you done with the blessings vouchsafed you? Are you satisfied with yourself and your life?'

'No, I loathe my life,' said Pierre with a frown.

'Thou loathest it. Then change it. Purify thyself, and as thou art purified, so shalt thou come to know wisdom. Look at your life, sir. How have you been spending it? In riotous orgies and debauchery, taking everything from society and giving nothing back. You have received wealth. How have you used it? What have you done for your neighbour? Have you given a thought to your slaves, tens of thousands of them? Have you succoured them physically and morally? No. You have profited from their labour to lead a dissipated life. This is what you have done. Have you chosen a career in the service where you might be of use to your neighbour? No. You have spent your life in idleness. And then you married, sir, taking responsibility for guiding a young woman through life, and what did you do? You did not help her, my dear sir, to discover the path of truth, you thrust her down into the abyss of deception and misery. Someone offended you and you shot him, and you now tell me that you know not God and you loathe your life. There is nothing strange in this, my dear sir.'

This said, the mason leant back again on the sofa and closed his eyes, as though exhausted by too much talking. Pierre gazed at that austere, unflinching, ancient, almost death-like face, and moved his lips without making a sound. What he wanted to say was, 'Yes, mine is a foul, idle, profligate life,' but he dared not break the silence. The mason sounded like an old man as he cleared his throat gruffly and called his servant.

'Any horses?' he asked, ignoring Pierre.

'They've got some that have just arrived,' answered the old man. 'But wouldn't you like to have a rest?'

'No, have them harnessed.'

'Surely he can't be just driving on, leaving me here all on my own, without telling me everything and offering me some help?' thought Pierre, getting to his feet with downcast head and beginning to pace up and down the room, casting occasional glances at the mason. 'Yes, I didn't see it, but I have been leading a despicably immoral life, but I didn't like it and I didn't want it,' thought Pierre. 'This man knows the truth, and if he wished to he could reveal it to me.' Pierre wanted to say this to the mason but he couldn't bring himself to do so. By now the traveller had stowed his things away with practised old hands and was buttoning up his sheepskin coat. When he had finished he turned to Bezukhov and said to him in a polite but casual manner, 'Where are you heading for now, sir?'

'Oh, er, Petersburg,' answered Pierre in a childlike tone, full of indecision. 'I must thank you. I agree with you completely. But please don't assume I've been as bad as all that. With all my soul I have longed to be what you would want me to be, but I've never had anyone to turn to for help . . . No, I know I was mostly to blame. Please help me, teach me, and perhaps I can . . .'

Pierre couldn't go on. He gulped and turned away.

The mason stood there in silence, apparently thinking things over.

'Help comes from God alone,' he said, 'but any measure of help that our order has power to give you, it will give you, sir. Go now to Petersburg and give this to Count Willarski.' Taking out his note-book, he jotted down a few words on a large sheet of paper folded into four. 'One piece of advice. When you reach the capital, the first thing you must do is devote some time to solitude and self-examination, and do not return to your old way of life. And now I wish you God speed, my dear sir,' he added, noticing that his servant had come in, 'and every success . . .'

The traveller was Osip Alexeyevich Bazdeyev, as Pierre discovered from the station-master's book. Bazdeyev had been a leading free-mason and Martinist since the days of Novikov.[3] For a long while after he had gone Pierre paced up and down the station room, neither lying down to sleep nor asking for horses. He was going over his depraved past, and thinking ecstatically of making a new start, imagining a blissful future, spotless and virtuous, which seemed so easy to achieve. He could see it now – he had been depraved simply because he had somehow forgotten how nice it is to be virtuous. His soul retained not a trace of its former doubts. He firmly believed in the

possibility of the brotherhood of all people, united in the aim of mutual
support along the path of virtue, and he now saw freemasonry as such
a brotherhood.

CHAPTER 3

When he got back to Petersburg, Pierre informed no one of his arrival,
never went out and spent many long days reading a volume of Thomas
à Kempis[4] which had been sent to him by some unknown person. One
thing and one thing only emerged from Pierre's understanding as he
read: he experienced a pleasure he had never known before – a belief
in the possibility of attaining perfection and the feasibility of practical
brotherly love between men, as revealed to him by Bazdeyev. A week
after his arrival the young Pole, Count Willarski, whom Pierre knew
slightly from Petersburg society, came into his room one evening with
the same solemn, official manner that Dolokhov's second had affected
when he had called on him. Closing the door behind him, and checking
that there was no one in the room but Pierre, he began to speak.

'I come to you with a message and a proposal, Count,' he said
without sitting down. 'Someone of very high standing in our brotherhood has been petitioning for you to be admitted to our fraternity
before the usual term and suggested that I be your sponsor. I consider
it my sacred duty to fulfil that person's wishes. Is it your desire under
my sponsorship to enter the brotherhood of the freemasons?'

Pierre was taken aback by the cold, austere tone of this man, whom
he had almost always seen before at balls smiling a pleasant smile in
the company of the most brilliant women.

'Yes, it is,' said Pierre.

Willarski bowed his head.

'One more question, Count,' he said, 'which I beg you, not as a
future mason but as an honest man, to answer in all sincerity. Have
you renounced your former beliefs? Do you believe in God?'

Pierre thought for a moment.

'Er, yes I do . . . I believe in God,' he said.

'In that case . . .' Willarski began, but Pierre interrupted him.

'Yes, I do believe in God,' he repeated.

'In that case, we can go,' said Willarski. 'My carriage is at your
disposal.'

Throughout the drive Willarski sat silent. When Pierre asked
what he would have to do and how he should respond to questions,

Willarski simply told him that brothers worthier than he would put him to the test, and all Pierre needed to do was tell the truth.

They drove in through the gates of a large house where the lodge had its quarters, and after climbing a dark staircase they came into a small, well-lit ante-room and took off their overcoats without the help of any servants. From there they walked through into another room. A man in strange attire appeared at the door. Advancing to meet him, Willarski whispered something to him in French and then went over to a small cupboard, where Pierre noticed articles of clothing like nothing he had ever seen before. Taking a scarf from the cupboard, Willarski placed it over Pierre's eyes and tied it in a knot behind, catching his hair painfully in the knot. Then he pulled him close, kissed him, took him by the arm and led him away. Pierre's hair still hurt, caught up in the knot; he was wincing from the pain and also grinning with a kind of embarrassment. He cut a huge figure with his arms dangling down at his sides as he tottered along uncertainly behind Willarski, his face all grin and grimace.

After leading him a dozen steps forward, Willarski stopped.

'Whatever happens to you,' he said, 'you must endure all things manfully if you are firmly resolved to enter our brotherhood.' (Pierre nodded his assent.) 'When you hear a knock at the door, you will take off the blindfold,' added Willarski. 'I wish you courage and success.' With that Willarski squeezed Pierre's arm and walked away.

Left alone, Pierre carried on grinning as before. Once or twice he shrugged and lifted a hand towards the scarf, as if wanting to take it off, but then put it down again. He spent five minutes with his eyes blindfolded but they seemed like an hour. His arms felt numb, his legs were wobbling and he seemed to be very tired. He was a prey to mixed feelings of the most complex kind. He was afraid of what was going to happen to him, but even more afraid of showing his fear. He wondered what was coming next, what would be revealed to him, but most of all he felt delighted that at long last the moment had come for him to step out along the path of regeneration towards a life of practical goodness – all those things he had been dreaming about since his meeting with Bazdeyev.

There were several loud knocks at the door. Pierre removed the blindfold and looked around. The room was in pitch-black darkness except for one place where a little lamp was burning in a white container. Pierre went over and saw that the little lamp stood on a black table where there was an open book. It was the Gospel and the white container was a human skull with its gaping eye-sockets and teeth. After reading the opening words of the Gospel, 'In the beginning

was the Word and the Word was with God . . .' Pierre walked round
the table and there before him was a large open box with some things
in it. It was a coffin full of bones. He wasn't in the least taken aback
by what he saw. Hoping to enter on a completely new life, totally
different from the old one, he was prepared for anything extraordinary, more extraordinary than what he was now seeing. The skull, the
coffin, the Gospel – he seemed to have been expecting all of this and
more. In an attempt to work up some emotion he looked all round.
'God . . . death . . . love . . . the brotherhood of man . . .' he kept saying
to himself, and with these words came an associated wave of vague
but joyful thoughts. The door opened and someone came in.

In the faint light, which Pierre had by now become accustomed to,
a small person entered the room. Blinded for a moment by coming
from light into darkness, this person stopped, then picked his way
cautiously towards the table, on which he then placed both of his
small, leather-gloved hands.

This short person was wearing a white leather apron that covered
his chest and upper legs. Around his neck he wore a kind of necklace,
with a tall white ruffle standing out from it, framing his equine face,
lighted from below.

'For what purpose have you come to this place?' The newcomer's
words were directed at Pierre, who had stirred with a slight rustling
noise. 'For what purpose have you, who believe not in the truth of the
light and who cannot see the light, for what have you come here?
What do you seek from us? Wisdom, virtue, enlightenment?'

The moment the door had opened and the unknown person had
come in, Pierre had experienced a sensation of awe and reverence the
like of which he used to feel at confession in childhood; here he was
face to face with a man who, according to the circumstances of everyday life, was a complete stranger, yet he was also a close neighbour
through the brotherhood of men. Pierre's heart was beating so fast
that he could hardly breathe as he turned to the 'tyler' (a masonic
term for a brother who prepares a 'seeker' for entry into the fraternity).
As he got nearer to the tyler, Pierre realized that he knew him – his
name was Smolyaninov – and he felt mortified to discover that the
newcomer was someone he knew; when he had entered he had been
nothing but a brother and mentor along the path of virtue. For a long
while Pierre could not get any words out, so the tyler had to repeat
his question.

'Yes. I . . . I . . . seek regeneration.' Pierre was forcing the
words out.

'Very good,' said Smolyaninov, and went on at once.

'Do you have any concept of the means by which our sacred order will assist you in achieving your goal? . . .' asked the tyler calmly but rapidly.

'I, er . . . hope for . . . guidance . . . er, help . . . in regeneration,' Pierre stammered, his voice quavering partly from emotion but also from not being accustomed to using Russian for abstract subjects.

'What concept do you have of freemasonry?'

'I presume that freemasonry means fraternity and the equality of men with virtuous aims,' said Pierre, embarrassed even as he spoke by the discrepancy between what he was saying and the solemnity of the occasion. 'I presume . . .'

'Very good,' said the tyler hastily, evidently happy with this response. 'Have you sought the means of achieving your goal in religion?'

'No. I regarded that as untrue and I have not followed it,' said Pierre, so quietly that the tyler could not hear, and asked what he was saying. 'I have been an atheist,' answered Pierre.

'You seek the truth in order to follow its laws in life, and therefore you seek wisdom and virtue, do you not?' asked the tyler after a moment's pause.

'Yes, yes,' Pierre agreed.

The tyler cleared his throat, folded his gloved hands across his chest and launched forth.

'I am about to reveal to you the main aim of our order,' he said, 'and if that aim coincides with yours, you shall enter our brotherhood with advantage. The first and principal aim and also the very basis of our order, on which it is established and which no human force can overturn, is the preservation and handing down to posterity of a certain solemn mystery . . . that has come down to us from the most ancient times, even from the first man, a mystery upon which depends, perhaps, the destiny of the human race. But since this mystery is such that no one can know it and profit from it without being prepared by prolonged and assiduous self-purification, not everyone can hope to acquire it rapidly. Thus we have a secondary aim, which consists in preparing our members as far as possible to reform their hearts, to purify and enlighten their minds by those means which have been revealed to us through tradition by men who have laboured to attain this mystery, and thereby to make them proper for reception of the same. Through the purification and regeneration of our members we endeavour, in the third place, to reform the whole human race by offering to it in our members models of piety and virtue, and thereby we commit all our strength to combat the evil that reigns throughout the world. Think on these things, and I shall come to you again.' This said, he left the room.

'To combat the evil that reigns throughout the world,' Pierre repeated, and he could see before him his future activity in that domain. He could see men such as he had been only two weeks before, and he began to address them in his mind as teacher and mentor. He imagined people who were sinful and unhappy but who could be helped in word and in deed, and also oppressors whose victims could be rescued. Of the three aims set out by the tyler it was the last one – the reformation of the human race – that particularly appealed to Pierre. The solemn mystery which the tyler had spoken of may have excited his curiosity, but it didn't strike him as really substantial, while the second aim, self-purification and personal regeneration, held little interest because at that moment he was relishing a sense of having completely renounced all his former vices and standing ready for nothing but goodness.

Half an hour later the tyler returned to instruct the seeker in the seven virtues, corresponding to the seven steps of the temple of Solomon, which every freemason must cultivate in himself. These were: 1 *Discretion* (safeguarding the secrets of the Order). 2 *Obedience* (to the higher authorities of the Order). 3 *Morality*. 4 *Love for mankind*. 5 *Courage*. 6 *Generosity*. 7 *The love of death*.

'And in the seventh place, strive,' said the tyler, 'through constant contemplation of death to bring yourself to think of it not as a dreaded enemy but as a friend . . . who delivers the soul grown weary in the labours of virtue from this life of torment and leads it to a place of recompense and peace.'

'Yes, that's as it should be,' thought Pierre as the tyler spoke these words and once again left him alone for contemplation. 'That's as it should be, but I'm so weak that I still love this life, and its meaning is only now being gradually revealed to me.' Pierre could remember five of the other virtues and as he counted them out on his fingers he felt he already possessed them in his soul: *courage* and *generosity*, *morality* and *love for mankind*, and most of all, *obedience*, which seemed to him more of a pleasure than a virtue. (He was utterly delighted at this time to be escaping from the arbitrary workings of his own nature and submitting his own will to those who had knowledge of the absolute truth.) Pierre had forgotten what the seventh virtue was and he simply couldn't bring it to mind.

The third time the tyler came back more quickly, and asked Pierre whether he was still determined to proceed and ready to submit to anything that might be demanded of him.

'I am ready for anything,' said Pierre.

'I must further inform you,' said the tyler, 'that our order conveys its teaching not by word alone but by other means that may be seen to work upon the true seeker after wisdom and virtue more powerfully than mere words. This temple and all that you see therein should already have suggested to your heart, if it be sincere, more than words can say, and it may be that in your coming initiation you will see further enlightenment of this kind. Our order reflects the practice of ancient societies which revealed their teaching in hieroglyphs. The word "hieroglyph",' said the tyler, 'is a term used to denote something beyond the senses that possesses qualities similar to the thing that it symbolizes.'

Pierre knew full well what a hieroglyph was but he dared not speak. He listened to the tyler in silence and what he heard made him think that his ordeal was about to begin.

'If you are fully resolved, I must proceed to your initiation,' said the tyler, coming closer to Pierre. 'As a sign of your generosity I now ask you to give me everything you have that is of value.'

'But I have nothing on me,' said Pierre, imagining he was being asked to give up everything he owned.

'Anything you have on you: your watch, money, rings . . .'

Pierre quickly took out his purse and his watch, taking ages to get the wedding ring off his fat finger. This done, the freemason said, 'As a sign of your obedience I now ask you to undress.' Pierre took off his coat, waistcoat and left boot as instructed by the tyler. The mason pulled Pierre's shirt open over his left breast and pulled his left trouser-leg up above the knee. Pierre made as if to remove his right boot and tuck both trouser-legs up to save this stranger the trouble, but the mason told him it wasn't necessary and gave him a slipper for his left foot. With a childlike grin of embarrassment tinged with doubt and self-mockery spreading over his face in spite of himself, Pierre stood there with his legs wide apart and his arms dangling down, facing the tyler and waiting for further instructions.

'And finally, as a sign of your sincerity, I ask you to reveal to me your chief temptation,' he said.

'Temptation! I used to have so many,' said Pierre.

'That temptation which more than any other has caused you to stumble on the path of virtue,' said the freemason.

Pierre paused, searching for a response.

'Wine? Gluttony? Frivolity? Sloth? Bad temper? Malevolence? Women?' He ran through his vices, weighing them in the balance and not knowing which one should have priority.

'Women,' said Pierre in a low voice, scarcely audible. The mason neither moved nor spoke for some time after this response. Eventually he walked up to Pierre, picked up the scarf lying on the table, and blindfolded him with it again.

'For the last time I say to you: turn all your attention in upon yourself, fetter your feelings and look for bliss not in your passions but in your heart. The source of all bliss is not without, it is within us . . .'

Pierre was beginning to sense this quickening source of all bliss welling up within him and flooding his soul with joyous emotion.

CHAPTER 4

Shortly after this someone came into the dark temple to fetch Pierre, not the tyler but his sponsor Willarski, whose voice he recognized. In response to further inquiries about the firmness of his resolve, Pierre answered, 'Yes, yes, I agree,' and with a beaming, boyish smile he walked forward, stepping cautiously and unsteadily in one boot and one slipper while Willarski held a sword against his bare breast. He was led out of the room and down several corridors, turning this way and that, until eventually he was brought to the doors of the lodge. Willarski gave a cough and was answered by a rapping of masonic gavels, after which the door opened before them. A bass voice (Pierre was still blindfolded) asked who he was, where and when he had been born, and further questions of that kind. Then he was led away again still blindfolded, and as he walked along they explained the allegorical meaning of his arduous journey, speaking of sacred friendship, the Great Architect of the Universe, the courage he would need in order to endure toil and peril. As the journey progressed Pierre noticed he was referred to in different ways, sometimes as 'the seeker', sometimes 'the sufferer' and sometimes 'the postulant', and various tapping sounds were made with gavels and with swords. As he was being led up to one object he sensed a certain amount of hesitation and uncertainty among his guides. He heard a whispered argument among the people around him, and one of them kept insisting that he must be made to walk on a particular carpet. After this they took his right hand and placed it on something, giving him a pair of compasses in his left hand to hold against his left breast, while they told him to listen to someone reading aloud and repeat an oath of fidelity to the laws of the Order. Then the candles were put out, a spirit-lamp was lit – Pierre could tell from the smell – and he was told that he would now see the lesser light. The blindfold was removed and in the dim glow of the burning spirit Pierre saw what looked like a dream-world, with several persons facing him, all dressed in aprons like the tyler's and pointing swords at his breast. Among them stood a man wearing a white bloodstained shirt. Seeing all this, Pierre thrust his chest forward towards the swords, wanting to be stabbed. But the swords were withdrawn and he was quickly blindfolded again.

'Now thou hast seen the lesser light,' said a voice. Then the candles were relit and he was told that he must now see the full light. Again the blindfold was taken off and a dozen voices suddenly chanted, '*Sic transit gloria mundi*.'[5]

Pierre gradually began to collect himself and look around at the room and the people in it. A dozen men, all dressed in the same garments that he had seen before, sat round a long table covered in black. Several of them were known to Pierre from Petersburg society. In the chairman's place sat a young man with a peculiar cross hanging from his neck; Pierre did not know who he was. To his right sat the Italian abbé whom Pierre had seen two years before at Anna Pavlovna's. The others included a very important dignitary and a Swiss tutor who had once been with the Kuragin family. All maintained a solemn silence as they listened to the Worshipful Master, who was holding a gavel. A blazing star had been cut into the wall; running along one side of the table was a narrow carpet depicting various figures, and on the other side stood something that looked like an altar with the gospel and skull on it. Round the table stood seven big church-like candlesticks. Two of the brothers led Pierre to the altar, placed his feet at right angles and told him to lie down prostrate before the gates of the temple.

'He ought to receive the trowel first,' whispered one of the brothers.

'Sh! Please be quiet,' said another.

Before complying Pierre squinted about short-sightedly, uneasy and suddenly assailed by doubt. 'Where am I? What am I doing? Aren't they laughing at me? Shall I be embarrassed to look back on this?' But the misgivings were short-lived. Pierre examined the serious faces of the people surrounding him, thought of everything he had just gone through and realized he couldn't stop half-way. He was horrified by his doubt and in a new attempt to evoke his earlier feeling of devotion he prostrated himself at the gates of the temple. And then the devotional feeling really did sweep over him, more strongly than ever. After lying there for some time he was told to get up and a white leather apron like everyone else's was put around him, and a trowel and three pairs of gloves were placed in his hands. And then the Grand Master addressed him. He told him he must try never to stain the whiteness of that apron, which stood as a symbol of strength and purity. Then he spoke of the unexplained trowel, saying that he must labour with it to scour all vice from his heart and to smooth the hearts of his fellow men with good grace. Then he turned to the first pair of gloves, a man's, and told him he could not know their significance, but must safeguard them; the second pair were to be put on at meetings, and as to the third pair, they were women's gloves, and he said of them, 'Dear brother, these woman's gloves are yours too. Give them to the woman whom you shall honour beyond all others. This gift will serve as a token of your purity of heart for the one woman you shall take unto yourself as a worthy helpmeet within masonry.' After a brief pause he added, 'But take care, dear brother, that these gloves never adorn hands that are unclean.'

As the Grand Master was pronouncing these last words, Pierre sensed embarrassment in him. He felt even more embarrassed himself, blushing like a child, on the point of tears, looking about him uneasily, and an awkward silence ensued.

The silence was broken by one of the brothers, who took Pierre over to the carpet and began reading from a note-book to interpret all the figures depicted on it: the sun, the moon, the gavel, the plumb-line, the trowel, the rough stone and the squared stone, the pillar, the three windows, and so on. Then Pierre was shown his assigned place and the signs of the lodge, told the password, and at long last allowed to sit down. The Grand Master began reading the statutes. These were very drawn out and Pierre in his joy, exhilaration and embarrassment was hardly in a state to take in what was being read. He managed to concentrate on just the last words of the statutes and these stuck in his memory.

'In our temples we acknowledge no degrees,' read the Grand Master, 'other than that between virtue and vice. Beware of making any distinction that may infringe equality. Fly to assist any brother whoever he may be, exhort him that goeth astray, raise him up that falleth and foster no malice or hatred towards any brother. Be thou kindly and courteous. In all hearts kindle the fire of virtue. Share thy happiness with thy neighbour, and allow no envy to mar the purity of that bliss. Forgive thine enemy, seek not to avenge thyself on him but by doing him good. By this fulfilment of the highest law thou shalt recover some traces of the ancient dignity thou hast lost.' When he had finished, he rose, took Pierre in an embrace and kissed him.

Pierre looked around with tears of joy in his eyes, not knowing how to respond to the congratulations and greetings coming from old acquaintances who now surrounded him. He recognized no one as an acquaintance; in all of these men he saw only brothers, and he burnt with impatience to start working with them. The Grand Master then rapped with his gavel, all of them sat down in their places and one brother began reading an exhortation on the need for humility.

The Grand Master proposed that the last duty be performed, and the important dignitary who bore the title 'Collector of Alms' began to go round all the brotherhood. Pierre felt like signing away all the money he possessed, but he thought that might look like pride, so he subscribed the same amount as everyone else.

The session was over, and Pierre, when he got back home, had a sense of returning from a long journey which had lasted dozens of years. He was a different man, who had renounced his old habits and his former way of life.

CHAPTER 5

The day after his initiation into the lodge Pierre was sitting at home reading a book and trying to fathom the significance of a square whose four sides symbolized God, morality, the physical world and unity through combination. Now and again he turned away from the book and the symbolic square to work out a new life plan in his imagination. The previous day he had been told at the lodge that word of his duel had reached the Emperor's ears, and it would be more sensible for him to leave Petersburg for a while. Pierre was thinking of going down to his southern estates and doing something for his serfs. He was dreaming blissfully of this new life when in walked Prince Vasily.

'My dear fellow, what have you been up to in Moscow? What's all this falling out with Hélène, dear boy? You've been getting it all wrong,' said Prince Vasily, as he came into the room. 'I've heard about it. I can assure you that Hélène is as blameless towards you as Christ was before the Jews.'

Pierre was about to respond but he went on.

'Now why didn't you just come and talk to me, treat me like a friend? I know all about it. I know what's going on,' he said. 'You have behaved quite properly for a man of honour, a bit hastily perhaps, but we won't go into that. There's one thing you must think about, though – where does this leave her and me in the eyes of society – and even the court?' he added, lowering his voice. 'She's down in Moscow and you're up here. Things have gone far enough, dear boy.' He drew him down by the arm. 'This is just a little misunderstanding, I'm sure you agree. Now why don't we sit down and write a letter, and she'll come up here, we can have things out and all the gossip will stop . . . Otherwise, my dear boy, to be quite candid, you might live to regret it.'

Prince Vasily gave Pierre a knowing look.

'I've learned from excellent sources that the Dowager Empress is taking a keen interest in this business. You know she is very graciously disposed towards Hélène.'

Several times Pierre had been on the point of replying, but, for one thing, Prince Vasily kept interrupting and wouldn't let him, and in any case Pierre was worried about striking the wrong note of final refusal, determined as he was to deny his father-in-law. Beyond that, he couldn't get yesterday's masonic precept out of his head: 'Be thou kindly and courteous.' He blinked and blushed, got to his feet and flopped down again, trying to force himself to do what he found hardest – say something unpleasant to a man's face, something he wasn't expecting, whoever he might be. He had become so used to complying with that offhand tone of authority which Prince Vasily affected that even now he felt he might not be able to resist it. But at the same time he sensed that his whole future would depend on what he said now, determining whether he would continue down the old path or start along the new one that the masons had shown to be so attractive, and that he was convinced would lead him towards self-regeneration and a new life.

'Come on, dear boy,' said Prince Vasily, full of good humour, 'just say yes, I'll do the writing, and then we'll kill the fatted calf.' But before Prince Vasily could finish his little joke, Pierre's face lit up with a fury all too reminiscent of his father, and without looking him in the eye he breathed out in a soft whisper, 'Prince, I did not invite you here. Go away. Please go away!' He leapt up and opened the door for him. 'Go away!' he repeated, amazed at himself and much enjoying the embarrassment and dismay written all over Prince Vasily's face.

'What's wrong with you? Are you ill?'

'Go away!' came the quavering voice once more. And Prince Vasily had to go, without a word of explanation.

A week later Pierre said goodbye to his new masonic friends, leaving them large sums of money for alms, and set off for his estates. His new brethren had given him letters addressed to masons in Kiev and Odessa, and they promised to write to him and guide him in his new way of life.

CHAPTER 6

Pierre's duel with Dolokhov had been hushed up, and in spite of the Tsar's strong disapproval of duelling at that time no one paid a price for it, neither the duellists nor their seconds. Nevertheless the whole affair, confirmed by Pierre's break with his wife, was much talked of in society. As an illegitimate son Pierre had been looked on most patronizingly; as the most eligible bachelor in all Russia he had been cosseted and praised; but now after his marriage, when young ladies and their mothers had lost all hope in him, he had declined steeply in society's esteem, especially since he had neither the wit nor the will to curry public favour. He was blamed for the whole affair. Hadn't he been insanely jealous, given to the same fits of bloodthirsty rage as his father? And when Hélène returned to Petersburg after Pierre's departure she was received on all sides not only warmly but with a touch of deference appropriate for someone in distress. Whenever the conversation touched upon her husband, Hélène would assume a dignified expression which she had mastered with all her usual *savoir faire*, though she had never quite worked out what it was supposed to mean. It seemed to imply that she was determined to survive her ordeal without a word of complaint, and her husband was a cross sent by God for her to bear. Prince Vasily was more open on the subject. He would shrug when the conversation came round to Pierre, point to his forehead and say, 'A bit touched. I've said it all along.'

'Yes, I said it was coming,' Anna Pavlovna would say about Pierre. 'I said it at the time, and I was the first to do so.' (She had to insist on being the first.) 'I said he was a young madman ruined by the depravity of our times. I said it when everyone else was in ecstasies over him, and he'd only just come home from abroad. Don't you remember? At one of my soirées he passed himself off as some kind of Marat?[6] And look how it's ended. I was against that marriage all along. I predicted everything that has happened.'

When she was free to do so Anna Pavlovna was still giving her soirées, soirées that only she could arrange, soirées which brought together what she described as 'the real cream of good society, the flower of Petersburg's intellectual élite'. Apart from their fine sense of social discrimination Anna Pavlovna's soirées were still famous for always parading some new and interesting personality and determining more clearly and unmistakably than anywhere else the exact political temperature of loyalist court society in Petersburg.

Towards the end of 1806, when all the grisly details were known –

Napoleon's rout of the Prussian army at Jena and Auerstadt, and the surrender of almost all the Prussian strongholds – and just when our troops had entered Prussia at the start of our second campaign against Napoleon, Anna Pavlovna was giving one of these soirées. Tonight 'the real cream of good society' consisted of the enchanting if unhappy Hélène, deserted by her husband; Mortemart; the fascinating Prince Hippolyte, just back from Vienna; two diplomats; the same old aunt; one young man described in that drawing-room as 'a man of much merit'; one newly appointed maid of honour and her mother, and several other persons of lesser standing.

Tonight's novelty, Anna Pavlovna's new offering to her guests for their delectation this evening, was Boris Drubetskoy, who had just arrived as a special messenger from the Prussian army, and it was in that same Prussian army that he served as adjutant to a personage of very high rank.

The political temperature taken at that soirée indicated the following:

'Whatever the European rulers and commanders may do by way of pandering to Bonaparte with the object of causing *me*, and *us* in general, maximum annoyance and mortification, our opinion in regard to Bonaparte cannot be changed. We shall never stop voicing our true opinion on this matter in the clearest terms, and all we have to say to the King of Prussia and everybody else is, "Hard luck. You got what you wanted, George Dandin."[7] And that's all we have to say.'

This is what was shown by the political temperature taken at Anna Pavlovna's soirée. When Boris, soon to be served up to the guests, entered the drawing-room, almost everyone who mattered was there and the conversation had been steered by Anna Pavlovna towards our diplomatic relations with Austria and the prospects of an alliance with her.

Boris cut a dashing figure in his adjutant's elegant uniform as he strolled into the drawing-room, fresh-faced and rosy-cheeked but now fully matured as a man. He was duly led across to pay his respects to the aunt before joining the general circle.

Anna Pavlovna offered him a desiccated hand to kiss and then introduced him to a number of people he didn't know, adding a whispered description of them one by one. Prince Hippolyte Kuragin was 'a young man of great charm', M. Krug, *chargé d'affaires* from Copenhagen, 'a serious intellectual', and the simplest description of all was applied to M. Shitov, a 'man of much merit' who was always referred to thus.

Thanks to a combination of his mother's exertions, his own tastes

and the peculiarities of his canny nature, Boris had by this time succeeded in obtaining a very advantageous position in the service. In his
capacity as an adjutant in the entourage of a high-ranking officer, he
had been given a very important assignment in Prussia, from where
he had just returned as a special messenger. He had mastered the
unwritten code that had pleased him so much at Olmütz, which allows
for a junior officer to outrank a general and says that what you
need to succeed in the service is not effort, hard work, gallantry or
perseverance, but simply the art of getting on well with people who
have promotion and awards in their gift. He often marvelled at his
own rapid advancement, and the fact that other people couldn't see
how it was done. This discovery had altered everything beyond recognition – his whole manner of life, his relationships with old friends,
all his plans for the future. Though not well off he would spend his
last kopeck to look better turned out than anyone else. He would have
deprived himself of many a pleasure sooner than permit himself to
drive in an inferior carriage or be seen on the streets of Petersburg in
an old uniform. He sought out and cultivated only people in higher
positions who might be of use to him. He loved Petersburg and
despised Moscow. The Rostov household and his childish passion
for Natasha were now unpleasant memories, and he had never been
back to their house since joining the army. Once admitted to Anna
Pavlovna's drawing-room, a development which he saw as an important step up in the service, he knew immediately how to act and let
Anna Pavlovna reap the benefits of any interest he might be able to
offer, which left him free to observe every face in detail and take stock
of any advantages or possibilities of intimacy with anyone there. He
sat down in the place indicated, next to the lovely Hélène, and opened
his ears to the general run of conversation, which was conducted in
French. The Danish *chargé d'affaires* was holding forth.

'"Vienna considers the bases of the proposed treaty so unattain-
able,"' he said, '"that they could not be secured even by a succession
of the most brilliant victories, and she doubts whether we have any
means at all of securing them." These are the actual words of the
Vienna cabinet.'

'The doubt is flattering,' put in the serious intellectual with a subtle
smile.

'We must make a distinction between the Vienna cabinet and the
Emperor of Austria,' said Mortemart. 'The Emperor of Austria can
never have thought up anything like this. It is the cabinet talking.'

'Alas, my dear vicomte,' said Anna Pavlovna, 'Europe will never be
a sincere ally of ours.' (She slightly mispronounced the first syllable of

the French word 'Europe' as if it were a nicety of pronunciation that
she could allow herself to use in the presence of a native speaker.)

Then Anna Pavlovna steered the conversation round to the courage
and determination of the Prussian King, so that Boris could be brought
into action.

Boris was listening carefully to each speaker, but as he waited for
his turn he managed to get in a few glances at the lovely Hélène, who
more than once smiled back into the handsome young adjutant's eyes.

It was perfectly natural when speaking of the Prussian situation
for Anna Pavlovna to invite Boris to describe his journey to Glogau,
and the situation of the Prussian army as seen by him. Boris took his
time, using his immaculate French to recount many a fascinating detail
about the armies, and the court, and studiously keeping any personal
opinion out of the facts he was narrating. Boris held their interest for
quite some time, which allowed Anna Pavlovna to feel that her novelty
item had gone down very well with the guests. Keenest of all to show
interest in Boris's account was Hélène. She asked him a number of
detailed questions about his trip and seemed particularly fascinated
by the situation of the Prussian army. The moment he had finished
she turned to him with her usual smile.

'You really must come and see me,' she said in a tone that implied
that this was absolutely essential, for reasons he couldn't begin to
understand. 'Tuesday, between eight and nine. It will give me great
pleasure.'

Boris promised that he would, and was about to plunge into further
conversation with her when Anna Pavlovna took him aside on the
pretext that her aunt wished to hear him.

'You know her husband, don't you?' said Anna Pavlovna, closing
her eyes and nodding lugubriously in the direction of Hélène. 'Oh
dear, such an unhappy woman and so exquisite! Don't mention him.
Please don't mention his name. It's too much for her!'

CHAPTER 7

When Boris and Anna Pavlovna rejoined the main company, Prince
Hippolyte was dominating the conversation. He was leaning forward
in his armchair and had just said, 'The King of Prussia!' with a guffaw.
Everyone turned towards him. 'The King of Prussia?' he asked with
another laugh before settling back, relaxed and serious-looking, into
the depths of his armchair. Anna Pavlovna waited for him to go on,

but since Hippolyte seemed determined not to add anything, she began to talk about the heathen Bonaparte, who had stolen Frederick the Great's sword at Potsdam.

'Yes, it's Frederick the Great's sword that I . . .' she began, but Hippolyte interrupted her by saying, 'The King of Prussia . . .' But again, as soon as everyone turned to listen to him he apologized and said no more. Anna Pavlovna frowned. Mortemart, Hippolyte's friend, gave him a stern look and said, 'Come on, what's all this about the King of Prussia?'

Hippolyte laughed, and seemed embarrassed to do so.

'No, it's nothing. All I meant was . . .' (He had been trying all evening to get in a joke he had heard in Vienna).[8] 'All I meant was that we are wrong if we go to war *for the King of Prussia*!'

Boris gave a cautious smile that could be taken either way, as a sneer or approval of the joke depending on how it was received. Everyone laughed.

'Your joke is a very bad one! Very clever but unfair,' said Anna Pavlovna, wagging a tiny wrinkled finger at him. 'We are going to war for sound principles, not for the King of Prussia. Oh, this Prince Hippolyte, he's such a naughty boy!' she said.

The conversation, mainly about politics and the latest news, went on all evening without flagging. Later on it took an even livelier turn when a new subject came up: rewards bestowed by the Tsar.

'Listen, only last year what's-his-name was given a snuff-box with a portrait on it,' said the serious intellectual. 'Why shouldn't so-and-so get the same?'

'Excuse me, a snuff-box with the Emperor's portrait on it is a reward, not a distinction,' said a diplomat. 'More like a present.'

'There are precedents for this. I would cite Schwarzenberg.'

'It's impossible,' someone else retorted.

'Do you want to bet? Now, the Grand Ribbon – that's something different . . .'

When everyone stood up to go, Hélène, who had had little to say all evening, turned to Boris and with a tender, knowing look exhorted him again to come and see her on Tuesday.

'It means a lot to me,' she said with a smile, looking round at Anna Pavlovna, and Anna Pavlovna, smiling her own lugubrious smile, the one she reserved for references to her royal patroness, spoke in support of Hélène's wishes. Something that Boris had said that evening about the Prussian army seemed to have inspired Hélène with a need to see him again. There was an implied promise that when he came on Tuesday she would explain what the need was. When Tuesday evening came and Boris entered Hélène's magnificent salon, however, he was not given any clear explanation of the necessity for his visit. There were other people present and the countess did not have a lot to say to him. It was only as he was saying goodbye and kissing her hand that she looked at him with a strangely unsmiling face and surprised him by whispering, 'Come to dinner tomorrow . . . tomorrow evening . . . please . . . you must.'

During that stay in Petersburg Boris became an intimate in the house of Countess Bezukhov.

CHAPTER 8

The conflict was flaring up and the theatre of war was moving closer to the boundaries of Russia. On all sides people could be heard cursing that enemy of the human race, Bonaparte. Militiamen and recruits were being called up from the villages and all sorts of news emerged from the theatre of war, all of it false as usual and therefore variously interpreted.

The lives of old Prince Bolkonsky, Prince Andrey and Princess Marya had changed a good deal since 1805.

In 1806 the old prince had been appointed one of the eight commanders-in-chief then appointed to direct recruitment all over Russia. Despite his age and infirmity, which had become more apparent during the period when he thought his son had been killed, the old prince felt he had no right to refuse a post to which he had been appointed by the Emperor himself, and this new field of activity gave him fresh energy and strength. He was continually away from home touring the three provinces under his command. Punctilious to the last degree in the performance of his duties, strict to the point of cruelty with his subordinates, he went into every last detail of his work. Princess Marya had stopped studying mathematics with her father, and now when she went into her father's room in the morning if he happened to be at home she was accompanied by the wet-nurse and little Prince Nikolay (as his grandfather called him). Baby Nikolay lived with his wet-nurse and the old nurse Savishna in the little princess's rooms, and Princess Marya spent most of her time in the nursery doing her best to be a mother to her little nephew. Mademoiselle Bourienne appeared equally devoted to the child, and Princess Marya often deprived herself to let her friend enjoy cuddling 'their little angel', as she called the baby, and playing with him.

In a little side-chapel near to the altar of the church at Bald Hills stood the tomb of the little princess, and there they had set up a marble monument ordered from Italy which depicted an angel with wings outspread ready to fly up to heaven. The angel's top lip curled up a little in a half-smile, and one day Prince Andrey and Princess Marya admitted to each other coming out of the chapel that the angel's face bore a curious resemblance to the face of the little princess. Even stranger – and this was something Prince Andrey did not admit to his sister – was the expression the sculptor had happened to put on the angel's face, because Prince Andrey could read in it the same words of gentle reproach that he had once read on the face of his dead wife, 'Oh, why have you done this to me?'

Soon after his return the old prince had made over to Prince Andrey a large estate called Bogucharovo just over twenty-five miles away. Partly to escape painful memories associated with Bald Hills, partly because Prince Andrey did not always feel like putting up with his father's eccentric behaviour and partly out of a need for solitude, Prince Andrey made much use of Bogucharovo, where he set up home and began to spend most of his time.

After the Austerlitz campaign, Prince Andrey had firmly resolved never to go back to the army, and when war broke out and everyone was obliged to serve, he avoided active involvement by working under his father in recruitment. Since the campaign of 1805 the old prince and his son had virtually exchanged roles. The old prince, spurred on by his new activity, was optimistic about the present campaign, whereas Prince Andrey, who was out of the war and secretly regretting it, looked on the black side.

On the 26th of February 1807 the old prince set off on a tour of the area. Prince Andrey was staying at Bald Hills, as he usually did when his father was away. Little Nikolay had been ill for the last three days. The coachman who had been driving the old prince returned with some papers and letters picked up in the town for Prince Andrey. The valet couldn't find the young prince in his study to give him the letters, so he went over to Princess Marya's apartment, but he wasn't there either. They told him the prince had gone to the nursery. 'If you please, your Excellency, Petrusha has brought some papers for you,' said one of the nursery-maids to Prince Andrey, who was busy, sitting on a child's little chair and squinting closely as he poured some drops from a medicine bottle into half a wine-glass of water with trembling hands.

'What is it?' he said angrily, and his hand shook so much that he accidentally poured too many drops from the bottle into the glass. He tipped the medicine out on to the floor and asked for more water. The maid gave him some.

The furniture consisted of a couple of armchairs, a baby's cot, two chests, two tables, one for a small child, and the tiny chair that Prince Andrey was sitting on. The curtains were drawn, and a single candle was burning on the table, screened by a bound musical score which shielded the cot from the light.

'My dear,' said Princess Marya, turning to her brother from the side of the cot, 'let's wait a bit . . . do it later on.'

'Oh, please. You do say some stupid things. You keep waiting for something to happen, and now look!' said Prince Andrey in an exasperated whisper, with every intention of hurting her.

'We'd better not wake him, my dear . . . he's gone to sleep,' the princess pleaded.

Prince Andrey got to his feet and tiptoed over to the cot, carrying the glass.

'Is that what you think? We ought not to wake him up?' he said, hesitating.

'Well, you know best . . . I, er . . . whatever you think,' said Princess Marya, all bashful and embarrassed that her opinion should prevail. She pointed to the maid, who was beckoning to him and whispering something.

This was their second sleepless night together watching over the feverish baby. Having no faith in the local doctor they had sent for another one in town, and as they waited for him they spent the long hours trying one remedy after another. Worried sick and weary from lack of sleep, they were taking out their anxiety on each other, finding fault and quarrelling.

'Petrusha has brought some papers from your papa,' whispered the maid. Prince Andrey went out.

'Damned papers!' he growled, but he listened to some verbal instructions from his father, received one or two envelopes and his father's letter, and then went straight back to the nursery.

'Any change?' he asked.

'No. Be patient, for heaven's sake. Karl Ivanych always says sleep is the best thing,' Princess Marya whispered with a sigh. Prince Andrey went over to the baby and felt him. He was burning hot. 'Damn you and your Karl Ivanych!' He took the wine-glass with the medicine drops in it and went back to the cot.

'Andrey, please don't!' said Princess Marya. But he scowled and glared with a mixture of anger and anguish, and bent over the baby with the glass.

'This is what I want,' he said. 'Come on, please, give him some.'

Princess Marya shrugged, but obediently took hold of the glass, beckoned the nurse over and started to give the baby his medicine. He wailed and wheezed. Prince Andrey winced, clutched at his head and went out of the room to sit down on a sofa in the next one.

He was still holding the letters. He opened them automatically and began to read. The old prince wrote as follows on blue paper in his large, looping hand, with the odd abbreviation here and there:

Have this moment received by special messenger most joyful news. If can be trusted, Bennigsen gained evidently complete victory over Bonaparte near Preussisch-Eylau. In Petersburg all jubilant and rewards galore sent to army. He's German, but must congratulate him. Commander in Korchevo, man called Khandrikov, can't make out what he's doing; reinforcements and stores not yet provided. Get over there at once and tell him I'll have his head off if it's not all here within the week. Have also had letter from Petya about Preussisch-Eylau battle in which he took part – it's all true. If people don't stick their nose in where it's not wanted, even a German has the beating of Napoleone Buonaparte. He's off, so they say, tail between legs. Get yourself over to Korchevo and carry out instructions – now!

Prince Andrey sighed and broke open the seal on the next letter. It was from Bilibin, two closely written pages. He folded it up without reading it, and reread his father's letter with the final injunction, 'Get yourself over to Korchevo and carry out instructions – now!'

'Oh no, I'm sorry, I'm not going anywhere until the baby's better,' he thought as he went over to the door and glanced into the nursery. Princess Marya was still standing by the cot, gently rocking the baby. 'Yes, what was that other nasty thing he said?' wondered Prince Andrey, harking back to his father's letter. 'Oh yes. Our troops have won a victory over Bonaparte, and I wasn't there. Yes, yes, he likes his little joke at my expense . . . Oh well, let him . . .', and he began to read Bilibin's letter, which was written in French. He read it through without taking half of it in, just to distract himself for a while from dwelling on certain obsessive and tormenting thoughts that had too long lingered in his mind.

CHAPTER 9

Bilibin was now on the diplomatic staff at military headquarters, and though he wrote in French, using little French witticisms and French turns of speech, he described the whole campaign with peculiarly Russian objectivity, which means not without self-criticism and self-mockery. Bilibin wrote that the need for tact and diplomacy was a torment to him, and he was happy to have in Prince Andrey a reliable correspondent to whom he could vent all the spleen that had been building up in him at the sight of what was going on in the army. It was an old letter, written in French and dating back to before the battle of Preussisch-Eylau.

Since our great successes at Austerlitz, my dear prince [wrote Bilibin], as you know, I have not left headquarters. I have acquired a real taste for warfare and I am much taken with it. What I have seen in these three months beggars belief.

I begin *ab ovo*. 'The enemy of the human race', as you know, is attacking the Prussians. The Prussians are our faithful allies, who have let us down no more than three times in three years. We take up the cause on their behalf. But as it turns out, the 'enemy of the human race' ignores our fine speeches, and with his usual rudeness and savagery he hurls himself at the Prussians without giving them time to finish the parade that they have just started, and hey presto! he gives them a good thrashing and moves into the palace at Potsdam.

'It is my most earnest wish,' writes the King of Prussia to Bonaparte, 'that your Majesty be received and treated in my palace in a manner congenial to you, and I have lost no time in taking every measure to that end which circumstances have permitted. If only I may be said to have succeeded!' The Prussian generals pride themselves on being polite to the French, and surrender at the first call.

The garrison commander at Glogau, in charge of ten thousand men, asks the King of Prussia what to do if he is called on to surrender ... This we know for a fact.

In short, hoping to impress by nothing more than a little military posturing, we find ourselves at war in all seriousness, on our own frontiers to boot, *with and for the King of Prussia*. We have everything in abundance except for one little thing – a commander-in-chief. Since it turns out that the successes at Austerlitz might have been more decisive if the commander-in-chief had not been so young, the octogenarians have been put on parade and the choice between Prozorovsky and Kamensky goes in favour of the latter. This general turns up in a covered wagon *à la* Suvorov and is greeted with acclamations of joy and triumph.

4th inst. First post from Petersburg. The mails are taken to the field-marshal's room – he likes to do everything himself. I am summoned to help sort the letters and take any intended for us. The marshal watches us at work and waits for any packets addressed to him. We search – there aren't any. The marshal loses patience, gets down to business himself and discovers some letters from the Emperor to Count So-and-so, Prince What's-his-name, and others. Then he flies into one of his rages. Thunder-bolts in every direction. He grabs hold of the letters, opens them and reads those from the Emperor to other people.

'So that's how they treat me! No confidence in me! Oh yes, ordered to keep an eye on me! All right then – get out, the lot of you!'

That's when he writes his famous order of the day to General Bennigsen:

'I am wounded, cannot ride, and cannot therefore command the army. You have brought your defeated *corps d'armée* to Pultusk. Here it stands exposed, no fuel, no provisions, in need of support, so, as reported by you to Count Buxhöwden[9] yesterday, you must consider withdrawing to our frontier, and this must be done today.'

To the emperor he writes:

'Too many journeys on horseback have made me saddle-sore, which now – on top of all my other dressings – quite prevents me from riding and commanding an army on such a wide front, and I have therefore transferred the said command to the general next in seniority to me, Count Buxhöwden, having despatched to him all my staff and appurtenances of the same, advising him, if bread runs out, to withdraw even further into Prussia, seeing that there is only one day's bread left and some regiments have none at all, as reported by regimental commanders Ostermann and Sedmoretsky, and any taken from the peasantry has been consumed, whilst I shall myself remain in hospital at Ostrolenka until I recover. In respect of which I most humbly beg further to report that if the army remains another fifteen days encamped as at present, by springtime not a man will be left in good health.

'I beg to be discharged from duty and allowed to retire to the country as an old man sufficiently shamed by his incapacity to fulfil the great and glorious destiny to which he was elected. I shall await here in the hospital your most gracious permission for the above, that I may not be reduced from the role of *commander* to that of *army clerk*. My retirement from the army will not involve the slightest danger to security – no more than a blind man leaving the army. In Russia there are thousands more like me.'

VOLUME II, PART II

The marshal is angry with the Emperor and punishes all of us. Nice logic, isn't it?

End of Act One. As you would expect, interest and amusement continue to increase in those that follow. After the departure of the field-marshal it turns out that we are within sight of the enemy and must fight. Buxhöwden is commanding officer by seniority, but General Bennigsen thinks differently, especially since he and his corps are the ones facing the enemy, and he wants a chance to fight a battle 'on his own hand', as the Germans put it. He does fight. It is the battle of Pultusk, which is seen as a great victory but in my view is nothing of the sort. We civilians, as you know, have a very crude way of deciding whether a battle has been won or lost. The side that does the retreating after the battle has lost, according to us, and by that token we lost the battle of Pultusk. To cut a long story short, we retreat after the battle, but we send a courier off to Petersburg with news of a victory, and the general does not transfer command to Buxhöwden because he is hoping to receive from Petersburg the title of commander-in-chief in acknowledgement of his triumph. During the interregnum we embark on manoeuvres of an extremely fascinating and original kind. Our aim is not what it should be – avoiding the enemy or attacking him – but avoiding General Buxhöwden, who by seniority ought to be our commanding officer. We pursue this goal with such vigour that even when we cross a river that cannot be forded we burn the bridges down in order to separate ourselves from the enemy, who for the time being is not Bonaparte but Buxhöwden. General Buxhöwden just missed being attacked and captured by superior enemy forces as a result of one of our splendid manoeuvres which saved us from him. Buxhöwden comes after us – we scuttle. The moment he crosses to our side of the river we cross back again. At last the enemy, Buxhöwden, catches up with us and attacks. The two generals have a row. There is even a challenge from Buxhöwden and an epileptic fit from Bennigsen. But at the critical moment the courier who took the news of our Pultusk victory to Petersburg brings back news of our man's appointment as commander-in-chief, and with enemy number one, Buxhöwden, disposed of, we are able to turn our attention to enemy number two, Bonaparte. But lo and behold! – at this juncture up rises enemy number three, the soldiers of *Russian Orthodoxy*, clamouring for bread, meat, biscuits, hay and I don't know what else! Nothing in the shops, roads impassable. Russian Orthodoxy goes on a looting spree the like of which you couldn't get a glimmering of from the last campaign. Half the regiments have turned themselves into gangs of free men rampaging through the countryside with fire and sword. Local inhabitants completely ruined, hospitals overflowing with sick people, famine everywhere. On two occasions headquarters have been attacked by marauding gangs and the commander-in-chief has had to put in a personal request for a battalion to drive them off. In one of these attacks my empty trunk and dressing-gown were stolen. The Emperor wants to authorize divisional commanders to shoot marauders, but I very much fear this will oblige one half of the army to shoot the other.

Prince Andrey began by skimming the letter, but unconsciously he became more and more absorbed in its contents (though he knew how far Bilibin could be believed). At this point he screwed up the letter and threw it away. It wasn't so much the contents of the letter that annoyed him; he was annoyed by the simple fact that that far-away life, now so alien to him, could bother him at all. He closed his eyes and wiped his forehead with one hand, as if to rid himself of any involvement in what he had been reading, and then listened again to what was going on in the nursery. Suddenly he thought he heard a strange sound coming through the door. He panicked, afraid that something might have gone wrong with the baby while he'd been reading the letter. He tiptoed back to the nursery door and opened it.

As he was going in he saw the nurse hiding something from him with a scared face. Princess Marya was no longer there beside the cot.

'My dear.' He heard Princess Marya's voice behind him whispering in what he took to be despair. As often happens after prolonged sleeplessness and great worry, he had panicked for no good reason and jumped to the conclusion that the baby was dead. Everything he saw and heard seemed to confirm his worst fears.

'It's all over,' he thought, and a cold sweat broke out on his forehead. He walked over to the cot in great distress, knowing he would find it empty – the nurse had been hiding the dead baby. He pulled the curtains aside, and for quite some time his worried eyes darted about without finding the baby. Then he saw him. The red-cheeked child was lying crosswise with his head lower than the pillow, smacking his lips in his sleep and breathing evenly.

Prince Andrey was overjoyed to see the child, having thought he had lost him. He bent down and touched the baby with his lips to check whether he was feverish, as his sister had shown him. The soft forehead was damp. He touched the head with his hand – even the hair was wet. The child was soaked with sweat. But he wasn't dead; no, the crisis was clearly over and he was getting better. Prince Andrey wanted to grab him, crush him, press the little helpless creature to his heart, but he didn't dare. He stood over him, gazing down at his head and his little arms and legs sticking up under the blanket. He heard a rustling sound at his elbow, and a shadow seemed to spread across under the canopy of the cot. He did not look round. He was still gazing at the baby's face and listening to his regular breathing. The dark shadow was Princess Marya, who had come over to the cot without making a sound, lifted the curtain and let it fall again behind her. Prince Andrey knew who it was without looking round and he held out his hand to her. She gave it a squeeze.

'He's covered in sweat,' said Prince Andrey.

'I was on my way to tell you.'

The baby stirred slightly in its sleep, gave a smile and rubbed its forehead against the pillow.

Prince Andrey looked at his sister. In the hazy half-light under the cot-hangings Princess Marya's luminous eyes shone brighter than ever with tears of happiness. She bent forward and kissed her brother, catching herself in the hangings. They shushed, wagging their fingers at each other, and lingered there in the half-light under the canopy, as if reluctant to leave the seclusion with the three of them, all alone, cut off from the rest of the world. Prince Andrey was the first to move away, catching his hair in the muslin hangings.

'Yes, it's all I have left,' he said with a sigh.

CHAPTER 10

Shortly after his initiation into the Masonic Brotherhood, Pierre set off for the Kiev province where most of his peasants lived, having written down for his own guidance a complete plan of action for the reform of his estates.

Once in Kiev, Pierre summoned all his stewards to a meeting in his main office, where he outlined his wishes and intentions. He told them that measures would soon be put in hand for the complete liberation of his peasants from serf rule,[10] and meanwhile his peasants were not to be overworked, women with children were not to be sent out to work, assistance was to be given to the peasants, corporal punishment was to be replaced by admonishment, and every estate must be furnished with hospitals, alms-houses and schools. Several of the stewards (including some overseers who were barely literate) listened in dismay, assuming the young count's remarks to imply that he was dissatisfied with the way they were running things and embezzling his money. Others soon got over the first shock of alarm and couldn't help laughing at Pierre's lisping speech and the new-fangled words that he used.

There were also some who were happy just to be hearing the sound of their master's voice. But one or two of them, including the head steward, listened to what he was saying and quickly worked out how to deal with the master and get what they wanted.

The head steward expressed great sympathy for Pierre's intentions, but observed that apart from these innovations things were in a bad way and needed a thorough sorting out.

Ever since Pierre had inherited Count Bezukhov's enormous wealth and with it an annual income of five hundred thousand, he had felt much worse off than he had been with an allowance of ten thousand from his father. He had formed a vague idea of his budget, which could be outlined as follows. About 80,000 roubles were being paid into the Land Bank. Another 30,000 went on the upkeep of his estate just outside Moscow together with his Moscow house and allowances for the three princesses. About 15,000 went into pensions, and a similar amount to charity. His countess was getting 150,000 for her maintenance. Interest on loans accounted for something like 70,000. The building of a new church had run to about 10,000 over the last couple of years. He hardly knew where the rest went – another 100,000 or so – but almost every year he was forced to take out new loans. And beyond that, every year the head steward wrote to him saying that fires had broken out, crops had failed and factories and workshops needing rebuilding. And so the first task Pierre had to face was the one he was least suited to and least fond of – to become a businessman.

Every day Pierre 'got down to business' with the head steward. But he couldn't escape the feeling that what he was doing didn't improve things one iota. He felt that what he was doing didn't affect the business side of things at all, business was beyond his grip and he wasn't making anything happen. On the one hand, the head steward put the bleakest construction on everything, insisting that Pierre had to go on paying his debts and starting up new projects based on serf labour, though this was something Pierre couldn't accept. On the other hand, Pierre kept demanding that they proceed with the business of liberating the serfs, to which the head steward objected by further insistence on the need to pay off debts to the Land Bank, which meant that things could not be hurried. He didn't say it was out of the question. He proposed to solve the problem by selling things off: the forests in the Kostroma province, some of the land lower down the river and the Crimean estate. But the way he put it, all these operations involved such complicated procedures concerned with the removal of distraints, proper authorization and all the rest that

Pierre soon lost the thread and was reduced to saying lamely, 'Yes, do that then.'

Lacking any practical ability or tenacity that might have made it possible for him to go into things properly, Pierre never took to management, and all he could do was keep up a pretence of business-like interest to impress the head steward. The steward maintained his own fiction, that what he was doing was of great benefit to the count, but a great nuisance to him.

Pierre knew some people in Kiev, where unacquainted persons moved quickly to make themselves acquainted by extending a warm welcome to the wealthy new arrival, the biggest landowner in the province. Temptations in the area of Pierre's major weakness, the one he had confessed to during his initiation into the lodge, proved quite irresistible. Once again whole days, weeks and months of his life went by with him busily doing the rounds of parties, dinners, lunches and balls. It was as bad as Petersburg for leaving him no time to think. Instead of the new life Pierre had hoped to lead, he was still living the old one, but in new surroundings.

Of the three precepts of freemasonry Pierre had to admit falling down on the one that said every mason must become a model of morality; and of the seven virtues he was completely deficient in two – good living and the love of death. He found some consolation in the belief that he was working on one of the other precepts, the improvement of the human race, and he did have other virtues such as loving his neighbour and generosity.

In the spring of 1807 Pierre made up his mind to go back to Petersburg. Along the way it was his intention to call in at each one of his estates to check for himself how far they had got with what he had told them to do and what was the current situation of the people whom God had entrusted to his care and whom he had been trying so hard to benefit.

The head steward, who thought that all the young count's silly schemes were bordering on madness and useless to them all – him, his master and all the peasants – had nevertheless made some concessions. While still insisting that liberation was impracticable, he did make arrangements on all the estates for the building of decent-sized schools, hospitals and alms-houses. During the master's various visits he arranged for him to be met not with pomp and ceremony, which he knew Pierre wouldn't like, but by little groups of religious and chari-table people, with plenty of icons and bread-and-salt hospitality, the sort of thing that would, according to his reading of the count, impress him and pull the wool over his eyes.

The southern spring, the swift and easy running of his Viennese carriage and the solitude of the open road all put Pierre in a good mood. The estates, which he had never visited before, became one by one more and more picturesque; all the peasants seemed to be thriving and they were touchingly grateful for his kindness to them. Everywhere Pierre was given a welcome that embarrassed him, yet deep down he found it all heart-warming. At one place the peasants brought him bread and salt and a icon of St Peter and St Paul, and then asked permission to build a new chapel in their church at their own expense in honour of these patron saints of his and as a gesture of love and gratitude for his kindness to them. At another stop he was welcomed by women carrying tiny babies, grateful for being released from hard physical work. In a third place he was met by a priest with a cross, surrounded by little children who were being taught reading, writing and religion because of the count's generosity. On all his estates Pierre saw with his own eyes stone buildings under construction or already built, all to the same plan – hospitals, schools and alms-houses, soon to be opened. Everywhere Pierre saw the steward's records showing a decrease in the amount of work done by the peasants for the benefit of the master, compared with previous years, and he heard the most moving expressions of gratitude from deputations of peasants dressed in their traditional blue kaftans.

What Pierre did not know was that the place where they brought him bread and salt and were building a new chapel to St Peter and St Paul was a trading village which held a fair every St Peter's day, and the chapel had been started long before by wealthy peasants of that village, where nine-tenths of the peasants lived in abject poverty. He did not know that as a result of his orders to stop sending nursing mothers out to work on the master's land, those same mothers had to work even harder on their own patches of land. He did not know that the priest who met him with the cross oppressed the peasants with his methods of extortion, and that the pupils gathered round him had been yielded up with much weeping and could be redeemed by their parents only for large sums of money. He did not know that the stone buildings were being put up, all to the same plan, by his own workers, which meant an actual increase in the forced labour of his peasants, but that didn't show up on paper. He did not know that where the steward's records showed a one-third reduction in rent, in accordance with his instructions, their compulsory labour had gone up by half. And so it was that Pierre returned from the tour of his estates delighted and fully restored to the mood of philanthropy in which he had left Petersburg, and he wrote most enthusiastically to his 'brother and mentor', as he called the Grand Master.

'How easy it is, what little effort it takes to do so much good,' thought Pierre, 'and how little we trouble ourselves to do it!'

He was pleased that so much gratitude had been shown him, but he felt embarrassed by this. Such gratitude only served to remind him how much *more* he could do for those kind and simple people.

The head steward, a very stupid man but with plenty of cunning, had the measure of his clever but simple-minded master, and he toyed with him. Noting the impact on the count of these carefully staged receptions, he redoubled and strengthened his arguments – it was impossible, and, what was more important, it was quite unnecessary to liberate the peasants, who were perfectly happy as things stood.

Deep down, Pierre had to agree with the steward that it would be difficult to imagine the people being any happier, and there was no telling what their future might be in freedom. However, not without reluctance, he continued to stick to what he thought was right. The steward promised to do everything in his power to carry out the count's wishes, knowing full well that the count would never be in a position to check whether everything possible had been done to speed up the sale of the forests and pay off the bank-loans, and he would probably never even ask about the buildings, let alone find out that when they were finished they just stood empty, and the peasants went on giving in labour and money exactly what other peasants gave to other masters – all that could be got out of them.

CHAPTER 11

Back from his southern tour in buoyant mood, Pierre did what he had been intending to do for some time; he went to visit his friend Bolkonsky, not having seen him for two years. At the last post-station he heard that Andrey was not at Bald Hills but at his new separate estate, so he went straight there.

Bogucharovo lay in flat, dull countryside covered with fields and stretches of birch and fir-trees, some felled and others growing wild. The manor house was at the end of a village that lay sprawled out down a long straight road. It stood in young woodland dominated by several large pine-trees, just above a newly dug pond filled to overflowing, with grass yet to grow on its banks.

The homestead consisted of a threshing floor, outbuildings, stables, a bath-house, a lodge and a large stone house with a semi-circular façade, still under construction. Around the house a new garden had recently been laid out. The fences and gates were solid and new, and in an open shed there were two fire-pumps and a water-butt painted green. The paths were straight, the bridges were strong and they had handrails. There was an air of efficiency and good house-keeping about the place. Some house serfs along the way, when asked where the prince was living, pointed to a small new lodge at the very edge of the pond. Prince Andrey's old servant, Anton, who had been with him since childhood, helped Pierre down from the carriage, said that the prince was at home and showed him into a clean little ante-room.

Pierre was struck by the modesty of this clean little house, after the splendid surroundings in which he had last seen his friend in Petersburg.

He walked quickly through into a little parlour, finished but not yet plastered and smelling of pine wood, and he would have gone on, but Anton tiptoed ahead and knocked at the door.

'What is it?' came a rough, unpleasant voice.

'A visitor,' answered Anton.

'Ask him to wait.' A chair was heard being scraped back.

Pierre hurried up to the door and suddenly found himself face to face with Prince Andrey, who was on his way out with a scowl on his face, looking older. Pierre hugged him, lifted his spectacles, kissed him on the cheeks and gave him a close scrutiny.

'Well, look who's here! I'm so pleased to see you,' said Prince Andrey.

Pierre said nothing; he was looking at his friend in some surprise and couldn't take his eyes off him. He was struck by how much Prince Andrey had changed. His words were welcoming enough, his face and his lips seemed to smile, but the lacklustre eyes had a dead look about them and despite his best efforts Prince Andrey seemed unable to make them shine with joy and happiness. It wasn't just that his friend looked thinner and paler, as well as being more mature; Pierre was shocked by Andrey's subdued look and his furrowed brow, both of which suggested obsessive worrying about something, and he was put off for a moment until he got used to it.

It always happens that when friends come together after a long separation the conversation jumps from one topic to another. Quick questions were met with short answers as they touched on things which they knew ought to be discussed at length. At last the conversation began to settle down, gradually returning to points that had been skimpily treated before, inquiries about how things had been going, any future plans, Pierre's travels and what he had been up to, the war and much more besides. The crestfallen look of worry which Pierre had noticed in Prince Andrey's eyes was even more noticeable in his smile as he listened, especially when Pierre spoke with joy and enthusiasm about the past and the future. The impression was that Prince Andrey wanted to involve himself in what Pierre was saying but couldn't manage to do so. Pierre began to feel it was somehow wrong to be talking to Prince Andrey so eagerly about his dreams and all his hopes of happiness and goodness. It would be too embarrassing for him to go into the new ideas he had got from the masons, and especially the way these had been refreshed and strengthened by his recent tour. He held back, afraid to seem naive, but at the same time he felt an urgent desire to show his friend without further ado that he was a changed man, better than the old Pierre that he had known in Petersburg.

'I can't begin to tell you what I've gone through since we met. I wouldn't recognize my old self.'

'Yes, we've both changed a lot since those days,' said Prince Andrey.

'Anyway, what about you?' asked Pierre. 'What are your plans?'

'Plans?' echoed Prince Andrey sarcastically. 'My plans?' he said again, as if surprised by the word and its meaning. 'Well ... you can see I've got some building going on. I should be able to move in next year ...'

Pierre said nothing; he was staring closely at Prince Andrey's face, which seemed to have aged so much.

'No, what I meant was ...' Pierre began but Prince Andrey cut him short.

'But let's not talk about me ... You do the talking. Tell me about your grand tour. What have you been up to on your estates?'

Pierre launched into a description of what he had been doing on his estates, trying as well as he could to play down his own involvement in the improvements that had been made. More than once Prince Andrey was able to anticipate what Pierre was going to say, as if all his efforts were old hat, and although he listened with some interest he did seem rather embarrassed at what he was hearing.

All of which made Pierre feel awkward and quite depressed sitting there with his friend. He stopped talking.

'I tell you what, my dear fellow,' said Prince Andrey, clearly depressed and ill at ease with his visitor, 'I'm just camped out here. I just came to have a look round. I'm going back to my sister today. I'll introduce you. Oh, but you've met before, haven't you?' he added, obviously trying to be pleasant to a guest he now had nothing in common with. 'We'll go back after dinner. And now would you care to look round my place?'

They went out and went for a good walk until dinner-time, talking politics and mentioning mutual acquaintances, like two people who were rather distant from each other. The only things that sparked any animation or interest in Prince Andrey were the new homestead and the building work, but even on this subject, when they were up on the scaffolding and Prince Andrey was describing the plan of the house, he suddenly stopped in mid-conversation. 'Oh, but this isn't very interesting,' he said. 'Let's have our dinner and get going.'

At dinner the conversation turned to Pierre's marriage.

'I was really surprised when I heard,' said Prince Andrey.

Pierre blushed as he always did when this subject came up, and he said hastily, 'I'll tell you the whole story one day. But you do know it's all finished, don't you?'

'For ever?' said Prince Andrey. 'Nothing's for ever.'

'But do you know what happened in the end? Have you heard about the duel?'

'Yes, you had to go through all that, didn't you!'

'The one thing I thank God for is that I didn't kill that man,' said Pierre.

'Why not?' said Prince Andrey. 'Killing a vicious dog is a good thing, really.'

'No, killing is wrong. It's bad.'

'What's wrong with it?' retorted Prince Andrey. 'What's right and what's wrong is something we can't decide. People keep making mistakes and they always will, especially when it comes to right and wrong.'

'Anything that harms someone else is wrong,' said Pierre, noticing with pleasure that for the first time since his arrival Prince Andrey was getting worked up about something and starting to speak out. He even seemed ready to make a clean breast of everything that had turned him into what he now was.

'And how do you know what's bad for somebody else?' he asked.

'Bad! Bad!' said Pierre. 'We all know what's bad for us.'

'Yes, you're right, but just because I know something is bad for me, it doesn't mean I can do the same harm to somebody else,' said Prince Andrey, getting more and more excited, and now evidently eager to let Pierre know all about his new attitude. (He was speaking in French.) 'I only know two really harmful things in life – remorse and illness. There is never any good unless these two things are absent. Living for myself and avoiding these two evils – that's my philosophy now.'

'What about loving your neighbour, and sacrificing yourself?' began Pierre. 'No, I can't agree with you! Living your life with the sole object of avoiding evil just so you won't regret anything afterwards – it's not enough. I used to live like that, I used to live for myself, and I ruined my life. And it's only now, when I'm living – or trying to live' (modesty called for this adjustment) 'for other people, it's only now that I've come to know any happiness in life. No, I just don't agree. And I don't think you believe what you're saying.'

Prince Andrey looked at Pierre with a sardonic smile and said nothing.

'Well, you'll soon see my sister, Marie. You two will get on together,' he said at last. 'You may be right as far as you're concerned,' he added, after a brief pause, 'but everyone's different. You used to live for yourself, and you tell me it almost ruined your life, and you've only found any happiness since you started living for other people. Well, my experience has been the other way round. I used to live for glory. (And what is glory? It's the same love for other people, wanting to do something for them, wanting praise from them.) In that kind of way I used to live for other people, and I did ruin my life, not almost – completely! And I've only found any peace of mind since I started living for myself.'

'But how can you think of living for yourself?' said Pierre, all worked up. 'What about your son, your sister, your father?'

'Yes, but they're the same as me. They're not other people,' said Prince Andrey. 'Other people – your "neighbours", as you and Marie call them – they're the source of all error and harm. Who are your "neighbours"? Your peasants down in Kiev that you want to do so much good for.' And he mocked Pierre with a challenging look, deliberately provoking him.

'You can't be serious,' said Pierre, more excited than ever. 'What error and harm can there be in my wanting to . . . well, I've not done much and I've done it very badly . . . but still, wanting to do good, and getting a little bit done? Where's the harm if miserable people like our peasants – and they are people like you and me, people living and dying with no idea of God and what truth is beyond icons and ridiculous prayers – now get some education and console themselves by believing in an after-life where there is retribution, reward and consolation? When nobody looks after people dying of disease while it's so easy to give them some real practical help, what harm and error can there be in my providing doctors, and a hospital and a home for old people? And isn't there tangible, incontestable good when a peasant with his wife and child have no rest day or night, and I give them some leisure and rest?' said Pierre, lisping as he gabbled. 'And I've done that – not very well, I admit, and not enough – but I have done something in that direction, and you're not going to persuade me I haven't done something good, and you're also not going to persuade me that you really believe what you're saying. And the main thing is this,' Pierre continued, 'I know, I know for an absolute certainty, that the pleasure of doing good like this is the only real happiness in life.'

'Oh well, if you put it like that, it's different,' said Prince Andrey. 'I'm building a house and garden – you're building hospitals. Either way it passes the time. But what's right and what's good – that'll have to be decided by somebody who knows everything. We can't decide. So, if it's an argument you want,' he added, 'you've got one.'

They got up from the table and sat out on the steps, because there was no verandah.

'Come on, then,' said Prince Andrey. 'You talk about schools,' he went on, bending one finger back. 'Education and all that. In other words, you want to bring him' (he pointed to a passing peasant who was doffing his cap) 'out of his animal condition and give him spiritual needs. Well, as I see it, the only form of happiness is animal happiness, and you want to take that away from him. I envy him, while you're trying to turn him into me, but without giving him my mind, my feelings and my money. Then you talk about giving him less work. But to my mind, he needs his physical labour, it's a condition of his existence, every bit as much as you and I need our intellectual work. You can't help thinking. I go to bed at nearly three in the morning, thoughts keep coming into my mind and I can't get to sleep. I toss and turn and I stay awake till morning because I'm thinking, and I can't help thinking, just as he can't help ploughing and mowing. If he stops he won't be able to go for a drink and he might fall ill. Just as I couldn't stand his terrible physical labour, it would kill me in a week, my idleness would be too much for him, he would grow fat and die. Then the third thing – what was the other thing you said?' Prince Andrey had bent back his third finger.

'Oh yes, I know. Hospitals, medicine. He has a stroke and he's dying, but no, you have him bled and he gets better. Now he's going to be an invalid for the next ten years, a burden to everybody. Let him die – it's a lot simpler and it's easier on him. Lots more like him are being born all the time – there's no shortage of them. I wouldn't mind if you were worried about losing a labourer – that's how I see him – but you want to cure him out of brotherly love. Well, he doesn't need it. And besides, who said medicine ever cured anybody? Killed lots of people – oh yes!' he said, scowling and turning away from Pierre.

Prince Andrey put his arguments so precisely that he had obviously gone through them many times before in his mind. And he was gabbling away like a man who has not spoken for a long time. His eyes shone brighter as his reasoning became more and more despondent.

'Oh, this is awful, awful!' said Pierre. 'I can't see how you can go on living with ideas like these. I used to have my moments when I thought like that, not all that long ago in Moscow or out on the road, but when it happens I feel so low and I'm not really living at all, everything seems vile . . . to me most of all. When it happens I can't eat and I don't wash . . . what's it like with you?'

'Oh, you ought to wash. It's unclean,' said Prince Andrey. 'It's the other way round. You have to try and make your life as enjoyable as you can. Here I am alive, and it's not my fault, so I have to try and get by as best I can without hurting anybody until death takes over.'

'But how do you live on with ideas like that? You could just sit there without moving, not taking part in anything . . .'

'Well, life won't leave you in peace, will it? I'd be glad to do nothing at all, but for one thing the local nobility have done me the honour of electing me marshal. I only just managed to wriggle out of it. They couldn't understand that I haven't got what it takes. I don't have the good-natured, fussy vulgarity that you must have for that sort of thing. Then there's this house. It had to be built so I could have a corner of my own to be quiet in. And now there's this recruiting.'

'Why aren't you in the army?'

'What, after Austerlitz?' said Prince Andrey darkly. 'No, thank you. I swore I'd never serve in the Russian army again. And I won't. If Napoleon was right here outside Smolensk threatening Bald Hills, I wouldn't serve in the Russian army,' Prince Andrey went on, pulling himself together. 'Anyway, as I was saying, there's this recruitment. My father's commander-in-chief of the Third District, and the only way I can get out of active service is to serve under him.'

'So you are in the service, then?'

'Yes.' He paused.

'May I ask why?'

'I'll tell you why. My father is one of the most remarkable men of his time. But he's getting old now, and he's not exactly cruel, but he's too forceful. He's too fierce. He's got used to having unlimited power, and now he has this new authority from the Emperor as a commander-in-chief of the recruiting. If I had arrived two hours later a couple of weeks ago he'd have strung up the registrar at Yukhnova,' said Prince Andrey with a smile. 'So I serve under him now because I'm the only one who has any influence over my father, and there are occasions when I can stop him doing something he'd come to regret.'

'So that's what it's all about!'

'Well, it's not quite what you think,' Prince Andrey went on. 'It's not that I wished him any good, that registrar, or do now. He's a crook who stole some boots from the recruits, and I wouldn't mind seeing him strung up, but I do feel sorry for my father, and that means for myself.'

Prince Andrey was still getting more and more animated. There was a feverish gleam in his eyes as he tried to show Pierre that he never did anything that was meant to do good to his neighbour.

'So, you want to liberate your serfs,' he went on. 'That's a very good idea, but not for you – I don't imagine you've ever had a man flogged or sent to Siberia – and certainly not for your peasants. Those who do get beaten, flogged or sent to Siberia – well, I don't imagine they're any the worse off for it. Out in Siberia they can go on living like cattle, the stripes on the body heal, and they'll be as happy as they ever used to be. The men it would be good for are those people who are morally bankrupt and eaten away by remorse, but they suppress the remorse and become callous just from having the ability to inflict punishment on all sides. These are the people I'm sorry for. They're the ones who make me want to see the serfs liberated. Maybe you haven't seen it, but I have, I've seen good men, raised in the old traditions of unlimited power, getting more and more irritable as the years go by, turning themselves into cruel brutes, aware of what's happening to them but unable to control themselves and just getting more and more miserable.'

Prince Andrey spoke with such feeling that Pierre couldn't help thinking that these ideas had something to do with his father. He did not respond.

'So that's who I'm sorry for, and I'm sorry for the loss of human dignity, good conscience and innocence – not for the backs and heads of these people, because those things don't change, however much you thrash them or shave them.'

'No, no, a thousand times no! I shall never agree with you,' said Pierre.

CHAPTER 12

That evening Prince Andrey and Pierre took the open carriage and set off for Bald Hills. Prince Andrey kept glancing at Pierre and breaking the silence now and then with remarks that showed he was in a good humour.

Pointing to the fields, he told him of the improvements he was making in the management of his land.

Pierre sat there morose and silent, answering in monosyllables and apparently absorbed in his own thoughts.

Pierre was reflecting on Prince Andrey's miserable state, how wrong he was, how ignorant of the true light, and thinking that he would have to help him out of this, show him the light and raise him up. But the moment he began working out what to say and how to say it, he could see Prince Andrey dashing his teaching to pieces with a single word, a single argument, and he was wary of even starting, wary of exposing to possible ridicule everything he held dear and sacred.

'No, but where do you get thoughts like these?' Pierre suddenly began, lowering his head like a charging bull. 'What makes you think like this? You ought not to think like this.'

'Think like what?' asked Prince Andrey in some surprise.

'About life. About the destiny of man. It can't be like that. I used to think that way but I found salvation – do you know where? In freemasonry. No, please don't smile. Freemasonry – it's not just a religious sect with lots of ceremonies, as I used to think. Freemasonry is the best expression, the only expression of mankind's noblest, eternal aspirations.' And he launched into a full account of freemasonry as he saw it.

Freemasonry, he claimed, was Christian doctrine freed from the bonds of politics and organized religion, the doctrine of equality, fraternity and love.

'Our holy brotherhood is the only thing that gives a true meaning to life. Everything else is a dream,' said Pierre. 'You must understand, my dear fellow, that outside this fraternity it's all lies and deceit, and I agree there's nothing left for an intelligent and kind man like you to do but go through the motions of living and try not to hurt anybody. But – accept our basic beliefs, enter into our brotherhood, give yourself to us, let us guide you, and straightaway you'll feel what I did, that you are part of a vast, unseen chain which starts in heaven,' said Pierre.

Prince Andrey listened to Pierre in silence, looking ahead. Once or twice he missed something because of the rumbling wheels and asked Pierre to repeat what he had said. Noting a peculiar glint in Prince Andrey's eyes and also his reluctance to speak, Pierre could see that his words were not falling on stony ground and Prince Andrey was not going to interrupt or laugh at anything he said.

They came to a river that had burst its banks, making it necessary for them to cross by ferry. While the men saw to the carriage and horses they walked on to the ferry-boat. Prince Andrey leant his elbows on the rail and gazed silently over the flood-water, which gleamed in the setting sun.

'Well, what do you think?' asked Pierre. 'Why don't you say something?'

'What do I think? I have been listening. What you say is all right,' said Prince Andrey. 'But you say, come into our brotherhood and we'll show you the meaning of life and the destiny of man, and the laws that govern the universe. But who are we? Just people. How do you come to know it all? Why am I the only one who can't see what you see? You see the earth as a kingdom of goodness and truth. I don't.'

Pierre interrupted him. 'Do you believe in the after-life?' he asked.

'Oh, the after-life,' repeated Prince Andrey.

But Pierre gave him no time for a proper answer, taking his response as a negative, especially in view of Prince Andrey's atheistic views, which he knew from the past. 'You say you can't see the earth as a kingdom of goodness and truth. Neither can I. Nobody can, not if you see our life as the end of everything. Here on *earth*, this earth here,' (Pierre pointed to the open country) 'there is no righteousness – it's all false and wicked. But in the universe, the whole vast universe, there is a kingdom of truth, and we are two things – children of earth here and now, and children of the universe in eternity. Don't I feel in my soul that I'm a part of that vast, harmonious whole? Don't I feel that I represent one link, one step on the ladder that runs from lower forms of existence to higher ones in that vast creative infinity which gives token of a Godhead, a Higher Power – call it what you will. If I can see, clearly see, a ladder rising from plants to men, why should I assume that this ladder, with its bottom end invisible, lost in the plant world, breaks off with me and doesn't keep on going up until it reaches higher forms of existence? I feel I can never disappear because nothing disappears in the whole universe, and more than that, I always shall be and always have been in existence. I feel that other spirits exist, far above me, and it's in their world that you will find truth.'

'Yes, this is Herder's doctrine,'[11] said Prince Andrey. 'But I'm not convinced by it, my dear fellow. I'm convinced by life and death. I'm convinced by seeing a creature dear to me, bound up with me, that I've treated badly . . . and just when I'm hoping to make it up to her,' (his voice shook and he turned away) 'suddenly she's in pain, she goes through agony and she ceases to be . . . Why? There must be an answer. And I believe there is one . . . That's what I find convincing. It convinced me,' said Prince Andrey.

'Yes, yes, of course' said Pierre, 'isn't that just what I'm saying?'

'No. My point is – you might be persuaded there is an after-life not by arguments, but by going through life hand-in-hand with somebody, and all at once that somebody vanishes *there, into nowhere*, and you are left standing over the abyss, staring down into it. And I have stared down into it . . .'

'Well, that's it then! You know there is a *there* and there is a *somebody*. *There* is the after-life. That *somebody* is God.'

Prince Andrey didn't answer. The coach and horses had long been taken over to the other bank and harnessed up again, the sun had half-set and the evening frost was sprinkling the pools near the ferry with stars, but – to the astonishment of the servants, coachmen and ferryhands – Pierre and Andrey were still on the boat, talking.

'If there is a God and an after-life, then there is truth and there is goodness; and man's greatest happiness lies in struggling to achieve them. We must live, love and believe,' said Pierre, 'believe that our life is not only here and now on this little patch of earth, but we have lived before and shall live for ever out there in the wholeness of things.' (He pointed up to the sky.) Prince Andrey was still standing with his elbows on the rail of the ferry, and as he listened to Pierre he never took his eyes off the sun's red reflection on the shining blue water. Pierre stopped talking. There was absolute stillness. The ferry had long since come to the bank, and the only sound came from the river, with waves plashing softly against the bottom of the boat. Prince Andrey half-imagined that the lapping of the water sounded like a chorus echoing what Pierre had been saying: 'This is the truth. Believe it.'

Prince Andrey sighed, and with a tender, radiant, child-like glow in his eyes he glanced at Pierre, whose face was flushed with triumph, though he was still diffident, conscious of his friend's superiority.

'Yes, if only it was true!' he said. 'Anyway, let's get back to the carriage,' added Prince Andrey, and as he walked off the ferry he looked up at the sky where Pierre had pointed, and for the first time since Austerlitz he saw it again, the lofty, eternal sky, just as he had seen it when he lay on the battlefield, and suddenly something inside him that had long lain dormant, something better than before, awoke in his soul with a feeling of youth and joy. It was a feeling that would vanish as soon as Prince Andrey got back to the normal run of everyday life, but he was sure, without knowing what to do with it, that this feeling was still there inside him. Pierre's visit marked a new age for Prince Andrey, a time when his life, although outwardly unchanged, began again in his own inner world.

CHAPTER 13

It was getting dark by the time Prince Andrey and Pierre drove up to the front entrance of the house at Bald Hills. As they were approaching, Prince Andrey had smiled and drawn Pierre's attention to a commotion going on at the back of the house. A bent little old woman with a bag on her back, and a short man with long hair, dressed in black, had seen the carriage driving and scuttled off back to the gate. Two more women ran out and all four of them hurried up the steps of the back porch, looking round at the carriage with scared faces.

'Those are the Servants of God. Masha's friends,' said Prince Andrey. 'They thought it was my father coming back. It's the one and only way she disobeys him. He says they've got to be sent away, these pilgrims, but she takes them in.'

'What do you mean "Servants of God"?' asked Pierre.

Prince Andrey had no time to answer. The house servants had come out to meet them, and he asked where the old prince was and whether he would be home soon. He was still in town, but expected back any minute.

Prince Andrey took Pierre to his own rooms, which were always waiting nicely prepared for him in his father's house, and then went off to the nursery.

'Let's go and see my sister,' he said to Pierre when he returned. 'I haven't seen her yet, she's hiding away, tucked up with her Servants of God. Serve her right. She's going to be really embarrassed, but you'll see her Servants of God. I'm telling you, it's something worth seeing.'

'Who are these "Servants of God"?' asked Pierre.

'You'll see.'

Princess Marya certainly was embarrassed, and her face went red and blotchy when she saw them coming in. Her room looked cosy, with the little lamps burning before the icon-stand, and next to her on the sofa, at the samovar, sat a young boy with a long nose and long hair, dressed in a monk's cassock. In an easy chair near by sat a thin, wrinkled old woman, with a gentle look on her child-like face.

'Andrey, why didn't you warn me?' she said in a tone of mild reproach, standing in front of her pilgrims like a mother hen with chickens.

'Delighted to see you. I am so glad to see you,' she said to Pierre, as he kissed her hand. She had known him as a child, and now his friendship with Andrey, his unhappy marriage and most of all his kindly, simple face, won her over. She looked at him with her lovely, luminous eyes, which seemed to say. 'I like you very much, but please don't laugh at *my people*.'

After the first exchanges of greeting, they sat down.

'I see Ivanushka's here,' said Prince Andrey with a smile, nodding towards the young pilgrim.

'Oh, Andrey, please!' said Princess Marya imploringly.

'I think you ought to know he's a woman,' Andrey informed Pierre in French.

'Andrey, for heaven's sake!' repeated Princess Marya.

It was clear that Prince Andrey's mockery of the pilgrims and Princess Marya's ineffectual way of standing up for them had become their normal way of carrying on with each other.

'Oh, my dear girl,' said Prince Andrey, 'it's the other way round – you ought to thank me for telling Pierre all about your close relations with this young person.'

'Indeed?' said Pierre, looking with curiosity and seriousness (for which Princess Marya felt especially grateful) at Ivanushka's face, while he, aware that he was the subject under discussion, watched them all with a crafty look in his eyes.

Princess Marya need not have felt any embarrassment on behalf of *her people*. They were not the slightest bit put out. The old woman had looked down, but now she kept stealing the odd sideways glance at the new arrivals, while she sat there unperturbed and quite still in her armchair, with her cup inverted on its saucer and a half-nibbled lump of sugar next to it, waiting to be offered another cup. Ivanushka, slurping his tea from the saucer, peeped about furtively with sly, feminine eyes and studied the two young men.

'Where have you been? In Kiev?' Prince Andrey asked the old woman.

'Oh yes, good sir,' answered the old woman, and once started she prattled on. ''Twas the very day of Christmas that I was deemed a worthy partaker in the holy, heavenly sacrament at the shrine of the

saints. But now I comes from Kolyazin, good sir, where a great blessing
has been revealed.'

'Did Ivanushka come with you?'

'No, I was travelling alone, benefactor,' said Ivanushka, putting on
a deep voice. 'I joined up with Pelageyushka at Yukhnovo . . .'

Pelageyushka cut in on her companion, evidently eager to describe
what she had seen. 'Yes, sir, it was in Kolyazin. A great blessing was
revealed.'

'What was it – found some more relics?' asked Prince Andrey.

'Stop it, Andrey,' said Princess Marya. 'Pelageyushka, don't tell
them.'

'Oh, why shouldn't I tell him, ma'am? I likes him. He's a good
gentleman, God's chosen, he's my benefactor. Gave me ten roubles,
he did, as I remember. When I was in Kiev, crazy Cyril, he says to me
(now there's a man of God, barefoot he goes winter and summer),
you're going the wrong way, he says, you go to Kolyazin, they got an
icon there, a holy Mother of God, works miracles it does, it's all just
been revealed. So I drops everything, I says goodbye to the good holy
people, and I'm off . . .'

Nobody spoke. The only sounds came from the pilgrim woman as
she sucked in her breath and droned on with her story. 'And when I
gets there, good sir, folks says to me as how a great blessing has been
revealed and drops of holy oil be trickling down the cheeks of the
Holy Mother of God . . .'

'Yes, yes, that's very good. We can hear the rest later,' said Princess
Marya, flushing.

'May I just ask her something?' said Pierre. 'Did you see it yourself?'
he asked.

'Bless you, good sir, to be sure I was found worthy enough. Such a
glow on the face, like the light of heaven, and all down the Holy
Mother's cheeks comes little drops, more and more little drops . . .'

'Well, it must be a trick,' said Pierre naively, after listening closely
to the old woman.

'Oh, sir, what are you saying?' said Pelageyushka, turning in horror
to Princess Marya for support.

'They do play tricks on ordinary people,' he repeated.

'Lord Jesus Christ!' said the pilgrim woman, crossing herself. 'Oh,
please don't talk like that, sir. There was a general once just like that,
didn't believe, and one day he says, "The monks is cheating us," and
the minute he says it, he was struck blind. And then the Holy Mother
of the Kiev catacombs comes to him in a dream and says: "Believe in
me and I shall make thee whole." And so he begged and prayed them,

"Take me to her, take me to her." This is the holy truth I tell you, which I've seen with my own eyes. They carried him to her, blind as he was. He came before her, fell down on his knees and said, "Make me whole and I shall give thee," says he, "all that the Tsar has bestowed on me." I saw it myself, good sir – the icon with a star fixed in it. And lo! – his sight was restored! It's a sin to speak as you do. God will punish you,' she admonished Pierre.

'How did the star get into the icon?' asked Pierre.

'Did the Holy Mother get promotion? They could have made her a general,' said Prince Andrey with a smile.

Pelageyushka suddenly turned pale, wringing her hands.

'Sir, sir, it's a great sin to talk like that, and you with a son!' she said, her pallor changing suddenly to bright red. 'Sir, may God forgive what you have said.' She crossed herself. 'May the Lord forgive him. Lady, what have we come to?' She turned to Princess Marya, got to her feet on the verge of tears and began picking up her little bag. She was obviously shocked and saddened by Andrey's words, full of shame for having accepted charity in a house where such things could be said, and sorry that from now on she would have to do without the charity offered here.

'What was all that about?' said Princess Marya. 'Why did you come in here?'

'Oh, come on, it was only a joke, Pelageyushka,' said Pierre. 'Princess, honestly, I didn't mean to upset her. I just . . . Please forget it. It was a joke,' he said with a diffident smile, trying to smooth things over and ease his conscience.

Pelageyushka stood there full of misgivings, but there was such a look of genuine regret on Pierre's face, and Prince Andrey seemed so meek and solemn as he glanced from her to Pierre, that she was gradually reassured.

CHAPTER 14

Reassured at last, the pilgrim woman was encouraged to talk, and she launched into some long stories, first about Father Amphilochus, whose life was so holy that his hands smelt of incense, and then about some monks she knew who had given her the keys to the catacombs on her recent pilgrimage to Kiev, and she had spent two days and nights in the catacombs among the saints with only a few crusts of bread. 'I says my prayers to one of them, I reads from the scriptures and then goes on to another one. I has a little nap, then I goes back to kiss the holy relics, and there's such peace, dearie, such blessedness, you never wants to come out into God's world again.'

Pierre listened with close and grave attention. Prince Andrey left the room. And then Princess Marya followed him out and took Pierre to the drawing-room, leaving the Servants of God to finish their tea.

'You're so kind,' she said to him.

'Oh, I really didn't mean to hurt her feelings. I know those feelings, and I value them highly.'

Princess Marya looked at him, saying nothing but smiling with affection.

'I've known you such a long time, haven't I? And I love you like a brother,' she said. 'How does Andrey strike you?' she followed on quickly, leaving him no time for a response to her warm words. 'He worries me. His health was better in the winter, but last spring his wound reopened, and the doctor told him to go away for proper treatment. And I worry about him in a moral sense. He doesn't have the kind of personality, like us women, to express his suffering and sorrow in tears. He bottles it all up. Today he is lively and cheerful. But that's your visit – it's already had an effect on him. He's not like this very often. If only you could persuade him to go abroad. He needs to be kept busy and this steady, quiet life is getting him down. Others don't notice it, but I can see it.'

It was nearly ten o'clock when the footmen rushed to the steps, hearing the old prince's carriage bells approaching. Prince Andrey went out on to the steps, and Pierre followed.

'Who's this?' asked the old prince, as he got out of the carriage and caught sight of Pierre.

'Ah! Pleased to see you! Kiss me!' he said when they told him who the young stranger was.

The old prince was in good spirits and he felt like being nice to Pierre.

Before supper, Prince Andrey returned to his father's study to find the old prince and Pierre having a heated discussion. Pierre was arguing that a time would come when there would be no more war. The old prince was enjoying a bit of good-humoured teasing.

'Drain all the blood out of men's veins and fill 'em up with water, then there'll be no more war. Women's talk. Women's talk,' he was saying, but he still gave him a friendly pat on the shoulder as he walked across to the table where Prince Andrey, happy enough to keep out of their conversation, was looking through some papers that the old prince had brought back from town. The old prince went over to him and began to talk business.

'That marshal, that Count Rostov, didn't send me half his contingent. Came to town and thought he'd invite me to dinner – I gave him dinner all right! . . . Anyway, look at this . . . Well, my boy,' said the old prince to his son, clapping Pierre on the shoulder, 'your friend is a good man. I like him! Gets me going. Some people talk sense and you can't bear to listen – he talks balderdash but he gets me going, an old man like me! Well go on, off you go,' he said. 'Maybe I'll come and sit with you while you have supper. We'll have another argument. Try to like my ignorant girl, Princess Marya!' he shouted after Pierre from the doorway.

It was only now on this visit to Bald Hills that Pierre felt the full value and charm of his close friendship with Prince Andrey. The charm went beyond his relations with Andrey himself to embrace all the family and all the staff. Despite hardly knowing them, Pierre felt immediately like an old friend when he was in the company of the harsh old prince and the gentle, diffident Princess Marya. Everybody liked him. It was not only Princess Marya, who had been won over by his gentle attitude to the pilgrims and now treated him to her most radiant gaze – even the tiny one-year-old Prince Nikolay, as the old prince called him, beamed at Pierre and came over to him to be picked up. And Mikhail Ivanych and Mademoiselle Bourienne looked on with smiling faces when he talked to the old prince.

When the old prince did emerge for supper that evening, it was obviously a gesture to Pierre. Throughout his two-day stay at Bald Hills he was extremely friendly towards him, and asked him to come and stay again.

When Pierre had left and all the family came together to talk about him, as people always do when a new guest has gone, everyone spoke well of him, and that is something people rarely do.

CHAPTER 15

It was on his return from leave on this occasion that Nikolay Rostov realized for the first time, and fully appreciated, the strong ties that bound him to Denisov and the regiment in general.

When Rostov was getting close to the regiment he began to experience the same kind of feeling that had come over him as he had approached his home in Moscow. When he saw his first hussar in his unbuttoned regimental uniform, when he recognized red-haired Dementyev and saw the tethered chestnut horses, when Lavrushka shouted gleefully to his master, 'The count's here!' and Denisov, who had been asleep on his bed, ran all dishevelled out of the mud-hut to embrace him, and the officers gathered round to welcome him, Rostov felt just as he had done when his mother had embraced him, and his father and his sisters, and the tears of joy welling up in his throat prevented him from speaking. The regiment was home too, a home as dependable, loving and precious as his parents' home.

After reporting to his colonel for reassignment to his squadron, doing a spell as orderly officer and going out on a foraging expedition, after resuming all the little regimental occupations and getting used to being deprived of liberty and pinned down within one narrow, set framework, Rostov had the same feeling of peace and moral support, the same sense of being at home, in the right place, that he had felt under his father's roof. There was none of the confusion of the outside world, where he could never find the right place to be and he kept getting things wrong. There was no Sonya to have things out with (or not, as the case may be). There was no possibility of deciding whether or not to go somewhere. There were no longer twenty-four hours in every day to be used up in so many different ways. There were no vast masses of people of medium significance, neither close nor remote. There were none of those obscure and uncertain money dealings with his father, and no reminders of that ghastly occasion when he had lost money to Dolokhov! Here in the regiment everything was straightforward and simple. The whole world could be divided into two unequal halves: our Pavlograd regiment and everything else. And everything else was no longer any concern of his. Here in the regiment everything was settled: you knew this man was a lieutenant and that one a captain, this man was a good fellow and that one was not, but, most importantly, everyone was your comrade. The manager of the field-canteen didn't mind giving credit, and your pay came through every four months. There was no need to think or choose for yourself; you just had to avoid doing anything that was wrong by Pavlograd standards, and when you were sent on any assignment, as long as you did what was clear and distinct, what you were told, all would be well.

Rostov was pleased and relieved to submit once again to the clear-cut conditions of regimental life; he felt like a weary man lying down to rest. During this campaign life in the regiment was all the more comforting to Rostov, because after his loss to Dolokhov (something for which he could never forgive himself despite his family's efforts to console him), he was determined to be a different soldier and to make amends by behaving well and by being a thoroughly good comrade, a good officer, in fact a good man – a hard task *out in the world*, but perfectly possible within the regiment.

Since his gambling loss Rostov had given himself five years to repay the debt to his parents. He was getting ten thousand a year from them, and he had made up his mind to spend no more than two thousand, putting the rest towards repayment.

After all the retreating, advancing and engaging with the enemy at Pultusk and Preussisch-Eylau, our army was now concentrated around Bartenstein awaiting the arrival of the Tsar and the start of a new campaign.

The Pavlograd regiment, as an army section which had taken part in the hostilities of 1805, had stayed behind in Russia to make up its numbers and did not arrive in time for action in the first skirmishes of the campaign. It took no part in the battles of Pultusk or Preussisch-Eylau, and when it did join the army in the field, in the second half of the campaign, it was attached to Platov's division.[12]

Platov's division was acting independently of the main army. Several times the Pavlograd hussars exchanged fire with the enemy, took prisoners and on one notable occasion captured Marshal Oudinot's carriages. In April the Pavlograd hussars had spent weeks on end encamped near a ravaged and deserted German village, and never stirred from that spot.

It was thawing, muddy and cold, the ice had broken up on the river, the roads were impassable, and for some days there had been no provisions, nothing for the horses or the men. With transport out of the question, the soldiers had dispersed about the abandoned and empty villages in search of potatoes, but very few were to be had.

Everything had been eaten up, and every last inhabitant had fled; those that remained were worse than beggars, and there was nothing to be taken from them; in fact the soldiers, not normally the most compassionate of men, often gave them what they had left.

The Pavlograd regiment had lost only two soldiers wounded in action, but almost half its men had gone down with hunger and disease. In the hospitals death was so certain that soldiers who became feverish or bloated from their bad diet preferred to stay on duty and drag themselves up and down the front line rather than go to any hospital. As spring came on the soldiers began to find a plant that looked like asparagus coming up out of the ground. For some reason they called it Mary's sweet-wort, and they scoured the fields and meadows in search of this Mary's sweet-wort (which was actually very bitter). They dug it up with their sabres and ate it, despite many warnings that it was dangerous and shouldn't be eaten. So that spring, when a new disease broke out among the soldiers, with swelling of the arms, legs and face, the doctors blamed it on this root. But no amount of warning could stop the soldiers of Denisov's squadron eating hardly anything but Mary's sweet-wort, because they had been eking out their last biscuits for a couple of weeks now, doled out at the rate of half a pound a man, and the last consignment of potatoes had arrived frozen and sprouting.

The horses, too, after two weeks feeding on nothing but thatch, looked shockingly thin and moth-eaten as their winter coats came away in tufts.

In spite of these appalling conditions, the soldiers and officers went on living just as usual, though their faces were pale and swollen and their uniforms were torn. They formed up on parade and numbered off, went out foraging, groomed their horses and cleaned their weapons, they fetched thatch for fodder and gathered round the cauldrons at dinner-time, only to walk away as empty as ever, joking about the awful food and going hungry again. Off duty the soldiers went on as before, lighting their fires, stripping off and steaming in front of them, smoking, sorting out one or two sprouting, rotten potatoes for baking, and swapping Potyomkin or Suvorov stories or sometimes tales about folk heroes like Alyosha, prince of rogues, or Mikolka who worked for the priest.

The officers lived as usual two or three to a roofless ruin of a house. The senior ones spent their time trying to get hold of straw and potatoes to feed the men, while the younger ones did the usual things, playing cards for money (which was plentiful, though there was nothing to eat), or enjoying innocent games like quoits and skittles. Nobody had much to say about the general run of the campaign, partly because nothing very positive was known, partly because of a vague idea that things were not going too well.

Rostov was living with Denisov again, and the bond of friendship between them had become even closer since they had been on leave. Denisov never mentioned any member of Rostov's family, but the commander's warm friendship towards his junior officer gave Rostov the impression that the older hussar's unhappy passion for Natasha had something to do with the strengthening of their friendship. There was no doubt that Denisov was shielding Rostov, keeping him out of danger as much as possible, and after any action he welcomed him back safe and sound with undisguised delight. Fetching up in a deserted and ruined village on one of his foraging expeditions, Rostov came across an old Pole and his daughter with a tiny baby. They had no proper clothes or food, they had been too weak to walk away and unable to pay for a ride. Rostov brought them back to camp and set them up in his own quarters, where he supported them for several weeks until the old man recovered. One of Rostov's comrades started kidding him once when they were talking about women, saying he was the cleverest fellow around and it wouldn't do any harm for him to introduce his comrades to the pretty little Polish woman that he'd rescued. Rostov took offence at this and flared up, saying such awful things to the officer that Denisov was hard put to stave off a duel between them. When the officer had gone away, and Denisov, who knew nothing about Rostov's relationship with the Polish woman, began to tell him off for over-reacting, Rostov said, 'You can say what you like . . . She's like a sister to me, and I can't tell you how much it hurt . . . because . . . well, you know . . .'

Denisov clapped him on the shoulder, and started pacing rapidly up and down the room without looking at Rostov, something he often did at times of high emotion. 'Oh weally,' he said, 'you Wostovs are such a cwazy bweed,' and Rostov could see that Denisov had tears in his eyes.

CHAPTER 16

In April the army was roused by the news that the Tsar was on his way. Rostov had no chance of taking part in the review conducted by him at Bartenstein; the Pavlograd hussars were posted well forward, a long way out of Bartenstein.

They were still encamped. Denisov and Rostov were living in a mud-hut dug out by soldiers and roofed over with branches and turf. The hut was built to a plan that had recently become very popular with the soldiers. A trench was dug just over three feet wide, nearly five feet deep and eight feet long. At one end of the trench steps were scooped out to form an entrance. The trench itself was the room, and in it the lucky officers, such as the squadron commander, had the benefit of a board mounted on four stakes at the opposite end to the steps – this was the table. Both sides of the trench were cut down a couple of feet to provide a surface usable as beds and couches. The roof was constructed so that a man could stand upright in the middle, and you could sit on the beds if you moved up close to the table.

Denisov, who always lived well because his men liked him so much, even had a board let into the front part of the roof with a broken but glued up window-pane in it. When it was very cold they used to bring red-hot embers over from the soldiers' camp-fires on a bent sheet of iron and put them near the steps (in the 'ante-room', as Denisov called that part of the hut), and this made it so warm that any visiting officers – and Denisov and Rostov were never short of visitors – could sit there in their shirtsleeves.

One April morning Rostov returned from a spell on duty. Arriving home just before eight o'clock after a sleepless night, he sent for some heat, changed his rainsoaked clothes, said his prayers, drank some tea, warmed himself, tidied things away in his corner and on the table, and with his face red from the wind outside and the warmth within, he lay down on his back with nothing on but his shirt and folded his hands behind his head. He was enjoying the pleasant thought that promotion ought to be his any day now following the last reconnaissance mission, while he waited for Denisov, who had gone off somewhere. He wanted to talk.

Suddenly he heard a thunderous voice outside the hut – unmistakably Denisov's. Rostov went to the window to find out who he was speaking to and saw that it was the quartermaster, Topcheyenko.

'I told you not to let them stuff themselves with that Mawy woot thing!' Denisov was roaring. 'I saw Lazarchuk with my own eyes bwinging it back fwom the field.'

'I did tell them, sir, lots of times, but they don't listen,' answered the quartermaster.

Rostov lay back down on his bed and thought with some pleasure. 'Let him sort it out. He's got his hands full now. I've done my day's work and I can have a lie-down. Marvellous!' Through the wall he could hear someone else speaking. It was Denisov's valet, Lavrushka, a clever rogue if ever there was one, and he was going on about some wagons and biscuits and oxen he'd seen while he'd been out scouting for provisions.

Then he heard Denisov's voice outside disappearing into the distance as he shouted, 'Second twoop! To horse!'

'I wonder where they're off to,' thought Rostov.

Five minutes later Denisov came into the hut, clambered on to his bed still wearing his muddy boots, lit his pipe angrily, rummaged through his things to find his riding-whip and sabre, and turned to leave the hut. When Rostov wanted to know where he was going he said vaguely and angrily that he had something to do.

'Let God be my judge in this – and our gweat Empewor!' said

Denisov as he went out. Outside, Rostov could hear the hoofs of several horses splashing through the mud. He didn't even bother to find out where Denisov was going. Warm and cosy in his corner, he soon fell asleep, and it was early evening before he emerged from the hut. Denisov was still out. The weather had cleared. Near the next hut two officers and a cadet were playing a form of quoits, with much laughter as they drove big radishes for pegs into the soft muddy ground. Rostov joined in. In the middle of a game the officers suddenly saw some wagons driving up, followed by more than a dozen hussars riding their skinny horses. The wagons trundled up with their hussar escort and stopped at the tethering rails, where they were immediately surrounded by more hussars.

'Hey, look! Denisov needn't have worried,' said Rostov. 'Fodder at last!'

'I'll say!' said the officers. 'The boys are going to like this!' Just behind the hussars came Denisov, still on horseback and accompanied by two infantry officers, all of them busy talking. Rostov went forward to meet Denisov.

'I'm warning you, Captain,' one of the officers was saying, a thin little man, visibly angry.

'Well, I've told you – I'm not giving them up,' answered Denisov.

'You'll answer for this, Captain. It's outrageous – stealing vehicles from your own side! Our men haven't eaten for two days.'

'Mine haven't eaten for two weeks,' countered Denisov.

'It's daylight robbery! You'll answer for it, sir!' repeated the infantry officer, raising his voice.

'Will you stop pestewing me? Eh?' roared Denisov, roused to fury. 'I'm wesponsible, not you. And buzz off you lot while you'we in a fit state to do so!' he shouted at the officers.

'All right then,' cried the little officer, refusing to be intimidated or to ride away. 'This is thieving, and I'm telling you . . .'

'Go away, damn you, move, at the double, while *you'we* in a fit state to do so!' And Denisov turned his horse towards the officer.

'All right, all right,' said the officer ominously. He turned his own horse away and trotted off, jolting in the saddle.

'Dog on a fence! You'we a weal dog on a fence!' Denisov called after him, this being the most insulting thing a cavalryman can say to an infantryman on horseback. He rode over to Rostov and roared with laughter.

'Gwabbed all this fwom the infantwy! Supewior stwength!' he said. 'Can't let the men die of starvation!'

The wagons that had just rolled up had been intended for an infantry regiment, but when he found out from Lavrushka that the wagon-train was unescorted, Denisov and his hussars had seized everything by brute force. Plenty of biscuits were issued to the men, and they even shared them with other squadrons.

The next day the colonel sent for Denisov, and, covering his eyes with open fingers, he said to him, 'This is how I see it. I know nothing, and I don't propose to take any action. But I advise you to ride over to HQ and sort things out with the provisions people. If possible say what stores you've had and sign for them. If you don't and they're put down against the infantry, it's bound to come out, and it could have a nasty outcome.'

Denisov left the colonel and went straight to HQ, genuinely keen to follow his advice.

That evening he came back to his hut in a terrible state; Rostov had never seen his friend like this. He was gasping and speechless. When Rostov asked him what was wrong, all he could do was whisper and croak, mouthing incoherent expletives and threats.

Alarmed at the state he was in, Rostov told him to get undressed, have a drink of water and send for the doctor.

'Me! Court-martialled for wobbewy! Give me a dwink of water. Well, let them twy me! I'll win! I'll get them, wotten swine! I'll tell the Empewor! Get me some ice,' he kept saying.

When the regimental doctor arrived he said it was essential to bleed him. A deep saucerful of black blood was extracted from Denisov's hairy arm, and only then was he in any state to tell them what had happened.

'I got there,' said Denisov. ' "Now then, where can I find your chief?" ' They showed me. "I twust you don't mind waiting?" "I'm hewe on business, I've widden twenty miles and I haven't time to wait. Announce me." Vewy good, but out comes the thief-in-chief and he wants to upbwaid me too. "This is wobbewy!" says he. "A wobber," I say, "is not someone who gwabs some wations to feed his men, it is someone who gwabs things to fill his own pockets." "Will you please be silent?" Vewy good. "Go and wite a weceipt," says he, "for the commissioner, but this will have to be weported." Off to the commissioner. In I go, and guess who's sitting at the table . . . No, guess! . . . Guess who's starving us all to death!' roared Denisov, banging the table with the fist of his recently bled arm so violently that it almost collapsed, and the glasses jumped. 'Telyanin! "What?" I shouted. "So it's you that's starving us all to death?" and I smashed his face in, gave him a wight one, I did. I called him every name under the sun and I laid into him. It was great fun, I can tell you,' cried Denisov, his white teeth gleaming under his black moustache in a smile of malicious glee. 'I'd have killed him if they hadn't pulled me off.'

'Don't shout. Calm down,' said Rostov. 'You've made it bleed again. Keep still. You need a bandage.'

Denisov was bandaged and put to bed. Next morning he woke up calm and cheerful.

But at midday the regimental adjutant called on Denisov and Rostov at their hut. His face was grave and full of regret as he painfully showed them the official form served on Major Denisov by the colonel in charge of the regiment, raising questions about the incidents of the previous day. The adjutant warned them that the affair seemed likely to take a very bad turn. There would be a court martial, and in view of current strictures against looting and insubordination the best he could hope for would be reduction to the ranks.

The case presented by the injured parties was that Major Denisov, after seizing the wagons, had come to the Chief Commissioner for Procurement on his own initiative and in a drunken state had called him a thief, issued physical threats and on being led out had rushed into the office and attacked two officials, one of whom ended up with a dislocated arm.

Rostov persisted with his questions and in response Denisov accepted that some other fellow did seem to have got involved, but anyway it was all complete rubbish, he wouldn't dream of worrying about any court, and that if those swine dared to pick on him he'd give them an answer they wouldn't soon forget.

This offhand manner was typical of Denisov's attitude to the whole affair, but Rostov knew him too well not to notice that deep down (though he hid it from everyone else) he was dreading the court martial and was desperately worried about the whole affair, which was clearly going to have terrible consequences. Documents began arriving daily, forms to be filled in and summonses, and Denisov was instructed to appear before the divisional staff on the 1st of May, having placed his squadron under the command of the officer next in seniority, for an inquiry into the fracas that had occurred in the commissioner's office. But on the day before the hearing Denisov was out on a reconnaissance mission organized by Platov and involving two Cossack regiments and two squadrons of hussars, as always well out in front, flaunting his courage, when a French marksman shot him in the fleshy part of his upper leg. At any other time, perhaps, Denisov wouldn't have left the regiment for a scratch like that, but on this occasion he took full advantage of it to excuse himself from appearing at Staff HQ, and went into hospital.

CHAPTER 17

The month of June saw the battle of Friedland,[13] in which the Pavlograd hussars did not take part. It was followed by a truce. Rostov, who was badly missing his friend and had had no news of him since he had left, was worried about the charge against him and his wound, so he took advantage of the truce and got permission to visit Denisov in hospital.

The hospital was located in a small Prussian town which had been ravaged twice by Russian and French troops. With the countryside around looking so pleasant in the early summer weather this little place looked particularly dismal, nothing but shattered roofs and fences, filthy streets and ragged inhabitants, and sick and drunken soldiers wandering about everywhere.

The hospital itself consisted of a stone house with bits of old fencing all over the yard, and many shattered window-frames and broken panes. Several soldiers swathed in bandages, with faces pale and swollen, were walking about or sitting around in the yard enjoying the sunshine.

The moment Rostov walked through the door he was assailed by the stench of hospital disinfectant and putrefying flesh. On the stairs he met a Russian army doctor with a cigar in his mouth. He was followed by a Russian medical assistant.

'I can't be everywhere at once,' the doctor was saying. 'Come and see me tonight. I'll be at Makar Alexeich's.' The assistant wanted to ask more questions. 'Oh, just do the best you can! What difference will it make?'

The doctor caught sight of Rostov coming up the stairs.

'What are you doing here, sir?' asked the doctor. 'What are you doing here? If you've missed all the bullets why would you want to catch typhus? This, sir, is a leper colony.'

'What do you mean?' asked Rostov.

'Typhus, sir. Go in there and you're a dead man. There's only the two of us still on our feet, Makeyev and me.' (He pointed to the assistant.) 'Five or six of us doctors have gone down. A new one comes in, give him a week and he's had it,' said the doctor with evident satisfaction. 'We've sent for some Prussian doctors, but our allies don't seem too keen to come.'

Rostov explained that he wanted to see one of the patients, Major Denisov of the hussars.

'I can't help you, my good sir. I don't know who's who. Listen, I'm on my own, looking after three hospitals, well over four hundred patients. It's a good job the Prussian charitable ladies send us a couple of pounds of coffee and some lint every month or we'd be lost.' He laughed. 'Four hundred, sir, and new ones every day. It is four hundred, isn't it?' He turned to the assistant.

The assistant looked worn out. It was all too obvious that he was squirming with irritation, just wanting the garrulous doctor to go away.

'Major Denisov,' repeated Rostov. 'He was wounded at Moliten.'

'Oh, I think he's dead. That's right, isn't it, Makeyev?' the doctor asked casually.

But the assistant did not confirm what the doctor had said.

'Long sort of fellow. Red-haired,' suggested the doctor.

Rostov described Denisov's appearance.

'Yes, there was someone like that,' the doctor declared with some delight. 'Must be dead by now, but I'll have a look. I used to have some lists. Have you got them, Makeyev?'

'They've gone to Makar Alexeich,' said the assistant. 'But if you'd like to go along to the officers' wards you can see for yourself,' he added, turning to Rostov.

'Ah, better not, sir!' said the doctor. 'You might end up staying here yourself.' But Rostov said goodbye to the doctor with a polite bow and asked the assistant to show him the way.

'Don't blame me!' the doctor shouted up the stairwell.

Rostov and the assistant turned into a dark corridor. The hospital stench was so strong there that Rostov held his nose and had to stop and pull himself together before going on. A door opened on the right, and out came a sallow, emaciated man limping along on crutches, dressed in his underclothes and with nothing on his feet. He leant against the door jamb and watched them as they approached, his eyes gleaming with envy. Rostov glanced in through the door and saw sick and wounded men lying about everywhere on the floor, on straw and greatcoats.

'What's in here?' asked Rostov.

'It's the privates' ward,' said the assistant. 'What can I do?' he added almost apologetically.

'Can I go in and have a look round?' asked Rostov.

'What is there to look at?' said the assistant. But the assistant's obvious desire to keep him out made Rostov all the more determined to go in, and he did so. Out in the corridor he had just about got used to the stench, but it was even stronger in here. It was different, more pungent, and you could tell that this was where it was coming from.

In the long room, which was brilliantly lit by sunshine streaming in through big windows, lay two rows of sick and wounded men with their heads to the wall, leaving an aisle down the middle. Most of them were unconscious, oblivious to the arrival of any outsiders. The conscious ones perked up, or at least lifted their sallow, emaciated faces, and every one of them stared closely at Rostov, all with the same expression, a silent and hopeful call for help mingled with resentment and envy of another man's health. Rostov went in as far as the middle of the room and then walked out, only to glance in through the open doors of the next two rooms, where he saw the same thing on both sides. He stood still, looking around. It was beyond words. He had never expected to see anything like this. Right in front of him sprawling across the empty central aisle on the bare floor was a sick man, probably a Cossack, to judge by the cut of his hair. He lay on his back, with his huge arms and legs outstretched. His face was a purply red, his eyes had rolled up leaving only the whites visible, and on his bare legs and arms, which were still red, the veins stood out like cords. He was banging his head on the floor, trying to say something in a hoarse whisper and repeating it over and over again. Rostov listened hard and at last he made out the one word that was being repeated. That word was, 'drink-a drink-drink!' Rostov looked round for anyone who might be able to move this sick man back into his place and give him water.

'Who looks after the patients in here?' he asked the assistant. At that moment a commissariat soldier working in the hospital as an orderly came in from the adjoining room, marched up, stamped and came to attention.

'Good day to you, sah!' bawled this soldier, goggling at Rostov and obviously mistaking him for some medical authority.

'Move that man. Give him some water,' said Rostov, pointing to the Cossack.

'Sah!' the soldier replied most obligingly, goggling harder than ever, still standing rigidly at attention and not offering to move away.

'No, nothing can be done here,' thought Rostov, looking down, and he was just about to walk away when he became aware of someone to his right giving him a special kind of look and he turned to see who it was. An old veteran sat there on a greatcoat, almost hidden in the corner, his harsh face all yellow, emaciated and cadaverous, his grey beard unshaven. He was staring closely at Rostov. The man next to him was whispering something and pointing to Rostov. Rostov could see that the old man wanted to ask him something. He went up closer and saw that the old veteran had only one leg bent under him, the other having been cut off above the knee. On the other side of the old man, a short distance away, lay a young private with his head thrown back, a waxen pallor on his snub-nosed, freckled face and his eyes rolled up under their lids. Rostov looked at this snub-nosed soldier and a chill ran down his spine.

'Hey, that one seems to be . . .' he said to the assistant.

'We've begged and begged, your Honour,' said the old soldier with a trembling jaw. 'He died early this morning. We're men, too, we're not dogs . . .'

'I'll see to it immediately. He'll be taken away, yes, er, taken away,' said the assistant hurriedly. 'This way, sir.'

'Come on, let's go,' said Rostov hastily, looking down, shrinking into himself and trying to pass unnoticed down the lines of those resentful and envious eyes which remained glued on him as he walked out of the room.

CHAPTER 18

The assistant walked down the corridor and led Rostov to the officers' wards, three rooms with doors opening between them. These rooms contained beds, and the sick or wounded officers were sitting or lying on them. Some were walking from one room to another in hospital dressing-gowns. The first person to meet Rostov in the officers' ward was a thin little man who had lost an arm. He was sucking on a stumpy pipe as he walked about the first room wearing a hospital dressing-gown and a night-cap. Rostov looked at him closely, trying to remember where he had seen him before.

'We meet again – by God's will – and what a place!' said the little man. 'Tushin, Tushin. You remember. I gave you a lift after Schöngrabern? Look, I've had a bit chopped off . . .' he said with a broad grin, showing the empty sleeve of his dressing-gown. 'Oh, you're looking for Vasily Denisov, are you? He's one of our room-mates,' he said, when he heard who Rostov wanted. 'Come through here,' and he led him into the next room, from which he could hear the sound of voices and several men laughing.

'How can they even live in this place, never mind laugh?' thought Rostov, with that stench of dead flesh from the privates' ward still in his nose. He had not yet escaped from those envious eyes following him on both sides, and the face of that young soldier with the eyes rolled upwards.

Denisov was asleep on his bed, with a quilt pulled up over his head, even though it was nearly midday.

'Hello, Wostov! How are you, how are you?' called the old familiar voice. But Rostov noticed with great sadness that behind this habitual show of breeziness lurked a new, secret and sinister feeling, just discernible in what Denisov said, the way he said it and the look on his face.

His wound was nothing much, but six weeks after the incident it still hadn't healed. His face was puffy and pallid like all the other hospital faces. But Rostov was struck by something else – Denisov didn't seem pleased to see him, and his smile was forced. He asked not a single question about the regiment or how the war was going, and when Rostov talked about these things Denisov wasn't listening.

Rostov even noticed that Denisov looked uncomfortable whenever he was reminded of the regiment, or of that other life of freedom outside the hospital. He seemed to be trying to forget the old life, as if he wanted to concentrate solely on his dealings with the commissariat officials. When Rostov asked how things were going in this direction, Denisov felt under his pillow and quickly pulled out a document which had recently come from the commission, and a first draft of his response to it. He got more and more excited as he read through his reply and he was particularly keen to emphasize for Rostov's benefit one or two clever barbs launched against his adversaries. Denisov's hospital companions, who had gathered round Rostov when they spotted a new arrival from the freedom of the outside world, began to drift away one by one as soon as Denisov started to read his text. Rostov guessed from the looks on their faces that all these gentlemen had heard the story many times before and they were getting bored with it. The only exceptions were his nearest neighbour, a fat Uhlan, who sat there on his bunk scowling darkly and smoking his pipe, and little one-armed Tushin, who never stopped listening, though he showed disapproval by shaking his head. The Uhlan interrupted Denisov in mid-flow.

'As far as I'm concerned,' he said, turning to Rostov, 'he ought to go straight to the Emperor and ask for a pardon. Everybody says there are big rewards on offer just now, and he'll get a pardon for sure . . .'

'What, me wequest a pardon fwom the Empewor!' said Denisov in a voice which he tried to invest with all his old energy and ardour, though there was a sense of impotence behind all the irritation. 'Why should I? If I was a wobber I'd ask for mercy, but hewe I am on a charge for twying to show who the wobbers are. Let them twy me. Nobody can fwighten me. I have twuly served my Tsar and my

country, and I'm not a thief! They can weduce me to the wanks, and
... Well anyway, this is stwaight talking. You listen to what I've
witten: "If I had wobbed the government . . ."'

'That's well put, no doubt about it,' said Tushin. 'But it's not the
point, Vasily,' he turned to Rostov, 'you have to give in to them, and
Vasily won't do it. You know the auditor said it doesn't look good.'

'So what?' said Denisov.

'The auditor wrote out a petition for you,' Tushin went on. 'All you
have to do is sign it and send it off. This gentleman will take it. He'
(Rostov was indicated) 'probably has influence up at HQ. This is your
best chance.'

'I've told you I'm not gwovelling to anybody,' said Denisov, cutting
in, and he went on reading his reply.

Rostov didn't dare argue with Denisov, though he felt instinctively
that the course proposed by Tushin and the other officers was the
safest. He would have been only too happy to help Denisov, but he
knew all about his obstinacy and his hot-tempered self-righteousness.

Denisov's vitriolic outpouring lasted more than an hour, and when
it was over Rostov said nothing. He spent the rest of the day, deeply
dispirited, in the company of Denisov's new friends, who had gathered
round him again, telling them everything he knew and listening to
other people's stories. Denisov looked on gloomily and said not a
word as the evening went on.

Late in the evening when Rostov was about to leave, he asked
Denisov if he had any jobs for him to do.

'Yes, hang on,' said Denisov. He looked round at the officers, took
his papers out from under the pillow and went over to the window
where there was an inkstand. He sat down to write.

'I can see it's no good knocking my head against a bwick wall,' he
said, coming away from the window and handing Rostov a large
envelope. It was the petition addressed to the Emperor which the
auditor had drawn up for him, and in it Denisov avoided references
to any wrong doing by officials in the commissariat, and simply asked
for a pardon. 'Please hand it in. I think . . .' He stopped short and
smiled a forced and sickly smile.

CHAPTER 19

Rostov returned to the regiment, reported to the commander on the progress of Denisov's case and then rode on to Tilsit with the letter to the Emperor.

On the 13th of June the French and Russian Emperors met at Tilsit. Boris Drubetskoy had asked the dignitary for whom he worked to include him in the entourage appointed for Tilsit.

'I'd like to see the great man,' he said, meaning Napoleon, having hitherto called him Bonaparte like everybody else.

'Do you mean Bonaparte?' said the general with a smile.

Boris looked quizzically at his general, but soon spotted that this was a little test in the form of a joke.

'I am speaking, sir, of the Emperor Napoleon,' he replied. The general smiled again and clapped him on the shoulder.

'You'll go far,' he said, and took him with him. Boris was one of the few people present at the Niemen on the day the two Emperors met. He saw the rafts decorated with royal monograms, watched Napoleon drive past the French guards on the far bank, saw the Emperor Alexander looking very pensive as he sat silent in the inn on the bank of the Niemen waiting for Napoleon's arrival. He watched as both Emperors got into boats, and saw Napoleon reach the raft first and walk forward rapidly to meet Alexander and shake him by the hand, whereupon both Emperors disappeared into a pavilion. Ever since he had begun to move in the highest circles, Boris had formed the habit of keenly observing everything that went on around him and writing it all down. During the meeting of the Emperors at Tilsit, he asked the names of the persons accompanying Napoleon, inquired about the uniforms they were wearing, and listened carefully to every word uttered by any person of consequence. At the precise moment the Emperors went into the pavilion he looked at his watch, and he didn't forget to look at it again the moment Alexander came out. The meeting had lasted one hour and fifty-three minutes, and he made a note of this that evening along with other details that he considered to be of historical importance. Since the imperial entourage was not very large, just to be present at Tilsit at the meeting of the two Emperors was a matter of real significance for a man who set so much store by succeeding in the service, and now that he had managed to get himself there Boris felt that henceforth his position was totally secure. He had not simply made himself known, he was now getting noticed and becoming a familiar figure. On two occasions he had been on assignments to the Emperor himself, so that the Emperor knew him by sight, and the people at court no longer kept him at arm's length, as they had done at first when they saw him as an upstart. Now, if he wasn't there people would be surprised.

Boris was lodging with another adjutant, a Polish count by the name of Zhilinsky. Educated in Paris, he was a wealthy man and a devoted Francophile, and while they were in Tilsit French guards officers and members of the French General Staff came round to lunch or dinner with Zhilinsky and Boris almost every day.

On the 24th of June Zhilinsky arranged a supper for his French acquaintances. Among the diners were one of Napoleon's aides – he was the guest of honour – several French guards officers, and a young boy of an old and aristocratic French line, a page of Napoleon's. That same evening Rostov took advantage of the darkness to avoid being recognized, came to Tilsit in civilian clothing and turned up at the quarters of Zhilinsky and Boris.

In one respect Rostov was like the whole army that he had just left behind – he was a long way from accepting the volte-face which had taken place at headquarters and in Boris concerning Napoleon and the French, suddenly transforming them from enemies into friends. In the army everyone still felt the same mixture of malevolence, fear and contempt for Bonaparte and the French. Only recently Rostov had been in an argument with one of Platov's Cossack officers over how Napoleon should be treated if ever he were taken prisoner – as an emperor or a criminal? And again quite recently Rostov had met a wounded French colonel on the road and had told him in no uncertain terms that peace could never be concluded between a legitimate emperor and a criminal like Bonaparte. So it seemed very odd to Rostov that there should be French officers in Boris's quarters wearing uniforms that he was used to looking at from a very different perspective on patrol out on the flank. He took one look at a French officer who happened to stick his head out of the door and was immediately seized by the feeling of warlike hostility that always came over him at the sight of the enemy. He stood there at the door and asked in Russian whether Boris Drubetskoy was a lodger here. Boris was in the ante-room and when he heard a strange voice he came out to see who it was. When he recognized Rostov, his face fell.

'Oh, it's you. Nice to see you, very nice,' he managed to say, and he smiled as he made a movement towards him. But Rostov had seen his first reaction.

'I seem to have come at a bad time,' he said. 'I wouldn't have come at all, but it's something important,' he said coldly.

'No, I was just a bit surprised to see you away from the regiment
... I'll be with you in a minute!' he added in French for the benefit of
someone who had called to him.

'I can see I've come at a bad time,' repeated Rostov.

Any trace of annoyance had vanished from Boris's face. Having
apparently weighed things up and decided how to proceed, he took
him by both hands and led him into the next room with studied
composure. Boris's eyes, gazing serenely but sharply at Rostov, seemed
to have disappeared behind some sort of veil or screen. It was as if he
had donned the sunglasses of their earlier life spent together – or so it
seemed to Rostov.

'Nonsense, you couldn't come at a bad time,' said Boris. Boris led
him into a room where supper was laid, introduced him to the guests
by name, explaining that he was not a civilian, but an officer in the
hussars, and an old friend of his. He named the other guests: 'Count
Zhilinsky, and from France Count N. N. and Captain S. S. . . .' Rostov
scowled at the Frenchmen, gave a grudging bow and said nothing.

Zhilinsky was by no means pleased to receive this unknown Russian
intruder, but he said nothing to Rostov. Boris seemed oblivious to any
embarrassment caused by the new arrival, and he made an attempt to
liven up the conversation with the same easy friendliness and the veiled
look that had come into his eyes when he had welcomed Rostov. With
typical French courtesy one of the French officers turned to Rostov,
as he sat there in grim silence, and said to him that he must surely
have come to Tilsit to see the Emperor.

'No, I came on business,' was Rostov's terse reply. Rostov had been
in a bad mood since the moment he had spotted the displeasure on
Boris's face, and like all people in bad moods, he imagined himself
surrounded by hostile glares and he felt *de trop*. Indeed, he was *de
trop*, and the only person to stay out of the general conversation,
which now took off again. 'What's he doing here?' was the question
posed by the eyes of the guests as they turned towards him. He got up
and went over to Boris.

'Listen, I'm getting in your way,' he whispered. 'If we could just
have a quick talk . . . I'll just go away.'

'No, no, you're not,' said Boris. 'But if you're feeling tired, come
and lie down and have a rest in my room.'

'No but really . . .'

They went into the little room where Boris slept. Rostov declined
to sit down and without further ado he launched into his business
with every appearance of being annoyed and somehow blaming it on
Boris. He told him about Denisov and asked whether he could and

would prevail on his general to intercede with the Emperor on
Denisov's behalf and get the letter presented. When they were alone
together Rostov became acutely aware for the first time that he felt
embarrassed to look Boris in the eye. Boris crossed one leg over the
other, and stroked the slender fingers of his right hand with his left as
he listened to Rostov, rather like a general listening to a report from
a subordinate, one minute glancing away and the next looking Rostov
straight in the face with the same cloudiness in his eyes. And every
time this happened Rostov felt awkward and looked down.

'I've heard of cases like this, and I know the Emperor is very strict
about these things. I think it might be better not to take this sort of
thing to his Majesty. To my mind, you'd be better off applying straight
to the corps commander . . . But my general view is . . .'

'You won't do it, will you?' Rostov almost shouted, avoiding
Boris's eyes.

Boris smiled.

'On the contrary, I'll do what I can. It's just that . . .'

At that moment Zhilinsky's voice came through the door, calling
Boris.

'Well, go on. Go on in,' said Rostov. He refused supper and stayed
there on his own in the little room, pacing up and down for quite
some time and listening to the cheery French chatter coming from the
next room.

CHAPTER 20

Rostov had arrived in Tilsit on the worst possible day for appealing
on Denisov's behalf. He could not go in person to see the general in
attendance, because he was not in uniform, and besides, he had come
to Tilsit without official permission, and Boris, even had he wanted
to, could not have gone the day after Rostov's visit. That was the day
(the 27th of June) when the preliminaries of peace were signed. The
Emperors exchanged decorations, Alexander receiving the Legion of
Honour, and Napoleon the Order of St Andrew (First Degree), and it
was also the day fixed for a banquet given by a battalion of the French
guards for the Preobrazhensky battalion, with both Emperors due to
attend.

Rostov felt so awkward and embarrassed with his old friend that
when Boris peeped in at him after supper he pretended to be asleep,
and next morning he left early to avoid seeing him. In tail-coat and

round hat Nikolay strolled round the town, staring at the French and their uniforms, and taking in the streets and the houses where the Russian and the French Emperors were staying. In the town square he watched as people began setting up tables and preparing for the banquet; he saw banners draped across the streets showing the Russian and French colours, and the letters A and N in huge monograms. There were flags and monograms in all the windows too.

'Boris isn't keen to help, and I don't want him to. That's settled then,' thought Nikolay. 'We're finished, but I'm not leaving here without doing everything I can for Denisov, and above all getting this letter through to the Emperor. The Emperor? . . . He's here!' thought Rostov, who had unconsciously found his way back to the house where Alexander was staying.

Saddled horses were standing at the entrance, and the entourage was assembling; clearly the Emperor would soon be setting off.

'Any minute now I might see him,' thought Rostov. 'If only I could give him the letter myself and talk to him about it . . . I can't be arrested for not being in uniform, can I? Surely not. He'd see the rights and wrongs of it. He understands everything. He knows everything. Is there anyone fairer and more gracious? And even if I did get arrested just for being here, so what?' he thought as he watched an officer climb the steps and go into the house where the Emperor was staying. 'Look, there are people going in and out. Oh! This is stupid. I'm going in and I'll give him the letter myself. Hard luck on Drubetskoy – he's driven me to it.' And then, with a sudden determination he didn't know he was capable of, Rostov walked straight into the house where the Emperor was staying, fingering the letter in his pocket.

'No, I can't miss this chance, not after Austerlitz,' he thought, expecting to meet the Emperor any minute and feeling his heart surge with blood at the very idea. 'I shall fall at his feet and implore him. He will raise me up, hear what I have to say and thank me.' 'I am always happy to do good, but to right a wrong is the greatest happiness,' Rostov could hear him saying. Curious eyes were upon him as he climbed the steps. At the top he saw a broad staircase leading straight up to a landing with a closed door on the right hand side. Below, under the stairs, was a door leading to the ground-floor rooms.

'Whom do you wish to see?' someone asked him.

'I have a letter. An appeal to his Majesty,' said Nikolay with a quavering voice.

'An appeal. You need the duty officer. This way, please.' (He motioned to the downstairs door.) 'Only it won't be accepted.'

At the sound of these casual words Rostov suddenly felt panic-stricken at what he was doing. The idea of meeting the Emperor at any moment was so wonderful that it scared him stiff, and he might have made a bolt for it but for an attendant who now came forward and opened the duty officer's door for him. Rostov went in.

There in the room stood a short, stout man of about thirty, dressed in white trousers, high boots and a cambric shirt which he seemed to have only just put on. A valet stood behind him buttoning his splendid new silk-embroidered braces, which made a strong impact on Rostov, though he couldn't have said why. The stout man was talking to someone in the next room.

'Good figure, and fiendishly pretty,' he was saying, but when he saw Rostov he stopped and frowned.

'What do you want? An appeal?'

'What is it?' asked someone from the next room.

'It's another appeal,' answered the man in the braces.

'Tell him to come back later. He'll be coming out any minute. We have to go.'

'Come back later, tomorrow. You're too late . . .'

Rostov turned to leave, but the man in the braces stopped him.

'Who is it from? Who are you?'

'It's from Major Denisov,' answered Rostov.

'Who are you – an officer?'

'A lieutenant, Count Rostov.'

'Damned cheek! Send it through the proper channels. Now get out . . . go away . . .' And he began putting on the uniform handed to him by the valet.

Rostov went out into the hall again, and saw there were lots of officers and generals in full dress uniform at the top of the steps, and he would have to walk right past them.

Cursing his own temerity and almost fainting away at the thought of meeting the Emperor at any minute and suffering the humiliation of being arrested before his very eyes, Rostov now saw the total folly of his bad behaviour, which he thoroughly regretted, and he was just squeezing through the splendidly attired entourage all round the front of the house, his eyes looking down at the ground, when a familiar voice called out to him, and a hand stopped him.

'Well, sir, what might you be doing here out of uniform?' asked a deep voice.

It was a cavalry general who had won special favour with the Emperor during the recent campaign; he had been the commanding officer of Rostov's division.

Rostov looked at him in dismay and tried to make some excuse, but once he saw that the general's face looked amused and benevolent he took him to one side and blurted out his story with great excitement, begging him to intercede for Denisov, who was known personally to the general.

The general heard Rostov's story and shook his head gravely. 'I'm sorry, very sorry. Such a gallant fellow. Give me the letter.'

Rostov had barely enough time to hand over the letter and tell him all about Denisov's plight when jingling spurs announced rapid movement down the stairs, at which the general left him and moved over on to the steps. The gentlemen of the Emperor's entourage ran down and took to their horses. The same groom who had been at Austerlitz, a man called Hayne, led the Emperor's horse forward, and when light footsteps came tripping down the staircase Rostov knew them at once. Forgetting any danger of being recognized, Rostov went along with a number of curious local people and moved up close to the steps, where once again, after a lapse of two years, he saw the adored features – the same face, the same glance, the same walk, the same blend of majesty and gentleness . . . And the feeling of rapturous adoration inspired by the Emperor was rekindled in Rostov's heart with all its old force. The Emperor was wearing the uniform of the Preobrazhensky regiment, white chamois leather breeches and high boots, and a star which Rostov didn't recognize. (It was the Legion of Honour.) He came out on the steps holding his hat under one arm and pulling on a glove. He stopped and had a look around, illuminating everything that met with his glance. He said a few words to one or two of the generals. Then he recognized Rostov's former divisional commander, smiled at him and beckoned him over.

All the entourage stood aside and Rostov watched as the general spoke to the Emperor for quite some time.

The Emperor said a few words in return and then took a step towards his horse. Once again the massed entourage and the spectators, Rostov among them, surged in closer to the Emperor. Standing by his horse with one hand on the saddle, the Emperor turned back to the cavalry general and said aloud obviously for all to hear, 'I cannot do it, General, and the reason I cannot do it is because the law is mightier than I am,' and he put his foot in the stirrup. The general bowed his head respectfully while the Emperor mounted his horse and galloped off down the street. Beside himself with excitement, Rostov ran on behind with the crowd.

CHAPTER 21

The Tsar rode off towards a square in which two battalions stood on parade ranged against each other: to the right, the men of the Preobrazhensky regiment and, to the left, the French guards in their bearskin caps.

As the Emperor rode up to one flank of the battalions, where the men presented arms, another group of horsemen was galloping up to the opposite flank, and at their head Rostov recognized Napoleon. It couldn't be anyone else. He galloped up, wearing a small hat and a blue uniform open over a white vest, with the St Andrew ribbon draped across his chest. He was riding a magnificent grey thoroughbred Arab caparisoned in crimson and gold. Riding up to Alexander, he half-raised his hat, a movement which immediately told Rostov, with his cavalryman's eye, that Napoleon was a poor and clumsy horseman. The battalions roared out their 'Hurrah!' and 'Long live the Emperor!' Napoleon said something to Alexander. Both Emperors dismounted and took each other by the hands. Napoleon's face wore an unpleasantly forced smile. Alexander was saying something to him with a warm and friendly expression on his face.

Despite the danger of being trampled by the horses of the French gendarmes controlling the crowd, Rostov followed every movement of the Emperor Alexander and Bonaparte, never taking his eyes off them. He was struck by something quite unexpected: Alexander was treating Bonaparte like an equal, and Bonaparte was completely relaxed, taking his familiarity with the Russian Tsar for granted as if it was something of long standing, and he seemed to be on equal terms with the Russian monarch.

Alexander and Napoleon, with their suite stretched out behind in a long train, moved towards the right flank of the Preobrazhensky battalion and ended up close to the crowd that was standing there. Suddenly the crowd found itself right next to the two Emperors, and Rostov, who was well to the front, began to be afraid of being recognized.

'Sire, I beg permission to award the Legion of Honour to the bravest of your soldiers,' said a clipped, grating voice, carefully articulating every letter.

It was the diminutive Bonaparte speaking, looking up straight into Alexander's eyes. Alexander listened attentively to what was being said, then inclined his head and gave an amiable smile.

'To the man who conducted himself with the greatest courage in this last war,' added Napoleon with precise enunciation of every syllable. He was scanning the ranks of Russian soldiers drawn up before him, still rigidly presenting arms but with their eyes fixed on the face of their own Emperor. Napoleon's air of authority and self-possession turned Rostov's stomach.

'If your Majesty will allow me to consult the colonel . . .' said Alexander, and he took a few hurried steps towards Prince Kozlovsky, the battalion commander. Meanwhile Bonaparte was peeling the glove off one of his little white hands, and he now tore it off and threw it away. An adjutant standing behind rushed forward eagerly and picked it up.

'Whom do we give it to?' the Emperor Alexander asked of Kozlovsky in Russian in a low voice.

'As your Majesty commands.'

The Emperor frowned with displeasure, glanced around and said, 'Well, we must give him an answer.'

Kozlovsky scanned the ranks in a businesslike manner, and his glance took in Rostov.

'Is it me?' thought Rostov.

'Lazarev!' The colonel scowled as he gave the command and Lazarev, their best marksman, stepped smartly forward.

'Where do you think you're going? Stand still!' voices whispered to Lazarev, who didn't know where to go. Lazarev came to halt, angling a scared look at his colonel, and his face twitched, as often happens to soldiers called out in front.

Napoleon half-turned his head and flapped a podgy little hand behind him, as if he was expecting to be handed something. Among the members of his suite, who knew immediately what was wanted, there was a great fuss and much whispering as something was passed from hand to hand, and then a page-boy, the same boy that Rostov had seen yesterday evening at Boris's house, trotted forward, bowed over the outstretched hand without keeping it waiting a second longer than was necessary, and placed in it a medal on a red ribbon. Without even looking, Napoleon squeezed two fingers together and there was the medal dangling between them. He then walked over to Lazarev, who stood there goggling, with eyes only for his own Emperor. Napoleon looked round at the Emperor Alexander to emphasize that what he was now doing he was doing for the benefit of his ally. The little white hand holding the medal brushed against a button on Private Lazarev's uniform. Napoleon seemed fully aware that all he had to do was deign to touch this private soldier on the breast and it would ensure that he would be for ever happy, well rewarded and distinguished from every other soldier in the world. He merely left the cross lying there on Lazarev's breast, dropped his hand and turned to Alexander apparently in no doubt that the medal would stick. And indeed it did, because many eager hands, Russian and French, were waiting to grab the cross and pin it to the uniform.

Lazarev scowled at the little man with white hands who had done something to him, and he continued to stand rigidly to attention, presenting arms, while staring straight at Alexander, as if asking for further instructions – should he just stand there, march off or do something else? No instructions were forthcoming so he stayed where he was for quite some time in the same state of rigidity.

The Emperors mounted their horses and rode away. The Preobrazhensky battalion was dismissed, and the men went to mingle with the French guards and sit down at the tables which had been set for them.

Lazarev was given a place of honour. French and Russian officers came to embrace him, congratulate him and shake him by the hand. Officers and common people crowded round just to have a look at Lazarev. There was a buzz of conversation in French and Russian and much laughter round the tables in the square. Two officers passed by near to Rostov, red-faced, merry and bright.

'How's this for a banquet, old man? Everything served up on silver,' one was saying. 'Seen Lazarev?'

'Yes.'

'I gather the Preobrazhenskys are going to give them a dinner tomorrow.'

'Yes, but what about Lazarev, lucky devil! Pension for life – twelve hundred francs.'

'How about this for a cap, boys!' yelled a Preobrazhensky soldier, putting on a French soldier's shaggy cap.

'Great stuff! It suits you!'

'Have you heard the latest response?' said one guards officer to another. 'The other day it was "Napoleon, France, Fortitude"; today it's "Alexander, Russia, Magnitude". Our Emperor calls, Napoleon responds. Tomorrow our Emperor's sending the St George to the bravest man in the French guards. Got to do it! Same response needed.'

Boris had come in with his comrade Zhilinsky to have a look at the banquet. On the way home he came across Rostov standing on the corner outside a house. 'Rostov! Hello there! We missed each other,' he said, and he had to ask what was wrong because Rostov looked a strange picture of gloom and despondency.

'Nothing's wrong. Nothing,' answered Rostov.

'You will drop in?'

'Yes.'

Rostov stood there on the corner for quite some time, watching the celebrations from a distance. His anguished mind was seething with problems that couldn't be resolved. His soul was alive with fearful doubts. He remembered Denisov with that new expression on his face and the way he seemed to have given in, and the hospital with all those torn-off arms and legs, the filth and disease. He remembered the stench of dead flesh in the hospital so vividly that he had looked round wondering where the smell was coming from. And he also kept remembering Napoleon with his little white hands, all smugness, and now being treated with affection and respect by the Emperor Alexander. What were all those torn-off legs and arms for, and why had those men been killed? Then he remembered Lazarev being rewarded, while Denisov got punishment instead of a pardon. He caught himself indulging in such strange ideas that they frightened him.

Hunger and the appetizing smell of the Preobrazhensky dinner brought him to his senses. He had to eat before going away. He went to a hotel he had seen that morning. There he encountered such a crowd of people and officers in civilian clothing like him that he had difficulty in getting dinner. Two officers of his own division joined him at his table. Naturally enough the conversation turned to the peace. Like most of the army Rostov's two officer comrades were dissatisfied with the peace concluded after the battle of Friedland. They kept on saying that if they could have held out just a bit longer Napoleon would have been done for – his troops were out of biscuits and ammunition. Nikolay ate in silence; most of the time he spent drinking. He polished off two bottles of wine by himself. He was agonized by an inner turmoil beyond any resolution. He was scared of his own reflections, but he couldn't get away from them. All of a sudden, in response to one of the officers who had said it was humiliating to look at the French, Rostov started shouting with a degree of violence that was quite uncalled for and shocked all the officers.

'How can you judge what would have been best!' he yelled with a rush of blood that reddened his face. 'How can you judge of the actions of the Emperor? What right have we to do any judging? We can't understand the aims or the actions of the Emperor!'

'I never mentioned the Emperor,' said the officer in self-justification, his only explanation of Rostov's outburst being that he was drunk.

Rostov wasn't listening.

'We're not officials in the diplomatic section, we're soldiers, that's what we are,' he went on. 'If they tell us to die, we die. And if we get punished, we must be in the wrong. Ours is not to judge. If his Majesty the Emperor feels like recognizing Bonaparte as an Emperor, and taking him on as an ally, that's the way it must be. If we started judging and criticizing at every end and turn, well, nothing will be sacred. Next thing we'll be saying there's no God, no nothing,' Nikolay continued, banging on the table and yelling at them, for no good reason according to his companions but, as he saw it, quite logically.

'We've got to do our duty, kill the enemy and stop thinking. And that's your lot!' he said.

'And drink,' put in one of the officers, not in an arguing mood.

'Yes, drink,' said Nikolay in full agreement. 'Hey, you!' he roared. 'Another bottle!'

PART III

In the year 1808 the Emperor Alexander visited Erfurt for another meeting with the Emperor Napoleon, and Petersburg high society had much to say about the splendour of this important meeting.

By 1809 the rapport between the two 'world sovereigns', as Napoleon and Alexander came to be called, had become so close that when Napoleon declared war on Austria, a Russian corps crossed the frontier for joint action alongside their old enemy Bonaparte against their old ally, the Austrian Emperor; so close indeed that high society began to talk of a possible marriage between Napoleon and one of Alexander's sisters. But, aside from foreign policy, Russian society was much preoccupied at this time with internal changes taking place in all government departments.

Meanwhile life itself, the ordinary life of real people with their personal involvement in health and sickness, hard work and relaxation, their involvement in thought, science, poetry, music, love, friendship, enmity and passion, went on as usual, far removed from political considerations, such as being for or against Napoleon, and all questions of reform.

Prince Andrey had been two years in the country without a single break. All the innovations introduced by Pierre on his estates without any concrete results, because of his continual flitting from one enterprise to another, had been carried through by Prince Andrey privately and without any noticeable effort on his part. He possessed in the highest degree the one quality that Pierre totally lacked: the practical application to get things going with no fuss or struggle.

On one of his estates three hundred serfs had been given the status of free farm-labourers (one of the first examples of this in Russia), and on the others forced labour had been replaced by the payment of rent. At Bogucharovo he was paying for a trained midwife to look after the peasant-women in childbirth, and a salaried priest was teaching the children of the peasants and house servants how to read and write. Prince Andrey spent half his time at Bald Hills with his father and his son, who was still being looked after by nurses. The other half he spent 'cloistered at Bogucharovo', as his father put it. For all the indifference to current events that he had shown to Pierre, he followed them closely, receiving a constant stream of books, and he was amazed to discover that when people came to see him or his father fresh from Petersburg, the very maelstrom of life, they were all miles behind him in their awareness of recent political developments at home and abroad, even though he had never left the countryside.

When not engaged in the management of his estates or voracious reading over a wide area, Prince Andrey had used the time to do a searching study of our last two military debâcles, and had also drafted a series of reforms in our service rules and regulations.

In the spring of 1809 Prince Andrey set off to visit the Ryazan estates, which now belonged to his son, with him as trustee.

Warmed by the spring sunshine, he drove along in his carriage, glancing at the first shoots of grass, the first leaves on the birch-trees and the first spring clouds looking fluffy and white as they floated through the bright blue sky. His mind was blank as he looked out on both sides, a picture of cheery unconcern.

They went over the crossing where he and Pierre had had their conversation a year before. They drove through a muddy village, past threshing floors and green winter crops, down and over a bridge still packed with snow, back uphill along a clay road gouged into hollows by the rain, past strips of stubble and a few bushes turning green, and then at last they drove into a wood with birch-trees on either side of the road. In the wood there was no wind and it was almost hot. The birches stood there with no sign of movement, spangled with their sticky green leaves, while lilac-coloured flowers and the first shoots of new green grass pushed up and peeped out from under last year's leaves. A scattering of baby firs stood out as coarse evergreens among the birches – a nasty reminder of winter. The horses neighed as they entered the forest, visibly perspiring.

Andrey's servant, Pyotr, said something to the coachman. He agreed, but his sympathy didn't seem to satisfy Pyotr, who turned on the box to face his master.

'Nice day, sir!' he said with a respectful smile.

'You what?'

'It's nice, isn't it, sir?'

'What *is* he talking about? . . . Oh, he must mean the spring,' thought Prince Andrey, glancing around. 'That's it. Everything's turning green . . . as early as this! The birch-trees, the wild cherries . . . even the alders are just on the turn. But not the oak, no sign there. Look, there's one.'

There at the roadside stood an oak-tree. It must have been ten times older than the birch-trees that made up the wood, ten times as thick and twice the height of any of them. That tree was enormous – it would have taken two men to join hands round its girth – with branches broken off it ages ago and its old, cracked bark all scarred and broken. There it stood among the beaming birches, with its great gnarled hands and fingers sprawling out awkwardly and unevenly, a truculent, sneering monster. He alone refused to submit to the charms of spring; he would not countenance either springtime or sunshine.

'Springtime, love and happiness!' this tree seemed to be saying. 'Aren't you fed up with it all, this stupid, senseless sham? It never changes, the same old trick! There *is* no springtime, sunshine or happiness. Just look at those dead fir-trees sitting there where they've been brought down, always the same every one of them, and look at me sticking out broken, peeling fingers wherever they care to grow – out of my back, out of my sides. That's how they've grown, and that's how I am, and I don't believe in any of your hopes and shams.'

Prince Andrey drove on through the forest, glancing back several times at the oak-tree as if he was expecting it to do something. Flowers and grass grew underneath it, but it just stood there among them, an ugly, awkward thing, stock-still and scowling.

'He's right, that tree, a thousand times right,' mused the prince. 'Other people, young people, they can keep that sham going, but he and I know what life is. Our lives are over and done with!' The tree had stirred up a host of new ideas in the prince's soul which held no hope, though their bitterness was sweet. On the journey there he seemed to have reconsidered his entire life and come right back to his first conclusion, which was as reassuring as it was devoid of hope – that he needn't bother with anything new, all he had to do was live out his life without doing any harm, free from worry and any kind of desire.

CHAPTER 2

As trustee of his son's Ryazan estates Prince Andrey needed to have a meeting with the local marshal of the nobility. Count Ilya Rostov was the marshal in question, and in mid-May Prince Andrey went to see him.

Spring was now at its hottest. The woodland was clothed in green, and everywhere was dusty and so hot that if you drove past any water you felt like going in for a swim.

Prince Andrey was in a miserable mood as he drove up the avenue towards the Rostovs' house at Otradnoye, mentally running through the bits of business that he would want to raise with the marshal. Through the trees on the right he heard happy female voices, and then he watched as a small crowd of young girls ran across his path. Out in front, dashing towards the coach came a black-haired, black-eyed girl, quite remarkably slender in her yellow print dress, with a white handkerchief on her head and stray locks of loose hair tumbling out of it. She was calling out, but once she saw a stranger she ran back laughing, without a glance in his direction.

For some reason Prince Andrey felt a sudden pang. It was such a lovely day, with sunshine and happiness on every hand, and here was this pretty slip of a girl who was oblivious to his existence and cared even less about it, and she was so pleased and happy with her own special life – a silly life, he had no doubt, but one that was merry and happy. 'What is she so glad about? What's in her mind? Not army regulations. Not Ryazan peasants and the rent they'll have to pay. What *is* in her mind, and why is she so happy?' Prince Andrey couldn't help wondering.

This year (1809) Count Ilya Rostov was living at Otradnoye exactly as he had always done, which meant entertaining virtually the whole province with hunting parties, theatricals, dinners and music. Always delighted to see a new guest, he gave Prince Andrey a warm welcome and almost forced him to stay the night.

Prince Andrey was bored during the day, left to the ministrations of an elderly host and hostess and some of the more notable guests amid the throng that filled the count's house in honour of an impending name-day. Several times Bolkonsky glanced across at Natasha, who never stopped laughing and enjoying herself with all the younger members of the company, and every time he wondered, 'What's in her mind? What is it that she is so glad about?'

That night, alone in a new place, he couldn't get to sleep. He read for a while, put out his candle and then lit it again. It was hot in his bedroom with the shutters closed on the inside. He felt angry with this stupid old man (his description of Count Rostov) who had detained him by claiming that the documents they needed were still in town, and he was annoyed with himself for having stayed.

Prince Andrey got out of bed and went over to open the window. The moment he pulled the shutters back, moonlight poured into the room as if it had been standing outside for ages waiting for this opportunity. He opened the window. The night was cool, still and bright. Just outside the window stood a row of pollarded trees, black on one side, gleaming with silver on the other. Beneath them there was a rambling kind of vegetation with lush, damp leaves and stems dappled with silver. Further away, beyond the silhouetted trees, some sort of sloping roof glistening with dew, and away to the right stood the rambling mass of a tall tree, with brilliant-white trunk and branches, and there above it was the moon, almost full, in a clear, almost starless spring sky. Prince Andrey leant out with his elbows on the window-ledge and fixed his gaze on that sky.

His room was on the middle floor; there were people in the room above, and they too were still awake. He could hear girls talking.

'Just once more,' said a female voice overhead, and Prince Andrey had no difficulty in recognizing it.

'Oh, when are you coming to bed?' came another voice.

'I'm not. I can't sleep. It's no use. Come on. Last time.'

The two female voices sang a musical line, the finale of some duet.

'Isn't it lovely! Anyway, it's time to go to sleep. Come on, that's it.'

'Oh, you go to sleep. I can't,' responded the first voice, now coming from somewhere nearer to the window. She must have been leaning right out because he could hear her dress rustling and even the sound of her breathing. Silence had descended and everything froze in the stillness of the moonlight and the shadows. Prince Andrey hardly dared to move for fear of giving himself away – not that he had intended any of this.

'Sonya! Sonya!' came the first voice again. 'How can you sleep? Come over here and look at this – it's gorgeous! Oh, it's just gorgeous! Sonya, wake up!' she said, almost with tears in her voice. 'This is the most gorgeous night there's ever been.'

Sonya made some grudging response.

'Oh, please come and look at this moon! . . . It's gorgeous! Come on. Darling, sweetheart, please come here. There you are, look at that!

Hey, if you rock back on your heels like this – watch – and squeeze
your knees together – hold them tight, as tight as you can – one big
squeeze and you could – fly away! . . . Like this – look!'

'Mind you don't fall out.'

He heard scuffling noises followed by Sonya's voice. She was not
pleased. 'Come on, it's past one o'clock.'

'Oh, you are a spoilsport. Go on then, you go to bed.'

Silence again, but Prince Andrey knew she was still sitting there.
Now and then he could still hear a soft rustling, and the occasional
sigh.

'Oh God! Oh God! What's it all about?' she cried suddenly. 'Oh
well, I suppose I'd better go to bed,' and the window banged as it
closed.

'Oblivious to my existence!' Prince Andrey had thought while he
was listening to her talk, inexplicably half-hoping and dreading that
she might say something about him. 'It's her again! It almost seems
planned!' he thought. And he was surprised to feel his spirit overwhelmed by a sudden surge of ideas and hopes that belonged to youth
and clashed with his whole way of life, so much so that his state of
mind was beyond all comprehension, and he went straight to bed and
fell asleep.

CHAPTER 3

Next morning Prince Andrey set off home before the ladies were up,
though not without taking leave of the count.

It was early June when, on his return journey, he drove once again
into the birch-wood where the gnarled oak-tree had made such a
strangely indelible impression on him. The harness-bells jingled in the
woodland with a more muffled sound than a month before, now that
everything was densely filled out and shady. The scattering of baby
firs, far from disrupting the overall beauty, blended their feathery
green shoots sweetly with the general mood.

All day it had been hot, with a storm brewing somewhere near by,
but only a few drops of rain from one small cloud had spattered the
dusty road and the lush greenery. The left-hand side of the forest was
in dark shade; the right-hand side glistened wet in the bright sunshine
and rippled in the breeze. Everything was in full bloom and the nightin-
gales were singing with sharp notes that echoed far and near.

'That oak-tree, it was somewhere near here in the forest. There was such an affinity between us,' he thought. 'But where was it?' As he wondered, he glanced across left and, unconsciously, without recognizing it, began to admire the very tree that he was looking for. The old oak was completely transformed, now spreading out a canopy of lush, dark foliage and stirring gently as it wallowed in the evening sunshine. No trace now of the gnarled fingers, the scars, the old sadness and misgivings. Succulent young leaves with no twigs had burst straight through the hard bark of a hundred years; it was almost incredible that this old fellow should have grown them.

'Oh yes, that's the one,' thought the prince, spontaneously overwhelmed by one of those surges of delight and renewal that belong to springtime. All the best times of his life came together sharply in his memory. The lofty sky at Austerlitz, the look of reproach on his dead wife's face, Pierre on the ferry and that young girl who had been so enthralled by the night's beauty, the night itself and the moon ... suddenly he remembered it all.

'No, life isn't over at thirty-one,' was his instant, final and irrevocable conclusion. 'It is not enough for me to know what is going on inside me. Everybody must know about it – Pierre, and that girl who wanted to fly up into the sky – they must all get to know me. My life must be lived for me but also for other people. They mustn't live like that girl, separated from me. My life must be reflected in them and they must live along with me, all of us together!'

Returning home from his travels, Prince Andrey decided he would go to Petersburg in the autumn, and he began dreaming up all sorts of reasons to justify the decision. A string of sensible, logical excuses for visiting the city, and even re-entering the service, was always at hand. Now, in fact, he could not begin to understand how he could ever have doubted the necessity of leading an active life, whereas a month before he would not have believed that the idea of ever leaving the country might occur to him. It now seemed absolutely clear that all his life experience would count for nothing if he failed to make practical use of it by starting to lead an active life again. He could not understand how such weak arguments could once have convinced him that he would be debasing himself if, after all he had learnt about life, he were to carry on believing in the possibility of doing something useful and the possibility of happiness and of love. Reason now spoke otherwise. After his journey to Ryazan Prince Andrey found country life tedious. His former interests had lost their appeal, and when he sat alone in his study he would often get to his feet, go over to the mirror and stare at his own face for minutes on end. Then he would turn to the portrait of Liza, looking out at him so sweetly and happily from her gilt frame with her Grecian hairstyle. Now, instead of saying those terrible words to her husband, she just looked at him with cheerful curiosity. Then he would clasp his hands behind his back and spend long minutes pacing up and down the room, frowning one moment and smiling the next, brooding on a series of strange ideas that lay beyond words, as secret as a hidden crime, ideas connected with Pierre, glory, the girl at the window, the oak-tree, the beauty of women, love – all the things that had changed the course of his life. And at moments like this if anyone came into his room his manner would be particularly abrupt, harsh, decisive, logical to a fault.

'Listen, my dear,' Princess Marya might say, coming in at just such a time, 'Little Nikolay can't go out for a walk today. It's too cold.'

'If it happened to be hot,' Andrey's tart response would be on such occasions, 'he would go out in his smock, but since it is cold you must dress him in warm clothing designed for that purpose. That's what happens when it's cold, not staying indoors when the child needs some fresh air.' He would pronounce all this with an exaggerated sense of logic, as if he needed to resolve his own inner illogicalities by secretly taking them out on someone else.

It was at times like this that Princess Marya thought how desiccated men's minds become with all that intellectual activity.

CHAPTER 4

Prince Andrey arrived in Petersburg in August 1809. This was the time when the young Speransky[1] was at the peak of his fame and his reforms were being carried through with the utmost vigour. It was in August that the Tsar was thrown out of his carriage, injured his leg and was laid up for three weeks at Peterhof, seeing Speransky and no one but Speransky every day. At that time the two famous decrees were being drafted – abolishing court ranks and making entry to two Civil Service grades (collegiate assessor and state councillor) dependent on examinations – and everyone was worried about them. Beyond that, the country's entire constitution was under review, with plans for radical reform of all government systems, legal, administrative and financial, from the State Council down to the district tribunals. Alexander had come to the throne with his head full of sketchy liberalism but now his dreams were taking shape and coming into practice. So far his efforts to implement them had been assisted by Czartoryski, Novosiltsev, Kochubey and Stroganov, a group of men that he jokingly referred to as his 'Public Welfare Committee'. They had recently been replaced at a stroke by two men: Speransky on the civilian side and Arakcheyev in charge of the military.

Soon after his arrival Prince Andrey, as a gentleman of the chamber, presented himself at court and at a levée. The Tsar met him on two occasions, but didn't favour him with a single word. Prince Andrey had long suspected that the Tsar had taken against him and disliked the look of him and his whole personality. The Tsar's look of cold aloofness bore out Prince Andrey's worst suspicions. Courtiers explained the Tsar's cold shoulder by saying that his Majesty was displeased at Bolkonsky's absence from active service since 1805.

'I know only too well that we have no control over our likes and dislikes,' thought Prince Andrey, 'so it's no use even thinking I might be able to hand over my note on army reform to the Tsar personally, but the thing will speak for itself.' He sent word of his note to an old field-marshal, a friend of his father's. The field-marshal gave him an appointment, received him with affection and promised to inform the Tsar. A few days later Prince Andrey received notice to call on the war minister, Count Arakcheyev.

At nine o'clock in the morning on the appointed day Prince Andrey entered Count Arakcheyev's reception-room.

Prince Andrey did not know Arakcheyev personally, never having met him, but everything he had heard had left him with little respect for this man.

'He is the war minister, someone trusted by the Tsar, and his personal qualities are his own business. He's been given the job of studying my note, so he must be the only person who can take it forward,' thought Prince Andrey, waiting his turn among the many important and unimportant persons in Count Arakcheyev's reception-room.

During his years of service, mostly as an adjutant, Prince Andrey had seen the waiting-rooms of many important people, and he was familiar with their distinctive characteristics. Count Arakcheyev's reception-room had its own special flavour. The faces of the unimportant people queuing for an audience with Count Arakcheyev betrayed nothing but obsequious humiliation, whereas the higher-ranking faces wore an expression of all-round embarrassment hiding behind a mask of unconcern and flippancy towards themselves, their situation and the person they were waiting to see. Some of them paced up and down deep in thought, others whispered and giggled, and Prince Andrey caught the nickname 'Mr Savage' and the words 'he's the boss and he can dish it out' applied to Count Arakcheyev. One general (a person of some significance), obviously offended at having to wait so long, sat with his legs crossed, smiling to himself with great disdain.

But each time the door opened, every face betrayed a single feeling – terror.

Prince Andrey asked the duty officer to mention his name again, but he was met with an amused look and told to wait his turn. After several persons had been ushered in and out of the minister's room by an adjutant, an officer with a particularly abject and panic-stricken face was admitted through the dreaded portal. His audience went on and on. Suddenly through the door came the roar of a thunderous voice, and the officer emerged white-faced and lips trembling, and walked off through the waiting-room with his head in his hands. It was then that Prince Andrey was ushered to the door and the adjutant whispered to him, 'Go to your right, over to the window.'

Prince Andrey walked into a rather ordinary, tidy study, and saw a man of about forty standing by a table, long in the body, with a long thin head and closely cropped hair. He was deeply wrinkled, his brows arched with a scowl over dull, greenish-hazel eyes, and a beaky red nose. Arakcheyev turned his head towards Prince Andrey without looking at him.

'What's your petition?' asked Arakcheyev.

'I'm . . . not petitioning, sir.' Prince Andrey spoke the words calmly. Arakcheyev's eyes turned to look at him.

'Sit down,' said Arakcheyev. 'Prince Bolkonsky?'

'I'm not petitioning, but his Majesty the Tsar has been kind enough to send your Excellency a memorandum submitted by me . . .'

'If you would kindly look here, my dear sir . . . I have read your note,' Arakcheyev interrupted, looking away again, any politeness not extending beyond his first words, his tone rising with impatience and contempt. 'You are proposing new army regulations? There are plenty of regulations already; the old ones get ignored. Nowadays everybody's drawing up new regulations. Writing's easier than doing something.'

'I come at his Majesty's will to learn from your Excellency how you propose to deal with my memorandum,' said Prince Andrey courteously.

'I have come to a decision about your memorandum and I have forwarded it to the committee. I do *not* approve it,' said Arakcheyev, getting to his feet and picking up a document from the desk. 'Here you are.' He handed it to Prince Andrey. Scrawled across the note was the following comment, badly spelt and with no punctuation or capital letters: 'unconvincing seeing its coppied from french army regulations and needlessly departs from our articles of war'.

'Which committee has the note been referred to?' asked Prince Andrey.

'The Army Regulations Committee, and I have recommended your Honour for membership. Unpaid.'

Prince Andrey smiled.

'I don't want any pay.'

'Unpaid membership,' repeated Arakcheyev. 'I bid you good day.' And he bawled out, 'Next!' as he bowed Prince Andrey out.

CHAPTER 5

While awaiting official confirmation of his committee membership, Prince Andrey looked up some old acquaintances, especially people he knew to be in power and therefore of possible use. Here in Petersburg he kept feeling as he had done before on the eve of a battle, when he was tormented by a restless curiosity and irresistibly attracted to higher spheres where the future was taking shape, a future that would determine the destiny of millions. Taking stock of everything – the angry irritability of the old guard, the caution of those who were in the know and the curiosity of those who were not, the fact that everyone was always in a hurry and anxious, the burgeoning of committees and commissions – not a day passed without him learning of a new one – he began to sense that now, in the year 1809, here in Petersburg, a momentous non-military campaign was beginning to build up, the commander-in-chief being a mysterious character he did not know, but someone he took to be a man of genius – Speransky.

And the whole reform movement, for all its vagueness, together with Speransky himself, the power behind it, captured his interest so keenly that his ideas on army regulations very soon began to take second place in his thinking.

Prince Andrey happened to be in a very favourable position for gaining a successful entrée into the broadest and highest circles of Petersburg society of the day. The reformist group welcomed him warmly and made every effort to attract him, firstly because he was considered clever and very well read, and secondly because he had already gained a reputation as a liberal by the freeing of his serfs. The miserable old guard welcomed him simply as his father's son, and expected him to sympathize with their condemnation of the reforms. The world of women that constituted *society* gave him a generous reception because he was a wealthy man of high rank and therefore a good match, as well as being a virtual newcomer in their midst surrounded by a romantic aura deriving from his brush with death and the tragic loss of his young wife. It was also the general opinion of all who knew him from days gone by that over the last five years he had changed a good deal for the better, softening his character and coming to full maturity. He was said to have lost his old affectation, pride and caustic cynicism, and to have gained the serenity that comes with years. He was talked about, a focus of interest, someone that people wanted to see.

The day after his interview with Count Arakcheyev, Prince Andrey happened to be at an evening reception at Count Kochubey's. He told him about his meeting with 'Mr Savage'. (This was how Kochubey referred to Arakcheyev, with the kind of sardonic amusement that Prince Andrey had observed in the war minister's waiting-room.)

'My dear fellow, even in this matter you can't do without Mikhail Mikhaylovich. He gets things done. I'll speak to him. He said he was coming this evening . . .'

'But what does Speransky have to do with army regulations?' asked Prince Andrey.

Kochubey shook his head with a smile, as if marvelling at Bolkonsky's naivety.

'He and I were talking about you the other day,' Kochubey continued, 'about your free tillers of the soil . . .'

'Oh, so you're the one, Prince, who freed the serfs?' said an old gentleman, a leftover from Catherine's day, turning towards Bolkonsky with great disdain.

'It was just a small estate and it wasn't profitable,' answered Bolkonsky, anxious not to annoy the old gentleman unnecessarily and therefore trying to minimize what he had done.

'You're afraid of being late,' said the old gentleman, looking at Kochubey.

'There's one thing I don't understand,' the old gentleman persisted. 'Who's going to farm the land if they are set free? It's easy to pass laws, but management is hard work. Same thing now – I ask you, Count, who will the department heads be when everybody has to take examinations?'

'Those who pass the examinations, I suppose,' answered Kochubey, crossing his legs and looking around the room.

'Look, what about Pryanichnikov, working for me, splendid man, salt of the earth, but he's sixty. Is he going to start taking examinations?'

'Yes, that's a difficult question, considering that education is not very widespread, but . . .'

Count Kochubey did not finish what he was saying. He got to his feet, took Prince Andrey by the arm and went over to meet a tall, fair-haired but balding man of about forty who had just come in. He had a large, open forehead and an elongated face of quite exceptional whiteness. He wore a dark-blue swallow-tail coat with a cross around his neck and a star on his left breast. It was Speransky. Prince Andrey knew who it was immediately, and he felt the kind of shock that comes upon people at critical moments in life. Whether it was respect, envy or anticipation he couldn't tell. Speransky's whole figure had a special character by which he could be immediately recognized. Nowhere in the society frequented by Prince Andrey had he seen such composure and self-assurance as in this man's clumsy and ungainly movements. Nowhere had he seen a glance that was so decisive and yet so gentle as in these half-closed, rather watery eyes. Never had he seen this kind of firmness in such a meaningless smile. Never had he heard a voice so delicate, smooth and soft. But what struck him most of all was the tender whiteness of the face, and especially the rather broad hands which were unusually puffy, soft and white. This kind of facial whiteness and softness Prince Andrey had seen only in soldiers who had spent a long time in hospital.

This was Speransky, secretary of state, confidential adviser to the Tsar, who had been at his side in Erfurt, and seen and spoken to Napoleon on more than one occasion. Speransky's eyes did not flit from one face to another as eyes do instinctively on first coming into a large company, and he was in no hurry to speak. When he did, he spoke softly, certain that he would be listened to, and looked only at the person to whom he was speaking.

Prince Andrey followed Speransky's every word and gesture with the closest attention. As people often do, particularly those who are highly critical of their fellow men, Prince Andrey, on meeting someone new – especially someone like Speransky whom he knew by reputation – always entertained the hope of discovering in him a perfect blend of human qualities.

Speransky apologized to Kochubey for not being able to come earlier, but he had been detained at the palace. He did not say that the Tsar had kept him. And this affectation of modesty was not lost on Prince Andrey. When Kochubey introduced Prince Andrey by name,

Speransky slowly transferred his eyes to Bolkonsky with the same smile on his face, and he gazed at him for a moment in silence.

'I am so pleased to meet you. I've heard about you. Everyone has,' he said.

Kochubey said a few words about Arakcheyev's reception of Bolkonsky. Speransky's smile broadened.

'The chairman of the Army Regulations Committee is a good friend of mine – Mr Magnitsky,' he said, carefully articulating every word and every syllable, 'and if you wish I can bring you together.' (He paused at the full stop.) 'I hope you may find him sympathetic and anxious to comply with anything reasonable.'

A small crowd had gathered around Speransky and the old gentleman who had been speaking about his clerk, Pryanichnikov, asked Speransky a question.

Without joining in the conversation Prince Andrey followed Speransky's every movement. Here was a man, thought Bolkonsky, who had only recently been a theology student, a nonentity, yet he now held in his hands, those puffy white hands, the very destiny of Russia. Prince Andrey was struck by the extraordinary disdain and composure with which Speransky responded to the old gentleman. He seemed to condescend from heights beyond measure. When the old man started talking too loud, Speransky smiled and said he couldn't judge the rights and wrongs of what the Tsar saw fit to do.

After chatting for a while in the general circle, Speransky got to his feet, went over to Prince Andrey and led him across the room. He obviously thought it best to take an interest in Bolkonsky.

'I've had no time to talk to you, Prince, because of the fascinating conversation that excellent old gentleman dragged me into,' he said, with a smile of gentle disdain, a smile that drew Prince Andrey and him together in recognizing the uselessness of the people he had just been talking to. This was flattering to Prince Andrey. 'I have known of you for some time, firstly from what you did with your serfs, an early example of something that needs to be followed, and, secondly, from your being one of those gentlemen of the chamber who did not consider themselves wronged by the new decree on court preferment that has been the cause of so much gossip and criticism.'

'You're quite right,' said Prince Andrey. 'My father didn't want me to take advantage of privilege. I began at the bottom.'

'Your father, a man of the old regime, clearly stands higher than those contemporaries of ours who condemn this measure, even though it is simply the embodiment of natural justice.'

'I imagine there is some basis, though, even for this kind of condemnation,' said Prince Andrey, trying to resist Speransky's influence, which he was beginning to notice. He was reluctant to agree with him in all respects; he wanted to put up a fight. Prince Andrey, whose speech was usually so easy and fluent, had some difficulty in expressing himself as he talked to Speransky. He was preoccupied with observing the personality of such a famous man.

'A basis of personal ambition perhaps.' Speransky spoke softly as he put in his word.

'And to some extent for the state,' said Prince Andrey.

'How do you mean?' said Speransky softly, looking down.

'I am an admirer of Montesquieu,'[2] said Prince Andrey. 'And his idea of honour as the principle of monarchy seems to me unchallengeable. I can see certain rights and privileges of the nobility as the means of maintaining that sentiment.'

The smile vanished from Speransky's white face, much to the advantage of his features. Prince Andrey's idea had probably struck him as particularly interesting.

'If you look at the question from that angle,' he began, speaking French with no little difficulty and enunciating even more elaborately than he had done in Russian, but still maintaining perfect composure. He said that honour (*l'honneur*) cannot be supported by privileges that get in the way of good service, that honour (*l'honneur*) is either a negative concept – the avoidance of reprehensible actions – or a known source of competition for commendation and rewards which are its fullest expression.

His arguments were concise, straightforward and clear. 'The institution that best underpins that honour, the source of proper competition, is an institution akin to the great Emperor Napoleon's Legion of Honour, which does not impede but actually promotes good government service, rather than class or court privilege.'

'I don't dispute that, but there's no denying that court privilege did the same thing,' said Prince Andrey. 'Every courtier considers himself bound to justify his position by worthy conduct.'

'But you decided not to take advantage of it, Prince,' said Speransky, his smile indicating that the argument was becoming embarrassing for his companion and he wanted to end it in the nicest way possible. 'If you will do me the honour of calling in next Wednesday, I shall have seen Magnitsky by then and I should have something to tell you that may be of interest, though it will also be a pleasure to continue our conversation.' At this he closed his eyes, bowed and left the drawing-room in the French manner, without saying goodbye, trying to slip away unnoticed.

CHAPTER 6

In the first weeks of his stay in Petersburg Prince Andrey sensed that the way of thinking he had worked out in his solitary life had been completely eclipsed by the petty concerns that now beset him in Petersburg.

When he got home in the evening he would jot down in his notebook four or five essential calls to be made or appointments at fixed times. The mechanical management of his life, arranging his day so as to get everywhere on time, absorbed most of his vital energy. He did nothing and thought nothing – he had no time to think. All he did was talk, and this he did successfully when dealing with ideas he had had time to think about before in the country.

He was sometimes annoyed to find himself saying the same thing on the same day to different audiences. But he kept himself so busy for days on end that he had no time to reflect that he wasn't actually doing anything. Speransky followed up their first meeting at Kochubey's with another long, confiding talk with Prince Andrey on Wednesday at his own home, where he received Bolkonsky alone and made a great impression on him.

Prince Andrey regarded the great bulk of humanity as contemptible and worthless creatures, and he was eager to find someone who embodied the ideal of perfection that he was striving for himself, so he was only too ready to believe that in Speransky he had found this ideal of a perfectly rational and virtuous man. Had Speransky come from the same background as Prince Andrey, with the same upbringing and moral code, Bolkonsky would soon have spotted his weak, human, unheroic sides, but he was so taken with this new, logical way of thinking that his understanding of the man remained incomplete. Besides this, Speransky, either because he was impressed by Prince Andrey's abilities or because he thought it prudent to recruit him as a supporter, toyed with him, flaunting his own dispassionate application of reason, and flattering him in honeyed tones bordering on the kind of arrogance that exists in a tacit assumption between two men that they are the only people capable of appreciating how stupid *everybody else* is and how wise and profound their own thoughts are.

In the course of their long conversation on Wednesday evening Speransky kept saying things like, 'With *us* anything that goes beyond the common run of established tradition is considered . . .', or (with a smile), 'But what *we* want is well-fed wolves with the sheep safe,' or '*They* can't get it into their heads . . .' – and always with a special inflection that said, 'The pair of us, you and I, we understand what *they* are and who *we* are.'

This first long conversation with Speransky served only to reinforce the feeling about him that Prince Andrey had had when they first met. He saw in him a thinking man of ruthless reason and enormous intellect, who had used nothing but his own energy and doggedness to gain power, which he was now using solely for the good of Russia. In Prince Andrey's eyes Speransky was just what he wanted to be – a man with a rational explanation for every aspect of human life, accepting reason as the only yardstick of validity and fully capable of applying this standard of reason to everything that came along. Everything came out so clear and straightforward in Speransky's exposition that Prince Andrey couldn't help agreeing with every word he said. If he raised objections and put up arguments it was only to assert his own independence and avoid being swamped by Speransky's ideas. Everything was as it should be, except for two things that disconcerted Prince Andrey. There was Speransky's cold, mirror-like stare, which blocked everything out of his soul, and also those flabby white hands of his, which Prince Andrey was drawn to magnetically, as people are to the hands of men who hold power. For some reason the mirror-like stare and the flabby hands irritated Prince Andrey. Another thing he disliked was Speransky's excessive contempt for other people, and then there was the changeability of his arguments when he was making a point. He would wield all possible weapons of thought other than metaphor, and when he changed from one to another it always seemed to Prince Andrey too much of a wrench. One moment he put himself forward as a practical man with no time for dreamy idealists, then he would take a satirical stance with ironical jeers at his opponents, before turning to ruthless logic or even soaring away into the realm of metaphysics. (This was one of his favourite weapons in any argument.) He would carry the question to the loftiest heights of metaphysical speculation, with digressions aimed at the defining of space, time and thought, and from here he would pluck a few arguments to crush his opponent, before swooping back down to terra firma with the original discussion. What did impress Prince Andrey as the great strength of Speransky's thinking was his totally unshakeable faith in the power and authority of the reasoning mind. One thing was clear: Speransky would never even think of acknowledging the idea that we all have thoughts beyond our power to express them, though this concept came naturally to Prince Andrey. Speransky never had any nagging doubts that everything he thought and believed in might be rubbish. And it was this quality of Speransky's mind that attracted Prince Andrey most of all.

In the first days of his acquaintance with Speransky, Prince Andrey regarded him with passionate admiration, not unlike the feelings he had once entertained for Napoleon. The fact that he was the son of a village priest, which was reason enough for foolish people to treat him with vulgar contempt, as many did, sneering at his humble origins, gave Prince Andrey a particular sensitivity in marshalling his own feelings towards Speransky, which were unconsciously strengthened in the process.

On the first evening that Bolkonsky spent with him they talked of the commission set up for the revision of the legal code, and Speransky told him sarcastically that the commission had now been sitting for a hundred and fifty years, was costing millions and had done nothing, except for Rosenkampf, who had stuck little labels on corresponding paragraphs of the different legal codes.

'And that's all the state gets for its millions!' he said. 'We want the senate to have new judicial powers, but we have no laws. That's why it's a sin for men like you, Prince, not to offer yourself for service.'

Prince Andrey observed that legal training was necessary for work like this, and he had none.

'Nobody else has. So what would you have us do? This amounts to a *circulus viciosus*, and it must be broken.'

Within a week Prince Andrey was on the Army Regulations Committee, and amazed to find himself also chairman of a sub-committee on the Commission for Revision of the Legal Code. At Speransky's request he took the first part of the Civil Code under current review, and used both the Napoleonic Code and the Institutes of Justinian to help revise the section on Personal Rights.

CHAPTER 7

A couple of years before this, at the beginning of 1808, Pierre had returned to Petersburg from visiting his estates, and had assumed (without seeking it) a prominent position among the freemasons of the city. He organized dinners and funerals in the lodges, recruited new members, took an active part in bringing different lodges together and in the acquisition of authentic charters. He paid for the building of temples, and did what he could to top up the collection of alms, since most of the members were stingy and late with their payments.

He stood virtually alone in maintaining the poorhouse built by their order in Petersburg.

Meanwhile his life went on as before, with the same kind of sudden passions and dissipation. He liked a good dinner and a lot to drink, and although he thought it was all immoral and degrading, he couldn't resist the temptations of the bachelor society in which he moved.

Although Pierre was thoroughly absorbed in his work and his life of pleasure, by the time a year had gone by he had begun to feel more and more as if the masonic ground on which he stood was giving way under his feet despite his best efforts to stand there ever more firmly. At the same time he felt that the more the ground gave way beneath his feet the more tightly he was trapped by it. When he had been working towards entry into the brotherhood he had felt like a man stepping confidently on to the flat surface of a bog. One foot down and in he went, so to convince himself he was still on firm ground he had stepped out with the other foot, sunk further in and got stuck in the mud. Now, despite himself, he was knee-deep in the bog and struggling.

Osip Bazdeyev was not in Petersburg. (He had recently withdrawn from all the activities of the Petersburg lodge and now stayed permanently in Moscow.) All his brother members in the lodge were people Pierre knew in everyday life, and it was difficult for him to see them as masonic brothers rather than Prince A or Ivan Vasilyevich B, most of them being, as he well knew from real-life encounters, weak and worthless personalities. For all their masonic aprons and secret signs he couldn't help seeing them in the uniforms and decorations they were working towards in ordinary life. Often after collecting the alms and counting no more than twenty or thirty roubles – and most of it only promised – from a dozen members, half of them as well off as he was, he thought of the masonic vow by which every brother undertook to give up all his worldly goods for his neighbour, and doubts stirred in his soul, though he tried not to dwell on them.

He divided all the brothers he knew into four categories. First, brothers who took no active part in the affairs of the lodges or humanity in general, but were obsessed with the secret mysteries of the order, questions about the threefold designation of God, or the three primordial elements – sulphur, mercury and salt – or the significance of the Square and all the figures on the Temple of Solomon. Pierre respected this category of masons, to which, by Pierre's reckoning, the elder brethren mainly belonged, including Osip Bazdeyev, though he didn't share their interests. His heart was not in the mystical side of freemasonry.

In the second category Pierre included himself and brothers like him who were seeking and wavering; they had not yet discovered in freemasonry a straight and clear path to follow, but still hoped to do so.

In the third category he included all the brothers (the majority of them) who saw nothing but external form and ceremonial in freemasonry, and who valued the disciplined execution of that external form without bothering too much about its content or meaning. Willarski and even the Grand Master of the lodge were two such people.

The fourth category was also rich in numbers, especially among the recent recruits to the brotherhood. These were men who, as far as Pierre could tell, believed in nothing and wanted nothing, having entered the brotherhood just to make contact with the numerous lodge-members who were young and wealthy, high-ranking or well connected and therefore powerful men.

Pierre began to feel dissatisfied with what he was doing. Freemasonry, at least in the form he knew here, sometimes seemed to rest on nothing but external show. He had no thoughts of doubting freemasonry itself, but he suspected that Russian freemasonry had taken a wrong turning and deviated from its source. So it was that at the end of the year he went abroad to devote himself to the higher mysteries of the order.

It was in the summer of 1808 that Pierre returned to Petersburg. From an exchange of letters between our freemasons and others abroad it was known that Bezukhov had managed to gain the confidence of many people in high positions abroad, that many mysteries had been revealed to him, he had been raised to a higher grade and was bringing back with him much that was of great value to the cause of freemasonry in Russia. The Petersburg freemasons all drove round to see him, doing their best to ingratiate themselves, and all of them sensed that he was holding something back and getting something ready.

They convened a solemn meeting of the lodge of the second degree, at which Pierre promised to convey what he had brought for the Petersburg brothers from the highest leaders of the order abroad. All the places were taken. After the usual ceremonies Pierre rose and launched into his speech.

'Dear brothers,' he began, blushing and stammering as he clutched his written address, 'it is not enough to observe our mysteries in the seclusion of the lodge – we must act, er . . . we need to act . . . We are slumbering, and we need to act.'

Pierre took up a large note-book and began to read from it.

'For the dissemination of pure truth and to ensure the triumph of virtue,' he read, 'we must get rid of prejudice, diffuse principles in harmony with the spirit of the times, undertake the education of young people, bind ourselves with indissoluble bonds to the wisest of men, boldly yet prudently overcome superstition, faithlessness and folly, and turn our devoted followers into men linked by a common cause and possessing power and authority.

'For the attainment of this goal we must ensure that virtue prevails over vice, we must exert ourselves so that honest men can obtain everlasting reward even in this world. But in these great undertakings we are severely hindered by existing political institutions. What is to be done in this situation? Are we to encourage revolution, overthrow everything, turn violence against violence? . . . No, we are very far from that. Any reform based on violence is to be deprecated, because it does little towards correction of evil while men remain as they are, and because wisdom has no need of violence.

'The whole plan of our order should be founded on the formation of strong character and virtue in men bound together in unity of conviction, a conviction that vice and folly should be suppressed in all places and by all means, while talent and virtue are fostered and deserving persons raised from the dust and united with our brotherhood. Only then shall our order achieve the power to tie the hands of the promoters of disorder without their feeling anything, and then control them without their being aware of it. In a word, our task is to create a form of supreme government which should spread across the world without affecting the responsibilities of citizenship, with all other governments continuing as before and doing anything they want as long as nothing hinders the great aim of our order, which is the triumph of virtue over vice. This has been the aim of Christianity itself. It has taught men to be wise and good, and to further their own advantage by following the precept and example of better and wiser men.

'When all was plunged in darkness, exhortation was, of course, sufficient in itself – the novelty of Truth gave her a special power – but in this day and age we need far more powerful methods. Nowadays a man guided by his senses needs to find virtue sensually attractive. Passion cannot be eradicated; all we can do is try to direct it towards a noble aim, so that everyone can satisfy his passions within the limits of virtue, and our order should provide the means to that end. As soon as we have a decent number of worthy men in every country, each of them educating two others, and all of them acting in concert, then nothing will be impossible for our order, which has already done so much in secret for the good of mankind.'

The speech not only made an impact, it produced uproar in the lodge. The majority of the brothers considered that the address smacked of Illuminism[3] and gave it a cold reception, much to Pierre's surprise. The Grand Master began to raise objections. Pierre began to expound his own views with more and more passion. It was a long time since a meeting had turned out to be as stormy as this one. There were two factions, one ranged against Pierre, accusing him of Illuminism, the other on his side. For the first time in his life Pierre was struck by the endless variety of men's minds, which guarantees that no truth is ever seen the same way by any two persons.

Even those members who seemed to be on his side interpreted him each in his own way, with provisos and amendments which he found unacceptable since his most urgent need was to transmit ideas to other people exactly as he saw them in his own mind.

At the end of the session, the Grand Master, sardonic and vindictive, rebuked Bezukhov for speaking with too much passion, remarking that he had been guided during the discussion not so much by love of virtue as by a taste for conflict.

Pierre refused to respond, except to inquire tersely whether his proposal would be accepted. They said no, it would not, so he left the lodge without waiting for the usual formalities and went home.

CHAPTER 8

Once again Pierre was afflicted by the kind of depression he so much dreaded. For three days after making his speech at the lodge he lay on a sofa at home, seeing no one and going nowhere. At this time he received a letter from his wife begging for a meeting; she wrote of her unhappiness on his account, and her wish to devote her whole life to him. At the end of the letter she informed him that she would be arriving in Petersburg from abroad in the next few days.

Shortly after reading the letter Pierre found his solitude invaded by one of the freemasons whom he least respected, and this man soon got round to the subject of Pierre's marriage, expressing his opinion by way of brotherly counsel that Pierre's harsh attitude to his wife was wrong, an infringement of the basic principles of freemasonry because he was withholding forgiveness from a penitent.

At the same time his mother-in-law, Prince Vasily's wife, sent a message begging him to call on her, if only for a few minutes, to discuss something very important. Pierre could see them ganging up against him in a plot to reunite him with his wife, and, given the state he was in, he found this not unpleasant. Nothing mattered now; nothing in life was of much consequence, and under the weight of his depression he set no store by his own freedom or relentless pursuit of further punishment for his wife.

'Nobody's in the right, nobody's in the wrong, so she can't be in the wrong,' he thought. If Pierre failed to give immediate consent to a reconciliation with his wife this was only because in his present despondency he was incapable of taking any action. If his wife had walked in at that moment he couldn't have sent her away. Compared with the weight on Pierre's mind, did it really matter whether he lived with her or not?

Without sending an answer to his wife or his mother-in-law, Pierre set off that same evening and drove down to Moscow to see Osip Bazdeyev.

This is what he wrote in his diary.

Moscow, 17 November
Just back from seeing my benefactor and hasten to write down all that transpired between us. Osip lives in poverty and for the last three years he has been suffering from a painful bladder condition. Not a moan or a word of complaint has been heard from him. From morning till late at night, except when he takes his frugal meals, he goes on with his academic work. He received me graciously and had me sit down on the bed where he was lying. I gave him the sign of the Knights of the East and Jerusalem and he did the same to me, and then he asked me with a gentle smile what I had learnt and acquired in the lodges of Prussia and Scotland. I told him the whole story as best I could, and I set out the principles for action that I had proposed in our Petersburg lodge, and told him about the hostile reception and the break between me and the brothers. At first he thought things over for quite some time and said nothing, then he gave me his own view of the whole matter, which enabled me to see things in a new light – everything that has happened and my way forward in the future. I was taken aback when he asked whether I remembered the threefold aim of the order: (1) the preservation and study of the mystery; (2) self-purification and self-improvement for its assimilation; and (3) the improvement of the human race through constant striving towards such purification. Which, he asked, is the first and greatest of these three aims? Obviously, self-improvement and self-purification. This is the only aim that we can always strive towards under any circumstances. But at the

same time this is the aim that calls for the greatest effort, and it follows that if we allow ourselves to be led astray by pride and lose sight of this aim we shall either strive towards a mystery we are not worthy to receive because of our impurity, or seek to reform the human race while setting an example of depravity and dissipation. Illuminism is a tarnished doctrine precisely because it has been seduced into social activity and has puffed itself up with pride. On this basis Osip condemned my speech and everything I have been doing. I agreed with him to the bottom of my heart. On the subject of my domestic affairs, he said to me, 'A mason's first duty, as I have told you, consists in self-perfection. But we often imagine that the best way to achieve this aim is to remove all the difficulties from our lives. Sir, it is the other way round,' he said. 'Only amidst the cares of this world can we achieve the three great aims of (1) self-knowledge, for a man can know himself only through comparison; (2) greater perfection, and this can be achieved only through struggle; and (3) the attainment of the greatest virtue – the love of death. Only the vicissitudes of life can show us all its vanity and promote our innate love of death, or rather rebirth into new life.' These words were particularly poignant coming from Osip, who never wearies of life in all his grievous physical pain. Yet he loves death, though he does not, for all the sublime purity of his inner self, feel properly prepared for it just yet. Then my benefactor explained to me the full meaning of the Great Square of Creation, and vouchsafed to me that the third and the seventh numbers are the basis of everything. He advised me not to withdraw from the society of the Petersburg brethren, to undertake only second-degree duties in the lodge and to do my best to distract the brothers from the seductions of pride and turn them towards the true path of self-knowledge and self-perfection. After this, for my own benefit, he advised me as a matter of first priority to watch myself carefully, and for this purpose he gave me a note-book, which I am now writing in with every intention of recording in it all my future actions.

Petersburg, 23 November

I am living with my wife again. My mother-in-law came round to see me in tears and told me that Hélène was here, begging to be listened to, that she was innocent, that she was miserable at my desertion of her, and much more besides. I knew that if I once gave in and saw her I wouldn't be able to hold out against her wishes. In my uncertainty, I didn't know who to turn to for help and advice. If only my benefactor had been here he would have told me what to do. I retired to my room, read through Osip's letters and recalled my conversations with him, all of which led me to the conclusion that I must not refuse a supplicant, I must extend a helping hand to anyone, especially someone close to me, and that I must bear my cross. But if I have forgiven her, this being the right thing to do, let my reunion with her have nothing but a spiritual purpose. This is my decision, and this is what I have written to Bazdeyev. I have told my wife I want her to forget the past, I have asked her forgiveness for any harm I might have done to her, and told her I have nothing to forgive her for. It gave me great joy to tell her that. She's not to know how hard it was for me to see her again. I have now installed myself on the top floor of this huge house, and I'm now experiencing a happy feeling of regeneration.

CHAPTER 9

At that time the high society people that came together at court and at the great balls broke down as always into several circles, each having a character of its own. The largest among them was the French circle of Count Rumyantsev and Caulaincourt which supported the Napoleonic alliance. Hélène had assumed a prominent position in this circle once she had become established in her husband's house in Petersburg. She received gentlemen from the French embassy and a great number of people famous for their wit and their polished manners who subscribed to that tendency.

Hélène had been at Erfurt for the famous meeting between the two Emperors and had returned well connected to all the notable pro-Napoleon figures in Europe. In Erfurt she had been brilliantly successful. Napoleon himself, seeing her at the theatre, had asked who she was and spoken well of her beauty. Her success as a beautiful and elegant woman came as no surprise to Pierre, for with the years she had become more beautiful than ever. What did surprise him was that over the last two years his wife had managed to gain a reputation as 'a charming woman with a mind as sharp as her beauty'. The celebrated Prince de Ligne wrote her letters eight pages long. Bilibin saved up his witticisms so as to issue them for the first time in the presence of Countess Bezukhov. To be received in her salon was to be certified as an intellectual. Young men read up on things before going to one of Hélène's soirées so they would have something to say in her salon, and embassy secretaries, even ambassadors, entrusted her with diplomatic secrets, all of which gave Hélène a certain authority. Pierre, knowing how stupid she really was, sometimes felt an odd mixture of bewilderment and alarm at her dinner-parties and soirées when the conversation turned to politics, poetry or philosophy. At soirées he

felt like a conjurer constantly expecting to have his tricks seen through
at any moment. But either because the successful management of a
salon like this depended on nothing but stupidity or because those who
were taken in found it all very amusing, the sham was never exposed
and the reputation of being 'a charming woman with a sharp mind'
stuck to Hélène Bezukhov so effectively that she could come out with
the most vulgar banalities and still find everyone hanging on her every
word and, more than that, discovering in what she said profound
meanings that she had never dreamt of.

Pierre was the ideal husband for such a brilliant society woman. He
was just an absent-minded eccentric, a *grand seigneur* of a husband
who kept out of the way and, far from lowering the high tone of her
drawing-room, acted as a useful foil to her by being his wife's exact
opposite in elegance and savoir-faire. In his wife's circle, which he found
utterly boring, Pierre's constant obsession with otherworldly considerations over the last two years, along with his genuine contempt for
everything else, gave him a special attitude of casual indifference and
all-round benevolence, the sort that cannot be acquired artificially and
therefore commands instant respect. He would walk into his wife's
drawing-room as if it was a theatre, he knew everybody there and he
treated them all with equal courtesy and equal indifference. From time
to time he would get into a conversation that sounded interesting and
then, without bothering to check whether or not there were any
embassy gentlemen present, he would bumble on, voicing opinions
which were sometimes quite embarrassing for that particular company.
But the general opinion of this eccentric man, married to 'the most
distinguished woman in Petersburg', was now so well established that
no one took his pronouncements at all seriously.

After Hélène's return from Erfurt, Boris Drubetskoy, now a great
success in the service, stood out among the many young men visiting
Hélène's house on a daily basis as the closest friend of the Bezukhov
household. Hélène called him her page and treated him like a child.
She smiled at him the way she smiled at everyone else, but sometimes
that smile grated on Pierre. Boris's attitude to Pierre was one of exaggerated dignity and lugubrious respect. This particular tone of respect
also worried Pierre. He had suffered so much humiliation three years
ago because of his wife, that now he was shielding himself against any
possibility of further humiliation, first by being a husband in name
only and then by not allowing himself to become suspicious.

'No, she's a blue-stocking now. She's renounced those old affairs for
good,' he said to himself. 'There's never been a case of a blue-stocking
having any passions of the heart,' he kept telling himself – a general

principle he had picked up somewhere and certainly believed in. But curiously enough the presence of Boris in his wife's drawing-room – and he was nearly always there – had a physical effect on Pierre. It tied him up in knots and destroyed all his instinctive freedom to move.

'Such a strange aversion,' thought Pierre, 'and at one time I used to be very fond of him.'

In society's eyes Pierre was a fine gentleman, something of a laughing stock, the purblind husband of a distinguished wife, a clever eccentric who never did anything but was quite harmless, a nice fellow with his heart in the right place. Meanwhile Pierre's spirit was undergoing a complex and difficult process of inner development that would be a revelation to him and lead to a host of spiritual doubts and delights.

CHAPTER 10

Pierre went on with his diary and this is what he wrote in it at that time:

24 November
Got up at eight, read the Scriptures, then went to my duties. (Following the advice of his benefactor Pierre was serving on a government committee.)

Came back for lunch and dined alone (countess had lots of guests I don't like), ate and drank with moderation, and spent the afternoon copying out passages for the brothers. In the evening I went down to the countess. Told a joke about B, and only realized I shouldn't have done when they all roared with laughter.

I go to my bed in a calm and happy frame of mind. Help me, O Lord, to walk in Thy ways: (1) to defeat anger through gentleness and deliberation; (2) to conquer lust through self-restraint and a sense of revulsion; (3) to withdraw from all worldly vanities without abandoning (a) government work, (b) family duties, (c) relations with friends, (d) care over finances.

27 November
Got up late after a long lie-in, complete idleness. O God, help me and strengthen me that I may walk in Thy ways. Read the Scriptures, but without any true feeling. Brother Urusov called – conversation about worldly vanity. Told me about the Tsar's new projects. I was on the point of coming out against them, but then remembered my principles and the words of my benefactor: a true mason should work hard for his country when his contribution is needed but watch quietly when not called upon.

My tongue is my enemy. More visitors: G, V and O – preparatory conversation about initiation of new brother. Duty of tyler laid upon me. Feel feeble and unworthy. Then talk of the full meaning of the seven pillars and steps of the Temple, the seven sciences, the seven virtues, the seven vices, the seven gifts of the Holy Spirit. Brother O was very eloquent. Initiation this evening. Newly decorated building added much to the splendour of the occasion. Boris Drubetskoy was admitted. I nominated him and acted as tyler. A strange feeling worried me all the time I was with him in the dark temple. I found myself hating him – am trying to control this feeling, without success. Which is why I would dearly like to save him from evil and lead him into the way of truth, but I couldn't get evil thoughts about him out of my own mind. It occurred to me that his only reason for joining the brotherhood was to make new contacts and curry favour with men in our lodge. He kept asking whether N or S were members of our lodge (which I couldn't answer) and he seems to me incapable of feeling any reverence for our holy order, because he is too preoccupied, and satisfied, with his own exterior to bother much about improving his spiritual being. Apart from all this I had no grounds for doubting him, though I did think he lacked sincerity and all the time we stood face to face in the dark temple I got the impression he was smiling and sneering at my words, and what I wanted to do was really stab him in his bare chest with the sword I was pointing at it. I wasn't at all fluent and I couldn't communicate my doubts as I should have done to the brothers and the Grand Master. O Great Architect of All Creation, help me find the true path that leads out of this maze of falsehood!

The next three pages of the diary were left blank, then it went on as follows:

Had a long and instructive private conversation with Brother V – he advised me to cleave to Brother A. Much was revealed to me, unworthy as I am. Adonai is the name of the Great Creator. Elohim is the name of the Ruler of All. The third name is the name unutterable, but its meaning is the *All*. These talks with Brother V strengthen and refresh me, and confirm me in the path of virtue. In his presence there is no room for doubt. I can see a clear distinction between the pathetic doctrines of worldly science and our sacred, universal teaching. Human science works by breaking everything down and kills everything off for the purpose of analysis. In the sacred science of our order all is one, everything is known by wholeness and vitality. The trinity – the three elements of matter – are sulphur, mercury and salt. Sulphur has the properties of oil and fire;

combined with salt it employs its fieriness to stimulate attraction, which draws in mercury, seizes it, retains it and combines with it to create various substances. Mercury is liquid and volatile, the spiritual essence – Christ, the Holy Ghost, Him.

3 December

Woke late, read the Scriptures, no feeling for it. Then went down and walked up and down in the big hall. Tried to meditate, but instead of that my imagination kept coming back to an incident that occurred four years ago. When Dolokhov met me after the duel in Moscow he said he hoped I was easy in my mind now, even though my wife had gone. At the time I didn't respond. Now I could remember every last detail of that meeting, and I replied to him mentally in the most vindictive and vitriolic words I could find. I pulled myself together and got rid of that idea, but only after I had caught myself livid with anger, and my remorse was inadequate. Then Boris Drubetskoy called with all sorts of stories to tell. The moment he arrived I felt unhappy about his visit and said something awful to him. He said something back. I lost my temper and gave him a terrible mouthful – some of it was very crude. He said nothing, and I came to my senses – but it was too late. My God, I just can't stand the man! But it's my vanity that causes all the trouble. I think I'm better than him, which makes me a lot worse, because he can condone my rudeness but I go on sneering at him. God grant that in his presence I may see my own vileness more clearly and act in such a way that even he may profit by it. Had a nap this afternoon, and as I was nodding off I distinctly heard a voice saying in my left ear, 'This is thy day.'

Dreamt I was walking along in the dark and suddenly there were dogs all round me, but I wasn't scared and I walked on. Suddenly a little dog sank its teeth in my left thigh and wouldn't let go. I tried to strangle it. But as soon as I yanked it away, another dog, a bigger one, leapt up and grabbed at my chest. I yanked this one away too, but then came a third one, bigger still, and he began to bite me. I lifted it off the ground, and the more I lifted the bigger and heavier it became. Then suddenly Brother A came up, took me by the arm, led me away and brought me to a building which you could only enter across a narrow plank. I stepped on to it but the plank bent and gave way, and then I found myself scrabbling up a wall which I just managed to get my hands on to. I made a huge effort and dragged my body up so that my legs dangled down on one side and my body on the other. I looked round and saw Brother A standing on the wall pointing to a great avenue and garden, and in the garden there was a huge, beautiful building. Then I woke up. O Lord, Great Architect of All Creation, help me to tear away these dogs, my evil passions, and especially the last one, the one that compounds the strength of all the others, and help me to enter into the temple of virtue which appeared to me as a vision in my dream.

7 December

Dreamt that Osip Bazdeyev was sitting in my house and I was very pleased to see him and wanted him to feel at home. But I kept chatting away constantly with other people, and all at once I realized this couldn't be to his liking and I wanted to get close to him and embrace him. But the moment I approached him I saw that his face had changed and had grown young, and he spoke to me softly, very softly, telling me something from the teachings of our order, but so softly that I couldn't hear. Then we all left the room, and something strange happened. We were either sitting or lying on the floor. He was telling me something. But I wanted to demonstrate what a sensitive person I was, so I wasn't listening. I began to picture the state of my own inner being, and the grace of God sanctifying me. And tears came into my eyes, and I was pleased to see he noticed. But he glanced at me in annoyance, jumped to his feet and broke off our conversation. I cowered away and asked him whether what he had been saying applied to me. He didn't answer, but he gave me a friendly look, and then all of a sudden we found ourselves in my bedroom, where there was a big double bed. He lay down on one edge, and I lay down too, burning with a desire to hug him. And in my dream he asked me, 'Tell me the truth, what is your worst temptation? Do you know what it is? I think you do.' Embarrassed by this question, I answered that idleness was my worst temptation. He shook his head in disbelief. And even more embarrassed, I told him that although I was living here with my wife, it was not like man and wife together. His response was that I had no right to deprive my wife of my embraces, and gave me to understand that this was my duty. I was just telling him that this was all very embarrassing when suddenly everything disappeared. And when I woke I had in my mind a biblical text: 'And the life was the light of men; and the light shineth in darkness; and the darkness comprehended it not.'

Osip Alexeyevich's face had looked young and radiant. That day I received a letter from my benefactor in which he wrote about responsibilities within marriage.

9 December

Dreamt again and woke up with a quaking heart. Dreamt I was in Moscow at home in the big sitting-room and Osip came in out of the drawing-room. I knew immediately that he had completed the process of regeneration, and I rushed to meet him. I kissed him on the face and hands, and he said, 'Do you not notice that my face is different?' I looked at him, still holding him in my arms, and I saw that his face was young, but he had no hair on his head and his features were quite different. And

I said to him, 'I would have recognized you if we had met by chance,' and as I said this I thought, 'Am I telling the truth?' Then suddenly I saw him lying there looking like a corpse, but he came round gradually and walked with me into the big study, holding a big book of drawing paper. I said, 'I drew all that.' And he answered by bowing his head. I opened the book, and all the pages were covered with splendid drawings. I knew that these pictures depicted the soul's erotic exploits with her lover. And I saw on those pages a wonderful drawing of a maiden with transparent clothes on her transparent body, soaring up into the clouds. And I knew that this maiden was nothing other than a representation of the Song of Songs. And as I looked at these pictures I felt I was doing something wrong but I couldn't tear myself away from them. Help me, Lord! Father, if it be Thy will to forsake me, then Thy will be done, but if I am the cause of these things, teach me what I am to do. I shall perish in my vileness if Thou shouldst utterly forsake me.

CHAPTER II

The Rostovs' financial position had not improved during the two years spent in the country.

Although Nikolay Rostov had stuck firmly to his resolution, and was still living on modest means in an obscure regiment, the way of life at Otradnoye, especially the way Mitenka ran things, was enough to ensure that their debts rose inexorably year by year. The only remedy that seemed at all obvious to the old count was for him to enter government service, and he had come to Petersburg now to look for a position, and at the same time, as he put it, to let his lassies have one last fling.

Shortly after the Rostovs' arrival in Petersburg, Berg proposed to Vera and his proposal was accepted. Although in Moscow the Rostovs were high society people, without ever realizing it, because their social standing could be taken for granted, in Petersburg their position was delicate and uncertain. In Petersburg they were provincials, too lowly for some people who had been their dinner-guests in Moscow and had never wondered then what level of society they belonged to.

The Rostovs were no less hospitable in Petersburg than they had been in Moscow; and a wide variety of people would foregather at their house for supper – there might be the odd country neighbour, an elderly gentleman with daughters but not much money, and an old maid-of-honour, Madame Peronsky, Pierre Bezukhov, anyone down to the son of their district postmaster, who was working in the city. Among the first of the men to become regular visitors at the Rostovs' house in Petersburg, you might say family friends, were Boris, Pierre, who had bumped into the old count in the street and been dragooned into coming, and also Berg, who now spent days on end with the Rostovs, fussing round Vera, the elder of the two young countesses, in the manner of a young man working himself up to make a proposal.

Berg had gone about flaunting his right arm, which had been wounded at Austerlitz, and brandishing a superfluous sword in his left hand – all to good effect. He had told his story to everybody with such conviction and authority that they all came to believe in his action as something portentous and very worthy – and Berg had received two decorations for Austerlitz.

He had also managed to distinguish himself in the Finnish campaign.[4] He had picked up a piece of shrapnel from the shell that had killed an adjutant close to the commander-in-chief and had taken it to the commander. Just as after Austerlitz, he went on and on about this incident and spoke again with such conviction that people ended up believing this was another task that had needed to be done – and Berg received two more decorations. By 1809 he was a captain in the guards with a chest full of medals, and he held one or two very lucrative posts in Petersburg.

The odd sceptic may have smiled at the mention of Berg's merits but it was not to be denied that Berg was a conscientious and gallant officer in good odour with the authorities, and a modest, good-living young man with a brilliant career ahead of him as well as a solid position in society.

Four years before, Berg had pointed out Vera Rostov to a German comrade he had met in the stalls of a Moscow theatre and said to him in German, 'She's going to be my wife.' That was the moment he had made up his mind to marry her. Now in Petersburg, after taking stock of the Rostovs' position and his own, he had decided the time had come to propose.

Berg's proposal was received at first with a reluctance that hardly flattered him. At first it seemed most unusual that the son of an obscure Livonian gentleman should ask for the hand of a Countess Rostov. But Berg's greatest quality was a kind of self-regard founded on such naivety and good will that the Rostovs came round to thinking it must be a good idea because he was completely convinced it was a good idea, in fact a very good idea indeed. Besides that, the Rostovs were in financial trouble which the suitor could hardly be unaware of, and the main thing was that Vera was now twenty-four years old and although she was undeniably good-looking and a sensible young woman who had been taken out everywhere no one had yet made a proposal. So consent was given.

'It's like this,' Berg said to a comrade, whom he described as a friend because he knew that everybody had friends, 'It's like this – I've weighed things up and I wouldn't be getting married if I hadn't given it a lot of thought, or if there had been anything wrong with it. But as things stand Papa and Mamma are reasonably secure – I've given them the income from that Baltic estate – and I can support a wife in Petersburg. I'm pretty careful, and with my pay and whatever she brings we can get along nicely. I'm not marrying for money – I think that's uncouth – but a wife ought to make her contribution and a husband his. I have my service career; she has good contacts and some small means. That's something nowadays, isn't it? But the thing is this: she's a lovely respectable girl, and she's in love with me . . .'

Berg blushed and smiled.

'And I love her because she has a nice personality and a lot of good sense. That other sister of hers, though – same family name but she's completely different, a horrible personality and she's not all that bright, you know what I mean . . . But my fiancée . . . You must come and see us. Come and have . . .' Berg went on. He was about to say 'dinner', but on second thoughts he said 'a cup of tea', and with a curl of his tongue he blew a tiny smoke ring, the very emblem of his dreams of happiness.

The parents' early reluctance to accept Berg's proposal had been followed by the usual celebrations and rejoicing, but the rejoicing was false and forced. Not a little discomfort and embarrassment was apparent in the attitude of the relatives towards this marriage. They seemed to feel guilty for not having given Vera enough affection and now being all too ready to get her off their hands. The old count was more disconcerted than anyone. Perhaps he couldn't have put his finger on what made him feel like that, but it had everything to do with his financial difficulties. He had no idea of what he was worth, how much he owed, or what he might be able to provide for Vera by way of a dowry. Both of his daughters at birth had been assigned an estate with three hundred serfs. But one of these had been sold, and the other mortgaged with the interest payments so far behind that it would have to be sold too, so she couldn't have this estate. And there wasn't any money.

Berg had been engaged for more than a month, and the wedding was only a week away, but still the count couldn't decide about the dowry, and he hadn't discussed it with his wife. Should he give Vera the Ryazan estate? Or sell off some forest-land? Or borrow on a bill of exchange?

Early one morning only a day or two before the wedding Berg walked into the count's study, smiled his nicest smile and politely asked his father-in-law to let him know what the Countess Vera was going to be given. The count was so taken aback by this long-expected inquiry that he just blurted out the first thing that came into his head.

'I like that. You're thinking ahead . . . Yes, I like it. You'll be well satisfied . . .'

He clapped Berg on the shoulder and got to his feet, with the conversation, he hoped, at an end. But Berg, still sweetly smiling, announced that if he didn't know for certain what Vera was being given, and didn't get some of it in advance, he would be obliged to call off the marriage.

'Look at it this way, Count, if I allowed myself to marry now with no definite security for the maintenance of my wife, that would be most irresponsible.'

The conversation ended when the count, anxious to demonstrate his generosity and avoid any more requests, said he would give him a note of hand for eighty thousand. Berg gave a pleasant smile, kissed him on the shoulder and said how grateful he was, but he couldn't make arrangements for his new life without getting thirty thousand in cash. 'Well, let's say twenty thousand at least, Count,' he added, 'plus a note for the other sixty thousand.'

'Yes, yes, very good,' babbled the count. 'Now you'll have to excuse me, dear boy. I'll let you have the twenty thousand – and a note for eighty thousand as well. So that's all right. Kiss me.'

CHAPTER 12

Natasha was now sixteen, and it was the year 1809, the year she had counted forward to on her fingers with Boris after they had kissed four years ago. She hadn't seen him since that day. When Boris's name came up she would speak about him quite openly to Sonya and her mother, as if what had passed between them was over and done with, a bit of childish nonsense long-forgotten not worth talking about. But in the depths of her soul she was still worried – was her engagement to Boris just a joke or was it a solemn and binding promise?

Ever since Boris had left Moscow in 1805 to go into the army he hadn't seen any of the Rostovs. He had been in Moscow several times and had sometimes passed quite close to Otradnoye, but he had never once dropped in on them.

Natasha sometimes suspected that he was avoiding her, and her suspicions were borne out by the lugubrious tone in which he was referred to by her elders.

'Old friends are soon forgotten nowadays,' the countess would say just after Boris's name had been mentioned.

Anna Mikhaylovna had also been a less frequent visitor of late. There was now a marked dignity in her bearing and she missed no opportunity to refer with gratitude but no little triumph to her son's abilities and the brilliant career he was cutting out for himself. When the Rostovs arrived in Petersburg, Boris did call to see them.

It was not without emotion that he drove to their house. Those memories of Natasha were Boris's most poetic memories. But at the same time, he was calling on them absolutely determined to make it clear to her and her relatives that the childish vows between Natasha and him could not be binding on either of them. Because of his closeness to Countess Bezukhov he now had a brilliant position in society, and he had a brilliant position in the service because of the patronage of a bigwig he was well in with, and now he was beginning to work on the possibility of marrying one of the richest heiresses in Petersburg, plans which might easily come to fruition. When Boris came into the Rostovs' drawing-room, Natasha was up in her room. Hearing of his arrival she almost ran down to the drawing-room, red in the face and radiant with a more than friendly smile.

Boris was still thinking of the little Natasha he had known four years ago dressed in a short frock, with brilliant black eyes darting out from under her curls, all wild whoops and girlish giggles, so when he saw a totally different Natasha coming into the room he was quite taken aback, and the surprise and delight showed on his face. Natasha was thrilled to see him looking like that.

'Well, do you recognize your little playmate and sweetheart?' said the countess. Boris kissed Natasha's hand and said he was surprised how much she had changed.

'You've grown so pretty!'

'I should hope so!' said the glint in Natasha's eyes.

'Does Papa look any older?' was what she asked.

Natasha sat there in silence, taking no part in the conversation between Boris and her mother but subjecting her childhood suitor to the minutest scrutiny. He could feel those eager, tender eyes boring into him, and once or twice he glanced across in her direction.

Boris's uniform, his spurs, his tie, his hairstyle – everything about him was the last word in fashion and absolutely *comme il faut*. Natasha took this in at a glance. He was sitting in a chair sideways on to the countess, his right hand smoothing the immaculate, close-fitting glove on his left hand, and he pursed his lips with marked refinement as he talked about the doings of Petersburg high society, with the occasional sweet but dismissive reference to the old days in Moscow and old Moscow acquaintances. Natasha sensed the deliberation with which he dropped one or two highly aristocratic names, alluding to the ambassador's ball, which he had attended, and invitations from So-and-so and What's-his-name.

Natasha sat there the whole time and never said a word, glancing across at him furtively. Boris became increasingly disconcerted and embarrassed under her gaze. He began to look round more frequently at Natasha, and his speech kept breaking down. He stayed no more than ten minutes before getting up to take his leave. Those quizzical, challenging and slightly mocking eyes had never left him. After this first visit Boris told himself that Natasha was as attractive as ever, but he mustn't give in to this feeling, because to marry her – a girl with virtually no fortune – would be the ruin of his career, and it would be dishonourable to pursue their old relationship with no intention of marriage. Boris made up his mind to avoid Natasha, but despite this decision he called again a few days later, and then he became a regular visitor, often spending whole days at the Rostovs'. He couldn't get it out of his mind that he ought to have things out with Natasha and tell her to forget the past – tell her that in spite of everything . . . she could never be his wife because he had no fortune and they would never let her marry him. But he could never quite bring himself to do it – the whole thing was too embarrassing. He became more and more involved with each passing day. Natasha – as far as her mother and Sonya could judge – seemed to be still in love with Boris. She sang him her favourite songs, showed him her album, got him to write things in it, stopped him talking about the old days because the new days were so wonderful, and every time he went back home in a fog of doubt not having said what he had meant to say, not knowing what he was doing, why he had come or how it would all end. He stopped visiting Hélène, received reproachful notes from her every day, and still spent days on end at the Rostovs'.

CHAPTER 13

One night the old countess was kneeling on the carpet in her bed-jacket, with her false curls discarded and a single thin wisp of hair escaping from under her white cotton night-cap, bowing to the floor and sighing and moaning as she said her prayers before going to bed, when the door creaked and in ran Natasha, also in a bed-jacket, with bare legs and slippers on her feet, and her hair done up in curl papers. The countess looked round with a frown on her face. She was saying her last prayer, 'And if this couch should be my bier . . .' Her devotional mood had been dispelled. Natasha, excited and red in the face, stopped in her tracks when she saw her mother praying and crouched down, automatically biting her tongue in self-reproach. Seeing that her mother had not finished praying, she tiptoed quickly over to the bed, slid one little foot against the other and pushed off her slippers before jumping up on to that very couch that the countess dreaded becoming her bier. It was a high feather-bedded couch, with five pillows ascending in size. Natasha slipped into bed, sank down into the feather mattress, turned over on one side and began snuggling down under the quilt, tucking herself in, bringing her knees up under her chin and kicking out with a tiny giggle as she alternately hid her face under the quilt and peeped out at her mother. The countess finished her prayers and came to bed looking all stern, but when she saw Natasha with her head under the covers she smiled her sweet, feeble smile.

'Now come on,' said her mother.

'Mamma, we can have a little talk, can't we?' said Natasha. 'Come on, one kiss under the chin, one more, and that's it.' And she put her arms round her mother's neck and kissed her under the chin. Natasha's general attitude to her mother could be quite brusque, but she behaved with such delicacy and sensitivity that whenever she put her arms round her mother she always did it without hurting her or doing anything unpleasant or embarrassing.

'Well, what is it this time?' asked her mother, settling down on the pillows and waiting for Natasha, who had been rolling backwards and forwards, to lie down next to her under the clothes, put her arms out and assume a serious attitude.

Natasha's late-night visits before the count came home from the club were a source of the sweetest pleasure for mother and daughter.

'Come on, what is it this time? And listen, I want to talk to you . . .' Natasha put her hand over her mother's mouth.

'About Boris . . . Yes, I know,' she said seriously. 'That's why I've come. Don't tell me – I know. No, do.' She took her hand away. 'Tell me, Mamma! He's a nice boy, isn't he?'

'Natasha, you're sixteen years old! I was married at your age. You say Boris is a nice boy. Yes, he is, very nice, and I love him like a son. But what do you want? . . . What do you think? I can see you've turned his head . . .'

She looked round at her daughter as she spoke. Natasha was lying there looking straight ahead at one of the mahogany sphinxes carved on the bedposts, so the countess could see her only in profile. Her face struck the countess as remarkably serious and full of concentration.

Natasha was listening, and her mind was working.

'Well?' she said.

'You've completely turned his head – but why? What do you want him to do? You know you can't marry him.'

'Why not?' said Natasha, with no change in her attitude.

'Because he's young, he's poor, he's related to you . . . oh, because you don't love him.'

'How do you know?'

'I just do. It's not right, my love.'

'But what if I want to . . . ?' Natasha began.

'Don't be silly,' said the countess.

'No, what if I want to . . . ?'

'Natasha, I'm being serious . . .'

Natasha didn't let her go on. She pulled the countess's large hand over and kissed it on the back and on the palm, then she turned it over again and started kissing it all over, one knuckle after another, and the spaces in between, then back to a knuckle, and as she did so she whispered, 'January, February, March, April, May.'

'Come on, Mamma, say something. Tell me,' she said, looking round at her mother, who was gazing at her daughter so fondly that she seemed to have forgotten what she was going to say.

'It won't do, darling. People are not going to understand your childish feelings for each other, and when they see you two so close together it could do you a lot of harm in the eyes of other young men who visit us, and anyway, what's more important, it's making him miserable for no good reason. He might have found someone who suits him, some girl with money, and now he's going crazy.'

'What do you mean, going crazy?' repeated Natasha.

'I'll tell you what happened to me. I used to have a cousin . . .'

'I know who you mean – Kirila Matveich. He's an old man.'

'Well he didn't used to be. But listen, Natasha, I'll have a word with Boris. He mustn't come here as often as he does . . .'

'Why mustn't he, if that's what he wants?'

'Because I know it won't lead anywhere.'

'How do you know? No, Mamma, please don't have a word with him. Don't you dare. It's so stupid!' said Natasha, in the tone of one being robbed of her property. 'Look, I'm not going to marry him, so let him come, as long as we both enjoy it.' Natasha looked at her mother, smiling. 'No marriage, but carry on as before,' said she, reinforcing her message.

'What do you mean, darling?'

'Just let's carry on as before. Yes, it's important that I never marry him, but . . . just let things carry on.'

'Carry on!' repeated the countess, and she surprised Natasha by bursting out laughing. It was well meant, the laughter of an old lady, and it made her shake from head to foot.

'Oh, please don't laugh,' cried Natasha. 'Look, the bed's shaking. You're just like me, we're both gigglers . . . Stop it . . .' She snatched her mother's hands, took one and kissed the knuckle on her little finger – that was June – and then she went on to the other one with July and August . . . 'Mamma, does he really love me? What do you think? Did men love you like this? And he's so nice, he really is nice! Though he's not really my type – he's a bit . . . sort of narrow, like a clock on the wall . . . Do you know what I mean? . . . Narrow, you know, all grey and pale . . .'

'You do say some silly things,' said the countess.

Natasha persisted. 'Don't you understand? Nikolay would. Now, take Bezukhov – he's blue, dark blue with a bit of red, and his shape is square.'

'You flirt with him, too,' said the countess with a laugh.

'No, I don't. He's a freemason. I've just found out. He's a very nice man – dark blue with some red. How can I explain it?'

'Little Countess!' came the count's voice through the door, 'are you still up?'

Natasha snatched up her slippers and skipped off to her room in her bare feet. But she couldn't get to sleep. She kept worrying about no one ever being able to understand everything that she understood, everything deep inside her.

'What about Sonya?' she wondered, looking at her friend sleeping there, curled up like a kitten with her great mass of hair. 'No, she wouldn't. She's too good. She's in love with dear Nikolay, and she's

not interested in anything else. Mamma – even she doesn't understand.
I'm amazingly clever . . . Oh, she's such a charming girl,' she went on,
speaking about herself in the third person and imagining that it was
some very clever man, the cleverest and best of all men, who was
talking about her . . . 'This girl has everything, absolutely everything,'
he continued. 'She's incredibly clever, so charming and so pretty –
she's out of this world, she moves so well, she can swim and ride like
nobody else, and that voice! – you've got to admit, that's a wonderful
voice!' She intoned a bit of her favourite music from a Cherubini
opera, flopped down on the bed, laughed out loud at the delightful
thought that she would soon be asleep, called across to Dunyasha to
blow out the candle, and before Dunyasha had left the room she was
in another world, the happier world of dreamland, where everything
was as light and beautiful as it was in the real world, only better
because it was all different.

Next day the countess sent for Boris and had a word with him, and
after that he gave up going to the Rostovs'.

CHAPTER 14

On New Year's Eve 1809 an old grandee who had been prominent in
Catherine's time gave a ball and a midnight supper. The Tsar and the
diplomatic corps were due to attend.

The well-known mansion of this grandee on the English Embankment was ablaze with innumerable lights. Policemen were deployed at
the brightly lit, red-carpeted entrance – not just constables but a police
chief and dozens of officers. As one carriage drove away another rolled
up, with grooms in red livery and grooms in plumed hats. Men in
uniforms with stars and ribbons emerged from the carriages, steps
clanged down and ladies in satin and ermine stepped out daintily and
hurried indoors passing noiselessly over the red baize.

Almost every time a new carriage drove up a whisper ran through
the crowd and caps were doffed. 'Is it the Emperor? . . . No, it's
only a minister . . . a prince . . . an ambassador . . . Look at those
plumes! . . .' came various voices in the crowd. One man better dressed
than anyone else seemed to know everyone, and as the dignitaries of
the day arrived he would say who they were.

A third of the guests were already there at the ball, but the Rostovs,
who had been invited, were still getting ready.

There had been many a discussion and much fuss in the Rostov family ahead of this ball, and much worrying that they might not be invited, that the dresses wouldn't be ready in time, and nothing would go right.

The Rostovs were to be accompanied to the ball by Marya Peronsky, friend and relative of the countess, a thin lady with a sallow complexion who, as maid-of-honour at the court of the Dowager Empress, was needed by the provincial Rostovs to guide them around the higher circles of Petersburg society.

The Rostovs were due to pick her up by ten o'clock at the Tavrichesky Garden, but it was now five to ten and the young ladies were still not ready.

Natasha was going to her first grand ball. She had got up that morning at eight o'clock, and spent the whole day in feverish worry and a whirl of activity. All her energies had been directed since early morning to the single aim of getting herself, her mother and Sonya turned out as nicely as they could possibly be. Sonya and her mother had placed themselves entirely in her hands. The countess was to wear a burgundy velvet dress, her two daughters white tulle dresses over pink silk slips with roses on their bodices. Hairstyles would be *à la grecque*.

The basic essentials were out of the way, everybody's feet, arms, necks and ears having been scrupulously scrubbed, powdered and perfumed in readiness for the ball. Legs and feet were adorned with open-work silk stockings and white satin shoes; everyone's hair was almost done. Sonya was at the stage of finishing touches, as was the countess, but Natasha had spent so much time looking after everybody else that she was now running late. She was still sitting at the mirror with a housecoat over her thin little shoulders. Sonya stood in the middle of the room, dressed and ready, fastening down one last recalcitrant ribbon and hurting her tiny finger as she pushed a pin squeakily through the silk.

'No, Sonya, not like that!' said Natasha, looking round, both hands clutching her hair, which the maid who was arranging it wasn't quick enough to let go of. 'It doesn't go like that. Come here.' Sonya squatted down. Natasha adjusted the ribbon.

'Please, miss, you mustn't move like that,' said the maid, still holding Natasha's hair.

'Oh, my goodness! Can't you wait a minute? There you are, Sonya.'

'Are you nearly ready?' came the countess's voice. 'It's nearly ten.'

'Yes, yes, two minutes . . . Are you ready, Mamma?'

'Only my cap to pin on.'

'Don't do it without me,' shouted Natasha. 'You don't know how!'

'But it's ten o'clock.'

They had agreed on half-past ten as a good time to arrive at the ball, and here was Natasha still not dressed – and they had to go via the Tavrichesky Garden.

With her hair done at last, Natasha, wearing her mother's dressing-jacket and a short petticoat, which made her dancing-shoes very noticeable, ran over to Sonya, examined her from head to foot, and then ran across to her mother. Turning her mother's head round, she pinned the cap on, gave her a quick peck on her grey hair and ran back to the maids, who were still taking the skirt up.

Natasha's skirt was the problem: it had been too long. Two maids were finishing the hem, hurriedly biting off the threads. A third one, with pins sticking out between teeth and lips, was running back and forwards between the countess and Sonya; a fourth was holding up the whole tulle creation in her arms.

'Mavrushka, darling, do please hurry!'

'Pass me that thimble, miss.'

'How much longer?' said the count from the doorway, as he started into the room. 'Get your perfume on. Madame Peronsky must be fed up with waiting.'

'Ready, miss,' said the maid, holding up the shortened tulle skirt between finger and thumb, blowing something off it, and shaking it out to show off the pure airy fluffiness of what she held in her hands.

Natasha began to get into the dress.

'In a minute, in a minute! Don't come in, Papa!' she shouted to her father as he opened the door, her face drowned in a sea of tulle. Sonya banged the door to. A moment later the count was allowed in. He was dressed in his blue swallowtail coat, long stockings and light shoes, all nicely perfumed and pomaded.

'Oh, Papa, you do look nice! You really do,' said Natasha, standing in the middle of the room, smoothing out the folds of her tulle.

'Just a minute, miss, if you don't mind . . .' said one of the maids, lifting the skirt and switching the pins from one corner of her mouth to the other with her tongue.

'You can say what you like!' cried Sonya in despairing tones as she gazed at Natasha's dress. 'You can say what you like – it's still too long!'

Natasha stepped back a little to inspect herself in the long glass. The skirt did seem too long.

'Lord bless 'e, ma'am, it bain't be too long at all,' said Mavrushka, scrambling along on her knees after her young lady.

'Well, if it is, we can tack it up. It'll only take a minute,' said

Dunyasha, getting a grip on things. And pulling a needle from the cloth on her chest she set to work again on the floor.

At this point the countess, arrayed in cap and velvet gown, walked diffidently back into the room, stepping softly.

'Oh, I say! Look at this beautiful woman of mine!' cried the count. 'She's prettier than all of you!' He made as if to embrace her, but she drew back with a blush on her face to avoid getting crumpled.

'Mamma, your cap should be at an angle,' said Natasha. 'Let me do it again,' and she darted forward. The maids turning up her skirt were not ready for a lunge like this and a piece of tulle was torn off.

'Mercy on us, what's happened? Hey, it wasn't my fault . . .'

'It's all right, I can run it up, it won't show,' said Dunyasha.

'Oh, my beauty, my little queen!' said the old nurse coming in at the doorway. 'And little Sonya, too. Oh, you beautiful girls!'

It was a quarter past ten when at last they were seated in their carriage and able to drive off. And they still had to go round by the Tavrichesky Garden. Madame Peronsky was there, ready and waiting. For all her age and plainness, she had been undergoing the same thing as the Rostovs, but without all the fluster, because it was all a matter of routine to her. Her ageing and unattractive body had been subjected to a similar process of scrubbing and scenting and powdering, she had been washed no less scrupulously behind her ears, and like the Rostovs' nurse, her old maid had gone into raptures over her mistress's outfit when she had come into the drawing-room dressed in her yellow gown adorned with the royal monogram. Madame Peronsky waxed lyrical about the Rostovs in their finery, and they did likewise about her fine dress and remarkable taste. Then, at eleven o'clock, fussing a good deal over their coiffures and their ballgowns, they seated themselves in the carriages and drove off.

CHAPTER 15

Natasha had not had a minute to herself all day, and it had never occurred to her to wonder what lay ahead.

In the damp, chill air and the semi-dark confines of the swaying carriage she now began to imagine for the first time what was in store for her there, at the ball, in the brightly lit halls – the music, the flowers, the dancing, the Tsar, all the brilliant young people of Petersburg. The prospect before her was so wonderful she couldn't really believe it would come true: it was all so out of keeping with the chilly darkness of the cramped carriage. Everything that lay ahead began to dawn on her only when she had walked across the red cloth, entered the vestibule, taken off her fur-coat and begun to walk up the brilliantly lit staircase with Sonya at her side, her mother just behind and flowers on all sides. It was then that she remembered how to behave on such an occasion, and she did her best to assume the majestic manner that she considered essential for a girl to adopt at a ball. But as luck would have it she was too dazzled to see anything clearly, her pulse thumped a hundred beats to a minute and the blood rushed to her heart, so she was unable to strike a pose that might have made her look silly. She walked on, almost swooning with excitement and struggling to hide it. And this was the manner that suited her best. Ahead of them and behind, guests were walking along dressed in similar ballgowns and talking to each other in similarly subdued tones. All the way up the staircase mirrors reflected ladies in white, blue and pink dresses, with diamonds and pearls on their bare arms and necks.

Natasha looked in the mirrors but couldn't make out her own reflection among all the others. Everybody blurred together in one glittering procession. At the entrance to the first room the steady hum of conversation, footsteps and greetings deafened Natasha; the light and the glare dazzled her still more. The host and hostess, who had been standing by the door for the last half-hour saying exactly the same thing, 'So pleased to see you,' to every new arrival, welcomed the Rostovs and Madame Peronsky with the same greeting. The two young girls in their white dresses, with identical roses in their black hair, made identical curtseys, but the hostess's eyes lingered instinctively on the slender figure of Natasha. She looked at her and gave her a special smile that went beyond her duty as a hostess. Looking at her, she was perhaps reminded of the golden days of her girlhood, now gone for ever, and her own first ball. The host too gave Natasha a close scrutiny, and asked the count which one of the girls was his daughter.

'Charming girl!' he said, kissing his fingertips.

The ballroom was full of guests crowding round the doorway where the Tsar was expected. The countess worked her way to the front of the crowd. Natasha could hear people asking who she was, and sense their eyes on her. She knew she was making a good impression on those who noticed her, and this helped to calm her nerves.

'There are plenty of people like us, and some of them are worse off,' she thought.

Madame Peronsky was pointing out to the countess the most distinguished persons at the ball.

'That's the Dutch ambassador, look, that grey-haired man over there,' Madame Peronsky was saying, indicating a little old gentleman with a mane of silvery grey curls, who was surrounded by ladies laughing at something he was saying. 'And look who's here, the Queen of Petersburg, Countess Bezukhov,' she said, pointing to Hélène, who had just come in.

'Isn't she gorgeous! She's the equal of Marya Antonovna. Look at all the men fussing round her, young and old. She's so pretty, and clever too . . . They say Prince So-and-so is wild about her. But look at these two – they're not pretty, but they've got even more followers.'

She pointed to two ladies crossing the room, a mother with her very plain daughter.

'Worth millions as a bride,' said Madame Peronsky. 'And here come the suitors . . . That's Countess Bezukhov's brother, Anatole Kuragin,' she said, pointing to a handsome horse guards officer, who raised his head and looked somewhere over the ladies' heads as he went by. 'Handsome, isn't he? They say he's going to marry that heiress. But your cousin, Drubetskoy, he's dancing round her too. She's worth millions, so they say. Oh, that's no less a person than the French ambassador,' she said when the countess saw Caulaincourt and asked who he was. 'Look at him strutting like a king. But they're so nice, you know, the French are so very nice. No nicer people in society. Oh, look, she's here! Yes, she's still the prettiest, our Marya Antonovna! What a simple outfit! Exquisite!'

'And that fat fellow with the glasses on, he's the great freemason,' said Madame Peronsky, indicating Bezukhov. 'Stand him alongside his wife and you'll see what a clown he is!'

Stout as ever, Pierre was waddling through the crowd, nodding to right and to left, with the easy sweetness of a man in a market crowd. He was squeezing through the throng evidently in search of a particular person.

Natasha was delighted to see the familiar face of the man described by Madame Peronsky as a clown, and she knew he was searching the crowd for them, and especially her. Pierre had promised to be there at the ball and find some partners for her. But on his way over Pierre stopped beside a very handsome, dark-haired man of medium height in a white uniform, who was standing by a window talking to a tall man with stars and a ribbon across his chest.

Natasha instantly recognized the splendid young man in white; it was Andrey Bolkonsky, looking altogether younger, happier and more handsome than before.

'There's someone else we know, Bolkonsky, over there, Mamma,' said Natasha, pointing him out. 'You remember, he stayed the night with us at Otradnoye.'

'Oh, do you know him?' said Madame Peronsky. 'I can't abide him. He's top dog at the moment. And so conceited – you wouldn't believe it! Takes after his father. And he's hobnobbing with Speransky, making all sorts of plans. And look how he treats the ladies! That lady over there was talking to him, and he just turned his back on her,' she said, pointing across. 'I'd give him a piece of my mind if he treated me like that.'

CHAPTER 16

There was a sudden stir, a murmur ran through the crowd, everyone surged forward and then moved back again, and through the space that had opened up in walked Tsar Alexander to the strains of a polonaise struck up by the orchestra. Behind him came the host and hostess. The Tsar strode in rapidly, bowing to right and left, as if he wanted to get through the preliminaries of the welcome as quickly as possible. This piece of music had become popular because new words had recently been set to it. They began, 'Alexander, Elisaveta, we rejoice to see you here . . .' The Tsar went into the drawing-room, the crowd swarmed over to the doorway, many of them hurrying across and coming straight back with their faces transformed. Again the crowd pressed back, away from the drawing-room door where the Tsar now appeared, talking to the hostess. An anxious-looking young man bore down on the ladies and begged them to move to one side. Several of them, with faces set to defy all etiquette, squeezed forward, at great risk to all their finery. Then the men began walking over to the ladies, forming couples for the polonaise.

There was a general stepping back, and out strode the Tsar, all smiles, leading the lady of the house with no attempt to follow the music. After him came the host along with Marya Naryshkin, and then the ambassadors, ministers and an assortment of generals, whose names Madame Peronsky never tired of reciting. More than half the ladies were already partnered and were moving off into the polonaise or preparing to do so.

Natasha sensed she was going to be left with her mother and Sonya, in the minority trapped at the side like wall-flowers. She stood there, with her thin arms dangling at her sides and her scarcely defined bosom steadily heaving, then she held her breath and gazed out with gleaming, frightened eyes, a picture of readiness for absolute joy or absolute misery. She wasn't bothered about the Tsar or any of the bigwigs being pointed out by Madame Peronsky; her only thought was, 'Isn't anybody going to come over to me? Am I going to be left out of the first dance? Am I going to be ignored by all these men? They don't seem to have noticed me, and if they do look at me they seem to be saying, "Not my type – not worth looking at". Surely not!' she thought. 'They must know I'm dying to dance, and I'm a good dancer and they'd really enjoy dancing with me.'

The polonaise had been going on for some time, and soon its strains began to fade away, echoing in Natasha's ears like an unhappy memory. She was almost in tears. Madame Peronsky had left them and the count was at the other end of the room, which left the old countess, Sonya and her stranded amid a crowd of strangers, of no interest, no use to anyone. Prince Andrey walked past with a lady on his arm, obviously without recognizing them. The handsome Anatole grinned as he spoke to his lady, and when he glanced at Natasha it was like someone glancing at a wall. Boris passed them twice, and each time turned away. Berg and his wife, who were not dancing, came over to them.

A family get-together here in the ballroom was particularly galling to Natasha – was there nowhere else for the family to talk but here at the ball? She didn't listen, and didn't look at Vera, who was going on about her green dress.

At last the Tsar stopped dancing and stood beside his latest partner (he had danced with three) as the music came to an end. A worried adjutant ran over to the Rostovs and begged them to move a bit further away, though they were already up against the wall, and then the orchestra struck up again, this time with the measured rhythm and inviting strains of a waltz. The Tsar glanced down the ballroom with a smile on his face. A moment passed; no one came out to begin. The adjutant who had been appointed Master of Ceremonies went over to Countess Bezukhov and asked her to dance. She gave a smile, raised a hand and placed it on the adjutant's shoulder without a single glance at him. The adjutant knew what he was doing. Taking a firm hold of his partner, he guided her casually, confidently, into a smooth gliding movement round the edge of the circle, then at the corner of the ballroom he turned his partner with an upward swoop of her left hand, and not a sound was heard against the quickening strains of the music beyond the measured jingle of the spurs on the adjutant's expertly flashing feet and the swish of his partner's swirling velvet skirt as every third beat brought her whisking through a turn.

Natasha watched them on the verge of tears, so disappointed that someone else was dancing that first round of the waltz.

Prince Andrey, wearing the white uniform of a cavalry colonel with white stockings and light shoes, was standing towards the front of the circle not far from the Rostovs, looking happy and excited. Baron Firhoff was talking to him about the first session of the State Council due to be held next day. As someone close to Speransky, involved in the work of the legislative commission, Prince Andrey could be relied on for sound information about that session, as opposed to the many rumours that were going round. But he wasn't listening to what Firhoff was saying; he was looking in turn from the Tsar to the gentlemen intending to dance but not yet bold enough to enter the ring. He was watching them closely, these gentlemen who had gone all shy in the presence of the Tsar, and the ladies who were dying to be asked to dance.

Pierre went over to Prince Andrey and took him by the arm.

'You're always dancing. Look, my protégée is here, the younger Rostov girl. Ask her,' he said.

'Where is she?' asked Bolkonsky. 'I'm sorry,' he said, turning to the baron, 'we'll finish this conversation somewhere else, but at a ball one must dance.' He went over in the direction indicated by Pierre. Natasha's desperately panicky face met his gaze. He knew her immediately and guessed what she was going through, realizing that this was her début. He remembered what she had said at the window, and with a look of delight on his face he approached Countess Rostov.

'Allow me to introduce my daughter,' said the countess, reddening.

'I've had the pleasure of meeting you all before, if the countess remembers,' said Prince Andrey, with a low bow of great courtesy, which belied Madame Peronsky's comments on his rudeness. He went up to Natasha and raised his hand to put it around her waist without negotiating an invitation to dance. He offered her the waltz. The timorous expression on Natasha's face, poised between despair and ecstasy, changed at once into a blissful, girlish smile of gratitude.

'I've been waiting so long for you,' came the message from that worried but happy young girl, a smile shining from her glistening eyes as she raised her hand to Prince Andrey's shoulder. They were the second couple to walk out into the ring.

Prince Andrey was one of the best dancers of his day. Natasha danced exquisitely. Her little feet in their satin slippers did what they had to do so easily and with no effort on her part, while her face glowed with pure happiness.

Her bared neck and arms were skinny, quite unattractive compared with Hélène's shoulders. Her little shoulders were narrow, her bosom was undefined, her arms were slender. But Hélène had been, so to speak, varnished by thousands of eyes that had caressed her form, whereas Natasha seemed like a young girl exposing her body for the first time, who would have been terribly embarrassed if she hadn't been assured on every side that it was all very necessary.

Prince Andrey loved dancing. He had been anxious to get away as fast as he could from the political or high-minded conversations that everyone was trying to draw him into, and also keen to break the irksome ring of constraint caused by the presence of the Tsar. This was why he had gone off to dance, and he had chosen Natasha as a partner because Pierre had pointed her out, and also because she was the first pretty girl to catch his eye. But the moment he put his arm round that slender, supple, quivering waist, and felt her stirring so close to him and smiling so close to him, the champagne of her beauty went to his head. He felt a thrill of new life and rejuvenation as he drew a deep breath, left her and stood there watching the other couples.

CHAPTER 17

After Prince Andrey, Boris came up and asked Natasha to dance, and he was followed by the dancing adjutant who had started the ball, and several other young men. Flushed with happiness, Natasha passed on her spare partners to Sonya, and never stopped dancing all evening. What fascinated everyone else at the ball she didn't notice and didn't even see. She didn't notice that the Tsar had a long conversation with the French ambassador, that he was unusually gracious towards one particular lady, that Prince So-and-so and Mr What's-his-name had said and done such and such, that Hélène had been a brilliant success, and that a certain somebody had paid her close attention. She didn't even see the Tsar, and she became aware that he had gone only when she noticed the ball livening up after his departure.

In one of the liveliest cotillions just before supper Prince Andrey danced again with Natasha. He reminded her of when he had first seen her on the avenue at Otradnoye, and how she couldn't get to sleep that night in the moonlight, and he told her he had unintentionally heard what she was saying. Natasha blushed at these reminders and tried to make excuses, as if there was something embarrassing in the emotion which Prince Andrey had unintentionally overheard her expressing.

Like all men who have grown up in society Prince Andrey was

pleased when he encountered something in that world that did not carry the usual society stamp. And Natasha was exactly that, with her sense of wonder, her enthusiasm, her diffidence and even the mistakes she made when she spoke French. His manner was particularly gentle and solicitous as he escorted her and talked to her. Sitting at her side, chatting about the simplest things, nothing in particular, Prince Andrey admired the radiant brilliance of her eyes and her smile, which had nothing to do with what she was saying but came from her own inner happiness. Natasha was chosen again and again, and whenever she got up with a smile and went off to dance, Prince Andrey particularly admired the mixture of timidity and gracefulness that she presented. In the middle of the cotillion Natasha was on her way back to her place, breathless at the end of a figure, when she was chosen yet again by another partner. Tired and panting, she demurred for an instant, on the point of refusing, but immediately put her hand on her partner's shoulder, beaming joyfully at Prince Andrey.

'I'd have been glad to have a rest and sit next to you. I am tired, but you see how they keep asking me, and I'm so pleased and happy, and I love everyone, including you, and I know all about it,' said the smile and more, much more besides. When her partner left her side, Natasha dashed across the room to choose two ladies for the next figure.

'If she goes to her cousin first and then to another lady, she's going to be my wife,' Prince Andrey said to himself – much to his own surprise – as he watched her. She went to her cousin first.

'The stupid things that sometimes come into your mind!' thought Prince Andrey. 'But one thing's for sure – that girl is so lovely and so unusual she'll be married before she's been out for a month since dancing here . . . She's something quite exceptional,' he thought, as Natasha seated herself beside him, adjusting a stray rose on her bodice.

At the end of the cotillion the old count in his blue swallowtail coat came over to the young people who had been dancing. He invited Prince Andrey to come and see them and asked his daughter whether she was having a good time. At first Natasha didn't answer; she just smiled a gently reproachful smile that said, 'How could you ask a question like that?' Then she said, 'I'm having the best time of my whole life!' and Prince Andrey watched as she half-raised her slender arms as if to embrace her father, and dropped them again at once. Natasha was indeed having the happiest time of her life. She was at the very peak of happiness, when a person is transformed into someone completely good and kind, and rejects the slightest possibility of evil, misery and grief.

*

It was at this ball that Pierre felt humiliated for the first time by the position his wife now occupied in the highest court circles. He was sullen and distracted. A deep furrow lined his forehead as he stood by a window, staring out over his spectacles and seeing no one. Natasha passed by near to him on her way to supper. She was struck by Pierre's dark and miserable appearance. She stopped and turned to face him. She so much wanted to help him, to let him have some of her own over-flowing happiness. 'What a lovely evening, Count,' she said, 'isn't it?'

Pierre gave a faraway smile, obviously not taking in what she was saying. 'Yes, I'm very glad,' he said.

'How could anybody be unhappy with anything tonight?' thought Natasha. 'Especially someone as nice as Bezukhov.'

In Natasha's eyes the people at the ball were all the same – nice, kind, beautiful people – and they all loved each other. Nobody would think of harming anybody else, so they must be happy, all of them.

CHAPTER 18

Next day Prince Andrey remembered the ball, but not for very long. 'Yes, it was a splendid ball,' he thought. 'And . . . oh yes, that Rostov girl is so sweet. There's something fresh about her, something unusual and distinctive – she doesn't seem to belong to Petersburg.' Then, with no further thoughts about yesterday's ball, he had a good drink of tea and got down to work.

But either from tiredness or lack of sleep he was in no mood for work, and he couldn't get anything done. He was for ever carping about his own work – something he often did – and he was delighted when he heard that someone had called to see him.

The visitor was Bitsky, a man to be found on every commission and at all levels of Petersburg society, a passionate devotee of all the latest ideas, especially Speransky's, an inveterate disseminator of metropoli-tan news, and one of those men who choose their opinions the way they choose their clothes – according to fashion – which only serves to make them seem more partisan than anyone else. Looking business-like and scarcely waiting to remove his hat, he ran over to Prince Andrey and began to blurt out what he had come to say. He had just heard details from the State Council that had sat that morning; the Tsar had opened the session and Bitsky waxed enthusiastic on the subject. The Tsar's speech had been quite remarkable. It had been the kind of speech that only a constitutional monarch could have delivered. 'The Emperor said quite bluntly that the Council and Senate are *estates of the realm*. He said that government must be founded not on arbitrary authority but on solid principles. The Emperor said that the fiscal system must be overhauled and the accounts made public,' Bitsky announced, emphasizing certain words, and widening his eyes knowingly. 'Yes, today's events mark a new epoch, the greatest epoch in our history,' he concluded.

Prince Andrey listened to this account of the opening of the State Council, which he had been looking forward to so keenly and had valued so much, amazed that now it had happened this event made no impact on him and struck him as less than insignificant. He listened to Bitsky's eloquent enthusiasm with secret scorn. The simplest idea in the world was taking over his mind. 'Why should I bother? Why should Bitsky?' he thought. 'Why should we bother about what the Emperor was pleased to say to the Council? Can any of that make me happier or better than I am?'

And with this simple reflection all of Prince Andrey's previous interest in the current reforms was suddenly destroyed. Later that day Prince Andrey was due to dine with Speransky in what the latter had described as 'a little get-together' as he issued the invitation. This dinner, in the intimate domestic circle of the man he so much admired, had seemed very enticing to Prince Andrey, especially since he had not yet seen Speransky at home. But now he didn't feel like going.

At the appointed hour, however, Prince Andrey was to be seen entering Speransky's house alongside the Tavrichesky Garden. It was a small place, almost monastic in its extraordinary cleanliness, and there in the parquet-floored dining-room Prince Andrey, arriving slightly late at five o'clock, found Speransky's 'little get-together' of close associates already assembled. There were no ladies present, except Speransky's little daughter (who had a long face like her father) and her governess. The guests were Gervais, Magnitsky and Stolypin. Out in the vestibule Prince Andrey had caught the sound of raised voices and someone with a loud, distinctive guffaw – a sort of stage laugh. Someone's voice – it sounded like Speransky's – was ringing with a clear '*haw-haw-haw!*' Prince Andrey had never heard Speransky laugh before, and this booming, resonant laughter coming from a great statesman struck him as odd.

Prince Andrey went into the dining-room. They were gathered in a group between two windows near to a little table laid with hors d'oeuvres. Speransky was standing by the table, a picture of joviality, wearing a grey swallowtail coat, with a star on his chest, and the same white waistcoat and high white stock that he had worn at the famous session of the State Council. His guests stood around him in a ring. Magnitsky had turned to face him and was half-way through a story. Speransky was listening, and laughing at what Magnitsky was going to say before he said it. As Prince Andrey walked in, Magnitsky's words were again drowned with laughter. Stolypin issued a deep-bass guffaw as he munched a piece of bread and cheese, Gervais gave a wheezy chuckle and Speransky laughed in his calculated staccato.

Still laughing, Speransky offered Prince Andrey a soft, white hand. 'So nice to see you, Prince,' he said. 'Just a minute . . .' He turned to Magnitsky, interrupting his story. 'We have a pact this evening. We're going to enjoy a good dinner. No talking shop.' He turned back to the story-teller and gave another laugh.

With a sense of surprise and sad disappointment, Prince Andrey listened to Speransky's ringing tones and watched him as he laughed. This wasn't Speransky, it was someone else, he thought to himself. Everything in Speransky that had seemed mysterious and attractive suddenly struck Prince Andrey as patently obvious and unpleasant.

At dinner the conversation, which never faltered, seemed like something out of a joke-book. Magnitsky had hardly finished his story when another guest announced his willingness to tell them a funnier one. For the most part, the stories centred around, if not the actual service, the people who worked in it. It was as if this little circle had decided once and for all they were a completely useless lot and the only possible attitude to them was one of cheerful hilarity. Speransky told them about a deaf statesman at the council that morning who was asked for his opinion and replied that he was of the same opinion. Gervais described one case under revision that was remarkable for the stupidity of all concerned. Stolypin spoke with a stammer as he intervened with a few impassioned words on the abuses of the old regime, but this threatened to give the conversation a serious turn, so Magnitsky responded by making fun of Stolypin's earnest attitude. Then Gervais came in with another joke, and the conversation soon resumed its bantering tone.

It was clear that Speransky liked to put his work behind him, relax and seek amusement in his little group of friends; meanwhile the friends themselves understood what he wanted, and they were doing their best to amuse him and themselves at the same time. But Prince Andrey found this kind of jollity laboured and anything but jolly. Speransky's refined tones grated on him, and his constant laughter struck such a false note that Prince Andrey's sensitivities were somehow offended. Prince Andrey was the only one not laughing, and he began to worry that he might be a drag on this party. But no one noticed his lack of sympathy with the general mood. They all seemed to be enjoying themselves.

Several times he tried to get into the conversation, but every time he did so his words were plucked away like a cork flung out of water. The jokiness of these people was quite beyond him. There was nothing crude or objectionable in what they were saying; it was all very witty and it might have been funny, but something was missing from it all, and whatever it was, it was the very essence of good humour – and they weren't even aware of its existence.

After dinner Speransky's daughter and her governess rose to leave the table. Speransky caressed his daughter with a white hand and gave her a kiss. Even this gesture was seen by Prince Andrey as something forced.

The men sat on and drank port like Englishmen. The talk turned to Napoleon's activities in Spain, of which they approved to a man, but in the middle of it all Prince Andrey suddenly came out against them. Speransky gave a smile, obviously wanting to change the subject, and launched into a completely irrelevant story. For some time everyone sat there in silence.

Ready at last to leave the table, Speransky replaced the cork in a bottle of wine and said, 'Costs a fortune nowadays, good wine!', gave it to the servant and got up. Everybody rose and went through into the drawing-room, chatting away as loud as ever. Speransky was handed two envelopes which had been delivered by a courier. He took them and went to his study. As soon as he had gone the party-like atmosphere subsided and the guests lapsed into a quiet and thoughtful conversation.

'On with the recitation!' said Speransky, coming out of his study. 'Remarkable talent!' he said to Prince Andrey. Magnitsky at once struck a theatrical pose and began to declaim some funny French poetry (composed by himself) ridiculing various well-known persons in Petersburg. Several times he was interrupted by applause. At the end of the recitation Prince Andrey went over to Speransky to take his leave.

'It's a bit early, isn't it? Where are you off to?' said Speransky.

'I promised to call in at a soirée.'

They said no more. Prince Andrey stared into those forbidding glassy eyes and felt how stupid he had been to expect anything from Speransky, or anything associated with him. How could he ever have set any store by what Speransky was doing? That measured, mirthless laugh of his rang in Prince Andrey's ears long after he had left Speransky's.

On reaching home Prince Andrey began to look back over his life in Petersburg during the last four months, and he saw it in a new light. He thought of all the trouble he had taken, the hoops he had jumped through, and the whole story of his project for army reform, which had been accepted in principle but was now being shelved because another scheme, a really dreadful one, had already been drawn up and presented to the Tsar. He thought of all those committee meetings, with Berg one of the sitting members. He thought of the long, pernickety discussions that took place over every last point of order and procedure and the short and non-pernickety treatment given to anything that mattered. He thought of his work on law reform, his painstaking translation of the Roman and French codes into Russian, and he felt thoroughly ashamed. Then came a vivid memory of Bogucharovo, his life in the country, his trip to Ryazan. He thought of his peasants, and Dron, the village elder. Relating these people to the section on Personal Rights which he had been paragraphing, he wondered how on earth he could have spent so much time on such useless work.

CHAPTER 19

The next day Prince Andrey went to various houses that he hadn't visited before, including the Rostovs', with whom he had renewed his acquaintance at the ball. Common courtesy called for a visit to the Rostovs, but Prince Andrey also wanted to have another look at that unusual, lively young girl who had made such a pleasant impression on him, and see her in her own home.

Natasha was one of the first to welcome him. She was wearing a plain dark-blue dress, and Andrey felt sure she looked prettier in that than she had done in her ballgown. She and all the family received Prince Andrey like an old friend, simply but very warmly. The entire family, once a target for Prince Andrey's harshest criticism, now seemed to consist of excellent, open-hearted, kindly people. The old count was so persuasive with his charitable nature and generosity of spirit – such rare and attractive qualities in Petersburg – that Prince Andrey could not refuse an invitation to stay for dinner. 'Yes, these are very nice, splendid people,' thought Bolkonsky. 'Of course they haven't the slightest idea what a treasure they possess in Natasha, but they're so nice, and they're the best possible background for her to stand out against, with all her poetry and charm and all that liveliness!'

Prince Andrey recognized in Natasha a strange and special new world, brimful of unknown joys, the same strange world that had tantalized him on the avenue at Otradnoye and on that moonlight night at the window. But now it was no longer so strange and tantalizing; he had stepped into it and was already tasting its new pleasures.

After dinner Natasha went over to the clavichord at Prince Andrey's request and began to sing. Prince Andrey stood by one of the windows talking to the ladies, and listened to her. In the middle of one phrase Prince Andrey stopped talking and suddenly felt close to tears, with a lump in his throat, something he had never known before. He watched Natasha as she sang, with a new and blissful sensation stirring in his soul. He was so happy, and at the same time so sad. He had nothing at all to weep about, but here he was on the verge of tears. What for? Past love? The little princess? Lost illusions? ... Future hopes? ... Yes and no. The main thing that was bringing him to the verge of tears was a sudden, vivid awareness of the dreadful disparity between something infinitely great and eternal that existed within him and something else, something constraining and physical that constituted *him* and even *her*. The disparity struck him with a mixture of anguish and bliss while she was singing.

When Natasha had finished she came over and wanted to know whether he liked her voice. Having said this, she felt embarrassed the moment the question was out of her mouth, realizing she ought never to have asked anything of the kind. He looked at her with a smile and said he liked her singing, as he liked everything else that she did.

It was late evening when Prince Andrey left the Rostovs'. He went to bed as habit dictated, but soon saw he wasn't going to get to sleep. He lit a candle and sat up in bed; he got out and in again, not at all worried about his insomnia. His soul was filled with a new feeling of bliss, as if he had emerged from a stuffy room into God's glorious daylight. It never occurred to him that he might be in love with the little Rostov girl. He wasn't even thinking about her. He was aware of her only as an image, but this opened up the whole of his life before him in a new light. 'Why do I go on struggling? Why do I keep on toiling at this narrow, cramped drudgery, when life lies open before me, the whole of life, with all its joys?' he kept asking himself. And now, for the first time in ages, he began to make happy plans for the future. He made a personal decision to sort out his son's education, find him a tutor and hand him into that man's care. Then he ought to retire from the army, go abroad and see something of England, Switzerland, Italy. 'I must take full advantage of my freedom while I'm still feeling young and strong,' he told himself. 'Pierre was right:

if you want to be happy, you have to believe in the possibility of happiness, and I do believe in it now. Let the dead bury the dead, but while ever there is life, you must live and be happy.' These were his thoughts.

CHAPTER 20

One morning Colonel Adolf Berg called on Pierre, who knew him as he knew everybody else in Moscow and Petersburg. He was immaculately turned out in a brand-new uniform, with his pomaded locks combed out at the temples in the style made popular by Tsar Alexander.

'I've just come from your good lady, the countess, and to my great misfortune, my request couldn't be granted by her. I'm hoping I shall be more fortunate with you, Count,' he said with a smile.

'What can I do for you, Colonel? I'm all yours.'

'Now that I'm nicely settled in my new quarters, Count,' Berg announced, obviously assuming that news of this development must be a matter for great rejoicing, 'I thought I might set something up, just a little soirée for a few people known to me and my wife. (He beamed with even greater benevolence.) I had in mind asking the countess and you to do me the honour of coming over for a cup of tea, and . . . a little supper.'

Only Countess Hélène, who considered it beneath her dignity to associate with nobodies like the Bergs, could have been cruel enough to turn down an invitation like this. Berg told him why he wanted to get together a small, select group of people at his new rooms, and why this would be a source of great pleasure for him, and although he would begrudge spending good money on cards or anything harmful, he didn't mind forking out for the sake of good company, and he explained it all so clearly that Pierre couldn't refuse, and he promised to come.

'Only please don't be late, Count, if I may make so bold. Ten minutes to eight, if I may make so bold. We'll have a few rounds of cards. Our general's going to be there. He's very good to me. And we'll have a bite to eat, Count. If you would be so kind.'

Contrary to his usual habit of always arriving late, Pierre got to the Bergs' not at ten minutes to eight, but at a quarter to.

The Bergs had everything ready for their little party and were quite ready to receive the guests.

Berg and his wife were sitting together in a clean, bright study, newly done out with little busts and pictures and new furniture. Berg sat beside his wife, neatly buttoned up in his new uniform, busily explaining the possibility, indeed the necessity, of cultivating people in higher stations – these were the only relationships that gave any pleasure. 'You pick things up, and you can ask the odd favour. Take me for instance – look where my life has gone since I started at the bottom. (Berg measured his life not in years but in awards and promotions.) My comrades have got nowhere, and I'll soon have my own regiment. And I'm fortunate enough to be your husband.' (He got to his feet and went over to kiss Vera's hand, stopping on the way to fold back the corner of a rug that was ruckled up.) 'And how did I get all this? Mainly by knowing how to cultivate the right people. Of course, you do have to behave properly and get things right as well.'

Berg smiled with a sense of his own superiority over a feeble woman. He paused and reflected that this charming wife of his was indeed a feeble woman, incapable of ever attaining any of the qualities needed for masculine prowess – 'ein Mann zu sein',[5] as the Germans put it. Meanwhile Vera was also smiling, with her own sense of superiority over a decent, well-behaved husband, who nevertheless, as she saw it, took such a wrong view of life – as all men did. Berg judged women by the standards of his own wife and considered all of them feeble and foolish. Vera judged men by the standards of her own husband and, extrapolating from him alone, she found all men conceited and self-centred, each convinced he was the only one with any sense whereas he didn't actually understand anything at all.

Berg got to his feet and gingerly embraced his wife, taking care not to squash the fine lace cape that had cost him a pretty penny, and he gave her a peck in the middle of her mouth.

'There's just one thing – we mustn't rush into having children,' he said, linking one thought to another at some subconscious level.

'No,' responded Vera. 'That's something I certainly don't want. We must live for society.'

'Princess Yusupov was wearing one just like that,' said Berg, smiling with pleasure and bonhomie as he pointed to the cape.

At that moment they were informed that Count Bezukhov had arrived. The young newlyweds smiled at each other with self-satisfaction on either side, each claiming unspoken credit for this visit.

'It's all a question of knowing how to cultivate the right people,' thought Berg. 'And knowing how to behave!'

'But, listen, when I'm looking after a guest,' said Vera, 'please don't interrupt me, because I know what they all need, and what needs to be said to different people.'

Berg was smiling too.

'Oh, we can't have that. Sometimes men need men's talk,' he said.

Pierre was shown into a small drawing-room where no one could sit down without disrupting the neat symmetry and tidiness, so it was perfectly natural and not the least bit strange that Berg, while magnanimously offering to disturb the symmetry of an armchair or a sofa for an honoured guest, found himself thoroughly uncomfortable and in several minds over how to do it, so he left his guest to resolve the matter of choice. Pierre shattered the symmetry by moving a chair up for himself, and with that the soirée was under way, with Berg and Vera falling over each other in their eagerness to look after the guest.

Vera had decided in her own mind that Pierre ought to be treated to conversation about the French embassy, so without further ado she launched forth on that subject. Berg then decided the conversation needed a touch of masculinity, so he cut across his wife's remarks with a reference to the subject of the war with Austria, followed by an instinctive switch from generalities to his own personal interests and the various proposals he had had, to persuade him to take part in the Austrian campaign, and his reasons for declining. Despite the desultory conversation and Vera's resentment of the interpolated masculine touch, both host and hostess were satisfied that, although there was only one guest present, the soirée had got off to a good start, that their soirée and all the other soirées were like peas in pod, with the same conversation, tea and lighted candles.

It wasn't long before Boris, an old comrade of Berg's, arrived. There was a tinge of patronizing high-mindedness in his attitude to Berg and Vera. Then came the colonel and his lady, then the general himself, then the Rostovs, by which time the soirée really had become exactly like every other soirée. Berg and Vera could hardly contain their smiles of rapture at the sight of all this traffic in their drawing-room, at the blurred murmur of conversation and the rustle of skirts as people curtsied and bowed. Everything was just like everywhere else, especially the general, who complimented them on their rooms, clapped Berg on the shoulder and then took charge in a fatherly way of arranging the table for a game of boston. The general sat down alongside Count Ilya Rostov, who was next in seniority to himself. The old folk were grouped together, and so were the youngsters, and with the hostess at the tea table, the cakes in their silver basket the image of the cakes at the Panins' soirée, absolutely everything was like everywhere else.

CHAPTER 21

Pierre, as one of the principal guests, had no choice but to sit down and play boston with the old count, the general and the colonel. In his position at the card table he happened to be sitting across from Natasha, and he was struck by a curious change that had come over her since the day of the ball. She was quiet, and not only was she less pretty than she had been at the ball, she would have looked rather plain but for her air of sweet indifference to everything.

'What's wrong with her?' Pierre wondered as he glanced across. She was sitting next to her sister at the tea table, grudgingly responding to Boris at her side without bothering to look at him. After playing out a whole suit and taking five tricks, much to his partner's satisfaction, Pierre was distracted by the sound of greetings and someone coming in, but he glanced at her again as he raked in his tricks.

'What can have happened to her?' he said to himself in even greater wonder.

Prince Andrey was standing in front of her, talking away with tender solicitude written all over his face. She was looking up at him, red as a beetroot and visibly trying to control her panicky breathing. And suddenly the flaming glow from some inner fire that had been doused until then was newly ablaze in her. She was utterly transformed. From being a plain creature she was once more the beautiful girl she had been at the ball.

Prince Andrey came over to Pierre, and Pierre noticed a new, youthful expression in his friend's face too. Pierre changed places several times during the play, sitting sometimes with his back to Natasha and sometimes facing her, and through all six rubbers he kept a close watch on her and his friend.

'There's something very serious going on between those two,' thought Pierre, suddenly assailed by a worrying feeling of joy mixed with bitterness that took his mind off the game.

At the end of six rubbers the general got to his feet, saying there was no point in playing like that, and Pierre was free to roam. Natasha was talking to Sonya and Boris on one side of the room. Vera was saying something to Prince Andrey with a subtle smile on her face. Pierre went over to his friend, asked whether he was intruding on any secrets and sat down beside them. Vera, having noticed Prince Andrey paying close attention to Natasha, felt that at a soirée, at a proper soirée, there really ought to be the odd gentle hint about the emotions, so she waited until Prince Andrey was on his own, struck up a conversation with him, mentioned emotions in general and then brought her sister into it. Dealing with such a clever man as Prince Andrey (which was how she saw him), she felt the need to handle this affair with tact and diplomacy. When Pierre came over and heard them talking he could see that Vera was getting carried away by her own self-confidence while Andrey seemed embarrassed – something that almost never happened to him.

'What's your opinion?' Vera was asking with a subtle smile on her face. 'Prince, you can see right through people. You can assess someone's character at a glance. What do you think about Natalie? Is she capable of being constant in her attachments? Could she be like other women (she had herself in mind), love somebody once and for all and stay faithful to him for ever? That's what I call true love! What do you think, Prince?'

'I don't know your sister all that well,' answered Prince Andrey with a sardonic smile intended to cover his embarrassment, 'so I can't settle a delicate question like that. In any case, I've always noticed that the less attractive a woman is, the more faithful she tends to be,' he added, looking round at Pierre as he joined them.

'Yes, Prince, you're quite right. In this day and age,' Vera persisted (talking of 'this day and age' in the way that persons of limited intelligence generally love to do, all too certain they have discovered and carefully considered what is special about their day and age, and that human characteristics change with the times), 'in this day and age a girl has so much liberty that the pleasure of receiving a lot of attention often suppresses her true feelings. And it has to be said that Natalie is very vulnerable in that area.'

This reversion to Natasha made Prince Andrey frown with annoyance. He made as if to get to his feet, but Vera persisted, with even greater subtlety in her smile.

'I'm sure no one has received more attention than she has,' Vera went on, 'but until quite recently she hasn't taken to anyone in particular. Now, you know, Count,' she said, turning to Pierre, 'not even our dear cousin, Boris, who, between ourselves, was very, very far gone in the land of tender feelings.' (She was referring to a map of love much in fashion at that time.)

Prince Andrey scowled, saying nothing.

'But you're a friend of Boris's, aren't you?' Vera said to him.

'Yes, I do know him . . .'

'He must have told you about his childish passion for Natasha.'

'Oh, was there a childish passion?' asked Prince Andrey with an unexpected rush of blood to his face.

'Oh yes. You know how it is – close intimacy between boy and girl cousins sometimes leads to love. Cousins, cousins, dangers in dozens. Don't you agree?'

'No doubt about it,' said Prince Andrey, and then, suddenly stimulated in the most awkward way, he started ribbing Pierre about the need to watch his step with his fifty-year-old lady cousins in Moscow, only to get to his feet in mid-joke, seize hold of Pierre's arm and take him to one side.

'What's going on?' asked Pierre, who had been watching his friend's strange agitation in some amazement, and had seen him glance across at Natasha as he got up.

'Listen, I must talk to you,' said Prince Andrey. 'You know that pair of women's gloves . . .' (He had in mind the masonic gloves given to a newly initiated brother for presentation to the woman he loved.) 'I . . . er, no, I'll talk to you later . . .' And with a strange glint in his eyes and a restlessness in his movements, Prince Andrey went over to Natasha and sat down beside her. Pierre watched as Prince Andrey asked her something and she blushed as she replied.

But at that moment Berg came over to Pierre, and insisted on his settling a dispute on Spanish affairs that had arisen between the general and the colonel.

Berg was pleased and happy. A smile of gratification was never off his face. The soirée was proving a great success, the exact image of all the other soirées he had ever been to. All the details were identical: subtle exchanges between the ladies, the card-playing and the general raising his voice as they played, the samovar, the cakes . . . only one thing was missing, something he had seen at every soirée and now wished to replicate. There had not yet been any shouting from the gentlemen or an argument about something serious and high-minded. The general had started just such a conversation and Berg now brought Pierre into it.

CHAPTER 22

Next day Prince Andrey went to lunch at the Rostovs', invited by Count Ilya, and spent the whole day there.

Everyone in the house could sense who Prince Andrey had really come to see, and he made no attempt to hide his efforts to spend the whole day with Natasha.

There was a feeling of dreadful anticipation everywhere, not only in Natasha's inner being – frightened, but happy and excited as she was – but permeating the whole household, as if some portentous event was just about to come to pass. The countess watched Prince Andrey closely, with an air of great concern and sorrow, whenever he talked to Natasha, and when he turned to look at her she would respond rather coyly, talking of this and that. Sonya was afraid to leave Natasha on her own, and equally afraid of being *de trop* if she stayed with them. Natasha's face was drained of all colour from fear and anticipation if she was left alone with him for a single moment. She was struck by Prince Andrey's diffidence. She could sense that he had something to say to her but couldn't get it out.

When Prince Andrey had gone home that night the countess went over to Natasha and whispered, 'Well?'

'Mamma, for heaven's sake don't ask me anything just now. It's not something I can talk about,' said Natasha.

Nevertheless, Natasha lay in her mother's bed for a long time that night, scared and excited, her darting eyes gradually settling into a stare. She told her everything he had said – he had lavished praise on her, talked about going abroad, asked where they were spending the summer, and wanted to know all about Boris.

'But all this, this . . . Oh, I've never felt like this before!' she said. 'But I feel so scared when I'm with him, I'm always scared when I'm with him. What does it mean? Is this the real thing? Is that what it means? Mamma, are you asleep?'

'No, darling, I'm scared too,' answered her mother. 'Go on, off you go to bed.'

'No, I shan't sleep. Oh, sleep is so stupid! Mamma, darling, I've never felt anything like this before,' she said, shocked and panicky at the feelings she recognized in herself. 'Who'd have thought . . . ?'

Natasha now had the impression she had fallen in love with Prince Andrey the first time she had seen him at Otradnoye. Sudden happiness seemed to have caught her unawares with all its dreadful strangeness – how odd that the man she had chosen there and then (as she now knew for certain), this very man should turn up again, apparently not indifferent to her.

'It all had to happen – he came to Petersburg just when we were here. And we met, as we had to, at the ball. It was all fate. We're obviously victims of fate. Everything's been leading up to this. That first time, the minute I saw him, I had a special feeling.'

'What was it he said to you? What was all that poetry about? Read it to me . . .' said her mother pensively, casting her mind back to some lines of verse that Prince Andrey had written in Natasha's album.

'Mamma, he's a widower – is there anything wrong in that?'

'Hush, Natasha. Don't forget to say your prayers. Marriages are made in heaven,' she said, quoting the French proverb.

'Mamma, darling, oh, I do love you! And I'm so happy!' cried Natasha, shedding tears of excitement and happiness, and hugging her mother.

At that very moment Prince Andrey was sitting with Pierre, talking about his love for Natasha and his absolute determination to marry her.

That evening Countess Hélène Bezukhov had given a reception attended by the French ambassador, a royal prince who had recently become a very frequent visitor at the countess's, and many brilliant ladies and gentlemen. Pierre had come down and wandered from room to room, unnerving all the guests by looking so tense, gloomy and preoccupied.

Ever since the night of the ball Pierre had been aware of an impending bout of nervous depression, and had been trying desperately to struggle against it. Since his wife's involvement with the royal prince Pierre had been unexpectedly made a gentleman of the bedchamber, and from that time he had felt a growing sense of weariness and embarrassment in court society, and his old thoughts about the vanity of all human life began to resurface more and more often. The affection he had recently noticed between his protégée, Natasha, and Prince Andrey had made him feel gloomier still because of the contrast between his position and his friend's. He made equal efforts to avoid two lines of thought: his wife, and the relationship between Natasha and Prince Andrey. Once again everything seemed meaningless on the scale of eternity; once again he faced the question, 'What's it all about?' Day after day, night after night, he forced himself to concentrate on masonic work, hoping to ward off any evil spirits. Shortly before midnight Pierre had come away from the countess's apartment and walked upstairs to his low-ceilinged room which reeked of tobacco smoke, where he had put on his tatty old dressing-gown and seated himself at the desk to carry on copying out the original transactions of the Scottish freemasons, when somebody came into the room. It was Prince Andrey.

'Oh, it's you,' said Pierre, looking distracted and none too pleased. 'I'm rather busy, as you can see,' he added, pointing to his note-book with the escapist look of a miserable man using work to get away from the trials of life.

Prince Andrey strolled in and stopped in front of Pierre with radiant bliss written all over his face, bursting with new life, and he beamed at his friend with the smugness of a happy man, never even noticing the gloomy face before him.

'Listen, dear boy,' he said, 'I tried to tell you yesterday, and I've come to tell you now. I've never felt anything like this. I'm in love, my friend.'

Pierre suddenly heaved a great sigh and flopped down ponderously on to the sofa next to Prince Andrey.

'With Natasha Rostov, I suppose,' he said.

'Yes, yes, who else could it be? I'd never have believed it, but the feeling's too strong for me. Yesterday I went through such torment and agony, but I wouldn't change that agony for anything in the world. I've never lived until now. I can't live without her. But can she love me? . . . I'm too old for her . . . Well, say something.'

'Me? Say something? Well, what did I tell you?' said Pierre, suddenly getting to his feet and beginning to pace up and down the room. 'It's what I've always thought. That girl's a real treasure . . . There's something special about her . . . My dear fellow, don't stop to think about it. Don't hesitate. Just get married, get married, get married! I know you'll be the happiest man on earth.'

'What about her?'

'She loves you.'

'Don't talk rubbish,' said Prince Andrey, beaming as he looked Pierre in the face.

'She does. I know she does,' Pierre cried angrily.

'No, listen,' said Prince Andrey, catching him by the arm and stopping him in his tracks. 'You can see what a state I'm in. I've got to talk to somebody about it.'

'Well, come on then, tell me all about it. I'm only too pleased to listen,' said Pierre, and his face changed perceptibly, the furrow of care on his forehead was smoothed away, and he listened with pleasure to what Prince Andrey had to say.

His friend was now just what he seemed to be, a new man, utterly changed. Where had his depression gone, his contempt for life, all that disillusionment? Pierre was the only person he could have spoken to so openly, and now he poured forth all that was on his mind. He began by planning his future well ahead with an easy spirit and great resolution, saying he wasn't prepared to sacrifice his own happiness for any silly ideas his father might have, and he would either make his father agree to the marriage and come to like her, or go ahead without his consent, and then he went on to marvel at the feeling that had overwhelmed him – something strange, new and beyond his control.

'I'd never have believed it, if anybody had said I could love like this,' said Prince Andrey. 'It's nothing like what I felt before. The whole world is split in two for me now: one half is *her*, and it's all happiness, hope and light; the other is *not her*, and it's all misery and darkness . . .'

'Darkness and gloom,' Pierre repeated. 'Oh yes, I know all about that.'

'I can't help loving the light. It's not my fault. And I'm *so* happy. Do you know what I mean? I know you're pleased for me.'

'Yes, I am,' Pierre agreed, and as he watched his friend, his eyes brimmed with sweet sadness. The brighter Prince Andrey's fate became, the gloomier his own seemed to be.

CHAPTER 23

If Prince Andrey was to marry he would need his father's consent, so the next day he set off to see him.

The old prince received his son's announcement with a show of outward equanimity which masked hidden fury. He couldn't understand how anyone could want to alter his way of living by introducing innovations when his life was drawing to its close. 'If they would only let me live my life out in my own way, and then do what they want . . .' the old man said to himself. Dealing with his son, however, he employed the kind of diplomacy that he reserved for special occasions. Adopting a calm tone, he discussed the whole matter.

First, the marriage was not a brilliant one in terms of birth, fortune or social standing. Second, Prince Andrey was not in the first flush of youth, his health was not good (the old man set great store by this), and the girl was very young. Third, there was his son; it would be a pity to entrust him to some slip of a girl. 'Fourth and last,' said the father to his son with a mocking glance, 'I appeal to you. Put it all off for a year, go abroad and see to your health, find a German tutor for Prince Nikolay – you've been wanting to do that – and then, if your love, passion, determination – whatever you want to call it – still matters to you, then get married. And that's my last word on the subject – I mean it, my very last word . . .' the old prince concluded, his tone clearly indicating that nothing was going to change his mind.

Prince Andrey could see through the old man: he was hoping that either Andrey's feelings or those of his fiancée would fail the test of a year's delay, or that he, the old prince, would be dead by the end of it, and he decided to fall in with his father's wish. He would make a proposal and then postpone the wedding for a year.

Three weeks after his last evening visit to the Rostovs' Prince Andrey returned to Petersburg.

After the conversation with her mother Natasha spent the whole of the next day waiting for Bolkonsky, but he didn't come. A second and a third day came and went – still no visit. Pierre stayed away too, and Natasha, unaware that Prince Andrey had gone off to see his father, didn't know what to make of his absence.

Three weeks went by like this. Natasha refused to go out. She walked the house like a ghost, gloomy and listless, weeping in secret at night, and she stopped going in to see her mother at bedtime. She was continually blushing and very touchy. She had the impression that her disappointment was an open secret and they were all laughing at her and feeling sorry for her. For all the intensity of her personal sorrow, it was hurt pride that made her misery even more painful.

One day she came in to see the countess and started to say something, only to collapse in tears. They were the tears of a child whose feelings have been hurt and it can't see why it is being punished. The countess did what she could to comfort her daughter. At first Natasha simply listened and listened, but then suddenly she interrupted her mother.

'Please don't, Mamma. I've stopped thinking about it – I don't want to any more! Oh why did he keep coming here and then suddenly stop?' There was a tremor in her voice and she was on the verge of tears, but she recovered her composure and went on to say, 'And now I don't want to get married at all. And besides I'm scared of him. Anyway, now I'm completely relaxed about everything.'

The day after this conversation Natasha put on one of her old dresses, one she knew she could rely on to feel good in all morning, and from first thing she resumed her old way of life, which had been abandoned ever since the ball. After morning tea she went out into the big hall, which she particularly liked because of its strong resonance, and did her singing practice, singing scales. When she had finished the first exercise she stood still in the middle of the hall and repeated one snatch of melody that particularly appealed to her. She listened enraptured, as if for the first time, by the charm of the notes as they swelled out to fill the vast spaces of the great room before slowly dying away, and suddenly she was happy again.

'Why should I bother about all that? I'm all right as I am,' she told herself, and she began walking up and down the room, not putting her feet down straight on to the echoing parquet, but doing a heel-and-toe at each step (she was wearing new shoes that she really liked), and listening as her heels clicked and her toes scraped rhythmically, which was just as nice as listening to the sound of her own voice. She glanced into a large mirror as she passed. 'Yes, that's me!' her expression seemed to say when she caught sight of herself. 'Very nice too. I don't need anybody else.'

A footman wanted to come in and clear something away, but she wouldn't let him. She shut the door on him and continued her promenade. This morning she was back at last in her favourite situation, that of loving herself and being her own best admirer. 'There goes Natasha – such a charming creature!' she said, referring to herself once again in the words of some third-person collective male figure. 'Pretty girl, good voice, young, not doing any harm, just leave her in peace.' But, however much people left her in peace now, she couldn't be at peace, and she sensed this immediately.

Out in the vestibule the front door opened, someone asked, 'Are they at home?' and footsteps could be heard approaching. Natasha was busy admiring herself in the glass, but suddenly she no longer saw herself. She was listening to the sounds coming from the vestibule. When she did see herself again she looked very pale. It was *him*. She knew for certain, though his voice was scarcely audible through the closed doors.

White-faced and panic-stricken, Natasha flew into the drawing-room.

'Mamma, it's Bolkonsky!' she said. 'Mamma, this is awful, I can't bear it! . . . I don't want . . . all this pain! What shall I do?'

The countess had no time to answer. Prince Andrey strode into the drawing-room looking worried and terribly serious. The moment he saw Natasha his face lit up. He kissed the countess's hand and Natasha's, and seated himself alongside the sofa.

'It's some time since we had the pleasure . . .' the countess began to say, but Prince Andrey cut right across her question with a quick response, obviously anxious to get out what he had come to say.

'I haven't been to see you all this time because I have been away seeing my father. I had something very important to discuss with him. I didn't get back till last night,' he said, glancing at Natasha. 'I must talk to you, Countess,' he added, after a moment's silence.

The countess looked down with a heavy sigh.

'I am at your disposal,' she managed to say.

Natasha knew she ought to go, but she couldn't bring herself to do it. There was a strangulated feeling in her throat, and she stood there goggling, staring quite rudely straight at Prince Andrey.

'Now? . . . This minute? . . . No, it can't be!' she was thinking.

He glanced at her again, and that glance told her she was not mistaken. Yes, here and now, this very minute, her fate was being decided.

'Run along, Natasha. I'll call you,' the countess whispered.

With frightened and imploring eyes Natasha glanced at Prince Andrey and her mother, and left the room.

'Countess, I have come to ask you for your daughter's hand,' said Prince Andrey.

The countess's face flared red, but at first she said nothing.

'Your proposal . . .' the countess began at last in measured tones. He sat there in silence, watching her face. 'Your proposal . . .' (she was painfully embarrassed) 'is, er, welcome, and . . . I accept your proposal. I'm glad of it. And my husband . . . I do hope . . . but the decision must rest with her . . .'

'I'll talk to her when I have your consent . . . Do I have it?' said Prince Andrey.

'Yes,' said the countess, extending her hand to him, and it was with mixed feelings of remoteness and tenderness that she pressed her lips to his forehead as he bent to kiss her hand. She dearly wanted to love him as a son, but he seemed like an alien spirit, and besides she was afraid of him.

'I'm sure my husband will consent,' said the countess, 'but what about your father . . . ?'

'I have kept my father informed of my plans, and he gives his consent with the sole proviso that the marriage does not take place for a year. I was going to tell you about that,' said Prince Andrey.

'Well, Natasha is very young, but – does it have to be such a long time?'

'There was no other way . . .' said Prince Andrey with a sigh.

'I'll send her in to you,' said the countess, and she went out of the room.

'Lord, have mercy on us!' she kept repeating as she searched for her daughter.

Sonya told her Natasha was in her bedroom. She was sitting on her bed, pale-faced and dry-eyed, gazing at an icon and murmuring something as she crossed herself rapidly. Seeing her mother, she leapt up and flew across to her.

'What is it, Mamma? . . . What is it?'

'Off you go, go and see him. He's asking for your hand,' said the countess – coldly, it seemed to Natasha . . . 'Go on . . . off you go . . .' her mother murmured with a mixture of sadness and disapproval, and she gave a deep sigh as her daughter ran off.

Natasha had no recollection of entering the drawing-room. As she came in and caught sight of him, she stopped short. 'This stranger, has he suddenly become *everything* to me?' she asked herself, and her answer was instantaneous. 'Yes, he has. He alone is dearer to me now than anything in the world.' Prince Andrey looked down as he advanced towards her.

'I fell in love with you the moment I first saw you. May I hope?' He glanced up at her and was struck by the solemn look on her passionate face, a face that seemed to say, 'Why do you ask? What's the point in feeling doubtful when you can't possibly know? What's the point in talking when words can't express your feelings?'

She came a little nearer, and stopped. He took her hand and kissed it.

'Do you love me?'

'Yes, yes,' said Natasha, with something near to impatience. She gave a deep sigh, then another, then the sighs came faster and faster until she burst into sobs.

'What is it? Is there anything wrong?'

'Oh, I am so happy,' she answered, smiling through her tears. She leant closer, thought for a second, as though wondering whether all this was really happening, and then kissed him.

Prince Andrey held her hand and gazed into her eyes, though in his heart he felt no trace of his former love for her. A change had come over his inner being. Gone was the former desire with all its poetry and mysterious charm. Now all he felt was pity for her feminine and childish frailty, dismay at her devotion and willingness to trust, and the hard, sweet taste of duty that must bind him to her for ever. This new feeling may have been less glorious and poetical, but it was stronger and more serious than before.

'Did your mamma tell you it cannot happen for a year?' said Prince Andrey, still gazing into her eyes.

'Is this really me, the "slip of a girl" that everyone used to call me?' Natasha was thinking. 'Am I really a *wife* from now on, the equal of this nice, clever man that I hardly know, someone that even my father looks up to? Is it really true? Is it really true that now I can't go on treating life like a joke, that now I'm a grown-up woman, now I'm fully responsible for every word and every action? . . . What did he ask me?'

'No,' she answered, without having understood his question.

'Please forgive me,' said Prince Andrey, 'but you're so young, and I've had so much experience. I'm afraid for you. You don't know yourself yet.'

Natasha concentrated hard on what he was saying, but she couldn't get the meaning of his words.

'Hard as that year will be for me, delaying my happiness,' continued Prince Andrey, 'you will use that time to make sure you know your own mind. I am asking you to make me a happy man in a year's time, but you are free – we shall keep our engagement secret – and if you were to find out you don't really love me, or if you fell in love with . . .' said Prince Andrey with a forced smile.

'Why are you saying all this?' Natasha interrupted. 'You know I've loved you since the day you first came to Otradnoye,' she said, certain she was telling the truth.

'In a year you'll learn all about yourself . . .'

'A who-ole year!' Natasha burst out, realizing for the first time that the wedding was to be delayed for a year. 'But why wait a year? . . . Why wait a year?'

Prince Andrey began to explain the reasons for the delay. Natasha wasn't listening.

'Is there no other way?' she asked. Prince Andrey said nothing in reply, but the impossibility of changing this decision was written on his face.

'Oh, that's awful! It's absolutely awful!' Natasha cried suddenly, breaking into sobs again. 'I'll die if I have to wait a year. It's impossible. It's awful.' She glanced at the face of her husband-to-be and saw his look of bewilderment and deep sympathy.

'No, it's all right, I'll do anything,' she said, suddenly in control of her tears, 'I'm so happy!'

Her father and mother came in and gave the engaged couple their blessing. From that day on Prince Andrey visited the Rostovs as Natasha's fiancé.

CHAPTER 24

There were no betrothal celebrations, and no announcement was made of Natasha's engagement to Bolkonsky; Prince Andrey insisted on that. He said that since he was responsible for postponing the wedding he ought to bear the whole burden of it. He said that although he was bound for ever by his word he did not want to bind Natasha, and he wanted her to feel completely free. If in six months' time she felt she didn't love him, she would have a perfect right to refuse him. Naturally enough, neither Natasha nor her parents would hear a word of this, but Prince Andrey was adamant. He came to their house every day, but he didn't behave like a fiancé; he addressed her formally and kissed her only on the hand. Since the day of his proposal the relationship between Prince Andrey and Natasha had changed completely into a new kind of uncomplicated closeness. It was as if they had not known each other before. Both of them loved to recall how they had treated one another when there was *nothing* between them. Now they both felt like utterly different creatures, no longer awkward and affected, but simple and sincere. At first Prince Andrey had been the cause of some embarrassment within the family. He had seemed like a man from another world, and Natasha worked hard at bringing them all round to him, declaring with no little pride that his unusual manner was all show, he was just like everybody else deep down – she wasn't scared of him and nobody else need be. It took only a few days for the rest of the family to get used to seeing him; any awkwardness soon disappeared and they went back to their old way of living, with him now accommodated to it. He could talk to the count about estate management, to the countess and Natasha about clothes, and to Sonya about albums and embroidery. There were times when the Rostovs, both privately and in front of Prince Andrey, expressed amazement at the way things had turned out, and how clear the omens had all been: Prince Andrey's coming to Otradnoye and their coming to Petersburg; the resemblance between Natasha and Prince Andrey that the old nurse had spotted during his first visit; the encounter between Andrey and Nikolay in 1805; and many other auguries, noted by various family-members, foreshadowing what was to come.

The house now had a special poetic atmosphere, the unchanging stillness that always goes with the presence of an engaged couple. They often sat together in a group without anyone talking. And if some of them got up and walked away, leaving them alone together, sometimes the engaged couple still sat there in silence. It wasn't often that they spoke of their future life together. Prince Andrey was too scared and embarrassed to talk about it. Natasha shared this feeling, as she shared all his feelings, being very good at guessing them. On one occasion Natasha began asking questions about his son.

Prince Andrey coloured up, as he often did at that time, which greatly endeared him to Natasha, and said that his son wasn't going to live with them.

'Why not?' said Natasha, somewhat taken aback.

'Oh, I can't take him away from his grandfather, and anyway . . .'

'Oh, I would have loved him so much!' said Natasha, quickly catching on to his line of thought, 'but I can see you don't want either of us to be blamed for anything.'

The old count sometimes came to Prince Andrey, kissed him and asked his advice about Petya's education or Nikolay's career. The old countess sighed as she watched them. Sonya was afraid at every end and turn of being *de trop*, and was always trying to find excuses for leaving them alone, even when it wasn't necessary. When Prince Andrey got going on a story – he was a splendid raconteur – Natasha listened to him with pride. When she was talking she noted with a mixture of joy and dread that he was watching her with close attention and a searching stare. She kept asking herself in some bewilderment, 'What does he see in me? What does he want when he stares like that? What if I haven't got what he's looking for?' Sometimes she slipped into one of her moods of happy abandon, and then she really loved to watch and hear Prince Andrey laughing at her. He seldom laughed, but when he did he did so with complete abandon, and she always felt closer to him when he had been laughing like that. Natasha's happiness would have been complete but for the dreadful thought of their impending separation, which was looming ever closer.

On the eve of his departure from Petersburg Prince Andrey brought Pierre along too; he hadn't been to the Rostovs' since the day of the ball. Pierre seemed absent-minded and embarrassed. He spent much of the time talking to the countess. Natasha sat down at a little chess table with Sonya, and invited Prince Andrey to join them. He came over.

'You've known Bezukhov quite some time, haven't you?' he asked. 'Do you like him?'

'Yes, he's very nice, but very odd.'

And she began doing what everyone always did when speaking of Pierre, telling stories about his absent-mindedness, stories that were largely fictional.

'I've told him our secret, you know,' said Prince Andrey. 'We've known each other since we were boys. He has a heart of gold. Please, Natalie,' he said, suddenly turning serious. 'I'm going away. Anything could happen. You might fall out of . . . Oh, I know I ought not to talk like that. But listen – if anything happens to you while I'm away . . .'

'What could happen?'

'If you get into any kind of trouble . . .' Prince Andrey persisted. 'Please, Mademoiselle Sophie, if anything happens, anything at all, go to him and nobody else for advice and help. I know he's terribly absent-minded and odd, but his heart's in the right place.'

None of them, father, mother, Sonya, not even Prince Andrey, could have foreseen the effect the separation would have on Natasha. She wandered the house all day long, red in the face, dry-eyed but wildly excited, fussing over little details as if she had no concept of what was about to descend on her. She didn't weep even when he kissed her hand for the last time and took his leave.

'Please don't go!' was all she could manage, in a voice that made him wonder whether he ought not to stay after all, a voice he would long remember. When he had gone she still didn't weep; she just sat in her room for days on end without crying, totally apathetic, saying nothing more than the occasional, 'Oh, why did he go?'

But then, two weeks after his departure, she amazed everyone around by just as suddenly recovering from her low morale and becoming her old self again, but with a change in her moral physiognomy much like the new look on a child's face at the end of a long illness.

CHAPTER 25

Over the last year, following his son's departure, old Prince Nikolay Bolkonsky's health and temper had got worse. He was now more irritable than ever, and it was generally Princess Marya who had to take the full fury of his unreasonable tantrums. He seemed determined to seek out all her vulnerable points and make her suffer the cruellest possible mental torment. Princess Marya had two passions and therefore two sources of pleasure: her nephew, little Nikolay, and religion, and both of these were favourite targets for the old prince's attacks and taunts. Whatever the topic of conversation, he would bring the subject round to superstitious old maids or children who were pampered and spoilt. 'You want to turn him' (Nikolay) 'into another old maid like yourself. You won't get away with it. Prince Andrey wants a son, not an old maid,' he would say. Or he would turn to Mademoiselle Bourienne when Princess Marya was with them and ask whether she liked our village priests and holy icons, subjects he always found so amusing.

He never stopped peppering Princess Marya with wounding remarks, but his daughter forgave him always and effortlessly. How could he be at fault, her own father, who (as she knew full well) loved her in spite of everything? How could he be considered unjust? What is justice anyway? Princess Marya never gave a thought to such a grand word as 'justice'. All the complex laws of humanity came together for her in one clear and simple law – the law of love and self-sacrifice, laid down by Him who suffered in His love for all humanity, though He was Himself truly God. Other people's justice or injustice – was that any concern of hers? Hers was to suffer and to love, and that she did.

That winter Prince Andrey had come back to Bald Hills full of high spirits, gentle and affectionate, the kind of brother Princess Marya had not known for many years. She had strongly suspected that something must have happened to him, but he had said nothing to his sister about falling in love. Before leaving, Prince Andrey had had a long conversation with his father, and Princess Marya noticed that they were unhappy with each other when the time came to part.

Soon after Prince Andrey had gone, Princess Marya wrote a letter from Bald Hills to her friend in Petersburg, Julie Karagin. (Princess Marya still dreamt – as girls do – of seeing Julie married to her brother.) She was currently mourning the loss of a brother killed in Turkey.[6]

Sorrow seems to be our common lot, my dear, lovely friend Julie.

Your loss is so awful that I can explain it to myself only as a special act of providence by God, who, in all His love for you, wishes to put you and your most excellent mother to the test.

Oh, my dear, religion, and religion alone can, if not comfort us, at least save us from despair. Only religion can make clear to us what man cannot comprehend without its aid: why and for what purpose good and noble beings capable of happiness, doing no harm to others, indeed essential for the happiness of other people, are called away to God, while wicked, useless and dangerous people are left among the living, a burden to themselves and everyone else. The first death I ever saw, which I shall never forget – the death of my dear little sister-in-law – left me with the same impression. You wonder why your noble brother was fated to die; like you I wondered why Liza had to die – an angel who had never done the slightest harm to anyone, and never had anything but kind thoughts in her heart. But do you know what, my dear friend? Five years have gone by, and even I, with my inferior intellect, am just beginning to understand clearly why it was necessary for her to die, and how that death was but an expression of the infinite goodness of the Creator, whose every action, though for the most part passing all understanding, is but a manifestation of His infinite love for His creation. Perhaps, I often think, she was too angelic, too innocent to have enough strength to perform all the duties of a mother. As a young wife, she was beyond reproach; perhaps she could not have been so in motherhood. As things stand, beyond all the pure memories and regrets she has left us, and particularly Prince Andrey, in the other world she will in all probability attain a place which I myself dare not hope for. But over and above her loss, that early and terrible death has actually come as a powerful blessing for me and my brother, in spite of all our grief. When it happened, at the moment of our loss, I could never have entertained thoughts like these; at that time I should have been horrified and dismissed them, but now it all seems so clear and certain. I write all this to you, my dear friend, simply to persuade you of a Gospel truth which has become a rule of living for me: not a hair of our head shall fall without His will. And His will is governed only by His infinite love for us, and so it is that whatever comes to pass, all is for our good.

You ask whether we shall spend next winter in Moscow. For all my desire to see you, I don't expect we shall, and I don't want to do so. And you may be surprised to hear that the reason for this is – Buonaparte. Let me explain: my father's health is noticeably declining; he cannot stand being contradicted and he's always so irritable. This irritability is, as you know, mostly directed towards politics. He cannot stand the idea of Buonaparte hobnobbing on equal terms with all the sovereigns of Europe, especially our own, the grandson of the great Catherine! As you know, I haven't the slightest interest in politics, but from my father and his conversations with Mikhail Ivanovich, I do get to know what is going on in the world, and in particular I keep hearing about all the honours bestowed on Buonaparte. Bald Hills seems to be the only place on the globe where he is not recognized as a great man, let alone Emperor of France. This is what my father cannot put up with. He seems very reluctant to talk about going to Moscow, and I have the feeling this is mainly due to his political views and the likelihood of him rubbing people up the wrong way, what with his general attitude and his habit of speaking his mind and not making any allowances for anybody. Whatever he gained from medical treatment in Moscow he would lose from arguing about Buonaparte, which would be inevitable. Anyway, it will all be settled soon.

Family life goes on in the same old way, except for my brother Andrey being away. As I wrote to you before, he has changed a lot recently. It is only now, this year, that he seems to have got over his grief at long last. He is just as I remember him when he was a boy, nice and kind, and more good-hearted than anyone I know. He seems to realize that his life is not over yet. But, despite the improvement in his morale, he has become very weak physically. He has kept on losing weight and he's more edgy than he used to be. I worry about him, and I'm so glad he is taking this foreign tour, which the doctors have been prescribing for ages. I hope he'll come back cured. You write to me that all Petersburg considers him one of the most capable, cultivated and intelligent young men. Forgive my family pride – this is something I have never doubted. The good that he has done here – to his peasants, the local nobility, everyone – is incalculable. When he arrived in Petersburg he simply got what he deserved. I'm amazed at the way rumours find their way from Petersburg to Moscow, especially groundless ones like the story you mentioned about my brother supposedly marrying the little Rostov girl. I don't think Andrey will ever marry anyone, and certainly not her. I'll tell you why. Firstly, I know that though he seldom speaks of his late wife, his sadness at her loss has penetrated his heart too deeply for him ever to consider arranging for a successor, and a stepmother for our little angel. And secondly, because, as far as I can tell, that girl is not the sort of woman who would appeal to Prince Andrey. I don't think Andrey can have chosen her to be his wife, and I must admit that I hope not.

But I've rambled on too long. Here I am finishing the second sheet.

Goodbye for now, my dear friend. God Almighty take you to His holy bosom. My dear companion, Mademoiselle Bourienne, sends her love.

MARIE

CHAPTER 26

In the middle of the summer Princess Marya was surprised to receive a letter from Prince Andrey in Switzerland with some strange and unexpected news. He informed his sister of his engagement to Natasha Rostov. His whole letter was suffused with ecstatic love for his fiancée, as well as tender and confiding affection for his sister. He wrote that he had never been in love like this before, and now at last he had a clear idea of what life meant. He asked her to forgive him for having kept quiet about his plans during his last visit to Bald Hills, though he had mentioned them to his father. He had said nothing because he knew she might go and persuade her father to give his consent, only to fail in the attempt, irritate her father and bring down on herself all the weight of his displeasure. 'Besides,' he wrote, 'things were not definitely settled then, and now they are. At that time our father insisted on a year's postponement, and now half of it, *six months*, have passed, and I remain firmer than ever in my resolution. If it weren't for the doctors insisting I stay here and take the waters I should be back in Russia by now, but, as things stand, I must delay my return for another three months. You know me, and how things are with Father. I don't need anything from him. I've always been independent, and I always shall be, but to go against his will, to incur his anger when perhaps he won't be with us much longer, would cut my happiness in half. I am writing to him now. Please choose the right moment, give him my letter, and let me know how he feels. Is there any hope of his agreeing to shorten the period by three months?'

After much hesitation, many misgivings and endless prayers, Princess Marya handed the letter to her father. The following day the old prince said to her calmly:

'Write and tell your brother to wait till I'm dead . . . He won't have long to wait. I'll soon set him free.'

The princess made as if to protest, but her father would have none of it, and he ranted on louder and louder. 'Go on, get yourself married, darling boy . . . Splendid family! . . . Clever people, eh? Plenty of money, eh? Oh yes, a nice little stepmother for Nikolay! Tell him not to wait – get married tomorrow . . . She'll be a stepmother for our little Nikolay, and I'll marry the little Bourienne girl! . . . He-he-he, can't have him doing without his own stepmother! Just one thing, no women-folk around this house from now on. Let him get married and go and live on his own. Why don't you go and live with him?' He turned to Princess Marya: 'Good luck to you! It's a cold world out there, a very cold world.'

After this outburst the prince never returned to the subject. But all his pent-up fury at his son's lack of spirit vented itself in the way he treated his daughter. To his former pretexts for taunting her he now added another one – snide remarks about stepmothers and being ever so nice to Mademoiselle Bourienne.

'Why shouldn't I marry her?' he would say to his daughter. 'She'd make a splendid princess!' And as the days went by, much to her surprise and bewilderment, Princess Marya began to notice that her father really was beginning to associate more and more with the French girl. Princess Marya wrote to Prince Andrey and described their father's reaction to the letter, but she consoled her brother with the hope that she might be able to bring him round.

Little Nikolay and his education, her brother Andrey and religion – these were Princess Marya's pleasures and consolations. But apart from them, since everybody has to have personal hopes, Princess Marya fostered, in the secret depths of her inner being, a private dream and a hidden hope from which she drew what consolation there was in her life. The consoling dream and hope came to her from her

'Servants of God' – the holy fools and pilgrims who visited her behind the prince's back. The longer Princess Marya lived, the more she observed life and experienced it, the more she marvelled at the short-sightedness of people who seek pleasure and happiness here on earth, toiling away, suffering and struggling, and doing so much harm to each other in pursuit of an impossible will-o'-the-wisp of happiness in iniquity. Prince Andrey had loved a wife and she had died, but that wasn't enough for him; he now wanted to bind his happiness to another woman. Her father was against it because he wanted a more distinguished or a wealthier match for Andrey. And all of them were struggling and suffering, tormenting themselves and tainting their souls, their eternal souls, to find themselves blessings that were only ephemeral. We are all well aware of this, but in any case Jesus Christ, the Son of God, came down to earth and told us that this life is but for a moment, it is a trial, yet we still cling to it and think to find happiness in it. 'Why can't people see this?' Princess Marya wondered. 'Well some people can – those despised Servants of God, who come to me up the backstairs with bags on their backs, scared of being seen by the prince, not because they're worried about persecution, but from fear of leading him into sin. To leave hearth and home, to renounce all thoughts of worldly blessings, and to wander the world, with nothing to cling to, in sackcloth and tatters, with a new name, doing no harm, but praying for people, praying equally for those who per-secute and those who give succour – there is no truth and no life higher than this truth and this life!'

There was one pilgrim by the name of Theodosia, a quiet little woman of fifty, with a pockmarked faced, who had been wandering the world for over thirty years barefoot and wearing heavy chains. Princess Marya was particularly fond of her. One evening when they were sitting together in a dark room lit only by an icon-lamp, Theodo-sia told her life-story. Princess Marya felt such a strong intuition that Theodosia was the one person who had found the right path in life that she decided she ought to go on a pilgrimage herself. When Theodosia had gone to bed Princess Marya thought things over well into the night and eventually came to the conclusion that – however strange it might look – she must go on a pilgrimage. She confided her intention to no one but a monk, Father Akinfi, and he gave her project his blessing. On the pretext of buying presents for pilgrim women, Princess Marya built up the complete outfit of a pilgrim – a rough smock, shoes of plaited bark, a kaftan and a black scarf. She would often go over to the secret chest where these things were hidden and hover there, undecided whether the time might not have come to carry out her plan.

Often as she listened to the pilgrim-women's stories she was so transported by their simple sayings – mechanical phrases to them, but powerful profundities to her ears – that she was more than once tempted ready to drop everything and run away from home. She could imagine herself alongside Theodosia, dressed in a rough smock, setting out on her pilgrimage with scrip and staff, trudging the dusty road, free from envy, free from earthly love, free from every desire, proceeding from one saint to another, and arriving at last where there is neither sorrow nor sighing, but everlasting joy and happiness.

'I shall come to a place and pray, but before I can grow used to it and love it, I shall move on. And I shall walk on till my legs give way under me, then shall I lie down and die, and come at last to that eternal haven of peace and quiet, where there is neither sorrow nor sighing!' thought Princess Marya.

But at the first sight of her father, and especially little Nikolay, she would falter, shed a few silent tears and feel like a woman of sin. Did she not love her father and her nephew more than God?

PART IV

According to biblical tradition the absence of work – idleness – was a condition of the first man's state of blessedness before the Fall. The love of idleness has been preserved in fallen man, but now a heavy curse lies upon him, not only because we have to earn our bread by the sweat of our brow, but also because our sense of morality will not allow us to be both idle and at ease. Whenever we are idle a secret voice keeps telling us to feel guilty. If man could discover a state in which he could be idle and still feel useful and on the path of duty, he would have regained one aspect of that primitive state of blessedness. And there is one such state of enforced and irreproachable idleness enjoyed by an entire class of men – the military class. It is this state of enforced and irreproachable idleness that forms the chief attraction of military service, and it always will.

Nikolay Rostov had been enjoying this blessed state to the full as he served on, after the year 1807, in the Pavlograd regiment, now commanding the squadron that had been Denisov's. Rostov had become a bluff, personable young man, likely to have been considered rather a bad egg by his old Moscow acquaintances, though he was loved and respected by his present comrades, subordinates and superiors, and he was enjoying life. But latterly, in the year 1809, he had begun to receive more and more letters from home full of complaints from his mother that things were going from bad to worse, and it was high time he came home to bring a little cheer and comfort to his old parents.

Reading these letters, Nikolay felt dismayed that anyone should want to extricate him from the environment in which he was living so quietly and comfortably, cut off from all the complexities of existence. He felt that sooner or later he might have to plunge back into that maelstrom of life, with all sorts of things going wrong and having to be put right, stewards' accounts, quarrels and intrigues, ties, society, to say nothing of Sonya's love and the promise he had made to her. It all seemed so terribly difficult and complicated that he took to answering his mother with frigid letters in very formal French, beginning 'My dear mamma', and ending 'Your obedient son', avoiding all mention of a time when he might return home. One letter in 1810 informed him of Natasha's engagement to Bolkonsky, and the year-long postponement of their wedding because the old prince wouldn't give his consent. This letter left Nikolay feeling worried and offended. For one thing, he would be sorry to lose Natasha from the household, because he cared for her more than anyone else in the family. Secondly, with his hussar's way of looking at things he regretted not having been there when all this had been going on; he'd have shown this Bolkonsky that linking up with him wasn't all that much of an honour, and if he really loved Natasha he would get married without his crazy old father's consent. For a moment he wondered whether to ask for leave, to see Natasha and find out how she was coping with her engagement, but they had manoeuvres coming up, and there was this business with Sonya, and everything was so complicated that he put it off again. But in the spring of that year he got another letter from his mother, written without his father's knowledge, and this was what decided him. She told him if he didn't come home and take charge, their whole estate would have to go under the hammer and they would be out on the street. The count was so weak, and he trusted Mitenka too much, and he was such a nice man that everyone took advantage of him, and things were going from bad to worse. 'I beg you in the name of God, please come home immediately, if you don't want me and all the family to be left utterly miserable,' wrote the countess.

That letter deeply affected Nikolay. He had an ordinary man's common sense and this told him what he simply *had* to do. He had to retire from the army, or at least to go home on leave. He had no real idea of why he had to go, but straight after his lunch-time nap he ordered his horse to be saddled, a grey by the name of Mars, a brute of a stallion that he hadn't ridden for ages. He galloped off, and when he returned, with the horse in a lather, he told Lavrushka, Denisov's old valet who had stayed on with him, and the comrades who dropped in that evening, that he had applied for leave and was on his way home. It all seemed so difficult, strange, quite unimaginable: he was going away without hearing from the staff about the only things that really mattered to him – was he being made up to captain or getting the Order of St Anne for the last manoeuvres? – he was going away without clinching the sale of his three roans to the Polish Count Goluchowski after all that haggling (with Rostov placing a side-bet that he would get two thousand for them); the ball would go ahead without him, the ball given by the hussars in honour of their favourite Polish belle, Madame Przazdziecka (one in the eye for the Uhlans, who had given a ball for their favourite belle, Madame Borzozowska) – but despite all this he simply knew he had to leave this lovely, clear-cut world for one that was nothing but messy nonsense. A week later his leave came through. His comrades – not only from the regiment, but from the whole brigade – gave Rostov a subscription dinner at fifteen roubles a head. There were two bands playing and two choruses singing, Rostov danced the trepak with Major Basov, the drunken officers tossed him in the air, hugged him and dropped him on the floor, followed by the men of the third squadron, who tossed him up again with a great 'Hurrah!' Then they put him in his sledge and went with him as far as the first post-station.

During the first half of the journey, from Kremenchug to Kiev, Rostov spent the whole time thinking back, as always happens on these occasions, to what he had left behind – in his case, to the squadron. But once he had jolted his bumpy way past the half-way point, he stopped thinking about his three roans, his quartermaster and Panna Borzozowska, and started to wonder rather anxiously how he would find things at Otradnoye. The nearer he got, the more intensely, much more intensely, his thoughts turned to home (as if inner feelings were also subject to the law of gravitation, varying in inverse proportion to the square of the distance). At the last station before Otradnoye he gave the sledge-driver a three-rouble tip, and soon he was racing up the steps of his home, all out of breath like a little boy.

After the excitement of the first meeting, and the odd feeling of being let down by expectations ('Everything's the same. Why was I in such a hurry to get here?'), Nikolay began to settle down and get used to the old way of living at home. His father and mother were just the same, though they had aged a little. The only thing new about them was a certain uneasiness and the occasional disagreement that hadn't been there before, deriving, as he was soon to learn, from the awful state of their affairs.

Sonya was now nearly twenty. She would grow no prettier than this; there was no more promise to be fulfilled, though what she had was quite enough. She had blossomed with love and happiness the moment Nikolay had come home, and this young girl's faithful, unshakeable love for him gladdened his heart. It was Petya and Natasha who surprised Nikolay most of all. Petya had grown into a tall, handsome boy of thirteen, full of happy fun, and his voice was breaking. Nikolay marvelled at Natasha for quite some time, and gave a laugh as he looked at her.

'My, how you've changed,' he told her.

'What do you mean "changed"? Am I uglier?'

'No, just the opposite. But there's a kind of dignity . . . A real princess!' he whispered to her.

'Yes, yes, yes!' cried Natasha gleefully.

Natasha ran through the story of her romantic attachment to Prince Andrey, and his visit to Otradnoye, and she produced his last letter.

'Well, aren't you pleased?' asked Natasha. 'I feel so calm and happy now.'

'Yes,' answered Nikolay. 'He's a splendid man. Are you very much in love with him?'

'What can I say?' answered Natasha. 'I've been in love with Boris, my teacher and Denisov, but this is completely different. I feel calm, settled. I know there's no better man in all the world, and so I feel calm and contented. It's completely different . . .'

Nikolay expressed his dissatisfaction at the marriage being delayed for a year, but Natasha turned on him in exasperation, arguing that this was the only possible way, it would have been awful to enter a family against the father's will, and anyway it was what she wanted herself.

'You just don't understand,' she kept saying.

Nikolay hesitated, and then said he agreed with her.

Her brother often wondered as he watched her. She just didn't seem like a young girl in love who was separated from her fiancé. She was calm, composed and as cheerful as ever, which didn't seem right to Nikolay, and he became very doubtful about her engagement to Bolkonsky. He couldn't bring himself to believe that her fate was sealed, especially without ever seeing her with Prince Andrey. He couldn't get it out of his head that there was something wrong with this proposed marriage.

'What's this delay all about? Why was there no announcement?' he thought.

In the course of a conversation with his mother about his sister, he discovered to his surprise, and somewhat to his satisfaction, that deep down his mother sometimes had her own doubts about the marriage.

'Look what he says,' she said, showing her son a letter from Prince Andrey with that hidden resentment that mothers always feel towards their daughters' future married happiness. 'He says he can't come before December. What could possibly keep him? Illness, I suppose! He's not very well. Don't mention this to Natasha. And don't be surprised if she's all bright and cheerful. It's just that she's playing out the last days of her girlhood, and I know how she reacts when she gets letters from him. Oh well, God willing, everything will turn out all right.' She ended as she always did by saying, 'He's a splendid man.'

CHAPTER 2

For some time after his arrival Nikolay was in a serious frame of mind bordering on depression. He was worrying about the impending need to tackle the ridiculous business affairs that had caused his mother to send for him. Then on the third day, in order to get this burden off his shoulders as soon as possible, he stormed off, scowling and saying nothing to Natasha when she asked where he was going, went straight to Mitenka's lodge and demanded *a full account of everything*. What was meant by *a full account of everything* Nikolay knew even less than the cowering, bewildered Mitenka. Neither the conversation nor Mitenka's run through the accounts lasted any length of time. The village elder, the peasant spokesman and the village clerk were waiting outside in the entrance hall, and they heard all that was going on with a mixture of horror and pleasure, first the rising bellow and thunder of the young count's voice, louder and louder, higher and higher, terrible words pouring out one after another.

'You thief! . . . Ungrateful swine! . . . I'll thrash you like a dog! . . . You've got *me* to deal with now! . . . Swindling pig!'

Then, with undiminished horror and pleasure, these people watched as the young count, purple with rage, his eyes bloodshot, dragged Mitenka out by the scruff of his neck, kneeing him and punctuating his own words with expert kicks up the steward's backside, and yelled, 'Get out of here! Get out and don't come back, you vile crook!'

Mitenka flew headlong down the half-dozen steps and shot off into the shrubbery. (This shrubbery was well known as a haven for all the delinquents of Otradnoye. Many a time Mitenka himself had come back from town roaring drunk and gone to ground in the shrubbery, and various denizens of Otradnoye anxious to keep clear of Mitenka had become familiar with its protective powers.)

Mitenka's wife and sisters-in-law peeped out in great alarm, scanning the passage from the doorway of their room, where a bright samovar was simmering away and the steward's high bedstead stood out with its patchwork quilt.

The young count ignored them as he strode past with firm steps, breathing deeply, and disappeared into the house.

Word of what had happened in the lodge reached the countess immediately through her maids. She was consoled by the thought that things were bound to improve from now on, though on the other hand she was worried about her son and how these events might affect him. Once or twice she tiptoed over to his door and listened; he sat within, smoking one pipe after another.

The next day the old count took his son to one side and said with a diffident smile, 'Listen, my dear boy, I think you may have gone a bit too far. Mitenka's told me the whole story.'

'I knew it,' thought Nikolay. 'I knew I'd never get to grips with anything in this crazy world.'

'You lost your temper because he didn't enter those seven hundred roubles in the book. But you see they were carried forward, and you never looked at the next page.'

'Papa, he's a thief and a swindler. That much I do know. And I've done what I've done. But if you prefer it that way, I won't talk to him again.'

'Oh no, dear boy!' The old count was embarrassed now. He was well aware that he had mismanaged his wife's estate and not done right by his children, but he hadn't the first idea how to make up for it all. 'No, please. Do go into everything. I'm an old man. I . . .'

'No, Papa, I'm sorry if I've upset you. You know more than I do.'

'Damn the lot of them, these peasants, and money problems and everything being carried forward,' he thought. 'Years ago I could add up with the best of them in a card school, but carrying things forward is beyond me,' he told himself, and from that time on he kept out of the business side of the family.

But one day the countess called her son in and told him she still held an IOU from Anna Mikhaylovna for two thousand roubles, and she asked Nikolay what he thought should be done with it.

'Well,' answered Nikolay, 'you say it's my decision. I don't like Anna Mikhaylovna, and I don't like Boris, but they were friends of ours, and they were poor. So that's what I'd do!' and he tore the note into pieces, which made the countess sob with tears of joy. After this, the young Rostov put all forms of business to one side and devoted himself with enormous enthusiasm to what was for him a new occupation – hunting – which the old count's estate catered for in the grand manner.

CHAPTER 3

The first signs of winter were in the air now, with morning frosts hardening the earth after its soaking by the autumn rain. The grass had gone tussocky and it stood out in splashes of bright green against patches of brown winter rye trodden down by the cattle, pale yellow corn stubble and reddish strips of buckwheat. The uplands and copses, which at the end of August had still been green islands among the black fields and stubble, had turned into golden and crimson islands in a sea of bright green early-winter crops. The hares had half-grown their winter coats, the fox-cubs were beginning to leave the den, and the young wolves had grown bigger than dogs. This was the best time of the year for hunting. Rostov, suddenly the keenest of country sportsmen, could see that his hounds were not quite hunting-fit and their pads were still tender, so when the hunters met they decided to rest the dogs for three days and then go out on a grand hunt on the 16th of September, starting at the Oak Grove, where there was an unhunted litter of wolves.

This was how things stood on the 14th of September.

All that day the hounds were kept in. There had been a sharp frost, but by evening the sky had clouded over and it had begun to thaw. On the morning of the 15th of September young Rostov stood at the window in his dressing-gown and gazed out on a morning that was perfect for hunting. There wasn't a breath of wind and the sky looked as if it was melting and dissolving into the ground. The only movement detectable in the air was the gentle descent of microscopic beads of moisture in a misty drizzle. Out in the garden bare branches were hung with limpid droplets dripping down on to newly fallen leaves. The kitchen-garden soil gleamed black and wet like the heart of a poppy, and only a few feet away it melted into the damp shroud of grey mist.

Nikolay went out on to the wet, muddy porch. There was a smell of dogs and rotting leaves. Milka, a stocky black and white bitch, lay there watching with her wide, bulbous black eyes, and when she caught sight of her master she got up, stretched back, lay down again like a hare and then suddenly jumped up to lick him on the nose and moustache. Another dog, a borzoi, suddenly spotted his master from the garden path, arched his back and shot up the steps, wagging his tail and rubbing up against Nikolay's legs.

There was a shout: 'Halloo!' It was the inimitable hunting call that somehow combines deep bass with reedy tenor. And round the corner

came the head huntsman and whipper-in, Danilo, all grizzled and
wrinkled, with his hair cut straight across his forehead Ukrainian-style.
He was holding a curved hunting-crop, and he had the air of aloofness
and total scorn that you only see in huntsmen. He greeted his master
by raising his Circassian cap while treating him to a look of great
disdain. Such scorn was not meant to offend his master. Nikolay knew
full well that this Danilo, for all his air of superiority and all-round
contempt, belonged to him, man and huntsman.

'Oh, it's you, Danilo,' said Nikolay rather shyly, sensing as he took
in the splendid hunting weather, the dogs and the huntsman that he
was being carried away by the kind of irresistible surge of pleasure
that makes you forget all your previous intentions, like a lover with
his mistress.

'What shall we do, sir?' The bass voice, hoarse from hallooing, rang
out like an archdeacon's, and a pair of furtive black eyes glinted at
the silent young master, two eyes that seemed to say, 'You can't resist
this, can you?'

'Nice day for it, eh? Go for a gallop? Spot of hunting?' said Nikolay,
scratching Milka behind the ears.

Danilo said nothing, but both his eyes were winking.

'I sent Uvarka out first thing to listen,' came his bass voice after a
moment's silence. 'According to what he says, *she's moved 'em on* to
Otradnoye land. Heard 'em howling.' (*'She's moved 'em on'* meant
that the she-wolf they both knew about had brought her cubs into the
Otradnoye copse, a little plantation not much more than a mile away.)

'Are we off then?' said Nikolay. 'Come on in, and bring Uvarka.'

'If that's what you want, sir.'

'Hold back on the feeding.'

'Yes, sir.'

Five minutes later Danilo and Uvarka were standing in Nikolay's
big study. Although Danilo was not a big man, seeing him in any room
was rather like seeing a horse or bear standing on the floor amongst
the furniture and bits and pieces of human life. Danilo was conscious
of this himself, and as usual he stood by the door and tried to speak
as softly as he could and avoid all movement for fear of doing any
damage in the master's apartment. He did his utmost to get everything
said as fast as he could so as to escape into the open air, to get out
from under a ceiling and find himself back under the sky.

After asking all his questions and getting Danilo to concede that
the dogs were fit (Danilo himself was dying to go hunting), Nikolay
told them to saddle the horses. But then, just as Danilo was about to
go, in tripped Natasha, not properly dressed, with her hair undone

and covered with a big scarf belonging to her old nurse. Petya ran in
with her.

'Are you going out hunting?' said Natasha. 'I knew you were! Sonya
said you wouldn't go. I knew you'd never be able to resist it on a day
like this!'

'Yes, we are,' Nikolay answered reluctantly. Today he wanted to
enjoy some serious hunting and he didn't want to take Natasha and
Petya. 'We are, but it's only a bit of wolf-hunting. You'd be bored.'

'You know that's what I like best,' said Natasha. 'You're awful –
going off on your own, getting the horses saddled and not telling us.'

'The Russians come and none shall bar the way!' declaimed Petya.
'Off we go!'

'But you can't. Mamma said you mustn't,' said Nikolay to Natasha.

'Oh yes I am. I've simply got to!' said Natasha brooking no resistance. 'Danilo, saddle some horses for us, and tell Mikhaylo to hunt
with my pack,' she said to the huntsman.

Simply to be there in the room was a dreadful ordeal for Danilo,
but for him to have any dealings with a young lady was beyond all
bounds. He looked down at the floor and scuttled away as if all of
this had nothing to do with him, desperately anxious to avoid inflicting
any damage on the young lady.

CHAPTER 4

The old count, who had always maintained a magnificent hunt, had
by now handed the whole thing over to his son, but on that day, the
15th of September, he was in a buoyant mood and he decided to ride
out with them. Within the hour the whole hunt was assembled in front
of the porch. Natasha and Petya wanted to say something to Nikolay,
but he brushed past them looking serious and solemn, as if to indicate
that this was no time for fooling around. He scanned the hunt from
side to side, sent a pack of hounds and huntsmen on ahead to go the
long way round, got on his chestnut Don horse, and whistling up his
own leash of borzois he set off across the threshing-ground and into
a field leading towards the Otradnoye wood. The old count's horse, a
sorrel gelding called Viflyanka, was led out by a groom, while he
himself was to drive over in a little trap and join the others at a
prearranged place, a break in the covert.

Fifty-four hounds were led out in the care of six grooms and
whippers-in. In addition to the family members eight men in charge

of more than forty borzois were going out – there must have been about a hundred and thirty dogs and twenty horsemen in all.

Every dog knew its master and its call. Every man in the hunt knew what was expected of him, where to be and what to do. Once past the fence, they all moved along steadily with no noise and no talking, straggling back along the road and stretching out across the field leading to the Otradnoye covert.

The horses trod the field gently as if they were walking over a thick carpet, and splashed through puddles as they crossed the road. The misty sky still seemed to be trickling slowly and imperceptibly down into the earth, the air was still and warm, and not a sound disturbed the silence except for the odd whistle from a huntsman, the snort of a horse, the smack of a whip or the whine of a dog who had lost his place. When they had gone about three-quarters of a mile, five more riders with their dogs emerged from the mist coming towards them. In front rode a fresh-faced, handsome old man with a big grey moustache.

'Morning, Uncle,' said Nikolay as the old man rode up to him.

'Fair for the chase! . . . I knew it would be,' was 'Uncle's' response. He was a distant relative who lived near by on modest means.

'I knew you wouldn't be able to resist it, and you were right to come out. Fair for the chase!' (Uncle's favourite saying.) 'I should get over to the covert straightaway. My Girchik tells me the Ilagins are out with their hounds over at Korniki. Fair for the chase! They'll pinch the litter from under your noses.'

'That's where I'm going. Shall we join forces?' asked Nikolay.

The hounds were brought together into a single pack, and 'Uncle' and Nikolay rode on side by side.

Natasha's eager face and gleaming eyes peeped out from her shawls and scarves as she galloped over to them, doggedly pursued by Petya and Mikhaylo, the huntsman and groom who had been detailed to look after her. Petya was laughing, whipping his horse and pulling back on the reins. Natasha sat on her jet-black Arabchick with easy confidence, controlling him with a gentle, steady hand.

The uncle looked askance at Petya and Natasha. For him, playing games and the serious business of hunting didn't go together.

'Good morning, Uncle. We're coming hunting too!' shouted Petya.

'Good morning to you. Mind you don't trample the dogs,' said the uncle sternly.

'Oh, Nikolay, darling, Trunila is such a nice dog! He knew me,' said Natasha, referring to her favourite hunting dog.

'Hmph, for one thing, Trunila's not a dog, he's a wolfhound,' thought Nikolay, glancing at his sister in an effort to put some noticeable distance between them at this particular time. Natasha took the hint.

'Oh, please don't think we're going to get in the way, Uncle,' said Natasha. 'We'll stay where we're put and we won't move a muscle.'

'Quite right too, little Countess,' said 'Uncle'. 'But don't fall off your horse,' he added, 'otherwise . . . Fair for the chase! . . . you won't have anything to sit on and watch.'

The little island of the Otradnoye covert hove into sight, a couple of hundred yards ahead. Rostov and his 'uncle' decided between them where best to loose the dogs, then Nikolay showed Natasha where to stand – in a spot where there was no chance of anything ever running out – and circled round above the ravine to close in from the rear.

'Listen, nephew, you're after a wise old bird,' said the uncle. 'One slip and she's gone.'

'Well, we'll see what happens. Karay! Here boy!' he shouted, this call being the best response he could think of. Karay was an old hound, misshapen and scabby, famous for having once taken on an old wolf single-handedly. Everyone was now in place.

The old count, knowing how keen his son was when it came to hunting, put on all speed so as not to arrive late, and the whippers-in were hardly in their places when Count Ilya Rostov, a picture of bonhomie, red in the face, jowls quivering, drove up behind his pair of fine black horses, crossed the green field and came to the place where the wolf might come out. Smoothing down his heavy coat and gathering everything he needed for the hunt, he was soon astride his glossy steed, the corpulent Viflyanka, who was gentle, sweet-tempered and, like himself, going grey. The horses and trap were sent back home. Count Ilya Rostov, no true sportsman at heart but a man familiar with every last rule of hunting, rode into the outskirts of the wood and took up a position near to some bushes, where he gathered the reins, settled down in his saddle, and, ready at last, looked around with a broad smile on his face.

Near by stood his personal attendant, Semyon Chekmar, a horseman of long standing, now rather heavy in the saddle. Chekmar held three wolfhounds on a leash, lively enough beasts, though they too had put on weight like their master and his horse. Two other dogs, old and wise, lay there off the leash. A hundred paces along the edge of the wood stood another of the count's grooms, Mitka, a daredevil rider and very keen hunter. The count had followed the old custom of toasting the hunt with a silver goblet of mulled brandy, followed by a light lunch washed down by half a bottle of his favourite claret.

Count Ilya was rather flushed from the wine and the effort of getting there. His watering eyes gleamed with a special brightness, and as he sat there in the saddle nicely swaddled in his heavy coat, he looked like a baby ready to be taken out on a trip in the open air.

With everything checked and in order, Chekmar, lean and gaunt, kept glancing across at his master, with whom he had lived on the best of terms these thirty years. He was clearly in a good mood and Chekmar could look forward to a pleasant chat. Then a third person rode towards them through the wood, very cautiously – clearly having been warned – and reined in behind the count. It was a grey-bearded old man in a woman's cloak, wearing a high peaked cap – the family fool with a woman's name, Nastasya Ivanovna.

'Listen, Nastasya Ivanovna,' whispered the count with a broad wink, 'scare that wolf away, and you'll get it in the neck from Danilo.'

'I knows what I be doing,' said Nastasya.

'Sssh!' hissed the count, and he turned to Semyon. 'Have you seen my Natasha?' he asked. 'Where's she gone?'

'Her Honour's with Master Petya, near them tall weeds over by Zharov,' answered Semyon with a smile. 'She may be a lady, but she don't half love her hunting!'

'You can't get over her being such a good rider, can you, Semyon?' said the count. 'She's as good as any man!'

'Course I can't. She's that quick and clever!'

'And where's our Nikolay gone? Up over Lyadov, eh?' the count asked, still whispering.

'Yes, sir. His Honour knows where to wait. Knows his hunting, he does. Sometimes me and Danilo can't believe how good he is,' said Semyon, who knew how to please his master.

'Good huntsman, eh? Looks good on a horse?'

'Perfect picture! The other day he run this fox out of yon patch at Zavarzino. Flew down that ravine, he did, sight for sore eyes – horse worth a thousand roubles, no price on the rider. Aye, you'd go a long way to find another like him!'

'Yes, a long way . . .' repeated the count, who seemed to be disappointed that Semyon's little speech hadn't lasted longer. 'A long way,' he said, turning up the skirt of his coat to get at his snuff-box.

'The other day he come out of church in all his finery, that Mikhail Sidorych . . .' Semyon stopped short, catching a distinct sound in the still air – hounds chasing, only two or three of them whining. Tilting his head, he listened carefully, wagging a cautionary finger at his master. 'Got the scent . . .' he whispered. 'Gone straight up Lyadov way.'

The count forgot to wipe the smile off his face as he looked out straight along the windbreak, holding his snuff-box in one hand without taking a pinch. After the baying of the hounds came the bass note of Danilo's horn – the wolf had been sighted! The pack joined the first three hounds, and their voices could be heard in full cry with the peculiar low howling sound that goes with the chase. The whippers-in had stopped hallooing now and taken up a wild whooping sound, with Danilo's voice ringing out above the others, deep and low one minute, shrill and piercing the next. Danilo's voice seemed to fill the whole forest, flood out beyond it and disappear far across the open fields.

After a few seconds of listening in silence the count and his groom felt certain the hounds had split into two packs, the larger one chasing off into the distance still in full cry, the other group coming through the woods past the count, and it was from this smaller pack that Danilo's voice could be heard with its great whoops. The sounds of the two chasing packs kept coming together and splitting apart again, but both were getting further away. Semyon gave a sigh and bent down to free up the leash where a young dog had got tangled up in it. The count gave a sigh too, noticed he was still holding the snuff-box and opened it to help himself to a pinch.

'Get back!' Semyon yelled at a dog that had poked his nose out through the bushes. This made the count jump, and he dropped his snuff-box. Nastasya Ivanovna got off his horse to pick it up. The count and Semyon looked on. Suddenly – this sort of thing tends to happen suddenly – the sound of the hunt was upon them. It was as if the baying dogs and Danilo's whooping cries were right there in front of them.

The count looked round to his right where he saw Mitka standing there, goggling, raising his cap and pointing back the other way.

'Look out!' he roared in a voice that suggested the words had long been struggling to get out. He let the dogs go and galloped over towards the count.

The count and Chekmar galloped out of the bushes, and there to the left they saw a wolf loping gently along with an easy swinging movement just to the left of the very thicket they had been standing in. The dogs yelped furiously, tore themselves free from the leash and flashed past the horses' hooves in pursuit of the wolf.

The wolf paused in his flight and staggered as if he was having a heart attack, but then he turned with his broad brow to face the dogs, loped off with the same gentle swinging movement, gave a couple of bounds and disappeared with a flick of his tail into the bushes. The same instant there was a great wailing sound, and out of the opposite bushes sprang a desperate hound, followed by another, and a third, and then the whole pack flew across the grass to the spot where the wolf had scrambled through and scuttled away. The hazel bushes parted behind the dogs, and Danilo's chestnut horse emerged, dark with sweat. There on its long back sat Danilo, hunched up and leaning forward. He had lost his cap and his grey hair straggled down over his red, perspiring face.

'Loo! loo! loo! . . .' came his whooping voice. When he caught sight of the count, his eyes flashed like lightning.

'Blast you!' he roared, brandishing his whip at the count. 'You let him go! . . . Call yourself a huntsman?' And evidently not willing to waste any more words on the embarrassed and frightened count, he turned away from him and took his fury out on the brown gelding, lashing its sweating and heaving flanks as he flew off after the dogs. The count stood there like a schoolboy after punishment, looking round on all sides and hoping his smile might summon up Semyon to sympathize with him in his dire situation. But Semyon wasn't there – he had galloped round outside the bushes to cut the wolf off from the wood. The men in the field had also galloped in on their prey, from two different sides. But the wolf had nipped off through the bushes, and not one of the party got anywhere near him.

CHAPTER 5

Meanwhile Nikolay Rostov was standing at his post, watching for the wolf. From the noise of the chase as it came up close and went away again, from the cries of the dogs that were familiar to him, from the voices of the huntsmen near by, far away and then suddenly getting louder, he could follow what was going on within the copse. He knew there were young and old wolves in the covert. He knew the hounds had split into two packs, and somewhere they had had sight of a wolf, but something had gone wrong. Every second he expected a wolf to come his way. He had worked things out in a thousand different ways – how the wolf would emerge, where it would happen and how he would deal with it. Hope gave way to despair. Several times he prayed to God for a wolf to run out on him. He prayed with the kind of passion and sincerity which often overwhelms people in moments of deep distress over trivialities. 'Oh, what would it cost Thee,' he asked God, 'to do this for me? I know Thou art great and it's a sin to pray for this, but for God's sake please let an old wolf come out on me, and let Karay catch him and get his teeth into his throat and finish him off right in front of 'Uncle', because he's watching me.' Rostov strained his eyes a thousand times during that half-hour, anxiously scanning the thickets at the edge of the copse, where a couple of scraggy oaks towered above the aspen undergrowth, an undercut bank led steeply down the ravine and 'Uncle's' cap peeped out from behind a bush on the right-hand side.

'No, I won't get that kind of luck,' thought Rostov. 'And it would cost Him so little! No chance! I'm always unlucky – at cards, fighting in the war, everything.' Clear visions of Austerlitz and Dolokhov flashed through his mind in rapid succession. 'Just once in my life to kill an old wolf. It's all I want!' he thought, straining eyes and ears, looking left, right and centre, and listening for the slightest variation in sound coming from the hunt. He looked to the right again, and this time he saw something running towards him over the open ground. 'No, it can't be!' thought Rostov, taking a deep breath, as men do when something long expected is finally achieved. This was a sheer fluke, and it had come about so simply, with no sound, no splendid flourish, nothing to mark its arrival. Rostov couldn't believe his eyes, and his doubts lasted more than a second. But the wolf was running on. She made a clumsy job of jumping across a little hollow that lay across her path.

It was an old she-wolf, grey-backed, with a well-filled, reddish belly. She wasn't in a hurry, apparently confident that no one could see her. Rostov held his breath and looked round at the dogs. Some were lying there, some were standing around, and they were oblivious to everything, not having seen the wolf. Old Karay had his head turned round and his yellow teeth bared as he rummaged angrily for a flea, snapping at his own haunches. 'Loo! loo! loo!' Rostov whispered, pursing his lips. The dogs leapt up, jingling the iron fittings on the leashes, and pricked up their ears. Karay stopped scratching his hind-leg and got up, cocking his ears and wagging his tail, with all its straggly tufts of hair.

'Shall I let them go?' Nikolay asked himself as the wolf moved away from the copse and came towards him. Suddenly the wolf was physically transformed. She shuddered – this was probably the first time she had felt human eyes upon her – turned her head slightly towards the huntsman and stopped, wondering whether to go on or go back. 'No difference. I'm going on!' the wolf seemed to say to herself, and she pressed on without looking round, treading softly and cautiously but with a firm and easy step. 'Loo! loo! . . .' Nikolay yelled in an unrecognizable voice, and his trusty horse hurtled off downhill of its own accord and leapt the watercourse to intercept the wolf, while the hounds ran even faster and overtook it.

Nikolay couldn't hear himself yelling and had no sense of galloping; he saw neither the dogs nor the ground he was covering. All he could see was the wolf, as she quickened her pace, bounding on in a dead straight line along the gully. The leading hound was Milka, the stocky black and white bitch, and she was closing on her. Nearer, nearer, almost there . . . But the wolf turned slightly sideways, and Milka, instead of putting on her usual final spurt, suddenly stiffened her fore-legs and pulled up with her tail in the air.

'Loo! loo! loo!' yelled Nikolay.

A red hound called Lyubim darted past Milka, dashed at the wolf and seized her by the hind leg, only to leap away immediately in terror. The wolf had squatted down, snarling, but now she got up again and raced away, followed a few feet behind by all the dogs, though they took care not to get too close.

'She'll get away! No, she can't!' thought Nikolay, still yelling in a husky voice.

'Karay! Loo! loo!' he yelled, looking for the old hound, his one last hope.

Karay summoned up all the strength left in his old frame and stretched out to his full length as he watched where the wolf was going and bounded slightly away from her to cut across her path. But it was clear from the wolf's speed and the dog's slowness that Karay had miscalculated. Nikolay could now see the copse not far ahead, and once the wolf got there she would be sure to escape. But suddenly in front of him some dogs appeared and a man with them, galloping almost straight at the wolf. There was still hope. A lanky, yellowish young borzoi, not one of the Rostovs' – Nikolay didn't know him – flew towards him straight at the wolf and almost knocked her down. The wolf recovered faster than might have been expected, snarled and savaged the young hound, which fell headlong on the ground with a piercing yelp, covered with blood from a gash in its side.

'Karay! Come on, old fellow!' Nikolay wailed.

Because of the wolf's setback the old dog, with tufts of matted hair dangling from his haunches, had managed to cut across the wolf's path and was now only five paces behind her. Sensing the danger, the wolf took one sideways glance at Karay, tucked her tail further down between her legs and ran on even faster. But then something happened to Karay – Nikolay couldn't see exactly what it was – and there he was on top of the wolf with the pair of them rolling down in a struggling heap into a gully just ahead.

That moment, the moment when Nikolay saw the dogs struggling with the wolf down in the gully, her grey coat visible at the bottom of the heap, one hind-leg sticking out, her ears flattened and her head gasping in terror (Karay had her by the throat) – the moment Nikolay saw all this was the happiest moment of his whole life. He had grasped the pommel of his saddle to get down and stab the creature when suddenly the wolf stuck her head up through the heaving mass of dogs and managed to get her fore-legs out on to the edge of the gully. With a snap of her teeth (Karay having let go of her throat), she heaved her hind-legs out of the hollow, tucked her tail back down, struggled free of the dogs and ran off again. Karay stumbled out of the gully with his hackles raised, hurt and perhaps badly wounded.

'Oh my God . . . No!' Nikolay shouted in despair. But then one of 'Uncle's' huntsmen cut across from the other side and his hounds ran the wolf to earth again. Again she was hemmed in on all sides.

Nikolay, his groom, 'Uncle' and his huntsman pranced round above the beast, whooping and howling, a second away from dismounting when the wolf cowered away, but starting forward again every time she shook herself free and edged towards the copse which might yet be her salvation.

At the beginning of this cruel scene Danilo, hearing the hunters' cries, had darted into the edge of the copse. He saw that Karay had the wolf at his mercy and checked his horse, assuming it was all over. But when he saw that the hunters were not dismounting and the wolf was shaking herself free and was off again, Danilo galloped his own horse, not towards the wolf, but straight towards the copse, like Karay, to cut her off. It was because of this manoeuvre that he was bearing down on the wolf when 'Uncle's' dogs brought her down for the second time.

Danilo galloped up in silence, holding a drawn dagger in his left hand and lashing the heaving flanks of his chestnut, using his riding whip as a kind of flail.

Nikolay didn't see Danilo and didn't hear him until the gasping chestnut flashed past and he heard the sound of a falling body and saw Danilo lying in the midst of the dogs on the wolf's back, trying to grab her by the ears. It was obvious to them all, dogs, hunters and wolf, that this was the end. The beast, flattening its ears in terror, tried to get up, but the dogs hung on. Danilo half-rose, then stumbled down, and as if he was going to bed collapsed with all his weight on top of the wolf and grabbed her by the ears. Nikolay was about to finish her off with the dagger, but Danilo whispered, 'No, don't. We'll string her up!' and he changed position to put his foot on the wolf's neck. They put a stick between the wolf's jaws and tied her up as if they were putting her on the leash, and also tied her legs. Danilo swung the she-wolf from side to side once or twice.

With weary, happy faces they tied the great beast, still alive, to a horse, which bridled and snorted, and with all the dogs milling round and yelping at her, they brought her to the place where they were all supposed to meet. The wolfhounds had taken two of the cubs, and the borzois the other three. The hunters were coming in now, proud of their booty and swapping stories, and everyone came over to have a look at the grand old wolf with her big broad head hanging down and the stick in her teeth, as she gazed with great, glassy eyes at the crowd of dogs and men around her. When they poked her, her tied legs jerked and she looked at them all, wild-eyed yet somehow innocent. Count Ilya Rostov rode over too, and had a poke at the wolf.

'Splendid beast!' he said. 'An old one, eh?' he asked.

'That she be, your Excellency,' answered Danilo, swift to doff his cap.

The count remembered the wolf he had missed, and his clash with Danilo. 'Have to do something about your temper, my boy,' said the count.

Danilo said nothing, but his nervous smile was as sweet and gentle as a child's.

CHAPTER 6

The old count went home. Natasha and Petya stayed on with the hunt but promised to follow immediately. It was still early in the day so the hunting party went on further. At midday they let the hounds loose in a ravine thickly overgrown with young trees. Nikolay stood at the top on some stubble land, from where he could see all his party.

Across from Nikolay was a field of winter rye, in which he could see one of his huntsmen standing alone in a hollow behind a hazel bush. No sooner had they loosed the hounds when Nikolay heard an intermittent baying sound coming from a dog he knew, Voltorn; other hounds joined in, pausing now and then, only to take up the same call. A moment later he heard from the ravine a call that told him they were on the scent of a fox, and the whole pack made off together along a narrow run, up towards the rye-field away from Nikolay.

He could see the whippers-in in their red caps galloping along the edge of the overgrown ravine. He could even see the dogs, and he was expecting the fox to come into sight at any moment now in the field across the ravine.

The huntsman standing in the hollow made a move and let his dogs go, and Nikolay saw an odd-looking red fox with stumpy legs and a big bushy tail scurrying across the green field. The hounds bore down on it, closing in, and the fox began to weave in and out in smaller and smaller circles, trailing its big brush, when all of a sudden a white dog – not one of ours – leapt on it, followed by a black one, and then there was a general hurly-burly which ended with the dogs standing over it, scarcely moving, their heads thrust in and behinds sticking out like the points of a star. Two huntsmen galloped over to the dogs, one in a red cap, the other, a stranger, in a green kaftan.

'Hello, what's this?' wondered Nikolay. 'Where did he come from? He's not one of "Uncle's" men.'

The huntsmen retrieved the fox, and stood there for quite some time without making any effort to tie it to a saddle. He could see the tethered horses and the outline of their empty saddles as they stood close to the huntsmen, and the dogs were there too, lying down. There was much waving of arms as the huntsmen did something to the fox. Someone blew a horn – which always signalled a fight.

'That's one of Ilagin's huntsmen, and he's having some sort of row with our Ivan,' said Nikolay's groom.

Nikolay told the groom to fetch his sister and Petya, and rode off at walking pace towards the spot where the whippers-in were rounding up the hounds. Several of the party galloped over to the scene of the squabble.

Nikolay dismounted, and when Natasha and Petya had ridden up he stood with them near the hounds waiting to hear how things had turned out. The huntsman who had been involved in the row soon came riding out of the bushes with the fox tied to the back of his saddle, and rode over to his young master. He had doffed his cap some way off and was making every effort to be polite, but he was as white as a sheet and gasping for breath, and fury was written all over his face. He had a black eye, though he seemed not to be aware of it.

'What was all that about?' asked Nikolay.

'Well, 'e was going to finish off our fox! And 'twas my bitch that caught it – the mouse-coloured one. I'll swing for him! Pinching my fox! Let 'im have it, I did – 'im and 'is fox. Here 'tis on my saddle. D'you want some of this?' said the huntsman, pointing to his hunting-knife, apparently under the delusion that he was still talking to his enemy.

Nikolay wasted no more words on this man; telling his sister and

Petya to wait there, he rode over to the place where the enemy hunt, under Ilagin, had collected.

The victorious Rostov huntsman rode over to join the others, and there, to a crowd of sympathetic and curious admirers, he recounted his noble deed.

The facts were clear. Ilagin, with whom the Rostovs were conducting a dispute that had gone to law, was hunting in places that belonged by custom to the Rostovs, and had now – deliberately, it seemed – sent his men to the very area where the Rostovs were hunting, and then allowed his man to snatch a fox being chased by other people's dogs.

Nikolay had never set eyes on Ilagin, but, never a man for half-measures when it came to judgements and feelings and having heard that their neighbour was an obstinate brute, he loathed him with every fibre of his being and considered him his bitterest foe. All worked up and spitting with rage, he was now on his way to have things out with him, clenching his riding-crop and ready for anything as long as it involved decisive action against his enemy.

He had scarcely emerged from the edge of the wood when he saw a stout gentleman in a beaver cap coming towards him on a splendid black horse, accompanied by two grooms. This was no enemy. Nikolay found Ilagin to be an impressive gentleman of great courtesy who seemed particularly anxious to make the young count's acquaintance. Ilagin raised his beaver cap as he approached, apologized profusely for what had occurred, said he would have the man punished for hunting someone else's fox, hoped that they could now become better acquainted and offered him the use of his own land for hunting on.

Natasha had followed on not far behind her brother, worried that his blood was up and he might do something terrible, but when she saw the two enemies exchanging friendly greetings she rode straight over to them. Ilagin raised his beaver cap even higher to Natasha, gave her the most affable of smiles and said the countess was worthy of Diana both in her love of hunting and in her beauty, of which he had heard so much.

By way of atonement for his huntsman's offence, Ilagin persuaded Rostov to ride up to his high land less than a mile away, which he preserved for his own shooting; it was, as he put it, swarming with hares. Nikolay consented, and the hunting party, swollen to twice its size, set off again. Their way led across several fields. The huntsmen fell back to move in line, while the gentry rode together. 'Uncle', Rostov and Ilagin kept stealing the odd furtive glance at each other's dogs, trying not to be noticed as they did so, and looking anxiously for any rivals that might outrun their own dogs.

Rostov was particularly struck by the beauty of one small and slender animal, a thoroughbred black-and-tan bitch belonging to Ilagin, with muscles like steel, a delicate muzzle and prominent black eyes. He had heard that Ilagin's dogs were a spirited lot, and in this handsome bitch he saw a rival to his Milka.

Ilagin started talking in a desultory way about this year's harvest, and in mid-conversation Nikolay pointed to the black-and-tan bitch.

'Nice bitch you have there!' he said casually. 'Is she a good mover?'

'That one? Oh yes, she's a good dog. Catches the odd hare,' Ilagin said in a voice that suggested indifference, though only a year ago he had given a neighbour three families of house serfs for Yerza, the black-and-tan bitch who was now his. 'So your people are none too pleased with the yield, then, Count,' he went on, resuming their previous conversation. And since it was only polite to return the young count's compliment, Ilagin had a good look at his dogs and settled on Milka, with her strikingly broad back.

'Now there's a splendid dog – the black-and-white one!' he said.

'Yes, she's all right. She can move,' answered Nikolay. ('I wouldn't mind seeing a good big hare run across that field, then I could show you what kind of dog she is!' he thought to himself.) Turning to his groom, he said he would give a rouble to the first man who could start up a hiding hare.

'What beats me,' Ilagin went on, 'is why some people are so jealous of each other when it comes to hunting and dogs. I'll tell you this, Count: I enjoy a good hunt, as you well know. Splendid company and all that . . . nothing better.' He doffed his beaver cap again to Natasha. 'But counting the kills and keeping score – I've no time for that sort of thing.'

'Certainly not!'

'Or getting worked up because somebody else's dog makes a kill and mine doesn't. All I'm interested in is the actual hunting. Are you with me, Count? I see it this way . . .'

At that moment a long drawn-out halloo, 'Over here! . . .', came from one of the dog-handlers. He was standing on a little rise amid the stubble with his whip held high, and he gave the call again, 'He's here! . . .' This cry, together with the raised whip, meant that he could see a hare squatting near by.

'I think he's spotted something,' said Ilagin casually. 'How about a little chase, Count?'

'Yes, we must get over there . . . Er, shall we go together?' answered Nikolay, with a close look at Yerza and 'Uncle's' red Rugay, the two rivals he had not yet had a chance of competing against. 'What if they're

miles faster than my Milka?' he thought, riding off with the two other
men in the direction of the hare.

'Nice big one, is he?' called out Ilagin as they came towards the
groom who had spotted the hare, and he looked round in some excitement, whistling to Yerza. 'Are you going to have a go, Mikhail Nikano-
rych?' he said to 'Uncle'. 'Uncle' scowled and rode on.

'I can't compete with you,' came the reply, 'Look at your dogs
... Fair for the chase! ... You've paid whole villages for your dogs
... They're worth thousands. Run yours against each other – I'll
watch!'

'Rugay! Here boy!' he shouted. 'Rugayushka!' he added, unwittingly conveying through this diminutive both his affection for the red
dog and all the hope he was investing in him. Natasha could see and
sense the hidden thrill of excitement affecting the two elderly men and
her brother, and she felt it too. The groom was still standing on the
rise with his whip in the air. The three gentlemen were riding towards
him at walking pace; the other hounds were up on the skyline, wheeling
away from the hare; the other huntsmen, the non-gentry, were also
riding away. Everything was happening slowly and methodically.

'Where is he pointing?' asked Nikolay, after riding another hundred
paces towards the groom. But there was no time for an answer: the
hare, sensing tomorrow morning's frost, decided it had lain there long
enough and was suddenly up and away. The hounds that were leashed
together flew downhill in full cry after the hare, while the unleashed
borzois sprinted from all directions towards the hounds or after the
hare. The meandering group of huntsmen and whips who had been
rounding the dogs up with shouts of 'Stay!' and the grooms who had
been directing the dogs by shouting 'Over here!' now galloped off
across the field. The imperturbable Ilagin, Nikolay, Natasha and
'Uncle' flew across the ground reckless of where and how they went
as long as they could keep the dogs and the hare in view, anxious not
to lose sight of the chase for a second. The hare turned out to be a
seasoned courser. When he had jumped up he had not just raced away,
he had pricked up his ears and listened to the cries and the thudding
of paws and hooves coming at him from every side. Now he made off
with a dozen bounds in his own good time, letting the dogs catch up
a little, and then suddenly, fixing his direction and finally sensing the
danger he was in, he put his ears back and was off like the wind. He
had come from the stubble, but now open fields lay ahead, and on
them marshy ground. The two dogs of the groom who had spotted
him were the closest and the first to pick up his scent, but they weren't
anywhere near to catching him when Ilagin's black-and-tan Yerza flew

past, got within a yard, pounced with awesome speed, going for the hare's tail, and rolled over, thinking she had him. But the hare arched his back and bounded off more smartly than ever, only for the stocky black-and-white Milka to come out from behind Yerza and sprint off in pursuit, rapidly gaining on the hare.

'Milushka! Gorgeous girl!' shouted Nikolay with a ring of triumph in his voice. It seemed for a moment that Milka couldn't miss, but she overran the hare and went flying past. The hare dropped back. The splendid Yerza came at him again, hovering over the hare's tail as if careful calculation was needed to avoid any mistakes this time and grab him by his hind-leg.

'Yerzynka, come on, darling!' wailed Ilagin, his voice unrecognizable. Yerza did not respond. Poised and about to seize the hare, she could only watch as he swerved and darted away to the ridge between the stubble and the green field. Again Yerza and Milka, running side by side like horses in double harness, flew after the hare; he was better off up on the ridge, and the dogs were taking longer to close him down.

'Rugay! Rugayushka! Fair for the chase!' This time it was another voice. And it was Rugay, 'Uncle's' hunched-up red dog, reaching out to his full length and curving his back, who caught up with the two leading dogs, flashed past and flung himself with complete abandon on the hare, toppling him from the ridge down into the green field, and leapt at him again even more savagely, sinking knee-deep in the boggy ground until all you could see was a rolling mass of dog and hare and the dog's back covered with mud. The other dogs gathered round, their behinds sticking out again like the points of a star. Within a few moments the whole party had pulled up alongside the horde of dogs. A delighted 'Uncle' was the only one to dismount, cut off a hare's foot and shake the blood away. He stared about edgily, eyes dancing, hands and legs almost out of control. He carried on talking, blurting out the first thing that came into his head and to no one in particular. 'Nice chase that one ... some dog! ... outstripped the lot of them ... one-rouble-dogs, thousand-rouble dogs ... Fair for the chase!' he gabbled, gasping and glaring aggressively, fulminating against the world in general, and all those enemies who had insulted him, and now at last he had a chance to get his own back. 'Do what you want with your thousand-rouble dogs ... Fair for the chase! Rugay, here's a nice little foot for you,' he said, dropping the hare's severed muddy foot for the dog. 'You've earned it ... Fair for the chase!'

'She was finished. She had three goes on her own,' Nikolay was saying. He too wasn't listening to anyone else and didn't mind whether he was being heard or not.

'Oh yes, cutting across like that!' said one of Ilagin's grooms.

'Course, once he'd been run down and missed like that, any old mongrel could have caught him,' Ilagin was saying at the same moment, red in the face and struggling to get his breath back after all the galloping and excitement. And also at the same time Natasha, who wasn't even trying to get her breath back, shrieked with such rapturous excitement that her scream rang in everyone's ears. It was a scream that said what the others were saying just by chattering all at once. It was the kind of weird scream that she would have been ashamed of, and the others would have been amazed to hear, at any other time. 'Uncle', meanwhile, had flung the hare neatly and tidily across his horse's hind-quarters and strapped him to the saddle, taunting them all by the very gesture, and with a strong hint that he had no wish to speak to anyone he got on his bay and set off home. Everyone else rode away too, he being the only one not suffering from a sense of injury and unhappiness, and it took some time for the rest of them to regain their previous outward show of indifference. For some time after, they kept looking askance at red Rugay, who trotted along behind 'Uncle's' horse with mud all over his hunched-up back, jingling the fittings on his leash, with the serene air of a conqueror.

'Look, I'm just like any other dog till it comes to a chase, but then – watch out!' was what the dog's demeanour conveyed, or so it seemed to Nikolay.

When, a good deal later on, 'Uncle' rode up to Nikolay and spoke to him, Nikolay felt quite flattered they were still on speaking terms after all that had happened.

CHAPTER 7

When Ilagin took leave of them in the early evening Nikolay, realizing he was a long way from home, accepted 'Uncle's' invitation for the hunting party to stay the night with him in the village of Mikhaylovka.

'You should come to my place . . . Fair for the chase!' said 'Uncle'. 'Best thing all round. Look, it's wet, you could have a nice rest, and we could send the little countess home in a trap.' The invitation was accepted, a huntsman was dispatched to Otradnoye for a trap, and Nikolay, Natasha and Petya rode over to 'Uncle's' house.

Men servants large and small, half-a-dozen of them, came running out on to the front steps to meet their master, while the women, old, large and small, slipped out in dozens round the back to watch the arrival of the huntsmen. The presence of Natasha – a woman, nay, a lady, on horseback – roused the curiosity of 'Uncle's' house serfs to such a pitch that many of them lost all inhibitions and went straight up to her, staring her in the face and voicing their opinions about her, as though she were some kind of exhibit rather than a human being, some wondrous object incapable of hearing and understanding what was being said about her.

'Arinka, sithee, she be sittin' sideways! Sideways sittin', an' 'er skirt all danglin' down . . . And look at yon little horn!'

'Lor' bless 'e, an' a knife too!'

'Reminds me o'them Tatar womenfolk!'

' 'Ow can tha do it wi'out fallin' off?' said the cheekiest one, straight in Natasha's face.

'Uncle' got off his horse at the steps of his little wooden house with its overgrown garden, surveyed the servant body and told them in no uncertain terms what to do – anyone not required was to disappear while the rest did everything necessary for the reception of his guests and the hunt servants.

They scurried away in every direction. 'Uncle' helped Natasha down from her horse, and gave her his arm up the rickety wooden steps.

The inside of the house, with its unplastered timber walls, was not the last word in cleanliness; nothing suggested that the main aim of its inhabitants was to keep the place spotless, though there were no signs of real neglect. There was a smell of fresh apples as you entered, and the walls were hung with the skins of wolves and foxes.

'Uncle' led his guests through into a little hall furnished with a folding-table and red chairs, then into a drawing-room with a round birch-wood table and a sofa, and on into his study, with its shabby sofa, threadbare carpet and several portraits – of Suvorov, 'Uncle' in military uniform and his father and mother. The study reeked of tobacco and dogs.

Once in the study 'Uncle' invited his guests to sit down and make themselves at home, and then left the room. Rugay came in, his back still plastered with mud, and went to lie on the sofa, cleaning himself with tongue and teeth. There was a corridor leading from the study, where they could hear the sound of women laughing and hushed voices coming from behind a screen with ragged curtains. Natasha, Nikolay and Petya took off their outdoor clothes and sat down on the sofa. Petya leant on one elbow and promptly fell asleep. Natasha and Nikolay sat there and said nothing. Their faces were burning and they were ravenous, but they felt very bright and cheerful. They glanced at each other. (Now the hunt was over and they were indoors, Nikolay felt no further need to demonstrate his masculine superiority over his sister.) Natasha winked at her brother, their mutual glee was uncontainable and they broke out into a great roar of laughter before they could think of a reason for doing so.

After a brief interval in came 'Uncle' wearing a Cossack coat, blue breeches and low boots. This mode of dress had left Natasha shocked and amused when 'Uncle' had appeared in it at Otradnoye, but now it seemed exactly right and in no way inferior to morning dress and frock-coats. Like the pair of them 'Uncle' was also in high spirits. Far from taking exception to their laughter – it never occurred to him that they might be laughing at his life-style – he joined in with the brother and sister, revelling like them in inexplicable glee.

'Will you look at this young countess here? Fair for the chase! I've never seen anyone like her!' he said, offering Rostov a long-stemmed pipe while filling his own stubby one, with three practised fingers.

'Out riding all day – enough to tax any man – and still as fresh as a daisy!'

Soon after 'Uncle's' reappearance the door was opened by a serving woman who from the sound of it was walking on bare feet, and in padded a plump, red-cheeked, good-looking woman of forty or so, with a double chin and full red lips, carrying a large heavily laden tray. Her eyes radiated good will and her every gesture spoke of warm hospitality as she looked round all the guests and treated them to a broad smile and a polite curtsey.

For all her exceptional stoutness, which made her bosom and her belly stick out and her head tilt back, this woman ('Uncle's' house-keeper) moved with surprising elegance. She walked over to the table, put the tray down, and with a few skilful movements of her puffy white hands transferred bottles, dishes and snacks to the table-top. This done, she walked off and paused in the doorway for a moment with a smile on her face. 'Take a good look – it's me! Now can you understand how "Uncle" lives?' was what her expression seemed to say to Rostov. Who could have failed to understand? Not only Nikolay, but even Natasha understood 'Uncle' now, and what had been meant by that furrowed brow and that smug smile of contentment hovering around his pursed lips as Anisya Fyodorovna had come into the room. On the tray were a bottle of home-made wine, several different kinds of vodka, tiny mushrooms, little rye-cakes made with buttermilk, oozing honey-combs, still and sparkling mead, apples and all sorts of nuts, raw, roasted and steeped in honey. Then Anisya came back in bringing preserves made with honey and sugar, along with ham and a freshly roasted chicken.

All these delicacies had been grown, picked and prepared by Anisya herself. Every smell, taste and flavour seemed redolent of Anisya, redolent of her plumpness, cleanliness, whiteness and her broad welcoming smile.

'Please help yourself, little Lady-Countess,' she kept saying, offering something to Natasha and following it immediately with something else. Natasha sampled everything. Never in her life, she thought, had she seen or tasted buttermilk cakes like these, such delicious preserves, such nuts in honey, or a chicken like this one. Anisya withdrew.

Rostov and 'Uncle', as they downed their cherry-flavoured vodka after supper, talked of hunts past and future, Rugay and Ilagin's dogs. Natasha sat up straight on the sofa, drinking in all that they were saying with a glint in her eyes. Several times she made an attempt to wake Petya and give him something to eat, but he just mumbled a few nonsensical words, obviously reluctant to come round. Natasha felt so happy at heart, so much at home in these new surroundings, that her only fear was that the trap would come for her too soon. When the conversation broke down for a moment, as it almost always does when you have friends in for the first time, 'Uncle' responded to what was in his guests' minds by saying, 'So there you have it . . . me in my last days . . . Soon be dead . . . Fair for the chase! Nothing left after that. So what's wrong with a bit of living in sin?'

'Uncle's' face had a knowing even rather handsome look and even a touch of beauty as he uttered these words. As he spoke Rostov was forcibly reminded of the many good things he had heard about this man from his father and the neighbours. From one end of the district to the other 'Uncle' was thought of as an eccentric but also the noblest and most selfless of men. He was brought in to abitrate in family disputes and chosen as executor. People told him secrets. He was invited to serve as a justice, and in other similar posts, but he had refused all public offices point-blank, spending autumn and spring out in the fields on his bay horse, winter indoors and summer stretched out in his overgrown garden.

'Why don't you work in the service, Uncle?'

'I used to once, but I gave it up. It doesn't suit me. Fair for the chase. Can't make head nor tail of it. May be all right for you – but it's beyond me. Now, take hunting – that's a different thing. Fair for the chase! Open that door there, will you?' he yelled. 'Why have you shut it?' A door at the end of the corridor (which 'Uncle' called a 'collidor', like the peasants) led to the 'huntsman's corner', as the room for the hunt servants was called. Bare feet padded along at some speed and an unseen hand opened the door into the huntsman's corner. Down the corridor came the distinct strains of a balalaika in the hands of an obvious expert. Natasha had been listening to this for some time, and now she went down the corridor to hear the music more clearly.

'That's Mitka, my coachman ... Bought him a decent balalaika. Very fond of it,' said 'Uncle'. He had built up a little tradition whereby every time he came home from the chase he liked to hear Mitka playing the balalaika in the huntsman's corner. This music was dear to his heart.

'He's good, isn't he? A really good player,' said Nikolay, with a touch of instinctive scorn in his voice, as if he was embarrassed to admit that this kind of music appealed to him.

'Good?' said Natasha, full of reproach as she sensed her brother's funny tone. 'It's more than good, it's absolutely magnificent!' She had considered 'Uncle's' mushrooms, honey and various vodkas the best in all the world, and now this playing struck her as the highest possible expression of music.

'More, please, more!' said Natasha in the doorway as soon as the balalaika stopped playing. Mitka retuned and launched again into a plangent version of 'My Lady', with many a trill and flourish. 'Uncle' sat there listening with his head on one side and the suggestion of a grin on his face. The 'My Lady' tune was repeated a hundred times over. With one or two more pauses for retuning, the same plangent notes came at them time and again, but no one found them at all tedious; they all clamoured for more. Anisya came in and leant her portly figure against the doorpost.

'Oh, little countess, just listen to that!' she said to Natasha, with a smile that was extraordinarily like 'Uncle's'. 'He's a marvellous player,' she added.

'He never gets that bit right,' said 'Uncle' suddenly with a wild gesture. 'He needs to draw it out more. Fair for the chase! ... A bit more drawn out ...'

'Do you play, then?' asked Natasha.

'Uncle' gave a smile instead of an answer.

'Anisya, old girl, go and see whether the strings on my guitar are all right, will you? It's a long time since I had it in my hands. Fair for the chase! Thought I'd given it up!'

Anisya, needing no second bidding, tripped off on her master's little errand and came back with his guitar. Without a glance at anyone 'Uncle' blew the dust off the instrument, tapped its body with his bony fingers, tuned up and settled himself down in an armchair. Thrusting out his left elbow somewhat theatrically, he gripped the guitar at the bottom of the neck, winked at Anisya and struck up, not with the first notes of 'My Lady' but a single chord of the purest tone followed by a smooth and gentle but sturdy rendition of the popular song, 'Coming down the high road . . .', picked out in very slow time. Nikolay and Natasha thrilled to the rhythm, the tune and the same steady spirit of joy that emanated from Anisya and her whole personality. Anisya blushed, hid her face in her handkerchief and left the room laughing. 'Uncle' went on playing, so sweetly, deliberately, sturdily, gazing with new inspiration at the spot vacated by Anisya. There was a hint of laughter down one side of his face under his grey moustache, and it broadened out as the song went on and the tempo quickened, while his flourishes tore at the heart-strings.

'Wonderful, Uncle, wonderful! Play it again!' cried Natasha the moment he had finished. She leapt up from her place and overwhelmed her 'uncle' with kisses and hugs. 'Oh, Nikolay, darling!' she said, looking round at her brother as if to say, 'How about that, then?'

Nikolay was equally delighted by 'Uncle's' playing, and 'Uncle' soon struck up again. Anisya's smiling face reappeared in the doorway, and other faces behind her.

> Fetching water sweet and clear,
> Maiden, stop and linger here . . .

played 'Uncle', breaking off with another wild flourish and a single strum, followed by a shrug of the shoulders.

'Oh, Uncle, darling, *please!*' cried Natasha, wailing and imploring as if her life depended on it. 'Uncle' got to his feet and suddenly it was as if there were two men in him – the first one treating his merry inner companion to a sombre smile, while the merry companion himself started on the simple but precise business of running through the steps of a folk-dance just about to begin.

'Come on, my little niece!' cried the uncle, beckoning to Natasha with the hand that had struck the last chord on the guitar.

Natasha threw off the shawl she had been wrapped in, ran round in front of her 'uncle', and stood there waiting, hands on hips, rhythmically jiggling her shoulders.

Here was a young countess, educated by a French *émigrée* governess – where, when and how had she imbibed the spirit of that peasant dance along with the Russian air she breathed, and these movements which the *pas de châle*[1] ought to have squeezed out of her long ago? But her movements and the spirit of them were truly Russian, inimitable, unteachable, just what 'Uncle' had been hoping for. The moment she took up her stance with such a confident smile, so proud of herself and full of mischievous fun, any misgivings that may have momentarily affected Nikolay and all the onlookers – would she get it all wrong? – were dispelled. Everyone was admiring her.

Her dancing was perfection itself, so beautiful that Anisya, who had been quick to give her the scarf she needed to dance with, chuckled tearfully as she watched the slender, graceful little countess, brought up in silks and velvet in a completely different world, demonstrate her instinctive understanding of all that Anisya stood for, and her father and her mother and her aunt and every last Russian soul.

'Oh yes, little Countess. Fair for the chase!' cried 'Uncle', laughing with delight as they came to the end of the dance. 'You're a niece to be proud of! All we need to do now is find you a nice husband, and then – fair for the chase!'

'We've found one,' said Nikolay with a smile.

'Oho!' said the uncle in some surprise, looking inquiringly at Natasha. Natasha nodded with her own happy smile.

'And a fine one too!' she said. But no sooner were the words out of her mouth than a new and different way of thinking and feeling surged up inside her. 'What did Nikolay's smile mean when he said, "We've found one"? Is he glad, or not? He seems to be thinking my Bolkonsky wouldn't approve of the fun we're all having now, or even understand it. Well, he would understand it. Where is he now?' Natasha wondered with a serious look on her face. But that lasted only a second. 'I'm not going to think about it. I'm just not,' she said to herself, and she sat down again with a new smile close to her 'uncle', begging him to play something else.

The 'uncle' played another song and then a waltz. Then, after a pause, he cleared his throat and launched into his favourite hunting song:

> Evening when the light is low,
> Deep and even falls the snow . . .

'Uncle' sang like a true peasant, with one simple thought in mind – in any song the words are the only thing that matters, the tune follows on, a tune on its own is nothing, a tune just brings it all together. And this gave 'Uncle's' natural way of singing a special charm, not unlike birdsong. Natasha went into ecstasies over 'Uncle's' singing. She made up her mind forthwith to drop the harp, take up the guitar and stick to it. She asked the uncle for the guitar and unhesitatingly picked out the chords of the song.

At about half-past nine a carriage arrived with a trap and three men on horseback who had been sent to fetch Natasha and Petya. The count and countess didn't know where they were and were very worried, said one of the men.

Petya was carried outside and laid in the carriage sleeping the sleep of the dead. Natasha and Nikolay got into the trap. 'Uncle' tucked Natasha in and said goodbye with new-found affection. He walked with them as far as the bridge, which could not be crossed, so they had to leave the road and cross by a ford, and told his huntsmen to ride on in front with lanterns.

'Goodbye, my dear little niece!' they heard him call through the darkness, and his voice was not the one Natasha had known before, but the one that had sung 'Evening when the light is low . . .'

Soon they were driving through a village where there were red lights shining and the smell of wood-smoke.

'Uncle's a real darling, isn't he?' said Natasha as they drove out on to the high road.

'Yes,' said Nikolay. 'Are you cold?'

'No, I'm fine, just fine. I'm so happy,' said Natasha, surprised to hear herself saying so. For some time neither of them spoke.

The night was dark and damp. The horses were invisible as they splashed through the unseen mud.

What was going on in that childlike, impressionable soul, so eagerly devouring and absorbing all the vast range of impressions that life can offer? How were they all shaping up in her mind? But there she was, a picture of happiness. They were nearly home when suddenly she began to hum the tune of 'Evening when the light is low . . .' She had just got it, after struggling to recall it all the way back.

'Got it at last?' said Nikolay.

'Penny for your thoughts, Nikolay,' said Natasha, something they loved to say to each other.

'Oh,' said Nikolay, thinking back. 'Er, I was just thinking about Rugay. Remember that red dog? He's just like 'Uncle'. If he was a man he'd keep 'Uncle' on all right, either for racing, or just because they get on together. 'Uncle's' easy to get on with, isn't he? Penny for yours.'

'Oh, er, wait a minute . . . I know. I was just thinking – here we are driving along and we assume we're heading for home, but we could be going anywhere, it's so dark, and all of a sudden we'll arrive somewhere and we'll see we're not at Otradnoye, we're in fairyland. And then I was thinking . . . oh, but that'll do.'

'Oh, you must have been thinking about *him*,' said Nikolay, and Natasha could hear the smile in his voice.

'No, I wasn't,' Natasha answered, though actually she had been thinking about Prince Andrey and how he would have taken to 'Uncle'. 'And I've been saying over and over again, all the way back, how nice Anisya looked when she walked, how very nice . . .' said Natasha. And Nikolay heard her ringing laughter, so spontaneous, so happy.

'Do you know what?' she said suddenly. 'I'm certain I'll never be as relaxed and happy as I am right now . . .'

'Don't talk such absolute rubbish!' said Nikolay. He was thinking, 'My Natasha's such a darling girl! I've never had a friend like her, and I never shall. Why does she have to go and get married? I could go on driving like this with her for ever!'

'Dear old Nikolay, he's such a darling!' Natasha was thinking.

'Look! The light's still on in the drawing-room,' she said, pointing to the windows of their house and the warm welcome that shone through the wet, velvety darkness of the night.

CHAPTER 8

Count Ilya Rostov had resigned as Marshal of the Nobility because the position involved too much expense, but still there was no improvement in his affairs. Natasha and Nikolay often came across their parents deep in private conversation and looking worried, and there was talk of having to sell off the Rostovs' magnificent family seat and the estate near Moscow. With the count no longer serving as Marshal lavish entertainment had become unnecessary and family life at Otradnoye was less hectic than in years gone by. But the huge house with its extensive wings was still teeming with people, and a couple of dozen still sat down to table. There were all manner of kith and kin going back years, family in all but name, the sort of people whose continued existence in the count's house seemed inevitable. There was Dimmler, the music-teacher, and his wife; Iogel, the dancing-master, and his family; an elderly resident lady known as Madame Belov, and many others – Petya's tutors, the girls' old governess, and one or two characters who just found it better, or cheaper, to live there than on their own. Entertainment was less lavish, but the Rostovs still lived on in a certain style, and anything else would have been unthinkable for the count and countess. There was the same hunting establishment, which had actually been expanded by Nikolay. There were still the same fifty horses and fifteen grooms in the stables, the same expensive presents on name-days, and the same sumptuous dinners involving the whole neighbourhood. The count still ran the same games of whist and boston, fanning his cards out for all to see and letting the neighbours bleed him of hundreds every day of the week until they came to regard the privilege of making up a rubber with Count Ilya Rostov as a handy source of revenue.

The count proceeded with his affairs like someone blundering into a huge animal trap, trying not to believe he had been caught but getting more and more entangled with every step he took, and not up to the task of either tearing himself free from the nets or disentangling himself with care and patience. The countess with her loving heart could sense that her children were being steadily ruined, though it was no good blaming the count, because he couldn't help being what he was, and he was desperately worried too (though he did his best to hide it) about the ruin that stared him and his children in the face, so she began to look for some way to put things right. To her woman's way of thinking there was only one way out – Nikolay must marry a wealthy heiress. This was their last hope, she felt, and if Nikolay refused the match she had found for him they would have to say goodbye to any possibility of restoring the family fortunes. This match was Julie Karagin, the daughter of splendid and virtuous parents known to the Rostovs since childhood; she had become a wealthy heiress on the recent death of her last surviving brother.

The countess had written personally to Madame Karagin in Moscow, suggesting a possible marriage between their two children, and the reply was favourable. Madame Karagin had replied that she herself was in agreement, but everything depended on how her daughter felt. She now invited Nikolay to Moscow. Several times the countess had told her son with tears in her eyes that with both of her daughters nicely settled her only wish now was to see him married. She said she could go peacefully to her grave once this was settled. Then she would add that she had an excellent girl in mind, and tried to sound him out on the subject of matrimony.

On other occasions she would sing Julie's praises and suggest that Nikolay might like to go down to Moscow and enjoy himself during the holidays. Nikolay soon guessed what his mother was driving at in these little confidences, and there came a time when he forced her out into the open. She came straight out with it: any hopes of restoring the family fortunes now depended on his marrying Julie Karagin.

'What do you mean, Mamma? If I loved a girl with no money would you really want me to sacrifice my feelings and my honour just to make us all rich?' he asked his mother, unaware of the cruelty in his question, but wanting to show off his own noble sentiments.

'No, no. You don't understand,' said his mother, not knowing how to put herself in the right. 'You don't understand, darling. It's your happiness I'm thinking about,' she added, sensing she was very much in the wrong, and floundering because of it. She burst into tears.

'Mamma, please don't cry. Just tell me this is what you want, and you know I'll give up anything, my whole life if necessary, for your peace of mind,' said Nikolay. 'I'll sacrifice anything, even my feelings.'

But the countess didn't want to hear the question put like that. She wanted no sacrifices from her son; she wanted to make sacrifices for him.

'No. You still don't understand. Let's talk about something else,' she said, wiping her tears away.

'Yes, maybe I am in love with a poor girl,' Nikolay said to himself. 'And what am I supposed to do – sacrifice my feelings and my honour to make us all rich? How could Mamma say such a thing? Sonya's poor, so I mustn't love her,' he thought, 'I mustn't respond to her faithful, devoted love. And one thing's certain – I'll be happier with her than any number of dolls like Julie. I can always sacrifice my feelings for the benefit of my family,' he said to himself, 'but I can't dictate what my feelings should be. If I do love Sonya, that feeling is stronger and more valuable to me than anything in the world.'

Nikolay did not go to Moscow and the countess did not take up the subject of marriage with him again. It was with great sadness, tinged with bitterness, that she watched the signs of a growing attachment between her son and Sonya, the girl with no dowry. She blamed herself for doing it, but she couldn't help picking on Sonya and nagging at her, often pulling her up for no good reason and addressing her as 'my dear young lady'. What infuriated the kind-hearted countess most of all was that this wretched, dark-eyed niece was so meek and mild, so good, so devoted and grateful to her benefactors, and so faithful, constant and unselfish in her love for Nikolay, that there was no fault to be found with her.

Nikolay was coming towards the end of his home leave. From Prince Andrey came a fourth letter, this time from Rome, informing them that he would have been on his way back to Russia long ago, but for the fact that his wound had suddenly reopened in the warm climate, which made it necessary to delay his return until early next year. Natasha was no less in love with her fiancé, no less consoled by her love, and no less eager to accept all the pleasures that life could offer, but by the end of the fourth month of their separation she began to suffer from fits of uncontrollable depression. She felt sorry for herself, sorry that all this time was being wasted, passing by uselessly, no good to anyone, while she felt so eager to love and be loved.

The Rostovs' was not a happy household.

CHAPTER 9

Christmas came, but apart from the High Mass, the tedious formality of exchanging greetings with neighbours and servants and everyone putting on new clothes, nothing unusual happened to mark the festival, whereas outside in the still air with twenty degrees of frost, the dazzling sunshine by day and the bright, starlit wintry sky at night seemed to be crying out for something special to celebrate the season.

On the third day of Christmas week, after lunch, all the members of the household went off to their various rooms. It was the day's lowest ebb of boredom. Nikolay, who had been out calling on neighbours that morning, gone for a nap in the sitting-room. The old count had retired to his study for a rest. In the drawing-room Sonya was sitting at a round table copying a pattern. The countess was playing patience. Nastasya Ivanovna, the buffoon, sat by the window with two old ladies, a picture of dejection. Natasha came in, walked over to Sonya to see what she was doing, then went across to her mother and stood there saying nothing.

'What are you doing wandering about like a lost soul?' said her mother. 'What do you want?'

'*Him* . . . I want him, now, this minute,' said Natasha, with a steely glint in her eyes and no smile. The countess looked up and stared at her daughter.

'Don't look at me like that, Mamma. Please don't. You'll make me cry.'

'Sit down here. Come and sit by me,' said the countess.

'Mamma, I want *him*. What am I doing here wasting away like this, Mamma?' Her voice faltered, tears fell from her eyes, and in order to hide them she turned away abruptly and went out of the room. She went into the sitting-room, where she stood for a moment in thought and then went on into the maids' room. There an old maid-servant was scolding a young girl who had just run indoors from the cold and was now out of breath.

'That's enough playing about,' she was saying. 'There's a time and a place for everything.'

'Oh, leave her alone, Kondratyevna,' said Natasha. 'All right, Mavrusha, off you go.' And after giving Mavrusha her freedom, Natasha crossed the great hall and went to the vestibule. An old footman and two young ones were playing cards. They broke off and got to their feet at the entrance of the young mistress. 'What shall I do with them?' Natasha wondered.

'Oh yes, Nikita, I want you to go somewhere ... (Where shall I send him?) Er, yes, go outside and fetch me a cockerel, please. And you, Misha, bring me some oats.[2]

'A few oats is it you want?' said Misha, with cheerful readiness.

'Just do as you're told, and do it now,' the old man urged him.

'Fyodor, you can get me a piece of chalk.'

Since she happened to be passing the butler's pantry she asked for the samovar to be lit, though it was nowhere near the right time for this.

The butler, Foka, was the grumpiest person in the house, and Natasha liked to test her authority over him. Only too ready to distrust her, he went off to find out whether he had heard aright.

'Young ladies nowadays!' said Foka, pretending to scowl in Natasha's direction.

There was no one in the house who sent more people scurrying around and gave the servants more work to do than Natasha. She couldn't set eyes on anyone without sending him or her on an errand. She seemed to be challenging any one of them to get angry or sulky, but no one's orders were more lovingly obeyed by the servants than Natasha's. 'What can I possibly do now? Where can I possibly go?' Natasha wondered as she ambled down the corridor.

'Nastasya Ivanovna, what sort of children am I going to have?' she asked the buffoon, who came towards her dressed in his woman's jacket.

'You'll have fleas, and dragonflies, and grasshoppers,' answered the buffoon.

'Oh, Lord! Same old story! Oh, where *can* I go? What can I do with myself?' And she clattered rapidly upstairs to see Iogel and his wife, who lived on the top floor. The two governesses were sitting with the Iogels and on the table were plates of raisins, walnuts and almonds. The governesses were discussing whether it was cheaper to live in Moscow or Odessa. Natasha sat down, listened to their discussion with a solemn, pensive air, and then got up again. 'The Island of Madagascar,' she said. 'Ma-da-gas-car,' she repeated, lingering long on all four syllables, and then, ignoring Madame Schoss, who wanted to know what she was talking about, she walked out of the room.

Petya, her brother, was upstairs too. He and his tutor were busy making fireworks to let off that night.

'Petya! Petya!' she yelled at him. 'Give me a piggy-back downstairs.' Petya ran over and presented his back, she jumped up on it and grabbed him round the neck with both arms, and he skipped off, prancing along the landing. 'No, don't . . . The Island of Madagascar,' she enunciated as she jumped down from his back and went downstairs.

Having inspected her kingdom, so to speak, and tested her authority, ensuring total obedience on all sides, but still bored out of her mind, Natasha went back to the great hall, took up her guitar and sat down with it in a dark corner behind a bookcase. She began to play on the bass string, picking out a melody remembered from an opera she had heard in Petersburg with Prince Andrey. For any passer-by who might have chanced to listen, the noise given off by her guitar would have been quite meaningless, but for her these sounds evoked a host of memories in her imagination. She sat there behind the bookcase with her eyes fixed on a shaft of light falling from the crack in the pantry door, listening to herself and remembering days gone by. She was in a reminiscing mood.

Sonya crossed the hall and went into the pantry carrying a small glass. Natasha glanced at her through the crack in the door, and suddenly she seemed to be remembering this scene from some time in the past, with the light falling through the crack in the pantry door, and Sonya walking across with the glass. 'Yes, yes, that's exactly how it was,' thought Natasha.

'What does this sound like, Sonya?' Natasha called out, plucking the thick string.

'Oh, there you are!' said Sonya, startled, and she came over to listen. 'I don't know . . . Is it a storm?' she said diffidently, afraid of getting it wrong.

'Yes, that's just how she jumped, just how she came over to me with that shy smile when it all happened before,' thought Natasha, 'and just like then . . . I thought there was something disappointing about her.'

'No, it's the chorus from *The Water-Carrier*.³ Listen.' And Natasha hummed through the tune of the chorus for Sonya to recognize. 'Where were you off to?' asked Natasha.

'I'm changing this glass of water. I've nearly finished that pattern.'

'You can always find something to do, and I can't, you know,' said Natasha. 'Where's Nikolay gone?'

'I think he's asleep.'

'Sonya, go and wake him up,' said Natasha. 'Tell him I want him to sing and I need him.'

She sat there a little while longer, wondering what it meant – this had all happened before – but she couldn't work it out, and didn't mind in the slightest, so she let herself glide back in imagination to the time when they had been alone together, and he had gazed at her with eyes full of love.

'Oh, I do wish he'd come! I'm afraid he never will!'

'And the worst thing is: I'm getting older. I really am. What's in me now won't be there soon. Perhaps he's coming today – now! Perhaps he's here already, sitting there in the drawing-room. Perhaps he did come yesterday, and I've forgotten about it.' She got up, put down her guitar, and went into the drawing-room. They were all there – tutors, governesses and guests, sitting at the tea table, and the servants standing behind them. But not Prince Andrey – he wasn't there, and life went on as before.

'Here she is,' said the count, seeing Natasha coming in. 'Come over here and sit with me.' But Natasha stayed by her mother, staring round the room as if she was looking for something.

'Mamma!' she said. 'Get him for me, Mamma, please get him. Hurry!' and again she could hardly stop herself sobbing. She sat down at the table and listened to them talking, the old folk and Nikolay, who had just come in for tea. 'Lord God in heaven! The same people, the same talk, Papa holding his cup and blowing his tea the same as he always does,' thought Natasha, with a terrible sense of revulsion welling up inside her at the sight of all these people, disgusting in their inevitable sameness.

When tea was over Nikolay, Sonya and Natasha went over to their favourite corner in the sitting-room, where their most intimate conversations always began.

CHAPTER 10

'Do you ever get that feeling,' said Natasha to her brother once they were settled in the sitting-room, 'that nothing's ever going to happen to you again, nothing at all, and anything good is in the past? And you don't feel bored exactly, but very, very sad?'

'I'll say!' he replied. 'It's happened to me. Everything's fine, everyone's happy, and suddenly you get this feeling of being fed up with everything, and realizing everybody's going to die. Once in the regiment I stayed in while they all went out celebrating. I could hear the music playing . . . and I had this empty feeling . . .'

'Yes, I know what you mean. I know that feeling. I really do,' said Natasha in full agreement. 'I was quite little when it first happened to me. Do you remember, once I got punished for pinching some plums, and you were all dancing, and I sat in the classroom sobbing. I just sobbed and sobbed – I'll never forget it. I felt so sad and sorry for everyone, sorry for myself and absolutely everybody. And the thing was – I hadn't done it,' said Natasha. 'Do you remember?'

'Yes,' said Nikolay. 'I remember coming to you afterwards, and I really wanted to comfort you, but you know, I felt too ashamed. We were so funny, weren't we? I had that little wooden doll, and I wanted to give it you. Do you remember?'

'And do you remember,' said Natasha, with a pensive smile, 'a long, long time ago, when we were really tiny, Uncle called us over into his study in the old house, and it was dark. We went in, and suddenly there was this . . .'

'Black man!' said Nikolay, finishing her sentence with a smile of delight. 'Of course I remember. I still don't know whether it really was a black man, or whether we dreamt it, or just heard about it.'

'He had grey hair. Do you remember? And white teeth, and he stood there looking at us . . .'

'Do you remember, Sonya?' asked Nikolay.

'Oh yes, I do remember something like that,' Sonya answered shyly.

'You know, I've often asked Papa and Mamma about that black man,' said Natasha. 'They say there wasn't any black man. But you remember him!'

'Of course, I do. I can see his teeth now.'

'Isn't it funny? Just like a dream. I like it.'

'And do you remember us rolling hard-boiled eggs in the big hall, and suddenly there were two old women there, going round and round on the carpet? Did that really happen or not? Remember the fun we had?'

'Yes. And do you remember Papa, in that heavy blue coat, firing his shot gun from the top of the steps?'

Smiling with happiness, they enjoyed going down memory lane; these were not the memories of old age, but the romantic memories of youth, images from the distant past where dreams and reality blur together. They laughed from pure pleasure.

Sonya, as always, couldn't keep up with them, even though she shared the same memories. She couldn't remember much of what they recalled, and what she could remember failed to evoke the same romantic response in her. She was just enjoying their enjoyment, and pretending to be part of it.

She could only come into it properly when they recalled Sonya's first arrival. Sonya said she had been scared of Nikolay because he had braid on his jacket and nurse had told her she was going to be tied up with braid.

'And I remember, they told me you'd been born in a cabbage-patch,' said Natasha. 'Yes, I remember, I had to believe them, even though I knew it wasn't true, and I had such an awkward feeling.'

While they were talking a maid popped her head in at the inner sitting-room door.

'Miss, they've brought you a cockerel,' she whispered.

'I don't want it now, Polya. Tell them to take it away,' said Natasha.

They resumed their conversation, but soon Dimmler came into the sitting-room, and walked over to the harp that stood in one corner. He removed the cloth cover, and the harp gave a discordant jangle. 'Herr Dimmler, please play my favourite nocturne, the one by Mr Field,'[4] came the voice of the old countess from the drawing-room.

Dimmler struck a chord, and turning to Natasha, Nikolay and Sonya he said, 'You youngsters are very quiet today.'

'Yes, we're in a philosophical mood,' said Natasha, glancing round for a moment before going on with the conversation. They were now on to dreams.

Dimmler began to play. Natasha tiptoed silently across to the table, picked up the candle and took it back to them, sitting down quietly in her place. It was dark in the room, especially where they were sitting on the sofa, but the silver light of the full moon shone in through the big windows and spread across the floor.

'Do you know what I think?' said Natasha, in a whisper, moving up closer to Nikolay and Sonya as Dimmler finished the nocturne and sat there faintly rippling the strings as if he didn't know whether to stop playing or begin a new piece, 'I think you can go on remembering, remembering and remembering until you can pre-remember things that happened before you were ever in this world . . .'

'That's metempsychosis,' said Sonya, who had been good at lessons and remembered everything. 'The Egyptians used to believe that our souls have been in animals, and will go back into animals again.'

'No, listen, I don't think we've ever been in animals,' said Natasha, still whispering even though the music had finished, 'but I do know for certain we were once angels somewhere beyond, and we came here, and that's why we can remember everything . . .'

'Please may I join you?' said Dimmler, coming over quietly and sitting down beside them.

'If we've been angels, why did we fall down so low?' said Nikolay. 'No, it's not possible!'

'It's not a question of being low . . . who said anything about being low? . . . The reason I know what I used to be is this,' Natasha replied with great conviction. 'You know the soul is immortal . . . Well, if I'm going to live for ever, that means I've lived before. I've been living all through eternity.'

'Yes, but it's hard for us to conceive of eternity,' said Dimmler, who had joined the young people with a slightly scornful smile, but was now talking just as quietly and seriously as they were.

'Why is it hard to conceive of eternity?' said Natasha. 'There'll be today, there'll be tomorrow, and there'll be always, and there was yesterday, and the day before . . .'

'Natasha! It's your turn! Sing something for me,' called the voice of the countess. 'What are you doing sitting there in a huddle like conspirators?'

'Oh, Mamma, I really don't feel like it!' said Natasha, but she got up as she spoke.

None of them, not even Dimmler, and he was no youngster, wanted to break off the conversation and come out of their corner of the sitting-room, but Natasha got to her feet, and Nikolay seated himself at the clavichord. Standing, as always, in the centre of the room, and choosing the best place for maximum resonance, Natasha began singing her mother's favourite piece.

She had said she didn't feel like singing, but she hadn't sung for a very long time, and it would be a long time in the future before she sang again as she sang that evening. Count Ilya heard her singing from his study, where he was in consultation with Mitenka, and he behaved like a schoolboy rushing through a lesson so he could get out to play, bungling his instructions to the steward until at last he stopped talking, and so did Mitenka, who just stood there before him silent and smiling, both of them listening. Nikolay never took his eyes off his sister, and breathed in and out when she did. Sonya, as she listened, thought of the vast difference between her and her friend, and the impossibility of her ever being anything like as enchanting as her cousin. The old countess sat there with a bitter-sweet smile on her face and tears in her eyes, shaking her head now and then. She was thinking about Natasha and her own youth, and she knew there was something terribly wrong about Natasha's impending marriage to Prince Andrey.

Dimmler had sidled up and sat down beside the countess, and now he listened with his eyes closed. 'No, Countess,' he said, at last, 'this is talent on a European scale. She's beyond all coaching . . . Such a gentle tone, such tenderness, and power . . .'

'Oh, I'm so worried about her, I really am,' said the countess, forgetting who she was speaking to. Maternal instinct told her there was something excessive about Natasha, something that would stop her ever being happy.

Natasha had not quite finished singing when fourteen-year-old Petya rushed in, wildly excited, to announce the arrival of the mummers. Natasha stopped abruptly.

'Idiot!' she yelled at her brother. She ran over to a chair, flopped down on to it and broke into such violent sobbing that it was a long while before she could stop.

'It's nothing, Mamma. Honestly, it's nothing. It's all right. Petya startled me, that's all,' she said, trying hard to smile, but the tears still flowed and she was still racked with sobs.

At first the mummers (house serfs dressed up as bears, Turks, tavern-keepers and fine ladies, monsters and clowns) huddled together timidly in the vestibule, though they had already brought in from outside a breath of cold air and a sense of fun. Then, hiding behind each other, they bumbled and bustled into the great hall, where things began rather uncertainly but soon became more and more hectic and friendly, with singing and dancing, and Christmas games. The countess, after working out who was who and having a good laugh at their costumes, went away to the drawing-room. Count Ilya sat there in the great hall beaming with pleasure and praising their performance. The youngsters had disappeared.

Half an hour later an old lady in a farthingale appeared amidst the other mummers in the hall – it was Nikolay. There was also a Turkish lady – Petya; a clown – Dimmler; a hussar – Natasha; and a Circassian boy with burnt-cork eyebrows and moustaches – Sonya.

After many a polite expression of surprise, bemusement and praise from those who were not dressed up, the young people began to think their costumes were so good they ought to be shown off to a wider audience.

Nikolay's first impulse was to put them all in his sledge and, with the roads in such good condition, drive over to 'Uncle's' along with a dozen house serfs in their costumes.

'No, why bother the old fellow?' said the countess. 'Anyway, you wouldn't have room to turn round there. If you must go, go to the Melyukovs'.'

Madame Melyukov was a widow living with several children of

various ages and their tutors and governesses in a house only a couple of miles down the road.

'Jolly good idea, my love,' the old count put in, his spirits rising. 'Just let me find a costume for myself and I'll come with you. I'll give Pashette something to look at.'

But the countess wouldn't let him go; for several days he had had a bad leg. It was decided that he must stay at home, but if Louisa Ivanovna (Madame Schoss) would agree to go with them the young ladies could go to Madame Melyukov's. Sonya, normally so shy and retiring, was the most vociferous in pleading with Louisa Ivanovna not to refuse.

Sonya's disguise was the best of them all. Her moustaches and eyebrows were particularly fetching. Everyone told her how pretty she looked, and she was taken right out of herself in a new mood of excitement and energy. An inner voice told her that now or never her fate would be decided, and dressed like a man she seemed like a completely different person. Louisa Ivanovna proved amenable, and half an hour later four troikas with merrily jingling bells and runners crunching and creaking over the frozen snow drove round to the front steps.

Natasha took the lead in setting the right tone of Christmas cheer, which passed quickly from one person to the next, grew wilder and wilder and came to a splendid climax as they all walked out into the frosty air, chatting and calling across to each other, with much laughter and shouting, and got into the sledges.

Two of the troikas were harnessed to workaday sledges, the third sledge was the old count's, with a trotter from Orlov's famous stud as the shaft-horse, while the fourth one belonged to Nikolay, and he had put his own short, shaggy black horse to the shaft. Nikolay, with a hussar's cloak belted over his old lady's farthingale, stood up tall in the middle of the sledge and held the reins. The light was so good that he could see the metal fittings on the harnesses glinting in the moonlight, and the horses eyes' goggling in alarm at the racket coming from the travellers in the dark shadow of the porch.

Sonya, Natasha, Madame Schoss and two maids got into Nikolay's sledge. Into the old count's went Dimmler, his wife and Petya, while the other mummers, the house serfs, took their places in the last two sledges.

'Zakhar, you go on ahead!' shouted Nikolay to his father's coachman, so that he could overtake him on the way. The old count's sledge with Dimmler and his party on board lurched forward, its runners creaking as if they were frozen to the snow, and the big bell clanging.

The trace-horses leant into the shafts and as their hooves plunged into the snow they kicked it up, hard and glittering like sugar.

Nikolay followed on behind the first sledge, and after him came the other two, crunching and grating. At first they drove down the narrow road at a slow trot. As they drove down past the garden, the leafless trees sometimes cast their shadows right across the road and hid the bright moonlight. But once they were out of the gates, the snowy plain, glittering with diamonds in a wash of midnight-blue, opened out on all sides, quiescent and bathed in moonlight. Now and again the first sledge would jolt over a pothole, followed by the next one and the one after that, and the sledges stretched out along the road, brutally assaulting the frozen stillness.

'Look, hare-tracks, lots of them!' Natasha's voice rang out through the frosty air.

'Isn't it bright, Nikolay?' said Sonya's voice.

Nikolay glanced round at Sonya, and bent down to take a closer look at her face. It was a new face, quite delightful with its black moustaches and eyebrows that peeped up at him from her furs – so close and yet so distant in the moonlight.

'That used to be Sonya,' thought Nikolay. He looked closer still and gave her a smile.

'What is it, Nikolay?'

'Nothing,' he said, turning back to his horses.

Once they were out on the well-travelled high road, smooth and shiny from sledge runners but lightly pitted by many a horseshoe-nail, with the marks visible in the moonlight, the horses needed no encouragement as they strained at the reins and quickened their pace. The left-hand trace-horse, bending his head down, jerked against his traces. The shaft-horse swayed from side to side, pricking up his ears as if to say, 'Shall we go now, or wait a bit longer?' Zakhar's sledge was well in front but it stood out distinctly, black on white, and they could hear the disappearing echo of its deep-toned bell. Yells and laughter and the sound of people talking floated back from his sledge.

'Right, my darlings!' shouted Nikolay, heaving the reins to one side, and cracking the whip. It was only the sudden onrush of wind straight in their faces and the straining new gallop of the trace-horses that told them the sledge was now hurtling along. Nikolay glanced back. The whooping and yelling and cracking of whips told him the other sledges were coming up fast, with the shaft-horses under the lash. Their own shaft-horse was swinging steadily along under his shaft-bow, with no hint of falling back and every promise of giving more and more if asked to do so.

Nikolay caught up with the first sledge. They were charging downhill on to a wide, well-travelled road through a meadow down by the river.

'Where are we now?' Nikolay wondered. 'Must be Kosoy meadow, I suppose. No, this is somewhere new. I've never seen this before. This isn't Kosoy meadow and that's not Dyomkin hill. Could be anywhere. It's somewhere new. It's a magical place. Who cares?' And yelling to his horses, he began to overtake the first sledge. Zakhar held his horses back and turned his face to them, white to the eyebrows with hoar-frost.

Nikolay gave his horses their head. Zakhar, reaching forward with both arms, clicked his tongue and did the same, calling out, 'Hold on, sir!'

The sledges flew along side by side, faster and faster, and the horses' hooves were a galloping blur. Nikolay pulled slightly ahead. Zakhar, with his arms still straining forward, raised one hand holding the reins.

'No chance, sir,' he yelled, but Nikolay got the last out of his three galloping horses and managed to get past Zakhar. The horses sprayed all their faces with powdery snow, close by they heard the ringing of the bells, and the horses' galloping legs blurred with the shadows of the sledge they were passing. Sounds came from all sides with the girls shrieking as the runners whistled over the snow.

Nikolay then brought his horses to a halt and looked around. Still the same enchanted plain all round them, bathed in moonlight, with a scattering of stars on its surface.

'Zakhar's shouting for me to turn left. Why should I?' thought Nikolay. 'Aren't we supposed to be going to the Melyukovs'? This can't be Melyukovka! We could be anywhere, and anything could be happening to us – and whatever *is* happening to us is very strange and very nice.' He peered back into the sledge.

'Look, his moustache and his eyelashes are all white,' said one of the strange, pretty, exotic figures sitting there, sporting fine moustaches and eyebrows.

'I think that person used to be Natasha,' thought Nikolay; 'and that was Madame Schoss, or maybe not. And that Circassian with the moustaches, I don't know who he is, but I love her.'

'Anybody feeling cold?' he asked them. The only answer was laughter. Dimmler yelled across from the next sledge, probably something funny, but they couldn't hear what he was shouting.

'Yes, yes,' other voices answered, raised in laughter.

But here they were in a kind of enchanted forest with shifting, black shadows and the glitter of diamonds, and a flight of marble steps, and the silvery roofs of enchanted buildings, and the yelp of wild animals. 'And if this really is Melyukovka,' thought Nikolay, 'it's a very funny thing that we've driven through a land that could have been anywhere and ended up here.'

It was indeed Melyukovka, and here came the footmen and maid-servants running out to meet them with lights and beaming faces.

'Who is it?' asked a voice from the entrance.

'It's the mummers from the count's. I can tell by the horses,' other voices answered.

CHAPTER II

Pelageya Melyukov, a broadly built, energetic lady, was sitting in her drawing-room, wearing spectacles and a baggy casual dress, sur-rounded by her daughters, doing what she could to keep boredom at bay. They were quietly dropping melted wax into water and watching the shadows of the shapes that came out, when suddenly they heard noises in the vestibule – footsteps and the voices of people arriving.

In from the vestibule trooped the hussars, fine ladies, witches, clowns and bears, clearing their throats and wiping the hoar-frost off their faces out in the hall, where candles were hurriedly lit. The clown – Dimmler – and the old lady – Nikolay – started a dance. Surrounded by the shrieking children, the mummers hid their faces and spoke in false voices as they bowed to their hostess and dispersed about the room.

'Bless me, they're all unrecognizable! Oh, that's Natasha! Look who she's pretending to be! Who is it she reminds me of? And here's Herr Dimmler – very handsome, too! I hardly knew him. Look at him dancing! Oh, my goodness, here's a Circassian! Little Sonya looks so nice like that! And who's this? Well, you've done us a power of good! Nikita, Vanya – take these tables away. And we were having such a quiet time! ... Ha-ha-ha! ... That hussar, look at that hussar! Just like a boy! And the legs! ... I can't see!' came the various calls.

Natasha, the young Melyukovs' favourite, disappeared with them into the back rooms, where burnt cork and various dressing-gowns and pieces of men's clothing were ordered, procured by the servants and received by bare, girlish arms reaching out through a half-open door. Within ten minutes all the young Melyukovs were ready to come out and join the mummers.

Mme Melyukov had given instructions for the guests to be given plenty of room and she had also arranged for them all to have refreshments, gentry and serfs; now she walked through the crowd of mummers, wearing her spectacles and a half-suppressed smile, scrutinizing them carefully but without recognizing anybody. Not only did she fail to spot the Rostovs and Dimmler, she couldn't even pick out her own daughters or recognize her late husband's dressing-gowns and the bits of his uniform they were wearing.

'Now who can this be?' she kept saying, addressing a governess but staring straight into the face of her own daughter disguised as a Kazan Tatar. 'Must be a Rostov, I suppose. Well, Mr Hussar, which regiment do you belong to?' she asked Natasha. 'Give that Turk a fruit pastille,' she said to a footman walking round with refreshments. 'His laws don't forbid it.'

Sometimes, as she watched the weird and laughable antics of the dancers, who were now letting themselves go on the strength of their undoubted anonymity, Mme Melyukov buried her face in her handkerchief while her elderly and portly figure shook from top to toe with irrepressible laughter and indulgence.

'My little Sasha, my little Sasha!' she cried out.

After several dances, some of them with singing, Mme Melyukov told everyone, servants and gentry alike, to form a large circle. Some string was provided along with a ring and a silver rouble, and they started playing games.

By the time an hour had passed all the costumes were crumpled and untidy. Corked moustaches and eyebrows were being smudged away from burning, perspiring and happy faces. Mme Melyukov was beginning to tell who was who among the mummers. She went into raptures over the clever costumes and the way they suited everyone, especially the young ladies, and she thanked them all for brightening their day. The guests were then invited to take supper in the drawing-room, while the servants were catered for in the hall.

'Oh no, you can't go fortune-telling in an empty bath-house – it's terrifying!' said one person over supper, an old maid who lived with the Melyukovs.

'What do you mean?' asked the Melyukovs' eldest daughter.

'Well, I can't see you doing it. It takes some courage . . .'

'I will,' said Sonya.

'Tell us what happened to that young lady,' said the second girl.

'Well, what happened was this,' said the old maid. 'This young lady went out, took a cockerel, set a table for two, everything just as it should be, and sat down. She sat there for a while, then suddenly what does she hear? Somebody coming – a sledge drives up jingling all sorts of bells. She can hear him coming. In walks a kind of human figure, something like an officer, and he sits down across from her in his proper place.'

'Ah! Ah!' screamed Natasha, goggling with horror.

'Go on. What did he do? Did he talk?'

'Oh yes, a human voice. Everything just as it should be, and he started to woo her with fine words, and she should have kept him going till the cock crowed, but she got scared – it was too much for her and she buried her face in her hands. And he grabbed hold of her . . . It was her lucky day – the maids ran in . . .'

'Go on with you, scaring them like that,' said Mme Melyukov.

'Oh, Mamma, you've done your share of fortune-telling,' said her daughter.

'What's this about fortune-telling in a barn?' asked Sonya.

'Oh, like now, for instance, you just go into a barn and listen. And it all depends on what you hear – if there's a rapping and a banging, that's bad, but if you hear a scattering of corn, it's good. But sometimes what you hear is . . .'

'Mamma, tell us what happened when you went into the barn.'

Mme Melyukov gave a smile.

'Oh, I've forgotten all that,' she said. 'Anyway, nobody here is going.'

'Yes, I will. Let me go. I want to,' said Sonya.

'Oh well, if you're not too scared.'

'Madame Schoss, may I?' asked Sonya.

Whether they had been playing the ring-on-the-string game or the rouble game or just talking as they were now, Nikolay had never left Sonya's side and now he looked at her in a completely new way. It was as if he was looking at her for the first time, all because of that corked moustache, and seeing her for what she really was. That evening Sonya certainly looked happier, livelier and prettier than Nikolay had ever seen her before.

'So, this is what she's like. What a fool I've been!' he kept thinking, looking at her sparkling eyes and the happy, rapturous smile dimpling her cheeks alongside that moustache, a smile he had never seen before.

'I'm not scared,' said Sonya. 'Can I go straightaway?' She got to her feet. They told her where the barn was, and how to stand, keep quiet and listen, and they gave her a heavy coat. She threw it over her head and glanced at Nikolay.

'That girl is gorgeous!' he thought. 'What have I been thinking about all this time?'

Sonya went out into the corridor to walk over to the barn. Nikolay hurried out on to the front steps, saying he was too hot. It certainly was stuffy indoors from the crowd of people.

Outside there was the same frosty stillness and the same moonlight, except that it was even brighter than before. The light was so bright, and there were so many stars sparkling in the snow that the sky was no attraction and the real stars were hardly noticeable. The sky was nothing but dreary blackness, the earth as bright as day.

'I'm a fool, a complete fool! What have I been waiting for all this time?' thought Nikolay, skipping down from the porch and scuttling round the corner of the house along the path leading to the back door. He knew Sonya would come this way. Half-way round he saw the dark shadow cast by a snow-covered stack of logs criss-crossed all over by a network of other shadows from the bare old lime-trees that fell on the snow and the path to the barn. The log wall and roof of the barn glittered in the moonlight, as if they had been hewn out of some precious stone. There was a crackling of twigs in the garden, and then everything relapsed into perfect stillness. Nikolay's lungs seemed to breathe in something more than air, something like the power and joy of eternal youth.

Footsteps could be heard tip-tapping down the steps of the back porch and crunching on the last step which was thick with snow, and an old maid-servant's voice called out, 'Straight down the path, miss. Mind you don't look round!'

'I'm not scared,' answered Sonya's voice, and her little feet in their thin slippers came rasping and crunching down the path towards Nikolay.

Sonya was walking along muffled up in the big coat. She was no more than a couple of paces away when she saw him. She saw him now not as he had always been, slightly intimidating. He was wearing his woman's dress, his hair was all tousled, and there was a blissful smile on his face, one that Sonya had never seen before. She rushed up to him.

'Totally different, and just the same,' thought Nikolay, staring down at her face, bright in the moonlight. He slipped his hands under the coat that she had thrown over her head, put his arms round her, pulled her close and kissed the lips, which sported a moustache and smelt of burnt cork. Sonya kissed him back full on the lips, freed her tiny hands and cupped his cheeks with them.

'Sonya!'

'Nikolay!'

That was all they said.

They ran over to the barn and when they returned to the house they went by different porches.

CHAPTER 12

As they were setting off home from Mme Melyukov's Natasha, who never missed anything worth noticing, managed to get them all to change places so that she and Mme Schoss got into one sledge with Dimmler, leaving Sonya to travel in another one with Nikolay and the maids.

No longer interested in overtaking, Nikolay drove smoothly all the way home, constantly gazing at Sonya through the flickering glow of the weird moonlight, searching beyond those eyebrows and moustaches for a glimpse of two different Sonyas, the old one and the new one from whom he had now resolved never to be parted. His eyes were constantly on her, and as both visions of Sonya impressed themselves upon him, recreating in his memory the smell of burnt cork that had blurred with the thrill of their kiss, he began to drink in great lungfuls of frosty air, he glanced down at the speeding earth and up at the glittering heavens, and he knew he was back in fairyland.

'Sonya, do you feel good?' he asked once or twice, with a meaningful shift to the intimate *ty* form.

'Oh yes. You too?' answered Sonya, also calling him *ty*.

Half-way home, Nikolay handed the reins to a coachman, ran over to Natasha's sledge for a moment and stood on the running-board.

'Natasha,' he whispered in French, 'listen, I've made up my mind about Sonya.'

'Have you told her?' asked Natasha, suddenly aglow with delight.

'Oh, Natasha, you do look funny with that moustache and those eyebrows! Are you pleased?'

'Of course I'm pleased. I really am! I was beginning to lose patience with you. I never told you, but you've been treating her very badly. A girl with a heart like that, Nikolay. Of course I'm pleased! I know I can be horrible, but I did feel awkward about being so happy on my own, and Sonya not being happy,' Natasha went on. 'Now, I really am pleased. Go on, get back to her.'

'I will in a minute. Oh, you don't know how funny you look!' said Nikolay, staring closely and discovering in her as well, his own sister, something strangely warm and enchanting that he had never seen before. 'Natasha, it's magic, isn't it?'

'Yes,' she answered, 'and you've done the right thing.'

'If only I'd seen her before as she is now,' Nikolay was thinking, 'I'd have asked her long ago what to do, and I'd have done anything she said, and everything would have been all right.'

'So, you are pleased, and I have done the right thing?' he asked.

'Of course you have! Mamma and I had a few words about it only the other day. Mamma said she was setting a trap for you. How could she say that? I almost lost my temper with her. I won't have a bad word said or thought about Sonya. There's nothing but good in her.'

'So it is the right thing to do?' said Nikolay, closely examining the look on her face to see whether she was telling the truth. Then he hopped off the sledge, crunched down into the snow and dashed back to his own troika. She was still sitting there, the same Circassian complete with moustache, happy smile and sparkling eyes, peeping out from under the sable hood, and this was Sonya, the Sonya who was now certain to become his happy and loving future wife.

When they got home the two young ladies described to the countess how much they had enjoyed their visit to the Melyukovs' and then went off to their room. They undressed for bed without washing off their moustaches, and then sat there for quite some time just talking about how happy they were. They told each other how they would live after they were married, and what good friends their husbands would be, and, again, how happy they would be. There were two mirrors on Natasha's table, set up earlier in the evening by Dunyasha.

'But when will it happen? I'm scared it won't ever happen . . . It's too much to hope for!' said Natasha, getting to her feet and going over to the mirrors.

'Sit down with the mirrors, Natasha. You might just see him,' said Sonya.

Natasha lit two candles and sat down. 'I can see somebody with a moustache,' said Natasha, catching sight of her own face.

'You mustn't laugh, miss,' said Dunyasha.

With the assistance of Sonya and the maid Natasha adjusted one of the mirrors, then she stopped talking and went all serious. For some time she sat there, staring down the row of disappearing candles reflected in the mirrors. Guided by the tales she had heard, she was expecting to see either a coffin, or perhaps *him*, Prince Andrey, in the very last blurred and smudgy square. But for all her eagerness to accept any dark outline as man- or coffin-shaped, she saw nothing. Her eyes began to water and blink, and she moved away from the mirror.

'Why do other people see things and I don't?' she said. 'You try, Sonya. Today you really must. Do it for me. I feel absolutely terrified today!'

Sonya sat down in front of the mirror, adjusted the angle and peered into it.

'Miss Sonya's bound to see something,' whispered Dunyasha. 'You laugh too much.'

Sonya heard these words, and also heard Natasha's whispered response: 'Yes, I know she'll see something. She did last year.' For two or three minutes nobody spoke.

'She's bound to . . .' Natasha began to whisper, but she never finished her sentence . . . Suddenly Sonya pushed the mirror away and put a hand over her eyes. 'Oh, Natasha!' she said.

'Did you see something? Come on, what was it?' cried Natasha.

'I told you she would,' put in Dunyasha, keeping the mirror from falling.

Sonya hadn't seen anything. She was just about to give in and start blinking and stand up when she had heard Natasha's voice saying, 'She's bound to . . .' She had no desire to hoodwink either Dunyasha or Natasha, but it was hard work sitting there. She couldn't imagine how or why she had cried out like that as she covered her eyes.

'Did you see *him*?' asked Natasha, catching at her arm.

'Yes. Wait a minute . . . I . . . yes I did.' Sonya couldn't stop herself saying it, though she wasn't sure whether Natasha's *him* had meant Nikolay or Andrey.

'Why shouldn't I say I saw something? Other people do. Anyway, who can tell whether I did or I didn't?' The thoughts flashed through Sonya's mind.

'Yes. I did see him,' she said.

'What was he doing? Standing up or lying down?'

'No, what I saw was, er . . . Well, first there was nothing, then I saw him lying down.'

'Andrey lying down? Is he ill?' asked Natasha, her eyes transfixed with terror.

'No, just the opposite, his face looked cheerful and he turned towards me.' And as she spoke these words she began to think she really had seen what she was talking about.

'Come on, Sonya, what happened next?'

'Well, it wasn't very clear. There was something blue and red . . .'

'Oh, Sonya, when will he come back? When shall I see him? Oh God! I'm so worried about him, and me. This whole thing scares me . . .' Natasha blurted out and without a word to Sonya, who was doing what she could to console her, she got into bed, and long after the candle had been put out she lay there motionless, watching the frosty moonlight with staring eyes as it poured in through the frozen window-panes.

CHAPTER 13

Not long after Christmas Nikolay told his mother about his love for Sonya and his absolute determination to marry her. The countess had long been aware of recent developments between Sonya and Nikolay, and she had been expecting this announcement. She listened to his words without comment, and then told her son he could marry anyone he wanted but neither she nor his father would give their blessing to any such marriage. For the first time in his life Nikolay felt that he had offended his mother, and despite all her love for him she was not going to give way. Coldly and without looking at her son she sent for her husband, and when he came in the countess set out there and then to give a brief and icy account of the situation, but she lost control, burst into tears of frustration and walked out of the room. The old count began by appealing to Nikolay, not very convincingly, and asked him to go back on his decision. Nikolay replied that his word was his bond, whereupon his father, sighing from obvious embarrassment, made no further comment and went off to see the countess. In every confrontation with his son the old count was plagued by a guilty conscience for having managed their affairs so badly, and he could hardly turn on his son for refusing to marry an heiress and choosing Sonya, the girl with no dowry. This served only to remind him all the more painfully that but for his mismanagement they could have wished for no better wife than Sonya for Nikolay, and that all the blame lay with him, Mitenka and his own uncontrollable bad habits.

Neither parent raised the subject again with their son, but a few days later the countess sent for Sonya, and with a viciousness that took them both by surprise accused her of inducement and ingratitude. Sonya looked down as she listened in silence to the countess's hurtful words, with no clear idea of what she was supposed to do. She would readily make any kind of sacrifice for her benefactors. The concept of self-sacrifice was dear to her heart, but in this instance she couldn't see who or what there was to sacrifice. She couldn't help loving the countess and all the Rostovs, but neither could she help loving Nikolay or believing that his happiness depended on their love. Sadly at a loss for words, she made no response. Nikolay felt he couldn't put up with this any longer and went in to have things out with his mother. First he asked his mother to forgive him and Sonya and consent to their marriage; then he warned her that if they kept on persecuting Sonya he would go straight out and marry her in secret. With an icy aloofness her son had never seen before the countess replied that he was now an adult, and Prince Andrey was marrying without his father's consent, and he could do the same thing, but she would never acknowledge that *scheming hussy* as her daughter.

Incensed by the words 'scheming hussy', Nikolay told his mother in no uncertain terms he had never expected her to try and make him prostitute his feelings, and if this was how things stood it was the last time he would ever ... But he never delivered the final word which his mother was now dreading, given the look on his face, and which would probably have remained a bitter memory between them for ever. He never delivered it because Natasha, who had been listening at the door, now ran in with a grave look on her pale face.

'Nikolay, darling, you don't know what you're saying. Shut up, shut up! I'm telling you now to *shut up!*' She was virtually screaming to drown him out.

'Mamma, darling, it's nothing to do with ... My poor, dear darling ...' she babbled at her mother, who was gazing in horror at her son, aware that a permanent break was staring them in the face, yet too stubborn and too worked up to give in. 'I'll sort things out later, Nikolay. Just go away. Listen to me, dear darling Mamma,' she said to her mother.

Her words may have been incoherent but they achieved the desired effect.

The countess gave a huge gasp and buried her face on her daughter's bosom, while Nikolay got to his feet, and walked out of the room clutching his head.

Natasha took it upon herself to effect a reconciliation, and she succeeded in so far as Nikolay received an undertaking from his mother that Sonya would not be put under pressure, and he for his part promised not to do anything without his parents' knowledge.

Fully determined to wind things up with the army, retire and come home to marry Sonya, Nikolay returned to his regiment at the beginning of January, chastened and unhappy about the clash with his parents, but, as he thought, still madly in love.

When Nikolay had gone the atmosphere in the Rostov household was more depressed than at any time in the past. The countess fell ill from all the emotional turmoil.

Sonya was saddened by having to part from Nikolay, and more so by the hostile attitude the countess couldn't help adopting towards her. The count was more worried than ever by the disastrous state of his finances, which now demanded decisive action. They were going to have to sell the town house and the estate near Moscow, and this meant going to Moscow. But because of the countess's illness he kept putting off his departure from one day to the next. Natasha, having originally endured separation from her fiancé fairly easily and even cheerfully, now grew increasingly impatient and restive with each passing day. The thought that the prime of her life, which could have been spent loving him, was draining away uselessly like this and benefiting no one, preyed upon her mind. Letters from Prince Andrey just made her angry. She was offended by the very idea that, while her life consisted of nothing but thinking of him, he was living a real life, seeing new places and new people that must be fascinating. The more interesting his letters were, the more they annoyed her. Her letters to him gave her no comfort; she looked on them as a tedious and formal obligation. She was no great writer, finding it impossible to set down adequately in a letter a thousandth part of what she was used to conveying by means of her voice, her smile and her eyes. She wrote him a series of dry, formal and identical missives to which she attached not the slightest importance, with spelling mistakes corrected by the countess at the rough copy stage.

The countess's health was not improving, but it was becoming impossible to put off the visit to Moscow any longer. There was the trousseau to see about and the house had to be sold, in addition to which Prince Andrey was due to go first to Moscow, where his father was spending the winter, and Natasha felt certain he was already there. The countess stayed behind in the country when, towards the end of January, the count left for Moscow, taking Sonya and Natasha with him.

PART V

CHAPTER I

After Prince Andrey's engagement to Natasha it dawned on Pierre, suddenly and for no obvious reason, that he couldn't possibly go on living as before. For all his staunch belief in the truths revealed to him by his benefactor, the old freemason, and the pleasure he had taken at first in striving so ardently towards the perfection of his inner self, after Prince Andrey's engagement to Natasha and the death of Osip Bazdeyev, news of which had reached him at almost exactly the same time, all the zest suddenly went out of that earlier way of living. He was left with nothing but the skeleton of a life: his house with his brilliant wife, now enjoying the favours of a very important person, entrée to all levels of Petersburg society and service at court with all its tiresome formalities. And now suddenly Pierre was shocked by the degree of disgust that he felt for that former life. He stopped keeping a diary, shunned the society of his brother-masons and went back to his old club, drinking too much, consorting with the bachelor set and adopting the kind of life-style that made Countess Hélène feel obliged to take him to task on the subject. Pierre felt she had right on her side, so he went down to Moscow to avoid compromising her.

Once in Moscow, the moment he set foot in his vast house with the faded and fading princesses and the hordes of servants, the moment he drove through the town and caught his first glimpse of the Iversky chapel with the lights of innumerable candles glinting and reflecting in the silver icon-covers and the Kremlin Square with its deep covering of untrodden snow, the sledge-drivers, the shanties of the Sivtsev Vrazhok slums, the old gentlemen of Moscow in the twilight of their lives, unhurried and set in their ways, and also the old ladies of Moscow, the Moscow ballrooms and the English Club – he felt he had come back home to a haven of peace. In Moscow he felt warm and welcome, comfortable and scruffy. It was like putting on an old dressing-gown.

All Moscow society, from the old ladies to the children, welcomed Pierre back like a long-awaited guest, whose place had always lain ready for him, never occupied by anyone else. In the eyes of Moscow society, Pierre was the nicest and kindest of men, the brightest and jolliest, the most generous of eccentrics, a hare-brained and warm-hearted Russian gentleman of the old school. His purse was for ever empty, being open to all.

Benefit performances, awful paintings and statues, charities, gypsy choirs, schools, subscription dinners, drinking parties, the masons, churches, book-publishing – everyone and everything met with his support, and had it not been for two of his friends, who had borrowed heavily from Pierre and set themselves up as his guardians, he would have given away his last kopeck. Not a single party or dinner took place at the club without him being there.

Once seen sprawling in his usual place on the sofa after a couple of bottles of Margaux he would be surrounded by a circle of friends and become the centre of all discussions, disputes and jokes. When people fell out, a friendly smile or a well-chosen *bon mot* from him was enough to bring peace. Masonic dinners were dull and dreary when he wasn't there.

When he got to his feet after a bachelor supper and yielded with a sweet smile to the entreaties of the revellers to drive off with them somewhere, the young men would raise the roof with yells of delight and triumph. In the ballroom he would dance if a partner was needed. He appealed to both young girls and the younger married ladies because he didn't flirt and was nice to everyone in just the same way, especially after supper. 'He's a delightful man with no sex,' they used to say of him (always in French).

This was Pierre – one among hundreds of retired gentlemen-in-waiting peaceably living out their days in Moscow. What horror he would have felt if he had been told on his return from abroad seven years ago that there was no point in searching or taxing his brains because the way forward was set for him, marked out in advance for all eternity, and it was no use fighting against it because he was bound to turn out exactly like every other man in his position. He wouldn't have believed it. Had he not put his heart and soul into so many things – setting up a republic in Russia, turning himself into another Napoleon, or a philosopher, or a master strategist capable of defeating Napoleon? Had he not considered it possible and highly desirable to work for the regeneration of sinful humanity and bring himself to the highest degree of perfection? Had he not gone about founding schools and hospitals and liberating his serfs?

But instead of all that, here he was now, the wealthy husband of an unfaithful wife, a retired gentleman-in-waiting, fond of his food and drink, not averse to unbuttoning his waistcoat after dinner and indulging in a little mild criticism of the government, a member of the Moscow English Club, and everyone's favourite on the Moscow circuit. It took him a long time to become reconciled to the idea that he was the very model of a retired Moscow gentleman-in-waiting, a type he had found so profoundly repellent seven years ago.

Sometimes he consoled himself with the idea that it didn't matter – this was only a passing phase – only to be struck by the horrifying thought that plenty of others had gone through the same 'passing phase', embarking on this kind of life and joining this club with all their teeth and hair and leaving when they were toothless and bald.

There were moments of pride when he took stock and it seemed to him that he wasn't like them, he was somehow different from the retired gentlemen-in-waiting he had once despised; they were vulgar and stupid men, given to complacency, 'whereas I'm still never satisfied, I really want to do things for humanity', as he put it when pride came upon him. 'Yes, but what if all of them, these comrades of mine, also struggled like me, looking for some new and original way of living, and only got as far as I have because they were beaten, like me, by the force of circumstances, society, breeding – a force of nature that renders a man impotent?' This is what he wondered when modesty came upon him. And when he had been some little time in Moscow he lost all contempt for his companions in destiny and even started to love them, respect them and feel as sorry for them as he did for himself.

Pierre no longer suffered from his earlier bouts of despair, disillusionment and loathing for life, but the same sickness that had once manifested itself in acute attacks had now been driven inwards, never to leave him for a single moment. 'What's the use of anything? What is it all about? What is going on in the world?' he asked himself in great bewilderment several times a day, allowing himself to be drawn forcibly into a search for meaning in all the phenomena of existence. But experience had taught him that there weren't any answers to these questions, so he made every effort to wrench himself away from them by turning to a book, nipping down to the club, or calling in at Apollon Nikolayevich's place for a good gossip.

'My Hélène has never cared for anything but her own body and she's one of the stupidest women in the world,' thought Pierre, 'yet everybody thinks she's the last word in intelligence and sophistication, and they all bow down to her. And take Napoleon – universally despised as long as he was a great man, and now he's just a pathetic clown the Emperor Francis wants to offer him his daughter for an illegal marriage. The Spaniards go down on their knees and thank God through their Catholic clergy for victory over the French on the 14th of June, and the French, through the same Catholic clergy, go down on their knees and thank God for victory over the Spaniards on the same day, the 14th of June. My masonic brothers take an oath in blood, swearing to sacrifice everything for their neighbour, but they won't cough up a rouble when you go round collecting for the poor, and meanwhile the Astraea lodge sets itself against the "Manna Seekers",[1] and they squabble over some authentic Scottish carpet or a completely superfluous Act which has no meaning any more, not even for the man who wrote it. We all profess the Christian laws of forgiveness of injuries and love for our neighbour – laws we have honoured by raising forty times forty churches in Moscow – but yesterday a deserter died under the knout, and it was a minister of these same laws of love and forgiveness, a priest, who had given the soldier a cross to kiss before his punishment.'

Thoughts like these were never far from Pierre's mind, and the whole of this universally accepted hypocritical sham, for all its familiarity, astonished him each time like something new. 'I understand this tangled mess of hypocrisy,' he thought, 'but how can I tell people everything I understand? I've tried, and I always find they understand it as well as I do at the bottom of their hearts, but there's something they're trying not to see. They won't see – *that*. Oh well, it's the way of things, I suppose. But here am I – what can I do with myself?' thought Pierre.

He had the unfortunate capacity that many men have, especially Russians, for seeing and believing in the possibility of goodness and truth, yet seeing the evil and falsehood in life too clearly to be capable of taking any serious part in it. Every aspect of human activity he saw as bound up with evil and deception. Whatever he tried to be, whatever he decided to do, he found himself repelled by evil and falsehood, with every avenue of activity blocked off. And meanwhile he had to live on and find things to do. It was too horrible to be ground down by life's insoluble problems, so he latched on to any old distraction that came along, just to get them out of his mind. He tried all kinds of society, drank a lot, bought pictures, built things and, most of all, he read.

He read and reread everything he could get his hands on. When he got home at night he would pick up a book and start on it before his valets had finished undressing him, and then read himself to sleep. From sleep he proceeded to drawing-room and club gossip; from gossip to wine, women and song; and from these back to more gossip, reading and wine. Wine was becoming more and more a mental and physical necessity. He defied the doctors who warned him that with his corpulence wine was a danger to his health, and kept on drinking heavily. The only time he felt good was when he had mechanically emptied several glasses of wine into his big mouth. Only then did he feel a pleasing sensation of warmth flowing through his whole body, along with a sentimental attachment to his fellow men, and enough wit to come out with an off-the-cuff response to any idea, as long as he didn't have to go too deeply into it. It was only after drinking a bottle or two of wine that he could vaguely accept that the horribly tangled skein of life, which had held such terrors for him, turned out to be less terrifying than he had imagined. As, with a ringing in his head, he chatted away, listened to people as they talked or read after dinner and supper, he couldn't get away from the sight of that tangled skein in one aspect or another. Only under the influence of wine could he say to himself, 'There's nothing to it. I'll soon get that disentangled. Look, I've got the solution here. But now's not the time. I'll sort it out later!' Except that 'later' never came.

Next morning at breakfast all the old questions resurfaced, as horribly insoluble as ever, so Pierre would dive into a book with all speed and rejoice when a visitor called.

Sometimes Pierre remembered what he had been told about soldiers in a shelter under fire with nothing to do, trying their best to keep busy and thus make the danger easier to bear. And Pierre pictured all men as soldiers like these, escaping from life through ambition, cards, law-making, women, little playthings, horses, politics, sport, wine, even government service. 'Everything matters, nothing matters, it's all the same. If I can only escape, one way or another!' thought Pierre. 'And not see *it*, the terrible *it*.'

CHAPTER 2

At the beginning of the winter old Prince Bolkonsky and his daughter moved to Moscow. He had become an object of special veneration in Moscow because of his past achievements, his powerful intellect and unusual character, and this, together with the current decline in the popularity of Tsar Alexander's regime, which coincided with a surge in anti-French sentiment and Russian patriotism, now made him the natural centre of opposition to the government.

The prince had aged a good deal that year. He had begun to show clear signs of senility: nodding off without any warning, forgetting very recent events while clearly remembering incidents from long ago, and the childlike vanity with which he assumed leadership of the Moscow opposition. Nevertheless, when the old man came down for tea, especially of an evening, wearing his powdered wig and a thick little coat, and responded to someone's challenge by launching forth into a series of sharp comments on the old days, or even sharper and more vitriolic criticism of the present day, he still evoked the same old feelings of respect and admiration in all his guests. For any visitors, that old-fashioned house, with its enormous mirrors, pre-Revolution furniture and powdered footmen, and the stern and shrewd old man, himself a relic from the past, along with his gentle daughter and the pretty Frenchwoman, both of whom doted on him, presented a magnificent and most appealing spectacle. But those same visitors never stopped to think that in addition to the couple of hours when they saw their hosts there were another twenty-two in the daily cycle during which the hidden private life of the household continued.

That private life in Moscow had recently become very hard for Princess Marya. In town she was deprived of her greatest pleasures – conversations with the pilgrims and the solitude, both of which she had found so refreshing at Bald Hills – and none of the advantages and delights of metropolitan life applied to her. She never went out into society; everyone knew that her father wouldn't allow her to go anywhere without him, and because of his failing health he couldn't go anywhere. People had stopped inviting her to dinner-parties or balls. Princess Marya had by now abandoned all hope of marriage. She had noted the frostiness and animosity with which the old prince received and dismissed any young men, possible suitors, who appeared at the house from time to time. Friends she had none; during this stay in Moscow she had lost faith in the two friends who had been closest to her. She had become disenchanted with Mademoiselle Bourienne, in whom she had never had complete confidence, and now she kept her at bay for a number of reasons. Julie Karagin, a regular pen-friend over five long years, was here in Moscow, but when they met face to face she struck Princess Marya as utterly alien. On the death of her brothers Julie had become one of the wealthiest heiresses in Moscow and was now making the most of the heady pleasures offered by high society and was surrounded by young men who seemed suddenly appreciative of her virtues. Julie had reached the stage when a young society lady no longer in the first flush of youth begins to sense that her last chance of getting married has come and her fate must soon be decided once and for all. Every Thursday Princess Marya smiled a lugubrious smile as she contemplated the prospect of having no one to write to because Julie was here on the spot and seeing her once a week, not that there was any pleasure to be derived from their meetings. Like the old French émigré who declined to marry the lady with whom he had spent all his evenings over many years because if he got married he wouldn't know where to spend his evenings, she regretted that with Julie being here she had no one to write to. In Moscow Princess Marya had no one to talk to either, and no one to share her troubles with, just at a time when many new troubles were adding themselves to the old ones. The time for Prince Andrey's return and marriage was fast approaching, and the task he had given her of bringing their father round was so far from completion that the whole thing seemed beyond hope – the slightest reference to young Countess Rostov simply enraged the old prince, who was almost always in a foul mood nowadays in any case. Another item in Princess Marya's store of recent troubles arose from the way she had been teaching her six-year-old nephew. In her attitude to little Nikolay she was shocked to find herself displaying the same signs of irritability as her father. However often she told herself not to lose her temper, almost every time she sat down to teach her nephew and pointed to letters of the French alphabet she felt such an urgent desire to make things easy and hurry the process of transferring knowledge from herself to the child (who was always scared stiff that his auntie might be about to come down on him), that at the slightest hint of inattention she quivered and gabbled and snapped at him, or shouted and sometimes grabbed him by his little hand and stood him in a corner. Once she had stood him there she would burst into tears at her own wicked and violent behaviour, whereupon little Nikolay, not to be outdone when it came to sobbing, would creep out of his corner without waiting for permission, walk over and pull her wet hands away from her face in an effort to console her. But the worst, easily the worst of her troubles was her father's terrible temper, which was invariably directed against his daughter and had recently reached the point of cruelty. Had he forced her to spend every night on her knees in supplication, had he beaten her, or made her chop wood and carry water, it would never have occurred that her lot was a hard one. But this loving tyrant – all the crueller for loving her so much and using that as a pretext for tormenting himself and her – was a past master at deliberate degradation and humiliation and convincing her she was always to blame for anything that happened. He had recently developed a new quirk, one which caused Princess Marya more misery than anything else – and this was his growing intimacy with Mademoiselle Bourienne. The idea that had occurred to him as a joke when he got the first news of his son's intentions – that if Andrey was going to get married, he might as well marry Mademoiselle Bourienne – clearly appealed to him, and in recent days he had gone out his way to shock her (as she saw it) by being particularly gracious to Mademoiselle Bourienne and demonstrating dissatisfaction with his daughter by a corresponding demonstration of love for the Frenchwoman.

One day, before her very eyes (she couldn't help thinking her father did it on purpose because she was there) the old prince kissed Mademoiselle Bourienne on the hand, then drew her close and gave her a passionate hug. Princess Marya blushed to the roots of her hair and fled from the room. A few minutes later Mademoiselle Bourienne breezed into Princess Marya's room, all smiles and chattering away merrily in her pleasant little voice. Princess Marya dried her tears hastily, marched over to the Frenchwoman and, without realizing what she was doing, turned on her in wild fury, gulping and screaming, 'You vile thing . . . it's inhuman . . . taking advantage of a feeble old . . .'

She couldn't go on. 'Get out of my room!' she yelled, breaking down in sobs.

Next day the old prince ignored his daughter, but she noticed that at dinner he gave orders for Mademoiselle Bourienne to be served first. Towards the end of dinner, when the footman served the princess with coffee first, from sheer habit, the old prince flew into a wild rage, flung his cane at Filipp and gave immediate orders for him to be sent off into the army.

'Insubordination . . . told him twice . . . and he still didn't obey! She's the first person in this house, she's my best friend,' roared the old prince. 'And as for you,' he fulminated, addressing Princess Marya for the first time, 'you dare ever again to do what you did yesterday . . . forget yourself in her presence, and I'll show you who's master in this house. Go on! Get out of my sight! Apologize to her!'

Princess Marya gave her apology to Mademoiselle Bourienne and also to her father, for what she had done and also for the behaviour of the footman, Filipp, who was begging her to intercede.

At moments like this Princess Marya's soul was afflicted by a sensation not far from the pride of self-sacrifice. And yet all of a sudden at moments like this, the very father she was censuring would either start looking for his spectacles, groping around close to them without seeing them, or completely forget what had just happened, or else he would take a single tottering step on his spindly legs and stare round to see whether anyone had noticed his feebleness, or – worst of all –

over dinner, when there were no guests to stimulate him, he would suddenly nod off, dropping his napkin and letting his shaking head droop down over his plate. 'Oh, he's so old and feeble, and I have the gall to criticize him!' she thought at moments like this in hateful self-reproach.

CHAPTER 3

In the year 1811 there lived in Moscow a French doctor by the name of Métivier, who was suddenly all the rage. He was very tall and handsome, he had the nice manners of a true Frenchman, and all Moscow had him down as a very accomplished physician. He was received in the very best houses, not merely as a doctor but as an equal.

Old Prince Bolkonsky had always poured scorn on medicine, but in recent days he had taken Mademoiselle Bourienne's advice, and allowed this doctor to see him, gradually getting used to his visits. Métivier came to see the old prince two or three times a week.

On St Nicholas's day, the old prince's name-day, all Moscow turned up at his front door, but he gave orders for no one to be admitted. Only one or two guests, whose names were on a list that he had given to Princess Marya, were to be invited to lunch.

Métivier turned up that morning with his greetings and considered it proper as the old prince's doctor to 'break the embargo', as he put it to Princess Marya, and go in to see the prince. As it happened, on the morning of his name-day the old prince was in one of his foulest moods. He had spent the whole morning tramping through the house, finding fault with everybody and pretending he couldn't understand anything that was said to him and nobody understood what he was saying. Princess Marya was all too familiar with this mood of nervous, simmering touchiness, which usually culminated in a furious outburst, and she went about that morning like someone staring down the barrel of a cocked and loaded gun and waiting for the inevitable big bang. The morning had gone off reasonably well – until the doctor arrived. After showing the doctor in, Princess Marya sat down with a book in the drawing-room not far from the door, through which she could hear everything that was going on in the prince's study.

At first the only voice she could hear was Métivier's, then came her father's, then both of them together. Then the door flew open, and in the doorway stood Métivier, a handsome figure of a man with his shock of black hair but terrified out of his wits, and behind him the old prince in skull-cap and dressing-gown, his face hideous with rage and the pupils of his eyes looking down at the floor.

'So, you don't know what's going on?' roared the old prince. 'Well I do! You French spy, you slave of Bonaparte. You're a spy! Get out, I tell you! Get out of my house!' And he slammed the door. Métivier gave a shrug and walked over to Mademoiselle Bourienne, who had come running in from the next room when she heard all the shouting.

'The prince is not quite himself – a touch of bile and a rush of blood to the brain. Don't be too concerned. I'll look in tomorrow,' said Métivier, and he scurried away putting a finger to his lips.

Through the door came the sound of shuffling slippers and a voice shouting, 'Spies and traitors! Traitors everywhere! No peace in your own house!'

When Métivier had gone the old prince summoned his daughter and deluged her with the whole fury of his passion. She was to blame for letting the spy in. Hadn't he told her, yes, told her, to put the names down on a list and not let anyone else in? Why had she let that scoundrel in? It was all her fault. He couldn't get a minute's peace with her in the house – he couldn't even die in peace.

'No, madam, we must part, we must part, I tell you! I can't take any more,' he said, storming out of the room. And as if to rob her of any crumb of consolation, he walked back in, did his best to look calm and collected, and added, 'And don't imagine that I've said this in the heat of the moment. Oh no, I'm perfectly calm and I've given it a lot of thought. It's going to happen. We must part. You can find yourself somewhere else to live! . . .' And he couldn't even leave it at that. With the vicious fury found only in a man inspired by love, and in obvious anguish himself, he shook his fists at her and roared, 'Oh! If only some fool would marry her!' With that he slammed the door, sent for Mademoiselle Bourienne and subsided in his study.

At two o'clock the six luncheon guests arrived and foregathered in the drawing-room to wait for him – the famous Count Rostopchin, Prince Lopukhin and his nephew, General Chatrov, a former army colleague of the prince's, and two representatives of the younger gener-ation, Pierre and Boris Drubetskoy. Boris, who had only recently come back to Moscow on leave, had been most anxious to meet Prince Nikolay Bolkonsky and had wormed his way in so effectively that for his sake the old prince had made an exception to his usual rule of keeping all young bachelors out of the house.

The prince did not receive 'society people' as such, but his house was the focal point of a small clique where – though there wasn't much talk of this in town – it was more flattering to be received than anywhere else. Boris had latched on to this a week previously when he had heard Rostopchin turn down an invitation from the commander-in-chief of Moscow, who had invited him to dinner on St Nicholas's day, with the words, 'That's the day when I always visit Prince Nikolay Bolkonsky to pay my devotion to the relics.'

'Oh yes, of course . . .' replied the commander-in-chief. 'How is he, by the way?'

The little party which had come together before luncheon in the old-fashioned drawing-room with its high ceiling and old furniture was much like a law-court in solemn session. They sat there in silence, and if they did speak it was in subdued tones. Prince Nikolay, when he came in, looked grim and reluctant to speak. Princess Marya seemed even more meek and mild than usual. The guests preferred to leave her out of the conversation, since it was obvious that she wasn't up to it. Count Rostopchin held the thread of the conversation all on his own, treating them to the latest news, first from the town and then the world of politics.

Lopukhin and the old general put in the odd remark now and then. Prince Nikolay presided like a judge receiving a submission, with nothing more than the occasional grunt or the briefest of words to indicate that he was taking stock of the facts laid before him. The tone of the conversation was based on the assumption that no one approved of what was being done in the political world. Events were described that clearly confirmed the idea of everything going from bad to worse, but in every account and every critical discourse it was remarkable how each speaker held back, or was held back by someone else, if he got anywhere near the borderline where criticism might have touched on the person of the Tsar himself.

Over the meal the conversation turned to recent political developments, in particular Napoleon's seizure of the Duke of Oldenburg's lands, and the Russian note, hostile to Napoleon, that had been sent to every European court.[2]

'Bonaparte sets about Europe like a pirate-king on a captured ship,' said Rostopchin, rehearsing a little saying he had had occasion to use before. 'One can only wonder that the ruling sovereigns are so tolerant – or so easily dazzled. The Pope is next in line. Bonaparte is brazen enough to try and depose the head of the Catholic Church, and no one says a word. Our Emperor is the only one who has protested against the seizure of the Duke of Oldenburg's lands. And even he . . .' Count Rostopchin broke off at this point, sensing that he was on the very brink of prohibited criticism.

'He's been offered other bits of land instead of the Duchy of

Oldenburg,' said the old prince. 'He shifts the dukes about anywhere
he likes ... It's like me sending my serfs from Bald Hills over to
Bogucharovo or down to Ryazan.'

'The Duke of Oldenburg bears his misfortune with admirable
strength of character and resignation,' said Boris in a polite contribution to the discussion. He could say this because on the way down
from Petersburg he had had the honour of being presented to the duke.
The old prince stared at the young man as if he wanted to take him
up on something, but he thought better of it, considering him too
young.

'I have read our protest against the Oldenburg affair, and I was
surprised at the poor wording of it,' said Count Rostopchin with the
offhand manner of one who can criticize something because he is
closely familiar with it.

Pierre looked at Rostopchin in innocent amazement, at a loss to
understand why he should be bothered about the poor wording of
the note.

'Does it matter how the note is worded, Count,' he said, 'if the
content is strong enough?'

'My dear fellow, with five hundred thousand men behind us, it
should be easy to get the style right,' said Count Rostopchin. Pierre
saw the point of Count Rostopchin's dissatisfaction with the wording
of the note.

'Plenty of scribblers everywhere,' said the old prince. 'Up in Petersburg they do nothing else but write – not just notes, they keep on
writing new laws. My Andrey up yonder, he's written a thick volume
of new laws for Russia. Everybody's at it nowadays!' and he gave a
weird kind of laugh.

The conversation ground to a halt, and then the old general drew
attention to himself by clearing his throat.

'Did you hear what happened at the review in Petersburg? Marvellous performance by the new French ambassador!'

'Eh? Oh yes, I did hear something. Blurted something out in his
Majesty's presence, didn't he?'

'His Majesty drew his attention to the grenadier division as they
marched past,' the general persisted, 'and it seems the ambassador
ignored him and had the gall to say "In France we don't bother with
stupid things like that." The Emperor vouchsafed no response. At the
next review his Majesty, so they say, gave him the cold shoulder.'

No one spoke. Here was a detail pertaining to the Tsar personally,
but it was beyond criticism.

'The cheek of the man!' said the old prince. 'Do you know Métivier?

I threw him out of the house today. He came here and they let him in, even though I asked for no one to be admitted,' said the old prince, glaring across at his daughter. And he went through the whole of his conversation with the French doctor and his reasons for believing Métivier was a spy. His reasons were very flimsy and obscure, but no one raised an objection.

After the main course champagne was served. The guests rose to congratulate the old prince. Princess Marya too went round to him. He treated her to a cold, spiteful glare, and offered her a clean-shaven, wrinkled cheek. There was a look on his face that said everything: their conversation that morning had not been forgotten, his decision still stood and only the presence of visitors prevented him from talking about it now.

When they proceeded to the drawing-room for coffee the old men sat down together. Prince Nikolay got more excited and began to expound his ideas on the impending war. He said that our wars against Bonaparte would always be lost while ever we went on seeking alliances with the Germans and meddling in European affairs that we couldn't get out of because of the Peace of Tilsit. 'We have no business fighting for or against Austria,' he went on. 'Our political interests are all to the east, and as far as Napoleon is concerned all we need is a well-armed force guarding the frontier and a strong policy, and he won't dare cross the Russian frontier again, as he did in 1807.'

'But how are we ever going to be able to fight the French, Prince!' said Count Rostopchin. 'How can we take arms against our teachers and our idols? Look at our young men, look at our ladies. The French are our gods, and Paris is our Paradise.'

He began to raise his voice so that everyone could hear.

'Our fashions are French, our ideas are French, our feelings are French! Look here, you sent Métivier packing because he's a Frenchman and a scoundrel, but our ladies go down on their knees and crawl after him. I was at a party yesterday evening, and, do you know, out of five ladies three were Catholics and they had a papal dispensation that allows them to do their embroidery on Sundays. And they sat there virtually naked, like signboards in a public bath-house – pardon me for saying so. Oh dear me, when you look at our young people today, Prince, you feel like taking Peter the Great's old cudgel[3] out of the museum and cracking a few ribs with it. Do it the Russian way! Soon knock the nonsense out of them!'

Nobody spoke. The old prince looked across at Rostopchin with a grin on his face and shook his head approvingly.

'Well, goodbye, your Excellency. Keep well,' said Rostopchin, jumping to his feet with his usual alacrity and extending a hand to the prince.

'Goodbye, my dear fellow ... Music to my ears. What a man – always worth listening to!' said the old prince, holding on to the hand and offering his cheek. The others rose when Rostopchin did.

CHAPTER 4

Sitting there in the drawing-room listening to the old men's chatter and tittle-tattle, Princess Marya couldn't understand a word of what she was hearing. The only thing she could think about was whether or not all the guests were aware of her father's hostility towards her. She hadn't even noticed that Drubetskoy – now on his third visit to their house – had been particularly attentive and amiable towards her all through dinner.

Princess Marya turned to Pierre with a far-away, inquiring look in her eyes, he being the last to go, after the prince had departed, leaving them alone together in the drawing-room. He had come over to her, hat in hand, with a smiling face.

'Can I stay on a bit?' he said, depositing his great bulk into a low chair alongside Princess Marya.

'Please do,' she said, but her eyes asked him, 'Didn't you notice?'

Pierre was in a happy after-dinner mood. He looked straight ahead and smiled a sweet smile. 'Have you known that young man very long, Princess?' he said.

'Which one?'

'Drubetskoy.'

'No, not very long ...'

'Do you like him?'

'Yes, he's a very nice young man. Why do you ask?' said Princess Marya, still thinking of her conversation that morning with her father.

'Because in my experience, when a young man comes from Petersburg to Moscow on leave, it is usually with the object of marrying an heiress.'

'Is that your experience?' said Princess Marya.

'Oh yes,' Pierre went on with a smile, 'and that young man is carrying on in such a way that wherever there are wealthy heiresses – that's where he is. I can read him like a book. At this moment he's wondering whether to mount an assault on you or Mademoiselle Julie Karagin. He's paying her a lot of attention.'

'Does he go there?'

'Yes, very often. And do you know the latest way of courting a woman?' said Pierre, beaming breezily, and obviously enjoying that jovial mood of ironical banter for which he had reproached himself so many times in his diary.

'No,' said Princess Marya.

'Well, nowadays, in order to please the girls in Moscow, you have to be melancholic. He's very melancholic just now with Mademoiselle Karagin,' said Pierre.

'Is he really?' said Princess Marya, staring into Pierre's kindly face but constantly preoccupied with her own troubles. 'I'd feel a bit better,' she was thinking, 'if I could just confide in somebody and tell them how I feel. And Pierre's the one to confide in. He's so kind and generous. I think I'd feel better. He would tell me what to do.'

'Would you ever marry him?' asked Pierre.

'Oh heavens, Count! There are times when I'd marry anybody,' Princess Marya said with tears in her voice, much to her own surprise. 'Oh! It's so hard when you love someone close to you and you feel . . .' she went on in a tremulous voice, 'you can't do anything for him that won't cause trouble, and you know you can't do anything about it. There's only one thing to do – go away, but where can I go?'

'What's wrong? What's happened, princess?'

But Princess Marya, instead of going into explanations, burst into tears.

'I don't know what's wrong with me today. Please don't take any notice. Forget what I've said.'

Pierre's breezy attitude was gone. He questioned the princess anxiously, begging her to make a clean breast of it and tell him all her troubles, but she just kept on repeating the same things – she wanted him to forget what she had said, she couldn't remember what she had said, and the only worry she had was the one he knew about – Prince Andrey's marriage, which looked like setting father against son.

'Have you heard anything about the Rostovs?' she asked, changing the subject. 'I believe they're due here soon. I'm expecting Andrey, too, any day now. I should have liked them to have their first meeting here.'

'And how does he look on things now?' asked Pierre, meaning the old prince. Princess Marya shook her head. 'Well, it can't be helped,' she continued. 'There are only a few months left now before the year is up. And it can't go on like this. All I'd like to do is spare my brother the first few minutes. Oh, I do wish they'd come. I'm hoping she and I can get to know each other . . . You've known them quite some time, haven't you?' asked Princess Marya. 'Give me your honest opinion, hand on heart. What sort of a girl is she? What do you make of her? But please tell me the whole truth, because, well, Andrey's taking such a risk going against his father. I just wanted to know . . .'

A vague instinct told Pierre that all this beating about the bush and the repeated insistence on hearing *the whole truth* rather suggested that Princess Marya was anything but well-disposed towards her future sister-in-law, as if she wanted Pierre to disapprove of Prince Andrey's choice, but Pierre said what he felt rather than what he thought. 'I don't know how to answer your question,' he said, colouring up without knowing why. 'I really don't know what sort of girl she is. I can't analyse her. She's fascinating. I don't know why. There's nothing more to be said about her.'

Princess Marya sighed, and her face seemed to say, 'Yes, just as I expected, just what I was dreading.'

'Is she clever?' asked Princess Marya. Pierre thought about this.

'I don't think she is,' he said. 'And yet, you know, perhaps she could be. She doesn't think it's worthwhile being clever . . . No, no, she's just fascinating, that's all.'

Princess Marya shook her head again, showing further disapproval.

'Oh, I do want to like her! You can tell her that if you see her before I do.'

'I have heard they'll be here in a day or two,' said Pierre.

Princess Marya told him about her plan of action: as soon as the Rostovs arrived she was going to form an attachment with her future sister-in-law and do what she could to bring the old prince round and get him to understand her.

CHAPTER 5

Boris had not succeeded in finding a wealthy heiress to marry in Petersburg, and it was with this in mind that he had come down to Moscow. In Moscow Boris found himself hesitating between the two wealthiest heiresses – Julie Karagin and Princess Marya. Although Princess Marya, for all her plainness, seemed more attractive than Julie, somehow he felt awkward about paying court to her. At their last meeting on the old prince's name-day every time he had begun to talk sentimentally her responses had been all over the place and she had obviously not been listening to him.

Julie, by contrast, was only too eager to receive his attentions, though she showed it in her own special way. Julie was now twenty-seven. On the death of her two brothers she had become extremely wealthy. By now she had lost what looks she had ever had, though she believed herself to be no less attractive, in fact far prettier than ever before. She had been confirmed in this delusion first by becoming a wealthy heiress but also because as she grew older she became less dangerous to men, which enabled them to approach her more easily and take full advantage of her suppers, her soirées and the lively society that gathered about her without incurring any obligations. A man who, ten years ago, would have been reluctant to visit a house with a seventeen-year-old girl in it for fear of compromising her and tying himself down would now call in cheerfully every day, treating her not as a good match but as a sexless acquaintance.

That winter the Karagins' house was one of the most open and welcoming in Moscow. Besides all the invitation-only dinner-parties and soirées, people gathered in large numbers at the Karagins' every day of the week, especially men, who took supper at midnight and stayed on till three in the morning. Julie never missed anything to do with the ballroom, the theatre or strolling in public. She dressed in the latest fashion. But in spite of everything, Julie was a picture of disillusionment, telling everyone she had lost all faith in love or friendship, or any of the joys of the here and now, and she looked only for the consolation to come – *up there*. She had adopted the tone of a girl who has suffered a great disappointment, a girl who has lost her lover or been cruelly deceived by him. Although nothing remotely like that had ever happened to her, she was looked upon as if it had, and it was her own firm belief that she had suffered a great deal in life. This melancholy never stopped her enjoying herself and never stopped young men enjoying themselves in her company. Every visiting guest took great care to acknowledge the melancholic state of mind that afflicted the hostess, and then went straight off to enjoy himself in society chit-chat, dancing, clever games, or a session of *bouts rimés*, which was all the rage at the Karagins'. There were only one or two young men, and they included Boris, who dipped below the surface of Julie's melancholy, and with these young men she held longer conversations in more secluded places on the vanity of everything in this world, and they were also privy to her albums, page after page of doleful sketches, sayings and poetry.

Julie was so sweet with Boris, sympathizing with his premature alienation from life, offering him what consolation she could as a good friend, she having suffered so much in her own life, and she opened up one of her albums for him. Boris drew a little sketch of two trees, and wrote underneath, 'O rustic trees, your sombre branches shed upon me darkness and melancholy.'

On another page he did a drawing of a tomb and inscribed below it:

> Our strength and stay is death; death brings us peace tomorrow.
> Ah me, no other power can shelter us from sorrow!

Julie thought this exquisite.

'There is something so delightful in a smile of melancholy,' she said to Boris, quoting verbatim from a book. 'It is a ray of light in the shadows, a subtle margin between sorrow and despair, demonstrating the possibility of consolation.'

Boris responded with the following verses in French:

> O poisoned fare by which my feeling soul is nourished,
> Thou single stay on which my happiness has flourished,
> Sweet melancholy, come to comfort and console,
> To calm the storms of my darkness and isolation
> And blend your hidden consolation
> With these my tears I cannot control.

Julie would go to her harp and play Boris the most plangent nocturnes. Boris would read aloud to her, more than once breaking down half-way through Karamzin's romantic story, *Poor Liza*, choking with emotion and unable to continue. When they met in society Julie and Boris would exchange lingering glances as though they were the only real people hailing each other in sympathy across a sea of indifference.

Anna Mikhaylovna, a frequent visitor, would play cards with Julie's mother and use every opportunity to gather all reliable information about Julie's expectations if she were to marry. (Her dowry would consist of two Penza estates and a large forested region near Nizhny Novgorod.) It was with deep emotion and complete resignation to the workings of Providence that Anna Mikhaylovna followed the exquisite sharing of sadness that united her son to the wealthy Julie.

'As charming and melancholic as ever, my dear sweet Julie,' she would say to the daughter. And to the mother, 'Boris tells me that here in your house he finds respite for his soul. He has been the victim of so many disappointments, and he's such a sensitive boy.'

'Oh, Boris dear, I have become so attached to Julie recently,' she would say to her son. 'I can't begin to tell you. But then, who could help loving her! A creature not of this world! Oh, Boris! Boris!' She would pause before going on. 'And I'm so sorry for her mamma,' she would then say. 'Only today she was showing me letters and accounts from Penza (they have a huge estate there), and, poor thing, she's all on her own. They all take advantage of her!'

Boris heard what his mother had to say with the ghost of a smile. He laughed lightly at her simple-minded scheming, but he did listen closely when she spoke about the Penza and Nizhny Novgorod estates, and sometimes followed up with penetrating questions.

Julie had long been expecting a proposal from her melancholic admirer, and was fully prepared to accept it, but Boris held back, secretly put off by the girl herself, her desperate desire to get married, her affectation and a horrible feeling that he would be giving up any last chance of true love. His leave was nearly up. Every day God sent, and sometimes several days at a time, he spent at the Karagins', and every single day Boris thought things over and decided that tomorrow was the day for him to propose. But when he was with Julie, watching her red face and chin, almost permanently powdered over, her watery eyes and that facial expression signalling instant readiness to switch from melancholy to artificial rapture inspired by conjugal bliss, Boris couldn't bring himself to say the word, even though he had long imagined himself owning those big estates, and had spent their profits several times over. Julie could see Boris hesitating, and sometimes it actually occurred to her that she might not be exactly to his taste, but feminine vanity soon came to her rescue, reassuring her that love must have made him go all shy. Even so, her melancholy was rapidly turning into exasperation, and shortly before the end of Boris's leave she thought of a positive plan of action. Just before Boris was due to go back who should appear in Moscow, and needless to say also in the Karagins' drawing-room, but Anatole Kuragin, whereupon Julie suddenly cast aside all melancholy, came over all cheerful and made a great fuss of the newcomer.

'Boris, my dear,' said Anna Mikhaylovna, 'I know from a reliable source that Prince Vasily has sent his son to Moscow to get him married to Julie. I have such a soft spot for Julie and this would make me very sorry. How do you feel about it, my dear?'

Boris was beside himself at the idea of being made a fool of, and having wasted a whole month of dogged melancholia on Julie, and seeing all the lovely money from those Penza estates which he had mentally assimilated and put to good use pass into somebody else's hands, especially the hands of an idiot like Anatole. He drove straight round to the Karagins absolutely determined to propose. Julie welcomed him with a breezy cheerfulness, just happening to mention how much she had enjoyed yesterday evening's ball, and she asked when he was leaving. Although Boris had come with every intention of declaring his love and therefore speaking tenderly, he launched forth irritably on the subject of feminine fickleness, observing how women could switch so easily from sadness to joy, and how their mood depended entirely on who happened to be running after them. Julie took offence at this, and said yes, it was perfectly true that a woman needed variety, and anyone would get bored if nothing ever changed.

'In that case, my advice to you . . .' But Boris, with a vitriolic word on the tip of his tongue, was suddenly struck by a galling thought – he might end up leaving Moscow without having achieved his goal, and after a great waste of effort, something he'd never experienced before. He cut himself short in mid-sentence, averted his eyes from her nasty look of exasperation and indecision, and said, 'But listen, I didn't come here to quarrel with you. Quite the opposite . . .' He glanced at her, wondering whether or not to go on. Every last sign of annoyance had instantly vanished from her face, and her restless, imploring eyes were glued on him in avid anticipation.

'I can always arrange not to see much of her,' thought Boris. 'In for a penny in for a pound!' He blushed to the roots of his hair, gazed into her face and said, 'You know how I feel about you!' That was enough. Julie was beaming with triumph and self-congratulation, but she still made Boris go through everything that is normally said on these occasions – that he was in love with her and had never loved any woman like this. She knew that her Penza estates and her forests near Nizhny Novgorod gave her every right to demand this, and she got what she wanted.

The newly engaged couple, dispensing now with all references to trees that enfolded them with darkness and melancholy, were soon making plans for setting up a brilliant future residence in Petersburg, going the rounds as necessary and making arrangements for a magnificent wedding.

CHAPTER 6

It was getting towards the end of January when Count Ilya Rostov arrived in Moscow with Natasha and Sonya. The countess was still too ill to travel, but it was no longer possible to put things off until she got better; any day now Prince Andrey was due to arrive in Moscow. In any case they had to order the trousseau, sell the estate just outside Moscow, and take advantage of old Prince Bolkonsky's presence in the city to arrange for his future daughter-in-law to be introduced. The Rostovs' town house had not been heated, and since this was only a short stay and the countess wasn't with them the old count elected to stay with Marya Dmitriyevna Akhrosimov, with whom the count had a long-standing offer of accommodation.

Late one night the Rostovs' four sledges drove into Marya Dmitriyevna's courtyard in Old Konyusheny Street. She now lived alone, having married off her daughter and seen her sons enter the service. She still had a good bearing, still spoke her mind, opining vociferously on all subjects, and her whole personality seemed like a reproach to everyone else for all kinds of weaknesses, passions and impulses that she happened to consider beyond the pale. She rose early, donned her house-jacket and saw to the housekeeping, before driving off, if it happened to be a saint's day, first to Mass and then on to the gaols and prisons, where she did good work that she never spoke about. On ordinary week-days she dressed and received petitioners from all classes – there was someone every day. Then she took lunch, a good rich meal, always with three or four guests in attendance. She would spend the afternoon playing boston, and during the evening she would have the newspapers and the latest books read to her while she sat there knitting. She rarely interrupted her routine to go out, and if she did it was only to visit the most important people in town.

She was still up when the Rostovs arrived and the pulley of the hall door creaked as it welcomed the Rostovs and their servants in from the cold. Marya Dmitriyevna was standing in the hall doorway, with her spectacles perched on the end of her nose and her head flung back, and she greeted the newcomers with a stern and angry look. Anyone might have thought she was annoyed at them for daring to come and was about to send them away again, but for the fact that she was simultaneously issuing detailed instructions to her servants for the accommodation of her guests and all their baggage.

'The count's things? Over here,' she said, pointing to the trunks without a word of welcome to anyone. 'The young ladies, over there on the left. All this fiddle-faddle!' she called to her maids. 'Get the samovar going! . . . Filled out nicely, very pretty,' she said to Natasha, catching her by the hood and drawing her close. Natasha was glowing red from the frosty air. 'Phoo! You're awfully cold! Come along, get those things off,' she shouted across to the count, who was wanting to come over and kiss her hand. 'You must be frozen too. Plenty of rum in the tea! Sonya, dear, *bonjour*,' she said to the other girl, this single French word bringing out the complex mixture of slight scorn and affection that determined her attitude to Sonya.

Eventually, when they had taken off their outer clothes, freshened up after the journey and come down to tea, Marya Dmitriyevna went round kissing them all.

'It does my heart good to see you. Thank you for coming to stay with me. It's been a long time,' she said, with a knowing glance at Natasha. 'The old fellow's here, and his son's due back any day now. You must make their acquaintance, you simply must. But we can talk about that later,' she added, glancing across at Sonya – a clear signal that she didn't want to talk about it in her presence.

'Now, listen,' she said, turning to the count. 'What are your plans for tomorrow? Who do you want me to send for? Shinshin?' She bent down one finger. 'That snivelling woman, Anna Mikhaylovna.' She bent down another. 'She's here with her son. He's getting married! Then Bezukhov, I suppose. He's here, too, with his wife. He ran away from her, but she came galloping after him. He had lunch here last Wednesday. Now, these people,' she went on, indicating the young ladies, 'I'll take them to the Iversky chapel tomorrow, and we'll call in on Madame Saucy Rascal.' (Her dressmaker's real name was Suzie Pascal.) 'You'll be getting all the latest things, I suppose. Don't look at me – sleeves are out here nowadays! Only the other day young Princess Irina Vasilyevna called in here, and what a sight! Looked as if she'd put two barrels on her arms. There's a new fashion every day now. And what will you be getting up to?' she asked the count abruptly.

'Everything's happened at once,' answered the count. 'All these rags to sort out, and now suddenly there's a buyer in prospect for the Moscow estate and the house. With your kind permission I'll pick my moment and slip over to the estate for a day or so. It would involve leaving the girls on your hands.'

'Splendid, splendid, they'll be all right with me. They'll be like wards of court. I'll take them wherever they ought to go – scold them a bit and spoil them a bit,' said Marya Dmitriyevna, extending a large hand to touch the cheek of her god-daughter and favourite, Natasha.

Next morning Marya Dmitriyevna took the young ladies off to the Iversky chapel and then to Madame Pascal, who was so intimidated by Marya Dmitriyevna that she always sold clothes to her at a loss in order to get rid of her as fast as she could. Marya Dmitriyevna ordered almost the whole trousseau. When they got home she sent everyone but Natasha out of the room, and called her favourite over to sit beside her armchair.

'Now, let's have a little chat. Congratulations on your engagement. He's a fine young man and you've hooked him! I'm very pleased for you. I've known him since he was so high,' she said, holding her hand a couple of feet from the floor. Natasha coloured up with pleasure. 'I'm very fond of him and all his family. But listen! I'm sure you know old Prince Nikolay was very much against his son getting married. He's a funny old devil! Of course, Prince Andrey is not a child any more; he can get by without him. But entering another family against the father's will is not a nice thing to do. It ought to be done with peace and love. You're a bright girl – you'll know how to cope. Just use your wits and your kind heart. Then everything will be all right.'

Natasha made no response, but her silence was not due to shyness, as Marya Dmitriyevna surmised. In point of fact, Natasha didn't like people poking their noses into anything to do with her love for Prince Andrey, which seemed to her so far removed from the ordinary run of human experience that in her view no one could possibly understand it. The only man she knew and loved was Prince Andrey; he loved her, and was due to return any day now and take her away. That was all she needed.

'I've known him such a long time, you see, and I do love your future sister-in-law, Masha. As they say, new sisters cause blisters, but she won't; she wouldn't hurt a fly. She's been asking me to bring you two together. You must go and see her tomorrow with your father. Try to be nice to her; she's older than you. By the time your young man gets back, you'll have got to know his sister and his father, and you'll have won them over. Am I right? This is the best way, isn't it?'

'Yes,' said Natasha without much enthusiasm.

CHAPTER 7

Next day, acting on Marya Dmitriyevna's advice, Count Rostov took Natasha to call on Prince Nikolay Bolkonsky. The count was unhappy about this; he was not looking forward to the visit and he approached it with dread in his heart. The last meeting with the old prince at the time of the recruitment levy was still fresh in his mind – he had invited Bolkonsky to dinner and in return he had been forced to sit through a furious diatribe for not having sent enough men. Natasha, by contrast, had put on her best dress and was in high spirits. 'They're bound to like me,' she thought. 'Everybody does. And I'm ready to do anything they want, and love them both for being his father and his sister. There can't be any reason for them not to like me!'

They drove up to the gloomy old house on the Vozdvizhenka and went into the vestibule.

'Oh well, God be merciful . . .' said the count, half-joking, half-serious, but Natasha could see that her father was all flustered as he went through into the entry-hall and inquired diffidently and in the softest tones whether the prince and the princess were at home. After they had been announced the prince's servants looked visibly embarrassed. One footman who was running over to announce them was stopped by another in the big hall, and whispered exchanges ensued. A maid-servant ran out to them in the hall and blurted out something to do with the princess. Then at last a curmudgeonly old footman emerged, only to inform the Rostovs that the prince could not receive anyone, though they were invited to go and see the princess. The first person to approach the visitors was Mademoiselle Bourienne. She greeted father and daughter with flamboyant politeness and led them off to the princess's apartment. The princess scuttled in to meet the visitors and tramped over to them, blotchy-faced, obviously worried and frightened, while struggling in vain to appear casual and welcoming. She took against Natasha at a single glance, seeing her as a creature of fashion, frivolous, flighty and vain. It never occurred to Princess Marya that before setting eyes on her future sister-in-law she was already prejudiced against her, subconsciously envying her beauty, youth and happiness, and resenting her brother's love for her. And besides this overwhelming feeling of antipathy, Princess Marya was still desperately worried because when the Rostovs had been announced the old prince had roared out that he wanted nothing to do with them – she could see them if she wanted to, but they mustn't be let in to see him. Princess Marya had decided to receive them, but she lived in constant dread of the old prince doing something outrageous, because he had seemed particularly upset by the arrival of the Rostovs.

'Well, here we are then. I've brought my little songstress to see you, Princess,' said the count, bowing and scraping, his eyes darting about anxiously in case the old prince came in. 'It will be nice for you to get to know each other. I'm so sorry the prince is still unwell . . .' and after one or two more such platitudes he got to his feet. 'With your permission, Princess,' he said, 'if I could just leave my Natasha on your hands for a short while . . . I'd rather like to pop round to Dogs' Square to see Anna Semyonovna – it's only round the corner – and then come back for her . . .'

Count Rostov had thought up this diplomatic ruse (as he told his daughter afterwards) to give the future sisters-in-law maximum freedom to talk, though it also reduced any risk of meeting the prince, who scared him stiff. This was something he refrained from telling his daughter, but Natasha realized how frightened and worried her father was, and she felt humiliated. She blushed because of her father, then felt furious with herself for having blushed, and she transfixed the princess with a bold, challenging glare intended to show that she wasn't afraid of anybody. The princess said she would be delighted, and asked him not to hurry back from Anna Semyonovna's, and then he was gone.

In defiance of several uneasy glances angled at her by Princess Marya, who wanted to talk to Natasha alone, Mademoiselle Bourienne stayed on and persisted in chattering about the pleasures of Moscow and the theatres. Natasha was still smarting from the embarrassing delay in the entry-hall, her father's edginess and the constrained attitude of the princess, who seemed to think she was doing them a favour by receiving her. The whole situation seemed unpleasant. She didn't like Princess Marya, who seemed very plain, pretentious and frosty. Natasha suddenly seemed to shrivel up, unconsciously adopting an offhand manner that alienated Princess Marya even more. Five minutes went by with the conversation laboured and constrained, and then came the sound of shuffling slippers speedily approaching. Terror was written all over Princess Marya's face as the door opened and in came the prince, wearing a white night-cap and dressing-gown.

'Ah, madam,' he began. 'Madam, Countess . . . Countess Rostov . . . if I'm not mistaken . . . I'm sure you'll forgive me, do forgive me . . . I didn't know, madam. As God's my witness, I didn't know you were honouring us with a visit. I came to see my daughter – which accounts for this costume. You'll have to forgive me . . . As God's my witness, I didn't know,' he repeated so unnaturally and so nastily, stressing the word 'God', that Princess Marya rose to her feet with her eyes glued to the floor, not daring to glance at her father or Natasha. Natasha rose too and gave a curtsey, also at a loss for something to do. Mademoiselle Bourienne was the only one capable of a sweet smile.

'You'll have to forgive me! You'll have to forgive me! As God's my witness, I didn't know,' muttered the old man, and after surveying Natasha from head to foot he walked out.

Mademoiselle Bourienne was the first to collect herself after this apparition, and she started to talk about the prince's poor health. Speechless, Natasha and Princess Marya gazed at each other and the longer they remained speechless and continued to gaze at each other, leaving unsaid all those things that ought to have been said, the greater was the mutual antipathy that rose between them.

When the count returned, Natasha, almost indecently pleased to see him, got away as fast as she could, with a feeling akin to loathing for that frigid old woman of a princess, who was capable of putting her in such an embarrassing position, and also of spending half an hour with her without saying a word about Prince Andrey. 'I just couldn't have been the first to talk about him with that Frenchwoman in the room,' thought Natasha. Meanwhile Princess Marya was tormenting herself in just the same way. She had known what needed to be said to Natasha, but she hadn't been able to bring herself to say it, partly because Mademoiselle Bourienne was in the way but also because she found it terribly difficult to begin talking about the marriage, though she couldn't have said why. The count was well on his way out of the room when Princess Marya scurried across to Natasha, seized her hand and said with a deep sigh, 'Wait a second. I think I should . . .' Natasha looked at Princess Marya with a kind of scorn, though she too couldn't have explained why.

'Dear Natalie,' said Princess Marya, 'I want you to know how glad I am my brother has found such happiness . . .' She paused, conscious of telling a lie. Natasha noted the pause and guessed the reason behind it.

'Princess, I don't think this is the right time to talk about it,' said Natasha, with a show of dignity and aloofness, though she was choking on tears.

'What have I said? What have I done?' she thought the moment she was out of the room.

Natasha kept them waiting for dinner that evening. She was still up in her room, crying like a child, sniffling and sobbing. Sonya stood over her, kissing her hair.

'Natasha, there's nothing to cry about,' she kept saying. 'Why do you bother about them? It'll soon pass, Natasha.'

'No, if only you knew how humiliating it was . . . As if I . . .'

'Natasha, don't say anything. It's not your fault, so why should you bother? Give me a kiss,' said Sonya.

Natasha looked up and kissed her friend on the lips, pressing her wet face against hers.

'I can't tell you. I don't know. It's nobody's fault,' said Natasha. 'It's my fault. But it hurts, it hurts so much. Oh, why doesn't he come?'

She went down to dinner with red eyes. Marya Dmitriyevna, fully aware of how the old prince had received the Rostovs, pretended not to notice Natasha's worried face and over dinner she kept a constant stream of loud jokes going with the count and the other guests.

CHAPTER 8

That evening the Rostovs went to the opera, where Marya Dmitriyevna had taken a box for them.

Natasha didn't feel like going, but it was impossible to refuse a treat that Marya Dmitriyevna had arranged especially for her benefit. When she was all dressed up and waiting for her father in the big hall, she glanced at herself in the big mirror and saw that she looked pretty, very pretty, which made her feel even sadder than before, though it was a sweet and tender sadness.

'Oh God, if only he was here with me now, I wouldn't be like I used to be, silly and shy, I'd be quite different, I'd give him a hug, cuddle up to him and force him to look at me with those searching, questioning eyes, the way he used to look at me before, and then I'd make him laugh, the way he used to laugh, and his eyes – oh, I can see those eyes!' thought Natasha. 'And why should I bother about his father and sister? I don't love anybody else but him, him, him, with that face and those eyes, with his smile, a man's smile yet also a little boy's . . . No, it's better if I don't think about him, don't think, forget him, completely forget him for the time being. I can't bear all this waiting. I'll be sobbing any minute now,' and she turned away from the mirror in a great effort to avoid tears. 'How can Sonya love Nikolay so calmly, so easily, and keep on waiting so patiently?' she wondered, looking at Sonya, who had just come in, smartly dressed and holding a fan. 'No, she's not a bit like me. I can't manage it.'

At that moment Natasha felt so overwhelmed by softness and tenderness that it wasn't enough for her to love and know she was loved in return – *now* was what mattered, she wanted to embrace the man she loved *now*, to talk about love and hear love-talk from him, because her heart was filled with words of love. As she sat there in the carriage beside her father, staring moodily at the lights of the street lamps as they flashed by the frozen window, she began to feel even sadder and more love-stricken, until she forgot where she was going and who she was with. The Rostovs' carriage fell into line with all the other carriages and trundled slowly up to the theatre, its wheels creaking over the snow. Natasha and Sonya hopped out holding up their skirts, followed by the count, assisted down by the footmen, and the three of them made their way through the stream of opera-goers and programme-sellers towards the corridor leading to the boxes. The music had started, as they could hear through the closed doors.

'Natasha, your hair!' whispered Sonya. The box-keeper slithered past the ladies deferentially, nipped ahead and opened the door into their box. The music was suddenly louder and clearer, and from the doorway they could see the brightly lit rows of boxes, the bare arms and shoulders of the ladies, and the stalls down below, noisy and glittering with uniforms. A lady going into a nearby box stole an envious woman's glance at Natasha. The curtain was still down but the overture was under way. Natasha smoothed down her dress, walked in with Sonya, sat down and gazed across at the brightly lit tiers of boxes opposite. Suddenly, there it was again, a sensation she had not experienced for some time – hundreds of eyes staring at her bare arms and neck; it was a pleasant and yet unpleasant sensation that brought back a swarm of associated memories, desires and emotions.

There they were: two extremely pretty girls, Natasha and Sonya, in the company of Count Ilya Rostov, who had been away from Moscow for some time, and all eyes were on them. Besides that, everybody had heard something of Natasha's engagement to Prince Andrey, they all knew the Rostovs had been living in the country ever since, and they looked with great curiosity at the girl who was about to make one of the best matches in Russia.

Natasha was even prettier after her stay in the country, as everyone had been telling her, and this evening, in her present state of excitement, she looked particularly attractive. She seemed to be brimming with life and beauty, and impervious to everything around her. Her black eyes scanned the crowd without looking for anyone in particular while her slender arm, exposed almost to the shoulder, rested on the velvet edge of the box and, quite unconsciously, her hand squeezed the programme rhythmically in time to the overture.

'Look, that's Alenina,' said Sonya, 'with her mother, isn't it?'

'Good heavens, Mikhail Kirillych has put some more weight on,' said the old count.

'Look! Anna Mikhaylovna. Fancy wearing a cap like that!'

'The Karagins are over there. Julie and Boris are with them. You can tell they're engaged.'

'Drubetskoy has proposed! Oh yes, I found out today,' said Shinshin, joining the Rostovs in their box.

Natasha glanced over where her father was looking, and there was Julie with a string of pearls round her thick red neck (which Natasha knew to be well-powdered), sitting next to her mother, a picture of contentment.

Behind them sat Boris, with his handsome, neatly brushed head of hair, all smiles as he lent an ear to what Julie was saying. He squinted across at the Rostovs and smiled again as he spoke to his fiancée.

'They're talking about us, me and him!' thought Natasha. 'And she's probably jealous of me, and he's reassuring her. They don't have a thing to worry about. If only they knew. I couldn't care less about any of them.'

Behind them sat Anna Mikhaylovna, decked out in a green head-piece; she was in celebratory mood, with happiness and resignation to the will of God written all over her face. Their box was full of the atmosphere generated by an engaged couple, which Natasha knew all about and was so fond of. She turned away from them, and suddenly all the events of that humiliating morning visit surged up in her mind again.

'What right has he to keep me out of his family? Oh well, better not think about it, till he comes back!' she said to herself, and she began to scan the faces, familiar and unfamiliar, down in the stalls.

There in the middle of the front stalls, leaning back against the orchestra-rail, stood Dolokhov, in Persian costume, with his curls brushed up into a huge shock of hair. He was standing in full view, deliberately inviting the attention of the whole audience, yet as casual as if he had been at home standing alone in his room. The most brilliant set of young Muscovites thronged round him, and he was clearly the cock of the roost.

Count Ilya laughed as he nudged the blushing Sonya and pointed out her former admirer.

'Didn't you recognize him?' he asked. 'But what's he doing here?' he asked, turning to Shinshin. 'I thought he'd gone off somewhere.'

'Yes, he did,' answered Shinshin. 'He went down to the Caucasus, then he ran away, and I believe he became a minister with some sort of ruling prince down in Persia, and he went and killed the Shah's brother. Anyway, all the Moscow ladies are crazy about him! "Dolok-hov – the man from Persia" – that's all you need to say. Nowadays you hear nothing but Dolokhov. They all kowtow to him. It's a rare treat to be asked to meet him,' said Shinshin. 'Dolokhov and Anatole Kuragin, they've got the ladies swooning all right.'

Into the adjoining box walked a gorgeous tall woman with a huge pile of hair, superb arms and shoulders ostentatiously exposed and a double string of large pearls round her neck. She took some time to settle down, with much rustling of her thick silk evening-dress.

Natasha couldn't resist staring at this lady's neck and shoulders, her pearls and her elaborate hairstyle and admiring the beauty of those shoulders and pearls. When she turned for a second look the lady glanced round, met the eyes of Count Ilya Rostov and gave him a nod and a smile. It was Countess Bezukhov, Pierre's wife. The count, who knew everyone in society, leant across and addressed a few words to her.

'Have you been here long, Countess?' he began. 'I've been meaning to call in and kiss your hand. I'm in town on business and I've brought my girls with me. I hear Semyonova's a wonderful actress,' the count went on. 'Your good husband never used to forget us. Is he here?'

'Yes, he did say he'd drop in,' said Hélène, with a close eye on Natasha.

Count Ilya sat back in his place.

'Lovely woman, isn't she?' he whispered to Natasha.

'Out of this world!' said Natasha. 'It would be easy to fall in love with her!'

At that moment the final chords of the overture rang out, and the conductor rapped on the stand with his baton. Late-comers scurried to their seats in the stalls, and the curtain rose.

Immediately a hush fell on boxes and stalls, and all the men, old and young, in evening-dress or uniform, and all the women with jewels draped across their exposed flesh turned with eager anticipation to watch the stage. Natasha too turned to watch.

CHAPTER 9

The stage consisted of flat boards down the middle with painted cardboard representing trees at both sides and cloth-covered boards at the back. Several young girls in red tops and white skirts were sitting in the middle of the stage. One very fat girl in a white silk dress sat to one side on a low bench with green cardboard glued on the back of it. They were all singing something. When they had finished their song the woman in white came forward to the prompter's box, and a man with fat legs squeezed into silk tights, with a feather in his hat and a dagger in his belt, came up to her and burst into song with much waving of his arms.

The man in tights sang alone, then she sang alone, then they both held back while the music played on and the man fingered the hand of the woman in white, obviously waiting for the right moment to start up again and sing a piece with her. They did sing together, after which the theatre erupted in applause and loud shouting, while the man and woman on the stage, representing two lovers, beamed as they held out their arms and took bows.

Just back from the country, and now in a serious frame of mind, Natasha saw all this as astonishingly grotesque. She couldn't follow the opera and couldn't hear any music; all she could see was painted cardboard and oddly dressed men and women, talking, singing and prancing about just as oddly under bright lights. She knew what it was supposed to represent, but it was all so grotesquely forced and unnatural that she found herself alternating between embarrassment and amusement at the actors' expense. She glanced round at faces in the audience, looking for signs of the same amusement and bewilderment that she was feeling. But all the faces were absorbed in what was happening on the stage, and they displayed a kind of rapture that Natasha could only assume to be affected. 'I suppose it has to be like this!' thought Natasha. She looked alternately at the rows of pomaded men's heads in the stalls and the half-naked women in the boxes, especially Hélène in the next box who was sitting there so openly exposed, staring fixedly at the stage with a quiet and serene smile on her face, and basking in the bright light that flooded the theatre and the close atmosphere warmed up by the crowd. Natasha was beginning to glide steadily into a state of light-headedness the like of which she hadn't experienced for some time. She lost all sense of what she was and where she was and what was going on before her eyes. She gazed ahead, letting her thoughts wander, and the weirdest of disconnected ideas suddenly flashed through her mind. One moment she felt like leaping over the footlights and singing along with the actress; then she felt an urge to dig an old gentleman sitting near by with her fan, or lean over towards Hélène and tickle her.

In a moment of silence on the stage with a new aria about to begin, a stalls door creaked open on the Rostovs' side of the theatre, and a man's footsteps could be heard padding over the carpet. 'That's him, Kuragin!' whispered Shinshin. Countess Bezukhov turned and beamed at the late arrival. Natasha followed Countess Bezukhov's eyes and saw a strikingly handsome adjutant walking towards their box with a confident stride and a courteous manner. It was Anatole Kuragin, whom she had seen and noticed some time before at a ball in Petersburg. He was wearing his adjutant's uniform, with one epaulette and a shoulder knot. He walked with a jaunty little swagger that would have looked ridiculous if he hadn't been so handsome, and if his fine features hadn't expressed such open-hearted self-assurance and high spirits. Although the performance was in full swing he didn't hurry as he strode down the sloping, carpeted aisle, his perfumed, handsome head held high and his spurs and sword gently jingling. With a quick glance at Natasha he went over to his sister, laid a tightly gloved hand on the edge of her box, nodded to her and leant over to asked her something, with a gesture towards Natasha.

'Delightful girl!' he said, obviously referring to Natasha, who could not hear his words but could read his lips. Then he proceeded to the front row and sat down beside Dolokhov, giving him a casual, friendly elbow in the ribs – and this was Dolokhov, the man who inspired such deference in everybody else. With a cheeky wink and a merry smile at him Anatole put one foot up on the orchestra-screen.

'Brother and sister, and they're so like each other,' said the count. 'Handsome pair!'

Shinshin lowered his voice and began telling the count about one of Kuragin's escapades in Moscow, and Natasha listened, not least because he had called her a delightful girl.

The first act came to an end. Everyone stood up in the stalls, they left their places and there was much coming and going.

Boris came over to the Rostovs' box, accepted their congratulations without any fuss, raised his eyebrows with a distracted smile, told Natasha and Sonya that his fiancée wished to invite them both to the wedding, and then left. Natasha had been chatting to him with a cheery, flirtatious smile on her lips, and she had congratulated him on his approaching marriage, the same Boris she had once been in love with. In the kind of light-headed mood she was in, everything seemed perfectly straightforward and natural.

Hélène was sitting near by in all her semi-nakedness, beaming at all and sundry, and Natasha beamed at Boris in exactly the same way.

Hélène's box had filled up inside and was surrounded from the stalls by the cleverest and most distinguished men, falling over each other in their eagerness to let everyone see that they were known to her.

Kuragin spent the entire interval standing with Dolokhov in front of the footlights staring across at the Rostovs' box. Natasha sensed that he was talking about her and the knowledge gave her a thrill of pleasure. She even adjusted her position so that he could see her in profile, which she considered her best angle. Before the beginning of the second act the figure of Pierre, whom the Rostovs hadn't seen since their arrival, appeared in the stalls. He had a sad look on his face, and he had put on even more weight since Natasha had last seen him. He walked down to the front rows without noticing anyone. Anatole went over to him and started talking, with the occasional glance and gesture towards the Rostovs' box. Pierre's face lit up when he saw Natasha and he hurried past rows of stalls towards their box. When he reached them he leant an elbow on the edge of their box and chatted to Natasha at some length, smiling all the time.

While she was talking to Pierre, Natasha heard the sound of a man's voice from Countess Bezukhov's box, and something told her it was

Kuragin. She glanced round and their eyes met. With a half-smile on his face and a look of such warmth and admiration he stared straight at her in such a way that it seemed odd for her to be standing so close to him and to be looking at him like that, absolutely certain that he liked her, without their knowing each other.

In the second act a cemetery was depicted on the painted cardboard, there was a hole in the back-cloth to represent the moon, the footlights were shaded, horns and double-basses sounded forth, and a number of people emerged from right and left dressed in black cloaks. These people began waving their arms about, with things that looked like daggers in their hands. Then some more people ran on and began dragging away the girl who had been in white but was now wearing a pale-blue dress. Instead of dragging her off straightaway they spent a long time singing with her, but then they did drag her away, and behind the scenes someone banged three times on a piece of iron, whereupon they all fell to their knees and sang a prayer. This action was interrupted more than once by wild cries from the audience.

All through the act, whenever Natasha glanced across at the stalls she saw Anatole Kuragin, with one arm flung along the back of his chair, staring up at her. She was delighted to see that he was so taken with her, and it never entered her head that there could be anything wrong with this.

When the second act came to an end Countess Bezukhov got to her feet, turned towards the Rostovs' box (with her bosom completely exposed), crooked a tiny gloved finger to beckon the old count over, ignored all the men crowding round her box, and engaged him in conversation with the sweetest of smiles.

'Oh, please introduce me to your lovely daughters,' she said. 'The whole town is singing their praises and I don't even know them.'

Natasha got up and curtsied to the magnificent countess. She was so delighted at being praised by such a brilliant beauty that she blushed with pleasure.

'I've every intention of becoming a Moscow resident myself,' said Hélène. 'Shame on you for burying pearls like these in the country!'

Countess Bezukhov's reputation as a woman of great charm was well founded. Saying what she didn't think, especially when it was flattering, came so naturally to her it was simplicity itself.

'No, my dear count, you must let me take your daughters in hand. Actually I'm not here for very long this time, and neither are you. But I'll do what I can to amuse them. I heard so much about you in Petersburg, and I've been wanting to meet you,' she said to Natasha, with that beautiful smile that never varied. 'I've heard of you from my page, too, Drubetskoy – you'll have heard that he's getting married – and also from my husband's friend, Bolkonsky, Prince Andrey Bolkonsky,' she said, with special emphasis and a strong hint that she knew how things stood between him and Natasha. She asked for one of the young ladies to be allowed to sit through the rest of the performance in her box so that they could get to know each other, and Natasha moved across.

The third act saw a palace depicted on the stage with lots of burning candles and walls hung with pictures of knights with beards. Two people, presumably a king and queen, stood at the front. The king waved his right hand in the air and sang something very badly – it was obviously his nerves – before sitting down on a crimson throne. The girl who had first been in white and then pale blue was now wearing a plain smock, and she had let her hair down. She was standing near the throne, singing something very doleful to the queen. But the king waved his hand harshly, and then some men with bare legs and women with bare legs came on from both sides and they all started dancing. Then the violins struck up with a light and happy tune, at which one of the actresses with thick, bare legs and thin arms detached herself from the rest, walked off the set to straighten her bodice, came back out into the middle of the stage and began to leap in the air, tapping her feet together very quickly. The stalls erupted with applause and shouts of 'bravo!' Then one man retreated into a corner of the stage. Louder and louder came the cymbals and horns in the orchestra, and this one man with his bare legs started leaping right up in the air and making fancy movements with his feet. (This was Duport, who took home sixty thousand silver roubles a year for this artistry.) The whole theatre from the stalls to the gods thundered their applause and yelled at the tops of their voices, and the man came to a halt and stood there beaming and bowing to all quarters. Then the bare legs were off again dancing, men and women, the king sounded off in time to the music and they all broke out in song. But suddenly a storm blew up, heralded by chromatic scales and diminished sevenths from the orchestra, and they all scurried away, dragging one of the company off stage, and the curtain fell. Once again the audience erupted with fearsome applause and they all stood there in blissful transports roaring out, 'Duport! Duport! Duport!'

It no longer seemed at all strange to Natasha. She looked round in delight, grinning with glee.

'Glorious, isn't he – Duport?' said Hélène, turning to her.

'Oh yes,' said Natasha in reply.

CHAPTER 10

During the interval there was a cool draught in Hélène's box as the door opened and in walked Anatole, stooping and trying not to brush against anyone.

'Allow me to introduce my brother,' said Hélène, her eyes shifting uneasily from Natasha to Anatole. Natasha turned her pretty little head towards the handsome adjutant and smiled at him over her bare shoulder. Anatole, who was just as handsome close to as he had been from a distance, sat down beside her and said this was a delight he had long been waiting for, ever since the Naryshkins' ball, where he had had the unforgettable pleasure of seeing her. Kuragin was much more astute and straightforward with women than he ever was in male company. He talked with an easy directness, and Natasha was agreeably surprised to discover that this man, the butt of so much gossip, had nothing formidable about him – quite the reverse, his face wore the most innocent, cheery and open-hearted of smiles.

Kuragin asked what she thought of the opera, and told her that at the last performance Semyonova had fallen down on stage.

'Oh, by the way, Countess,' he said, suddenly treating her like a close friend of long standing, 'we're getting up a fancy-dress ball. You must come – it's going to be great fun. They're all getting together at the Arkharovs'. Please come. You will, won't you?' As he spoke he never took his smiling eyes off Natasha, her face, her neck, her exposed arms. Natasha knew for certain he was besotted with her. She liked this, yet she could feel the temperature rising and she was beginning to feel somehow cornered and constrained in his presence. When she wasn't looking at him she could sense him gazing at her shoulders, and she found herself trying to catch his eye to make him look at her face. But when she looked into his eyes she was shocked to realize that the usual barrier of modesty that existed between her and other men was no longer there between the two of them. It had taken five minutes for her to feel terribly close to this man, and she scarcely knew what was happening to her. Whenever she turned away she bristled at the thought that he might seize her from behind by her bare arm and start kissing her on the neck. They were going on about nothing in particular, yet she felt closer to him than she had ever been to any other man. Natasha kept glancing round at Hélène and her father for help – what did it all mean? – but Hélène was deep in conversation with a general and didn't respond to her glance, and her father's eyes conveyed nothing but their usual message, 'Enjoying yourself? Jolly good. I'm so pleased.'

There was an awkward silence, during which Anatole, the personification of cool determination, never took his voracious eyes off her, and Natasha broke it by asking whether he liked living in Moscow. She coloured up the moment the question was out of her mouth. She couldn't help feeling there was something improper about even talking to him. Anatole smiled an encouraging smile.

'Oh, I didn't like it much at first. Well, what is it that makes a town nice to live in? It's the pretty women, isn't it? Well, now I do like it, very much indeed,' he said, with a meaningful stare. 'You will come to the fancy-dress ball, Countess? Please come,' he said. Putting his hand out to touch her bouquet he lowered his voice and added in French, 'You'll be the prettiest woman there. Do come, dear Countess, and give me this flower as your pledge.'

Natasha didn't understand a word of this – any more than he did – but she felt that behind his incomprehensible words there was some dishonourable intention. Not knowing how to respond, she turned away as if she hadn't heard him. But the moment she turned away she could feel him right behind her, very close.

'Now what? Is he embarrassed? Is he angry? Should I put things right?' she wondered. She couldn't help turning round. She looked him straight in the eyes. One glance at him, standing so close, with all that self-assurance and the warmth of his sweet smile, and she was lost. She stared into his eyes, and her smile was the mirror-image of his. And again she sensed with horror there was no barrier between the two of them.

The curtain rose again. Anatole strolled out of the box, a picture of composure and contentment. Natasha went back to her father's box, completely taken by the new world she found herself in. All that was happening before her eyes now seemed absolutely normal. By contrast, all previous thoughts of her fiancé, Princess Marya, her life in the country, never even crossed her mind. It was as if it all belonged to the distant past.

In the fourth act there was some sort of devil who sang and waved his arms about till the boards were taken away beneath him and he disappeared down below. That was all Natasha saw of the fourth act. She felt worried and excited, and the cause of all the excitement was – Kuragin; she couldn't keep her eyes off him. As they came out of the theatre Anatole walked over to them, called their carriage and helped them into it. As he was assisting Natasha he squeezed her forearm just above the wrist. Natasha glanced round at him, thrilled and flushed with pleasure. He gazed at her with gleaming eyes and a tender smile.

Natasha was back home before she could form any clear impression of what had happened. Suddenly she had a horrible feeling as she remembered about Prince Andrey, and in front of them all as they sat there drinking a cup of tea after the theatre she gave a loud moan, blushed to the roots of her hair and rushed out of the room. 'My God! It's the end of me!' she said to herself. 'How could I have let him go as far as that?' she thought. She sat there for some time, burying her crimson face in her hands, trying to get a firm grip on what had been happening but quite incapable of grasping anything, either what had happened or what she now felt. It all seemed dark, confusing and dreadful. Back in that huge open space under the bright lights, when Duport with his bare legs and his little spangled jacket had just finished leaping about to the music over those damp boards, and those young girls and the old men, and Hélène, too, beaming proudly and serenely in all her naked glory, had gone wild and roared 'Bravo!' – there, in the shadow of Hélène herself, everything had been plain and simple, but now, as she sat there in solitude, it was beyond all understanding. 'What's it all about? Why did I feel so scared of him? What are all these guilty feelings?' she thought.

Her mother, the old countess, was the only person to whom Natasha could have confided all that was on her mind – at night and in bed. She knew Sonya was straight-laced and clear-minded about these things; she would either have got the wrong end of the stick or just been shocked by any confession. Natasha would have to try and solve these agonizing problems on her own.

'Am I finished with Prince Andrey's love or not?' she wondered, and then reassured herself with an ironical smile. 'Silly girl, asking things like that!' she thought. 'What's happened to me? Nothing. I haven't done anything. I didn't ask for this. No one will ever know, and I shan't see him again,' she told herself. 'So, this much is clear: nothing has happened, there's nothing to apologize for, and Prince Andrey can love me *for what I am*. But am I really *what I am*? Oh God, Oh God, why isn't he here?' Natasha's consolation was short-lived. Once again, in her imagination, she ran through her conversation with Kuragin, and she could still see his features, his every gesture and the kind smile on the face of a brave handsome man squeezing her arm.

CHAPTER 11

Anatole Kuragin was staying in Moscow because his father had sent
him away from Petersburg, where he had been getting through twenty
thousand roubles a year in cash and running up debts for a similar
amount, and his creditors had begun to demand payment from his
father. Prince Vasily informed his son that for one last time he would
pay half his debts, on condition that he went down to Moscow, where
a post had been found for him (with no little effort) as adjutant to the
commander-in-chief, and finally made every effort to find a good
marriage-partner. He suggested either Princess Marya or Julie Karagin.

Anatole had consented and gone down to Moscow, where he stayed
with Pierre. At first Pierre was reluctant to receive Anatole, but it
wasn't long before he got used to him being there, started going out
with him on some of his wild jaunts, and gave him money, ostensibly
as a loan.

Shinshin had been quite right to say that Anatole had driven all the
Moscow ladies crazy, especially by his offhand attitude and his obvious preference for gypsy girls and French actresses – he was said to be
having an affair with the queen of them all, Mademoiselle George.[4]
He never missed a party at Dolokhov's, or with any other member of
the fast set in Moscow, he hit the bottle for nights on end, outdrinking
everybody else, and attended every high-society ball and soirée. He
was said to have had several affairs with Moscow ladies, and he was
given to flirting with one or two of them in the ballroom. But he had
steered clear of unmarried girls, especially wealthy heiresses, most of
whom were not very pretty, and for one good reason known to none
but a few of his closest friends: for the last two years he had been
married. Two years before, while his regiment was stationed in Poland,
a small-time Polish landowner had forced Anatole to marry his
daughter.

It had not taken long for Anatole to walk out on his wife, but by
agreeing to send a regular cash remittance to his father-in-law he had
preserved the right to pass himself off as a bachelor.

Anatole was quite happy with his situation, himself and other
people. With every fibre of his being he was convinced of what his
instincts told him: there was no other way to live than the way he was
living, and he had never done anything wrong in his life. He had no
capacity for reflecting on how his actions might affect other people,
or what the consequences of this or that action might be. He took it
for granted that just as the duck was created to live on water, he was

created by God to live on thirty thousand a year and occupy a high
station in society. So strong was this conviction that when other people
looked at him they accepted it and wouldn't have dreamt of denying
him either his high station in society or the money that he borrowed
right and left, obviously with no thought of paying it back.

He was not a gambler – at least he was never bothered about winning
money and he was a good loser. He wasn't vain. He didn't care what
people thought about him. Still less could he have been accused of
ambition. More than once he had infuriated his father by ruining his
own prospects, and he laughed at honours of every kind. He wasn't
mean, and he never refused anyone who turned to him for help. What
he loved was having a good time and chasing women, and since,
according to him, these tastes were in no way dishonourable, and he
was incapable of considering how his gratification of them might affect
other people, he genuinely considered himself beyond reproach, he
felt a real contempt for rogues and scoundrels, his conscience was
clear and he walked tall. Men of pleasure, masculine versions of Mary
Magdalene, are secretly convinced of their own innocence, and like
their feminine counterparts they base this on the hope of forgiveness.
'She shall be forgiven because she was full of love; he shall be forgiven
because he was full of fun.'

Dolokhov, back in Moscow that year after his exile and his Persian
adventures, now spent his time wallowing in luxury, gambling and
the pleasures of the flesh, and he had his own good reasons for
renewing his friendship with his old Petersburg comrade Kuragin.

Anatole had a genuine liking for Dolokhov because of his sharp wit
and bold spirit. Dolokhov needed Anatole's name, contacts and social
standing to attract wealthy young men into his gambling circles, so he
was using Kuragin without him being aware of it, though at the same
time he found him amusing. As well as having a calculated need for
Anatole, the very process of manipulating another man soon became
a regular source of enjoyment for Dolokhov, even a necessity.

Natasha had made a big impact on Kuragin. Over supper after the
opera he gave Dolokhov the benefit of his expert appraisal of her
arms, shoulders, legs and hair, and announced his intention of having
a bit of a fling with her. The possible outcome of such an entanglement
was beyond Anatole's powers of comprehension, just as he could never
see the outcome of any of his actions.

'She's a pretty girl, old man, but not for the likes of us,' Dolokhov
said to him.

'I'll tell my sister to ask her to dinner,' said Anatole. 'How about
that?'

'Better wait till she's married . . .'

'Do you know something?' said Anatole. 'I do like little girls. It's so easy to turn their heads.'

'You've been in trouble with one little girl already,' put in Dolokhov, who knew about Anatole's marriage. 'Watch what you're doing!'

'Well, it can't happen again, can it?' said Anatole with a good-humoured laugh.

CHAPTER 12

The day after the opera the Rostovs stayed in, and no one came to see them. Marya Dmitriyevna had a long talk with Natasha's father, keeping it secret from her. Natasha put two and two together and guessed they were talking about the old prince and hatching something between them, and this made her feel worried and offended. She was expecting Prince Andrey any minute, and twice that day she sent someone to Vozdvizhenka to find out whether he had arrived. He hadn't. She now felt worse than she had done during their first days in Moscow. Her impatience and longing for him were now exacerbated by the unpleasant memory of her encounter with Princess Marya and the old prince, and an anxious, worried feeling that she couldn't account for. She kept on imagining either that he wouldn't ever come or that something would happen to her before he did. She couldn't just sit there quietly hour after hour, as she had once done, thinking about him. The moment he came into her mind, the memory of him blended with memories of the old prince and Princess Marya, the opera and Kuragin. Once again she wondered whether she might not have been to blame and whether she could be said to have broken faith with Prince Andrey, and again she found herself analysing every last word, gesture and change of expression on the face of that man who had somehow managed to arouse her in such a dreadful way. To the rest of the household Natasha seemed livelier than usual, but she was far from being as happy and contented as before.

Sunday morning came, and Marya Dmitriyevna invited her guests to go to morning service at her parish church, the Church of the Assumption.

'I don't like those modern churches,' she said, obviously fancying herself as something of a free-thinker. 'God is the same everywhere. Our parish priest is an excellent man and he puts on a nice service, it's all very dignified, and his deacon's just the same. What's holy about giving concerts in the choir? I don't like it. It's too much like entertainment!'

Marya Dmitriyevna enjoyed her Sundays, and knew how to celebrate them. Her house had always been washed and cleaned on the Saturday, she and the servants all had a day off, and everybody put on their Sunday best and went to church. There was more food on the mistress's table, and the servants had vodka and roast goose or pork at theirs. But nothing in the house marked the holiday more clearly than Marya Dmitriyevna's broad, stern face, which assumed for the day a look of unwavering solemnity.

After church, when they had finished their coffee in the drawing-room, with the covers taken off the furniture, a servant announced that the carriage was ready and Marya Dmitriyevna, dressed in her best shawl, which she wore for visiting, got to her feet and solemnly announced that she was going to call on old Prince Bolkonsky to speak to him about his attitude to Natasha. After she had gone one of Madame Pascal's dressmakers called and Natasha, only too glad of the distraction, went into an adjoining room, closed the door and began trying on her new dresses. Just as she had put on a sleeveless basted bodice and was bending her head to look in the mirror and see what it looked like from the back, she suddenly heard her father's voice in the drawing-room in eager conversation with someone else – it was a woman's voice, one that made her blush. It was Hélène. Before Natasha had time to take off the bodice she was trying on, the door opened and in walked Countess Bezukhov, wearing a dark-heliotrope velvet dress with a high collar, and smiling her sweet and friendly smile.

'My dear girl, you look so lovely!' she said to the blushing Natasha. 'So charming! No, Count, this is too much,' she said to Count Ilya, who had followed her in. 'How can you live in Moscow without going out? No, I'm not letting go of you! This evening Mademoiselle George is giving a recitation at our house and we have one or two people coming. If you don't bring your lovely girls, who are much prettier than Mademoiselle George, I shall disown you! My husband's away in Tver, or I should have sent him to invite you. You have to come. Yes, you must. Between eight and nine.'

She nodded to the dressmaker, who knew her and was curtseying politely, and seated herself in an armchair next to the mirror, decoratively rearranging the folds of her velvet dress. She kept up a constant flow of pleasant chit-chat interspersed with enthusiastic admiration of Natasha's beauty. She inspected her dresses and spoke highly of them, speaking no less highly of a new dress of her own made from 'metal gauze', which she had just received from Paris and strongly recommended to Natasha.

'But you'd look nice in anything, my lovely darling!' she declared. A grin of pleasure had settled permanently on Natasha's face. She felt so happy, blossoming under the praises of this nice lady, Countess Bezukhov, who had once seemed so remote and important and was now being so kind. Natasha's spirits rose, and she felt almost in love with this kind and beautiful woman. As for Hélène, her admiration of Natasha was quite genuine, and she really did want to see her enjoying herself. Anatole had asked her to bring Natasha and him together, and this was why she had come to the Rostovs'. She found the thought of bringing her brother and Natasha together most amusing.

Although Hélène had once resented Natasha's ability to take Boris away from her in Petersburg, she now dismissed that from her mind, and as far as she was able she wished Natasha nothing but good. On her way out she took her protégée to one side and said, 'My brother came to dinner last night. We almost died with laughter – he won't eat, all he does is sigh for you, my lovely darling! He's crazy about you, my dear, simply crazy.'

Natasha blushed to the roots of her hair when she heard this.

'Look how she's blushing! Dear lovely girl!' Hélène went on. 'But do come. Even if you're in love that's no reason to lock yourself away. Even if you're engaged, I'm sure your fiancé would want you to go out rather than die of boredom while he's away.'

'So she knows I'm engaged. So they've been talking and laughing about it, she and her husband, Pierre, and Pierre's as straight as a die. So it can't be all that important.'

And once again, under the spell of Hélène, something that had seemed dreadful now struck her as straightforward and normal behaviour. 'And she's such a fine lady, she's so nice to me, and she seems to have taken to me in a big way,' thought Natasha, gazing at Hélène, wide-eyed and wondering. 'And why shouldn't I have a bit of fun?'

Marya Dmitriyevna came back in time for dinner, looking all serious and saying nothing, which suggested defeat at the hands of the old prince. She was too upset by the argument that had occurred to be able to sit down and talk calmly about it. When the count ventured a question she replied that all was well and she would tell him about it tomorrow. On hearing of Countess Bezukhov's visit and the evening invitation, Marya Dmitriyevna said, 'I don't care to associate with Countess Bezukhov, and I advise you not to do so, but now that you've promised, you'd better go. It will be a nice distraction,' she added, addressing Natasha.

CHAPTER 13

Count Rostov took his two girls to Countess Bezukhov's evening recitation. There were quite a few people there, but Natasha knew hardly anybody. The count noted with some displeasure that the company consisted almost entirely of men and women who were notorious for their free and easy life-style. Mademoiselle George was standing in one corner of the drawing-room surrounded by young men. There were several Frenchmen there including Métivier, who had been a regular visitor at Countess Bezukhov's ever since her arrival in Moscow. The count made up his mind not to play cards, not to let his daughters out of his sight and to go home the minute Mademoiselle George finished her performance.

Anatole was standing by the door, rather obviously on the look-out for the Rostovs. He welcomed the count, went straight up to Natasha and followed her in. At the first sight of him Natasha had the same feeling that had come over her at the opera: she felt flattered that he was so taken with her but scared by the absence of any moral barrier between them.

Hélène gave Natasha a rapturous welcome, lavishing praise on her beauty and her appearance. Shortly after their arrival Mademoiselle George left the room to put on her costume.

The chairs were rearranged and people began to sit down. Anatole moved a chair aside for Natasha and was about to sit down next to her, but the count, who was keeping a wary eye on his daughter, sat down there himself. Anatole took his place behind them.

Mademoiselle George came out with a red scarf flung over one shoulder and her bare, fat, dimpled arms on show. She walked into the empty space reserved for her between the chairs, and struck a theatrical pose. There was a murmur of excited anticipation.

Mademoiselle George surveyed her audience sternly with her gloomy eyes before launching forth into a French poem about the guilty love of a mother for her son. In some places she raised her voice, in others she dropped to a whisper, raising her head triumphantly or pausing now and then to spit out her words with a throaty hiss and much rolling of the eyes.

'Exquisite, divine, so lovely!' came the voices on all sides. Natasha was watching the fat lady, but she couldn't hear anything, see anything or take in anything that was happening. She had no feelings other than being borne away irrevocably back to that strange, crazy world so remote from the world she had known before, a world in which there was no telling right from wrong or good sense from madness. Behind her sat Anatole; conscious of his proximity, she squirmed between anxiety and expectation.

After the first monologue the whole company rose and surrounded Mademoiselle George in rapturous acclamation.

'Isn't she beautiful!' said Natasha to her father, as he got up with the rest and struggled through the crowd towards the actress.

'I would say no, looking at you,' said Anatole, following behind Natasha. He picked his moment to say it, when she was the only one who could hear. 'You're so lovely . . . from the moment I saw you I haven't stopped . . .'

'Come on, Natasha, over here!' said the count, turning back for his daughter. 'How beautiful she is!'

Natasha didn't speak as she caught up with her father and stared at him with eyes full of wonderment and unanswered questions.

Several recitations later Mademoiselle George departed and Countess Bezukhov invited all the guests into the great hall.

The count tried to get away, but Hélène pleaded with him not to spoil their impromptu ball. The Rostovs stayed on. Anatole asked Natasha for a waltz, and while they were dancing he squeezed her waist and her hand and told her she was enchanting and he was in love with her. During the écossaise, which she also danced with him, when they were on their own Anatole said nothing – he just stared at her. Natasha doubted herself – could she have dreamt what he had said to her during the waltz? At the end of the first figure he squeezed her hand again. Natasha looked up nervously into his face, but there was so much assurance and warmth in his fond look and smile that as she glanced at him she couldn't bring herself to say what had to be said. She looked down again.

'Please don't say things like that. I'm engaged to be married, and I love someone else . . .' she gabbled. She glanced up. Anatole was not in the least disconcerted or embarrassed by what she had said.

'Don't tell me about that. What difference does it make?' he said. 'Listen – I'm in love with you, madly in love. Is it my fault you're so irresistible? . . . Look, it's our turn to start . . .'

In her state of high excitement and alarm Natasha stared round, wide-eyed and fearful, though apparently enjoying herself more than usual. She remembered almost nothing of what took place that evening. They had danced the écossaise and the Grossvater. Her father had wanted them to go, and she had begged him to let them stay on. No matter where she went and who she talked to, she could feel his eyes on her. Then she had asked her father's permission to leave the room in order to rearrange her dress, and Hélène had followed her out, chatting away and laughing at her brother's passion, and then she remembered coming across Anatole again in the little sitting-room, and Hélène had somehow disappeared, they were left alone, and Anatole had taken her by the hand and said to her so tenderly, 'I can't come and see you, but can I really never see you again? I'm madly in love with you. Can I never . . . ?' and barring her way, he had brought his face up close to hers.

His big, gleaming, manly eyes were so close to hers that she could see nothing else.

'Natalie?' His question had dropped to a whisper, and her hands were being squeezed until they hurt. 'Natalie?'

'I don't understand. There's nothing I can say.' The response was written in her eyes.

Burning lips were pressed against hers, then she was instantly free again – and with a shuffling of shoes and a rustling of silks Hélène was back in the room. Natasha had glanced round at her, then, red-faced and quivering, looked back at him, full of alarm and unanswered questions, before walking over to the door.

'One word, for God's sake, just one,' Anatole was saying. She stopped. She was longing to hear one word from him, one word to tell her what had happened and give her something to respond to.

'Natalie, one word . . . just one . . .' was all he could repeat, evidently not knowing what to say, and he kept on repeating it till Hélène reached them.

Hélène accompanied Natasha back into the drawing-room. The Rostovs declined the offer of supper and went home.

When she got home Natasha was in for a sleepless night. She was tormented by a question that had no answer: which one did she love – Anatole or Prince Andrey? She certainly loved Prince Andrey – the strength of her love for him was still a clear memory. But she loved Anatole too – there could be no doubt about that. 'If not, how could all these things have happened?' she thought. 'If I could still smile at him as he smiled at me when we were saying goodbye, if I could let things go that far, surely I must have fallen in love with him at first sight. He must surely be a kind man, noble and good, and I couldn't help falling in love with him. What shall I do if I love them both?' she asked herself, but there were no answers to these terrible questions.

CHAPTER 14

Morning came with its bustle and trouble. Everyone got up and soon the house was abuzz with movement and chatter. In came the dressmakers once again. Down came Marya Dmitriyevna, and tea was served. Natasha kept glancing round at everyone, uneasy and wide-eyed, as if she wanted to anticipate every glance that came her way, while struggling to keep up a pretence of normality.

After breakfast – always her best time of the day – Marya Dmitriyevna seated herself in her armchair and called for Natasha and the old count.

'Now listen, friends, I've been thinking things over, and this is my advice to you,' she began. 'Yesterday, as you know, I went to see Prince Bolkonsky. Well, I did manage a little talk with him . . . He thought fit to shout at me. But I can shout with the best. I gave as good as I got.'

'But what was he like?' asked the count.

'What was he like? He's off his head . . . He just won't listen. I won't go on. We've given this poor girl enough to worry about as it is,' said Marya Dmitriyevna. 'But my advice to you is – finish your business, go back to Otradnoye . . . and wait.'

'Oh no!' cried Natasha.

'Yes, go back home,' said Marya Dmitriyevna, 'and wait. If your fiancé comes here now there's bound to be a row, but if he's on his own he can sort things out man to man with his father and then come on to you.'

Count Rostov could see the wisdom of this proposal, and it met with his approval. If the old man eventually came round it would be better to visit him later in Moscow or at Bald Hills. If he didn't, the wedding would have to go ahead against his will, and it would have to be at Otradnoye.

'Yes, it's absolutely true,' said he. 'I'm only sorry I went to see him and took her with me,' said the count.

'There's nothing to be sorry about. Once you were here, you could hardly avoid paying your respects. If he didn't like it, that's his business,' said Marya Dmitriyevna, looking for something in her handbag. 'And with the trousseau nearly ready there's nothing to hold you up. I can send on the bits that aren't ready. I'll be sorry to see you go, but, God bless you, it's the best thing to do.' She found what she was looking for in her bag and handed it to Natasha. It was a letter from

Princess Marya. 'She's written to you. She's really suffering, poor girl! She's afraid you might think she doesn't like you.'

'Well, she doesn't,' said Natasha.

'Don't talk such nonsense,' cried Marya Dmitriyevna.

'I just don't believe it. I know she doesn't like me,' said Natasha impudently, taking the letter with a look of such cold and grim determination that Marya Dmitriyevna peered at her more sharply and frowned.

'Don't answer back, young lady,' she said. 'What I say is true. Make sure you write back to her.'

Without replying Natasha went up to her own room to read Princess Marya's letter.

Princess Marya wrote that she was in despair at the misunderstanding that had arisen between them. Whatever her father's feelings might be, wrote Princess Marya, she asked Natasha to believe that she was bound to love her – she was the girl chosen by her brother, and for the sake of his happiness she would make any sacrifice.

'And another thing,' she wrote, 'please do not think that my father has taken against you. He is an old man and quite poorly, and allowances have to be made for him. But he is kind-hearted and generous, and he will come to love the woman who makes his son happy.' Finally Princess Marya asked Natasha to arrange a time when they could come together again.

After reading the letter Natasha sat down to the writing-table to write back. She began by jotting down an automatic 'Dear Princess . . .' in French, and then stopped. How could she go on after all that had happened the day before? Yes, yes, it really had happened, and now everything was different, she thought, sitting over the letter she had barely begun. 'Should I turn him down? Should I? Oh, it's too awful!' And to get away from horrible thoughts like these she went in to see Sonya and went through some embroidery patterns with her.

After dinner Natasha went back to her room and took up Princess Marya's letter again. 'Is it all over?' she thought. 'Has it all happened just like that and ruined everything that went before?' She could remember the full force of her love for Prince Andrey, but she still felt she was in love with Kuragin. She conjured up a picture of herself living happily as Prince Andrey's wife, a picture she had so often dwelt on in her imagination, but at the same time, burning with excitement, she brought back to mind every detail of yesterday's encounter with Anatole.

'Why couldn't that happen too?' she kept wondering in her fog of bewilderment. 'That's the only way I could be completely happy. With things as they are I have to choose, and I can't be happy unless I have both of them. I know one thing,' she thought. 'Telling Prince Andrey what's happened and hiding it from him are equally impossible. But with *him* nothing's been spoilt. But how could I say goodbye to Prince Andrey's love and all the happiness I've been living on for so long?'

'Please, miss,' whispered a maid, coming into the room looking all secretive, 'a man told me to give you this.' She handed her a letter. 'But please, miss, for the love of Jesus . . .' said the girl, as Natasha, not giving it a thought, broke the seal automatically and began reading a love-letter from Anatole, without taking in a word of it, aware of one thing only – it was a letter from him, the man she loved. Yes, she did love him. Otherwise, how could what had happened have happened? How could she have ended up with a love-letter from him in her hand?

Natasha's hands were shaking as she held on to that passionate love-letter, composed for Anatole by Dolokhov, and as she read it through she discovered in it echoes of everything that she herself seemed to be feeling.

'Since yesterday evening my fate is sealed: to be loved by you or to die. There is no other way . . .' the letter began. He went on to say that he knew her family would never give her to him, for secret reasons that he could reveal only to her in private, but if she loved him, she had only to say the word *yes*, and no human power could mar their bliss. Love would conquer all. He would snatch her away and carry her off to the ends of the earth.

'Yes, yes, I do love him!' thought Natasha, reading the letter for the twentieth time and discovering some new deep meaning in every word.

That evening Marya Dmitriyevna was going to the Arkharovs', and proposed taking the young ladies with her. Natasha pleaded a headache and stayed behind at home.

CHAPTER 15

Late that night when she got back Sonya went into Natasha's room and to her surprise found her fast asleep on the sofa, still dressed. On the table next to her lay Anatole's letter, open. Sonya picked it up and read it.

As she read she kept glancing down at Natasha, who was still asleep, watching her face in the hope of discovering some explanation of what she was reading, but finding nothing. Natasha's face was peaceful, gentle and happy. Clutching at her chest to stop herself choking, Sonya sank down into an armchair, pale-faced and trembling with emotion and horror, and burst into tears.

'Why didn't I see this coming? How can it have gone so far? Has she lost all her love for Prince Andrey? And how could she have let Kuragin go as far as this? He's a liar and a scoundrel, that's for sure. What will Nikolay do – dear, noble Nikolay – when he gets to know? So that's what it meant, that funny look on her face, all determined and excited, the other day, and yesterday, and today,' thought Sonya. 'But she can't possibly have fallen in love with him! She's probably opened that letter without knowing who it was from. She probably feels insulted by it. Surely she couldn't do that!'

Sonya wiped away her tears and went over to Natasha, looking closely at her face again.

'Natasha!' she said in a barely audible voice.

Natasha woke up and saw Sonya.

'Oh, you're back.'

And with the warm impulsiveness that can come over people at the moment of waking she hugged her friend. But when she saw Sonya's embarrassment she was embarrassed too, and suspicious.

'Sonya, you've read the letter, haven't you?' she said.

'Yes,' said Sonya softly.

Natasha gave a smile of triumph.

'No, Sonya, I can't go on like this!' she said. 'I can't hide it from you any longer. You know we love each other! . . . Sonya, darling, he writes . . . Sonya . . .'

Sonya goggled at Natasha as if she couldn't believe her ears.

'What about Bolkonsky?' she said.

'Oh, Sonya, oh, if you knew how happy I am!' said Natasha. 'You don't know what love . . .'

'But, Natasha, do you mean to say it's all over?'

Natasha gazed wide-eyed at Sonya as if she didn't understand the question.

'Are you breaking it off with Prince Andrey, then?' said Sonya.

'Oh, you don't understand. Don't talk nonsense. Just listen,' said Natasha, with a flash of irritation.

'No, I don't believe it,' repeated Sonya. 'I can't understand you. Look, you've been in love with one man for a whole year, and now suddenly . . . I mean, you've only seen him three times, Natasha. I don't believe it. This is some kind of joke. Three days, and you've forgotten everything, and . . .'

'Three days,' said Natasha. 'I seem to have been in love with him for a hundred years. I'm sure I've never been in love before. You wouldn't understand. Sonya. Wait a minute – come and sit here.' Natasha hugged and kissed her. 'I've heard it can happen this way – you probably have too – but this is the first time I've felt love like this. It's not what I've felt before. The moment I set eyes on him, I knew he was my master and I was his slave, and I couldn't help loving him. Yes, his slave! I'll do whatever he commands. You wouldn't understand. Well, what can I do? What *can* I do, Sonya?' said Natasha, her face full of rapture and alarm.

'Well, stop and think what you're doing,' said Sonya. 'I can't leave things like this. These secret letters . . . How could you let him do all that?' she said, with scarcely concealed horror and revulsion.

'I've just told you,' answered Natasha, 'I have no will of my own. Can't you get it into your head? I'm in love with him!'

'Well, I can't let it go on like this. I'm going to tell on you,' cried Sonya, bursting into tears.

'You what? For heaven's sake . . . If you tell on me, we're enemies,' said Natasha. 'You want me to be miserable. You want them to come between us . . .'

Seeing Natasha in such a state of alarm, Sonya wept tears of shame and sorrow for her friend.

'But what's happened between the two of you?' she asked. 'What's he been saying to you? Why doesn't he come to the house?'

Natasha ignored her.

'For heaven's sake, Sonya, don't tell anybody. Don't torment me,' Natasha implored her. 'Remember, you shouldn't get mixed up in things like this. I've told you . . .'

'But why all this secrecy? Why doesn't he come to the house?' Sonya persisted. 'Why doesn't he ask for your hand straight out? Look, Prince Andrey gave you a completely free hand in case this sort of thing . . . But I just can't believe it. Natasha, have you thought about the *secret reasons* behind it?'

Natasha looked at Sonya in amazement. This was obviously the first time the question had occurred to her, and she didn't know how to respond.

'Well, I don't know what the reasons are. But there must be some!' Sonya sighed and shook her head distrustfully.

'If there were any reasons . . .' she started to say, but Natasha, anticipating her misgivings, interrupted in some alarm.

'Sonya, you can't start having doubts about him, you really can't! Don't you see that?' she cried.

'Does he love you?'

'Does he love me?' parroted Natasha, beaming indulgently at her friend's obtuseness. 'Well, you've read his letter, haven't you? And you have seen him.'

'But what if he's a dishonourable man?'

'*Him*? How could he be dishonourable? If you only knew!' said Natasha.

'Well, if he's not dishonourable, he ought to do one of two things – either say what his intentions are or stop seeing you. And if you won't do it, I will. I'll write to him. And I'll tell your papa,' said Sonya, full of determination.

'But I can't live without him!' cried Natasha.

'Natasha, I don't understand you. What exactly are you saying? Think of your father. Think of Nikolay.'

'I'm not bothered about anybody else. He's the only one I love. How dare you call him dishonourable? Don't you know I'm in love with him?' cried Natasha. 'Sonya, go away. I don't want to quarrel with you. Go away, for heaven's sake. Just go away. You can see how miserable I am,' cried Natasha viciously, in a voice of barely controlled exasperation and near-despair. Sonya ran out of the room sobbing her heart out.

Natasha went over to the table and without a moment's thought sat straight down and wrote the reply to Princess Marya that she hadn't been able to write all morning. In the letter she told Princess Marya in a word or two that any misunderstandings between them were now at an end. She was going to take full advantage of Prince Andrey's magnanimity in giving her complete freedom as they parted from each other. She asked her to forget everything and forgive her if she had anything to apologize for, but she couldn't be his wife. Just for the moment everything seemed so easy, straightforward and clear-cut.

The Rostovs were due to leave town on Friday, and on Wednesday the count took a prospective purchaser down to his estate near Moscow.

On the day he left, Sonya and Natasha were invited to a grand dinner-party at Julie Karagin's; Marya Dmitriyevna went with them. At the dinner Natasha met Anatole again, and Sonya watched as she said something to him, taking great care not to be overheard, and all through the meal Natasha looked more excited than ever. When they got home it was Natasha who started the conversation that Sonya had been waiting for.

'Listen, Sonya, you've been saying all sorts of silly things about him,' Natasha began in a tiny voice, the kind of voice that children put on when they are looking for praise. 'Well, I've had it all out with him tonight.'

'Well, what did he say? Come on, what did he say? Natasha, I'm so glad you're not angry with me. Tell me the whole story. Tell me the truth. What did he say?'

Natasha considered what to say.

'Oh, Sonya, if you knew him as I do! He said . . . He asked me what kind of promise I had given Bolkonsky. He was so glad I'm in a position to refuse him.'

Sonya gave a bleak sigh.

'But you haven't refused Bolkonsky, have you?' she said.

'Well, maybe I have! Maybe it's all over with Bolkonsky. Why do you think so badly of me?'

'I don't think anything. I just don't understand . . .'

'Just wait, Sonya, and you'll understand. You'll see the sort of man he is. Don't think too badly of either of us.'

'I don't think badly of people. I like everybody and I'm sorry for everybody. But what can I do?'

Sonya was not won over by Natasha's ingratiating tone. The softer and more appealing Natasha's face grew, the more serious and severe Sonya's became.

'Natasha,' she said, 'you asked me not to talk to you, and I haven't done. But now you've started things off. Natasha, I don't trust him. Why this secrecy?'

'Again, again!' interrupted Natasha.

'Natasha, I'm afraid for you.'

'What is there to be afraid of?'

'I'm afraid you'll be ruined,' said Sonya firmly, horrified to hear her own words.

Natasha's face looked angry again.

'All right then, I'll be ruined, I will, I'll be ruined for ever. But it's nothing to do with you. You won't suffer for it, I will. Leave me alone, just leave me alone. I hate you!'

'Natasha!' Sonya appealed to her in great distress.

'I hate you, I hate you! You're my enemy for ever!' And Natasha ran out of the room.

Natasha avoided Sonya and didn't speak to her again. With the same mixture of excitement, wonder and guilt on her face she wandered through the rooms seizing on one thing after another, and throwing everything down as soon as she picked it up.

Hard as it was on Sonya, she kept watch over her friend and never let her out of her sight.

The day before the count was due to return Sonya happened to notice that Natasha had spent all morning sitting at the drawing-room window, as if she was waiting for something, and suddenly she gave a signal to a passing officer whom Sonya assumed to be Anatole.

Sonya kept an even closer watch on her friend, and she noticed that all through dinner and afterwards during the evening Natasha was in a strange mood, most unlike her usual self. When people asked her questions she gave silly answers, she started sentences and never finished them, and she kept laughing all the time.

After tea Sonya saw a timid-looking maid waiting for her to go past Natasha's door. She let her go in, listened at the door and found out that another letter had arrived. Suddenly it dawned on Sonya that Natasha was hatching some dreadful plan for that evening. She knocked at the door, but Natasha wouldn't let her in.

'She's going to run away with him!' thought Sonya. 'She's capable of anything. There's been a pitiful kind of look on her face today and real determination. And she cried when she said goodbye to Papa,' Sonya remembered. 'Yes, that's it, she's going to run away with him. What can I do about it?' wondered Sonya, remembering all the signals given off by Natasha showing clearly that she had some terrible plan in mind. 'Count Rostov isn't here. What can I do? I could write to Kuragin and demand an explanation. But who says he's bound to answer? I could write to Pierre – that was what Prince Andrey asked me to do if there was any trouble . . . But perhaps she really has broken things off with Bolkonsky – she did send that letter to Princess Marya yesterday. And Uncle's not here.'

To tell Marya Dmitriyevna, who had such faith in Natasha, seemed a terrible thing to do.

'Well, one way or another,' thought Sonya, standing in the dark corridor, 'now or never it's time for me to show my appreciation of all the benefits I've had from this family and my love for Nikolay. No, if I have to go three nights without sleep, I'm not leaving this corridor, and I'll stop her going by brute force. I'm not going to stand by and see this family ruined and disgraced,' she thought.

CHAPTER 16

Anatole had recently moved in with Dolokhov. A plan for abducting the Rostov girl had been thought up and worked out in detail by Dolokhov over several days, and the evening when Sonya had listened at Natasha's door and made up her mind to keep guard over her was the very day when the plan was due to be carried out. Natasha had promised to come out at ten o'clock and meet Kuragin by the back porch. Kuragin would be waiting for her with a troika, get her on board and drive her from Moscow to the village of Kamenka forty miles away, where an unfrocked priest would be standing by ready to marry them. At Kamenka a relay of horses would be waiting to take them down to the Warsaw road, from where they would use post-horses to take them out of the country.

Anatole had secured a passport, an order for post-horses, ten thousand roubles borrowed from his sister and another ten thousand raised by Dolokhov.

The two necessary witnesses – Khvostikov, a low-grade civil servant now retired and regularly exploited by Dolokhov at the card-table, and Makarin, a former hussar, a pleasant man with no backbone, whose devotion to Kuragin knew no bounds – were now sitting in Dolokhov's front room drinking tea.

In Dolokhov's big study, adorned with Persian rugs, bearskins and weaponry right up to the ceiling, Dolokhov sat waiting, fully rigged out in travelling cloak and high boots, in front of an open bureau with accounts and bundles of banknotes lying around on it. Anatole, with his uniform unbuttoned, was stalking about, going from the room where the witnesses were sitting through the study into a back room, where his French valet and one or two other servants were doing the last of the packing. Dolokhov was counting notes and jotting down figures.

'Well,' he said, 'you'll have to give Khvostikov two thousand.'

'Well, give him it, then,' said Anatole.

'Makarka –' (their name for Makarin) 'well, he'd go through fire and water for you and not ask for any reward. That's it then, the accounts are finished,' said Dolokhov, showing him a note. 'Does that look all right?'

'Yes, of course it does,' said Anatole, obviously not listening, just staring into space with a permanent grin on his face.

Dolokhov slammed the bureau shut, and turned to Anatole with a sardonic smile.

'Hey, listen – why don't you drop all this while there's still time?' he said.

'Idiot!' said Anatole. 'Stop talking rubbish. If only you knew ... It's hellishly important to me!'

'I still think you should drop it,' said Dolokhov. 'It's serious, this scheme of yours. No laughing matter.'

'You will have your little joke. To hell with you! Do you hear?' said Anatole, frowning. 'I'm not in the mood for your stupid jokes.' And he walked out of the room.

As he did so Dolokhov was smiling a lofty, rather contemptuous smile.

'Hang on a minute,' he called after Anatole. 'I'm not joking. This is serious. Come back in here! Come on!'

Anatole came back into the room, trying to concentrate as he looked at Dolokhov and obviously reluctant to submit.

'Listen. I'm saying this for the last time. Why would I want to joke with you? Have I ever got in your way? Who made all the arrangements? Who found you a priest? Who got you a passport and all this money? It was me.'

'All right. Thank you very much. Do you think I'm not grateful?' Anatole sighed and embraced Dolokhov.

'So I have helped you, but I've still got to tell you the truth. This is a dangerous business, and when you come to think of it, it's stupid. You take her away – well and good. Do you think they'll leave it at that? It'll come out that you're already married. Then they'll have you up on a criminal charge . . .'

'Oh, rubbish, rubbish!' said Anatole, scowling again. 'I've gone through this time and again, haven't I?' And Anatole, with the stubborn attachment that you tend to find in small-minded people to any conclusion stemming from their own mental processes, outlined the argument he had already gone through a hundred times with Dolokhov.

'Let me go through it again. I've decided that if this marriage turns out to be invalid,' he said, bending one finger back, 'that means I'm not responsible. And if it is valid, it won't matter. Anyway, abroad nobody's going to know anything about it. See? It's all right, isn't it? And you will go on and on and on about it!'

'Oh, please, why don't you drop the whole thing? You'll only get yourself into a mess . . .'

'To hell with you!' said Anatole, and he strode off into the next room clutching his hair, but he was soon back and he sat down in an armchair with his feet tucked up, right in front of Dolokhov. 'I'm in a hellish state! Do you know what I mean? How's that for a heartbeat?' He took Dolokhov's hand and placed it on his heart. 'But oh, that foot, my dear boy, those eyes! A goddess!' he rhapsodized in French. 'Can you hear what I'm saying?'

Dolokhov watched him with a cold smile, a gleam in his handsome eyes and a hard stare, obviously minded to get more fun out of him.

'What will you do when the money runs out?'

'When the money runs out? Eh?' Anatole parroted, genuinely taken aback by any thoughts for the future. 'What shall we do when the money runs out? I don't know ... You do say some stupid things!' He looked at his watch. 'Time to get going!' Anatole disappeared into the back room.

'How much longer? Do get a move on!' he shouted at the servants.

Dolokhov cleared away the money, called a servant and told him to fetch them something to eat and drink before the journey, and then went through to where Khvostikov and Makarin were sitting.

Anatole was lying on the study sofa, propped up on one elbow, smiling to himself and mouthing tender pleasantries.

'Come in here and have a bite to eat. And a drink!' Dolokhov called from the next room.

'I don't feel like it,' answered Anatole, still wrapped up in his own smiles.

'Come on. Balaga's arrived.'

Anatole got to his feet and went through into the dining-room. Balaga was a well-known troika driver, who had known Dolokhov and Anatole for the last six years and had often driven them around in his sledges. More than once, when Anatole's regiment had been stationed at Tver, he had picked him up in Tver of an evening, got to Moscow by dawn, and driven him back the next night. More than once he had driven Dolokhov out of trouble. More than once he had driven them round the town with gypsies and 'the little ladies', as he called them, on board. More than once he had run pedestrians and other vehicles off the Moscow roads in their service, always relying on his 'gentlemen', as he called them, to get him out of trouble. Many a horse of his had been ridden into the ground with them in the sledge. More than once they had thrashed him; more than once they had got him drunk on champagne and madeira, which was much to his taste, and he knew things about both of them that would have dispatched any ordinary man to Siberia ages ago. They often brought Balaga in on things when they were out on the town, getting him to drink and dance with the gypsies, and their money had passed through his hands in thousands. In their service he risked his life and his skin twenty times a year, and he wore out more horses than their over-generous payments could ever make up for. But he liked them, liked the furious pace of their driving – they could cover twenty miles in an hour and a half – liked driving coachmen off the road and running down pedestrians in Moscow, and hurtling along the Moscow streets. He liked to hear the wild shouts and drunken voices behind him, yelling,

'Get a move on!' when they were already going flat out, and he liked to lash the occasional passing peasant across the neck when he was already reeling back more dead than alive. 'Real gentlemen!' he thought.

Anatole and Dolokhov liked Balaga – he drove like a Jehu and he liked what they liked. With other customers Balaga drove a hard bargain, squeezing twenty-five roubles out of them for a two-hour drive, and he seldom went out himself, generally sending one of his young boys. But when it came to 'his own gentlemen' he always did the driving, and he never asked for payment.

Only two or three times a year, when he happened to know through their valets that there was money around, would he turn up in the morning, quite sober, bow down and ask them to help him out. The gentlemen always invited him to sit down.

'I was wondering whether you might be able to oblige, Fyodor Ivanovich, sir,' or, 'Your Excellency,' he would say, 'I'm right out of horses, and I need to go the fair. If you could just lend me something, whatever you can manage . . .'

And whenever they were in funds Anatole and Dolokhov would give him a thousand or two.

Balaga was a fair-haired, short, snub-nosed peasant in his late twenties, with a red face and a particularly red, thick neck, bright little eyes and a short beard. He wore a fine blue silk-lined kaftan over a sheepskin jacket.

He turned to the icon corner, crossed himself, and went over to Dolokhov, extending a small black hand.

'My respects to you, Fyodor Ivanovich!' said he with one of his bows.

'Good day to you, my friend. Ah, here's the man himself!'

'Good day, your Excellency!' he said to Anatole as he came in, and once again he extended a hand.

'I say, Balaga,' said Anatole, placing a hand on each of his shoulders, 'do you care for me or not? Eh? Now's the time for stalwart service. What sort of horses have you brought? Eh?'

'Did what your man said – brought your favourite beasts,' said Balaga.

'Right, listen, Balaga. Ride them to death if needs be, only get there in three hours. All right?'

'If they're all dead, 'ow are we going to get there?' said Balaga with a wink.

'Don't get funny with me. I'll smash your face in!' cried Anatole suddenly, glaring at him.

'Just my little joke,' chuckled the driver. 'Do anything for my gentle-men I would. We'll get you there as fast as horses ever galloped.'

'All right,' said Anatole. 'Come and sit down.'

'Sit down here,' said Dolokhov.

'I think I'll stand, Fyodor Ivanovich.'

'Nonsense! Sit down and have a drink,' said Anatole, and he poured him out a stiff glass of madeira. The driver's eyes lit up at the sight of the wine. After one polite refusal he tossed it off and wiped his mouth with a red silk handkerchief which he took out of his cap.

'Right, your Excellency, when do we start?'

'Er . . .' Anatole consulted his watch. 'Time we were off now. Listen to me, Balaga. You will get us there in time?'

'Oh yes, off to a good start and we'll get there all right,' said Balaga. 'Got you to Tver, didn't we? In seven hours. I bet you've not forgotten that, your Excellency!'

'D'you know, one Christmas I drove back from Tver . . .' Smiling at the memory of it, Anatole was talking to Makarin, who gazed back, lost in admiration. 'It was incredible, Makarka, we flew the whole way – you could hardly breathe. We crashed into a line of wagons and jumped two of 'em! How about that?'

'They was real horses,' said Balaga, picking up the story. 'Two young 'uns at the sides and that bay with the shaft' – he turned to Dolokhov – 'and you wouldn't believe it, sir, forty miles them beasts galloped. There was no 'olding 'em back, me hands was frozen stiff it was that cold. I let go o' the reins. "You 'old them yourself, sir," says I, and I rolled back down in the sledge. Didn't need no driving. Couldn't 'old 'em back till we got there. Hell's teeth, they got us there in three hours. Only one of 'em died, 'im on the left.'

CHAPTER 17

Anatole left the room and came back a few minutes later wearing a fur jacket with a silver belt, and a sable cap tilted at a jaunty angle, a good match for his handsome face. He paused for a look in the mirror and then turned to Dolokhov with the same mirror-pose and took a glass of wine.

'Well, Fedya, I'll say goodbye. Thanks for everything, and goodbye,' said Anatole. 'Well now, comrades, friends . . .' he thought for a moment, '. . . of my youth . . . goodbye to you all.' He had turned to Makarin and the others.

Although they were all going with him, Anatole evidently wanted to turn this address to his comrades into a moving and solemn ceremony. His speech was loud and measured, his chest was square and he was swinging one of his legs.

'Raise your glasses everybody. You, too, Balaga. So . . . comrades . . . friends of my youth, we've had some fun together, seen a bit of life, had lots of fun. Haven't we just! So, when shall we meet again? I'm off abroad! We've seen a bit of life, so goodbye, boys. I drink to you! Hurrah!' This said, he drained his glass, and smashed it on the floor.

'Your health!' said Balaga. He, too, drained his glass and wiped his lips on his handkerchief.

Makarin embraced Anatole with tears in his eyes.

'Oh dear, Prince, it breaks my heart to part from you,' he said.

'Come on! Let's get going!' shouted Anatole.

Balaga was half-way out of the room.

'No, hang on,' said Anatole. 'Shut that door. We've got to sit down. That's the way.' The door was closed, and they all sat down.[5]

'Right boys, quick march!' said Anatole, getting to his feet.

Joseph, the valet, handed Anatole his sabretache and sabre, and they all went out into the hall.

'What about the coat?' said Dolokhov. 'Hey, Ignatka! Slip over to Matryona Matveyevna, and ask her for that sable coat. I've heard what elopements can be like,' said Dolokhov with a wink. 'She'll come tripping out more dead than alive, still dressed for indoors. Stop for a second and it'll be all tears, and "dear Papa" and "dear Mamma", then she's frozen stiff and she wants to go back in – so you've got to wrap her up straightaway in a big coat and get her into the sledge.'

The valet came back with a woman's fox-fur coat.

'Idiot, I said sable. Hey, Matryosha, the sable coat!' he shouted, his loud voice echoing through every room.

A pale, thin, good-looking gypsy woman with gleaming black eyes and curly black hair with a hint of grey ran out wearing a red shawl, with a sable coat over her arm.

'Here you are. You're welcome, I'm sure,' she said, visibly afraid of her master, but ruing the loss of her coat.

Instead of replying Dolokhov took the coat, put it round Matryosha's shoulders and wrapped her up in it.

'That's how it's done,' said Dolokhov. 'And then like this,' he said, turning the collar up round her head, leaving only her little face exposed. 'And then like this, see?' and he pushed Anatole's head forward towards the inside of the collar and the flash of Matryosha's smile.

'Well, goodbye, Matryosha,' said Anatole, giving her a kiss. 'Oh dear, no more fun over here! My regards to Styoshka. Goodbye then. Goodbye, Matryosha. Wish me luck.'

'God grant you all the luck in the world, Prince,' said Matryosha with her strong gypsy accent.

There by the steps stood two troikas, the horses held by two of the best young drivers. Balaga got into the first one, and raised his elbows high, taking his time to sort out the reins. Anatole and Dolokhov got in behind him. Makarin, Khvostikov and the valet got into the other sledge.

'All set?' asked Balaga. 'Away!' he yelled, wrapping the reins round his hands, and the sledge hurtled off down Nikitsky Boulevard.

'Wheee! . . . Garn! . . . Move! . . . Grrrh!' yelled Balaga and the young driver on the box, the only sounds in the night.

In Arbatsky Square the sledge bumped into a carriage with a dreadful crunch and shouts rang out, but off they flew down the Arbat. After driving the full length of Podnovinsky Boulevard, reining in and turning back, Balaga stopped the horses at the crossing by Old Konyusheny Street.

The keen young man on the box jumped down to hold the horses by the bridle. Anatole and Dolokhov walked off down the footpath. When they got to the gates, Dolokhov whistled. An answering whistle echoed back and a maid-servant ran out.

'Come on into the courtyard, or you'll be seen. She'll be here in a minute,' she said.

Dolokhov stayed by the gate. Anatole followed the maid into the courtyard, turned a corner and ran up the steps.

He was met by Gavrilo, Marya Dmitriyevna's giant of a footman.

'This way, sir. The mistress wants to see you,' said the groom in his deep bass voice, blocking the approach to the door.

'Whose mistress? Who are you?' Anatole asked in a breathless whisper.

'This way, sir. My orders are to show you in.'

'Kuragin! Get back here!' shouted Dolokhov. 'Traitors! Come on back!'

By the little back gate where he had stopped Dolokhov was wrestling with a porter, who was trying to shut the gate and lock Anatole in. Dolokhov bundled the porter away with a last desperate shove, grabbed Anatole, heaved him out through the gate and ran off with him back to the sledge.

CHAPTER 18

Marya Dmitriyevna had come across a very tearful Sonya in the corridor and forced a confession out of her. She had seized Natasha's note from Anatole and read it, and now she marched in to see Natasha, still holding the letter.

'You shameless little hussy!' she said to her. 'I don't want to hear a word!' Thrusting Natasha away while the girl gazed at her dry-eyed but speechless with amazement, she locked her in, ordered the porter to admit certain persons who were due to turn up that night, but not let them out again, and told her footman to show these persons up, and then she sat down in the drawing-room to wait for the abductors. When Gavrilo came in to inform Marya Dmitriyevna that the persons had turned up but had got away, she rose to her feet with a scowl on her face, clasped her hands behind her back, and wandered from room to room, considering what to do. It was nearly midnight when she set off for Natasha's room, feeling the key in her pocket. Sonya was in the corridor still sitting there sobbing. 'Marya Dmitriyevna, please, for heaven's sake, let me in to see her!' she said.

Instead of replying Marya Dmitriyevna opened the door and went in. 'Hateful, disgusting girl, in my house, the vile little hussy! It's her father I'm sorry for,' Marya Dmitriyevna had been thinking, trying to control her fury. 'Hard as it may be, I shall silence the lot of them and hide it from the count.' She now strode imperiously into the room.

Natasha was lying perfectly still on the sofa with her head buried in her hands. She had been lying in exactly the same position when Marya Dmitriyevna had left her.

'You're a very nice girl, aren't you?' said Marya Dmitriyevna. 'Using my house to arrange meetings with your lovers! Let's put our cards on the table. And you listen to me when I'm speaking.' Marya Dmitriyevna touched her on the arm. 'Listen to me when I'm speaking! You've shamed yourself like a common little slut. I know what I'd do with you, but I'm sorry for your poor father. I shall hide it from him.'

Natasha didn't change position, but her whole body was racked with noiseless, convulsive sobs and a terrible choking. Marya Dmitriyevna glanced round at Sonya and sat down on the edge of the sofa next to Natasha.

'He's lucky I didn't catch him, but I shall,' she said, coarsening her voice. 'Do you hear what I say, eh?' She put a large hand under Natasha's face and turned it towards her. Both Marya Dmitriyevna and Sonya were shocked by the sight of Natasha's face. Her eyes were dry but gleaming, her lips were tightly compressed and her cheeks looked hollow.

'Leave me . . . a-lone . . . I . . . just let me die . . .' was all she could manage to say before wrenching herself viciously away from Marya Dmitriyevna and flopping back down into her former position.

'Natalya! . . .' said Marya Dmitriyevna. 'This is for your own good. Now just lie still. Come on, lie still like that. I won't touch you. But listen to me . . . I'm not going to go on about how bad you've been. You're aware of that yourself. But your father's due back tomorrow, and I want to know what I'm supposed to tell him. Do you hear me?'

Once again Natasha's body was convulsed with sobs.

'If he gets to know, what will your brother do, and your fiancé?'

'I have no fiancé. I've broken it off,' cried Natasha.

'It makes no difference,' Marya Dmitriyevna insisted. 'I mean, if they do find out, do you think they'll leave it at that? I know your father – he could easily challenge him to a duel. That will be all right, will it?'

'Oh, just leave me alone. Why did you have to interfere? Why? Why? Who asked you to?' cried Natasha, sitting up on the sofa and fixing Marya Dmitriyevna with a vicious glare.

'So what did you want?' screamed Marya Dmitriyevna, roused to fury again. 'I mean, you weren't exactly locked away, were you? Did anybody stop him coming to the house? Why did he have to carry you off, like some gypsy girl? . . . And if he'd managed it, do you imagine they wouldn't have caught him? Your father, your brother, your fiancé? He's a swine and a scoundrel, and that's all there is to it!'

'He's better than any of you,' cried Natasha, raising herself up. 'If you hadn't got in the way . . . Oh my God, what now? Sonya, why . . . ? Oh, go away! . . .' And she sobbed with the kind of despair that people feel when they weep for troubles they know they have brought upon themselves.

Marya Dmitriyevna was about to speak again, but Natasha suddenly yelled, 'Go away, go away! You all hate me and despise me!' And she flung herself back down on the sofa.

Marya Dmitriyevna went on for some time pouring shame on Natasha, drumming it into her that everything had to be hidden from the count, and no one would know anything about it if only she would undertake to forget the whole thing, and not give off any signs that something might have happened. Natasha wouldn't respond. She had stopped sobbing, but she was now seized with bouts of shivering and trembling. Marya Dmitriyevna put a pillow under her head, covered her with two blankets, and brought her some lime-water with her own hands, but Natasha wouldn't respond to anything she said.

'Oh well, let her sleep,' said Marya Dmitriyevna, and she left the room, thinking Natasha must have dropped off. But she hadn't. Her staring eyes gazed out vacantly from her pale face. She never slept a wink all night long, she didn't cry and she never said a word to Sonya, who got up several times and went in to see her.

Next day Count Rostov arrived back from his estate, as promised, in time for lunch. He was in a very good mood, being on the point of agreeing terms with the purchaser, and there was now nothing to keep him in Moscow away from his countess, and he had begun to miss her dearly. Marya Dmitriyevna came to welcome him with the news that Natasha had been quite poorly the previous day, but they had sent for the doctor and now she was feeling better. Natasha had not left her room all morning. With pinched, cracked lips, and dry, staring eyes, she sat by the window, uneasily watching people drive past down the street, and looking round nervously at anyone who entered the room. She was obviously waiting for news of him, waiting for him to come or at least write to her.

When the count walked in to see her, she turned uneasily at the sound of his man's heavy tread, and her face resumed its earlier cold, even vindictive expression. She didn't even get up to greet him.

'What is it, my angel. Are you ill?' asked the count.

Natasha was silent for a moment.

'Yes, I am,' she answered.

When the count asked anxiously why she was so depressed and whether anything had happened to her fiancé she assured him that nothing had, and told him not to worry. Marya Dmitriyevna confirmed Natasha's insistence that nothing had happened. This imaginary illness, his daughter's agitated state and the embarrassment written all over the faces of Sonya and Marya Dmitriyevna told the count all too clearly that something must have happened while he had been away. But it was just too awful for him to imagine that anything scandalous might have happened to his beloved daughter, and he valued his present good humour and peace of mind so much that he shied away from further inquiries and tried to reassure himself that nothing very unusual could have happened, his only regret being that her indisposition would delay their return to the country.

CHAPTER 19

Ever since the day of his wife's arrival in Moscow Pierre had been intending to leave town, if only to get away from her. Shortly after the Rostovs' arrival, the deep impression made on him by Natasha caused him to carry out his intention with all speed. He left for Tver to see Osip Bazdeyev's widow, who had promised some time ago to hand over her late husband's papers.

When Pierre got back to Moscow he was handed a letter from Marya Dmitriyevna asking him to call because something very important had come up concerning Andrey Bolkonsky and his fiancée. Pierre had been avoiding Natasha. He could sense that his feelings towards her were stronger than they ought to be between a married man and a young girl engaged to one of his friends. But somehow fate kept bringing them together.

'What's happened now? What do they want me for?' he kept thinking as he dressed to go to Marya Dmitriyevna's. 'Oh, if only Prince Andrey would hurry up and come home and get married to her,' thought Pierre on the journey there.

In the Tverskoy Boulevard somebody hailed him.

'Pierre! When did you get back?' called a familiar voice. Pierre looked up. A sledge flew by behind a pair of trotting greys kicking up snow all over the front board – it was Anatole and his constant companion Makarin. Anatole was sitting bolt upright in the classic pose of a dashing army man, the lower part of his face muffled in a beaver collar and his head bent slightly forward. His face was fresh and glowing, his hat sported white feathers and sat at a jaunty angle, showing off pomaded curls with a sprinkling of fine snow.

'Now that's what I call worldly wisdom!' thought Pierre. 'He can't see beyond the pleasure of the moment, nothing worries him, so he's always happy and contented. What wouldn't I give to be like him?' he mused, full of envy.

In Marya Dmitriyevna's entrance-hall, as the footman helped Pierre off with his coat he said that his mistress wanted him to go up to her bedroom.

As he opened the hall door Pierre caught a brief glimpse of Natasha sitting by the window looking thin, pale and crabby. She glanced round at him, scowled and left the room with an air of icy aloofness.

'What's happened?' asked Pierre, going into Marya Dmitriyevna's room. 'A nice turn of events!' answered Marya Dmitriyevna. 'Fifty-eight years I've lived on this earth and never seen anything so disgraceful.'

And after making Pierre swear not to breathe a word of what was to follow Marya Dmitriyevna told him that Natasha had broken off her engagement without telling her parents, all because of Anatole Kuragin, Pierre's wife having brought the two of them together, and Natasha had tried to elope with him while her father was away and get married in secret.

Pierre sat there with his shoulders hunched and his mouth wide open, listening to what Marya Dmitriyevna had to say, and he could hardly believe his ears. What, Prince Andrey's beloved fiancée, Natasha Rostov, always such a charming girl hitherto, had given up Bolkonsky for that fool Anatole, who was already married (Pierre knew his secret), fallen in love with him and agreed to elope? It was beyond Pierre's imagination or understanding! The lovely image of Natasha that was so dear to his soul – and he had known her since childhood – didn't fit with this new picture of her as someone depraved, stupid and cruel. He thought of his own wife. 'They're all the same,' he told himself, reflecting that he was not the only man to be tied by the unhappy hand of fate to a dreadful woman. But even so he could have wept for Prince Andrey, wept for his pride. And the more he felt for his friend, the more his feeling of contempt and revulsion grew as he thought of Natasha, who had just walked past him with that air of icy aloofness. He was not to know that Natasha's heart was overflowing with despair, shame and humiliation, and she could hardly be blamed for her face happening to look all calm, aloof and austere.

'What do you mean get married?' cried Pierre when he heard Marya Dmitriyevna's words. 'He can't get married – he's married already.'

'It never rains but it pours,' said Marya Dmitriyevna. 'What a splendid young man! Absolute swine! And she's still expecting him to come – she has been for two days! We've got to stop her waiting for him. We must tell her.'

Once Pierre had told her all about Anatole's marriage, and she had vented her fury in the strongest language, Marya Dmitriyevna got round to letting Pierre know why she had sent for him. She was terrified that either Count Rostov or Prince Bolkonsky, who might arrive at any moment, could easily get to know about this affair despite her best efforts to conceal it and challenge Kuragin to a duel, so she now wanted Pierre to act on her behalf and kick his brother-in-law out of Moscow with clear instructions never to darken her door again. Pierre promised to do what she wanted, suddenly recognizing the danger that threatened the old count, and Nikolay and Prince Andrey.

After outlining her wishes in a few precise words, she let him go through into the drawing-room.

'Keep the count in the dark. Behave as if you know nothing,' she said. 'And I'll go and tell her she needn't bother waiting for him! Oh, and do stay on for dinner, if you feel like it,' she called after Pierre.

Pierre met the old count. He seemed nervous and upset. That morning Natasha had told him she had broken off her engagement to Bolkonsky.

'Trouble, nothing but trouble, my dear fellow,' he said to Pierre, 'when these girls are away from their mother. I'm sorry I ever came. I won't beat about the bush. Maybe you've heard – she's broken off her engagement without a word to a soul. I must admit I never did like the idea of them getting married. Oh, I know he's a fine man, but there was never going to be much happiness with them going against his father like that, and Natasha will never be short of suitors. Still, it had been going on for such a long time . . . but how could she do such a thing without a word to her father and mother? And now she's ill, and God knows what's wrong with her. It's an awful thing, Count, a really awful thing to take your daughters away from their mother . . .'

Pierre could see the count was terribly upset, and he kept trying to change the subject but the count came back time and again to his woes.

Sonya came into the drawing-room, long in the face.

'Natasha's not too well. She's up in her room and would like to see you. Marya Dmitriyevna's with her and she wants you there too.'

'Yes, of course, you're such a great friend of Bolkonsky's. She probably wants to send him a message,' said the count. 'Oh dear, oh dear! Everything was going so well!' And the count walked out of the room clutching at his few grey hairs.

Marya Dmitriyevna had told Natasha that Anatole was already married. Natasha didn't believe her, and insisted on confirmation from Pierre's own lips. Sonya told Pierre this much as she led him down the corridor to Natasha's room.

Natasha was sitting beside Marya Dmitriyevna, looking pale and serious, and she met Pierre at the door with a quizzical glare of feverish intensity. She neither smiled nor nodded, she just stared at him and her look asked a simple question: was he a friend or an enemy like the rest of them, as far as Anatole was concerned? Pierre the man clearly didn't exist for her.

'He knows the whole story,' said Marya Dmitriyevna to Natasha. 'Let him say whether I'm telling the truth or not.'

Like a wounded animal at bay watching the dogs and the hunt close in, Natasha looked from one to the other.

'Natalya,' Pierre began, looking down with a feeling of pity for her and revulsion at the operation he had to perform, 'true or not, what difference does it make? You see . . .'

'So it's not true that he's married?'

'I'm afraid it is.'

'He *is* married! Since when?' she asked. 'Word of honour?'

Pierre swore on his word of honour.

'Is he still here?' she gabbled.

'Yes. I saw him a few minutes ago.'

Speech being clearly beyond her, she gestured with both hands for them to go away and leave her alone.

CHAPTER 20

Instead of staying to dinner Pierre drove away immediately after leaving Natasha's room. He scoured the town in search of Anatole Kuragin. At the very thought of this man the blood rushed to his heart and he could hardly breathe. He was nowhere to be found, not on the ice-hills, not at the gypsies', not at Comoneno's. Pierre drove to the club. In there it was just like any normal day with members coming in for dinner and sitting around in groups. They greeted Pierre and went on talking about the city and the latest news. A footman well accustomed to Pierre's friends and habits greeted him, and said several things: a place had been left for him in the small dining-room, Prince Mikhail Zakharych was in the library, and Pavel Timofeich had not yet come in. One of Pierre's acquaintances broke off from chatting about the weather to ask if he'd heard about Kuragin's abduction of young Countess Rostov, which was the talk of the town, but was it true? Pierre laughed it off as a bit of nonsense, having just come from the Rostovs'. He asked after Anatole; one man said he wasn't in yet, another said he was expected for dinner. It felt strange for Pierre to look round at that quiet crowd of uninvolved people, who had no knowledge of what turmoil his spirit was going through. He wandered from room to room, waited for everyone to arrive, and then, with no sign of Anatole, he abandoned dinner and set off for home.

His prey, Anatole, was dining that day with Dolokhov, and the pair of them were trying to work out how the plan that had ended in failure could be made to succeed. According to Anatole it was vital for him to see Natasha, so that evening he went round to his sister's to discuss with her how another meeting could be arranged. When Pierre got back home after his fruitless tour of the city his valet told him that Prince Anatole was in with the countess. The countess's drawing-room was full of guests.

Pierre completely ignored his wife even though he hadn't seen her since his return – at that moment he loathed her more than ever – strode into the drawing-room, spotted Anatole and went over to him.

'Oh, hello, Pierre,' said the countess, coming over to her husband. 'You've no idea what a predicament our Anatole finds himself in . . .' She stopped short at the sight of her husband's lowered head, the fire in his eye, the resolute tread – she had recognized the look of towering rage and dreadful power that she knew only too well from personal experience following the duel with Dolokhov.

'Wherever you are, there's bound to be vice and evil,' said Pierre to his wife. 'Anatole, come with me. I want a word with you,' he said in French. Anatole glanced round at his sister, but got to his feet compliantly, ready to follow Pierre.

Pierre grabbed him by the arm, jerked him forwards and walked out of the room.

'Please, not in my drawing-room . . .' Hélène whispered, but there was no response from Pierre. He had gone.

Anatole followed on with his usual jaunty swagger. But there was an uneasy look on his face. Pierre went into his room, shut the door behind them and spoke to Anatole without looking at him. 'Did you tell Countess Rostov you would marry her? Did you try to elope with her?'

'My dear fellow,' answered Anatole, in French (as was the whole conversation), 'I do not feel obliged to answer questions addressed to me in that tone of voice.'

Pierre's face, already pale, was now contorted with rage. With one huge hand he grabbed Anatole by the collar of his uniform, and proceeded to shake him from side to side until a sufficient degree of terror had registered on his face.

'When I say *I want a word with you* . . .' Pierre insisted.

'I say. This is ridiculous, isn't it?' said Anatole, fingering his collar where a button had been ripped away with a piece of cloth.

'You're a vile swine, and I have no idea what prevents me from permitting myself the pleasure of braining you with this,' said Pierre. (The awkwardness of his speech was because it was in French.) He had picked up a heavy paperweight and was now wielding it ominously, but he soon put it back down again.

'Did you promise to marry her?'

'I, er . . . I never thought . . . I didn't actually, er . . . because . . .'

Pierre cut him short.

'Have you got any letters from her? Have you got any letters?' Pierre repeated his question, bearing down on Anatole. Anatole took one look at him, stuffed his hand in his pocket and took out a wallet.

Pierre took the proffered letter, shoved a table out of the way and flopped down on the sofa.

'Don't worry, I'm not going to get violent,' said Pierre in response to Anatole's gesture of alarm. 'Letters – that's number one,' said Pierre like a child going through a lesson. 'Number two –,' he went on after a moment's silence, getting to his feet again and starting to pace up and down, 'you're leaving Moscow tomorrow.'

'But how can I? . . .'

'And three . . .' Pierre ignored him and went on, 'you never breathe a word of what went on between you and the young countess. I know I can't stop you, but if you have a grain of conscience . . .'

Pierre paced up and down the room several times without saying anything. Anatole sat there at the table, scowling and biting his lips.

'When all's said and done surely you can get it into your head that there is such a thing as other people's happiness and peace of mind beyond your own pleasure – can't you see you're ruining someone's whole life just for a bit of fun? Go and amuse yourself with women like my wife. You're within your rights there – they know what you want from them. They're armed against you because they've experienced the same kind of depravity, but promising marriage to a young girl, pulling the wool over her eyes, carrying her off! . . . Can't you see – it's so sordid, it's like attacking an old man or a child! . . .'

Pierre paused and glanced at Anatole, with more curiosity now than anger.

'Well, I'm not too sure about that, you know,' said Anatole, regaining self-confidence as Pierre controlled his fury. 'I'm not too sure about that – and I don't want to be,' he said, avoiding Pierre's eyes and speaking with a slight tremor of the jaw, 'but you've called me names – "sordid" and suchlike – which as a man of honour I can't accept from anyone.'

Pierre looked at him in amazement, at a loss to understand what he could possibly want.

'I know it's all been in private,' Anatole persisted. 'But I'm afraid I can't . . .'

'What is it you want – satisfaction?' said Pierre sarcastically.

'Well, the least you could do is take it back, what? If you're asking me to do what you want. How about that?'

'Yes, yes, I take it all back,' said Pierre, 'and please forgive me.' Pierre couldn't take his eyes off the dangling button. 'Yes, and here's some money too. You might need it for the journey.'

Anatole smiled.

The look on his face, the mean, cringing smile that he knew so well from his wife, was the last straw for Pierre. 'You're a vile and callous breed!' he cried, and stormed out of the room.

Next day Anatole left for Petersburg.

CHAPTER 21

Pierre drove round to let Marya Dmitriyevna know that her wishes had been carried out – Kuragin had been banished from Moscow. The whole house was in a state of turmoil and alarm. Natasha was very poorly and Marya Dmitriyevna told him why on the quiet: once she had been told Anatole was married, that same night she had poisoned herself with arsenic, which she had got hold of by some secret means. After swallowing just a little she had become so scared she had woken Sonya up and told her what she had done. The necessary antidotes had been administered in good time and now she was out of danger, but still too weak even to think of being taken back to the country, and the countess had been sent for. Pierre saw the count in his terrible distress, and Sonya constantly in tears, but he wasn't allowed to see Natasha.

That day Pierre dined at the club and heard gossip on all sides about the attempted abduction of young Countess Rostov. He strenuously denied all such stories, assuring everyone there was nothing in them beyond the fact his brother-in-law had proposed to Natasha and been refused. It had occurred to Pierre that his duty lay in covering up the whole affair and restoring the young countess's reputation.

He was dreading Prince Andrey's return, but every day he drove round to the old prince to catch up on the latest news about him.

Mademoiselle Bourienne had kept old Prince Bolkonsky abreast of all the rumours flying about the town, and he had read the note to Princess Marya in which Natasha had broken off the engagement. He seemed more cheerful than usual and couldn't wait to see his son again.

A few days after Anatole's departure Pierre received a note from Prince Andrey letting him know he was back and inviting him over.

The first thing his father did when Prince Andrey arrived home in Moscow was hand over Natasha's note to Princess Marya breaking off the engagement. (Mademoiselle Bourienne had filched the note from Princess Marya and handed it on to the old prince.) From his father's lips he heard a rather embellished account of Natasha's elopement.

Prince Andrey had arrived in the evening, and Pierre had come to see him the very next morning. He was expecting to find Prince Andrey in virtually the same state as Natasha, and so it came as a surprise for him to walk into the drawing-room and hear the sound of Prince Andrey's voice in the study, holding forth enthusiastically on the subject of some affair going on up in Petersburg. The old prince and some other voice kept cutting across him from time to time. Princess Marya came out to meet Pierre. She sighed, looking back towards the door of the room where Prince Andrey was talking, in an obvious gesture of sympathy for him in all his grief, but Pierre could tell from her face that she was pleased by what had happened and also by her brother's acceptance of his fiancée's unfaithfulness.

'He says he's been expecting it,' she commented. 'I know his pride won't let him tell us what he feels, but I must say he's taken it better, far better, than I ever expected. It obviously wasn't meant to be . . .'

'So it really is all over, is it?' said Pierre.

Princess Marya looked at him in some surprise, genuinely at a loss to understand how anyone could ask a question like that. Pierre went on into the study. Prince Andrey had changed a good deal and looked altogether healthier, but there was a new furrow running down between his brows. He stood there dressed in civilian clothes, arguing vehemently face to face with his father and Prince Meshchersky, and making bold gestures.

The topic of conversation was Speransky, news of whose sudden banishment and alleged treachery had just broken in Moscow.

'Now he's being criticized and censured by people who were raving about him only a month ago,' Prince Andrey was saying, 'and by other people incapable of understanding what he's been aiming at. It's too easy to criticize a man when he's out of favour, and make him shoulder the blame for everybody else's mistakes. But I tell you this: if any good has been done in the present reign it's been done by him, and him alone . . .' He saw Pierre and stopped. His face twitched and took on a nasty look. 'And posterity will see justice done to him,' he said, winding things up before turning to Pierre.

'Now then, how are you? Still putting the weight on?' he said with some warmth, though the new furrow had etched itself deeper still on his forehead. 'Yes, I'm very well,' he said, responding to Pierre's inquiry with a smile. Pierre could see all too clearly what his smile meant: 'I'm very well, but nobody's bothered about the state of my health.'

After commenting on the dreadful state of the road from the Polish frontier, and mentioning some people he had met in Switzerland who knew Pierre, and talking about Monsieur Dessalles, whom he had brought from Switzerland to be his son's tutor, Prince Andrey plunged eagerly back into the conversation about Speransky, which was still preoccupying the two old gentlemen.

'If there had been any treachery, and any proof of a secret relationship with Napoleon, this would have come out in public,' he was quick to argue, with no little passion. 'Personally I don't much care for Speransky – I never did – but I do care for justice.'

Pierre now recognized in his friend something he knew only too well, a need to get involved in a heated dispute about some neutral topic, purely to drown out thoughts that were too near the heart and too painful.

When Prince Meshchersky had gone, Prince Andrey seized Pierre by the arm and took him along to the room that had been prepared for him. A bed had been made up and open trunks and cases stood around. Prince Andrey went over to one of them and took out a box. Out of the box he took a bundle of letters. All this he did very rapidly and in silence. Then he got to his feet again and cleared his throat. There was a scowl on his face, and his lips were set.

'I'm sorry to trouble you . . .' Pierre could see that Prince Andrey wanted to talk about Natasha, and his broad face glowed with sympathy and pity. It was an expression that infuriated Prince Andrey, and although he carried on talking his tone was clipped, sharp and bad-tempered. 'I've received a rejection from Countess Rostov, and I've heard rumours about your brother-in-law seeking her hand, or something like that. Is it all true?'

'Well, it is and it isn't,' began Pierre, but Prince Andrey cut him short.

'Here are her letters,' he said, 'and her portrait.' He picked up the little bundle and handed it to Pierre.

'Give this to the countess . . . if you happen to see her.'

'She's very ill,' said Pierre.

'Oh, so she's still here?' said Prince Andrey. 'And what about Prince Kuragin?' he snapped.

'He left a long time ago. She's been at death's door.'

'I'm very sorry to hear of her illness,' said Prince Andrey. He laughed a cold, harsh, nasty laugh not unlike his father's.

'So Mister Kuragin has not bestowed his hand on Countess Rostov?' said Prince Andrey. He snorted several times.

'He couldn't have married her, because he's married already,' said Pierre. Prince Andrey gave another nasty laugh, again recalling his father. 'And where is he now, your brother-in-law, may I ask?' he said. 'He's gone to Peters . . . oh, I really don't know,' said Pierre.

'Well, it's not important,' said Prince Andrey. 'Please tell Countess Rostov from me that she was and is perfectly free, and I send my best wishes.'

Pierre took the bundle with both hands. Prince Andrey, as if trying to remember whether he had anything more to add, or half-waiting for Pierre to come out with something, looked at him steadily.

'Listen. Do you remember that difference of opinion we had in Petersburg?' said Pierre. 'Remember what we . . . ?'

'Yes, I do,' Prince Andrey answered hastily. 'I said that a fallen woman should be forgiven, but I didn't say I could forgive her, and I can't.'

'Surely, there's no comparison, is there?' asked Pierre.

Prince Andrey cut him short. He cried harshly, 'Oh yes, go and ask for her hand again, be magnanimous, all that sort of thing? . . . Well, that's all very noble, but I'm not up to following on in that gentleman's tracks. And if you value my friendship, don't talk to me ever again about that . . . well, all this business. Goodbye then. You will hand that on? . . .'

Pierre left him, and went in to see the old prince and Princess Marya.

The old man seemed livelier than usual. Princess Marya was just the same as ever, but through all her sympathy for her brother Pierre could see she was delighted that his marriage plans had collapsed. Looking at them, Pierre could sense the degree of contempt and antipathy all three of them felt for the Rostovs, and he realized that from now on in their presence it would be impossible even to mention the name of a girl capable of giving up Prince Andrey for anyone else in the world.

Over dinner they talked about the war that was clearly coming. Prince Andrey never stopped talking and arguing, first with his father then with Dessalles, the Swiss tutor, and although he seemed more animated than usual Pierre well knew the deeply hidden cause that lay behind all the animation.

CHAPTER 22

That evening Pierre called at the Rostovs' to carry out Prince Andrey's commission. Natasha was in bed, the count was out at the club, and Pierre, once he had handed the letters over to Sonya, went in to see Marya Dmitriyevna, who was keen to hear how Prince Andrey had taken the news. Ten minutes later Sonya came in to speak to Marya Dmitriyevna.

'Natasha insists on seeing Count Bezukhov,' she said.

'Well, we can't take him upstairs, can we? I mean, you're not very tidy up there,' said Marya Dmitriyevna.

'No, she's put some clothes on and come down to the drawing-room,' said Sonya.

Marya Dmitriyevna could only shrug. 'Oh, how long till the countess comes? I'm quite worn out with her. Listen, keep some of it back,' she said to Pierre. 'One hasn't the heart to scold her, she's so pathetic, poor thing.'

Natasha was standing in the middle of the drawing-room, looking pale, composed and much thinner (though hardly the picture of contrition that Pierre had expected). When Pierre appeared in the doorway she lurched forward a little, clearly unsure whether to walk over to greet him or wait for him to come across to her.

Pierre hurried over. He was expecting her to offer her hand as usual but instead she came close and stopped in front of him, breathing hard and letting her arms dangle down lifelessly, in the very pose she had so often taken up in the middle of the hall when she was about to sing, except that the look on her face was quite different.

'Count Bezukhov,' she began, gabbling her words, 'Prince Bolkonsky was your friend. Well, he still is,' she corrected herself. (She thought of everything as belonging to the past, and now quite different.) 'He once told me I should turn to you . . .'

Pierre looked at her, speechless and choking. Until then he had reproached her in his heart, and made every effort to despise her, but now he felt so sorry for her there was no room in his heart for reproach.

'He's back now. Please ask him . . . to for . . . forgive me.' She stopped short and her breath came even faster, but she wasn't weeping.

'Yes . . . I will tell him,' said Pierre, 'but . . .' He didn't know how to go on.

Natasha was visibly alarmed at a certain idea that might well have occurred to Pierre.

'No, I know it's all over,' she hastened to say. 'No, it can't ever happen now. What upsets me is the harm I've done to him. There's only one thing I ask – I want him to forgive me, forgive me, forgive me for everything . . .' Her whole body was convulsed. She sat down on a chair.

Pierre felt a heart-breaking surge of pity for her, the like of which he had never known before.

'Yes, I will tell him, I'll go through it all again,' said Pierre. 'But . . . well, there's just one thing I'd like to know . . .'

'What's that?' was the question in Natasha's eyes.

'I'd like to know whether you were in love with . . .' Pierre didn't know what to call Anatole, and he coloured up at the very thought of him, 'with that vile man.'

'Please don't call him vile,' said Natasha. 'I don't . . . know. I just don't know . . .' She burst into tears again, and Pierre was overwhelmed with an even stronger sensation of pity, tenderness and love. He could feel tears trickling down under his spectacles, and hoped no one would see them.

'We won't say another word about it, my dear girl,' he said. His voice was so gentle, tender and full of feeling that it had a strange effect on Natasha. 'Not another word, my dear. I'll tell him everything. I'll just ask you one thing: please look on me as a friend, and if you ever need any help or advice, or if you just want to pour out your soul to somebody – not now, but when you've had a chance to get things clear – please think of me.' He took her hand and kissed it. 'I'll be only too happy to . . .' Pierre was suddenly embarrassed.

'Don't talk to me like that. I'm not worth it!' cried Natasha, and she made as if to leave, but Pierre held her back by the arm. He knew he had more to say. But when he spoke he was surprised at the way it came out.

'Hush, don't say things like that. You have your whole life ahead of you,' he told her.

'Oh no I don't! It's all gone wrong for me,' she said, full of shame and humiliation.

'All gone wrong?' he repeated. 'If I was somebody else, the handsomest, the cleverest, the best man in the world, and if I were free, I'd be down on my knees right now begging for your hand and your love.'

For the first time in many days Natasha wept tears of gratitude and emotion as she took a quick glance at Pierre and walked out of the room.

Pierre went out after her, almost running down to the vestibule, fighting down tears of affection and happiness that gave him a lump in his throat. He flung his fur coat over his shoulders, unable to find his way into the sleeves, and got into his sledge.

'Where to now, your Excellency?' asked the coachman.

'Where to?' Pierre asked himself. 'Where can I go? I can't face the club or visiting people.' All of humanity seemed so pathetically poor compared with the tenderness and love that he now felt, compared with the new softness and gratitude shown by Natasha as she had turned at the last moment and glanced at him through her tears.

'Home,' said Pierre, defying ten degrees of frost by flinging aside the bearskin coat from his great chest and taking in deep, joyous lungfuls of air.

It was clear and frosty. A dark, starlit heaven looked down on the black roofs and the dirty, dusky streets. Only by looking up at the sky could Pierre distance himself from the disgusting squalor of all earthly things as compared with the heights to which his soul had now been taken. As he drove into the Arbat a vast firmament of darkness and stars opened out before Pierre's eyes. And there in the middle, high above Prechistensky Boulevard, amidst a scattering of stars on every side but catching the eye through its closeness to the earth, its pure white light and the long uplift of its tail, shone the comet, the huge, brilliant comet of 1812, that popular harbinger of untold horrors and the end of the world. But this bright comet with its long, shiny tail held no fears for Pierre. Quite the reverse: Pierre's eyes glittered with tears of rapture as he gazed up at this radiant star, which must have traced its parabola through infinite space at speeds unimaginable and now suddenly seemed to have picked its spot in the black sky and impaled itself like an arrow piercing the earth, and stuck there, with its strong upthrusting tail and its brilliant display of whiteness amidst the infinity of scintillating stars. This heavenly body seemed perfectly attuned to Pierre's newly melted heart, as it gathered reassurance and blossomed into new life.

VOLUME III

PART I

The latter part of 1811 saw a new build-up in the concentration and arming of troops in Western Europe, and in 1812 these forces – millions of men if you include those in transport and provisioning – moved from west to east, closing in on the frontiers of Russia, where the Russian forces had been similarly gathering since 1811.

On the 12th of June the forces of Western Europe crossed the Russian frontier, and war began. In other words, an event took place which defied human reason and all human nature. Millions of men set out to inflict on one another untold evils – deception, treachery, robbery, forgery, counterfeiting, theft, arson and murder – on a scale unheard of in the annals of law-courts down the centuries and all over the world, though at the time the men responsible did not think of these deeds as crimes.

What led to this extraordinary occurrence? What causes lay behind it? Historians, in their simple-minded certitude, tell us that the causes of this event were as follows: the violence done to the Duke of Oldenburg; non-observance of the Continental System;[1] Napoleon's megalomania; Alexander's obstinacy; mistakes made by diplomats, and so on.

It follows, then, that all Metternich, Rumyantsev or Talleyrand[2] would have had to do, between getting up in the morning and partying in the evening, was exert themselves just a little and make a nice job of phrasing some diplomatic note, whereupon all Napoleon would have had to do was write to Alexander saying, 'Esteemed brother, I consent to the Duke of Oldenburg having his duchy back,' and there would have been no war.

We can well understand why contemporaries might have seen things that way. We can understand why Napoleon might have attributed the cause of the war to the machinations of the English (indeed, he said as much from St Helena). We can further understand why English members of parliament thought the war had been caused by Napoleon's megalomania; why the Duke of Oldenburg blamed the war on the violence done to him; why those in trade explained the war in terms of the Continental System, which was bringing Europe to its knees; why veterans and old-world generals blamed it all on their being called up for service again; why legitimists of the period would insist on the necessity of getting 'back to basics', and diplomats of the day put it down to the 1809 alliance between Russia with Austria not being properly concealed from Napoleon, plus the clumsy wording of Memorandum No. 178. We can well understand how these – and other causes, endless in number, infinite in their proliferation because of the endless points of view available – might have appeared to contemporaries. But for us, the descendants of these people, as we contemplate this vast accomplishment in all its enormity and seek to penetrate its dreadful simplicity, these explanations seem inadequate. It is beyond our comprehension that millions of Christian men should have killed and tortured each other just because Napoleon was a megalomaniac, Alexander was obstinate, the English were devious and the Duke of Oldenburg was badly done by. We can see no connection between these circumstances and the stark reality of murder and violence; we cannot see how an affront to a duke could have induced thousands of men to rampage through the other end of Europe, slaughtering the inhabitants of Smolensk and Moscow and getting slaughtered in return.

We, their descendants – those of us who are not historians seduced by the pleasures of research and can therefore review events with unclouded common sense – find ourselves faced with an incalculable multiplicity of causes. The more deeply we go into the causes, the more of them there are, and each individual cause, or group of causes, seems as justifiable as all the rest, and as false as all the rest in its worthlessness compared with the enormity of the actual events, and its further worthlessness (unless you combine it with all the other associated causes) in validating the events that followed. For instance, Napoleon's refusal to withdraw his troops beyond the Vistula and restore the Duchy of Oldenburg seems to us no more valid as a cause than the willingness or unwillingness of any old French corporal to serve a second term, for had he refused to serve, and a second and a third and a thousand corporals and soldiers along with him, Napoleon's army would have been reduced by that number and there could have been no war.

If Napoleon had not taken umbrage at the demand for him to withdraw beyond the Vistula and had not given the order to advance, there would have been no war. But if every last sergeant had refused to go back into the army there could have been no war either. And war would also have been impossible if there had been no deviousness from England, no Duke of Oldenburg, no offence taken by Alexander, no autocracy in Russia, no French Revolution with its consequent dictatorship and empire, nor any of those things that led up to the French Revolution, and so on and so forth. If any one of these causes had been missing, nothing could have happened. It follows therefore that all of these causes, billions of them, came together to bring about subsequent events, and these events had no single cause, being bound to happen simply because they were bound to happen. Millions of men, abandoning all human feelings and common sense, were bound to march from west to east and slay their fellows, just as a few centuries ago hordes of men had marched from east to west, slaying their fellows.

The actions of Napoleon and Alexander, whose word seems to have dictated whether anything should or should not happen, were no more self-determined than the actions of any common soldier drafted in by lot or conscription. This has to be so, for one good reason: in order for the will of Napoleon or Alexander (who appear to have dictated events) to prevail, it would have been necessary for a countless number of disparate circumstances to coincide, and without any one of them those events could never have occurred. It was necessary for those millions of men who wielded the real power – soldiers shooting or bringing up supplies and guns – to do what they were told by one or two feeble individuals, and to have been brought to this point by an infinite number of complex and disparate causes.

Historical fatalism is the only possible explanation of irrational phenomena like these (phenomena with a rationale beyond our comprehension). The more we try to explain away such phenomena in rational terms, the more irrational and incomprehensible they become for us.

Each man lives for himself, using his freedom to get what he wants, and he feels with every fibre of his being that at any particular time he is free to perform an action or refrain from doing so, but the moment any action is taken it becomes an irrevocable piece of history, with a significance which has more to do with predetermination than freedom.

There are two sides to life for every individual: a personal life, in which his freedom exists in proportion to the abstract nature of his interests, and an elemental life within the swarm of humanity, in which a man inevitably follows laws laid down for him.

Although on a conscious level a man lives for himself, he is actually being used as an unconscious instrument for the attainment of humanity's historical aims. A deed once done becomes irrevocable, and any action comes together over time with millions of actions performed by other people to create historical significance. The higher a man stands on the social scale, the more contact he has with other men and the greater his impact on them, the more obvious are the inevitability and the element of predestination involved in everything he does.

'The hearts of kings are in the hands of God.'

Kings are the slaves of history.

History – the amorphous, unconscious life within the swarm of humanity – exploits every minute in the lives of kings as an instrument for the attainment of its own ends.

At that time, in the year 1812, Napoleon believed more strongly than ever that it was for him 'to shed or not to shed the blood of his peoples' (as Alexander had put it in his most recent letter), though he was in fact more subject than ever to those laws which forced him, for all his apparent and self-styled freedom of action, to do what had to be done for the world in general, for the sake of history.

The men of the west went east to kill each other. And the law of causal coincidence determined that thousands of minor causes colluded and coincided to produce this movement and the coming war: an angry reaction to non-observance of the Continental System; the Duke of Oldenburg; the advance into Prussia, undertaken, as Napoleon saw it, solely in the interests of securing an armed peace; the French Emperor's taste and passion for going to war, which caught the mood of his people; the excitement of preparing things on a grandiose scale; the vast expenditure on such preparations, and the necessity of getting something back for one's money; the dizzying effect of honours given and received in Dresden; all those diplomatic negotiations which were then seen as directed by a genuine desire for peace, though all they did was wound people's self-esteem on both sides; along with millions and millions of other causes, colluding and coinciding with each other to produce the impending events.

When a ripe apple falls, what makes it fall? Is it gravity, pulling it down to earth? A withered stalk? The drying action of the sun? Increased weight? A breath of wind? Or the boy under the tree who wants to eat it?

Nothing is the cause of it. It is just the coming together of various conditions necessary for any living, organic, elemental event to take place. And the botanist who finds that the apple has fallen because of the onset of decay in its cellular structure, and all the rest of it, will be no more right or wrong than the boy under the tree who says the apple fell because he wanted to eat it and prayed for it to fall. Anyone who claims that Napoleon went to Moscow because he wanted to, and eventually lost because Alexander wanted him to lose, will be no more right or wrong than the man who claims that thousands of tons of earth in an undermined hill collapsed because of the last blow from the last pick-axe of the last workman. When it comes to events in history, so-called 'great men' are nothing but labels attached to events; like real labels, they have the least possible connection with events themselves.

Every action they perform, which they take to be self-determined and independent, is in a historical sense quite the opposite; it is inter-connected with the whole course of history, and predetermined from eternity.

CHAPTER 2

On the 29th of May Napoleon left Dresden, where he had spent three weeks surrounded by a court made up of princes, dukes, kings and even an emperor. Before leaving, Napoleon spoke pleasantly to the princes, kings and emperor who had earned his favour, and unpleas-antly to the kings and princes who had not quite come up to scratch. He presented the Empress of Austria with some diamonds and pearls of his own (which means stolen from other kings). He warmly em-braced his Empress, Marie-Louise, who thought of herself as his wife despite the existence of another one back in Paris, and left her behind, as his historian tells us, deeply distressed by the almost unendurable separation. With the diplomats still believing firmly in the possibility of peace and working strenuously towards it, and even though the Emperor Napoleon had just written a personal letter to the Emperor Alexander calling him his 'esteemed brother' and assuring him in good faith that he had no wish to go to war and would always treat him with affection and respect, he set off to join the army, stopping from time to time to issue further instructions guaranteed to speed up the eastward march of his men. Surrounded by pages, adjutants and an armed escort, he was travelling in a comfortable carriage drawn by six horses along the Posen–Thorn–Danzig–Königsberg road. In each of these towns he was welcomed by thousands of people with a mixture of enthusiasm and anxiety.

The army was moving from west to east, and he was driven in the same direction by continual relays of six horses. On the 10th of June he caught up with the army and spent the night in specially prepared quarters in the Wilkowiski forest, which belonged to a Polish count.

Next day Napoleon drove on ahead of the army as far as the river Niemen, where he put on a Polish uniform and rode out on to the river bank to find a good place for the crossing of the river.

One glimpse of the Cossacks posted on the far bank and the steppe disappearing into the distance, where, far away, lay the holy city of Moscow, capital of an empire just like the Scythian empire invaded by Alexander the Great, and Napoleon ordered an immediate advance, confounding the diplomats and breaking every last rule of strategy, and next day his troops began crossing the Niemen.

Early on the morning of the 12th of June he came out of his tent, which had been pitched that day on the steep left bank of the Niemen, and watched his troops through a telescope as they poured out of the forest and swarmed over three bridges thrown across the river. The troops knew of the Emperor's presence, and were on the look-out for him. When they caught sight of a figure in a greatcoat and hat standing apart from his suite in front of his tent on the opposite hillside, they threw their caps in the air and shouted, 'Long live the Emperor!' And one after another in an unbroken stream they flowed out of the immense forest that had hitherto concealed them and split up at the three bridges to march across. 'Now we'll get somewhere. He'll warm things up when he gets involved. My God he will! . . . There he is! . . . Long live the Emperor! So this is the Steppe-land of Asia! Nasty bit of country, though. *Au revoir*, Beauché – I'll keep a nice palace for you in Moscow. Goodbye and good luck! . . . Have you seen the Emperor? Long live the Emperor! . . . ror . . . ror! When I'm Governor of the Indies, Gérard, I'll make you Minister for Kashmir – you can count on it. Long live the Emperor! Hurrah! Hurrah! Hurrah! Cossack rabble, look at 'em running away! Long live the Emperor! There he is! Can't you see him? I've seen him twice, as close as you and me. The little corporal . . . Saw him giving the cross to one of the veterans . . . Long live the Emperor!' Voices rang out on all sides, from old and young, people of every character and social standing. And all their faces looked the same, blissfully happy as they set out at last on the long-awaited campaign, glowing with enthusiasm and devotion to the man in the grey coat up on the hill.

On the 13th of June Napoleon mounted a small thoroughbred Arab horse and galloped down towards one of the bridges over the Niemen to deafening roars of acclamation, which he obviously had to put up with, because there was no way of silencing men determined to express their love for him by roaring their heads off. But all this shouting, which accompanied him wherever he went, was hard to bear, and it distracted him from the military considerations that had dogged him ever since he had joined up with the army. He rode across a bobbing pontoon bridge to the other side of the river, turned sharp left and galloped off towards Kovno, preceded by ecstatic horse guards breathless with delight as they galloped on ahead to clear the way. When he got to the broad river Wilja, he pulled up alongside a regiment of Polish uhlans deployed on the bank.

'Long live the Emperor!' roared the Poles with the same kind of wild enthusiasm, breaking ranks and jostling to get a glimpse of him. Napoleon took a long look up and down the river, got off his horse and sat down on a log lying on the bank. At a silent signal from him he was handed a telescope, which he rested on the back of a page only too pleased to run over and help. After studying the far bank he looked down and concentrated all his attention on a map spread out between the logs. Without looking up again he said something, and two of his adjutants galloped off towards the Polish uhlans.

'What was that? What did he say?' came the cry from the Polish ranks as an adjutant galloped over to them. The order was to find a fording-place and cross the river. The elderly Polish colonel, a fine figure of a man, blushed and stammered from sheer excitement as he asked permission to swim straight across the river without bothering to find a ford. In fear and trembling at the very thought of a refusal, like a little boy asking permission to get on a horse, he asked them to let him swim across the river before the Emperor's eyes. The adjutant told him the Emperor would probably not be displeased at such an excessive display of zeal.

The words were hardly out of his mouth when the old officer, with his big bristling moustache, radiant face and gleaming eyes, brandished his sabre in the air with a loud 'Long live the Emperor!', ordered his men to follow, put spurs to his horse and galloped off down to the river. Once there he gave a vicious kick to a reluctant horse, and plunged into the depths, heading out into the fastest part of the river. Hundreds of uhlans galloped down and followed him in. Out in the middle of the fast-flowing current it was shockingly cold. The uhlans were soon sliding off their horses and clinging on to one another. Some of the horses were drowned, and so were some of the men, while the others struggled to swim across, clinging to the saddle or hanging on to their horse's manes. They swam forward manfully, and although there was a crossing-place only a few hundred yards away they were proud to swim on and drown in the river under the eyes of that man sitting on the log who wasn't even watching what they were doing. When the adjutant, back with the Emperor, picked his moment and bravely drew attention to the Poles' devotion to his Majesty, the little man in the grey coat got to his feet, summoned Berthier, and began pacing up and down the bank with him, issuing instructions and glancing sourly from time to time at the drowning uhlans, who were proving such a distraction.

This was nothing new for him; he needed no reminding that his presence anywhere on earth, from Africa to the steppe-land of Muscovy, always had the same devastating effect on men, sometimes driving them to acts of madness and self-sacrifice. He sent for his horse and rode back to his quarters.

Some forty uhlans had drowned in the river even though boats had been sent out to help. Most of them struggled back to this side. The colonel and one or two of his men did manage to swim right across and scramble out on the other bank. And their first thought on clambering out, with their soaking clothes flapping and streaming, was to roar, 'Long live the Emperor!' and look back in triumph at the place where Napoleon had been standing. He was no longer there, but for one moment they thought that happiness was theirs.

That evening between the issuing of two orders – one for speeding up the arrival of counterfeit rouble notes printed for circulation in Russia, and the other for the execution of a Saxon caught with a letter on him containing a report on the disposition of the French troops – Napoleon issued a third instruction: the colonel who had charged into the river for no good reason was to be enrolled in the Legion of Honour, of which Napoleon himself was the head.

As Euripides once said, 'Those whom God wishes to destroy he first drives mad.'

CHAPTER 3

Meanwhile the Russian Emperor had been living in Vilna for more than a month, inspecting the troops and observing manoeuvres. Nothing was ready for the war that everyone was expecting, and the Tsar had come from Petersburg to help prepare for it. There was no general plan of action. Hesitancy over the need to adopt one plan from the many that had been proposed was worse than ever at the end of the Tsar's month at headquarters. Each of the three armies[3] had its own separate commander-in-chief, but there was no commander with over-all authority, and the Tsar showed no sign of undertaking that role himself.

The longer the Tsar stayed on in Vilna, the fewer preparations were made for the war by men grown weary of waiting for it. Every effort of those who surrounded the Tsar seemed to be directed towards ensuring that his Majesty enjoyed himself and forgot all about the coming war.

In June, after a round of balls and other celebrations given by Polish magnates, members of the court and the Tsar himself, it occurred to one of the Polish generals seconded to the Tsar that all the generals on the staff should give a dinner and a ball in honour of his Majesty. The proposal was taken up joyfully on all sides. The Tsar gave his consent. The generals set about raising the money by subscription. The lady considered most likely to appeal to the Tsar was invited to act as hostess for the ball.

Count Bennigsen, a local landowner, offered a house for this cele-bration and the 13th of June was the day fixed for a ball and a dinner, with a regatta and fireworks at Zakreto, Count Bennigsen's country seat.

On the very day when Napoleon ordered his men across the Niemen, and the vanguard of his army pushed the Cossacks aside and crossed the Russian frontier, Alexander spent a long evening at Count Bennigsen's house enjoying the ball given by the generals on his staff.

It was a glittering, happy occasion. According to the connoisseurs rarely had so many beautiful women been gathered together in one place. Countess Bezukhov, one of the Russian ladies who had followed the Tsar from Petersburg to Vilna, was there, and her massive charms – what people liked to call her Russian beauty – put the more dainty Polish ladies in the shade. She got herself noticed, and the Tsar favoured her with an invitation to dance.

Boris Drubetskoy ('one of the boys again', as he liked to put it), having left his wife behind in Moscow, was also there; although not a staff general himself, he had subscribed a large sum towards the ball. Boris was now rich in money and honours, and had no further need of patronage, being on equal terms with the most distinguished men of his generation.

They were still dancing at midnight. Finding herself without a suit-able partner for the mazurka, Hélène herself offered to dance with Boris. They made up the third couple. Boris allowed his cool gaze to stray towards Hélène's naked shoulders, emerging so splendidly from a dark-coloured, gold-embroidered gauze dress, as he chatted about old acquaintances, but, although no one was aware of it, least of all Boris himself, he never took his eyes off the Tsar while he was there in the same room. The Tsar was not dancing; he was standing in the doorway, stopping people at random with the kind of gracious remark that only he could utter.

At the beginning of the mazurka, Boris watched as a staff general, Balashev, one of the Tsar's closest confidants, went over and defied court etiquette by stopping near by while his Majesty was still in conversation with a Polish lady. After saying a few more words to the lady, the Tsar glanced quizzically at Balashev, and then, suddenly aware there must be a good reason for him to behave like this, he nodded gently to the lady and gave Balashev his full attention. The first words were hardly out of Balashev's mouth when a look of astonishment came over the Tsar's face. He took Balashev by the arm and walked across the room with him, unconsciously clearing a swathe several yards wide as people drew back on either side. Boris could see that Arakcheyev's face displayed the same excitement as the Tsar walked away with Balashev. Arakcheyev glanced rather furtively at the Tsar, sniffing with his red nose, and edged forward out of the crowd as if he was expecting the Tsar to turn in his direction. (Boris observed that Arakcheyev, already jealous of Balashev, was annoyed to see any piece of news, let alone something of obvious importance, reach the Tsar without going through him.) But the Tsar and Balashev walked straight past Arakcheyev without noticing him and went out through the door into the illuminated garden. Arakcheyev, grasping his sword and staring around balefully, followed on twenty paces behind.

Boris worked his way through the figures of the mazurka in a state of anguish, wondering what news Balashev could possibly have brought, and how he could find out before anyone else did. When they came to the figure in which he had to choose his ladies, he whispered to Hélène that he wanted to choose Countess Potocka, who seemed to have gone out on to the balcony, and gliding over the dance-floor he flew across to the doorway into the garden, from where he could see the Tsar and Balashev coming back on to the terrace, and this stopped him in his tracks. The Tsar and Balashev were heading for the doorway. Boris bustled about as if he couldn't quite get out of the way, squeezing back respectfully against the door-post with his head bowed. The Tsar was coming to the end of an outburst that made him sound like someone who had been personally offended. 'Entering Russia without declaring war!' he was saying. 'I shall not make peace until every last enemy under arms has left my country.'

Boris had the impression that the Tsar had enjoyed saying these words, and was happy with the way his thoughts had come out, but not at all happy that Boris had overheard them.

'Nobody must know about this!' the Tsar added, with a scowl.

Boris could tell this was directed at him, so he closed his eyes and bowed his head slightly again. The Tsar went back into the ballroom and stayed there for another half-hour or so. Boris had become the first person to hear the news that French troops had crossed the Niemen, which now gave him a golden opportunity to demonstrate for the benefit of certain very important people that he had access to many things that were hidden from others, and thus an opportunity to rise even higher in the esteem of these persons.

The unexpected news that the French had crossed the Niemen was unexpected largely because it came at the end of a month's unfulfilled expectations, and at a ball! At the first moment of indignation and resentment after hearing the news, Alexander had hit on the pronouncement that has since become famous – one that appealed to him as a true expression of his feelings. Returning home after the ball at two in the morning, the Tsar sent for his secretary Shishkov[4] – and told him to write an order to the troops and an open letter to Field-Marshal Prince Saltykov, with the necessary inclusion of words to the effect that he would never make peace until every last enemy under arms had left Russian soil.

Next day the following letter was written, in French, to Napoleon:

Esteemed brother,

I learnt yesterday that, notwithstanding the fidelity with which I have met my obligations towards your Majesty, your troops have crossed the frontiers of Russia, and I have this moment received from Petersburg a note in which Count Lauriston advises me with reference to this invasion that your Majesty has considered himself to be in a state of war with me ever since Prince Kurakin asked for his passports. The reasons given by the Duke of Bassano for refusing to release the passports would never have led me to suppose that this incident could ever have served as grounds for aggression. In point of fact, he never received any authorization for his action, as he himself has acknowledged, and as soon as I was informed of it I immediately acquainted him with the full extent of my disapproval by ordering him to remain in post. If your Majesty is not seeking to shed the blood of our subjects over a misunderstanding of this kind, and will consent to withdraw his troops from Russian territory, I shall disregard what has occurred, and an accommodation between us will be possible. In the contrary case, I shall be compelled to repulse an invasion which has been entirely unprovoked on my side. It is still within your Majesty's power to preserve humanity from the disasters of another war.

I am, etc.,

(Signed) ALEXANDER.

CHAPTER 4

At two o'clock in the morning on the 14th of June the Tsar sent for Balashev, read out his letter to Napoleon, and ordered him to take the letter and deliver it personally to the French Emperor. As he sent Balashev on his way, he repeated his words about not making peace until every last enemy under arms had left Russian soil, and told him he must be *absolutely certain* to communicate those words to Napoleon. The Tsar had not included them in his letter to Napoleon because he felt with his usual sensitivity that any such words would be out of place at a time when one last attempt at conciliation was being made, but he told Balashev he must be absolutely certain to communicate them to Napoleon in person.

Balashev rode off in the early hours of the 14th, with a bugler and two Cossacks in attendance, and by dawn he had reached the French outposts at the village of Rykonty on the Russian side of the Niemen. He was stopped by the French cavalry sentries.

A French hussar subaltern in crimson uniform and shaggy cap challenged Balashev and told him to stop. Balashev did not do so immediately, but came on along the road at walking pace.

The subaltern scowled, swore under his breath, turned his horse front on towards Balashev, laid a hand on his sword and inquired with a coarse shout whether the Russian general was deaf and couldn't hear what people were saying. Balashev gave his name. The subaltern dispatched a soldier to his superior officer.

Completely ignoring Balashev, the subaltern fell into conversation with his comrades about regimental matters, not even glancing across at the Russian general. It was a very peculiar sensation for Balashev, accustomed as he was to all the courtesies of office close to the highest power and authority – scarcely three hours before he had been conversing with the Tsar himself – to stand here on Russian soil and watch this hostile, and, worse still, disrespectful, display of brute force.

The sun was just emerging from some dark clouds; the air was fresh and dewy. A herd of cattle was being driven along the road from the village. Across the fields, one after another, larks were popping up trilling and rising like bubbles in water.

Balashev looked all round, expecting an officer to ride out from the village. The Russian Cossacks, the bugler and the French hussars glanced at each other now and then in silence.

A French colonel of hussars, evidently fresh from his bed, came riding up from the village on a handsome sleek grey horse, accompanied by two hussars. The officers, the soldiers and the horses all had a swaggering smugness about them.

This was the earliest stage of a campaign, when the troops were still in a state of peaceful activity and good order, virtually ready for parade, with the right touch of military stylishness in their dress and the spirited bravado that always accompanies the start of a campaign.

Despite a struggle to suppress his yawns the French colonel was courteous enough, and the full significance of Balashev's arrival was not lost on him. He conducted him through the lines and informed him that his wish for an audience with the Emperor was likely to be immediately satisfied, since he had been led to believe the Emperor's quarters were not too far away.

They rode through the village of Rykonty, past French tethered horses, sentries and soldiers, who saluted their colonel, goggling at the sight of a Russian uniform. They came out on the other side of the village, and the colonel told Balashev they were not much more than a mile from the divisional commander, who would receive him and take him on to his destination.

The sun was now well up in the sky, shining merrily down on the bright green countryside.

They had just passed an inn on an uphill slope when a group of horsemen came riding down towards them led by a tall figure of a man sporting a plumed hat, a scarlet cloak, and shoulder-length black hair. His black horse bore trappings that glittered in the sun and he rode in the French manner, sticking his long legs out in front. This rider bore down on Balashev, ablaze in the bright June sunshine and aflutter with feathers, jewellery and gold lace trimmings.

This stately and theatrical galloping rider, a mass of bracelets, plumes, necklaces and gold, was within a couple of horse-lengths of Balashev when Julner, the French colonel, said to him in an awe-struck whisper, 'The King of Naples'.[5] It was actually General Murat, but he was now called the 'King of Naples'. It was beyond all understanding how he could have become the King of Naples, but that was what they had called him and he, far from entertaining any doubts, behaved with more stateliness and gravity than ever before. He was so convinced of his standing as the King of Naples that when some Italians shouted 'Long live the King!' as he walked the streets with his wife just before leaving Naples, he turned to her with a poignant smile and said, 'These poor people, they don't know I'm leaving them tomorrow.'

But despite his firm belief that he was King of Naples, and his sympathy for his subjects in their grief at losing him, in recent days, after he had been ordered back into service, and especially after his meeting with Napoleon at Danzig, when his most eminent brother-in-law had said, 'I have made you a king for you to rule my way, and not yours,' he had resumed his familiar duties with all enthusiasm and now behaved like a well-fed but not overweight stallion feeling the touch of his harness and prancing about in the shafts; festooned with all colours and expensive trinkets, he now galloped the highways of Poland without the slightest idea where he was going or why.

Suddenly catching sight of a Russian general, he made a splendid royal gesture with his head, tossing back his mane of wavy curls, and looked quizzically at the French colonel. The colonel told his Majesty politely about Balashev and his mission, without being able to get his tongue round the name. 'De Bal-macheve!'[6] said the King, sweeping aside the colonel's difficulty by sheer determination, and adding, with regal magnanimity, 'Delighted to make your acquaintance, general.' As soon as the King started speaking more loudly and quickly, his regal bearing deserted him in an instant, and, without noticing it, he lapsed into his natural tone of bonhomie and familiarity. He rested a hand on the withers of Balashev's horse.

'Well, General, it looks very much like war,' he said, ruefully implying that this was a matter that demanded his impartiality. 'Your Majesty,' answered Balashev, 'the Emperor, my master, has no desire for war, and as your Majesty can see . . .' Balashev was ringing all the grammatical changes of 'your Majesty', using the title with the affectation that is inevitable when addressing a personage for whom the title in question is still a novelty.

Murat's face beamed with idiotic smugness as he listened to 'Monsieur de Balacheff'. But royalty imposes obligations. As King and ally, he felt compelled to engage Alexander's envoy in conversation about matters of state. He dismounted, took Balashev by the arm and walked a few steps away from his entourage, who stayed behind waiting patiently, only to pace up and down with him, trying to say serious things. He mentioned that the Emperor Napoleon had been much offended by the demand for the withdrawal of his troops from Prussia, especially since news of the demand had leaked out, thus impugning the dignity of France. Balashev began to say that the demand was in no way offensive, because . . . but Murat cut across him.

'So you don't consider the Emperor Alexander to be the instigator?' he said suddenly, with a pleasant but fatuous smile.

Balashev told him precisely why he thought Napoleon was the war-monger.

'Ah, my dear general,' said Murat, interrupting again. 'I hope with all my heart the Emperors will come to some arrangement, and the war that has started by no desire of mine is brought to an end as soon as possible,' he said in the tone used by servants who want to go on being good friends even though their masters have quarrelled. Changing the subject, he inquired after the health of the grand duke, and recalled a most enjoyable time spent with him in Naples. Then, suddenly aware once again of his regal standing, Murat drew himself up into the splendid pose he had adopted for his coronation, and said with a wave of his right arm, 'I will detain you no longer, General. I wish you every success in your mission.' And, awhirl with plumes and embroidered scarlet cloak, and glinting with jewellery, he rejoined his patiently waiting entourage.

Balashev rode on, fully expecting from what Murat had said that he would be presented to Napoleon himself in no time at all. But instead of being taken straight to Napoleon he was detained at the entry to the next village by sentries from Davout's infantry corps, just as he had been at the front line, and an adjutant of the corps commander was summoned to take him into the village for a meeting with Marshal Davout himself.

CHAPTER 5

Davout was Napoleon's Arakcheyev, without his cowardice, but just as demanding and cruel as Alexander's Arakcheyev, and equally incapable of expressing his devotion by anything other than viciousness.

The organism of any state needs men like these in the way that the organism of nature needs wolves, and they are always there, showing themselves and holding their own, no matter how incongruous their presence and proximity to the head of the state may seem. This law of inevitability is the only way of explaining the fact that such a vicious man, capable of ripping out grenadiers' moustaches yet running scared of all danger because of his nerves, a man as uncultivated and boorish as Arakcheyev, managed to enjoy lasting authority alongside a sovereign like Alexander, with all his gentle, chivalrous and noble character.

Balashev found Davout sitting on a tub in the indoor shed of a peasant's hut. He was busy writing, checking some accounts. An adjutant stood at his side. Better quarters could have been found, but Marshal Davout was one of those people who deliberately get themselves into the gloomiest circumstances in order to have the right to be gloomy. For the same reason they are always pressed for time and overburdened with work. 'Oh, it's all right for you thinking about the bright side of life, but look at me sitting on this tub in a filthy shed, hard at work!' said the expression on his face.

The greatest pleasure and sole requirement of people like this when they come across someone enjoying a busy life is to throw their own plodding and gloomy activity straight in his face. Davout allowed himself this pleasure when Balashev was brought before him. He plunged deeper into his work when the Russian general came in, though he did glance up through his spectacles at Balashev's face, a picture of excitement deriving from the loveliness of the morning and his talk with Murat; he did not rise, he did not budge, but he darkened his scowl with a nasty sneer.

Noting that Balashev's face had fallen at this reception, Davout looked across and asked him icily what he wanted.

Balashev could only imagine that he was being received like this only because Davout was unaware that he was a general on Alexander's staff, and his personal representative before Napoleon, so he lost no time in stating his rank and his mission. Against all expectations, when Davout had listened to what Balashev had to say he became even more uncouth and surly.

'Where's your dispatch?' he snapped. 'Give it to me. I'll send it to the Emperor.'

Balashev said he was under orders to hand the document to the Emperor in person.

'Your Emperor's orders are obeyed in your army, but here,' said Davout, 'you'll do as you're told.'

And, as if to make the Russian general even more conscious of being subject to brute force, Davout sent the adjutant to fetch the duty officer.

Balashev took out the packet containing the Tsar's letter and laid it on the table (a table consisting of a door laid across two tubs with the torn-off hinges still dangling from it). Davout took the envelope and read the address.

'You are perfectly at liberty to show me respect or not,' said Balashev, 'but, allow me to observe that I have the honour to serve as a general on his Majesty's staff . . .'

Davout glanced at him without saying a word, obviously delighted to observe signs of emotion and embarrassment on Balashev's face.

'You'll be given appropriate treatment,' he said, before putting the envelope in his pocket and walking out of the barn.

Shortly afterwards an adjutant of the marshal's by the name of Monsieur de Castrés came in and escorted Balashev to the quarters that had been prepared for him.

That day he took dinner in the barn with the marshal at the same 'table' on the tubs.

Next day Davout went off early in the morning, but before doing so he sent for Balashev, and told him in no uncertain terms that he wanted him to stay there, to go on with the baggage-train if ordered to do so, and to talk to nobody but Monsieur de Castrés.

After four tedious days of solitary confinement, with a strong sense of impotence and insignificance all the more agonizing because he had been so recently at the centre of power, and after several relocations along with the marshal's baggage and the French troops, who by now had taken the whole district, Balashev was brought back to French-occupied Vilna, and he re-entered the town by the same gate he had ridden out through four days before.

Next day one of the Emperor's gentlemen-in-waiting, Count Turenne, came to Balashev and told him the Emperor Napoleon was disposed to grant him an audience.

Four days before, sentries of the Preobrazhensky regiment had stood guard in front of the very house to which Balashev was now conducted, and this time two French grenadiers stood there, in their fur caps and blue uniforms open down the front, along with an escort of hussars and uhlans, and a brilliant entourage of adjutants, pages and generals, all waiting for Napoleon to come out, gathered together at the bottom of the steps round his saddle-horse and his Egyptian bodyguard, Rustan. Napoleon was to receive Balashev in the very house in Vilna from which Alexander had sent him on his way.

CHAPTER 6

Balashev, no stranger to imperial pomp, was astounded by the luxury and splendour of Napoleon's court.

Count Turenne led him into a large reception-room, where a number of generals, gentlemen-in-waiting and Polish magnates were waiting patiently, many of them people Balashev had seen at the court of the Russian Emperor. Duroc told him the Emperor Napoleon would receive the Russian general before going out for his ride.

Balashev was kept waiting for a few minutes before a gentleman-in-waiting came into the great room, bowed politely and walked off again, inviting him to follow.

Balashev went through into the small reception-room with only one other door, leading into the study, the room where the Russian Emperor had given him his orders and dispatched him. He stood there alone for a couple of minutes waiting. There was a rush of footsteps on the other side of the door, both halves of which were then flung open by a gentleman-in-waiting who came to a halt and stood there respectfully in attendance. In the ensuing silence someone else could be heard moving about in the study with a firm and resolute tread – Napoleon. He had just finished dressing for his ride and was wearing a blue uniform, open over a white waistcoat which covered his round belly, high boots and white doeskin breeches, stretched tightly over fat thighs and stumpy legs. His short hair looked as if it had just been brushed, but one lock had been left curling down in the middle of his broad forehead. His plump white neck stood out sharply against the black collar of his uniform. He smelt of eau-de-cologne. His full, young-looking face with its prominent chin shone with the graciousness of a monarch welcoming a visitor with regal splendour.

He emerged from the study at a quick pace, wobbling as he walked, with his head tilted slightly back. The whole of his tubby, dumpy figure, with his broad, fat shoulders and his chest and belly sticking out whether he liked it or not, had the impressive stateliness of a forty-year-old used to his creature comforts. It was also obvious that today he was in a particularly good mood.

He nodded in acknowledgement of Balashev's deep, deferential bow, walked over to him and started talking immediately like a man who values every moment of his time, and does not stoop to preparing anything in advance because he is confident of always speaking well and saying just what needs to be said.

'Good day to you, General!' he said. 'I have received the Emperor

Alexander's letter brought by you, and I am very pleased to see you.' His large eyes took one glance at Balashev's face, and then he immediately looked straight past him.

It was obvious that Balashev's personality was of no interest to him. Clearly, the only thing that held any interest for him was anything going on in *his own* mind. Nothing outside his person held any significance because, as he saw it, everything in the world was dependent on his will.

'I do not, and did not, desire war, but you have forced me into it. *Even now,*' he continued, emphasizing the phrase, 'I stand ready to receive any explanations you may be able to give me.' And he held forth with a concise and lucid exposition of his reasons for being displeased with the Russian government.

Judging by the tone of gentle restraint and friendliness adopted by the French Emperor, Balashev became quite convinced that he wanted peace and was prepared to negotiate.

'Your Majesty! Emperor and master,' said Balashev, launching into his long-prepared speech the moment Napoleon had stopped talking and had levelled a quizzical look at him, but he felt disconcerted with the Emperor's eyes upon him. 'You look confused. Pull yourself together,' Napoleon seemed to be saying, as he examined Balashev's sword and uniform with the ghost of a smile. Balashev did manage to pull himself together and start speaking. He told him that the Emperor Alexander did not see Kurakin's demand for his passports as sufficient grounds for war, that Kurakin had been acting on his own initiative and without the Tsar's approval, and that the Tsar had no desire for war, and no relations with England.

'Not *yet*,' Napoleon put in, and, as if wary of his own feelings, he frowned and gave a slight nod for Balashev to continue.

After running through all he had been told to say, Balashev asserted that the Emperor Alexander wanted peace, and was prepared to negotiate – on one condition ... At this point Balashev demurred, remembering the words Tsar Alexander had left out of his letter, but had insisted on having included in the open letter to Saltykov, and had instructed Balashev to repeat to Napoleon. Balashev recalled them: '... until every last enemy under arms has left Russian soil,' but he was held back by a feeling of some complexity. He couldn't bring himself to utter those words, however much he wanted to. He faltered and said, '... that all French troops withdraw beyond the Niemen.'

Napoleon could see how uneasy Balashev had been over those last words. The Emperor's face twitched, and his left calf began to pulsate rhythmically. He remained rooted to the same spot and his speech became louder and faster than before. During the ensuing outburst Balashev found himself continually looking down to stare at the pulsating twitch in Napoleon's left calf, which intensified as his voice grew louder.

'I am no less desirous of peace than the Emperor Alexander,' he began. 'I'm the man who has spent eighteen months doing everything possible to obtain it! For eighteen months I have been waiting for an explanation, but before negotiations can begin what demands are placed upon me?' he said with a scowl, stabbing the air with a puffy little white hand by way of a question.

'The withdrawal of your forces beyond the Niemen, sire,' said Balashev.

'Beyond the Niemen?' echoed Napoleon. 'So you now want me to withdraw beyond the Niemen – only beyond the Niemen?' he repeated, looking Balashev straight in the eyes.

Balashev bowed his head respectfully.

Four months before he had been told to withdraw from Pomerania; now they wanted no more than withdrawal beyond the Niemen. Napoleon spun on his heel and started pacing up and down the room.

'You tell me I am required to withdraw beyond the Niemen before negotiations can begin. But you made the same demand two months ago for me to withdraw beyond the Oder and the Vistula, and yet you are still willing to negotiate.'

Silently he paced the floor from one corner of the room to the other and then came to a halt right in front of Balashev. His face seemed to have set hard and his left leg was twitching faster than ever. Napoleon was well aware of his twitch. 'The pulsation in my left calf is a great sign with me,' he would say in days to come.

'Demands like these – for me to abandon the Oder and the Vistula – can be made to a prince of Baden, but not to me!' Napoleon almost shrieked, taking himself by surprise. 'If you gave me Petersburg and Moscow I wouldn't accept conditions like that. Are you saying I started this war? Well, who was the first to go out and join his army? The Emperor Alexander, not me. And here you are offering to negotiate when I have spent millions, when you are an ally of England, and when you're in a weak position – now you offer me negotiations! What's the purpose of your alliance with England? What has she given you?' he snapped. He was obviously no longer concerned with the benefits of a peaceful settlement and the discussion of any such possibility; his sole intention was to demonstrate his own righteousness, his own power, and to demonstrate Alexander's wrongness and error.

His opening words had clearly been intended as an indication of his own advantageous position, and his willingness to negotiate despite it. But here he was in full flow, and the more he talked the less capable he became of controlling what he was saying.

His whole purpose was now clearly centred on the need to exalt himself and insult Alexander, precisely what he had had the least intention of doing at the outset of the interview.

'They tell me you have made peace with the Turks.'

Balashev bent his head in token of affirmation.

'Yes, we have . . .' he began. But Napoleon wouldn't let him go on. He himself was clearly the only person who needed to speak, and on he went with all the volubility and uncontrolled testiness characteristic of spoilt people.

'Yes, I know you've made peace with the Turks without gaining Moldavia or Wallachia. And I would have given your Emperor those provinces just as I gave him Finland. Oh yes,' he went on, 'I gave my promise, and I would have given the Emperor Alexander Moldavia and Wallachia, but now he'll have to do without those fair provinces. He could have joined them on to his empire, and in one reign he would have extended the frontiers of Russia from the Gulf of Bothnia to the Danube delta. Catherine the Great couldn't have done better,' Napoleon declared, getting more and more worked up as he paced the room, and repeating for Balashev's benefit more or less the same words he had used to Alexander himself at Tilsit. 'All of that he would have owed to my friendship. Oh, what a splendid reign! What a splendid reign! . . .' he kept on repeating. He stopped, pulled a gold snuff-box out of his pocket and took a greedy sniff from it. 'What a splendid reign Emperor Alexander's *might have been!*'

He glanced with some pity at Balashev, and since Balashev showed signs of making some comment he hastened to interrupt him again.

'What could he have wanted or looked for that he wouldn't have got from my friendship? . . .' said Napoleon, with a shrug of bemusement. 'But no, he has preferred to surround himself with my enemies. And who precisely?' he went on. 'He has recruited the Steins, Armfeldts, Wintzengerodes and Bennigsens! Stein – a traitor, driven out of his own country; Armfeldt a lecher and conspirator; Wintzengerode a renegade French subject. Bennigsen may be a bit more of a soldier than the rest of them, but he's still useless; he couldn't do anything in 1807, and he must have given your Emperor nothing but terrible memories . . . Granted, if they had the slightest ability they might have been put to some use,' Napoleon went on, his words barely keeping up with the ceaseless torrent of ideas proving his right or his might (the same thing, in his mind), 'but even that's too much to ask! They're useless for war or peace! I hear that Barclay is more capable than the lot of them, but I wouldn't be too sure about that, judging by his first efforts. And what are they doing, what are all these courtiers doing? Pfuel makes propositions, Armfeldt argues, Bennigsen ponders, and when Barclay is brought in to take some action, he can't decide what to do – and time is slipping away. Bagration is the only real soldier. He's a stupid man, but he does have experience, a good eye and some backbone . . . And what part does your young Emperor play in this unseemly mob? They compromise him and make him responsible for everything that happens. A monarch ought not to be with the army unless he's a general,' he said, obviously launching these words as a bare-faced challenge to the Tsar. Napoleon was well aware of Alexander's longing to be a military commander.

'It's a week since hostilities began and you haven't even managed to defend Vilna. You've been split in two and driven out of the Polish provinces. Your troops are complaining . . .'

'No, sir, quite the opposite,' said Balashev, who was having difficulty in assimilating all that was coming at him and keeping up with the verbal pyrotechnics, 'the troops are full of enthusiasm . . .'

'I know all there is to know,' Napoleon cut him short. 'There's nothing I don't know, and I know the number of your battalions as well as I know my own. You have less than two hundred thousand men, and I have three times as many. I give you my word of honour,' said Napoleon, oblivious to the fact that his word of honour carried no weight, 'I give you my word of honour that I have five hundred and thirty thousand men this side of the Vistula. The Turks will be of no use to you; they are good for nothing, which they have proved by making peace with you. The Swedes? They're destined to be ruled by mad kings. They had one king who was mad, and they replaced him with another, Bernadotte,[7] who soon went mad; being a Swede, you would have to be mad to form alliances with Russia.'

Napoleon gave a nasty laugh, and took another sniff from his snuff-box.

Balashev was waiting with a ready response to every one of Napoleon's phrases. Many times he made as if to reply, but Napoleon always cut him short. For instance, on the subject of Swedish insanity Balashev wanted to say that, with Russia behind her, Sweden was effectively an island, but Napoleon drowned him out with an angry outburst. Napoleon was in such a state of high indignation that he needed to talk, talk, talk in order to prove to himself that he was in the right. Balashev was making heavy weather of it. As an envoy he was anxious not to lose face, and he felt duty-bound to raise objections, but as a man he cringed before the numbing onslaught of mindless fury which had Napoleon in its grip. He was now aware that anything said by Napoleon would be meaningless and an embarrassment to the speaker himself when he eventually pulled himself together. Balashev stood there looking down at Napoleon's fat legs working away, and did all he could to avoid his eyes.

'And what are your allies to me?' said Napoleon. 'I have allies of my own, the Poles, eighty thousand of them and they fight like lions. And soon there'll be two hundred thousand.'

Probably even more annoyed with himself at stretching the truth in such an obvious way and at Balashev standing there before him meekly resigned to his fate and saying nothing, he turned on his heel, strode over to Balashev, gesticulating wildly with his white hands, and almost shouted straight in his face, 'I tell you this – you turn Prussia against me . . . and . . . I tell you this – I'll wipe her off the map of Europe!' he said, his face contorted and white with fury, as he punched one little hand sharply with the other. 'Oh yes, I'll shove you back across the Dvina and the Dnieper, and I'll put back the frontier that Europe was criminal and blind to let you come across. Yes, that's what you've got coming to you. That's what you've gained by alienating me,' he said, and he paced the room in silence several times, his podgy shoulders heaving. He put the snuff-box back into his waistcoat pocket, took it out again, held it to his nose several times, and came to a halt facing Balashev. He paused, stared Balashev straight in the face with a look of mockery and said in a soft voice, 'And to think what a fine reign your master *might have had*.'

Balashev, feeling obliged to respond, told him that from Russia's point of view things did not look so bleak. Napoleon made no comment; he was still sneering and obviously not listening. Balashev said that in Russia they were expecting the war to end well. Napoleon gave a patronizing nod of the head as if to say, 'I know it's your duty to say that, but you don't believe it. My arguments have won you over.'

When Balashev had said his piece Napoleon took out his snuff-box once again, had a good sniff and gave a signal by stamping his foot twice on the floor. The door opened and a gentleman-in-waiting weaved his way in deferentially and handed the Emperor his hat and gloves, while another handed him a pocket-handkerchief. Napoleon ignored them and turned to Balashev.

'Please assure the Emperor Alexander from me,' he said, taking his hat, 'that I am devoted to him as before. I know him thoroughly, and have the highest opinion of his noble qualities. I shall detain you no longer, General. You will receive my letter to the Emperor.' And

Napoleon walked rapidly over to the door. Everyone in the outer reception-room rushed forward and down the stairs.

CHAPTER 7

After everything Napoleon had said to him, after those furious outbursts, and after those acidic last words, 'I shall detain you no longer, General. You will receive my letter,' Balashev felt certain that from now on not only would Napoleon not want to see him again, he would go out of his way to avoid seeing him, an envoy who had been so badly treated, and, more to the point, someone who had witnessed such degrading and intemperate behaviour on his part. But, much to his surprise, Balashev received through Duroc an invitation to dinner that evening with the Emperor.

Bessières, Caulaincourt and Berthier were present at the dinner.

Napoleon welcomed Balashev with a display of good humour and friendliness. Far from showing any signs of embarrassment or self-reproach for his tantrum that morning, he did all he could to put Balashev at his ease. It was clear that Napoleon had convinced himself long before this that he was incapable of error and that everything he did was good, not because it conformed with any general concept of right or wrong, but simply because *he* was the one who did it.

The Emperor was in buoyant mood after his ride through Vilna, where he had been hailed and pursued by cheering crowds. Every window in every street he drove down was hung with rugs and banners displaying his monogram, and welcoming Polish ladies had waved their handkerchiefs at him.

At dinner he placed Balashev at his side and treated him well – treated him in fact like one of his own courtiers, like someone who could be counted on to sympathize with his plans and celebrate his successes. Amongst other things he talked about Moscow, and asked Balashev many questions about the Russian capital, speaking not just out of curiosity like a traveller wanting to know about a new place he intends to visit, but with the certain knowledge that since Balashev was Russian he must be flattered that anyone should be so interested.

'How many people are there in Moscow? How many houses? Is it really known as "Holy Moscow"? Are there many churches in Moscow?' he asked.

And when told there were over two hundred he said, 'Why do you need so many churches?'

'Russians are very religious people,' replied Balashev.

'And yet a large number of monasteries and churches is always a sign of backwardness in a people,' said Napoleon, glancing at Caulaincourt to see what he made of this remark.

With great respect Balashev begged to differ from the French Emperor.

'All countries have their own customs,' he observed.

'But there's nothing like that anywhere else in Europe,' said Napoleon.

'Begging your Majesty's pardon,' said Balashev, 'it's not only Russia. Spain has a large number of churches and monasteries too.' Balashev's reply, a veiled reference to recent French defeats in Spain, proved very popular when Balashev came to repeat it back at the court of the Emperor Alexander, though at the time it was little appreciated at Napoleon's dinner-table, where it passed unnoticed.

From the looks of indifference and bemusement on the faces of the marshals it was clear that they couldn't make head or tail of the witticism implied by Balashev's intonation. 'If this is a joke we don't get the point, or else it's just not very funny,' their expressions seemed to say. The impact of his response was so small that Napoleon did not notice, and he went on naively to ask Balashev which cities lay along the most direct road from there to Moscow. Balashev, always on the qui vive, said that just as all roads lead to Rome, all roads lead to Moscow – there were a lot of roads, including the road to Poltava chosen by Charles XII.[8] Balashev felt an instinctive surge of pleasure at the sharpness of this reply, but the word 'Poltava' was scarcely out of his mouth when Caulaincourt launched forth on the awful state of the road from Petersburg to Moscow and his personal memories of Petersburg.

After dinner they withdrew for coffee into Napoleon's study, which had been Emperor Alexander's study only four days before. Napoleon sat down, toying with his Sèvres coffee cup, and motioned for Balashev to sit down beside him.

There is a well-known after-dinner state of mind which is more effective than the dictates of reason in making a man feel at peace with himself and well disposed to everyone else. Napoleon was now in this state. He felt surrounded by worshipping admirers. He was convinced that after his dinner even Balashev was a friend and admirer. Napoleon turned to him with a benevolent smile which had only a touch of mockery.

'They say this is the room that belonged to the Emperor Alexander. Strange, isn't it, General?' he said, obviously taking it for granted that this comment could not be other than acceptable to the Russian, demonstrating as it did the superiority which he, Napoleon, enjoyed over Alexander.

Balashev, incapable of any response, bowed his head in silence.

'Yes, this is the room where Wintzengerode and Stein were conferring four days ago,' Napoleon went on, smiling the same confident and ironic smile. 'What I can't understand,' he said, 'is why the Emperor Alexander had to surround himself with all my personal enemies. That's something . . . I simply don't understand. Did it never occur to him that I might do the same thing?' he asked Balashev, and this reversion clearly set him off again on the trail of that morning's furious outburst, still fresh in his memory. 'And I want him to know I shall do just that,' said Napoleon, getting to his feet and pushing away his cup with one hand. 'I'll drive every last relative of his out of Germany – all those Württembergs, Badens and Weimars . . . Oh yes, I'll drive them all out. Let him get a bolt hole ready for them in Russia.'

Balashev bowed his head in an effort to imply that he would be glad to take his leave of them, and if he was listening it was only because he had no alternative but to hear what was being said. Napoleon didn't notice his expression. As he spoke to Balashev, he saw him not as an enemy envoy but as one of his devoted admirers who must surely rejoice at the humiliation of his former master.

'And why has the Emperor Alexander taken personal command of his troops? What's all this about? War is my business, but his job is to reign as a monarch, not command armies. What can have induced him to take charge like that?'

Once again Napoleon took out his snuff-box and paced the room several times in silence, only to surprise Balashev by walking rapidly over to him. With the ghost of a smile on his face and in one easy, firm, quick movement, as if he was doing something not merely momentous but also pleasurable to Balashev, he reached up to the forty-year-old Russian general's face, took hold of one ear and tweaked it with a smile on his lips that wasn't in his eyes.

To have your ear tweaked by the Emperor was regarded as the greatest honour and the highest mark of favour at the French court.

'So, you have nothing to say, admirer and courtier of the Emperor Alexander?' he said, as if it was amusing for someone in his company to be a courtier and admirer of anyone who was not Napoleon. 'Are the horses ready for the general?' he added, with a slight nod in acknowledgement of Balashev's bow. 'Give him mine. He has *a long way to go* . . .'

The letter brought back by Balashev was Napoleon's last letter to Alexander. Every last detail of the conversation was communicated to the Russian Emperor, and they were at war.

CHAPTER 8

After his meeting with Pierre in Moscow Prince Andrey went up to Petersburg, telling his family it was a business trip, though in fact he was going there to meet Anatole Kuragin, something that he felt simply had to be done. But when he got to Petersburg and asked after him, Kuragin was gone. Pierre had let his brother-in-law know that Prince Andrey was after him. Anatole Kuragin had lost no time in obtaining a commission from the war minister, and he'd gone off to join the army in Moldavia. But while he was in Petersburg Prince Andrey came across Kutuzov, his old general, who had always had a soft spot for him, and Kutuzov invited him to go with him to Moldavia, where the old general had been placed in command of the army. Once Prince Andrey had received an appointment on the commander's staff he travelled down to Turkey.

Prince Andrey did not think it was right for him to get in touch with Kuragin and challenge him formally. He thought that any challenge from him, without some new pretext for a duel, might compromise young Countess Rostov; so he wanted to meet Kuragin face to face in order to fabricate a different excuse for a duel. But even down in the Turkish army Prince Andrey missed Kuragin, who had gone back to Russia soon after Prince Andrey's arrival. There, in a new country and new surroundings, Prince Andrey found life easier. After his fiancée's unfaithfulness, which hurt him more and more as he strove to conceal the effect it was having on him, the very circumstances that had recently made him so happy now became unbearable, especially the freedom and independence he had come to value so much. He had abandoned those ideas that had first come to him on the battlefield at Austerlitz, the thoughts he had enjoyed discussing with Pierre and had relied on to fill his empty hours first at Bogucharovo, then in Switzerland and Rome, and in fact he now dreaded them and the boundless vistas of light they had once opened up. Now, all he had time for were matters of immediate and practical relevance, quite different from his former interests, and he seized on these with an eagerness that grew in proportion to his success in suppressing the earlier ones. It was as if the infinitely receding firmament that had once arched above him had suddenly turned into a low, fixed vault bearing down on him, perfectly clear but containing nothing eternal or mysterious.

Of all the activities open to him military service was the most straightforward and familiar. He carried out his duties as a staff general with great diligence and enthusiasm, amazing Kutuzov by his appetite for work and his eye for detail. Despite his failure to catch up with Kuragin in Turkey Prince Andrey did not feel impelled to gallop after him back to Russia. Nevertheless, he was certain of one thing: however long it took, whatever his contempt for Kuragin, however many times he could prove to himself that Kuragin wasn't worth stooping to quarrel with, he knew that when they did meet he would be no more able to resist challenging him than a starving man could resist grabbing at food. And it was this continual awareness that the insult had not been avenged, and his heart was still overflowing with unassuaged fury, that poisoned the spurious tranquillity Prince Andrey was managing to enjoy in Turkey by keeping inordinately busy displaying his ambition and expending a great deal of useless energy.

In 1812, when news of the war with Napoleon reached Bucharest (where Kutuzov had spent two months day and night alongside his Wallachian mistress), Prince Andrey asked to be transferred to the western army. Kutuzov, by now thoroughly sick of Bolkonsky's constant activity, which he took personally as an accusation of idleness, was only too ready to let him go, and sent him off with a commission to Barclay de Tolly.

Before joining the western army, which in May of that year was encamped at Drissa, Prince Andrey called in at Bald Hills, which was only a couple of miles off the Smolensk high road and therefore not out of his way. The last three years of Prince Andrey's life had been so full of ups and downs, and he had experienced so much change in outlook, thought and feeling (after many travels in the west and the east), that it seemed weird and amazing to find life going on at Bald Hills exactly as it always had done, down to the last detail. He drove up the avenue to the stone gates of the house like someone approaching a castle sleeping under an enchanter's spell. It was all as staid as ever, with the same cleanliness, the same silence about the house, the same furnishings, the same walls, the same sounds, the same smell and the same timid faces, just a little older. Princess Marya was just the same plain and timid girl, beginning to show her age, watching her best years go by in a state of dread and constant moral affliction, with no sense of benefit or happiness. Mademoiselle Bourienne was the same self-sufficient, flirtatious young girl, enjoying every moment of her life and brimming with happy hopes for the future. But she did seem to have grown in confidence, thought Prince Andrey. The tutor he had brought back from Switzerland, Dessalles, was wearing a coat of Russian cut and he could now converse with the servants in broken Russian, but he was just the same well-intentioned, educated but narrow-minded and nit-picking preceptor. Only one physical change was noticeable in the old prince: he had lost a tooth and the gap showed at one side of his mouth. His character was the same as ever, but his irritability had grown worse, along with his misgivings about the way the world was going. Little Nikolay was the only one who had really changed: he had grown taller, his cheeks were rosier and his hair was a mass of dark curls. When he was happy and laughing he had an unconscious habit of pursing his pretty little mouth and raising his upper lip, just as his dead mother, the little princess, had once done. He was the only who did not conform to the law of no change in this enchanted sleeping castle. But although superficially everything looked the same, deep down the relationships between all the various personalities had altered since Prince Andrey had last observed them. The household was divided into two separate camps who were at daggers drawn, though they had changed their way of living and come together now purely for his benefit. One consisted of the old prince, Mademoiselle Bourienne and the architect; Princess Marya, Dessalles, little Nikolay, along with all the nannies and nurses, made up the other.

During his stay at Bald Hills all the family dined together, but they were ill at ease, and Prince Andrey could sense them making allowances for him as if he was a guest whose presence was an embarrassment. Prince Andrey couldn't help picking this up at dinner on the first day, and he sat at the table saying not a word. The old prince soon noted his strange behaviour and he, too, sat there in sullen silence before stalking off to his room the moment dinner was finished. When Prince Andrey called in to see him later in the evening and tried to stimulate him by talking about young Prince Kamensky and his campaign, the old prince surprised him by launching forth on the subject of Princess Marya, fulminating about her silly superstitions and her dislike of Mademoiselle Bourienne, the only person, according to him, who had his interests at heart.

The old prince would always claim that if he was ill it was Princess Marya's fault; she went out of her way to torment him and make him angry; she was spoiling little Prince Nikolay by being too soft with him and telling him silly stories. The old prince knew only too well he was a torment to his own daughter, and she had a hard life, but he knew just as well that he couldn't help it, and anyway she deserved what she got. 'Prince Andrey can see all this. Why doesn't he say something about his sister?' the old prince was wondering. 'Does he have me down as a villain or an old fool, with no cause to alienate my daughter and take to this Frenchwoman? He has no idea, so I must have things out with him and he's got to listen,' thought the old prince, and he plunged into a lengthy explanation of why he couldn't put up with his daughter's stupidity.

'If you want my opinion,' said Prince Andrey, avoiding his father's eyes (now that he was about to find fault with him for the very first time), 'I wasn't going to say anything, but if you want my opinion I'll be quite candid about the whole thing. If there's any misunderstanding or incompatibility between you and Masha, I don't think it's her fault. I know how she loves you and respects you. If you want my opinion,' Prince Andrey went on, flying off the handle, as he had been doing all too easily in recent days, 'there's only one thing to be said: if there are any misunderstandings, they're caused by that worthless woman, who is no fit companion for my sister.'

The old man's darting eyes settled into a fixed stare directed at his son, and his forced smile revealed the gap of his lost tooth, something Prince Andrey had not yet managed to get used to.

'So, it's companion, is it, my dear fellow? Aha! You've been talking about it, haven't you? Eh?'

'Father, I had no wish to pass judgement,' said Prince Andrey in a hard and bitter tone, 'but you put me up to it, and I've said what I shall always say – it's not Marie's fault, it's other people ... it's that Frenchwoman's fault ...'

'But this is judgement! ... It is judgement!' said the old man in a low voice, and Prince Andrey thought he detected some embarrassment, but suddenly the old man leapt to his feet and yelled at him, 'Get out! Go on, get out of my house!'

Prince Andrey was all for setting off at once, but Princess Marya persuaded him to stay on one more day. During that day Prince Andrey didn't see his father, who stayed in his room and wouldn't let anyone in but Mademoiselle Bourienne and Tikhon, though he kept asking whether his son had gone. Next morning before setting out Prince Andrey went over to his son's part of the house. The little boy, curly-haired like his mother and a picture of good health, sat on his knee. Prince Andrey started telling him the story of Bluebeard, but his mind began to wander before he got to the end. He wasn't thinking about the pretty little boy sitting on his knee who was his son – he was thinking about himself. He cast around in his mind and was horrified not to discover the slightest feeling of remorse for upsetting his father, or any regret at leaving him with bad blood between them for the first time in his life. Worst of all, he also failed to discover in himself any trace of the tender affection he used to feel for his boy, and had hoped to rekindle by cuddling him on his knee.

'Well, go on,' said the little boy. Prince Andrey put him down without a word and walked out of the room.

The moment Prince Andrey had given up his daily pursuits, and especially when he had gone back to the old surroundings in which he had once been so happy, his old world-weariness had returned with all its intensity, and he now felt an urgent need to flee from these memories and find something to do as soon as possible.

'Are you really going, Andrey?' his sister said to him.

'Thank God I can,' said Prince Andrey. 'I'm just sorry you can't.'

'How can you say such a thing?' said Princess Marya. 'How can you say that, when you're off to that awful war, and he's so old? Mademoiselle Bourienne has told me he keeps on asking about you . . .' At the very mention of these things her lips trembled and tears fell from her eyes. Prince Andrey turned away and began to pace up and down the room.

'Oh, my God! My God!' he said. 'Just think . . . what . . . who . . . what trash can cause so much misery!' he said in a venomous outburst that alarmed Princess Marya.

She understood that when he said 'trash' he meant not only Mademoiselle Bourienne, the cause of her misery, but also the man who had ruined his own happiness.

'Andrey, please, one thing I beg of you,' she said, catching him by the elbow and looking at him with eyes shining through tears. 'I understand you.' (She looked down.) 'You mustn't think sorrow is the work of men. Men are His instruments.' Her eyes darted across slightly above Prince Andrey's head; it was the kind of easy, familiar glance with which you glance over to a place where a favourite portrait hangs. 'Sorrow is sent by Him, and not by men. Men are His instruments. The fault is not theirs. If you think someone has done you wrong you must forgive and forget. We have no right to punish others. And you will know the joy of forgiveness.'

'If I was a woman, Marie, I would do that. It's a woman's virtue. But a man must not, and cannot, forgive and forget,' he said, and although until then he had not been thinking of Kuragin, all his unassuaged fury surged up again in his heart. 'Marie's trying to talk

698

VOLUME III, PART I

me into forgiveness – that means I ought to have punished him ages ago,' he thought.

And with no further response to Princess Marya, he let his mind stray to the happy moment of vindictive delight when he caught up with Kuragin. He knew he was in the army.

Princess Marya tried to persuade her brother to stay on for one more day, telling him she knew how miserable her father would be if Andrey went away without patching things up. But Prince Andrey said it probably wouldn't be all that long before he came back again from the army, and he would be sure to write to his father, and if he stayed on now their quarrel would only be more embittered.

'Goodbye, Andrey! Remember – sorrows come from God, and men are never to blame.' These were the last words he heard from his sister as they said their goodbyes.

'That's how it has to be!' thought Prince Andrey as he drove down the avenue leaving Bald Hills behind. 'Poor innocent creature, she has to stay there at the mercy of an old man who has outlived his wits. The old man can tell he's in the wrong, but he can't help it. My boy is growing up and enjoying life, but life will let him down, and he'll let other people down just like everybody else. And I'm off to the army. But why? I don't know, but here I am longing to catch up with a man I despise, to give him a chance to kill me and sneer at me!' He had known circumstances like these before, but then they had been all intertwined, and now they were all unravelled, a series of disparate and senseless eventualities coming upon him one after another.

CHAPTER 9

Prince Andrey reached General Headquarters at the end of June. The first army, with the Tsar attached to it, was encamped at Drissa behind fortifications. The second army was in retreat, attempting to rejoin the first army, from which, according to reports, it had been cut off by huge numbers of French troops. Everyone was dissatisfied with the way things were going in the Russian army, but no one even dreamt that the Russian provinces were in danger of being invaded, or imagined the war might be carried beyond the frontiers of the Polish provinces in the western region.

Prince Andrey caught up with Barclay de Tolly, to whom he was being sent, on the bank of the Drissa. Since there was no large village or settlement anywhere near the camp, the vast numbers of generals and courtiers attached to the army were billeted over a wide area in the best houses of villages scattered along several miles on both sides of the river. Barclay de Tolly's quarters were a couple of miles from the Tsar. His welcoming words were curt and frigid, but he did say in his German accent that he would mention Bolkonsky's name to the Tsar so that he could be given a specific appointment, and meanwhile he was to stay on as a member of his staff. Anatole Kuragin, whom Prince Andrey had hoped to find here, had gone. He was in Petersburg, and Bolkonsky was pleased to hear it. Thoroughly absorbed in being at the centre of a huge, burgeoning war, he was glad to enjoy a brief respite from the vexation caused by the very thought of Kuragin. For four days no demands were made on him so he spent his time riding right around the entire fortified camp, gathering intelligence and talking to people in the know so that he could form a sound overall impression of things. But he couldn't decide whether a camp like this was of any use or not. If he had learnt one lesson from his military experience it was that in matters of war the most carefully considered plans count for nothing (as he had seen at Austerlitz); everything depends on how you react to unexpected and unpredictable enemy action; everything depends on who takes charge, and how. In order to clarify this last question in his own mind Prince Andrey used his rank and his contacts to penetrate the character of army control and any people and parties who had a hand in it. His overall conclusion about how things stood ran as follows.

Before the Tsar had left Vilna the troops had been divided into three armies, one under the command of Barclay de Tolly, a second under Bagration, and a third under Tormasov. The Tsar was with the first army but not as commander-in-chief. In the official announcement there was no mention of his taking command; it was simply stated that the Tsar would remain with the army. Besides that, he was attended not by the staff of a commander-in-chief, but by men of the imperial headquarters.

Quartermaster-General Prince Volkonsky was the head of his staff, which included generals, aides, diplomatic officials and a large number of foreign nationals, and they were not military personnel. The Tsar could also call on the various services of ex-war minister Arakcheyev; Count Bennigsen, his senior general; the Tsarevich, Konstantin Pavlovich; Count Rumyantsev, the chancellor; Stein, the former Prussian minister; Armfeldt, the Swedish general; Pfuel, his chief campaign planner; Adjutant-General Paulucci, a Sardinian émigré; Wolzogen; and many others. These people may have been without specific army duties, but rank carried influence, and it often happened that a corps commander or even a commander-in-chief couldn't tell whether full authority lay behind some recommendation or inquiry from Bennigsen or the Tsarevich or Arakcheyev or Prince Volkonsky, or whether some command in the form of a recommendation came from the individual concerned or from the Tsar, and whether or not it had to be obeyed. But all this was on the surface; the actual significance of the presence of the Tsar and all these men was as clear as crystal to any courtier – and in the presence of a monarch all men become courtiers. It went as follows: although the Tsar refrained from calling himself commander-in-chief, he was actually in charge of all three armies, and the men around him were his assistants. Arakcheyev was a tried and trusted guardian of law and order, and the Tsar's bodyguard. Bennigsen, as a local landholder, was there ostensibly just to honour the Tsar, though in fact he was a good general, a wise councillor and a useful stand-by replacement for Barclay. The Tsarevich was there because it seemed the right thing for him to do. The former Prussian minister, Stein, was there because his advice might be useful, and the Emperor Alexander valued his personal qualities. Armfeldt was a sworn enemy of Napoleon, and his self-confidence always rubbed off on Alexander. Paulucci was there because he was a powerful speaker who knew his own mind. The adjutant-generals were there because the Emperor was never without them. Last but by no means least, Pfuel was there because he had created the plan of action against Napoleon and persuaded Alexander of its validity, and he was now running the whole campaign. Pfuel was assisted by Wolzogen, a specialist in translating Pfuel's ideas into a more accessible form than Pfuel himself ever could, he being an abrasive academic theorist, full of his own importance and contempt for everyone else.

Besides these Russians and foreigners – the foreigners were a special case, men acting in an alien sphere, who had the nerve to keep coming up with bright ideas every day of the week – there were many more secondary figures, who were with the army because their principals were there.

From all the ideas and opinions circulating in this vast, brilliant, proud and restless realm, Prince Andrey was able to make out the following clearly defined sub-divisions into factions and parties.

The first party consisted of Pfuel and his disciples, military theorists who believed there was such a thing as a science of warfare, a science with its own immutable laws – the law of oblique movement, the law of outflanking, etc. Pfuel and his disciples demanded that the army should retreat into the depths of the country in accordance with the precise laws laid down by the pseudo-science of warfare, any departure from which they saw as outright barbarity, ignorance or evil intent. To this party belonged the Germanic princes Wolzogen, Wintzengerode and others, most of them also Germans.

The second party was diametrically opposed to the first one. As always, where there was one extreme, the opposite extreme found its own representatives. Ever since Vilna men of this party had been demanding the invasion of Poland and the abandonment of all previous plans. Representatives of this party were also representatives of strong action, and beyond that representatives of nationalism, which made them more and more one-sided in this dispute. They were the Russians: Bagration, Yermolov, whose career was now in the ascendant, and others. Yermolov's well-known joke was on everyone's lips at the time – he claimed to have asked the Tsar for promotion to the rank of German. Men of this party harked back to Suvorov: all you had to do was stop thinking, stop sticking pins in maps, just go out and fight, thrash the enemy, keep him out of Russia and keep the men's spirits up.

To the third party, which the Tsar trusted most of all, belonged the courtiers, who kept trying to reconcile the first two tendencies. Men of this party – mainly civilians, including Arakcheyev – spoke and reasoned like men pretending to have convictions they did not possess. They admitted that war, especially with a genius like Bonaparte (by now they had stopped calling him Buonaparte), did undoubtedly call for profound theoretical consideration and profound scientific knowledge, at which Pfuel was a genius. But at the same time you had to admit that theorists could often be a bit narrow-minded, so you couldn't trust them completely; you had to lend an ear to what Pfuel's opponents were saying, and also to what was being said by practical men who had experience of war, and then go for a happy medium. Men of this party insisted on sticking to Pfuel's plan for holding the camp at Drissa, but changing his disposition of the other two armies. This meant that neither one thing nor the other could be achieved, but the men of this party still thought this was the best plan.

The fourth tendency was the one that had as its leading representative the grand duke and heir-apparent, who had been brought down to earth unforgettably at Austerlitz, having ridden out at the head of his guards in helmet and white jacket as if he was reviewing the troops, fully expecting to slay the French with great panache, only to find himself unexpectedly caught up in the front line, from the turmoil of which he had no little difficulty in extricating himself. The men of this party displayed sincerity with all its merit and deficiencies. They were scared of Napoleon, they were aware of his strength and their own weakness, and they readily admitted it. What they said was, 'Nothing but sorrow, disgrace and ruin can come of this war! We've lost Vilna, we've lost Vitebsk, and we're about to lose Drissa. The only sensible thing left for us to do is sue for peace, and as soon as possible, before we get driven out of Petersburg!'

This view was widespread throughout the higher echelons of the military, and it had its supporters in Petersburg too – one of them being the chancellor, Rumyantsev, who had his own reasons of state for supporting the peace movement.

The fifth group were those who supported Barclay de Tolly, not so much as a man, but as war minister and commander-in-chief. 'Whatever he may be,' they would say, always beginning with this proviso, 'he's an honest, practical man, and there's no one better. Give him the real power, because you can't win a war without unity in the high command, and he'll show what he's made of, as he did in Finland. If our army is still strong and well organized, and has pulled back to the Drissa without being defeated, we owe it all to Barclay. If Barclay is replaced by Bennigsen now, all will be lost. Bennigsen showed how useless he is as early as 1807.' This was the line taken by the fifth party.

The sixth party, the Bennigsenites, said the exact opposite: in the last analysis there was no one more capable and experienced than Bennigsen, and wherever you turned you always came back to him. The men of this party claimed that the Russian retirement to Drissa had been nothing less than a humiliating defeat, one mistake after another. 'The more mistakes they make,' these men said, 'the better things will be. It'll take them less time to realize we can't go on like this. We want none of your Barclays, we want someone like Bennigsen, who showed his mettle in 1807, and even Napoleon gave him his due. He's a man people would be glad to see in power. There's only one Bennigsen.'

The seventh class were the sort of people who always circulate around monarchs, especially young ones, and there were plenty of them around Alexander – generals and adjutants, not only passionately devoted to the Tsar as Emperor, but sincerely and disinterestedly worshipping him as a man, just as Nikolay Rostov had worshipped him in 1805, and seeing him as the embodiment of every virtue and human quality. These persons admired the Tsar's modesty in declining command of the army, but thought he was taking modesty too far. They shared a single purpose and demand: their adored Tsar should set aside his needless diffidence, and publicly proclaim that he was placing himself at the head of the army and taking over the staff of the commander-in-chief, and from now on he would listen as necessary to advisers steeped in theory and practice but he personally would lead the troops, and they would be roused by him to new heights of enthusiasm.

The eighth and largest group, vast in size, outnumbering the others ninety-nine to one, consisted of people who didn't want peace or war, offensive action or defensive camps at Drissa or anywhere else, or Barclay, or the Tsar or Pfuel or Bennigsen; all they wanted, the only thing that mattered to them, was making as much money as they could and enjoying themselves. The troubled waters of intrigue that swirled round the Tsar's headquarters offered many possibilities for success that would have been inconceivable at any other time. One courtier in a lucrative post and not wanting to lose it would find himself in agreement with Pfuel today and his opponents tomorrow, and the day after tomorrow he would disclaim any views on the same question, in order to avoid responsibility and please the Emperor. Another, with an eye to the main chance, would seek the Tsar's attention by bellowing out something his Majesty had hinted at the previous day, or taking people on at the council, arguing vociferously, beating his breast and challenging anyone who disagreed to a duel as a demonstration of his readiness for self-sacrifice in the common good. A third would simply take advantage of a gap between councils and the absence of enemies to apply for an extraordinary grant in respect of faithful service, knowing that time was on his side and he would not be refused. A fourth would ensure that the Tsar kept coming across him up to his eyes in work. A fifth would strive towards a long-desired goal – dinner at the Emperor's table – by taking up some new cause and arguing it one way or the other with tremendous passion, marshalling all sorts of arguments with every shade of strength and fairness.

All the men in this party were out for roubles, honours and promotion, and to help them in the chase they simply followed royal favour like a weather-vane; if the vane swung one way all the drones of the Russian army swarmed off in that direction, which made it more difficult for the Tsar to swing back. In all the current uncertainty, with the threat of serious danger hanging over them and the resulting sense of dire alarm, in this maelstrom of intrigue, vanity, competition, conflicting emotions and opinions, involving people from so many different nationalities, this eighth and largest party, obsessed with self-interest, served only to compound the sense of disorder and confusion. Whatever question arose, this cloud of drones, still sounding off on the last topic, would swarm over to a new one, buzzing loud enough to drown and obscure what was being said by honest people.

At the time when Prince Andrey reached the army another group – a ninth party – had just emerged from all the others and was beginning to make its voice heard. It was the party of older, more reasonable men, experienced politicians, who were able to stand back from the many conflicts of opinion, take an objective view of all that was going on at headquarters and consider various ways of getting out of the mess of uncertainty, confusion and weakness.

The members of this party said what they thought: the trouble was caused mainly by the Tsar's presence in the army along with his military court. This transferred into the army a loose system of short-term, fluctuating and insecure relationships that may be all right within the court itself, but was ruinous to an army; the Tsar's job was to govern the country, not lead the troops; the only solution would be for the Tsar and his court to get out of the army; the presence of the Tsar immobilized fifty thousand troops earmarked for the guarantee of his personal security; and the worst possible commander-in-chief, given his freedom to act, would be better than the best commander-in-chief hamstrung by the presence and authority of the Tsar.

While Prince Andrey was staying at Drissa with time on his hands, Shishkov, secretary of state and chief representative of this last group, wrote a letter to the Tsar with Balashev and Arakcheyev as willing fellow-signatories. In it he took advantage of the Tsar's permission for him to offer an opinion on the general course of events, used a clever pretext – the absolute necessity of his Majesty's being in the capital to rouse public feeling for the war effort – and respectfully suggested that the Emperor should leave the army.

An appeal by the Emperor to his people and a call for them to defend their fatherland – the very appeal that would turn out to be the main reason for Russia's eventual triumph, insofar as this was actually affected by the Tsar's presence in Moscow – were proposed to his Majesty, and accepted by him, as a pretext for leaving the army.

CHAPTER 10

This letter had yet to be handed to the Tsar when Barclay informed Prince Andrey over lunch that his Majesty would be pleased to grant him a personal interview in order to ask him about Turkey, and Prince Andrey was to present himself at Bennigsen's quarters at six o'clock that evening.

That very day news had reached the Tsar's quarters that Napoleon's troops were on the move again, threatening the army – though this would turn out to be wrong. And that same morning Colonel Michaud had accompanied the Tsar on a tour of the Drissa fortifications, systematically pointing out that Pfuel's fortified camp, which had been seen as a tactical masterpiece guaranteed to destroy Napoleon – this camp was a stupid idea that would be the downfall of the Russian army.

Prince Andrey proceeded to Bennigsen's quarters, a small manorhouse right down on the river-bank. Neither Bennigsen nor the Tsar was there, but Chernyshev, the Tsar's aide-de-camp, received Bolkonsky and told him the Tsar had gone off for the second time that day with General Bennigsen and Marchese Paulucci on an inspection of the Drissa fortifications, about which they were beginning to have the most serious doubts.

Chernyshev was sitting by a window in the outer room with a French novel in his hand. This had probably once been the ballroom; the organ was still there, though it was piled with rugs, and a camp-bed belonging to Bennigsen's adjutant took up one corner. The adjutant himself was there, sitting on his rolled-up bedding; he looked dozy and exhausted either from work or from too much partying. There were two doors leading out of the room, the old drawing-room door straight ahead and another one opening into the study on the right. Through the first door came the sounds of conversation mainly in German but with the odd burst of French. A meeting had been convened in the old drawing-room at the Tsar's behest, not a council of war – the Tsar liked to keep things vague – just a few people he considered worth consulting over their imminent difficulties. Not a council of war, but an impromptu council convened for the Tsar's personal benefit in order to clarify a number of questions. Invitations to this semi-council had been sent to the Swede, General Armfeldt, Adjutant-General Wolzogen, Wintzengerode (described by Napoleon as a renegade French subject), Michaud, Toll, Count Stein – anything but a military man – and finally Pfuel himself, the mainspring of everything, according to what Prince Andrey had heard. Prince Andrey managed to get a good look at this man when Pfuel came in shortly after him and lingered for a while exchanging a few words with Chernyshev before going on into the drawing-room.

At first sight Pfuel, in his sloppy Russian general's uniform, which fitted him badly and looked like fancy dress, seemed familiar to Prince Andrey, though he had never seen him before. He was in the run of Weierother, Mack, Schmidt, and many other German generals obsessed with theory; Prince Andrey had seen them all at work in 1805, but Pfuel was a perfect specimen of the type. Prince Andrey had never before set eyes on a German theorist who so completely combined all the characteristics of the other Germans.

Pfuel was short and skinny but big-boned, coarse and robust, with broad hips and protruding shoulder-blades. He had a wrinkled face with deep-set eyes. His hair had obviously been hastily brushed back from his temples, but it stuck up behind in funny tufts. He looked worried and angry as he glanced round before walking into the large room, and he seemed to be scared of everything in there. Grasping his sword rather clumsily, he turned to Chernyshev and asked where the Tsar had gone. He made it clear that he wanted to walk straight through the rooms, get the formalities over as fast as he could and sit down at a map, where he would feel at home. He responded to Chernyshev with a few quick nods, and he gave a sarcastic smile when they told him the Tsar had gone out to inspect the fortifications that he, Pfuel, had laid down in accordance with his theory. He muttered something under his breath, growling in the sharp tones always used by arrogant Germans: 'Stupid man . . .' or 'To hell with the whole damn thing . . .' or 'A nice mess this is going to be . . .' Prince Andrey didn't quite catch what he said and was about to move on, but Chernyshev introduced him to Pfuel, mentioning that he had just come on from Turkey, where the war had ended so well. Pfuel launched a fleeting glance at Prince Andrey, or rather through him, and said with a laugh: 'A war of splendid tactics, I'm sure!' With that he gave another contemptuous laugh and walked through into the room from which the sounds of voices were coming.

It was clear that Pfuel, testy and sarcastic at the best of times, was particularly incensed today at their effrontery in going out without him to inspect his camp and subject it to criticism. Prince Andrey was able to draw on his experiences at Austerlitz and use this brief encounter with Pfuel to form a clear impression of the man's personality. Pfuel was one of those hopelessly opinionated, arrogant men who would go to the stake for their own ideas, self-assured as only a German can be, because only a German could be self-assured on the basis of an abstract idea – science, the supposed knowledge of absolute truth. A Frenchman is self-assured because he sees himself as devastatingly charming, mentally and physically, to men and women alike. An Englishman is self-assured on the grounds that he is a citizen of the best-organized state in the world, and also because as an Englishman he always knows the right thing to do and everything he does, because he is Englishman, must be right. An Italian is self-assured because he gets excited and easily forgets himself and everybody else. A Russian is self-assured because he knows nothing, and doesn't want to know anything because he doesn't believe you can know anything completely. A self-assured German is the worst of the lot, the most stolid and the most disgusting, because he imagines he knows the truth through a branch of science that is entirely his invention, though he sees it as absolute truth.

Pfuel was clearly this kind of man. He had his science – the theory of oblique movement – which he had deduced from the wars of Frederick the Great, and everything he came across in today's military history seemed to him the most preposterous barbarity, a series of ugly confrontations with so many blunders on both sides that these wars were not worthy of the name of war because they didn't conform to his theory, did not lend themselves to scientific study.

In 1806 Pfuel had been one of those behind the plan of campaign that ended in Jena and Auerstadt, but he failed to see in the outcome of that war the slightest indication that his theory might be flawed. On the contrary, by his reckoning the entire debacle was due to infringements of his theory, and he used to say with typical relish and sarcasm, 'I told you the whole damn thing would go wrong.' Pfuel was one of those theorists who love their theory so dearly they lose sight of the aim of all theory, which is to work out in practice. He was so much in love with theory that he hated all practice and didn't want to know about it. He positively rejoiced in failure, because failure was due to practical infringements of his theory, which went to show how right the theory was.

He exchanged a few words about the present war with Prince Andrey and Chernyshev, his attitude being that of a man who knows in advance it's all going to go wrong, and who doesn't particularly mind if it does. This was eloquently confirmed by the uncombed tufts of hair sticking up on the back of his head, and the hurriedly brushed locks at his temples.

He strode off into the next room, where his deep voice could soon be heard growling away.

CHAPTER 11

Prince Andrey's eyes were still on the departing Pfuel when Count Bennigsen came bustling into the room, gave Bolkonsky a passing nod and walked straight through into the study, issuing some instructions to his adjutant as he went. The Tsar was not far behind, and Bennigsen had hurried on ahead to get one or two things ready and be there to receive him. Chernyshev and Prince Andrey went out on to the porch. The Tsar was there looking weary as he dismounted. The Marchese Paulucci was speaking to him. The Tsar was listening with his head tilted to the left, but he didn't look pleased with Paulucci, who was holding forth with tremendous passion. The Tsar took a step forward, obviously anxious to bring the conversation to an end, but the excited Italian followed him in, red in the face and still chattering away in defiance of all etiquette.

'And the man who advised this camp at Drissa . . .' Paulucci was addressing the Tsar in French as his Majesty climbed the steps, saw Prince Andrey and stared closely at a new face. 'As for him, sire,' Paulucci persisted in sheer desperation, hardly able to contain himself, 'the man who devised this camp at Drissa, I see no alternative to the madhouse or the gallows.' The Tsar was not prepared to go on listening and didn't seem to have heard what the Italian had been saying. He now recognized Bolkonsky and addressed him graciously:

'I'm so pleased to see you. Go on in where they are meeting and wait for me there.'

The Tsar proceeded into the study. He was followed by Prince Pyotr Volkonsky and Baron Stein, and the door closed behind them. Prince Andrey took advantage of the Tsar's permission and went through into the drawing-room where the council had assembled accompanied by Paulucci, whom he knew from Turkey.

Prince Pyotr Volkonsky was a kind of acting head of the Tsar's staff. Volkonsky emerged from the study carrying some maps, which he spread out on the table before outlining a series of questions on which he wished to hear the opinions of the gentlemen present. During the night, it seemed, word had been received (falsely, as it turned out) that the French were on the march, threatening the Drissa camp with a pincer movement.

General Armfeldt spoke first, and he came out with a quite unexpected proposal for resolving the present difficulty, a brand-new suggestion, inexplicable except in terms of his eagerness to demonstrate that he too was not without opinions: that the army should form up in a position some distance from the Petersburg and Moscow roads and wait there for the enemy. Clearly, this was a plan that Armfeldt had thought up some time before, and he was putting it forward now not really as a solution to the present problem, because it had lost all relevance, but merely because he had spotted an opportunity for speaking. It was one suggestion among millions, all of them perfectly reasonable as long as no one had any real idea of how the war would work out. His proposal had its detractors and supporters. Young Colonel Toll was the Swedish general's most vociferous detractor, and in the course of the ensuing argument he took a well-filled note-book out of his side pocket and asked permission to read from it. In a rambling discourse Toll put forward yet another plan of campaign – totally different from Armfeldt's and Pfuel's. Paulucci countered with a proposal for immediate advance and attack, which he saw as the only way out of the present uncertainty and the trap that we were now in – his description of the Drissa camp. During these heated discussions not a word came from Pfuel or his interpreter Wolzogen (the bridge between him and the court world). Pfuel limited himself to the occasional contemptuous snort, and then he turned his back on them to indicate that he wasn't going to demean himself by responding to the rubbish he was hearing. But when Prince Volkonsky, who was chairing the debate, called upon him to voice an opinion, all he said was, 'Why me? General Armfeldt has proposed an excellent position with the rear exposed. Or there's this Italian gentleman with his attack – a splendid idea! Or a retreat? Just as good. Why ask me?' he said. 'Oh no, you all know better than I do.'

But when Volkonsky said with a scowl that he was asking his opinion on the Tsar's behalf, Pfuel got to his feet, roused himself and launched forth.

'You've messed it all up and ruined everything. You would have it you knew better than I did, and now you come running back for me to put things right. Well, nothing needs to be put right. All you have to do is carry on exactly according to the principles laid down by me,' he said, rapping on the table with his bony fingers. 'Where's the difficulty? Nonsense – it's child's play!' He went over to the map and began poking at it with a desiccated finger, jabbering away as he demonstrated that the effectiveness of the Drissa camp was immune to all contingencies, every development had been foreseen, and if the enemy did try a pincer movement, the enemy must face inevitable destruction.

Paulucci, who had no German, started asking questions in French. Wolzogen came to the rescue of his leader, who didn't speak much French, and began translating what was said, but he could hardly keep up with Pfuel, who was speeding ahead with his demonstration that everything – not only what was happening now but anything that could possibly happen – was covered by his plan, and if trouble had arisen, this was due entirely to missing out on some of its details. He gave one sardonic laugh after another as he rambled on with his demonstration, and then brought it to an end with the contempt of a mathematician who refuses to use any other methods to establish a proof that has already been conclusively demonstrated. Wolzogen then took over in French, developing his own ideas with the occasional 'Don't you agree, your Excellency?' addressed to Pfuel. But Pfuel was now like a soldier lashing out at his own men in the heat of battle, and he yelled furiously at everybody, including Wolzogen, 'I ask you, what more is there to explain?' Paulucci and Michaud sang in concert as they rounded on Wolzogen in French. Armfeldt was going on at Pfuel in German. Toll was giving Prince Volkonsky a Russian version of events. Prince Andrey held back, watching and listening.

Of all these men it was the fulminating, single-minded and absurdly arrogant Pfuel that Prince Andrey felt most sympathy for. He was clearly the only man there who wanted nothing for himself and knew no personal malevolence; all he wanted was to see his plan carried out, the plan that had cost him years of hard toil as his theory had evolved. He looked ridiculous, his sarcasm was offensive, but you had to admire his boundless devotion to an idea.

Besides that, with the single exception of Pfuel, all the speeches of those present had one thing in common that had been absent from the council of war in 1805 – a mixture of fear and panic at Napoleon's genius, which betrayed itself in every protestation, however much they tried to hide it. Napoleon was assumed to be capable of anything; he was expected from all sides at once, and they were able to destroy one another's proposals by the mere mention of his dreaded name. Pfuel seemed uniquely capable of treating even Napoleon like a barbarian, on a par with everyone else who opposed his theory. And apart from admiration, Pfuel also aroused a feeling of pity in Prince Andrey. The courtiers were beginning to adopt a new tone towards him, Paulucci had spoken out to the Tsar, and, more significantly, a kind of desperation was edging its way on to Pfuel's own features, all of which made it clear that others already knew what he was beginning to feel – his downfall was not far away. And for all his self-assurance and sarcastic German bombast, he looked pathetic with his hair plastered down at the temples and sticking up in tufts at the back. Try as he might to conceal it with a great bluster of irritation and contempt, he was visibly in despair that the one chance of putting his theory to the test on a colossal scale and demonstrating its infallibility to the whole world was slipping away from him.

The debate went on and on, and the longer it went on the more animated it became, with raised voices and name-calling, and the less possible it was to draw any kind of overall conclusion from what was being said. Listening to this polyglot babel of shouted proposals, plans and counter-proposals, Prince Andrey stood back amazed at what they were all saying. Ideas which he had long held and often thought about during his military service – that there was no such thing as a science of warfare, and never could be, and therefore there could be no such a thing as 'military genius' – struck him now as entirely true and self-evident. 'What kind of theory and science can there be when conditions and circumstances are indeterminate and can never be defined, and the active strengths of the warring parties are even more indefinable? No one can, no one ever could, know what the positions of our army and the enemy will be at this time tomorrow, and no one can know the relative strengths of the various detachments. Sometimes, when there is no coward up front to run away shouting, "We've been cut off!", but there is a brave and cheery soul shouting, "Hurrah!", a detachment of five thousand is a match for thirty thousand, as happened at Schöngrabern, and on other occasions fifty thousand will run away from eight thousand, as they did at Austerlitz. What kind of science can there be when, as in all practical matters, nothing can be defined, and everything depends on an incalculable range of conditions which come together significantly at a moment that no one can know in advance? Armfeldt says our army has been cut off, but Paulucci says we have the French army caught between two fires; Michaud says the big disadvantage of the Drissa camp is that the river is behind us, while Pfuel says this is its strength. Toll proposes one plan, Armfeldt proposes another; they are all equally good and bad, and the advantages of any one proposition will only become clear after the event. So why all this talk about military genius? Does it take genius to get the biscuits delivered on time or know when to march the troops right or left? People are called geniuses only because of the pomp and power invested in the military, and because there are always plenty of wheedling rogues ready to fawn on power and credit it with the spurious quality of genius. It's the other way round – the best generals I've ever known have been stupid or absent-minded. Bagration was the best – Napoleon himself admitted that. And as for Bonaparte! I remember his smug look and tight little face on the field at Austerlitz. A good military commander has no need of genius or any outstanding qualities; quite the reverse, he needs to be devoid of the finest and noblest of human attributes – love, poetry, affection, a philosophical spirit of inquiry and scepticism. He needs to be narrow-minded, totally convinced that what he is doing is very important (otherwise he would never have enough staying-power), and only then will he become a valiant military commander. God forbid that he should be like a human being, a prey to love and compassion, hesitating over right and wrong. It is obvious why a theory of genius should have been fabricated for them by people of old – such men and power are the same thing. Credit for any success in battle belongs not to them, but to some soldier in the ranks who shouted "Hurrah!", just as blame for failure belongs to one who shouted, "We've had it!" And it's only there in the ranks that anyone can serve and be absolutely certain he is doing something useful!'

This is what Prince Andrey was thinking about as he listened to the buzz of chatter, and he came to his senses only when Paulucci called across to him just as the meeting was breaking up.

Next day at the review the Tsar asked Prince Andrey where he wished to serve, and Bolkonsky wrote himself off for ever in court circles by opting for army service when he could have requested a post in attendance on the Tsar's person.

CHAPTER 12

Before the campaign began Nikolay Rostov had received a letter from his parents with a few words about Natasha's illness and the breaking off of her engagement, which they described as a rebuff from her, and another plea for him to retire from the army and come home. On receiving this letter Nikolay made no attempt to apply for leave or retirement; he wrote back to say how very sorry he was that Natasha was ill and had broken off her engagement, and he would make every effort to do what they wanted. To Sonya he wrote separately.

'My beloved, companion of my soul,' he wrote. 'Nothing but honour could keep me from going back to the country. But now, at the outset of a campaign, I would feel a sense of dishonour not only towards my comrades, but also in my own eyes, were I to put my own happiness ahead of my duty and my love for our fatherland. But this is our last separation. Believe me, once this war is over, if I am still alive and still loved by you, I shall cast everything aside and fly to you, to press you for ever to my ardent breast.'

And indeed, it was only the outbreak of war that had detained Rostov and kept him from going back home, as he had promised, to marry Sonya. The autumn and winter at Otradnoye with the hunting, the Christmas celebrations and Sonya's love had opened up the prospect of a nice quiet life as a country gentleman, full of pleasures he had never known before, which now beckoned alluringly. 'A nice wife, children, a decent pack of hounds, a dozen quick borzois, managing the estate, visiting the neighbours, get myself elected to something,' he mused. But now there was a war on, and he had to stay with his regiment. And since he had to, Nikolay Rostov, being what he was, managed to make the most of regimental life and ensure that this life was a pleasant one.

Nikolay had been given a warm welcome by his comrades on his return from leave and had then been sent off to Ukraine on a procurement mission, from where he came back with some splendid horses, which was gratifying for him and the source of much praise from the top brass. While he had been away his promotion to captain had come through, and when the regiment was placed on a war footing with an increased complement he was given his old squadron to command.

With the new campaign under way the regiment was sent to Poland on double pay, with new officers, new men and fresh horses. Best of all, the happy mood of excitement that comes at the beginning of a war permeated everything, and Rostov, conscious of his privileged position in the regiment, gave himself up body and soul to the business and pleasure of soldiering, though he knew that sooner or later he would have to give it all up.

For a variety of complex reasons, administrative, political and tactical, the army was in retreat from Vilna. Every retreating step was taken against a complex interplay of self-interest, argumentation and high passion at headquarters, but for the hussars of the Pavlograd regiment the whole business of retreating, in high summer and with everything in good supply, was the simplest and most agreeable of tasks. Low spirits, worry and intrigue might have been rampant at headquarters, but the army rank and file never gave a thought to where they were going or why. If there were any misgivings about retreating they were focused on moving out of nice familiar quarters and leaving behind a pretty Polish lady. And if it ever occurred to anyone that things were not going too well he would do his best, like a good soldier, to put a brave face on things, ignoring the general course of events and concentrating on personal affairs close at hand. At first they had been very pleasantly ensconced just outside Vilna, where they had got to know the local Polish gentry, and they had prepared for inspections that were then conducted by the Tsar or various members of the high command. Then came the order to retreat to Swienciany and destroy all stores that couldn't be carried away. Swienciany was remembered by the hussars for two reasons only: it was 'the drunken camp', so called by every soldier who stayed there, and it was also the cause of many a complaint against the troops for their over-zealous application of orders to remove all stores, since they took 'all stores' to include horses, carriages and carpets seized from the Polish gentry. Rostov remembered Swienciany as a village in the backwoods where, on his first day, he had sacked his quartermaster and lost control of the men of his squadron, who had drunk themselves stupid on five barrels of old beer brought along without his knowledge. From Swienciany they had fallen back further and further as far as Drissa, and from Drissa the retreat had continued until they were almost back at the Russian frontier.

On the 13th of July the Pavlograd hussars saw serious action for the first time.

On the 12th of July, the night before the action, there had been a thunderstorm with torrential rain. The summer of 1812 was a bad one for thunderstorms.

The two Pavlograd squadrons were encamped in the middle of a rye-field which had been standing in full ear but was now thoroughly trampled by cattle and horses. The rain came down in torrents, and Rostov was sitting with one of his protégés, a young officer by the name of Ilyin, in a little shelter that had been knocked up for them. A fellow-officer with mutton-chop whiskers, delayed by the rain on his way back from headquarters, dropped in on Rostov.

'Hello, Count. I'm on my way back from headquarters. Have you heard about Rayevsky's amazing feat?' And the officer launched into a detailed account of the battle of Saltanov that he had picked up at headquarters.

Rostov went on smoking his pipe, wriggling his neck where the rainwater was trickling down, listening with half an ear and glancing from time to time at the young Ilyin who was squeezed up close by. Ilyin, a boy of sixteen new to the regiment, looked up to Nikolay just as Nikolay had looked up to Denisov seven years before. Ilyin tried to imitate everything Rostov did, and adored him like a girl.

The officer with mutton-chop whiskers, Zdrzhinsky, was going on about the dam at Saltanov, portentously described by him as the Russian Thermopylae,[9] and the heroic deed performed there by General Rayevsky, a deed worthy of the ancients. Zdrzhinsky told how Rayevsky had gone out on to the dam with his two sons under a terrible hail of fire and charged forward with them at his side. Rostov listened but, far from encouraging Zdrzhinsky in his transports with a sympathetic word or two, he assumed the air of a man who was embarrassed by what he was hearing but had no intention of raising any objections. With Austerlitz and the campaign of 1807 behind him, Rostov knew from personal experience that everybody lies, as he had done, when it comes to describing deeds of war. Secondly, he was too experienced not to be aware that everything happens on a battlefield in a way that totally transcends our imagination and powers of description. For these reasons he didn't like Zdrzhinsky's story, and didn't like Zdrzhinsky himself, with his way of bending right down and thrusting his moustaches straight in the face of the person he was talking to. It was a tight squeeze in the little shelter and he was squeezing them more. Rostov watched him and said not a word. 'In the first place, the dam they were charging must have been so crowded and chaotic that if Rayevsky really had gone forward with his sons it couldn't have had any effect on anybody beyond the ten or twelve men closest to him,' thought Rostov. 'Nobody else could have seen Rayevsky on the dam or who was with him. But even the ones who did see him couldn't have got much of a boost from it – why should they bother about Rayevsky's warm fatherly feelings when their own skins were at stake? Anyway, the fate of Mother Russia didn't depend on the Saltanov dam being taken or not taken, as was the case at Thermopylae, so they say. So why make a sacrifice like that? What's the point in getting your own children mixed up in a battle? I wouldn't expose my brother, Petya, to any danger, or even Ilyin, and he's nothing to me, though he's a nice boy – I'd do what I could to keep them somewhere safe and sheltered.' These were the thoughts that ran through Rostov's mind as he listened to Zdrzhinsky. But he didn't say a word about them, being too experienced even for that. He knew that stories like this redounded to the glory of our war effort, so it was best to pretend not to doubt them. This is what he did.

'Well, that's it. I've had enough,' said Ilyin, noticing that Rostov didn't like Zdrzhinsky's talk. 'Stockings, shirt, the lot – I'm soaked. I'm off to find somewhere else to shelter. I think the rain may have eased off.'

Ilyin walked out and Zdrzhinsky rode away.

Five minutes later Ilyin was back, splashing through the mud as he ran towards the shelter.

'Hurrah! Rostov, let's get going. Guess what I've found – an inn, a couple of hundred yards away, and our boys are there already. It's a chance to dry out, and Marya Genrikhovna's there too.'

Marya Genrikhovna was the regimental doctor's wife, a pretty young German girl whom he had married in Poland. Being short of money or reluctant to part from his young wife in the early days of their marriage, the doctor took her with him everywhere; she was part of the regiment and his jealousy made him the butt of many a joke among the hussar officers.

Rostov flung a cape over his shoulders, yelled across to Lavrushka to follow on with their things, and set off with Ilyin, slipping in the mud and splashing straight through pools in the drizzling rain with intermittent flashes of lightning in the distance searing through the evening darkness.

'Rostov, where are you?'

'Over here . . . Look at that lightning!' they called to one another.

CHAPTER 13

The doctor's little covered cart stood waiting by an abandoned inn; inside there were half a dozen officers. Marya Genrikhovna, a buxom little German blonde, was sitting on a broad bench in the front corner wearing her short dressing-gown and night-cap. Her husband, the doctor, lay asleep just behind her. Rostov and Ilyin came in to a raucous welcome of shouting and happy laughter.

'Hey! You're having a wonderful time in here!' said Rostov with a laugh.

'Well, don't just stand there gawping at us!'

'Look at them! Dripping all over the place! Do you want to flood us out? Don't drip all over Marya Genrikhovna's clothes,' came the various voices.

Rostov and Ilyin looked round quickly for some little corner where they could get out of their wet clothes without offending the modesty of Marya Genrikhovna. They headed for a little partition to go behind it and change, but the tiny space was completely filled by three officers who sat there playing cards by the light of a single candle on an empty box and refused to budge. Marya Genrikhovna yielded up a petticoat for use as a curtain and with that for a screen Rostov and Ilyin, assisted by Lavrushka, who had followed on with their kit-bags, got out of their wet things and came out in dry clothes.

A fire had been lit in the broken-down stove. They got hold of a board, rigged it up across a couple of saddles, covered it with a horse-cloth and then produced a small samovar, a hamper and half a bottle of rum. They all crowded round Marya Genrikhovna, asking her to be mother. One of them offered her a clean handkerchief to wipe her pretty little hands; somebody else spread his tunic under her little feet to keep them out of the damp; a third man hung his cape over the window to keep the draught out; a fourth wafted the flies away from her husband's face so he wouldn't wake up.

'Leave him alone,' said Marya Genrikhovna with a shy, happy smile. 'He won't have any trouble sleeping – he's been up all night.'

'Oh no, Marya Genrikhovna,' answered the officer, 'we've got to look after the doctor! Anything could happen, and I want him to be nice to me when he cuts my leg off, or my arm.'

There were only three glasses, the water was so dirty you couldn't tell whether the tea was strong or weak, and the samovar only held enough water for six glasses, but all this added to the pleasure of waiting, in order of rank, until it was your turn to receive a glass from Marya Genrikhovna's chubby little hands with their short and not too clean nails. All the officers seemed to have really fallen in love with Marya Genrikhovna for one evening. Even the officers who had been playing cards behind the screen soon abandoned their game and came to gather round the samovar, catching the general mood and flirting with Marya Genrikhovna. She, seeing herself surrounded by such brilliant and solicitous young men, was beaming with delight despite her best efforts to conceal it, and the obvious way she jumped every time her husband stirred in his sleep behind her. There was plenty of sugar but only one spoon, so no one could have a proper stir. It was decided that Marya Genrikhovna would stir everybody's glass in turn. Rostov received his glass, topped it up with rum and asked Marya Genrikhovna to do the stirring.

'But you don't take sugar, do you?' she said, and the smile never left her face, seeming to suggest that everything she said and everybody else said was wildly amusing and had a double meaning.

'I'm not bothered about the sugar, I just want you to stir it with your little hand.'

Marya Genrikhovna accepted this and looked round for the spoon, but someone had snatched it away.

'Use one of your little fingers, Marya Genrikhovna,' said Rostov. 'It'll taste nicer.'

'Too hot,' said Marya Genrikhovna, colouring up with pleasure.

Ilyin fetched a bucketful of water, topped it up with a little rum, walked over to Marya Genrikhovna and asked her to stir it with her finger.

'This is my cup,' he said. 'Dip your finger in and I'll drink the lot.'

When the samovar had been emptied Rostov reached for the cards and proposed a game of 'kings' with Marya Genrikhovna. They drew lots to decide who was going to be her partner. Rostov proposed new rules: whoever was 'king' would have the right to kiss Marya Genrikhovna's hand, and the 'knave' would have to get the samovar going again for the doctor when he woke up.

'Yes, but what if Marya Genrikhovna is king?' asked Ilyin.

'She's already our queen! And her word is law.' The game had hardly started when the doctor's dishevelled head suddenly loomed up behind his wife. He had been awake for some time, listening to what they were saying, and it was clear that he could see nothing enjoyable, diverting or the least bit funny in what was being said and done. His face was a picture of sorrow and anguish. Without greeting the officers he scratched himself and asked them to let him through because they were standing in his way. The moment he had left the room all the officers erupted in great bellows of laughter, and Marya Genrikhovna blushed till her eyes watered, which made her even more alluring to all the officers. When he came back in from the yard the doctor turned to his wife (who had wiped the radiant smile off her face and was now watching him apprehensively, waiting to see what his verdict would be) and told her it had stopped raining and they would have to spend the night in their covered cart if they didn't want all their things to be stolen.

'No, I'll put a guard on it . . . two guards!' said Rostov. 'Don't say another word, doctor.'

'I'll guard it myself!' said Ilyin.

'No, gentlemen, you've had plenty of sleep, but I've had two sleepless nights,' said the doctor, and he sat down moodily at his wife's side to wait for the end of the game.

One look at the doctor's moody expression as he stole shifty glances at his wife, and the officers became rowdier than ever; many of them laughed uncontrollably and had to work hard at thinking up decent excuses for doing so. When the doctor had gone, taking his wife with him, and the pair of them had settled down in their little cart, the officers took to the inn floor and snuggled down under their damp coats. But sleep didn't come; they chatted away for quite some time, harking back to the worried doctor and his blissful wife, and even running out on to the steps to report back on what was going on in the cart. Several times Rostov buried his head in his coat and tried to get to sleep, only to be distracted by some new comment, and then the conversation would start up again, and the room would soon be ringing with great guffaws of ridiculous laughter like that of happy children.

CHAPTER 14

It was past two o'clock and they were all still awake when the quarter-master appeared with orders for them to proceed to a little place called Ostrovna. The officers buckled to immediately, getting their things together, with no pause in the laughter and banter, and the samovar was refilled with dirty water. But Rostov set off for his squadron without waiting for tea. It was getting light, the drizzle had cleared up and the dark clouds were thinning. It was a damp morning, the chill made worse by clothes that had not had time to dry out. As they came out of the inn into the half-light of early morning Rostov and Ilyin both glanced under the leather cover of the doctor's cart, still glistening from the rain. The doctor's feet stuck out from under the apron. In the middle of the cart they caught a glimpse of his wife's night-cap on a pillow, and they could hear sleepy breathing.

'Lovely little thing, isn't she?' said Rostov to Ilyin, close behind.

'A delightful woman!' responded Ilyin, with all the gravity of a sixteen-year-old.

Half an hour later the squadron was on parade along the road. They were given the order to mount, and they did so, crossing themselves. Rostov rode off, ordering them to move forward, and the hussars came after him four abreast, to the sound of hooves splashing through mud, jingling sabres and subdued exchanges between the men, trotting down the broad highway between two rows of birch-trees after the infantry and artillery, which had gone on ahead.

The broken clouds, violet-coloured and tinged red by the rising sun, scudded before the wind. It was getting lighter by the minute. They could now clearly see, still wet from yesterday's rain, the feathery grass that is a permanent feature of all country roadsides. The birch branches hung down, swaying in the wind, with glittering droplets showering right and left. The soldiers' faces became clearer and clearer. Rostov, with Ilyin sticking beside him, rode down one side of the road between the two rows of birches.

On active service Rostov allowed himself the indulgence of riding a Cossack horse instead of an ordinary regimental animal. A connoisseur and lover of horses, he had recently managed to acquire a big chestnut-and-white charger from the Don steppe, a lovely beast with a fine spirit, who was never outgalloped. Rostov found him a delight to ride. He was thinking about his horse now, and the morning, and the doctor's wife, but the approaching danger never crossed his mind.

In earlier days Rostov had always felt scared as he rode into battle;

now he felt not a flicker of fear. He was fearless not because he had got used to being under fire (you never get used to danger) but because he had learnt how to master his own spirit in the face of danger. He had formed the habit, when riding into battle, of thinking about anything except the one thing that ought to have been more fascinating than anything else – the danger that lay ahead. However earnestly he had struggled to do this, and however many times he had bitterly called himself a coward in the early days, he had never been able to manage it. But it had come by itself with the passing years. He rode on now between the birch-trees with Ilyin at his side, occasionally stripping the leaves from twigs that came to hand, sometimes touching his horse's flank with one foot, finishing a pipe and handing it back without turning round to a hussar following on, all with the cheery breeziness of someone out for a ride. He felt for Ilyin with his over-excited face and his persistent, worried chatter. He knew from experience what an agonizing state the cornet must be in, racked by forebodings of terror and of death, and he knew that nothing could help him but the passage of time.

Once the sun had appeared in the clear band of sky just below the stormclouds the wind died down, as if it would not presume to spoil the beauty of a summer morning after a storm; the branches still dripped, but the droplets fell straight to the ground, and a hush lay over everything. The sun was now fully up just above the horizon, though it soon vanished into a long, narrow strip of overhanging cloud, only to emerge brighter still a few minutes later on top of the cloud, breaking out through its edges. Everything was bright and shining. And coinciding with the bright sunlight, as if in response to it, the first shots rang out ahead.

Rostov had no time to think things over and work out how far away these shots had been; one of Count Ostermann-Tolstoy's adjutants was suddenly on him, galloping up from Vitebsk with an order to advance down the road at a steady pace.

The squadron overtook the infantry and the battery, even though they had also picked up speed, and then the hussars trotted down a hill, through an empty village which had lost all its inhabitants, and up the other side. The horses were beginning to lather and the men were red in the face.

'Halt! Dress ranks!' called the divisional commander ahead of them. 'By the left, forward! Walk on!'

And the hussars made their way past the lines to the left flank of our position, coming to a halt behind our uhlans, who formed the front line. To the right was a dense column of infantry – the reserves – and behind them further up the hill on the line of the horizon where the air was so sweet and clear our cannons stood, picked out in the angled rays of the bright morning sunshine. Ahead of us, across the valley, we could see the enemy's columns and guns. In the valley itself our advance line had gone into action and was merrily exchanging fire with the enemy.

These shots were music to Rostov's ears, music he had not heard for such a long time, and he felt his spirits rise. *Tra-ta-ta-ta!* More shots rang out, volleys and rapid single fire. Then – silence, but not for long; more bursts, like the sound of fire-crackers underfoot.

The hussars stayed where they were for an hour or so. The cannons opened up. Count Ostermann rode up with his suite behind the squadron, stopped for a quick consultation with the colonel of the regiment and rode on uphill towards the big guns.

Just after he had gone a command was roared out among the uhlans.

'Columns! fall in! Prepare to charge!'

The infantry platoons ahead of them parted to let the cavalry through. The uhlans surged forward, with fluttering streamers atop their lances, and proceeded downhill at a steady pace towards the French cavalry, just now emerging down below on the left.

As soon as the uhlans had moved off down the slope the hussars were ordered uphill to cover the battery. As they moved round to take up the positions vacated by the uhlans, they heard the fizzing and whining of musket-shot from the front, falling short of its target.

This sound, which he had not heard for many a long day, had an even more joyous and energizing effect on Rostov than the musket-shots before them. He rose in the saddle and scanned the battlefield opening out before him as he rode uphill, and his heart went out to the uhlans as they pressed forward. They flew down on the French dragoons, there was some kind of hurly-burly in the smoke and five minutes later the uhlans were dashing back, not towards the spot they had come from, but further left. In among the orange-coloured ranks of uhlans on their chestnut horses, and behind them, a huge mass of blue French dragoons mounted on their greys could now be seen.

CHAPTER 15

Rostov, with the sharp eye of a hunting man, was one of the first to spot these blue dragoons pursuing our uhlans. Nearer and nearer came the scattered hordes of uhlans and the pursuing French dragoons. He could now see individual figures, men that had looked so small at the bottom of the hill, fighting, chasing each other, waving arms and brandishing sabres.

For Rostov it was like watching a hunt. Instinct told him that if his hussars were to attack the French dragoons now they would give in, but the attack would have to come now, this very minute, or it would be too late. He looked round. The captain standing beside him also had his eyes glued on the cavalry down the hill.

'Andrey Sevastyanych,' said Rostov, 'we could get them couldn't we?'

'It would be a nice piece of work,' said the captain, 'but as a matter of fact . . .'

Rostov waited no longer for his response; he spurred his horse and galloped off in front of his squadron. He hardly had time to give the command – the whole squadron, feeling as he did, dashed after him. Rostov couldn't have said how or why he did it. It was like hunting; he did what he did without thinking or weighing things up. He could see the dragoons were getting close and galloping all over the place, he knew they couldn't withstand a charge, and he also knew that this was their moment, and it wouldn't come again if he missed it. He felt exhilarated by the sound of bullets whistling and whining on all sides, and his horse was straining forward so strongly he couldn't hold him back. He spurred him on, gave the command and instantly set off downhill at a half-gallop heading towards the dragoons, hearing the thudding hooves of his squadron coming on behind, properly deployed. They flew downhill, went into a full gallop, faster and faster, getting nearer and nearer to their uhlans and the pursuing French. The dragoons were not far away now. Those in front took one look at the hussars and turned back; the ones behind came juddering to a halt. It was just like diving across to cut off a wolf – Rostov urged his Don horse forward, giving him his head, and shot across to intercept the dragoons in their tattered ranks. One uhlan stopped in his tracks, another one, on foot, flung himself to the ground to avoid being ridden down, and a riderless horse joined in with the charging hussars. Almost all the dragoons were now riding away. Rostov picked out one of them on a grey and flew after him. There was a bush in the way, but his gallant horse took it in his stride, and Nikolay was hardly straight in the saddle again when he saw that it would take him only a second or two to catch up with his chosen enemy. The Frenchman, an officer to judge by his uniform, sat hunched up on his grey horse, urging it on with his sword. The next moment Rostov's horse ran straight into the grey's hindquarters and nearly brought it down while Rostov surprised himself by raising his sword and aiming a blow at the Frenchman.

But then, in an instant, Rostov's enthusiasm suddenly drained away. The officer fell to the ground, not really from the sword cut, which gave him no more than a scratch above the elbow, but from the bump between horses and sheer terror. As Rostov reined in, his eyes were searching for his foe to see whom he had brought down. There was the French officer, hopping along with one foot caught in his stirrup. He was terrified, wincing from immediate expectation of another blow, and he looked up at Rostov, recoiling in horror. This pale, mud-stained face of a fair-haired young man with a dimple on his chin and bright blue eyes had no business with battlefields; it was not the face of an enemy; it was a domestic, indoor face. Before Rostov could make up his mind what to do with him, the officer called out in French, 'I surrender!' He was still in a panic, vainly struggling to extricate his foot from the stirrup and still staring up at Rostov with fear in his eyes of blue. Then some hussars galloped over, freed his foot and got him up into the saddle again. The hussars had their hands full on all sides dealing with the dragoons: here was a wounded man with blood streaming down his face who wouldn't let go of his horse; there was another man who had scrambled up on to a colleague's horse and was clasping him round the waist; a third was helping another hussar up on to his own horse. The French infantry were just ahead, loosing off shots as they ran. The hussars hurried away with their prisoners. Rostov galloped along with the rest, conscious of a nasty feeling inside, an aching round his heart. It was as if he had suddenly seen something, something vague and confused that he couldn't account for, in capturing that French officer and hitting him with his sword.

Count Ostermann-Tolstoy was there to welcome them back. He sent for Rostov, thanked him and told him he would report his gallant action to the Tsar and recommend him for a St George's Cross. When the summons had come for him to appear before Count Ostermann, Rostov could only recall that he had gone on the attack without any orders to do so, and he was certain his commanding officer had sent for him to discipline him for being out of order. Ostermann's honeyed words and the prospect of getting a medal should, therefore, have come as a pleasant surprise to Rostov, but he still felt sick at heart, troubled by the same vague but nasty feeling. 'What is it? What's worrying me?' he wondered as he rode away from seeing the general. 'Ilyin? No, he's all right. Did I do anything I should be ashamed of?

No, that's not it!' Something else was worrying him, a kind of remorse. 'Yes, I know, it's that French officer with the dimple. I can remember holding back just when I'd lifted my arm.'

Rostov suddenly noticed that the prisoners were being led away, and he galloped after them to have a look at his Frenchman with a dimple in his chin. He was sitting astride one of their pack-horses dressed in his funny uniform, staring around uneasily.

The scratch on his arm wasn't really a wound. He looked at Rostov with a forced smile and waved a greeting. Rostov still felt embarrassed and somehow ashamed.

All that day and the next Rostov's friends and comrades noticed that, without being exactly morose or snappy with them, he was quiet, pensive and in a world of his own. He was reluctant to accept a drink, he wanted to be left alone and he seemed permanently preoccupied.

Rostov couldn't take his mind off the brilliant exploit which, to his astonishment, had won him the St George's Cross and a heroic reputation. There was something odd about it. 'It turns out they're even more scared than we are,' he thought. 'Is this it then? Is this what they mean by heroism? Did I really do it for my country? And what has he done wrong with his dimple and his blue eyes? He was so scared! He thought I was going to kill him. Why should I want to kill him? My hand shook. And they've given me the George Cross! I can't see it, I just can't see it!'

But even as Nikolay turned these things over in his mind without being able to work out what was wrong with him, the wheel of fortune was turning, as it so often does in the army, and turning in his favour. After Ostrovna he came to prominence and was put in command of a battalion. From now on they called on him whenever there was a need for an officer of outstanding bravery.

CHAPTER 16

The moment Countess Rostov received news of Natasha's illness, even though she was still poorly and had little strength, she left for Moscow immediately with Petya and the whole household; the other Rostovs moved over from Marya Dmitriyevna's house and they all settled down together in their own home.

Natasha's illness was so serious that, fortunately for her and her parents, all thoughts of what lay behind it, her conduct and the breaking off of her engagement, had faded into the background. She was too ill for anyone to start bothering about how far she was to blame for what had happened; after all, she could neither eat nor sleep, she was growing thinner by the day, she had a bad cough and according to the doctors her life was in danger. The only thing to concentrate on was how to get her well again. Doctors kept rolling up to see Natasha individually and in consultant groups. They rattled away in French, German and Latin, criticized each other and wrote out prescriptions for all sorts of medicine guaranteed to cure every imaginable disease, but not one of them hit on the simple idea that Natasha's affliction was beyond them, just as all diseases affecting any living person are beyond our comprehension because every living person has his own peculiarities, every complaint is unique, new, complex, unknown to medicine – not a disease of the lungs, kidneys, skin, heart, et cetera, long recorded in the annals of medicine, but a disease that happens to be one possibility from an infinite number of afflictions affecting those organs. An idea as simple as this could never have occurred to the doctors (just as a wizard could never accept the idea that magic is beyond him), because their business in life had always been the curing of disease, that's what they'd always been paid for, and that's what they'd spent the best years of their life doing. But the real reason why this idea could never have occurred to the doctors was because they could see that now they were being really useful here, definitely useful to the entire Rostov household. Useful, not because they were making the patient swallow predominantly noxious substances (the harm they were doing was scarcely perceptible because the noxious substances were administered in tiny doses), no, they were useful, necessary, you might say indispensable (in the same way that the world has always been full of mountebanks, miracle-men, homoeopaths and allopaths, and always will be), because they satisfied the psychological yearnings of the patient and those who loved her. They satisfied the eternal human need to go on hoping for relief, the need for sympathy and for someone to do something that is felt by any suffering individual. They satisfied the eternal human need – seen at its simplest in a little child – to be rubbed where it hurts. When a child gets hurt he rushes into the arms of his mother or nurse for them to kiss or rub him where it hurts, and he feels better when the tender spot gets rubbed or kissed. The child cannot believe that these infinitely strong and wise friends of his lack the power to ease his pain. The very hope of relief and the sympathy shown by his mother as she rubs him are a source of comfort. The doctors helped Natasha by kissing and rubbing her poorly place and telling her she would soon be better if the coachman just drove down to the chemist's on the Arbat and spent one rouble, seventy kopecks on a few powders and some pills in a pretty little box, as long as she took the powders in boiled water at two-hourly intervals on the dot.

What would they have done, Sonya, the count and countess – they couldn't just stand there watching their feeble Natasha fade away – if they hadn't been able to minister to her with hourly pills, warm drinks, little cuts of chicken, and all the vital necessities laid down by the doctors that kept them so busy and consoled them one and all? As the rules laid down became ever more strict and complicated, so their consolation grew. How could the count have borne his beloved daughter's illness without knowing it was costing him a thousand roubles and being ready to find thousands more if it would do her any good; without knowing that, if by any chance she didn't get better, he would find thousands more again to take her abroad to consult foreign doctors; without being able to tell people in great detail how Métivier and Feller had got it all wrong, but Friez had got it right, and Mudrov had produced an even better diagnosis? What would the countess have done if she hadn't been able to go to her sick Natasha and tell her off now and then for not following the doctor's instructions to the letter?

'How can you expect to get better,' she would say, fussing with annoyance to hide how worried she was, 'if you won't do what the doctor says and take your medicine properly? We can't have all this silliness, can we? You might get *pneumonia*,' said the countess, much consoled by the very sound of that solemn word, which like everyone else she had no understanding of.

And what would Sonya have done without the happy knowledge that in those early days she hadn't taken her clothes off for three nights running so she could be on hand to carry out the doctor's orders down to the last detail, and now she couldn't sleep for fear of missing the right time to administer a few none-too-noxious pills from the little golden box? Even Natasha herself, despite many a protestation that medicine wouldn't do her any good and it was all nonsense, was delighted to see so many sacrifices being made for her, and to be forced to take medicine at certain times, and no less delighted to demonstrate by ignoring the doctor's instructions that she didn't believe in medicine and set little store by her own life.

The doctor rolled up every day, came and took her pulse, looked at her tongue, ignored her distraught face and made little jokes. But afterwards, when he had gone out into the next room followed hastily by the countess, he would assume a grave expression and inform her with a thoughtful shake of his head that her daughter was not yet out of the wood, though this latest medicine ought to do the trick, and all they could do was wait and see, the illness being more in the mind than the body, and yet . . .

The countess would slip him a piece of gold, trying to hide the deed from herself and from him, and she always went back to the poorly patient with more hope in her heart.

The symptoms of Natasha's illness were loss of appetite, sleeplessness, a cough and continual depression. The doctors had insisted she must never be far from medical attention, so they kept her there in the stifling atmosphere of the city. The whole summer of 1812 passed without the Rostovs going down to the country.

Despite the huge number of pills, drops and powders Natasha swallowed from enough little jars and boxes for Madame Schoss to build up a nice little collection (she had a passion for such things), despite Natasha's being deprived of her normal country life, youth prevailed, her affliction gradually became overlaid with the business of everyday life and an agonizing pain was lifted from her heart, receding into the past and giving her physical health a chance to improve.

CHAPTER 17

Natasha was calmer, but not happier. Not only did she avoid all outward forms of amusement such as balls, skating, concerts and the theatre, but she never even laughed without a suggestion of tears behind the laughter. She was incapable of singing. Whenever she began to laugh or tried to sing all alone, she was choked with tears: tears of remorse, tears of regret for a lost time of pure happiness, tears of annoyance at herself for so wantonly destroying her young life that might have turned out to be so happy. It was particularly laughter and singing that seemed like a profanation of her sorrow. Flirtation was far from her mind; here there was no temptation to resist. She said at the time that all men were no more to her than Nastasya Ivanovna, the buffoon, and she meant it. Some kind of inner sentinel seemed to guard against all pleasure. And indeed she appeared to have lost all her old girlish interests, which now belonged to a carefree former life once full of hope. Her bitterest and most recurrent memory took her back to those autumn months – the hunting, 'Uncle', the Christmas holidays spent with Nikolay at Otradnoye. She would have given anything to bring back a single day of that time! But it was all gone for ever. Her misgivings at the time had not been wrong; a time of freedom like that with such capacity for every kind of enjoyment would never come again. And yet life had to go on.

She took some pleasure in the thought that far from being better than everybody else, as she had once imagined, she was worse, much worse than anybody in the whole world. But this had little meaning. She knew it was true, but she kept on wondering, 'What's next?' only to find there was nothing next. There wasn't any joy in life, but life was passing. Natasha was clearly determined not to be a burden to anybody and not to get in anybody's way, but she wanted nothing for herself. She kept away from everyone in the house, and her brother Petya was the only person she felt at ease with. She liked being with him more than anyone else, and when she was alone with him there were occasions when she laughed. She hardly ever went out, and among the visitors she welcomed only one person – Pierre. No one could have been gentler, more caring, and yet more serious-minded than Count Bezukhov in his dealings with her. Natasha took in this tenderness at a subconscious level, and this was what made him so nice to be with. But she felt no gratitude towards him on this account: being good seemed to come naturally to Pierre and cost him no effort. Pierre seemed to be so spontaneously good-natured there was no merit in his kindness. Sometimes Natasha noticed some embarrassment or awkwardness in Pierre when she was with him, especially when he was trying to do her a favour or could see something looming up in the conversation that might bring back painful memories. Noting this, she put it down to his kind personality and the same kind of diffidence which she imagined he showed to everybody else. After uttering those unexpected words – if only he had been free to do so he would have been down on his knees asking for her hand and her love – which had come out at a moment of high emotion directed towards her, Pierre had said nothing of his feelings to Natasha, and she could only assume that those words, so comforting at the time, had been said like the usual bits of nonsense you come out with to console a weeping child. Not because Pierre was married, but because Natasha could sense a moral barrier between them – the very thing she had not felt with Kuragin – it never crossed her mind that her relationship with Pierre might one day develop into love on her side, even less on his, or even into the kind of tender, fully acknowledged romantic friendship between a man and a woman of which she had seen several examples.

Towards the end of the fast of St Peter, Agrafena Ivanovna Belova, a country neighbour of the Rostovs, came to Moscow to worship at the shrines of the saints. She suggested to Natasha that she should fast and prepare for Holy Communion, and Natasha seized on the idea with some relish. In defiance of the doctors' prohibition on going out in the early morning, Natasha insisted on keeping the fast and preparing for Communion not the way it was done in the Rostovs' household – by attending three services at home – but by following in the footsteps of Agrafena Ivanovna for a whole week, which meant not missing a single service, Matins, Vespers or Mass.

The countess was pleased to see this kind of zeal in Natasha. After all the unsuccessful medical treatment, deep down she was now hoping that prayer might do her daughter more good than medicine, so despite terrible misgivings she fell in with Natasha's wishes, said nothing to the doctors and handed her into the care of Madame Belova.

Agrafena Ivanovna used to come in to wake Natasha at three in the morning, and more often than not she found her already awake. Natasha was afraid of sleeping in and being late for Matins. After a quick wash she meekly pulled on her shabbiest dress and an old shawl before walking out into the deserted streets, shivering as she met the chill air and the limpid half-light of early morning. On the advice of Agrafena Ivanovna Natasha was preparing for Communion not at her own parish church, but at a church where the priest was described by the devout Madame Belova as someone with a particularly austere and righteous way of living.

There were never many people in church. Natasha and Madame Belova stood side by side always in the same place before an icon of the Mother of God which formed part of the screen behind the left choir, and at this unusual morning hour Natasha was overwhelmed by a new sense of humility before the sublime mystery as she gazed up at the black face of the Blessed Virgin lit up by candles burning in front and the morning light coming in through a window. She listened to the words of the service, trying hard to follow and understand. When she did understand, her personal emotions merged in every shade with her prayers; when she didn't, she had an even sweeter sense that the desire to understand everything amounted to pride, no one could ever understand everything, and all she had to do was believe and give herself up to God, and at moments like this she had a sense of Him guiding her soul. She crossed herself, bowed low, and when she didn't understand she simply yielded in disgust to a sense of her own vileness and prayed for forgiveness, total forgiveness, and mercy. The prayers she said most of all were prayers of repentance. Walking home in the early morning, when the only people they encountered were bricklayers on their way to work or men cleaning the streets, and the houses were full of sleeping people, Natasha glimpsed the first fresh possibility of redemption from sin and a new life of purity and happiness.

She spent a whole week leading this kind of life and the feeling grew stronger with each passing day. And the joy of Holy Communion (or holy communication, as Agrafena Ivanovna liked to call it, enjoying the pun) was so enormous she thought that blissful Sunday would never come.

But come it did, that happy, unforgettable Sunday when Natasha returned from Holy Communion dressed in her white muslin frock, experiencing peace of mind for the first time in many months and no longer oppressed by the life that lay ahead.

The doctor called to see Natasha the same day and his instructions were to keep on with the powders he had prescribed two weeks before. 'Oh, keep taking them, yes definitely, morning and evening,' he said, visibly and genuinely gratified by his own success. 'Now you mustn't forget. Countess, you have nothing to worry about,' said the doctor with great good humour, deftly palming his gold. 'We'll soon have her singing and dancing again. This last medicine has done the trick all right. She's so much better.'

The countess looked down at her fingernails and spat a little for luck before returning to the drawing-room with a smile on her face.

CHAPTER 18

At the beginning of July Moscow was awash with rumours about the progress of the war, and they were getting more and more alarming; there was talk of the Tsar making an appeal to the people, and the Tsar himself was said to be on his way back to Moscow from the army. And with no manifesto and no appeal to the people having been issued, by the 11th of July these communications and the overall position of Russia had become the subject of even wilder speculation. It was claimed that the Tsar was leaving because the army was in danger; it was also claimed that Smolensk had fallen, Napoleon had a million troops at his disposal, and nothing short of a miracle could save Russia.

On Saturday, the 11th of July, the manifesto was out but not yet circulating in print, and Pierre, who happened to be at the Rostovs', promised to come back to dinner the following evening, Sunday, and bring with him the manifesto and appeal, which he would have got by then from Count Rostopchin.

That Sunday the Rostovs attended divine service as usual in the private chapel of the Razumovskys. It was a hot July day. Even at ten in the morning, as the Rostovs descended from their carriage by the chapel, the sultry atmosphere, the shouts of the street hawkers, the bright, gaily coloured summer clothing of the crowd, the dusty leaves on the trees along the boulevard, the martial music and white-trousered battalion marching past to go on parade, the rumble of traffic and the blazing-hot sunshine, all conspired to produce that feeling of summer lassitude, that happiness and unhappiness with things as they stand, which are at their sharpest on a bright, hot day in town. All the fashionable world of Moscow, all the Rostovs' acquaintances were there in the chapel. (This year, as if anticipating something in the air, very many of the wealthy families who usually went down to the country for the summer had stayed on in Moscow.)

As Natasha walked in beside her mother behind a footman in livery who was clearing their way through the crowd she heard the voice of a young man talking about her in an audible whisper.

'That's young Countess Rostov. Didn't she . . .'

'She's looking thin, but she's still pretty!'

She caught several comments and thought she heard the names of Kuragin and Bolkonsky mentioned. But she was always thinking things like that. She couldn't get it out of her mind that anybody who so much as glanced at her must surely be thinking about what had happened to her. With a heavy feeling and a sinking heart, as always in a crowd nowadays, Natasha walked on in her lilac silk dress trimmed with black lace, bearing herself as only a woman can, with poise and dignity totally belying the pain and shame in her heart. She knew she was pretty, there was no mistaking that, but this was no longer a source of pleasure for her. On the contrary, it had hurt her more than anything else in recent days, and it was particularly painful on this bright, hot summer's day in town. 'Another Sunday, another week,' she said to herself, thinking back to the previous Sunday, 'and still the same life that isn't life, the same conditions that used to make life seem so easy. I'm still young and pretty, and now I know I'm a good person. I was wicked before, but now I'm good,' she thought, 'but these are the best years of my life and they're slipping by, completely useless.' She stood there next to her mother, nodding to people they knew who were standing near by. From force of habit Natasha watched the ladies to see how well turned-out they were, and looked disapprovingly at a lady not far away who held herself badly and crossed herself with a little cramped gesture. Then came the annoying thought that she was still being judged, and here she was, judging other people, so by the time the first sounds of the service rang out she was disgusted at the vileness of her character, disgusted that she had lost what purity of heart she had had before.

A venerable old priest with a gentle air about him took the service with the kind of peaceful solemnity that has such an inspiring and calming effect on the souls of worshippers. The sanctuary doors were closed, the curtain came slowly across and from within came a low voice uttering solemn words. Natasha felt herself inexplicably choking on tears, and she was swept by a feeling of blissful lassitude.

'Teach me what to do . . . how to find righteousness for ever and ever . . . what to do with my life!' she prayed. A deacon came out in front of the altar screen, and with his thumb sticking out he drew his long hair from under his robes, made the sign of the cross on his breast, and began the litany in loud and solemn tones:

'In peace let us pray to the Lord.'

'As a single community, all people together with no distinction of class, free from all enmity, united in brotherly love, let us pray . . .' thought Natasha.

'For peace from above and for the salvation of our souls . . .'

'For the world of angels and the souls of all spiritual beings who dwell above us,' prayed Natasha.

When they prayed for the army she thought of her brother and Denisov. When they prayed for all who travel at sea and on land she thought of Prince Andrey, prayed for him and prayed that God might forgive her for the wrong she had done him. When they prayed for all who love us, she prayed for her family, her father and mother and Sonya – newly aware of her wickedness towards them and the full strength of her love for them. When they prayed for those who hate us, she made herself think of enemies and people full of hatred so she could pray for them. In the category of enemies she included her father's creditors and everybody who had any business dealings with him, and every time her mind strayed to enemies and those who hate us she thought of Anatole, who had done her so much harm, and although he hadn't actually hated her she was delighted to have him as an enemy to pray for. Only when praying could she think clearly and calmly about Prince Andrey or Anatole, conscious that her feelings towards them dwindled away to nothing compared with her fear and love of the Lord God. When they prayed for the Royal Family and the Synod, she bowed very low and crossed herself even more devoutly, telling herself that although it was all above her head she couldn't have any doubts – she just loved the ruling Synod and wanted to pray for it.

When the litany was over, the deacon crossed his stole over his breast and said, 'Let us commit ourselves and our whole lives to Christ the Lord.'

'Commit ourselves to the Lord,' Natasha repeated in her heart. 'O Lord God, I commit myself to Thy will,' she thought. 'I ask for nothing. I want nothing. Teach me what I must do, how to exercise my will! Take me unto Thee. Please take me!' Natasha said, eager and full of emotion. She stood there without crossing herself, her slender arms dangling down, as if she expected to be seized at any moment by an unseen force that would deliver her from herself, from her misgivings and urges, her remorse, hopes and sins.

Several times during the service the countess stole a glance at her daughter's radiant face and glittering eyes, and prayed for God to help her.

To everyone's surprise, the deacon made a sudden departure from the liturgy that Natasha knew so well by bringing out the little footstool reserved for the priest to kneel on when he reads out the prayers on Trinity Sunday, and placing it in front of the sanctuary gates. Then out came the priest wearing his lilac-coloured velvet skullcap; he adjusted his hair and flopped down on his knees. The congregation also knelt, exchanging glances in some surprise. What they then heard was a new prayer just received from the Synod, a prayer for the protection of Russia against enemy invasion.

'Lord God of all power, God of our salvation,' intoned the priest in the soft, clear, restrained voice that is only heard in churches of the Slavs and makes such a devastating impact on the Russian heart.

'Lord God of all power, God of our salvation! Look down this day with mercy and blessings on Thy humble people. Graciously hear us, spare us and have mercy on us. Thy land is confounded by the foe, and he would fain lay waste the whole earth. These lawless men are gathered together to overthrow Thy kingdom and destroy Thy holy Jerusalem, Thy Beloved Russia, to defile Thy temples, overturn Thine altars and desecrate our holy shrines. How long, O Lord, how long shall the wicked prevail? How long shall they wield their unlawful power?

'Almighty God, hear us when we pray to Thee, strengthen with Thy might our most gracious and supreme Sovereign Lord, Emperor Alexander Pavlovich; be mindful of his virtue and gentleness; reward him according to his righteousness and long may it preserve us, Thy chosen Israel. Bless his counsels, his undertakings and all his deeds; strengthen his kingdom with Thine Almighty hand, and vouchsafe him victory over the enemy, even as Thou gavest Moses victory over Amalek, and Gideon over Midian, and David over Goliath. Preserve his army; put bows of brass into the hands of those that have gone to war in Thy name, and gird their loins with strength for the fight. Take up Thy sword and shield, arise and come to our aid; confound and put to shame those who devise evil against us, and let them be scattered before the face of Thy faithful warriors like dust before the wind; may Thy mighty angel confound them and put them to flight. May the net that they know not ensnare them, and their plots hatched in secret be turned against them. And let them fall beneath the feet of Thy servants and be laid low by our hosts. O Lord, Thou art able to save both great and small, Thou art God, and no man shall prevail against Thee.

'God of our Fathers, remember Thy blessings and mercy of old. Turn not Thy face from us; be gracious to us in our unworthiness; spare us in Thine infinite mercy, and in Thy bounteous goodness forgive us our transgressions and iniquity. Create in us a pure heart, and renew a righteous spirit within us; strengthen us all in our faith in Thee; fortify us with hope; inspire us with true love for one another; arm us with unity of spirit in the righteous defence of the inheritance Thou hast given to us and to our forefathers; and let not the sceptre of the unrighteous be raised against the destiny of Thy holy people.

'O Lord our God, in Whom we believe and trust, confound us not in our hope for Thy mercy, and give us a sign of Thy blessing, that those who hate us and our Orthodox faith may see it and be put to shame and confusion, and may all lands know that the Lord is Thy Name and that we are Thy people. Show Thy mercy upon us this day, O Lord, and grant us Thy salvation. May the hearts of Thy servants rejoice in Thy mercy. Strike down our enemies and be swift to destroy them beneath the feet of Thy faithful servants. For Thou art the defence, the succour, and the victory of those that put their trust in Thee; and to Thee be the glory, to Father, Son and Holy Ghost, as it was in the beginning, is now and ever shall be, world without end. Amen.'

In her state of heightened religious sensitivity Natasha was deeply affected by this prayer. She hung on every word about the victory of Moses over Amalek, and Gideon over Midian, and David over Goliath, and about the destruction of 'Thy Jerusalem', and she prayed with all the emotion and tenderness that filled her heart to overflowing, though she couldn't quite make out what she was praying for. She felt wholeheartedly involved in prayers for a righteous spirit, the fortifying of hearts with faith and hope, and the inspirational power of love. But she couldn't pray for her enemies to be trampled underfoot when only a few minutes earlier she had been wishing for more enemies to love and pray for. Yet neither could she doubt the righteousness of the prayer recited by the priest on his knees. She felt a thrill of dread at the awesome punishments due to be meted out to mankind for its sins, especially her sins, and she prayed that everyone should be forgiven, including her, and that she and everybody else should enjoy peace and happiness in their lives. And it seemed to her that God heard her prayer.

CHAPTER 19

Ever since the day Pierre had driven home from the Rostovs with Natasha's look of gratitude still fresh in his mind, stared up at the comet in the sky and felt the range of new possibilities opening up before him, he had stopped worrying about the agonizing problem of the vanity and senselessness of all earthly things. The terrible questions, 'Why?' 'What's it all about?', which had always assailed him whatever he was doing, had now been replaced, not by different questions or answers to the old ones, but by an image of *her*. If he heard people prattling on about nothing, or did so himself, if he read or heard about something that reminded him of human wicked- ness or folly, he no longer despaired; he had stopped wondering why people bothered with anything at all when life was so short and uncertain. He had only to think of her as he had last seen her, and all his doubts melted away, not because she had any answers to the questions that had been haunting him, but because her image trans- ported him instantly into another realm of sweetness, light and active spirituality, where there was no question of being in the right or in the wrong, a region of beauty and love well worth living for. If he came across some worldly abomination he would say to himself, 'So- and-so's robbing the state and the Tsar while the state and the Tsar weigh him down with honours, is he? Well, let him get on with it – *she* smiled at me yesterday, she asked me round, and I love her, and nobody will ever know.'

Pierre still went out a good deal, he hadn't stopped drinking and he led the same kind of idle, dissipated life, because apart from a few hours spent with the Rostovs he had to get through the rest of his time somehow, and the habits and friendships formed in Moscow kept drawing him back inexorably to the same old life. But in recent days, with rumours from the theatre of war sounding more ominous by the day, and with Natasha's health much improved, which meant that she no longer required the same degree of sympathy and pity, he had found himself increasingly overwhelmed by an inexplicable feeling of restlessness. His present position was untenable, he thought, and, sensing the approach of some disaster that was going to change the whole course of his life, he cast around impatiently on all sides watching for signs of it. One of his brother masons had revealed to Pierre a certain prophecy concerning Napoleon, taken from the Revelation of St John the Divine, where, in chapter xiii, verse 18, we read:

> Here is wisdom. Let him that hath understanding count the number of the beast: for it is the number of a man; and his number is Six hundred threescore and six.

And in the fifth verse of the same chapter:

> And there was given unto him a mouth speaking great things and blasphemies; and power was given unto him to continue forty and two months.

The French alphabet, laid out alongside the Hebrew (or Arabic) numerical system, with the first nine letters representing units, the next tens, and so on, gives the following values:

a b c d e f g h i k l m n o p q r s t u v w x y z
1 2 3 4 5 6 7 8 9 10 20 30 40 50 60 70 80 90 100 110 120 130 140 150 160

If you use this system to write out the words *l'empereur Napoléon* numerically, the sum of the letter-numbers comes to 666 (allowing 5 for the *e* omitted from *le*), which makes Napoleon the beast prophesied in the Apocalypse. More than that, if you apply the same system to the French number forty-two, *quarante-deux* (the span of months allotted to the beast that spoke 'great things and blasphemies'), you get 666 once again, from which it emerges that Napoleon came to a peak in 1812, a French Emperor forty-two years old. This prophecy made a great impression on Pierre, and he began wondering what could possibly put an end to the power of the beast that was Napoleon. Using the same system of taking the numerical values of letters and adding them up, he set out to solve this problem. He wrote down possible answers: *l'empereur Alexandre? La nation russe?* He added up the letters, but they came to much more or much less than 666. Once he applied the system to his own name in its French version, 'Comte Pierre Besouhof', but the total was miles out. He changed the spelling, substituting *z* for *s* added *de* and the article *le*, but he still couldn't get what he wanted. Then it occurred to him that if the

answer he was looking for was to be found in his name, surely his
nationality ought to be mentioned as well. He tried *Le russe Besuhof*
and this came to 671, only five too much and 5 was the value of *e*,
the letter dropped from the definite article in *l'empereur Napoléon*.
Dropping the *e* again (quite unjustifiably) Pierre got the answer he was
after in the phrase *l'russe Besuhof* – exactly 666! This discovery shook
him. How, and by what means, he was connected with the great event
predicted in the Apocalypse, he couldn't tell, but the connection was
there beyond doubt. It was all there: his love for Natasha, the Antichrist, Napoleon's invasion, the comet, the number 666, *l'empereur
Napoléon* and *l'russe Besuhof* – all these things were going to gestate
together and something would suddenly emerge from them to help
him break out of that vicious circle created by the petty concerns of
Moscow that had so enthralled him, and lead him forth to some
mighty achievement and true happiness.

The day before the Sunday when the new prayer was read out, Pierre
was due to carry out his promise to the Rostovs by calling on Count
Rostopchin to collect a copy of the Tsar's appeal to the country and
also pick up any late news from the army. On his arrival at Count
Rostopchin's that morning Pierre ran straight into a special courier
just back from the army. The courier was a familiar figure on the
Moscow ballroom scene and Pierre knew him well.

'For heaven's sake, can you take something off me?' said the courier.
'I've got a sackful of letters to parents.'

These included a letter from Nikolay Rostov to his father. Pierre
took that, and Count Rostopchin gave him a copy of the Tsar's appeal
to Moscow, fresh off the press, the last army orders and his own most
recent bulletin. A quick glance through the army announcements,
including lists of the dead and wounded, and also recent honours, told
Pierre that Nikolay Rostov had been awarded the Order of St George,
Fourth Class, for outstanding bravery at Ostrovna, and that Prince
Andrey Bolkonsky had been placed in command of a regiment of
chasseurs. Although reluctant to reawaken the Rostovs' memories of
Bolkonsky, Pierre couldn't resist the temptation to raise their spirits
by handing on the news of their son's decoration, so he sent the printed
announcement and Nikolay's letter straight round to the Rostovs,
holding back the Tsar's appeal, Rostopchin's bulletin and the other
announcements so he could take them along at dinner-time.

The conversation with Rostopchin, who looked so worried and
hard-pressed, Pierre's encounter with the courier, who had let it drop
so casually that the army was in a terrible state, rumours of spies being

caught in Moscow and a pamphlet in circulation stating that Napoleon had sworn to be in both capitals by autumn, together with the Tsar's impending arrival the next day – all things conspired to rekindle with new intensity in Pierre that feeling of excitement and anticipation that had never really left him since the appearance of the comet, and had flared up again at the beginning of the war.

The idea of doing some military service had occurred to Pierre long before this, and he would have done something about it but for two things: in the first place, he was a sworn member of the Masonic brotherhood committed to peace on earth and the abolition of war, and secondly, one look at the great mass of Muscovites who had gone into uniform as self-proclaimed patriots, and for some reason he squirmed with embarrassment at the idea of doing the same thing. But the main reason for not carrying out his intention to join up was the rather vague idea that he, *l'russe Besuhof*, was associated with the number of the beast, 666, and his role in putting an end to the power of the beast 'speaking great things and blasphemies' had been pre-determined from time immemorial, which meant that his was not to go about doing things, his was to sit there and wait for the inevitable to happen.

CHAPTER 20

As usual on Sundays the Rostovs were having a few close friends in for dinner. Pierre arrived early in order to catch them alone.

During the past year Pierre had put on so much weight he would have looked grotesque but for his great height, big limbs and the solid strength that enabled him to carry his enormous bulk with evident ease.

He mounted the stairs, puffing and panting and muttering under his breath. His driver no longer bothered to ask whether to wait. He knew that when the count was at the Rostovs' he would be there till midnight. The Rostovs' footmen ran forward with a warm welcome, eager to help him off with his cloak, and take his stick and hat. Pierre always stuck to his club habit of leaving his stick and hat behind in the vestibule.

The first person he saw at the Rostovs' was Natasha. Before actually seeing her, while he was taking off his cloak he heard her. She was practising her scales in the hall. He knew she had given up singing during her illness, so he was surprised and delighted by the sound of her voice. He opened the door softly, and there was Natasha, in the lilac-coloured dress she had worn at the service, walking up and down the room singing.

She had her back turned to him as he opened the door, but when she made a sharp turn and saw the look of surprise on his chubby face she coloured up and walked quickly over to him.

'I want to start singing again,' she said. 'It's something to do, isn't it?' she added by way of an excuse.

'A splendid thing to do!'

'Oh, I'm so glad you've come! I'm feeling so happy today,' she said with the old enthusiasm that Pierre hadn't seen for many a long day. 'Did you know darling Nikolay has won the George Cross? I'm so proud of him.'

'Of course I do. I sent the announcement. Well, I mustn't stop you,' he added, and made as if to walk through into the drawing-room.

Natasha stopped him.

'Count, I shouldn't really be singing, should I?' she said, blushing, her eyes fixed quizzically on Pierre's face.

'Yes . . . Why not? You've got things the wrong way round. But why do you ask me?'

'I really don't know,' Natasha answered hastily. 'I just wouldn't want to do anything you wouldn't like. I trust you completely. You've no idea what you mean to me, how much you've done for me!' She was gabbling away and didn't notice Pierre colouring up at these words. 'I saw something else in that announcement – *he*, Bolkonsky,' – she blurted the word out in a rapid whisper – 'he's here in Russia, back in the army. What do you think,' she said hurriedly, obviously anxious to get it all out before her strength failed her, 'will he ever forgive me? Will he always think badly of me? What do you think? What do you think?'

'What I think is . . .' said Pierre. 'There's nothing for him to forgive . . . If I was him . . .' By association, Pierre was instantly transported back in memory to the time when he had comforted her and said that if he was somebody else, the best man in the world and free, he would be down on his knees asking for her hand, and the same feeling of compassion, tenderness and love came over him, and the same words rose to his lips. But she didn't give him enough time to say them.

'Yes, you, you,' she said, breathing out the word *you* with much enthusiasm, 'you're different. Anyone kinder, more generous, better than you I have never known – no one could be! If it hadn't been for you then, and even now . . . I don't know what would have become of me, because . . .' Suddenly her eyes were watering; she turned away, held her music up to her eyes, started singing and set off again to walk up and down the room.

At that moment Petya ran in from the drawing-room.

By now Petya was a handsome, rosy-cheeked boy of fifteen, with full red lips, very like Natasha. He was studying for university entry, but in recent days he and his comrade, Obolensky, had made up their minds to go into the hussars.

Petya rushed over to his namesake, Pierre, to talk business.

He had asked him to find out whether he would be accepted into the hussars.

Pierre was walking around the drawing-room, oblivious to Petya.

The boy plucked him by the sleeve to attract his attention.

'Hey, Pyotr Kirilych, talk to me about my plan, for heaven's sake! You're my only hope,' said Petya.

'Oh yes, your plan . . . Going into the hussars . . . I will mention it. Yes, I'll mention it today . . .'

'Well now, my dear fellow, did you get the manifesto?' asked the old count. 'My little countess has been to church at the Razumovskys'. She heard the new prayer. Very nice too, she says.'

'Yes, I did,' answered Pierre. 'The Tsar's coming here tomorrow . . . There's to be an extraordinary meeting of the nobility and a new levy – ten men per thousand, they say. Oh, by the way, my congratulations.'

'Yes, indeed, thank God. Well, any news from the army?'

'Our boys are in retreat again. They are just outside Smolensk, they say,' answered Pierre.

'Oh Lord! Oh Lord!' said the count. 'Where's the manifesto?'

'The Tsar's appeal? Oh yes!' Pierre went through his pockets looking for the papers, but he couldn't find them. Still patting his pockets, he kissed the countess's hand as she came in, and looked round anxiously, evidently expecting Natasha, who had stopped singing by now but hadn't come through into the drawing-room.

'Good heavens, I don't know what I've done with it,' he said.

'There you are, he's always losing things,' said the countess.

Natasha came in. Her face had softened but she still looked worried as she sat down, without a word, watching Pierre. The moment she had come into the room Pierre's face, a picture of gloom, had lit up, and although he went on scrabbling for the documents, he stole several glances at her.

'Oh, for goodness' sake, I'll go back home. That's where I must have left them. No doubt about it . . .'

'But you'll be late for dinner.'

'Oh dear! The driver's gone.'

But Sonya had gone back into the vestibule to look for the papers and found them in Pierre's hat, where he had studiously tucked them under the lining. Pierre set about reading them.

'No, no. After dinner,' said the old count, who was obviously looking forward to the reading as a great treat.

At dinner they drank champagne and toasted the new chevalier of St George, and Shinshin told them the latest city gossip – an old Georgian princess had fallen ill, Métivier had disappeared from Moscow, and some German had been dragged before Rostopchin by the people, who claimed he was a French spy. According to Count Rostopchin they were calling him a *champignon*, but he told them to let the *champignon* go, because he was nothing more than an old German toadstool.[10]

'There are so many arrests,' said the count. 'I keep telling the countess not to speak French so much. It's not the right time.'

'And have you heard the latest?' said Shinshin. 'Prince Golitsyn's hired a Russian teacher – he's learning Russian.'

'It's getting dangerous to speak French in the streets,' he added – in French.

'Well, Count Pyotr Kirilych, if there's a general call-up we'll have to get you on a horse, won't we?' said the old count to Pierre.

Pierre had been quiet and pensive throughout dinner. Faced with this question he just stared at the count as if he couldn't understand what he was saying.

'Yes, yes, everybody's off to the war,' he said. 'No! A fine soldier I'd make! And yet you know, it's all so strange, so strange! Well, I can't understand it. I don't know, I've no taste for the military life, but nowadays nobody can answer for himself.'

After dinner the count settled down in a comfortable chair, took on a serious air and asked Sonya, who was thought to be a very good reader, to read the Tsar's appeal.

'To Moscow, our foremost capital city.

'The enemy has crossed our frontiers with huge forces. He comes to lay waste our beloved country . . .'

Sonya's thin little voice rang out. She was reading with close concentration. The count was listening with his eyes closed, sighing heavily at certain passages.

Natasha, bolt upright, directed searching looks at her father and Pierre.

Pierre felt her eyes on him and had to struggle to stop himself looking round. The countess looked angry and censorious, shaking her head at the manifesto's every solemn pronouncement. In all these words she could see only one thing: the danger menacing her son would not soon be over. Shinshin had twisted his lips into a sardonic smile and was obviously getting ready to make a joke when the first suitable opportunity came along – at the expense of Sonya's reading, the count's next comment, even the manifesto itself if no better chance came up.

After reading about the dangers threatening Russia, the hopes invested by the Tsar in Moscow, and especially its illustrious nobility, Sonya came to the concluding words and read them with a quavering voice due mainly to the close attention being paid by all the listeners:

'We shall appear without delay amidst our people in the capital, and in other parts of our dominion, for consultation and the supervision of all levies and recruitment, both those which are already barring the way to our enemy, and those newly formed to bring about his defeat wherever he appears. And may the ruin with which he threatens us rebound upon his own head, and may Europe, delivered from bondage, glorify the name of Russia!'

'Quite right!' cried the count, opening his moist eyes, choking and snuffling once or twice, as if a strong vinaigrette had been held to his nose. He went on, 'One word from the Tsar and we shall make every sacrifice, and spare nothing.'

Shinshin was prevented from saying something funny about the count's patriotism by Natasha, who leapt up from her seat and ran over to her father.

'Papa, you're such a darling!' she cried, kissing him, but she glanced round at Pierre again with the touch of flirtation that had returned with her new excitement.

'What a girl! Some patriot!' said Shinshin.

'No, I'm not, I'm just . . .' Natasha began, stung to the quick. 'You think everything's funny, but this is no joke . . .'

'Of course it's no joke,' repeated the count. 'Just let him say the word, and we'll be off . . . We're not a bunch of Germans!'

'Did you notice what he said?' said Pierre, ' "For consultation".'

'Yes, yes, for anything that turns up . . .'

Meanwhile Petya, who was being ignored, went over to his father, red in the face, and in a voice that wobbled between gruff bass and shrill treble he said, 'Now, listen, Papa, I'm telling you straight, and Mamma too, say what you will, I'm telling you straight, you *must* let me go into the army, because I can't . . . well, that's it . . .'

The countess turned her eyes to heaven in dismay, clasped her hands and turned on her husband in anger.

'Now look what you've done with all your clever talking!'

But the count was quick to reassert himself amidst all the excitement.

'Now listen,' he said. 'It's a bit early for you to be a soldier! Stop this silly nonsense. You've got some studying to do.'

'It isn't nonsense, Papa. Fedya Obolensky's younger than me, and he's going. Anyway, I can't study now, when . . .' Petya came to a halt, beetroot-red and perspiring, though he managed to get out, '. . . when our country's in danger.'

'That'll do, that'll do. You're being silly . . .'

'But you said yourself we would make any sacrifice.'

'Petya! Shut up, I tell you!' cried the count, looking round at his wife, who was watching her younger son, white-faced and staring.

'No, I'm telling you . . . Listen to Count Bezukhov. He'll tell you . . .'

'Nonsense, I tell you! The milk's hardly dry on his lips and he wants to go into the army! That's enough, I tell you,' and the count collected the papers, probably to read them through again in the study before his nap, ready to walk out.

'Pyotr Kirilych, shall we have a smoke?'

Pierre was too embarrassed to know what to do. It was Natasha, with an unusually radiant and eager look in her eyes, as she stared at him with something more than affection, that had reduced him to this state.

'Er, no. I ought to be going home . . .'

'Going home? But you were going to spend the evening with us . . . You don't come very often as it is. And this little girl of mine,' said the count with great good humour and a sideways glance at Natasha, 'needs you to keep her happy . . .'

'Er, no. I've forgotten something. I really must be going home . . . Business . . .' Pierre blurted out.

'All right, I'll say goodbye then,' said the count, and he left the room.

'Why are you going home? Why are you so upset? What's it all about?' Natasha asked Pierre, with a new challenge in her eyes.

'Because I love you!' he wanted to say; but didn't. He blushed till the tears came, and looked down.

'Because I think I ought to come and see you a bit less often . . . Because . . . no, it's just er . . . a bit of business . . .'

'But *why*? Tell me, please,' Natasha was about to insist, but suddenly she stopped.

The two of them looked at each other in dismay and embarrassment. He tried to force a laugh, but it wouldn't come. There was agony in his smile as he kissed her hand and left without a word.

Pierre made up his mind to stop visiting the Rostovs.

CHAPTER 21

After receiving such a categorical refusal Petya went off to his room, locked himself in and wept bitter tears for some time. When he came down to tea, gloomy, unspeaking and tear-stained, the family pretended not to notice.

Next day, the Tsar arrived in Moscow. Several of the Rostovs' servants asked permission to go out and see the Tsar. That morning Petya took a lot of trouble with himself, combing his hair scrupulously and adjusting his collar like an adult. He screwed his eyes up in front of the mirror, gesticulated, shrugged, and then at last, without a word to anyone, pulled on his cap and left the house by the back steps to avoid being noticed. Petya had made up his mind to go down to where the Tsar was and have a straight talk with some gentleman-in-waiting (he thought the Tsar was always surrounded by gentlemen-in-waiting), making it clear that he, Count Rostov, in spite of his youth, wished to serve his country, and youth shouldn't be seen as an obstacle to devotion, and he was ready for ... Petya had composed many a splendid phrase while he was getting ready and now he was off to communicate them to a gentleman-in-waiting.

Petya felt certain his presentation to the Tsar would succeed if only because he was still a child (he could just see them all, amazed at his youth), and yet with his nicely adjusted collar arrangement, his neat hair and a slow, sedate way of walking he was hoping to look like a grown-up man. But the further he walked, the more fascinated he became with the growing crowds advancing on the Kremlin, and he soon forgot about maintaining the adult slowness and sedateness. As he closed in on the Kremlin he had to stop himself being jostled out of the way, so he stuck both elbows out with grim determination. But determined or not, when he got to Trinity Gate the crowd, seemingly oblivious to his patriotic purpose in going to the Kremlin, shoved him up so close against a wall that he had to give in and stop walking while carriages trundled in through the archway. Near Petya stood a peasant woman, a footman, two tradesmen and a retired veteran soldier. After waiting for a while wedged in the gateway, Petya decided not to wait for all the carriages to go through and he tried to shove through and get ahead of all the others by flailing away with his elbows. The peasant woman next to him was the first to feel the force of them, and she yelled, 'Hey, who d'you think you're shoving, young sir? Can't you see we're all stuck? You'll never get through there.'

'We can all get through like that!' said the footman, also quick with his elbows, and he shoved Petya back into a stinking corner of the gateway.

Petya wiped his sweaty face with his hands, and straightened the damp collar arrangement he had taken so much trouble with at home to make it look like an adult's.

By now Petya was feeling far from presentable, and he was afraid that if he showed himself to the gentlemen-in-waiting in this state they would never let him in to see the Tsar. But the crush was so bad there was no possibility of straightening himself out or moving somewhere else. One of the generals who came riding through was a friend of the Rostov family, but, although Petya would have dearly loved to ask him for help, he thought this wouldn't be a manly thing to do. When all the carriages had gone in, the crowd rushed forward and Petya was swept along with it into the square, which was already full of people. Not only the square, but the slopes and even the rooftops were covered with people. The moment Petya set foot on the square he heard the ringing of bells and the happy murmur of the crowd that thronged the whole Kremlin.

The crush eased off for a while, but then suddenly all heads were bared and the crowd surged forward again. Petya was squashed so tight he couldn't breathe, and then came the cheering: 'Hurrah! Hurrah! Hurrah!'

Petya stood on tiptoe, shoving and squeezing, but he couldn't see anything beyond the surrounding crowd.

Deep emotion and great rapture were written on every face. A shopkeeper's wife standing near Petya was sobbing, and her face was streaming with tears.

'Father! Angel! Lord and Master!' she kept chanting, using her fingers to wipe away the tears.

'Hurrah!' rose from the crowd on every side.

For a minute the crowd stayed where it was, then there was another surge forward.

Petya was wild with excitement. With gritted teeth and a ferocious glare in his rolling eyes, he hurled himself forward, elbowing his way through and yelling 'Hurrah!' as if he was ready to die and kill everybody else, but faces no less ferocious than his, yelling just as loud, were hemming him in on both sides.

'So this is it. This is the Tsar!' thought Petya. 'No, I could never give him the petition myself. It would be outrageous!'

Nevertheless, he kept on forcing himself forward as desperately as ever, and over the backs of the people in front he caught a glimpse of an open space and a strip of red carpet, but then the crowd swayed

back again. The police were forcing people back because they were
encroaching too close on the procession. The Tsar was making his
way from the palace to the Cathedral of the Assumption. Suddenly
Petya got a terrible blow in the ribs and he was so badly crushed that
his eyes misted over and he fainted. When he came round a clergyman
in a shabby blue cassock, with shaggy grey hair down his back –
probably a deacon – was propping him up with one arm and fending
the crowd off with the other.

'Hey, there's a young gentleman here – he's been crushed!' the
deacon was saying. 'Watch what you're doing! Steady on . . . You're
squashing him to death!'

The Tsar had entered the cathedral. The crowd fanned out again,
and the deacon manœuvred Petya, white-faced and scarcely breathing,
over towards the big Tsar-Cannon.[11] Several people took pity on Petya
and before long quite a crowd had gathered round attentively. The
nearest bystanders took him under their wing, unbuttoning his coat,
hoisting him up on top of the cannon, and shouting at other people
who were squeezing up too close.

'You could kill somebody, squashing like that! What do you think
you're doing? Murderers! Look at 'im, poor little fellow, he's as white
as a sheet,' said voices.

Petya soon came round and the colour came back to his face. The
pain had gone, and this unpleasant little setback had gained him a
seat on top of the cannon, from where he hoped to see the Tsar,
because he had to come back that way. Petya had abandoned any idea
of submitting his petition. Now he just wanted to see him – then he
would be able to say he'd had a lucky day!

While the service went on inside the Cathedral of the Assumption,
marking both the Tsar's arrival and the peace concluded with Turkey,
the crowd scattered about the square, and hawkers came round selling
kvass, gingerbread and poppy-seed sweets (Petya's favourite), and
the people chatted about all the usual things. A shopkeeper's wife
showed her torn shawl and told them how much it had cost; another
one complained that nowadays the prices of everything silk had
gone through the roof. The deacon who had rescued Petya was talking
to an office-worker about the different priests who were officiating
today with the most reverend bishop. The deacon made several uses
of the word 'conciliar', which meant nothing to Petya. Two young
apprentices were having fun with some servant-girls, cracking nuts
with their teeth. All this talk, especially the chit-chat with the girls,
which would normally have been fascinating to someone of Petya's
age, had no appeal for him today. He sat there enthroned on his

cannon, still excited at the thought of the Tsar and his love for him. The mixture of pain and panic when he was being crushed, together with the general rapture, had produced in him a passionate sense of occasion.

Suddenly cannon shots were heard from the embankment to mark the peace with Turkey, and the crowd swarmed over to the embankment to watch the firing. Petya would have liked to run across too, but the deacon, who had taken charge of his young gentleman, wouldn't let him go. They were still firing when a number of officers, generals and gentlemen-in-waiting came running out of the cathedral. Others followed at a slower pace, caps were doffed and the people who had run across to watch the cannons rushed back again. Eventually four men in uniforms and ribbons came out through the cathedral doors to a great 'Hurrah! Hurrah!' from the crowd.

'Which is the Tsar? Which one?' Petya asked around in a tearful voice, but there was no answer; everybody was too excited. Petya picked one of the four, and although he could hardly see him through his tears of joy, he focused all his passionate attention on him, though in fact this wasn't the Tsar. He roared 'Hurrah!' in a frenzied voice, and made up his mind once and for all that tomorrow nothing would stop him joining the army.

The crowd ran after the Tsar, went with him as far as the palace, and then began to break up. It was getting late, Petya had had nothing to eat, and he was sweating profusely, but he had no intention of going home. He stayed on with a smaller though still considerable crowd in front of the palace while the Tsar was at dinner. He gazed up at the palace windows waiting for something to happen, and envying both the grand personages driving up to the entrance to dine with the Tsar and the servants waiting at table, who could be glimpsed now and then at the windows.

Over dinner with the Tsar Valuyev glanced through the window and said, 'The people are still out there, hoping for another sight of your Majesty.'

When dinner was over the Tsar got to his feet, still munching a biscuit, and walked out on to the balcony. The crowd swept forward, taking Petya with it, and rushed towards the balcony.

'Angel! Father! Hurrah! Lord and master!' Petya roared along with the crowd. Some women and even a few of the more sensitive men, including Petya, wept for joy.

A fair-sized piece of biscuit fell from the Tsar's hand, hit the balcony railing and bounced down to the ground. A coachman in a jerkin, who was nearest to it, pounced on the piece of biscuit and snatched it up. Several people surged towards the coachman. When he saw this the Tsar asked for a plate of biscuits, and started tossing them down from the balcony. Petya goggled at this and the blood rushed to his head. Exhilarated more than ever by the danger of the crush, he dived towards the biscuits. He couldn't have said why, but he felt he must get one of the biscuits dropped from the Tsar's hands, and nothing must stop him. He leapt forward, knocking over an old woman who was just about to grab a biscuit. Down on the ground the old woman wouldn't admit defeat; she was still scrabbling after the biscuits but couldn't quite get hold of one. Petya shoved her hand away with his knee, grabbed a biscuit, and roared a hoarse 'Hurrah!' as fast as he could so as not to miss the Tsar.

The Tsar went in, and after that most of the crowd began to disperse.

'Told you it was worth waiting – and it was,' came delighted voices from all parts of the crowd.

Happy as he was, Petya felt reluctant to go home, because this would mean admitting that his day's pleasure was over. He walked away from the Kremlin, but instead of going home he went to see his pal, Obolensky, another fifteen-year-old who was keen to enlist. When he did get home, Petya made an announcement that brooked no denial: if they wouldn't let him go he was going to run away. And the following day, without actually giving in, Count Ilya Rostov went and made a few inquiries to see whether there was somewhere not too dangerous that Petya might be posted to.

CHAPTER 22

Two days later, on the 15th of July, an endless line of carriages could be seen standing outside the Sloboda palace.

The great halls were teeming. The first one was full of uniformed noblemen, the second with bearded merchants in blue, full-skirted coats, wearing all their medals. The hall selected for the Council of the Nobility was abuzz with movement and noise. The real big-wigs were sitting on high-backed chairs round a large table under a portrait of the Tsar, but most of the other noblemen were strolling about the hall.

These noblemen, people Pierre was used to seeing every day at the club or in their homes, were all in uniform, some dating back to the ages of Catherine or Paul, some new ones belonging to Alexander's reign, others nothing more than the standard uniform of the nobility, but the overall effect of these costumes was to impart a weird fantasy quality to this diverse assembly of faces, both young and old, many of them familiar. It was the older men who stood out with their half-seeing eyes, toothless mouths, bald heads, thin bodies, and faces all wrinkled, sallow or bloated. For the most part they just sat there in silence, and if they did get up to walk about and talk to people they would generally attach themselves to someone a bit younger. These faces were like the ones Petya had seen on the square, full of expectancy, waiting for some solemn event, totally different from their everyday selves and yesterday's faces, when all that mattered was a game of boston, Petrushka the cook, the state of Zinaida Dmitriyevna's health, and things like that.

Pierre was there. He had felt uncomfortable since early morning after squeezing himself into a nobleman's uniform that wouldn't fit. He was in a state of high excitement; this extraordinary assembly, of both nobles and merchants, the States General that transcended class, had reawakened in him a whole series of ideas about Rousseau's *Social Contract* and the French Revolution, ideas long abandoned but still engraved on his soul. The words he had spotted in the manifesto, about the Tsar coming to the capital for *consultation* with his people, had confirmed that he was on the right lines. Acting on the assumption that something really important of that order was almost upon them, something he had long been waiting for, he walked up and down watching and listening intently. Nowhere did he pick up the slightest sign of the ideas that now obsessed him.

The Tsar's manifesto was read out to enthusiastic applause, and then they all scattered about the rooms deep in conversation. Apart from everyday chit-chat, Pierre heard deliberations about where the marshals would have to stand when the Tsar came in, the best time to put on a ball for the Tsar, whether they should be broken down by districts or act together as a province, and so on. But the moment anyone so much as touched on the war and the purpose of their meeting, everything became vague and uncertain. Everyone, it seemed, would sooner listen than speak.

In one of the rooms a middle-aged man cutting a handsome, virile figure in his retired naval officer's uniform was holding forth to a little crowd that had gathered round him. Pierre moved over to the growing circle, and listened to the speaker. Count Ilya Rostov, wearing a uniform from the days of Catherine, had been sauntering about beaming at all and sundry, since he knew everyone, but now he too came over to this group and lent an ear with a pleasant smile on his face, as always when he was listening, nodding with approval when he agreed with the speaker. The retired naval officer was coming out with some outrageous things, as was evident from the listeners' faces and the fact that some people Pierre knew to be meek and timid souls were recoiling in disapproval or standing up to him. Pierre gradually elbowed his way into the middle of the circle, listening closely, and got the impression the speaker was a true liberal, but not in the sense that Pierre was interested in. The naval officer had the strong, melodious baritone of a Russian nobleman, with the pleasant addition of a guttural French *r* and slurred consonants, the kind of voice you hear when men shout, 'Be a good fe'ow, bwing me a pipe!' and phrases like that. His tone suggested an easy authority and long experience of the good life.

'What if the peopuh of Smolensk have offahd to waise militia for the Empewah? Are the peopuh of Smolensk going to lay down the law fow us? If the good noble peopuh of the Moscow pwovince think fit, they can show their loyalty to the Empewah by othah means. Have we fo'gotten the militia of 1807? Only the pwiests' sons and thieves and wobbahs made any money out of that . . .'

Count Ilya Rostov smiled his bland smile and nodded in approval.

'And was ah militia any good to the state? Not the swightest! Bwought the wuwal economy to wack and wuin. Bwing back conscwiption, that's what I say . . . othahwise a man comes back to you neithah soldiah no' peasant, nothing but only a mowal weck. We nobuhls are pwepared to wisk our lives. Evwy man jack of us will dwum up wecwuits. One word fwom our sov'weign and we'll go out and die for him,' added the orator, warming to his theme.

Count Rostov was drooling with pleasure, and he nudged Pierre, but Pierre wanted to speak too. He moved forward, full of excitement, without knowing why he was excited or what he was going to say. He opened his mouth to launch forth, only to be interrupted by a wily, crotchety senator without a tooth in his head, standing near to the orator. Obviously a veteran of the debating chamber well accustomed to formulating an argument, he spoke out in a low, clear voice.

'I would imagine, my dear sir,' said the senator, his toothless mouth champing, 'that we have been summoned here not to discuss the relative merits of conscription and the militia for our country today. We have been summoned to make a response to the appeal graciously placed before us by our sovereign the Emperor. As to the decision between conscription and the militia – we can leave that to a higher authority . . .'

Suddenly Pierre had found a target for all his excitement. He was furious with the senator for taking such a pernickety and narrow-minded view of the nobility and what they were being asked to do.

Pierre stepped forward and stopped him in his tracks. Without actually knowing what he was going to say, he launched forth in rather bookish Russian, with the occasional lapse into French.

'Excuse me, your Excellency,' he began. (Pierre was well acquainted with this senator, but on this occasion he felt it best to address him formally.) 'Although I don't agree with this gentleman . . .' (Pierre hesitated, on the point of referring to him as 'the honourable previous speaker') 'with this gentleman – I'm afraid I don't know your name, sir – but *I* would imagine that those of us who are of noble estate, apart from any expression of sympathy and zeal for the cause, have also been convened to consider what measures we can take to assist our country. I would imagine,' said Pierre, warming to his task, 'that the Tsar himself would not be too pleased to find us being nothing more than the owners of peasants whom we have given up to him, and er, cannon-fodder . . . sort of . . . that we are willing to be – instead of finding us full of good c . . . cou . . . counsel.'

Many people shuffled away from the circle when they noticed the derisive smile of the senator and Pierre's outspokenness. Count Rostov was the only person who liked what Pierre said, just as he had liked what the naval officer had said and the senator. He always liked what the last speaker had said.

'I would imagine that before we get down to discussing these questions,' Pierre continued, 'we ought to ask the Emperor, his Majesty, with the greatest respect to communicate to us the numbers of our troops, the positions of our troops and our army, and only then . . .'

These words were hardly out of Pierre's mouth when he was roundly attacked from three sides at once. The most violent onslaught came from an old and well-disposed acquaintance by the name of Stepan Stepanovich Apraksin, who had often been his partner at boston. But Stepan Stepanovich was in uniform, and because of this or perhaps for some other reason, Pierre saw before him a completely changed man. Stepan Stepanovich yelled at Pierre with an old man's anger on an old man's face: 'In the first place, I'm telling you we have no right to put questions like that to the Emperor, and secondly, if the Russian nobility did have such a right, the Emperor would be in no position to reply. Troop movements depend on enemy manoeuvres. We put men in and we take them out . . .'

Another voice cut across Apraksin. It belonged to a forty-year-old man of medium height known to Pierre from earlier days at the gypsies' entertainments, when he had been no good at cards. He too was a different man in uniform, and he now moved up closer to Pierre.

'Anyway, this is no time for deep discussions,' said this nobleman.

'Action's the word! There's a war on. The enemy's on the march and he's coming to destroy Russia, to desecrate the tombs of our fathers, and get our wives and children.' He thumped himself on the chest. 'We shall arise. To a man we shall arise and follow our father the Tsar!' he roared, his eyes bloodshot and rolling. A murmur of approval ran through the group. 'We are Russians, ready to put our lives on the line for the defence of our faith, our throne, our country. But we must leave off our idle dreaming if we are true sons of our fatherland. We'll show them in Europe – Russia shall defend Russia!' roared this gentleman.

Pierre wanted to reply, but he couldn't get a word out. He could sense that the sound of his words, irrespective of any meaning, would be drowned out by the other's excited voice.

Count Rostov was nodding in agreement at the back. Some of the listeners had been quick to align themselves shoulder to shoulder with the speaker as he wound up, and there was a chorus of approval: 'Oh yes. Quite right. Yes indeed!'

Pierre wanted to say that he was by no means averse to sacrificing money, or his peasants, or himself, but you needed to know exactly what was what if you wanted to help . . . but he couldn't speak.

Voices were yelling and shouting together, too many for Count Rostov to nod to. And the group was continually growing, collapsing and re-forming until at last there came a general surge, accompanied by the buzz of conversation, towards the big table in the big room. Pierre was given no chance to speak. They talked him down, jostled him aside and turned their backs on him as if he was the common enemy, not because they didn't like what he had said (which had been lost by now in the torrent of further speeches), but because a crowd is always at its liveliest when it has a tangible object to love and another one to hate. Pierre had provided the latter. Many speakers said their piece after that excited gentleman, all in the same tone. There were some very fine and original speeches.

Glinka, the owner of *The Russian Messenger*, who had been immediately recognized and hailed with shouts of 'Author! Author!', announced that it would take hell to repulse hell, and he had seen a child smile at thunder and lightning, but we would not be that child.

'No, no, not when it thunders here!' came the encouraging noises from the back.

They all drifted over towards the large table where the bald grey-bearded seventy-year-olds sat decked out in their uniforms and decorations. Pierre had seen virtually all of these men at home with their personal buffoons, if not playing boston at the club. The crowd advanced to the table, still with no lapse in the buzz of conversation. Various speakers, squashed up against the high chair-backs by the surging crowd, were holding forth one after the other and sometimes two at a time. Those at the back noted what the speaker had not managed to say and lost no time filling the gaps. Others, suffering in the heat and the crush, were racking their brains in search of any idea that could be blurted out. The bigwigs with familiar faces sitting at the table kept looking round at each other, and in most cases the expressions on those faces all said the same thing – they were feeling the heat. Pierre, however, was feeling all worked up; even he had caught the general mood, the urge to demonstrate that they could take anything in their stride, a mood that expressed itself in tone and attitude rather than in the meaning of anything said. He was sticking to his own ideas but he still felt somehow in the wrong, and he was keen to defend himself.

'All I said was – we could make better sacrifices when we know what the needs are,' he announced to the world, trying to shout the others down.

One old man sitting near by looked round, only to be immediately distracted by an outburst at the other end of the table.

'Yes, Moscow will fall! It's the price we'll have to pay!' came one voice.

'He's the enemy of mankind!' came another.

'If I could just say . . .'

'Gentlemen, you're squashing me! . . .'

CHAPTER 23

At that moment the crowd parted and Count Rostopchin, with his jutting chin and sharp eyes, came bustling in dressed in a general's uniform with a sash over his shoulder.

'Our sovereign the Emperor will be here immediately,' said Rostopchin. 'I have just come from him. I am assuming that, given our present situation, there is not much to discuss. The Emperor has graciously seen fit to summon us along with the merchants,' said Count Rostopchin. 'Millions will flow from that quarter.' He pointed to the merchants' hall. 'Our task is to raise men and not spare ourselves . . . It's the least we can do.'

The only consultation was with the bigwigs at the table. To say it was conducted quietly would be an understatement; the atmosphere was positively lugubrious when, after the racket that had gone before, all that could be heard were a few old men's voices reciting one at a time, 'Yes, I agree,' or, just to be different, 'Yes, I'm of the same opinion.'

The secretary was instructed to write down the resolution of the Moscow nobility, to wit: the nobles of Moscow, like those of Smolensk, shall furnish a levy of ten men per thousand serfs, fully kitted out.

The gentlemen got to their feet with an air of relief when the session was over, scraped their chairs back and strolled round the room, stretching their legs, taking their friends by the arm and having a good chat.

'The Tsar! The Tsar!' came the sudden call through every room, and the whole crowd swarmed towards the entrance.

The Tsar walked in down a wide aisle formed by two lines of noblemen. Every face was a picture of reverence mixed with alarm and curiosity. Pierre was some way away, and he couldn't quite catch everything said by the Tsar. He could tell from what he did hear that the Tsar was speaking of the danger that threatened the empire, and his great faith in the Moscow nobility. In response another voice informed the Tsar of the resolution just passed by the assembly.

'Gentlemen!' The Tsar's voice trembled as he spoke.

A ripple of anticipation passed through the crowd, then there was silence and Pierre could hear the Tsar quite clearly. He sounded caring, compassionate and deeply emotional as he said:

'I have never doubted the loyalty of you Russian noblemen. But this day it has surpassed my expectations. I thank you in the name of the fatherland. Gentlemen, we must act! Time is of the essence . . .'

The Tsar stopped talking, everyone crowded in on him, and cries of delight echoed on all sides.

'Yes indeed, of the essence . . . from the mouth of the Tsar!' came the sobbing voice of Count Rostov from the back. He hadn't heard a word, but in his own way he seemed to understand.

The Tsar then went on from the nobility's room to the merchants' room. He was there for ten minutes or so. Pierre watched with the rest as the Tsar came back from the merchants' room full of emotion and with tears in his eyes. They learnt afterwards that the Tsar had hardly begun to speak to the merchants when he broke down in tears and finished what he had to say in a trembling voice. When Pierre saw the Emperor he was on his way out with two merchants. Pierre knew one of them, a portly tax-farmer; the other was the mayor, a man with a pinched, sallow face and narrow beard. Both were in tears. The thin man's eyes were watering, but the portly tax-farmer was blubbering like a child and he kept repeating:

'Life, property, take it all, your Majesty!'

At that moment Pierre had only one thought in mind: the urge to show that nothing was too much for him and he would make any sacrifice. The constitutional implications of his speech were on his conscience, and he now wanted a chance to smooth things over. When he heard that Count Mamonov was furnishing a regiment, Bezukhov lost no time in informing Count Rostopchin that he would furnish and maintain a thousand men.

Old Rostov couldn't hold back his tears as he told the whole story to his wife. He agreed to Petya's request on the spot and set off personally to register his name.

The Tsar left Moscow the next day.

The noblemen went back from the assembly to their homes and clubs, took off their uniforms, and with deep misgivings issued orders to their stewards to start raising the levy. They were amazed at what they had done.

PART II

Napoleon went to war with Russia because he could not resist going to Dresden, could not resist the adulation, could not resist the idea of donning the Polish uniform, and giving in to the stimulating feel of a June morning, and could not contain his petulant outbursts in the presence of Kurakin and later on Balashev.

Alexander refused all negotiations because he felt personally insulted. Barclay de Tolly tried to command the army as best he could so as to do his duty and earn a glorious reputation as a great general. Rostov attacked the French because he could not resist the temptation to gallop across a flat field. And all the countless numbers of people involved in this war acted like this, each according to his own peculiarities, habits, circumstances and aims. Moved ostensibly by fear or vanity, pleasure, indignation or reason, and acting on the assumption they knew what they were doing and were doing it for themselves, they were actually nothing more than unwitting tools in the hands of history, performing a function hidden from themselves but comprehensible to us. This is the unavoidable fate of all men of action, and the higher they stand in the social hierarchy the less freedom they have.

As we write, the leading figures of 1812 are long gone from the scene, their personal interests have vanished without trace, and all we have to go on are the historical results of that period.

But if we assume that the people of Europe under Napoleon's leadership somehow *had* to go over and die in the depths of Russia, all the senseless, cruel and self-contradictory actions of the participants in this war become intelligible.

It was Providence that compelled all those men, striving for the realization of their own personal ambitions, to work co-operatively towards an outcome of immense significance, of which no single individual (not Napoleon, not Alexander, even less anybody actually involved in the fighting) had the slightest inkling.

We write now with a clear view of what caused the rout of the French army in 1812. It is beyond argument: two things caused the rout of Napoleon's French forces – on the one hand, they were badly prepared for a winter campaign in the Russian heartland, and they set out too late; on the other hand, the war took on a special character after the burning of Russian towns and the build-up of Russian hatred for the enemy. But at the time no one foresaw what now seems obvious: this was the only way the best army in the world, eight hundred thousand strong and led by the best general, could have lost to a Russian army wet behind the ears, half as strong and led by inexperienced generals. Not only was this *entirely unforeseen*, but *on the Russian side* every last effort was made to prevent the only thing that could have saved Russia, and *on the French side*, despite Napoleon's depth of experience and supposed military genius, every effort was made to push on to Moscow in late summer, the one thing that would guarantee disaster.

In historical works on the year 1812 French writers like to claim that Napoleon was well aware of the danger of extending his line, that he wanted to fight, and that his marshals advised him to call a halt at Smolensk. By arguing along these lines they seek to demonstrate that even at that stage of the campaign the real danger had been spotted. Russian historians are even keener to claim that from the outset there existed a plan of campaign borrowed from the Scythians which involved luring Napoleon into the heart of Russia, and some writers attribute this plan to Pfuel, some to an unknown Frenchman, some to Toll, while others attribute it to the Emperor Alexander himself, on the basis of notes, draft schemes and letters containing real hints at this course of action. But all these hints that what eventually happened was foreseen on both sides, the French and the Russian, are put forward now only because they have been justified by subsequent events. If the events had not occurred these hints would have been forgotten like the thousands, nay millions, of other contradictory hints and speculative ideas prevalent at the time that turned out to be wrong and were soon forgotten. The outcome of any event is always accompanied by such a range of speculative ideas about its cause that irrespective of the outcome there will always be somebody who can say, 'Look, I told you that's how it would turn out,' conveniently forgetting the vast number of other speculative ideas, many of which predicted the exact opposite.

Clearly, any suggestions that Napoleon was aware of the danger of extending his line, and that the Russians had a plan to lure the enemy into the heart of their country, fall into to this category, and only the most biased of historians could attribute any such thoughts to Napoleon and his marshals, or any such plans to the Russian generals. Speculative ideas like these fly in the face of the facts. From the moment of the invasion and during the whole course of the war, far from attempting to lure the French into the heart of Russia, the Russians did everything they could to stop them in their tracks; and Napoleon, far from worrying about extending his line, celebrated every step forward as a triumph, and did not seek opportunities to engage the foe with anything like the same eagerness as he had done in his previous campaigns.

At the outbreak of war our armies were cut off from each other and the only aim we had in mind was to unite them, though if our plan was to retreat and lure the enemy into the heart of the country, there would have been no advantage in bringing them together. The Emperor was out with the army to boost morale by defending every inch of Russian soil, not with some idea of retreat. Pfuel's huge camp at Drissa meant: thus far and no further. The Tsar called the commander-in-chief to account for every retreating step. The Emperor could never have anticipated the enemy's taking of Smolensk let alone the burning of Moscow, and when the armies had been reunited the Tsar was furious to learn that Smolensk had been taken and burnt without a pitched battle being fought outside its walls. This was the Tsar's attitude, but the Russian generals and the Russian people as a whole were even more incensed at the very idea of our men retreating into the heartland.

Napoleon split our armies and moved straight on, deep into the country, spurning several chances to force an engagement. By August he was in Smolensk and his only thought was to keep on going even though, as we can now see, marching forward spelt disaster.

The facts are clear: Napoleon foresaw no danger in pressing on to Moscow, and neither Alexander nor his generals had the slightest thought of luring Napoleon on – they thought the very opposite. Napoleon was drawn on into Russia not by a preconceived plan – no one dreamt of any such possibility – but by some complex interplay of desires, motivation and machinations on the part of the warring contenders, who had no idea of how things would turn out and what would be Russia's sole salvation. The whole thing was a fluke. Our armies were split up early on. We tried to bring them together, with every intention of joining battle and stopping the enemy's advance, but, for all these attempts at unification, while managing to avoid battle with a far stronger enemy, we were forced into retreat at a sharp angle, thus drawing the French along with us to Smolensk. But there is more to it than that. We were retreating at a sharp angle not just because the French were moving in between the two armies; the angle was made sharper and we retreated further because Barclay de Tolly, an unpopular German, was loathed by Bagration, who was due to come under his command, and Bagration employed every delaying tactic in the book with the second army to avoid joining up with him only to hand over control. He delayed unification for as long as he could, even though unification was the main aim of everyone in authority, because he thought that marching his men would expose them to danger, and it would be best for him to edge to the left, southwards, harassing the enemy's flank and rear and building up his army from Ukraine. But it seems likely that his real reason for thinking along these lines was to avoid placing himself under the command of Barclay, the hated German who was his junior in rank.

The Emperor was out with the army to boost morale but his presence there, his vacillation and the vast numbers of counsellors and plans available rendered the first army inactive, so it had to retreat.

The camp at Drissa was where they proposed to draw the line, but up rose Paulucci, with his eye on the commander-in-chief's job, and his tireless efforts finally prevailed on Alexander, with the result that Pfuel's entire scheme was abandoned and the whole thing was handed over to Barclay. But since Barclay failed to inspire complete confidence, limitations were placed on his power. The armies were split up, there was no unity of command and Barclay remained unpopular. But this mess arising from all the divisiveness and the unpopularity of the German commander-in-chief led to two things: on the one hand, vacillation and a reluctance to stand and fight, which could not have been avoided if the armies had been united and led by anyone but Barclay, and on the other hand, rising impatience with the Germans and a surge of patriotism.

At long last the Tsar withdrew from the army, on the pretext – the only convenient one available – of boosting morale in the two capitals in order to guarantee nationwide support for the war. And the Emperor's visit to Moscow did succeed in trebling the Russian military strength. The Tsar had left the army so as not to cramp the style of the overall commander-in-chief, in the hope that more decisive action could be taken. But no, army command became even more confused and enfeebled. Bennigsen and the Tsarevich stayed on with a swarm of adjutants-general, to keep an eye on the commander-in-chief and urge him on to greater activity, but Barclay, more constrained than ever with all these 'eyes of the Tsar' on him, became increasingly wary of decisive action and ever more reluctant to fight.

Barclay insisted on caution. The Tsarevich hinted at treachery and demanded a general engagement. Lyubomirsky, Bronnitsky, Wlocki[1] and others of that ilk raised such a hue and cry that Barclay got rid of the Polish generals on the pretext of sending some documents to the Tsar in Petersburg, and from now on it was open war with Bennigsen and the Tsarevich.

Down in Smolensk, despite Bagration's best efforts to the contrary, the armies had come together at last.

Bagration drove up in his carriage to the house occupied by Barclay. Donning his sash, Barclay came out to welcome his superior officer and present his report. Bagration, not to be outdone when it came to displays of magnanimity, ignored his own higher rank and placed himself under Barclay's command, though in doing so he agreed with him less than ever. He still reported directly to the Tsar, as he had been ordered to do. In a letter to Arakcheyev he wrote:

> My sovereign's will is supreme, but I can do nothing with this 'minister' [Barclay]. For heaven's sake send me somewhere else if only to command a regiment. I cannot stay here. Headquarters is swarming with Germans, so no Russian can live here, and nothing makes any sense. I used to think I was serving my sovereign and my country, but as things have turned out I am serving Barclay. To be quite candid, I don't like it.

Relations between the two commanders were further poisoned by the swarm of Bronnitskys, Wintzengerodes, and their like, so there was now less unity than ever. Preparations were made to attack the French outside Smolensk. A general was sent to take stock of the situation. This general, detesting Barclay, went to see a friend of his, a corps commander, spent a day with him and came back to condemn point by point a proposed battlefield that he hadn't even seen.

In the midst of these arguments and all this intrigue over a proposed battlefield, while we were looking round frantically for the enemy, having somehow lost his location, the French happened upon Neverovsky's division and soon found themselves at the very walls of Smolensk.

We were surprised into sudden action at Smolensk to save our lines of communication. Battle was joined, with thousands of deaths on both sides.

Contrary to the wishes of the Tsar and all his people Smolensk was abandoned. But Smolensk was set on fire by its own inhabitants, who had been let down by their governor, and these ruined people set an example for the rest of Russia to follow by transferring themselves to

Moscow obsessed with all that they had lost and seething with hatred of the enemy. On went Napoleon, with us in retreat, and *this* was how the one thing that would destroy Napoleon came about.

CHAPTER 2

The day after his son's departure Prince Nikolay Bolkonsky sent for Princess Marya.

'Well, I hope you're satisfied,' he said to her. 'Causing a row between me and my son! Does that satisfy you? Just what you wanted! I hope you're satisfied . . . It hurts me, hurts me a lot. I'm old and weak, but you've got what you wanted. Well, that's it. I don't blame you for gloating . . .' And after that Princess Marya didn't see her father again for a week. He was ill and never came out of his study.

Princess Marya was surprised to see that during this illness the old prince even excluded Mademoiselle Bourienne from his room. Tikhon was the only person who attended him.

A week later the prince re-emerged and resumed his old way of life, getting closely involved in the new buildings and the gardens, and severing relations with Mademoiselle Bourienne. His tone was frigid and he adopted a funny attitude to Princess Marya that seemed to say, 'Look, you made up stories about me, you lied to Prince Andrey about my relations with that Frenchwoman, and you caused a row between us. Well, now you can see – I can do without the pair of you, you and that Frenchwoman.'

Princess Marya spent half the day with little Nikolay, following his progress, teaching him Russian and music, and talking to Dessalles. The rest of the day she spent in her rooms, reading or passing the time with her old nurse and her 'Servants of God', who came up the back stairs to see her now and then.

Princess Marya's attitude to the war was that of all women. She feared for her brother who was out there fighting, and she was horrified at the unbelievable cruelty that led men to go out and kill each other. She could make nothing of this war, which seemed just like all the others. She could make nothing of it despite the efforts of Dessalles, her constant companion, who followed the war with a keen interest and did his best to put over his version of events, and her 'Servants of God', who had their own hair-raising way of reporting rumours among the peasantry about an invasion by the Antichrist, and even though Julie, now Princess Drubetskoy, had started writing again and was sending a stream of patriotic letters from Moscow. One of them read like a literal translation from the French:

> I am writing to you in Russian, my good friend, because I have a hatred for all the French people and equally for their language that I cannot support to hear spoken . . . In Moscow we are all excited through enthusiasm for our adored Emperor.
>
> My poor husband is enduring travail and hunger in horrible Jewish taverns, but the news that I have only enthuses me even more.
>
> You have doubtless heard of the heroic action of Rayevsky, who has embraced his two sons and said, 'I shall die at their side, but we shall not yield!' And although the enemy was twice as strong, indeed we did not yield. We pass the time here as best we can, but in war, as in war! Princess Alina and Sophie spend entire days with me, and we, the unhappy widows of living husbands, have delightful conversations while we make lint. We want only for you, my darling . . .

and so on.

But the main reason why Princess Marya could make nothing of the war was that the old prince never mentioned it, refused to acknowledge its existence, and laughed in Dessalles' face when he brought the subject up over dinner. The prince spoke with such easy assurance that Princess Marya suspended judgement and believed what he said.

Throughout the whole of July the old prince was unusually energetic, even vivacious. He laid out another new garden and began a new building for the servants. The only thing that worried Princess Marya was that he slept badly. He had given up his habit of sleeping in his study and now slept in a different place every night. First he would have his camp-bed set up in the gallery, then he would use the sofa or a high-backed armchair in the drawing-room, dozing the hours away while young Petrushka acted as a replacement for Mademoiselle Bourienne and read to him. After that he would try a night in the dining-room.

On the 1st of August a second letter came from Prince Andrey. The first one, received soon after his departure, had contained an abject apology from Prince Andrey for having spoken out of turn, and a request to be restored to favour. The old prince had responded in terms of affection, and from then on he had kept away from the Frenchwoman. Prince Andrey's second letter came from just outside Vitebsk, after it had fallen to the French, and it consisted of a brief account of the whole campaign, including a sketch-map by way of illustration, and some speculation on the future course of the campaign. In this letter

Prince Andrey pointed out to his father the awkwardness of his situation at Bald Hills close to the theatre of war, in the direct line of the enemy's advance, and advised him to move to Moscow.

At dinner that evening, when Dessalles said he had heard that the French had taken Vitebsk, the old prince remembered Prince Andrey's letter.

'I've heard from Prince Andrey today,' he said to Princess Marya. 'Have you read the letter?'

'No, Father,' the princess answered diffidently. There was no possibility that she could have read the letter; this was the first she had heard of it.

'He writes about this war,' said the prince, with the sneering smirk that had become second nature to him nowadays when speaking about the war.

'Very interesting, I'm sure,' said Dessalles. 'Prince Andrey is in a position to know . . .'

'Oh yes, very interesting!' put in Mademoiselle Bourienne.

'Go and get it,' said the old prince to Mademoiselle Bourienne. 'You know where it is, on that little table under the paperweight.' Mademoiselle Bourienne jumped up eagerly.

'No, wait,' he called out with a scowl. 'You go, Mikhail Ivanych!'

Mikhail Ivanych got to his feet and set off for the study. But he was scarcely out of the room when the old prince glanced round edgily, threw down his napkin and walked out himself, muttering, 'Can't trust them to do anything. Always get things wrong.'

As he went out, Princess Marya, Dessalles, Mademoiselle Bourienne and even little Nikolay exchanged glances, though no one said a word. Back came the old prince, bustling in with Mikhail Ivanych. He put the letter and the plan down at his side, but dinner passed without him handing it to anyone to read.

It was only when they had gone through into the drawing-room that he handed the letter to Princess Marya, then he unfolded the plan of his new buildings in front of himself, stared down at it and told her to read the letter out loud. When she had done so, Princess Marya looked quizzically at her father. He was still staring down at the plan, apparently in a world of his own.

'What do you make of it, Prince?' Dessalles ventured to inquire.

'Make of it? What do I make of it?' said the old prince, as if shocked into listening, his eyes still riveted on the building-plan.

'It is very possible that the theatre of war may move in our direction . . .'

'Ha-ha-ha! The theatre of war!' said the old prince. 'I've told you before, and I tell you again – the theatre of war is Poland, and the enemy will never get beyond the Niemen.' Dessalles looked in amazement at the prince, who was going on about the Niemen when the enemy was already at the Dnieper.[2] But Princess Marya could not remember where the Niemen was geographically so she assumed that what her father had said was true.

'When the snow thaws they'll drown in the marshes of Poland. They're the only ones who can't see it,' said the old prince, clearly harking back to the 1807 campaign, which seemed like yesterday to him. 'Bennigsen should have gone into Prussia before that, then things would have taken a different turn . . .'

'But, Prince,' Dessalles ventured, 'the letter mentions Vitebsk . . .'

'Oh, the letter. Yes . . .' said the prince, with some irritation. 'Yes . . . yes . . .' His face went all gloomy. He paused. 'Yes, he says the French have been beaten at, er, what river was it?'

Dessalles looked down.

'The prince doesn't say anything about that,' he said gently.

'He doesn't what? Well, I didn't invent it, that's for sure.'

There was a long silence.

'Yes . . . yes . . . Well then, Mikhail Ivanych,' he snapped, looking up suddenly and pointing to the building-plan, 'tell me how you're going to change this . . .'

Mikhail Ivanych went over to the drawing. The old prince had a few words with him about the new building, then he glared at Princess Marya and Dessalles and walked off to his room.

Princess Marya could see shock and embarrassment written all over Dessalles' face as he watched her father go. She noted his silence and was struck by the fact that her father had left his son's letter behind on the drawing-room table. But she could not bring herself to speak, to ask Dessalles what lay behind his embarrassed silence; she could not even think about it.

That evening Mikhail Ivanych was sent by the prince to Princess Marya to ask for the letter left behind in the drawing-room. Princess Marya handed it over, and with extreme reluctance she ventured to ask what her father was doing.

'Still very busy,' said Mikhail Ivanych with a mixture of politeness and irony in a smile that drained the colour from her face. 'He's very worried about the new building. He did a bit of reading, but now . . .' – Mikhail Ivanych lowered his voice – 'he's at his bureau, going through his will, I imagine.' (In recent days one of the old prince's favourite occupations had been going through the papers he wanted to leave behind at his death, a collection that he called his 'will'.)

'And is Alpatych being sent to Smolensk?' asked Princess Marya.
'Oh yes. He's been waiting for ages.'

CHAPTER 3

When Mikhail Ivanych came back to the study with the letter the old prince was sitting at the open bureau wearing his spectacles and an eye-shade, holding a fistful of papers at arm's length and reading them in the light of a shaded candle. His pose was one of high seriousness: these papers, which he called his 'remarks', were to be delivered to the Tsar after his death.

When Mikhail Ivanych came in there were tears in the prince's eyes as he remembered writing what he was now reading. He took the letter from Mikhail Ivanych, stowed it in his pocket, folded up his papers and called to Alpatych, who had been waiting by the door for some time.

He had written down on a piece of paper a list of things he wanted from Smolensk, and now he began pacing the floor as he issued instructions to the ever-patient Alpatych, still standing by the door.

'First, writing paper – d'ye hear? Eight quires of *this* quality, gilt-edged . . . Take this sample. Make sure you get the right kind. Some varnish, sealing-wax – it's all on Mikhail Ivanych's list.'

He took a few more paces and consulted his memorandum.

'Then go to the governor and give him the letter about the deed, in person.'

Then bolts were needed for the doors of the new building, and they had to be of a special kind designed by the old prince himself. Then a strongly bound box had to be ordered to keep his will in.

By now the issuing of instructions to Alpatych had taken more than two hours, but still the prince wouldn't let him go. He sat down, deep in thought, then his eyes closed and he was off into a doze. Alpatych shifted position.

'Well, go on then, off you go,' said the prince. 'If there's anything else, I'll send a message.'

Alpatych went out. The prince went back to the bureau, glanced inside, riffled through his papers, closed the top and sat down at the table to write to the governor.

It was late by the time he got to his feet with the letter written and sealed. He felt tired, but he knew he would never get to sleep: it was in bed that nasty thoughts came to him. He called Tikhon and went through the rooms with him, to let him know where to make up his bed for tonight. He prowled around, assessing the merits of every corner.

Nowhere suited him, but the worst place of all was his usual couch in the study. That couch filled him with dread, probably because of the horrible thoughts he had had, lying on it. Nowhere was quite right, but the best spot was a little corner in the sitting-room behind the piano, a place he hadn't yet slept in.

With the help of a footman Tikhon brought all the things in and began to make up the bed.

'No, no, not like that!' cried the old prince. With his own hands he eased the bed a fraction away from the corner, and then back again.

'Well, at last, I've done everything that can be done. Now I shall get some rest,' thought the prince, and he let Tikhon undress him.

Frowning with annoyance at the effort involved in taking off his coat and trousers, the prince undressed, flopped down on his bed and was soon, to all intents and purposes, lost in thought, as he stared down with disgust at his desiccated yellow legs. In fact he wasn't thinking at all, he was just gathering himself for the enormous effort of lifting his legs up and rolling over on the bed. 'Ugh, it's so hard! Ugh, I'll be glad when this struggle is over. If only *you* would let me go!' he kept thinking. Tightening his lips, he made that effort for the twentieth time, and there he was, lying down. But hardly had he managed this when the bed started moving gently backwards and forwards beneath him, as though it was breathing by itself, rocking and knocking. This happened nearly every night. His eyes had been steadily closing; now they were open.

'Leave me alone, damn you!' he growled, raging against some unknown presence. 'Ye-es, there was something important, something very important . . . I saved it up to think about in bed. Was it the bolts? No, I got that off my chest. No, there was something else, something in the drawing-room . . . Princess Marya said something stupid. Dessalles was going on about it, blithering idiot . . . Something in my pocket . . . Oh, I can't remember.'

'Tishka! What did we talk about over dinner?'

'Prince Andrey, Mikhail Ivanych . . .'

'Shut your mouth.' The prince slapped his hand down on the table. 'Yes, I've got it, Prince Andrey's letter. Princess Marya read it out. Dessalles was going on about Vitebsk. I'll read it now.'

He told Tikhon to get the letter out of his pocket and push the little table with the lemonade and the spiral wax candle on it a bit nearer the bed. Then he put his glasses on and started reading. Only now, in the still of the night, as he went through the letter under the pale glow emanating from the green shade, did he get a momentary glimpse of its meaning.

'The French are at Vitebsk, and that could mean four days from Smolensk. Maybe they're already there . . .'

'Tishka!'

Tikhon leapt up.

'No, no, it doesn't matter!' he cried.

He tucked the letter away under the candlestick and closed his eyes. And in his mind's eye there it was again – the Danube, high noon, reeds, the Russian camp, and him a young general without a line on his face, a merry, dashing, ruddy-faced figure, striding into Potyomkin's gaily coloured tent. Again he burns with envy of this highly favoured man, and it hurts as much as it did at the time. And he goes through every word uttered at that first interview with Potyomkin. Then another vision – a dumpy woman, yellowing and jowly, the Dowager Empress, her smiles, all that she said at her first gracious reception of him. And then her face as she lay on the catafalque, and the clash with Zubov over her coffin for the right to go and kiss her hand.

'Oh, hurry me away, back to that time. Hurry me out of here and now, so I can be left in peace!'

CHAPTER 4

Bald Hills, the estate of Prince Nikolay Bolkonsky, was situated forty miles east of Smolensk, and a couple of miles off the Moscow road.

On the evening of the day when the old prince had taken so long to give Alpatych his instructions Dessalles asked if he could have a word with Princess Marya, and told her that since the prince was not quite himself and wasn't taking any precautions to guarantee his own safety, even though Prince Andrey's letter had made it clear that staying on at Bald Hills would not be without risk, he respectfully advised her to write on her own account, and send a letter via Alpatych to the provincial governor in Smolensk, asking for a statement of how things stood and the degree of risk they were running at Bald Hills. Dessalles had written the letter to the governor and Princess Marya had signed it; now it was handed to Alpatych, who was told to give it to the governor and come back as soon as possible if there was danger.

When he had received all his commissions, Alpatych put on his white beaver hat (a present from the prince), took his stick, just like the prince, walked out to be seen off by the servants, and got into the leather gig harnessed to three sleek roans.

The big bell was tied up and the little ones had been muffled with paper. The prince didn't allow them to drive with bells at Bald Hills, though out on the road Alpatych loved to hear them all jingling. Alpatych was like a king with his courtiers: there to see him off were the land-office clerk, a scullery maid and a cook, two old women, a boy servant dressed like a Cossack, several coachmen and one or two other servants.

His daughter was busy stuffing chintz-covered feather cushions down behind his back and under his bottom. His old sister-in-law slipped a little bundle in on the sly. One of the coachmen helped him in.

'All these women making a fuss! Women, women!' said Alpatych, babbling his words just like the old prince, as he got into the little trap. Dropping his imitation of the prince, he gave the clerk some final instructions about work, then raised his hat over a bald pate and crossed himself three times.

'If anything happens ... you come back, Yakov Alpatych. In the name of Jesus, spare a thought for us,' called his wife with an ear to the rumours of war and the enemy.

'Women, women, all this fuss!' Alpatych muttered to himself as he drove off, glancing round at the fields. He could see the rye turning yellow, thick oats that were still green, and black stretches where the second ploughing was only just under way. Alpatych drove on, admiring the corn crop that had turned out so well this year, scanning the rye fields, some of which were already being reaped, and thinking all the time like a true manager about sowing and reaping, and whether he might have forgotten any of the prince's instructions. He stopped twice to feed the horses, and got to town in the late afternoon of the 4th of August.

On the way Alpatych had encountered and overtaken wagons and troops, and as he drove into Smolensk he could hear gunfire in the distance, though it didn't worry him. What did worry him more than anything was that just outside Smolensk he had seen a splendid field of oats being mown down by some soldiers apparently for fodder, and they had pitched camp in the middle of it. This really worried him, but he soon forgot it when his mind went back to his own business.

All the interests in Alpatych's life had been bounded by the will of the prince for over thirty years, and he had never strayed beyond those bounds. As far as Alpatych was concerned anything not connected with carrying out the prince's orders was of no interest, in fact it didn't exist.

Arriving in Smolensk, then, on the evening of the 4th of August, Alpatych stayed where he had made a habit of staying for the last thirty years, at an inn kept by Ferapontov on the other side of the Dnieper in the suburb of Gachina. Twelve years before, Ferapontov, tipped off by Alpatych, had bought some woodland from the old prince and gone into trade; by now he owned a house, an inn and a corn-merchant's shop all in the same province. Ferapontov was a portly, dark, red-faced forty-year-old peasant with thick lips, a big knobbly nose, a knobbly forehead overlooking bunchy black brows, and a round belly.

He was standing there in a cotton shirt and waistcoat outside his shop, which opened on to the street. As soon as he saw Alpatych he came forward to meet him.

'You're very welcome, Yakov Alpatych. Folks is leaving town, and 'ere you are comin' in,' he said.

'What do you mean leaving town?' said Alpatych.

'Yes, I'm tellin' you – folks is stupid. Dead scared o' the French.'

'Women's talk, women's talk!' replied Alpatych.

'I'm with you there, Yakov Alpatych. What I say is – there's orders not to let him through – so they won't. But the peasants is charging three roubles for a horse and cart. No conscience!'

Yakov Alpatych was only half-listening. He ordered a samovar, and hay for the horses, then he drank some tea and lay down to sleep.

All night long there was a constant flow of troops down the street past the inn. Next morning Alpatych put on a jacket that he kept for town wear and went about his business. It was a sunny morning, and it had been hot since eight o'clock. 'Good day for harvesting,' he thought.

Gunfire had been heard outside the town first thing, and since eight o'clock cannon-fire had been mingling with the rattle of muskets. The streets were crowded with people in a hurry, including soldiers, but drivers still plied for hire, shopkeepers stood at their shops, and church services were being held as usual. Alpatych went shopping, called at the government offices, went to the post and then on to the governor's. The offices, shops and post office were abuzz with talk of the war and the enemy attack. The people were all asking what to do and trying to calm each other's fears.

Outside the governor's house Alpatych came across a large group of people including some Cossacks, and there at the entrance stood a travelling carriage belonging to the governor. On the steps Yakov Alpatych ran into two gentlemen, one of whom he knew, a former police-captain, who was holding forth with some passion.

'Well, it's no joke now,' he was saying. 'You're all right if you're on your own. One mouth to feed's not too bad, but if you've got thirteen in the family and a bit of property . . . This is it . . . we've all had it. I blame the government . . . Brigands, dammit, I'd hang the lot of them . . .'

'Shh! You don't know who's listening,' said the other.

'I don't care! Let him hear! We're not dogs, are we?' said the former policeman, looking round and catching sight of Alpatych.

'Hey, Yakov Alpatych, what are you doing here?'

'His Excellency's orders. I'm to see the governor,' answered Alpatych, stretching up proudly to his full height and putting one hand to his bosom, as he always did when he spoke the old prince's name . . . 'His Excellency bade me inquire about the present state of affairs,' he said.

'May as well tell you, then,' cried the gentleman. 'It's come to this – you can't get a cart or anything else! . . . There it goes again – hear that?' he said, pointing in the direction of the gunfire.

'This is it . . . we've all had it . . . brigands!' he said, repeating himself, and went off down the steps.

Alpatych shook his head and went on up. The waiting-room was full of merchants, women and clerks, looking at each other in complete silence. The door of the governor's room opened, at which they all stood up and pressed forward. A clerk hurried out, spoke to a merchant, told a tubby official with a cross round his neck to follow him, and vanished again, obviously anxious to avoid all the looks and questions coming his way. Alpatych edged forward, and the next time the clerk came out he put one hand inside his buttoned coat and spoke to him, handing over the two letters.

'For his Honour Baron Asch from General-in-Chief Prince Bolkonsky,' he boomed out with so much portentousness and heavy meaning that the clerk turned and took the letters. A few minutes later the governor received Alpatych and said to him hurriedly, 'Please tell the prince and the princess I knew nothing about it . . . I was acting on orders from above . . . and that's . . .'

He gave Alpatych a printed notice.

'And by the way, since the prince is not well I advise them to leave for Moscow. I'm off myself very soon. Tell them . . .' But the governor never finished his sentence. An officer covered in dust and drenched with sweat rushed in and blurted out something in French. Horror was written all over the governor's face.

'You can go,' he said, nodding to Alpatych, and then he turned to the officer with more questions. Horrified, helpless eyes turned eagerly towards Alpatych when he came out of the governor's room. No longer could Alpatych ignore the gunfire, which was getting closer and louder by the minute, as he hurried back to the inn. The document handed to Alpatych by the governor read as follows:

Be assured that at present the town of Smolensk is not in the slightest danger, nor is it likely to be so threatened. I shall proceed from one side, and Prince Bagration from the other, and we shall join forces outside Smolensk on the 22nd inst., after which our two armies with their combined forces will defend their compatriots in the province entrusted to your governance until their efforts shall have driven back the enemies of our country, or until their gallant ranks be destroyed down to the last warrior. You will hereby take note that you have a perfect right to reassure the inhabitants of Smolensk, since those who are defended by two such valiant armies may be confident of their victory. (Directive from Barclay de Tolly to the Civil Governor of Smolensk, Baron Asch, 1812.)

Crowds of people were scurrying nervously about the streets.

Carts piled high with household crockery, chairs and little cupboards were pouring out through gates in a constant stream and trundling down the streets. There were carts outside the entrance to the house next-door to Ferapontov, and women were howling as they said goodbye. A yapping yard dog frisked around the harnessed horses.

Alpatych put on more speed than usual as he hurried into the yard and went straight in under the shed roof to his horses and trap. The coachman was asleep. He woke him up, told him to get the horses ready, and went over to the house. In the family quarters he could hear children wailing, a woman sobbing uncontrollably, and Ferapontov yelling himself hoarse with rage. The cook burst into the passage flapping like a frightened hen, just as Alpatych walked in.

'It's the mistress. He's beating her up. He'll be the death of her! . . . He's beat her up, smashed her face in! . . .'

'What for?' asked Alpatych.

'She wanted to go. It's just a woman's way! Take me away, she says. Don't finish me off with all my little ones. Folks has all gone, she says. What about us? And he's just beat her up . . . beat her and smashed her!'

Alpatych nodded to signify some kind of approval, but he didn't want to hear any more so he strode straight across towards the opposite door into the room where his purchases had been left.

'You brute! You murderer!' yelled a thin, pale woman rushing out with a baby in her arms and the scarf torn off her head. She ran down the steps into the yard. Ferapontov came after her, but when he saw Alpatych he pulled his waistcoat down, smoothed his hair back, gave a yawn and followed Alpatych across into the room.

'Not going already, are you?' he asked.

Without answering or looking round, Alpatych gathered up his purchases and asked how much he owed.

'We can sort that out later. Been to the governor's, eh?' asked Ferapontov. 'What have they decided to do?'

Alpatych replied that the governor had told him nothing definite.

'How can we pack up and go with our business to look after?' said Ferapontov. 'Cost us seven roubles for cartage to Dorogobuzh. I keeps on saying it: they've no conscience! Now, Selivanov, he pulled a good trick on Friday, sold flour to the army at nine roubles a sack. Quick drink of tea?' he added. While the horses were being harnessed, Alpatych and Ferapontov drank tea together and had a good chat about the price of corn, the crops and good weather for the harvest.

'I think it's calming down a bit,' said Ferapontov, getting to his feet after the third cup of tea. 'I imagine our boys had the best of it. They said they wouldn't let them through. That's our strength for you ... The other day they were on about Matvey Ivanych Platov – seems he drove 'em into the river Marina. Eighteen thousand drowned in a day.' Alpatych scooped up his purchases, handed them to the coachman who had just come in and settled up with Ferapontov. From the gateway came the sound of wheels, hooves and jingling bells as a little trap drove out.

Now, well into the afternoon, half the street lay in shadow, with the other half in bright sunshine. Alpatych glanced through the window and went to the door. Suddenly they heard the strange sound of a faraway hiss and crump, followed by booming cannon-fire blending into one dull roar that made the windows rattle.

Alpatych went out into the street; two men were running down the street towards the bridge. From different sides came the whistle and thud of cannonballs and the crash of grenades exploding as they rained down on the town. But these almost inaudible sounds were hardly noticed by the inhabitants against the roaring cannons they could hear just outside the town. This was it, the bombardment ordered by Napoleon and launched on the town by one hundred and thirty cannons at just after four o'clock. It was a bombardment with a significance that the people were slow to appreciate.

At first the crashing cascade of grenades and cannonballs excited nothing but curiosity. Ferapontov's wife, who had been howling incessantly out in the shed, now walked down to the gate carrying the baby, and stared in silence at the people as she listened to all the noises.

The cook and a shopkeeper also came out to the gate. They were all bright and cheerful, eager to get a glimpse of the shells flying overhead. Several people came round the corner chatting away.

'Some force!' one was saying. 'Roof and ceiling smashed to bits.'

'Like a pig's snout digging the ground up!' said another voice.

'Terrific stuff! Keeps you on your toes!' he went on with a laugh. 'Lucky you skipped to one side or you'd have been flattened.' Others joined them. They slowed to a stop and talked about cannonballs raining down next door to them. Meanwhile other missiles – hurtling cannonballs with an ominous hiss, or sweetly whistling grenades – were flying incessantly overhead, though none of them fell anywhere near; they all flew on somewhere else. Alpatych was getting into his trap. The innkeeper stood by the gate.

'Haven't you seen enough?' he shouted to the cook, who had come out in her red skirt, with her sleeves rolled up and her bare elbows working away, and was now going down to the corner to listen to what people were saying.

'Marvellous, isn't it?' she said time after time, but as soon as she heard her master's voice, she came back, pulling down her tucked-up skirt.

Something whistled over their heads again, this time very near, like a little bird swooping down on them, there was a flash of fire in the middle of the street, a big bang and smoke all over the place.

'Stupid girl, what do you think you're doing?' yelled the innkeeper, running over to the cook.

Immediately women on all sides gave a pathetic, 'Oh no!', the baby screamed with shock, and the people crowded round the cook with ashen faces. The cook's groans and cries rose above the rest of the crowd.

'A-agh! My lovely friends, dear lovely friends! Don't let me die! My dear lovely friends! . . .'

Five minutes later the street was deserted. The cook had had her thigh broken by shrapnel from a grenade, and they carried her off into the kitchen. Alpatych, his coachman, Ferapontov's wife and children and the porter were down in the cellar, all ears. The roar of the cannons, the whistling shells, and the pathetic whimpering of the cook, loudest of all, were unrelenting. Ferapontov's wife, rocking and crooning at her baby, asked everybody who came down into the cellar in a frightened whisper where her husband had gone after he had stayed out on the street. A newly arrived shopkeeper told her he had gone off with the crowd to the cathedral, where they were raising on high the holy icon of Smolensk, which had power to work miracles.

Towards dusk the cannonade eased off. Alpatych came out of the cellar and stood in the doorway.

The evening sky, recently so clear, was blotted out with smoke. A new crescent moon stood high in the heavens, weirdly distorted through the smoke. After the terrible roar of the cannons a hush seemed to have settled on the town, broken only by footsteps that seemed to echo everywhere, the sound of groans and distant cries, and the crackle of buildings on fire. The cook had stopped moaning. On two sides palls of black smoke rose up from fires and drifted away. Out on the streets soldiers in their various uniforms marched or scurried all over the place, not in formation but like creatures from a shattered anthill. Several of them ran straight into Ferapontov's yard before Alpatych's very eyes. He went back to the gate. The street was blocked by a bustling, scurrying regiment in retreat.

'They've surrendered the town. Get out while you can,' said an officer noticing him standing there. Then he turned straight back to the soldiers and yelled, 'I'll give it you, running through the yards!'

Alpatych went back into the house, called out for the coachman and told him to get going. Alpatych and the coachman were followed out by Ferapontov's entire household. When they saw smoke coming from burning houses and sometimes even flames, clearly visible despite the gathering gloom, the women, who had kept quiet until now, broke down and howled as they gazed at the fires. Similar cries came like echoes from other parts of the street. Alpatych's hands shook as he and the coachman sorted out the tangled reins and traces of the horses under the shed-roofing.

As Alpatych was driving out through the gate he saw a dozen loud-mouthed soldiers in Ferapontov's open shop helping themselves to wheat flour and sunflower seeds, and filling their bags and knapsacks. Ferapontov chose this moment to arrive home and come back into his shop. When he saw the soldiers his first impulse was to yell at them, but he stopped himself, clutched at his hair, and broke down, half-laughing, half-sobbing.

'Help yourselves, boys! Don't leave it for those devils,' he shouted, grabbing sacks with his own hands and hurling them into the street. Some of the soldiers ran away because they were scared; others went on filling their bags. Ferapontov caught sight of Alpatych and turned in his direction.

'Russia's had it!' he roared. 'Alpatych! We've had it! I'll set fire to it myself. We've had it!' Ferapontov ran into the yard.

A solid moving mass of soldiers blocked the whole steet; Alpatych could not get through and had no alternative but to wait. Ferapontov's wife and children were also sitting there on top of a cart, waiting for a chance to get going.

By now night had fallen. There were stars in the sky, and from time to time the new moon shone down through the pall of smoke. Alpatych's trap and his hostess's cart trundled slowly along amidst rows of soldiers and other vehicles, and where the road sloped down to the Dnieper they came to a complete stop. Down a lane not far from the crossroads where they had halted some shops and a house were on fire. The fire had almost burnt itself out. The flames were dying down, lost in black smoke, but then they would suddenly flare up again, picking out the faces of the milling crowd held up at the crossroads with a peculiar clarity. Black figures flitted in and out near the fire, and people could be heard talking and shouting above the unceasing crackle of the flames. Alpatych could see it would be some time before his trap would be able to move on, so he got out and walked back to the lane to have a look at the fire. Soldiers were nipping in and out near the fire, and Alpatych saw two of them hard at work with a man in a rough coat, hauling burning beams from the fire across the street to a yard opposite, while others carried armfuls of hay.

Alpatych joined a large group of people standing in front of a tall barn that was well on fire. Flames were licking up the walls, the back one had collapsed, the boarded roof was falling in, and the beams were all ablaze. The crowd were obviously waiting for the roof to come down. Alpatych waited with them.

'Alpatych!' The old man suddenly heard a familiar voice calling to him.

'Glory be, it's your Excellency,' answered Alpatych, instantly recognizing the voice of the young prince.

Prince Andrey, mounted on a black horse and wearing a cape across his shoulders, was there at the back of the crowd, looking down at Alpatych.

'What are you doing here?' he asked.

'Your . . . your Excellency!' was all Alpatych could get out, his voice choking with sobs . . . 'Your, your . . . have we really had it? Your father . . .'

'What are you doing here?' Prince Andrey repeated.

The flames flared up and in the bright light Alpatych caught a momentary glimpse of his young master's face, pale and worn. Alpatych told him the full story of how he had been sent to town and was now finding it hard to get away.

'Anyway, your Excellency, do you think we've had it?' he asked again.

Instead of replying Prince Andrey took out his note-book, propped up one knee, and scribbled a pencilled message on a torn-out page. He wrote this to his sister:

Smolensk is surrendering. Bald Hills will be occupied by the enemy within a week. Go to Moscow immediately. Let me know the moment you leave. Send special messenger to Usvyazh.

When he had given Alpatych this written message he gave him some more instructions about getting the old prince, the princess, his son and the tutor on the road, and how and where he could be contacted once this was done. The words were hardly out of his mouth when a staff officer, complete with entourage, galloped up to him.

'You're a colonel, aren't you?' shouted the staff officer in a voice that Prince Andrey recognized, with its German accent. 'Houses are being set on fire under your very nose and you just stand there! What's the meaning of this? You will answer for it!' shouted Berg, who was now assisting the Head of Staff commanding the First Army infantry, left flank – a good position, 'nice and prominent', as Berg put it.

Prince Andrey glanced at him without any reaction, and carried on talking to Alpatych.

'So, tell them that I shall wait for an answer until the 10th, and if I don't receive news by the 10th that they've all gone away, I shall have to drop everything and go over to Bald Hills in person.'

By now Berg had recognized Prince Andrey.

'Prince,' he said, 'I spoke like that purely because it's my duty to carry out instructions ... and I'm a stickler for ... I do beg your pardon.' Berg was most apologetic.

There was a great crash in the middle of the fire. The flames died down for a second or two, and clouds of black smoke swirled out from under the roof. This was followed by another fearful crash and a massive collapse.

'Oooh!' roared the crowd as the roofing of the barn came crashing down and a smell of baking wafted up from the burning grain. The flames flared up again, lighting up the happy, careworn faces of the crowd round the fire.

The man in the rough coat raised both arms and yelled out, 'That's it! There she goes! Well done, boys!'

'He's the owner,' went the word.

'There you have it then,' said Prince Andrey. 'Tell them everything I've told you.'

This was addressed to Alpatych. Without a word to Berg, who was standing speechless at his side, he put spurs to his horse and rode off down the lane.

CHAPTER 5

The troops continued their retreat from Smolensk. The enemy came on behind. On the 10th of August, as the regiment under Prince Andrey's command marched along the main road, they went past the avenue leading off to Bald Hills. There had been more than three weeks of hot weather and drought. Every day fleecy clouds floated across the heavens, now and then hiding the sun, but the sky always cleared in the late afternoon and the sun went down in a deep red haze. The earth got its only refreshment from a heavy dew at night. Any wheat left in the fields was scorched and scattered. The marshes had dried up. The cattle bellowed from hunger, finding nothing to graze on in the sun-baked meadows. Only at night and in the woods was there any cool air, and then only while the dew lasted. Out on the road, the high road where the troops were marching, there was never any cool air, not even at night, not even when the road went through a wood. No dew touched the six inches of churned-up sandy dust. They were on the road at first light. Axle-deep, the wagons and big guns trundled on without a sound, while the infantry marched up to their ankles in soft, choking, burning dust that never cooled off overnight. Sandy dust stuck to feet and wheels, and rose in a cloud over the marching men, getting into eyes and hair and nostrils and, worst of all, down into the lungs of man and beast moving down the road. The higher the sun, the higher the cloud of dust, and through the filter of tiny, burning dust-particles you could look straight at the sun, hanging there like a huge crimson ball in a sky devoid of clouds. There wasn't a breath of wind, and men were left gasping in the thick, still atmosphere. They marched with cloths over their mouths and noses. Whenever they got to a village there was a rush for the wells. They fought over the water, and drank it down to the mud.

Prince Andrey was a regimental commander, and as such he was committed to the management of the regiment, the welfare of his men, the need to receive and transmit orders. For him the burning and abandonment of Smolensk were an epoch-making event. A new feeling, a burning hatred of the enemy, made him transcend his personal sorrow. He was wholly committed to his regiment, he looked after his

officers and men, and he treated them with kindness. The regiment
called him 'our prince', they were proud of him, and he was well-
liked. But his kindness and friendliness were confined to the regiment,
Timokhin and other such men, different people from an alien sphere,
people with no knowledge or understanding of his past. The moment
he brushed up against anyone from the old days, or any of the staff
officers, he became all prickly, full of venom, derision and contempt.
Anything that linked him with memories from the past he found
repulsive, so, when it came to dealings with that old world, all he
wanted was to avoid unfairness and *do his duty*.

Indeed, all was darkness and gloom for Prince Andrey, especially
after Smolensk had been abandoned on the 6th of August, though
he believed it could and should have been defended, and after his ail-
ing father had been forced to flee to Moscow, leaving his beloved
Bald Hills open to plundering, the estate that he had loved so much,
developed and settled with peasants. Because of his position, Prince
Andrey had others things to think about – he was bothered about his
regiment. However, on the 10th of August the column which included
his regiment marched past the turn-off to Bald Hills. Two days before
Prince Andrey had been informed that his father, his son and his sister
had left for Moscow. Even though there was nothing for him to do on
the estate, he decided, with a typical urge to rub salt into his own
wounds, that he must ride over to Bald Hills.

He had his horse saddled and rode off down the side-road towards
his father's house, where he had been born and spent his childhood.
As he rode past the pond, where there had always been dozens of
peasant women gossiping as they pounded the washing or rinsed the
clothes, Prince Andrey could see there was no one there, and the little
wooden pier was torn away and floating sideways, half-sunk in the
middle of the pond. He rode to the keeper's lodge. There was no one
anywhere near the stone gates, and the door had been left open. The
paths of the garden were overgrown, and calves and horses could be
seen wandering about all over the English park. Prince Andrey rode
over to the conservatory, where some of the glass panes were broken
and the trees in tubs were either knocked over or dried up. He called
Taras, the gardener. No response. Going round the conservatory into
the open garden, he saw that the ornamental fence was in ruins, and
plum-tree branches had been ripped off with the fruit. An old peasant
(Prince Andrey had seen him by the gate since childhood) was still
there on a little green bench making a shoe from bark-fibre.

He was too deaf to hear Prince Andrey coming up. He just sat there
on the seat where the old prince had been fond of sitting, with the

bark-fibre hanging from the branches of a broken down and dried-up magnolia.

Prince Andrey rode on to the house. Several lime-trees in the old garden had been cut down, and a piebald mare was wandering about with her foal among the rose bushes right in front of the house. The windows were all shuttered, except for one downstairs that was open. A little serf-boy dashed indoors the moment he saw Prince Andrey.

Alpatych had sent his family away, and was staying on alone at Bald Hills. He was sitting in the house, reading *The Lives of the Saints*. On hearing that Prince Andrey had come, he walked outside with his spectacles on his nose, buttoning himself up, hurried over to the prince, and without saying a word burst into tears as he kissed him on the knee.

Then he turned away, annoyed with himself for being so soft, and went into a full account of how things stood. Everything of real or sentimental value had been moved to Bogucharovo. Some grain had been carted away, anything up to a hundred quarters, but the hay and spring corn – a wonderful crop this year, according to Alpatych – had been commandeered by the troops and cut while still green. The peasants were ruined; some had gone to Bogucharovo, but a few had stayed on. Prince Andrey cut him short and asked when his father and sister had left, meaning when had they set off for Moscow. Alpatych assumed he was talking about the move to Bogucharovo; he said they had set off on the 7th, and then he was off again into problems of management, and he wanted instructions.

'Am I under your Honour's orders to let the oats go and get a receipt from the officers?' he asked. 'We've still got six hundred quarters.'

'What can I tell him?' Prince Andrey wondered, looking down at the old man's bald head shining in the sun. He could tell by the look on his face that Alpatych knew full well how irrelevant these questions were; he was only asking them to allay his own grief.

'Yes, let it go,' he said.

'If your Excellency noticed that the garden's a bit untidy,' said Alpatych, 'there was nothing I could do to stop it. Three regiments have been through and spent the night here. The dragoons were the worst. I wrote down the CO's name and rank so we can file a complaint.'

'But what about you? What are you going to do? Are you staying on if the enemy occupies the place?' Prince Andrey asked him.

Alpatych turned to Prince Andrey, looked him straight in the face, and then all at once, he pointed heavenwards with a solemn gesture.

'He is my refuge. His will be done!' he said.

A group of peasants and house serfs were coming across the field, baring their heads as they got near to Prince Andrey.

'Well, goodbye!' said the prince, bending down towards Alpatych. 'You should go. Take whatever you can, and tell the peasants to go to one of the other estates – Ryazan or Moscow.'

Alpatych was clinging to his leg and sobbing his heart out. Prince Andrey eased him away, spurred his horse and galloped away down the avenue.

The old man was still there, squatting over his last and tapping away at his new shoe, as inconsequential as a fly on the dead face of a loved one. Then two little girls came haring out of the conservatory with their skirts full of plums picked from the trees, only to run straight into Prince Andrey. The elder girl took one horrified look at the young master, grabbed her younger playmate by the hand and nipped off to hide behind a birch-tree, scattering green plums and not stopping to pick them up.

Prince Andrey was startled, and he turned away hoping they might not notice he had seen them. He felt sorry for the pretty little girl that he had frightened. He was wary of glancing in her direction, yet he felt an overwhelming urge to do just that. He was swept by a lovely, heart-warming sensation that was quite new to him; the sight of those two little girls had suddenly made him aware that there were such things as other human interests, a million miles from his own but no less legitimate. The little creatures had one burning ambition: to pinch those green plums and scoff them without getting caught, and Prince Andrey wished them well in their enterprise. He could not resist another glance. Feeling safe at last, they had nipped out of their hiding-place and they were off, singing out in shrill little voices, holding their skirts up and dashing merrily across the grassy field as fast as their bare, sunburnt little feet would carry them.

Prince Andrey was feeling quite refreshed by his escape from the dusty realm of the high-road that the troops were marching along. But not far from Bald Hills he turned back on to the road, and caught up with his regiment at their halt near a dam at the end of a small pond. It was about two in the afternoon. The sun, a red ball seen through the dust, baked and scorched his back intolerably through his black coat. The dust was still there, standing immobile over the halted, chattering troops. There wasn't a breath of wind. As he rode towards the dam, Prince Andrey caught a whiff from the pond, a fresh, muddy smell. He felt an urge to dive in, however muddy it might be. He glanced over at the pond, where he could hear nothing but shrieks and laughter. It wasn't very big, it was covered with thick green slime, and it had obviously gone up a couple of feet, enough to overflow the dam, by being full of white, naked human bodies, soldiers with brick-red hands, faces and necks, all larking about in the water. All this bare, white human flesh, whooping and roaring with laughter, was thrashing around in the muddy pool like carp in a bucket. These were the sounds of men having fun, and that gave it all an air of special sadness.

One blond young soldier of the third company with a thin strap round his ankle – Prince Andrey knew who he was – crossed himself, stepped back to get a good run-up and plunged in with a huge splash. Another man, a swarthy-skinned NCO with an unruly head of hair, stood waist-deep in the water, flexing his muscular figure and snorting with delight as he poured the water over his head with hands that were black to the wrists. The place rang to the sound of back-slapping, whooping and roaring.

Out on the banks, up on the dam, down in the pond, everywhere was a picture of white, healthy, muscular flesh. Timokhin, the officer with the little red nose, towelling himself on the dam, was embarrassed at the sight of Prince Andrey, but he decided he must speak.

'It's really good, sir. You ought to have a go!' he said.

'Too dirty,' said Prince Andrey, pulling a face.

'We'll clear it for you. Give us a minute.' And naked as he was Timokhin ran off to clear the boys out.

'The prince's coming in.'

'What prince? *Ours?*' several voices cried, and they were all so keen to get out of the way that Prince Andrey could hardly manage to pacify them. He could not help feeling it would have been better to have a sponge-down in a shed.

'Flesh, bodies, cannon fodder . . .' he thought, looking down at his own naked body and shuddering, not so much from the cold as from an inexplicable feeling of revulsion and horror that had come over him at the sight of that great throng of bodies splashing about in the dirty pond.

On the 7th of August Prince Bagration, halting at Mikhaylovka on the Smolensk road, had written in the following terms to Arakcheyev:

Dear Count Aleksey Andreyevich,
[He was writing to Arakcheyev, but he knew the letter would be read by the Tsar, so he weighed every word, to the best of his ability.]

I imagine the minister [Barclay de Tolly] will have reported the abandonment of Smolensk to the enemy. It is painful, it is sad, and the whole army is in despair that such a crucially important place has been so wantonly abandoned. I for my part tried to persuade him in the most urgent terms, and in the end I wrote to him, but he was not to be convinced. On my word of honour, Napoleon was in deeper trouble than ever before, and he might have lost half his army, but he would never have taken Smolensk. Our troops have fought and are fighting as never before. I kept the enemy at bay with fifteen thousand men for thirty-five hours and beat them, but he wouldn't hold out for fourteen hours. It is shameful, a stain on our army, and as far as he is concerned, I don't think he should still be in the land of the living. If he reports that we sustained great losses, it is not true; four thousand maybe, not even that. And if it had been ten thousand, what then? We're at war. And besides, the enemy's losses were incalculable.

What would it have cost him to hold out for a couple of days? To say the least, they would have gone away of their own accord, for they hadn't a drop of water for man or horse. He gave me his word he would not retreat, then all of a sudden he sends a dispatch that he is withdrawing that very night. You cannot fight like this, and we may soon have brought the enemy right through to Moscow . . .

Rumour has it that you are thinking of suing for peace. God forbid that you should! After all those sacrifices and so many insane retreats – in suing for peace you will turn the whole of Russia against you, and every man jack of us will be too ashamed to wear the uniform. If it comes to it, we must go out and fight while ever Russia can, while ever there's a man still standing . . .

There must be one man in charge, not two. Your minister may be a good man in the ministry, but as a general he's not just useless, he's beneath contempt, and the destiny of all our country has been left in his hands . . . I really am going insane with frustration; you must forgive me for putting it so strongly. It is quite clear that anyone who recommends suing for peace and putting this minister in charge of the army does not love his sovereign, and wants to see us all ruined. So, what I say is right and proper: get the militia ready. For the minister is exercising the greatest skill in leading our visitor on to the capital. Aide-de-camp Wolzogen is looked on with great suspicion by the whole army. They say he is Napoleon's man more than ours and the minister follows his advice in all things. I am always civil to him, in fact I obey him like a corporal, even though I am his senior. It hurts me to do so, but out of love for my sovereign and benefactor, I obey him. But I grieve for the Tsar that he entrusts a gallant army to men like this. Don't forget that by retreating we have lost more than fifteen thousand men, through fatigue or left sick in the hospitals, and if we had gone on the attack this would not have happened. Tell me for God's sake, what will our mother Russia have to say about this defeatism, and why are we abandoning our good and gallant country to such rabble and sowing the seeds of hatred and shame in every Russian? Have we no guts? Who are we afraid of? Don't blame me if the minister is a dithering idiot, a yellow-bellied, dilatory fool with the worst character defects. There is weeping and wailing throughout the army; they curse him and wish he was dead . . .

CHAPTER 6

All the infinite sub-divisions into which the phenomena of life can be broken down can be reduced into those in which content predominates and those in which form predominates. To the latter group we may safely assign life in Petersburg, especially in the salon, as distinct from the life in the country, the district, the province, even in Moscow. Salon life does not change.

In the aftermath of 1805 we had several times made peace with Napoleon and fallen out with him again, and we had made and un-made new constitutions, but the salons of Anna Pavlovna and Hélène were the same as they had been, respectively, seven and five years before. Anna Pavlovna's circle went on in the same old way, non-plussed by Bonaparte's successes, which they saw as linked to indul-gence on the part of the sovereigns of Europe in a spiteful plot aimed solely at upsetting and worrying the court circle of which Anna Pavlovna was the representative. Hélène's circle went on in the same old way, flattered by the gracious presence from time to time of no less a person than Rumyantsev, a great admirer of his hostess's sharp intelligence; in 1812 these people waxed eloquent, as they had done in 1808, about a 'great nation', and a 'great man', much regretting the break with France, which, according to Hélène's regular visitors, was bound to end in peace very soon.

With the Tsar's return from the army a stir of excitement had run through these rival salons in recent days, resulting in the occasional manifestation of mutual hostility, but each salon remained true to itself. Anna Pavlovna's set excluded anyone who was French (except for one or two dyed-in-the-wool legitimists), and their idea of patriot-ism extended to a boycott of the French theatre, and insistence that the French company playing there cost as much to maintain as a whole army corps. They were avid followers of the latest news from the front, encouraging any amount of rumours that greatly favoured our army. In the French circle of Hélène and Rumyantsev any reports of enemy atrocities or the cruelty of war were discounted, and much was made of Napoleon's repeated attempts at conciliation. This group roundly condemned as premature any suggestion that it was time to plan the evacuation to Kazan of the court school and the girls' college patronized by the Dowager Empress. Hélène's salon looked on the whole process as men going through the motions of war, with peace not far away at all, and the general view was that best expressed by Bilibin, who had happened to find himself in Petersburg and was now almost one of the family at Hélène's, as befitted a man of intelligence: things would be decided not by gunpowder but the brains behind it. The effusions of Moscow, news of which reached Petersburg along with the Tsar, were looked on in Hélène's salon with knowing irony and a measure of discreetly handled scorn.

In Anna Pavlovna's circle, by contrast, the same effusions were greeted with much enthusiasm and spoken about gravely; it was like Plutarch speaking of the ancients. Prince Vasily, who had managed to maintain his hold on all the important positions, constituted the one connecting link between the two circles. He used to visit both 'my good friend Anna Pavlovna' and 'my daughter's diplomatic salon', and it wasn't uncommon, with all his comings and goings, for him to get things mixed up and say something at Anna Pavlovna's that should have been said at Hélène's.

Soon after the Tsar's arrival Prince Vasily was deep in conversation about the progress of the war at Anna Pavlovna's, and he came out strongly against Barclay de Tolly, adding that he could not make up his mind who should be given overall command. One of the guests, acknowledged as 'a man of real ability' (and they said that in French), told them he had seen the newly elected commander of the Petersburg militia, Kutuzov, presiding that very day over the enrolment of new recruits at the Treasury, and he would go so far as to suggest with all due caution that Kutuzov might be the man to satisfy all requirements.

Anna Pavlovna gave a lugubrious smile, and observed that Kutuzov had caused the Tsar nothing but trouble.

'I've said it time and again in the Assembly of the Nobility,' Prince Vasily put in, 'but nobody listens. I said that electing him to the command of the militia wouldn't find favour with his Majesty. They don't listen.

'It's this mania for dissent,' he went on. 'Don't ask me why they do it. It's all because we are trying to ape the stupid effusions of Moscow,' said Prince Vasily, losing the thread for a moment and forgetting that the effusions in question should be ridiculed at Hélène's, not at Anna

Pavlovna's, where the right thing to do was admire them. He was quick
to put himself in the right. 'Is it decent for Kutuzov, the oldest general in
Russia, to be presiding in those chambers? It won't get him anywhere!
You can't have a man like him as commander-in-chief. He can't ride a
horse, he falls asleep at meetings, and he's completely immoral! He
earned a marvellous reputation in Bucharest! Never mind his qualities
as a general, at a time like this how can we appoint a man who's on his
last legs and blind? Yes, blind! What a splendid idea – a blind general!
He can't see a thing. All right for a spot of blind-man's buff! . . .'

No one dissented.

On the 24th of July this was a perfectly correct thing to say. But on
the 29th Kutuzov received the title of prince. This ennoblement might
have been a signal for him to be put out to grass, so Prince Vasily's
judgement was still a perfectly correct thing to say, though now he
was in no great hurry to say it. But on the 8th of August a committee was convened, consisting of Field-Marshal Saltykov, Arakcheyev,
Vyazmitinov, Lopukhin and Kochubey, to discuss the progress of the
war. This committee decided that the various failures had been caused
by high-level dissension, and, although the committee members were
aware that the Tsar was not well-disposed towards Kutuzov, they
didn't take long to propose his appointment as overall commander.
Before the day was out Kutuzov had been appointed commander-in-
chief of all military forces, and plenipotentiary in charge of the whole
occupied region.

On the 8th of August Prince Vasily came across the 'man of real
ability' once again at Anna Pavlovna's. The 'man of real ability' was
making a great fuss of Anna Pavlovna herself, with a view to using
her influence to get himself appointed as chief administrator in one of
the Empress Maria's institutions of female education. Prince Vasily
strode into the room with the air of a conquering hero, a man who
has just achieved his life's ambition.

'Well, have you heard the great news? Prince Kutuzov is our field-
marshal! No more dissension. I am so pleased, absolutely delighted!'
said Prince Vasily. 'A real man at last!' he declared with a knowing
look and a forbidding glare at everyone in the room. For all his desire
to secure the job, the 'man of real ability' could not resist the impulse
to remind Prince Vasily about his earlier judgement. (This was a double
faux pas, in relation to Prince Vasily in Anna Pavlovna's drawing-
room, and also to Anna Pavlovna herself, because she had received
the news with no less delight – but he couldn't resist it.)

'But, Prince, they say he's blind,' he said, reminding Prince Vasily
of his own words.

'Get away with you. He can see well enough,' growled Prince Vasily, speaking quickly with the deep voice and intermittent cough that he always used to sweep away difficulties. 'He can see well enough,' he repeated. 'And what pleases me,' he went on, 'is that the Emperor has given him unlimited authority over all the forces and all the region – that's something no other commander-in-chief has ever had. That makes two autocrats,' he concluded with a triumphant smile.

'I hope so in God's name,' said Anna Pavlovna.

The 'man of real ability', still a novice in court society, was keen to ingratiate himself with Anna Pavlovna, so he wanted to protect her original stance on this issue.

'They say the Emperor was reluctant to appoint Kutuzov,' he commented. 'They say he blushed like a young lady listening to the naughty bits of La Fontaine when he heard the Tsar say, "Your sovereign and your country bestow this honour upon you."'

'Perhaps his heart wasn't really in it,' said Anna Pavlovna.

'No, no, no,' Prince Vasily protested with some vigour. Kutuzov was now second to none. In his eyes, Kutuzov, as well as being a good man in himself, was worshipped by all and sundry. 'No, that cannot be right. The Tsar has always had a high opinion of him,' he added.

'In God's name I hope Prince Kutuzov will take full control,' said Anna Pavlovna, 'and not let *anybody* put a spoke in his wheel.'

Prince Vasily soon cottoned on: he knew what 'anybody' meant. He spoke in a whisper.

'I know for a fact that Kutuzov made one stipulation: the Tsarevich must not go with the army. Do you know what he said to his Majesty?' And Prince Vasily trotted out certain words attributed Kutuzov: 'I can neither punish him if he gets things wrong nor reward him if he does well. Oh! He's got his head screwed on has old Kutuzov. What a character! I've known him for ages.'

'They do say,' observed the 'man of real ability', who had yet to acquire the diplomatic skills of a courtier, 'that his Excellency even stipulated that the Emperor himself was not to go with the army.'

The words were hardly out of his mouth when Anna Pavlovna and Prince Vasily spun on their heels, looked sadly at each other and sighed at his simple-mindedness.

CHAPTER 7

While all this was going on in Petersburg the French had gone straight through Smolensk and were closing in on Moscow. Adolphe Thiers is one Napoleonic historian among many who has sought to justify his hero by asserting that Napoleon was brought to the walls of Moscow against his will. He is no less correct than any other historian who attributes historical events to the will of a single man, and no less correct than Russian historians who assert that Napoleon was brought to Moscow by the skills of our Russian generals. Apart from the law of retrospective vision (or hindsight) which makes everything in the past seem like a preparation for eventual developments, there is here another complicating factor – the question of interaction. A good player who loses at chess is genuinely convinced that he lost because he made a mistake, and he goes back to the opening gambits to find what the mistake was, forgetting that his every move throughout the whole game involved similar errors, no move being perfect. The mistake that he concentrates on attracts his attention only because it was exploited by his opponent. How much more complex than this is the game of war, which has to be played out within specific time-limits, and where there is no question of one man's will directing events through his control of soulless machinery, because everything develops from the interplay of infinitely varied and arbitrary twists and turns!

After Smolensk Napoleon tried to force a battle east of Dorogobuzh, just outside Vyazma, then again at Tsarevo-Zaymishche, but as it happened through the interplay of infinitely varied circumstances the Russians were not able to stand and fight until Borodino, about seventy miles short of Moscow. After Vyazma Napoleon had given the order for a direct advance on Moscow.

Moscow, the Asiatic capital of this great empire, the sacred city of the peoples of Alexander, Moscow, with its countless churches built like Chinese pagodas!

This Moscow gave Napoleon's imagination no rest. Along the road from Vyazma to Tsarevo-Zaymishche Napoleon was riding his bob-tailed light bay ambler, flanked by guardsmen, bodyguards, pages and aides-de-camp. His chief of staff, Berthier, had dropped back to interrogate a Russian prisoner taken by the cavalry. Now, taking the interpreter, Lelorgne d'Ideville, with him, he galloped after Napoleon, caught him up and reined in looking very pleased with himself.

'Well?' said Napoleon.

'He's one of Platov's Cossacks. He says his detachment is joining the main army, and Kutuzov has been appointed commander-in-chief. He's a bright fellow and very talkative!'

Napoleon smiled, and bade them give the Cossack a horse and bring him along. He wanted to talk to him himself. Several adjutants galloped away, and within an hour Denisov's serf Lavrushka, who had been handed on to Rostov, rode up to Napoleon on a French cavalry saddle, wearing his orderly's jacket, with the merry, mischievous air of a man who has had a few drinks. Napoleon bade him ride alongside and asked him some questions.

'Are you a Cossack?'

'Yes, sir, your Honour.'

Thiers' version of events goes as follows: 'The Cossack, unaware of the company he was keeping, since Napoleon's ordinary appearance contained nothing that might suggest to the Oriental mind the presence of a monarch, was extremely outspoken in what he said about his experience of war on the ground.'

The real version is this: Lavrushka had got blind drunk the night before and left his master without dinner, so he had been thrashed on the spot and sent to the village to get some chickens, only to be distracted by a little looting, whereupon he had been caught by the French. Lavrushka was one of those rough and ready, insolent lackeys who have seen a thing or two and feel obliged to do everything in a mean, underhand way; they would do anything to keep on the right side of their masters, and they are especially good at sniffing out any baser instincts such as vanity and meanness. When brought to Napoleon Lavrushka recognized him immediately, without any doubt; he was not the least bit intimidated and did everything he could to win over his new masters.

He knew full well that this was Napoleon, and he was no more intimidated by Napoleon than by that Rostov or the sergeant-major with his whip, because there was nothing that either of them, sergeant-major or Napoleon, could have taken away from him.

He rattled away with all the latest gossip among the orderlies. Much of it was true. But when Napoleon asked him whether or not the Russians were expecting to defeat Napoleon, Lavrushka screwed up his eyes and thought about it.

He saw this as a trick question – people like Lavrushka see trickery round every corner – so he knitted his brows, and for a while he didn't respond.

'It's like this,' he said thoughtfully, 'if it comes to a battle pretty soon your lot will win. But you wait a couple of days and if there's a battle then, it'll go on a bit.' A beaming Lelorgne d'Ideville gave the following translation: 'If battle is engaged within three days the French would win, but if it was later God knows what would come of it.' Napoleon was not beaming, though he did seem to be in the highest of spirits, and he had the words repeated.

This did not escape Lavrushka, who decided to provide further amusement by pretending not to know who he was talking to.

'We know you've got your Bonaparte and he's beaten everybody in the world, but we're a different kettle of fish . . .' he said, without knowing how and why this bit of chauvinism slipped into his concluding words. The interpreter translated his speech, omitting the last bit, and Bonaparte gave a smile. 'The young Cossack brought a smile to the lips of his all-powerful interlocutor,' says Thiers. Napoleon rode on a few paces in silence, then turned to Berthier and said he wanted to see what effect it would have on 'this son of the Don' when he found out that the man who the son of the Don was talking to was the Emperor himself, the man who had carved his victorious name on the Pyramids for all time.

The news was broken.

Lavrushka could tell this was being done to fox him and Napoleon expected him to be in a state of panic, so he tried to please his new masters by putting on a great show of dumbfounded amazement and stupefaction, with much rolling of the eyes, and the kind of face he always pulled whenever he was being taken away for a thrashing. 'The word were scarcely out of the interpreter's mouth,' Thiers informs us, 'when the Cossack was so stricken with amazement that he did not utter another word, but rode on with his eyes glued on this conqueror, whose fame had reached him across the steppes of the Orient. All his loquacity was suddenly stemmed and replaced by a simple-minded and reverent silence. Napoleon gave him a reward and ordered him to be set free like a bird returned to the fields that witnessed its birth.'

Napoleon rode on, dreaming of Moscow, his obsession, while the bird returning to the fields that had witnessed its birth galloped back to our outposts, working out in advance a version of events that had not taken place but could be told to his comrades. He wasn't keen on the idea of telling them what had really happened, for the simple reason that it didn't seem worth talking about. He rode back to the Cossacks, asked where he could find his regiment, now part of Platov's detachment, and by evening he had found his master, Nikolay Rostov, encamped at Yankovo. Rostov had just got on his horse to ride round the local villages with Ilyin. He gave Lavrushka another horse and took him along too.

CHAPTER 8

Prince Andrey was wrong in thinking that Princess Marya was in Moscow and out of danger.

After Alpatych's return from Smolensk, the old prince began to behave as if he had suddenly woken up. He gave orders for the militia to be called up from the villages and supplied with arms, then he wrote to the commander-in-chief informing him that he had every intention of staying on at Bald Hills and defending himself to the last; it was for the commander-in-chief to decide whether or not steps should be taken for the defence of Bald Hills, where one of the oldest surviving Russian generals would soon be taken prisoner or die. He announced to his household that he was staying on at Bald Hills.

But although he was determined to stay, the prince made arrangements for sending the princess, along with Dessalles and the little prince, first to Bogucharovo and then on to Moscow. Alarmed by her father's outburst of feverish, sleepless activity so soon after his earlier despondency, Princess Marya could not bring herself to leave him behind on his own, so for the first time in her life she made so bold as to disobey him. She refused to go, and brought down on her head a horrific storm of fire and fury. The prince raked up all his righteous grievances against her. He was full of accusations: she had tormented him, she had caused trouble between him and his son, she had harboured the vilest suspicions about him, she had made it her one goal in life to poison his existence. He drove her out of his study, telling her he didn't care one way or the other whether she stayed or went. He said he didn't want to know of her existence, and gave her fair warning to keep right out of his sight. This came as a relief to Princess Marya, because she had been afraid he would have her forcibly removed from Bald Hills, and all he had done was banish her from his sight. She knew the meaning of this: deep down in his heart he was secretly glad she was staying on and not going away.

The day after little Nikolay went off the old prince got up early and put on his full dress uniform, fully intending to go and see the commander-in-chief. The carriage stood ready. Princess Marya watched as he strode out in his uniform resplendent with all his medals, and went down the garden to inspect an armed guard of peasants and house serfs. She sat by the window listening to his voice floating in from the garden. Suddenly some men came running up from the avenue with a terrified look on their faces.

Princess Marya ran down the steps, along the path through the flower-beds and out on to the avenue. There, coming towards her, was a great crowd of militiamen and servants, and in the midst of the crowd several men were supporting a little old man in a uniform and medals and helping him along. Princess Marya ran towards him, but in the play of sunlight filtering down through the shady lime-trees in tiny round patches she could not quite make out whether there had been any change in the way he looked. The one thing she could see was that his earlier expression of grim determination had changed into shrinking submissiveness. When he caught sight of his daughter he tried to move his lifeless lips and he gave a hoarse croak. It wasn't clear what he wanted. He was lifted up, carried through into the study and laid out on the dreaded couch that had bothered him so much in recent days.

A carriage was sent to fetch the doctor, who bled him that evening and diagnosed a stroke with right-side paralysis.

Bald Hills was becoming a more and more dangerous place to stay in, so next day they moved the prince to Bogucharovo. The doctor went with him.

By the time they got to Bogucharovo Dessalles had already gone to Moscow with the little prince.

For three weeks the old prince lay there paralysed in the new house built by Prince Andrey and his condition showed no change for better or worse. Comatose, grotesque and corpse-like, he kept muttering non-stop, his eyebrows and lips twitching, and there was no telling whether or not he recognized where he was. Only one thing was certain: he was suffering and he urgently wanted to say something. What it was no one could tell: some quirky idea in a sick, half-crazy mind, perhaps, or something to do with public affairs, or was it a family matter?

The doctor said that this restlessness didn't mean anything; it was pure physiology. But Princess Marya felt sure (and her suspicion was confirmed by the fact that her presence seemed to make things worse) that he wanted to tell her something. His sufferings were clearly both physical and mental.

There was no hope of recovery. He could not be moved. What if he died out on the road? 'Wouldn't it be better if it was all over and done with?' Princess Marya sometimes thought. She watched him day and night, almost without sleeping, and the awful thing was that she often watched him not looking for signs of recovery, but often *longing* for signs that the end was near.

It came as a shock for the princess to admit this to herself, but this is what she felt. And Princess Marya was troubled by something even more terrible, the fact that ever since her father's illness (if not before that, when she had decided to stay on in the vague expectation that something might happen) a series of long-forgotten hopes and desires slumbering within her had come to life again. Thoughts that had not entered her head for years – dreams of a new life free from the perpetual dread of her father, even of the possibility of love and a happy marriage – haunted her imagination like temptations of the devil. It was no good trying to banish these thoughts; her mind seethed with questions about the kind of life she would lead *when it was all over*. These were temptations sent by the devil, and Princess Marya knew it. She knew that the only weapon against *him* was prayer, and she tried to pray. She adopted a prayerful attitude, gazed at the holy icons, recited prayers, but she could not actually pray. She felt as if she had been transported into a new world of real life, hard work and freedom of movement, the complete opposite of the spiritual world where she had been incarcerated for so long with prayer as her only consolation. Prayers and tears were now beyond her, and her mind was full of practicalities.

The danger of staying on at Bogucharovo was increasing. On all sides there was word of the French getting near, and in one village, barely a dozen miles away, a house and estate had been looted by them. The doctor insisted that the prince must be moved on, and the local marshal sent one of his officials to persuade Princess Marya to get away as soon as possible. The police-chief called and said the same thing: the French were twenty or thirty miles away, French proclamations were circulating in the villages, and if the princess didn't take her father away before the 15th, on their heads be it.

The princess decided to leave on the 15th. She was busy all the previous day with preparations and the issuing of instructions, with everyone now turning to her. Without changing for bed, she spent the night of the 14th as usual in the room next to the one where the old prince lay. Several times she woke hearing a groan or a muttered sound, a creak from the bed, or the footsteps of Tikhon and the doctor going in to turn him over. Several times she listened at the door; he seemed to be more agitated than ever and muttering louder than before. She couldn't sleep, and several times when she went to the door to listen she was tempted to go in, but couldn't bring herself to do so. Even though he could not speak, Princess Marya could tell, and in any case she knew, how he hated any display of anxiety on his behalf. She had noticed him turning away instinctively to avoid her eyes, which, just as instinctively, had been glued on him. She knew that if she were to go in at night at an unusual time it would upset him.

And yet she had never felt more sorry for him, never felt such a dread of losing him. She recalled the whole of her life with him, and in his every word and every action she saw an expression of love for her. Occasionally these memories were encroached upon by temptations of the devil, thoughts about what would happen after his death, and what she would do with her new-found freedom. But she drove these thoughts away with a feeling of revulsion. By morning he had settled down, and she had fallen asleep.

She woke late. The innocence that often comes with the moment of waking showed her only too clearly what worried her most about her father's illness. She woke, listened to what was happening on the other side of the door, heard him still muttering, and told herself with a sigh that nothing had changed.

'But what did I expect? What did I want? I want him to die,' she cried in a fit of self-loathing.

She washed and dressed, ran through her prayers, and went out on to the steps. There were carriages at the entrance, without the horses, and their luggage was being stowed.

The morning was warm and grey. Princess Marya hung about on the steps, still horrified at her own wickedness, and trying to get her thoughts into some kind of order before going in to see him.

The doctor came downstairs and walked out to see her.

'He's a little better this morning,' said the doctor. 'I've been looking for you. You can just about make out what he's saying. His head's a bit clearer. Come on in. He's asking for you . . .'

Princess Marya's heart leapt at this news and the colour drained from her face; she had to lean against the door to keep herself from falling. The thought of seeing him, talking to him, feeling his eyes on her now, when her soul was brimming with these awful, criminal temptations, filled her with an agonizing feeling of delight mixed with horror.

'Shall we go in?' said the doctor.

Princess Marya went into her father's room and walked over to his bed. He was lying well propped up, and his little bony hands with their knotted purple veins were laid across the quilt. His left eye stared straight ahead, while the right eye looked askew, and his lips and eyebrows were without any movement. He looked pathetically small and thin. His face with its shrunken features seemed to have shrivelled up or melted away. Princess Marya went over and kissed him on the hand. His left hand seized hers; he had clearly been waiting for her. He tugged at her hand, and his eyebrows and lips quivered with an angry tremor.

She looked at him in dismay, trying to make out what he wanted of her. When she shifted position so his left eye could see her face he calmed down and for some seconds he kept that one eye glued on her. Then, with a stirring of his lips and tongue, sounds emerged as he struggled to speak, still fixing her with a meek, imploring gaze as if he was worried that she might not understand.

Princess Marya stared back at him, concentrating as hard as she could. The sad comedy of his struggle with his tongue forced Princess Marya to look down, and it cost her an effort to swallow the deep sobs rising in her gorge. He said something, and repeated it several times. Princess Marya could not catch what it was, but she tried to guess by repeating his words and making them sound like questions.

'O-o . . . a-ay,' he said over and over again . . . His words were beyond all understanding. The doctor thought he might have guessed, so he repeated them.

'Don't be afraid?'

The prince shook his head, and said it again.

'Soul – a soul in pain!' came Princess Marya's interpretation. With a mumble of approval he took her hand and pressed it to different parts of his chest as if he could not find the right place for it.

'Thinking! . . . About you!' he managed to get out, much more clearly than before, now that he felt sure he was being understood. Princess Marya pressed her head against his arm, fighting down her sobs and tears.

He stroked her hair.

'I've been calling for you . . . all night . . .' he managed to say.

'If only I'd known . . .' she said, through her tears. 'I was scared to come in.'

He squeezed her hand.

'Weren't you asleep?'

'No, I couldn't sleep,' said Princess Marya, shaking her head.

Instinctively following her father, she was even speaking like him and gesturing with sign language, as if she could not get her words out.

'Dear girl!' Or was it, 'darling! . . .'? Princess Marya could not tell, but the look in his eyes told her beyond doubt it was something full of warmth and affection that she had never heard from him before.

'Why didn't you come?'

'And all I wanted was for him to die!' thought Princess Marya.

There was a short silence.

'Thank you . . . my dear daughter . . . for everything . . . Forgive me . . . Thank you . . . Please forgive me . . .' And tears ran down from his eyes. 'Bring Andrey,' he blurted out, though even as he spoke a look of childish shyness and uncertainty came over his face. He seemed to realize his request was meaningless. Or so she thought.

'I've had a letter from him,' answered Princess Marya.

He seemed taken aback and he gave another shy glance.

'Where is he?'

'He's with the army, Father, at Smolensk.'

He was silent for some time now, lying there with his eyes closed. Then he rallied as if challenged by his own doubts, and, anxious to convince them he could remember and understand, he nodded and opened his eyes.

'Oh yes,' he said, softly but distinctly. 'Russia's gone! Done for!'

And again he was convulsed with sobs, and tears ran down from his eyes. It was too much for Princess Marya; she wept with him, looking him in the face.

He closed his eyes again. He had stopped sobbing. He pointed to his eyes, and Tikhon, quick on the uptake, wiped his tears away.

Then he opened his eyes and said something that no one could understand for quite some time, until Tikhon finally picked it up and told them.

Princess Marya was looking for a meaning in the way he had been speaking a few minutes earlier. It must surely be something about Russia, or was it Prince Andrey, her, his grandson, his imminent death? This was why she could not work out what he was saying.

'Put your white dress on. I like it,' he had said.

When she understood these words Princess Marya sobbed louder than ever, so the doctor took her by the arm and walked her out on to the terrace, calming her down and reminding her she had to get ready for the journey. When Princess Marya had gone, the prince started talking again about his son, the war and the Tsar. His eyebrows twitched with anger, his croaky voice got louder, and this was when he had his second and final stroke.

Princess Marya stayed out on the terrace. Morning had broken into a day of hot sunshine. She could take nothing in, think of nothing, and feel nothing beyond her passionate love for her father, a love that seemed to have escaped her understanding until this moment. She hurried out into the garden sobbing, and ran down the paths between Prince Andrey's recently planted lime-trees that led to the pond.

'Oh no . . . I was . . . I . . . I was longing for him to die! Yes, I wanted to get it over and done with . . . I wanted some peace *for myself* . . . And now what's going to happen to me? What can I do with peace when he's gone?' Princess Marya murmured out loud, tripping rapidly through the garden, and holding her hands to her chest, which was racked with convulsive sobs. She walked right round the garden in a circle that brought her back to the house again, and there coming towards her were Mademoiselle Bourienne (who was still at Bogucharovo, and had no desire to move away) and an unknown gentleman. It was the district marshal, who had come to persuade the princess how urgent it was for them to leave immediately. Princess Marya listened without taking it in. She led the way indoors, offered him lunch, and sat down with him. Then she left the table with an apology, and went to the old prince's door. The doctor came out looking very agitated and said she could not go in.

'Go away, Princess! Please go away!'

Princess Marya went down the garden again, and there by the pond she sat down on the grass at the bottom of a slope where nobody could see her. She was unaware of the time passing. She was brought to her senses by the sound of a woman's footsteps hurrying down the path. She got to her feet and there was Dunyasha, her maid, who had obviously rushed out to find her only to be stopped in her tracks, shocked by the sudden sight of her mistress.

'Please, Princess, you must come . . . the prince . . .' said Dunyasha in a trembling voice.

'Yes, I'm coming, I'm coming!' the princess blurted out, giving Dunyasha no time to finish. Looking away from her, she ran back to the house.

'Princess, this is the will of God! Please prepare yourself for the worst,' said the marshal, meeting her at the door.

'Leave me alone. It's not true!' she shouted angrily.

The doctor tried to stop her. She fended him off and ran to the door. 'Why are they stopping me, all these people who look so scared? I don't need them! What are they doing here?' she thought. She opened the door, and as bright daylight flooded into a room that had been kept in semi-darkness, she was suddenly horrified. There were some women in there, including her old nurse. They all pulled back from the bed to let her through. He was still there lying on the bed, but the forbidding look on his calm face brought Princess Marya to a halt in the doorway.

'No, he's not dead. He can't be!' Princess Marya said to herself. She went over to him, and struggling against a surge of horror she pressed her lips to his cheek. But she recoiled immediately. In an instant all the warm affection she had been feeling for him was gone, replaced by a terrible fear of what lay ahead. 'Oh, no! He's gone! He's gone, and here where he was, there is something different, something sinister, some ghastly, horrible, repulsive mystery!' Burying her face in her hands, Princess Marya sank into the arms of the doctor, who held her up.

With Tikhon and the doctor looking on, the women washed what was left of the prince, tied a cloth round his head to stop his mouth stiffening while wide open, and tied another cloth round his sprawling legs. Then they dressed him in his uniform and medals, and his little desiccated body was laid out on the table. Heaven knows when all the arrangements had been made, or by whom; they seemed to take place of their own accord. By nightfall candles had been lit all around the coffin, a pall was spread over it, juniper had been strewn across the floor, a printed prayer had been tucked under the dead man's withered head, and a deacon sat in a corner reading aloud from the Psalms.

Like shying, snorting horses crowding round over a dead horse a large group of people, outsiders and family, had gathered round the coffin in the drawing-room – the marshal, the village elder, some peasant women, all with darting eyes that settled into apprehensive stares as they crossed themselves and bowed down to kiss the old prince on his cold, stiff hand.

CHAPTER 9

Before Prince Andrey settled down there, Bogucharovo had never had an owner who lived on the estate, and the Bogucharovo peasants were very different from the peasants at Bald Hills. They differed in speech, dress and attitude. They claimed to be people from the steppe. The old prince applauded their stamina whenever they came over to Bald Hills to help out with the harvesting, or to dig ponds and ditches, but he didn't like them because they were an uncivilized lot.

Prince Andrey's last stay at Bogucharovo, and his innovations – hospitals, schools and rent reductions – far from mollifying them, had intensified those aspects of their character that the old prince had identified as uncivilized. Rumour-mongering was rife amongst them: one day they were all going to be enrolled as Cossacks, the next they were going to be forced into a new religion, then there was something about proclamations by the Tsar, or the oath of allegiance to Tsar Paul in 1797 (which was supposed to have given the peasants their freedom, only it was withdrawn later on by the gentry), or Tsar Peter Fyodorovich, who was expected to return to the throne in seven years' time, ushering in an age of complete freedom with everything so straightforward that you wouldn't need any government. Rumours about the war, Napoleon and his invasion became linked in their minds with vague notions of Antichrist, the end of the world and complete freedom.

The vicinity of Bogucharovo consisted mainly of large villages belonging either to the crown or to absentee owners with quit-rent peasants. Very few landowners actually lived there, so there were not many house serfs and literacy was low, and so the peasants of this locality were especially prone to these mysterious undercurrents of Russian country life which have origins and meanings that baffle the modern mind. This had shown up about twenty years ago in a movement that caused the peasants of this district to uproot themselves and move off to a place with warm rivers. Hundreds of peasants, including those from Bogucharovo, had suddenly started selling off their cattle and moving away with their families down to the south-east. Like birds flying out across the ocean these men, women and children set off for the south-east, where none of them had ever been before. They bought their freedom one by one, or just ran away. They formed up in cavalcades, and away they went on foot or in wagons, bound for the land where the warm rivers flowed. Many were caught and sent to Siberia, many others died of cold and hunger on the road, many came back of their own accord, and the movement petered out just as it had begun – for no obvious reason. But the undercurrents still flowing deep down among the people were now welling up into some new elemental force waiting to erupt just as weirdly and unexpectedly, yet with primitive simplicity and power. In 1812 anyone living close to the peasants must have been aware that the undercurrents were boiling up, ready to burst forth very soon.

Alpatych, who had come over to Bogucharovo shortly before the old prince's death, soon became aware of mounting agitation among the peasants, and he noticed that, unlike the Bald Hills district, where all the peasants within a forty-mile radius had moved away, abandoning their villages to destruction at the hands of the Cossacks, in the steppe country of Bogucharovo the peasants were said to have made contact with the French, accepted leaflets from them and passed them round, and then stayed on in their homes. He had learnt through some of his trusty serfs that only a day or two before, a peasant called Karp, whose voice counted for something in village politics, had returned from a trip away as an official driver with the news that the Cossacks were destroying the deserted villages, whereas the French weren't going to touch them. He knew that only yesterday another peasant had come over from Visloúkhovo, a nearby hamlet occupied by the French, with a proclamation from the French general that the inhabitants would come to no harm, and anything taken from them would be paid for, if they stayed on. As proof of this, the peasant brought with him from Visloúkhovo a one-hundred-rouble note (counterfeit money, but he didn't know that), which he had received as a deposit for hay.

Last but not least, Alpatych knew that on the day when he had ordered the village elder to collect some carts and move the princess out of Bogucharovo, a village meeting had been held at which a decision was taken to stay there and wait. Meanwhile, time was pressing. On the day of the prince's death, the 15th of August, the marshal had urged Princess Marya to move on immediately because things were getting dangerous. He had told her he wouldn't be responsible for anything that happened after the 16th. He had driven away the same evening, with a promise to come back next morning for the funeral. But next day he could not come because he was suddenly informed that the French were on the move, and he only just managed to get his own family and their valuables moved out.

For the best part of thirty years Bogucharovo village affairs had been handled by the elder, Dron, known to the old prince as Dronushka.

Dron was one of those peasants strong in body and mind who grow a big beard as soon as they can and don't look any different at sixty or seventy, when they still have no grey hair, all their teeth and the straightness and strength of a thirty-year-old.

Shortly after the warm rivers trek, in which he took part with everybody else, Dron was appointed village elder and overseer of Bogucharovo, and he had carried out his duties fastidiously for twenty-three years. The peasants were more scared of him than they were of the master. He commanded the respect of both princes, old and young, as well as the steward, and they jokingly called him 'the minister'. During his period of office Dron had never got drunk or had a day's illness. Even after a sleepless night or any amount of hard labour he had never shown a flicker of fatigue, and although he could not read or write he never forgot a monetary item or an ounce of flour, though he sold it in great wagonloads, nor did he miss a single wheatsheaf anywhere on the fields of Bogucharovo.

It was Dron that Alpatych, now back from the ruined estate at Bald Hills, summoned on the day of the prince's funeral. He told him to get twelve horses ready for the princess's carriages, and eighteen wagons for the onward move from Bogucharovo. Although the peasants paid rent instead of working as serfs, Alpatych was not anticipating any difficulty in having this order carried out because there were two hundred and thirty households down in Bogucharovo, and the peasants were not short of a rouble or two. But when Dron heard the order he looked down and said nothing in reply. Alpatych gave him the names of some peasants he knew; Dron was to take the carts from them.

Dron told him the horses belonging to those peasants were away working. Alpatych named some other peasants, but they too, according to Dron, had no horses available: some were working in government transport, some had gone lame, and some had died of starvation. The way Dron saw it, there wouldn't be any horses, not even for the princess's carriages, let alone the baggage transport.

Alpatych fixed his man with a close stare and a dark scowl. Dron was the very model of a village elder, but Alpatych had not spent twenty years managing the prince's estates for nothing, and he was himself a model steward. He had a remarkable capacity for sensing the needs and instincts of the peasants he was dealing with, and this made him an outstanding steward. One glance at Dron told him that these responses were not an expression of his own thinking, but that of a general mood that had permeated the Bogucharovo community and captured his imagination. At the same time, he knew that Dron, who had feathered his own nest and was loathed in the village, must surely be vacillating between the two camps – the masters and the peasants. He could see equivocation in his very eyes, so he came up close and scowled at Dron.

'Now listen, Dronushka,' he said, 'don't give me that nonsense. His Excellency Prince Andrey gave me the orders personally – to move the people away, and not leave them behind with the enemy, and the Tsar has said the same thing in a decree. Anyone who stays behind is a traitor to the Tsar. Do you hear what I say?'

'Yes,' said Dron, still looking down.

This was not enough for Alpatych.

'Listen, Dron, there's going to be trouble!' said Alpatych with a shake of his head.

'You're in charge!' said Dron gloomily.

'Dron, that's enough!' repeated Alpatych, taking his hand out of his coat-front and pointing down at the floor under Dron's feet with great solemnity. 'I can see straight through you. Nay, son, I can see three yards down underneath you,' he said, staring at the floor beneath Dron's feet.

Dron, visibly disconcerted, managed one quick glance at Alpatych before looking down again.

'Now you can just drop this nonsense, and tell everybody to get packed and ready to leave for Moscow, and get some carts ready tomorrow morning for the princess's things. And don't you go to the meeting. Do you hear what I say?'

Suddenly Dron fell at his feet.

'Yakov Alpatych, let me go! Take my keys. Let me go, for the love of Christ!'

'That's enough!' cried Alpatych sternly. 'I can see three yards down underneath you,' he repeated, knowing that his wizardry with bees, his uncanny instinct for sowing at just the right time, and his skill in pleasing the old prince over twenty years had long ago given him the reputation of a magician, and folk knew that the ability to see three yards down underneath people was something only magicians can do.

Dron got to his feet and was about to speak, but Alpatych cut him short.

'Where did you get such an idea? Eh? What are you thinking about? Eh?'

'What can I do with the people?' said Dron. 'They're all worked up. I've tried to tell them . . .'

'Tried to tell them!' said Alpatych. 'Are they drinking?' he asked abruptly.

'They're all worked up, Yakov Alpatych. Yes, they've got another barrel.'

'Then you listen to me. I'm off to the police. You tell them that. And tell them to stop all this nonsense and get the carts ready.'

'Yes sir,' answered Dron.

Yakov Alpatych had had his say. He had been handling peasants for many a long year, and he knew that the best way to bring them into line was not to give them the slightest inkling they could do anything other than obey. Alpatych was happy enough with the submissive 'Yes sir' that he had got out of Dron, though he still had his doubts, amounting to near-certainty that the carts would not be forthcoming without the intervention of the military authorities.

And indeed, when evening came there were still no carts. Another village meeting had been held outside the tavern, and a decision had been taken to drive the horses out into the woods and not provide any carts. Without a word of this to the princess, Alpatych ordered his own things to be unloaded from the wagons from Bald Hills and those horses to be harnessed to the princess's carriage. Meanwhile he went to the police.

CHAPTER 10

After her father's funeral Princess Marya locked herself away in her room and wouldn't let anyone in. A maid came to the door to say that Alpatych had come to ask for instructions about their departure. (This was before Alpatych had spoken to Dron.) Princess Marya half-rose from the sofa where she was lying, and shouted through the closed door that she was never going anywhere, and would they please leave her alone.

The windows of the room Princess Marya was lying in looked west. She lay on the sofa with her face towards the wall, and as she fingered the buttons on a leather cushion she could see nothing but that cushion, and for all her vagueness there was only one thing on her mind. She was thinking about the finality of death and her own vileness of spirit, which she hadn't known about until now, until it had emerged during her father's illness. She wanted to pray, but hadn't the courage to do so; she could not turn to God in her present spiritual state. She lay like this for a very long time.

The sun had gone round to the other side of the house and the slanting rays of evening light filtered in through the open window, casting a glow across part of the morocco cushion Princess Marya was staring at. Suddenly her train of thought was broken. She sat up without knowing what she was doing, smoothed her hair back, got to her feet and walked over to the window, instinctively inhaling the fresh cool air of a fine, if rather breezy, evening.

'Yes, now you can enjoy a beautiful evening! He's gone. No one's going to stop you,' she said to herself, sinking down on to a chair and resting her head on the window-sill.

A soft and tender voice spoke her name out in the garden and she felt someone kiss her on the head. She looked up. It was Mademoiselle Bourienne dressed in black with tokens of mourning. She had stolen up on Princess Marya, kissed her with a sigh and promptly burst into tears. Princess Marya looked round at her. All their nasty encounters, and her jealousy of the young Frenchwoman, came flooding back into Princess Marya's mind. She also remembered that *he* had changed towards Mademoiselle Bourienne in recent days until he could not stand the sight of her, which just went to show how unfair she had been in rebuking her. 'Yes, and who am I, who am I – the one who wanted him dead – to pass judgement on anyone else?' she thought.

Princess Marya had a sudden vision of Mademoiselle Bourienne's predicament, debarred from her company while still dependent on her, and living on among strangers. And she felt sorry for her. She gave her the benefit of a gentle, quizzical gaze and held out her hand. Mademoiselle Bourienne burst into tears again as she took her hand, kissed it, and went on to talk about the princess's grief, with which she so much wanted to associate herself. She said her only consolation in her grief was that the princess was letting her share it with her. She said that all their former contretemps must pale into insignificance before their overwhelming grief, that she felt a new sense of purity before other people, and that *the one above* now looked down on her with love and gratitude. The princess listened without taking anything in, though she did glance at her now and then, and her ears were attuned to the sound of her voice.

'Your position is doubly dreadful, dear Princess,' said Mademoiselle Bourienne after a short silence. 'I know you could not think about yourself and you still can't, but my love is such that I must do it for you . . . Has Alpatych been to see you? Has he talked to you about leaving?' she asked.

Princess Marya didn't answer. She could not work out who was moving or where to. 'How can anyone start doing new things now, or thinking about anything? Nothing makes any difference now, does it?' she was wondering. She didn't answer.

'Dear Marie, you do know, don't you?' said Mademoiselle Bourienne, 'that we're in danger, we're surrounded by the French, and it's dangerous to go anywhere. If we do move we're almost sure to be taken prisoner, and God knows . . .'

Princess Marya looked at her companion, with not the slightest idea what she was saying.

'Oh, if only people knew – it makes no difference now,' she said. 'Of course, I wouldn't dream of leaving *him* . . . Alpatych said something about going away . . . Have a word with him . . . I can't do anything. I don't want to . . .'

'I've had a word with him. He's hoping we may get away tomorrow, but I think we'd be better off staying here,' said Mademoiselle Bourienne. 'Because . . . you must agree, dear Marie, that to fall into the hands of soldiers or rioting peasants out on the road would be absolutely awful.'

Mademoiselle Bourienne took a sheet of unusual, non-Russian paper out of her tiny handbag. It was the proclamation by General Rameau telling people not to leave their homes because they would be given full protection by the French commanders. She handed it to the princess.

'I think it might be best to throw ourselves on the mercy of this general,' said Mademoiselle Bourienne. 'I'm sure you'd be treated with proper courtesy.'

Princess Marya read the paper and her face crumpled with tearless sobbing.

'Where did you get this?' she asked.

'They probably guessed I was French from my name,' said Mademoiselle Bourienne, colouring up.

Proclamation in hand, Princess Marya rose from the window, walked out of the room, ashen-faced, and went straight into Prince Andrey's former study.

'Dunyasha! Send for Alpatych, Dronushka, anybody!' said Princess Marya. 'And tell Mademoiselle Bourienne to keep away,' she added, hearing the Frenchwoman's voice. 'We must be on the road! On the road as soon as possible!' said Princess Marya, horrified at the thought of falling into the hands of the French.

Oh, if Prince Andrey ever found out she was in the hands of the French! That she, the daughter of Prince Nikolay Andreich Bolkonsky, should be reduced to asking General Rameau for protection, and accepting favours from him! The very idea horrified her and gave her the shudders. She turned bright red and felt a surge of malevolence and sheer pride the like of which she had never felt before. She had a sudden vision of her present position: the difficulty was bad enough, but, oh, the humiliation! 'They, the French, will settle down in this house. General Rameau will take over Prince Andrey's study, and amuse himself by going through his letters and papers. Mademoiselle Bourienne will give them an honourable welcome to Bogucharovo. I shall get a little room as a special favour. The soldiers will break into father's new grave to steal his crosses and medals. They'll go on and on about their victories over the Russians, with lots of hypocritical sympathy for me in my grief . . .' These thoughts did not come naturally to Princess Marya, but it was now her bounden duty to think like her father and brother. As far as she was concerned she could stay anywhere and do anything, but no, she must think like a true representative of her dead father and Prince Andrey. Instinctively she had begun to think their thoughts and feel their feelings. She felt the inevitability of saying and doing whatever they would have said or done. She went into Prince Andrey's study, tried to get right inside his way of thinking, and considered her predicament.

The practicalities of life that had seemed so insignificant since her father's death rose up again before Princess Marya with new, unparalleled intensity, and became an obsession.

Red in the face and over-excited, she paced the room, sending first for Alpatych, then Mikhail Ivanych, then Tikhon, then Dron. Dunyasha, the old nurse and the maids could not tell her how far Mademoiselle Bourienne had been right in what she said. Alpatych wasn't in; he had gone to the police. A sleepy-eyed Mikhail Ivanych, the architect, came when he was sent for, but he had nothing to say to her. In response to her questions all he could do was smile the same smile of acquiescence he had got used to over fifteen years of responding non-committally to the old prince's comments, so there were no definite answers to be got from him. The old valet, Tikhon, also came when called, his pinched and sunken features a picture of inconsolable grief; all he did was answer 'Yes, ma'am,' to every question put to him by Princess Marya, and as he looked at her he could scarcely contain his sobs.

At long last Dron, the village elder, turned up, and with a deep bow to the princess he stationed himself near the door.

Princess Marya paced the room and came to a halt face to face with him.

'Dronushka,' she said. Here was a staunch friend, the dear old Dronushka who had gone to the fair at Vyazma every year and come back smiling, with the same old gingerbread, his speciality, just for her. 'Dronushka, ever since our sad loss . . .' she began, and then stopped, unable to continue.

'We are all in God's hands,' he said with a sigh.

Neither of them spoke.

'Dronushka, Alpatych has gone off somewhere, and I've no one to turn to. Is it true what they say – I can't get away?'

'Why not, your Excellency? Of course you can,' said Dron.

'I've been told it's too dangerous because of the enemy. My dear friend, there's nothing I can do. I can't tell what's happening. I have nobody. I want to go, definitely, tonight, or first thing in the morning.'

Dron didn't speak. He looked up rather furtively at Princess Marya.

'There aren't any horses,' he said. 'I've just been telling Yakov Alpatych.'

'What do you mean, there aren't any horses?' said the princess.

'It's a punishment sent by the Lord,' said Dron. 'Some horses has gone off for the troops, and some be dead. What a year we've had. We'll be lucky if we don't die of hunger ourselves, never mind feeding the horses! As things is, some of 'em goes three days without a bite to eat. There's nothing left. We're all ruined.'

Princess Marya listened carefully to what he was saying.

'The peasants are ruined? They have no bread?' she asked.

'They are dying of hunger,' said Dron. 'No use talking about horses and carts.'

'But why didn't you say, Dronushka? Can't someone help them? I'll do whatever I can . . .' It seemed curious to Princess Marya that at a moment like this, when her heart was full of grief, there could be such a thing as rich and poor, and the rich weren't helping the poor. She had a vague recollection of hearing about a special store, 'the master's grain', that was sometimes given out to the peasants. She also knew that neither her brother nor her father would refuse the peasants in their hour of need; she was just a little worried about not saying quite the right thing about distributing this grain. She was pleased to have an excuse for getting involved in something for which she could forget her own grief with a clear conscience. She wanted Dronushka to tell her all about the peasants' needs, and whether there was any of 'the master's grain' at Bogucharovo.

'By the way, does my brother have any of that "master's grain" here?' she asked.

'Yes. It's not been touched,' Dron declared with no little pride. 'The prince didn't give me no orders about selling it.'

'Give it to the peasants. Give them all they need. You have my brother's permission,' said Princess Marya.

Dron heaved a deep sigh but said nothing.

'Go and distribute that grain, if there's enough to go round. Give it all away. You have my brother's permission, and tell them – what's ours is theirs. We begrudge them nothing. Tell them from me.'

Dron watched the princess closely all the while she was speaking. 'Let me go, ma'am, for God's sake. Please have my keys taken away,' said he. 'I have served these twenty-three years, and never done anything wrong. Let me go, for God's sake.'

Princess Marya could not make head or tail of what he wanted and why he was asking to be let go. She told him she had never doubted his loyalty, and she was ready to do anything for him and the peasants.

CHAPTER 11

An hour later Dunyasha came in and told the princess that Dron had come back, and all the peasants were gathered together outside the barn just as the princess had ordered, and they wanted to hold some discussions with the mistress.

'But I never sent for them,' said Princess Marya. 'I only told Dronushka to give them the grain.'

'Oh, please, ma'am . . . in God's name, Princess, have them sent away and don't go out to see them. It's a trick,' said Dunyasha. 'Yakov Alpatych will be here soon and we can leave . . . and if I may say so . . .'

'What do you mean a trick?' asked the princess in some surprise.

'Oh, I'm sure it must be . . . Please do what I say, in God's name. Ask nurse. They say they won't leave now, even when you've ordered them to go.'

'There must be some mistake. I haven't ordered them to go away . . .' said Princess Marya. 'Send for Dronushka.'

Dron duly appeared and confirmed what Dunyasha had said. The peasants had come in response to orders from the princess.

'But I never asked them to come,' said the princess. 'You must have given them the wrong message. I just told you to give them the grain.'

Dron gave a sigh, but said nothing.

'If you give the word, they'll go away,' he said.

'No, no, I'll go and see them,' said Princess Marya.

Despite the best efforts of Dunyasha and the old nurse, who wanted to dissuade her, Princess Marya walked out on to the steps. Dronushka, Dunyasha, the old nurse, and Mikhail Ivanych followed on behind.

'They probably think I'm offering them grain to keep them here while I go away and leave them at the mercy of the French,' thought Princess Marya. 'I'll promise them monthly provisions and somewhere to live on the Moscow estate. I'm sure Andrey would have done even more if he'd been here,' she thought as she walked forward in the gathering dusk towards the crowd waiting in the paddock near the barn.

The crowd huddled together and a stir went through them as they rapidly doffed their hats. Princess Marya came closer, looking down at her feet as they kept catching in her gown. With so many different eyes, old and young, glued on her, and a sea of so many different faces, Princess Marya could not see them as individuals; she would have to address them all at once, and she didn't know how to get going. But once again the sense that she was representing her father and brother came to her aid, and she launched forth with full confidence.

'I'm very glad you have come,' she began with a racing, thumping heart, and not yet looking up. 'Dronushka has told me that you've been ruined by the war. We are all in the same boat, and I shall spare no effort to help you. I'm going away, because it's too dangerous here

... and the enemy's not far away ... because ... Well, I'm giving you all we have, my friends, and I want you to take everything, all our grain, so that you don't go hungry. But if you've been told that I'm giving you grain to keep you here, that is not true. It's the other way round – I'm asking you to move out with all your things and go to our Moscow estate, and there I shall take full responsibility for you, and I promise you won't go hungry. You will have somewhere to live and something to eat.'

The princess stopped. No comment came from the crowd, only sighs.

'I'm not doing this on my own,' the princess went on. 'I do it in the name of my dead father, who was a good master to you, and my brother and his son.'

She paused again. No one broke the silence.

'We are all in the same boat, and we shall share our troubles equally. All that is mine is yours,' she said, looking round at the faces before her. All eyes were on her and all faces held the same inscrutable expression. Whether it was curiosity, loyalty, gratitude, or fear and mistrust, the expression on every face was the same.

'Thank ye kindly, only we'm not for taking the master's grain,' said a voice at the back of the crowd.

'Why not?' said the princess. There was no reply, and Princess Marya scanned the crowd, noticing that every eye that met hers soon looked away.

'Why won't you take it?' she asked again.

There was no reply.

Princess Marya found the silence increasingly oppressive; she struggled to catch somebody's eye.

'Why don't you say something?' she said to a very old man standing right in front of her, leaning on his stick. 'Tell me if you think you need more than this. I'll do anything,' she said, catching his eye. But he seemed to be stung by her approach and he bent his head right down, mumbling, 'Why should we do what you say? We don't want your grain.'

'Why should we cut and run? We're not going to ... We're not, you know ... We're not having it. Sorry about you, but we're not having it. Go on. You go. Go away on your own ...' The voices came from all parts of the crowd. And again every face in the throng wore the same expression, only now it was clearly not one of curiosity and gratitude – it was an expression of bloody-minded truculence.

'I don't think you quite understand,' said Princess Marya with a despondent smile.

'Why won't you move out? I promise I'll get you settled and provide for you. If you stay here the enemy will ravage you . . .' But her voice was lost in the shouting of the crowd.

'We're not having it! Let 'em ravage us! We're not taking your grain! We're not having it!'

Princess Marya tried again to catch someone's eye in the crowd, but no one's eyes were on her; all were averted. She felt awkward and embarrassed.

'That's a good 'un, that is! . . . Follow her – and give up your freedom! Burn your house down and go and be a slave. Nice idea, that! "Have some grain," she says!' came voices from the crowd.

With downcast eyes Princess Marya left the group and went back into the house. For Dron's benefit she repeated her order for the horses to be ready for an early start in the morning, then she went off to her room and stayed there, alone with her thoughts.

CHAPTER 12

Well into the night Princess Marya sat by the open window of her room listening to the sound of peasants' voices floating across from the village, but she wasn't thinking about them. She felt she would never understand them however much thought she gave to them. There was only one thing on her mind – her grief, which, after the break forced upon her by having to worry about the present, now seemed part of the past. Now at last she could remember, and weep, and pray. After sunset the wind had dropped. The night was cool and still. Towards midnight the voices in the village were beginning to die down, somewhere a cock crowed, the full moon rose slowly behind the linden-trees, a cool, white, dewy mist came up from the ground, and stillness reigned over village and house.

One after another images from the recent past – her father's illness and his last moments – rose up in her imagination. And with the taste of sweet melancholy she lingered over those images, suppressing with a feeling of horror only the final death scene, which she could not bear to contemplate even in her imagination at that quiet and mysterious hour of the night. And those images rose before her with such clarity and detail that they seemed to blur in and out between reality, the past and the future.

She had a vivid recollection of the moment when he had had his first stroke and was being brought back in from the garden at Bald

Hills, supported under the arms, and with his grey eyebrows twitching away he had given her a shy, uneasy glance and muttered something. 'Even then he was trying to tell me what he did tell me the day he died,' she thought. 'What he told me then, he had always thought.'

And then she remembered every detail of the night at Bald Hills before his stroke, when she had had a premonition of disaster, and had insisted on staying put. She hadn't slept, and during the night she had stolen downstairs on tiptoe, gone to the door of the conservatory where her father was spending that night and listened to his voice. He was saying something to Tikhon in a weary, worried voice. He clearly wanted to talk. 'Why didn't he send for me? Why didn't he let me be there instead of Tikhon?' The thought had occurred to Princess Marya then, and it did so again now. 'Now he'll never be able to tell anyone the full story, all that was in his heart. Neither of us can ever return to that moment when he could have told me all that was on his mind, and with me listening instead of Tikhon it might have been heard and understood. Why didn't I go in?' she wondered. 'He might have said it to me then – the things he said the day he died. Even then he asked about me twice while he was talking to Tikhon. He was longing to see me, and I just stood there, outside the door. He felt sad and weary talking to Tikhon – Tikhon could not understand him. I remember him talking about Lise as if she was still alive – he'd forgotten she was dead – and Tikhon reminded him she had passed away, and he shouted out, "You fool!" He was so miserable. Through the door I could hear him groaning as he lay back on the bed and shouted out, "Oh God!" Why didn't I go in then? What could he have done to me? What could I have lost? Maybe he would have calmed down. Maybe he would have said it then.' And Princess Marya repeated the affectionate word he had said to her the day he died. 'Dar-ling!' As she said it Princess Marya broke down in sobs and tears that were balm to her soul. She could see his face now. Not the face she had known for as long as she could remember and had always seen from a distance, but the other one, the feeble, timid face she had seen on the last day when she had bent down near to his lips to catch what he was saying and had, for the first time, examined it close to, with all its wrinkles and little features.

'Darling,' she repeated.

'What was he thinking when he said that word? What is he thinking now?' The question just came to her, and in response to it she caught a quick image of him with the same expression she had seen on his face in the coffin, tied round with a white cloth. And the same horror that had overcome her the moment she had touched him, and felt that this wasn't him, that it was something mysterious and repulsive, came over her now. She tried to think about something else, tried to pray, but she could not do anything. She stared wide-eyed across at the moonlight and into the shadows, half-expecting at any moment to see his dead face, and she could feel herself falling under the spell of the stillness that reigned in and around that house.

'Dunyasha!' she whispered. 'Dunyasha!' she screamed like a wild thing, and tearing herself out of the stillness, she ran towards the maids' room straight into the arms of the old nurse and the maids who had come rushing out to meet her.

CHAPTER 13

On the 17th of August Rostov and Ilyin, accompanied by Lavrushka, just back from imprisonment by the French, and a hussar orderly left Yankovo, ten miles or so from Bogucharovo, and went out for a ride to put Ilyin's newly acquired horse through its paces and find out whether there was any hay to be had in the local villages.

For the last three days Bogucharovo had found itself in between the two hostile armies, and it was equally likely that the Russian rearguard or the French vanguard might arrive in the village, so Rostov, scrupulous squadron commander that he was, wanted to steal a march on the French in acquiring any provisions that might still be there.

Rostov and Ilyin were in the best of moods. On the way to Bogucharovo, which they knew only as an estate belonging to some prince, with a manor house where they hoped to find a lot of staff including, perhaps, one or two pretty servant-girls, they asked Lavrushka all about Napoleon and laughed at what he told them, or else they raced each other to put Ilyin's new horse under pressure. Rostov was completely unaware that the village they were riding towards belonged to the very Prince Bolkonsky who had been engaged to his sister.

Rostov and Ilyin raced their horses flat out one last time along the uplands outside Bogucharovo and Rostov was the winner, the first to gallop down the village street.

'You win,' said Ilyin, all red in the face.

'Yes, I usually do, flat fields, here, anywhere,' answered Rostov, stroking and patting his foaming Don horse.

'I could have won on my Frenchy, your Excellency,' Lavrushka called from well back, referring to his own miserable nag, more suited to hauling carriages, 'but I didn't want to embarrass you.'

They slowed to a walking pace and made their way towards a big crowd of peasants standing in front of a barn. Some of them doffed their caps; others, who didn't, just stared as they rode up. Two spindly old peasants with wrinkled faces and thin beards emerged from the tavern with grins all over their faces, staggering about and singing out of tune, and they came over towards the officers. 'Good boys, these!' said Rostov with a laugh. 'Hey there, have you got any hay?'

'Two peas in a pod,' said Ilyin.

'Verree merree-ee-ee . . . !' they intoned, beaming beatifically.

One peasant detached himself from the crowd and came across to Rostov.

'Oose side be you on?' asked the peasant.

'The French,' answered Ilyin with a laugh. 'And this here is Napoleon,' he said, pointing to Lavrushka.

'So, you be Russians then?' the peasant inquired.

'You got many men 'ere?' asked another stocky peasant, making his way over.

'Yes, plenty,' answered Rostov. 'But what are you all doing here?' he added. 'Some kind of holiday?'

' 'Tis the old 'uns. Village business,' answered the peasant, edging away.

At that moment two women appeared with a man in a white hat, walking down from the prince's house towards the officers.

'The pink one's mine. Hands off!' said Ilyin, with an eye on Dunyasha, who was striding purposefully in their direction.

'Do for us!' said Lavrushka, winking at Ilyin.

'What can I do for you, gorgeous?' said Ilyin with a grin.

'The princess has sent me. Her Excellency wishes to know what regiment you are from, and who you are.'

'This is Count Rostov, squadron commander, and I am – your humble servant.'

'Merree bee-ee-ee!' warbled the drunken peasant with the blissful grin, staring across at Ilyin as he chatted to the girl. Just behind Dunyasha Alpatych doffed his hat to Rostov as he drew near.

'Begging your pardon, your Honour,' he said, putting one hand in his coat-front and speaking with deference tinged with contempt for the officer's youthfulness. 'My mistress, the daughter of General-in-Chief Prince Nikolay Andreich Bolkonsky, who died on the 15th of this month, finding herself in some difficulty through the stupid ignorance of these persons' – he nodded towards the peasants – 'invites you into the house . . . If you wouldn't mind coming this way, sir,' said Alpatych with a sad smile. 'It's not far, and out here things are not quite, er . . .' Alpatych nodded to the two peasants, who were hovering at his back like gadflies round a horse.

'Garn, Alpatych! . . . Hey, Yakov Alpatych! You all right then? Oops, for Jesus Christ's sake, sorry old boy. You all right?' cried the peasants beaming at him with sublime delight.

Rostov looked at the drunken peasants and gave a smile.

'Unless your Excellency finds this amusing?' said Yakov Alpatych with grave sobriety, pointing to the old peasants with his free hand.

'No, it's not very amusing,' said Rostov, and he moved his horse along. 'What's wrong exactly?' he inquired.

'Begging your pardon, sir, these peasant brutes here won't let their mistress off the estate. They keep threatening to unharness the horses. Everything has been packed since early morning, but her Excellency can't get away.'

'Impossible!' cried Rostov.

'I'm telling you the absolute truth, sir, and it's an honour to do so,' said Alpatych.

Rostov dismounted, handed his horse to the orderly and walked up to the house with Alpatych, asking for further deatils.

In point of fact, the princess's offer of grain and her confrontation with Dron and the deputation of peasants had brought things to such a pitch that Dron had finally handed in his keys and gone over to the peasants, refusing to turn up when Alpatych sent for him, and that morning when the princess had ordered the horses so they could get on the road, the peasants had held a big meeting outside the barn and sent word that they were not going to let the princess out of the village, and there was an edict that people were not to move out, so they would have to unharness the horses. Alpatych went to have things out with them; they responded (Karp being the principal speaker, with Dron skulking at the back of the crowd) by stating that the princess would not be allowed through, there was an edict forbidding it, so she should stay on and they would serve and obey in all things as they always had done.

At the very time when Rostov and Ilyin were galloping into the village, Princess Marya was defying the best efforts of Alpatych, the old nurse and the maid to dissuade her from ordering the horses. She was ready to start. But one look at the cavalrymen bearing down on them at a good gallop and the coachmen scattered, assuming them to be Frenchmen, and left the women bewailing their lot inside the house.

'Kind sir! Father to us all! God has sent thee!' The voices rang with emotion as Rostov walked in through the entrance hall. Princess

Marya was sitting in the big hall, helpless and at her wits' end, when Rostov was shown in to see her. She had no idea who he was, why he was here or what would become of her. One look at his Russian face and his general demeanour, together with the very sound of his opening words, told her she was dealing with someone of her own station; she glanced at him with her deep, radiant eyes, and spoke, though her voice shook with emotion. Rostov's romantic imagination immediately dramatized the situation. 'A defenceless grief-stricken young woman, all alone and left to the mercy of brutal peasants up in arms! Ah, what quirk of fate has landed me here?' thought Rostov as he listened and watched her. 'And oh, the gentle poise, the nobility of her features and her eyes!' he mused as she told her diffident story.

When she started to say that this had all happened the day after her father's funeral, her voice shook. She turned away, worried that Rostov might think she was trying to play on his feelings, then gave him a quick, quizzical look full of apprehension. There were tears in his eyes. Princess Marya noticed them and looked at him with a radiance in her eyes that took away the plainness of her face.

'I cannot begin to tell you how glad I am, Princess, that I happened along and can now place myself at your disposal,' said Rostov, getting to his feet. 'If you would care to start your journey now, I pledge my honour that no man shall dare do you a discourtesy if only you will allow me to escort you,' and, after performing the kind of deep bow normally reserved for royalty, he made for the door.

Rostov's deferential manner seemed calculated to suggest that although he would consider it a great pleasure to make her acquaintance he did not wish to take advantage of her plight to force his attentions upon her.

Princess Marya sensed this with real appreciation.

'I really am most grateful to you,' she said to him in French, 'but I do hope it was all a mistake and no one is really to blame.' And she burst into tears.

'Please forgive me,' she said.

Rostov was frowning as he gave another deep bow and left the room.

CHAPTER 14

'Nice, isn't she? Oh yes, my little pink girl's a beauty. Her name's Dunyasha . . .' But then, with one glance at Rostov's face, Ilyin stopped short. He could see that his revered commanding officer was in a very different frame of mind.

Rostov took one dark look at Ilyin, made no reply and strode off rapidly towards the village.

'I'll show them a thing or two. Let me get at them, the swine,' he muttered to himself. Alpatych trotted on behind, gliding along just short of running pace and struggling to keep up with Rostov.

'What have you decided to do, your Honour?' he said, coming alongside.

Rostov stopped, clenched his fists and turned on Alpatych, bristling.

'Do? What am I going to do, you stupid old fool?' he shouted. 'Where have you been all this time. Eh? The peasants are up in arms and you're in a blue funk! You're a traitor yourself. I know you lot. I'll flay every man jack of you . . .' And then, as if this was a waste of good fire and fury, he turned away from Alpatych and stormed off. Alpatych swallowed his wounded pride and came gliding on behind, still with plenty to say. He told Rostov the peasants were in a very awkward mood just now, and it might be a good idea not to put their backs up without military assistance, and wouldn't it be best to send for help?

'I'll give them military assistance . . . I'll put their damned backs up . . .' Nikolay was burbling, out of his mind and choking with savage fury and the need to vent it. With no idea of what he would do when he got there, he strode out, impelled by instinct, bearing down on the crowd. And the nearer he got to them the more Alpatych began to feel that this hot-headed approach might just pay off. The peasants in the crowd seemed to think the same thing as they watched him stride resolutely in their direction with a dark scowl on his face.

Once the hussars had ridden into the village and Rostov had gone up to see the princess the crowd had lost its certainty and solidarity. Some peasants started complaining that the men who had ridden in were Russians, and they might not take too kindly to the idea that they were refusing to let their young lady go. Dron was of that opinion, but the moment he voiced it Karp and others rounded on their former village elder.

'How many years have you fattened your belly on this village?' shouted Karp. 'You don't care! You'll dig up your crock of gold and scram. You're not bothered whether our homes are burnt down or not!'

'Everythin' under control, they says, no one leaves, nothin' moves out – and 'ere she is flittin' with all 'er stuff!' shouted someone else.

'Your son should've been called up, but you saw 'im all right, didn't you?' put in a little old man, suddenly turning on Dron, 'and 'twas my Vanka got took and 'ad 'is head shaved. Oh, I don't know . . . we've all got to die!'

'Oh yes, we've all got to die!'

'I'm not one to go against the commune,' said Dron.

'Go against it? You've fattened your belly on it!'

Two lanky peasants said their piece. When Rostov accompanied by Ilyin, Lavrushka and Alpatych were almost up to the crowd Karp stuck his thumbs into his belt and stepped forward with the suggestion of a smile on his face. Dron did the opposite; he skulked off to the back, and the crowd closed round him.

'Hey there! Who's your village elder?' snapped Rostov, striding quickly up to the crowd.

'Elder? What do you . . . ?' asked Karp. But before he could finish his cap was sent spinning and his head jerked back from a hard punch.

'Caps off, traitors!' roared Rostov in a voice that told them his blood was up. 'Where's the elder?' he yelled furiously.

'The elder! 'E wants the elder. Mr Dron, 'tis you 'e wants,' came various voices from peasants quick to knuckle under, while caps were being doffed.

'No rioting here. We'm keeping good order,' declared Karp. And several other voices called out at the same time from the back:

'It's like what the old 'uns says . . . too many be givin' out orders.'

'Don't you argue with me! Mutiny! You thieving swine! Traitors!' Rostov's voice was unrecognizable, a mindless screech, as he grabbed Karp by the collar. 'Tie this man up!' he shouted, though there was no one but Lavrushka and Alpatych to do the tying up.

Lavrushka, however, ran over to Karp and grabbed him by the arms from behind.

'Shall I call our boys up, your Honour?' he shouted.

Alpatych turned to the peasants and called two of them out by name to come and tie Karp's hands. The peasants were quick to obey, stepping out of the crowd and undoing their belts as they came.

'Where's the village elder?' shouted Rostov.

Dron, frowning and pallid, stepped out too.

'Are you the elder? Tie him up, Lavrushka,' shouted Rostov in a voice that brooked no opposition. And sure enough, two more peasants set about tying Dron's hands, and he obligingly took off his belt and handed it over.

'Now listen to me, all of you,' Rostov turned to the peasants. 'Quick march! Go back to your homes this instant. I don't want to hear another word from you.'

'Hey, we 'aven't done nothin' wrong. We bin a bit daft. Just a bit o' nonsense, though . . . Told you things was gettin' out o' hand,' came various incriminatory voices.

'Didn't I tell you?' said Alpatych, coming into his own. 'It was wrong, boys.'

'We bin a bit daft, Yakov Alpatych,' came other voices, and the crowd began to break up and scatter about the village.

The two tied-up peasants were taken up to the manor house. The two drunken peasants followed on behind.

'Hey, look at 'e now!' said one of them, addressing Karp.

'Thinks you can talk like that to your betters? What d'ye think you was doing? You're a fool,' put in the other man, 'a right fool.'

Within two hours the horses and wagons were standing in the courtyard of the Bogucharovo house. The peasants were scurrying in and out, stowing the family things in the carts, and Dron, released at Princess Marya's behest from the lumber-room where they had locked him up, was out in the yard directing the men.

'Hey, watch what you're doing,' said one of the peasants, a tall man with a round, beaming face, taking a casket from a housemaid's hands. 'That's worth a bit, that is. If you just chuck it in like that or shove it under the rope it'll get scratched. I don't like that sort of thing. Everything should be done properly. Do it by the book. Look, like this, place it under the matting and cover it up with hay. There you are. Splendid job!'

'Lord have mercy on us, look at all these books,' said another peasant, bringing out Prince Andrey's book-cases. 'Hey, mind you don't slip! They weighs a ton, boys. Nice books these!'

'All them pages, took 'em ages!' said a tall, round-faced peasant nodding with a knowing wink in the direction of some big fat dictionaries sitting on top.

Rostov had no desire to force himself on the princess, so he didn't go back to see her, preferring to stay down in the village and wait for her to drive out. Eventually Princess Marya's carriages drove away from the house, whereupon Rostov got on his horse and rode alongside as far as the road occupied by our troops, seven or eight miles from Bogucharovo. At the inn at Yankovo he parted from her with a show of courtesy and allowed himself to kiss her hand for the first time.

'Please don't mention it!' he said, colouring up in response to Princess Marya's protestation of gratitude for her salvation, which is what she called it. 'Any old policeman would have done the same thing. If all we had to do was wage war against the peasants, we wouldn't have let the enemy come as far as he has,' he said, inexplicably embarrassed and eager to change the subject. 'I'm only too happy to have had the opportunity of making your acquaintance. Goodbye, Princess. I wish you good luck and you have my sympathy, and I hope we shall meet again under happier circumstances. Please, spare my blushes – not a word of thanks.'

But if the princess had now stopped thanking him in words, she went on thanking him with the look on her face, which glowed with gratitude and affection. She could not believe she had nothing to thank him for. Quite the reverse, she saw it as beyond doubt that but for him she would surely have been lost, a prey to the rebellious peasants and the French, and that in saving her *he* had exposed *himself* to obvious and terrible danger. Even more certain was the fact that he was a man of noble and lofty soul who had proved immediately sensitive to her situation and distress. His kindly, innocent eyes, watering with sympathy when she had spoken tearfully about her loss, haunted her imagination. When she was on her own with the goodbyes behind them, Princess Marya suddenly felt her eyes brimming with tears again, and she began to wonder, not for the first time, whether she might have fallen in love with him. On the way to Moscow, even though the princess's situation could hardly be described as a happy one, Dunyasha, who was travelling with her in the carriage, noticed several times that her mistress's face as she bent forward to look through the window wore a secret smile of pleasant wistfulness.

'Oh dear, what if I have fallen in love with him?' Princess Marya was thinking.

It was awkward for her to admit even secretly to herself that she had fallen in love with a man who would possibly never love her in return, but she consoled herself with the thought that no one would ever know, and she would bear no blame for this love, as long as it remained unspoken, even if it was her first and last love, and it went on for a lifetime.

Sometimes she remembered the way he had looked at her, the sympathy he had shown, what he had said, and then happiness seemed not beyond the bounds of possibility. And it was then that Dunyasha caught her looking through the window with a real smile.

'And to think he should have come to Bogucharovo, and just at that time!' thought Princess Marya. 'And to think it was his sister who refused Andrey!' In all of this Princess Marya saw the workings of Providence.

Princess Marya had made a very favourable impression on Rostov. Whenever he brought her to mind he felt happy. And when his pals heard about his adventures in Bogucharovo and poked fun at him for having gone out to look for hay and ended up hooking one of the richest heiresses in Russia, it made him angry. It made him angry for the simple reason that the idea of marrying the gentle, and, as he recalled, delightful Princess Marya with her huge fortune had occurred to him spontaneously on more than one occasion. For him personally Princess Marya as a wife left nothing to be desired. Marrying her would make the countess, his mother, so happy and would mend his father's fortunes. And it would even – Nikolay could feel it in his bones – make the princess herself very happy.

But what about Sonya? What about his promise? This was why it made him angry when they poked fun at him about Princess Bol-konsky.

CHAPTER 15

After his appointment as army commander-in-chief Kutuzov re-membered Prince Andrey and asked him to report to headquarters.

Prince Andrey reached Tsarevo-Zaymishche on the very day and at the very time when Kutuzov was making his first inspection of the troops. Prince Andrey stopped in the village at the priest's house, where the commander-in-chief's carriage was waiting outside, and he sat down on a bench by the gate to await 'his Serene Highness', as everyone now called Kutuzov. Floating across the fields beyond the village came the music of a regimental band, and the roar of a huge crowd shouting 'Hurrah!' to the new commander-in-chief. By the gate a dozen paces away from Prince Andrey stood two orderlies, a courier and a major-domo, enjoying the fine weather while their masters were away. A swarthy little lieutenant-colonel of hussars with prodigious whiskers and sideboards rode up to the gate, glanced at Prince Andrey and asked whether his Serene Highness was staying here and whether he would be back soon.

Prince Andrey told him he was not on his Highness's staff, and he too had only just arrived. The lieutenant-colonel of hussars turned to an immaculate orderly, the orderly of the commander-in-chief himself, who spoke to him with that special kind of aloofness with comes naturally to a commander-in-chief's orderly when speaking to officers:

'His Highness? Yes, he should be back soon. What is it you want?'

The officer grinned through his whiskers at the orderly's tone, dismounted, gave his horse to a servant, and walked over to Bolkonsky with a slight bow.

Bolkonsky made room for him on the bench. The hussar sat down beside him.

'You, too? Waiting for the commander-in-chief?' he began. 'They say he's weady to weceive evewybody, thank God! Not like those widiculous kwauts! No wonder Yermolov talked about being pwomoted to the wank of German. Now p'whaps the Wussians will get a word in. God knows what they think they've been up to. Just one wetweat after another. Have you seen any action?' he asked.

'I have had the pleasure,' said Prince Andrey, 'not only of taking part in the retreat, but also of losing everything I held dear during that retreat – not to speak of my property, the house where I was born . . . and my father – he died of grief. I'm from near Smolensk.'

'Oh, you must be Pwince Bolkonsky! Delighted to meet you. Lieutenant-Colonel Denisov, better known as Vaska,' said Denisov, shaking hands with Prince Andrey and looking him in the face with warm friendliness. 'Yes, I heard about that,' he said with some sympathy, and after a brief pause he went on, 'Yes, we're fighting like the Scythians. It's all vewy well, except for those who bear the bwunt of it. So you're Pwince Andwey Bolkonsky!' He shook his head. 'Yes, I'm vewy, vewy pleased to meet you,' he added, shaking his hand with a wistful smile.

Prince Andrey knew about Denisov from Natasha's stories of when she was first wooed. The bitter-sweet memory brought back the heart-ache he hadn't even thought about in recent days, though it still lay buried in his soul. In recent days so many different things had happened, some of them vitally important, like the abandonment of Smolensk, his visit to Bald Hills and the news of his father's recent death, and he had gone through so many trials that these particular memories had left him alone for long periods, and when they did come to mind they didn't hurt with anything like the old intensity. And as far as Denisov was concerned, the associations evoked by the name of Bolkonsky belonged to a romantic time in the distant past, when one evening after supper, much affected by Natasha's singing, he had proposed to a little fifteen-year-old girl without really knowing what he was doing. He smiled at the thought of those days and his love for Natasha, and then went straight on to the one thing that had become an outright obsession with him. This was a plan of action that had come to him while he had been on duty at the outposts during the retreat. He had laid the plan before Barclay de Tolly, and now he had every intention of laying it before Kutuzov. It was based on the fact that the French operations line was over-extended, and his idea was that, instead a frontal attack blocking the French advance (or maybe along with an attack of that kind), they ought to concentrate on their communications. He began explaining his plan to Prince Andrey.

'They can't defend the whole of that line. It's not possible. I guawantee I could bweak thwough it. Give me five hundwed men and I'll cut their communications, for sure I will! There's only one system that'll work – guewilla warfare.'

Denisov got to his feet and began to elaborate for Bolkonsky's benefit, with much waving of the arms. He was in mid-flow when suddenly they heard the soldiers shouting again, ragged sounds this time that blended with music and song over a wide area near the parade-ground. Hoofbeats and cheering soon could be heard in the nearby village.

'He's coming! He's coming!' shouted the Cossack from the gate.

Bolkonsky and Denisov walked over to the gate, where a little group of soldiers formed a guard of honour, and there was Kutuzov coming down the street on a little bay horse. An immense suite of generals followed on. Barclay was riding almost level with him, and a great crowd of officers was scurrying about behind them and on every side with loud cries of 'Hurrah!'

His adjutants were first into the yard. Kutuzov dug his heels into his horse, which was ambling along so slowly under his weight, and all the time he kept nodding right and left and raising a hand to his white horseguard's cap with its red band and no peak. When he got to the guard of honour, to be saluted by a set of elite grenadiers, most of them sporting decorations, he paused for a moment in silence and looked at them very closely with the steady gaze of a true commander before turning to the group of generals and other officers standing round him. There was a subtle change in his expression, and he shrugged with an air of bemusement.

'What, with men like these nothing but retreat after retreat?' he said. 'Well, goodbye, General,' he added, and urged his horse in through the gateway right past Prince Andrey and Denisov.

'Hurrah! Hurrah! Hurrah!' went the roaring voices behind him.

Since the last time Prince Andrey had seen him Kutuzov had put on even more weight and now he looked really flabby, bloated with fat. But some things about him had not changed – the familiar scar, the wall-eye and the overall impression of weariness in face and figure. As well as the white horse guard's cap he was wearing a military greatcoat with a whip on a narrow strap slung across his shoulder. He sat on his game little horse very badly, a ponderous, wobbly load.

'Ugh! . . . ugh! . . . ugh!' he wheezed, though the sound was barely audible, as he rode into the courtyard. His face shone with the relief of a man looking forward to a nice rest after being a long time in the limelight. He withdrew his left foot from the stirrup with a lurch of his big body and scowled with exertion as he brought it up on to the saddle, used his knee to steady himself and flopped down with a groan into the supporting arms of his Cossacks and aides.

He pulled himself together, looked round with his eyes half-closed, glanced at Prince Andrey, seemed not to recognize him, and shambled off tubbily in the direction of the steps.

'Ugh! . . . ugh! . . . ugh!' he wheezed, and turned to take another look at Prince Andrey. As often happens with old men, the impression of Prince Andrey's face had taken some seconds to trigger a memory of his personality. 'Oh, hello there, my dear fellow, hello there. Do come along . . .' he said wearily, lumbering up the steps that creaked under his weight. He unbuttoned his coat and sat down on a bench in the porch.

'Well then, how's your father keeping?'

'News of his death reached me yesterday,' said Prince Andrey tersely.

Kutuzov looked at him wide-eyed with dismay, then he took his cap off and crossed himself. 'God rest his soul! And may God's will be done with all of us!' He heaved the deepest of sighs and paused. 'I loved him deeply and had great respect for him, and you have my heartfelt sympathy.' He put both arms round Prince Andrey, hugged him to his fat chest and held on for quite some time. When he released him, Prince Andrey could see Kutuzov's thick lips quivering, and there were tears in his eyes. He gave another sigh and pushed down on the bench with both hands to help himself up.

'Come in, do come in, and we'll have a chat,' he said, but at that moment Denisov, who cringed before the authorities as little as he did before the enemy, ignored the indignant whispering of adjutants trying hard to stop him, and walked boldly up the steps, spurs a-jangle. Kutuzov still had his hands pushing down on the seat, and he gave Denisov a resentful glance. Denisov stated his name and then announced that he needed to apprise his Highness on a matter of vital importance for the good of the country. Kutuzov levelled a weary eye at Denisov, raised both hands in a gesture of annoyance before folding them across his stomach, and repeated what he had heard: 'The good

of the country? Well, what do you mean? Out with it.' Denisov
coloured up like a young girl (it was most odd to see a blush spreading
over that hairy, ageing, hard-drinking face), and launched into a confident exposition of his plan for cutting the enemy's line of operations
somewhere between Smolensk and Vyazma. Denisov came from that
region, and he knew the locality well. His plan seemed unquestionably
sound, primarily because of the strength of conviction in his delivery.
Kutuzov stared at his feet, occasionally glancing up towards the courtyard of the house next-door, as if he was expecting something nasty
to emerge from it. What did emerge from next-door while Denisov
was in mid-flow was a general with a briefcase under his arm.

'What's this?' asked Kutuzov in the middle of Denisov's exposition.
'It didn't take you long to get things ready.'

'Indeed not, your Serene Highness,' said the general. Kutuzov shook
his head as if to say, 'How can one man be so efficient?' and turned
his mind back to Denisov.

'On my word of honour as a Wussian officer,' Denisov was saying,
'I shall cut wight thwough Napoleon's communications.'

'Are you related to Intendant-General Kirill Denisov?' asked
Kutuzov, interrupting.

'He's my uncle, sir.'

'Oh! We used to be friends,' said Kutuzov breezily. 'Very good, very
good, dear boy. You stay here on the staff, and we'll have a little talk
tomorrow.' Nodding to Denisov, he turned away and reached out for
the papers that Konovnitsyn had brought over.

'If your Highness would like to come through into the house, you
would be most welcome . . .' said the disgruntled duty general. 'There
are plans to be gone over and some papers to sign.' An adjutant
appeared in the doorway and announced that all was in readiness
within. But Kutuzov seemed not to want people with him when he
went inside. He scowled . . .

'No, have a table brought out here, dear boy. I'll go through them
here,' he said. 'Don't you go away,' he added, turning to Prince Andrey.
Prince Andrey stayed there in the porch listening to what the duty
general had to say.

While they were busy with the report Prince Andrey detected a
woman's voice whispering on the inside of the doorway, and he caught
the rustle of a woman's silk dress. Several times glancing across, he
noticed behind the door a good-looking woman with red cheeks and
a full figure, wearing a pink dress with a lilac silk scarf over her
head. She was holding a dish, and she seemed to be waiting for
the commander-in-chief to come in. Kutuzov's adjutant explained to

Prince Andrey in a whisper that this was the priest's wife, it was her house, and she was going to welcome his Highness with the traditional bread and salt. Her husband had met his Serene Highness with a cross in church, and now it was her turn in the house . . .

'She's very pretty,' added the adjutant with a smile. Kutuzov glanced round at these words. He was listening to the duty general's report (mostly a critique of the position at Tsarevo-Zaymishche) just as he had listened to Denisov, and just as he had listened to the debate at the council of war before Austerlitz seven years ago. He was obviously listening only because he had ears to listen with, and, even though one of them was packed with tow for his earache, they could not help hearing, but it was obvious that nothing that general could possibly say was going to be of any interest, let alone surprise him, because he had heard it all before, and if he was listening it was only because he had to, just as you have to listen to a service in church. Every word spoken by Denisov had been businesslike and sensible. What the general was now saying was even more businesslike and sensible, but Kutuzov clearly had no time for knowledge or intellect, because he knew something different that would win the day – something different, independent of intellect and knowledge. Prince Andrey kept a close watch on his face, and all he could make out on it was a look of boredom mixed with curiosity about the female voice whispering inside the door, and a desire to observe decorum. It may have been obvious that Kutuzov had no time for intellect or learning, or even the eager patriotism shown by Denisov, but his distaste was not based on intellect, or sentiment, or knowledge (none of which he had any pretensions towards), it came from something else – old age and long experience. The only amendment to the report made by Kutuzov himself had to do with looting by the Russian soldiers. The last item in the general's report was a document presented for his Highness's signature relating to a landowner's claim for compensation from the army authorities for the commandeering of his green oats.

Kutuzov smacked his lips and shook his head as he listened to this claim.

'Chuck it in the stove . . . Into the fire with it! And I tell you once and for all, my dear fellow,' he said, 'chuck everything like that into the fire. Let them cut corn and burn wood to their hearts' content. I haven't told them to, and they don't have my permission, but I can't investigate this sort of thing. It can't be helped. You can't make omelettes without breaking eggs.' He glanced down at the paper again. 'Pernickety devil, he's just like a German,' he muttered with a shake of his head.

CHAPTER 16

'Well, that's that then,' said Kutuzov as he signed the last document and lumbered to his feet. He smoothed out the rolls of fat on his podgy white neck and walked over to the door with a more buoyant look about him.

The priest's wife, with the blood rushing to her face, grabbed the dish, but although she had been rehearsing for ages, she missed the right moment to present it. She went ahead anyway and offered it to Kutuzov with a low bow. Kutuzov screwed up his eyes, gave a smile, chucked her under the chin and said, 'Oh what a pretty face! Thank you, my pet!'

He took some gold coins out of his trouser pocket and put them on her dish.

'Well now, how is life treating you?' he said, walking through to the room that had been set aside for him. The priest's wife, with a dimpled smile on her rosy-cheeked face, followed him in. The adjutant came out to Prince Andrey in the porch, and invited him to lunch. Half an hour later Kutuzov sent for Prince Andrey. He was sprawling in an armchair, still wearing his unbuttoned military coat. He was holding a French novel, and when Prince Andrey came in he marked his place with a paper-knife and put it down. Prince Andrey saw from the cover it was *The Knights of the Swan*, a romantic tale by Madame de Genlis.

'Do sit down, sit down here, and let's have a little talk,' said Kutuzov. 'It's sad, very sad. But don't forget, dear boy, you can look on me as a father, a second father!'

Prince Andrey told Kutuzov everything he knew about his father's death, and what he had seen at Bald Hills during his recent visit.

'Is this what we've been reduced to?' Kutuzov cried suddenly, deeply disturbed, accepting Prince Andrey's account as a vivid picture of the plight Russia was in.

'Give me time. Just give me time!' he added with a vicious glare, but he seemed reluctant to dwell on such a disturbing subject, and he went on to say, 'I've sent for you to keep you here with me.'

'I thank your Highness,' answered Prince Andrey, 'but I'm afraid I'm no good for staff work any more,' he said, with a smile that was not lost on Kutuzov, who looked back quizzically. 'No, the thing is,' added Prince Andrey, 'I've got used to my regiment. I like the officers, and the men seem to like me. I wouldn't want to leave the regiment. If I decline the honour of being in attendance on you, please believe . . .'

Kutuzov's podgy face glowed with a shrewd, kindly expression and a suggestion of irony. He cut Bolkonsky short.

'I'm sorry. You would have been useful to me. But you're right, you're quite right. It's not here that good men are needed. There's never any shortage of counsellors, but good men are hard to come by. The regiments wouldn't be what they are if all the counsellors served in them like you. I remember you at Austerlitz. Yes I do, I remember you with that flag!' said Kutuzov, and Prince Andrey's face flushed with pleasure at the memory of it. Kutuzov drew him close, offering him a cheek to kiss, and again Prince Andrey caught a glimpse of tears in the old man's eyes. Even though Prince Andrey knew Kutuzov was prone to tears, and he was being especially nice to him in order to show sympathy for his recent loss, he still felt pleased and flattered by this reminder of Austerlitz.

'Make your own way, then, and God go with you. I know your way is the way of honour!' He paused. 'I missed you at Bucharest. I needed someone to send . . .' And he was off on to another subject, the Turkish war, and the peace that had been concluded. 'Oh yes, I've had my share of criticism,' he said, 'for the war and the peace . . . but everything fell into place at the right time. "Everything falls into place for the man who knows how to wait,"' he said, quoting the French proverb. 'And there were just as many counsellors there as there are here . . .' he went on, falling back on the subject of counsellors that had become an obsession with him. 'Ugh, counsellors, counsellors!' he said. 'If we'd listened to them all we'd still be in Turkey, without any peace and with the war still on. Too much of a hurry. More haste, less speed, I say. Kamensky would have come to grief there, if he hadn't died first. He went about storming fortresses with thirty thousand men. Taking fortresses is easy enough, the hard part is winning the war. And you don't get that by storming and attacking – what you need are *time* and *patience*. Kamensky used his soldiers to attack Rushchuk. I used those two, time and patience, and I took more fortresses than he did, and I soon had the Turks eating horse-meat!' He shook his head. 'And I'll have the French doing it too. Take my word for it,' cried Kutuzov, warming to his task and patting himself on the chest, 'I'll have them eating horse-flesh!' And again his eyes were misty with tears.

'But we shall have to fight, shan't we?' said Prince Andrey.

'Oh yes, if that's what people want they'll have to have it . . . But mark my words, dear boy! There's nothing stronger than those two old soldiers – *time and patience*. There's nothing they can't do, but our wise counsellors are deaf in one ear, and that's where the trouble is. Some want action, others don't. So what am I to do?' he asked, evidently expecting a reply. 'Come on, what would you have me do?' he repeated, and his shrewd eyes shone with deep meaning. 'I'll tell you what to do,' he said, with no answer forthcoming from Prince Andrey. 'I'll tell you what to do, and what I do. When in doubt, my friend,' – he paused – 'hold back.' He said this in French, slowly, syllable by syllable.

'Well, goodbye, my dear fellow. I feel for you with all my heart in your great sorrow, and don't forget – as far as you're concerned I'm not his Highness, or a prince, or a commander-in-chief, I'm a father to you. If you need anything come straight to me. Goodbye, my dear boy!' Again he hugged and kissed him.

And Prince Andrey was hardly out of the room when Kutuzov heaved a sigh of relief and settled down to Madame de Genlis and *The Knights of the Swan*.

How or why it came about Prince Andrey could never have explained, but after this encounter with Kutuzov he returned to his regiment greatly reassured about the way things were going and the man they had been entrusted to. The more clearly he registered the absence of all personal interest in this old man, who seemed to have reduced himself to going through the motions of old passions, and had replaced an active mind capable of organizing things and coming to conclusions with a capacity for calm contemplation as events unfolded, the more confident he felt that everything would work out as it should. 'He has no axe to grind. He won't have any ideas or hatch any schemes,' Prince Andrey told himself, 'but he'll listen to everybody and miss nothing, he'll put things in their proper places, he won't get in the way of anything useful or allow anything that might do any harm. He knows there is something stronger and more important than his will – the inexorable march of events – and he has the knack of watching events and seeing what they mean, and when he sees what they mean he knows how to stand back from them and redirect his will somewhere else. But the main reason for believing in him,' thought Prince Andrey, 'is that he's Russian – never mind Madame de Genlis and a few French proverbs – and his voice shook when he said, "Is this what we've been reduced to?" and he choked when he said he would "soon have them eating horse-flesh!"'

It was this feeling, shared more or less dimly by everyone, that underpinned the unanimity and general approval which accompanied the appointment of Kutuzov as commander-in-chief, the people's choice whatever misgivings may have been felt in court circles.

CHAPTER 17

After the Tsar's departure from Moscow life went on in the same old
way, and its course seemed so normal that it was soon hard to recall
the days of fervour and heady patriotism, and hard to believe the
country was in real danger, and the members of the English Club were
also sons of Mother Russia, ready for any sacrifice. The one thing that
brought back the general mood of patriotic fervour during the Tsar's
Moscow visit was the call for contributions of men and money, which
soon turned from offers into officially formulated demands that had
every appearance of being legal and binding.

As the enemy closed in on Moscow the attitude of the inhabitants to
their situation, far from becoming all serious-minded, actually became
more frivolous, as always happens with people who can see a terrible
danger bearing down on them. At the first approach of danger two
voices always speak out with equal force in a man's heart: one tells
him very sensibly to consider the exact extent of the danger and any
means of avoiding it; the other says even more sensibly that it's too
wearisome and agonizing to contemplate the danger, since it is not in
a man's power to anticipate future events and avoid the general run
of things, so you might as well turn away from the nastiness until it
hits you, and dwell on things that are pleasant. Left to himself a man
will usually listen to the first voice; out in society he listens to the
second one. This is what was now happening to the good people of
Moscow. It was years since there had been so much fun in the city.

Rostopchin's broadsheets were the talk of the town, rivalling Vasily
Pushkin's[3] latest *bouts rimés* in popularity. They featured a drinking-
house at the top, a tapster and a Moscow citizen, Karpushka Chigirin,
*an ex-militiaman who, when he has had a drop too much to drink,
hears that Napoleon is bent on marching on Moscow, whereupon he
flies into a rage, curses the French up hill and down dale, walks out
of the drinking-house and speaks to the assembled people under the
sign of the eagle.*

The club members got together in the corner room to peruse these
posters, and some of them were greatly amused by Karpushka's being
so rude to the French and saying things like *they'll get bloated on
Russian cabbage, burst their bellies on Russian porridge and choke to
death on the cabbage soup, and anyway they're all dwarfs and any
village lass could fork 'em away three at a time.*

There were others, though, who did not approve of this tone, which
they called vulgar and stupid. Rumour had it that Rostopchin had

expelled all Frenchmen, in fact all foreigners, from Moscow, and some of them had turned out to be spies and agents of Napoleon. But the main reason for putting this about was to be able to keep repeating the funny things Rostopchin said as he dispatched them. As the foreigners were being shepherded on board a barge heading for Nizhny, Rostopchin had said to them in French, 'Keep yourselves to yourselves, get on this barge, and make sure it doesn't turn into Charon's ferry.'[4] The word went round that all government offices had been evacuated from Moscow, which inspired Shinshin's much-repeated little joke that at last Napoleon had given Moscow something to be grateful for. It was claimed that Mamonov's regiment was costing him eight hundred thousand, and Bezukhov was stumping up even more, but the best thing about him was that he was going to get into uniform and ride at the head of his regiment, and spectators were welcome without paying at the gate.

'You never say nice things about anybody,' said Julie Drubetskoy, picking up a handful of lint and squeezing it between slender fingers that glittered with rings.

Julie would be leaving Moscow the following day, and she was giving a farewell soirée.

'Bezukhov does look ridiculous, but he's very nice, and his heart's in the right place. How can you take pleasure to be so *caustique*?'

'You're fined!' said a young man in a militiaman's uniform, referred to by Julie as her knight in shining armour – he was going with her to Nizhny.

In Julie's circle, as in many others in Moscow, the unwritten rule was to speak nothing but Russian, and anybody who slipped up and spoke some French had to pay a fine into the coffers of the Committee for Voluntary Donations.

'A double fine for Frenchified Russian,' said a Russian writer who happened to be within earshot. You can't say "take pleasure to be . . ."'

'You never say nice things about anybody,' Julie persisted with the militiaman, ignoring the author and his remark.

'I plead guilty to *caustique*,' she said, 'and I'll even pay up for *taking pleasure to tell* the truth. But I won't be held responsible for Frenchified Russian,' she said, turning now to the scribbler. 'I have neither the time nor the money to hire a teacher and learn Russian like Prince Golitsyn. Oh, but here he comes!' added Julie. '*Quand on* . . . Oh no,' she protested to the militiaman, 'you can't catch me like that. *When one* talks of the sun, out it comes! We were just talking about you.' She gave a sweet smile as she welcomed Pierre with the easy lapse into falsehood that comes naturally to women in high society. 'We were saying your regiment's bound to be better than Mamonov's.'

'Oh, don't talk to me about the regiment,' answered Pierre, kissing his hostess's hand and sitting down beside her. 'I've had enough of it!'

'You will, er, take command personally, won't you?' said Julie, exchanging a sly, mocking glance with the militiaman.

Face to face with Pierre the militiaman had lost some of his causticity, and Julie's smile now left him looking nonplussed. For all his good-natured absentmindedness Pierre had the kind of personality that soon put an end to any attempt to make a fool of him.

'Oh no,' Pierre chuckled with a glance down at his huge, bulging figure. 'Too much for the French to aim at here, and I'm afraid I could never get up on a horse.'

Of all the people available as subjects for gossip Julie's guests hit on the Rostovs.

'I hear their finances are in a bad way,' said Julie. 'And the count's not being very sensible. The Razumovskys did want to buy his house and their local estate, but it's going on for ever. He's asking too much.'

'No, I think the sale will go through any day now,' said someone. 'Though you'd have to be crazy to buy anything in Moscow just now.'

'Why do you say that?' asked Julie. 'Do you really think Moscow's in danger?'

'Well, why are you going away?'

'Why am I going away? That's a funny thing to ask. I'm going because . . . well, everybody's going, and I'm not Joan of Arc or an Amazon.'

'Quite so. Would you mind passing me a bit more of that linen?'

'If he plays his cards right he ought to be able to pay off all his debts,' said the militiaman, reverting to the subject of Count Rostov. 'He's a good-hearted old fellow, but a very poor specimen.'

'Anyway, why have they stayed on as long as this? They were meaning to leave for the country quite some time ago. Natalie is her old self now, I imagine?' Julie asked Pierre with a devious smile.

'They're waiting for their younger son,' said Pierre. 'He joined up with Obolensky's Cossacks, and they sent him to Belaya Tserkov. That's where the regiment is being formed. But now they've had him transferred to my regiment, and he's expected any day now. The count's been dying to get away for ages, but nothing would induce the countess to leave Moscow till her son gets back.'

'I saw them the day before yesterday at the Arkharovs. Natalie looks pretty again and she's in much better spirits. She sang for us. Some people get over things so easily!'

'What kind of things?' asked Pierre with a disgruntled look. Julie smiled at him.

'Oh, Count, really, chivalrous knights like you don't exist outside the pages of Madame de Souza's novels.'

'Chivalrous knights? What can you possibly mean?' asked Pierre, colouring up.

'Come now, my dear count. It's all over Moscow. Honestly, I do admire you!'

But her last words had come out in French and they brought cries of 'Fined again! Fined again!' from the militiaman.

'Oh, all right. You can't even talk now. It's such a bore!'

'What's all over Moscow?' said Pierre getting to his feet with some resentment.

'Oh, come on, Count, you know very well!'

'I know absolutely nothing,' said Pierre.

'I know how close you've been to Natalie, so . . . Actually, I was always closer to Vera myself. Such a darling girl, Vera.'

'No, madame,' Pierre persisted, still disgruntled. 'I have certainly not assumed the role of Countess Rostov's knight. I haven't been near the place for nigh on a month. How could you be so cruel? . . .'

'I think you do protest too much,' cried Julie with a smile, brandishing her lint. Determined to have the last word, she promptly changed the subject. 'By the way, I've just heard that poor Marie Bolkonsky arrived in Moscow yesterday. You know she's lost her father?'

'Has she really? Where is she? I'd very much like to see her,' said Pierre.

'I spent yesterday evening with her. Today or tomorrow morning she's taking her nephew down to their Moscow estate.'

'Well, how is she? How's she getting on?' said Pierre.

'Oh, she's all right, just feeling very sad. You'll never guess who came to her rescue! It's so romantic. Nikolay Rostov! She was surrounded, they were trying to kill her and the servants had been wounded. He just rushed in and saved her . . .'

'Another romance,' said the militiaman. 'All this running away has a clear purpose: to get all our old maids married off. There's Katish for one, and now Princess Bolkonsky.'

'You know what I think? She's just a little *amoureuse*. Just a little in love with that *jeune homme*.'

'Fined again! Fined again! Fined again!'

'But how can you say things like that in Russian?'

CHAPTER 18

When Pierre got home he was handed two new Rostopchin posters that had been brought in during the day.

The first denied the rumour that Count Rostopchin had stopped people leaving Moscow: on the contrary, he was glad to see that ladies and merchants' wives were going. 'Less panic and less rumour,' said the notice, 'but on one thing I stake my life: that scoundrel will never set foot in Moscow.'

On reading these words Pierre realized for the first time that the French were going to set foot in Moscow. The second poster announced that our headquarters were at Vyazma, and Count Wittgenstein had defeated the French, but also, since many Muscovites wished to arm themselves, weapons had been provided and had only to be collected from the arsenal: swords, pistols and guns were available to all citizens at cut-down prices.

The tone of this poster was noticeably less humorous than the earlier Chigirin discourses. The two posters gave Pierre pause for thought. He could now see clearly that the menacing stormcloud he had been invoking so wholeheartedly, even though he instinctively recoiled from it in horror, was now almost upon him.

'What shall I do: join up and go out to the army, or wait here?' Pierre asked himself for the hundredth time. He picked up a pack of cards which happened to be lying there on the table and settled down to play patience.

'If this deal comes out,' he told himself, holding the pack in one hand and shuffling with the other as he turned his eyes upwards, 'if it comes out that will mean . . . what will it mean? . . .' Before he could decide what it would mean he heard the voice of the eldest princess outside the study door, asking for permission to come in. 'So, it will mean I've got to go off and join the army,' Pierre told himself. 'Yes, do come in,' he said to the princess.

The eldest of his cousins, she of the long thin waist and stony face, was the only one still living in Pierre's house, the two younger sisters having both got married.

'Oh, Cousin, please forgive me for coming in to see you.' She seemed excited and her tone was disparaging. 'But I hope you realize some decisions have to be taken. What on earth is going to happen? Everyone has left Moscow, and the people are up in arms. Why are we staying on?'

'Quite the reverse, dear cousin, everything seems to be most satisfactory,' said Pierre in the bantering tone he usually adopted with his cousin to dispel the embarrassment he always felt towards her in his role as benefactor.

'Oh yes, satisfactory ... highly satisfactory, I'm sure. Varvara Ivanovna has been telling me how well our troops are doing. And much credit it does them, I must say. And the people, too, they've taken to the streets and they won't obey any orders. My own maid has turned against me. If things go on as they are they'll soon be after our blood. You can't walk down the street. But what bothers me is that the French will be here in a day or two. Why are we waiting for them? Please, Cousin, just do me one favour,' said the princess, 'give orders for me to be taken to Petersburg. Say what you will about me, I could not live under Bonaparte.'

'My dear cousin, that's quite enough. Where do you get your information from? You've got things the wrong way round ...'

'I will not submit to your Napoleon. Others may do as they like ... If you won't do this for me ...'

'But I will, I'll give the orders straightaway.'

The princess was obviously quite put out by having no one to vent her anger on. Muttering under her breath she perched on the edge of a chair.

'But what you've heard is not right,' said Pierre. 'Everything's quiet down town, and there's no danger. Look what I've just been reading ...' Pierre showed her the posters. 'The count says here he'll stake his life on it the enemy will never set foot in Moscow.'

'Oh, you and your count,' the princess spat out spitefully. 'He's a hypocrite and a villain. He was the one who brought them out on to the streets. Didn't he write on his stupid posters that they should grab the world and his wife by the scruff of the neck and dump them in the lock-up? Stupid man! Honour and glory, says he, to anyone who does. Look where it's got us, all his fine talk! Varvara Ivanovna told me she was almost strung up by the mob for speaking a few words of French.'

'Well, I know how it is ... But you do take things too seriously,' said Pierre, dealing out his cards for a game of patience.

That hand did come out, but rather than going off to join the army Pierre stayed on in a Moscow that was getting emptier by the day, and his mood was the same – a mixture of excitement, indecision and delicious dread of impending doom.

By the following evening the princess had gone, and Pierre's head steward came in to report that the money needed for the equipment of his regiment could not be raised without selling one of his estates. He did his best to persuade Pierre that all these silly ideas about a regiment would be the ruin of him. Pierre could hardly conceal a smile as he listened to the steward.

'Well, go on, sell it,' he said. 'It can't be helped. There's no going back on what I said!'

The worse things got, especially things that mattered to him, the happier Pierre was, and the clearer it became that the long-awaited catastrophe was almost upon them. Hardly any of Pierre's acquaintances were still in town. Julie had gone, Princess Marya had gone. Of the people closest to him only the Rostovs were left, but Pierre didn't go to see them.

That day for a little relaxation Pierre drove out to the village of Vorontsovo to have a look at a huge balloon that was being built by Leppich[5] for devastating use against the enemy, and the test balloon due for launching the following day. The balloon wasn't quite ready, but Pierre found out it was being built with the Tsar's approval. The Tsar had written to Count Rostopchin (in French) as follows:

> As soon as Leppich is ready select a crew of good, clever men for his gondola, and dispatch a courier to General Kutuzov to give him due warning. I have told him about this. Please ensure that Leppich is strongly advised to be very careful where he comes down for the first time lest he go off course and fall into the hands of the enemy. It is essential that he co-ordinate his movements with those of the commander-in-chief.

On the way home from Vorontsovo Pierre was driving through Bolotny Square when he saw a crowd at the Place of Execution, so he stopped and got out of his carriage. A French chef accused of espionage was being flogged. The flogging was over, and the executioner was at the flogging-bench untying a stout man with red sideburns, blue stockings and a green jacket stripped off his back, who was moaning grievously. Another criminal, frail, thin and pale, was waiting for his turn. To judge by their faces both of them were Frenchmen. Pierre shoved his way through the crowd looking every bit as terrified and sickly as the skinny Frenchman.

'What's happening? Who are they? What have they done?' he kept asking. But the crowd – clerks, tradesmen, shopkeepers, peasants, women in cloaks and jackets – were so fascinated by what was happening at the Place of Execution that nobody answered. The stout man got to his feet wincing, twisted his shoulders and tried his best with a show of bravery to pull on his jacket without looking round at everybody, but suddenly his lips trembled and he burst into tears, furious with himself, as sometimes happens with grown men, however full-blooded. There were loud comments from the crowd as people stifled their feelings of sympathy – or so Pierre liked to think.

'Some chef belonging to a prince . . .'

'Hey, monsewer, Russian sauce a bit sharp for a Froggy? . . . Makes you wince a bit!' said a wrinkled clerk standing near Pierre at the moment the Frenchman burst into tears. The clerk looked round, obviously expecting applause. Some people did laugh, but others were so dismayed they could not take their eyes off the executioner, who was in the process of stripping the second Frenchman.

Pierre was choking. He screwed up his face, turned away sharply, went back to his carriage and got in, all the time muttering under his breath. As they drove on he got the shudders several times, and yelled out so loud that the coachman asked what he wanted.

'Where are you going?' Pierre shouted to the coachman as he turned into Lubyanka Street.

'You told me to go to the governor general's,' answered the coachman.

'You stupid idiot!' roared Pierre, a man who rarely abused his coachman. 'I told you to drive me home. Get going, you blockhead!' and under his breath he muttered, 'I've got to leave town this very day.'

It was the sight of the tortured Frenchman and the crowd all round the Place of Execution that had brought Pierre to a final decision: he simply could not stay on in Moscow, he must set off that very day to join the army, and as he saw it either he must have told the coachman, or the coachman ought to have known.

When he got home Pierre told his omniscient and omnipotent head coachman, Yevstafyevich, who was famous throughout Moscow, that he was leaving for Mozhaysk that night to join the army and his saddle horses should be sent down there. This was more than could be arranged in a single day, so Pierre yielded to Yevstafyevich's ministrations and delayed his departure till next day so there would be time for relays of horses to be sent on ahead.

The morning of the 24th dawned bright after a spell of bad weather, and that day after dinner Pierre set out from Moscow. Changing horses during the night at Perkhushkovo, Pierre heard that there had been a huge battle that evening (the battle of Shevardino). He was told that even at Perkhushkovo the ground had been shaking from the cannon-fire. No one could answer Pierre when he asked whether the battle had been won or lost. Dawn was breaking when Pierre got to Mozhaysk.

Every house in Mozhaysk had been taken over by the military, and at the inn where Pierre was met by his coachman and groom there wasn't a room to be had. The place was full of officers.

The whole of Mozhaysk and the surrounding area was swarming with soldiers standing around or on the march. Cossacks, infantrymen, cavalrymen, wagons, gun-carriages and cannons were all over the place. Pierre pressed on as fast as he could, and the further he moved away from Moscow and the more deeply he became immersed in this ocean of troops, the stronger he was gripped by a thrilling sense of excitement and a totally new feeling of exhilaration. It was not unlike the sensation he had experienced at the Sloboda palace during the Tsar's visit, a sense of the urgent need to do something positive and make sacrifices. He rejoiced in a new awareness that everything that makes for happiness in life – comfort, wealth, even life itself – was nothing but trash to be thrown away with pleasure when you compare it with ... well, something else ... What that something else was Pierre could not have said, and he didn't even try to work out who or what he was taking such exquisite pleasure in honouring by the ultimate sacrifice. He wasn't at all worried about why he wanted to start making sacrifices, but the idea of sacrifice itself was a source of new delight.

CHAPTER 19

On the 24th the battle of the Shevardino redoubt was fought; on the 25th not a shot was fired by either side; on the 26th came the battle of Borodino.

For what reason and in what way was battle offered and accepted at Shevardino and Borodino? Why *did* they join battle at Borodino? There was no sense in it for the French or the Russians. The immediate outcome was a clear inevitability: we Russians were brought one step closer towards the destruction of Moscow (the thing we dreaded most in all the world), and the French were brought one step closer towards the destruction of their entire army (the thing they dreaded most in all the world). At the time this outcome was as plain as a pikestaff, yet Napoleon offered battle and Kutuzov accepted.

If the military leaders had been guided by principles of reason it ought to have been clear to Napoleon that in marching nearly fifteen hundred miles and offering to fight, with a fair chance of losing a quarter of his men, he was heading for certain destruction, and it ought to have been just as clear to Kutuzov that in accepting the offer, also with a good chance of losing a quarter of his men, he was sure to lose Moscow. For Kutuzov it was a mathematical certainty, as clear as a game of draughts in which I am a piece down and if I go on exchanging pieces I am bound to lose, so I must avoid any exchanges. When my opponent has sixteen pieces and I have fourteen I am only one eighth weaker, but by the time we have exchanged thirteen pieces he will end up three times stronger than I am.

Before the battle of Borodino our forces were about five-sixths the strength of the French, but when it was over they were only half as strong; in other words before the battle a hundred thousand faced a hundred and twenty thousand, and when it was over fifty thousand faced a hundred thousand. Nevertheless, a leader as shrewd and experienced as Kutuzov took on the battle, which had been offered by Napoleon, who is generally described as a military genius, though it lost him a quarter of his men and extended his line of communications even further. It may be said that he thought he could end the campaign by taking Moscow, as he had done by taking Vienna, but there is a lot of evidence against this. Napoleon's own historians tell us he had wanted to call a halt as far back as Smolensk, realizing how dangerously extended he was and knowing full well that the taking of Moscow would not be the end of the campaign, because he could see from Smolensk the dreadful state of the abandoned Russian towns, and he had received not a word of reply to repeated announcements of his desire to open negotiations.

The actions of Kutuzov and Napoleon in offering and accepting battle at Borodino were involuntary and meaningless. But later on, with the battle a *fait accompli*, historians have come forward with every kind of specious argument to demonstrate the foresight and genius of these generals, who of all the involuntary agents in the history of the world were surely the most enslaved and involuntary.

The ancients have left us examples of epics with all the historical interest focused on particular heroes, and nowadays we cannot get used to the idea that this kind of history is meaningless at the present stage of human development.

In response to the other question, of how battle was offered and accepted at Borodino and before that at Shevardino, there exists another clearly defined, universally familiar and totally false account. All the historians describe events as follows:

In retreat from Smolensk, they say, the Russian army scouted around to find the best location for a general engagement, and just such a location was discovered at Borodino. The Russians, they say, fortified this location in advance, on the left-hand side of the Moscow–Smolensk road and at right angles to it, all the way from Borodino to Utitsa, and that is where the battle was fought.

In front of this location, we are told, a fortified earthwork was thrown up on the rising ground at Shevardino as an outpost for the observation of enemy movements.

On the 24th, so the story goes, Napoleon attacked this outpost, and took it. On the 26th he attacked the whole Russian army, which had taken up position on the field of Borodino.

This is the historical version of events, and it is totally wrong, as anyone can tell if he is prepared to go into the matter.

The Russians did not scout round to find the best location; quite the reverse, as they retreated they had by-passed many locations better than Borodino. They did not take a stand at any of these positions, partly because Kutuzov refused to take up a position not chosen by himself personally, partly because the popular clamour for a battle was not yet strong enough, partly because Miloradovich had yet to arrive with the militia, and for lots of other reasons.

The fact is, there had been stronger positions earlier on, and the Borodino location where the battle took place was no improvement on anywhere else in the Russian empire that might have been chosen at random by sticking a pin into a map.

Far from fortifying a location on the left-hand side at right angles to the road, the place where the battle was fought, the Russians never even dreamt of fighting a battle on that spot until the 25th of August 1812. This is proved firstly by the fact that there were no fortifications there before the 25th, and the earthworks begun on that day had not been completed by the 26th; and secondly, proof is provided by the situation of the Shevardino redoubt itself, out in front of the battlefield, which rendered it valueless. For what purpose was this redoubt more strongly fortified than any other post? And for what purpose was every effort made and were six thousand men sacrificed to defend it until last thing on the 24th? A Cossack patrol would have been enough to keep track of enemy movements. And a third way of proving that the position of the battlefield was not anticipated, and the Shevardino redoubt was not an advance post of that position, lies in the fact that until the 25th Barclay de Tolly and Bagration were convinced that the Shevardino redoubt was the *left* flank of the position, and Kutuzov himself, in a report jotted down in haste immediately after the battle, speaks of Shevardino as the *left* flank of their position. It was only much later on, when reports of the battle came to be written down at leisure, that a curiously inaccurate statement was invented (probably to gloss over errors made by the commander-in-chief, who had to be seen as infallible) to the effect that the Shevardino redoubt served as an *advance* post, whereas it was nothing more than a fortified post on the left flank, and the battle of Borodino was undertaken by us in a fortified location selected in advance, whereas it was really fought in an unexpected place that was virtually without fortification.

What happened is clear. A location was chosen on the river Kolocha, which cuts across the high road not at ninety degrees, but at an acute angle, with the left flank at Shevardino, the right flank near the village of Novoye, and the centre at Borodino, near the confluence of the Kolocha and the Voyna. Anyone looking at the field of Borodino and disregarding the actual course of the battle would consider this location, conveniently covered by the Kolocha, the obvious one to be adopted by an army that wanted to check the advance of an enemy marching down the road from Smolensk towards Moscow.

Napoleon, riding towards Valuyevo on the 24th, did not (according to the history books) see the position of the Russians between Utitsa and Borodino (he could not have seen it since it didn't exist), and did not see the advance posts of the Russian army, but in his pursuit of the Russian rearguard he stumbled upon the left flank of the Russian position at the Shevardino redoubt, and surprised the Russians by taking his troops across the Kolocha. And since it was too late for a general engagement the Russians withdrew the left flank from their intended position and took up a new one, which had not been anticipated and was not fortified. By crossing the Kolocha on the left-hand side of the road Napoleon shifted the whole battle-to-be from right to left (looked at from the Russian side) and transferred it to the fields that lie between Utitsa, Semyonovsk and Borodino – fields with nothing more to offer in the way of military advantage than any others in Russia – and it was here that the whole battle of the 26th took place.[6]

If Napoleon had not reached the Kolocha on the evening of the 24th and had not ordered an immediate attack on the redoubt, if he had launched his attack the following morning, no one would have had any doubt that the Shevardino redoubt was the left flank of the Russian position, and the battle would have gone ahead as anticipated. In that case we would probably have defended the Shevardino redoubt even more stubbornly, it being our left flank; we would have attacked Napoleon in the centre or from the right, and the general engagement would have been fought out on the 25th in a location that had been anticipated and fortified. But since the attack on our left flank occurred in the evening following the retreat of our rearguard, that is, immediately after the action at Gridneva, and since the Russian generals would not or could not undertake a general engagement that same evening, the 24th, the first and most important action in the battle of Borodino was already lost on the 24th, a loss that clearly led straight to the débâcle that occurred on the 26th.

Following the loss of the Shevardino redoubt, on the morning of the 25th we found ourselves without a position for the left flank, and we were forced to let the left wing curl back, fortifying it where and when we could.

So it wasn't just a question of our Russian troops being protected on the 26th of August by nothing but flimsy, unfinished earthworks; the disadvantage of their position was aggravated by the Russian generals' failure to grasp what had actually happened (the loss of the left-flank position, and the whole field of the battle-to-be swinging from right to left), which left them holding their extended line all the way from Novoye to Utitsa, and that meant they had to transfer troops from right to left in mid-battle. As a result of this, throughout the entire battle the Russians had to face the whole French army bearing down on our left wing, with our forces doubly disadvantaged.

(Poniatowski's action against Utitsa and Uvarov's action against the French on the right flank were outside the general course of the battle.)

And so the battle of Borodino was fought quite differently from the way it is normally described (by historians so anxious to gloss over the blunders of our generals they detract from the glorious achievements of the Russian army and the Russian people). The battle of Borodino was not fought out in a carefully selected and well-fortified location with some slight disadvantage in numbers on the Russian side. Following the loss of the Shevardino redoubt the battle of Borodino was fought out in an open location with almost no entrenchments, with Russian forces doubly disadvantaged vis-à-vis the French, in other words under conditions that made it unthinkable even to get through three hours without the army being utterly defeated and put to flight, let alone keep on fighting for ten hours and still leave the issue in doubt.

CHAPTER 20

It was the morning of the 25th, and Pierre was on his way out of Mozhaysk. When he got to the point where the road out of town meandered steeply downhill, Pierre got out of his carriage and walked past a cathedral on the right-hand side at the top of the slope, where a service was being held and the bells were ringing. One of the cavalry regiments was following him downhill, with the singers out in front. Coming up the hill towards them was a train of carts filled with casualties from the previous day's engagement. The peasant drivers were running this way and that, urging the horses on and wielding their whips. The carts, each carrying three or four wounded soldiers stretched out or sitting up, jolted over the stones that had been thrown down to make some sort of road up the hill. The wounded men, white-faced and bandaged with rags, clung to the sides wincing and scowling as they were shaken and thrown about in the carts. Almost all of them gawped at Pierre in his white hat and green swallowtail coat with the simple-minded curiosity of children.

Pierre's driver yelled furiously at the casualty convoy to keep to one side of the road. The cavalry regiment marching on downhill in step with the singers soon caught up with Pierre's carriage and this blocked the road. Pierre stopped and squeezed back to the edge of the road that had been dug into the hill. The slope of the hillside kept the sun off the cutting, and it was cold and damp down there, but overhead the bells sang out merrily on a bright August morning. A cart with wounded men on it came to a standstill at the edge of the road right in front of Pierre. The driver in his bark-fibre shoes ran round the back of his cart, and with much puffing and panting shoved some stones under the back wheels, which had no tyres on them; then he set to tightening his horse's harness.

A wounded veteran with his arm in a sling, who had been walking along behind the cart, took hold of it with his good arm, and looked round at Pierre.

'You from these parts?' he said. 'Are they dropping us here or taking us on to Moscow?'

Pierre was so preoccupied that he didn't hear. He was engrossed in watching the cavalry regiment that had come up against the casualty convoy, and the cart right in front of him with its three wounded men, two sitting up, one lying down. One of the pair sitting up seemed to have been wounded in the cheek. His whole head was swathed in rags, and one cheek had swollen up as big as a baby's head. His mouth and nose had been skewed to one side. He was looking over at the cathedral and he crossed himself. Another soldier, a conscript, only a boy, with blond hair and a thin white face that seemed to have been drained of all blood, was watching Pierre with a friendly smile. The third man was lying on his belly so you could not see his face. The cavalry singers were now level with the cart. They were belting out a good soldier's song that had the men dancing along.

My hair's all gone, I've got a spiky head,
And here I am a-wanderin' far from home . . .

A kind of echo, joyous in a very different way, came ringing down
from the metallic clanging of the bells. And joyous in a different way
again was the hot sunshine that bathed the top of the opposite slope. But
under the hillside where Pierre stood next to the cart with the wounded
soldiers and the gasping little nag, it was miserably damp and dismal.

The soldier with the swollen cheek looked savagely at the singing
cavalrymen.

'All right for that lot, showing off!' he growled resentfully.

'It's not just soldiers now, you know, there's peasants, too, I've seen
'em! Oh yes, the peasants, they're gettin' dragged in as well,' said the
soldier standing by the cart and talking to Pierre with a lugubrious
smile on his lips. 'No pickin' and choosin' now . . . Chuck everybody
at 'em. It's all about Moscow, you know. Get it all over an' done
with.' Although the soldier didn't express himself clearly, Pierre got
his meaning and nodded in agreement.

Now at last the road was clear, so Pierre walked to the bottom of
the hill and drove off again.

On he went, searching for familiar faces on either side of the road,
but all he saw were unfamiliar ones, fighting faces from all over the
military, every one of them staring in amazement at his white hat and
green swallowtail coat.

He had gone two or three miles before he came across someone he
knew, and he hailed him with great delight. It was a doctor, a senior
member of the army medical staff. He was coming towards Pierre in
a covered gig, with a young doctor at his side, and the moment he
spotted Pierre, he called out to the Cossack who had taken over as his
driver, and told him to stop.

'Count! Your Excellency, what are you doing down here?' asked
the doctor.

'Oh, I just felt like having a look . . .'

'Well, there's going to be plenty to look at . . .' Pierre got out of his
carriage, and stopped to exchange a few words with the doctor, telling
him he had every intention of taking part in the battle.

The doctor advised Bezukhov to go straight to Kutuzov.

'What do you think you're doing, wandering off out of sight, God
knows where on the battlefield?' he said, exchanging a quick glance
with his young colleague, 'and his Serene Highness does know you,
so you'll get a warm welcome. That's what you must do, my friend,'
said the doctor.

The doctor had an exhausted and harassed look about him.

'So you think . . . Anyway, there's just one more thing I wanted to ask – where exactly is our position?' said Pierre.

'Our position?' said the doctor. 'Not really my cup of tea. Get yourself down past Tatarinova. There's a fair amount of digging going on there. Some high ground. You can see a lot from there,' said the doctor.

'Can you really? . . . If you could just . . .'

But the doctor had cut him short and was walking back to his gig.

'I would have taken you there, but I'm up to here, for heaven's sake . . .' (The doctor pointed to his throat.) 'Must rush. I'm off to see the corps commander. Do you know how bad things are? . . . Listen, Count, there's going to be a battle tomorrow with a hundred thousand troops. We can count on twenty thousand casualties at the very least, and we haven't enough stretchers, beds, dressers or doctors for six thousand. We have got ten thousand carts, but we need lots of other things. Just have to do what we can.'

Pierre was greatly affected by the curious idea that of all those thousands of men, alive and kicking, young and old, who had been staring at his hat with such easy amusement, twenty thousand were inexorably destined to be wounded or killed, maybe men he had seen with his own eyes.

'They may be going to die tomorrow. How can they think of anything but death?' And suddenly, by some mysterious association of ideas, he had a vivid recollection of walking down the hill outside Mozhaysk, with the carts and the wounded men, the clamour of the bells, the slanting rays of sunshine, and the cavalrymen singing.

'All those cavalrymen marching into battle, coming across wounded soldiers, never stopping to think what's in store for them – they just march past winking at their wounded comrades. And of all those men, twenty thousand are doomed to die – and they think my hat's funny! It's weird!' thought Pierre, moving on towards Tatarinova.

Outside some gentleman's house on the left side of the road there were carriages, wagons and orderlies and sentries in droves. This was where his Serene Highness, the commander-in-chief, was staying. But when Pierre arrived he was out, and so were most of the staff. They had all gone to church. Pierre pressed on towards Gorki, where he drove uphill and found himself on the little village street. There he had his first sight of conscripted peasants in their white shirts, with crosses on their caps. Brimming with energy and running with sweat, there they were on the right-hand side of the road working away at a huge grass-covered mound with raucous comments and roars of laughter. Some were digging, some were wheeling the earth away in barrows, while a third lot stood around doing nothing.

Two officers stood on the knoll telling them what to do. At the sight of these peasants, so obviously revelling in their new-found status as soldiers, Pierre thought again of the wounded men at Mozhaysk, and now he could see what the soldier had meant with his 'Chuck everybody at 'em'. The spectacle of these bearded peasants toiling on the field of battle with their funny, clumsy boots, their sweaty necks, one or two of them with shirts open from top left to bottom right showing their sunburnt collar-bones, told Pierre more about the primacy and solemn meaning of the here and now than anything he had yet seen and heard.

CHAPTER 21

Pierre got out of his carriage, walked past the toiling peasants and climbed up the mound which according to the doctor offered a good view of the field of battle.

It was about eleven in the morning. The sun was behind Pierre a little to his left, and it shone down brightly through the clear, rarefied air on the huge vista sprawling before him like an amphitheatre on rising ground.

The main road from Smolensk cut through the amphitheatre upwards at the top left, and in its meandering course it passed through a village with a white church five or six hundred yards away at the bottom of the hill. This was Borodino. The road cut down below the village, crossed over a bridge and then rose steadily, weaving up and down and in and out, until it got to the hamlet of Valuyev, clearly visible about four miles away – and that's where Napoleon was now. Beyond Valuyev the road disappeared into yellowing woodland on the horizon. In among those trees, far away amidst the birches and the firs on the right-hand side of the road, stood the gleaming sunlit cross and belfry of the Kolotsky monastery. At various places in the blue distance, to the right and left of the woodland and the road, smoke rose up from camp-fires and you could see the indistinct outline of massed troops, ours and the enemy's. Off to the right, the rivers Kolocha and Moskva ran through countryside that was broken and hilly. The villages of Bezzubovo and Zakharino could be seen through gaps in the hills. Over to the left the ground was flatter, with fields of corn, and smoke rose from a single village that had been set on fire – Semyonovsk.

Everything Pierre saw on either hand looked so indistinct that, glancing left or right over the landscape, he could find nothing that quite lived up to his expectations. Nowhere was there a field of battle as such, the kind of thing he had expected; there was nothing but ordinary fields, clearings, troops, woods, smoking camp-fires, villages, mounds and little streams. Here was a living landscape, and try as he might he could not make out any military positioning. He could not even tell our troops from theirs.

'I've got to ask someone who knows about these things,' he thought, and he turned to an officer who was much taken with the sight of his huge, unmilitary figure.

'Excuse me,' said Pierre. 'What's that village down there?'

'I think it's called Burdino, isn't it?' said the officer, turning to ask his comrade.

'Borodino,' said the other man, putting him right.

The officer was obviously delighted at the chance to have a chat, and he came over to Pierre.

'Is that where our men are?' asked Pierre.

'Yes, and that's the French, a bit further away,' said the officer. 'There you are, you can see them, just over there.'

'And are our men over yonder?' asked Pierre.

'Yes, you can see them with the naked eye . . . Look, there they are!' The officer pointed to columns of smoke on the left rising up beyond the river, and his face had the same stern and serious expression that Pierre had noticed on many of the faces he had come across.

'Ah, that's the French! What about those over there?' Pierre was now pointing to a slight rise on the left with some troops moving round it.

'No, they're ours.'

'Oh, are they? What about there?' Pierre pointed to another mound in the distance, with a big tree on it, near to a village just visible in a hollow, where you could see the smoke from camp-fires and a black shape of some kind.

'It's *him* there too!' said the officer. (It was the Shevardino redoubt.) 'Yesterday it was ours, now it's *his*.'

'So where is our position, exactly?'

'Our position?' said the officer, with a grin of delight. 'I can give you every detail, because I've been involved in almost all our fortifications. That's our centre, down there in Borodino.' He was pointing to the village with the white church straight ahead. 'That's where we cross the Kolocha. There, where you can see those rows of hay down in that hollow, that's where the bridge is. And that's our centre. Our right flank is out over there.' He pointed sharply to the right, off into the broken country. 'That's the Moskva river, and we've built three redoubts there, good strong ones. Now, er, the left flank . . .' He faltered. 'Well, it's a bit difficult to explain . . . Yesterday our left flank was out there, over at Shevardino. See that oak-tree? Near there. But now we've pulled the left wing back a bit. Can you see over there? That village and all the smoke – that's Semyonovsk. That's where it is.' He pointed to Rayevsky's redoubt. 'But I don't think there's going to be a battle there. *He*'s moved his troops in, but it's a blind; he'll probably come round from the right of the river. Anyway, wherever it happens, a lot of us will be missing at roll-call tomorrow!' said the officer.

A veteran sergeant had walked up during this conversation and stood there in silence waiting for the officer to finish speaking. But at this point he broke in, obviously resenting this last remark.

'We need to send for some gabions,' he said grimly.

The officer looked rather embarrassed, as if he knew full well that it might be all right to think how many men would be missing next day, but you ought not to talk about it.

'Yes, well, er, send the third company again,' he said hastily. 'And who might you be? Not one of the doctors, are you?'

'No, no, I just happen to be here,' answered Pierre. And he went back down the hill and walked past the working peasants again.

'Ugh, filthy swine!' said the officer from behind Pierre, holding his nose and hurrying past them.

'Look, they're coming! They're here! They've got her . . . They'll be here in a minute . . .'

The sudden calls soon had officers, soldiers and peasants scurrying down the road.

A church procession was winding its way up the hill from Borodino. It was headed by a regiment of infantry marching smartly along the dusty road, shakos off and trailing arms. From behind the infantry came the sound of chanting.

Bareheaded soldiers and peasants raced past Pierre in their rush to meet the processing people.

'They're bringing her! Our defender . . . the Holy Mother of Iversk!'

'Smolensk,' came the voice of correction.

Militiamen – those who had been in the village and those who had been working at the battery – had flung down their spades and run down towards the procession. The battalion marching along the dusty road was followed by priests in their church robes, a little old man in a hood with attendant clergy and choristers. Behind them came soldiers and officers carrying a huge holy icon with a black face in a setting of silver. This was the icon that had been brought away from Smolensk and taken around by the army ever since. Behind it, ahead of it and on all sides came crowds of soldiers with bared heads, walking, running or bowing down to the ground.

The procession came to a halt at the top of the hill. The men who had kept the icon aloft by its linen holdings were relieved by others, the deacons relit their censers and the service began. The scorching sunshine beat straight down on them, a cool and gentle breeze toyed with the hair on many a bared head, and stirred the ribbons that decked the holy icon, and the singing had a subdued sound under the open sky. The icon was surrounded by a huge crowd of people – officers, soldiers and men of the militia, all with bared heads. An open space had been reserved for the top brass to the rear of priest and deacon. A bald-headed general wearing the order of St George round his neck stood immediately behind the priest, and he never crossed himself during the service – he was obviously a German – but nevertheless, listened carefully through to the end, knowing it was necessary to arouse the patriotism in the Russian peasant. Another general stood there in a martial pose and as he made the sign of the cross he flapped a hand in front of his chest and looked round on all sides. Pierre was standing among the peasants, and he recognized in this group of officials several persons he knew. But he didn't look at them; he was fascinated by the grave expressions on the faces in the crowd of soldiers and peasant militiamen, all gazing with equal intensity at the holy icon. As soon as the weary choristers, singing out now for the twentieth time, launched into their leisurely, mechanical rendition of, 'O Mother of God, save Thy servants from all adversities', and priest and deacon chimed in with, 'For to Thee under God every man doth flee as to a steadfast bulwark and defence', every face was lit up with a special awareness of the solemnity of the coming moment, the same expression he had seen on the hill at Mozhaysk and then flickering again on so many, many faces that he had come across that morning. Ever more urgently came the bowing of heads, the tossing back of hair, the sounds of deep sighing and the beating of breasts as the soldiers crossed themselves.

The crowd round the icon suddenly parted and Pierre was squashed back. Someone was walking over to the holy icon, probably someone of real consequence, to judge by the alacrity with which people made way for him.

It was Kutuzov, on his way back to Tatarinova after a tour of our position, and he had come to take part in the service. Pierre knew him at once by his peculiar figure, which marked him out from everyone else.

With a long overcoat draped over his enormous bulk and his slightly stooping back, with his white head bared and his blind white eye all too noticeable in a puffy face, Kutuzov lurched and staggered his way out into the ring and stood behind the priest. He crossed himself in a practised way, bent down to touch the earth, gave a deep sigh and bowed his grey head. Kutuzov was followed by Bennigsen and his entourage. Although the commander-in-chief attracted the attention of all the top brass, the militiamen and soldiers ignored him and went on with their prayers.

When the service was over Kutuzov went up to the holy icon, flopped down heavily on his knees, bowed down to the ground, and then found he could not get up, despite several attempts to do so, because of his great bulk and general feebleness. His grey head quivered with the effort. At last he managed it, and thrusting out his lips like a simple child he kissed the icon, and gave another bow with one hand touching the ground. The other generals duly followed, then the officers, and after them came the soldiers and militiamen, breathless with excitement, pushing and shoving, falling over each other in one mad scramble.

CHAPTER 22

Caught in the crush and reeling back off balance, Pierre looked about him.

'Count! Count Bezukhov! What are you doing here?' said a voice. Pierre looked round.

Boris Drubetskoy, wiping his knees with one hand (he must have dirtied them going down before the icon), was walking over to Pierre with a smile on his face. Boris was immaculately turned out, with the slightest hint of the battle-ready soldier about him. He wore a long military coat with a riding-crop slung across one shoulder à la Kutuzov.

Meanwhile Kutuzov had reached the village, and he now sat down in the shade of the nearest house on a bench swiftly provided by one Cossack and covered with a rug by another. He was immediately surrounded by a vast and glittering entourage.

The icon moved on, and the crowd with it. Pierre stood there talking to Boris no more than thirty paces from Kutuzov. He explained his determination to take part in the battle and inspect the position.

'I tell you what,' said Boris. 'I shall honour you with the freedom of the camp. You'll get the best view from where Count Bennigsen is going to be. I'm in attendance on him. I'll put him in the picture. And if you want to go round the position you'd better come along with us. We're just off to the left flank. And when we get back you can stay the night with me, and we'll have a game of cards. I'm sure you know Dmitriy Sergeich. He's staying over there.' He pointed to the third house in Gorki.

'Oh, it's the right flank I wanted to see. They say it's very strong,' said Pierre. 'I wanted to start at the river Moskva and go round the whole position.'

'Well, you can do that later on. It's the left flank that matters . . .'

'Yes, I see. And where's Prince Bolkonsky's regiment? Could you point it out to me?' asked Pierre.

'Prince Andrey's regiment? We're going right past it. I'll take you to see him.'

'What was that about the left flank?' asked Pierre.

'Well, to be quite candid, just between ourselves, the left flank's in a bit of a spot,' said Boris, lowering his voice confidingly. 'Count Bennigsen had something quite different in mind. His idea was to fortify that mound over there, but certainly not, er . . .' He gave a shrug. 'His Serene Highness wouldn't have it, or maybe they talked him out of it. Anyway . . .' But Boris never finished what he was saying because at that moment one of Kutuzov's adjutants came over to have a word with Pierre. 'Ah, Kaysarov,' Boris said to him with the broadest of smiles, 'I was just trying to tell the count here about our position. It's amazing how well his Serence Highness can read the enemy's mind!'

'Oh, you mean the left flank?' said Kaysarov.

'I do indeed. Our left flank is now very, very strong.'

Kutuzov had purged his staff of everyone surplus to requirements, yet Boris had wangled his way through the changes and stayed on at headquarters. He had made his mark with Count Bennigsen. Count Bennigsen was no different from everyone else served by Boris; he now looked upon young Prince Drubetskoy as indispensable.

Among the army chiefs there were two clearly delineated parties: Kutuzov's party and the party of Bennigsen, chief of staff. Boris belonged to the latter, and there was no one more accomplished at sucking up to Kutuzov while managing to imply that the old fellow was no good, and Bennigsen was in charge. Now the chips were down, battle was on them, and there could only be one of two results: either Kutuzov would be annihilated and power transferred to Bennigsen, or if by any chance Kutuzov managed to win, the implication would be that it was all due to Bennigsen. Either way, major honours would be flying around for deeds done on the morrow and new men would see their careers advanced. So Boris felt excited and edgy all day.

After Kaysarov Pierre was joined by other people that he knew, and he was powerless to deal with all the questions about Moscow that were showered upon him, or listen to all the tales they had to tell. Every face was a picture of excitement and worry. But what struck Pierre was that the reason for all the excitement on some of the faces had to do with questions of personal success, and he could not get out of his mind a different kind of excitement seen on other faces that had to do with universal questions rather than personal ones, questions of life and death. Kutuzov noticed the figure of Pierre and the group gathered round him.

'Call him over,' said Kutuzov.

An adjutant passed on the message, and Pierre proceeded towards the bench. But someone else was there before him, a militiaman. It was Dolokhov.

'How did that man get here?' asked Pierre.

'Little swine, he creeps in everywhere!' came the answer. 'He was reduced to the ranks, you know. Now he wants to bounce back. He comes up with all sorts of ideas, but he has been going over to the enemy lines at night . . . You've got to hand it to him . . .' Pierre removed his hat and bowed politely to Kutuzov.

'Sir, I decided that if I told you what I know you could send me away or tell me you knew it already, and I had nothing to lose . . .' Dolokhov was saying.

'Yes, quite.'

'And if I'm right, I shall be helping my country, for which I am ready to die.'

'Yes, quite. Quite.'

'And, sir, if you happen to need a man who would not spare his own skin, be kind enough to remember me . . . Perhaps I could be of some service . . .'

'Yes, yes. Quite,' repeated Kutuzov, with an amused twinkle in the narrowing eye that now surveyed Pierre.

Meanwhile Boris, with all the deftness of a practised courtier, had moved in on the commander-in-chief along with Pierre, speaking to the count in the easiest manner and the softest voice, as though they were in mid-conversation.

'Those peasant militiamen, they've put clean shirts on to die in,' he was saying. 'How's that for heroism, Count?'

This was said with the obvious intention of being overheard by his Serene Highness. Boris knew Kutuzov would prick up his ears at these words, and sure enough, his Highness did speak to him.

'What was that about the militia?' he said to Boris.

'They have put clean shirts on, sir, for tomorrow, ready for death.'

'Ah ... Wonderful people ... Nobody like them,' said Kutuzov, eyes closed, shaking his head. 'Nobody like them!' he said again with a sigh.

'So, you want a whiff of gunpowder?' he said to Pierre. 'Yes, it's a nice smell ... I have the honour of being a great admirer of your wife. I do hope she's well. My quarters are at your service.' And then Kutuzov began behaving as old people often do, gazing around vacantly as if he could not remember what to say or do next. But suddenly he seemed to remember what he was after, and he beckoned to Andrey Kaysarov, the brother of his adjutant.

'What was that thing? How does it go? You know, that bit of poetry by Marin. How does it go? He was on about Gerakov[7] ... "You'll stay a teacher in the corps ..." Go on, you remember,' said Kutuzov, his face ready for a good laugh. Kaysarov recited the poem; a beaming Kutuzov nodded in time to the rhythm.

When Pierre walked away from Kutuzov, Dolokhov came over and took him by the arm.

'I'm so pleased to meet you here, Count,' he said in a loud voice, ignoring all bystanders and speaking with assertiveness and the utmost gravity. 'On the eve of a day which, God knows, not all of us will be destined to survive, I'm glad of an opportunity to tell you that I regret any past misunderstandings between us, and I would like to think you hold nothing against me. Will you please forgive me?'

Pierre looked at Dolokhov with a smile, not knowing what to say. Dolokhov's eyes were watering with tears as he embraced Pierre and kissed him.

Boris put a word in with his general, and Count Bennigsen spoke to Pierre, offering to take him along on their tour of the lines.

'You'll find it interesting,' he said.

'I'm sure I shall,' said Pierre.

Half an hour later Kutuzov had set off back to Tatarinova, while Bennigsen and his entourage, now including Pierre, went off to look at the lines.

CHAPTER 23

Bennigsen went down the high road from Gorki and made for the bridge which the officer on the mound had pointed out to Pierre as being the centre of the position, where rows of new-mown grass were turning into sweet-smelling hay down by the riverside. They crossed the bridge and went on to the village of Borodino, where they turned left, rode past vast numbers of men and cannons, and climbed up to the high mound where militiamen were digging earthworks. This was the redoubt, so far without a name, that would come to be called Rayevsky's redoubt, or 'the battery on the mound'.

Pierre took no special notice of this redoubt. He wasn't to know that for him this spot would turn out to be more unforgettable than any other part of the Borodino plain. Then they rode down through a ravine to Semyonovsk, where the soldiers were hauling the last logs away from shacks and barns. On they went, first downhill then up again across a field of rye, all trampled and flattened as if a hail-storm had passed over it, along a track recently laid down across the ploughed furrows by the artillery, until they got to some more earthworks, pointed ones known as flèches, which were also still under construction.

Bennigsen stopped at the flèches and peered across at the Shevardino redoubt, which had been ours only yesterday, where you could see several men on horseback. The officers told him Napoleon and Murat were over there. Everybody gazed intently at the little group of horsemen. Pierre stared with the rest, trying to work out which one of the barely discernible figures was Napoleon. Eventually the group of horsemen went off down the hill and rode away.

Bennigsen turned to a general who had just ridden up and launched into a description of our entire troop disposition. Pierre listened to what he was saying, straining every nerve to grasp the essential features of the impending battle, but he was forced to the disappointing conclusion that his brain was not up to it. He could not understand a word. Bennigsen stopped speaking, and noticing that Pierre was all ears he spoke to him rather curtly.

'Not very interesting, I imagine.'

'Oh, it is. It's really interesting.' Pierre echoed his word at some cost to the truth.

From the flèches they rode off further to the left down a road that wound its way through a thick copse of small birch-trees. In the middle of the wood a brown hare with white paws hopped out on to the road just in front of them, startled by the sound of so many hoofbeats. Panicking, it skipped along the road for quite some time to general amusement and much laughter, and it was only when several voices shouted at it that it darted off to one side and disappeared into a thicket. After a mile and a half of woodland they emerged into a clearing, where Tuchkov's corps had been stationed to defend the left flank.

At this point, on the outer edge of the left flank, Bennigsen had much to say and do, and he spoke with some passion; Pierre took this to be of signal importance from the military point of view. Just ahead of Tuchkov's troops there was a little hill, a little hill unoccupied by troops. This, according to the vociferous Bennigsen, was a bad mistake: it was madness to leave a commanding height unoccupied and station troops down below it. Several generals were of the same opinion. One in particular waxed eloquent, aggressively asserting that they would just get slaughtered. Bennigsen took personal responsibility for moving the troops uphill.

This adjustment on the left flank gave Pierre even more pause for thought on the subject of warfare. Listening to Bennigsen and the other generals as they castigated the disposition of the troops at the bottom of the hill, Pierre could see what they were getting at and he fully shared their view. But for this very reason he could not imagine how the man who had placed them there at the bottom of a hill could have made such a terrible and obvious mistake.

Pierre was not to know that these troops had been stationed where they were not to defend the position, as Bennigsen had assumed; they had been hidden away out of sight to catch the enemy unawares, to keep under cover and suddenly lash out at him as he moved forward. Bennigsen had no knowledge of this, and he moved the men up for his own reasons, without informing the commander-in-chief.

CHAPTER 24

It was bright that evening (the 25th of August), and Prince Andrey was lying propped up on one elbow in a dilapidated barn in the village of Knyazkovo, out at one end of his regiment's encampment. Through a gap in a broken-down wall he was looking out on a row of thirty-year-old pollarded birch-trees running along a hedge, a field with piles of oats all over it, and some bushes where he could see camp-fires smoking as the soldiers got down to their cooking.

For all his present consciousness of life as something oppressive, irrelevant and wearisome, Prince Andrey felt no less excited and edgy than he had done at Austerlitz seven years previously on the eve of battle.

He had done all that was necessary in the receiving and issuing of orders for tomorrow's battle. There was nothing more to be done. But he was haunted by certain thoughts, the simplest, clearest and therefore the most painful of thoughts, that refused to leave him in peace. He was well aware that tomorrow's engagement would be the most ghastly battle he had ever taken part in, and for the first time in his life the possibility of death presented itself, not in relation to the living world, or any effect it might have on other people, but purely in relation to himself and his own soul, and it seemed so vivid, almost a dependable certainty, stark and terrible. And from the heights of this vision everything that had once tormentingly preoccupied him seemed suddenly bathed in a cold, white light with no shadows, no perspective, no outline. His whole life seemed like a magic-lantern show that he had been staring at through glass by artificial light. Now suddenly the glass was gone, and he could see those awful daubings in the clear light of day. 'Yes, yes, here they are, these false images that I used to find so worrying, enthralling and agonizing,' he told himself, giving his imagination a free rein to run over the main pictures in the magic lantern of his life, looked at anew in the cold, white daylight brought on by a clear vision of death. 'Here they are, these crudely daubed figures that used to seem so magnificent and mysterious. Honour and glory, philanthropy, love of a woman, love of Fatherland – how grand these pictures used to seem, filled with such deep meanings! And now it all looks so simple, colourless and crude in the cold light of the morning I can feel coming upon me.' There were three main regrets in his life that had a special claim on his attention: his love for a woman, the death of his father, and the invasion of the French, who now held half of Russia. 'Love! . . . That little girl who seemed to be overflowing with mysterious energies. Oh, how I loved her! And I made all those romantic plans about love and happiness with her! Oh, what a nice little boy I was!' he spat out aloud. 'To think I believed in some ideal kind of love that would keep her faithful while I went away for a whole year! Like the gentle turtle-dove in the fable, she was supposed to pine away waiting for me! And now everything's so much simpler . . . it's all so horribly simple and ghastly!'

'My father, too, did all that building at Bald Hills, and he thought it was his place, his land, his air, his peasants. But then along came

Napoleon, and without even knowing of his existence he swept him away like a wood-chip on the path, and left Bald Hills and all his life in ruins. Princess Marya says it's a trial sent from above. What's the trial for when he's gone and will never return? Never again! He's gone for ever! So who's the trial for? Our country lost and Moscow destroyed! Anyway, tomorrow I'll get killed, and probably not by a Frenchman, maybe by one of our own men, like that soldier who let his gun go off right next to my ear yesterday, and the French will come along and pick me up by the head and feet and chuck me into a pit so I don't stink them out, and a whole new way of living will come about, everybody will get used to it, and I shan't know anything about it because I shall have gone.'

He glanced at the row of birch-trees impassive in their yellows and greens, with their white bark gleaming in the sunshine. 'To die . . . let me get killed tomorrow and have done with it . . . let everything else carry on, but with me gone.' He had a clear vision of his own non-existence in this life. And suddenly those birch-trees, with their light and shade, the wispy clouds and the smoke-plumes rising from the fires, everything around him seemed to have been transformed into something terribly ominous. A cold shiver ran down his back. He got quickly to his feet, strode out of the barn and went for a walk.

Back in the barn he heard voices outside.

'Who's that?' called Prince Andrey.

The red-nosed Captain Timokhin, once in charge of Dolokhov's company but now promoted to battalion-commander because of a shortage of officer material, came in diffidently. He was followed by an adjutant and the regimental paymaster.

Prince Andrey got rapidly to his feet, listened to what the officers had come to talk about, issued one or two instructions, and was just about to send them on their way when he heard a voice outside the barn and its sibilant tones seemed familiar.

'What the devil was that?' said the voice of someone in mid-stumble.

Prince Andrey looked out just in time to see Pierre reeling; he had tripped over a stake lying on the ground, and almost lost his feet. Prince Andrey had a great distaste for seeing people from his own circle, and Pierre was particularly unwelcome as a reminder of the moments of anguish he had gone through on his last visit to Moscow.

'Well I never!' he cried. 'What quirk of fate brings you here? You're the last person I expected.'

As he was saying this his eyes and his whole expression displayed more than coldness, they displayed outright hostility, and it was not lost on Pierre. He had approached the barn in a state of high excitement, but now after one look at Prince Andrey's face he felt crushed and embarrassed.

'Well, I've come ... er, you know ... just ... come along ... I think it's interesting,' said Pierre, parroting the meaningless word 'interesting' for the umpteenth time that day. 'I wanted to watch the battle.'

'Oh yes? What about your masonic brethren? What do they say about the war? What would they do to stop it?' said Prince Andrey sardonically. 'Oh well, tell me about Moscow. Do you know anything about my people? Did they get to Moscow all right?' he asked in all seriousness.

'Yes. Julie Drubetskoy told me they did. I went to see them, but they weren't there. They'd gone out to your Moscow estate.'

CHAPTER 25

The officers would have been happy to leave, but Prince Andrey seemed reluctant to be left alone with his friend, and he invited them to stay on and have a drink of tea. Benches were brought in, and tea was provided. The officers stared in bemusement at Pierre's big bulky figure, and listened as he talked first about Moscow and then the disposition of our troops, which he had been lucky enough to see round. Prince Andrey said nothing, and there was such an intimidating look on his face that Pierre found himself talking to the good-hearted Timokhin rather than Bolkonsky.

'So, you now understand the whole disposition of our troops?' said Prince Andrey, cutting him short.

'Yes ... Well, it depends what you mean,' said Pierre. 'I'm not a military man, so I can't say I've got the last detail, but, yes, I do understand the general arrangement.'

'In which case you know more than anybody else does,' said Prince Andrey.

'Oh!' said Pierre, taken aback, looking over his spectacles at Prince Andrey. 'Well, anyway, how do you feel about Kutuzov's appointment?'

'I was very pleased about it, and that's all I know,' said Prince Andrey.

'Well, what's your opinion of Barclay de Tolly? All sorts of things were being said about him in Moscow. What do you make of him?'

'Ask them,' said Prince Andrey, indicating the officers.

Pierre looked across at Timokhin with the condescendingly quizzical smile that everyone adopted towards him.

'It was a moment of *serendipity*, sir, when his *Serene* Highness took over,' said Timokhin diffidently, hardly able to take his eyes of his colonel.

'Why do you say that?' asked Pierre.

'Well, take firewood or fodder ... I tell you what ... All the way back from Swienciany you daren't lay hands on a twig, or a wisp of hay, or anything at all. We were in retreat, you see, so *he* was going to get the lot. Isn't that right, sir?' he said, turning to his prince. 'But no, for us it was hands off. In our regiment two officers were court-martialled for things like that. Well, ever since his Serene Highness has been in charge, it's all been dead simple. Serendipity I call it.'

'But why had he been forbidding it?'

Timokhin looked round in embarrassment, not knowing how to respond to a question like that. Pierre turned to Prince Andrey and asked him the same thing.

'Why, so as not to ravage the country we were leaving behind for the enemy,' said Prince Andrey, a bitter and sardonic man. 'It's a matter of principle: never allow pillage or let your men get used to looting. Oh yes, Barclay was right about Smolensk as well, in his judgement that the French might outflank us – they were so much stronger. But what he could not see was this,' yelled Prince Andrey in a voice grown suddenly strident as if he had lost control, 'he just could not see that for the first time ever we were fighting for Russian soil, and there was a kind of spirit in the men that I'd never seen before, and we had held them off for two whole days, and the success of it had made us ten times stronger. But he ordered a retreat, and all our efforts and all our losses went for nothing. He had no thought of treachery. He was trying to do everything in the best possible way and he did think things through. But that's precisely why he was no good. He's no good now precisely because he thinks things through very carefully as a matter of principle, as befits a German. How can I put it? ... Let's say your father has a German valet, and he's a first-rate valet who fulfils all his needs better than you could. Let him carry on the good work. But if your father falls ill and takes to his death-bed, you'll send the valet packing and look after your father yourself with your own clumsy hands that are not used to doing things, and you'll bring him more comfort than any stranger, however skilled. That's what we've done with Barclay. While ever Russia was doing well she could be served by a stranger, and an excellent minister he was too, but the moment she's in danger she needs her own flesh and blood. So, your people at the club have him down as a traitor! The fact that they are calling him a traitor now makes it all the more likely that later on they'll feel ashamed of their false charges and then they'll promote him from treachery to glory, honour and genius, and that would be an even greater injustice. He's just an honest German, a stickler . . .'

'They say he's a clever general, though,' said Pierre.

'I don't know what you mean by a clever general,' said Prince Andrey, flashing a smile.

'A clever general . . .' said Pierre, 'well, it's somebody who foresees every contingency . . . who can read the enemy's mind.'

'Oh, that's impossible,' said Prince Andrey, as if this were a long-established certainty. Pierre looked at him in surprise.

'Hang on,' he said. 'They do say war is a bit like playing chess.'

'Yes, it is,' said Prince Andrey, 'but there's one little difference. In chess you can take as long as you want over every move. You're beyond the limits of time. Oh, there is one other difference: a knight is always stronger than a pawn and two pawns are always stronger than one, whereas in war a battalion can sometimes be stronger than a division, and sometimes weaker than a company. You can never be sure of the relative strengths of different forces. Believe me,' he went on, 'if anything really depended on what gets done at headquarters, I'd be up there with them, doing things, but no, I have the honour of serving here in this regiment along with these gentlemen, and I'm convinced that tomorrow's outcome depends on us, not on them . . . Success never has depended, never will depend, on dispositions or armaments, not even numbers, and position least of all.'

'Well, what does it depend on?'

'On the gut feeling inside me and him,' he indicated Timokhin, 'and every soldier.'

Prince Andrey glanced across at Timokhin, who was staring at his commanding officer in alarm and bemusement. In contrast to his former silence and reserve, Prince Andrey now seemed to be all worked up. He seemed unable to stop himself blurting out every thought that came into his head.

'A battle is won by the side that is absolutely determined to win. Why did we lose the battle of Austerlitz? Our casualties were about the same as those of the French, but we had told ourselves early in the day that the battle was lost, so it was lost. And we said that because then we had nothing to fight for. We wanted to get off the battlefield as fast as we could. "All is lost! Let's run away!" And run we did. If we had waited till evening before saying that, God knows what might have happened.

'But we shan't be saying that tomorrow. You talk about our position. The left flank's weak, and the right flank's too spread out,' he went on. 'It's all nonsense. Irrelevant. So what is in store for us tomorrow? A hundred million contingent factors, and they'll all be determined by what happens on the day – who's run away and who's going to run away, us or them, who gets killed, one man or another. But what's going on right now is just fooling about. The point is this: those people who took you round the positions don't help things along, they actually get in the way. They're completely absorbed in their own petty interests.'

'At a time like this?' said Pierre, full of reproach.

'*Yes. At a time like this,*' repeated Prince Andrey. 'They think this is a good time to get one over on a rival and win themselves another cross or ribbon. The way I see it, tomorrow looks like this: a hundred thousand Russians and a hundred thousand Frenchmen have come together to fight, and the fact is these two hundred thousand men *will* fight, and the side that fights hardest and spares itself least will come out on top. And if you like, I'll tell you something else: whatever happens, however much the top brass mess things up, we shall win tomorrow. Tomorrow, whatever happens, we are going to win!'

'Yes sir, it's true what you say, absolutely true,' put in Timokhin. 'Who would spare himself now? The soldiers in my battalion, believe it or not, have refused their vodka. Not the right day for it, they say.'

Nobody spoke.

The officers got to their feet. Prince Andrey went to see them out, giving one or two last instructions to the adjutant. When the officers had gone, Pierre moved up closer to Prince Andrey, and was just about to start talking when they heard hoofbeats coming from three horses not far down the road, and glancing in that direction Prince Andrey recognized Wolzogen and Clausewitz, with a Cossack in attendance. They were talking as they rode past, and Pierre and Prince Andrey could not help overhearing the following snatches of conversation in German:

'The war must to be conducted over a very wide area. This is a policy I cannot endorse highly enough,' came one voice.

'Yes indeed,' said the other, 'and since the aim is to weaken the enemy the loss of private individuals must be ignored.'

'Quite so,' confirmed the first voice.

'Conducted over a very wide area!' Prince Andrey snorted furiously when they had gone. 'It was in that "very wide area" that I had a father, a son and a sister at Bald Hills. He's not bothered about that. It's just what I was saying: these German gentlemen won't win tomorrow, they'll only mess things up as much as they can, because a German head like that man's contains nothing but calculations no more useful than a sucked egg, and his heart lacks the one thing that's needed for tomorrow, the thing that Timokhin has. They've given *him* the whole of Europe, and they come over here to give us lessons – wonderful teachers!' he added, his voice rising again to screaming pitch.

'So you do think we're going to win tomorrow?' said Pierre.

'Oh yes,' said Prince Andrey distractedly. 'One thing I would do if I was in power,' he began again. 'Stop taking prisoners. What's the sense in taking prisoners? It's just medieval chivalry. The French have destroyed my home and they're on their way to destroy Moscow. They've injured me and they're still doing it with every second that passes. They're my enemies, they're all criminals – that's the way I see it. It's also what Timokhin thinks, and all the army with him. They must be put to death. If they're my enemies they can't be my friends, whatever might have been said at Tilsit.'

'Yes, yes,' said Pierre, his eyes shining as he looked at Prince Andrey. 'Oh yes, I'm with you all the way!'

The one question that had been haunting Pierre all day, ever since Mozhaysk in fact, now struck him as quite clear and settled once and for all. Now he could sense the full significance of the war and the impending battle. Everything he had seen during the day, all the sober and serious faces he had caught glimpses of, came back to him now in a new light. He had observed what the physicists call latent heat in the patriotic spirit of the men that he had seen, and this explained why they were all preparing for death with such composure and what passed for light-heartedness.

'Taking no prisoners,' said Prince Andrey. 'That alone would transform the whole war and would make it less cruel. But playing at war, that's what's so vile, being magnanimous and all that sort of thing. That kind of magnanimity and sensitivity reminds me of the magnanimity and sensitivity of a posh lady who feels sick at the sight of a calf being slaughtered – she's such a nice person she can't stand the sight of blood, but she does enjoy a nice dish of fricasséed veal. They go on and on about the rules of war, chivalry, flags of truce, showing mercy to the afflicted, and so on. It's a load of rubbish. I saw enough chivalry and flags of truce in 1805. They cheated us, and we cheated them. They loot people's homes, issue counterfeit money and, worst of all, they kill my children and my father, and they still go on about the rules of war, and being magnanimous in victory. Don't take any prisoners! Kill and be killed! Anyone who has got this far, as I have, through suffering . . .'

Prince Andrey, who had been thinking he didn't mind one way or the other whether they took Moscow as they had taken Smolensk, was stopped sharply in mid-flow by a sudden tremor and a lump in his throat. He walked up and down once or twice without saying anything, but his eyes had a feverish glint in them and his top lip quivered as he launched forth again.

'If we didn't have all this business of magnanimity in warfare, we would only ever go to war when there was something worth facing certain death for, as there is now. Nobody would go to war just because Pavel Ivanych had insulted Mikhail Ivanych. But if there's going to be a war like this one, let there be war. And besides, the intensity of military commitment would be of a different order. All these Westphalians and Hessians brought over here by Napoleon would never have followed him into Russia, and we wouldn't have gone off to fight in Austria and in Prussia without knowing what for. War is not being nice to each other, it's the vilest thing in human life, and we ought to understand that and not play at war. It's a terrible necessity, and we should be strict about it and take it seriously. It comes down to this: no more lying, war means war and it's not a plaything. Otherwise war will be a nice hobby for idle people and butterfly minds . . . The military class gets all the honours. And what is war, what is necessary for success on the battlefield, what is the moral basis of a military society? The aim of war is murder, the weapons of war are spying, treachery and the fostering of further treachery, the destruction of people, looting their property and stealing from them to keep the army on the road, falsehood and deceit, which go by the name of clever tactical ploys, and the moral basis of the military class is the curtailment of freedom through discipline, linked with idleness, ignorance, cruelty, debauchery and drunkenness. And in spite of all that, it's still the highest class, universally respected. All heads of state except the Chinese wear military uniforms, and the biggest rewards go to the man who has killed the most people . . . People come together to murder one another, as they will do to-morrow; men get slaughtered and crippled in their tens of thousands, and then services of thanksgiving are held to celebrate the killing of vast numbers of men (they even exaggerate the numbers), and victory is proclaimed, on the basis that the more men slaughtered, the greater the achievement. How can God look down from heaven and listen to it all?' Prince Andrey called out in a shrill voice that set the teeth on edge. 'Listen, old fellow, life's become unbearable for me just lately. I

can see I've come to understand too much. And it's not a good thing
for man to taste of the tree of the knowledge of good and evil . . . Oh,
well, not much longer!' he added. 'But I can see you're nodding off,
and it's time I went to bed. Off you go back to Gorki,' said Prince
Andrey suddenly.

'Oh no!' answered Pierre, his deeply sympathetic eyes lighting up
with alarm as he looked at Prince Andrey.

'Time you were on your way. You need a good night's sleep before
a battle,' repeated Prince Andrey. He went quickly over to Pierre,
embraced him and kissed him. 'Goodbye, then. Off you go,' he cried.
'Maybe we'll meet again . . . maybe not . . .' and he turned on his heel
and hurried off back into the barn.

By now it was dark, and Pierre could not make out the expression on
his face, so he never knew whether it was intimidating or affectionate.

He stood there for some time in silence, wondering whether to
follow him in or go back to Gorki. 'No, he doesn't need me!' Pierre
told himself, 'and I know this is our last meeting!' He gave a deep sigh
and rode off back to Gorki.

Back in the barn Prince Andrey lay down on a rug, but he could not
get to sleep.

He closed his eyes. One image followed another. There was one that
gave him pleasure, and he lingered over it. He vividly recalled one
evening in Petersburg. Natasha's face was a picture of eager excitement
as she told him how she had gone mushrooming the previous summer
and got lost in a big forest. She was describing in any old order the
depths of the forest, her own sensations, and her chat with a bee-keeper
she had come across, and she never stopped interrupting herself to
say, 'No, I can't do it. I'm not telling it properly. No, you can't possibly
understand,' even though Prince Andrey kept trying to reassure her
that he was taking it in and he really had understood everything she
had been trying to say. Natasha was dissatisfied with her own words.
She felt they didn't do justice to the poetical and romantic feelings she
had experienced that day and now wanted to turn inside out. 'It was
all so wonderful, that old man, the darkness in the forest . . . and his
nice, kind . . . no, I can't describe it,' she had said, all worked up and
red in the face.

Prince Andrey smiled now the same happy smile he had smiled then
as he gazed into her eyes. 'I did understand her,' thought Prince
Andrey. 'It was more than understanding. That spiritual energy, that
sincerity, that open-heartedness, the very soul of her that seemed to
be bound up in her body, I loved the soul in her . . . My love was so
deep and blissful . . .' And then suddenly he remembered how their

love had ended. '*He* didn't care for any of that. He didn't see any of it. It didn't register on him. All he saw in her was a pretty little girl, *nice and fresh*, but it would have been below him to unite his destiny with hers. And what about me? . . . And there he is, still alive and enjoying life.'

Prince Andrey leapt to his feet like a scalded cat, and began walking up and down again outside the barn.

CHAPTER 26

On the 25th of August, the eve of the battle of Borodino, Napoleon's quarters were at Valuyevo. M. de Bausset, prefect of the French Emperor's palace, and Colonel Fabvier, arrived there, the former from Paris, the latter from Madrid.

M. de Bausset had changed into court uniform and ordered the package he had brought for the Emperor to be carried in before him; now he walked into the outer section of Napoleon's tent, and chatted to an aide as he set about unpacking the box.

Fabvier stopped at the entrance and stayed outside, talking to some generals that he knew.

The Emperor Napoleon was still in his bedroom, finishing his toilet. With much snorting and harrumphing he twisted this way and that, offering first his fat back and then his flabby, hairy chest to the flesh-brush wielded by a valet who was rubbing him down. Another valet held one finger over the mouth of a little bottle as he sprinkled the Emperor's pampered person with eau de cologne, and the look on his face suggested that he was unique in knowing where and how much to sprinkle. Napoleon's short hair was wet and matted down over his forehead. But his face, for all its sallow puffiness, glowed with physical pleasure. 'Go on, harder, keep at it . . .' he kept saying amidst further shrugs and harrumphing as the valet brushed away. An adjutant who had come into the bedroom to report the number of prisoners taken in yesterday's action stood by the door; he had delivered his message and was waiting for permission to leave. Napoleon glanced up at him with a scowl.

'No prisoners?' he exclaimed, repeating what the adjutant had said. 'They're forcing us to destroy them. Too bad for the Russian army . . . Go on, harder . . .' he said, hunching up his podgy shoulders for the valet. 'Good. Send de Bausset in, and Fabvier too,' he said to the adjutant with a nod.

'Yes, sir.' And the adjutant was out of the door.

It took no time at all for the two valets to get his Majesty into his blue guards uniform, and soon he was striding through into the reception-room with a bold and rapid tread.

De Bausset meanwhile was busy fussing with the present he had brought from the Empress, which he wanted to arrange across a couple of chairs right in front of the Emperor's doorway. But his Majesty had taken less time than expected to get dressed and come out, so the surprise wasn't quite ready.

Napoleon spotted immediately what they were up to, and guessed they weren't ready for him. Not wishing to deprive them of the pleasure of preparing a nice surprise for him, he pretended he hadn't seen M. de Bausset, and called Fabvier over. Napoleon arranged his face into a severe frown as he listened in silence to Fabvier's discourse on the courage and devotion of his men fighting at Salamanca, the other end of Europe, whose only thought was to be worthy of their Emperor, and whose only dread was to incur his displeasure. The battle had been a disaster. Napoleon made one or two sarcastic comments during Fabvier's account, to the effect that no more could have been expected in view of his absence.

'I must put things right in Moscow,' said Napoleon. 'Goodbye for now,' he added, and summoned de Bausset, who had now had enough time to get his surprise ready; something had been placed across the chairs and covered with a cloth.

De Bausset gave a very low bow in true French courtly fashion, the special bow of the older Bourbon retainers, and came closer to hand over a letter.

Napoleon addressed him breezily, and tweaked his ear.

'It hasn't taken you long. I'm delighted to see you. Well, come on then, what's the word from Paris?' he said, his earlier dark glare switching instantly to a look of warm cordiality.

'Sire, the whole of Paris regrets your absence,' answered de Bausset, going through the motions. But even though Napoleon knew de Bausset was obliged to say this or something like it, even though in his brighter moments he knew it wasn't true, he was still gratified to hear it. He was gracious enough to give the man's ear another tweak.

'I'm so sorry to have made you do so much travelling,' he said.

'Sire, I expected nothing less than to find you at the gates of Moscow,' said de Bausset.

Napoleon gave a smile, looked up distractedly and glanced to his right. An adjutant glided forward with a gold snuff-box, which he offered up. Napoleon took it.

'Yes, it's all worked out well for you,' he said, bringing the open snuff-box up to his nose. 'You and your wanderlust. In three days' time you'll get your first sight of Moscow. I'm sure you weren't expecting to see the Asiatic capital. It'll be a nice trip for you.'

De Bausset bowed in appreciation of this sympathetic interest in his wanderlust (though this was the first he had heard of it).

'Well now, what have we here?' said Napoleon, observing that all the courtiers were staring at the object hidden under the cloth. De Bausset, practised courtier that he was, performed a nifty backward two-step, half-twisting but not once turning his back, and in one movement whipped off the cover and proclaimed, 'A present to your Majesty from the Empress.'

It was a brightly coloured portrait, painted by Gérard, of the son born to Napoleon and the daughter of the Austrian Emperor, the little boy known for some reason as the King of Rome.

He was a very pretty child with curly hair and eyes like those of Christ in the Sistine Madonna, and he had been portrayed playing cup and ball. The ball represented the earth and the stick in his other hand was meant as a sceptre.

Although the painter's message (with the so-called King of Rome skewering the earth on a sceptre) was not altogether clear, the allegory seemed to strike Napoleon in the same way that it had struck everyone who had seen it in Paris, as something perfectly understandable and most appealing.

'The King of Rome!' he exclaimed, with an elegant gesture towards the portrait. 'Admirable!' He had an Italian's knack of changing his facial expression at will, and by the time he had walked over to the portrait his air was one of contemplative tenderness. He could sense the moment; whatever he might say or do now would be history in the making, and it occurred to him that the best thing to do, with him at the height of his power, enough for his child to be playing cup and ball with the earth itself, would be to go for the opposite extreme and put on a show of fatherly affection at it simplest. His eyes were misty with emotion as he moved closer, looked round for a chair (one was under him in a flash), and sat down facing the portrait. One gesture from him and everybody tiptoed out, leaving the great man alone with his feelings.

After sitting there for a while and reaching out, for no particular reason, to feel the rough texture of a highlight in the painting, he got to his feet and recalled de Bausset and the officer on duty. He gave orders for the portrait to be taken outside and placed in front of his tent so that the old guard stationed near him should not miss the pleasure of seeing the King of Rome, son and heir of their adored Emperor.

And sure enough, as expected, while he sat breakfasting with M. de Bausset, who had joined him by gracious invitation, they could hear the officers and men of the old guard cheering with delight as they dashed up to look at the portrait.

'Long live the Emperor! Long live the king of Rome! Long live the Emperor!' came the rapturous cries.

After breakfast, in the presence of de Bausset, Napoleon dictated his order of the day to the army.

'Short and sweet!' was Napoleon's assessment of it when he had read through the text of his proclamation, which had been written down at one go and needed no corrections. It ran as follows:

> Soldiers! The battle you have been longing for is upon us. Victory depends on you. It is essential for us; it will give us all that we need: comfortable quarters and a speedy return home. Behave as you did at Austerlitz, Friedland, Vitebsk and Smolensk. May posterity long recall with pride your achievements this day! And may it be said of each one of you: he was there at the great battle before Moscow!

'Before Moscow,' Napoleon repeated, and inviting M. de Bausset, the devotee of travel, to go with him on his ride, he left the tent and walked over to the horses that stood waiting ready saddled.

'Your Majesty is too kind,' was de Bausset's response to the invitation. He was dead on his feet, he was not a good rider and he was frightened of horses.

But Napoleon nodded to the traveller, and de Bausset had no option but to mount. The moment Napoleon came out of the tent the cheering of the guards gathered round his son's portrait was redoubled. Napoleon gave a frown.

'Take him away,' he said, pointing to the portrait with a stylish, magnificent gesture. 'It is too early for him to look upon the battlefield.'

De Bausset lowered his eyelids and bowed his head with a deep sigh. It was his way of showing how well he understood the Emperor's words and how much he appreciated them.

CHAPTER 27

History tells us that Napoleon spent the whole of that day, the 25th of August, on horseback, inspecting the locality, going over plans submitted by his marshals, and issuing personal instructions to his generals.

The Russians' original battle-line along the Kolocha had been broken, and the loss of the Shevardino redoubt on the 24th had caused them to pull back on the left flank. This section had not been entrenched, it was no longer protected by the river, and it was the only part of the front that gave on to flat, open ground. This was the obvious place for the French to attack, as any man, military or non-military, could have seen. One might have thought that this conclusion could have been reached without too much cogitation, without all the fuss and bother now indulged in by the Emperor and his marshals, and certainly without recourse to the remarkable and lofty faculty that goes by the name of genius, which is so lovingly ascribed to Napoleon. Yet the historians who later described the battle, the men surrounding the Emperor at the time and Napoleon himself all thought otherwise.

Napoleon rode up and down the field, examining the countryside with an air of profound introspection, nodding or shaking his head to himself as a register of approval or uncertainty but keeping his thoughts to himself, and, without a word to the surrounding generals about the profound thought processes that lay behind his decisions, he transmitted only his final conclusions, and these took the form of instructions. He listened carefully to a proposal from Davout, now the Duke of Eckmühl, that they should turn the Russian left flank, and then announced that there was no need for this, though he never explained why not. But when General Compans (who was due to attack the flèches) proposed taking his division through the woods, Napoleon signified his approval, even though the so-called Duke of Elchingen (Marshal Ney) ventured to observe that moving troops through woodland was a risky business that might break up the formation of the division.

Napoleon scrutinized the countryside across from the Shevardino redoubt, thought things over for a while in silence and then indicated two places where batteries were to be set up for tomorrow's action against the Russian fortifications, and the line running from them along which the field artillery was to be deployed.

After issuing these orders, along with a number of others, he went back to his tent, and the battle-disposition of the troops was written down from his dictation.

This disposition, which French historians describe in rapturous terms and others treat with the greatest of respect, went as follows:

At daybreak two new batteries set up during the night on the plateau occupied by the Duke of Eckmühl to open fire on the two enemy batteries opposite.

At the same time General Pernetti, commander of the 1st Corps artillery, with thirty pieces from Compans' division and all the howitzers from Desaix's and Friant's divisions, to advance, open fire and mount an intense bombardment of the enemy's battery, which will then be under attack from the following:

Guards artillery	24 guns
Compans' division	30 guns
Friant and Desaix's divisions	8 guns
Total	62 pieces

General Fouché, commander of the 3rd Corps artillery, is to deploy all sixteen howitzers of the 3rd and 8th Corps on both flanks of the battery detailed to bombard the left-side entrenchment, bringing the total of guns ranged against it to 40.

General Sorbier to stand ready and, when ordered, to advance with all the guards artillery howitzers deployed against one or other of the enemy entrenchments.

Prince Poniatowski to advance on the village through the wood during the bombardment, and turn the enemy's position.

General Compans to advance through the wood and take the first fortification.

With the battle thus under way further instructions will be issued in response to enemy movements.

Bombardment on the left flank to begin as soon as the cannons on the right are heard firing. Marksmen from the divisions of Morand and the Viceroy to open heavy fire the moment they see the attack on the right wing has begun.

Viceroy to take the village (Borodino) and cross by the three bridges, then keep level with Morand's and Gérard's divisions, all three advancing on the redoubt under his command and coming into line with the rest of our troops.

All this to be carried out in good order, protecting the reserve as far as possible.

Imperial Camp at Mozhaysk,
6th September (25th August Old Style) 1812.

These arrangements, obscure and confused as they are in this written form – if we can take time off from worshipping Napoleon's military genius and look at his actual instructions – boil down to four points, four basic instructions, none of which was carried out, or ever could have been.

In the disposition the first thing said is: *Batteries installed in locations chosen by Napoleon, along with cannons of Pernetti and Fouché, coming into line with them, one hundred and two pieces in all, to open fire and bombard the Russian flèches and redoubts.* This could never have happened because from the locations set by Napoleon the Russian earthworks were out of range, and these one hundred and two pieces were wasting their fire until the nearest officer ignored Napoleon's instructions and had them moved forward.

The second instruction was: *Poniatowski to advance through the wood, take the village and turn the Russian left flank.* This was not done, and never could have been, because as Poniatowski advanced through the wood towards the village he found his way blocked by Tuchkov, which meant that he could not and did not turn the Russian position.

The third instruction was: *General Compans to advance through the wood and take the first fortification.* Compans' division did not take the first fortification; it was forced back because as it emerged from the wood it had to re-form under a hail of grapeshot, which Napoleon knew nothing about.

The fourth instruction was: *Viceroy to take the village (Borodino) and cross by the three bridges, then keep level with Morand's and Gérard's divisions* (nothing about when and where they were to move), *all three advancing on the redoubt under his command and coming into line with the rest of our troops.*

As far as we can tell, not from the meanderings of this senseless prose but from the Viceroy's actual attempts to carry out his orders, he was supposed to advance through Borodino and attack the redoubt from the left, while the divisions of Morand and Gérard advanced simultaneously from the front.

All of this, like the other instructions, failed to come about, and never could have come about. The Viceroy did get through Borodino, but was driven back at the Kolocha, and could make no further progress. The divisions under Morand and Gérard failed to take the redoubt; they were driven back, and at the end of the day the redoubt was seized by the cavalry (something almost certainly unforeseen by Napoleon, and never reported to him).

So it turns out that not one of the Emperor's instructions was carried out, and none of them ever could have been. But in the disposition it was stated that with the battle under way further instructions would be issued in response to enemy movements, so you might well imagine that all necessary arrangements were actually made by Napoleon in mid-battle. But this was not the case, and never could have been, because during the battle Napoleon was so far away that (as it later emerged) he could not have known how things were going, and not a single instruction issued by him during the battle could possibly have been carried out.

CHAPTER 28

Many historians tell us that the French failed to win the battle of Borodino because Napoleon had a cold, and if he hadn't had a cold the orders he issued before and during the battle would have marked him out even more clearly as a genius, and Russia would have been destroyed and the face of the world would have been changed. To those historians who maintain that Russia was formed by the will of a single man, Peter the Great, and France was turned from a republic into an empire, and the French army marched into Russia all by the will of a single man, Napoleon, the argument that Russia retained power because Napoleon had a bad cold on the 26th of August must seem highly persuasive.

If it was a matter of Napoleon's will determining whether or not there was to be a battle at Borodino, a matter of his will determining that such-and-such orders were given, then clearly the cold that had an effect on the manifestation of his will might have been the saving of Russia, though that means that the valet who forgot to give Napoleon his waterproof boots on the 24th must have been the saviour of Russia. By that reckoning the conclusion is inescapable, as inescapable as the conclusion arrived at jokingly by Voltaire (without knowing who the joke was on) that the Massacre of St Bartholomew's Night was due to Charles IX suffering a touch of indigestion. But to anyone who cannot accept that Russia was formed by the will of a single man, Peter the Great, and the French empire was created, and the war with Russia set up, by the will of a single man, Napoleon, this kind of argument will seem not just weak and unreasonable, but contrary to all human experience. The question of what causes historical events will call for a very different answer, that the course of worldly events is determined on high and it depends on the complex combined will of all the participants, Napoleon's influence on these particular events being no more than peripheral and fictitious.

Strange as it may seem on the face of it, this proposition that the Massacre of St Bartholomew's Night, for which the order was given by Charles IX, was not the result of his will – he only thought he was ordering it to happen – and that the slaughter of eighty thousand men at Borodino was not the result of Napoleon's will (even though he gave the order for battle to commence and other orders for it to continue), and he only thought he was ordering it to happen – strange as this proposition may seem, the same human dignity which tells me that each one of us is neither more nor less of a man than the great Napoleon forces us towards this kind of solution to the problem, and historical research provides abundant justification for it.

At the battle of Borodino Napoleon never fired a shot and didn't kill anyone. All of that was done by the soldiers; hence he did no killing of his own.

The soldiers of the French army set out to slay Russian soldiers at Borodino not because of Napoleon's orders, but because they wanted to. The whole army, Frenchmen, Italians, Germans and Poles, hungry men dressed in rags and weary from the long campaign, took one look at the army that barred the way to Moscow and came to one conclusion: if the wine was uncorked it had to be drunk. If at that point Napoleon had told them not to fight the Russians they would have killed him and gone on to fight the Russians, because by now it had become inevitable.

When they heard Napoleon's proclamation offering consolation for getting themselves maimed or killed in the knowledge that posterity would say they had been at the battle before Moscow, they shouted, 'Long live the Emperor!' in the same way that they had shouted, 'Long live the Emperor!' at the sight of the picture with the little boy skewering the earth on a stick, and would have shouted, 'Long live the Emperor!' at any bit of nonsense he might care to pronounce. They had nothing left to do but shout, 'Long live the Emperor!' and go off to fight in order to get themselves the victor's food and rest in Moscow. It was not as a result of orders from Napoleon, therefore, that they set about the business of killing their fellow men.

And it was not Napoleon who determined the course of the battle, because none of his instructions were carried out, and during the battle he had no knowledge of what was happening out in front of him. This is to say that the manner in which these men slaughtered one another was not the result of Napoleon's will; the killing went on independently, resulting from the will of all the participants in their hundreds of thousands. It only *seemed* to Napoleon that everything was due to his will. For this reason the question whether Napoleon did or didn't have a cold that day is of no greater interest to history than whether the humblest soldier in transport command had a cold or not.

Napoleon's health on the 26th of August gains no greater significance from the quite unjustified contention of some writers that his cold rendered his instructions and dispositions on the day less effective than before. The instructions reproduced above are certainly no worse, indeed they are better, than many a similar disposition that had brought him victory in the past. The instructions he is supposed to have issued in mid-battle were certainly no worse than any orders he had given before; they were much the same as usual. But these instructions and dispositions are now seen as inferior, for the simple reason that Borodino was the first battle that Napoleon didn't win. The finest and profoundest of orders and dispositions will seem very weak, and open to criticism with a knowing air by every last student of military history, when the battle they were written for hasn't been won. Conversely, the stupidest of orders and dispositions will seem very shrewd, and serious authors will write volume after volume to demonstrate their virtues, if only the battle they were written for has been won. The dispositions put together by Weierother at Austerlitz have given rise to perfect examples of works like this, and even they have come in for some criticism, if only for their perfectionism, their excess of detail.

At Borodino Napoleon played his part as the representative of authority as well as he had done in previous battles, perhaps even better. He did nothing to impede the progress of the battle, he gave ear to reasonable opinion, he never lost his grip or contradicted himself, he didn't panic or run away; he just used his good sense and military experience to stay calm, behave with dignity and go through the motions of exercising masterful control.

CHAPTER 29

On his return from a second meticulous tour of inspection Napoleon said, 'The board's set up. The game begins tomorrow.'

He ordered some punch, sent for de Bausset and began to talk to him about Paris, and the various changes he had in mind for the Empress's household. His recollection of the tiniest details of court life came as a surprise to the prefect.

He showed interest in all sorts of silly little things, he made jokes about de Bausset's wanderlust and he carried on a casual conversation like some famous surgeon, experienced and self-confident, chatting away as he rolls his sleeves up and dons his apron while the patient is being strapped to the operating-table. 'My hands and my brain have everything under control. When it's time to start I'll do the job better than anyone, but for the moment I can crack a few jokes. The more jokes you hear from me and the calmer I am, the greater your confidence, peace of mind and admiration for my genius should be.'

Napoleon drained a second glass of punch, and then went off to get some rest in anticipation of the serious business that surely awaited them in the morning.

He was so preoccupied with this business that he could not get to sleep, and although he could feel his cold getting worse in the damp night air he got up at three o'clock and walked out into the main section of the tent, sneezing violently. He asked whether the Russians had gone away. No, the enemy camp-fires were still in the same places. He nodded with approval.

The duty adjutant came in.

'Well, Rapp, do you think our business will go well today?' Napoleon asked him.

'Without a shadow of doubt, sire!' answered Rapp.

Napoleon looked at him.

'Sire, do you remember what you were kind enough to say to me at Smolensk?' said Rapp. 'When the wine is uncorked it has to be drunk.'

Napoleon frowned, and sat there in silence for some time with his head propped up on one hand.

'This poor army,' he suddenly burst out. 'It's gone down a lot since Smolensk. Lady Luck is nothing but a whore, Rapp. I've always said so, and now it's coming home to me. But the guards, Rapp, the guards are all still there, aren't they?'

'Yes, sire,' replied Rapp.

Napoleon took a lozenge, put it in his mouth, and looked at his watch. He didn't feel sleepy, morning was still a long way away, and he could not kill time by giving any orders because they had all been given and were now being carried out.

'Have the guards regiments been issued with biscuits and rice?' Napoleon asked sternly.

'Yes, sire.'

'Are you sure about the rice?'

Rapp responded by saying that he had passed on the Emperor's orders about the rice, but Napoleon shook his head unhappily, as if he could not trust them to have carried out his order. A servant came in with punch. Napoleon called for another glass for Rapp, and stood there sipping at his own in silence. 'I can't taste anything or smell anything,' he said, sniffing at the glass. 'I'm fed up with this cold. They go on and on about medicine. What good is medicine when they can't cure a cold? Corvisart gave me these lozenges, but they're not doing me any good. What can they cure? They can't cure anything. Our body is a machine for living. That's the way it's organized, and that's its nature. The life inside should be left alone. Let the life inside defend itself. It will get on better like that, instead of paralysing it and clogging it with remedies. Our body is like a perfect watch with only a fixed time to run. The watchmaker has no power to get inside it, he can only fumble with it blindfold. Our body is a machine for living, and that's all there is to it.' And once launched into defining things – Napoleon had a weakness for coming out with definitions – he seemed suddenly impelled to produce a new one. 'Do you know, Rapp, what the military art is?' he asked. 'It's the art of being stronger than the enemy at a given moment. That's all it is.'

Rapp made no reply.

'Tomorrow we shall have Kutuzov to deal with,' said Napoleon. 'Let's see what happens! You remember – he was in command at Braunau, and not once in three weeks did he get on a horse and go round his entrenchments! Let's see what happens!'

He looked at his watch. It was still only four o'clock. He didn't feel sleepy, the punch was finished, and there was still nothing to do. He got to his feet, paced up and down, put on a warm overcoat and hat and walked out of his tent. The night was dark and clammy; you could almost feel the dampness seeping down from on high. Near by, the French guards' camp-fires had burned down, but far away you could see the Russian fires burning smokily all down their line. The air was still, but there was a faint stirring and a clear rumble of early-morning movement as the French troops began the business of taking up their positions.

Napoleon paced up and down outside his tent, glanced across at the fires, listened to the sounds of movement, and as he was walking past he stopped in front of a tall guardsman in a shaggy cap on sentry-go outside his tent, who drew himself up like a big black post when he saw the Emperor.

'Been long in the service?' he asked, with that mixture of a military man's straight talk and forced camaraderie that he always affected when talking to soldiers. This soldier gave his answer.

'Ah! An old campaigner! Has your regiment had any rice?'

'Yes, your Majesty.'
Napoleon nodded and walked away.

By half-past five Napoleon was on his way over to the village of
Shevardino.

It was getting light, and the sky had cleared. A solitary stormcloud
lay in the eastern sky. The deserted camp-fires were going out in the
pale light of morning.

A single deep cannon-shot roared out on the right. The boom
whooshed past and died away in the stillness. Several minutes passed.
A second shot rang out, then a third, and the air shook. Then came
the solemn boom of the fourth and a fifth, not far away on the right.

The first shots had barely died away when another one came, then
another and another, more and more, some blending into a single
sound, others bursting in alone.

Napoleon and his entourage continued their way to the Shevardino
redoubt, where he got down from his horse. The game had begun.

CHAPTER 30

When he got back to Gorki from visiting Prince Andrey, Pierre told
his groom to get the horses ready and call him early the following
morning, and then he fell fast asleep behind a screen in a corner made
available by Boris.

By the time Pierre was properly awake next morning the hut was
empty. The little window-panes were rattling in their frames. His
groom was there at his side, giving him a good shake. 'Your Excellency!
Your Excellency! Your Excellency! . . .' the groom kept repeating over
and over again as he shook him by the shoulder without looking at
him, with little apparent hope of ever waking him up.

'Eh? Have they started? Is it time?' said Pierre, coming round.

'Hark at the guns, sir,' said the groom, himself an old soldier. 'All
the gentlemen have gone, and his Serene Highness went past ages ago.'

Pierre threw on some clothes and ran out on to the porch. It was a
bright, fresh, dewy, cheerful morning. The sun had just broken through
a covering of cloud, and its half-filtered rays poured down through the
gaps, streaming over the rooftops opposite to light up the dew-sodden
dust on the road, the walls of the houses, the fence-palings and Pierre's
horses standing in front of their hut. Outside, the cannons boomed
louder. An adjutant and his Cossack passed by at a sharp trot.

'Come on, Count, it's time!' cried the adjutant.

Telling his groom to come on behind with a horse, Pierre walked down the street and over towards the mound which had given him such a good view of the battlefield yesterday. There on top stood a crowd of military men. Pierre could hear staff-officers speaking French, and he soon saw Kutuzov, with his grey head, topped with a red and white cap, hunched down into his shoulders. Kutuzov was looking through a telescope down the main road that stretched before him.

At the top of the steps up on to the mound Pierre took one look ahead and was transfixed by the sheer splendour of the view. It was the same place, the same vista that he had enjoyed yesterday, but now the entire landscape was covered with troops and gunsmoke, and in the clear morning air, as the bright sun came up over Pierre's left shoulder, it bathed the whole scene with slanting rays of piercing light, touching everything with gold and pink, and leaving long, dark shadows. Far away along the curving edge of the horizon the scene was bounded by stretches of woodland that might have been carved out of some yellowy-green precious stone, and up over Valuyevo they were broken by the Smolensk high road, swarming with troops. Down below, fields dotted with copses glittering with gold. And everywhere, right, left and centre, there were soldiers. It was a vibrant scene, astonishing in its splendour, but what struck Pierre most forcibly was the battlefield itself, Borodino, and the hollow winding its way along both sides of the Kolocha.

The ground above the Kolocha, in Borodino itself, and out on both sides but especially over on the left where the Voyna empties itself through marshy ground into the Kolocha, was overhung by the kind of mist that seeps down and thins out to let the bright sun come shimmering through, revealing the landscape and painting it in magical colours. Gunsmoke wreathed its way in, and the intermingling smoke and mist was everywhere shot through with lightning-flashes of early-morning sunlight glinting on water, dew and bayonets in the hands of soldiers swarming along the river banks and through Borodino. Through the mist you could make things out: a white church here, there the roofs of shacks in Borodino, with fitful glimpses of great masses of men, the odd green-coloured ammunition-box, an occasional cannon. And the whole scene was writhing, or it looked as if it was, because of the mist and smoke drifting across the entire landscape. All across the misty hollows close to Borodino, and outside the village on higher ground, especially to the left down the line, from copse and meadow puffs of smoke curled up out of thin air, either singly or in clusters, sporadically or in big, rapid bursts, weaving together on high then swelling, billowing out, seeping away and merging together in all over the landscape. Curiously enough, it was this swirling gunsmoke, with the ensuing bangs, that gave the whole spectacle its special beauty.

'*Pooff!*' Suddenly a thick, round ball of smoke rose up, shot through with flashes of purple, grey and a milky-white hue, followed a second later by the inevitable '*boom!*'

'*Pooff-pooff!*' Two clouds of smoke this time, jostling and merging in mid-air.

'*Boom-boom!*' came an echo confirming what the eye had seen.

Pierre took a long look at the first puff of smoke, watching it grow rapidly from a thick, round ball into bigger round palls of smoke drifting off to one side, and *pooff* . . . (then a pause) *pooff-pooff* . . . then three more, and another four all at once, each puff of smoke followed, after the same time-lapse, by another *boom . . . boom-boom-boom*, each sound beautiful, strong and true. Sometimes the smoke-clouds seemed to be scudding across the plain, sometimes they seemed to stand still and let everything fly by – copses, fields and glinting bayonets. These big palls of smoke rose up in an unceasing stream from the left, soaring over fields and bushes, each one followed by a triumphant boom. Much nearer, over the low ground and woodland, tiny puffs of smoke floated up from the musket-fire, hardly enough to form into balls of smoke, though each had its tiny after-echo too. '*Tra-ta-ta-ta!*' came the persistent crackle of the muskets, but they sounded thin and sporadic compared with the steady booming of the cannons.

Pierre felt a sudden longing to be down there amidst all the smoke, the glinting bayonets, the movement and the din. He looked round at Kutuzov and his entourage to measure his own impressions against theirs. Like him they were all looking ahead, staring down at the battlefield, and they seemed to share his feelings. Every face glowed with that sensation of *latent heat* that Pierre had noticed the day before, and fully understood after his talk with Prince Andrey.

'Go on, my dear fellow, off you go, and God go with you!' Kutuzov was saying to a general at his side, though his eyes never left the battlefield. The general in question heard the order and walked past Pierre towards the downward steps.

'Down to the crossing,' said the general with icy severity when one of the staff-officers asked where he was going.

'Oh yes, me too,' thought Pierre, and he set off in the same direction.

The general was mounting a horse brought up by his Cossack. Pierre went over to his own groom, who was standing there holding his horses. Asking for the easiest mount, Pierre got on, grabbed the horse by its mane, turned out his toes, dug his heels into the animal's belly, and trotted off after the general with a desperate feeling that his spectacles were slipping down and he daren't let go of the mane or the reins, much to the amusement of the staff-officers watching him from the mound.

CHAPTER 31

The general who was leading the way galloped downhill and turned sharp left at the bottom. Pierre lost sight of him and careered straight into the ranks of some infantrymen marching just ahead. He turned left and right in an attempt to extricate himself, but there were soldiers everywhere, and they all had worried faces as they went forward on some unseen business that was obviously no laughing matter. They all looked puzzled and annoyed to see this fat man in a white hat who was trampling them under his horse's hooves for no apparent reason.

'What's 'e think 'e's doin' in the middle of a battalion?' one man shouted for his benefit. Another gave his horse a good shove with his gun-butt, and Pierre, leaning forward in the saddle with his plunging steed almost out of control, managed to gallop through a space and out in front of the soldiers.

Ahead lay a bridge, and by the bridge there were some more soldiers, firing away. Pierre rode towards them. Without knowing it, he had hit upon the one bridge over the Kolocha, on the road from Gorki to Borodino, which had come under French attack in one of the first advances after they had taken the village itself. Pierre could see there was a bridge in front of him, and the soldiers were doing something in the smoke on both sides of the bridge, and also out in the meadow among the rows of new-mown hay he had noticed the day before. But despite the incessant hail of fire it never occurred to him that this was it, the actual battlefield. He didn't hear the bullets whizzing past on all sides, or the shells flying overhead; he didn't see the enemy on the other side of the river, and it was quite some time before he saw any men killed or wounded, though they were dropping all round him. He was taking a careful look around, and the smile never left his face.

'What's 'e doin' out in front?' came another call intended for his benefit.

'Turn left!', 'Go right!' came the various voices. Pierre did turn right, and happened upon one of General Rayevsky's adjutants, a man he knew. The adjutant fixed him with a furious glare, and by all appearances he was about to yell at him too, but then he recognized him, and nodded in acknowledgement.

'What are you doing down here?' he said, and galloped on. Pierre, feeling out of his depth, quite useless, and worried about getting in the way again, galloped after him.

'What's happening here? Can I go with you?' he asked.

'Hang on a minute,' answered the adjutant. He galloped over to a portly colonel waiting in the meadow, handed something to him, and only then spoke to Pierre. 'What brings you here, Count?' he asked with a smile. 'Still curious about things?'

'Yes, yes,' said Pierre. But the adjutant had turned his horse and was riding on.

'Things are not too bad over here, thank God,' said the adjutant, 'but it's pretty hot out there on the left flank with Bagration.'

'Is it?' said Pierre. 'Where's that, then?'

'Come up on the mound with me. We can see a lot from up there. And our battery's not doing too badly,' said the adjutant. 'Are you coming?'

'Oh yes, I'll come with you,' said Pierre, looking round on all sides in search of his groom. Now for the first time Pierre began to see wounded men, some staggering about, others being carried away on stretchers. And out there in the meadow with the rows of sweet-smelling hay that he had ridden through the day before there was one soldier who was lying crosswise, perfectly still, with his shako off and his head awkwardly thrown back. 'Why haven't they taken him?' Pierre was on the point of asking, until he saw the adjutant looking grimly in the same direction, and this made him swallow his words.

Without finding his groom Pierre rode with the adjutant up a hollow towards the Rayevsky redoubt. His horse lagged behind, and kept bumping into the adjutant's horse at every step.

'I can see you don't do much riding, Count,' said the adjutant.

'No, but I'm all right. Her action is a bit awkward, though,' said Pierre, rather bemused.

'I'm not surprised ... Look, she's wounded!' said the adjutant. 'Right fore-leg, just above the knee. Must have been a bullet. Congratulations, Count,' he said. 'Your baptism of fire.'

They rode through the smoke of Sixth Corps territory right behind the artillery, which had been moved forward and was keeping up a deafening bombardment, and out into a small copse. Here under the trees it was cool and quiet, with a smell of autumn. Pierre and the adjutant got down from their horses and proceeded uphill on foot.

'Is the general here?' asked the adjutant when they got to the redoubt.

'No, you've just missed him. He went that way,' someone answered, pointing off to the right.

The adjutant glanced round at Pierre as if he wasn't sure what to do with him.

'Oh, please don't bother about me,' said Pierre. 'I'll go up on the mound, if I may.'

'Yes, do. You can see everything from up there, and it's not too dangerous. I'll come and get you later.'

Pierre went up to the battery, and the adjutant rode away. They never saw each other again, and only much later on did Pierre learn that the adjutant had lost an arm that day.

The mound on which Pierre now stood – afterwards known to the Russians as the mound battery, or the Rayevsky redoubt, and to the French as the great redoubt, fatal redoubt or centre redoubt – was the famous place that the French looked on as the key position, where tens of thousands fell.

It consisted of a mound with trenches dug outwards on three sides. In the entrenchments there were ten cannons that fired out through gaps.

There was a line of further cannons on either side of the redoubt, and they also kept up a constant barrage. The infantrymen were stationed just behind this line. When Pierre got to the top of the mound he hadn't the slightest idea that this place with its little trenches and one or two cannons firing away was the very heart of the battle. Quite the reverse: he assumed (by the very fact that he happened to be there) that it was one of the least important locations on the battlefield.

Pierre sat down at one end of the earthwork that enclosed the battery and watched what was going on with an instinctively happy smile. He got up from time to time and strolled about the battery with the same smile on his face, trying not to get in the way of the soldiers forever running past with pouches and ammunition, or loading the cannons and hauling them into position. The cannons never stopped firing, one after another, with a thunderous, deafening roar, and they smothered the surrounding countryside in blankets of powder-smoke.

Among the infantrymen providing cover for the battery fear was rampant and it showed, but here inside, by contrast, where only a small number of men toiled away together in seclusion, cut off from the rest of the trench, there was a shared camaraderie that could be sensed all round, a kind of family feeling.

At first the sudden appearance of Pierre's unmilitary figure in a white hat made a bad impression on this little group. As they ran by the soldiers were surprised, even shocked, by the sight of him and he attracted many a sidelong glance. The senior artillery officer, a tall, lanky man with a pock-marked face, came right up to Pierre on the pretext of checking the action of the end cannon, and took a close look at him.

A boyish officer with a little round face, still wet behind the ears and obviously just out of cadet school, feeling very protective towards the two cannons they had given him charge of, spoke sharply to Pierre.

'I'm sorry, sir, I'll have to ask you to move,' he said. 'You can't stay here.'

The soldiers shook their heads disapprovingly as they looked at Pierre. But once they were satisfied that the man in the white hat wasn't doing any harm, as he either sat quietly on a slope, or politely got out of the soldiers' way with a shy smile on his face as he walked about the battery, under full fire, like someone calmly strolling down a boulevard, suspicion and resentment gradually gave way to the kindly spirit of friendly banter that soldiers tend to reserve for their animals: the dogs, cockerels, goats and other creatures who happen to share the fortunes of the regiment. The soldiers soon made the mental adjustment and accepted Pierre into their family, calling him one of their own, and they gave him a special name. 'Our gent', as they called him, caused many a good-humoured laugh among them.

A cannonball ploughed the earth up a couple of paces from Pierre, spattering him with dirt. He looked round with a smile as he brushed it off his clothes.

'How come you ain't scared, sir?' said a broad, red-faced soldier with a strong, white, toothy grin.

'Are you, then?' asked Pierre.

'You bet I am!' answered the soldier. 'She don't show no mercy. Bang, guts everywhere. You got to be scared, sir,' he said with a laugh.

One or two soldiers had stopped beside Pierre looking all amused and friendly. It was as if they hadn't expected him to talk like other people, and when he did they were delighted.

'Yes, but this is our job. We're soldiers. You're a gentleman. Takes the biscuit that does, you bein' a gentleman an' all that!'

'Back to your stations!' called the little boy officer to the soldiers who had gathered round Pierre. This boy could not have been doing more than his first or second turn of duty and he was taking things very seriously and being very officious towards the men and his senior officer.

The constant thunder of the cannons and the rattle of musketry were getting louder all over the field, especially on the left in the region of Bagration's flèches, but from where Pierre was standing almost nothing could be seen because of the smoke. In any case, he was completely absorbed in observing this little family group up on their battery, cut off from the rest of the world. His first instinctive surge of excitement at the sights and sounds of the battlefield had given way to another feeling, especially since he had seen that soldier lying all alone in the hayfield. He now sat there on his slope and took stock of the figures moving about him.

By ten o'clock a couple of dozen men had been stretchered away, two cannons had been put out of action, shells continued to rain down on the battery, and bullets came howling and whistling from afar. But nobody there seemed to notice; from every corner all you could hear was a stream of breezy repartee and jokes.

'Here's a beauty!' yelled one of the soldiers as a grenade came whistling over.

'Not down here! You want the infantry!' another added with a chuckle, watching the grenade soar across and land in the middle of the covering troops.

'Bowing to a friend?' said another soldier, jeering at a peasant who had ducked down at the sight of a flying cannonball.

One or two soldiers came together at the trench wall to have a look at what was going on out front.

'The line's gone down there, look, they're coming back,' they said, pointing down.

'None of your business,' the old sergeant yelled to them. 'If that's right, it means they're needed for a job at the back.' And the sergeant grabbed one soldier by the shoulder and kneed him in the thigh. They all laughed.

'Forward number five!' came the call from one side.

'Come on, boys, all together, *heave!*' came the happy voices of the men shoving the cannon forward.

'Phew, almost had our gent's hat off!' said the red-faced joker with a laugh, showing his toothy grin. 'Ooh! Nasty bitch that one!' he added, cursing a cannonball as it smashed into a wheel and took a man's leg off.

''Ere comes the little foxes!' another soldier laughed as he saw the peasant militiamen who had come for the wounded crouching down and creeping along. 'Not your cup o' tea, is it? Look at 'em, gawping! That's stopped 'em!' they shouted at the militiamen, who had halted in their tracks at the sight of a soldier with his leg torn off. 'Diddums do it, sonny,' they cried, making fun of the peasants. 'Don't like it, do 'e?'

Pierre noticed that with every ball that fell, with every loss, the level

of excitement went up and up. The faces of these men blazed with
fire from within, defiantly rejecting reality even as it happened, like
lightning flashes licking round a stormcloud, faster and faster, brighter
and brighter, as it continued to build up.

Pierre wasn't looking ahead at the field of battle; he no longer had
any interest in what was going on down there. He was completely
absorbed in observing the build-up of that inner fire, and he could feel
the same fire building up in his own soul too.

By ten o'clock the infantry that had been out in front of the battery
in the bushes and on the banks of the Kamenka were in retreat. From
the battery they could see the men running back past them, using their
guns to carry the wounded. A general with his entourage came up to
the redoubt, exchanged a few words with the colonel, glared furiously
at Pierre and rode off downhill again, having told the covering infantry
behind the battery to lie down so as to be less exposed to fire. After
that from the infantry ranks over on the right came the sound of a
drum and shouts of command, and from inside the battery they could
see the footsoldiers moving forward.

Pierre looked over the top of the trench. One particular figure caught
his eye – an officer with a pale young face who was walking backwards,
holding his sword down and looking round uneasily.

The ranks of infantrymen vanished into the smoke, but they could
still be heard calling across to each other and firing continuously with
their muskets. It took only a few minutes for hordes of wounded men
and stretcher-bearers to start coming back. Shells rained down on the
battery even more furiously. There were men lying around who were
not being picked up. Round the cannons the toiling soldiers had
redoubled their efforts. Pierre was now being ignored. Two or three
times people yelled at him furiously for getting in the way. The senior
officer strode rapidly from cannon to cannon with a dark scowl on his
face. The boy officer, with even more red in his cheeks, issued his orders
more conscientiously than ever. The straining soldiers did everything –
passing on the charges, turning round, loading and all the rest – more
urgently, with a new swagger and a new spring in their step.

The stormcloud was now on them, and the flickering fire that Pierre
had been watching lit up their faces more brightly than ever. He was
standing beside the senior officer. The little boy officer ran up and
saluted.

'Colonel, sir, I have the honour to inform you we have only eight
rounds left. What shall we do, continue firing?' he asked.

'Grapeshot!' yelled the senior officer, still peering out over the trench
top.

Suddenly something happened. The boy officer cried out, doubled up and sat down on the ground, like a bird shot on the wing. Pierre's vision blurred; everything looked weird and dark.

The cannonballs came whistling down one after another, smashing into eveything – breastwork, soldiers, cannons. These sounds had barely registered on Pierre before; now he could hear nothing else. To one side of the battery, the right-hand side, some soldiers were shouting 'Hurrah!', but they seemed to be running back rather than going forwards.

A cannonball thudded into the very edge of the trench where Pierre was sitting and sent the earth flying; a little black ball flashed past him and smacked into something soft. The militiamen who were just about to come into the battery ran back.

'Grapeshot! Everybody!' shouted the officer.

The sergeant ran up to the officer and said in a timorous whisper (like a butler informing the dinner host that the wine he wanted has run out) there was nothing left to fire.

'Swine! What do they think they're doing?' shouted the officer, turning to Pierre. Sweat ran down the senior officer's red face. He scowled. There was a glint in his eye. 'Get down to the reserves. Fetch some ammunition-boxes!' he shouted, looking furiously past Pierre at the soldier.

'I'll go,' said Pierre. There was no response from the officer, who was off, striding down to the other end.

'Hold your fire! . . . Wait!' he called.

The soldier who had been told to go for ammunition bumped into Pierre.

'Listen, sir, this is no place for you,' he said as he ran away.

Pierre ran after him, making a detour round the spot where the boy officer was sitting.

A cannonball flew past him, then another, and another; they were raining down on all sides as he charged downhill. 'Where am I going?' he was beginning to wonder, when suddenly he was there beside the green ammunition-boxes. He hesitated – should he run back or go on? Suddenly a terrific bang sent him reeling backwards down to the ground. At the same instant he was dazzled by a great searing flash, and deafened by a terrible hissing sound and a thunderous roar that banged in his ears.

When he came to, Pierre found himself sitting on his bottom resting back on his hands. The ammunition-box that had been at his side had disappeared; all that was left were a few charred green bits of board and some rags littering the scorched grass. A horse was galloping away still attached to some shattered bits of shaft. Another horse lay like Pierre on the ground, letting out prolonged and piercing whinnies.

CHAPTER 32

Out of his mind with terror, Pierre leapt to his feet and ran back up to the battery, the one place where he might be safe from the horrors around him.

As he walked into the redoubt he realized there wasn't any firing from the battery, but there were some men in there busy doing something or other. He could not make out who they were. He caught a quick glimpse of the senior officer slumped over the earth wall with his back towards him, as if he was staring down at something, and he saw another soldier, someone he knew from before, struggling to free himself from some men who were holding him, and yelling 'Brothers! Help me!' And he saw something else that struck him as odd.

The colonel had been killed, the soldier shouting for help was a prisoner, and here at his feet was another soldier bayoneted in the back – but he had no time to take it all in. He had scarcely set foot in the redoubt when a thin man in a blue uniform with a sallow, sweaty face charged at him brandishing a sword and shouting. Pierre's instinct was to ward off the shock as they crashed blindly into each other, so he put out both hands and grabbed the man (it was a French officer) by the shoulder and the throat. The officer dropped his sword and seized Pierre by the scruff of his neck.

For a few seconds they stared with terrified eyes at one another's foreign faces, both of them suddenly unnerved, uncertain what they had done or were going to do next. 'Am I being taken prisoner or am I taking him prisoner?' they were both wondering. But the French officer was clearly more inclined to think he'd been captured, because Pierre's strong hand, an instrument of primitive terror, was tightening its grip on his throat. The Frenchman was trying to say something, when suddenly a cannonball zoomed across viciously low over their heads, and the Frenchman ducked down so sharply he seemed almost to have been decapitated by it.

Pierre had ducked too, and let go of his man. With no further thoughts about who was capturing whom, the Frenchman rushed back inside the battery, and Pierre tore off downhill, tripping over the dead and wounded, who seemed to be catching at his feet.

But before he got to the bottom of the hill he ran into vast hordes of Russian soldiers falling over each other and whooping with glee as they charged up to storm the battery. (This was the famous attack for which Yermolov claimed all the credit, on the grounds that without his courage and good luck this feat of arms would have been impossible, the attack when he is supposed to have scattered the redoubt with George Crosses that he happened to have in his pocket.)

The French, who had taken the battery, now fled, pursued so far beyond the battery by our soldiers, yelling 'Hurrah!', that there was almost no stopping the Russians.

Prisoners were brought down from the battery, including a wounded French general, who was soon surrounded by our officers. Down came a stream of wounded men, some known to Pierre, some not, French and Russian, walking, crawling or carried on stretchers, their faces hideously contorted by pain.

Pierre went back up on to the mound where he had spent more than an hour, and there was no one left from the little family group that had accepted him as one of their own. Dead bodies were everywhere, people he didn't know. But one or two he did know. The little boy officer was still sitting there huddled up against the earth wall in a pool of blood. The ruddy-faced soldier's body was still twitching, but nobody picked him up.

Pierre ran back down the slope.

'Oh, surely they'll stop now. They'll be horrified at what they've done!' he thought, aimlessly following on behind crowds of stretchers moving away from the battlefield.

But the sun stood high in the sky, veiled by a pall of smoke, and ahead of them, especially on the left, over by Semyonovsk, the smoke was alive with movement, and the clamour of cannon and musket, far from dying away, was getting louder, in mounting desperation, like a man in terrible agony putting all his effort into one last scream.

CHAPTER 33

The main action at the battle of Borodino was fought out in the seven-thousand-foot space between Borodino and Bagration's flèches. (Outside this area, there was action on one side by Uvarov's cavalry in the middle of the day, and on the other side, beyond Utitsa, there was a skirmish between Poniatowski and Tuchkov, but these two isolated outbursts were insignificant compared with what was going on in the centre of the battlefield.) The main action was fought out in the simplest, most unsophisticated manner in the open space, visible from both sides, that separated Borodino from the flèches by the wood.

The battle began with a barrage mounted by hundreds of guns on both sides. Then, when the whole plain was covered with smoke, the French brought forward two righthand divisions under Desaix and Compans to attack the flèches, while the Viceroy's regiments advanced on Borodino from the left. The flèches were not much more than half a mile from the Shevardino redoubt, where Napoleon was standing, but Borodino was nearly two miles further away in a straight line, so Napoleon could never have seen what was going on over there, especially with the intermingling of smoke and fog that completely obscured the whole locality. The soldiers of Desaix's division moving in on the flèches remained visible only as far as the hollow between them and their target, where they dropped out of sight, and the smoke from cannon and musket in the flèches became dense enough to screen the whole slope on the far side. Through the smoke you could catch odd glimpses of black shapes likely to be men, and the occasional glint of a bayonet. But from the Shevardino redoubt you could not tell whether they were standing still or moving, or whether they were French or Russian.

The sun was now shining brightly, and its angled rays shone straight on Napoleon's face as he looked over towards the flèches, shielding his eyes with one hand. Smoke wreathed over the ground in front of the flèches; at one moment the smoke itself seemed to move, the next it was the troops who seemed to be moving through the smoke. You might have heard the occasional shout through all the firing, but no one could tell what was going on over there.

Napoleon stood on his mound and peered through a telescope. There in the tiny circle of glass he could see smoke and soldiers, sometimes his own men, sometimes Russians, but when he looked again with the naked eye he could not find the place he had just been looking at. He walked down the mound, and started pacing up and down at the bottom.

From time to time he would stand still, listen carefully to the firing and peer out intently across the battlefield.

It was just not possible to work out what was happening in the flèches, not from down here where he was standing, not from the top of the mound where some of his generals were standing, not even inside the flèches themselves, because they were now constantly changing hands, occupied now by French, now by Russian soldiers, living, dead or wounded, panicking and scared out of their wits. For hours on end this was a scene of incessant cannon- and musket-fire, with control shifting between Russians and French, infantry and cavalry. They surged forward, fell, fired their guns, fought hand to hand, not knowing what to do with each other; all they could do was yell out and run back again.

Adjutants sent out by Napoleon and orderlies dispatched by the marshals were continually galloping in from the field with reports on the progress of the battle, but they were all false, partly because in the heat of battle no one can say what is actually happening at a given moment, partly because many of the adjutants never got to the battle-field as such, all they did was hand on what they had heard from other people, and also because in the time it took for an adjutant to ride the couple of miles that separated him from Napoleon circumstances would have changed, and the news he was bringing was already out of date. Thus an adjutant came galloping in from the Viceroy with news that Borodino had been taken and the bridge over the Kolocha was in French hands. What the adjutant wanted to know from Napoleon was: should the troops cross the bridge? Napoleon sent an order for them to form up on the far side and wait, but even as he issued it, in fact moments after the adjutant had set out from Borodino, the bridge had been retaken by the Russians and burnt down, in the very skirmish Pierre had become involved in first thing that morning.

Another adjutant galloped in ashen-faced and scared stiff from the region of the flèches, bringing word that the attack had been repulsed, Compans was wounded and Davout had been killed, while in actual fact the flèches had been captured by a different French unit just as the adjutant was being told they were lost, and Davout was alive and well except for a bit of bruising. Working on the basis of false reports like these, Napoleon issued a stream of instructions which had either been carried out already, or were not carried out at all, and never could have been.

Napoleon's marshals and generals were nearer the battle scene but, like him, they were not actually involved, and only now and then did they find themselves under fire; these men issued their own instructions without consulting Napoleon, telling people where to stand and what to fire at, where the cavalry should ride and the infantry run. But even these instructions, just like Napoleon's, were almost never followed, and if they were it was only to a tiny extent. More often than not, what happened was the opposite of what had been ordered. Soldiers told to advance would suddenly find themselves under a hail of grape-shot, and come running back. Soldiers told to stand still would suddenly see the Russians right in front of them, and either run away or surge forward, and the cavalry would charge off unbidden to catch up with any running Russians. In this way two cavalry regiments galloped through the Semyonovsk hollow and right up the hill, where they turned round and galloped flat out all the way back again. The same thing applied to the infantry, which was prone to run off in any direction other than the one they were supposed to go in.

All the real instructions – when and where to move the field-guns, when to send the infantry in and tell them to start firing, when to send Russian horses to ride down Russian infantry – all instructions of this kind were issued by officers on the spot, out in the ranks, without consulting Ney, Davout or Murat, let alone Napoleon himself. They were not scared of getting into trouble for disobedience or acting independently, because on the field of war what is at stake is the thing that matters most to any man – the saving of his own skin – and sometimes this means running away, sometimes it means rushing forward, and all those men that found themselves in the thick of the action did what they did on the spur of the moment.

And as it happened, all this rushing to and fro did little to relieve or even affect the position of the troops. All this charging at each other on foot and on horseback didn't do a great deal of harm; the harm, the death and the maiming were caused by cannonballs and bullets flying about all over that open space and men running into them. If ever they managed to get out of the area where balls and bullets were flying about, a superior officer, standing at the rear, would soon bring them back into line, reimpose discipline, and use it to get them back under fire, where once again, scared to death, they would lose all discipline and stampede anywhere on the spur of the moment.

CHAPTER 34

Napoleon's generals, Davout, Ney and Murat, who were situated not far from the field of fire, and even ventured into it once or twice, repeatedly directed vast masses of well-ordered troops back into that area. But, contrary to what had invariably happened in all their previous battles, instead of them duly reporting back that the enemy had been put to flight, the well-ordered masses of troops kept coming back in disorganized, panic-stricken mobs. They were soon brought back into line, but their numbers were dwindling. In the middle of the day Murat sent an adjutant to Napoleon with a request for reinforcements.

Napoleon was sitting at the foot of his mound drinking punch when the adjutant galloped in with a positive assurance that the Russians would be finished if his Majesty would just let them have another division.

'What do you mean reinforcements?' was Napoleon's astonished reaction, and he looked daggers at the adjutant, a handsome young man with a mane of black curly hair not unlike Murat's own locks, as if he could not understand what he was saying. 'Reinforcements!' he was thinking. 'How can they want reinforcements when they've already got half the army ranged against one weak Russian flank that hasn't got any support?'

'Tell the King of Naples,' said Napoleon stiffly, 'that it is still not midday, and I cannot yet see my chess-board clearly. You may go.'

The handsome young man with the curly black mane gave a deep sigh, backed away with one hand to his hat, and galloped off back to the killing field.

Napoleon got to his feet, sent for Caulaincourt and Berthier, and started to chat about things that had nothing to do with the battle.

In mid-conversation, just when Napoleon was getting interested, Berthier's eye was caught by a general galloping over to their redoubt on a steaming horse followed by his entourage. It was Belliard. He got down from his horse, strode rapidly across to the Emperor, and at the top of his voice he began explaining in no uncertain terms the absolute necessity for reinforcements. He gave his word that the Russians would be killed off if the Emperor would just let them have another division.

Napoleon gave a shrug, and continued to pace up and down without giving any answer. Belliard turned to the other generals in his entourage, who were standing round him, and spoke to them eagerly in the same loud voice.

'You're being rather hot-headed, Belliard,' said Napoleon, coming back to speak to his roving general. 'It's too easy to get things wrong in the heat of battle. Go back and have another look, then you can come and talk to me.' Belliard was scarcely out of sight when another messenger came galloping in from the battlefield.

'Well, what do you want?' said Napoleon, with the air of a man thoroughly annoyed by constant pestering.

'Sire, the prince . . .' the adjutant began.

'Wants reinforcements?' growled Napoleon with an angry gesture. The adjutant confirmed this with a nod, and was about to go into detail, but the Emperor turned away, took a couple of steps, stopped, turned back, and called Berthier over. 'The reserves are needed,' he said with a slight spreading of the hands. 'Who shall we send in? What do you think?' he asked Berthier, whom he would later describe as 'that gosling I've turned into an eagle'.

'Claparède's division, sire,' said Berthier, who knew all the divisions, regiments and battalions by heart.

Napoleon nodded in agreement.

An adjutant galloped off to Claparède's division. Within minutes the young guards drawn up behind the redoubt were on the move. Napoleon gazed in their direction without saying a word. Then suddenly he said to Berthier, 'No. I can't send Claparède. Send Friant's division.'

Although there was nothing to be gained by sending Friant's division in preference to Claparède's, and in fact it would now be awkward and time-consuming to bring Claparède to a halt and dispatch Friant, the order was carried out to the letter. Napoleon could not see that as far as his troops were concerned he was acting like a doctor issuing prescriptions that would slow down the patient's progress, a function he knew well and roundly condemned.

Friant's division vanished like the rest into the smoke of the battlefield. Adjutant after adjutant now came galloping in from every side, all with the same message, as if they were working in collusion. They all asked for reinforcements, and they all told the same story: the Russians were sticking to their posts and keeping up a hellish barrage of fire, so bad that the French troops were melting away.

Napoleon sat on a camp-stool, and thought things over.

M. de Bausset, the great traveller, hadn't had a bite to eat since early morning, so he now came over to the Emperor and ventured respectfully to propose a little lunch.

'I was hoping by now to be able to congratulate your Majesty on a victory,' he said.

Napoleon's only response was to shake his head. Taking the negative gesture as a reference to victory rather than lunch, M. de Bausset risked a respectful little joke: surely there was no reason in the world that ought to get in the way of lunch when lunch was at hand.

'Oh, go away,' snapped Napoleon with a dark glare, turning his back on the man. M. de Bausset's face positively glowed with a beatific smile that blended sympathy, regret and delight, as he glided back to the other generals.

Napoleon's heart was sinking, like that of a lucky gambler who has been throwing his money about senselessly and always won, only to find himself more and more certain to lose just at the point when he has carefully calculated all the possibilities and worked out his system.

His men were the same, the generals were the same, the same preparations had been made, the same dispositions, the same 'short and sweet' proclamation, and he was the same – he knew that, he knew he was even more experienced and skilful now than before – and even the enemy was the same as at Austerlitz and Friedland. But the wave of a hand that had once inspired such dread seemed to have been magically deprived of its power.

All the old tactical ploys that always brought success – concentrating his batteries on a single point, use of reserves to break the line, cavalry attack by 'men of iron' – all these had been used, but they weren't bringing victory, and, worse still, the same reports came pouring in from all quarters: generals killed or wounded, the need for reinforcements, the Russians standing their ground and the French troops in disarray.

Hitherto, it had only taken a few words of command, just a sentence or two, for marshals and adjutants to come galloping back with congratulations, radiant faces and stories of trophies captured: entire divisions taken prisoner, sheaves of enemy colours and eagles, cannons and stores, and the only request from Murat was to let the cavalry go and get the baggage-trains. It had been like this at Lodi, Marengo, Arcola, Jena, Austerlitz, Wagram and everywhere else. But now something unusual was happening to his men.

Despite the reported capture of the flèches Napoleon could see that things were definitely not working out as they had done in previous battles. He could see that his own feelings were shared by all the men around him, battle-hardened as they were. Faces were gloomy; eyes were shifty. De Bausset was the only one with no grip on what was happening. With his long experience of war, of course, Napoleon knew full well what it meant for the attacking side not to smell victory after eight hours slogging it out on the field. He knew this was virtually a defeat, and the slightest mischance might now, with the outcome of the battle on a knife-edge, finish him off and his troops with him.

When he let his mind run over the whole of this strange Russian campaign, which hadn't seen a single victory, or a single flag, cannon or corps taken in two solid months, when he looked at the disguised misery on the faces around him, and listened to reports that the Russians were still standing their ground – a kind of nightmare feeling came over him, and his head was filled with all the nasty eventualities that might bring him down. The Russians might attack his left wing, or break through in the centre; he could be killed by a stray cannonball. Anything was possible. In previous battles he had only ever dwelt on successful eventualities; now a vast number of nasty eventualities loomed before him, and he expected them all to happen. Yes, it was just like a nightmare in which a man dreams he is being attacked and in his sleep he lashes out with one arm and hits his assailant with the kind of force he knows is bound to flatten him, only to feel his arm go dead and flop down as limp as a rag, leaving him helpless before the inexorable, horrible hand of death.

The news that the Russians were indeed attacking the left flank of the French army gave Napoleon a taste of that very horror. He sat there on his camp-stool at the bottom of the mound, elbows on knees, with his head in his hands, saying nothing. Berthier came over and proposed a ride down the line to take stock of the position.

'What's that? What did you say?' said Napoleon. 'Yes, tell them to bring my horse.' He mounted the horse and rode off in the direction of Semyonovsk.

In the slowly thinning powder-smoke which hung over all the terrain that Napoleon was now riding through, horses and men, singly and in heaps, were lying around in pools of blood. Neither Napoleon nor any of his generals had ever seen horror on this scale, so many men killed in such a small space. The roar of the big guns that had not stopped for ten hours was so excruciating it gave a new meaning to the whole spectacle (like the music that accompanies *tableaux vivants*). Napoleon rode up to the high ground at Semyonovsk, and through the smoke he could just make out ranks of soldiers in uniforms of colours he was not used to seeing. They were the Russians.

The Russians stood in serried ranks just beyond Semyonovsk village and the redoubt, and all down their lines their guns thundered and smoked without end. It was not a battle now; it was just a long-drawn-out massacre, of no conceivable benefit to either side. Napoleon reined in his horse, and sank back into the pensive mood that Berthier had just shaken him out of. He had no power to stop this thing that was being enacted before his eyes and on every side, even though he was supposed to be in charge of it and it was supposed to depend on him, and now for the first time, following the experience of failure, it all seemed so futile and horrible.

A general rode up and took the liberty of making a suggestion: Napoleon should send in the old guard. Ney and Berthier were standing close by, and they looked at each other with withering smiles to hear such a reckless suggestion coming from a general.

Napoleon looked down, and sat there for some time without saying a word.

'Here we are eight hundred leagues from France, and I'm not having my guard torn to pieces,' he said at last, wheeling his horse round, and he set off back to Shevardino.

CHAPTER 35

Kutuzov sat on the same rug-covered bench where Pierre had seen him that morning, with his grey head slumped on his chest and his big heavy body sprawling. He was not giving any orders; all he did was say yes or no to suggestions.

'Yes, yes, you do that,' he would say when various proposals were made. 'Yes, yes, dear boy, you go over there and have a look,' he would respond to one or other of the nearby adjutants, or, 'No, don't, we'd better wait.' He listened to reports as they came in and responded to any requests for instructions from his subordinates, but as he listened he didn't seem very committed to what was being said; he seemed more interested in some aspect of the speaker's facial expression or tone of voice. Long years of military experience, confirmed by the wisdom of old age, had told him that one person cannot control hundreds of thousands of men fighting to the death, and he knew that the fate of battles is not decided by orders from the commander-in-chief, nor by the stationing of troops, nor the number of cannons or enemies killed, it is decided by a mysterious force known as the 'spirit of the army', and his lot was to keep track of that force and direct it as best he could.

The general impression conveyed by Kutuzov's face was one of quiet but intense concentration, just strong enough to overcome the feebleness of his ageing body.

At eleven o'clock a report came in that the French had been driven back out of the flèches they had taken, but Bagration had been wounded. Kutuzov gave a groan and shook his head.

'Ride over to Prince Bagration and find out what's what,' he said to an adjutant, and then turned to the Prince of Württemberg, who was standing behind him, and said, 'Would your Highness mind taking charge of the First Army?'

Very soon after the prince's departure – he could not have got as far as Semyonovsk – his adjutant came back to Kutuzov with a request for more troops.

Kutuzov frowned, and sent orders for Dokhturov to take the charge of the First Army, and for the prince to come back because he could not do without him when things were so fraught. News came in that Murat had been taken prisoner, and the staff-officers gathered round with congratulations, but Kutuzov merely smiled.

'Hold on, gentlemen,' he said. 'The battle is won, and taking Murat prisoner is nothing out of the ordinary. But we must delay our celebrations.' Nevertheless he dispatched an adjutant to take the news round the troops.

When Shcherbinin galloped in from the left flank to report that the French had taken the flèches and Semyonovsk, Kutuzov could sense the bad news in advance from the sounds coming from the battlefield and the look on Shcherbinin's face, so he got to his feet as if he wanted to stretch his legs, took Shcherbinin by the arm and drew him to one side.

'Go on down, dear boy,' he said to Yermolov, 'and see whether anything can be done.'

Kutuzov was in Gorki, the centre of the Russian position. Napoleon's attack on our left flank had been beaten back several times. In the centre the French never advanced beyond Borodino. And on the left flank Uvarov's cavalry had put the French to flight.

Not long after two o'clock the French attacks ceased. As he read the faces of men who had ridden back from the battlefield, and those around him, Kutuzov could see nothing but the tense expressions of men strained to the limit. He was satisfied; the day had succeeded beyond his expectations. But the old man's physical strength was being sapped. His head was drooping; soon he was nodding and dropping off to sleep. They brought him some dinner.

Adjutant-General Wolzogen, the man whom Prince Andrey had overheard saying that the war ought to be 'conducted over a very wide area' and whom Bagration could not stand, rode up to Kutuzov while he was eating. Wolzogen had come from Barclay de Tolly to report recent developments on the left flank. Barclay was a sensible man, and when he saw hordes of men running back wounded and the Russian ranks in disarray he weighed things up and decided the battle was lost. He then sent his favourite adjutant to go and tell the commander-in-chief.

Kutuzov was having a bit of trouble with a mouthful of chicken, but his wincing eyes looked rather more cheerful now, as he glanced up at Wolzogen.

Wolzogen walked over to Kutuzov with an air of nonchalance and a slightly insolent smile on his face. His saluting hand barely touched his cap.

He treated his Serene Highness with an affected touch of off-handedness, intended to demonstrate that he, a highly trained military man, was prepared to let the Russians idolize a useless old codger like this, but he knew the measure of his man. 'The old gentleman' (as Wolzogen's German circle always called Kutuzov) 'is not doing too badly for himself,' he thought, and with a pointed glare at the dishes laid out before Kutuzov he launched into his report on the present situation along the left front, giving the old gentleman Barclay's version of events and also what he himself had seen and assimilated. 'Our position is in enemy hands at every point, and we cannot counterattack because there aren't enough troops to do it. The men are running away and there's no stopping them,' he submitted.

Kutuzov stopped chewing and stared at Wolzogen in amazement, as if he could not understand what he was saying. Wolzogen noticed the old gentleman's agitation and went on with a smile:

'I felt I had no right to conceal from your Highness what I have seen . . . The troops are all over the place . . .'

'Seen? What you have seen? . . .' said Kutuzov with a scowl, getting rapidly to his feet and marching up close to Wolzogen. 'How . . . how dare you! . . .' he fulminated, choking with emotion and making threatening gestures with his trembling hands. 'How dare you, sir, say that to *me*? You know nothing. Tell General Barclay from me that his information is wrong, and that I as commander-in-chief know more about the real course of the battle than he does.'

Wolzogen made as if to protest, but Kutuzov cut him short.

'The enemy has been halted on the left flank and defeated on the right. If you have been looking in the wrong place, sir, do not allow yourself to talk about things you do not understand. Kindly return to General Barclay and inform him of my utter determination to attack the French tomorrow,' said Kutuzov sternly.

There was complete silence, broken only by the heavy wheezing and gasping of the old general. 'They have been repulsed at all points, for which I thank God and our brave men. The enemy is defeated, and tomorrow we shall drive him from the sacred soil of Russia!' said Kutuzov, crossing himself, and he gave a sudden shuddering sob through rising tears.

Wolzogen gave a shrug, pursed his lips and walked away in silence, marvelling at the old gentleman's stubbornness.

'Ah, here he is. This is my hero!' said Kutuzov as a rather corpulent, handsome, black-haired general came walking up the hillside. It was Rayevsky, who had spent the whole day in the key position during the battle.

Rayevsky reported that the men were staunchly standing their ground, and the French dared not mount another attack.

Kutuzov listened to what he had to say and then asked him in French, 'So, *unlike the others*, you do not think we are now obliged to retreat?'

'On the contrary, your Highness, when matters are undecided it is always the most determined who come through to victory,' answered Rayevsky; 'and it is my belief . . .' 'Kaysarov!' Kutuzov called to his adjutant. 'Sit down and write tomorrow's order for the day. And you,' he said, turning to another, 'ride down the line and tell them tomorrow we attack.'

While Kutuzov was talking to Rayevsky and dictating the order Wolzogen came back from Barclay and announced that General Barclay de Tolly would like to have written confirmation of the order issued by the field-marshal.

Without looking at Wolzogen, Kutuzov ordered an adjutant to write down the order, which the former commander-in-chief was justified in asking for in order to avoid all personal responsibility.

And through that mysterious, indefinable bond that maintains morale across an entire army, the very 'spirit of the army' and its nerve-centre in time of war, Kutuzov's words, his order for them to go into battle again next day, were instantly flashed from one end of the army to the other.

The words themselves, the phrasing of the order, were by no means the same when they got out to the last links in the chain. The stories that went from mouth to mouth in the outer reaches of the army bore no resemblance to what Kutuzov had actually said, but the sense of his words penetrated everywhere, because what Kutuzov had said was not the result of subtle thought and long consideration, but a surge of emotion that lay deep in the heart of the commander-in-chief, and deep in the heart of every Russian.

And hearing the word – tomorrow we attack the enemy – together with confirmation from the highest spheres of the army of what they most wanted to believe, exhausted men whose courage had been faltering felt a sense of relief and new inspiration.

CHAPTER 36

Prince Andrey's regiment was among the reserves, which were kept back behind Semyonovsk completely inactive and under heavy artillery fire until going on for two o'clock. Then the regiment, which had already lost more than two hundred men, was moved forward into a trampled field of oats in the area between Semyonovsk and the Rayevsky redoubt, where thousands of men were to fall during the day. At that very time, just before two, the concentrated fire from hundreds of enemy guns was actually being intensified in this area.

Without moving an inch or firing a shot the regiment lost another third of its men on this spot. Ahead of them, especially over to the right, the cannons boomed away through the never-thinning smoke, and from the mysterious pall that blanketed all the countryside up front came an unending stream of hurtling, hissing cannonballs, and grenades, which whizzed across more slowly. Sometimes there was a kind of breathing space for a quarter of an hour when all the cannonballs and grenades overshot them, but sometimes it took less than a minute for several men to be torn down, and we were for ever dragging away the dead and carrying off the wounded.

With every new hit the chances of staying alive grew less and less for anyone not yet killed. The regiment was split into battalion columns three hundred paces apart. It made no difference; morale was the same all over the regiment. All the men were the same: miserable and silent. There wasn't much talking in the ranks, and what talking there was soon stopped when the next big bang came and the call of 'Stretcher!' Most of the time the men followed their orders and just sat there on the ground. One man would take off his shako, loosen the gathers and tie them up again; another would crumble up some dry clay to clean his bayonet; another would adjust a buckle or tighten a strap on his shoulder-belt; someone else would re-roll his leg bandages with infinite care and pull his boots back on again. Some men built tiny houses out of clods of earth, or plaited together stubble straw. They all seemed thoroughly engrossed in what they were doing. When men got killed or wounded, when stretchers were dragged past, when our troops started coming back, when massed ranks of the enemy suddenly appeared through the smoke, all these developments were completely ignored. Whenever our artillery or cavalry moved forward or the infantry was on the move, encouraging noises came from all sides. But quite the most interesting things were incidental events that had nothing to do with the battle. It was as if these morally exhausted men could find some relief in the ordinary events of everyday life. An artillery battery trundled across in front of their line. A horse pulling an ammunition cart had got one leg outside the traces.

'Hey! Watch that trace-horse! . . . Get her leg out! She'll go down! . . . Look! They haven't seen it!' A great cry rose from all the ranks.

Another time everybody homed in on a small brown dog with a stiff little tail, which had sprung out of nowhere and was fussing around, trotting up and down in front of the ranks. Suddenly a cannonball fell near by, and it yelped and ran off with its tail between its legs. The whole regiment came alive with yells and shrieks of laughter. But these distractions lasted no more than a minute, and the men had been eight hours with no food and nothing to do, in constant fear of death, and their pale and haggard faces grew paler and more haggard.

Prince Andrey, haggard and pale like everybody else in the regiment, paced the meadow next to the field of oats from one boundary-ditch to the next with his hands behind his back and his eyes on the ground. He had no orders to give and nothing to do. Everything took care of itself. The dead were dragged back behind the line, the wounded were carried away, and the ranks closed up. If any soldiers ran away they soon doubled back. At first Prince Andrey had felt duty-bound to keep his men's spirits up and set an example, so he walked the ranks, but it wasn't long before he realized he had nothing to teach them. All his energy, like every soldier's, was instinctively concentrated on distracting himself from the horror of his situation. He paced the meadow, dragging his feet and rustling through the grass, and he watched the dust thickening on his boots. First he would lengthen his stride and try to follow in the footsteps left behind by the mowers, then he would count his steps and work out how many times he would have to walk from one ditch to another to cover half a mile; or he would strip the flowers from some wormwood growing in the ditch, rub them in his palms and sniff the acrid, bitter-sweet scent. Of yesterday's thoughts not a trace remained. His mind was blank. Wearily he listened to the all too familiar sounds, the whine of the shells so different from the booming of the guns, he glanced at the faces of the men of the first battalion that he had seen a thousand times before, and waited. 'Here she comes. This one's for us!' he thought, listening closely as something whistled over from the hidden region of the smoke. 'One! Two! Here come some more! That one's down . . .' He stopped short and glanced down the ranks. 'No, it must have gone over. Oh, that one *is* down!' And he set off for another walk, lengthening his pace to try and get to the ditch in sixteen strides.

A whistling sound followed by a thud! Five paces away a cannon-ball smacked into the dry soil and buried itself. A chill ran down his back. Again he glanced down the ranks. That one could have got quite a few of them; there was a bunch of men along by the second battalion.

'Mr Adjutant!' he shouted. 'Tell them not to stand too close together!'

The adjutant did as instructed and started to walk over towards Prince Andrey. From the other side a battalion commander came riding up.

'Look out!' yelled a terrified soldier as a grenade came over like a little bird zooming down with whirring wings on the look-out for a landing place, and plopped down with a dull thud next to the major's horse a couple of paces away from Prince Andrey. The horse was the first to move. Unconcerned about the rights and wrongs of showing fear, it gave a snort, reared up, almost throwing the major and galloped away. The men latched on to the horse's terror.

'Get down!' yelled the adjutant, flinging himself to the ground. Prince Andrey hesitated. The smoking shell was spinning like a top between him and the prostrate adjutant, near a clump of wormwood growing in the ditch between meadow and field.

'Is this death then?' Prince Andrey wondered, and he was swept by a new sense of longing as he gazed down at the grass, the wormwood and the spiral of smoke swirling up from the spinning ball. 'I can't die. I don't want to die. I love life. I love this grass, the earth, the air . . .'

These thoughts flashed through his mind, though he was still aware that eyes were on him.

'Shame on you, Mr Adjutant!' he called to the officer. 'What kind of . . .' But he didn't finish. In one terrific bang shrapnel flew like matchwood with an overwhelming smell of gunpowder and Prince Andrey was sent flying to one side with one arm in the air, and he fell to the ground face-down.

Several officers ran up. He was bleeding from the stomach on the right-hand side, and a great stain was oozing out all over the grass.

The militiamen were called over and they stood there behind the officers holding a stretcher. Prince Andrey lay on his chest with his face buried in the grass, gasping as he struggled for air.

'Don't just stand there! Come on!'

The peasants came up and got hold of him by the shoulders and feet, but he gave such a terrible cry they looked at each other and put him down again.

'Pick him up! Get him on the stretcher. You can't do any harm!' yelled a voice. They lifted him by the shoulders again and put him on the stretcher.

'Oh, my God! My God! What's happened to him? . . . Stomach! . . . He's had it! Oh, my God!' came the officers' voices.

'Went right past my ear,' the adjutant was saying.

The peasants settled the stretcher across their shoulders and hurried off to the dressing station down the path that they had trampled flat.

'Get in step! . . . Blast these peasants!' cried an officer, grabbing them by the shoulders as they bumbled along, jolting the stretcher.

'Get it right, Fyodor. 'Ow be 'e?' said the leading peasant.

'Got 'e now!' said the one at the back, delighted with himself as he fell into step.

'Your Excellency! Prince! Are you all right, sir?' came the trembling voice of Timokhin as he ran up and peeped over the stretcher.

Prince Andrey opened his eyes and looked up at the speaker from deep in the stretcher where his head had sunk down, but his eyelids soon closed again.

The militiamen carried Prince Andrey to the dressing station at the edge of a wood, where there were wagons waiting. The station – three tents with their flaps turned back – stood under a few birch-trees. Just inside the wood were the wagons and horses. The horses were munching oats in their nose-bags and sparrows kept swooping down to pick up any dropped grains. One or two crows, scenting blood, cawed impatiently as they flitted about among the birch-trees. Tents were spread out over four or five acres, with bloodstained men outside them, lying on the grass, standing up or sitting around, dressed in all kinds of clothing. They were surrounded by hordes of long-faced stretcher-bearers who were watching carefully. In the interests of good order the officers kept shooing them away, but it was no good. The soldiers ignored them and stood there leaning on their stretchers with a close eye on what was happening under their noses, as if it might help them fathom the difficult meaning of this spectacle. From inside the tents came a variety of sounds, from wild and angry screaming to heart-rending moans and groans. Now and then dressers would come rushing out to get water and say who was next. The wounded men stood in line by the tent, gasping for breath, moaning, weeping, yelling and cursing, or asking for vodka. Some were delirious. Prince Andrey, a colonel no less, was whisked through the crowd waiting for treatment and taken straight to one of the tents, where his bearers stopped, awaiting instructions. Prince Andrey opened his eyes and for some time could not make out what was happening around him. The meadow, the wormwood, the whirling black ball, and that deep surge of love for life all flashed again through his mind. A couple of paces away stood a tall, handsome, dark-haired sergeant with a bandage round his head, leaning against a branch. He had bullet-wounds to the head and leg, and his loud voice made him the centre of attention. Quite a crowd of wounded men and stretcher-bearers had gathered round him, hanging on his words.

'Give 'im a right thumpin', we did. 'E soon packed it in. Got the king 'imself, we did,' the soldier was shouting, glaring round with a feverish glint in his black eyes. 'If only them preserves had got there in time, old boy, there wouldn't have been nothin' left of 'im. God's truth, I'm telling you . . .'

Prince Andrey was no different from all the other bystanders; he gazed across at him with shining eyes, and felt some relief. 'But it doesn't make any difference now, does it?' he thought. 'What will it be like over there – and what's it been like down here? Why did I feel so sorry to let go of life? There's been something in this life I never understood, and still don't.'

CHAPTER 37

A doctor in a bloodstained apron came out of the tent, holding a cigar between the thumb and little finger of one of his bloodstained hands to keep the blood off it. He threw his head back and had a good look round over the heads of the wounded men. He obviously wanted a short break. He spent a few minutes turning his head right and left, after which he gave a sigh and looked down again.

'Come on, then,' he said to a dresser who was pointing to Prince Andrey, and told the bearers to bring him into the tent.

A murmur ran through the waiting wounded.

'Oh yes, posh people first. Just the same up in heaven,' said one.

Prince Andrey was carried in and laid on a recently vacated table that had just been washed down by an assistant. He could not see anything very clearly inside the tent, distracted as he was by pathetic groans coming from every side and the excruciating pain in his thigh, his stomach, and his back. Everything he saw blended into a single overall impression of naked, bloodstained human flesh, which seemed to fill the low tent in the way that naked human flesh had filled that dirty pond on the Smolensk road a few weeks before on a hot day in August. Yes, it was the same flesh, the same cannon-fodder, the sight of which had horrified him then, perhaps as a portent of things to come.

There were three tables in the tent. Two were occupied; Prince Andrey was laid on the third. For some time he was left alone with no choice but to watch what was happening on the other two tables. On the nearest one sat a Tatar, most likely a Cossack, going by the uniform thrown down at his side. Four soldiers were holding him down while a doctor in spectacles cut into his muscular brown back.

'Ugh! Ow! Ouch!' the Tatar grunted, and then with a sudden upward jerk of his broad, swarthy, sunburnt face he bared his white teeth and started writhing convulsively, his cries building up into one long ringing, piercing scream. On the other table, which had a lot of people standing round it, a big, well-built man lay supine with his head flung back. There was something about the colour of the curls and the shape of the head that seemed strangely familiar to Prince Andrey. Several of the dressers were holding him tight and bearing down on his chest. One of his big chubby white legs was constantly on the move, jerking convulsively all over the place. This man was a shuddering mass, sobbing and choking. Two doctors, one of them pale and trembling, were working silently on the other, gory leg. The doctor in spectacles finished dealing with the Tatar, who soon had a coat thrown round him, and came over to Prince Andrey, wiping his hands.

He took one glance at his face and quickly turned away.

'Don't just stand there. Get him undressed!' he roared at the dresser.

His earliest, remotest recollections of childhood came back to Prince Andrey as the dresser, with his sleeves rolled-up, moved quickly to undo his buttons and take off his clothes. The doctor bent down over the wound, probed it, and gave a deep sigh. Then he signalled to somebody. And the terrible agony in his stomach made Prince Andrey lose consciousness. When he came round, the broken splinters of his thigh-bone had been removed, the bits of torn flesh cut away, and the wound bandaged. Water was sprinkled on his face. Just as Prince Andrey opened his eyes the doctor bent over him, kissed him on the lips without saying anything, and hurried away.

After all the pain he had endured Prince Andrey now felt blissfully at peace; he had not felt like this for a very long time. The nicest and happiest moments of his life, especially his earliest childhood, when he had been undressed and put to bed, and his nurse had sung lullabies over him, and he had burrowed down under the pillows feeling happy just to be alive, floated through his imagination, and instead of seeming like past events they seemed like the here and now.

The other doctors were still working on the wounded man whose head had struck Prince Andrey as somehow familiar; they were lifting him now and trying to calm him down.

'Show me ... Oh! Ooh! ... Oooh!' The man was scared stiff, moaning in agony and racked with sobs. These moaning sounds made Prince Andrey feel like crying too. Whether it was because he was dying an inglorious death, or because he was sorry to let go of life, or because of the memories of his lost childhood, or because he was in pain, and many others were too, and this man was moaning so pathetically, he wanted to cry, to break down like a child in tears of innocence and something near to happiness.

They showed the wounded man his amputated leg, still wearing its boot and covered with coagulated blood.

'Oh! Oo-ooh!' He was sobbing like a woman. The doctor who had been standing beside him, blocking the view, now moved away.

'My God! What's all this? What's *he* doing here?' Prince Andrey wondered.

He knew this wreck of a man who was moaning so pathetically, the poor devil who had just had his leg off: it was Anatole Kuragin. It was Anatole who was being propped up and encouraged to have a drink of water, though his trembling, swollen lips could not get a hold on the rim of the glass. Anatole took a deep breath, gagging and sobbing. 'Yes, it's him. Yes, and that man is somehow connected with me, closely and painfully connected,' thought Prince Andrey, with no clear grasp of what he was looking at. 'What kind of contact is there between that man and my childhood, my life?' he wondered, and could find no answer. And suddenly another unexpected memory from that childhood world of innocence and love flashed through his mind. He remembered Natasha as he had seen her for the first time at the ball in 1810, with her slender neck and slender arms, and her startled, happy face, so eager for ecstatic pleasure, and in his heart he felt a pang of love and tenderness stronger and deeper than ever before. Now he recalled the point of contact between him and this man who was peering vaguely across at him through tears welling up in his swollen eyes. Everything came back to him, and his heart filled with a blissful surge of passionate pity and love for this man.

It was all too much for Prince Andrey; he broke down in tears of love and tenderness for his fellow men, himself, his own silly misdoings and everybody else's. 'Sympathy and love, for our brothers, those who love us and those who hate us, for our enemies. Yes, the kind of that love God preached on earth, that Marie told me about and I could not understand – that's why I was so sorry to let go of life, that's what would have been left for me if I had lived. But now it's too late. I know it is.'

CHAPTER 38

The ghastly sight of a battlefield littered with corpses and wounded men, together with the feeling of heaviness in his head, the news that a score of generals known to him personally were among the dead or wounded, and the knowledge that his once mighty army had lost its power, all of this had a curious effect on Napoleon, who was usually not averse to surveying the dead and wounded, because (he imagined) it showed his dauntless spirit. This time the horror of the battlefield was too much for his dauntless spirit, which he had always looked on as a virtue and his greatest claim to fame. He was quick to leave the battlefield and head back to Shevardino. There, he sat down on a camp-stool with his heavy face all yellow and puffy, his eyes dim, his nose red, and his voice hoarse, looking down but forced to listen to the sounds of battle. Feeling sick at heart, he was waiting for the action to end, convinced he had started the whole thing off and now he could not stop it. For one brief moment personal, human feelings won out over the artificial apology for a life that he had been leading for such a long time. He gave himself up to the agony and death he had seen on the battlefield. The heaviness in his head and chest delivered a sharp reminder of his own vulnerability to agony and death. At that moment he didn't want Moscow, victory or glory. (Why would he need any more glory?) All he wanted was to be left alone in peace and quiet. But when he had been on the high ground above Semyonovsk the artillery commander had asked permission to take several batteries up there in order to increase fire on the masses of Russian troops just outside Knyazkovo. Napoleon had agreed, and told them to let him know whether these batteries had any effect. Now here was an adjutant reporting that the Emperor's orders had been carried out, two hundred guns had been directed at the Russians, and they were still standing their ground.

'Our fire is mowing them down in rows, but they won't budge,' said the adjutant.

'They want more!' said Napoleon in his husky voice.

'Sire?' repeated the adjutant, who had missed what he said.

'They want more!' Napoleon croaked hoarsely, with a scowl. 'Give them more.'

As things stood, without any orders from him, what he wanted done was being done, and he carried on issuing instructions simply because he thought it was expected of him. And back he went once again into his old world of artificiality with its fantasies of greatness, and once again (like a horse on a treadmill that thinks it's doing something for itself) he humbly resumed the cruel, unhappy, burdensome, inhuman role that was his destiny.

And this would not be the only hour or day of his life when darkness afflicted the mind and conscience of this man, who had assumed more responsibility for what was going on than any other participant, though he never, to the end of his days, had the slightest understanding of goodness, beauty, truth or the significance of his own deeds, which were too far removed from truth and goodness, too remote from anything human for him to be able to grasp their significance. Unable to renounce his own deeds, which were highly praised by half the world, he was forced to repudiate truth, goodness and everything human.

As he had ridden round the edge of the battlefield piled with corpses and mutilated men (the product of his will, as he saw things) he had taken a good look at all these men, and this would not be the only day of his life when he tried to work out how many Russians had fallen for every Frenchman; he took great pleasure in deceiving himself with the false belief that there were five Russians for every Frenchman. This would not be the only occasion in his life that he wrote a letter to Paris describing the battlefield as 'superb' because there were fifty thousand corpses on it. Even on the island of St Helena, in the peace and solitude where he said he intended to devote his leisure to an account of the great things he had achieved, he would one day write:

The Russian war should have been the most popular war of modern times: it was a war of good sense and tangible benefit fought for the peace and security of all; it was purely pacific and conservationist.

It was fought for a great cause, the end of uncertainty and the beginning of security. A new horizon, new labours were to unfold, bringing nothing but welfare and prosperity for all. The European system had already been established; all that remained was to organize it.

Satisfied on these great points and at peace on all sides, I too might have had my Congress and Holy Alliance – ideas that were stolen from me. In this assembly of great sovereigns we would have been able to talk over our interests like members of one family and make ourselves accountable to our peoples like clerks reporting to their masters.

In this way Europe would soon have come to be truly a single people, and everyone who travelled around would always have found himself in one common fatherland. They would have insisted that all rivers be open to everyone, and the seas common to all, and the great standing armies reduced henceforth simply to the role of royal bodyguards.

Back in France, in the bosom of the great, strong, magnificent, peaceful and glorious fatherland, I would have declared its frontiers immutable, any future war purely *defensive*, and any further aggrandizement *anti-national*. I would have involved my son in the Empire, my *dictatorship* would have been at an end, and his constitutional reign would have begun . . .

Paris would have been the capital of the world, and the French the envy of the nations! . . .

My leisure and my declining years would then have been devoted, in company with the Empress and during the royal apprenticeship of my son, to taking our own horses, like a real couple from the country, on a leisurely tour of every corner of the Empire, receiving complaints, redressing wrongs and scattering monuments and great works on every side.

This man, predestined by Providence for the unhappy, involuntary role of butcher of nations, actually convinced himself that the motivation behind his deeds had been the welfare of nations, and that he could control the destinies of millions, and bring them benefits by the exercise of power. Subsequently he wrote as follows about the Russian war:

Of the four hundred thousand men who crossed the Vistula, half were Austrians, Prussians, Saxons, Poles, Bavarians, Württembergers, Mecklenburgers, Spaniards, Italians, Neapolitans. The Imperial Army, which lived up to its name, was one-third composed of Dutch, Belgians, inhabitants of the Rhineland, Piedmontese, Swiss, Genevese, Tuscans, Romans, inhabitants of the Thirty-second military division, of Bremen, Hamburg, etc. It included barely a hundred and forty thousand French-speakers. The Russian expedition cost France itself less than fifty thousand men. In the various battles during the retreat from Vilna to Moscow the Russian army lost four times as many men as the French army. The burning of Moscow cost the lives of one hundred thousand Russians, who died of cold and hunger in the forests; and finally, in its march from Moscow to the Oder, the Russian army also suffered the inclemency of the season: it numbered no more than fifty thousand men on reaching Vilna, and less than eighteen thousand at Kalisch.

He really imagined that the war with Russia had come about by his will, and the horror of what was done left no impression on his soul. He boldly assumed full responsibility for what had occurred, and in his darkened mind found justification in the fact that of the men who perished in their hundreds of thousands there were fewer Frenchmen than Hessians and Bavarians.

CHAPTER 39

Tens of thousands of men lay dead in various attitudes and different uniforms all over the fields and meadows belonging to the Davydov family and a few crown serfs, fields and meadows where for hundreds of years the peasants of Borodino, Gorki, Shevardino and Semyonovsk had harvested their crops and grazed their cattle. For a couple of acres around the dressing-stations the grass and earth were soaked with blood. Hordes of scared-looking men of various allegiances, wounded and unwounded, were shambling away from the scene, back to Mozhaysk on one side, on the other back to Valuyevo. Other hordes, weary and famished, were being led forward by their officers. There were others too who still stood their ground and had not stopped firing.

The whole plain, which had looked so lovely and bright earlier in the day with all those puffs of smoke and the bayonets glinting in the morning sunshine, was now shrouded in a cloud of dark, damp mist and smoke reeking with the strange, pungent smell of saltpetre and blood. One or two dark clouds had come up, and a fine drizzle was sprinkling the dead, the wounded, the fearful, the weary and the wavering. 'Good people, that's enough,' it seemed to say. 'Stop and think. What are you doing?'

The men on both sides, exhausted and in need of food and rest, began to have the same kind of doubts about whether they should go on slaughtering each other; hesitation was written on every face, and in every soul the same question asked itself: 'Why – for whose benefit – should I kill and be killed? Go on, kill who you want, do what you want – I've had enough!' By late afternoon this same thought had dawned on every spirit there. Any minute now all of these men might suddenly see the horror of what they were doing, pack it in and run off anywhere.

But even though the battle was nearing its end and the men could sense all the horror of their actions, even though they would have been glad to stop, they were still in the grip of an inexplicable, mysterious force which kept the surviving gunners – they were down to one in three – running with sweat, filthy with powder and blood, stumbling about and gasping with exhaustion, as they went on bringing up charges, loading the guns, taking aim and lighting the fuses, so that the cannonballs, as fast and as vicious as ever, flew across from both sides to splatter human flesh, keeping the whole ghastly business going – not by the will of man, but by the will of the one who governs men and worlds.

Anyone looking at the disarrayed rear of the Russian army would have said that with one last push from the French the Russian army would have been done for, but anyone looking at the rear of the French army would have said that one last push from the Russians would have finished off the French army. Neither French nor Russians mounted that last push, and the flame of battle burnt slowly down.

The Russians never made the push because they were not attacking the French. At the start of hostilities all they had done was stand across the Moscow road, blocking it off to the French; and here they were at the end of the battle standing their ground just as they had done at the beginning. But even if it had been the aim of the Russians to drive the French back, they could never have mounted this final push, because the Russian troops were shattered, no part of the army had avoided losses during the battle, and the Russians, by standing their ground, had lost *one half* of their entire army.

As for the French – with fifteen years of military success behind them, confident of Napoleon's invincibility, happy in the knowledge that they had taken part of the battlefield without losing more than a quarter of their men, and still with a reserve of twenty thousand untouched guardsmen – they could have made this last push with something to spare. The French had attacked the Russian army with the aim of displacing it, and they ought to have made this last push, because, while ever the Russians continued to bar the way to Moscow, their aim had not been achieved, and all their efforts and losses had been in vain. But they did not. Some historians claim that all Napoleon had to do was send in the old guard, and victory would have been assured. To talk about what might have happened if Napoleon had sent his guard in is to talk about spring coming in autumn. It could never have happened. It wasn't a case of Napoleon choosing not to send the guards in; he could not possibly have done so. Every general, officer and man in the French army knew it could not be done, because the spirit of the army had failed and wouldn't allow it.

Napoleon wasn't alone in his nightmare sensation of a mighty arm losing its power; every general, every soldier in the French army, combatants and non-combatants, with all their experience of previous battles (when they had made only one-tenth of the present effort but the enemy had always run away), was equally horrified to encounter an enemy that could lose *one half* of its strength and still stand its ground with undiminished ferocity. The morale of the attacking French army had been sapped. The victory that was won was not marked by the capture of a few tattered rags on sticks called colours, or by measuring the ground where the troops stood before and after;

it was a moral victory – the kind that forces the enemy to acknowledge the moral superiority of his opponent, and his own impotence – and at Borodino that victory was won by the Russians. The French invaders were like a mortally wounded ravening beast that knew its end was near, though it couldn't stop, any more than the Russian army, half as strong, could have helped giving way. The French army still had just enough impetus to struggle on to Moscow, but there, with no new challenge from the Russian army, it was bound to perish, bleeding to death from the wound sustained at Borodino. The direct consequences of the battle of Borodino were these: Napoleon's unprovoked flight from Moscow, his return down the old Smolensk road, the destruction of his five-hundred-thousand-strong invading force, and the collapse of Napoleonic rule in France, a country on which, at Borodino, for the very first time, the hand of an opponent stronger in spirit had been laid.

PART III

For the human mind absolute continuity of motion is inconceivable. The laws behind any motion become comprehensible to man only when he breaks that motion down into arbitrarily selected units and subjects these to examination. But at the same time this arbitrary sub-division of continuous motion into discontinuous units is the cause of much human error.

We all know the fallacy (a 'sophism' to the ancients) whereby a tortoise that has a start on Achilles will never be caught up by him, even though Achilles is walking ten times faster than the tortoise. While Achilles is busy covering a certain distance between him and the tortoise, the tortoise leading the way will have covered another one-tenth of that distance. Achilles covers that tenth, by which time the tortoise has covered another hundredth, and so on ad infinitum. This problem was considered by the ancients to have no solution. The absurdity of the conclusion (that Achilles will never overtake the tortoise) arises from the arbitrary decision to sub-divide the motion into discrete units, whereas the motion of both Achilles and the tortoise was continuous.

By adopting smaller and smaller units of motion all we do is get closer and closer to a solution to the problem without ever reaching it. Only by allowing for an infinitely small quantity and a progression rising from it up to a tenth, and by taking the sum of that geometrical progression, can we arrive at a solution of this problem. A new branch of mathematics taking account of infinitely small quantities can now consider other more complex problems of motion and provide solutions to problems that once seemed insoluble. When applied to these problems of motion, this new branch of mathematics (unknown to the ancients) allows for infinitely small quantities and by doing so creates the basic condition of motion – absolute continuity – thus correcting the inevitable mistake that the human intellect is bound to make when it rejects continuous motion in favour of discrete units of motion.

In the search for laws of historical movement exactly the same thing occurs.

The movement of humanity, arising from a countless series of actions arbitrarily performed by many individuals, is a continuous phenomenon.

The aim of history is to work out what laws lie behind this movement. But in its attempt to establish the laws behind the continuous movement that arises from all those arbitrary individual actions taken together, the human mind accepts a sub-division into arbitrarily determined discrete units. The first thing history does is to take an arbitrary series of continuous events and examine it separately, whereas in fact no event can *ever* have a beginning, because an individual event flows without any break in continuity from another. The second thing history does is to treat the actions of a single person, king or commander, as the sum total of everybody else's individual will, whereas in fact the sum of individual wills never expresses itself in the actions of a single historical personage.

In the development of historical science, smaller and smaller units are selected for analysis, as if this is the path that leads to truth. But however small the units determined by history, we feel that the acceptance of any discrete unit, or of a *beginning* to any phenomenon, or the idea that multiple individual wills express themselves in the actions of any one historical personage, is intrinsically wrong.

Criticism can effortlessly ensure that every conclusion of history gets blown away like dust, leaving no trace behind, simply by selecting a greater or smaller discrete unit for analysis – and criticism has every right to do this, because the selection of historical units is always an arbitrary business.

Only by adopting an infinitely small unit for observation, the differential in history otherwise known as human homogeneity, and perfecting the art of integration (the adding up of infinitesimals) can we have any hope of determining the laws of history.

The first fifteen years of the nineteenth century in Europe present an extraordinary spectacle – millions of men in movement. Men drop their normal occupations and rush from one end of Europe to the other, plundering, slaughtering one another, experiencing triumph and despair, and the whole business of life is disrupted for years to come as the movement accelerates and builds up before tailing off again.

What was it that caused all this movement? By what laws did it develop? This is what human intelligence wants to know.

When historians reply to these questions they present the sayings and doings of a few dozen men in one building in the city of Paris, and sum up these doings and sayings in a single word – revolution. Then they launch into detailed biographies of Napoleon and one or two persons for and against him; they also tell us how some of these persons were influenced by others, and they conclude by saying this is what caused all the movement, and these are the laws that governed it.

But human intelligence not only balks at this explanation, it declares categorically that the whole method is faulty because in the course of this explanation a very slight phenomenon is taken as the cause of a much greater one. It was the sum total of men's individual wills that caused both the revolution and Napoleon, and nothing but this sum total of wills went on to suffer them and ultimately destroy them.

'But whenever there have been conquests there have always been great conquerors; whenever states have been rocked by revolution there have always been great politicians,' says history. 'Yes, indeed, whenever there have been great conquerors there have been wars,' replies human intelligence, 'but this doesn't prove that the conquerors actually caused the wars, or that the laws behind wars can be discovered in the personal doings of a single man.'

Whenever I look at my clock and see the little hand get to the number ten, bells start ringing in the church next door and I hear them, but the fact that the bell-ringing always starts when the hands get to ten o'clock doesn't give me the right to assume that the position of the hands on my clock actually causes the movement of the bells.

Whenever I see a steam-engine move, I hear the whistle, and see the valves opening and the wheels turning, but I have no right to assume that the blowing of the whistle and the turning of the wheels actually cause the movement of the engine.

Peasants say that in late spring a cold wind blows because the oak-buds are coming out, and it is certainly true that every spring there is a cold wind blowing just as the oak-tree puts out its shoots. But even though I don't know what causes a cold wind to blow just when the oaks are bursting forth, I cannot agree with the peasants that the cause of the cold wind is the budding of the tree, because wind power is not affected by buds. All I am seeing here is a coincidental series of events common enough in all walks of life. What I can see is this: however often and however closely I scrutinize the hands on the clock, or the valves and the wheels on the engine, or the oak-buds, I shall never discover what makes bells ring, the engine move, or the wind blow in springtime. In order to do that I shall have to change my angle of approach completely and study the laws that govern the motion of steam, the ringing of bells, and the blowing of the wind. History must do the same thing. And some efforts have already been made in this direction.

In order to study the laws of history we must change the subject completely, forget all about kings, ministers and generals, and turn to the homogeneous, infinitesimal elements that move the masses to action. No one can say how far it is within man's grasp to arrive at the laws of history in this way, but it is obvious that this is the only possible way of discovering any historical laws, and human intelligence has hitherto not devoted to this way of thinking a millionth part of the effort that historians have put into describing the doings of various kings, ministers and generals, and expounding their own opinions of those doings.

CHAPTER 2

An armed force speaking a dozen different European tongues has invaded Russia. The Russian army and population pull back to avoid a confrontation, first to Smolensk, then from Smolensk to Borodino. The French army moves on towards Moscow, its goal, accelerating all the time. The advance gathers momentum as the army nears its goal, just as the speed of a falling body increases as it nears the ground. Behind them lie hundreds of miles of hunger and hostility; ahead, only a few dozen miles separate them from their goal. This is sensed by every soldier in Napoleon's army, and the invading force, propelled by its own momentum, needs no driving.

Among the retreating Russian troops bitter hostility and hatred of the enemy flare up more and more furiously as they go; every step back concentrates the mind and builds determination. At Borodino the armies come together. Neither is destroyed, but immediately after the conflict the Russian army pulls back; this is inevitable, just as a billiard-ball automatically recoils when hit by another ball travelling faster towards it. And just as inevitably, even though the ball of the invading army has discharged its energy in the collision, there is just enough left for it to go trundling on a short distance further.

The Russians fall back through Moscow and end up eighty miles beyond the city; the French reach Moscow and come to a halt. Five weeks pass without so much as a skirmish. The French don't make a move. Like a wild beast mortally wounded, bleeding and licking its wounds, they stay there in Moscow for five weeks without actually doing anything, and then suddenly, with no new reason for leaving, they are up and off, scurrying down the Kaluga road, with a victory to their credit too, for they win the field after the battle of Maloyaroslavets, after which they avoid all other confrontations and run off as fast as their legs will carry them, first to Smolensk, then Vilna, the Berezina and beyond.

On the evening of the 26th of August Kutuzov and the whole Russian army were convinced they had won the battle of Borodino. Kutuzov wrote as much to the Tsar. He ordered the troops to prepare for another battle to finish off the enemy, not because he was trying to fool people but because he knew the enemy was beaten, as did anyone who had been in the battle.

But that evening and all the next day one report after another came in, telling of unheard-of losses, the loss of half the army; another battle was a physical impossibility.

There could be no question of going into battle before all the information was in, before the wounded had been picked up, the ammunition stores replenished, the dead counted, new officers appointed to replace those who had been killed, and the men had been given food and time to sleep. Meanwhile, the very next morning after the battle, the French army moved against the Russians, carried along by its own impetus, now accelerating in inverse proportion to the square of the distance from its goal. Kutuzov had wanted to attack that next day, and the whole army wanted to as well. But in order to mount an attack it is not enough to want to do it; there must also be the possibility of doing it, and now there was no such possibility. It was impossible to do anything but fall back a day's march, after which it was as impossible to do anything but fall back a second and a third day's march, until finally, on the 1st of September, when the army got to Moscow, despite a growing strength of feeling in the troops, sheer force of circumstances compelled the troops to fall back beyond Moscow. And the troops fell back one last day's march, abandoning Moscow to the enemy.

Anyone disposed to imagine that campaign strategy and battle-plans are drawn up by the high command the way one of us might do it, sitting in his study poring over a map and working out what he would have done and how he would have done it under the various circumstances of war, must face some awkward questions. Why didn't Kutuzov do this or that when he was forced to retreat? Why didn't he dig in somewhere before Fili? Why didn't he miss out on Moscow and go straight down the Kaluga road? And so on ... People who think like that forget – or maybe they never knew – the extent to which commanders-in-chief are constrained by circumstances. The circumstances encountered by a commander-in-chief in the field bear no resemblance to any circumstances we may dream up as we sit at home in a cosy study, going over a campaign on the map with a given number of soldiers on either side, in a known locality, and starting out at a specific moment in time. The general never experiences anything like the *beginning* of an event, which we are always privy to. The general always finds himself in the midst of events as they unfold, which means he is never at any moment in a position to contemplate the full significance of what is taking place. Each event carves out its own significance imperceptibly, moment by moment, and at any point in this gradual and uninterrupted carving-out of events the commander-in-chief finds himself in the very midst of a most complex interplay of intrigue and worry, dependence and authority, planning, advice, threats and trickery; he finds himself constantly called upon to respond to an endless flow of suggestions, all contradictory.

Academics specializing in military history tell us with a perfectly straight face that Kutuzov ought to have turned his army down the Kaluga road long before Fili, and that someone actually suggested such a plan. But an army commander has before him, especially in a crisis, not one plan, but dozens of them. And each of them, although well founded in terms of strategy and tactics, contradicts all the others. It seems simple enough: all the commander has to do is pick one of them, but even this is beyond him. Time and events will not wait. Imagine him receiving a suggestion on the 28th to cross over to the Kaluga road, but on the instant up gallops an adjutant from Miloradovich asking whether they should immediately engage with the French or fall back. An instant response and clear instructions are required. But an order to fall back would mean not turning off to the Kaluga road. After the adjutant comes the quartermaster asking where to take the stores, and the chief medical officer wants to know where to send the wounded, then a courier rides in from Petersburg with a letter from the Tsar ruling out any possibility of abandoning Moscow, and here is one of the commander's rivals, anxious to undermine his authority (there's never any shortage of people like that) with a new scheme diametrically opposed to the plan of cutting across to the Kaluga road. Besides which, the commander's own expenditure of energy demands sleep and sustenance. But a worthy general who has been bypassed when the medals were being given out has come to complain, and the local inhabitants are begging for protection. Meanwhile the officer sent out to inspect the locality comes back with a report totally different from the one just submitted by another officer, while a spy, a prisoner and a general who has been out on reconnaissance all give completely different descriptions of the enemy's position. People who forget, or who never understood, circumstances like these under which any commander is inevitably compelled to operate will bring up, say, the position of the troops at Fili and use it to assume that on the 1st of September the commander-in-chief was at liberty to decide whether or not to abandon Moscow, whereas, given the position of the Russian army only three or four miles from Moscow, there was no question to be decided. When *was* this question decided? In many places: at Drissa, and Smolensk, and most palpably on the 24th of August at Shevardino, then on the 26th at Borodino, and at every minute of every hour of every day during the retreat from Borodino to Fili.

CHAPTER 3

The Russian army, pulling back from Borodino, halted at Fili. Yermolov, who had ridden out to take stock of the position, came over to the commander-in-chief.

'There is no possibility of fighting in this position,' he said.

Kutuzov looked at him in some surprise, and got him to repeat what he had said. When he had done so, he offered his hand.

'Give me your hand, my dear fellow,' he said, and, turning it over to feel his pulse, he went on, 'You're not well, dear boy. Think what you are saying.'

On Poklonnaya hill, four miles short of the Dorogomilov gate, Kutuzov got out of his carriage and sat down on a bench by the side of the road. A great crowd of generals gathered around. Count Rostopchin, who had come out from Moscow, joined them. The brilliant company broke up into small groups, chatting among themselves about the pros and cons of the present position, the state of the army, the plans that had been submitted, the general situation in Moscow, and all things military. Everybody felt that, although they had not been summoned for this purpose, and nobody was prepared to call it by its proper name, this was a council of war. Conversation was restricted to topics of general interest. If anyone imparted or received any personal news it was communicated in a whisper, and the talk swiftly returned to general topics. Not a joke, laugh or smile passed between these people. They were all obviously struggling to keep on top of things. All the groups, as they chatted away, did their level best to stick close to the commander-in-chief, whose bench was the centre of interest, and they spoke out to make themselves heard. The commander-in-chief listened, and sometimes made an inquiry about something said near by, but he didn't enter into any conversation or express an opinion. More often than not he would listen to one group talking, only to turn away in disappointment as if they were saying things he had no desire to hear. Some of them were discussing the position, criticizing not so much the position itself as the intellectual calibre of those who had selected it. Others argued that the real mistake had been made earlier on; they should have gone into battle two days before. A different set was going on about the battle of Salamanca, which was being described by a newly arrived Frenchman by the name of Crosart, dressed in a Spanish uniform. (This Frenchman, along with one of the German princes serving in the Russian army, was analysing the siege of Saragossa, in the belief that Moscow might have to be defended in the same way.) In the fourth group, Count Rostopchin was saying that he and the Moscow city guard were ready to die at the city walls, but he still felt it proper to complain that he had been kept in the dark, and if only he'd known earlier on everything would have been different ... A fifth group was demonstrating a profound level of strategic awareness by discussing the right direction for the troops to go in. A sixth group was talking utter nonsense.

Kutuzov's face looked ever more worried and dejected. From all this talk Kutuzov drew a single conclusion: defending Moscow was *a physical impossibility* in the fullest sense of the phrase, so utterly impossible that even if some crazy commander gave the order to go into battle there would be nothing but chaos, and no battle would be fought. No battle would be fought because it wasn't just a question of all the commanding officers acknowledging the impossibility of their position; the only topic of conversation now in every group centred around what was going to happen after the position had been necessarily abandoned. How could commanding officers lead their men out to fight a battle that they believed couldn't be won? The junior officers, and even the soldiers (who were capable of thinking for themselves), knew the position couldn't be held, and they couldn't go into battle with any confidence of winning. Bennigsen could go on and on about defending the position, and others could discuss it till the cows came home, but this issue no longer mattered; it was nothing but a pretext for argument and intrigue. Kutuzov was aware of this.

Bennigsen, who had chosen the present position, was waxing eloquent in a great show of Russian patriotism – Kutuzov couldn't listen to him without wincing – and insisting on the defence of Moscow. His purpose was as clear as daylight to Kutuzov: if the defence failed it was Kutuzov's fault – he had brought the army all the way to the Sparrow hills without fighting the enemy – but if it was successful he wanted the credit, and if they opted out he washed his hands of the crime of abandoning Moscow.

But the old man had no time now for this kind of chicanery. There was only one terrible question on his mind, a question to which he heard no answer. The question was: 'How can I have let Napoleon get as far as Moscow, and when did I do it? When did it happen? Yesterday, when I sent word to Platov to fall back, or the evening before when I had a nap and let Bennigsen take over? Or was it before that? . . . When, oh when did this ghastly thing happen? Moscow has to be abandoned. The army must fall back. The order must be given.'

To issue such a dreadful order seemed like resigning his command of the army. And apart from the fact that he loved power and had got used to it (he had been galled by the honours lavished on Prince Prozorovsky, under whom he had served in Turkey), he was convinced that he was destined to be the saviour of Russia, and this was why he had been appointed commander-in-chief, against the Tsar's wishes but by the will of the people. He was convinced that in these difficult times he was the only man who could hold out as head of the army, and the only man in the world capable of taking on Napoleon without flinching. Now he dreaded having to give this order. But he had to do something; he had to stop this idle chatter that was getting out of hand.

He summoned his senior generals.

'For good or ill, it is in my head that the decision must be made,' he said in French, getting up from his bench, and he rode off to Fili, where his carriages were waiting.

CHAPTER 4

A council of war had been convened for two o'clock in a spacious room at the best end of a wooden house belonging to a prosperous peasant by the name of Andrey Savostyanov. His large family, men, women and children, were all huddled together in a dark room across the passage. His Serene Highness had taken to Andrey's six-year-old granddaughter, Malasha, and given her a sugar-lump while he drank his tea; she alone was allowed to stay behind in the large room, tucked away on top of the big stove. Malasha was a picture of delight, peeping down timidly at all the faces and uniforms, and the decorations worn by the generals, as they strode in one after another and took their places on the broad benches in the special corner under the icons. Kutuzov ('Grandad' to Malasha in her mind) was sitting on his own in a dark corner just past the stove. He was slumped down in a folding armchair, constantly clearing his throat and pulling at his coat-collar, which seemed too tight for his neck, even though it was unbuttoned. The generals came in one after another and presented themselves to the field-marshal; he shook hands with some of them, and nodded to the others.

Adjutant Kaysarov made as if to open a curtain covering the window opposite Kutuzov, but his Highness waved him away angrily, and Kaysarov got the point: Kutuzov didn't want his face to be seen.

The peasant's deal table, covered with maps, plans, pencils and papers, was so crowded that the orderlies brought another bench in, and put it near the table for Yermolov, Kaysarov and Toll to come over and sit on. In the place of honour under the icons sat Barclay de Tolly, with the Order of St George round his neck; his high forehead merging into a bald pate crowned the pallid face of a sick man. He had been feverish for the last two days, and he was all aches and pains. Beside him sat Uvarov, talking in hushed tones like everyone else and making rapid gestures with his hands. Chubby little Dokhturov was listening intently with raised eyebrows, clasping his hands over his stomach. Sitting opposite was the clean-cut, bright-eyed Count Ostermann-Tolstoy, with his broad head propped up on one hand, keeping his thoughts to himself. Rayevsky sat there, as usual twisting the black hair at his temples into curls, and looking from Kutuzov to the door and back again. Konovnitsyn's strong, handsome face was shining warmly with a shrewd and kindly smile. He caught Malasha looking his way and made funny signals with his eyes, bringing a smile to the little girl's face.

They were waiting for Bennigsen, who was supposed to be out on a tour of inspection but was actually finishing a jolly good lunch. From four till six they waited, and in all that time they held back from serious deliberations, limiting themselves to side-issues discussed in hushed tones.

Only when Bennigsen came in at last did Kutuzov stir from his corner and move over to the table, taking good care to ensure that his face kept out of the candle-light thoughtfully provided.

Bennigsen opened the proceedings with a question: were they to abandon the holy and ancient capital of Russia without a struggle, or stand and defend it?

A long silence ensured. Brows were furrowed, and the only sounds that broke the stillness came from Kutuzov, who kept clearing his throat and coughing irritably. All eyes were on him. Even Malasha couldn't take her eyes off 'Grandad'. She was nearer than anyone, and she could see his face crumpling; he was on the verge of tears. But not for long.

'*The holy and ancient capital of Russia!*' he suddenly called out, with fury in his voice, parroting Bennigsen's words to bring out the false note in them. 'Allow me to inform your Excellency that this question has no meaning for a Russian.' (He lunged forward with his huge bulk.) 'You cannot put the question like that. There's no sense in it. The question I have brought these gentlemen together to discuss is a military question. It goes like this: the salvation of Russia rests with the army; which is better – to risk the loss of the army and Moscow by fighting, or to abandon Moscow without any fighting? This is the question on which I wish to hear your opinion.' He flopped back down into his low chair.

The debate began. As far as Bennigsen was concerned the game was not yet lost. He took the point made by Barclay and others that it would not now be possible to take a defensive stand at Fili, but went on to demonstrate the depth of his Russian patriotism and devotion to Moscow by proposing to switch the army during the night from right to left and attack the French the next day on their right flank. Opinions were divided, with arguments for and against this proposal. Yermolov, Dokhturov and Rayevsky sided with Bennigsen. Whether they were guided by a feeling that some sacrifices ought to be made before the city was abandoned, or by other, personal, considerations, these generals seemed incapable of understanding that this session of the council could not turn back the inexorable tide of events, and Moscow was already an abandoned city. The other generals accepted this, put the question of Moscow to one side, and discussed the best direction for the retreating Russian army to take.

Malasha watched all that was going on with rapt attention, though she had her own version of events at the council. For her it came down to a straight fight between 'Grandad' and 'Longcoat', her name for Bennigsen. She could see them getting all animated when they spoke to each other, and she was on 'Grandad's' side. In the middle of the conversation she watched 'Grandad' fix Bennigsen with a sharp and clever stare, and straight after that she noted with glee that 'Grandad' had beaten 'Longcoat' by saying something special, and Bennigsen had gone red in the face and was now walking furiously up and down the room. The words that had made such an impact on Bennigsen were Kutuzov's carefully considered and softly delivered comments on the pros and cons of his proposal to move the troops from right to left during the night and attack the French on their right flank.

'Gentlemen,' said Kutuzov, 'I cannot endorse the count's plan. Troop movements close to the enemy are always a risky business, as military history shows. Take, for instance . . .' (Kutuzov seemed to pause for thought as he searched for an example, watching Bennigsen with a bland and innocent expression) '. . . well, take the battle of Friedland, which, I'm sure the count will remember, was not . . . entirely successful, and that was because the troops were redeployed too close to the enemy . . .'

A momentary silence that followed seemed to go on for ever.

The debate was resumed, but with more and more breaks in it, until finally they could all sense there was nothing more to be said.

During one of the breaks Kutuzov gave a deep sigh and seemed about to speak. Everybody turned in his direction.

'Well, gentlemen, I can see I'm going to have to pay for the broken pots,' he said. He got slowly to his feet and walked across to the table. 'Gentlemen, I have heard your arguments. Some of you will not agree with me. But I . . .' (he paused) 'by the authority invested in me by my Tsar and country, I hereby order you to retreat.'

Whereupon the generals began to disperse with the solemn and silent wariness of people going their separate ways at the end of a funeral. One or two of the generals spoke to the commander-in-chief, pitching their comments in quite a different tone from the one they had used at the council table.

Malasha, who was late for supper, climbed down from the stove backwards, her bare toes clinging to the knobs and bumps, then she was off, wriggling her way between the generals' legs and skipping out through the door.

Kutuzov dismissed the generals and sat there for some time with his elbows on the table, thinking over one or two dreadful questions. When did it happen? When was it certain that Moscow had to be abandoned? When did something happen that made it inevitable, and whose fault was it?

'Well, I didn't see it coming!' he said to the adjutant, Schneider, who had come in to see him. It was now well into the night. 'I never expected it! I never thought it would come to this!'

'You must get some rest, your Highness,' said Schneider.

'But it's not over yet. They'll end up eating horse-meat like the Turks!' Kutuzov shouted, ignoring Schneider and bringing his podgy fist crashing down on the table. 'They will, you know . . . if only . . .'

CHAPTER 5

Meanwhile, there was something to attend to that was even more important than the retreat of the army without putting up a fight: the evacuation of Moscow and the burning of the city. Count Rostopchin, whom we usually take to be the motive force behind this event, was acting in a very different manner from Kutuzov.

After the battle of Borodino, this event – the evacuation and burning of Moscow – became as inevitable as the retreat of the army without putting up a fight.

Every Russian could have predicted the outcome, not by intellectual effort but from the gut-feeling that lies within us as it lay within our fathers.

What had happened in Moscow was happening now in every town and village on Russian soil from Smolensk onwards, and without the assistance of Count Rostopchin and his posters. The people were waiting philosophically for the enemy to arrive. There was no rioting, no disturbance of the peace, and nobody was torn to pieces; they calmly awaited their fate, sensing within themselves sufficient strength to do what was necessary when the crisis came. And once the enemy began to get near, the wealthier elements of the population went away, leaving their property behind, while the poorer people stayed on, setting fire to all that was left and destroying it.

An awareness that this was the way things were going, and always would go, was, and is, deeply implanted in every Russian heart. This awareness, along with a foreboding that Moscow was going to be taken by the enemy, lay deeply implanted in Russian society in the Moscow of 1812. Those who had started to leave the city in July and early August had shown they were expecting it. Those who left the city taking with them only what they could carry, and leaving their houses and half their property behind, were acting out of patriotism, but the *latent* kind that does not show itself in fine phrases, in killing one's children for the sake of the fatherland, or any number of unnatural reactions like these, but comes out inconspicuously, in the most simple and natural way, and therefore always gets the best results.

'Shame on you, running away from danger. Only cowards are

deserting Moscow,' they were told. In his posters Rostopchin kept drumming it into them that it was disgraceful to leave Moscow. They felt ashamed when they heard themselves described as cowards; they felt ashamed to be going away, but they still went, and they knew they had to. Why did they go? They couldn't possibly have been scared off by Rostopchin's accounts of atrocities carried out by Napoleon in conquered countries. As they streamed away the first to go were the wealthy, educated people, who knew full well that Vienna and Berlin had survived intact, and that throughout the occupation the inhabitants of those cities had enjoyed themselves with all those utterly charming Frenchmen, whom all Russians, and especially the ladies, found so attractive at that time.

They were leaving because for the Russians it wasn't a question of how easy life might or might not be under French rule in Moscow. It was just not possible to live under French rule; this was the worst thing that could possibly happen. They were leaving before Borodino; and after Borodino the movement speeded up, notwithstanding calls to defend the city, notwithstanding any number of proclamations from the governor of Moscow about going into battle with the wonder-working Icon of Iversk and the air-balloons that would finish off the French, and all the other rubbish that Rostopchin splashed all over his posters. They knew it was the army's job to fight, and if the army proved incapable it would be no good marching out with young ladies and house serfs to fight Napoleon on the Three Hills; no, they must get away, however much it hurt to leave their property behind knowing it would be destroyed. Away they went, without a passing thought for the solemn significance of Muscovites abandoning this huge, thriving capital city, and obviously consigning it to the flames. (A large city of wooden buildings, once abandoned, would be certain to burn down.) They went away for personal reasons, yet it was their departure that brought about the splendid achievement that will always redound to the glory of the Russian people. The lady who moved out in June and took her black servants and her entertainers from Moscow down to Saratov, with a vague determination that she would never be a servant of Bonaparte, and a real fear of being stopped by orders from Rostopchin, was actually doing nothing less than partaking of that great action that saved Russia.

As for Count Rostopchin, one day he would pour scorn on those who were leaving, but the next he would evacuate all the government offices; he distributed weapons that wouldn't work to the drunken rabble; one day he would raise aloft the holy icons, the next he would ban the movement of all holy relics and images by Father Augustin;

he commandeered all the private vehicles left in Moscow, then used one hundred and thirty-six of them to transport Leppich and his air-balloons; at one time he dropped hints that he might set fire to Moscow and described how he had burnt his own house down, then he wrote a proclamation to the French in which he solemnly accused *them* of destroying his childhood home; he would sometimes claim the credit for setting fire to Moscow, then later he would disclaim any knowledge of it; he told the people to capture all spies and bring them in, then censured the people for doing just that; he expelled all French residents from the city, but allowed Madame Aubert-Chalmé, who formed the centre of French society in Moscow, to stay on; he ordered the arrest and banishment of the old and venerable post-master Klyucharyov, who had done nothing wrong; he brought people together on the Three Hills to fight the French, and then, to get rid of them, he gave them a man to murder, and slipped away by the back gate. He swore he would perish with Moscow, but he survived to scribble French verses in ladies' albums about his role in the affair. One went roughly as follows:

> I am by birth Tatarian,
> But Rome – I am your man!
> The French call me barbarian,
> The Russians – George Dandin.

This man had no idea what was happening. He just wanted to be seen doing something, to take people by surprise, to do a heroic deed that was gloriously patriotic, and he behaved like a little boy amusing himself while events of enormous magnitude – the abandonment and burning of Moscow – were inexorably taking shape, and he kept raising his tiny little fist first to urge on, then to turn back the mighty tide of popular will that swept him along as it went.

CHAPTER 6

Hélène had returned with the court from Vilna to Petersburg, where she found herself in an embarrassing situation.

Here in Petersburg Hélène had enjoyed the special patronage of an important dignitary, who occupied one of the highest positions in the government. Out in Vilna she had formed a liaison with a young foreign prince. When she got back to Petersburg prince and dignitary were both in town, both were asserting their rights, and Hélène was faced with a problem she had not previously encountered in her career: how to preserve her intimacy with both, without offending either.

What might have seemed to any other woman a difficult task verging on the impossible Countess Bezukhov took in her stride, and without sacrificing her reputation as a highly intelligent lady. Had she attempted to cover things up, or had she tried to wriggle out of her awkward situation by being shifty and clever, she would have ruined everything by acknowledging that she was in the wrong. But no, Hélène behaved like a great personality who can get away with anything; convinced of her innocence, she assumed the moral high ground, and looked down on everybody else as guilty people.

The first time the young foreigner came out with an objection to her behaviour, she tilted back her beautiful head with some pride, half-turned towards him and put him in his place.

'So this is it,' she said. 'The selfishness and cruelty of men! Just what I was expecting. A woman sacrifices herself for you, she suffers, and this is her reward. What right have you to ask me, monseigneur, to account for my friendships and affections? This man has been more than a father to me!'

The prince began to protest, but Hélène cut him short.

'Well, yes, maybe his feelings for me do go beyond those of a father, but that's no reason for me to shut the door in his face. Not being a man, I cannot show ingratitude. What you must realize, monseigneur, is that as far as my personal feelings are concerned I am accountable only to God and my own conscience!' she concluded, raising a hand to her sublimely beetling bosom as she glanced up to heaven.

'No, for God's sake listen!'

'Marry me, and I'll be your slave!'

'No, it's impossible.'

'I'm not good enough for you to marry, you . . .' And she broke down in tears.

The prince did his best to soothe her, but Hélène had every appearance of being inconsolable. She insisted tearfully that nothing could stop her remarrying, and there were precedents for this. (There were very few at that time, but Hélène cited Napoleon and one or two exalted personages.) She had never been a wife to her husband. She had been sacrificed into marriage.

'But what about the law? Religion?' murmured the prince, half won-over.

'Religion, laws . . . what were they invented for if they can't manage something like this?' said Hélène.

The prince was amazed that such a simple idea had never occurred to him, and he consulted the holy brethren of the Society of Jesus, with whom he had close contacts.

A few days later, at one of the wonderful parties given by Hélène at her summer villa on Stone Island she was introduced to a M. Jobert, a fascinating middle-aged man with snow-white hair and brilliant black eyes, a lay member of the Jesuit brotherhood (a 'short-robed', lay member), who spent a long time in conversation with Hélène out in the garden under the illuminations and to the strains of music about the need to love God, and Jesus, and the Sacred Heart, and the consolations afforded by the one true Catholic faith in this life and the next. Hélène was deeply moved, and several times both of them found themselves on the verge of tears, with their voices trembling. A dance partner then called Hélène away, breaking the thread of the conversation with her future 'director of conscience', but the following evening M. Jobert called on Hélène alone, and soon after that he became a regular visitor.

One day he took the countess along to a Catholic church, and there she was led forward to kneel at an altar. The fascinating, middle-aged Frenchman laid his hands on her head, and she experienced a sensation that she later described as something akin to a breath of fresh air wafting into her soul. This, they explained, was the 'grace of God'.

Then a long-robed abbé was brought to her; he heard her confession, and absolved her from her sins. Next day she took delivery of a casket containing the Sacred Host, which was left with her for use in her own home. Some days later Hélène learnt with pleasure that she had been admitted into the true Catholic Church, and in a day or two the Pope himself would hear about her and send her some sort of document.

Everything that was done to her, and around her, during this period; all the attention lavished on her by so many clever men, gratifying and refined as it was in all its forms; and the dovelike purity of her present condition (she wore nothing but white dresses and white ribbons throughout) was most enjoyable, but not for a moment did she let the enjoyment distract her from her goal. And since this was a matter of low cunning, in which the stupid person always wins out over the bright one, Hélène had soon cottoned on to the main motivation behind all the fine words and splendid ceremonies involved in her conversion to Catholicism, which was to get good money out of her for the Jesuit cause (hints had already been heard), and she now refused to pay up until she had undergone the various formalities necessary to free her from her husband. To her way of thinking, the real purpose of every religion was to preserve the decencies and still satisfy human desire. And with this in mind she took advantage of a consultation with her spiritual adviser to ask how far she was bound by her marriage.

They were sitting together in an alcove by a drawing-room window. It was dusk. The scent of flowers wafted in through the window. Hélène was wearing a white dress, transparent over shoulders and bosom. The sleek, well-fed abbé, with his podgy, clean-shaven chin, his good strong mouth and his white hands clasped unthreateningly round his knees, was sitting close to Hélène. A subtle smile played on his lips, a discreet admiration of her beauty shone from his eyes, and he looked her in the face once or twice as he outlined his attitude to this problem. Hélène grinned warily as she stared back at his curly hair and his clean-shaven, dark-shadowed cheeks, and waited anxiously for the conversation to move in a new direction. But the abbé, even as he made no secret of drinking in the beauty of his companion, was also much enjoying his own skilful handling of the situation.

The director of conscience explained his thinking, which went as follows.

'Without knowing the full significance of what you were undertaking, you took a vow of conjugal fidelity to a man who, for his part, was committing an act of sacrilege when he entered into holy wedlock with no faith in its religious significance. That marriage did not have the dual significance it should have had. Nevertheless, your vow was binding upon you. You have broken it. What kind of sin did you commit? A venial sin or a mortal sin? A venial sin, because you committed it without malice aforethought. If now, with the object of bearing children, you were to marry again, your sin could be forgiven. But still the question has two aspects to it. In the first pl . . .'

'No, the way I see it,' Hélène cut in with a smile of bewitching beauty as she wearied of the way things were going, 'once converted to the true religion, I cannot be bound by anything imposed upon me by a false religion.' Her director of conscience was astounded at being presented with a Columbus's egg[1] of such stark simplicity. He rejoiced at his pupil's unheralded speed of development, and yet he could not relinquish the towering structure of reasoned argument he had worked on so hard.

'We must come to an understanding,' he smiled, and looked for ways of undermining his spiritual daughter's contention.

CHAPTER 7

Hélène had come to the conclusion that in ecclesiastical terms her situation was plain and simple, but her spiritual counsellors kept raising difficulties for the simple reason that they were worried about how things might seem to the worldly authorities. So she decided to go out into society and prepare the ground. She provoked the jealousy of the elderly dignitary by telling him what she had told her other suitor: the issue was straightforward – the only way of obtaining exclusive rights over her was to marry her. At first the elderly dignitary was just as shocked as his younger counterpart had been to receive a proposal of marriage from a wife with a husband who was still alive. But Hélène's absolute certainty that the whole thing was as simple and natural as marrying a young girl had its effect on him too. If she had shown the slightest twinge of hesitation, embarrassment or reticence her case would undoubtedly have been lost, but not only did she avoid showing any such twinge, she spoke openly about this business to her intimate friends (and that meant all Petersburg), informing them with disarming innocence that the prince and the dignitary had proposed to her, and since she loved both men she was afraid of hurting either of them.

A rumour swept the city, not that Hélène wanted a divorce from her husband (if the rumour had said that, many people would have come out against any such impropriety), but simply that the ill-starred and ever-fascinating Hélène was agonizing over her two suitors, wondering which one to marry. There was no interest in the extent to which this might or might not be feasible; the only questions were who would be the better match, and how would the court look on things. True, there were one or two puritans incapable of rising to the occasion who saw this as a desecration of the sacrament of marriage, but they were few in number, and they kept their own counsel, while most people concentrated on the upturn in Hélène's fortunes, and who would be the better choice. Whether it was a good thing or a bad thing for a wife to remarry during her husband's lifetime was not up for discussion, because clearly this question must have been settled once and for all by 'wiser heads than ours' (as the saying went), and to doubt the validity of the decision would be to risk parading one's ignorance and lack of savoir-faire.

The only person to come out with an opinion that departed from the general view was Marya Dmitriyevna Akhrosimov, who had come up to Petersburg that summer to see one of her sons. Chancing across

Hélène at a ball, this lady stopped her in the middle of the room, and spoke out in a harsh voice with everyone listening.

'So, I hear it's in order now for women to go from one living husband to another! I suppose you think this is something new. But they've beaten you to it, madam. It's a very old idea. It's done in every brothel.' This said, Marya Dmitriyevna fluffed up her capacious sleeves in a familiar gesture of intimidation, glared round at the company and strode off across the ballroom.

Although people were wary of Marya Dmitriyevna, she was looked on in Petersburg as a kind of comic figure, so the only word that got noticed was the last vulgar expression, which was passed on in whispers as if it was the only important thing that had been said.

Prince Vasily, who had become rather forgetful of late, tended to repeat a phrase over and over again, and every time he came across his daughter he would say the same thing.

'Hélène, a word in your ear,' he would say, drawing her to one side and jerking her arm downwards. 'A little bird tells me about certain plans for . . . you know what. Well, my dear child, you know how my father's heart rejoices to hear you are . . . You've had so much suffering. But, my dear child, listen only to the promptings of your heart. That's all I have to say.' And each time, stifling the same surge of emotion, he would embrace his daughter cheek to cheek and then wander off on his own.

Bilibin, who had lost none of his reputation as a wit, was a friend of Hélène's, one of those disinterested allies who can always be seen circulating round brilliant women, men friends who are never going to change into lovers. One day, in what he called 'a little sub-committee', Bilibin gave his friend Hélène the benefit of his views on the subject.

'Listen here, Bilibin,' said Hélène – she always addressed friends in the Bilibin category by their surnames – allowing her white fingers glittering with rings to brush against his jacket-sleeve. 'I want you to tell me what to do, as a brother would to a sister. Which one?'

Bilibin puckered up the skin just above his eyebrows, and gave it some thought with a smile hovering about his lips.

'This comes as no great surprise, you know,' he said. 'As a true friend of yours, I have been thinking, and rethinking, about this whole business. Look at it this way. If you marry the prince . . .' Bilibin bent one finger back to mark off the younger suitor '. . . you lose for ever the opportunity of marrying the other man, *and* you displease the court. (Some kind of connection there, as you well know.) But if you marry the count you'll be making an old man very happy, and eventually as the widow of the great . . . you would be no mismatch for the prince . . .' At this Bilibin dissolved the wrinkles on his brow.

'This is friendship indeed!' said Hélène, beaming radiantly as she brushed Bilibin's sleeve again. 'But I do love them both, and I wouldn't want to hurt either of them. I would give up my life for the happiness of them both,' she declared.

Bilibin gave a shrug: for worries of this order even he had no cure to offer.

'Wife and mistress together!' thought Bilibin. 'That's what I call plain speaking. She wants to marry them all at once.'

'But do tell me – what will your husband's attitude be?' he said, relying on the strength of his reputation to save him from disaster in asking such a naive question. 'Will he give his consent?'

'Oh, he's so fond of me!' said Hélène, who was under the strange impression that Pierre also adored her. 'He'll do anything for me.' Bilibin began a puckered wrinkle to indicate the imminent arrival of a telling phrase.

'Including divorce?' he said.

Hélène gave a laugh.

One of the people bold enough to question the propriety of the proposed marriage was Hélène's mother, Princess Kuragin. She had always been painfully jealous of her daughter, and now, with the subject of her jealousy so close to her own heart, she couldn't come to terms with even the thought of it.

She consulted a Russian priest about the extent to which divorce and remarriage during the husband's lifetime was feasible, and the priest said it was impossible. To her delight he referred her to a Gospel text in which (under his interpretation) remarriage during the lifetime of the husband was explicitly forbidden.

Furnished with these arguments, which she considered incontestable, Princess Kuragin drove round to see her daughter early one morning to make sure of finding her alone.

Hélène listened patiently to her mother's objections, and then gave a smile of gentle irony.

'Look, it spells it out: "Whoso marrieth her that is divorced . . ."' said the old princess.

'Oh, Mamma, don't be so silly. You don't understand. In my position I have certain duties . . .' Hélène began, switching from Russian to French, because in Russian she always felt her case lacked a certain clarity.

'But, darling . . .'

'Oh Mamma, surely you must understand that the Holy Father, who has the power to issue dispensations . . .'

At this point the lady companion who lived in with Hélène came in to announce that his Highness was out in the hall, hoping to see her.

'No, tell him I won't see him. I'm furious with him for not keeping his word.'

'Countess, there is mercy for every sin,' said a fair-haired young man, long in face and nose, as he walked into the room.

The old princess rose politely and curtsied. The young man ignored her. Princess Kuragin nodded to her daughter, and floated across to the door.

'Yes, she's right,' thought the old princess, all of her certainties having dissolved at his Highness's sudden arrival. 'She is right, but how can our youth have gone by and been lost for ever without our knowing about it? And it was such a simple thing,' thought Princess Kuragin as she climbed into her carriage.

The issue was settled once and for all for Hélène by early August, and she wrote to her husband (who was still very fond of her, or so she thought), informing him of her intention to marry N. N., and her conversion to the one true faith, and asking him to deal with the necessary formalities for obtaining a divorce, further details to be conveyed by the bearer of this letter.

'Whereupon, my dear friend, I pray to God that He may have you in His holy and powerful keeping. Your friend, Hélène.'

This letter was delivered to Pierre's Moscow house while he was out on the field at Borodino.

CHAPTER 8

When the battle of Borodino was over Pierre ran down from the Rayevsky redoubt for the second time that day, and walked up the ravine leading to Knyazkovo along with hordes of soldiers. He came to the dressing-station, took one look at all the blood and heard all the men screaming and groaning, and hurried on, swept along in a mob of soldiers.

The one thing Pierre wanted now with all his heart and soul was to get away from the ghastly sensations he had lived through that day, to get back to his ordinary life-style, go indoors and settle down to sleep in his own bed. He could sense that life would have to get back to normal before he could begin to understand himself and all he had seen and experienced. But around him there were no signs of normality.

Although there were no bullets or shells whistling down on the road he was walking along, all the things he had seen and heard on the battlefield were still in evidence on every side. Everywhere he saw the same agonized, exhausted, sometimes curiously vacant faces, the same blood, the same soldiers' overcoats, the same sounds of firing no less horrifying for being a bit further away. Beyond that, it was all heat and dust.

Pierre walked a couple of miles down the Mozhaysk road and sat down at the side of the road.

It was dusky now, and the firing had stopped. Pierre stretched out, leaning on one elbow, and lay there for ages watching the shadows walk past in the evening twilight. He kept imagining a shell hurtling down on him with a weird screaming sound. This would give him the shudders and make him sit up. He had no idea how long he had been there. In the middle of the night, three soldiers came up with firewood, settled down near by and lit a fire.

The soldiers kept glancing across at Pierre as they got the fire burning up, stuck a cooking-pot on it and dropped in their broken biscuits, followed by some lard. The delicious aroma of the greasy stew mingled with the smell of smoke. Pierre pulled himself half-way up and gave a sigh. The soldiers (there were three of them) were eating and chatting away, completely ignoring Pierre.

'What mob do you belong to, then?' one of the soldiers suddenly asked Pierre, the question clearly suggesting that he was thinking along the same lines as Pierre. He seemed to be saying, 'If you're hungry we'll give you some grub, only tell us if you're a good man first.'

'Who, me? . . .' said Pierre, sensing a need to lower his social standing as much as he could so he could feel closer to the soldiers and more within their range of experience.

'Actually, I'm an officer with the militia, but my men have disappeared. I went out on the battlefield and we got separated.'

'Is that right?' said one of the soldiers.

Another shook his head.

'Well, you can have some of this muck if you fancy it!' said the first man. He licked his wooden spoon clean and handed it to Pierre.

Pierre squatted down nearer the fire, and weighed into the brew in the pot. It tasted like the most delicious food he had ever eaten. As he bent over the pot, helping himself to huge spoonfuls and wolfing them down one after another, the soldiers watched him in silence. Then one of them spoke again.

'Where you off to, then, eh?'

'Mozhaysk.'

'You a gent, then?'

'Yes.'

'What's your name?'

'Pyotr Kirillovich.'

'All right, Pyotr Kirillovich, you come with us, we'll get you there.'

In the dead of night the soldiers walked to Mozhaysk and Pierre went with them.

The cocks were crowing by the time they arrived and started climbing the uphill slope into the town. Pierre walked on with the soldiers oblivious to the fact that his inn was at the bottom of the hill and he had gone right past it. He might never have noticed – his thoughts were miles away – if he hadn't happened to run into his groom half-way up the hill. The groom had been out looking for him up in the town, and was on his way back to the inn when he recognized Pierre by the whiteness of his hat, which stood out in the dark.

'Your Excellency!' he cried. 'We was getting worried about you. What are you doing walking? And where are you heading for, for heaven's sake?'

'Er, yes . . .' said Pierre.

The soldiers came to a halt.

'Right, found your own people, have you?' said one of them.

'We'll say goodbye, then. Pyotr Kirillovich, wasn't it?'

'Goodbye, Pyotr Kirillovich!' came the other voices.

'Goodbye!' said Pierre, and he turned off towards the inn with the groom.

'Should I tip them?' thought Pierre, feeling for his pocket. 'No, better not,' an inner voice told him.

There wasn't a room to be had at the inn; every one was taken. Pierre went out into the yard, muffled his head up and lay down in his carriage.

CHAPTER 9

Pierre's head had hardly hit the cushion when he felt himself dropping off to sleep. Then immediately he could hear, just like the real thing, the cannons going *boom, boom, boom*, men groaning and screaming, and the thump of falling shells, he could smell the blood and gunpowder, and a feeling of horror, the fear of death, swept over him. He opened his eyes in panic and stuck his head out of the cloak. The yard was quiet. The only sounds came from somebody's servant chatting to the porter at the gate as he squelched through the mud. Over Pierre's head, under the dark, wooden eaves, he could hear pigeons fluttering, startled by the movement of him sitting up. The whole yard reeked as a tavern should, of hay, dung and tar, and the smell of it all lifted Pierre's spirits. Between two dark buildings he could see the pure, starlit sky.

'Thank God it's all over!' thought Pierre, burrowing down again. 'Fear – what a terrible thing it is. It got to me straightaway. I feel so ashamed! But they . . . *they* were rock-solid and perfectly calm all the way through,' he thought. *They*, in Pierre's mind, were the soldiers, soldiers on the battery, soldiers who had fed him, soldiers who had prayed to the icon. *They* – those strange people, completely unknown to him before – *they* stood out from everybody else, etched clearly and sharply in his mind.

'Oh, to be a soldier, just an ordinary soldier!' thought Pierre as he nodded off. 'To enter into that communal life with your whole being, to be absorbed into whatever it is that makes them what they are. But how can you cast off everything that doesn't matter, everything sent by the devil, the whole burden of the outer man? There was a time when I could have been one of them. I could have run away from my father. God knows I wanted to. And after that duel with Dolokhov I could have signed on as a soldier.'

And in his imagination Pierre pictured that dinner at the club when he had challenged Dolokhov, and then his benefactor at Torzhok. And in his mind he saw another picture: a grand dinner at the lodge. In the English Club. And someone he knew, someone close to him, some dear friend, was sitting at the end of the table. Yes, him! My benefactor. 'But isn't he dead?' thought Pierre. 'Yes, he did die, and I didn't know he was still alive. I'm so sorry he died, and I'm so glad he's alive again!' Down one side of the table sat Anatole, Dolokhov, Nesvitsky, Denisov and others of that ilk (this category of people was as sharply delineated in Pierre's dream as the other category of men that he had referred to as *them*), and that lot, Anatole and Dolokhov, were shouting and singing at the tops of their voices, but through all their racket he could just hear the voice of his benefactor that refused to be drowned out, and the sound of his voice was as insistent and meaningful as the roar of the battlefield, though also sweet and soothing. Pierre couldn't make out what his benefactor was saying, but he knew (the category of his ideas was also sharply delineated in his dream) that he was talking about virtue, and the possibility of being like *them*. And *they* with their simple, good, stolid faces stood all round his benefactor.

They meant well, but they took no notice of Pierre; they didn't know him. Pierre wanted them to notice him, and he wanted to speak. He tried to get up, but instantly his legs felt cold and all exposed.

He felt embarrassed, and covered his legs with one arm. In the real world his coat had slipped down. As he pulled it back up Pierre opened his eyes for an instant and caught sight of the same roofs and posts, and the yard, but it was all bathed in a blueish light, and there was a twinkling of dew or frost.

'It's getting light,' thought Pierre. 'But that's not it. I've got to listen to the benefactor and understand what he's saying.'

Again he burrowed down under his coat, but the masonic dinner and his benefactor had gone. He was left with mere thoughts, coming out in words, ideas, a voice speaking them, or was it Pierre himself thinking them?

When he remembered these thoughts afterwards, although they had been stimulated by the impressions of that particular day, Pierre was certain they had come to him from outside. He really believed that in his waking moments he could never have thought those thoughts or expressed them in that form.

'War is the subjection of man's will to the law of God at its most agonizing extreme,' said the voice. 'Simplicity is submitting to God's will. You cannot escape Him. And *they* are simple. *They* don't talk, they do things. Spoken words are silver, unspoken words are gold. A man can be master of nothing while ever he fears death. And the man that fears not death possesses everything. Without suffering a man would know not his limits, would know not himself. The hardest thing . . .' (Pierre was thinking, or hearing, in his dream) '. . . is to know how to unite in your soul the meaning of the whole. Unite the whole?' Pierre said to himself. 'No, not unity. You can't unite your thoughts, you can *harness* thoughts, all of them together. Yes, that's what you have to do. *Harness* them together, *harness* them.' Pierre repeated the words with a thrill of delight, feeling that they, and they alone, said what he wanted to say, and solved the whole problem he had been agonizing over.

'Yes, we must get them *in harness*. No time to lose.'

'Time to get them in harness. Time to harness the horses, your Excellency! Your Excellency . . .' A voice was saying it over and over again. 'Harness the horses, harness the horses . . . Time to go, sir . . .'

It was the groom waking Pierre. The sun was shining straight in Pierre's eyes. He glanced at the filthy inn and its yard, where soldiers were watering their skinny horses at the well, and wagons were trundling out through the gate.

He turned away in disgust, closed his eyes and quickly sank back down into the carriage-seat. 'No, I don't want that. I don't want to see that and understand it. I want to know what was coming out in my dream. In another second I would have seen it all. What can I do now? Harness things? How can I harness things together?' And Pierre was horrified to realize that the entire meaning of what he had seen and thought during his dream had slipped away.

And here were the groom, the coachman and the porter all telling Pierre the same story: an officer had brought word that the French were advancing on Mozhaysk and our troops were retreating.

Pierre got out, ordered them to pack the carriage and follow on and walked through the town on foot.

The troops were on the march, leaving behind not far from ten thousand wounded men. You could see the wounded sitting by the windows in the houses, and thronging the yards and streets. Out on the streets you could hear men screaming, swearing and banging on the carts detailed to take the wounded away. When Pierre's carriage caught up with him he gave a lift to a wounded general that he knew, all the way to Moscow. On the way he learnt that his brother-in-law, Anatole, and Prince Andrey had both been killed.

CHAPTER 10

Pierre got back to Moscow on the 30th. Almost at the city gates he was met by one of Count Rostopchin's adjutants.

'Hey, we've been looking for you everywhere,' said the adjutant. 'The count needs to see you as a matter of urgency. He wants you to come and see him straightaway. It's something very important.' Instead of going home, Pierre took a cab and drove round to the governor's.

Count Rostopchin had come back into town from his summer villa at Sokolniki that very morning. The ante-room and reception-room in the count's house were crammed with officials, some of them called in by him, others wanting instructions. Vasilchikov and Platov had already been in and informed the count that defending Moscow was out of the question; the city would have to be surrendered. This news was being kept from the people, but the top officials and the heads of the various departments knew that Moscow would soon be in enemy hands, as did Count Rostopchin himself. And to avoid personal responsibility all of them had come to the governor to ask what to do with the sections they were in charge of.

At the moment when Pierre walked into the waiting-room an army courier was on his way out from an interview with the count. With an air of hopelessness he waved away the questions coming at him, and walked across the room.

While he was waiting Pierre cast a weary gaze over the roomful of various officials, young and old, military and civilian, important and insignificant. Every last one of them seemed worried and unhappy. Pierre went over to one group that contained someone he knew. They welcomed him and went on with their conversation.

'No, sending them away and bringing them back again won't do any harm, but as things stand we don't know where we are.'

'But look what he's written here,' said another, pointing to a printed paper he was holding in his hand.

'That's different. We need that sort of thing for the common people,' said the first man.

'What is it?' asked Pierre.

'It's the latest poster.'

Pierre took it and started to read.

'His Serene Highness Prince Kutuzov has withdrawn through Mozhaysk to join up more quickly with troops heading his way, and he has now taken up a strong position which the enemy will find it hard to attack. Forty-eight cannons and supplies of ammunition have been sent out to him, and his Serene Highness has vowed to defend Moscow to the last drop of blood and fight in the streets. Brother citizens, do not misunderstand the closing of the Law Courts; this step was unavoidable, but be assured that we shall still have our own ways of dealing with criminals! When the time comes I shall need some good men, from town and country. I shall give the call a day or two beforehand, but for the moment there's no need, and I say no more. You will find axes useful, and hunting spears are pretty good too, but the three-pronged fork is the best of the lot – Frenchmen weigh no more than a sheaf of rye. Tomorrow afternoon I shall take the Iversk icon of the Mother of God to the wounded men in Catherine's Hospital. There we shall have the water blessed, and they will get better more quickly. I'm feeling better myself. I did have trouble with one eye, but now I'm on the lookout with both.'

'But I was told by the military,' said Pierre, 'there couldn't be any fighting in the town, and the position . . .'

'Yes, yes, that's what we're saying,' said the first speaker.

'And what does it mean when he says, "I did have trouble with one eye, but now I'm on the lookout with both"?'

'The count had a stye on his eye,' said the adjutant smiling, 'and he was very upset when I told him people were coming up to ask what was wrong with him. Oh, by the way, Count,' he said suddenly, turning to Pierre with a smile on his face, 'we've been hearing about your family problems. The word is that your wife, the countess . . .'

'I haven't heard anything,' said Pierre indifferently. 'What have you heard?'

'Oh, you know how it is – stories go the rounds. I'm just telling you what I've heard.'

'What have you heard?'

'Well, people are saying,' said the adjutant with the same unwavering smile, 'that your wife, the countess, is getting ready to go abroad. I'm sure it's all nonsense.'

'Maybe it is,' said Pierre, looking round absentmindedly. 'Who's that?' he asked, pointing to a little old man with a big snow-white beard, eyebrows of the same colour and a ruddy face, wearing a clean blue coat.

'Him? Oh, he's just a local tradesman. He runs an eating-place. It's Vereshchagin. You must have heard the story about the proclamation.'

'Oh, that's Vereshchagin, is it?' said Pierre, staring closely at the old man's calm, steady face, searching for signs of treachery.

'That's not *the* Vereshchagin. That's the father of the fellow who wrote the proclamation,' said the adjutant. 'His son's in gaol. Got it coming to him, I shouldn't wonder.'

A little old gentleman wearing a star and another official, a German with a cross round his neck, came over to join them.

'Well, it's a long story really,' the adjutant was saying. 'There was this proclamation that came out a couple of months ago. It was sent to the count, and he ordered an inquiry. Well, Gavrilo Ivanych here looked into things and he found out the proclamation had gone through exactly sixty-three pairs of hands. He goes to one fellow and asks where he got it from. Oh, so-and-so. Where did *he* get it from? So-and-so. And it went on like that until they traced it all the way back to Vereshchagin . . . Bit of a tradesman, not much education, you know, makes a bit on the side,' said the adjutant with a smile. 'So they asked him where he got it from. Not that we didn't know. There was only one man he could have got it from – the postmaster. But there must have been some kind of deal between them. Nobody, he says – he wrote it himself. No good threatening him or asking questions. He sticks to his story. He wrote it himself. So they told the count, and he had him in. "Where did you get this proclamation?" "Wrote it myself." Well, you know what the count's like,' said the adjutant, enjoying himself and smiling with pride. 'Came down on him like a ton of bricks ... called him a brazen liar and a stubborn idiot!'

'I see! The count needed him to point the finger at Klyucharyov,' said Pierre.

'Well no, he didn't,' said the adjutant in dismay. 'Klyucharyov had sins enough to answer for without that. That's why he was banished. Anyway, the count was furious. "How could you have written this?" says he. He picks up a copy of the *Hamburg Gazette* from the table. "Here it is. You didn't write this, you translated it, and you made a rotten job of it because you're a stupid fool and you don't know any French." Can you imagine it? "No," says he, "I haven't read no gazettes. I just wrote it." "Well if you did, you're a traitor, and I'm handing you over to the court, and they'll string you up. Just tell us where you got it from." "I haven't seen no gazettes. I wrote it." And that's where it stands. The count had the father in. Same story. So they had him tried and sentenced. I think he got hard labour. That's why the father's here now – interceding for his son. But he's a useless layabout! You know the type – spoilt brat, tradesman's son, fancy-man seducer of women, been to a few classes and let it go to his head. Ugly customer! His father runs that eating-house down by the Stone Bridge, with that huge icon, God the Father – you know, a sceptre in one hand and an orb in the other – well, he took that home for a day or two, and do you know what he did with it? He got somebody from the gutter who could paint a bit, and ...'

CHAPTER 11

In the middle of this new story Pierre was called in to see the governor-general.

He walked into Count Rostopchin's study. As he did so Rostopchin was scowling and rubbing his forehead and eyes with one hand. There was a little man with him and he was speaking, but the moment Pierre came in he stopped talking and left the room.

'Ah! See the conquering hero comes,' said Rostopchin as soon as he had gone. 'We've been hearing about your valiant deeds! But that's by the way. Tell me, my dear fellow, just between the two of us – are you a freemason?' said Count Rostopchin, looking all serious as if this was some kind of criminal activity that he might just be prepared to condone. Pierre made no response. 'I keep my ear to the ground, old man, and I do know there are masons and masons. I just hope you're not one of those who use the salvation of mankind as an excuse to destroy Russia itself.'

'Yes, I am a mason,' answered Pierre.

'Well then, listen to me, dear boy. I imagine you're not unaware that Messrs Speransky and Magnitsky have been sent away to their proper places, and Mr Klyucharyov has got the same treatment, along with all the others who have used the building of Solomon's temple as an excuse to bring down the temple of Russia. You may take it from me there are good reasons behind this. I could never have banished our Postmaster General if he hadn't been a danger to the community. It has now come to my notice that it was you who sent a carriage to get him out of town, and his papers have been sent to you for safe-keeping. I like you, and I wish you no harm, and since you're half my age, I'm going to give you a bit of fatherly advice. Sever all contacts with that kind of person, and get out of here as fast as you can.'

'But what has Klyucharyov done wrong?' asked Pierre.

'That's my business. I'm not answerable to you!' Rostopchin burst out.

'If he's accused of circulating Napoleon's proclamations, you have no proof,' said Pierre, avoiding Rostopchin's eyes. 'And as for Vereshchagin . . .'

'Ah, there you have it!' Rostopchin cut in, scowling again and shouting louder than before. 'Vereshchagin is a snake in the grass, a traitor who will get what's coming to him,' he said, speaking with all the vindictiveness of someone recalling an old grievance. 'But I didn't call you in to talk about my affairs – I brought you here to give you some advice, or your marching orders, if that's the way you prefer it. I'm asking you to sever all contacts with the likes of Klyucharyov and get out of town. I'm going to beat the nonsense out of anybody stupid enough to . . .' But then suddenly he seemed to realize he was bawling at a man who hadn't done anything wrong, so he took Pierre by the hand in a friendly way and added: 'We're on the eve of a public disaster, and I haven't time for niceties when people come in to talk business. Sometimes my head fair spins. Anyway, what are you up to now, my dear fellow, you personally?'

'Oh, nothing,' answered Pierre, still refusing to look up. His face looked preoccupied, and its expression didn't change.

The count frowned.

'Listen to me, old man. Get away as soon you can. That's my friendly advice to you. Nothing more to be said. A word to the wise

. . . Goodbye, dear boy. Oh, by the way,' he shouted after Pierre as he walked out through the doorway, 'is it true the countess has fallen into the clutches of the holy fathers of the Society of Jesus?'

Pierre did not respond to this. He stormed out of Rostopchin's room with the darkest, angriest scowl that had ever been seen on his face.

By the time he reached home it was getting dark. That evening more than half-a-dozen assorted visitors came to see him – a committee secretary, the colonel of his militia battalion, his steward, his butler, and several other petitioners. All of them had business to discuss with Pierre, and he had decisions to make. He hadn't the slightest idea what they were on about, not the slightest interest in any of them, and to each man in turn he blurted out the first thing that came into his head just to get rid of him. Alone at last, he broke open his wife's letter and read it through.

'*The men* – the soldiers in the battery, Prince Andrey killed . . . the old man . . . Simplicity is submitting to God's will. The need to suffer . . . the meaning of the whole . . . harnessing things together . . . my wife is going to be married . . . The need to forget and understand . . .' And he went over to his bed, flung himself down on it without taking his clothes off, and fell fast asleep.

When he woke up the following morning his butler came in with the news that an official from the police department had been expressly ordered by Count Rostopchin to come round and find out whether Count Bezuhov had already left, or was on his way.

A dozen assorted visitors were waiting downstairs in the drawing-room to see Pierre on business. Pierre threw on some clothes, but instead of going down to see the waiting throng, he ran down the back stairs and slipped out through the gate.

From that moment on, until after the destruction of Moscow, despite many attempts to trace him, no member of Bezukhov's household staff saw him again, or knew where he had gone.

CHAPTER 12

The Rostovs stayed on in Moscow until the 1st of September, the day before the enemy entered the city.

Once Petya had joined Obolensky's Cossack regiment and gone off to Belaya Tserkov, where the regiment was forming, the countess panicked. For the first time that summer the realization that both of her sons were away at war, both had flown the nest, and today or tomorrow either one of them might get killed, possibly both of them at the same time, which had happened to the three sons of a lady she knew, struck her with painful clarity. She tried to get Nikolay back, she wanted to run off after Petya and get him posted to Petersburg, but neither was possible. Petya couldn't be brought back unless his regiment came back too, or unless he was transferred to another regiment on active service. Nikolay was away at the front somewhere, and not a word had been heard from him since his last letter, which had contained a detailed description of his encounter with Princess Marya. The countess couldn't sleep at night, and when she did sleep she dreamt that both of her sons had been killed. After much deliberation and consultation the count eventually hit on a way of soothing the countess. He got Petya transferred from Obolensky's regiment to Bezukhov's, which was in training near Moscow. True, Petya was still in the army, but this transfer gave the countess the consolation of seeing at least one of her sons under her wing again, and she was hoping to arrange for Petya never to go away, and always to be sent to serve in places where there would be no risk of his going into battle. While ever Nikolay had been the only one in danger the countess had imagined, not without some qualms of conscience, that she loved her eldest child more than the others, but now that her younger boy, naughty little Petya, bad at his lessons, the clumsy boy who broke everything in the house and drove them all wild, her Petya, with his turned-up nose, laughing black eyes and fresh rosy cheeks with only a bit of fluff on them, had got in with those huge, awful, violent men who had gone away somewhere fighting over something or other, and enjoying it too – now as a mother she seemed to love him more, much more, than all the rest. The nearer they got to the time when her longed-for Petya was due back in Moscow, the more worried the countess became. She felt certain she would never live to see such happiness. The close proximity of Sonya, or her favourite Natasha, or even her husband simply irritated the countess. 'I don't need them. All I want is Petya!' she thought.

One day towards the end of August, the Rostovs received another letter from Nikolay. He was writing from the province of Voronezh, where he had been sent to procure fresh horses. This letter brought no comfort to the countess. The knowledge that one son was out of danger just made her more apprehensive about Petya.

Although by the 20th of August virtually everyone they knew had left Moscow in dribs and drabs, and although everybody was trying to persuade the countess to get away as soon as she could, she wouldn't hear of leaving until the treasure of her life, her adored Petya, had come back. On the 28th of August he arrived. The sixteen-year-old officer was anything but delighted to be welcomed by his mother with such a morbid display of affection and soppiness. Though his mother concealed her intention of never letting him escape from under her wing again, Petya soon guessed what she was up to and instinctively recoiled from the idea that his mother might make him too soft and turn him into a silly woman (as he put it to himself), so he kept her at arm's length and avoided her, devoting himself during his stay in Moscow exclusively to Natasha. His brotherly affection was so strong he was almost in love with her.

Even as late as the 28th the count, with his usual negligence, had made no preparations for leaving, and it was the 30th of the month before the wagons that were due to come in from the Moscow and Ryazan estates and pick up their property at the house finally arrived.

From the 28th to the 31st Moscow was seething with movement. Every day thousands of war casualties from Borodino were brought in through the Dorogomilov gate and taken all over Moscow, while thousands of carts piled high with residents and their belongings trundled out through other gates. Rostopchin's posters made no difference; either independently of them, or maybe because of them, the town was alive with the weirdest and most contradictory rumours. Some said there was a ban on leaving the city; others claimed the opposite – the churches had been stripped of their icons, and everybody was going to be forced out of Moscow. Some said there had been another battle after Borodino, and the French had been routed; others claimed the opposite – the entire Russian army had been wiped out. Some said the Moscow militia was going to march out to the Three Hills, led by the clergy; others whispered that Father Augustin had been told he couldn't leave, traitors had been caught, the peasants were up in arms and they were robbing anybody who left town, and so on and so forth. But this was all talk. In point of fact, even though the council at Fili still lay in the future, so no decision to abandon Moscow had yet been taken, absolutely everyone – those who were leaving and those who were staying – felt that, although no one could say so openly, Moscow was lost and it was up to everybody to get out as soon as they could and save their own property. There was a feeling of change in the air, as if they were sitting on a powder-keg, yet everything went on unchanged until the 1st of September. Like a criminal on his way to the scaffold, who knows he has only minutes to live but still looks round at everything and straightens the untidy cap on his head, Moscow continued to go through the motions of everyday life, fully aware that the hour of doom was at hand when the normal way of life that they had grown so used to would be blasted away.

During the three days leading up to the occupation of Moscow all the Rostovs went about their various bits of family business. The head of the family, Count Ilya Rostov, drove from one end of the town to the other in search of every last rumour, and when he was at home he went round giving out trivial and ill-considered instructions to those who were getting things ready for the departure.

The countess was in charge of the packing, finding fault with everybody and forever chasing after Petya because she resented him spending all his time with Natasha. Sonya was the only person who got down to the actual business of getting things packed. But Sonya had been particularly sad and silent of late. She had been there at the reading of Nikolay's letter, when the mention of Princess Marya had set the countess off on an ecstatic train of thought based on the idea that the encounter between Nikolay and the princess showed the workings of Divine Providence.

'I was never very happy,' said the countess, 'when Bolkonsky was engaged to Natasha, but I always longed for Nikolay to marry the princess, and I've a feeling it might just happen. Oh, how wonderful that would be!'

Sonya could see the justice of this. The only possibility of easing the Rostovs' plight was by marrying Nikolay to an heiress, and the princess would be an excellent match. But this was a bitter pill to swallow. In spite of her grief, or perhaps because of it, she took on all the hardest jobs in sorting things out and stowing them away, and kept herself busy for days on end. The count and countess consulted her when there were instructions to be given. Petya and Natasha, by contrast, never lifted a finger to help; they just got in the way and irritated everybody. All day long the house rang with their flying footsteps, yells and shrieks of laughter about nothing at all. They were happy and laughing not because there was any reason for laughter. It was the other way round: they were so full of high spirits and great glee that everything seemed reason enough for joy and laughter. Petya was flying high because he had left home a boy, and come back (so everyone told him) a splendid young man, because he was back home again, because he had left Belaya Tserkov, where active service had seemed such a remote prospect, and come back to Moscow, where the fighting would start any day now, but most of all because Natasha, who always set the pace for him, was flying high herself. And she was like that because she had spent too much time being sad, and now, with no more reminders of why she had been so sad, she was well again. And also because there was someone to adore her; being adored was like greasing the wheels that turned her into a smooth-running machine, and Petya certainly adored her. But most of all they were flying high because war was at the walls of Moscow, there would be fighting at the gates, arms were being given out, everybody was rushing about and running away, and something quite sensational was happening, which is always a source of delight, especially for young people.

CHAPTER 13

On Saturday, the 31st of August, the Rostov household looked as if it had been turned upside down. Every door was wide open, every stick of furniture had been carried outside or shifted around, and all the mirrors and pictures had been taken down. The rooms were littered with trunks, straw, wrapping-paper and string. Peasants and house serfs clomped across the parquet floors as they took things outside. The courtyard was crowded with carts, some of them stacked with goods and roped up, others yet to be filled.

Courtyard and house were alive with voices and footsteps, and swarming with house servants and peasants who had come in with the carts. The count had gone off somewhere first thing. The countess had gone down with a headache from all the racket and the hurly-burly, and she was lying flat out in the new sitting-room with a vinegar poultice across her forehead. Petya was out. (He had slipped away to see a young friend; the pair of them were planning to get themselves transferred from the militia into a front-line regiment.) Sonya was out in the big hall, supervising the stowage of glass and china. Natasha was sitting in the middle of the floor amidst the wreckage of her room, in a sea of scattered dresses, ribbons and scarves. She was staring down at the floor as she clutched an old ballgown, the one she had worn at her first Petersburg ball – and how unfashionable it looked now.

Natasha felt embarrassed that she was doing nothing when everyone else was so busy, and several times that morning she had tried to get involved, but her heart wasn't in it. Mentally and physically she was incapable of undertaking anything unless her heart and soul were in it. She had stood over Sonya for a few minutes while she packed the china, and she had tried to help, but not for long; soon she was off to her room to see to her own packing. At first it was fun to be giving away some of her dresses and ribbons to the maids, but when it came to packing what was left, it was too much trouble.

'Dunyasha, would you pack my things, darling? Please. Would you?'

Only too readily Dunyasha promised to do everything, whereupon Natasha sat herself down on the floor with the old ballgown in her hands, and let her thoughts wander – anything to avoid what should have been on her mind there and then. Natasha was jolted out of her reverie by the sound of the maids chattering in the next room and then clattering out of their room and down the back stairs. Natasha got to her feet and looked out of the window. There on the street was a huge train of wagons that had come to a halt, full of wounded men.

Maids, footmen, housekeeper, the old nurse, cooks, coachmen, grooms, and kitchen-boys – they were all out there at the gates, staring at the wounded men.

Natasha flung a white pocket-handkerchief over her hair, and held the corners with both hands as she went down to the street.

Mavra, the old housekeeper, had walked out from the crowd by the gate and gone over to one wagon that had a covering of fibre matting. She was now talking to a pallid young officer who was lying in it. Natasha tiptoed forward one or two steps, and stood there shyly, holding on to her handkerchief and listening to what the housekeeper was saying.

'So. None of your people left in Moscow?' Mavra was saying. 'You'd be better off in somebody's house . . . This one, for instance. The masters are all moving out.'

'Don't suppose they'd allow that,' said the officer in a feeble voice. 'There's our senior officer . . . Ask him,' and he pointed to a corpulent major who was walking back past the carts lined up along the street.

Natasha glanced fearfully at the wounded officer's face, and went straight up to the major.

'Would you please allow the wounded men to stay in our house?' she asked.

The major smiled and raised one hand to his cap.

'Which one do you want, mam'selle?' he said, screwing his eyes into a smile.

Natasha calmly repeated her request, and her face and her whole manner, even though she was still hanging on to the corners of the handkerchief, seemed so serious that the major wiped the smile off his face and gave some thought to this new possibility before saying yes to it.

'I don't see why not,' he said.

Natasha gave him a tiny nod, and skipped back to Mavra, who was standing over the young officer and talking to him with a great show of sympathy.

'He said yes. He said they can!' whispered Natasha.

The officer in the covered cart turned into the Rostovs' courtyard, and dozens of carts carrying wounded men were soon accepting invitations from good citizens to drive up to the entries of other houses in Povarsky Street. Natasha was obviously delighted to be dealing with different people under totally new circumstances. She worked alongside Mavra, getting as many people as possible to drive into their yard.

'We must ask your papa, though,' said Mavra.

'Don't be silly. It makes no difference now! We can move into the drawing-room just for one day. They can have our part of the house, all of it.'

'Oh, miss, what are you talking about? They can go into the outbuildings, the men's room and old nurse's room, but even then you'll have to ask.'

'All right, I will.'

She ran indoors. The sitting-room door was ajar; there was a strong smell of vinegar and Hoffmann's drops. Natasha tiptoed in.

'Are you asleep, Mamma?'

'How can anybody sleep?' said the countess, who had just been nodding off.

'Mamma, darling!' said Natasha, kneeling down and bringing her face close up to her mother's. 'I'm so sorry, please forgive me. I'll never do it again. I've woken you up. Mavra sent me. They've brought some wounded soldiers, officers. You will let them in, won't you? They've got nowhere to go. I know you will,' she gabbled without pausing for breath.

'Officers? Who's been brought in? I don't understand what you're saying,' said the countess.

Natasha laughed, and even the countess managed a thin smile.

'I knew you would . . . Right, I'll go and tell them.' And Natasha gave her mother a kiss, got to her feet and went to the door.

Out in the hall she ran into her father, who had just got back, the bearer of bad news.

'We've stayed on too long!' said the count, unable to hide his resentment. 'The club's closed, and the police are leaving.'

'Papa, I've invited some wounded soldiers into the house. You don't mind, do you?' said Natasha.

'Of course not,' said the count, his mind on other matters. 'But that's by the way. I'm asking you now to stop messing about. Please help with the packing. We ought to be on the road. We must be off tomorrow . . .'

And the count issued the same instructions to his butler and the servants.

Petya was back by dinner-time, and he also brought news. He said the people had been out today collecting weapons in the Kremlin, and although Rostopchin's poster said he would give the call a day or two beforehand, there was a clear understanding that tomorrow everybody had to go with their weapons to the Three Hills, because a great battle was going to be fought there.

The countess was horrified. As he was saying all this she kept a nervous watch on her son's eager, excited face. She knew it: one word from her about Petya staying away from this battle (she could see he was relishing the prospect of it), and he would go on at her about being a man, honour, the fatherland – the bone-headed obstinacy of men that brooked no opposition – and all would be lost. So, in the hope of getting away beforehand and taking Petya along as their guard and protector, she said nothing to her son, but as soon as dinner was over she took her husband to one side, burst into tears and begged him to take her away as soon as possible, that night if it could be done. Until this moment she had been a model of self-control, but now with all the guile and affection that come naturally to a woman, she said she would die of fright if they didn't get away that very night. For once she was not pretending; everything scared her now.

CHAPTER 14

Madame Schoss, who had been out walking on a visit to her daughter, added to the countess's fears by describing what she had seen outside a public house in Myasnitsky Street. That thoroughfare was on her way home, but she hadn't been able to walk down it because there was a drunken mob rampaging round the public house. She had taken a cab and driven home by a roundabout route; the driver had told her that the mob had been breaking barrels open, and they had been told to do so.

After lunch all the Rostov household were only too eager to resume the business of packing and preparing for their departure at top speed. The old count jumped to it, and spent the whole day trotting in and out of the courtyard, shouting meaningless instructions to the hurrying servants, and trying to get them to go even faster. Petya directed operations outside. Sonya couldn't make head or tail of the count's contradictory orders, and she didn't know which way to turn. The servants were running about all over the place, inside and out, shouting, arguing and making a terrible racket. Natasha now joined the fray, with her usual enthusiasm. At first her sudden involvement was viewed with some suspicion. Everybody expected nothing but silliness from her and they wouldn't do what she said, but she stuck to her guns and urgently insisted on being obeyed, losing her temper and almost weeping from frustration because they wouldn't listen, and at last she won them round. Her first solid achievement, which cost her much effort but finally established her authority, had to do with packing the rugs. The house contained a number of expensive Gobelin tapestries and Persian carpets. When Natasha got to work she found two boxes standing open in the ballroom, one almost full of china, the other full of rugs. There was a lot more china stacked on the tables and more still coming in from the pantry. What they needed was a third box, and the servants had gone to get one.

'Sonya, don't do that. We'll get it all in,' said Natasha.

'We won't, miss. We've already tried,' said the under-butler.

'No, wait a minute, please.' And Natasha started taking the paper-wrapped plates and dishes out of the box.

'It would be better to wrap the dishes in with the rugs,' she said.

'But, for goodness' sake, we've still got enough rugs left to fill three boxes,' said the footman.

'Just wait. Please.' And Natasha began sorting things out. She moved swiftly and with an expert hand. 'We don't need these,' she said, handling some Kiev plates. 'We do need this lot. They can go in the rugs,' she decided, fishing out the Saxony dishes.

'Oh, Natasha, please don't. Leave us alone. We'll get it all packed,' Sonya chided.

'What a young lady!' exclaimed the butler.

But Natasha was determined. She pulled everything out and quickly started repacking, deciding that the poor-quality rugs and spare crockery needn't be taken at all. When everything had been emptied out she began the repacking, and lo and behold, by throwing out all the cheaper stuff that wasn't worth taking the valuable items were easily squeezed into two boxes. There was only one problem: the lid of the rug box wouldn't shut. A few things could have been taken out, but Natasha wanted to do it her way. She unpacked, repacked, squashed it down, got one of the servants to help Petya, now pressed into service, force the lid down, and added her own desperate efforts.

'It's no good, Natasha,' Sonya said. 'I can see you're right, but you'll have to take the top one out.'

'I will not,' yelled Natasha, using one hand to flick her tousled hair away from her sweating face and the other to press down on the rugs. 'Come on, Petya, squash it down! Press hard!' she cried. The rugs sank down and the lid snapped to. Natasha clapped her hands and shrieked with delight while the tears came to her eyes. But that lasted no longer than a second. She was off on another job, and now the servants trusted her completely, the count didn't object when he heard that his daughter had told them to ignore his instructions, and the servants started coming to Natasha to ask whether a cart was properly loaded and could they rope it down. It was all going swimmingly now, with Natasha in charge. Anything useless was left behind and the things that mattered were stowed with maximum efficiency.

But despite their best efforts night came and they were still not quite packed and ready. The countess had fallen asleep, and the count put off the departure till morning and went off to bed.

Sonya and Natasha slept in the sitting-room, without taking their clothes off.

That night another wounded officer was driven along Povarsky Street, and Mavra, who was standing at the gate, had him brought into the Rostovs' yard. She could only surmise that he must be a man of some importance. He was being transported in a four-wheeled carriage with the hood down and the apron all across the front. Up on the box sitting alongside the driver was a venerable-looking old valet. A doctor and two soldiers were following this carriage in a smaller one.

'Please come in here, come on in. The masters are on their way out. The whole place is empty,' said the old woman to the old servant.

'Well,' answered the valet with a sigh, 'we're not going to make it. We have our own house in Moscow, but it's a long way out, and there's no one there.'

'Well, do come in here, our masters have got plenty of everything, and you're very welcome,' said Mavra. 'Is the gentleman very bad, then?' she asked.

The valet's gesture spoke volumes.

'He won't make it. Better ask the doctor.' And the valet got down and went to the vehicle behind.

'Very good,' said the doctor.

The valet came back to the front carriage, took a look inside, shook his head, told the coachman to turn into the yard, and stood there at Mavra's side.

'Oh, Lord Jesus Christ!' she murmured.

Mavra told them to bring the wounded man indoors.

'The masters won't mind . . .' she said.

But they had to avoid carrying him up any steps, so they took the wounded man to the lodge, and put him in the room that had been Madame Schoss's.

The wounded man was Prince Andrey Bolkonsky.

CHAPTER 15

Moscow's last day had dawned. The autumn weather was bright and clear. It was Sunday. As on any other Sunday church bells were summoning the faithful. By all appearances no one could have been anticipating what was in store for the city.

There were only two social indicators that reflected the position Moscow was in: the activity of the poor people or hoi polloi, and prices. Early that morning factory workers, house serfs and peasants came flocking out on to the Three Hills, mingling with clerks, divinity students and members of the gentry. They lingered there for a while waiting for Rostopchin, but his non-appearance told them for certain that Moscow was going to be surrendered, so they swarmed back into the city and dispersed among all the taverns and public houses of Moscow. Prices, too, were a good indicator of how things stood that day. The prices of weapons, horses and carts and the value of gold rose steadily, while the value of paper money and household goods was in steep decline, so that by early afternoon there were instances of drivers going halves over any luxury goods like cloth that they were delivering, and whereas a peasant's horse would fetch five hundred roubles, furniture, mirrors and bronzes could be had for nothing.

The sudden collapse of normal life made little impact on the staid, old-fashioned house of the Rostovs. In relation to people, it is true that three servants from their immense retinue had disappeared overnight, but nothing had been stolen; in relation to prices, it transpired that the Rostovs with their thirty carts brought in from the country now owned something of enormous value that many people envied and some were offering to purchase for enormous sums of money. And it was not only a question of being offered enormous sums of money; all the previous evening and now early in the morning of the 1st of September orderlies and servants started turning up in the Rostovs' courtyard, sent there by wounded officers, and wounded men themselves would come limping in from the Rostovs' own house and other houses nearby to implore the servants to try and get them a lift out of Moscow. The butler who received these requests, although sympathetic, turned them all down point-blank, saying that he would never even dare pass this on to the count. However grievous the situation of these abandoned casualties, it was obvious that if you gave them one cart there would be nothing to stop you giving them another, and another, until they were all gone – and the carriages too. Thirty wagons weren't enough to save all the wounded, and in a general catastrophe you had to put you and yours first. This was how the butler reasoned on his master's behalf.

Count Rostov woke up that morning and slipped quietly out of his bedroom so as not to disturb the countess, who had been awake most of the night, and walked out on to the front steps in his lilac silk dressing-gown. The wagons were standing there in the courtyard loaded and roped. The carriages waited at the bottom of the steps. The butler was out at the entrance talking to an old orderly and a pale-faced young officer with his arm in a sling. The moment the butler caught sight of his master he made it clear in no uncertain terms that they had better be on their way.

'Ah, Vasilich, is everything ready, then?' asked the count, rubbing his bald head as he gave the officer and the orderly a friendly glance and a quick nod. (The count liked seeing new faces.)

'We can harness immediately, your Excellency.'

'Splendid. Once the countess is up and about we'll be on our way, God willing! What can I do for you two gentlemen?' he said, addressing the officer. 'Are you staying in the house?'

The officer came nearer. His pallid face had suddenly flushed crimson.

'Count, would you do me a great favour? Please . . . for God's sake . . . could you squeeze me into one of your wagons? I've nothing with me . . . I could get in with the luggage . . .'

Before the officer had finished speaking the orderly was there with a similar request for his master.

'Oh, yes, yes, yes,' gabbled the count. 'Only too glad to help. Vasilich, see to this, will you? Have one or two wagons cleared. Er, that one maybe? What's, er . . . Oh . . . just do what's necessary . . .' The count's instructions consisted of vague ramblings. But the warm glow of gratitude on the officer's face instantly set the seal on his order. The count took a look round. On all sides – in the courtyard, at the gates, at the lodge windows – he could see wounded men and orderlies. They were all looking his way and beginning to head for the steps.

'Sir, I wonder if you would mind coming with me to the gallery. We

need you to decide about the pictures,' said the butler. And the count
went indoors with him, repeating his instructions that any wounded
men who wanted a lift were not to be refused.

'Well, we can take a few things out, can't we?' he added in a low,
conspiratorial voice, as if he didn't want to be overheard.

The countess woke at nine, and Matryona, who had been her maid
before her marriage and now guarded her like a police-chief, came in
to report that Madame Schoss was most annoyed, and the young
ladies' summer dresses couldn't possibly be left behind. When the
countess wanted to know what had upset Madame Schoss it emerged
that this lady's trunk had been taken down from its cart, and all the
carts were being unroped and the luggage was being taken out to make
room for wounded men who had been invited along by the count, in
all his innocence. The countess sent for her husband.

'What's this I hear, my dear? They're unloading the luggage?'

'Oh yes, my love. I've ... I've been meaning to tell you ... Dear
little countess ... This officer came up to me asking for a couple of
carts for the wounded. I know it's our property, but think about them
being left behind! ... They're out there in the yard. We invited them
in. Some of them are officers ... You see, my love ... The way I see
it ... I mean ... I think we should take them. We're not in too much
of a hurry.'

The count's tone was diffident, as always when it came to money.
The countess knew the tone well, the inevitable harbinger of some
new piece of business likely to be ruinous for the children, like the
building of a new gallery, or a conservatory, getting up a new theatre
in the house, or forming an orchestra, and it was now a matter of
habit and duty for her to resist anything that came to her in that
diffident tone.

Assuming her attitude of tearful resignation, she spoke to her
husband.

'Listen, Count, you've brought us so low we're getting nothing for
the house, and now you want to get rid of all our things – *the children's
property*. It was you who told me we have a hundred thousand roubles'
worth of valuables in this house. I won't have it, my dear, I won't
have it. What do you think you're doing? It's the government's job to
look after the wounded, and they know full well. Look at the Lopukh-
ins across the street – they cleared out every stick only the other day.
That's how other people do things. We're the only fools. You may
have no consideration for me, but at least think about the children.'

The count threw up his hands, and went out of the room without
saying a word.

'Papa! What's all this about?' asked Natasha, who had followed him to her mother's room.

'Nothing! You keep out of this!' the count said angrily.

'But I heard,' said Natasha. 'Why is Mamma objecting?'

'Keep out of it!' cried the count.

Natasha walked over to the window, looking thoughtful.

'Oh, Papa, look. Berg's come to see us,' she said, looking out of the window.

CHAPTER 16

By this time Berg, the Rostovs' son-in-law, was a colonel, with the orders of Vladimir and Anne round his neck, and he was still enjoying his nice little sinecure as assistant head of staff to the assistant chief officer commanding the Second Corps first division.

On the 1st of September he had come back to Moscow from the army. He had nothing to do in the city, but he had noticed that everyone else in the army was going to Moscow on leave, and they were finding things to do there. So he decided that he too ought to apply for some leave on domestic and family grounds.

Berg drove up to his father-in-law's house in his neat little trap drawn by a pair of sleek roans, an exact copy of those belonging to a certain prince. He took a long look at the carts in the yard, and as he ran up the steps he took out a clean pocket-handkerchief and tied a knot in it.

Berg glided speedily from the ante-room to the drawing-room, where he embraced the count, kissed Natasha's hand and Sonya's, and lost no time inquiring after Mamma's health.

'Never mind people's health at a time like this! Come on, tell us what's going on in the army!' said the count. 'Are they retreating, or will they stand and fight?'

'Our Eternal Father is the only power that can decide the fate of our country, Papa,' said Berg. 'The army burns with the spirit of heroism, and at this very moment our leaders have, so to speak, foregathered in council. No one knows the outcome. But in general I can say this, Papa – that heroic spirit, the authentic and time-honoured valour of our Russian army that they – I mean *it*,' he said, correcting himself, ' – showed in the battle of the 26th . . . well, no words can do justice to it.' (He smote himself on the breast in the manner of a general he had heard holding forth, but his timing was out – the blow on the chest should have been delivered along with the phrase 'our Russian army'.) 'I can say quite openly that we officers, far from having to urge the soldiers on, or anything like that, were hard put to hold back this . . . those brave deeds of ancient valour,' he gabbled. 'General Barclay de Tolly risked his life all over the place at the head of his troops, I can assure you. Our particular corps was stationed on a hillside . . . Imagine the scene . . .' And off he went into all the stories he had committed to memory from the many circulating at a time of good stories. Natasha embarrassed Berg by watching him closely as if the solution to some problem was hidden in his face.

'Such widespread heroism as was demonstrated by the Russian soldiers is beyond description and worthy of the highest praise!' said Berg, looking at Natasha, and in an attempt to mollify her he answered her sharp stare with a smile . . . 'Russia is not to be found in Moscow, she dwells in the hearts of her sons! Isn't that right, Papa?'

At this moment the countess came in from the sitting-room looking weary and thoroughly annoyed. Berg leapt to his feet, kissed the countess's hand, asked after her health, and stood at her side, exuding sympathy with much shaking of his head.

'Yes, Mamma, the truth is, these are hard and anxious times for every Russian. But why are you looking so worried? There's still time to get away . . .'

'I can't work out what the servants are up to,' said the countess to her husband. 'They've just told me we're nowhere near ready. Someone will have to go and take charge. It's at times like this that one misses Mitenka. I can't see an end to it.'

The count was on the verge of a reply, but he bit it back with a visible effort, got to his feet and walked over to the door.

Berg, meanwhile, had taken out his handkerchief as if he was going to blow his nose, and when he saw the knot in it, he paused for a moment's thought, shaking his head in a lugubrious, meaningful way.

'By the way, Papa, I have a great favour to ask you . . .' he began.

'Hm?' said the count, pausing.

'I was going past Yusupov's place just now,' said Berg with a laugh, 'when their steward, a man I know, came running out and asked whether I might like to buy any of their things. I popped in, you know, just out of curiosity, and there was this sweet little chiffonier and a dressing-table. You remember, the very thing my dear Vera wanted, and we quarrelled about.' (At the mention of the chiffonier and dressing-table Berg had slipped unconsciously into a tone that showed how delighted he was with his lovely domestic set-up.) 'And such a delightful piece! It's got a secret English drawer – you know the sort.

Just what my little Vera has been wanting. I'd love to give it to her as a nice little surprise. I noticed you have lots of peasants down in the yard. Please could I borrow one of them? I'll pay him well, and . . .'

The count scowled and cleared his throat.

'Ask the countess. I don't give the orders.'

'If it's any trouble please don't bother,' said Berg. 'Only, I'd love to get it for Vera.'

'Oh, to hell with the lot of you! Hell and damnation! Hell and damnation!' roared the old count. 'My head's spinning.' And he walked out of the room.

The countess burst into tears.

'Yes, indeed, these are terrible times, Mamma!' said Berg.

Natasha had left the room with her father, and she seemed to be in two minds. First she followed him, then she turned back and ran downstairs.

Petya was standing on the steps busily issuing weapons to the servants who were leaving Moscow. The loaded carts were still there in the courtyard. Two had been unroped, and the wounded officer was clambering aboard one of them with some assistance from his orderly.

'What's it all about?' Petya asked Natasha. (Natasha knew what he meant: why were their father and mother at loggerheads?) She didn't answer.

'I know. Because Papa wanted to give all the carts to the wounded men,' said Petya. 'Vasilich told me. If you want my opinion . . .'

'My opinion!' Natasha turned a furious face on Petya, virtually yelling at him. 'In my opinion, it's all so horrible! It's vile! . . . Oh, I don't know. We're like a load of Germans! . . .' Her throat was racked with sobs, but she didn't want to break down or waste the full effect of her fury, so she turned and flew back up the steps.

Berg was sitting beside the countess, summoning up all his powers of filial consideration in an effort to soothe her. The count was pacing up and down the room, pipe in hand, when Natasha stormed into the room, her features contorted with fury, and raced across to her mother.

'It's horrible! It's just vile!' she screamed. 'You can't possibly have given orders like that!'

Berg and the countess stared at her in alarm and bewilderment. The count had come to a halt by the window, and he was listening.

'Mamma, it's impossible. Look what's happening down in the yard!' she cried. 'They're being left behind!'

'What's wrong with you? Who are? What do you want?'

'The wounded men! It's impossible, Mamma. It's outrageous . . . No listen, Mamma, darling, it's all wrong. I'm sorry, but please, darling . . . Mamma, it doesn't matter what we take with us. Just look down there in the yard . . . Mamma! . . . You can't do it!'

The count stood by the window, listening to Natasha without looking round. All at once he choked, and pressed his face against the window.

The countess glanced at her daughter, saw she was ashamed of her own mother, saw her agitation, suddenly realized why her husband wouldn't look round at her, and stared about with a distracted air.

'Oh, do what you want! I'm not stopping anybody doing anything,' she said, giving in gradually.

'Mamma, darling, I am sorry.'

But the countess pushed her daughter away, and went over to the count.

'You give the orders, dear. You tell them . . . I don't know what I'm doing,' she said, looking down shamefacedly.

'Out of the mouths of babes . . .' murmured the count through tears of joy, and he hugged his wife, who was only too pleased to bury her face of shame on his breast.

'Papa, Mamma! Let me give the orders. May I?' asked Natasha. 'We'll still take all the really important things,' she added.

The count nodded, and Natasha was off, racing away like a chasing child across the big hall, through the ante-room and down the front steps to the courtyard.

The servants gathered round Natasha, reluctant to believe the curious instructions she was giving out, until the count himself appeared and on behalf of his wife confirmed that all the carts were to be made available for the wounded and the boxes put into storage. Once they understood this, the servants set to with a new will and much enthusiasm. The new development no longer seemed strange; it seemed the most natural thing in the world, just as a quarter of an hour earlier they hadn't thought it the least bit strange to be leaving wounded men behind and taking the furniture – that too had seemed the most natural thing in the world.

The entire household rallied round and tackled the business of getting the wounded into the wagons, as if they wanted to make up for having neglected it earlier. The wounded soldiers came crawling out of their rooms and crowded round the wagons, pale-faced but happy. The news that there was transport available soon got round the neighbouring houses, and wounded men started trickling into the yard from other places. Many of the wounded soldiers asked them not to take out the boxes – just let them sit on top. But once the unloading process was under way there was no stopping it. It made no difference whether they left everything or only half the stuff behind. Cases full of china, bronzes, pictures and mirrors, so carefully stowed the night before, now lay neglected in the yard, and still they continued to find new ways of taking more and more things out and leaving more and more wagons for the wounded.

'We can take four more,' said the steward. 'They can have my trap too, or anything might happen to them.'

'Oh, do let them have our wardrobe cart,' said the countess. 'Dunyasha can come with me in the carriage.'

The wardrobe wagon was unloaded and dispatched to pick up wounded men two houses away. Family and servants were bubbling with excitement. Natasha was ecstatic, much happier than she had been for a very long time.

'What can we fasten this to?' said a servant, struggling with a trunk wedged on the narrow footboard at the back of the carriage. 'It's got to go on a cart.'

'What is it?' asked Natasha.

'The count's books.'

'Oh, leave it. Vasilich will take care of that. We don't need it.'

With the big carriage full of people the question was: where was Petya going to sit?

'He'll go up on the box. You'll go up on the box, won't you, Petya?' Natasha called out.

Sonya was working flat out too, but her aim was the opposite of Natasha's. She was seeing to the stowage of everything left behind, drawing up an inventory at the countess's request, and trying to get them to take as much as possible with them.

CHAPTER 17

Just before two o'clock the Rostovs' four carriages, packed and ready for the road, stood waiting by the front door. One by one wagon-loads of wounded men were trundling out of the courtyard.

A vehicle carrying Prince Andrey was on its way past the front steps when it was noticed by Sonya, who was helping one of the maids to arrange comfortable seating for the countess in her huge, high carriage.

'Whose carriage is that?' asked Sonya, popping her head out of the carriage window.

'Oh, haven't you heard, miss?' answered the maid. 'It's the wounded prince. He stayed here last night, and he's coming on with us.'

'Oh, who is he? What's his name?'

'It's our intended that was ... Prince Bolkonsky!' answered the maid with a sigh. 'They say he's dying.'

Sonya jumped out of the carriage and ran in to see the countess. The countess, dressed for the road in hat and shawl, was pacing wearily up and down the drawing-room, waiting for the rest of the household to come in and sit down behind closed doors for the usual silent prayer before starting out. Natasha wasn't there.

'Mamma,' said Sonya, 'Prince Andrey's here. He's wounded and dying. He's coming on with us.'

The countess's eyes widened in alarm; she snatched at Sonya's arm, and took a look round.

'What about Natasha?' she said.

For both of them this news could have only one meaning. They knew their Natasha, and worrying about how this news might affect her overrode any sympathy for the man himself, however much affection they might have for him.

'Natasha doesn't know yet, but he is coming with us,' said Sonya.

'You say he is dying?'

Sonya nodded.

The countess hugged Sonya and burst into tears. 'God moves in a mysterious way!' she thought, sensing in this turn of events the hand of the Almighty, hitherto hidden from the eyes of man.

'All right, Mamma, we're completely ready! What's wrong? ...' asked Natasha, rushing in all excited.

'Oh, nothing,' said the countess. 'If we're ready, let's be on our way.' And the countess bent over her reticule to conceal her worried face. Sonya gave Natasha a hug and a kiss.

Natasha looked puzzled.

'What's all this? What's happened?'

'Nothing's happened ... Nothing ...'

Natasha was not to be fooled.

'It's something awful, and it affects me ... What is it?' she asked.

Sonya gave a sigh, but said nothing. The count, Petya, Madame Schoss, Mavra and Vasilich trooped in, the doors were closed and they all sat down to spend a few moments in silence avoiding each other's eyes.

The count was the first to stand up. He gave a deep sigh and crossed himself before the icon. All the others did the same. Then the count proceeded to embrace Mavra and Vasilich, who were staying on in Moscow, and while they caught his hand and kissed him on the shoulder, he patted them on the back and mumbled a few vague words of affection and encouragement. The countess went off to the icon-shrine, where Sonya found her kneeling before the few holy images that were still left up on the walls. (All the best icons, family heirlooms, were going with them.)

Out on the steps and down in the courtyard the servants who were travelling with the family, armed to the teeth with swords and daggers issued by Petya, were standing around with their trousers tucked in their boots, belts and straps good and tight, saying goodbye to those who were staying behind.

As always at the start of a journey, many things had been forgotten or wrongly stowed, and the two grooms, one at each side of the open carriage door, had to stand there for quite some time waiting to help the countess up the steps, while maids flew back and forth with cushions and little bundles between house, carriages, coach and gig.

'They'll go on forgetting things as long as they live!' said the countess. 'Oh, you know I can't sit like that.' Dunyasha gritted her teeth and looked all offended, but instead of saying anything she got quickly up into the carriage to rearrange the cushions.

'Oh, these servants!' said the count, shaking his head.

Old Yefim, the only coachman the countess would trust as a driver, sat perched up on his box, not bothering to look round at what was happening at the back. Thirty years of experience had taught him it would be some time yet before he would hear the magic words, 'Off we go, and God go with us!' and even when they were uttered he would be stopped again at least twice to send back for something that had been forgotten, after which he would still have to pull up one last time for the countess herself to stick her head out of window and beg him for heaven's sake to take care going downhill. Knowing all this, he waited philosophically, more patiently than his horses, especially the near one, Falcon, a chestnut who wouldn't stop pawing the ground and champing the bit. At long last they all were on board, the steps were folded away, doors slammed, a forgotten travelling-case was sent for, and there was the countess with her head out the window saying what was expected of her. Only then did Yefim remove his hat with a deliberate gesture and make the sign of the cross. Likewise the postilion and all the servants.

'Off we go, and God go with us!' said Yefim, putting his hat back on. 'Pull, me beauties!'

The postilion urged the horses. The right shaft-horse took the strain, the high springs creaked and the carriage rocked. A footman ran alongside and jumped up on the box. The carriage lumbered out of the courtyard on to the bumpy road, others jolted out behind and they set off down the street in a long procession. In carriages, coach and gig all the travellers made the sign of the cross towards the church opposite. The servants who were staying on walked along on both sides of the carriages to see them off.

Rarely had Natasha felt such a thrill of delight as the one she felt now, sitting in the carriage next to the countess and looking out at the slow-moving walls of poor, forsaken Moscow. From time to time she would stick her head out of the carriage window to glance back, and then look ahead at the long train of wagons full of wounded soldiers that were leading the way. Almost at the front she could see the raised hood of Prince Andrey's carriage. She didn't know who was inside, but every time she surveyed the procession of wagons her eyes searched for that coach. She knew it would be right in front.

In Kudrino, and from every street, from Nikitskaya, Presnya and Podnovinskaya, came other trains of vehicles, just like the Rostovs', and by the time they got to Sadovaya the carriages and carts were two abreast all down the road.

As they turned past the Sukharev water-tower, Natasha, who was keeping a sharp eye on the walking crowds and passing vehicles, gave a cry of delight and surprise.

'Good Heavens! Mamma, Sonya, look over there! It's him!'

'Who? Who?'

'Look! For heaven's sake, it's Pierre Bezukhov,' said Natasha, leaning right out to get a good look at a tall, corpulent figure in a coachman's long coat, obviously, from his bearing and his walk, a gentleman in borrowed clothing. There he was, going through the Sukharev tower-arch, walking along with a sallow-faced, beardless little old man in a rough overcoat.

'Saints above! Bezukhov dressed like a driver, with that funny old boy,' said Natasha. 'Look! Look!'

'That's not him. Don't be so silly!'

'Mamma,' shouted Natasha. 'I'll bet you anything it's him. I tell you it is. Stop, stop!' she yelled to the coachman; but the coachman couldn't stop, because carts and carriages were pouring out of Meshchansky Street, and people were shouting at the Rostovs to get a move on and stop holding everybody up.

And in fact, even though he was further away now, the Rostovs did get a glimpse of Pierre, or someone remarkably like him: there he was in his coachman's coat, walking down the street with his head bowed and a serious look on his face, side by side with a little, beardless old man who looked like a servant. The old fellow, suddenly aware of being looked at by a face poking out of a carriage window, nudged

Pierre on the elbow politely and said something, pointing towards the carriage. Pierre's thoughts were miles away, and it took some time for him to grasp what the old man was saying. Eventually he got the message and looked in the direction indicated. The moment he saw Natasha he followed his instinct and strode quickly towards the carriage. But he had hardly gone a dozen steps when he pulled up, obviously with something on his mind. Natasha's beaming face looked back at him from the carriage window glowing with amusement and affection.

'Come on, Pyotr Kirillych! We knew it was you! Isn't it marvellous?' she shouted, holding a hand out to him. 'How are things with you? What are you doing like that?'

Pierre took her outstretched hand and kissed it clumsily as he bumbled along beside the carriage, which was still moving.

'Is anything wrong, Count?' the countess asked, sounding surprised and sympathetic.

'Huh? What do you mean? Don't ask,' said Pierre, and he glanced up at Natasha, though without having to look he had felt warmed by the glow of her radiant, laughing eyes.

'What are you doing, then? Staying on in Moscow?'

For a moment Pierre said nothing.

'Staying on?' he then asked. 'Er, yes, that's what I'm doing. Goodbye, then.'

'Oh, I wish I was a man. I'd stay on with you. I think it's wonderful!' said Natasha. 'Mamma, please can I stay?'

Pierre looked blankly at Natasha, trying to say something, but the countess cut him short.

'We hear you were at the battle.'

'Yes, I was,' answered Pierre. 'Tomorrow there's going to be another battle . . .' he was starting to say, but it was Natasha's turn to interrupt.

'But there's something wrong, isn't there, Count? There's something different about you.'

'Oh, don't ask. Please don't ask. I can't tell you. Tomorrow . . . No! . . . Goodbye, then. Goodbye,' he said. 'Terrible times!'

Letting the carriage go, he stepped back on to the pavement.

Natasha's head was still sticking out of the carriage window. For some time her smiling face beamed fondly back at him, glowing with happiness tinged with amusement.

CHAPTER 18

Since his disappearance from home Pierre had been living for a couple of days in the empty house of his deceased benefactor, Osip Bazdeyev. This was how it came about.

When he woke up the morning after his return to Moscow and his meeting with Count Rostopchin, it took Pierre some time to realize where he was and what was required of him. When he was told that the names of the persons waiting so patiently to see him had been added to by that of a Frenchman who had come along with a letter from his wife, the Countess Hélène, he felt suddenly overwhelmed by the sense of alienation and hopelessness that was his weak spot. He had a sudden feeling that everything was finished, all over the place, broken down, there was no right or wrong, no future to look forward to, no way out of his present situation. A strange smile came to his face and he started muttering under his breath. One minute he would flop down on the sofa in an attitude of utter dejection, the next he would get to his feet, go over to the door and peep through the crack into the ante-room where the visitors were waiting, only to turn back with a wave of his arms and snatch up a book. The butler came in for the second time to say that the Frenchman who had brought the letter from the countess was most anxious to see him if only for a minute, and someone had come from Osip Bazdeyev's widow to ask him to take charge of his books because she was leaving for the country.

'Oh, er, yes, hang on, I'm coming . . . Or shall I . . . ? No . . . All right, go and tell them I'll be there in a minute,' said Pierre.

But as soon as the butler had gone Pierre picked up his hat, which was lying on the table, and left by the other door. He found no one in the corridor. Pierre walked the whole length of the corridor to the staircase and went down as far as the first landing, frowning and rubbing his forehead with both hands. The hall porter was standing by the front door. But there was another staircase leading down from the landing to the back entrance. Pierre went down the back stairs and out into the yard. He had not been seen. But once outside, the moment he got to the gate the drivers standing by their carriages and the gate porter saw the master coming and doffed their caps. Aware of their scrutiny, Pierre behaved like an ostrich sticking its head in a bush to avoid being seen; bowing his head and quickening his pace, he hurried away down the street.

Of all the business waiting for Pierre's attention that morning the task of sorting out Osip Bazdeyev's books and papers seemed more urgent than anything else.

He hailed the first cab that came along and told the driver to take him to Patriarch's Ponds, where Bazdeyev's widow lived.

With his eyes glued on the lines of loaded carts coming from all directions and trundling out of Moscow, Pierre felt as happy as a truant schoolboy as he braced his big frame to make sure he didn't fall out of the rickety old droshky and chatted away to his driver.

The driver told him they were issuing arms in the Kremlin, and tomorrow they were sending everybody out through the Three Hills gate, and there was going to be a terrific battle.

When he got to Patriarch's Ponds, Pierre managed to rediscover Bazdeyev's house, which he hadn't visited for some time. There was the little garden gate. It was Gerasim, the same little sallow-skinned, beardless old man Pierre had seen with Bazdeyev five years before at Torzhok, who answered his knock.

'Anybody in?' asked Pierre.

'Owing to present circumstances, Madame Bazdeyev and her children have gone to the country house at Torzhok, sir.'

'I'd still like to come in. I want to look through the books,' said Pierre.

'Yes sir, you are most welcome,' said the old servant. 'Makar Alekseyevich, the brother of my late master, God rest his soul, has stayed on, but he's not too strong, your Honour.'

Pierre knew full well that Bazdeyev's brother, Makar, was a drunken half-wit.

'Yes, I know about that. Come on, let's go in,' said Pierre, and he went inside. There in the vestibule stood a tall, bald-headed old man in a dressing-gown, with a red nose and galoshes on his bare feet. When he saw Pierre he muttered something irritably and walked off down a corridor.

'He had a fine mind once, but you can see he's not as strong as he was, your Honour,' said Gerasim. 'Would you care to go into the study?' Pierre nodded. 'It's been sealed up, and nothing has been touched. Madame Bazdeyev gave orders that if you sent for the books I was to let them go.'

Pierre went into the gloomy study which he had entered with such trepidation when his benefactor was still alive. Untouched since the death of Bazdeyev, it was now thick with dust, and gloomier than ever.

Gerasim opened one of the shutters, and tiptoed out. Pierre took a walk round the room, and then went over to a cupboard where the manuscripts were kept, and took one lot out. It was something of great importance that had been one of the most sacred treasures of their order: a set of original Scotch Acts with Bazdeyev's notes and commentaries. He sat down at the dusty desk, laid out the manuscripts, opened them up and closed them again before pushing them to one side. With his elbows on the desk and his head in his hands he sat there thinking.

Gerasim peeped in cautiously several times only to see Pierre sitting always in the same position.

More than two hours passed. Gerasim ventured to make a little noise from the doorway to get Pierre's attention. Pierre didn't hear him.

'Sir, should I let the driver go?'

'Oh yes,' said Pierre, rousing himself and starting to his feet. 'Listen,' he added, taking Gerasim by one of the buttons on his coat and looking down at the little old man with moist eyes that were glinting with excitement. 'Listen. You know tomorrow there's going to be a battle . . .'

'I have heard tell . . .' answered Gerasim.

'Please don't tell anybody who I am. And do what I say . . .'

'Oh yes, sir,' said Gerasim. 'Can I get you something to eat, sir?'

'No, but I do want something else. I want some peasant clothing and a pistol,' said Pierre, suddenly colouring up.

'Oh yes, sir,' said Gerasim, after a moment's thought.

Pierre spent the whole day alone in his benefactor's study. Gerasim could hear him pacing restlessly up and down, and talking to himself. He spent the night there too, on a bed specially made up for him.

Unruffled by Pierre's decision to move in, Gerasim took it with the composure of a servant who had seen many weird things in his time; in fact, he seemed delighted to have someone to serve. That same evening, without even wondering what they were for, he managed to acquire a coachman's long coat and cap, and he promised to get the necessary pistol the next day. Twice during the evening Bazdeyev's brother shuffled up to the door in his galoshes, and stood there fawning as he stared in at Pierre. But the moment Pierre turned to face him he gathered up his dressing-gown, looking embarrassed and angry, and scuttled away.

Pierre put on the coachman's coat that Gerasim had got hold of, once it had been disinfected with steam, and the two of them went out together to buy a pistol at the Sukharev market. It was then that Pierre ran into the Rostovs.

CHAPTER 19

During the night of the 1st of September Kutuzov ordered the Russian troops to fall back through Moscow and go down the Ryazan road.

The first troops moved that night, marching at an easy pace and in good order. But at dawn, when the retreating troops got to the Dorogomilov bridge, they saw endless masses of soldiers hurrying across, herding together on the other side, struggling up slopes, blocking the streets and alleys, while masses more bore down on them from the rear. And for no good reason they panicked and rushed forward. There was a great surge towards the bridge, up on to the bridge itself, down to the fords and into the boats. Kutuzov had arranged to be driven through the back streets right round to the other side of Moscow.

By ten o'clock on the morning of the 2nd of September the only troops left in the suburb of Dorogomilov were some members of the rearguard, and they had plenty of space. The army itself was now beyond Moscow, out on the other side.

At that time, ten o'clock on the morning of the 2nd of September, Napoleon was standing amidst his troops up on Poklonny hill, gazing down on the spectacle that lay before him. From the 26th of August to the 2nd of September, from the battle of Borodino to the entry of the French into Moscow, throughout that anxious but memorable week, there had been a spell of that extraordinarily beautiful autumn weather that always takes us by surprise, when the low sunshine is warmer than in spring; when the air is pure and thin, everything sparkles enough to sting the eyes; when you breathe deep and feel refreshed, drinking in the fragrant autumn air; when even the nights are warm, and on dark, warm nights like these golden stars startle or delight us by scattering themselves endlessly down the sky.

The weather was like this at ten o'clock on the 2nd of September. The morning light was magical. Down below Poklonny hill lay the sprawl of Moscow with her river, her gardens and her churches; she seemed to be living a life of her own, and her domes shimmered like stars in the sunlight.

Looking down on this strange city, with its weird forms of unfamiliar architecture, Napoleon felt a touch of envy and a pang of niggling curiosity as men do when they come across an alien way of life that knows nothing of them. Here was a town that was obviously living life to the full. From the elusive signs that tell you unmistakably even at a distance whether a body is dead or alive, Napoleon, far away on Poklonny hill, could feel the life pulsating through this town, and almost hear the big, beautiful creature breathing. Every Russian looking at Moscow feels her to be a mother; every foreigner who sees her, although probably ignorant of her significance as the mother city, is bound to sense her femininity, as did Napoleon.

'This Asiatic city with churches beyond number, holy Moscow! Here she is at last, the famous city! Not before time,' said Napoleon. Dismounting from his horse, he told them to open a plan of Moscow before him, and sent for his interpreter, Lelorgne d'Ideville.

'An occupied city is like a girl who has lost her virtue,' he thought (something he had said to Tuchkov at Smolensk).

And this was how he looked on the oriental beauty that he was seeing for the first time as she lay there before him. He had a strange feeling now that the desire burning in him for so long like an impossible dream had been gratified. In the clear morning light he looked first at the town and then at the plan, checking its details, excited and overawed by the certainty of possessing it.

'But how could it be otherwise?' he thought. 'Here is this capital at my feet awaiting her fate. Where is Alexander now, and what must he be thinking? A strange, beautiful, magnificent city! And a strange and magnificent moment for me! I wonder how I seem to them,' he mused, thinking of his soldiers. 'Here is the city – a reward for all these men of little faith,' he thought, looking round at his entourage and the troops who were marching up and falling into line.

'One word from me, one wave of my arm, and the ancient capital of the Tsars would be no more. But my clemency is ever ready to descend upon the vanquished. I must be magnanimous and truly great. But no, it isn't true – I am not yet in Moscow,' he suddenly realized. 'Still, here she lies at my feet with her golden domes and crosses glinting and shimmering in the sun. But I shall spare her. On the ancient monuments of barbarism and despotism I shall inscribe great words of justice and mercy . . . That will hurt Alexander more than anything else. I know him.' (Napoleon seemed to think that amidst all these events the most important thing was the rivalry between him and Alexander.) 'From the heights of the Kremlin – yes, there it is, the Kremlin, yes – I shall give them the laws of justice, I shall teach them the meaning of true civilization, I shall make generations of boyars[2] speak their conqueror's name with love. I shall tell their deputation that I have not sought, and do not seek, war; my war has been waged against the dishonest policy of their court; I love and respect Alexander, and in Moscow I shall accept terms of peace worthy of myself and my peoples. I have no wish to use the fortunes

of war to humiliate a monarch deserving of respect. "Boyars," I shall
say to them, "I have no desire for war. I desire peace and prosperity
for all my subjects." And I know I can count on being inspired by
their very presence, and I shall speak to them as I always do, clearly
but solemnly, like a great man. But am I really in Moscow? Yes, there
she is!'

'Bring me the boyars,' he said to his entourage. Immediately a
general galloped off with his own brilliant suite to fetch the boyars.

Two hours passed. Napoleon took lunch, and returned to the same
spot on Poklonny hill, waiting for the deputation to arrive. His speech
to the boyars had by now taken definite shape in his mind. It was a
speech full of dignity and majesty, as seen by Napoleon.

Napoleon was carried away by the attitude of magnanimity which
he had every intention of striking in Moscow. In his own mind he had
already scheduled certain days for assemblies in the Tsars' palace at
which the great Russian nobles would mingle with the courtiers of
the French Emperor. Mentally he saw himself appointing a governor
capable of winning the hearts of the people. Having heard that Moscow was full of religious institutions, he imagined himself showering
them with blessings. As he saw it, when he had been in Africa he had
had to sit in a mosque wearing one of their capes, and now in Moscow
he must be like the Tsars and show mercy. And since, like all Frenchmen, he couldn't conceive of anything at all emotional without some
reference to his poor mother sweet and tender, he decided to have an
inscription put on all these charitable foundations in capital letters
saying: THIS ESTABLISHMENT IS DEDICATED TO MY DEAR MOTHER
or simply MY MOTHER'S HOUSE. 'Am I really in Moscow? Yes, there
she is lying before me. But why is the deputation from the city taking
so long?' he wondered.

Meanwhile, at the rear of the suite, heated exchanges were going
on in whispers between the generals and marshals. The adjutants that
had gone to fetch the deputation had come back with the news that
Moscow was empty; whether they had driven off or just walked away,
everybody had gone. The faces of those conferring looked pale and
worried. It wasn't the fact that Moscow had been abandoned by its
inhabitants (bad enough in itself) that alarmed them; it was the prospect of having to tell the Emperor, and how to tell him. Without
putting his Majesty into the terrible situation that the French see as
being 'open to ridicule', how could they tell him that it had been a
waste of time waiting for the boyars, and there was nobody left in
Moscow apart from a few drunken mobs? Some of them said come
what may they would have to scrape up some kind of deputation;

others said no, the Emperor must be properly prepared by skilful persuasion, and then told the truth.

'We'll have to tell him eventually,' said some members of the entourage . . . 'But gentlemen . . .'

The situation was made worse by the fact the Emperor, thoroughly absorbed in his magnanimous plans, was strolling patiently to and fro in front of the city map, shading his eyes now and then to look down the Moscow road, with a proud and happy smile on his face.

'It can't be done . . .' the gentlemen-in-waiting kept repeating with a shrug. They couldn't bring themselves to utter the terrible words that haunted all their minds: 'open to ridicule . . .'

Meanwhile, the Emperor was getting tired of waiting in vain, and his strong histrionic sense told him that the magnificent moment, by going on too long, was beginning to lose its magnificence, so he gave a sign to his men. A solitary cannon boomed out the signal, and the occupying army marched into Moscow from several sides at once, through the Tver, Kaluga and Dorogomilov gates. In they went, faster and faster, falling over each other, accelerating to a quick trot, occupying troops disappearing in their own clouds of dust and filling the air with their ringing, deafening shouts.

Drawn on by the forward movement of the army, Napoleon himself went as far as the Dorogomilov gate, but there he came to a halt, got off his horse and took a long stroll under the Kamer-Kollezhsky rampart, still waiting for the deputation to arrive.

CHAPTER 20

Meanwhile Moscow was empty. Some people were still there – up to one in fifty of the inhabitants had stayed behind – but in essence it was empty.

It was as empty as a dying beehive with no queen.

All life has gone from a hive without a queen. Yet a superficial glance at that kind of hive suggests it has as much life as any other.

Under the hot rays of the midday sun the bees circulate just as happily round a queenless hive as they do round other hives that still have life; at a distance it still smells of honey, and the bees fly in and out just the same. Yet you only have to watch it for a while to see there is no life there. The flight of the bees is not the same as in living hives; the beekeeper is met with a smell and sounds that are different. When the beekeeper taps on the wall of a sick hive, instead of getting an immediate and unanimous response in the ominous lifting of stings and the buzzing of bees in their tens of thousands as they fan their racing wings into a healthy, living roar, he is greeted by a desultory buzzing from odd corners of an empty hive. The entrance no longer gives off a heady whiff of sweet-smelling honey and venom; there is no smell of fulness from within. The scent of honey intermingles with an odour of emptiness and decay. There are no guards round the entrance raising their stings, sounding the alarm, ready to die in defence of the hive. Gone is the low, even tenor of toil that sounds like water on the boil; all you hear is the broken, desultory noisiness of nothing. Long, black, honey-smeared scavenger-bees fly in and out, timid and shifty; instead of stinging they sneak away at the first sight of danger. Where once they flew in with nectar and flew out empty, now they fly out with honey. The beekeeper opens the lowest section and peers into the bottom of the hive. Instead of clusters of fat black bees clinging to each other's legs, subdued by their hard toil and hanging down to the floor while they work away with a ceaseless murmur to draw out the wax, sleepy, desiccated bees listlessly roam the roof and walls of the hive. What should have been a floor nicely polished with glue and swept clean by bees' wings is now a spattering of wax, excrement, bees in their last throes waggling their legs, and dead bees that haven't been cleared away.

The beekeeper opens the top section of the hive and examines the super. Instead of tightly packed rows of bees sealing every gap in the combs and keeping the brood warm, he sees the cunning complexity of the combs themselves, without the virginal purity of their earlier days. It is a picture of filthy neglect. Black scavenger-bees buzz around busily looking for plunder while the home bees, a desiccated, shrunken, shrivelled up and listless lot, old before their time, drag themselves about, putting up no opposition, having lost all desire and any sense of being alive. Drones, hornets, bumblebees and butterflies flit about aimlessly, their wings tapping against the walls of the hive. Now and then the cells containing the dead brood and honey are stirred by an angry buzzing; somewhere a couple of bees have reverted to their old ways without knowing why and started cleaning the hive, straining every nerve to drag away dead bees and bumblebees, and it is all beyond their strength. In a different corner another pair of old bees are going through the motions of fighting or cleaning themselves or feeding each other, though they don't know whether they are taking on friends or enemies. Somewhere else a crowd of bees squeezes up close together and picks on a victim, beating it and smothering it. The victim, dead or dying, then drops slowly down, light as a feather, on to a pile of corpses. The beekeeper parts the two centre frames to look in on the nursery. Instead of seeing thousands of black bees sitting back to back in tightly packed rings guarding the lofty mysteries of generation, all he sees are miserable shells, a few hundred somnolent bees more dead than alive. Almost all of them have died unawares, sitting there in the sanctuary which was once theirs to guard but has now ceased to exist. They reek of death and decay. One or two of them manage to stir themselves and rise up to fly across feebly and settle on the hand of the invader, but they lack the will to sting him and die. The rest are dead; they flutter down as airy as fish-scales. The beekeeper closes the section and puts a chalk-mark on the hive; in his own good time he will return to break it open and burn it out.

Moscow was as empty as this, and Napoleon, weary, restless and scowling, could be seen pacing up and down under the Kamer-Kollezhsky rampart as he waited to perform that purely formal but (to his mind) very necessary ritual – the receiving of a deputation.

There were still a few people stirring themselves in odd corners of Moscow, aimlessly reverting to their old ways without knowing what they were doing.

When, with all due delicacy, Napoleon was informed that Moscow was empty, he glared at his informant, turned his back on him and went on pacing up and down in silence.

'My carriage,' he said.

He got in beside the duty adjutant, and drove through into the suburbs.

'Moscow deserted! What an incredible thing to happen!' he said to himself.

Instead of driving straight into town he put up at an inn in the Dorogomilov suburb.

His *coup de théâtre* had not come off.

CHAPTER 21

The long march of the Russian troops through Moscow went on from two o'clock at night to two o'clock the following afternoon, and they took with them the last departing citizens and the wounded soldiers.

The greatest crush during the troop movement took place on the Kamenny, Moskva and Yauza bridges. With the troops dividing into two streams to go round the Kremlin and backing up from the Moskva and Kamenny bridges, a huge number of soldiers took advantage of the hold-up and congestion to turn back, steal past St Basil's and through the Borovitsky gate, and sneak uphill into Red Square, where instinct told them there would be easy pickings. It was like sale-time at the Gostiny Bazaar with every aisle and alley swarming with crowds. But there were none of the usual honeyed voices tempting and cajoling the passer-by, no hawkers, no crowds of brightly dressed women shoppers – just uniforms and greatcoats everywhere (no guns), as the soldiers went in empty-handed and came back out tight-lipped and loaded with plunder. The traders and salesmen (what few there were) wandered among the soldiers in a kind of daze, opening their stalls, relocking them, even helping the war heroes to carry things away. Outside in the square a military drummer summoned them to muster. But the drum-roll did not affect the rampaging soldiers as once it had; instead of bringing them in it made them run away. Dotted among the soldiers in the shops and aisles were some men with the grey coats and shaven heads of convicts. Two officers, one with a scarf over his uniform, astride a scraggy dark grey horse, the other on foot, dressed in a military overcoat, stood talking on the Ilyinka corner. A third officer rode up.

'Orders from the general. Whatever we do, we've got to get them moving. It's outrageous! Half the men have run away.'

'Hey you! And you two! Where do you think you're going?' he shouted to three unarmed infantrymen who were sneaking past into the bazaar, holding up the skirts of their greatcoats. 'Stop, you swine!'

'Well, you try rounding them up,' answered another officer. 'It can't be done. All we can do is push on faster so the last ones don't scarper!'

'Push on? They're stuck there up on the bridge. Nobody's moving. Could we cordon them in? Might stop them running away.'

'Well go on in there! Get them out!' shouted the senior officer.

The officer in the scarf dismounted, called up a drummer and went with him into the arcade. There was surge of running soldiers. A shopkeeper with red pimples on his cheeks near his nose, and something on his well-fed face that spoke of steady determination in the pursuit of profit, came bustling up to the officer waving his arms in a great display of anxiety.

'Your Honour!' said he. 'We need your protection. We can be quite generous . . . any little thing that catches your eye . . . our pleasure! Hang on, I'll fetch you a nice piece of cloth – a couple of nice pieces for a gentleman like you, sir. Our pleasure! We do understand, you know, but this is daylight robbery! Please, your Honour! Put somebody on guard . . . Give us a chance to lock up, at least . . .'

More shopkeepers crowded round.

'No good moaning about it,' said one of them, a thin man with a stern face. 'When your head's chopped off you don't worry about your hairstyle. Let 'em have what they want!' And he turned away with a great sweep of his arm.

'It's all right for you, Ivan Sidorych!' The first shopkeeper turned on him angrily. 'Your Honour, *please*.'

'What's that supposed to mean?' shouted the thin man. 'I've got three shops – goods worth a hundred thousand. How can you guard that lot when the army's gone? Listen everybody. God's will is with us still!'

'*Please*, your Honour,' said the first shopkeeper with a polite bow.

The officer was taken aback; it was obvious from his face that he didn't know what to do. 'What's it got to do with me?' he cried suddenly, and strode off rapidly down one of the aisles. In one open shop he heard people fighting and swearing, and as the officer got near a man in a grey overcoat with a shaven head was bundled out of the door.

This man squeezed down and slipped past the shopkeepers and the officer. The officer pounced on the soldiers who were still in the shop. But then the most awful shouting and screaming came from a huge crowd down near the Moskva bridge, and the officer ran out into the square.

'What is it? What's happening?' he asked, but his comrade was already riding off in the direction the screams were coming from, beyond St Basil's. He got on his horse and followed. When he reached the bridge he saw two cannons ready for firing, the infantry marching across, one or two broken-down wagons, some frightened faces and some soldiers roaring with laughter. Near the cannons stood a wagon with a pair of horses in harness. At the back behind the wheels huddled four borzois in collars. The wagon was piled high with goods and right on top, next to a little child's chair stowed upside down, sat a peasant woman at her wits' end, screaming. The officer learnt from his comrades that the roaring of the crowd and the woman's shrieks were due to the fact that General Yermolov had come across this crowd, and when he found out the soldiers were wandering off into the shops and crowds of citizens were blocking the bridge, he had ordered the cannons down from their carriages so they could go through the motions of firing at the bridge. The crowd had surged forward, overturning wagons, trampling one another and yelling desperately in the crush, but the bridge had been cleared and the troops had moved on.

CHAPTER 22

Meanwhile the city itself was deserted. There was virtually no one out on the streets. All the gates and shops were closed; only the odd drinking-house rang with solitary shouts or drunken singing. No one was out driving and there was hardly a footstep to be heard. Povarsky Street stood silent and deserted. The vast courtyard of the Rostovs' house was littered with a few bits of straw and some dung left behind by horses; not a soul was to be seen. Inside the Rostovs' house, now abandoned with all its contents, there were two people in the great drawing-room: the porter, Ignat, and the page-boy, Mishka, Vasilich's grandson, who had stayed on with his grandfather. Mishka had opened the clavichord and was picking out notes with one finger. The porter was standing hands on hips in front a huge mirror with a huge grin on his face.

'Listen to me play, Uncle Ignat! Isn't that good?' said the little boy, thumping down on the keys with both hands.

'Get away with you!' answered Ignat, watching his own face with amazement as the grin on it stretched wider and wider.

'Oh, you ought to be ashamed of yourselves! You really should!' came a voice from behind them. Mavra had glided in silently. 'Look at old fat-face with his stupid grin! So this is what you get up to! And there's work to be done down there. Vasilich is dead on his feet. Just you wait!'

Ignat stopped grinning, hitched up his belt and looked down at the floor as he walked out, humiliated.

'Auntie, I was only having a little play . . .' said the boy.

'I'll give you having a little play, you little horror!' shouted Mavra, shaking her fist at him. 'Go and put the samovar on for your grandad.'

Wiping some dust away, she closed the clavichord, gave a sigh and walked out of the drawing-room, shutting the door behind her. Back down in the yard Mavra wondered what to do next: go and have a drink of tea in the lodge with Vasilich, or pop down to the store-room and tidy up some of the things that still needed putting away.

From the quiet street came the sound of rapid footsteps. They paused at the gate, and the latch rattled as someone tried to open it.

Mavra went over.

'Who do you want?'

'The count, old Count Rostov.'

'And who might you be?'

'I'm an officer. I really would like to see him,' said a cheery voice, the voice of a Russian gentleman.

Mavra opened the gate, and in walked a round-faced officer, a boy of eighteen, with features not unlike the Rostovs'.

'They've gone away, sir. Went away last night, sir, their Honours did,' said Mavra welcomingly. The young officer stood there in the gateway and clicked his tongue as he wondered whether to come on in or stay where he was.

'Oh, how annoying!' he said. 'I should have come yesterday . . . Oh, what a pity!'

Mavra was watching him sympathetically as she took in the young man's face with its familiar Rostov features, his tattered greatcoat and worn-out boots. 'What was it you was wanting to see the count for?' she asked.

'Oh dear . . . Now what shall I do?' the officer muttered in annoyance, reaching for the gate as if he intended to go away. Then he stopped again, still hesitating.

'You see,' he went on suddenly, 'I'm related to the count, and he's always been so good to me. You see how I am . . .' (He looked down with a wry smile at his coat and boots.) 'I'm in rags. I haven't a penny to my name . . . I was just going to ask the count . . .'

Mavra cut him short.

'If I could ask you to wait just a minute, sir. Only a minute,' she said. And the moment his fingers dropped from the latch she was off, tripping round to her lodge in the back court on her nippy old lady's legs.

As she trotted off on her errand, the officer walked round the court-yard, looking down at his tattered boots with a thin smile on his face.

'What a pity I have missed Uncle Ilya! What a nice old lady! I wonder where she's gone. And how can I find out the shortest way back to my regiment? By now they'll be at the Rogozhsky gate . . .' All these thoughts went through the young officer's mind while she was away. Then Mavra came back round the corner looking scared but very determined; she was carrying something wrapped up in a check handkerchief. A few steps away from him she undid the handkerchief, took out a white twenty-five rouble note, and thrust it into the officer's hand.

'If his Excellency had been at home . . . I know he would have . . . well, er, blood's thicker than water . . . but with things as they are . . . you might be able to, er . . .' Mavra was squirming with shyness and embarrassment. The officer did not refuse; neither did he hurry to take the note. He thanked her. 'If only the count had been here,' murmured

Mavra apologetically. 'Christ be with you, sir. God keep you,' she said, bowing to him and showing him the way out. The officer, smiling and shaking his head in what looked like self-mockery, jogged away down the empty streets to catch up with his regiment at the Yauza bridge.

Mavra's eyes were moist as she stood there outside the closed gate for some time, shaking her head pensively and feeling a great flood of maternal affection and sympathy for the unknown boy officer.

CHAPTER 23

From a half-built house in Varvarka, where the ground floor served as a drinking-shop, came the sounds of drunken revelry and singing. A dozen factory workers were sitting on benches at tables in a dirty little room. Woozy with drink, sweating and bleary-eyed, they were belting out some kind of a song through gaping mouths. They were putting everything into it, singing their hearts out, completely out of tune, not because they really wanted to sing, but just to let the world know they were out on the town and getting gloriously drunk.

One of them, a tall, fair-haired young man in a clean blue coat was up on his feet, standing over them. He might have been handsome, with his fine, straight nose, but for his tight thin lips that never stopped twitching and a pair of lacklustre, staring, scowling eyes. He was standing over the singers, obviously transported as he solemnly and jerkily beat time over their heads with a bare, white arm and awkward fingers stuck out at all angles. His coat sleeve kept slipping down, and the young boy kept rolling it up again with his left hand, scrupulously, as if there was something special about that sinewy white arm, and it had to be kept bare for waving at them. In the midst of all the singing the outer passage and the porch erupted in sounds of fighting and shouting. The tall young man gave one final flourish.

'That's it!' he shouted magisterially. 'A fight, boys!' And he went out to the porch still rolling his sleeve up.

The workmen followed. They had brought the tavern keeper some skins from the factory that morning, he had treated them to wine, and they had stayed there drinking under the leadership of the tall young man. Some blacksmiths working not far away had heard the sounds of revelry coming from the drinking-house, and jumped to the conclusion that it had been broken into. They wanted to smash their way in as well. There was fighting in the porch.

The tavern keeper was scrapping with a blacksmith in the doorway, and the factory workers came out just in time to see the smith reel away from the tavern keeper and fall flat on his face on the pavement.

Another blacksmith was shoving the tavern keeper with his chest as he struggled to get through the door.

The young man with the rolled-up sleeve came at this intruder, hit him in the face and roared to his men, 'Come on! Our boys are getting beaten up!'

By now the first blacksmith, back on his feet, was scratching blood from his battered face, and wailing.

'Police! Murder! They're killing people! Over here, boys!'

'Holy saints! He's been beaten to death! There's a man here dead!' screamed a woman coming out of the gate next door. A crowd soon gathered round the bleeding blacksmith.

'Not satisfied with ruining people and fleecing everybody?' someone asked the tavern keeper. 'Now you've done it. You've gone and killed him, you swine!'

The tall young man, now standing by the porch, looked blearily from tavern keeper to blacksmiths and back, spoiling for a fight but not knowing which way to turn.

'You murderer!' he roared suddenly at the tavern keeper. 'Tie him up, boys!'

'Come on then. I'd like to see you try!' roared the tavern keeper, tearing himself away from his attackers. He snatched off his cap and hurled it down on the ground. It was as if this action carried some deep and ominous meaning: the factory workers crowding in on him stood where they were, unsure of themselves.

'You listen to me, mate. I knows the rules. I'm going to the police. You think I won't find them? Nobody gets away with robbery, not nowadays they don't!' bawled the tavern keeper, picking up his cap.

'We'll go too, damn you!'

'Come on then, damn you!'

The tavern keeper and the tall young man were gabbling the same things one after another, and they both moved off down the street. The bloody-faced blacksmith was keeping pace with them. The workmen and a mob of bystanders came on behind with much chattering and shouting.

Standing on the corner of Maroseyka, opposite a big house with closed shutters and a cobbler's signboard, were a couple of dozen miserable-looking boot-makers, a skinny, weary lot dressed in loose smocks and torn coats.

'Owes us our money, 'e does!' a thin workman with a straggly beard and severe scowl was saying. 'Sucks the blood out of us, and then he's off. Strung us along he has, all this week, and now look – 'e's gone.'

He stopped when he saw the mob and the bloody-faced blacksmith. The boot-makers watched them with interest, only too eager to join in with the moving crowd.

'Where's everybody going then?'

'I'll tell you where. They're going to the police.'

'Is it true our lot's had it?'

'Well, what do you think? Listen to what folks is saying!'

The air was thick with questions and answers. As the rabble grew the tavern keeper saw his chance, dropped away and went back to his house.

The tall young man never noticed his foe slipping from him; his bare arm was working away as he gabbled on, attracting everybody's attention. The mob were homing in on him in particular, somehow assuming he might have the answers to the questions that worried them.

'"What we wants is law and order!" he says. "That's what the government's for!" Isn't that right, good Christian folk?' said the tall young man, with the ghost of a smile on his face.

'Does he think there's no government? How could we get by without a government? We'd all get robbed, wouldn't we?'

'We've been listening to rubbish!' went the word through the crowd. 'They're not going to let Moscow go just like that! They been spoofing, and you've swallowed it. Plenty of troops, aren't there? They're not going to let *him* in. That's the government for you. You listen to what folks is saying!' they said, pointing to the tall fellow.

By the China-town wall another knot of people was gathering round a man in a rough coat holding a piece of paper.

'It's a decree. They're reading a decree!' came voices from the crowd, and the mob surged round the reader.

The man in the coat was reading the poster for the 31st of August. As the mob crowded round he seemed disconcerted but, under pressure from the tall young man, who had shoved his way through, he started to read the notice. There was a tremor in his voice.

'First thing tomorrow I shall go and see his Serene Highness, the prince,' he read ('*Serineinous*!' parroted the tall young man, with a triumphant smile and a deep frown), 'to hold talks, go into action and give every assistance to the troops in exterminating the enemy swine. Root and branch we too shall . . .' the reader went on, and then paused for a moment ('Hear that?' roared the tall young man triumphantly. 'He's got the measure of them!'), 'we too shall destroy them and send these visitors to hell. I'll be back by dinnertime, and we shall kick them, stick them and lick them, the enemy swine.'

These last words were delivered to a background of complete silence. The tall man's head dropped in dismay. It was obvious that nobody had taken these last words in. It was the phrase 'I'll be back by dinnertime tomorrow' that seemed to affect everybody, reader and audience alike. The sensitivities of the crowd were strained to breaking point and this was too ordinary, too down-to-earth, not what they wanted. Any one of them could have said it, and therefore it was something that should never have been said by higher authority.

They stood there, all of them, silent and crestfallen. The tall man's lips were moving, and he was swaying.

'Look! He's the one to ask! . . . It's him, isn't it? . . . Ask him! Go on . . . He'll tell us . . .' came sudden voices from the back of the crowd, and the general attention switched to a little carriage that had just driven into the square with an escort of two mounted dragoons. It was the police-chief.

The police-chief, who had received orders that morning from Count Rostopchin (along with a large sum of money that was still in his pocket) to go out and set fire to the wooden barges on the river, ordered his driver to stop when he saw a crowd bearing down on him.

'Who are these people?' he shouted, watching them sidle forward diffidently in ones and twos. 'Who are all these people? I'm asking you,' repeated the police-chief when he got no reply.

'Your Honour,' said the man in the rough coat, 'after his Excellency's proclamation, sir, they wanted to be of service, risking life and limb, not making any trouble, sir, as his Excellency said . . .'

'The count has not gone. He is still here, and he will soon be making arrangements for you,' said the police-chief. 'Get going!' he said to the driver. The crowd stood still, clustering round those who had heard the words of authority, and watching the little carriage as it drove away.

Meanwhile the police-chief looked round in alarm and said something to his driver. The horses put on speed.

'They've done us! Take us to the count!' roared the voice of the tall man. 'Don't let him go, boys! What's he got to say for himself? Hold him!' roared various voices, and the crowd rushed off after the carriage.

The mob pursued the police-chief all the way to Lubyanka, a noisy rabble.

'Oh yes, the nobs and the tradesmen have all gone, and we're left here to go under. Treat us like dogs, don't they?' went the ever-growing murmur through the crowd.

CHAPTER 24

On the evening of the 1st of September Count Rostopchin had come away from his meeting with Kutuzov feeling humiliated and offended that he had not been invited to the council of war, and that Kutuzov had completely ignored his offer to play a role in the defence of the city, and also amazed at the new way of thinking he had picked up at the camp whereby the tranquillity of the capital and its patriotic fervour were being treated as secondary considerations, if not altogether irrelevant and trivial. Thus humiliated, offended and amazed, Count Rostopchin had returned to Moscow. After supper he lay down on a sofa without getting undressed, and just before two in the morning he was woken up by a courier with a letter from Kutuzov. The letter said that since the troops were retreating to the Ryazan road on the other side of Moscow would the count kindly send some police officials to escort the troops through the town? There was nothing new in this. He had known Moscow was going to be surrendered not just since yesterday's meeting with Kutuzov on the Poklonny hill, but ever since the battle of Borodino, and the time when all the generals arriving back in Moscow had declared unanimously that another battle was impossible, and he himself had approved the evacuation of government property by night, and half the inhabitants had dribbled away. Nevertheless this communication, in the form of a simple note containing instructions from Kutuzov, received at night when he had just got to sleep, took the governor by surprise and annoyed him.

In days to come Count Rostopchin would explain his actions during this period by writing more than once in his memoirs that his main aim at the time was twofold: to maintain the peace in Moscow and to get the citizens out. If this double purpose is admitted, everything Rostopchin did seems beyond reproach. You ask why the holy relics, arms, ammunition, gunpowder and grain supplies were not taken away; why thousands of citizens were cheated into believing that Moscow was not going to be abandoned – and thus ruined? 'To keep the peace in Moscow,' comes the explanation from Count Rostopchin. Why were piles of useless papers from government offices, Leppich's balloon and things like that evacuated? 'To leave the town empty,' comes the explanation from Count Rostopchin. The mere mention of a threat to public order is enough to justify any action.

All the horrors of the Reign of Terror in France were based on nothing more than a need to keep the peace.

What foundation was there for Count Rostopchin's dread of

popular disturbance in Moscow in 1812? Was there any reason for presupposing a tendency towards revolution in the city? The inhabitants were leaving; Moscow was filling up with retreating troops. Why would the people be likely to rebel in these circumstances?

As the enemy approached nothing resembling a rebellion took place anywhere, neither in Moscow nor anywhere else in Russia. On the 1st and 2nd of September more than ten thousand people were left behind in Moscow, and apart from a crowd that gathered in the commander-in-chief's courtyard, at his instigation, nothing happened. It is clear there would have been even less reason to expect popular disturbances if after the battle of Borodino, when the surrender of Moscow had become a certainty, or at least a strong probability, Rostopchin had taken steps for the evacuation of all the holy relics, gunpowder, ammunition and money, and told the people to their faces that the town was being abandoned, instead of working them into a frenzy by putting up posters and issuing weapons.

Rostopchin, a hot-headed and impulsive man, had always moved in the highest spheres of the administration, and although he was a patriot at heart he didn't have the slightest knowledge of the people he thought he was governing. From the moment the enemy first entered Smolensk Rostopchin had formed a mental picture of himself as the leader of popular feeling – the very heart of Russia. Not only did he imagine (as do all administrators) that he was directing the actual behaviour of all Muscovites, he really believed he was shaping their mental attitude by means of his appeals and posters, which were written in the kind of vulgar slang that is despised by the people in everyday situations and incomprehensible when it comes at them from on high. This rather grand role as the leader of popular feeling was so agreeable that Rostopchin simply grew into it, and was therefore caught unawares by the sudden need to drop the role and surrender Moscow without any heroic posturing. The ground was cut from under him, and he had no idea what to do. He could see it coming, but he refused to believe in the surrender of Moscow until the very last minute, and he made no preparations. The inhabitants who were leaving were going against his wishes. If government offices were being evacuated it was only at the insistence of the officials and with Rostopchin's reluctant approval. He was himself entirely absorbed in his self-appointed role. As often happens with over-imaginative people, he had known for ages that Moscow was going to be surrendered, but his knowledge was of the intellectual kind; deep down he refused to believe it, and couldn't make the mental adjustment to a new situation.

All his efforts and energy (whether or not these were successful or had any effect on the people is another question) had gone into inspiring the people with his own feelings – a hatred of the French and self-confidence.

But when the catastrophe began to assume its truly historic proportions; when it was no longer enough to express hatred of the French in words alone; when it became impossible to express that hatred even by fighting; when self-confidence became irrelevant to the one issue facing Moscow; when the population rose as one man, abandoned their property, and streamed out of Moscow in a negative demonstration of their positive patriotic feeling – then the part picked out for himself by Rostopchin suddenly lost its meaning. All at once he felt forsaken, feeble and foolish, with no ground to stand on.

When they woke him up to read Kutuzov's curt missive with its peremptory tone, Rostopchin felt annoyed largely because he knew it was all his fault. Moscow was still full of things entrusted to him, government property that should have been removed. There was no chance now of getting it all away. 'Who's responsible for this? Who has let all this come about?' he wondered. 'Not me, of course. I had everything ready. I had Moscow, like this, in the palm of my hand! Now look what's happened! Villains, traitors!' he thought, without defining too precisely who these villains and traitors were, but feeling a deep need to hate some treacherous people who must be to blame for the false and ludicrous position he now found himself in.

Rostopchin spent the whole night issuing instructions, and he had men coming in from all over Moscow. Those close to him had never seen the count so depressed and touchy.

'Your Excellency, there's someone here from the Provincial Registrar's Department – the director is waiting for instructions . . . From the Consistory . . . the Senate . . . the University . . . the Foundling Hospital . . . The Suffragan has sent someone . . . he wants to know . . . Oh, the Fire Brigade – any orders for them? The prison governor . . . the superintendent of the lunatic asylum . . .' All night long the count was faced with a relentless stream of visitors reporting in.

His responses to all these inquiries were curt and tetchy, as if to say that instructions from him were now no longer necessary because all his careful preparations had been ruined by somebody, and that *somebody* would have to answer for anything that might happen from now on.

'Oh, tell that idiot,' he replied to the inquiry from the Registrar's Department, 'to stay on and guard his own archives. And what's all this nonsense about the Fire Brigade? If they have any horses, let them go off to Vladimir. Don't leave them behind for the French to get hold of.'

'Sir, the superintendent of the lunatic asylum is here. What are your orders for him?'

'Orders? Tell them all to go, that's all . . . And let the lunatics out into the town. We've got madmen in charge of our armies, so God must want this lot out as well.'

When asked about the convicts in the gaol, the count roared furiously at the overseer:

'What, do you want me to give you two non-existent battalions to escort them? Just let them go, and have done with it!'

'Sir, there are some political prisoners – Meshkov, Vereshchagin . . .'

'Vereshchagin! Haven't they hanged him yet?' cried Rostopchin. 'Bring him in here.'

CHAPTER 25

By nine o'clock next morning, with the troops on their way through Moscow, people had stopped coming to Rostopchin for instructions. Anyone who could get away was doing so without any prompting, and those who stayed behind were making their own decisions about what needed to be done.

Count Rostopchin had himself driven to Sokolniki, where he sat down in his study with his arms folded and a dark scowl on his sallow face, and waited in silence.

In moments of untroubled repose every administrator feels that the entire population working under him is kept going only by his efforts; this feeling of being absolutely indispensable gives every administrator his greatest sense of reward for all the hard work that he puts in. It is easy to understand that while ever the ocean of history remains calm, a pilot-administrator in a little bobbing boat holding on to the ship of the people with a tiny boathook, and moving along with it, might easily think *he* is driving the ship that he is clinging to. But the moment a storm comes up, with the sea heaving and the ship tossing about, this kind of delusion immediately becomes impossible. The great ship on its vast course is a free agent, the boathook can no longer reach the moving vessel, and the pilot who had been in charge, providing all the power, finds himself transformed into a creature that is pathetically useless.

Rostopchin could sense this, and he was infuriated. The police-chief who had been confronted by the crowd arrived to see him just as an adjutant walked in to tell him his horses were ready. Both men were pale, and the police-chief, after reporting that he had carried out his assignment, told Count Rostopchin there was a huge crowd of people out in the courtyard wanting to see him.

Without saying a word Rostopchin got to his feet and walked out quickly into his airy, luxuriously appointed drawing-room, where he crossed to the balcony door and took hold of the handle, only to let go of it and move across to a window that gave a better view of the whole crowd. The tall young man was standing at the front, with a serious look on his face, waving his arms in the air and saying something. The bloody-faced blacksmith stood next to him looking truculent. The roar of raised voices came in through the closed windows.

'Is the carriage ready?' said Rostopchin, moving back from the window.

'Yes, your Excellency,' said the adjutant.

Rostopchin went back to the balcony door.

'Well, what do they want?' he asked the police-chief.

'Sir, they say they are following your orders and they have come together to go and fight the French. There was some shouting about treachery. But they are a rough lot, your Excellency. I only just managed to get away. Your Excellency, if I may advise you . . .'

'Please go. I know what to do without any help from you,' cried Rostopchin angrily. He stood at the balcony door looking down at the crowd. 'Look what they've done to Russia! Look what they've done to me!' he thought, feeling a great surge of uncontainable fury against the persons unknown who must be to blame for what was happening. As is often the case with hot-headed people, the fact that he was in a foul temper meant that he needed someone to vent his fury on. 'There they are – the mob, the dregs,' he thought, looking down at the crowd. 'This is the rabble they have stirred up by their folly. What they need is a victim,' it occurred to him as he watched the tall man in front with his arm in the air. And why did it occur to him? Because he too needed a victim, some object to vent his fury on.

'Is the carriage ready?' he asked again.

'Yes, your Excellency. What are your orders in relation to Vereshchagin? He is waiting by the steps,' answered the adjutant.

'Oh is he?' cried Rostopchin, as if he had suddenly remembered something.

He flung open the door and strode purposefully out on to the balcony. The roar of voices instantly died down, caps and hats were doffed, and all eyes looked up at the governor.

'Good day, men!' said the count, raising his voice and speaking quickly. 'Thank you for coming here. I'll be with you in a moment, but first we have to deal with a criminal. We have to punish the villain who has brought Moscow to its knees. Wait there for me!' And he strode back inside, slamming the door behind him.

A murmur of approval and pleasure ran through the crowd. 'He'll sort 'em out, all them traitors. Talk about the French . . . he's got the measure of that lot!' said the people, only too keen to blame everybody else for their own lack of faith.

A few minutes later an officer hurried out of the main entrance, and brought the dragoons to attention. The crowd surged eagerly across from the balcony to the front steps. An angry-looking Rostopchin emerged rapidly at the top of them, and glanced round quickly as if he was looking for somebody.

'Where is he?' he said, and the moment he said it he caught sight of a young man with a long, thin neck, and the shaven half of his head covered with a short stubble, coming round the corner of the building between two dragoons. This young man was wearing a thin blue coat with a fox-fur lining that had once looked very smart, and a filthy pair of rough and baggy convict's trousers with the bottoms shoved down into a pair of dirty boots that had worn thin. His feeble and spindly legs were heavily shackled and he was finding it difficult to walk properly.

'Ah!' said Rostopchin, hurriedly averting his eyes from the young man in the fur-lined coat and pointing to the bottom step. 'Place him there.'

Clanking his shackles, the young man struggled to his appointed place on the step. Running a finger round the inside of his coat-collar, which was too tight, he turned his long neck this way and that, and then gave a deep sigh as he folded his thin hands (not the hands of a workman) over his stomach in a gesture of resignation.

For several seconds, while the young man was getting himself up on to the step, there was complete silence. Only at the back of the crowd, with everybody pressing forward in the same direction, was there any noise: some grunting and groaning amid all the pushing and shoving.

Rostopchin scowled and passed a hand over his face as he waited for him to arrive at the appointed spot.

'Listen, men!' he said, with a metallic ring to his voice. 'This man, Vereshchagin, is the swine that has lost Moscow for us.'

The young man in the fur-lined coat, stooping a little and showing no resistance, stood there with hands still clasped together over his stomach. His haggard young face, with its look of despair and hideously disfigured by the half-shaven head, hung down. At these opening words he slowly raised his head and looked up at the count from below, as if he wanted to say something to him, or at least to catch his eye. But Rostopchin kept his eyes away from him. A blue vein behind the young man's ear stood out like a cord on his long, thin neck, and suddenly his face coloured up.

All eyes were on him. He stared out at the crowd, and, as if detecting signs of encouragement on the faces before him, he gave a pathetic little smile and looked down again, shuffling his feet on the step.

'He is a traitor to his Tsar and his country. He went over to Bonaparte. He is the only Russian to have disgraced a Russian name. It is because of him that we are losing Moscow,' said Rostopchin in a grating monotone, and suddenly he took a quick glance down at Vereshchagin, who was still standing there in the same attitude of resignation. As if to indicate that one look at him was the last straw, he raised a fist in the air and virtually screamed at the crowd:

'You judge him! Do what you want with him!'

The people were silent; all they did was squeeze up closer. Clutching at each other, struggling to breathe in that highly charged, stifling atmosphere, unable to move, vaguely sensing the approach of some indescribable horror, the mob could not take much more. The men at the front who had seen and heard all that had gone on before them stood there horror-stricken with wide eyes and gaping mouths, straining their backs to resist the pressure from behind.

'Give him a thrashing! . . . Let this traitor die and no longer disgrace the name of a Russian citizen!' screamed Rostopchin. 'Kill him! That's an order!'

No one could hear what Rostopchin was saying, but the fury in his voice was enough to send a deep groan through the mob and make them surge forward. But then once again they stopped.

'Count!' Vereshchagin's timid yet theatrical voice cut across the momentary silence. 'Count, God above is our only . . .' said Vereshchagin, looking up, and again the thick vein pulsated with blood on his thin neck. The colour raced to his cheeks and just as quickly faded. He never finished what he had started to say.

'Kill him! That's an order!' yelled Rostopchin, suddenly as white as Vereshchagin himself.

'Sabres at the ready!' shouted the officer to the dragoons, drawing his own weapon.

Another wave, now overwhelming, swept through the crowd from back to front, shoving everybody forward, and sent those at the front staggering over to the bottom steps. The tall young man, with a stony look on his face, found himself right next to Vereshchagin, with his fist still rigid in the air.

'Hit him!' the officer said to the dragoons in a voice not much more than a whisper, and one of the soldiers, his face suddenly contorted with fury, lashed Vereshchagin on the head with the flat of his sword.

Vereshchagin gave a quick gasp of surprise, and looked round in alarm, as if he couldn't understand why they had done this to him. An echoing gasp of surprise and horror ran through the crowd.

'O Lord in heaven!' came a pathetic call from one side. But Vereshchagin's instinctive gasp of surprise was followed by a heartbreaking howl of pain, and this was his undoing. The thread of human sympathy that had been holding the mob in check had been stretched to breaking point, and now it snapped. The crime was begun; it must run its full course. A plaintive cry of reproach was submerged in the menacing, furious roar of the mob. Like the legendary seventh wave that shatters a ship, one last, devastating wave surged from the back of the crowd right through to the front, swept people off their feet and engulfed everything. The dragoon who had hit Vereshchagin was gathering himself for a second blow. Vereshchagin gave a scream of terror, hid his face in his hands and dashed out into the crowd. He ran straight into the tall young man, who grabbed Vereshchagin's slender neck with both hands, and roared like a wild animal as they went down together under the feet of the stampeding, trampling mob.

Some hands lashed out and tore at Vereshchagin, others at the tall young man. And the screams coming from people getting crushed in the crowd and from some who were trying to rescue the tall young man only increased the frenzy of the mob. It took the dragoons some time to get the bleeding, half-dead factory worker out of the crowd. And all this time, however frantically the mob tried to finish off what had been started, the men who were beating and throttling Vereshchagin, intent on tearing him limb from limb, couldn't manage to kill him. The crowd pressed in on all sides, squashing them in the middle, surging back and forth like one great heaving mass, and they could neither finish him off nor leave him alone.

'Give him one with an axe, eh? ... Look, he's been trampled to death ... Traitor! Judas! No, he's still alive ... he is, you know ... He had it coming to him ... Try this hatchet! ... Isn't he dead yet?'

It was only when the victim had stopped struggling, and his screams had fizzled out into a drawn-out, rhythmic gurgling sound, that the mob began to step gingerly away from the bleeding corpse that lay there on the ground. Everybody came up to have a look at what had been done, and they all shrank back in horror, amazed and accusing.

'Oh Lord, the people are like wild animals. He couldn't have lived through that!' came the voices in the crowd. 'Only a boy . . . Looks like he's a merchant's son . . . Oh, the people! . . . Somebody said they've got the wrong man . . . No, he's not the right one! . . . Oh Lord! . . . Another man's been beaten up too . . . half-dead, they do say . . . Oh, the people! They don't think about sin any more . . .' It was the same men speaking, now full of pain and pity as they looked down at the dead body with its blue face filthy with matted dust and blood, and its long, slender, half-severed neck.

A punctilious police official, thinking it wasn't very nice to leave a dead body lying around in his Excellency's courtyard, told the dragoons to haul the body out into the street. Two dragoons took hold of the mangled legs, and dragged the body away. The dead head, shaven, gory and grimy, trailed along the ground, bumping from side to side on its long neck. The crowd shrank back from the corpse.

When Vereshchagin fell to the ground, and the crowd of yelling savages closed in and surged over him, Rostopchin suddenly went pale, and instead of going through to the back entrance where his horses were waiting, he scuttled off down a corridor that led only to some ground-floor rooms, looking down and without the slightest idea where he was going or why. The count's face was white, and he couldn't control a feverish trembling in his jaw.

'Er, this way, your Excellency . . . Where are you going, sir? . . . Would you like to come this way?' said a quavering, timorous voice behind him. Words were beyond Rostopchin as he turned back and went where he was shown. There was his carriage at the back entrance. Even here they could hear the distant roar of the howling mob. Count Rostopchin scrambled up into his carriage, and told them to drive to his country house at Sokolniki. When they got to Myasnitsky Street and the shouting of the mob fell away, the count began to have second thoughts. The emotion and panic he had displayed before his subordinates were now a source of embarrassment. 'Ghastly, hideous rabble! They're like wolves. Only flesh will satisfy them,' he thought. '*Count, God above is our only . . .*' Vereshchagin's words suddenly came back to him, and a horrible chill ran down his spine. But it soon passed, and Count Rostopchin smiled at himself with some scorn. 'I had other things to do. The people had to be satisfied. Many other victims have perished, and are still perishing, for the public good,' he thought; and he started to run through the range of obligations he owed to his family, the city entrusted to his care, and himself – not as Fyodor Rostopchin (Fyodor Rostopchin may be considered to have sacrificed himself for 'the public good') – but as governor of Moscow, the representative of state power fully authorized by the Tsar. 'If I had been just plain Fyodor Rostopchin, my line of action might have been totally different, but I was duty bound to preserve the life and the status of the governor.'

Rocking gently in the softly sprung carriage, out of range of the mob and its ghastly noises, Rostopchin found himself physically comforted, and, as always, along with the physical relief came help from his intellect, which was busy fabricating good reasons for moral comfort too. The thought that reassured Rostopchin was hardly original. Since time began and men started killing each other, no man has ever committed such a crime against one of his fellows without comforting himself with the same idea. This idea is 'the public good', a supposed benefit for other people.

No person in control of his passions is ever aware of this benefit, but a man fresh from committing such a crime always knows for certain where the benefit lies. Rostopchin knew.

Far from reproaching himself in his own mind for what he had just done, he congratulated himself on having made the most of a fleeting opportunity to punish a criminal, and at the same time placate the mob. 'Vereshchagin had been tried and sentenced to death,' Rostopchin reflected (though the Senate had sentenced Vereshchagin to nothing more than hard labour). 'He was a spy and a traitor. I couldn't have let him go unpunished, and so I got two birds with one stone. I satisfied the mob by giving them a victim, and I executed a villain.'

By the time he had arrived home at his country house and got involved in some domestic arrangements, the count's peace of mind was complete.

Within half an hour he was off again, speeding across the Sokolniki plain, no longer absorbed in the recent past, but thinking and planning ahead. He was heading for the Yauza bridge, where he had been told he would find Kutuzov. In his imagination he was rehearsing one or two angry, caustic phrases for use in tearing a strip off Kutuzov for his deception. He would make it clear to this foxy old courtier that all the responsibility for the calamities that were bound to follow the surrender of Moscow, and the ruin of Russia (as he cared to put it), lay upon his doddery old head. Running through what he was going to say, Rostopchin twisted furiously back and forth inside the carriage, glaring fiercely out of both windows.

The Sokolniki plain was deserted. Only at the far end, by the almshouse and the lunatic asylum, did they begin to see little knots of people in white clothing, and one or two similarly dressed individuals, walking about on the plain, shouting and waving their arms.

One of them was running across to intercept Count Rostopchin's carriage. The count, his driver and all the dragoons stared with a confused feeling of horror mixed with curiosity at these madmen who had been given their freedom, and especially the one who was cutting across them. Wobbling along on his long, spindly legs, with his dressing-gown flapping behind him, this madman ran flat out with his eyes glued on Rostopchin, shouting something in a hoarse voice and waving him down. He had a dark and solemn look on his thin, sallow face with its patchy bits of straggly beard. His agate-black eyes with their rolling saffron whites jumped and jerked. 'Stop! I tell you! Stop!' came his thin, shrill voice, and he followed this up with another wheezy call accompanied by other weird sounds and insistent hand-movements.

He caught up with the carriage and ran alongside.

'Thrice they have slain me. Thrice did I rise again from the dead. I have been stoned and crucified . . . I shall rise again . . . rise again . . . rise again . . . My body they have torn to pieces. The kingdom of heaven shall be cast down . . . Thrice shall I cast it down, and thrice shall I raise it up again,' he wailed, his voice getting higher and louder. Suddenly Count Rostopchin turned as white as he had done when the crowd had fallen upon Vereshchagin. He looked away. 'G-g-get going, faster!' he called to his driver in a quavering voice.

The carriage put on all speed. But Count Rostopchin kept on hearing somewhere at his back the mindless scream of despair as it echoed away into the far distance, while up ahead his eyes saw nothing but the shocked and scared, bleeding face of the traitor in the fur-lined coat.

For all the newness of that image, Rostopchin suddenly realized it was deeply imprinted on his heart, etched in blood. He knew the bloody imprint of that memory would never be healed, and the more distant it became, the more cruelly and viciously the dreaded memory would survive in his heart to the end of his days. He seemed to hear the sound of his own words coming back: 'Kill him, or you'll answer with your heads!' 'Why did I utter those words? They just came out . . . I needn't have said them,' he thought, 'and then *nothing at all* would have happened.' He saw again the face of the dragoon who had struck the first blow, scared to begin with but then suddenly roused to a frenzy, and the diffident glance of unspoken reproach levelled at him by that young man in the fur-lined coat. 'But I didn't do it for myself. I was duty bound to do what I did. The rabble . . . the traitor . . . the public good,' he thought to himself.

There were still hordes of troops near the bridge over the Yauza. It was hot. Kutuzov cut a weary, brooding figure as he sat on a bench not far from the bridge, and he was doodling with his whip in the sand when a noisy carriage came rattling up. A man in a general's uniform complete with plumed hat came over to Kutuzov and spoke to him in French, his eyes darting about between fury and fear. It was Count Rostopchin. He told Kutuzov he had had to come here, because Moscow was no more, the capital city had gone, and only the army was left. 'It might have been different if your Serene Highness had not assured me you would never surrender Moscow without a fight. None of this would have happened!'

Kutuzov stared at Rostopchin as if he couldn't make head or tail of what he was saying and had to concentrate hard in the hope of picking out some special meaning flickering for a moment on the face of the man addressing him. Rostopchin wound down in some embarrassment. Kutuzov gave a slight shake of his head and murmured quietly, with his searching eyes still glued on Rostopchin's face, 'No, I won't surrender Moscow without a fight.' Whether Kutuzov was otherwise preoccupied when he uttered these words, or said them deliberately, knowing how meaningless they were, Count Rostopchin hurried away without replying. And lo and behold! The governor-general of Moscow, the proud Count Rostopchin, picked up a whip, walked over to the bridge, and began directing the carts that were blocking the way.

CHAPTER 26

It was getting on for four o'clock in the afternoon when Murat's troops entered Moscow. Out in front rode a detachment of the Württemberg hussars; behind them came the King of Naples himself with a large suite of men.

Half-way down the Arbat, near to St Nicholas's Church, Murat called a halt and waited for a report from the advance detachment on the present situation at *le Kremlin*, the Moscow citadel.

A little knot of remaining Muscovites gathered round Murat. They stared in polite bemusement at the curious figure of the long-haired commander all decked out in feathers and gold.

'What's 'e supposed to be then? Is it 'im? Is 'e their Tsar? Not bad, is 'e?' came a few quiet voices.

An interpreter came over to the group of onlookers.

'Hey, caps . . . take your caps off,' went the word in the little crowd as people turned to each other. The interpreter asked an old porter how far it was to the Kremlin. The porter listened blankly to a stream of Russian coming at him with a weird Polish accent, couldn't tell that the interpreter was speaking his language and didn't understand a word of it, so he dived behind the others for safety.

Murat came over to the interpreter and told him to ask where the Russian troops had gone. One of the Russians understood what they were after, and soon several voices were answering the interpreter all at the same time. A French officer from the advance detachment then rode up to Murat and reported that the gates into the citadel had been barricaded, and there was probably an ambush there.

'Good,' said Murat. He turned to one of the gentlemen of his suite and ordered him to bring up four light cannons and open fire on the gates.

The artillery came trotting out from the column of troops behind Murat, and rode off down the Arbat. When they got to the end of Vozdvizhenka the artillery came to a halt and formed up in the square. Several French officers supervised the siting and spacing of the cannons, and looked across at the Kremlin through a telescope.

The Kremlin bells were ringing for evening service, and the sound of them worried the French. They could only take this as a call to arms. A few infantrymen ran over to the Kutafyev gate. The entry was barricaded with beams and planks. Two musket shots rang out from the gateway the moment it was approached by an officer with some of his men. The general standing by the cannons yelled across some words of command, and the officer and the soldiers ran back.

Three more shots came from the gate. One grazed the leg of a French soldier, and a few voices could be heard uttering strange cries from behind the barricade. The faces of the French general, the officers and men changed in a flash, as if someone had given an order, expressions of quiet good humour giving way to looks of grim determination, close concentration and readiness for action and suffering. To every last man from the marshal to the humblest soldier, this was now not one of the streets in Moscow or the Trinity gate; it was another battlefield, and bloodshed was likely. They all stood ready to fight. The shouting on the other side of the gateway died down. The cannons were brought forward. The gunners blew the ash off their burnt-down linstocks. An officer shouted 'Fire!' and two canister-shots whistled over one after another. The shot rattled against the stone gateway, the beams and barriers, and two wavering smoke-clouds rose above the square.

A few seconds after the echoes of the shots had died away over the stonework of the Kremlin, the French heard a strange sound overhead.

Thousands of jackdaws soared up from the walls and circled round in the air with raucous cawing and a great flapping of wings. Along with this sound a solitary human cry was heard from the gate, and through the smoke emerged the figure of a bare-headed man wearing a long peasant's coat. He held up his musket and took aim at the French. 'Fire!' repeated the artillery officer, and a musket shot and two cannon shots rang out simultaneously. Once again the gate was enveloped in smoke.

There was now no movement from behind the barricade, and the French infantrymen approached the gate with their officers. There in the gateway lay seven Russians, three wounded and four dead. Two men in long peasant coats were seen running away along the walls down towards Znamenka.

'Get rid of this lot,' said the officer, pointing to the beams and the dead bodies. The French soldiers finished off the wounded, and threw the dead bodies over the parapet. Who these men were nobody knew. They were dismissed in a few words, 'Get rid of this lot', thrown down below and later cleared away to avoid a stink. The historian Thiers is unique in devoting a few eloquent lines to their memory: 'These wretched men had invaded the sacred citadel, taken weapons from the arsenal and fired on the French (the wretches). Some of them were dispatched with swords, and the Kremlin was purged of their presence.'

Murat was informed that the way had been cleared. The French came in through the gate and began to set up camp on Senate Square. The soldiers threw chairs down into the square from the Senate House windows and lit fires with them.

Other detachments marched past the Kremlin and pitched camp along Moroseyka, Lubyanka and Pokrovka. Others set themselves up in Vozdvizhenka, Znamenka, Nikolsky and Tverskoy. With no hosts available, the French decided not to take over any houses; instead, they pitched camp as normal, but out in the town.

The French were a ragged lot, hungry and exhausted, and their numbers were down by two-thirds, but their soldiers entered Moscow in good order. It was a harassed and exhausted army, though still ready for action and a real threat. But it remained an army only up to the point when its soldiers scattered themselves all over the town. Once the soldiers began to find their various ways into wealthy, deserted houses, the army had gone for ever, to be replaced by men who were neither citizens nor soldiers, but in-between creatures of the type known as looters. Five weeks later these same men would set out from Moscow, and by then they had ceased to be an army. They were a mob of looters, all of them carrying or wheeling piles of things they considered valuable or useful. The aim of these departing men was not what it had been before, to acquit themselves well in battle, but simply to keep all the loot they had managed to get their hands on. Like a monkey who slips his hand down the narrow neck of a jug and grabs a handful of nuts, and then refuses to open his fist for fear of dropping his treasure, even if it costs him his life, the departing French were obviously bound to come to grief because of all the loot they were carrying, and it was no more possible for them to abandon their loot than for the monkey to let go of his handful of nuts. Ten minutes after the dispersal of the French regiments all over the various districts of Moscow, not a soldier or officer was left. At the windows of houses men in greatcoats and Hessian boots could be seen laughing as they strolled about the rooms. Down in the cellars and out in the store-rooms the same sort of men were taking over any provisions; in the yards the same sort of men were unlocking or breaking into coach-houses and stables; in the kitchens they were lighting fires, and rolling up their sleeves to start mixing, kneading and baking, and they were either scaring the women and children out of their wits or amusing them and being nice. And men like these were all over the place, in all the shops and houses. They existed in great numbers, but there wasn't any army.

Throughout that first day the French commanders issued order after order forbidding the troops to disperse about the town, strictly prohibiting violent behaviour towards any inhabitants and looting, and calling everybody to a general roll-call that evening. But in defiance of all such measures the men who had so recently made up an army drained away all over this wealthy, deserted city, so richly supplied with goods and luxuries. Like a ravening herd of cattle that sticks together while crossing a barren plain but scatters unstoppably in all directions as soon as they get to green pastures, the army scattered unstoppably throughout this wealthy town.

Moscow had no inhabitants, and the soldiers were rapidly absorbed like water soaking into sand, as they drained away unstoppably in all directions radiating out starwise from the Kremlin, their first point of entry. Cavalry soldiers would find their way into a merchant's house abandoned with all its belongings, where there was more than enough stabling for their horses, yet still go on to occupy another house because it seemed better. Many took several houses, chalking the occupier's name outside, there were quarrels with other companies over possession and they even came to blows. The soldiers had barely settled in before they rushed out to have a look round the town, and when they heard about places where everything had been abandoned they charged off to pick up valuable items that could be had for the taking. Officers who followed on to stop this behaviour couldn't help getting involved themselves. In Carriage Row there were shops still stocked with carriages, and generals flocked there to choose coaches and carriages for their own use. The few remaining citizens invited officers into their homes in the hope of protecting themselves against robbery. These were days of bonanza, with no end to the wealth available. Everywhere, in all the places surrounding the districts occupied by the French, there were new regions as yet unexplored and unoccupied which the French imagined to be teeming with more good things. And Moscow steadily absorbed them. But it was like water flowing over dry soil when the water and the soil mingle into mud; when the ravenous army entered the wealthy, deserted city, both the army and the wealth soon disappeared, and the result was a place of filth, burning buildings and gangs of looters.

The French attributed the burning of Moscow to Rostopchin and his 'ferocious patriotism'; the Russians to French barbarism. In point of fact, there never has been, and never could be, any satisfactory explanation of the burning of Moscow, not in terms of attributing responsibility to any one person or group of people. Moscow burnt because she found herself in a situation in which any town of wooden construction was bound to burn, whether or not it had a hundred and thirty pretty useless fire-appliances at its disposal. Once her inhabitants had gone away Moscow was bound to burn, just as a pile of wood-shavings is bound to catch fire if you scatter sparks all over it for days on end. A town of wooden buildings where something catches fire almost every day during the summer, even when the owners are still there and the police are at hand, is sure to burn when the property-owners have gone away and been replaced by pipe-smoking soldiers who use Senate House chairs as firewood in Senate Square and cook themselves a meal twice a day. Even in peace-time whenever troops are billeted in villages the number of fires in the district goes up straightaway. How much greater the likelihood of fire in an abandoned town built of wood and occupied by foreign troops! There is no point in blaming it on Rostopchin's 'ferocious patriotism' or French savagery. Moscow was set on fire by men smoking pipes, kitchen stoves and camp-fires, by the careless behaviour of enemy soldiers living in houses they didn't own. If there was any arson (which is very doubtful because no one had any reason to go round starting fires, and in any case that is a tricky business and also very dangerous), we cannot claim this as the real cause because the same thing would have happened without it.

However convenient it may have been for the French to blame the ferocious Rostopchin, and for the Russians to the blame that villain Napoleon, or at a later date to hand the heroic torch to their patriot peasantry, we cannot hide the fact that there could never be one single reason behind the fire, because Moscow was as certain to burn as any village, factory or house abandoned by its owners and taken over by strangers to live in and cook their porridge. Yes, it is true that Moscow was burnt by its inhabitants, but it was burnt by those who went away rather than those who stayed behind. Moscow was not like Berlin, Vienna and other cities that emerged unscathed from the enemy occupation. The difference was that her inhabitants, instead of welcoming the French with the keys of the city and the traditional bread and salt, preferred to walk away.

CHAPTER 27

It was not until the evening of the 2nd of September that the process of absorbing the French into Moscow by spreading out starwise finally reached the district where Pierre was staying.

After two days spent in isolation and unusual circumstances Pierre was in a state bordering on insanity. He was wholly obsessed by a single idea. He didn't know when or how it had come about, but he was now so completely obsessed that he remembered nothing from the past, and understood nothing of the present. Everything he saw and heard seemed dreamlike as it passed before him.

Pierre had left his own house simply to escape from the challenging and complex tangle of everyday demands that he could not unravel in his current state of mind. He had gone to Osip Bazdeyev's house ostensibly to sort out the dead man's books and papers, but actually in search of peace and quiet amidst all the turmoil of his life. In his heart and memory he associated Bazdeyev with a different realm of quietude and ideas that seemed solemn and eternal, the exact opposite of the tangled web of anxiety that he could feel himself being drawn into. He sought a quiet refuge, and he certainly found one in Bazdeyev's study. Sitting there in the deathlike stillness of the study with his head in his hands and his elbows on the dead man's dusty desk, one by one he brought back to mind all the impressions of the last few days, considering them calmly and with full understanding,

especially the battle of Borodino and that overwhelming sense of his
own insignificance and hollowness compared with the righteousness,
simplicity and strength of character of those few people who had left
a mark on his soul and whom he thought of as 'them'. When Gerasim
had interrupted his reverie Pierre's first thought was that he might go
out and join the people in their defence of Moscow. (He knew such a
proposal was in the air.) This was why he had asked Gerasim to get
him a peasant's coat and a pistol, and why he told him he was going
to hide his identity and stay on in Bazdeyev's house. Then throughout
his first day of solitude and idleness (Pierre made several attempts to
concentrate on the masonic manuscripts, but to no avail) his mind
had been drawn back repeatedly to a vague recollection of an idea
that had been nagging at him for some time: the cabbalistic significance
that linked his name with Napoleon's. But as yet the idea that he,
l'russe Besuhof, was fated to put an end to the power of *the Beast*,
was nothing more than one of those dreams that pop up in the mind
spontaneously and are immediately gone without trace. When Pierre
had bought the peasant's coat, with the sole object of joining the
people in the defence of Moscow, and then met the Rostovs, and
Natasha had said, 'Are you are staying on? I think it's wonderful!' it
occurred to him that it really might be wonderful, even if they took
Moscow, for him to stay on and fulfil his destiny.

The next day he had followed the people out to the Three Hills gate
with one idea in mind: to spare no effort in keeping up with *them* in
everything they did. But when he came back, certain that Moscow
was not going to be defended, he suddenly felt that what had seemed
like an outside possibility before had now become an unavoidable
necessity. He had to stay on in Moscow, hide his identity, meet
Napoleon and kill him. He had to put an end to the misery of Europe,
all of which in Pierre's estimation could be laid at Napoleon's door,
or die in the attempt.

Pierre knew every detail of the German student's attempt on
Napoleon's life in Vienna in 1809,[3] and he also knew that the student
had been shot. But the danger to which he was exposing himself in
fulfilling his purpose acted only as a further stimulus.

Two emotions of equal intensity drove him inexorably on. The first
was the impulse towards sacrifice and suffering stemming from his
sense of the common calamity, the feeling that had induced him to go
down to Mozhaysk on the 25th and find his way into the very thick
of the battle, and had now made him give up his life of ease and
luxury, run away from home, sleep in his clothes on a hard sofa and
eat the same food as Gerasim. The other was that vague, exclusively

Russian, feeling of contempt for everything conventional, artificial, rooted solely in human experience, a contempt for everything that most people would consider the best things in the world. Pierre had felt this strangely attractive emotion for the first time in the Slobodskoy palace, when it suddenly occurred to him that wealth, power, life itself, all the things that men put so much effort into building up and maintaining, if they have any value at all, are never worth more than the pleasure to be had by renouncing them.

It was the feeling that makes a volunteer-recruit spend his last farthing on drink, or a drunken man smash mirrors and windows for no good reason, even though he knows it will cost him what little he has; the feeling that impels a man to do things that the common mentality would write off as insane, in order to take the measure of his own independence and strength by maintaining the existence of a higher code transcending everyday experience by which human life is to be judged.

Ever since the day when Pierre had experienced this emotion for the first time in the Slobodskoy palace it had exerted a strong hold on him, but only now did he feel able to give it its head. More than that, Pierre now found himself confirmed in his purpose, and prevented from abandoning it, by everything he had already done towards its fulfilment. His running away from home, the peasant coat, the pistol, his meeting with the Rostovs when he had told them he was staying on in Moscow – it would all seem so humiliating and ridiculous (something Pierre cared about) if after all that he had turned round and left Moscow like everybody else.

As always, Pierre's physical condition corresponded to his state of mind. The rough diet that was so new to him, all the vodka he drank during those days, the absence of wine and cigars, his dirty unchanged linen, and two nights without much sleep on a short sofa with no bedclothes, all kept Pierre in a state of nervous tension not far from madness.

It was getting on for two o'clock in the afternoon. The French were now in Moscow. Pierre knew this, but instead of doing anything he just sat there thinking about the task that lay ahead of him, going over it in minute detail. In his daydreams Pierre never had a clear picture of himself carrying out the murder, nor of Napoleon dying, but he could imagine with stark vividness and wistful enjoyment his own demise and his manly heroism.

'Yes, one for all. I must do it or die in the attempt!' he thought. 'Yes, I'll get near him . . . and then suddenly . . . Pistol or dagger?'

thought Pierre. 'Well, it doesn't make any difference ... "You are being executed not by me but the Hand of Providence," I shall say.' (Pierre was wondering what to say at the moment of killing Napoleon.) 'Go on then. Take me. Execute me,' Pierre would go on to say, bowing his head with a sad but resolute expression on his face.

While Pierre was standing there in the middle of the room thinking along these lines the door of the study opened, and there in the doorway stood Makar Bazdeyev. Before, he had always looked so diffident, but now he was completely transformed.

His dressing-gown hung open. His face was red and hideously contorted. He had obviously been drinking. When he saw Pierre he was taken aback for a moment, but then, noticing that Pierre was as shocked as he was, he rallied and tottered out into the middle of the room on his spindly legs.

'They're not up to it,' his hoarse voice said confidingly. 'I'm telling you. I shall not surrender. Is that not right, sir?' He paused and thought for a moment, then he took one look at the pistol lying on the table, grabbed it with surprising speed and rushed out into the corridor.

Gerasim and the porter, who had been following Makar, stopped him in the hallway and tried to take the pistol from him. Pierre came out of the study and watched the half-insane old man with a mixture of revulsion and compassion. Makar was frowning with exertion as he struggled to hold on to the pistol, and he called out in his hoarse voice, obviously dreaming up some great adventure.

'To arms! Prepare for boarding! Oh no you don't! You're not getting this!' he was shouting.

'Everything's going to be quite all right. Please let go, sir. There you are, sir. Please ...' Gerasim was saying, trying to steer Makar gently by his elbows towards the door.

'Who are you? Napoleon!' roared Makar.

'That's not very nice, sir. Just come into your room, please, and have a little lie-down. Give me that little pistol.'

'Be gone, you scurvy knave! Don't touch me! See this?' screamed Makar, brandishing the pistol. 'Prepare for boarding!'

'See if you can grab it,' Gerasim whispered to the porter.

They seized Makar by the arms and dragged him off towards the door.

The hallway rang with the unseemly sounds of a scuffle and a drunken voice, wheezy and gasping.

Then there was another cry, a woman screaming out in the porch, and the cook came running into the vestibule.

'Look who's here! Lord in heaven! Four of 'em, on horses!' she screamed.

Gerasim and the porter let go of Makar. The corridor was quiet for a moment, then it echoed with a loud knocking as several hands pounded on the front door.

CHAPTER 28

Pierre had made up his mind it would be better for him not to reveal his title or his knowledge of French until his purpose had been achieved, so he stood by the half-open door into the corridor, determined to hide as soon as the French came in. But when they did Pierre stayed by the door, held there by an irresistible curiosity.

There were two of them. One was an officer, tall and handsome, a fine figure of a man; the other, obviously a common soldier or an orderly, was a short, thin, sunburnt man with sunken cheeks and a blank look on his face. The officer limped in first, leaning on a stick. He took only a few steps before apparently deciding that these would make good quarters; he stopped, turned round and bawled in an authoritative voice to the soldiers standing in the doorway to put up the horses. Having seen to this, he crooked an elbow and raised it on high ostentatiously, smoothing his moustache and touching his hat.

'Good day to you one and all!' he said in French with a cheery smile, taking a good look around.

There was no response.

'Are you the master of the house?' the officer asked Gerasim.

Gerasim gave the officer an anxious, quizzical look.

'Quarters. Quarters. Lodgings,' said the officer, peering down at the little man from his great height with a cheery, ingratiating smile. 'The French are good fellows. No harsh words between us, old fellow,' he went on in French, looking at Gerasim, who was too scared to speak, and clapping him on the shoulder. 'I say, are there no French-speakers in this establishment?' he added, looking round and meeting Pierre's eyes. Pierre shrank back from the door.

The officer turned back to Gerasim, and asked to be shown over the house.

'Gone master . . . no savvy . . . me you . . .' said Gerasim, trying to add meaning to his words by saying them in the wrong order.

The French officer gave a smile, waved his hands in front of Gerasim's nose to let him know he didn't understand either, and limped over towards the door where Pierre was standing. Pierre made a move, intending to go and hide, but at that very moment he caught a glimpse of Makar Bazdeyev, who had appeared at the open kitchen door with a pistol in his hand. With a madman's cunning Makar eyed the Frenchmen, raised his pistol and took aim.

'Prepare for boarding!' yelled the drunken man, squeezing the trigger. The French officer spun round at this cry, and at the same instant Pierre flung himself at the drunkard. As Pierre grabbed the pistol and jerked it up in the air, Makar finally managed to get his finger on the trigger, there was a terrific bang and they were all enveloped in a cloud of smoke. The Frenchman turned pale and rushed back to the door.

Forgetting his intention of hiding his knowledge of French, Pierre snatched the pistol away and threw it down, before running over to the officer and speaking to him in French. 'You're not wounded, are you?' he asked.

'No, I don't think so,' answered the officer, checking all over his body, 'but it was a near thing,' he added, pointing to a hole in the plaster on one wall.

'Who is this man?' he asked with a grim look at Pierre.

'Oh, I really am in despair at what's happened,' Pierre blurted out, forgetting the part he was supposed to be playing. 'He's a madman, a wretched creature. He didn't know what he was doing.'

The officer went over to Makar and fingered his collar.

Makar's lips were pouting as he leant shakily against the wall; he seemed almost to be falling asleep.

'You brigand! You're going to pay for this!' said the Frenchman, letting go of him. 'We are merciful in victory, but we do not pardon traitors,' he added with a splendid flourish, looking all grave and gloomy.

Pierre carried on in French, trying to persuade the officer not to be too hard on this drunken imbecile. The Frenchman listened in silence with the same gloomy air, and then suddenly turned to Pierre with a smile on his face. He stared at him for several seconds without saying anything. Then his handsome face melted into an expression of histrionic sentimentality, and he held out his hand.

'You saved my life. You are French,' he said. For this Frenchman there could be no other conclusion. Heroic deeds could only be performed by Frenchmen and saving the life of Monsieur Ramballe, captain of the Thirteenth Light Brigade, had been an unmistakably heroic deed.

But, for all the sureness of the officer's conclusion and his absolute certainty, Pierre felt he had to disillusion him.

'I'm Russian,' he said quickly.

'Tut-tut-tut! Tell that to other people,' said the Frenchman, smiling and waving a finger before his nose. 'You can tell me all about it later on,' he said. 'Delighted to meet a fellow countryman. Well then, what shall we do with this man?' he added, treating Pierre like a brother-in-arms. The French officer's expression and tone seemed to imply that if Pierre really wasn't a Frenchman he would hardly want to disavow the designation once it had been bestowed, this being the most honourable title in the world. Pierre dealt with his last question, and explained again who Makar Bazdeyev was. He also explained that just before the officer's arrival the drunken imbecile had managed to snatch a loaded pistol and they had been unable to get it off him. Pierre begged him to let his action go unpunished.

The Frenchman stuck out his chest, and made a regal gesture with one hand.

'You saved my life! You are a Frenchman. You ask me to pardon him. I grant you his pardon. Take this man away.' The French officer spoke quickly and with strong emphasis. He had latched on to Pierre, promoting him to French citizenship for having saved his life, and now walked with him further into the house.

The soldiers, who had heard the shot out in the yard, had come into the passage to find out what was happening, only too keen to help punish any offenders, but the officer stopped them in their tracks.

'You will be sent for when you are needed,' he said. The soldiers withdrew. The orderly, who had found his way to the kitchen, came in to report to the officer.

'Captain, they have soup and a leg of mutton in the kitchen,' he said. 'Shall I serve them up?'

'Yes, and the wine,' said the captain.

CHAPTER 29

The French officer walked further in with Pierre, who felt duty bound to repeat for the captain's benefit that he wasn't French; he also made an attempt to go his own way, but the captain wouldn't hear of it. He was so courteous, polite, affable and genuinely grateful to him for saving his life that Pierre hadn't the heart to refuse, so he sat down with him in the first large room they came to. When Pierre kept on insisting he wasn't French, the captain, plainly at a loss to understand how anyone could repudiate such a flattering title, gave a shrug and said that if he insisted on passing himself off as a Russian, so be it, but it made no difference – he would still feel a special bond between them that would last for ever, eternal gratitude to Pierre for saving his life.

If this man had shown even the slightest sensitivity towards the feelings of others, and had had the faintest inkling of what Pierre was going through, Pierre might well have walked away at this point. But since the man was a bundle of energy and impervious to anything beyond himself he was too much for Pierre.

'Frenchman or Russian prince incognito,' said the Frenchman with a glance at Pierre's dirty but obviously high-quality linen, and the ring on his finger. 'I owe my life to you, and I offer you my friendship. A Frenchman never forgets an insult or a favour. I offer you my friendship. That's all I have to say.'

The officer's smile, tone of voice, facial expression and hand-movements spoke so eloquently of open-heartedness and nobility (in the French sense) that Pierre instinctively smiled back as he accepted the outstretched hand.

'Captain Ramballe of the Thirteenth Light Brigade, Chevalier of the Legion of Honour following the business of the 7th of September,'[4] he said by way of introduction, an irrepressible smile of self-satisfaction curling the corners of his mouth under the moustache. 'Will you now please tell me with whom I have the honour of conducting this pleasant conversation when I might have been lying in an ambulance with that madman's bullet in my body?'

Pierre said he wasn't in a position to give his name, and he coloured up as he tried to think of another name and started to give reasons for not being in a position to name himself, but the Frenchman cut him short.

'Please!' he said. 'I understand your reasons. You're an officer . . . maybe a staff-officer. You have taken up arms against us. That's none of my business. I owe you my life, and that's what counts. I am at your service. You are a nobleman, aren't you?' he added rather quizzically. Pierre gave a bow.

'Well, please tell me your Christian name. I ask no more than that . . . Monsieur Pierre, you say? Splendid. That's all I want to know.'

When they had served up the mutton, an omelette, a samovar, vodka, and some wine taken from a Russian cellar and brought along by the French, Ramballe invited Pierre to share his meal, and then he set to work himself with the greedy appetite of a healthy, hungry man, munching away with his strong teeth, and continually smacking his lips and exclaiming, 'Splendid! Delicious!' His reddened face was soon running with perspiration. Pierre was feeling hungry too, and he joined in with a will. Morel, the orderly, brought some hot water in a sauce-

pan and put a bottle of claret in it to warm. He returned with a bottle
of kvass for them to taste. This drink was already known to the French,
and it had its own nickname. They called it 'pig's lemonade' and
Morel, who had found it in the kitchen, praised it to the skies. But
since the captain had his wine, acquired on the way across Moscow,
he let Morel have the kvass while he attended to the bottle of Bordeaux.
He wrapped a napkin round the neck of the bottle and poured out a
glass of wine for himself and Pierre. With his appetite satisfied and
the wine going to his head the captain became livelier than ever, and
he chatted away incessantly throughout dinner.

'Oh yes, my dear Monsieur Pierre, I owe you a candle in church for
saving me from that madman. I've got quite enough bullets in my
body, you know. Here's one from Wagram,' (he pointed to his side)
'and two from Smolensk' (the scar on his cheek). 'And there's this leg
that won't walk, as I'm sure you've noticed. I got that at the great battle
outside la Moskova on the 7th.' (The reference was to Borodino.) 'My
God, that was a splendid day! You should have seen it – a deluge of
fire. You gave us a tough time there. Something to be proud of, I'll
say! And do you know? I might have caught a bit of a cold, but I'd do
it all over again. I'm sorry for anyone who wasn't there.'

'I was,' said Pierre.

'Were you really?' pursued the Frenchman. 'Oh well, all the better
then. You are proud enemies, though. The big redoubt was well held,
for goodness' sake. And you made us pay for it too! I went at it three
times, sure as I'm sitting here. Three times we were right on top of the
cannons, and three times we were driven back like men of cardboard.
Oh, it was splendid, Monsieur Pierre. Your grenadiers were superb, by
God. I watched them close ranks six times in succession and march as if
they were out on parade. Wonderful men. Our king of Naples, who
knows it all backwards, yelled out, "Bravo!" 'Aha! Soldiers like us!' he
said after a moment's silence. 'All the better, Monsieur Pierre, all the
better. Terrible in war . . . chivalrous with the fair sex.' (He gave a wink
and a smile.) 'There you have the French, M. Pierre. Isn't that right?'

The captain was so simple-hearted and good-humoured, so cheery,
self-contained and pleased with himself that Pierre almost winked
back as he enjoyed watching him. It was probably the mention of
chivalry that brought the captain round to contemplating the state of
things in Moscow.

'By the way, do tell me, is it true that all the women have left
Moscow? What a curious idea! What were they frightened of?'

'Wouldn't the French ladies leave Paris if the Russians came?' said
Pierre.

'Ha-ha-ha!' The Frenchman burst out in a roar of spirited laughter, clapping Pierre on the shoulder. 'That's a good one, that is!' he went on. 'Paris ... But Paris ... Paris ...'

'Paris is the capital of the world,' said Pierre, finishing the sentence for him.

The captain looked at Pierre. He had the habit of stopping in mid-conversation and staring closely with his gentle, laughing eyes.

'Well, if you hadn't told me you're a Russian I would have laid odds you came from Paris. You have that indefinable quality ...' and after this compliment he stared at him again in silence.

'I have been in Paris. I spent years there,' said Pierre.

'I can see that! Paris! A man who doesn't know Paris is a barbarian ... You can spot a Parisian a mile off. Paris is ... Talma, la Duchénois, Potier, the Sorbonne ... [5] the boulevards.' But, suddenly aware that this conclusion was becoming rather anti-climactic, he hastened to add, 'There is only one Paris in the world ... You've been in Paris, but you stayed Russian. Well, I don't think any the less of you for that.'

Pierre was now feeling the effect of the wine, and after several days spent alone with his gloomy thoughts he found himself drawn irresistibly into enjoying this conversation with such a cheerful and good-hearted person.

'To return to your ladies – I hear they are very beautiful. What a ridiculous idea to go and bury themselves out on the steppe when the French army is in Moscow. What a lost opportunity! Your peasants are different, but you civilized people ought to know us better than that. We have taken Vienna, Berlin, Madrid, Naples, Rome, Warsaw – every capital in the world. We are feared, but we are also loved. We are worth knowing. And as for the Emperor ...' he started to say, but Pierre cut across him.

'The Emperor,' he repeated, his face looking suddenly sombre and embarrassed. 'Is the Emperor ... ?'

'The Emperor? He is generosity, mercy, justice, order, genius – that's what the Emperor is. I can vouch for it ... I, Ramballe, the man you see before you, was an enemy of his eight years ago. My father was an émigré count. But he has won me over, that man has. Taken hold of me. I couldn't resist the spectacle of the greatness and glory he was heaping on France. When I understood what he wanted, when I saw he was preparing a bed of laurels for us, I said to myself, you know, "This is a monarch!" And I gave myself up to him. Oh yes, he is the greatest man of past centuries and those to come.'

'But is he here in Moscow?' Pierre asked, hesitantly, with a shifty look.

'No, he will make his entry tomorrow,' said the French officer, and he went on with his chatter.

Their conversation was interrupted by voices from the gate, followed by Morel coming in to tell the captain some Württemberg hussars had arrived and they wanted to put up their horses in the yard where the captain's were already put up. The worst thing was that the hussars couldn't understand what was being said to them.

The captain sent for the senior NCO and asked him sternly which regiment he belonged to, who his commanding officer was, and on what basis he allowed himself to start taking over quarters that were already occupied. He was a German who knew very little French, and although he managed answers to the first two questions, he replied to the last one, which he hadn't understood, in a mixture of broken French and German, saying that he was quartermaster of his regiment, acting under orders from his superior officer to occupy all the houses one after another. Pierre was a German-speaker, and he translated the German's words for the captain, and then translated the captain's response for the benefit of the Württemberg hussar. Once he understood what was being said to him, the German gave way and went off with his men.

The captain went out to the entrance and barked out a few orders.

When he came back in Pierre was sitting in the same place, with his hands clasped around his head. His face was a picture of anguish. He really was going through it at that moment. The moment the captain had gone out and Pierre had been left alone, he suddenly came to and realized what a situation he was now in. It wasn't just that Moscow had been taken, or that these lucky conquerors were making themselves at home and patronizing him, that tormented him at that time, painful though all this was in itself. He was tormented by a sudden awareness of his own weakness. One or two glasses of wine and a chat with this genial man had destroyed the mood of sombre concentration he had been living in for the last few days, and this mood was essential to him if he was going to carry out his mission. His things were ready, the pistol, the dagger and the peasant's coat. Napoleon was making his entry tomorrow. Pierre felt just as convinced it would be the right and proper thing to do to slay this villain, but he now had the feeling he was not going to do it. Why not? He didn't know – it was just a vague presentiment that he wasn't going to carry out his mission. He was fighting against this awareness of his own weakness, knowing somehow he wasn't going to overcome it, and his dark ideas of yesterday – vengeance, murder and self-sacrifice – had been blown away like dust at the first contact with another human being.

The captain came back in, limping a little and whistling to himself.

The Frenchman's chatter that Pierre had found so amusing now seemed revolting. His whistling, his walk, and his way of twirling his moustache all seemed like an insult to Pierre now.

'I'll go. I won't say another word to him,' thought Pierre. He may have thought this, but he still sat there, transfixed by a strange feeling of weakness. He longed to get up and go, but he couldn't do it.

The captain, by contrast, seemed in high spirits. He paced the room a couple of times. There was a gleam in his eye and a slight twitch in his moustache as if he was smiling to himself at some secret joke.

'Charming fellow, the colonel of these Württembergers,' he blurted out. 'He's German, but a good fellow if ever there was one. Still, he is German.'

He sat down facing Pierre.

'By the way, I see you're a German-speaker.'

Pierre looked at him in silence.

'What's the German for "shelter"?'

'Shelter?' parroted Pierre. 'Shelter in German is *Unterkunft*.'

'Say again.' The captain spoke quickly and doubtfully.

'*Unterkunft*,' repeated Pierre.

'*Onterkof*,' said the captain, and he stared at Pierre for several seconds with laughter in his eyes. 'Awful fools these Germans, aren't they, Monsieur Pierre?' he concluded.

'Oh well, another bottle of this Moscow claret, eh? Morel, warm us another bottle! Morel!' the captain shouted cheerily.

Morel came in with candles and another bottle of wine. The captain glanced at Pierre in the candle light, and was visibly struck by the look of anguish on his companion's face. Ramballe came over to Pierre and bent towards him with all the appearance of genuine sympathy and regret.

'Oh dear, we are looking gloomy!' he said, touching Pierre on the arm. 'Have I offended you in some way? No, tell me, please, have you anything to hold against me?' He was full of questions. 'Maybe it's just the present situation?'

Pierre said nothing, but he looked warmly into the Frenchman's eyes. He liked his display of sympathy.

'My word of honour, apart from being in your debt, I feel we are friends. Is there anything I can do for you? I am yours to command. In life and death. I say so hand on heart,' he said, slapping himself on the chest.

'Thank you,' said Pierre. The captain looked closely at Pierre just as he had done when learning the German for 'shelter', and his face suddenly brightened.

'Very well, then. Here's to our friendship,' he cried breezily, pouring out two glasses of wine.

Pierre took the glass and drained it. Ramballe did the same, gave Pierre's arm another squeeze, and leant forward with his elbows on the table in an attitude of wistful contemplation.

'Yes, my dear friend, such are the vagaries of fortune . . .' he began. 'Who would have said I would one day be a soldier and captain of dragoons in the service of Bonaparte, as we used to call him? Yet here I am with him in Moscow. I must tell you, my dear fellow,' he continued in the doleful rhythmic tones of a man about to embark on a long story, 'our name is one of the oldest in France . . .'

And with the easy-going simplicity and openness of a Frenchman, the captain told Pierre the history of his ancestors, his childhood, adolescence and manhood, and everything to do with his relations, his fortunes and his family. Naturally enough, 'my poor mother' played a prominent part in the recital.

'But that's only the stage-setting of life. The real thing is love. Love! Isn't that right, Monsieur Pierre?' he said, warming to his theme. 'Another glass.'

Pierre drained his glass again, and filled up a third one.

'Ah, women! Women!' And the captain gazed at Pierre with brimming eyes as he launched into the subject of love and his erotic exploits. There had been a lot of them, and this was easy to believe if the officer's rather smug but handsome face and the eager enthusiasm with which he talked about women were anything to go by. Although all Ramballe's accounts of his love affairs had that degrading quality that the French see as the uniqueness and poetic charm of love, the captain told his stories with such genuine certainty that he was the only man who had ever tasted and known the delights of love, and he described women in such alluring terms, that Pierre could not help but be a good listener.

Clearly, the Frenchman's favourite version of love was neither that mean, straightforward kind of love that Pierre had once felt for his wife nor the romantic love, blown up out of all proportion by himself, that he now felt for Natasha.

Ramballe treated both these kinds of love with equal contempt – one was for working men, the other for morons. The 'love' that this Frenchman celebrated consisted mainly in having an unnatural relationship with a woman, and in combinations of outrageous behaviour that set the highest premium on sensuality.

Thus the captain related the moving story of his love for a seductive thirty-five-year-old marquise, which had gone on at the same time as an affair with a charming, innocent child of seventeen, the daughter of the said seductive marquise. The battle between mother and daughter as to who could be the more generous ended with the mother sacrificing herself and offering her daughter in marriage to her lover, an outcome that even now, as a distant memory, was capable of moving the captain deeply. Then he related an episode in which the husband played the part of the lover, and he – the lover – the part of the husband, and several comic episodes among his memoirs of Germany, the land where *Unterkunft* means 'shelter', husbands eat nothing but cabbage soup, and the young girls are excessively blonde.

The last episode, dating back only to Poland, was still fresh in the captain's memory and described with rapid hand movements and a face ablaze with passion. He had saved the life of a Pole – saving people's lives was a constant theme running through the captain's stories – and this man had entrusted him with his seductive wife, a Paris girl at heart, while he himself went off to serve with the French. The captain had been delighted, and the seductive Polish lady had wanted to run away with him, but the captain had been moved by a sudden feeling of generosity and restored the wife to the husband with the words, 'I once saved your life. Now I save your honour!'

At the repetition of these words the captain wiped his eyes and gave himself a shake, as if to rid himself of the weakness that had come over him at the onset of this touching memory.

As often happens late in the evening when the effects of the wine are making themselves felt, Pierre was able to follow and understand every detail of what the captain was saying while also following his own train of personal memories that happened to have popped up in his imagination. As he listened to all these love stories, his own love for Natasha suddenly came into his mind, and as he ran through all the tokens of that love in his imagination, he was mentally comparing them with Ramballe's stories. As he listened to a story of conflict between love and duty, Pierre could see before him every last detail of that meeting with the object of his own love at the Sukharev water-tower. At the time he had not been much affected by it, and not once had it come to mind since. But now he thought he could see something deeply significant and very romantic in that meeting.

'Come on Pyotr Kirillych! I knew it was you!' He could hear her words now. He could see her eyes, her smile, her travelling cap with a stray curl peeping out from under it . . . and it all seemed so sad and moving now.

When the captain got to the end of his tale about the seductive Polish lady he turned to Pierre and asked whether he had had any experiences like this; did he know of any examples of someone sacrificing himself for love while envying a lawful husband?

Roused by this question, Pierre looked up and felt an irresistible urge to talk about what was on his mind. He started off by explaining that he looked upon love for a woman rather differently. He said that in all his life he had only ever loved one woman, and he still loved her, and this woman could never be his.

'You don't say!' said the captain.

Pierre went on to explain that he had loved this woman from her earliest years, but had not dared to think of her because she was then too young, and besides he had been an illegitimate son with no name of his own. Then, when he had received a name and great riches, he had not dared think of her because he loved her too much, because he put her on a pedestal high above the whole world, and especially above himself. When he got to this point in his story Pierre asked the captain whether he could understand all this.

The captain gestured for him to go on with the story even if he couldn't understand it.

'Platonic love . . . Passing clouds . . .' he muttered. It may have been the wine, or an urge to speak out, or the thought that this man didn't know, and never could know, any of the people in his story, or all of these things together, but something loosened Pierre's tongue. With trembling lips and a faraway look in his brimming eyes he came out with the whole story: everything about his marriage, and the story of Natasha's love for his best friend, and her unfaithfulness, and his own uncomplicated relationship with her. In response to questions from Ramballe he also told him what he had at first been at pains to hide, his position in society, and he even disclosed his name.

The part of the story that really impressed the captain was the fact that Pierre was a very rich man with two palatial houses in Moscow, and when he had abandoned everything, instead of leaving Moscow he had stayed on in the town hiding his name and social standing.

Late at night they went outside together. The night was warm and clear. Over on the left there was a glow from the first fire to break out in Moscow, out in Petrovka. On the right a young crescent moon stood high in the sky, and across the firmament in the opposite direction hovered the shining comet that was connected in Pierre's heart with his love. At the gateway into the yard stood Gerasim, the cook and two Frenchmen. They could be heard laughing as they carried on a mutually incomprehensible conversation. They were looking across towards the glow of the fire burning in the town.

A small fire a long way away in a huge city was nothing to worry about.

Gazing up at the lofty, starlit sky, the moon, the comet and the glow from the fire, Pierre felt a thrill of joyous and tender emotion. 'How splendid it all is! What more could anyone want?' he thought. And then suddenly, when he remembered what his mission was, his head seemed to spin, and he felt so nauseous that he had to lean against a fence to avoid falling down.

Without saying goodnight to his new friend Pierre tottered away from the gate and found his way back to his room, where he lay down on the sofa and fell fast asleep.

CHAPTER 30

The glow from the first fire to break out, on the 2nd of September, was watched from various roads and with mixed feelings by citizens streaming out of Moscow on foot and in vehicles, and also the retreating troops.

That night the Rostovs had stopped at Mytyshchi, about fifteen miles outside Moscow. They had set out so late on the 1st of September, the road had been so blocked with traffic and troops, so many things had been forgotten and servants sent back to get them, that they had decided to stop for the first night when they were only two or three miles out of town. They were late setting out the next morning, and again there were so many delays they got no further than Great Mytishchi. At ten o'clock the Rostov family, and the wounded soldiers travelling with them, had all found places for themselves in the yards and huts of the village, which was quite a large one. The Rostovs' servants and drivers, along with the orderlies of the wounded officers, settled their masters for the night, had some supper, fed the horses and came out on to the wooden steps of one of the huts.

In the next hut lay one of Rayevsky's adjutants, who was moaning and groaning in the most piteous way from the pain of a fractured wrist – a terrible sound that cut through the darkness of the autumn night. At the first stop this adjutant had spent the night in the same yard as the Rostovs. The countess claimed she had never closed an eye all night because of all the moaning, and at Mytyshchi she had moved into a less comfortable hut just to get further away from the wounded man.

It was one of the servants who noticed something in the dark night sky up above the body of a tall carriage by the entry: another small glow from a fire. They had seen one glow some time before, and everybody knew it came from Little Mytyshchi, where Mamonov's Cossacks had set the place on fire.

'Hey, look, boys! Another fire!' said the orderly. They all looked across at the glow.

'Yes, but they told us Mamonov's Cossacks had set fire to Little Mytyshchi.'

'Get away! That's not Mytyshchi, it's further in.'

'Get an eyeful of that. Looks like it's in Moscow.'

Two of the men went down the steps, walked round in front of the carriage and squatted on the step.

'Yon's too far left! Look, Mytyshchi's way over there, and that's miles away on the other side.'

More servants joined them.

'That's got going, that has,' said one. 'Gentlemen, Moscow's on fire. It's in Sushchovsky or mebbe Rogozhsky.'

There was no response. For some time all the servants stared in silence at the distant flames of this new conflagration. Old Danilo, the count's valet (as he was called), came up to the crowd and shouted at little Mishka.

'Stupid boy! Don't stand there gawping! The count might want something and there'd be nobody there. Go and sort them clothes out.'

'Hey, I only run out for some water,' said Mishka.

'What do you think, Danilo? Moscow's on fire, isn't it?' asked one of the footmen.

Danilo said nothing, and again for quite some time they all stood there in silence. The blaze was moving; the glow was spreading.

'Lord have mercy on us! ... The wind's gettin' up, after all that drought . . .' said the same voice.

'That's well on, that is. O Lord in heaven! Look, you can see the jackdaws! Lord, have mercy on us miserable sinners!'

'Don't worry. They'll soon put that out.'

'Who will?' came the voice of Danilo, silent until then. His voice was gentle and deliberate. ''Tis Moscow sure enough, boys,' he said. 'There she be, our mother, the white . . .' his voice faltered and he broke down in choking sobs, sounding like the old man he was. And this seemed to be all that was needed for the others to take in the full meaning of the glow they were watching. All that could be heard were people sighing and saying prayers, and the old valet choking and sobbing.

CHAPTER 31

The valet went back in and told the count Moscow was on fire. The count put on his dressing-gown and came out to have a look. Sonya, who was still dressed, came out with him and so did Madame Schoss. Natasha and the countess were left alone indoors. (Petya was no longer with the family, having gone on ahead to join his regiment on the march to Troitsa.)

The countess burst into tears when she heard that Moscow was in flames. Natasha's lively eyes had settled as she sat, pale-faced, on the same bench under the icons that she had gone straight to when they had arrived, and she ignored what her father was saying. She was listening to the never-ending moan coming from the adjutant, which could be heard three huts away.

'Oh, it's so awful!' cried Sonya, coming in from the yard chilled and frightened. 'I'm sure the whole of Moscow will be burnt down. There's a terrible glow over everything! Natasha, come and have a look. You can see through the window,' she said to her cousin, obviously trying to distract her. But Natasha stared back as if she couldn't understand what was being asked of her, and she turned round to stare again at the corner of the stove. Natasha had been in this frozen state since that morning, when Sonya, to the amazement and annoyance of the countess, had for some unknown reason seen fit to tell Natasha about Prince Andrey's wound, and the fact that he was there with them in their convoy. Sonya had rarely suffered such fury from the countess. Sonya had wept and asked to be forgiven, and she now seemed to be trying to smooth things over by being unfailingly nice to her cousin.

'Look, Natasha, it's on fire. It's awful!' said Sonya.

'What's on fire?' asked Natasha. 'Oh yes, Moscow.'

And to get rid of Sonya without giving offence by ignoring her she moved her head nearer the window and looked through it from an angle that made it impossible for her to see anything, and then went back to her former position.

'Did you see it?'

'Yes, I really did,' she said in a voice that pleaded to be left in peace.

Neither the countess nor Sonya had any trouble understanding why Moscow, even in flames, or anything else in the world, might not be of the slightest interest to Natasha.

The count came back in and lay down behind the partition. The countess went over to Natasha, rested the back of her hand on her head, as she always did when her daughter was ill, and then brushed her forehead with her lips as if to find out whether she was running a temperature, before giving her a kiss.

'You've got a chill. You're shaking all over. You ought to lie down,' she said.

'You what? Oh yes, all right, I will. In a minute,' said Natasha.

When Natasha had been told that morning that Prince Andrey was seriously wounded and was travelling with them, her instinctive response had been to ask lots of questions. Where were they taking him? How had it happened? Was he badly hurt? Could she see him? But once she had been told she couldn't see him, and his wound was serious but his life wasn't in danger, even though she clearly didn't believe them, she could see she would get the same answers whatever she said, so she stopped asking questions and refused to speak at all. All day long Natasha had sat there rigidly in the corner of the carriage with a special look in her wide, staring eyes that the countess knew only too well and always dreaded, and she was still sitting like that now on the little bench in the hut. She was hatching something. She was making her mind up; perhaps she had already done so. The countess knew full well, but she had no idea what Natasha had decided to do, and this was a terrible source of worry.

'Natasha, do get undressed, darling. Come into bed with me.'

The countess was the only one to have had a proper bed made up. Madame Schoss and the two girls were having to sleep on the floor on piles of hay.

'No, Mamma, I'll lie down here on the floor,' said Natasha irritably. She went over to the window and opened it. The moaning adjutant sounded much louder with the window open. She put her head out into the humid night air, and the countess could see her slender shoulders racked with sobs heaving against the window frame. Natasha knew it wasn't Prince Andrey moaning. She knew Prince Andrey was in their yard, in the next hut just across the passage, but still, that terrible, never-ending moaning and groaning was making her sob. The countess exchanged a glance with Sonya.

'Come to bed, sweetheart. Do come to bed, darling,' said the countess, reaching out to touch Natasha gently on the shoulder. 'It really is time for bed.'

'Yes, all right . . . I'll go to bed now, straightaway,' said Natasha, getting undressed so quickly she broke some of the strings on her petticoats. Slipping off her dress and putting on a bed-jacket, she sat down with her feet tucked under her on the bed made up on the floor, jerked her short pigtail of very fine hair forward over her shoulder and started to re-plait it. Her long, thin, practised fingers moved quickly and skilfully as she separated the hair, braided it and tied it up again. Natasha was moving her head from side to side as she always did, but she stared fixedly ahead the whole time and her wide eyes had a feverish look about them. When she had finished getting ready for bed she lowered herself gently down on to the sheet spread over the hay on the side nearest the door.

'Natasha, you go the middle,' said Sonya.

'No, I'll stay here,' said Natasha. 'And please come to bed your-selves,' she added irritably before burying her face in the pillow.

The countess, Madame Schoss and Sonya got undressed very quickly and were soon in bed. Only the icon-lamp was left burning. But outside, the fire at Little Mytyshchi lit up the landscape for more than a mile around, there was a lot of noise coming from some drunken peasants at the tavern across the street where Mamonov's Cossacks had broken in, and the adjutant could still be heard moaning and groaning.

Natasha lay there for a long time listening to the sounds coming to her from within and without, and she never moved a muscle. First she heard her mother praying and sighing, then her bed creaking under her, then Madame Schoss whistling and snoring as she always did, then Sonya breathing softly. The countess called out to Natasha. Natasha didn't respond.

'I think she's asleep, Mamma,' whispered Sonya.

The countess waited for a while in silence and then spoke again, but this time nobody answered.

It wasn't long before Natasha caught the sound of her mother's steady breathing. Natasha still didn't move, though her little bare foot, sticking out from under the blanket, felt frozen on the uncovered floor.

A cricket chirped in a cranny, as if he was king of the world. A cock crowed a long way away, and others answered close by. The shouting had died away in the tavern. Only the adjutant's moaning went on as before. Natasha sat up.

'Sonya! Are you asleep? Mamma!' she whispered.

No answer. Slowly and cautiously Natasha got up, crossed herself and stepped cautiously with her slender, supple, bare feet on to the dirty, cold floor. A floorboard creaked. With nimble movements she skipped forward one or two steps like a little kitten, and took hold of the cold door-handle.

Something seemed to be thumping on every wall of the hut with a heavy, rhythmic thudding sound; it was the beating of her own heart, which was bursting with dread, love and panic.

She opened the door, stepped over the threshold and out on to the damp, cold earth of the passage beyond. She felt refreshed by the chill air that met her. Her bare foot brushed against a sleeping body; she stepped over it, and opened the door into the hut where Prince Andrey was lying. It was dark inside. There was a bed with something lying on it, and in the far corner on a little bench a guttering tallow candle with a huge wick.

Ever since yesterday morning when she had been told that Prince Andrey was with them, wounded, Natasha had decided she had to see him. She couldn't have said why precisely, but she knew their meeting would be an agonizing experience, and this reinforced her certainty that it couldn't be avoided.

All day long she had lived in the hope of seeing him that night. But now the moment had come she was horrified at the thought of what she might see. Had he been disfigured? What was left of him? Was he something like that never-ending moan of the adjutant? Yes, that's what he was like. In her imagination he was the personification of that awful moaning. When she caught sight of a dark mass in the corner, and mistook a pair of raised knees under the blanket for someone's shoulders, she imagined it to be some ghastly body, and she stopped in terror. But an irresistible urge drew her on. She took one cautious step, then another, and there she was in the middle of the small hut, which was cluttered with baggage. There was another figure (Timokhin), lying on a bench under the icons, and two more down on the floor (the doctor and the valet).

The valet sat up whispering. Timokhin couldn't sleep because of a painful wound in his leg, and he goggled at this weird apparition – a girl in a white chemise, bed-jacket, and nightcap. The only effect of the valet's scared and sleepy reaction, 'Who's that? What do you want?' was to make Natasha hurry across to the object lying in the corner. Horribly inhuman though it looked, she simply had to see that body. As she slipped past the valet the guttering candle flared up a little, and she could see Prince Andrey quite clearly, lying there just as she had always seen him, with his arms stretched out on top of the blanket.

He was just the same as ever, but the feverish flush on his face, his glittering eyes, rapturously glued on her, and most of all his neck, as soft as child's where his nightshirt collar was turned down, gave him a special look of boyish innocence that she had never before seen in Prince Andrey. She ran over to him and in one smooth, youthful movement dropped quickly down on her knees.

He smiled, and held out his hand to her.

CHAPTER 32

Seven days had passed since Prince Andrey had come round in the ambulance station on the field of Borodino. All that time he had been in a state of almost continual unconsciousness. The fever and inflammation of his damaged intestines, were, according to the doctor travelling with the wounded man, sure to finish him off. But on the seventh day he enjoyed eating a piece of bread with a drink of tea, and the doctor noticed his temperature was down. Prince Andrey had regained consciousness that morning. The first night after leaving Moscow had been fairly warm, and Prince Andrey had spent the night in his carriage, but at Mytishchi the wounded man himself had asked to be taken indoors and given some tea. The pain caused by moving him had made Prince Andrey groan aloud and lose consciousness again. When he had been stretched out on his camp-bed he lay there quite still for a long time with his eyes closed. Then he opened his eyes and whispered softly, 'What about the tea?' The doctor was struck by this sudden ability to remember little details of everyday life. He took his pulse, and to his surprise and dissatisfaction found that it was stronger. His dissatisfaction was due to the fact that experience told him Prince Andrey couldn't survive, and if he didn't die now he would die later on, in even greater agony. Travelling with Prince Andrey was Timokhin, the red-nosed major from his regiment, who had joined him in Moscow; he had been wounded in the leg, also at Borodino. They were accompanied by the doctor, the prince's valet, his driver and two orderlies.

They gave Prince Andrey some tea. He gulped it down, looking with feverish eyes at the door in front of him, as if there was something he couldn't quite understand or remember.

'That's enough. Is Timokhin here?' he asked.

Timokhin dragged himself along the bench towards him.

'Yes, sir.'

'How's your leg?'

'Oh, I'm all right. What about you?'

Again Prince Andrey thought for a while, as if he was trying to remember something.

'I need a book,' he said.

'What book?'

'The Bible. I haven't got one.'

The doctor promised to get hold of a bible, and began asking the prince how he felt. Prince Andrey answered all the doctor's questions rationally, though reluctantly, and then said he wanted a bolster pushed under him because he felt uncomfortable and was in a lot of pain. The doctor and the valet removed the greatcoat that was covering him, winced at the nauseating smell of putrefying flesh coming from the wound, and began to examine that terrible place. Something was worrying the doctor. He made a few adjustments that involved turning the wounded man, but the pain was such that Andrey gave another groan and lost consciousness again. He began to ramble, and kept asking for them to bring the book and push it under him. 'Is it too much trouble?' he kept saying. 'I haven't got it. Fetch one, please, and shove it under me, here. Just for a minute,' he said pathetically.

The doctor went out to wash his hands.

'You are a shameless lot,' the doctor was saying to the valet, who was pouring water over his hands. 'I can't take my eyes off you for a minute. You've laid him right on top of his wound. He's in such agony I wonder he can stand it.'

'I thought we had pushed things under him, by the Lord Jesus Christ,' said the valet.

For the first time Andrey knew where he was and what was happening to him. He knew he had been wounded and remembered asking to be taken indoors when the carriage had stopped at Mytishchi. He had lost consciousness from the pain and come round again properly in the hut while he was drinking tea. Now here he was again trying to recall everything that had happened to him, and his most vivid recollection was that moment in the ambulance station when, at the sight of a man he had not liked suffering terrible agony, he had been struck by new ideas, ideas that brought the promise of happiness. And these same ideas – vague and fuzzy though they now were – had taken possession of his soul again. He remembered that some new kind of happiness was within his grasp, and it had something to do with the Bible. This was why he had asked for a bible. But the position they had laid him in, which was so bad for his wound, and the agony of being moved, had caused him to drift away again, and it was only in the complete stillness of the night that he had come round for the third time. They were all asleep. A cricket chirped across the passage, there was shouting and singing in the street, cockroaches rustled across the table-top and up the icons, and a big fat autumn fly was buzzing between his pillow and the tallow candle that stood near by with its big wick smouldering.

His mind was not functioning normally. A healthy man usually thinks, feels and remembers a vast number of different things all at the same time, but he has the power and ability to pick out one track of ideas or phenomena and concentrate all his attention on that. A healthy man can break off from really serious thinking to exchange courtesies with anybody who comes in, and then go straight back to where he was in his thinking. It was in this respect that Prince Andrey's mind was not functioning normally. His mental powers were as clear and active as ever, but they were acting independently of his will. His mind was overwhelmed by the widest possible range of ideas and images all emerging at the same time. Sometimes an idea would suddenly start up in his mind, working away with the kind of strength, clarity and depth that he hadn't experienced when he had been well, but suddenly the thought would break off half-way through, giving way to some new and unexpected image, and there was no way back.

'Yes, a new kind of happiness was revealed to me, one of the inalienable rights of man,' he thought to himself as he lay there in the quiet semi-darkness of the hut, staring ahead with wide eyes that had settled but still held a feverish look. 'Happiness beyond materialism, beyond all external, material influences, happiness known only to the soul, the happiness of loving! It is within the conception of all men, but it can be fully determined and ordained by God alone. But how did God ordain this law? And what about His son? . . .' And then suddenly his chain of thoughts was broken, and Prince Andrey heard a noise (he couldn't tell whether this was part of a delirious dream or something real), a kind of soft voice whispering something insistent and rhythmical. '*Pitty-pitty-pitty*,' and then, '*itty-itty*,' and again, '*pitty-pitty-pitty*,' and again, '*itty-itty*.' And all the time, lulled by this sweet susurration, Prince Andrey felt as if a strangely ethereal edifice of delicate needles or splinters was rising up above his face, in the very middle of it. He felt he had to keep things in balance (though it was terribly difficult) so that this soaring structure didn't collapse, and yet it was collapsing, and slowly rising up again to the rhythmic murmur of the music.

'It's stretching up and spreading out, stretching and spreading!' Prince Andrey said to himself. As he listened to the whispering murmur and sensed the edifice of needles stretching and rising Prince Andrey caught glimpses of a red halo round a candle, and he could hear cockroaches rustling and a fly buzzing round his pillow and his face. And every time the fly brushed against his face it gave him a burning sensation, and he was surprised that the fly could hit him right in the middle of the soaring edifice without bringing it down. And besides this, there was something else that was terribly important to him, something white over by the door. Was that a statue of the sphinx pressing down on him?

'Must be my shirt on the table,' thought Prince Andrey, 'and there are my legs, and that's the door. But what's all this stretching and straining and *pitty-pitty-pitty*, and *itty-itty* and *pitty-pitty-pitty*. No more, please. Stop it. Leave me alone,' Prince Andrey begged wearily. And then suddenly thought and feeling floated to the surface again with the utmost clarity and strength.

'Yes, it's love . . .' (his thoughts were lucidity itself), 'but not the kind of love that loves for a reason, a purpose, a cause, but the kind of love I felt for the first time when I was on my death bed and I saw my enemy and loved him. I experienced the feeling of love that is the essence of the soul, love that seeks no object. I can feel it now, that blessed feeling. To love your neighbour and love your enemy. To love everything, to love God in all His manifestations. You can love someone dear to you with human love, but it takes divine love to love your enemy. *That's* why I felt such joy when I knew I loved that man. I wonder what happened to him. Is he still alive? . . . When you love with human love you can change from love to hatred, but divine love cannot change. Nothing, not even death, nothing can destroy it. It is the essence of the soul. How many people I have hated in the course of my life! And there's nobody I have loved more and hated more than her.' And he formed a clear mental image of Natasha, though not as he had seen her in the past, with all the charm that had given him such joy. For the first time he caught an image of her soul. And he could understand all her feelings, suffering, shame and remorse. For the first time he could sense the full cruelty of his rejection of her, the break between them. 'If I could only see her one last time . . . just once, to look into her eyes and say . . .'

And then *pitty-pitty-pitty*, *itty-itty*, *pitty-pitty* – ugh, the fly had settled on him . . . And his attention slid away into another realm half-way between reality and delirium where something very special was going on. Here the edifice was still intact, still rising; there was still something straining upwards, the candle was still burning, the red halo was still there, and the same shirt-that-was-a-sphinx was still there over by the door. But there was something else. There was a creaking sound, a breath of fresh air, and a different white sphinx stood in the doorway. This sphinx had a white face and in it the gleaming eyes of Natasha, the very girl who had just been in his thoughts.

'Oh, this terrible delirium – it goes on for ever!' thought Prince Andrey, trying to rid himself of this face. But the face stayed there in all its reality; the face was coming closer. Prince Andrey tried to get back to the earlier realm of pure thought, but he couldn't manage it. His delirium kept dragging him back. The softly murmuring voice kept up its rhythmic whisper, he could still feel something pressing down on him, and something rising up, and there was the strange face right in front of him. Prince Andrey gathered all his strength in an effort to bring himself round; he stirred a little, but then there was a sudden ringing in his ears, his eyes went dim, and he fainted away like a man disappearing under water.

When he came round there was Natasha, the very living Natasha that of all people in the world he was dying to love with that newly revealed, pure, divine love, down on her knees before him. He knew it was the real, living Natasha, and this came as no surprise; he was quietly happy. Natasha was kneeling, terrified but rooted to the spot (she couldn't have moved a muscle), gazing at him and trying so hard not to sob. Her pale face showed no movement other than a slight tremor in her lips and chin.

Prince Andrey gave a sigh of relief, smiled and held out his hand.

'Is it you?' he said. 'Real happiness!'

In one quick movement Natasha carefully shuffled up closer, still on her knees, and took his hand equally carefully, bending her face down over it, kissing it, caressing it with her lips.

'Oh please forgive me!' she whispered, looking up and glancing at him. 'Please do forgive me!'

'I love you,' said Prince Andrey.

'Forgive . . .'

'What is there to forgive?' asked Prince Andrey.

'Forgive me for what I . . . what I . . . did to you,' Natasha murmured in a barely audible broken whisper, and she kissed his hand more and more, covering it with caresses from her lips.

'I love you, darling, more than I did, better than before,' said Prince Andrey, lifting her face with his hand so he could look her in the eyes.

Those eyes, brimming with happy tears, were gazing at him with gentle compassion and the joy of love. Natasha's pale thin face with its puffy lips was worse than unattractive – it looked terrible. But

Prince Andrey couldn't see her face; he saw only the glittering eyes, and they were beautiful. They heard voices behind them.

Pyotr, the valet, was now wide awake, and he had woken the doctor. Timokhin, who had not slept at all because of the pain in his leg, had long been a witness to all that was happening, and he had shrunk down on his bench, carefully pulling the sheet right across his bare body.

'What's all this then?' said the doctor, getting up from his low bed. 'I must ask you to withdraw, madam.'

At that moment there was a knock at the door; it was a maid sent by the countess, who had noticed that her daughter was missing.

Natasha left the room like a sleepwalker woken up in mid-trance, walked back to her hut, and sank down on her bed sobbing.

From that day on, at every stop and overnight stay throughout the rest of the Rostovs' journey, Natasha never left Bolkonsky's side, and the doctor was forced to admit that he had not expected to see such fortitude in a young girl, nor that kind of skill in nursing a wounded man.

Awful as it was for the countess to think that Prince Andrey might (and according to the doctor probably would) die on the road in her daughter's arms, she was no match for Natasha. Even though the rapprochement between Prince Andrey and Natasha raised the possibility that if he happened to survive their old engagement might be renewed, nobody – least of all Natasha and Prince Andrey – ever mentioned it. The unresolved question of life and death still hung in the balance, not only over Prince Andrey, but over the whole of Russia, and this precluded all other considerations.

CHAPTER 33

Pierre woke late on the 3rd of September. He had a headache, the clothes he had slept in hung heavily on him, and he had a vague recollection of something reprehensible that he had done the evening before. That reprehensible something was yesterday's conversation with Captain Ramballe.

It was eleven o'clock by his watch, but it was very dark outside. Pierre got to his feet, rubbed his eyes, and the moment he saw the pistol with its engraved stock back on the desk where Gerasim had put it he remembered where he was and what was in store for him that day.

'I wonder if I'm too late,' he thought. 'No, surely that man won't make his entry into Moscow before midday.'

Without stopping to think about what was in store for him he got down to business straightaway.

Pierre straightened his clothes, picked up the pistol and was on the point of leaving when he realized for the first time he couldn't just walk down the street brandishing a pistol, so how could he carry it? Even under his loose coat it would be difficult to hide a big pistol. It couldn't be tucked in his belt or under his arm without being noticeable. Besides, the pistol had been fired, and Pierre hadn't had time to reload it. 'Never mind, I'll have to use a dagger,' Pierre decided, even though he had told himself repeatedly when wondering how to fulfil his mission that in 1809 the student's biggest mistake had been to try and kill Napoleon with a dagger. But by now Pierre's main aim seemed to be not so much to carry out his mission as to prove to himself that instead of backing away from it he was doing all he could to see it through. Pierre grabbed the blunt, jagged dagger in a green scabbard that he had bought with the pistol at the Sukharev tower, and hid it under his waistcoat.

Pierre tightened the sash round his peasant's coat, pulled his cap down over his eyes, and walked down the corridor, trying not to make a noise or run into the captain, and slipped out into the street.

The fire he had watched so indifferently yesterday evening had spread noticeably during the night. Moscow was blazing at several different points. The buildings in Carriage Row, the Bazaar, across the river and on Povarsky Street, as well as the barges on the river Moskva and down at the timber yards near the Dorogomilov bridge were all on fire.

Pierre's route was to take him down various side-streets to Povarsky Street, and then on to St Nicholas' church on the Arbat, where he had long before picked out in his mind a suitable spot for the doing of his deed. Most of the houses had their gates locked and shutters up. The streets and alleys were deserted. The air was full of smoke and the smell of burning. Now and then he had come across Russians looking all anxious and apprehensive, and Frenchmen with an out-of-town look of camp-life about them, walking down the middle of the road. Both sorts of people looked surprised when they saw Pierre. It wasn't just his height and his fat body, or the sombre look of concentrated suffering that affected his face and whole figure; the Russians stared at Pierre because they couldn't work out what class he belonged to.

As for the French, they were surprised to see that, whereas all the other Russians stared at them with curiosity and trepidation, Pierre simply ignored them.

At the gates of one house three Frenchmen trying to communicate with some Russians who couldn't understand what they were saying stopped Pierre to ask if he spoke French. Pierre shook his head and walked on. Down a side-street a sentry guarding a green caisson hailed him, and it was only when his menacing shout was repeated and his gun rattled as he picked it up that Pierre suddenly realized he was supposed to be walking on the other side of the street. He heard nothing and saw nothing. He hurried along, horrified to be harbouring such a strange and terrible intention, yet dreading – if last night's experience was anything to go by – that he might lose his grip on it. But he was not destined to get to the place he was heading for without a new shock to his frame of mind. As it happened, even if he hadn't been distracted en route he could never have carried out his plan, because Napoleon had gone down the Arbat four hours earlier on his way from the Dorogomilov suburb to the Kremlin, where he was now ensconced in the royal study in a foul mood, issuing detailed instructions for immediate steps to be taken to put the fire out, stop any looting and reassure the citizens. But Pierre knew nothing of this. Totally absorbed in what lay ahead, he was agonizing as men do when they attempt the impossible, and the thing is impossible not because of any intrinsic difficulty, but because it requires them to act out of character. He was tormented by a terrible dread that he would weaken at the critical moment, and then lose all self-respect.

Even without seeing or hearing anything he was finding his way by instinct, and he moved unerringly down the back-streets leading to Povarsky.

As Pierre got nearer, the smoke got thicker, and thicker, and he could actually feel the heat from the conflagration. Tongues of flame licked up here and there along the roof-tops. He came across more and more people in the streets, and they were getting more excited. But although Pierre could sense that something unusual was going on around him, he didn't realize he was walking towards the fire. He was going along a path across a large open space which had Povarsky Street running down one side and Prince Gruzinsky's gardens on the other when he suddenly heard a woman near by crying with despair. He stopped as if he had come round from a dream, and looked up.

On the parched and dusty grass down one side of the path lay piles of household things: feather-beds, a samovar, icons and some trunks.

There on the ground by the boxes sat a skinny woman, no youngster, with long, protruding upper teeth, wearing a black cloak and cap. She was sobbing and weeping fit to burst, rocking to and fro and muttering to herself. Two little girls, ten- or twelve-year-olds, in dirty little dresses and cloaks were staring at their mother with fear written all over their pale faces, not knowing what to make of her. The youngest child, a little boy of about seven, in a thick coat and a huge cap, obviously somebody else's, was howling in the arms of an old woman who was cradling him. A dirty, bare-legged servant-girl was sitting on a trunk; she had let down her blonde locks, and was tidying them up, sniffing at her singed hair. The husband, a stooping little man in uniform, with side-whiskers curling round like little wheels and smooth hair peeping out from under a square-set cap, looked impassive as he shifted the piled-up trunks and sorted through them to drag out some kind of clothing.

The woman almost threw herself down at Pierre's feet the moment she saw him.

'Mercy on us, good Christian folk! Save me. Help me, kind sir! ... Please, somebody help!' she managed to get out through her sobs. 'It's my little girl! ... My daughter! ... My youngest girl. She's been left behind! ... She's in the fire! Oo-oh! After all that nursing! ... Oh-oh-oh!'

'Don't go on about it, Marya Nikolayevna,' the husband said softly to his wife, obviously wanting to justify himself in the presence of an outsider. 'Your sister must have taken her. Where else could she be?' he added.

'You monster! You villain!' the woman screamed furiously in mid-wail. 'You've got no heart, no feeling for your own child. Any other man would have rescued her from the fire. He's a monster, not a man, not a father. You're a gentleman, sir,' gabbled the woman, turning to Pierre and choking with sobs. 'The whole row was on fire. It just came at us. The girl shouted, "Fire!" We grabbed a few things and ran out in what we stood up in ... This is all we could bring ... the holy icons, and my marriage bed. Everything else has gone. We grabbed the children too, but not little Katechka. Oh Lord! Oh-oh!' and again she broke down sobbing. 'My sweet little baby! She's burnt to death! Burnt to death!'

'But where? Where did you leave her?' asked Pierre.

His face had lit up with sympathy, and the woman saw that this man might be able to help.

'Good, kind sir!' she howled, clutching at his legs. 'Be kind to us! Set my mind at rest if you can't do anything else ... Aniska, you little slut, show him where to go,' she screamed at the servant-girl, opening her mouth wide in her fury so that her long teeth stuck out even more.

'Show me where to go. Just show me. I . . . I'll go and do something about it,' Pierre blurted out in a panic.

The dirty servant-girl came out from behind the trunk, put up her hair, gave a deep sigh and stumped off down the path ahead of him on her rough bare feet.

Pierre felt as if he had fainted away and suddenly come back to life. He raised his head higher, his eyes began to gleam with the light of life, and he hurried after the girl, overtook her and came out on to Povarsky Street. The entire street was enveloped in clouds of black smoke, with tongues of flame licking out here and there. A big crowd had gathered in front of the fire. In the middle of the street stood a French general, talking to some people standing round him. Pierre went with the servant-girl and they tried to get through to the place where the French general was standing, only to be stopped by some French soldiers.

'No way through!' shouted a voice.

'This way, Uncle,' bawled the girl. 'Down that lane past the Nikulins.'

Pierre turned back, skipping into a trot now and then just to keep up with her. The girl ran across the street, turned left down a side-street, went past three houses and turned in through a gateway on the right.

'Just in here,' she said before running across a yard to open a little gate in a paling-fence, where she stopped and pointed to the small wooden end-section of a building that was blazing away merrily. One side of it had collapsed, the other was on fire, and flames were licking out of the window-holes and up under the roof.

As Pierre went in through the little gate he ran into a wall of heat, and instinctively stopped in his tracks.

'Which one? Which is your house?' he asked.

'Oooh!' wailed the servant-girl, pointing to the end-section. 'That's it. That's where we been livin'. Burnt to death, you 'ave, our little treasure, Katechka, my dear little missy. Ooh!' wailed Aniska at the sight of the fire, feeling it was her turn to give vent to her feelings.

Pierre darted across to the end-section, but the heat was so great that the only thing he could do was skirt round close to the big house, which was burning only on one side, and at roof-level. A group of French soldiers were swarming round it. At first he couldn't work out what they were doing as they carried things out of the house, but when he saw a French soldier just in front hitting a peasant with the flat of his sword and pinching his fur-lined coat, Pierre got a vague impression they were after loot, though he had no time to stop and think about it.

The sounds of walls and ceilings breaking apart and crashing down; the sizzling hiss of the flames and the wild shouts of the crowd; the sight of billowing clouds of smoke belching out in great black swirls or shooting up and scattering showers of gleaming sparks; flames licking up the walls in big, thick red sheaves or covering them with what looked like golden fish-scales; the blistering heat, the choking smoke and the speed of everything roused Pierre in the way that only a huge fire can. The effect was particularly strong on Pierre, because now, at the sight of the fire, he felt suddenly liberated from all the ideas that had been weighing him down. He felt young and carefree, ready and resolute. He ran round to the end-section from the house side, and was about to dash into the bit that was still standing when he heard people calling out just above his head, and something heavy came crashing down close by.

Pierre looked up at the windows of the house and saw some French soldiers who had just thrown down a drawer out of a chest, full of metal objects. Other French soldiers waiting down below walked over to the drawer.

'Hey there, what does that fellow want?' shouted one of the French soldiers, looking at Pierre.

'There's a child in that house. Have you seen a child?' said Pierre.

'What's he on about? Go on, get out of here!' came various voices, and one of the soldiers, evidently worried that Pierre might take it into his head to pinch their bits of silver and bronze, pounced on him ominously.

'A child?' shouted another Frenchman from above. 'I did hear something squawking in the garden. Perhaps it was the brat this fellow's looking for. Got to be nice to each other, haven't we?'

'Where is it?' asked Pierre.

'Round there! Over there!' the French soldier shouted down from the window, pointing to the garden at the back of the house. 'Hang on, I'll come down.'

And sure enough, a minute later the Frenchman, a black-eyed young man with a mark on his cheek, working in his shirt-sleeves, hopped out of a window on the ground floor, clapped Pierre on the shoulder, and ran round with him to the garden. 'Get a move on, you fellows,' he shouted to his comrades, 'it's getting hot.' Running down a sandy path round to the back of the house, the Frenchman jogged Pierre by the arm, and pointed to a little round space. Under a garden seat lay a little three-year-old girl in a pink dress.

'Here's your little kid. Oh, it's a girl. Better still,' said the Frenchman. 'So long, then, old boy. Got to be nice to each other. We're all mortal, aren't we?' And the Frenchman with the mark on his cheek ran back to his mates.

Breathless with joy, Pierre ran up to the child, and tried to pick her up. But when she saw a stranger, the little girl – a consumptive-looking, ugly little thing, very like her mother – screamed and ran away. But Pierre soon caught her, and lifted her up in his arms. Screeching in desperate fury, she tried to wrench herself away from Pierre using her tiny little hands, and bite him with her slobbering little mouth. Pierre felt a pang of horror and disgust, as if he was in contact with some nasty little wild animal. Fighting down an impulse to throw the child away, he ran back with it to the big house. But now it was impossible to get out that way. Aniska, the servant-girl, was nowhere to be seen, and it was with a mixture of pity and disgust that Pierre held on to the sopping wet, pitifully howling baby as tenderly as he could, and rushed across the garden to find another way out.

CHAPTER 34

Pierre ran round via many a back-street and courtyard, but when he got back to the Gruzinsky garden at the corner of Povarsky Street carrying his little burden, for a moment or two he didn't recognize the place he had set out from to go and look for the baby; it was so crammed with people and all the bits and pieces they had carried out from the houses. Apart from Russian families who had run away from the fire with a few belongings, there were also one or two French soldiers wearing different uniforms. Pierre ignored them. He was anxious to find the civil servant's family, and give the child back to its mother, so he could go off and save somebody else. Pierre somehow felt he had a lot more to do, and it must be done quickly. Well warmed up by the heat from the fire and all the running about, at this point Pierre was full of energy and determination, enjoying the same thrill of youth that had surged through him when he had rushed off to save the baby, but now it was even stronger. The baby had gone quiet, and she sat there on his arm hanging on to Pierre's coat with her tiny hands, and looking round like a little wild animal. Pierre glanced at her once or twice with a half smile. He thought he could see something pathetically innocent and angelic in that frightened, sickly little face.

Neither the official nor his wife was anywhere to be seen in the place where he had left them. Pierre strode quickly through the crowd, scanning the various faces as he came across them. He couldn't help noticing a Georgian or Armenian family consisting of a very old man with fine oriental features wearing a new, cloth-covered sheepskin coat and new boots, an old woman who looked rather similar and a much younger woman, the very image of an oriental beauty, with black eyebrows arching in sharp lines and a beautifully impassive oval face that looked remarkably soft and tender. Among the bits and pieces scattered all over the ground and all the people crowding into that open space, she stood there in her rich satin mantle with a bright lilac shawl over her head, looking for all the world like a tender hot-house plant that had been thrown out in the snow. She was sitting on some bundled up things just behind the old woman, and her big black almond eyes with their long lashes were glued to the ground. She seemed conscious of her beauty, and it scared her. Pierre was much taken by her face, and even though he was in a hurry he glanced round at her several times as he made his way over to the fence. When he got there and still couldn't find the people he was looking for, he stopped and took a good look around.

Pierre stood out now with a baby in his arms, and several Russians, men and women, soon gathered round him.

'Have you lost somebody, good sir? You're a gentleman, aren't you, sir? Whose baby is that?' they asked him.

Pierre told them the baby belonged to a woman in a black cloak who had been sitting on this very spot with her children, and he asked who she was and where she might have gone.

'Must be the Anferovs,' said an old deacon to a peasant woman with a pockmarked face. 'Lord, have mercy! Lord, have mercy!' he added, in his characteristic bass growl.

'No, not the Anferovs,' said the woman. 'Oh no, the Anferovs went off first thing this morning. It'll either be Marya Nikolayevna's or Ivanova's.'

'He called her a woman, and Marya Nikolayevna's a lady,' put in a house serf.

'You know who she is, then? Thin woman. Long teeth,' said Pierre.

'Yes, that's Marya Nikolayevna. Her lot moved out into the garden when we got attacked by these wolves,' said the woman, nodding towards the French soldiers.

'O Lord, have mercy upon us!' the deacon added again.

'Try down there. I'm sure it's her. She was crying her eyes out,' said the woman again. 'I'm sure it's her. Look, down there.'

But Pierre was no longer listening. For some seconds he had been absorbed in something that was going on only a few steps away. He was watching the Armenian family and two French soldiers who had come over to them. One of them, a fidgety little man, was wearing a blue greatcoat, with a piece of string tied round his middle. He had a nightcap on his head, and his feet were bare. The other soldier made a stronger impression on Pierre. A tall, skinny, round-shouldered man with fair hair, he lumbered about with a moronic look on his face. He was dressed in a rough tunic, blue trousers and big worn boots. The little Frenchman in the blue coat who had nothing on his feet had gone up to the Armenians, spoken to them, and grabbed at the old man's legs, which soon had him pulling off his boots as fast as he could. The other soldier in the tunic had stopped right in front of the beautiful Armenian girl, and he stood there with his hands in his pockets, starting at her without saying a word or moving a muscle.

'Here, you take the baby,' said Pierre, speaking forcefully and shoving the child on to the peasant woman. 'You take her back. Go on, take her!' His voice had risen almost to a shout, and he put the screaming child down on the ground before turning back to watch the Frenchmen and the Armenian family. By now the old man was sitting on the ground with nothing on his feet. The little Frenchman had just taken the second boot, and was slapping the boots together. The old man was sobbing as he spoke, but Pierre noticed all this only in passing. His eyes were riveted on the Frenchman in the tunic, who had taken his hands out of his pockets, sidled up to the young woman with a deliberate little swagger, and was now fingering her neck.

The beautiful Armenian girl sat there as before, completely immobile, with her long eyelashes drooping downwards, apparently not seeing or feeling what the soldier was doing to her.

In the short time it took for Pierre to cover the few steps separating him from the Frenchmen, the tall, thin marauder in the tunic managed to tear a necklace from the Armenian beauty's neck, which left the young woman clutching at her neck with both hands and screaming.

'Leave her alone!' Pierre roared in a voice that sounded hoarse with rage. He grabbed the tall, stooping soldier by his round shoulders and gave him a good shove. The soldier fell down, scrambled to his feet and ran away. But his comrade threw the boots to one side, and bore down on Pierre drawing his sword threateningly.

'Let's not do anything stupid, now,' he shouted.

Pierre was in the kind of furious rage that made him oblivious to everything, and he had the strength of ten men. He flung himself at the barefoot Frenchman before the man could finish drawing his sword, flattened him and began hammering him with both fists. Roars of encouragement came from the crowd, but just then a patrol of French lancers came riding round the corner. The lancers trotted up to Pierre and the Frenchman, surrounding them both. Pierre never remembered what happened next. He had a vague recollection of hitting somebody and being hit back until eventually he found himself with his hands tied, being searched by a group of French soldiers standing all round him.

'Lieutenant, he's got a dagger,' were the first words Pierre recognized.

'Aha, a weapon,' said the officer, and he turned to the barefoot soldier, who had been taken along with Pierre. 'All right. You can tell your story at the court martial,' said the officer. Then he turned and said to Pierre, 'Listen you. Do you speak French?'

Pierre looked around with bloodshot eyes, and said nothing. His face must have looked terrible, because the officer whispered something, and four more lancers detached themselves from the rest, came over and stationed themselves next to Pierre on both sides.

'Do you speak French?' The officer repeated the question, but kept his distance as he did so. 'Get the interpreter.'

A little man in Russian civilian clothing emerged from the ranks. Pierre could tell immediately from the way he dressed and spoke that he was a French salesman from a Moscow shop.

'He doesn't look like a common man,' said the interpreter, eyeing Pierre.

'Oh no? He looks very much like an arsonist to me,' said the officer. 'Ask him who he is.'

''Oo are you?' asked the interpreter in very Frenchified Russian. 'You must answer ze officer.'

'I'm not saying who I am. I'm your prisoner. Take me away,' Pierre blurted out in French.

'Aha!' commented the officer with a scowl. 'All right, march him away!'

A crowd had collected round the lancers. Nearest of all to Pierre stood the peasant woman with the pockmarked face, who now had the baby. As the patrol moved off she came forward.

'Hey, where are they taking you, dearie?' she said. 'The baby! What shall I to do with the baby if it's not theirs?' she cried.

'What does this woman want?' inquired the officer.

Pierre was behaving as if he had been drinking. His blood was up and his spirits soared at the sight of the little girl he had saved.

'What is she talking about?' he said. 'She's bringing me my daughter. I've just saved her from the fire,' he declared. 'Goodbye!' And he strode off solemnly between the Frenchmen, wondering why on earth he had blurted out such a pointless lie.

The lancers' patrol was one of the ones Durosnel had ordered out on to the streets of Moscow to stop any looting, and, more importantly, to catch the arsonists who, according to a widespread opinion mooted among the top-ranking French officers that day, were behind all the fires. In the course of patrolling a few more streets the lancers arrested another half-dozen suspicious characters, all Russian – a shopkeeper, a couple of theology students, a peasant and a house serf – along with several people caught looting. But of all these suspicious characters Pierre seemed more suspicious than anyone.

When they had all been taken away for the night to a large house on the Zubov rampart, where a guardhouse had been set up, Pierre was separated from the rest and placed under close guard.

VOLUME IV

PART I

Meanwhile in Petersburg a complex struggle was not only continuing
in the highest circles, it was gaining in intensity. The parties involved
– those of Rumyantsev, the French set, Marya Fyodorovna, the Tsarevich and others – found themselves drowned out as always by the
buzzing of the court drones. But life in the city went on as before, an
easy life, full of luxury, disturbed only by phantoms and reflections of
real life, and this meant that a great effort of will was needed for them
to realize just how dangerous and difficult the situation of the Russian
people was. There were the same receptions and balls, the same French
theatre, the same interests pursued at court, the same interests and
intrigues pursued in government service. Only in the very highest
circles was an effort made to bear in mind the full difficulty of the
present situation. It was whispered that the two Empresses had
adopted polarized attitudes towards these difficult circumstances. The
Dowager Empress, Marya Fyodorovna, worried about the welfare of
the charities and educational institutions of which she was patron,
had made arrangements for them all to be evacuated to Kazan, and
all their belongings were now packed. But when the younger Empress,
Yelizaveta Alexeyevna, was asked what arrangements she might like
to make, she replied graciously enough, with the patriotic spirit that
was now her byword, that she couldn't make any arrangements for
state institutions, since they were the Tsar's business, but as far as she
personally was concerned, she stated in the same gracious way that
she would be the last person to leave Petersburg.

On the 26th of August, the very day of the battle of Borodino, a
soirée was held at Anna Pavlovna Scherer's house, the high point of
which was to be a reading of the Metropolitan's letter written to
accompany the icon of Saint Sergiy, which was being sent to the
Tsar. This letter was considered a model of ecclesiastical and patriotic
eloquence. It was to be read by no less a person than Prince Vasily,

who was famous for his powers of declamation. (He was one of the Empress's readers.) His declamatory skill consisted in delivering a torrent of words in sonorous tones and a sing-song voice that plunged up and down between a gentle murmur and a despairing wail irrespective of meaning, which meant it was entirely a matter of chance whether any particular words attracted a murmur or a wail. This reading, as always with Anna Pavlovna and her hospitality, was not without political significance. She was expecting a number of bigwigs, and she wanted to embarrass them for continuing to visit the French theatre, and appeal to their patriotic spirit. A lot of people had already arrived, but not all of the ones she was waiting for, so Anna Pavlovna delayed the reading and went about encouraging general conversation.

The hottest news in Petersburg concerned Countess Hélène Bezukhov, who was ill. The countess had fallen sick a few days ago, and missed a number of occasions at which she would normally have been the finest adornment. The word was that she refused to see anyone, and instead of engaging the famous Petersburg physicians who usually attended her, she had placed herself in the hands of some Italian doctor, who was giving her some new and unusual treatment.

Everybody knew only too well that the lovely countess's indisposition arose from the difficulties of marrying two husbands at the same time, and the Italian doctor's cure amounted to getting rid of the difficulties. But in the presence of Anna Pavlovna no one was bold enough to think thoughts like that; it was as if they knew nothing at all about it.

'I hear the poor countess is very ill. The doctor says it's angina pectoris.'

'Angina? Oh, that's an awful thing to have.'

'They do say the rivals have been reconciled, thanks to the angina.' They took great pleasure in mouthing the medical term.

'I'm told the old count's reaction was very moving. He cried like a baby when the doctor told him how serious it was.'

'Oh, it would be a terrible loss. She's such a charming woman.'

'You're talking about the poor countess,' said Anna Pavlovna, sidling up. 'I've sent for news of her. I did hear she was a bit better. Oh, there's no doubt about it, she's the loveliest woman in the world,' said Anna Pavlovna, smiling at her own solemn words. 'We do belong to different camps, but that doesn't stop me giving the countess her due. She's so unhappy.'

Taking these last words as a slight lifting of the veil of mystery that hung over the countess's illness, one rather impetuous young man felt emboldened to voice surprise that the best-known doctors hadn't been called in, and the countess was being looked after by some quack, who might be giving her dangerous medicine.

'Well, you're better informed than I am!' cried Anna Pavlovna, rounding on the callow young man with sudden viciousness. 'But I have it on the best authority that this doctor is a very learned and skilful man. He is private physician to the Queen of Spain.'

And leaving the young man annihilated, Anna Pavlovna turned to Bilibin, who was talking about the Austrians over in a different group, with his forehead all puckered up and ready to relax in the delivery of some *bon mot*.

'I thought it was rather charming!' He was talking about a diplomatic note that had gone to Vienna along with the Austrian banners captured by Wittgenstein, 'the hero of Petropolis', as they called him in Petersburg.

'What is? What do you mean?' Anna Pavlovna inquired, thus creating a silence for the *bon mot*, even though she had heard it before.

And Bilibin repeated the precise wording of the diplomatic dispatch that he had composed.

'The Emperor returns the Austrian flags,' said Bilibin, 'friendly banners gone astray, found by him along the way,' Bilibin concluded, relaxing his wrinkles.

'Charming, charming!' commented Prince Vasily.

'I suppose you mean the way to Warsaw,' said Prince Hippolyte in a very loud voice, much to everyone's surprise. All eyes turned to him; no one knew what he meant. Prince Hippolyte stared around as well in breezy bemusement. He had no more idea than anyone else what his words were supposed to mean. He had often noticed in his career as a diplomat that an off-the-cuff remark like that was considered very witty, so he had blurted out the first words that came into his head, just in case. 'It might come out all right,' he had thought, 'and if it doesn't they'll know what to do with it.' As it happened the awkward silence that ensued was broken by the arrival of the inadequately patriotic person Anna Pavlovna was wanting to tackle, so she smiled, wagged her finger at Prince Hippolyte, called Prince Vasily over to the table, set him up with two candles and a manuscript, and asked him to start. There was a general hush.

'Most gracious sovereign Emperor!' thundered Prince Vasily with a dark glare at the audience as if inviting anyone to challenge him. But nobody said a word. 'Moscow, our ancient capital, the New Jerusalem, receives *her* Messiah' – the emphasis was sudden and misplaced – 'like unto a mother that embraces her zealous sons, and sees through the gathering darkness a vision of thy dominion in all its dazzling glory, raising her voice in triumph and singing, "Hosanna! Blessed is he that cometh forth!" ' Prince Vasily uttered these last words in the most plangent tones.

Bilibin was examining his nails very closely, and many in the audience shrank back visibly, as if wondering whether they might have done something wrong. Anna Pavlovna was mouthing the words in advance, as old women whisper the next prayer in the communion service. 'Let the flagrant and brazen Goliath . . .' she whispered.

Prince Vasily continued:

'Let the flagrant and brazen Goliath who comes from the borders of France visit upon the realm of Russia all the horrors of death. Our humble faith, the sling of the Russian David, shall send a swift blow to the head of his pride that so thirsteth for blood. This icon of the venerable Saint Sergiy, in ancient times a jealous champion of our country's weal, is hereby borne to your Imperial Majesty. I grieve that my failing powers prevent me from rejoicing in the sight of your most gracious countenance. I offer up to Heaven my most fervent prayers, that the Almighty may in His mercy exalt the generation of the righteous and fulfil the hopes of your Majesty . . .'

'Such power! And what a delivery!' came various voices praising reader and author alike. Newly inspired by this rousing appeal, Anna Pavlovna's guests stayed on for some time discussing the country's present situation, and there was a variety of opinions as to how the battle that must be fought any day now would turn out.

'You will see,' said Anna Pavlovna. 'Tomorrow is the Emperor's birthday, and we shall hear something. I have a funny feeling it will be something good.'

CHAPTER 2

Anna Pavlovna's funny feeling was amply justified. Next day, during a special service held at court in honour of the Tsar's birthday, Prince Volkonsky was called out to receive a message from Prince Kutuzov. It was a report written by Kutuzov at Tatarinova on the day of the battle. Kutuzov wrote that the Russians had not given an inch, French losses had been greater than ours, and this message was being dashed off on the actual battlefield without waiting for all the latest intelligence to come in. So there had been a victory. There on the spot, without leaving church, the congregation rendered thanks to the Creator for His help with their cause, and for victory.

Anna Pavlovna's funny feeling had been justified, and all that morning the town was in a happy holiday mood. Everyone assumed the victory to have been conclusive, and there was talk of Napoleon having been taken prisoner and deposed, and a new sovereign being chosen for France.

Far away from the scene of action and amid the distractions of court life it is quite difficult for events to be properly reflected and kept in proportion. Public events are automatically centred around some event of personal significance. Here, for instance, the courtiers were celebrating not just because a victory had been won, but equally because news of it had arrived on the Tsar's birthday. It was like an arranged surprise that had come off well. Kutuzov's report had also mentioned some Russian losses, including names as such as Tuchkov, Bagration and Kutaysov. So it was that, quite unconsciously in this Petersburg world, the sad side of things also centred around a single incident – the death of Kutaysov. Everybody had known him, the Tsar had liked him, and he had been an interesting young man. All that day people said to each other when they met, 'What a marvellous coincidence! Just like that, in the middle of the service. Oh, but what a loss – Kutaysov! Terrible pity!'

'What did I tell you about Kutuzov?' Prince Vasily said now, with the pride of a prophet. 'I always said he was the only man capable of beating Napoleon.'

But next day there was no news from the army, and the public voice began to waver. The courtiers felt for the Tsar in the agony of suspense that he was suffering.

'What a dreadful situation for the Empreror to be in!' said the courtiers. They stopped singing the praises of Kutuzov as they had done the other day; now they rounded on him as the cause of the Tsar's present plight. Prince Vasily stopped boasting about his beloved Kutuzov, and kept quiet when the commander-in-chief's name came up. To make matters worse, by that evening everything had seemingly conspired to plunge the Petersburg world into deep distress and anxiety: a dreadful piece of news came to add to their woes. Countess Hélène Bezukhov had died quite suddenly of the dreadful illness which they had so much enjoyed chatting about. At large gatherings the official word was that Countess Bezukhov had died from a terrible attack of angina pectoris, but in close circles people went into great detail, telling how the personal physician to the Queen of Spain had prescribed small doses of a certain medicine for Hélène that were supposed to have a special effect on her, but Hélène, tormented by the old count's suspicions and her husband's failure to respond to her letter (that wretched profligate Pierre), had suddenly taken an overdose and died in agony before any help could be given. According to the story, Prince Vasily and the old count had rounded on the Italian, but he had produced notes left by the unhappy deceased, and these were so explicit they had promptly let him go.

Conversation now centred around three sad developments – the Tsar's state of uncertainty, the loss of Kutaysov and the death of Hélène.

On the third day after Kutuzov's dispatch a country gentleman arrived from Moscow, and soon the news that the city had been surrendered to the French was all over town. This was awful! What a position for the Emperor to be in! Kutuzov was now a traitor, and when Prince Vasily talked to visitors calling in to express their condolences over his daughter's death, if there was any mention of Kutuzov (whom he had so recently praised to the skies, though allowances had to be made for the fact that in all his grief he had forgotten his earlier comments), he said you couldn't have expected anything different from a blind and dissipated old man.

'The thing that surprises me,' he would go on to say, 'is how on earth we could have entrusted the fate of Russia to the likes of him.'

While ever the news remained officially unconfirmed, it was still possible to doubt it, but next day the following message arrived from Count Rostopchin:

Prince Kutuzov's adjutant has brought me a letter demanding a police escort for the army down the Ryazan road. He says he is regretfully abandoning Moscow. Sire! Kutuzov's action decides the fate of the capital and your whole empire. Russia will shudder to learn that this city, where the greatness of Russia is concentrated and the ashes of your forefathers lie, has been surrendered. I shall follow the army. I have had everything taken away. All that remains is for me to weep over the fate of my country.

On receiving this message, the Tsar dispatched Prince Volkonsky to Kutuzov with the following response:

Prince Mikhail Ilarionovich! I have received no reports from you since the 29th of August. Meanwhile I have received, by way of Yaroslavl, from the governor-general of Moscow, writing on September 1st, the sad tidings that you have decided to take the army away and abandon Moscow. You can well imagine the effect this news has had upon me, and your silence exacerbates my astonishment. I am sending herewith

Adjutant-General Prince Volkonsky to ascertain from you the present situation of the army and the reasons that lie behind such an unhappy decision.

CHAPTER 3

Nine days after the abandonment of Moscow a courier from Kutuzov reached Petersburg with an official announcement of the surrender of the city. He was a Frenchman, Michaud, who, as he put it, 'may have been a foreigner but called himself a Russian heart and soul'.

The Tsar was quick to receive the messenger in his study in the palace on Kamenny Island. Michaud had never set eyes on Moscow before the campaign and knew not a word of Russian, yet he wrote that he was deeply moved when he came before 'our most gracious sovereign' with the news of the burning of Moscow, the flames of which had lit up his route.

Though the origins of M. Michaud's sorrow must have been different from those that lay behind the grief of Russian people, Michaud had such a gloomy look about him when he was shown into the Tsar's study that the Tsar asked him at once:

'Do you bring me sad news, Colonel?'

'Very sad, sire,' answered Michaud, looking down with a sigh. 'The surrender of Moscow.'

'Can they really have surrendered my ancient capital without a fight?' the Tsar asked sharply, suddenly roused.

Michaud respectfully gave the message Kutuzov had asked him to give: there had been no possibility of fighting just outside Moscow, and since they had been left with a straight choice – either to lose the army and Moscow together or to lose only Moscow – the commander-in-chief had been forced to go for the latter option.

The Tsar listened without a word, avoiding Michaud's eyes.

'Is the enemy now inside the city?' he asked.

'Yes, sire, and by now the city is reduced to ashes. I left it all in flames,' said Michaud decisively, but one glance at the Tsar made him feel horrified at what he had done. The Tsar's breathing was rapid and laboured, his lower lip was quivering, and for one moment his handsome blue eyes were moist with tears.

But this lasted no more than a moment. The Tsar's sudden frown was a gesture of self-reproach for showing weakness. He looked up and spoke firmly to Michaud.

'I can see from all that is happening, Colonel, that Providence requires great sacrifices of us. I am ready to submit to His will in all things, but tell me, Michaud, how did you leave the army, seeing my ancient capital abandoned just like that without striking a blow? Did you see any alarm and despondency?'

Once he saw that his most gracious sovereign had regained his composure, Michaud was able to do the same, but the Tsar had asked a straight, factual question calling for a straight answer, and he didn't have one ready yet.

'Sire, will you permit me to speak frankly, as a loyal soldier?' he said, playing for time.

'Colonel, that is what I always insist upon,' said the Tsar. 'Hide nothing from me. I really do want to know how things stand.'

'Sire!' said Michaud, with the delicate hint of a smile on his lips now that he had had time to prepare his answer. It was polite, but it involved a little word play. 'Sire! I left the whole army, from the commanders to the lowest soldier without exception, in fear and trembling.'

'What can you mean?' the Tsar cut in with a dark scowl. 'Would my Russians allow themselves to lose heart in the face of misfortune? . . . Never!'

This was just what Michaud was waiting for to work his little trick.

'Sire,' he said, still respectful but now looking rather playful, 'their only dread is that your Majesty might be persuaded to sue for peace through sheer goodness of heart. They are spoiling for a fight,' said this representative of the Russian people, 'and eager to prove their loyalty to your Majesty by laying down their lives . . .'

'Aha!' said the Tsar, much reassured, with a gleam of affection in his eyes as he clapped Michaud on the shoulder. 'Colonel, you put my mind at rest . . .'

The Tsar looked down, and for a while he said nothing.

'Well, off you go back to the army,' he said at last, drawing himself up to his full height and addressing Michaud with a warm, regal gesture, 'and tell our good men, tell all our loyal subjects wherever you go, that when I am left without a single soldier I shall put myself at the head of my beloved nobility and my splendid peasants, and drain the last resources of my empire. I have more at my disposal than my enemies imagine,' said the Tsar, getting more and more excited. 'But if it were ever to be written in the decrees of Divine Providence,' he said, with his gentle, handsome eyes shining with emotion and raised towards heaven, 'that my dynasty should cease to reign on the throne of my ancestors, then after exhausting every means in my power I shall grow my beard down to here' (the Emperor placed his hand half-way down his chest) 'and go and eat potatoes with the humblest of my peasants rather than underwrite the shame of my country and my dear people, whose sacrifice I fully appreciate.'

Uttering these words in a voice full of feeling, the Tsar turned away brusquely as if he didn't want Michaud to see his eyes filling with tears, and walked to the other end of the study. After standing there for a while, he strode back to Michaud, and gripped his arm warmly below the elbow. The Tsar's gentle and handsome face was flushed, and his eyes smouldered with determination and fury.

'Colonel Michaud, don't forget what I am saying to you here. One day, perhaps, we shall recall it with pleasure . . . It's Napoleon or me,' he said, touching his breast. 'We can no longer rule together. I have come to know him. He will not deceive me again . . .' And the Tsar paused, frowning. At these words, seeing the look of gritty determination in the Tsar's eyes, Michaud, the foreigner who was a Russian heart and soul, felt truly inspired at that solemn moment by what he had heard (as he would later recount), and he felt he was expressing not only his own feelings but those of the Russian people as a whole, since he considered himself to be their representative, as he coined the following phrases:

'Sire! At this moment your Majesty is underwriting the glory of the nation and the salvation of Europe!'

The Tsar dismissed Michaud with a slight nod.

CHAPTER 4

With half of Russia in enemy hands, the inhabitants of Moscow scurrying away to remote provinces, and one levy of militia after another being raised for the defence of the country, we who were not living at that time are bound to think that all the Russian people, great and small, were wholly occupied in sacrificing themselves, saving their country, or weeping over its downfall. Every last story and description that has come down to us from that period tells of nothing but self-sacrifice, patriotism, despair, grief and heroic conduct on the part of the Russians. In real life, of course, it wasn't like that. It seems so to us, because all we see from the past is the general historical interest of the period; what we don't see are all the personal human concerns of people at that time. Yet in real life personal concerns of immediate relevance are so much more important than the general public interest that they prevent the public interest from ever being sensed, or even noticed. Most people at that time ignored the general course of events because they were wrapped up in their immediate personal concerns. And these same people were the prime movers of their day.

The ones who were actually making an effort to follow the general course of events, and trying to get involved through self-sacrifice and heroic conduct, were the least useful members of society; they looked at things the wrong way round, and everything they did, with the best of intentions, turned out to be useless and absurd, like the regiments provided by Pierre and Mamonov that went off to loot Russian villages, like the lint scraped by the ladies that never got through to the wounded, and so on. Even people who just liked to think things through and talk them over couldn't discuss the current situation of Russia without unconsciously lapsing into hypocrisy, falsehood or useless victimization and animosity levelled against individuals they were eager to blame for things that weren't anybody's fault.

Historical events illustrate more clearly than anything the injunction against eating of the Tree of Knowledge. The only activity that bears any fruit is subconscious activity, and no one who takes part in any historical drama can ever understand its significance. If he so much as tries to understand it, his efforts are fruitless.

The more intimately anyone was involved in the unfolding Russian drama of the day, the more easily its meaning escaped him. In Petersburg, and out in the provinces a long way from Moscow, ladies and gentlemen put on their militia uniforms, bewailed the fate of Russia and the loss of her ancient capital and talked of self-sacrifice, and so on. But in the army, which had retreated beyond Moscow, scarcely anybody talked or thought about Moscow, or gazed at the burning city and vowed to get his own back on the French, because they were all thinking about pay-day, or the next halt, or Mary the canteen-girl, or things like that.

Nikolay Rostov never had any idea of self-sacrifice; it was only because war happened to break out while he was still a serving soldier that he found himself with a direct and lengthy part to play in the defence of his country, and consequently able to look on what was happening in Russia without falling into despair or coming to pessimistic conclusions. If he had been asked his opinion of Russia's present situation he would have said it wasn't his job to think about things like that, that's what Kutuzov and the rest of them were there for, but he had heard the regiments were being topped up, so there must be a lot of fighting still to do, and with things as they were he ought to make colonel within a couple of years.

Since this was his general attitude he felt no misgivings at having to absent himself from the coming battle when he was suddenly directed to go down to Voronezh and get hold of fresh horses for the division. In fact he received the news with the greatest satisfaction, which he didn't seek to hide, and his comrades fully understood.

A few days before the battle of Borodino Nikolay was issued with money and travel documents, and off he went to Voronezh, using post-horses, having sent some hussars on ahead.

Only someone who has been through the same thing, someone who has spent months on end in the atmosphere of an army in the field, could possibly imagine the feeling of bliss that Nikolay experienced when he escaped from a region crawling with troops, foraging parties, trains of supply-wagons, and field-hospitals, when he left behind all the soldiers, army vehicles, the squalid conditions of camp life, and started to see villagers with working men and peasant women, fine country houses, cattle grazing in the fields and posting-stations with their sleepy masters. He was ecstatically happy; it was as if he was seeing it all for the first time. And what really surprised him, and pleased him, was the sight of women, healthy young women, who didn't have dozens of officers hovering around them, women who were delighted and flattered to meet a travelling officer and share a joke with him.

Nikolay was in buoyant mood when he arrived at his hotel in Voronezh late at night. He ordered everything he hadn't been able to get hold of for ages in the army, and the following morning he gave himself a really close shave and put on the full-dress uniform that he hadn't worn for many a long day, before driving over to present himself to the authorities.

The commander of the local militia was a civilian general, an old gentleman who was obviously enjoying his military status and rank. His attitude to Nikolay was rather truculent – he thought he knew the right attitude for a military man to adopt – and he interrogated him very seriously, as if it was his right to do so, and to find out how things were going, without showing approval or disapproval. Nikolay was in such a good mood that all this struck him as amusing.

From the militia commander he went to see the governor. The governor was a fussy little man, warm-hearted and as straight as a die. He told Nikolay about various stud-farms where he might be able to get horses, recommended a horse-dealer down town and a gentleman farmer fifteen miles away who had the best horses, and said he would help in any way he could.

'Are you Count Ilya Rostov's son? My wife was a great friend of your dear mamma's. We offer a little entertainment on Thursdays, and today is Thursday. Do come and see us. Take us as you find us,' said the governor, seeing him out.

Nikolay took a carriage with post-horses, invited his quartermaster to get in beside him and galloped off to see the gentleman with the best horses who lived fifteen miles away.

In those early days in Voronezh everything Nikolay undertook was enjoyable and easy, and, typically for a man in a really good mood, it all went like clockwork.

The country gentleman Nikolay had been sent to see turned out to be an old cavalry officer, a bachelor, an expert on horses who loved his hunting and owned many good things: a smoking-room, a century-old herb-brandy, vintage Hungarian wines and some quite superb horses.

It took Nikolay no time to agree terms: six thousand roubles bought him seventeen prime stallions, ideal, as he put it, for presentation as remount samples. Rostov stayed for dinner, drank rather too much Hungarian wine and exchanged kisses with the country gentleman, having struck up a warm relationship with him, before driving back down the vilest of roads in the happiest of moods, constantly badgering the coachman to get a move on so they wouldn't be late for the governor's evening reception.

Nikolay changed his clothes, washed his head in cold water, splashed himself with scent and turned up at the governor's, only slightly late, ready with the phrase 'Better late than never'.

It wasn't a ball as such, and not a word had been said about dancing, but they all knew Katerina Petrovna would play waltzes and schottisches on the clavier, so there would be some dancing, and everyone, counting on this, had come dressed for a ball.

Provincial life in the year 1812 went on exactly as before, except that the provincial towns were enlivened by the sudden appearance of wealthy families from Moscow, and also, as in everything else that was going on in Russia at that time, there was a noticeable attitude of devil-may-care resignation – we're in it up to our knees, and nothing makes any difference now – and the inevitable small talk, instead of limiting itself to the weather or mutual acquaintances, was now extended to include Moscow, the army and Napoleon.

The gathering at the governor's consisted of the cream of Voronezh society.

There were lots of ladies there, and quite a few people known to Nikolay from Moscow, but among the men there was no one to compete with a chevalier of St George, a dashing hussar and a young man as good-natured and well-bred as Count Rostov. Among the men there was an Italian prisoner, an officer in the French army; and Nikolay felt that the presence of this prisoner added to his stature as a Russian hero. He was a kind of trophy. Nikolay could sense this, and as far as he could tell everybody looked on the Italian in the same way. He went out of his way to treat the foreign officer with dignity while keeping him at arm's length.

As soon as Nikolay entered the room in his hussar's uniform, exuding a fragrance of scent mingled with wine, and pronounced the words, 'Better late than never,' which then echoed round the room, people clustered around him. All eyes were on him, and he felt immediately at home in this provincial town, taking his rightful place as a universal favourite, which was always an agreeable position to be in, but now amounted to a heady pleasure after long days of abstinence. At every posting-station, in all the taverns, in the horse-breeder's smoking-room, he had encountered servant-girls flattered by his attention, but here at the governor's evening party it was even better: Nikolay seemed to see before him an inexhaustible supply of young married ladies and pretty girls just waiting to be noticed by him. They all flirted with him, the ladies and the girls, and the elderly among them took it upon themselves from this first evening to try and get this gallant young rake of a hussar married off and settled down. The latter group included no less a person than the governor's wife, who treated Rostov like a close relative, using affectionate language and calling him 'Nicolas'.

Katerina Petrovna did what was expected of her, striking up with waltzes and schottisches, and the dancing began, an opportunity for Nikolay to charm the company even further by his nimble-footedness. He took them all by surprise by his free-and-easy dancing style. He even surprised himself by the way he danced that evening. He had never danced like that in Moscow – he would have considered it improper, sheer bad taste, to career about with such abandon – but here he felt it necessary to amaze them all by producing something out of the ordinary, something they would assume to be the way they did things in the capital, though it hadn't yet got out to the provinces.

Nikolay spent the whole evening concentrating his attention on a pretty little blonde, blue-eyed and buxom, the wife of a local official. With the naive certainty enjoyed by young men out on the town that other men's wives were created for their special benefit, Rostov never left this lady's side, and he was also very friendly towards her husband, treating him conspiratorially, as if they both knew an unspoken truth: they were made for each other – Nikolay and his wife, that is. The husband didn't seem persuaded of this, however, and he tried giving

Rostov a dark look or two. But Nikolay was brimming with such innocent good humour that now and then even the husband fell prey to his exuberance. Towards the end of the evening, however, as the wife's face grew redder and livelier, the husband's grew steadily paler and sadder. It was as if they had been issued with a limited amount of vivacity between them, and as the wife's share of it rose, the husband's dwindled away.

CHAPTER 5

With a smile that never left his lips Nikolay leant forward a little in his armchair, and bent down over his blonde beauty, searching classical mythology for suitable compliments to pay her.

Breezily shifting the position of his legs in his tight riding-breeches, still wafting his perfume all over the room, and full of admiration for his fair companion, himself and the splendid curves of his own legs encased in their tight boots, Nikolay told the little blonde there was a lady here in Voronezh he was planning to abduct.

'What's she like?'

'Charming. Divine. Her eyes' (Nikolay gazed at his companion) 'are blue, her lips are coral, pearly-white . . .' (he glanced down at her shoulders) 'a figure like Diana's . . .'

Her husband came over and asked his wife sullenly what they were talking about.

'Ah, Nikita Ivanych!' said Nikolay, getting to his feet in a courteous gesture. And as though anxious for Nikita Ivanych to share the joke he began to tell him, too, about his plan to run away with a blonde lady.

The husband smiled grimly, the wife radiantly.

The kindly governor's wife came over wearing a look of disapproval.

'Anna Ignatyevna wishes to see you, Nicolas,' she said, pronouncing the words 'Anna Ignatyevna' with such emphasis that Rostov was left in no doubt that Anna Ignatyevna was a very important person. 'Come along, Nicolas. You don't mind if I call you that, do you?'

'Please do, Auntie dear. Who is she?'

'Anna Ignatyevna Malvintsev. She's heard about you from her niece. Apparently you rescued her . . . You know who I mean?'

'Well, I've rescued lots of young women!' cried Nikolay.

'Her niece is Princess Bolkonsky. She's here in Voronezh with her aunt. Oh ho! Do I see a little blush? What's all this then?'

'No, I just wasn't thinking. Please, Auntie dear.'

'Very well, very well. Oh dear, you're such a funny boy!'

The governor's wife led him over towards a tall, very stout lady wearing a little blue cap, who had just finished playing cards with the top people in town. It was Madame Malvintsev, Princess Marya's aunt on her mother's side, a wealthy, childless widow, who had lived all her life in Voronezh. She was standing there totting up her losses when Rostov approached.

Full of self-importance, she gave a grim frown, took one glance at him and went on chiding a general who had won money from her.

'My dear boy, I'm so pleased to meet you,' she said at last, holding out her hand to him. 'Do come and see me.'

After saying a few words about Princess Marya and her late father, who had evidently not been in Madame Malvintsev's good books, and asking after Prince Andrey, who was apparently no favourite of hers either, the dignified old lady dismissed him, but not before she had repeated her invitation for him to call on her.

Nikolay promised to do so and blushed again as he took his leave. At the mere mention of Princess Marya's name Rostov experienced an inexplicable feeling of shyness, even dread.

As he walked away from Madame Malvintsev Rostov had every intention of going back for some more dancing, but the little governor's wife laid her plump little hand on his sleeve, told him she wanted to have a word with him, and led him off into her sitting-room. One or two people who were already there soon slipped out so as not to be in her way.

'Do you know something, dear boy,' said the governor's wife with a serious expression on her kindly little face. 'She'll be just the match for you. Would you like me to fix things up?'

'Who are you talking about, Auntie dear?' asked Nikolay.

'I'll pair you off with the princess. Katerina Petrovna goes on about Lili, but I say, no – it must be the princess. Is that what you want? I'm sure your mamma will be most gratified. Really, she's such a nice girl, so charming! And she's not as plain as all that.'

'I'll say she isn't,' said Nikolay, apparently offended at the very idea. 'As for me, Auntie dear, like a good soldier I don't force myself on anyone, but neither do I refuse anything that turns up,' Rostov blurted out unthinkingly.

'All right. But do remember – this is no joking matter.'

'Of course it isn't!'

'Yes, yes . . .' said the governor's wife, apparently to herself. 'Oh, there is one other thing, dear boy. You're making rather too much of that other lady – the blonde. I know the husband's a pathetic creature, but really . . .'

'Oh no, he and I are the best of friends,' said Nikolay in all his simple-heartedness. It had never crossed his mind that what he saw as a pleasant pastime could be offensive to anybody else.

But over supper he remembered what had happened.

'I was a bit stupid saying things like that to the governor's wife!' he thought. 'She's going to start fixing things up, and what do I do about Sonya?'

When the time came for him to take his leave of the governor's wife, and she said to him once again with a smile, 'You won't forget, will you?' he took her to one side.

'There is just one thing . . . To be quite candid, Auntie dear . . .'

'What's all this then? Come on over here, my dear, and sit down with me.'

Nikolay felt a sudden urge, a need even, to pour out all his innermost feelings (those things he would never have spoken about to his mother, his sister, or even a close friend) to this woman, who was virtually a stranger. Later on, whenever Nikolay remembered this inexplicable, spontaneous outpouring, even though it was to have highly important consequences for him, it seemed to have come about by a sudden silly impulse, as things like this always seem to have done. But at the same time this outburst of plain speaking, along with one or two other little things, really were to have consequences of massive importance to him and his whole family.

'It's like this, Auntie dear. Mamma has been trying for ages to get me married off to an heiress, but I hate the idea of marrying for money.'

'Oh, yes, I can see that,' said the governor's wife.

'But Princess Bolkonsky's different. For one thing, I can honestly say I like her very much. I feel close to her. And apart from that, ever since I happened across her in such an odd situation, I know it sounds weird, but I can't help thinking fate had a hand in it. I mean, just think: Mamma has been dreaming about this for ages, but she and I have never happened to meet before. Something has always happened to stop us meeting. Then, while ever my sister, Natasha, was engaged to her brother, it was obvious there couldn't be any question of my marrying her. I had to meet her first just at the time when Natasha's engagement had been broken off, and after that, well . . . So you see how it is. I've never said this to anyone before, and I never shall again. You're the only one.'

The governor's wife thanked him by squeezing his elbow.

'Do you know my cousin, Sonya? I'm in love with her. I've promised to marry her, and I'm going to marry her . . . So you see. It's out of the question.' Nikolay was bright red and becoming incoherent.

'My dear, dear boy, you mustn't talk like that. Why, Sonya hasn't a penny to her name, and you told me yourself your papa's affairs are in a terrible state. And what about your mamma? Well, it would kill her, for one thing. And for another, Sonya, if she has any heart at all, what kind of life would it be for her? Your mother at her wits' end. The family facing ruin. Oh no, my dear, you and Sonya will have to understand how things are.'

Nikolay said nothing. It came as a great relief to hear these arguments.

'Anyway, Auntie dear, it's not to be,' he said with a sigh after a brief silence. 'And in any case, would the princess have me? Don't forget she's still in mourning. It's unthinkable, isn't it?'

'What makes you think I'm going to get you married off here and now? There are different ways of going about things,' said the governor's wife.

'I can see you know a thing or two about matchmaking, Auntie dear . . .' said Nikolay, placing a kiss on her plump little hand.

CHAPTER 6

When she had arrived in Moscow not long after her encounter with Rostov at Bogucharovo, Princess Marya had found her nephew there with his tutor, and a letter from Prince Andrey telling her how to get to her aunt, Madame Malvintsev, in Voronezh. The whole business of making arrangements for the journey while worrying about her brother, the organization of her life in a new home, new people, bringing her nephew up – all these things had drowned out the siren voices that had called to Princess Marya's heart and tormented her during her father's illness and after his death, especially in the aftermath of her encounter with Rostov. She felt depressed. Now after a month spent in quiet seclusion she began to feel the loss of her father more and more poignantly, and in her heart it was bound up with the downfall of Russia. She was terribly anxious; the thought of the danger to which her brother was now exposed – he being the only close contact left to her now – was a source of continual torment. She was also worried about bringing her nephew up properly, a task she constantly felt she wasn't up to. But at the bottom of her heart she was at peace with herself, conscious that she had managed to suppress the dreams and hopes of personal happiness that had threatened to erupt in relation to her encounter with Nikolay Rostov.

When the governor's wife called on Madame Malvintsev the day after her evening reception, she outlined her plans and talked them over, insisting that although present circumstances precluded the usual processes of matchmaking, there was nothing to stop them bringing the young people together, and letting them get to know one another, and so, with the full approval of the aunt, she began to talk about Rostov in Princess Marya's presence, singing his praises, and describing how he had coloured up at the mention the princess's name, though this caused Princess Marya more pain than joy. Her inner peace was gone; desires, doubts, self-reproach and hope had risen again.

For two whole days before Rostov called, Princess Marya never stopped thinking about the best way to react to his visit. First she would make up her mind not to come down into the drawing-room when he came to see her aunt; it would be improper for her to receive visitors while she was still in deep mourning. Then she thought no, this would be churlish after what he had done for her. Then the possibility occurred to her that her aunt and the governor's wife were cooking something up for her and Rostov, a suspicion seemingly confirmed at times by particular words of theirs and some odd looks. Then she would tell herself that only her own depravity could have led her to think this of them: surely they must realize that in her situation, still wearing the heaviest mourning, that kind of matchmaking would be an offence both to her and to her father's memory. Working on the supposition that she would go down to see him, Princess Marya tried to anticipate what he would say to her, and what she would say to him, but her words either seemed too frigid, something he didn't deserve, or else they struck her as fraught with too much meaning. Worst of all she dreaded the embarrassment that was sure to overwhelm her, and betray her, the moment she saw him.

But when Sunday came and the footman entered the drawing-room after matins to announce the arrival of Count Rostov, the princess showed no sign of embarrassment, nothing more than a slight reddening of the cheeks, and her eyes gleamed with a radiance that was new.

'You've seen him, haven't you, Auntie?' Princess Marya asked in a calm voice, not knowing herself how she could put on such a good show of being so calm and natural.

When Rostov came in the princess looked down for a moment, giving their visitor time to exchange greetings with her aunt, but then, at the precise moment when Nikolay turned to her, she looked up again and met his gaze with shining eyes. Smiling with pleasure, she half-rose in a single movement full of dignity and grace, offered a slender, delicate hand, and spoke to him in a vibrant contralto new to her repertoire. Mademoiselle Bourienne was there with them, and she stared at Princess Marya in total amazement. Skilled as she was in matters of flirtation, she couldn't have improved on this tactical display of how to greet a man you want to win over.

'Either black is her colour, or else she's grown quite pretty, and I never noticed. Where did she get that poise and style?' thought Mademoiselle Bourienne.

Had Princess Marya been capable of reflection at that moment, she would have been more amazed than Mademoiselle Bourienne at the change that had come over her. The moment she set eyes on that dear, sweet face a new kind of vitality seemed to take possession of her, removing her conscious will and telling her what to say and do. From the time Rostov entered the room her face was transformed. It was like a new light in a carved and painted lantern, suddenly bringing out in breathtaking beauty all the detailed work on its panels that until then had looked rough, dark and devoid of all meaning. This was the kind of transformation that had come over Princess Marya's face. For the first time in her life all the pure, inner spirituality that she had worked so hard to achieve was revealed for all to see. All her hard-won spirituality and self-criticism, suffering, striving for goodness, humility, love and capacity for self-sacrifice flowed from her now in the glow of her radiant eyes, her gentle smile and every feature of her tender face.

None of this was lost on Nikolay Rostov; it was as if he had known her all her life. Here before him was a creature totally different from anyone he had ever met before, and better than anyone, someone much better than himself, and this mattered most of all.

The conversation was quite inconsequential. They talked about the war, automatically exaggerating, like everybody else, how sad they were about it, they recalled their last meeting, though this made Nikolay anxious to change the subject, and they spoke of the governor's nice wife, and their two families.

Princess Marya said nothing about her brother; it was her turn to change the subject whenever her aunt mentioned Prince Andrey. Clearly, she could speak out and put on a show of being worried about Russia's troubles, but her brother was a subject too close to her heart, and she was neither willing nor able to mouth pleasantries about him. Nikolay noticed this, as indeed he noticed, with newly developed powers of observation, every nuance of Princess Marya's character, all of them adding to his certainty that she was someone special and altogether original.

Nikolay had been just like Princess Marya, blushing with embarrassment when he heard her name mentioned or even thought about her, but now he was with her he felt perfectly at ease; completely forgetting all his carefully prepared phrases, he felt able to blurt out the first thing that came into his head, and it was always the right thing to have said.

Nikolay did not stay long. During a pause in the conversation he did what people always do when there are children about: he turned to Prince Andrey's little son. Giving him a cuddle, he asked whether he wanted to grow up to be a soldier. He picked the little boy up and whirled him round joyously, sneaking a glance at Princess Marya. Her gentle, happy, unassuming eyes were watching the child she loved in the arms of the man she loved. Her special look, and its meaning, were apparently not lost on Nikolay; he flushed with pleasure, and delightedly smothered the child with affectionate kisses.

Because she was still in mourning Princess Marya was not going out into society, and it did not seem right for Nikolay to call on them again, but the governor's wife was determined to go on with her matchmaking. She kept on telling Nikolay all the nice things Princess Marya had said about him, and vice versa, and she tried to persuade Rostov to declare himself to Princess Marya. With this in mind, she arranged for the young people to come together at the bishop's house before morning service.

Rostov made it clear to the governor's wife that he was not going to make a declaration of any kind to Princess Marya, but he did promise to be there.

He felt as if he was back at Tilsit. On that occasion Rostov had not allowed himself to doubt whether what everybody else accepted as right really was right, and now, after a brief but genuine struggle between his efforts to think out his life in terms of pure reason and meekly giving in to circumstances, he went for the latter, handing himself over to a power that seemed to be inexorably sweeping him along. He knew that after his promise to Sonya any declaration of his feelings to Princess Marya could only be described as dishonourable. And he knew he would never do anything dishonourable. But he also knew (though it wasn't a question of knowing, more a feeling at the bottom of his heart), that by surrendering to circumstances and to the people who were now guiding him, he was not doing anything wrong, he was just doing something very, very serious, more serious than anything he had ever done before.

After his meeting with Princess Marya, although his outward way of life stayed the same, all his former pleasures had lost their charm, and she was often in his mind. But he never thought of her as he had thought of all the young girls he had ever met in society, nor as he had got used to thinking about Sonya, rapturous though those thoughts had sometimes been. Like virtually every honest young man, he had seen every young girl as a possible future wife, mentally measuring them against all the usual details of married life: the white house-coat, the wife at the samovar, the wife with her own carriage, the patter of tiny feet, his mamma and papa, their attitude to her, and so on and so forth. And he had always enjoyed these images of the future. But when he thought of Princess Marya and being engaged to her, which was what the matchmakers were after, he couldn't form the vaguest outline of his future married life. If he so much as tried, it all seemed so false and incongruous. And it filled him with nothing but dread.

CHAPTER 7

The dreadful news about the battle of Borodino and so many men killed and wounded, and the even more dreadful news about the loss of Moscow reached Voronezh in the middle of September. It was only from the newspapers that Princess Marya learnt of her brother's wound, and since she had no definite details about him she was prepared to go off and find Prince Andrey. (This was what Nikolay heard, though he hadn't seen her himself.)

When he heard about the battle of Borodino and the surrender of Moscow, Rostov was not seized with despair, rage, a desire for revenge or anything like that, he suddenly felt jaded, irritated with everything in Voronezh, ill at ease and also rather guilty. All the conversations he was privy to had a ring of hypocrisy. He didn't know what to make of it all, and he sensed he would have to get back to the regiment before everything became clear again. He speeded up the purchase of the horses, and started being rough with his servant and quartermaster, often for no good reason.

Several days before Rostov's departure a thanksgiving service was held in the cathedral to mark the victory gained by the Russian armies, and Nikolay went along. He stood throughout just behind the governor, in an attitude of prim decorum befitting a military man, letting his mind roam freely over a wide range of topics. At the end of the service the governor's wife beckoned him over.

'Have you seen the princess?' she said, nodding towards a lady in black standing behind the choir.

Nikolay recognized Princess Marya immediately, not so much by the profile he could see under her hat as by the sudden sense of concern, trepidation and sympathy towards her that swept over him. Princess Marya looked deeply preoccupied as she made the last signs of the cross before leaving the church.

Nikolay looked at her face in some surprise. It was the same face he had seen before, with the same general appearance of refined, inner spirituality and suffering, but it was now suffused by a quite different light. It had a pathetic look compounded of sadness, prayer and hope. Behaving exactly as he had done before in her presence, Nikolay walked straight over without waiting to be urged by the governor's wife and without wondering about the rights and wrongs of addressing her while they were still in church. He told her he had heard of her grief and wanted to express his heartfelt sympathy. The moment she heard his voice her face lit up in response, instantly glowing with a mixture of joy and sorrow.

'There's just one thing I wanted to say, Princess,' said Rostov. 'If Prince Andrey was not still alive it would have been in the gazettes. After all, he is a colonel.'

The princess gave him a blank look, but she was clearly comforted by the deep compassion written all over his face.

'And I know from much experience that a shrapnel wound' (the papers had mentioned a shell) 'tends to be either instantly fatal or not too serious,' Nikolay went on. 'We must hope for the best. I'm confident . . .'

Princess Marya interrupted him.

'Oh, it would be so aw . . .' she exclaimed, but she was too emotional to finish what she was saying. Bowing her head with the kind of graceful gesture that typified her every movement in his presence, she thanked him with her eyes and walked out after her aunt.

That evening Nikolay didn't go out; he decided to stay in and finish off some book-keeping work that had to do with the horse-dealers. By the time he had finished it was too late to go out, but still too early to go to bed, so Nikolay spent a long time pacing up and down the room, thinking about his life, something he rarely did.

Princess Marya had made a favourable impression on him when they had first met at Bogucharovo. Their coming together under such unusual circumstances, together with the fact that his mother had actually singled her out as a wealthy heiress who might be a good match for him, had made him look at her very closely. During his stay in Voronezh the favourable impression had turned into a very strong one. Nikolay was deeply affected by the singular moral beauty that he could now see in her. But here he was getting ready to leave, and he hadn't yet considered how painful it would be to go away from Voronezh and give up any chance of seeing her. Yet the experience of meeting Princess Marya that morning in church had, he felt, pierced his heart more deeply than he had anticipated, and more deeply than was good for his peace of mind. The delicacy of that sad, pale face, those radiant eyes, those gentle and graceful movements, but most of all the deep and tender sadness pervading all her features, disturbed him and moved him to compassion. In men Rostov couldn't stand an appearance of spirituality and loftiness (which was why he hadn't liked Prince Andrey), and he dismissed any such thing as otherworldly philosophizing, but in Princess Marya it was that very air of sadness, revealing the full depth of her spiritual world, a new experience for Nikolay, that so irresistibly attracted him.

'She must be a wonderful girl! A positive angel!' he said to himself. 'Oh, if only I was free! Why did I have to rush into things with Sonya?' And he couldn't help but compare the two of them: one was very poor and the other very rich in those spiritual gifts that Nikolay himself lacked and therefore prized so highly. He tried to imagine what might have happened if he had been free. How would he have proposed, and would she have become his wife? No, it was too much for his imagination. He shivered with dread and couldn't picture anything very clearly. With Sonya he had long ago formed an image of the future; everything was clear-cut and straightforward because it was all carefully thought out and he knew everything there was to know about Sonya. But with Princess Marya he couldn't picture any future life, because he had no understanding of her; he just loved her.

His dreams of Sonya had a light-hearted quality about them; they were full of fun. But dreaming about Princess Marya was no easy matter; it was rather frightening.

'I remember her praying!' he thought. 'You could tell she was putting all her soul into her prayers. Yes, that's the kind of faith that moves mountains. I'm sure her prayers will be answered. Why shouldn't I pray for something that I want?' he wondered. 'What do I want? Freedom. Freedom from Sonya. She was right,' he thought, remembering what the governor's wife had said. 'There'll be nothing but misery if I end up marrying her. A mess, heartache for Mamma . . . our finances . . . a mess, a terrible mess! Besides, I don't even love her. Not the way I should. O God! Get me out of this terrible, hopeless situation!' He had suddenly found himself praying. 'Yes, faith will move mountains, but you do have to believe. You can't pray the way

Natasha and I did when we were children. We used to pray for the
snow to turn into sugar, and then run outside to see whether it had
done. Oh no. But I am not praying for silly little things now,' he said,
putting his pipe down in a corner and standing in front of the holy
icon with his hands held together. His heart melted at the thought of
Princess Marya, and he began to pray as he had not prayed for a very
long time. He was standing there with tears in his eyes and a lump in
his throat when Lavrushka walked in with some papers.

'Stupid fool! Bursting in when you're not wanted!' said Nikolay,
quickly changing his demeanour.

'A cullier's come from the governor,' said a sleepy Lavrushka. 'Letter
for you.'

'Right. Thank you very much. Now get out!'

Nikolay took the two letters, one from his mother, the other from
Sonya. He could tell by the handwriting, and he broke the seal on
Sonya's letter first. He had hardly read a few lines when his face turned
white and his eyes goggled with a mixture of dismay and sheer delight.

'No, it's not possible!' he said out loud. Unable to stay sitting down,
he started to pace up and down the room, holding the letter in both
hands and reading it. He skimmed the letter once, then read it through
a couple more times. With a shrug of his shoulders and his hands in
the air, he stood transfixed in the middle of the room, open-mouthed
and staring. His prayer, which he felt sure God would answer, had
been answered, but Nikolay was just as shocked as if it had been
something outrageous and completely out of the blue; the very quick-
ness of the event seemed to prove the letter hadn't come from God as
an answer to his prayers, it was pure coincidence.

The apparently undoable knot that had kept him tied down had
been cut by Sonya's letter, which was so unexpected and (Nikolay
couldn't help thinking) completely uncalled-for. She wrote that in view
of their recent misfortunes, including the loss of almost all the Rostovs'
Moscow property, and the countess's constantly reiterated longing for
Nikolay to marry Princess Bolkonsky, as well as his silence and coldness of late, taking one thing with another she had decided to release
him from his promise and set him completely free.

I couldn't bear to think I might be the cause of any anguish or discord
within the family which has shown me so much kindness [she wrote], the
one aim of my affection being the happiness of those I love, and so,
Nicolas, I beg you to consider yourself a free man, and to know that in
spite of everything no one could love you more than

Your Sonya

Both letters had been sent from Troitsa. The other was from the countess. It contained a description of their last days in Moscow, the departure, the fire and the loss of all their property. Among other things the countess also mentioned that Prince Andrey had been in the convoy of wounded soldiers travelling with them. He was still in a critical condition, but the doctor now said that there was more hope. Sonya and Natasha were nursing him.

Next day Nikolay went to see Princess Marya, and took the letter with him. Neither of them uttered a word about the possible implications of the words, 'Natasha is nursing him',[1] but this letter had the effect of suddenly bringing Nikolay and the princess into an intimate relationship since they were now virtually members of the same family.

Next day Rostov saw Princess Marya off on her journey to Yaroslavl, and a few days after that he set off himself to rejoin his regiment.

CHAPTER 8

Sonya's letter to Nikolay that had answered his prayer had been written from Troitsa. This is how it came about. The old countess had become more and more obsessed with the idea of Nikolay marrying a wealthy heiress. She knew that Sonya was the biggest obstacle in the way of this. And in recent days, especially after Nikolay's letter describing his meeting with Princess Marya at Bogucharovo, Sonya's life had become more and more difficult in the countess's house. The countess missed no opportunity for turning on Sonya with a cutting or humiliating remark.

But a few days before they set out from Moscow the countess, distressed and overwrought by everything that was going on, sent for Sonya, and instead of bullying and insisting she had begged her with tears in her eyes to repay everything they had ever done for her by making the sacrifice of breaking off her engagement to Nikolay.

'I shan't have a moment's rest until you give me your word,' she said.

Sonya sobbed hysterically and answered through her sobs that she would do anything, she was ready for anything, but she stopped short of giving an actual promise, and in her heart she couldn't bring herself to do what they wanted. She was required to sacrifice herself for the happiness of the family that had nurtured her and brought her up. Making sacrifices for other people was Sonya's way of life. Her position in the household was such that this was the only way for her to demonstrate her good qualities. She was used to making sacrifices and actually enjoyed it. But with every sacrifice she had had to make, until now she had been blissfully aware that it was raising her stock, in her own eyes and other people's, and also making her a worthier match for Nikolay, whom she loved more than anything in life. But now things were different: it would mean giving up everything that made sacrifice itself worth while, and the meaning of her entire life. For the first time in her life she felt bitterness against the people who had done so much for her only to torture her more agonizingly: she envied Natasha, who had never had to go through anything like this, never been asked to make sacrifices of her own, only ever got other people to make sacrifices for her and ended up by being loved by everybody. And for the first time in her life Sonya could sense her pure and gentle love for Nikolay turning into a wild passion that rose above all principles, virtue and religion. And under pressure from this passion, Sonya, with a lifetime of dependence and dissembling behind her, knew instinctively how to fob off the countess with general comments and vague responses, and she also managed to avoid talking to her, but she was now determined to wait for a private meeting with Nikolay, when she would use the occasion not to set him free, but, the very opposite, to bind him to her for ever.

The ghastly upheaval of the Rostovs' last days in Moscow had repressed all the dark thoughts that Sonya now found so burdensome. She was glad to find temporary relief in practicalities. But when she heard of Prince Andrey's presence in their house, in spite of all the genuine sympathy she felt for him and Natasha, she was seized by a wonderful superstitious feeling that God did not want her to be parted from Nikolay. She knew Natasha loved no one but Prince Andrey, and had never stopped loving him. She knew that now they were together, reunited under such terrible circumstances, they would fall in love again, and then Nikolay, being a relative, wouldn't be able to marry Princess Marya. Despite all the horrors of the last days in Moscow and the first days of the journey, this feeling, this awareness that Providence was intervening in her private life, made Sonya feel happy.

It was at the Troitsa monastery that the Rostovs made the first break in their journey.

In the monastery hostel three large rooms were assigned to the Rostov family, one exclusively for Prince Andrey. On that first day there the wounded man was feeling much better. Natasha was sitting with him. In the next room the count and countess were in polite conversation with the father superior, who had called in to see his old acquaintances and benefactors. Sonya was sitting there with them, dying to know what Prince Andrey and Natasha were talking about. She could hear their voices through the door. The door of Prince Andrey's room opened. Natasha came out looking all excited and didn't see the monk getting to his feet to greet her and pulling a baggy sleeve up to free his right hand. She went straight over to Sonya and took her by the arm.

'Natasha, what do you think you're doing? Come over here,' said the countess.

Natasha walked across to receive a blessing, and the old monk counselled her to turn to God, and also their patron saint, whenever she needed help. As soon as the father superior had gone, Natasha took her friend by the hand, and walked out with her into the empty third room.

'Sonya, he is going to live, isn't he? Do say yes,' she said. 'Sonya, I'm so happy, and so miserable too! Sonya, darling, everything's back to where it was. I want him alive. He just can't . . . because . . . be . . . cause . . .' And Natasha collapsed in tears.

'Yes! I knew it! Thank God,' said Sonya. 'He is going to live.' Sonya was just as excited as her friend, experiencing the same mixture of anguish and dread, as well as one or two personal reflections that she was keeping to herself. She sobbed as she kissed and comforted Natasha. '*I* want him alive!' she kept thinking. After shedding their tears and chatting together as they wiped them away, the two friends went over to Prince Andrey's door. Natasha opened it carefully and glanced in. Sonya stood next to her by the half-open door.

Prince Andrey was lying there, raised up on three pillows. His pale face looked peaceful, his eyes were closed, and they could see his steady breathing.

'Oh, Natasha!' Sonya cried suddenly, stifling a shriek as she grabbed her cousin by the arm, and backed away from the door.

'What is it? What's wrong?' asked Natasha.

'It's that thing . . . You know . . .' said Sonya, with a white face and quivering lips.

Natasha gently closed the door and walked over to the window with Sonya, not yet understanding what she was saying.

'You remember,' said Sonya, looking scared and serious. 'You remember. That time when I looked in the mirror instead of you . . . at Otradnoye. At Christmas time . . . Do you remember what I saw?'

'Yes, I do,' said Natasha, goggling. She had a vague recollection of Sonya telling her something about seeing Prince Andrey lying down.

'You remember!' Sonya went on. 'I saw him. I told you, all of you, you and Dunyasha. I saw him lying on a bed,' she said, emphasizing every detail by gesturing with a lifted finger, 'and he had his eyes shut, and he was covered with a pink quilt, and he had his hands folded,' said Sonya, with growing certainty, as she ran through the details they had just set eyes on, that she had *actually seen* them before. At the time she hadn't seen anything at all; she had blurted out the first thing that came into her head. But what she had invented then now seemed as real as any other actual memory. What she had said at the time – that he had looked round and smiled at her, and he was covered with something red – she remembered clearly now, and she was absolutely certain about what she had seen and said: he had been covered with a pink quilt – yes, it was pink – and his eyes had been closed.

'Yes, it was pink,' said Natasha, who also seemed to have an inkling that it had been a pink quilt, and this little detail was the oddest thing, the real mystery behind the prophetic vision.

'What does it mean?' said Natasha, thinking about it.

'I don't know! It's all so weird!' said Sonya, clutching at her head.

A few minutes later Prince Andrey rang his bell, and Natasha went in to see him while Sonya, in a rare state of excitement and emotion, stayed behind by the window, contemplating the weirdness of the way things had turned out.

That day there was an opportunity of sending letters to the army, and the countess was writing to her son.

'Sonya,' she said, looking up from her letter as her niece walked past. 'Sonya, you will write to Nikolay, won't you?' She spoke in a gentle voice with a tremor in it. Sonya could read her meaning in the weary eyes that peered out over her spectacles. It was a look that contained a strong plea, a dread of refusal, shame at having to beg and a capacity for implacable hatred if there was a refusal.

Sonya went to the countess, knelt by her and kissed her hand.

'Yes, Mamma, I will,' she said.

Sonya was feeling chastened, excited and deeply moved by all that had happened that day, especially the mysterious way in which her prophetic vision had come true. Now, knowing that the rapprochement between Natasha and Prince Andrey meant that Nikolay wouldn't be able to marry Princess Marya, she welcomed a resurgence of the self-sacrificing spirit she was used to, and liked to live by. She sat down with a gratifying sense of doing something truly magnanimous, and although her velvet-black eyes were blinded with tears so that she had to keep breaking off, she managed to write the poignant letter that was to have such a strong impact on Nikolay when he received it.

CHAPTER 9

In the guardroom where Pierre had been taken the officer and soldiers who had arrested him treated him with hostility but not without a certain respect. Their attitude was one of doubt about his identity – could he possibly be someone of importance? – mixed with hostility inspired by their recent struggle with him.

But when the guard changed next morning Pierre could sense that the new detail – officers and men – did not find him as interesting as he had been to the soldiers who had brought him in. And, indeed, the next day's guard, looking at this big, stout man in a peasant's coat, saw nothing of the beefy character who had fought so desperately with the pillaging soldier and the convoy, and had uttered those solemn words about saving a child; he was nothing more than prisoner No. 17 in a group of Russians who were being detained for some reason at the pleasure of the higher authorities. If there was anything odd about Pierre it was his gritty air of deep concentration, together with his excellent French, which greatly surprised his captors. Nevertheless, during the day Pierre was put in with all the other suspicious characters who had been arrested, because his room was wanted for an officer.

All the Russians detained with Pierre were the dregs of society. And without exception, once they knew he was a gentleman and a French-speaker to boot, they kept away from him. Pierre listened gloomily as they joked about him.

The following evening Pierre learnt that all the prisoners (probably including him) were to be tried for arson. On the third day Pierre was taken into a house along with the others to be confronted by a French general with white moustaches sitting there with two colonels, and some other Frenchmen with scarves on their sleeves. They put a series of questions to Pierre and the others with the correctness and scrupulous care that is used with all defendants and is supposed to eliminate human fallibility: they wanted to know who he was, where he had been, what he had been doing there, and so on.

These questions were like all questions posed in a courtroom: they ignored any essence of living truth – in fact, they made it impossible for any such essence ever to be discovered – and their sole purpose was to provide a conduit down which the court officials wanted to channel any answers from a defendant so as to bring him straight to the end of the inquiry – conviction. The moment he began to say anything not conducive to this end they would simply remove the conduit and let the flow go anywhere. Besides that, Pierre felt what all defendants feel in court, a sense of bafflement that left him wondering why he was being asked all these questions. He had a distinct feeling they were patronizing him, and just going through the motions of civility by providing a conduit that was nothing more than a subterfuge. He knew he was in their power; their power and that alone had brought him here, their power and that alone gave them the right to make him answer their questions, and the only purpose of the proceedings was to convict him. It followed, then, since they had all the power and a strong desire to convict him, there was no need for the subterfuge of questions and answers in a courtroom. It was perfectly obvious that the questioning was bound to lead to a guilty verdict. When asked what he had been doing when he was arrested Pierre assumed what tragic dignity he could and replied that he was taking a child he had rescued from the flames back to its parents. Why had he been fighting with a looter? Pierre said he had been defending a woman, the defence of a woman under attack being every man's duty, and so on . . . They stopped him; this was out of order. Why had he been in the courtyard of a burning house, where he had been seen by several witnesses? He said he had gone out for a walk to see what was happening in Moscow. They stopped him again. The question wasn't where was he going, but what was he doing so near to the fire. Who was he? They were repeating the first question put to him, which he had refused to answer. Again he replied that he couldn't give them an answer.

'Make a note of that. That's bad. Very bad,' came the stern comment from the general with the white whiskers and the purple-red face.

On the fourth day fire broke out in several places along the Zubovsky rampart.

Pierre was transferred with thirteen of the others to a coach-house belonging to a merchant's mansion near the Crimean Ford. As he walked down the streets Pierre could hardly breathe for the smoke that seemed to hang over the whole city. Fires were raging on all sides. Until then Pierre had not grasped the significance of the burning of Moscow, and he was horrified as he gazed at the fires.

Pierre spent four more days in the coach-house of the mansion near the Crimean Ford, and in the course of them he learnt by listening to a conversation between the French soldiers that any day now the prisoners detained here could expect to hear their sentences handed down by a marshal. Which marshal, Pierre couldn't find out from the soldiers. As far as the soldiers were concerned this marshal clearly represented power at its highest and most esoteric.

For Pierre these first days, ending on the 8th of September when the prisoners were arraigned and interrogated for the second time, were the hardest to bear.

CHAPTER 10

On the 8th of September into the prisoners' coach-house walked an officer of some considerable standing, if the deference shown to him by the guards was anything to go by. This man, probably a staff-officer, held out a piece of paper and read through a list of all the Russian names. He had Pierre down as 'the one who won't give his name'. Almost too lazy even to glance at the prisoners, he told the officer on guard to have them tidied up and decently dressed before bringing them before the marshal. An hour later a squad of soldiers turned up, and Pierre was taken out with another thirteen men and marched over to the Virgin's Field. It was a lovely day, sunny after rain, and the air was exceptionally clear. There was no pall of smoke as there had been on the day when Pierre had been taken out from the guard-room in the Zubovsky rampart; any smoke rose straight up in a column through the pure air. There were no flames anywhere, but columns of smoke rose up on all sides, and the whole of Moscow, as far as Pierre could tell, had burnt down in one huge conflagration. All over the place he could see empty spaces with nothing but stoves and pipes still standing, interspersed in a few places with the blackened walls of stone-built houses. Pierre stared at the ruins without recognizing parts of the town he knew well. Odd churches seemed to have survived here and there. The Kremlin had escaped; its towers and the belfry of Ivan the Great shone white in the distance. They could see the gleaming dome of the Novodevichy convent not far away, and the chiming of the bells was extraordinarily clear. The bells reminded Pierre that it was Sunday, and a special one: the Nativity of the Virgin. But there seemed to be no one there to celebrate. On every side there was nothing but charred ruins, and the only Russians they came across were a few ragged, scared-looking people, who scuttled away the moment they spotted the French.

Clearly the Russian nest had been ruined and destroyed, but Pierre felt instinctively that Russian order, thus annihilated, had been superseded in its nest by another, different kind of order, the rigorous order of the French. He could sense this in the serried ranks of marching soldiers stepping out boldly and breezily as they escorted him and the other prisoners. He could sense it in the sudden appearance of an important French official coming towards them, driven by a soldier in a carriage and pair. He could sense it in the merry strains of military music floating across the meadow from over on the left. And he had sensed it, too, with a sudden insight into what it was all about, when the list of names had been read out to them that morning by the newly arrived French officer. Pierre had been arrested by one set of soldiers, taken to one place and transferred to another along with dozens of different people. He could so easily have been forgotten or mixed up with other people, but no, his own answers under interrogation came back to him in the form of a new title: 'the one who won't give his name'. And under this title, which filled Pierre with dread, they were taking him somewhere, with absolute certainty on their faces that he and the other prisoners were the right ones, going to the right place. Pierre felt like a meaningless speck trapped in the wheels of some well-oiled machinery working away in a manner that he didn't understand.

He and the other prisoners were escorted across to the right-hand side of the Virgin's Field, not far from the convent, and taken up to a big white house with a huge garden. It was Prince Shcherbatov's house; Pierre had often been there in former days as a guest of its owner. Now, he gathered from what the soldiers said, it was occupied by a marshal, the Duke of Eckmühl.

They were brought to the entrance and taken in one by one. Pierre was the sixth to be led in. Through the glass gallery they went, through the ante-room and the hall, all of them familiar to Pierre, until they came to the long, low study, where an adjutant stood waiting by the door.

Davout was sitting at a desk at the far end of the room with his spectacles on his nose. Pierre walked over to him. Davout was too busy with a document in front of him to look up. So, without looking up, he asked in the gentlest of tones, 'Who are you?'

Pierre didn't respond; he couldn't have said a word. Davout was more than a French general to Pierre; to Pierre Davout was a man renowned for his cruelty. Looking into Davout's icy features – he was behaving like a martinet of a teacher with limited patience who was waiting for an answer – Pierre sensed that a second's delay could cost him his life, but he had no idea what to say. He couldn't bring himself to say what he had said at the first interrogation, but to reveal his identity and social standing might be humiliating and even dangerous.

Pierre was speechless. Before he had time to decide on a course of action, Davout looked up, pushed his spectacles up on his forehead, screwed up his eyes and stared closely at Pierre.

'I know this man,' he said, in an icy, even tone, clearly calculated to put the fear of death into Pierre. The chill that had been running down Pierre's spine now seemed to crush his head in a vice-like grip.

'You cannot know me, General, I have never seen you.'

'He's a Russian spy,' Davout interrupted, speaking to another general whom Pierre had not noticed. Davout turned away. With an unexpected tremor in his voice Pierre launched forth and was soon in full flow.

'No, monseigneur,' he said, suddenly remembering that Davout was a duke. 'You couldn't know me. I'm a militia officer, and I haven't been out of Moscow.'

'Your name?' Davout repeated.

'Bezukhov.'

'What proof is there that you're not lying?'

'Monseigneur!' cried Pierre more in supplication than annoyance.

Davout looked up again and stared closely at Pierre. For several seconds they looked at one another, and it was this look that saved Pierre. The business of staring at each other took them beyond the realm of warfare and courtrooms; they were two human beings and there was a bond between them. There was a single instant that involved an infinite sharing of experience in which they knew they were both children of humanity, and they were brothers.

When Davout had first glanced up from the document that had the lives and actions of men numbered off in columns, Pierre was nothing more than a chance occurrence, and Davout could have had him shot without the slightest qualm of conscience, but now he recognized him as a man. He thought for a moment.

'How will you prove the truth of what you say?' asked Davout icily.

Pierre thought of Ramballe, and gave his name, his regiment and the street and house where he was staying.

'You are not what you say,' Davout said again.

Pierre's voice shook and trembled as he struggled to find proof that his testimony was true.

But at that moment an adjutant came in and said something to Davout.

Davout beamed at the adjutant's news and began buttoning up his jacket. He seemed to have completely forgotten about Pierre. When the adjutant reminded him about the prisoner, he scowled, nodded in Pierre's direction, and told them to take him away. But where they were taking him Pierre couldn't tell: was it back to the shed or over to the place of execution that his companions had pointed to on their way past the Virgin's Field?

He looked round and saw that the adjutant was checking something.

'Yes, of course,' said Davout. But Pierre had no idea what the 'yes' meant.

Pierre would never remember where he went, how they got there or how long it took. In a state of total stupefaction and bemusement, taking nothing in, he made his legs move in step with the others until they all stopped, and he stopped. And all this time Pierre's head was obsessed with a single thought, a simple question: who had condemned him to death? Who was it?

It wasn't the men who had interrogated him at the first session; clearly, none of them had wanted to, or had the authority. It couldn't have been Davout, who had put such humanity into his look. Davout had been no more than a minute away from understanding that things had gone badly wrong, but that had been prevented by the arrival of the adjutant. The adjutant had obviously had no evil intent, though he could have stayed outside. Who was it, then, when all was said and done, who was punishing him, killing him, taking his life, Pierre's life, with all his memories, yearnings, hopes and ideas? Who was doing this? And Pierre felt he knew the answer: no one was.

It was the way of things. A pattern of circumstances.

It was some kind of system that was killing him, killing Pierre, taking his life, taking everything away, destroying him.

CHAPTER 11

From Prince Shcherbatov's house the prisoners were taken straight down to the Virgin's Field, past the convent on the left and into a kitchen garden where a post had been dug into the ground. A big pit had been excavated behind the post, and there was a pile of newly dug earth to one side. A large crowd of people stood round the pit and the post in a semi-circle. The crowd consisted of a small number of Russians and a large number of Napoleon's off-duty soldiers, Germans, Italians and Frenchmen in a variety of uniforms. To the right and left of the post stood rows of French soldiers wearing blue uniforms with red epaulettes, high boots and shakos. The prisoners were lined up in order as listed by name (Pierre was sixth) and led out towards the post. There was a sudden drum-roll on both sides; the sound of it made Pierre feel as if part of his soul had been torn from him. He lost all power of thought and imagination. All he could do was look and listen. And he had only one thought in mind: some dreadful deed had to be accomplished and he wanted it over and done with as soon as possible. Pierre looked round at his companions and studied them.

The two men at the end were convicts with shaven heads, one tall and thin, the other a dark, hairy muscular man with a flat nose. The third was a house serf, a man in his mid-forties with greying hair and a plump, well-fed figure. The fourth man was a big handsome peasant with a full, light-brown beard and black eyes. The fifth was a factory worker, a thin, sallow boy of eighteen or so in a loose coat.

Pierre heard the Frenchmen discussing whether to shoot them one by one or two at a time. 'Two at a time,' answered the senior officer, calm and cool. There was a stirring in the ranks, and everybody seemed to be hurrying things on, not like people making a quick job of something familiar to all, but like men hurrying through some nasty and incomprehensible duty that had to be done.

A French official wearing a scarf came up to the right-hand end of the line of prisoners, and read out the sentence in Russian and in French.

Then two pairs of French soldiers came up to the criminals, and acting on orders from an officer took hold of the two convicts standing at one end. The convicts walked over to the post, stopped in front of it, and, while they were waiting for bags to be brought, they looked round dumbly like wild animals at bay. One of them kept crossing himself, the other scratched his back and worked his lips into something like a smile. The soldiers made a quick job of blindfolding them, putting bags over their heads and tying them to the post.

A dozen marksmen with muskets marched steadily out of the ranks and came to a halt eight paces from the post. Pierre turned away to avoid seeing what was going to happen. There was an ear-splitting bang that seemed louder than any thunderclap, and Pierre looked round. There was a cloud of smoke, and some French soldiers with trembling hands and pallid faces were busy doing something at the side of the pit. The next two were brought forward. It was the same again: these two men looked at everybody in the same way, without a hope, saying nothing, but with eyes begging for protection. Clearly they could neither understand nor believe what was coming to them. It was beyond belief: they were the only ones who knew what life meant to them, so they couldn't understand, or believe, that it could be taken away.

Trying not to look, Pierre turned away again, but again his hearing was shattered by a fearsome bang, and with the sound he saw smoke, blood and the pallid, scared faces of the Frenchmen, busy doing something again at the post, getting in each other's way with their trembling hands. Pierre's breathing was laboured; he looked round as if to ask, 'What's it all about?' The same question was written in all the eyes that met Pierre's. On all the faces, Russian and French, the faces of officers and men, all of them without exception, he could read the same sense of shock, horror and conflict that he felt in his own heart. 'But who *is* doing it? They're all suffering like me! Who is it? Who?' flashed through Pierre's mind in a split-second.

'Marksmen of the Eighty-sixth, forward march!' someone called. The fifth prisoner standing next to Pierre was led forward – alone. Pierre didn't realize he had been spared; he and all the rest had been brought here just to witness the execution. With mounting horror and no sense of joy or relief he watched what was being done. The fifth prisoner was the factory worker in the loose coat. The moment they laid hands on him he recoiled in terror and grabbed at Pierre. (Pierre shuddered and tore himself away.) The factory hand couldn't walk. They held him under his armpits, and he yelled as they dragged him along. When they got him to the post he suddenly went quiet. He seemed to have realized something. Whether he realized it was no good screaming, or thought these people couldn't possibly kill him, he stood there at the post waiting to be blindfolded just as the others had done, and stared round with the glittering eyes of a wounded animal.

This time Pierre couldn't bring himself to look away and close his eyes. At this fifth murder curiosity and emotion were at fever pitch for him and the whole crowd. Like the others this fifth man seemed calm enough. He pulled his coat tighter, and rubbed one bare foot against the other.

As they were putting his blindfold on he shifted the knot himself because it was digging into the back of his head, then, when they backed him up against the bloodstained post, he half-fell into an awkward position, pulled himself together, squared his feet and settled back comfortably. Pierre never took his eyes off him and didn't miss the slightest movement he made.

There must have been a word of command followed by the sound of eight muskets being fired. But, however hard he tried to remember it afterwards, Pierre never heard the slightest sound of a shot. All he saw was the factory hand slumping down on the ropes for some reason, spurts of blood in two places and the ropes themselves giving way under the weight of the sagging body as the factory hand slid down into a sitting position, his head drooping gawkily and with one leg buckled up underneath him. Pierre ran over to the post. No one stopped him. Frightened men with pallid faces were busy doing something round the factory hand. One old Frenchman with a moustache couldn't stop his jaw trembling as he undid the ropes. The body flopped down. Scrabbling soldiers hurried to heave it past the post and start shoving it down into the pit.

Every last man of them clearly knew beyond doubt they were all criminals, and they had to move quickly to hide all traces of their crime.

Pierre took a glance down into the pit and saw the factory hand lying there with his knees tucked up close to his head, and one shoulder higher than the other. That shoulder was rising and falling rhythmically, and twitching as it did so. But earth was already raining down in shovelfuls all over the body. One soldier roared at Pierre in a voice of savage and feverish fury, ordering him back into line. But Pierre didn't take it in; he just stood there by the post, and no one drove him away.

Once the pit had been filled up an order rang out. Pierre was taken back to his place, and the French troops that were lined up in ranks on both sides of the post performed a half-turn and set off marching in step past the post. The twenty-four marksmen standing in the middle of the circle with their recently fired muskets doubled back into line as their companies marched past.

Pierre stared now with glazed eyes at these marksmen running out of the circle two by two. They had soon rejoined the ranks – all but one of them. A young soldier, his face deathly white, was still there facing the pit, standing on the spot he had fired the shot from; his shako was skewed back, and his musket rested on the ground. He reeled like a drunken man, staggering a few steps forward and a few steps back to keep himself from falling. A veteran NCO ran out, grabbed the young soldier by the shoulder and hauled him back into the ranks. The crowd of Frenchmen and Russians began to disperse. They all walked off in silence, with their heads bowed.

'Teach 'em a thing or two about fire-raising . . .' said one of the Frenchmen. Pierre glanced round at the speaker, and saw it was a soldier trying to console himself somehow for what had been done, and not managing to do so. He left his sentence unfinished, waved his hand and marched on.

CHAPTER 12

After the execution Pierre was separated from the other prisoners and left alone in a little church that had been ruined and befouled.

In the late afternoon a patrol sergeant came into the church with two soldiers and informed Pierre he had been pardoned and would now be going to a special barracks set aside for prisoners of war. Without taking in a word of this, Pierre got to his feet and walked off with the soldiers. He was escorted to the top end of the field where some sheds had been knocked together out of charred planks, beams and other bits of wood, and taken into one of them. It was dark inside, and he was suddenly surrounded by a diverse group of men, about twenty of them. He stared at them without the slightest idea who they were, why they were there, or what they wanted from him. He could hear words coming at him, but they seemed inconclusive and irrelevant; he had no idea what they meant. He gave some answers to the questions put to him, but with no clear idea of who was listening or how his answers would go down with them. He was looking at faces and bodies, but they all seemed equally meaningless.

From the moment Pierre had witnessed the grisly murder carried out by men who hadn't wanted to do it he had felt as if the mainspring of his soul that kept everything in him balanced and working and gave him a semblance of life had been torn out, and it all seemed to have collapsed into a pile of meaningless rubbish. Without Pierre fully realizing it, all his faith had been undermined, faith in the good order of the universe, in the souls of men, in his own soul, even in God. This was something Pierre had experienced before, but never with this kind of intensity. Whenever he had been assailed by doubts like these in the past they had arisen from a sense of his own guilt, and at the bottom of his heart Pierre had always known that salvation from this kind of despair and doubt lay in his own hands. But now he felt he wasn't to blame for the world collapsing before his eyes and leaving nothing but meaningless ruins behind. He felt powerless; there was no way back to his old faith in life.

There were men all round him in the darkness. He seemed to be an interesting distraction for them. They were telling him something and asking questions, then they took him away and he ended up in a corner of the shed next to some men who were talking on all sides, and laughing.

'Anyway, me old mates, that same prince *who-oo* . . .' (with great stress on this word) came a voice from across the shed.

Sitting in the straw with his back against the wall, still and silent, Pierre kept opening and closing his eyes. The moment he closed them he could see the terrible face of the factory hand, terrible because of its sheer simplicity, and the faces of the men forced into murder, and they were even more terrible because of the anguish written all over them. So he would open his eyes again and stare blankly into the surrounding darkness.

Next to him sat a stooping little man who made his presence felt by the stench of sweat that came wafting from him every time he made any movement. This man was fiddling around with his feet in the darkness, and, although Pierre couldn't see his face, he could sense him continually glancing his way. As his eyes grew more used to the dark Pierre realized that this man was unwrapping his footcloths, and the way he was doing it caught Pierre's imagination.

After unwinding the strings from one of his legs he tidied them away and then tackled the other leg, glancing up at Pierre. While one hand was still hanging up the first leg-string, the other hand was busy unwinding the string on the other leg. With this meticulous procedure, in a swift succession of neat and tidy circular movements, the man unrolled his footcloths and hung them up on pegs in the wall overhead, took out a knife, cut off a piece of something, snapped the knife shut, put it away at the head of his sleeping-place, eased himself into a more comfortable position and sat there with his arms clasped round his knees, staring straight at Pierre. Pierre was aware of something rather pleasant, something rounded and reassuring, in those neat, circular movements, the man's nicely tidied corner, even the very smell of him. He couldn't take his eyes off him.

'Seen a lot o' trouble in your time, sir, 'ave you?' said the little man suddenly. And there was so much concern and such simplicity in the sing-song voice that Pierre couldn't get an answer out through the trembling of his jaw and his rising tears. Barely a second later, leaving no time for Pierre to start looking embarrassed, the little man went on in the same pleasant tones:

'There you are, sweetie, don't you worry,' he said, in the gently soothing sing-song voice of an old Russian peasant woman. 'Don't you worry, old pal. Trouble's short, life's long! Oh yes, me dear. And we're gettin' on fine, thank God. No nastiness 'ere. They'm all men same as you an' me, bad and good among 'em,' he said. He was still speaking as he got nimbly to his knees and then to his feet, and walked off somewhere, coughing to clear his throat.

'So that's where you've got to, you little rogue!' Pierre heard the same soothing voice at the other end of the shed. ''Ere she be, little devil. She remembers me! Go on with you, that's enough!' Pushing down a dog that was jumping up at him, the soldier came back to his place and sat down. He was holding something wrapped up in a bit of rag.

''Ere you are, sir. You taste these,' he said in the same tone of respect he had used before, unwrapping his little bundle and handing Pierre a few baked potatoes. 'We had soup for dinner. But these potatoes is a real treat!'

Pierre had had nothing to eat all day, and the smell of the potatoes was out of this world. He thanked the soldier and set about them.

'No, not like that, sir,' said the soldier with a grin, and he took one of the potatoes from him. 'Try 'em like this.' He got out his clasp-knife again, cut the potato in the palm of his hand into two equal halves, sprinkled them with a pinch of salt from the rag, and gave them back to Pierre.

'Real treat they is,' he repeated. 'You try 'em like that.' Pierre would have sworn he had never eaten better in his life.

'No, I am all right,' said Pierre, 'but why did they have to shoot those poor men? ... That last boy couldn't have been more than twenty.'

The little man gave a soothing tut-tut. 'Oh yes, the sin of it ...' he added quickly, and went straight on talking as if he always had a mouthful of words at the ready so they could come flying out by pure chance.

'How d'you come to stay on in Moscow, sir?'

'I didn't think they'd get here quite so quickly. I stayed on by accident,' said Pierre.

'Just come in your house an' got you, did they, old darlin'?'

'No, I went out to see the fire, and they got me then. Tried me for arson.'

'No justice in a courtroom,' put in the little man.

'How long have you been here?' asked Pierre, munching his last potato.

'Me? Took me out of the 'orspital in Moscow last Sunday they did.'

'Are you a soldier then?'

'Yes, we're all from the Apsheron mob. Dyin' of fever I was. Never told us nothin'. Must've been twenty of us layin' there sick. Never 'ad a thought, we didn't, no idea 'ow things was.'

'You've had a bad time in here then?' asked Pierre.

'Not too good, me old darlin'. My name's Platon. Platon Karatayev,' he added, obviously wanting to smooth the path for Pierre to talk to him. 'The boys used to call me their little mate. Bound to get you down a bit, isn't it, matey? Moscow – mother of all cities. Sight like that's bound to get you down a bit. But you know what they says: "A worm be in the cabbage, but 'e dies before 'e's done,"' he added quickly.

'What was that? What did you say?' asked Pierre.

'You what?' said Karatayev. 'What I says is this: we're at large but God's in charge,' he said, quite sure he was repeating what he had just said. And he plunged on. ''Ave you got your own family estate then, sir? Your own 'ouse? My goodness, your cup was runnin' over! Little wife, too? Your old mum and dad still alive?' he asked and though Pierre couldn't see it in the dark, he felt sure the soldier's lips were squeezed up in a wincing little smile of good will as he asked these questions. Karatayev was quite distressed to learn that Pierre had no parents, and especially that he had never had a mother.

'Wives give advice, and their mothers are nice, but there's nobody like your own mother!' said he. 'And have you any little ones?' he continued. Pierre's negative response seemed to come as another disappointment, and he was quick to add, 'Oh well, you're a young man. Please God, you'll 'ave some. One day you will. The great thing is to get on with other people . . .'

'Doesn't make any difference now, does it?' Pierre couldn't help saying.

'Ah, you're a lovely man,' Platon countered. 'The beggar's bowl or the prison hole, you have to take what comes.' He settled down more comfortably, and cleared his throat, obviously ready to launch into a long story. 'Now take me, for instance, my dear friend. When I was still livin' at home,' he began, 'we 'ad a nice family place, lots of land, lovely 'ouse – we was well off, something to thank God for. Seven of us when we went out reapin' with our dad. Nice life. Good Christian peasants we was. Now what d'you think happened? . . .' and Platon Karatayev went into a rambling story about how he had gone into somebody else's copse to get wood, and been caught by the keeper, how he had been flogged and tried, and sent off to join the army. 'And do you know, me old darlin',' said he with a smile in his voice, 'we thought it was the end of the world, but it turned out for the best. My brother would've had to go if I hadn't got into trouble. And my younger brother, he had five little ones, see, and I only 'ad a wife to leave behind. We did 'ave a little girl, but God took her to him before I went in the army. Went home on leave, I did, and I'm tellin' you, they was livin' better than ever. Yard full of beasts, womenfolk at home, two brothers off earnin' good money. Only Mikhaylo, the youngest, still at home. Father says all his kids matters to him; bite any finger, it hurts just the same. And if they hadn't shaved Platon for a soldier that time, Mikhaylo would've had to go. Got us all together he did – would you believe it? – stood us right in front of the holy icons. "Mikhaylo," says he, "come you 'ere and bow down at his feet. You women, you bow down as well. And you grandchildren, you bow down. Understand?" says he. So there we 'ave it, me old dear. Fate picks you out. And 'ere we be, always passing judgement – that's not right, doesn't suit us. Our 'appiness, me dear, be like water in a drag-net. Swells out lovely when you pulls; take it out and it's empty. Yes, that's the way things be.' And Platon shifted position in the straw.

After a short pause he got up.

'Bet you could do with some shut-eye,' he said, and he began rapidly crossing himself and intoning, 'Lord Jesus Christ, holy Saint Nikola, Fraula and Laura![2] Lord Jesus Christ, holy Saint Nikola, Fraula and Laura! Lord Jesus Christ, have mercy and save us!' he concluded, bowing down to touch the ground with his forehead. Then he got to his feet, gave a sigh and sat down again on his straw. 'That's it, then. Lord, make me lie down like a stone, and rise like new bread!' he murmured before lying down and pulling his greatcoat over him.

'What were you reciting just then?' asked Pierre.

'Huh?' said Platon, already half asleep. 'Recitin'? I was just sayin' my prayers. Don't you say your prayers, then?'

'Yes, I do,' said Pierre. 'But what was all that about Fraula and Laura?'

'Oh, them,' Platon answered quickly. 'They be the 'orses' saints. Got to think o' the poor beasts, too,' he said. 'Look at this little 'ussy, she be all curled up nice an' warm, daughter of a bitch!' he said, reaching down to touch the dog at his feet. With that he turned over again and went straight to sleep.

Somewhere outside there were distant sounds of people calling out and crying, and the glow from a fire could be seen through cracks in the shed-walls, but inside it was all dark and quiet. Pierre couldn't get to sleep for some time. He lay where he was with his eyes open in the darkness, listening to Platon's steady snoring at his side, and he could feel his ruined world rising up again in his soul with a new kind of beauty, and its new foundations were unshakable.

CHAPTER 13

In the shed, where Pierre spent four weeks, his fellow prisoners consisted of twenty-three soldiers, three officers and two government officials.

Later on Pierre would remember them as nothing more than misty figures, but Platon Karatayev would always stay in his mind as a most vivid and precious memory, the epitome of kind-heartedness and all things rounded and Russian. When Pierre took a look at his neighbour next day at dawn his first impression of something rounded was fully confirmed. Everything about Platon's figure, in his French military coat with a piece of string round his waist, his soldier's cap and bark-fibre shoes, was rounded. He had a perfectly round head, and his back, chest, shoulders, even his arms, which he always held out as if he was just about to embrace something, had rounded lines; his open smile and big, soft, brown eyes were round as well.

Platon Karatayev must have been on the wrong side of fifty if the stories of his old campaigns were anything to go by. He didn't know his own age and had no means of working it out. But he had strong, white teeth that gleamed in two full semi-circles whenever he laughed, which was often, and they were all good and sound; there wasn't grey hair in his beard or on his head, and his whole figure gave an impression of suppleness combined with remarkable toughness and stamina.

His face, for all its web of rounded wrinkles, shone with the innocence of youth, and his voice had a pleasant lilt. But the great thing about his way of talking was its spontaneity and shrewdness. Clearly, he never thought over what he had said or worked out what he was going to say, and this gave his sharp utterances a ring of truth and a special stamp of irresistible persuasiveness.

In the first days of his imprisonment his physical strength and agility were such that he didn't seem to know the meaning of illness or fatigue. Every night as he lay down to sleep he said, 'Lord, make me lie down like a stone and rise like new bread,' and every morning when he got up he would stretch his shoulders always in the same way and say, 'Sleep deep, wake with a shake.' And that's how it worked out: he only had to lie down to fall asleep like a stone, and when he woke, one shake saw him instantly ready to tackle anything without a second's delay, like a child wanting to play with his toys straightaway. There was nothing he couldn't do, if not brilliantly, then at least tolerably well. He could bake, cook, sew, work wood and cobble boots. He was always busy with something, and it was invariably late evening before he allowed himself a little conversation, which he loved, and some singing. He sang not like a singer who knows he has an audience, but more like a bird: obviously, he just needed to sing, in the way that sometimes you just have to stretch your limbs or go for a walk, and the sound of his singing was always light, sweet, plangent, almost feminine, and his face as he sang was very serious.

Now that he was in prison, letting his beard grow, he seemed to have cast off all the unnatural military behaviour that had been forced upon him, and reverted instinctively to his old peasant ways.

'A soldier back home leaves his shirt hanging out,' he used to say. He was reluctant to talk about his life as a soldier, though he never complained, and he kept on repeating that in all his years of service he'd never once been hit. Whenever he got going on a story he inevitably drew on a series of distant memories, obviously very dear to him, taking him back to a former life that he referred to as 'Christian' (*Khristiansky*), though what he meant was 'a peasant's' (*krestyansky*). The proverbs with which his speech was so liberally salted were not the coarse, usually indecent, expressions common among soldiers, but popular sayings that seem almost meaningless on their own, though they suddenly take on the profound significance of real wisdom when heard in a proper context.

Often he would come out with something that flatly contradicted what he had said before, yet both sayings were true. He loved talking, and he spoke well, embellishing his speech with warm diminutives and proverbial sayings that Pierre thought he had invented himself. But the best thing about his way of speaking was that the simplest of incidents, some of them witnessed but not really noticed by Pierre, in Karatayev's version assumed a new depth of meaning and dignified stature. He liked listening to the folk tales that one soldier used to tell in the evenings, always the same ones, but he preferred stories from real life. He beamed with delight listening to stories of this kind, contributing words of his own and asking questions aimed at bringing out clearly the full meaning and stature of the deeds recounted. Karatayev enjoyed no attachments, no friendships, no love in any sense of these words that meant anything to Pierre, yet he loved and showed affection to every creature he came across in life, especially people, no particular people, just those who happened to be there before his eyes. He loved his dog, his comrades, the French, and he loved Pierre, his neighbour. But Pierre felt that for all the warmth and affection Karatayev showed him (an instinctive tribute to Pierre's spirituality), he wouldn't suffer a moment's sorrow if they were to part. And Pierre began to feel the same way towards Karatayev.

To all the other men Platon Karatayev was just an ordinary soldier; they called him their mate or Platosha, made fun of him all the time, and sent him on errands. But as far as Pierre was concerned, that first-night impression of Karatayev as simplicity and truth roundly epitomized for all time in some mysterious way stayed with him for ever.

Platon Karatayev never learnt anything by heart except his prayers. When he spoke, he would always launch forth without any idea of how he was going to finish what he was saying.

Sometimes Pierre was particularly impressed by what he had said and asked him to repeat it, but Platon could never remember what he had said even a minute before, just as he could never run through the words of his favourite song for Pierre's benefit. How did it go? 'My own dear mother . . .', 'my little birch-tree . . .', 'my sickening heart . . .' – a few words, but no meaning. It was beyond him. He simply couldn't understand the meaning of any words out of context. Every word and every action of his was the outward manifestation of the unfathomable process of ongoing activity that made up his life. But that life, as he saw it, had no meaning out of its own broader context. Its only meaning was as one small part of a greater whole that he was conscious of at all times. Words and actions flowed from him as smoothly, inevitably and spontaneously as fragrance from a flower. He couldn't see any value or meaning in an action or word with no context.

CHAPTER 14

As soon as she heard from Nikolay that her brother was in Yaroslavl with the Rostovs, Princess Marya defied all her aunt's best efforts to dissuade her by getting ready straightaway to go and see him, and rather than going alone she was to take her nephew along too. She didn't stop to ask whether it would be difficult or not difficult, possible or impossible; she didn't want to know. Her duty was not only to be at the side of her brother, who might be on his deathbed, but to do all she could to take his son to see him, and she was ready to go. If Prince Andrey had not been in touch, Princess Marya had her own explanation: either he was too weak to write, or he thought the long journey would be too difficult and dangerous for her and his son.

It took only a day or two for Princess Marya to make preparations for the journey. Her party would travel in the huge coach that had brought her to Voronezh, and they were also taking a covered trap and a baggage-wagon. She would be accompanied by Mademoiselle Bourienne, little Nikolay and his tutor, her old nurse, three maids, Tikhon, a young footman and a courier sent along by her aunt.

There could be no question of taking the direct route through Moscow, and the detour that Princess Marya would have to make, through Lipetsk, Ryazan, Vladimir, and Shuya, was a long way round; it would also be difficult because there would be no posting horses, and down in the region of Ryazan, where the French had been seen, it might even be dangerous.

Throughout this arduous journey Mademoiselle Bourienne, Dessalles and Princess Marya's servants were amazed at her display of vitality and strength. She was the last to go to bed and first up in the morning, and nothing could stop her. Thanks to her infectious vitality and energy they were getting near to Yaroslavl by the end of the second week.

The end of her stay in Voronezh had provided Princess Marya with the happiest days of her whole life. Her love for Rostov was no longer a source of torment or worry. That love had now filled her whole soul and become an inseparable part of her, and she had stopped struggling against it. Latterly Princess Marya had managed to persuade herself – though clearly not in so many words – that she was in love and loved in return. It was her last meeting with Nikolay that had finally convinced her, when he had come over to tell her that her brother was with the Rostovs. Nikolay did not venture so much as hint at the possibility of Prince Andrey's engagement to Natasha being renewed (if he were to recover), but Princess Marya could tell from his face that he was aware of this and was thinking about it. Nevertheless, his attitude to her – so considerate, tender and loving – certainly didn't change; indeed Princess Marya sometimes thought he seemed delighted at the new kinship between them because it gave him more freedom to express his loving friendship. Princess Marya knew she was in love for the first and last time in her life, she could sense she was loved in return, and this gave her a settled form of happiness.

But this happiness affected only one aspect of her inner life and had no effect on the intensity of her deep concern for her brother. The reverse was true: there was a sense in which her inner contentment made it possible for her to put everything into her feelings for her brother. These feelings were so intense as they set out from Voronezh that all the people travelling with her took one look at her careworn, despondent face and felt certain she would fall ill on the way. But it was the difficulties and setbacks of the journey itself, tackled with such determination by Princess Marya, that rescued her for the time being from her grief and gave her strength.

As always when you are out on the road, Princess Marya fixed her mind exclusively on the actual journey, and lost track of its purpose. But as they got near to Yaroslavl and she had a new vision of what was in store for her, not at some future date but that very evening, her anxiety knew no bounds.

A courier had been sent on ahead to find out where the Rostovs were staying in Yaroslavl and what sort of condition Prince Andrey was in, and when he met the huge travelling coach at the city gate, he was dismayed by the sight of the ashen face that looked out at him through the window.

'I've got it all, your Excellency. The Rostovs are staying in the square, at the Bronnikovs' house – he's a merchant. Not far away, just down there by the Volga,' said the courier.

Princess Marya stared at him with a scared and quizzical look, taking nothing in. Why didn't he answer the only question that mattered: How was her brother? Mademoiselle Bourienne put the question for her.

'How is the prince?' she asked.

'His Excellency is staying with them in the same house.'

'He must be alive, then,' the princess thought to herself, and she asked in a quiet voice, 'How is he?'

'The servants said there was no change.'

She didn't ask what 'no change' was supposed to mean. With a fleeting, barely perceptible glance at little seven-year-old Nikolay, who was sitting opposite, much enjoying the sight of a new town, she looked down, and didn't look up again until the great rumbling carriage stopped jolting and swaying and came to a standstill. The carriage steps came clattering down.

The carriage doors were opened. There was water on the left, a broad expanse of river; on the right, the entrance steps. There was a welcoming party that included the servants and a rosy-cheeked girl with a thick coil of black hair, who was looking at her with an unpleasant, rather forced smile on her face, or so it seemed to Princess Marya. (This was Sonya.) The princess ran up the steps, and the girl with the forced smile said, 'Here you are! Come in here!' and the princess found herself in the hall looking at an elderly woman with oriental features distorted with anguish, who was advancing rapidly to meet her. It was the countess. She put her arms round Princess Marya, and proceeded to kiss her.

'My dear child,' she said, 'I love you. I have known you for such a long time.' Princess Marya was thoroughly distraught, but she knew this was the countess, and she ought to say something. Without knowing how she did it, she managed to get out a few polite French phrases pitched in the same tone as those addressed to her, and then she asked, 'How is he?'

'The doctor says he's out of danger,' replied the countess, but even as she said it, she sighed and her eyes rolled upwards, negating her own words.

'Where is he? Please can I see him?' asked the princess.

'Yes, of course, Princess. Directly, my dear. Is this his son?' she said, turning to little Nikolay, who was on his way in with Dessalles. 'There's plenty of room for everybody. It's a nice big house. Oh, what a delightful boy!'

The countess conducted the princess into the drawing-room. Sonya spoke to Mademoiselle Bourienne. The countess petted the little boy. The old count came in to welcome the princess. He had changed enormously since Princess Marya had last seen him. Then he had been a bouncy, cheery, confident little old man; now he looked like some pathetic creature that had lost its way. As he talked to the princess he glanced round shiftily all the time, as if to check with other people that he was behaving himself properly. After the destruction of Moscow and the loss of his property, knocked out of his usual groove, he had clearly lost all sense of his own importance, and now felt he no longer had a place in life.

Despite all her anguish, her one desire to see her brother without further ado, and her sense of annoyance that at a time like this, when all she wanted was to go and see him, they were exchanging pleasantries and saying nice things about her nephew, the princess was taking everything in, and she could see that for the time being she had no alternative but to fall in with the new system she was now entering. She realized it was unavoidable, and this was hard to bear, but she didn't hold it against them.

'This is my niece,' said the count, introducing Sonya. 'You haven't met her, have you, Princess?'

Princess Marya turned towards her, doing her best to stifle a rising feeling of hostility at the sight of this girl, and kissed her.

But the strain of feeling that her mood was different from everybody else's was beginning to tell.

'Where is he?' she asked again, turning to face them all.

'He's downstairs. Natasha is with him,' answered Sonya, colouring up. 'We've sent someone to ask . . . Princess, you must be very tired.'

Tears of annoyance were stinging Princess Marya's eyes. She turned away and was just about to ask the countess again which way to go when she heard a noise at the door, the light, eager footsteps of someone who seemed to be tripping along quite cheerfully. She looked across and saw someone almost running into the room. It was Natasha, the same Natasha she had so heartily disliked when they had met such a long time ago in Moscow.

But Princess Marya took one look at Natasha's face and immediately recognized a comrade in adversity, and therefore a friend. She flew across, took her in her arms and burst into tears on her shoulder.

The moment Natasha, sitting at Prince Andrey's bedside, had heard of her arrival, she had tiptoed out of the room and run up to see Princess Marya. It was her tripping footsteps that had sounded so cheerful.

As she ran in, there was only one expression on her worried face, an expression of love, infinite love for him, for her, for anything the man she loved held dear, an expression of pity, compassion for others, and a deep desire to give herself up entirely to helping them. At that moment there was clearly not the slightest thought of self, of her relationship with him, in Natasha's heart.

With her refined sensitivity Princess Marya took this in with a single glance at Natasha's face, and wept with sweet sorrow on her shoulder.

'Come on, Marie, let's go and see him,' said Natasha, drawing her away into the next room.

Princess Marya looked up, wiped her eyes and turned to Natasha. She felt sure she would get to know everything from her and find out what was going on.

'What is . . .' she began to ask, only to stop short. She felt that no question and no answer could be put into words. Natasha's face and eyes would be sure to give her the clearest and deepest version of the truth.

Natasha glanced at her with a scared and doubtful look, wondering whether or not to tell all she knew. She seemed to sense that with those luminous eyes piercing her to the bottom of her heart, it was impossible not to tell the whole, whole truth as she saw it. Natasha's lip suddenly trembled, ugly creases came at the corners of her mouth, and she broke down in sobs, burying her face in her hands.

Princess Marya now knew.

But she went on hoping, and managed a few words, though she had little faith in them.

'But how is his wound? What sort of state is he in?'

'You . . . you'll see for yourself,' was all Natasha could say.

They sat for a while downstairs outside his room, to bring their tears under control and go in with calm faces.

'How has his illness progressed? When did it worsen? When did *that* happen?' Princess Marya asked.

Natasha told her that at first he had been in danger from a high temperature and a great deal of pain, but that that had passed away at Troitsa, and the doctor had only been worried about one possibility – gangrene. But even the risk of that had gone. When they had got to Yaroslavl the wound had begun to fester (by now Natasha knew all about festering wounds, and much more besides), and the doctor had said the festering might take its normal course. Fever had set in. The doctor had said that the fever itself wasn't too serious. 'But two days ago,' Natasha began, 'all of a sudden *this thing* came over him . . .' She struggled with her sobs. 'I don't know why, but you'll see what he's like.'

'Is he weaker? Has he lost weight? . . .' asked the princess.

'No, he hasn't. It's worse than that. You'll see. Oh, Marie, he's too good . . . he can't, he can't possibly live, because . . .'

CHAPTER 15

When Natasha opened the door with a practised hand for Princess Marya to go in first, the princess could feel the sobs rising in her throat. There was no way of preparing for the encounter or composing herself; she knew she wouldn't be able to see him without tears.

She understood what Natasha had meant when she had said, '*This thing* came over him two days ago.' She took it to mean that a sudden relaxation had come over him, and this process of relaxing and mellowing was a harbinger of death. As she approached the door her imagination conjured up a picture of Andrey as a little boy, when his face had been so soft and sweet and full of feeling. On the rare occasions she had seen that look in later life it had always affected her deeply. She knew he would say some soft, loving words to her just as her father had done on his deathbed, and it would be unbearable, and she would break down in sobs when she heard them. But sooner or later it had to be, and she went into the room. Her sobs seemed to rise higher and higher in her throat as her short-sighted eyes began to make out his figure and his features more and more clearly, and now at last she saw his face, and their eyes met.

He was lying on a couch, propped up with cushions, wearing a dressing-gown lined with squirrel-fur. He looked thin and pale. One thin hand of transparent whiteness held on to a handkerchief; with the other he was softly fingering his delicate moustache, which had grown quite long. His eyes sought out the newcomers as they came in.

The moment she saw his face and met his eyes Princess Marya immediately checked her stride, her tears dried up and her sobbing stopped. As she caught the expression on his face and the look in his eyes she felt suddenly timid and guilty.

'What have I got to feel guilty about?' she asked herself. The answer came from him in a hard, icy stare: 'Being alive and thinking about the living world, while I . . .'

Andrey's deep stare, inward- rather than outward-looking, contained something not far from hostility as he slowly scanned his sister and Natasha. He kissed his sister while they held hands, something they had always done.

'Hello, Marie. How did you get here?' he said, and his voice was as flat and otherworldly as the look in his eyes. If he had screamed in sheer despair, the scream would have been less ghastly than the sound of his voice.

'Have you brought Nikolay?' he said in the same slow, flat tone, obviously finding it difficult to remember where he was.

'How are you now?' said Princess Marya, surprising herself by what she was saying.

'You'll have to ask the doctor, my dear,' he said. Making a big effort to put on a show of affection, he managed to mouth a few more words (obviously without the slightest idea of what he was saying): 'Thank you for coming, my dear.'

Princess Marya squeezed his hand. He winced at her touch, though his reaction was barely noticeable. He was silent now, and she couldn't think of anything to say. She understood what had happened to him two days before. In his words, in his tone of voice, above all in his eyes – so cold, verging on the hostile – there was that sense of remoteness from all earthly things that seems so horrible to a living person. Clearly, he was having the greatest difficulty in understanding anything to do with the living world, yet it seemed that his inability to understand the living world was not due to any loss of comprehension, it was because he could now comprehend something different, something beyond the understanding of living people, something that was gradually absorbing his whole being.

'Funny how fate has brought us together again,' he said, breaking the silence and pointing to Natasha. 'She's looking after me.'

Princess Marya heard what he said, but she couldn't understand him. How could Prince Andrey, with all his warmth and sensitivity, talk like that in the presence of the girl he loved, and who loved him? If he had any thought of living he wouldn't have spoken in such a cold and offensive tone. If he didn't know he was dying, how could he have been so callous, talking like that while she was there? There was only one explanation: nothing mattered to him now, and the reason nothing mattered was that something new and much more important had been revealed to him.

The conversation was incoherent, lacking warmth, continually breaking down.

'Marie came round through Ryazan,' said Natasha.

Prince Andrey didn't notice she had called his sister Marie. And Natasha as she did so became aware of it for the first time.

'Did she?' he said.

'She had heard that Moscow has been burnt to the ground, every bit of it. It looks as though . . .'

Natasha stopped. Conversation was impossible. He was obviously straining to listen, but not managing to do so.

'Yes. Burnt down. That's what they say,' he said. 'Terrible pity,' and he stared straight ahead, his fingers playing distractedly with his moustache.

'So you met Count Nikolay, Marie?' said Prince Andrey all of a sudden, evidently trying to say something nice. 'He said in his letter how much he liked you,' he went on, speaking so frankly and easily; he was obviously incapable of understanding the complexity and deep significance his words would have for living people. 'If you ever found you liked him too, it might be a good idea . . . to get married,' he added, gabbling a little as if he was glad to hit on just the words he had been struggling to find. Princess Marya heard him speak, but his words didn't mean anything; they just showed how terribly remote he now was from anything to do with the living world.

'Don't talk about me,' she said calmly, with a glance across at Natasha. Natasha, could feel her eyes upon her, but she didn't look back. Another silence ensued.

'Andrey, would you . . .' Princess Marya began with a catch in her voice, 'would you like to see Nikolay? He never stops talking about you.'

For the first time Prince Andrey smiled the ghost of a smile, but Princess Marya, who knew his face so well, was horrified to realize it was not a smile of joy, not of tender affection for his son, it was a smile of quiet, gentle mockery as his sister made one last desperate attempt to bring him back to sensitivity.

'Yes, I would like to see little Nikolay. Is he well?'

When they brought the little boy in he was scared by the sight of his father, but he didn't cry, because nobody else was crying. Prince Andrey kissed him, but he obviously didn't know what to say.

When they had taken the child away Princess Marya went over to her brother once more, kissed him, finally lost all self-control, and burst into tears.

He stared at her.

'Are you sorry for Nikolay?' he asked.

Princess Marya nodded through her tears.

'Marie, you know it says in the Bib . . .' he began, but suddenly stopped.

'What were you saying?'

'Nothing. You can't cry in here,' he said, giving her the same icy look.

When Princess Marya had burst into tears Andrey knew she was weeping for little Nikolay, who was going to be left without a father. He made a huge effort to return to this life, and see things from their point of view.

'Yes, it must seem sad to them,' he thought. 'But it's really so straightforward! The fowls of the air sow not, neither do they reap, yet your heavenly Father feedeth them,' he said to himself, and he wanted to say it to his sister. But no, they would only take it their way. They wouldn't understand at all! 'What they can't understand is that all these feelings they make so much of – all these thoughts and feelings of ours that seem so important – they're of no consequence! We can't understand each other!' And he said no more.

Prince Andrey's little son was seven years old. He could barely read, and he knew nothing. He would go on to see a lot more of life, gaining in knowledge, curiosity and experience. But if he had had access then to all the faculties acquired in later life, he couldn't have had a truer, deeper understanding of the drama he had just seen enacted between his father, Princess Marya and Natasha. He took in the whole thing, and left the room without shedding a tear. Without saying a word he went up to Natasha, who had followed him out, and glanced timidly up at her with his lovely dreamy eyes. His pink top lip with the little arch in it was trembling as he leant his head against her and burst into tears.

From that day on he gave Dessalles a wide berth, and also avoided the countess, who wanted to smother him with kindness, and either sat somewhere on his own, or timidly sought out Princess Marya or Natasha, whom he now seemed to love even more than his aunt, and cuddled up to them in his quiet, shy little way.

When Princess Marya left her brother's side she understood everything that Natasha's face had been trying to tell her. She and Natasha said nothing more about the possibility of his life being saved. They took turns at his bedside, and Princess Marya abandoned her tears in favour of continual prayer, turning in spirit to the immortal, invisible presence that could now be so palpably experienced as it hovered over the dying man.

CHAPTER 16

Prince Andrey not only knew he was going to die, he could feel himself dying; he already felt half dead. He was experiencing a sense of remoteness from all earthly things, and a strangely joyful lightness of being. Neither impatient nor anxious, he lay there waiting for what was to come ... The ominous, eternal, remote and unknown presence he had been conscious of throughout the whole of his life was now closing in on him, and becoming – through the strange lightness of being that he was now experiencing – almost intelligible and tangible ...

In the past he had dreaded the end. Twice in his life he had experienced that ghastly, agonizing feeling, the fear of death, the end, but now he couldn't understand why he had been so afraid of it.

The first time he had had that feeling was when the shell was spinning like a top right in front of him, and he had looked round at the stubble and the bushes, and up at the sky, fully aware that he was staring death in the face. When he had come round after sustaining his wound it was as if he had been suddenly freed from the oppressive constraints of life, and he had felt love blossoming in his soul, a love that seemed to be eternal, free-ranging, invested with a life of its own, and from then on, far from fearing death, he had never even thought about it.

During the hours that followed, hours of solitude, constant pain and semi-delirium, the more he edged his way mentally towards this newly discovered principle of eternal love, the stronger his unconscious renunciation of earthly life became. Loving everything and everybody, always sacrificing oneself for the sake of love, meant loving no one person, and not living this earthly life. And the more he absorbed this principle of love, the easier he found it to renounce life, and the more effectively he destroyed the dreadful barrier that the absence of love sets up between life and death. During that first period, whenever he remembered he was going to die, he said to himself, 'All right, then. Couldn't be better!'

But after that night at Mytishchi, when in his semi-delirious state the one woman he had been longing for had appeared before him, and he had pressed her hand to his lips and wept sweet tears of joy, the love for one woman had crept back unseen into his heart, and restored him to life. He began thinking again; some of his thoughts were pleasant, others disturbing. He remembered the moment at the ambulance station when he had caught sight of Kuragin, but he couldn't find his way back to the feelings he had experienced then. He was longing to know whether Kuragin was still alive or not. But he was too scared to ask.

His illness had been taking its normal physical course, but then suddenly, two days before Princess Marya's arrival, what Natasha called 'this thing' had come over him. It was the last spiritual struggle between life and death, with death coming out on top. It was a sudden awareness that life, seen through his love for Natasha, was still precious, and it came with a final shock of defeat mixed with fear of the unknown.

It happened in the evening. As usual after dinner he was slightly feverish, though his thoughts were remarkably clear. Sonya was sitting at the table. He fell into a doze. He was swept by a sudden surge of happiness.

'Oh good, she's here!' he thought.

And sure enough, Natasha had tiptoed in unheard and was sitting there in Sonya's place.

Ever since she had started looking after him he had always had a strong sense of her physical presence. She was sitting sideways-on in a low chair, screening him from the light of the candle, and she was knitting a stocking. (She had learnt to knit after hearing Prince Andrey once say that the best people to care for the sick are old nannies knitting stockings, because knitting always has such a soothing effect on people.) Her slender fingers flashed and the speeding needles clicked. He could clearly see the sharp silhouette of her pensive, lowered head. She made a slight movement, and the ball rolled down off her knee. She gave a start, glanced round at him, bent down to pick up the ball in one careful, smooth and deliberate movement, screening the light with her other hand, and sat back as before.

He watched her without stirring, and he could see that after this movement she needed to draw a deep breath, but was determined not to do so, forcing herself to breathe evenly.

At the Troitsa monastery they had talked about the past, and he had said that if he lived he would always thank God for his wound, because that had brought them together again, though since then they had never talked about the future.

'Could it have happened, or not?' he was wondering now as he watched her and listened to the slight clicking of the steel needles. 'Can fate have brought us together so strangely only for me to die? . . . Can the truth about life have been revealed to me only to show I've been living a lie? I love her more than anything in the world! But what can I do if I do love her?' he said, and suddenly he gave an instinctive groan, a habit he had fallen into while suffering so much pain.

Hearing the sound, Natasha put her knitting down, leant closer, and suddenly saw that his eyes were gleaming. She tripped across and bent over him.

'You're not asleep, are you?'

'No. I've been watching you for ages. I felt you come in. You're the only one who can give me that kind of gentle peace . . . and such lovely light. I could cry with happiness!'

Natasha moved closer. Her face was radiant with bliss.

'Natasha, I love you too much! More than anything in the world!'

'What about me?' She turned away for a second. 'But why do you say too much?' she said.

'Too much? . . . Well, what do you think, what do you feel in your heart, in your heart of hearts? Am I going to live? What do you think?'

'I'm sure you are. Yes, I'm sure!' Natasha almost cried out, seizing both of his hands in a passionate gesture.

It was some time before he spoke.

'Wouldn't it be wonderful?' He took her hand, and kissed it.

Natasha felt happy and deeply moved, but then she came to her senses. This wouldn't do; he had to be kept quiet.

'But you haven't had enough sleep,' she said, suppressing her feeling of joy. 'Do try to get some sleep. Please.'

He squeezed her hand and let it go, and she moved back near to the candle, where she sat down again as before. Twice she glanced across at him; he looked back with shining eyes. She fixed on a certain amount of stocking to knit, and told herself not to look round until it was done.

And sure enough, it was not long before his eyes closed and he dozed off. But his sleep did not last. He woke up suddenly in a cold sweat, deeply alarmed.

As he had been going to sleep he had been thinking about what now obsessed him all the time – living and dying. Most of all, dying. He felt closer than ever to death.

'Love? What is love?' he thought.

'Love gets in the way of death. Love is life. Every single thing I understand, I understand only because I love. Everything is – everything exists – only because I love. Everything is bound up with love, and love alone. Love is God, and dying means me, a tiny particle of love, going back to its universal and eternal source.' These thoughts seemed comforting enough, but they were only thoughts. There was something missing. They seemed lop-sided, too personal, too rational; they should have been blindingly obvious. Besides, there was still something worrying him, something he couldn't get to grips with. He fell asleep.

In a dream he sees himself lying there in the same room he is actually lying in, but he hasn't been wounded, he is fit and well. Lots of people, all different kinds, people who don't matter and aren't worried about him, appear before him. He is talking to them, arguing about nothing at all. They seem to be getting ready to go on a journey. Prince Andrey is vaguely aware that none of this matters, there are other things of much greater importance for him to bother about, but he keeps on talking, impressing them with his casual, witty comments. They begin to slip away imperceptibly one by one, and all that is left is the question of closing the door. He rises to his feet and goes over to the door to get it locked and bolted. *Everything* now depends on whether or not he will get there in time to shut it. He is walking forward, hurrying, but his legs won't move, and he knows he is not going to get the door locked, though he strains agonizingly to do so. And he is filled with a ghastly feeling of terror. This terror is the fear of death: beyond the door there is *It*. But while he is flailing helplessly towards the door, that horrible *something* is already pushing from the other side, forcing the door open. Something inhuman – death – is pushing on the door, and he must hold it back. With one last effort he grabs at the door – it can't now be shut – to try and hold it back, but his efforts are feeble and clumsy. Under pressure from the ghastly thing outside, the door opens and shuts again.

More pushing from the other side. His last, inhuman struggles are fruitless. Both leaves of the door open without a sound. *It* comes in. *It* is *death*. And Prince Andrey has died.

But at the very moment of death Prince Andrey realized he was dreaming; at the moment of death itself he summoned all his strength and forced himself back to consciousness.

'Yes, that was death. I have died and woken up again. But that's what death is – a reawakening!' His soul was suddenly ablaze with light, and the veil that had hidden the unknown from him was half lifted for his spirit to see beyond. He had sensed the releasing of pent-up forces within him, and he felt the curious lightness of being that had not left him since.

When he woke up in a cold sweat and stirred on the couch Natasha went over and asked him what was wrong. He didn't answer, he couldn't understand what she was saying, and he gazed at her with a strange look in his eyes.

This was the change that had come over him two days before Princess Marya's arrival. From that day on, according to the doctor, the wasting fever took a turn for the worse, but Natasha ignored him; she could see the terrible signs emanating from Andrey's spirit, and their message was beyond doubt.

For Prince Andrey that day marked more than a reawakening from sleep; it was a reawakening from life. And in relation to his own life-span it seemed to take no longer than waking up does in relation to the span of a dream. It was a relatively slow reawakening, but there was nothing violent or terrible about it.

His last days and hours were spent in a simple, down-to-earth way. Princess Marya and Natasha, who never left his side, both felt that. They did not weep; they did not shudder. And towards the end they both felt they were not looking after him (he was no more, he had gone away), they were cherishing the most immediate memory of him – his body. Both of them felt emotions so strong they were unaffected by the horrible outward aspect of death, and they felt no need to work at their grief. They never wept, with him or without him, and when they were together they didn't even talk about him. They felt that no words could express what they now understood.

They could both see him slowly and gently slipping further and further down into another realm. They knew this had to be, and it was good. He received absolution and was given communion. Everybody came in to say goodbye. When his son was brought in to see him he pressed his lips to the boy's flesh and then turned away, not because he was in any pain or anguish (Princess Marya and Natasha could see this clearly), but simply because he thought he had done all that was necessary. When they told him to give the boy his blessing he did what was required of him and then looked round as if he was wondering whether there was anything else that needed to be done. When the body suffered its final spasms and gave up the ghost, Princess Marya and Natasha were there.

'It's all over, isn't it?' said Princess Marya, after the body had lain there, quite still, for some moments, going cold before their eyes. Natasha came up close, glanced down at the dead eyes, and closed them with a quick movement. She closed them without kissing them, hanging on to her closest memory of him.

'Where has he gone? Where is he now? . . .'

When the body lay washed and dressed in the coffin on the table, everybody came in to take leave of him, and everybody wept. Little Nikolay wept from agonizing, heart-breaking bewilderment. The countess and Sonya wept because they were sorry for Natasha, and because he had gone from them. The old count wept because he could see himself taking the same terrible step before much longer.

Natasha and Princess Marya now also gave way to tears, but not from personal sorrow. They wept with a melting sensation of reverence gripping their very souls as they contemplated the simple and solemn mystery of death that had been accomplished before their eyes.

PART II

The human intellect cannot grasp the full range of causes that lie behind any phenomenon. But the need to discover causes is deeply ingrained in the spirit of man. And so the human intellect ignores the infinite permutations and sheer complexity of all the circumstances surrounding a phenomenon, any one of which could be individually construed as the thing that caused it, latches on to the first and easiest approximation, and says, 'This is the cause!' When it comes to histori-cal events, where the actions of men are the object of study, the will of the gods used to serve as a primeval approximation to underlying cause, though this was eventually superseded by the will of a few men occupying the historical foreground – the heroes of history. But one glance below the surface of any historical event, one glance at the actions of the mass of humanity involved in it, is enough to show that the will of the historical hero, far from controlling the actions of the masses, is itself subject to continual outside control. You might think it doesn't matter very much whether historical events are interpreted one way or another. But between the man who says that the peoples of the west marched on the east because Napoleon willed them to do so, and the man who says this movement took place because it was bound to take place, there is the same yawning gap as there is between men who used to claim that the earth stood still while the planets revolved around it, and other men who said they didn't know what keeps the earth in place, but they did know there were laws controlling its motion and the motion of the other planets. There are no single causes behind historical events, and there never can be, other than the one grand cause behind all causes. But there are laws controlling events, some of them beyond our ken, some of them within our groping grasp. The discovery of these laws becomes possible only when we stop looking for causes in the will of individual men, just as the discovery of the laws of planetary motion became possible only when men stopped believing in the earth as a fixed entity.

After the battle of Borodino, the enemy occupation of Moscow and the burning of the city, the most important episode of the war of 1812, according to the historians, was the movement of the Russian army across from the Ryazan to the Kaluga road and on to the camp at Tarutino, the so-called flanking manœuvre beyond the river Krasnaya Pakhra. Historians credit a number of different people with this stroke of genius, and argument continues about its rightful attribution. Foreign historians, even the French, acknowledge the genius of the Russian military command when they discuss this flanking manœuvre. But why military commentators, and all subsequent writers, should see this *flanking* manœuvre as the profoundly significant brain-child of some individual, something that saved Russia and destroyed Napoleon, is very difficult to understand. For one thing, it is difficult to see any profound wisdom or genius in this manœuvre: it requires little mental effort to work out that the best position for an army not under attack is where its supplies are most readily available. And anybody, down to the stupidest thirteen-year-old boy, could have easily guessed that the most advantageous position for the army in 1812, after the retreat from Moscow, would be down the Kaluga road. So, in the first place, it is impossible to understand the thought processes that have led historians to descry deep wisdom in this ploy. Secondly, it is even more difficult to understand why historians treat this development as the saving of Russia and the destruction of the French; if the circumstances before, during and after this flanking manœuvre had been slightly different it could well have led to the destruction of the Russian army and salvation for the French. Even if the position of the Russian army did begin to improve from the time of that manœuvre, it doesn't follow that the improvement was necessarily caused by it.

The flanking manœuvre might well have brought no advantage; worse than that, it could easily have led to the destruction of the Russian army if other circumstances had prevailed. What would have happened if Moscow had not burnt down? If Murat had not lost sight of the Russians? If Napoleon had decided to do something? If the Russians had followed the advice of Bennigsen and Barclay and gone into battle at the Krasnaya Pakhra? What would have happened if the French had attacked the Russians when they were marching on the other side of the Pakhra river? What would have happened later on if Napoleon had got to Tarutino and attacked the Russians with even a tenth of the energy he had put into the attack at Smolensk? What would have happened if the French had marched on Petersburg? ... If any of these developments had occurred, the flanking manœuvre could have led to disaster rather than salvation.

The third point is the most difficult to understand: students of history seem determined to ignore the possibility that this march cannot be attributed to any one individual; no one ever predicted it, and, like the retreat to Fili, this ploy was, in fact, never fully worked out in advance by anybody. It came about step by step, incident by incident, moment by moment, emerging from an infinitely varied set of unimaginably different circumstances, and was perceived in its entirety only when it had become a reality, a past event.

At the Fili council the idea uppermost in the minds of the Russian high command was the blindingly obvious course of retreat straight down the road to Nizhny Novgorod. Evidence of this can be seen in the council's majority vote in favour of this route, and especially the commander-in-chief's famous conversation afterwards with Lanskoy, the head of supplies. Lanskoy reported to the commander-in-chief that the main army stores were stockpiled along the river Oka in the provinces of Tula and Kazan, and if they retreated down the Nizhny road the army would be cut off from its supplies by the broad river, which couldn't be crossed in the early winter. This was the first signal of the need to abandon the route that had at first seemed the most natural one to take – retreat down the Nizhny road. The army was steered further south, down the Ryazan road, closer to its supplies. As time went by, the inactivity of the French, who actually lost sight of the Russian army, together with the worrying need to defend the ordnance factory at Tula, and especially the advantage of going in the direction of their own supplies, pushed the army even further south, down the Tula road. As they made their way in one desperate lunge over to the Tula road beyond the Pakhra, the generals of the Russian army were intending to call a halt at Podolsk. They never gave a thought to stopping at Tarutino. But our army was forced even further south by countless other developments, including the re-emergence of the French troops (who really had lost them), new battle plans and, most importantly, the availability of generous supplies in Kaluga, and they switched again from the Tula to the Kaluga road and marched on to Tarutino, right in the middle of their own supply lines. Just as there is no precise answer to the question, 'When was Moscow abandoned?' it is impossible to say exactly when the decision was taken to move the army to Tarutino, or who took it. It was only when the army had got there, impelled by a boundless variety of infinitesimally small forces, that people began to convince themselves this was what they had wanted and predicted all along.

CHAPTER 2

The famous flanking manœuvre comes down to this: the Russian army had been retracing its steps in full retreat, and when the French stopped attacking, they deviated from the straight line they were following, saw they were not being pursued and moved off naturally in a new direction, attracted that way by the availability of plentiful supplies.

If we imagine, not generals of genius in charge of the Russian army, but a leaderless army acting alone, even that kind of army would have had no alternative but to head back towards Moscow, coming round in a big arc through the richest countryside to an area where maximum supplies were available.

So natural was this switching across from the Nizhny road to the Ryazan, Tula and Kaluga roads that this was the very direction taken by looting stragglers from the Russian army, and the very direction insisted on by the authorities in Petersburg for Kutuzov's next move. At Tarutino Kutuzov received what amounted to a reprimand from the Tsar for moving the army to the Ryazan road, and he was ordered into the very position across from Kaluga which he had taken up by the time the Tsar's letter reached him.

The Russian army reacted like a billiard ball: recoiling in the direction imparted by the shock of the whole campaign and particularly the battle of Borodino, the army absorbed the energy of the collision, encountered no further shocks and simply rolled away into the most natural position.

Kutuzov's merit had nothing to do with military genius, or what they call strategic manœuvring; his merit was to have been the only person to grasp the full significance of what had happened. He was the only one who grasped the significance of the French army's lack of activity; he was the only one who kept on insisting they had won the battle of Borodino; he – the commander-in-chief who might have been expected to be thirsting for battle – was the only one who did everything in his power to restrain the Russian army from rushing into futile encounters.

The wild beast wounded at Borodino lay around where the fleeing huntsman had left him, but whether it was alive, and whether it still had any strength and was lying low, the huntsman didn't know.

Suddenly a moan came from the creature. The moan from the wounded beast (the French army) that gave away the secret of its hopeless plight was the decision to send Lauriston to Kutuzov's camp with overtures for peace.

Napoleon, with his certainty that the right thing to say was not the right thing to say but the first thing that came into his head, wrote to Kutuzov the first words that came into his head, and these happened not to make any sense. They went as follows:

Monsieur le Prince Kutuzov [he wrote],
I am sending one of my aides to discuss with you various topics of interest. I beg your Highness to have faith in what he says, *especially when he expresses the sentiments of esteem and particular consideration that I have long entertained for your person.* This letter having no other object, I pray God, Monsieur le Prince Kutuzov, to maintain you in His holy and powerful keeping.

(Signed) NAPOLEON.

Moscow, 3rd October 1812.

Kutuzov replied as follows:

I should be cursed by posterity if I were regarded as the initiator of any kind of settlement. *Such is the present spirit of my nation.*

And he carried on doing everything in his power to hold the Russian army back from any attack.

A month of French army looting in Moscow, together with Russian army quietude at Tarutino, had brought about a change in the relative strengths of the two armies, a change in morale and sheer numbers, all of which told in favour of the Russians. Although the position of the French army and its numerical strength were unknown to the Russians, as soon as this change came about the inevitability of an eventual attack soon made itself felt in all manner of ways. These were: Lauriston's mission; the availability of generous supplies at Tarutino; persistent reports of inactivity and poor discipline in the French army; new recruitment bringing our regiments up to strength; the fine weather; the long spell of rest enjoyed by the Russian soldiers, and the usual eagerness of well-rested troops to finish the job they were there to do; curiosity about what was happening in the French army, which had been out of sight for so long; the sheer audacity shown by the Russian outposts nipping in and out among the French encamped at Tarutino; stories about easy victories over the French enjoyed by peasants and guerrilla groups, and the envy that this caused; a desire for revenge that lay in every heart while ever the French remained in Moscow; and, what mattered most of all, a vague awareness rising in every soldier's heart that there had been a shift in the relative strength of the armies, and the advantage now lay with us. A substantial change of this nature really had come about, and advance was now inevitable. And straightaway, as surely as a clock begins to chime and strike when the minute hand has completed a full circle, this change was reflected among the top brass in increased activity, the whirring of wheels within wheels.

CHAPTER 3

The Russian army was commanded by Kutuzov and his staff, and also by the Tsar from Petersburg. Before the news of the abandonment of Moscow reached Petersburg, a detailed plan for the whole campaign had been drawn up and sent to Kutuzov for him to follow. Even though this plan had been put together on the assumption that Moscow was still in our hands, it was endorsed by the staff and accepted as the basis for action. Kutuzov's response was limited to a comment that movements planned at a distance were always difficult to put into practice. In order to resolve any difficulties as and when they arose, further instructions were issued, and new staff were sent down to Kutuzov with the sole duty of keeping an eye on his movements and reporting back.

Besides this, the high command of the Russian army was completely reshuffled. The places of Bagration, who had been killed, and Barclay, who had stalked off in high dudgeon, had to be filled. Much serious thought went into consideration of the best thing to do: whether A should take over from B, and B from D, or whether it ought to be the other way round, with D taking over from A, and so on, as if this had an impact on anything at all beyond the self-esteem of A and B.

Given Kutuzov's hostility towards his chief of staff, Bennigsen, the presence of the Tsar's confidential advisers and all these various new appointments, party in-fighting at headquarters was even more complicated than usual. A was trying to undermine B's position, D was getting at C, and so on, in all conceivable combinations and permutations. And everybody was undermining everybody else mainly over the course of the war, which all these men thought they were in control of, though in practice the war ignored them and went its own inevitable way. In other words, it never corresponded with what they were thinking; it was the essential outcome of interacting forces among the masses. And all these machinations, with everybody at daggers drawn and cross-purposes, were accepted at high command as a true reflection of developments that were inevitable.

Prince Kutuzov! [wrote the Tsar on the 2nd of October in a letter received by Kutuzov after the battle of Tarutino]

Ever since the 2nd of September Moscow has been in enemy hands. Your last reports were dated the 20th, and in all this time not only has no attempt been made to act against the enemy and liberate our ancient capital, according to your last reports you have actually retreated even further. Serpukhov has now fallen to an enemy detachment, and Tula, with its famous ordnance factory that means so much to the army, is in danger. From reports received from General Wintzengerode I note that an enemy force of ten thousand men is marching up the Petersburg road. Another one, thousands strong, is closing in on Dmitrov. A third has advanced along the Vladimir road. A fourth force of some considerable strength is stationed between Ruza and Mozhaysk. Napoleon himself was in Moscow on the 25th. In view of this intelligence, with the enemy's forces split up into sections, and Napoleon himself with his guard in Moscow, is it possible that the enemy forces confronting you are too strong for you to go on the offensive? The opposite assumption seems far more probable: you are being harassed by detachments (a corps at the most) greatly inferior to the army entrusted to your command. It would seem possible for you to have profited from these circumstances and attacked a weaker enemy and destroyed him, or at least forced him into retreat and kept in our hands decent parts of the provinces now under enemy occupation, thus diverting danger away from Tula and the other towns of the interior. You will be responsible if the enemy manages to send a considerable force up to Petersburg and threaten this capital, where it has not been possible to maintain troops in any great numbers, since the army entrusted to your command, acting with energy and determination, provides you with ample means to avert this new calamity. Remember you have still to answer to your humiliated country for the loss of Moscow. You have had experience of my readiness to reward you. That readiness will remain undiminished within me, but Russia and I have the right to expect from you all the energy, determination and success betokened by your intellect, your talent as a military man, and the bravery of the troops operating under your leadership.

This letter demonstrates that a sense of the changing relative strength of the armies was now making itself felt as far away as Petersburg, but while it was in transit Kutuzov had been unable to hold his army back, and a battle had already been fought.

On the 2nd of October, a Cossack by the name of Shapovalov out on a scouting mission shot one hare and wounded another. Shapovalov pursued the wounded animal deep into the forest, and there he stumbled across the left flank of Murat's army, encamped and unprotected. He laughingly told his mates how he had nearly walked straight into the hands of the French. An ensign overheard the story and told his commanding officer.

The Cossack was sent for and interrogated. His officers wanted to seize the opportunity and get some horses from the French, but one of them had contacts with the army high command, and he mentioned the incident to a staff general. In recent days relations on the staff had been strained almost to breaking point. Only a few days before this Yermolov had gone to Bennigsen and implored him to use all his influence with the commander-in-chief to go on the offensive.

'If I didn't know you I would imagine you didn't want what you are asking for,' replied Bennigsen. 'I have only to recommend one line of approach for his Serene Highness to be sure to do the opposite.'

The news brought in by the Cossacks, soon confirmed by mounted scouts, was proof enough: the time was ripe. The cord slipped, the wheels whirred and the chiming started. For all his supposed authority, intellect, experience and knowledge of people Kutuzov looked at all the indicators – the note from Bennigsen, who was reporting personally to the Tsar, the unanimity of opinion among the generals, his own assessment of what the Tsar wanted to happen and the intelligence brought in by the Cossacks – and he could no longer hold back the inexorable momentum. By issuing orders for something he considered both useless and pernicious he was giving his blessing to what had now become a *fait accompli*.

CHAPTER 4

Bennigsen's note stating the need to go on the offensive, and the report from the Cossacks that the enemy's left flank was unprotected, were merely the latest indicators that the signal to attack could be delayed no longer, and the attack was scheduled for the 5th of October.

On the morning of the 4th Kutuzov signed the documents of disposition. Toll read them to Yermolov, and invited him to see to the detailed arrangements.

'Very good, very good, but not just now. I haven't time,' said Yermolov, and walked out of the hut. The overall disposition of the troops as drawn up by Toll was a splendid one. Everything was neatly written out, as it had been at Austerlitz, but this time not in German. 'Column Number One marches here, then there. Column Number Two marches there, then here . . .' And so on.

On paper every one of these columns arrived in position dead on time, and they destroyed the enemy. As always on these occasions everything had been meticulously thought through, but as always on these occasions not a single column arrived anywhere on time. When enough copies of the disposition were ready, an officer was summoned and sent to Yermolov to hand them over for implementation. A young officer of the horse guards, one of Kutuzov's personal staff, set off for Yermolov's quarters, thrilled to be carrying out such a vital commission.

'He's not in,' Yermolov's servant told him. The horse guards officer set off for a general's quarters where Yermolov was often to be found.

'No, he's not here. Neither is the general,' he was told.

The officer remounted and rode off to another general's.

'No, he's gone out.'

'I hope they don't blame me for slowing things up! It's infuriating!' thought the officer.

He rode all over the camp. For every man who claimed to have just seen Yermolov riding off with some other generals there was another who said he must be back home by now. The officer stayed out searching until six o'clock in the evening, and never stopped to eat. Yermolov was nowhere to be found, and nobody knew where he was. The officer had a quick meal with a comrade before setting off back to the vanguard to report to Miloradovich. Miloradovich was out too, but here at least they did tell him the general had gone to a ball at General Kikin's and Yermolov was probably there too.

'Well, where is it?'

'At Yechkino, over yonder,' said an officer of the Cossacks, pointing towards a country house in the far distance.

'What, right over there! Outside our lines?'

'Two regiments of our boys have been sent over to the outposts. There's a right party going on out there now, I'll tell you! Two bands, three lots of singers.'

The officer rode out through our lines and on to Yechkino. Some way off he could hear the happy sounds of soldiers dancing and singing merrily together.

'In the country . . . in the countree . . .' went the song, to a lot of whistling and the sound of a balalaika, swamped now and again by a great roar of voices. The officer's own spirits rose when he heard these sounds, but he was still worried about being blamed for taking so long to hand over the vital message that had been entrusted to him. It was getting on for nine o'clock. He dismounted and walked up to the entrance of a big, completely undamaged manor house situated half-way between the French and the Russian lines. Footmen were trotting in and out of the vestibule and buffet bearing wine and food. The singers stood by the windows. The officer was taken across to a door, and there before him all of a sudden were all the top generals in the army, including the big, imposing figure of Yermolov. All the generals were standing round in a half-circle with their coats unbuttoned, pictures of merriment, red in the face and laughing their heads off. There in the middle of the room a handsome general, red-faced and not very tall, was dancing a trepak with much energy and not a little style.

'Ha, ha, ha! Good for you, Nikolay Ivanovich! Ah, ha, ha!'

The officer felt doubly guilty for bursting in on them at a moment like that with an important message, and he would have waited, but one of the generals spotted him, heard why he had come and told Yermolov. The latter came across to the officer with a scowl on his face, listened to his story, and took the documents from him without a word.

'Do you reckon he just happened to be out?' said a comrade of the horse guards officer, a staff man himself, later that evening, referring to Yermolov. 'Not on your life! That was deliberate. He was getting at Konovnitsyn. You watch the fur fly tomorrow!'

CHAPTER 5

The next morning Kutuzov, decrepit old man that he was, rose early, said his prayers, got dressed and, with a sinking feeling that he had to go out and take command of a battle he didn't approve of, he got into his carriage and drove out from Letashovko, a village two or three miles from Tarutino, to the place where the attacking columns were supposed to have been drawn up. Kutuzov trundled along, nodding off, waking up again, and cocking an ear. Wasn't that the sound of shots over on the right? Could this be the start of the action? But no, everything was still quiet. A damp and overcast autumn day was just dawning. As he got near to Tarutino Kutuzov spotted some cavalry-men leading their horses to water down the road he was driving along. Kutuzov had a good look at them, then he stopped his carriage and asked what regiment they came from. They came from a column which ought to have been a long way ahead, setting up an ambush.

'Must be a mistake,' thought the old commander-in-chief. But as he drove on, Kutuzov saw infantry regiments with their arms stacked, and the soldiers standing around in their underclothes, busy cooking porridge and fetching wood. He sent for their commanding officer. The officer contended that no order to advance had been received.

'I don't see . . .' Kutuzov began, but he checked himself at once, and sent for the senior officer. He got out of his carriage, hung his head and paced up and down in silence, breathing heavily. He had sent for Eykhen, an officer on the General Staff, and when he arrived Kutuzov turned purple with rage, not because this officer was to blame for the mistake, but because he was an object worthy of his fury. The old man staggered and spluttered as he fell into the kind of rage that would some-times have him rolling about on the ground in a frenzy, and he fell upon Eykhen, shaking his fists at him, yelling and shouting abuse in the lan-guage of the gutter. Another officer, Captain Brozin, also quite blame-less, happened to turn up, and he suffered the same fate.

'Here's another filthy swine! I'll shoot the lot of you! Vermin!' he shouted hoarsely, waving his arms and reeling about. His pain was actually physical. There he was, his Serene Highness, the commander-in-chief, constantly assured that no one in Russia had ever had his kind of power, put in a position like this – reduced to a laughing-stock throughout the whole army! 'All that worry, all my prayers for today, a night without sleep, thinking things over. Why do I bother?' he thought to himself. 'When I was a young officer wet behind the ears nobody would have dared make a fool of me like this . . . And now look!' He was actually suffering physical pain, as if he had been subjected to corporal punishment, and the only way for him to express it was in fulminating cries of agonized rage. But soon his strength ebbed away. He took a look round, conscious that he had rather overdone the bad language, got into his carriage and drove back in silence.

His fury was spent, and it did not return. Kutuzov blinked feebly as he listened to the excuses and explanations (Yermolov kept out of sight till next day), and the assurances from Bennigsen, Konovnitsyn and Toll that the movement that had miscarried would take place the following day. Once again all Kutuzov could do was give his consent.

CHAPTER 6

Next day the massed troops were in position by evening, and they marched off during the night. It was an autumn night with a purple tinge to the black clouds, but there was no rain. The ground was damp without being muddy, and the troops made no noise as they advanced, apart from the odd clank of artillery. No talking above a whisper was allowed, no smoking of pipes or striking of lights; they had to keep the horses from neighing. Secrecy added to the fun of it all. The men marched on in high spirits. Several columns halted, stacked their guns and lay down on the chilly ground, assuming they had got to where they should be. Other columns (most of them) marched all night and got to places where they clearly shouldn't have been.

Count Orlov-Denisov with his Cossacks (the least important detachment of them all) was the only one that fetched up in the right place at the right time. They halted at the edge of a forest, on a path that led from the village of Stromilova to Dmitrovsk.

Count Orlov nodded off, but they woke him before dawn. A deserter from the French camp was brought to see him. It was a Polish NCO from Poniatowski's corps. He explained in Polish that he had deserted because he had felt humiliated in their service; he should have been commissioned long ago, he was braver than anybody else, so he had come over to them and he wanted to get his own back. He said Murat was camping for the night less than a mile away, and if they would give him a hundred men he would go and take him alive. Count Orlov-Denisov consulted his fellow officers. The offer was too tempting to refuse. They were all eager to go; they all said yes, we must have a shot at it. After much argument and further consultation it was decided that Major-General Grekov would take two regiments of Cossacks and go with the Polish deserter.

'Don't you forget,' said Count Orlov-Denisov to the Polish deserter, as he sent him on his way. 'If you've been lying, I'll have you hanged like a dog, but if it's true there's a hundred gold pieces in it for you.'

The deserter said nothing as he got on his horse with grim determination and rode off with a hurriedly mustered group of Grekov's men. They disappeared into the forest. Count Orlov watched them go, shivering from the chill of the early dawn and greatly excited by the scheme he had launched on his own initiative. He came back out of the wood and peered across at the enemy camp, which was just visible in the tricky first light of dawn amid the dying camp-fires. There was a stretch of open rising ground to Count Orlov-Denisov's right, and that's where our columns ought to have been. He looked in that direction, but even though you could have seen them miles away, there was no sign of these columns. Meanwhile Count Orlov-Denisov thought he could see things beginning to stir over in the French camp, and this was confirmed by his sharp-eyed adjutant.

'It's too late, isn't it?' said Count Orlov, staring across at the camp. And suddenly – as so often happens when a man we trust is gone from our sight – the picture became perfectly clear: that deserter had been stringing them along, lying through his teeth, he would ruin the whole attack by taking out two regiments, and God alone knew where he was leading them! How could you hope to capture the commander-in-chief in amongst masses of his own troops?

'Swine. He was lying,' said the count.

'We could call them back,' said one member of his suite, full of the same misgivings as he stared across at the camp.

'What? . . . Well, what do you think? Let them go on? Or bring them back?'

'Is that your order – bring them back?'

'Yes, yes, bring them back!' Count Orlov said, suddenly decisive, glancing at his watch. 'We'll be too late. It's light now.'

An aide galloped off into the wood after Grekov. When Grekov came back, Count Orlov-Denisov, roused to a state of high excitement by his decision to abandon the initiative, and from waiting and waiting for infantry columns that never turned up, and also by the enemy's close proximity (which was affecting every man in his detachment), decided to attack.

The command came out in a whisper.

'To horse!'

The men fell in, crossing themselves . . .

'Go! And God go with you!'

A great 'Hurrah!' rang through the woods, and platoon after platoon of Cossacks, trailing their lances, soared merrily across the stream as if they were being poured out of a sack, and set off for the enemy camp.

One desperate, terrified yell from the first French soldier to spot the coming Cossacks, and every man jack of them, half-dressed and half-asleep, took to his heels, abandoning cannons, muskets and horses.

If only the Cossacks had ignored the things behind them and around them, and gone after the French, they would have captured Murat and everything that went with him. That's what their commanding officers wanted them to do. But there was no shifting the Cossacks once they had got their hands on some loot and some prisoners. The word of command went unheard. There on the spot they had taken fifteen hundred prisoners, thirty-eight cannons, some regimental colours and, what mattered most to the Cossacks, horses, saddles, blankets and all kinds of things like that. All of this needed sorting out. They had to secure the prisoners and the cannons, share out the loot, yell at each other and even fight over the spoils, and the Cossacks got down to it.

When the French realized they were not being pursued they rallied, fell back in and opened fire. Orlov-Denisov was still waiting for the other columns to turn up, and he made no further attacks.

Meanwhile, following the disposition, 'Column Number One marches here . . .' and so on, the infantry regiments of the missing columns, under Bennigsen's command and Toll's direction, had set off in good order and, as always, arrived somewhere, but not where they were supposed to arrive. As always too, soldiers who had set off in high spirits began to drag their feet, there were murmurs of discontent, they knew they were in a mess, and they retraced some of their steps. Adjutants and generals galloped up and down, yelling furiously, arguing with each other, telling everybody they had come the wrong way and were going to be late, swearing at everybody, and so on, until eventually they gave up in despair, and marched on for the sake of it, just to get somewhere. 'We've got to arrive somewhere or other!' And yes, they did arrive somewhere, but it wasn't where they were needed; just a few managed to arrive in the right place, but so late they were utterly useless except as cannon-fodder. In this battle Toll played the part of Weierother at Austerlitz, galloping indefatigably all over the place, and everywhere he went he found everything at sixes and sevens. For instance, he came across Bagovut's corps in the forest in broad daylight when these men ought to have been miles away long ago, combining forces with Orlov-Denisov. Shocked and stung by this lapse, Toll could only think that somebody must be to blame, so he galloped over to the corps commander and tore strips off him, telling him he deserved to be shot. General Bagovut, a phlegmatic military man of the old school, had been just as worried by all the delays, chaos and contradictory orders. To everyone's amazement, he flew into a towering rage, quite out of character for him, and said some very nasty things to Toll.

'Nobody's telling me how to go about my own business, but I'm as ready as the next man to lay down my life with my men,' he said, and he marched ahead with one division. Emerging on to the battlefield under French fire, the valiant Bagovut was too worked up to wonder whether or not his sortie with a single division was likely to do any good at this point in the action. He marched his men straight ahead directly into the line of fire.

Danger, shells, bullets – this was what he was after in all his fury. One of the first bullets killed him; others followed, killing many of his men. And for quite some time his division stayed there under fire, serving no purpose.

CHAPTER 7

Meanwhile, another column was scheduled to mount a frontal attack on the French, but this column had Kutuzov in charge. He was only too aware that nothing but chaos would come out of this battle, which had been entered into without his approval, so he did all he could to hold his forces back. He made no move.

Kutuzov kept his own counsel, riding his little grey horse and giving leisurely responses to any proposals for the launching of an attack.

'Say what you will about attacking. What you can't see is that these complex manœuvres are beyond us,' he said to Miloradovich, who was eager to advance.

'We missed taking Murat alive this morning, and we didn't get to our places in time, so now there's nothing we can do!' he said to somebody else.

When Kutuzov was informed there were now two battalions of Poles to the rear of the French, whereas earlier on the Cossacks had reported no one there, he glanced back over his shoulder at Yermolov (not having spoken to him since the previous day).

'They're dying to attack, they propose all sorts of ideas, but when you get down to it there's nothing ready, the enemy's had plenty of warning, and he knows what to do.'

Yermolov screwed up his eyes and gave a faint smile when he heard these words. He knew the storm had passed, and Kutuzov would be satisfied with that little hint.

'He's amusing himself at my expense,' Yermolov said quietly to Rayevsky at his side, digging him in the knee.

Shortly afterwards, Yermolov moved forward to Kutuzov and put in a polite proposition.

'There's still time, your Highness. The enemy is still here. A word from you and we could mount an attack ... If we don't our guards won't have seen any smoke.'

Kutuzov said nothing, but when he received a report that Murat's troops were in retreat he gave the order to advance, but every hundred yards he halted for three-quarters of an hour.

The entire battle was limited to what had been achieved by Orlov-Denisov's Cossacks; the rest of the troops simply lost a few hundred men for no good reason.

This battle resulted in Kutuzov receiving a diamond decoration, Bennigsen being rewarded also with diamonds plus a hundred thousand roubles, and many other people getting many nice things, according to rank. It also resulted in lots more changes on the staff.

'That's *our way of doing things*, always the wrong way round!' said the Russian officers and generals after the battle of Tarutino. They still say it nowadays, on the assumption that some idiot has got everything the wrong way round, and that's something we would never have done. But people who say things like this either don't know what they are talking about, or they are deliberately fooling themselves. Every single battle – Tarutino, Borodino, Austerlitz – works out differently from the way it was scheduled by the planners. This is inevitable.

The course of a battle is affected by an infinite number of freely operating forces (there being no greater freedom of operation than on a battlefield, where life and death are at stake), and this course can never be known in advance; nor does it ever correspond with the direction of any one particular force.

If there are many forces acting simultaneously and from different directions on a given body, the direction of its motion can never correspond with any one of the forces; it will always turn out to be the middle way, the shortest route, the line defined in mechanics by the diagonal of a parallelogram of the forces involved.

If in the accounts provided by historians, especially the French ones, we find a claim that wars and battles tend to follow a predetermined plan, we can only conclude that the accounts are untrue.

The battle of Tarutino obviously failed to achieve Toll's purpose, which was to lead the army into action in strict accordance with his troop dispositions; or perhaps that of Count Orlov-Denisov, who wanted to capture Murat; or the destruction of the whole corps at a stroke, which was perhaps the purpose of Bennigsen and others; or the purpose of an individual officer eager to get into battle and cover himself with glory; or the Cossack who was hoping for more loot than he actually got, and so on. But if we regard the purpose of the battle as what was actually achieved, and what was the universal desire of every Russian (the expulsion of the French from Russian soil, and the destruction of their army), it will be perfectly clear that the battle of

Tarutino, not in spite of, but because of, its inconsistencies, was exactly what was needed at that point in the campaign. It would be difficult, nay impossible, to imagine any outcome of that battle more expedient than the one that occurred. With only the slightest effort, despite maximum confusion, and at the cost of the most trifling losses, we got the best results of the whole campaign, we saw retreat turn into attack, we exposed the weakness of the French, and gave them a shock, the one thing needed to put Napoleon's army to flight.

CHAPTER 8

Napoleon enters Moscow after a brilliant triumph, the victory *de la Moskowa*; there can be no doubt about this since the French emerge as masters of the field. The Russians retreat, abandoning their capital city. Moscow, replete with provisions, arms, ammunition and untold riches, is in Napoleon's clutches. The Russian army, half the strength of the French, lets a whole month go by without making the slightest effort to attack. Napoleon's position couldn't be more brilliant. One would have thought it called for no great genius to fall upon a Russian army of half your strength and finish them off; or negotiate an advantageous peace; or, should they refuse, make a threatening move towards Petersburg; or, if that fails, go back to Smolensk or Vilna; or just stay on in Moscow – in other words, to maintain the brilliant position in which the French army now found themselves. To do all this it was only necessary to take the simplest and easiest of steps: prevent the soldiers from looting, prepare winter clothing, of which Moscow had enough for the whole army, and requisition provisions on a regular basis – according to French historians there was enough food in Moscow to feed the entire army for more than six months. Napoleon, that genius of geniuses who, according to the historians, enjoyed control of his army, did none of these things.

Not only did he fail to do any of these things, he did the opposite; he used all his powers to go through the full range of courses open to him and opt for the stupidest and most disastrous of them all. Of all the possibilities – wintering in Moscow, marching up to Petersburg, or over to Nizhny Novgorod, or back by a more northerly or southerly route, perhaps down the road eventually taken by Kutuzov – it would have been hard to imagine a more stupid and disastrous policy than the one adopted by Napoleon: staying on in Moscow until October, thus giving the troops every opportunity to rampage through the city, then vacillating for some time before leaving a well-fortified place and marching out of Moscow, advancing towards Kutuzov and then abstaining from battle, turning to the right and marching on to Maloyaroslavets, again making no attempt at a breakthrough, and finally retreating, not down the road taken by Kutuzov, but back up to Mozhaysk and down the Smolensk road through countryside that had been devastated. It would be hard to conceive of a more stupid course than this, anything more disastrous for the army, as events would show. It would have been a stiff challenge for any expert strategist, assuming Napoleon's object to be the destruction of his own army, to devise a series of actions which, without relying on any steps taken by the Russian forces, could have guaranteed the complete destruction of the whole French army with such certainty as the course taken by Napoleon.

This was done by Napoleon, the man of genius. And yet to say that Napoleon destroyed his own army because he wanted to, or because he was a very stupid man, would be just as wrong as claiming that Napoleon got his troops to Moscow because he wanted to, and because he was a very clever man and a great genius. In both cases his individual contribution, no stronger than the individual contribution of every common soldier, happened to coincide with the laws by which the event was being determined.

Historians utterly falsify the past when (simply because Napoleon's actions were not vindicated by subsequent events) they represent Napoleon in Moscow as a man whose powers were in decline. He was behaving exactly as before, and afterwards in 1813 – exerting all his strength and skill to do the best for himself and his army. Napoleon's actions at this time were no less spectacular than in Egypt, Italy, Austria and Prussia. We cannot say with any certainty what degree of real genius Napoleon showed in Egypt, where forty centuries looked down on him in his glory, because all his famous exploits in that country are described for us exclusively by Frenchmen. We can arrive at no certain judgement of his genius in Austria and Prussia, since any information about his achievements in those places has to be extracted from French and German sources. And the inexplicable surrender of entire formations without a fight, and fortresses without a siege, is bound to predispose the Germans towards the concept of genius as the sole explanation of the war as it was waged in Germany. But we, thank God, have no reason to invoke his genius to cover our shame. We have paid for the right to look the facts simply and squarely in the face, and we are not going to give up that right.

His actions in Moscow are as spectacular and redolent of genius as anywhere else. He never stops issuing order after order and plan after plan from the time he enters Moscow to the time he leaves. He is in no way inhibited by the absence of citizens and deputations, or even the burning of Moscow. He never loses sight of the welfare of his army, the actions of the enemy, the welfare of the peoples of Russia, the conduct of affairs in Paris or the diplomatic considerations involved in the anticipated peace.

CHAPTER 9

With regard to military matters, immediately after his arrival in Moscow Napoleon issues General Sebastiani with strict orders to keep a watch on all movements of the Russian army, sends detachments down all the various roads, and gives Murat the job of finding Kutuzov. He then gives meticulous instructions for the fortification of the Kremlin. Then he draws up the kind of plan for a future campaign over the whole map of Russia that only a genius could have conceived. On the diplomatic side, Napoleon sends for Captain Yakovlev, who has been robbed and reduced to rags and doesn't know how to get out of Moscow, outlines his whole policy in close detail and shows great magnanimity before writing a letter to the Emperor Alexander, in which he considers it his duty to inform his friend and brother that Rostopchin has managed affairs very badly in Moscow, and then sending Yakovlev with it to Petersburg.

After parading his views and his magnanimity in the same kind of detail to Tutolmin, he sends this little old fellow off to Petersburg as well, to open negotiations.

With regard to legal matters, orders are issued, as soon as the fires break out, for the guilty persons to be found and executed. And the villainous Rostopchin is punished by having his various houses burnt down.

With regard to administrative matters, Moscow is presented with a constitution. A municipal council is set up, and the following proclamation is issued to the populace:

CITIZENS OF MOSCOW!

Your sufferings have been harsh, but his Majesty the Emperor and King wishes to stop them in their course. Terrible examples have shown you how he punishes disobedience and crime. Serious steps have been taken to put an end to civil disorder and to restore public security. A paternal administration, elected from your own numbers, will comprise your municipality or city council. It will look after you, and all your needs and interests. Its members will be distinguished by a red ribbon worn across the shoulder, and the city mayor will wear a white sash over it. But when they are not on duty they will wear only a red ribbon around the left arm.

A city police force has been re-established on its former footing, and its operations are already improving public order. The government has appointed two general commissioners, or police-chiefs, and twenty commissioners, or police inspectors, responsible for all the different districts. You will recognize them by a white ribbon worn around the left arm. Several churches of various denominations remain open, and divine service goes on unhindered. Your fellow citizens are returning daily to their homes, and orders have been issued for their assistance and protection once they are there, which is their entitlement in misfortune. The aforesaid are the steps which the government has taken to restore order and alleviate your condition, but for this to be achieved it is necessary for you to combine your efforts with those of the government, to forget, if possible, any misfortunes you have suffered, to look forward to a less cruel future, to be assured that a shameful death inevitably awaits anyone guilty of violating your persons or your surviving property, and by virtue of this entertain no doubt that they will be safeguarded, since this is the will of the greatest and most righteous of monarchs. Soldiers and citizens of whatever nation, restore public confidence, the source of all prosperity within the state. Live like brothers. Render aid and protection one to another. Combine to frustrate the intentions of the wicked in mind. Obey all authorities military and civil, and soon your tears shall cease to flow.

With regard to supplying the army, Napoleon issued orders for all troops to enter Moscow by rota and plunder all necessary supplies for the army to be properly provisioned for the immediate future.

With regard to religion, Napoleon issued an order for the priests to be brought back, and services held again in the churches.

With regard to commerce, and in order to guarantee supplies for the troops, the following notice was pasted up everywhere:

PROCLAMATION

You peace-loving citizens of Moscow, artisans and working men who have been driven from the city by the troubles, and you, scattered sons of the soil kept in the fields by unwarranted fears, hear this! Calm is returning to this capital, and order is being restored. Your fellow countrymen are emerging confidently from their hiding-places and finding themselves treated with respect. Any violence perpetrated against them or their property meets with summary punishment. His Majesty the Emperor and King offers his protection, and considers none among you his enemies save those who go against his orders. He wishes to end your troubles, and restore you to your homes and families. Co-operate with his beneficent purposes, therefore, and come to us without any risk of danger. Citizens, return with confidence to your habitations. You will soon find ways to satisfy your needs! Craftsmen and hard-working artisans, return to your occupations. Your houses, shops, and guards to protect them, await you, and you will receive due payment for your labour! And lastly, you too, peasants, come out of the forests where you have hidden in terror, and return without fear to your huts in all certainty of finding protection. Markets have been established in the city, where peasants can bring their surplus stores and country produce. The government has taken the following steps to guarantee freedom to trade: (1) From this day forth, peasants, farmers and those living on the outskirts of Moscow can without risk of danger bring goods of whatever kind to two appointed markets, to wit – those on Moss Street and Hunter's Row. (2) The said goods shall be bought from them at such prices as may be agreed between seller and buyer, but if the seller cannot get what he is asking as a fair price for them, he shall be at liberty to take his goods back to his village, without let or hindrance on any pretext whatever. (3) Every Sunday and Wednesday are fixed as the main market days for each week, in accordance with which a sufficient number of troops shall be stationed on Tuesdays and Saturdays along all the high roads at such a distance from the town as to protect carts coming in. (4) Similar steps will be taken to ensure that peasants with their horses and carts meet with no hindrance on their homeward journey. (5) Immediate steps will be taken to reintroduce normal trading.

Citizens and country people, and you, workmen and craftsmen of whatever nationality, you are called upon to realize the fatherly intentions of his Majesty the Emperor and King, and to work with him for the public good. Lay your respect and trust at his feet, and lose no time in *joining with us!*

With regard to maintaining morale among the troops and people, parade after parade was held, and decorations were bestowed.

The Emperor rode about the streets reassuring the citizens, and despite being very busy with affairs of state he found time for personal appearances at theatres set up at his behest.

With regard to philanthropy – philanthropy being a monarch's greatest gallantry – Napoleon did all that could have been expected of him. He had 'My Mother's House' inscribed on all the charitable institutions, thus combining warm filial sentiment with the majesty of a virtuous monarch. He visited the foundling home, and as he gave the orphans saved by him his white hands to kiss, he indulged Tutolmin with gracious conversation. Then he ordered his soldiers to be paid in forged Russian money. Thiers waxes eloquent on this subject:

> Reinforcing the effectiveness of these methods by an action worthy of both him and the French army, he had relief distributed to the fire victims. But since food was too precious to be given away to foreigners mostly treated like enemies, Napoleon preferred to issue them with money so that they could provide for themselves from outside, and he had them paid in roubles notes.

With regard to army discipline, orders were continually being issued prescribing severe punishment for dereliction of military duty, and an end to all looting.

CHAPTER 10

But, strange to relate, all these arrangements, efforts and plans, not the least bit inferior to many others made before under similar circumstances, never got through to what mattered. Like the hands on a clock-face detached from the workings, they went round aimlessly and arbitrarily without engaging with the cogs.

With regard to the military, the plan of campaign, this work of genius – on which subject Thiers claims that 'his genius never devised anything more profound, skilful or admirable', and goes on to take issue with Monsieur Fain over the date of this work of genius, which was not the 4th, but the 15th of October – this plan never was and never could have been put into practice, because it was utterly remote from reality. The idea of fortifying the Kremlin, which would have entailed pulling down 'the Mosque' (as Napoleon called the Cathedral of Vasily the Blessed), turned out to be quite useless. The mining of the Kremlin was merely to satisfy the Emperor's desire on leaving Moscow to have the Kremlin blown up, which was like having the floor beaten because a child has hurt himself on it. The pursuit of the Russian army, one of Napoleon's major preoccupations, gave rise to an incredible phenomenon. The French generals managed to lose sight of the sixty-thousand-strong Russian army, and it took what Thiers refers to as the 'skill', nay the 'genius', of Murat for them to rediscover this sixty-thousand-strong needle in a haystack.

With regard to diplomacy, all Napoleon's insistence on magnanimity and justice when speaking to Tutolmin and Yakovlev (whose main concern was to find himself a greatcoat and a carriage to travel in) came to nothing. Alexander refused to receive these envoys, and did not respond to the messages they brought.

With regard to law and order, the execution of the so-called incendiaries was followed by the other half of Moscow burning down.

The establishment of a municipal council did not stop the looting, and benefited nobody beyond the few people who sat on it, and were able to use the maintenance of public order as a pretext for plundering Moscow for themselves, or protecting their own property against other plunderers.

With regard to religion, Napoleon's simple trick in Egypt of making a personal appearance in a mosque cut no ice when it was attempted here. Two or three priests picked up in Moscow made an attempt to carry out Napoleon's wishes; but one of them was hit in the face by a French soldier during the service, and another was referred to as follows by a French official: 'The priest whom I had discovered and invited to resume saying Mass cleaned the church and then closed it. During the night the doors were forced open, padlocks were smashed, books were torn to pieces and other desecrations occurred.'

With regard to commerce, the proclamation to 'hard-working artisans and peasants' fell on deaf ears. There were no hard-working artisans left in Moscow, and the peasants seized any messengers who ventured too far out of the town with this proclamation and killed them.

With regard to entertainment, attempts to provide theatres for the people and the troops were equally unsuccessful. Theatres set up in the Kremlin and in Poznyakov's house were immediately closed down, because the actors and actresses were being stripped of their possessions.

Even philanthropy failed to achieve the desired results. Moscow was full of paper money, genuine and counterfeit, and the notes were valueless. The French were assiduously piling up their loot, and they cared for nothing but gold. It was not only Napoleon's generously bestowed banknotes that lost their value; even silver went down in relation to gold.

But the most striking example of the ineffectiveness of all the authorities' efforts was Napoleon's vain attempt to stop the looting and restore discipline.

Here are some reports submitted by the military authorities:

'Looting goes on in the city despite all the orders to stop it. Public order has not yet been restored, and there isn't a single merchant trading within the law. Only the canteen-keepers venture to sell things, and they are dealing in stolen goods.'

'Part of my district continues to be a prey to looting by the soldiers of the Third Corps, who, not satisfied with going down into the cellars and stripping the poor wretches of what little they have left, are vicious enough to stab them in the process, as I have seen on more than one occasion.'

'Nothing new to report, apart from further stealing and looting by the soldiers. October 8th.'

'Stealing and looting continue. A gang of robbers is operating in our district, and they will have to be stopped, though it will take strong guards to do it. October 11th.'

'The Emperor is exceedingly displeased that, in defiance of strict orders to stop all looting, bands of pillaging guardsmen can be seen continually returning to the Kremlin. In the old guards, indiscipline and looting have been worse than ever last night and today. The Emperor notes with regret that soldiers of the elite, appointed to guard his person, who ought to be setting an example to the other ranks, are so lax in their discipline that they have started breaking into cellars and store-rooms prepared for the army. Others have sunk so low they have been ignoring sentries and officers on guard duty and even swearing at them and hitting them.'

'The grand marshal of the palace complains bitterly [wrote the governor] that despite repeated prohibitions the soldiers continue to obey the call of nature in all the courtyards, and even under the Emperor's own windows.'

The army, like a herd of cattle running wild and trampling underfoot the very fodder that might have saved them from dying of hunger, was falling apart and getting closer to disaster with every extra day that passed as they stayed on in Moscow.

But it never stirred.

It panicked and ran only when it was suddenly shocked and horrified by the capture of wagon-trains on the Smolensk road and the battle of Tarutino. News of the battle of Tarutino reached Napoleon unexpectedly in mid-parade, and, according to Thiers, filled him with an urge to punish the Russians, and he gave the army the marching orders they had long been clamouring for.

In their flight from Moscow the soldiers took with them everything they had been able to lay their hands on. Even Napoleon took his own personal treasure-trove. Thiers tells us he was shocked to see all those wagons groaning under army loot, but, for all his experience of war, he decided against ordering all the extra wagons to be burnt, as he had done with a marshal's baggage on the way to Moscow. He took one look at all these carts and carriages filled with soldiers, and said it was all right, these vehicles would come in handy for transporting food and also the sick and the wounded.

The plight of the army was like the plight of a wounded beast that realizes the end is near, but doesn't know what it's doing. Studying the subtle manœuvres and general aims of Napoleon and his army from the time they entered Moscow to the moment of their destruction is rather like looking for meaning in the jumping and twitching of a mortally wounded animal. Very often the wounded creature will hear a slight movement and rush towards the shooting huntsman, lurching forward, then back again, hastening its own end. This is what Napoleon was now doing, under pressure from his entire army. Rumours of the battle of Tarutino shocked the wild beast into action, and it rushed headlong towards the shooting, got as far as the huntsman, darted back, then forward again, and eventually, like any wild beast, ran away down a familiar track that happened to be the worst and most disastrous of all ways out.

The Napoleon that comes down to us as the motive force behind this movement (just as primitive people saw the figurehead on the prow of a ship as the motive force driving the ship), the Napoleon who was active at this time was like a child in a carriage who pulls on the straps inside and thinks he is doing the driving.

CHAPTER 11

Early in the morning of the 6th of October Pierre walked out of the shed, turned back and stood in the doorway playing with the lavender-grey mongrel bitch with a long body and short bandy legs that was frisking round him. She lived in their shed, sleeping with Karatayev; now and then she took herself off into town, though she always came back again. She had probably never belonged to anybody, she was nobody's now, and she didn't even have a name. The French called her Azor, the story-telling soldier called her Femgalka, but Karatayev called her Greycoat, or sometimes Floppy. She was just a lavender-grey dog, apparently quite unconcerned at having no master, no name, no particular breed, not even a definite colour. She had a fluffy tail that stood up straight in a little round tuft; her bandy legs served her so well she seemed not to need all four of them, because quite often she would gracefully cock a back-leg up, and nip around expertly on three. For her, everything was a source of fun. One moment you would catch her rolling on her back yelping with joy, then you would see her basking in the sunshine, looking all dreamy and solemn, then she was off again, frisking around with a splinter of wood or a bit of straw.

Pierre's clothing now consisted of a dirty, tattered shirt, the only thing left from what he had been wearing, a pair of soldier's drawers tied round the ankles with pieces of string on Karatayev's advice, to keep the warmth in, and a peasant's coat and cap. Physically Pierre had changed a great deal during this period. He didn't look fat any more, though he still retained the Bezukhovs' bulk and strength. A beard and moustache covered the lower part of his face; his long, matted hair, crawling with lice, gave him a thick cap of curls. There was a firm, calm look in his eyes, the kind of sharpness and alertness that Pierre's face had never shown before. All his old lassitude, which had shown itself even in his eyes, had given way to a new vitality; he looked instantly ready for action and resistance. His feet were bare.

Pierre looked across the meadow at the steady movement of wagons and men on horseback, then right out over the river, then at the dog, who was making a good show of really wanting to bite him, then down at his bare feet, twisting them about with enormous pleasure, and wriggling his big, thick, dirty toes. And every time he looked at his bare feet his face lit up with a bright smile of contentment. The sight of those bare feet reminded him of all he had gone through and all he had learnt during this period, and the memory was sweet.

For several days the weather had been calm and clear, with just a light frost in the mornings; it was a real Indian summer.

It was warm outside in the sunshine, and the warmth was particularly pleasant, with a bracing freshness still in the air after the early-morning frost.

Over everything, all objects near and far, lay the magic crystal brightness you will only ever see at this time in the autumn. The Sparrow hills were visible in the distance, along with a village, a church and a big white house. And the leafless trees, the sand, the stones and the rooftops of houses, the green church-steeple and the sharp corners of the white house in the distance all stood out with remarkable clarity, delicately etched in the limpid air. Nearer in stood the familiar ruins of a half-burnt mansion, occupied by French soldiers, with lilac bushes still showing dark-green by the fence. And even this charred and grimy house, such a hideous sight in bad weather, looked lovely, even comforting, in all the stillness and brightness.

A French corporal with a night-cap on his head and his coat casually unbuttoned, came round the corner of the shed, sucking on a stubby pipe, gave Pierre a friendly wink, and walked over to him.

'Nice bit of sunshine, eh, Monsieur Kiril?' (This was what all the French soldiers called Pierre.) 'Just like spring.'

And the corporal leant against the door, offering Pierre his pipe, even though he was always doing this, and Pierre always refused.

'If we were out on the road in weather like this . . .' he began.

Pierre asked him some questions, hoping to find out whether he had heard anything about the French moving out, and the corporal told him nearly all the troops were going, and they were expecting orders today about what to do with the prisoners. In the shed that Pierre lived in there was a Russian soldier by the name of Sokolov who was so ill he was near to death, and Pierre told the corporal something had to be done about him. The corporal told Pierre not to worry: they had field stations and proper hospitals for cases like that, they would be told what to do with the sick, and all possible contingencies had been anticipated by the powers that be.

'Anyway, Monsieur Kiril, all you have to do is say the word to the captain, you know. He's a you know what, but he doesn't forget things. Talk to the captain when he comes round. He'll do the necessary.'

The captain in question had had many a long conversation with Pierre, and done him all sorts of favours.

' "Mark my words, St Thomas," he was saying to me only the other day, "that Kiril's an educated man, speaks French he does, he's a Russian lord who's been through a bad patch, but he's a real man. And he knows what's what . . . If he wants anything, he only has to ask, nobody will refuse him nothing." When you've done your own bit of studying, see, you have a lot of time for education and posh people. I'm telling you this for your own good, Monsieur Kiril. That bit of business the other day – but for you it could have turned very nasty.'

The corporal chatted on for a few more minutes and then went away. (The other day's bit of business had been a set-to between the prisoners and the French soldiers, which Pierre had managed to sort out by persuading his companions to calm down.)

Several of the prisoners had heard Pierre talking to the corporal, and now they wanted to know what he had said. Pierre was busy telling his companions what had been said about the French moving out of Moscow when a thin, sallow, ragged French soldier came up to the door of the shed. With one quick, uncertain gesture he put his fingers to his forehead in a kind of salute, looked at Pierre, and asked whether Private Platoche, who was making a shirt for him, lived in this shed.

The French soldiers had been issued with linen and leather a week or so before this, and had got the Russian prisoners to make boots and shirts for them.

'Oh yes, me old darlin', 'tis ready all right!' said Karatayev, emerging with a neatly folded shirt. Because of the heat, and to make it easier for working, Karatayev was wearing nothing but a pair of drawers and a tattered shirt, as black as the soil. He had tied his hair up with a strip of bark-fibre like a factory-worker, and his round face looked rounder than ever and even more genial.

'A deal's a deal. Friday, I said, and I've done it,' said Platon with a broad smile, unfolding the shirt he had made.

The Frenchman looked round nervously. He seemed full of misgivings, but he overcame them, slipped off his jacket and put the shirt on. Under his uniform he hadn't been wearing a shirt; next to his yellow, thin body he wore a long, greasy, flowery silk waistcoat. He was obviously worried that the prisoners might take one look at him and fall about laughing, and he shoved his head quickly through the neck-hole. None of the prisoners said a word.

'Nice fit, that,' said Platon, easing the shirt down. The Frenchman got his head and arms through, and inspected the fit of the shirt, checking the needle-work without once looking up.

'Well, me dear, this ain't no tailor's shop, you know, and I didn't have no proper sewing kit, and they do say you can't kill a louse without the right kit,' said Karatayev, admiring his own handiwork.

'No, it's very good. Thank you very much. But you must have some stuff left over . . .' said the Frenchman.

'It'll bed in as you wears it,' said Karatayev, still revelling in his achievement. 'There you are. Nice and comfortable, that's what you'll be.'

'Thank you, thank you very much, old fellow, but what about the offcuts?' repeated the Frenchman, handing Karatayev a banknote. 'Have you got the offcuts?'

Pierre could tell Platon was determined not to understand what the Frenchman was saying in his own language, and he watched the pair of them without interfering. Karatayev thanked him for the money, but he was still lost in admiration of his own work. The Frenchman insisted, and asked Pierre to translate.

'What does he want with the offcuts?' said Karatayev. 'Nice set of leg-bands they'd have been. Oh well, it doesn't worry me.'

And so, with a sudden saddening of his features, Karatayev took a bundle of remnants out of his shirt and handed them over without looking at the Frenchman. 'Oh, dearie me!' he cried, and walked away. The Frenchman looked down at the linen, nonplussed, glanced quizzically in Pierre's direction, and seemed to pick up a message from the way Pierre looked back.

'Hey, Platoche!' he called in a thin, shrill voice, suddenly blushing. 'You can keep these,' he said. He gave him the remnants, turned away and walked off.

'Now, just look at that,' said Karatayev, shaking his head. 'Not supposed to be Christians, but they've got souls too. Like what the old folks always said: a sweaty hand's an open hand, a dry fist is tight. Not a stitch to his back, and 'e gives me this lot.' Karatayev stood there for a while, saying nothing, just smiling thoughtfully to himself and staring at the offcuts. 'Nice set of leg-bands these'll be, me dear,' he said, walking off back into the shed.

CHAPTER 12

Four weeks had passed since Pierre had been taken prisoner. Although the French had offered to transfer him so he could be with the officers, he had stayed on in the same shed they had first put him in.

In the burnt-out ruins of Moscow Pierre had passed through degrees of hardship and deprivation that tested a man to the limit, but, because of his strong constitution and good health, which he had taken for granted until now, and especially because the privations had come upon him so gradually he couldn't have said when they had started, he was able to stand the strain not only with something to spare, but with real pleasure. And it was now that he attained the peace of mind, the feeling of being at ease with himself, that he had been struggling vainly to achieve for so long. He had spent so much of his life casting around in all directions for the kind of tranquillity and self-certainty that had impressed him so much in the soldiers at Borodino. He had sought for it in philanthropy, freemasonry, a dissipated life in high society, wine, heroic deeds of self-sacrifice, and romantic love for Natasha. He had sought it through the power of thought, and all his struggles and various experiments had ended in frustration. And now without noticing it he had gained that inner peace and harmony simply through the horror of death and hardship together with what he had observed in Karatayev. Those ghastly moments he had lived through during the execution seemed to have blotted out of his imagination and his memory once and for all a whole series of worrying thoughts and anxious feelings that had once seemed so important. No thoughts now about Russia, the war, politics or Napoleon. None of this seemed to matter any more; it was not his responsibility, and his was not to sit in judgement. 'Russia, warm weather – they don't go together,' he would say to himself, repeating Karatayev's words, which he found strangely reassuring. His plans for killing Napoleon, all his cabbalistic calculations and his ideas about the beast of the Apocalypse now seemed senseless and positively ludicrous. His bitterness towards his wife, and the fear of having his name dragged through the mud, now seemed not just petty – they were hilarious. What did it matter to him if that woman chose to go away somewhere and lead the kind of life that appealed to her? What did it matter to anybody – least of all him – whether or not they found out that this prisoner's name was Count Bezukhov?

Nowadays he often remembered his conversation with Prince Andrey, and he completely agreed with his friend, though with some slight distortion of his meaning. Prince Andrey had thought, and said, that happiness exists only in a negative sense, and he had said so with more than a touch of bitterness and irony, as if he was saying something else besides: that all our instinctive strivings towards positive happiness were implanted only for us to be let down and tormented by them. But Pierre recognized the truth of the basic idea without having to qualify it. Pierre now saw the absence of suffering and the satisfaction of our basic needs, followed up by freedom to choose an occupation, or lifestyle, as the highest and most dependable form of human happiness. It was only here and now that Pierre had fully appreciated for the first time in his life the enjoyment of eating when you are hungry, drinking when you are thirsty, sleeping when you are tired, keeping warm when it is cold and talking to a fellow creature when you feel like talking and you want to hear men's voices. Through deprivation Pierre now saw the satisfaction of his basic needs – good food, cleanliness and freedom – as the ultimate happiness, and the choice of an occupation or lifestyle, now that this choice was so restricted, seemed such a simple matter that he forgot that a surfeit of luxury takes all the pleasure out of satisfying our basic needs, and maximum freedom in the choice of occupation, which had been provided for him through education, wealth and his position in society, makes the actual choice of an occupation extraordinarily difficult, because it destroys the need and desire for any such thing.

Pierre now dreamt of nothing but his coming freedom, though in years to come he would think and talk about that month of incarceration with much enthusiasm, recalling all the intensely pleasurable sensations that were now gone for ever, and especially the complete peace of mind and inner freedom that he had known only at that time.

On that first morning, when he had got up at first light, come out of the shed and seen the dark domes and crosses on the Novodevichy Convent, then the grass with its dusting of hoar-frost, then the slopes of the Sparrow hills and the wooded river-banks meandering away into the purple distance, when he had felt the chill touch of the morning air and heard the cawing of jackdaws flying across the fields away from Moscow, and then seen a sudden glint of light in the east followed by the sun's rim rising majestically from behind a cloud, and the domes and crosses, the hoar-frost, the horizon and the river all merrily sparkling in the new light – Pierre had felt a new surge of strength and vitality, the like of which he had never known before.

And that feeling had never left him during the whole period of his incarceration; on the contrary, it had expanded within him as the hardships of his plight had gone on increasing.

This feeling that Pierre had of being ready for anything, of moral alertness, was reinforced by the high esteem in which he came to be held by his companions very soon after he entered the shed. His knowledge of foreign languages, the courtesy shown to him by the French, his readiness to give away anything he was asked for (as an officer he was given three roubles a week), the physical strength he showed by hammering nails into the hut wall, his gentle attitude towards them all, and his incredible ability to sit there for ages doing nothing but think, made him seem like a superior being enveloped in mystery. The very qualities that had proved inhibiting, if not actually destructive, in the society he had lived in before – his physical strength, disdain for luxury, absent-mindedness, open-heartedness – gave him virtually heroic status here among these men. And Pierre felt that this view of him imposed its own obligations.

CHAPTER 13

In the early hours of the 7th of October the exodus of the French army began. Kitchens and sheds were taken down, wagons were loaded, and off went the troops and the baggage-trains.

At seven in the morning a convoy of French soldiers stood in marching order outside the sheds wearing their shakos and waiting with knapsacks, muskets and huge sacks, and the whole line was abuzz with the chatter of Frenchmen, which included a lot of colourful language.

In the shed they stood ready, dressed, belted and shod, waiting for the word to move. The sick man, Sokolov, looking pale and thin, with blue rings round his eyes, sat in his place all on his own, the only one not wearing boots or outdoor clothing. His eyes protruded from an emaciated face as he stared round quizzically at his mates, who were all ignoring him, and he moaned quietly at regular intervals. Clearly, it wasn't so much the pain of his dysentery as the fear and worry of being left behind that was making him moan.

Pierre was wearing a piece of string round his waist and a pair of light shoes that Karatayev had cobbled up from the covering of a tea-chest that a Frenchman had brought in to have his boots soled with. He went over to the sick man and squatted down beside him.

'Come on, Sokolov, they're not all going at the same time, you know. They've got a hospital here. As like as not you'll be better off than the rest of us,' said Pierre.

'Oh God! I'm a dead man! Oh God!' The soldier redoubled his moaning.

'Hang on, I'll ask them again. Give me a minute,' said Pierre. He got to his feet and went over to the shed door. While he was making his way across, the corporal who had offered Pierre a pipe the day before came up outside with two soldiers. All three, corporal and privates, were in marching order, with shakos and knapsacks in place and chinstraps buttoned, which altered their familiar faces.

The corporal was on his way to lock the door in accordance with orders received. The prisoners had to be counted before they could be let out.

'Corporal, what's going to happen to the sick man?' Pierre launched forth, but at the moment of doing so he began to have doubts. Was this the same corporal that he knew so well or another person? He looked totally different at that moment. To make matters worse, Pierre found himself speaking against a sudden drum-roll that rattled out on two sides. The corporal scowled at Pierre's words, uttered a few meaningless oaths and slammed the door. Left in semi-darkness inside the shed, they could hear the crisp drum-roll coming from two sides and drowning out the sick man's moans.

'This is it! . . . It's back again!' Pierre said to himself, and an involuntary shiver ran down his spine. In the change that had come over the corporal's face, the sound of his voice and the rousing, deafening drum-tattoo Pierre recognized the mysterious, inhuman force that drove people against their will to murder their fellow men, the force he had seen working to full effect during the execution. There was no point in panicking, or trying to avoid this force, or appealing on bended knee to the men who were acting as its implements. This much Pierre had learnt. You just had to wait and stick it out. Pierre didn't go anywhere near the sick man and didn't look round at him. He stood there in silence by the shed door, scowling.

When the doors of the shed were flung open, and the prisoners crammed the doorway, scrambling over one another like a flock of sheep, Pierre elbowed his way to the front, and got through to the captain, the man who was ready to do anything for him, if the corporal's words were anything to go by. The captain was also in marching order, and his icy features betrayed *the thing* Pierre had recognized in the corporal's words and the drum-roll.

'Come on! Get a move on!' the captain was saying, grim-faced and scowling, as he watched the prisoners scramble past.

Pierre knew it wasn't worth trying, but he still went up to him.

'Well, what is it?' said the officer, scanning him coldly, as if he didn't recognize him. Pierre mentioned the sick prisoner.

'He can walk, damn him!' said the captain.

'Come on! Get a move on!' he kept on calling out, ignoring Pierre.

'Well, no, he's in terrible pain!' Pierre was trying to say.

'Get out of the way!' shouted the captain with a vicious scowl.

Trum-ti-ti-tum-tum-tum went the rattling drums. Pierre could see that the mysterious force now had total control over these men, and there was no point in saying anything more.

The officers among the prisoners were split off from the men and ordered to march in front.

There were about thirty officers, including Pierre, and a good three hundred men.

The officers, who had emerged from the other sheds, were all strangers to Pierre, and much better dressed than he was. They looked at him in his funny foot-gear with cold eyes full of suspicion. Not far

from Pierre walked a portly major with a bloated, sallow, irritable-
looking face. He was wearing a Kazan dressing-gown, with a towel
for a belt, and he was obviously looked up to by his fellow prisoners.
He had one hand thrust inside his dressing-gown, clutching a tobacco-
pouch, while the other gripped his pipe by its stem. Puffing and panting, he growled at them all and rounded on them angrily for shoving
against him, as he saw it, and for rushing on when there was nowhere
to rush to, and gawping in amazement when there was nothing to
gawp at. Another officer, a thin little man, spoke to all and sundry,
holding forth about where he thought they were being taken, and
how far they would get that day. A commissariat official wearing his
uniform and a pair of high felt boots kept running from side to side
to have a good look at what was left after the burning of Moscow,
opining in a loud voice on what had been burnt and telling them what
district of the town they were in as it hove into view. A third officer,
of Polish extraction to judge by his accent, took issue with the commissariat official, pointing out that he was getting things wrong as he
identified the various districts of Moscow.

'Why bother?' said the major testily. 'Makes no difference whether
it's St Nikolay or St Vlas. Look, it's all burnt down, and that's it . . .
And will you stop shoving? There's plenty of road,' he said, turning furiously on a man walking behind him who certainly hadn't
pushed him.

'Oh, no, no, no. Look what they've done!' came the prisoners'
voices from every side, despite the major, as they stared at the charred
ruins. 'Look over there across the river. Zubovo. Inside the Kremlin
. . . Look, half of it's gone! I told you it was like that across the river,
and I was damn well right.'

'All right, so it's all burnt down. No point in going on about it,'
said the major.

On their way through Khamovniki (one of the few Moscow districts
that had survived the fire), walking past the church, the whole throng
of prisoners suddenly surged to one side, calling out in shock and
horror.

'Absolute swine!'

'Heathen lot!'

'Yes he's dead. It's a dead man . . . And they've wiped something
all over him.'

Pierre, too, moved over towards the church to get nearer the thing
that was causing the outcry, and he could just make out something
leaning on the church fence. Some of his companions had a better view,
and from what they said he learnt it was a dead body propped up

against the fence in a standing position, with its face smeared with soot.

'Come on, damn you, get going! Move, you devils, all thirty thousand of you!' They could hear the escort swearing, and the French soldiers flailed the flat of their swords with a new viciousness to disperse the prisoners who had stopped to stare at the dead man.

CHAPTER 14

The prisoners and their guards were on their own as they marched through the back-streets of Khamovniki, with the soldiers' carts and wagons straggling on behind, but as they emerged near the provision shops they found themselves caught up in a huge, lumbering train of artillery intermingled with private vehicles.

At the bridge they ground to a halt, waiting for those in front to get across. Once on the bridge the prisoners got a good view of the endless trains of baggage-wagons stretching out in front and coming on behind. To their right, where the Kaluga road loops round by the Neskuchny gardens, endless lines of troops and wagons disappeared into the distance. These were the troops of Beauharnais's corps, who had been the first to leave. Behind them came Marshal Ney's troops and transport, stretching back down the embankment and right across the Stone Bridge.

Davout's troops, which included the prisoners, were crossing by the Crimean Ford, and some of them were already out on the Kaluga road. But the baggage-trains straggled back so far that Ney's leading troops came streaming out of Bolshaya Ordynka before the last carts of Beauharnais's corps had got through to the Kaluga road on their way out of Moscow.

Once over the Crimean Ford the prisoners found themselves moving only a few steps at a time before they ground to a halt, and then they would move on again, while masses of vehicles and men thickened on all sides. It took them more than an hour to cover the few hundred yards that separate the bridge from the Kaluga road and when they got to the square where the outlying streets converge on the Kaluga road, the prisoners were squashed in and kept standing for several hours at the crossroads. On all sides there was a constant roar that sounded like the sea, coming from rumbling wheels and marching men, with angry voices calling out and plenty of swearing. Pierre stood there crushed against the wall of a charred house, listening to this noise as it blurred in his imagination with the roll of drums.

Some of the Russian officers scrambled up on to the wall of the burnt house where Pierre was standing so they could get a better view.

'Hey, the crowds! Huge crowds everywhere! . . . They've even got stuff stacked up on the cannons! Look at them furs!' came the voices. 'Look what they've been pinching, the swine . . . See what he's got on the back of that cart? . . . a mounting from an icon that is, by God! . . . They must be Germans. Hey, there's one of our peasants! . . . Vile scum! Look at him. He can hardly move! My God, those little carriages, they've even got hold of them! . . . He's all right, perched up there on those trunks. Good God, they're at it hammer and tongs. It's a fight! . . . Go on, give him one in his face! We'll be here all night at this rate. Look at that lot! . . . Must be Napoleon's! Can you see those horses! Monograms and a crown! It's like a house on wheels. Hey look, he's dropped a bag, and he hasn't seen it. Another fight over there . . . Woman here with a baby. Not bad looking either! Go on, love, they'll let you through like that! Goes on for ever, this does! Hey, there's some Russian wenches! They are, you know. Nice and cosy in them carriages!'

And what had happened at the church in Khamovniki happened again: a wave of eager curiosity swept all the prisoners forward towards the road, and because of his height Pierre was able to peer across over the heads and see what the prisoners were so keen to look at. Three carriages had come to halt, stuck between some ammunition carts, and they were carrying a number of women who were heavily made up and decked out in garish colours, sitting there all squashed together, yelling something in shrill voices.

From the moment Pierre had recognized the return of that mysterious force nothing had seemed strange or terrible any more, not even a corpse with its face smeared with soot for a joke, or these women who seemed to be in such a hurry to get somewhere, or the burnt ruins of Moscow. Pierre was now impervious to virtually anything he saw. It was as if his spirit, girding itself up for a hard struggle, was refusing to take in any impressions that might sap its strength.

The carriages of women drove on. Then the rest trundled off, carts, soldiers, baggage-wagons, soldiers, carriages, soldiers, caissons, more soldiers and a few women here and there.

Pierre could not see these people as individuals; he saw them all together and in movement.

All these men and horses seemed to be pressing on, impelled by some invisible force. During the hour Pierre spent watching them they kept on streaming out of the various streets all with a single idea in mind: to get through as fast as they could. They were all the same, crashing into each other, getting angry, spoiling for a fight. White teeth snarled, faces scowled, the same curses flew back and forth, and all these men had the same look of gallant determination and cold callousness that Pierre had seen on the corporal's face that morning while the drums had been beating.

In the late afternoon the officer commanding their escort rallied his men, and with much yelling and forceful persuasion got in among the baggage-trains and fetched the prisoners, surrounded on all sides, out on to the Kaluga road.

They set off at a quick pace, took no breaks and only halted when the sun was going down. The baggage-carts were shunted up close together, and the men began to bed down for the night. Every man jack of them seemed irritable and unhappy. The cursing, angry bellowing and fighting went on and on. A carriage had driven into one of their carts from behind and run a shaft through it. Soldiers rushed up from all sides, some lashed the carriage horses across their heads as they turned them round, others scrapped among themselves, and Pierre saw one German badly wounded by a blow to the head from a short sword.

Now they had come to a standstill out in the country on a dismal and chilly autumn evening, all these men seemed to have been struck by the same sensation, a nasty awakening from the sense of urgency that had carried them along as they left the city. Now they were at a halt it seemed to have dawned on them they had no idea where they were going, and that there was a lot of pain and hardship ahead of them along the way.

During this halt the prisoners came in for rougher handling by the soldiers in charge than they had had when they set off. For the first time they were given horse-meat to eat.

Every single member of the escorting force, from the officers down to the commonest soldier, now harboured a kind of personal animosity towards every one of the prisoners, all of which was in stark contrast to their earlier friendly relations.

This animosity was redoubled when the roll was called and it was discovered that in the hurly-burly of getting out of Moscow one Russian soldier had managed to escape by pretending he was ill with stomach pains. Pierre had watched a Frenchman lash out at a Russian soldier for wandering too far from the road and heard the captain who had been friendly with him reprimanding an NCO for letting the prisoner escape, and threatening him with court martial. When the NCO argued that the prisoner was too ill to walk the officer told him their orders were to shoot anyone who couldn't keep up. Pierre felt that the fateful force that had laid him low during the execution, and had been nowhere apparent during his imprisonment, had now taken over his existence again. It made him feel scared, but he also felt that even as this fateful force did its best to crush him, a new, independent, vital strength was building up in his soul all the time.

Pierre's evening meal, as he chatted to his companions, consisted of rye flour and horse-meat soup.

Neither Pierre nor any of his companions made any mention of what they had seen in Moscow, or the harsh treatment they were now getting from the French, or the orders to shoot stragglers they had just heard about. All of them seemed determined to defy their worsening circumstances by remaining particularly cheerful and lively. They reminisced and talked about funny things they had seen on the march, steering well clear of anything to do with their present situation.

It was long after sunset. A few stars were lit up across the sky, the rising full moon had painted a red glow along the horizon as if it was on fire, and the huge red ball hung there in the grey darkness, shimmering strangely. There was more and more light. It was the end of the evening, but night had not yet begun. Pierre got up and walked away from his new companions, wandering off between the camp-fires to the other side of the road, where he had been told the common prisoners were camping. He wanted to talk to them. On the road a French sentry stopped him and told him to go back.

Pierre did go back, but not to his companions by the camp-fire; he went over to an unharnessed wagon where there was nobody about. Tucking his legs up under him, and lowering his head, he sat down on the cold ground, leant back against a wagon wheel, and spent a long time sitting there quite still, just thinking. More than an hour went by. No one disturbed him. Suddenly he burst out laughing, and his heavy, good-humoured laughter was so loud that men looked round in astonishment on every side to hear such a burst of weird hilarity evidently coming from a man sitting there on his own.

'Ha, ha, ha!' laughed Pierre. And he talked to himself out loud. 'The soldier wouldn't let me through. They've taken me and locked me up. They keep me prisoner. Me? *What me?* My immortal soul! Ha, ha, ha! . . . Ha, ha, ha!' he laughed, and his eyes filled with tears.

A man got up and came over to see what this strange, big fellow was laughing about all by himself. Pierre stopped laughing, got to his feet and walked away from the inquisitive intruder, taking a good look round.

The vast makeshift camp that seemed to go on for ever had been abuzz with the sounds of fires crackling and men talking, but now it was settling down. The red camp-fires were burning down and going out. The full moon stood high in the limpid sky. Far away forests and fields that had been invisible beyond the confines of the camp were now coming into sight. And out there beyond the forests and fields lay all the shimmering, beckoning distance of infinity. Pierre glanced up at the sky and the play of the stars receding into the depths. 'And it's all mine, and it's all within me, and it all adds up to *me*!' thought Pierre. 'And they caught all that, shut it up in a shed and boarded it in!'

He smiled as he walked back to bed down with his companions.

CHAPTER 15

At the beginning of October another messenger came to Kutuzov from Napoleon bearing overtures for peace in a letter purporting to have been written from Moscow, though in fact Napoleon was slightly ahead of Kutuzov down the old Kaluga road. Kutuzov's response was the same as before, when Lauriston had been the messenger: peace was out of the question.

Soon after this a report came in from Dorokhov's guerrilla army to the left of Tarutino claiming that French troops had been spotted at Fominsk, troops belonging to Broussier's division, which was cut off from the rest of the army and could be easily destroyed. The soldiers and officers were spoiling for a fight. The staff generals, buoyed up by the memory of an easy victory at Tarutino, urged Kutuzov to act on Dorokhov's proposal. Kutuzov could see no reason to go on the attack. The inevitable compromise was decided on, and a small detachment was sent to Fominsk to attack Broussier.

By a strange turn of events this task, which would turn out to be both difficult and highly significant, was entrusted to Dokhturov, a modest little general, nobody's idea of a master planner or a regimental commander, who dashed around showering military crosses on batteries, and such like, a man looked on and spoken of as indecisive and ineffective, even though in every Russian war against the French, from Austerlitz to the year 1813, we always find him taking command where the situation is at its toughest. At Austerlitz he was the last to abandon the Augezd dam, and he rallied the regiments, saving what he could from flight and disaster when there were no other generals left in the rearguard. Stricken with fever, he marched twenty thousand men over to Smolensk to defend the town and take on the whole of Napoleon's army. Once there, he had barely nodded off at the Molokhov gate, shivering with fever, when he was woken up by the roar of a cannonade directed against Smolensk, and he held the city for a whole day. At Borodino, with Bagration killed and nine-tenths of our left flank lying dead, and the full fire of the French artillery raining down on them, it is our indecisive and ineffective Dokhturov who is sent there by a Kutuzov only too anxious to make up for sending the wrong man in the first place. Off he goes, the quiet little Dokhturov, and Borodino ends up as the greatest glory in Russian military history with many of its heroes celebrated in poetry and prose, but scarcely a word about Dokhturov.

So Dokhturov is now sent to Fominsk, and then to Maloyaroslavets, where the French are engaged for the last time, and where, quite clearly, the final downfall of the French army really begins. And once again we have many accounts of heroes and geniuses at this point in the campaign, but of Dokhturov nothing – a few words at the most, and those of faint praise. The silence surrounding Dokhturov is the clearest endorsement of his merit.

It is natural for a man who doesn't understand how a machine works to imagine, when he sees it in action, that a chip that has fallen in by accident and is now jumping about and stopping things working properly is the most important part of the whole mechanism. Anyone who doesn't understand the construction of the machine cannot conceive that this chip is just jamming up the works and reining them, unlike one little cog-wheel, spinning away quietly, which is one of the most essential parts of the machine.

On the 10th of October, by the time Dokhturov had marched half-way to Fominsk and halted at the village of Aristovo, making careful preparations for carrying out his orders to the letter, the whole of the French army had made its way in fits and starts to the position occupied by Murat, ostensibly to give battle, but suddenly and for no apparent reason it then lunged off left down the new Kaluga road, and began marching into Fominsk, where until now Broussier had been standing alone. At this time Dokhturov had at his disposal nothing more than Dorokhov's troops and the two small detachments of Figner and Seslavin.

On the evening of the 11th of October Seslavin brought a captured French guardsman to the headquarters at Aristovo. The prisoner said that the troops that had entered Fominsk that day were the advance guard of the whole army, Napoleon was with them, and the whole army had marched out of Moscow five days before. That same evening a house serf coming in from Borovsk brought word that he had seen a huge army entering the town. Some of Dorokhov's Cossacks reported that they had seen French guardsmen marching along the road to Borovsk. All of this intelligence made one thing clear: in the place where they had been expecting to encounter a single division they were faced with the entire French army, marching away from Moscow in an unexpected direction – down the old Kaluga road. Dokhturov insisted on holding back since it was not clear now where his duty lay. He had been ordered to attack Fominsk, but at that time only Broussier had been in Fominsk, and now the whole French army was there. Yermolov wanted to take the initiative, but Dokhturov kept on insisting that he must have instructions from his Serene Highness, General Kutuzov. They decided to report back to staff headquarters.

For this purpose they chose a capable officer, Bolkhovitinov, who was given the task of delivering a written report and explaining the whole thing in words. It was just before midnight when Bolkhovitinov received his dispatch and verbal instructions, and galloped off to headquarters, accompanied by a Cossack with spare horses.

CHAPTER 16

The autumn night was dark and warm. It had been drizzling for the last four days. With two changes of horses Bolkhovitinov covered twenty miles in an hour and a half on a muddy, sticky road and got to Letashovko not much after one in the morning. Dismounting at a peasant's hut with a wattle fence bearing the inscription *General Staff*, he dropped the reins and walked into the dark entry.

'Quick. The duty general! Very important!' he cried as someone jumped to his feet, snorting in the darkness.

'His Honour has been ill since yesterday evening. He hasn't slept for three nights,' an orderly's voice pleaded in a whisper. 'You'll have to wake the captain first.'

'It's urgent. I'm from General Dokhturov,' said Bolkhovitinov, groping his way in through an open door.

The orderly was ahead of him, waking somebody up. 'Your Honour, your Honour, there's a cullier.'

'You what? What? Who from?' said a sleepy voice.

'From Dokhturov and Alexey Petrovich. Napoleon is at Fominsk,' said Bolkhovitinov. He couldn't see the speaker in the darkness, but he could tell from the voice that it wasn't Konovnitsyn.

The man who had been woken up was yawning and stretching. 'I'm not keen on waking him up,' he said, fumbling with something. 'He's not at all well. Could be a rumour, couldn't it?'

'Here's the report,' said Bolkhovitinov. 'My instructions are to hand it straight to the duty general.'

'Hang on. Let me strike a light. Why do you keep hiding things away, damn your eyes?' said the man who had been doing all the stretching, to his orderly. It was Shcherbinin, one of Konovnitsyn's adjutants. 'Oh, here we are. I've got it,' he added.

The orderly struck a light, and Shcherbinin felt for a candlestick.

'Oh, the swine!' he said with disgust. By the light of the sparks Bolkhovitinov caught a glimpse of Shcherbinin's youthful face as he held the candle, and there was another man there asleep in a corner. It was Konovnitsyn.

When the sulphur splinters kindled by the tinder had flared up into a blue flame, then a red one, Shcherbinin lit a tallow candle, which sent the cockroaches that had been gnawing at it scurrying away, and looked at the messenger. Bolkhovitinov was spattered all over with mud, and his face was smeared where he had wiped it with his sleeve.

'Who is it from?' asked Shcherbinin, taking the packet.

'It's true all right,' said Bolkhovitinov. 'Prisoners, Cossacks, spies, they all tell the same story.'

'That's it, then. We'll have to wake him,' said Shcherbinin. He got to his feet and went over to the sleeping man, who was wearing a night-cap and was covered with a greatcoat. 'Sir!' he said. Konovnitsyn did not stir. 'You're wanted at headquarters!' he said with a smile, knowing these words would be sure to wake him. And sure enough, the head in the night-cap came up in a flash. For a moment Konovnitsyn's strong, handsome face, with its cheeks feverishly inflamed, wore a far-away, dreamy look, but he gave a sudden start and his face resumed its usual expression of composure and strength.

'Well, what is it? Who wants me?' he asked at once, but with no haste, blinking at the light. Konovnitsyn listened to the officer, then broke open the seal and read the dispatch. Without waiting to finish reading he lowered his feet in their worsted stockings to the earth floor and started pulling on his boots. Then he took off his night-cap, ran a comb down both sides of his head, and put on his forage cap.

'How long did it take you to get here? We must go and see his Highness.'

Konovnitsyn had not been slow to realize that this news was of vital importance, and there was no time to be lost. It never crossed his mind to wonder whether it was good news or bad. This was not the point.

His whole attitude to the war was based on something other than intellect or reason. Deep in his heart he had an unspoken conviction that all would be well, but it was not his job to entertain any such belief, let alone talk about it; his job was to go on doing his duty. He was doing his duty, and putting all his energy into it.

Like Dokhturov, General Konovnitsyn gets only a passing mention in the 1812 roll of honour, alongside the Barclays, Rayevskys, Yermolovs, Platovs and Miloradoviches. Like Dokhturov, he was dismissed as a man of very limited ability and knowledge. Again like Dokhturov, he was no compiler of battle-plans, but he was always there in the thick of things. Ever since being appointed duty general he had slept with his door open, and given orders to be woken up if a messenger arrived. In battle he was always under fire, so much so that Kutuzov told him off about it, and was reluctant to send him out. Like Dokhturov, he was one of those inconspicuous cog-wheels that never judder or rattle; they just go on working as the most essential parts of the machine.

As he walked out of the hut into the damp, dark night, Konovnitsyn gave a scowl, partly because his headache was getting worse, and partly from a nasty thought that had occurred to him: this news would create a stir in the nest of all these important staff people, and especially with Bennigsen, who had been at daggers drawn with Kutuzov ever since the battle of Tarutino. They were in for a stream of proposals, arguments, orders and counter-orders. He could see it all coming, and although it gave him no pleasure, he knew it had to be.

And sure enough, Toll, to whom he reported the new developments, launched forth immediately with his version of events for the benefit of the general who shared his quarters, until Konovnitsyn, after listening for some time in weary silence, reminded him they ought to go and see his Serene Highness.

CHAPTER 17

Like all old people Kutuzov was a poor sleeper. During the day he would often nod off unexpectedly, but at night he would lie there on his bed without getting undressed, and more often than not he just lay awake, thinking.

He was lying on his bed like that now, with his huge, heavy, disfigured head resting on a fat hand. He was thinking, with his one eye wide open, staring into the darkness.

Since he was being cold-shouldered by Bennigsen, the one man who was in correspondence with the Tsar and carried more weight than anybody else on the staff, Kutuzov was more at ease with himself in one respect: he didn't have to lead his soldiers into attack when it was useless to do so. And he could only imagine that the lesson learnt at Tarutino and the day before the battle, a painful memory for Kutuzov, must surely have an effect on them too.

'They've got to understand we can only lose by going on the offensive. Patience and time, these are my heroes of the battlefield!' thought Kutuzov. He knew better than to pick apples while they are still green. An apple will fall when it's good and ripe, but if you pick it while it's still green you spoil the apple and the tree and you set your teeth on edge. Like a good hunter, he knew the beast had been wounded, wounded as only the whole might of Russia could have wounded it, but the question of whether it was mortally wounded was still open. Now from the overtures made through Lauriston and Barthélemy, and from the reports coming in from guerrillas, Kutuzov was virtually certain the wound was a deadly one. But more proof was needed. They must wait.

'They want to run off and watch him die. Better to wait and see. Nothing but new manœuvres, new attacks . . .' he thought. 'And what's it all for? Anything to cover themselves with glory. As if it's fun to go out fighting. They're like children who won't tell you what really happened because they all want to show themselves off as the best fighters. And that's not the point now. Oh, and what wonderful manœuvres these people keep coming out with! They think when they've thought about two or three contingencies (he had in mind the general plan sent down from Petersburg) there aren't any more to think about. But there's no end to them!'

The open question of whether the wound administered at Borodino was or was not a mortal wound had been hanging over Kutuzov's head for a whole month. On the one hand, the French had taken possession of Moscow. On the other hand, it was surely beyond doubt, and Kutuzov felt this with every fibre of his being, that the terrible blow that he had summoned all his strength to administer, along with all the Russians, must have been a deadly one. But in the last analysis proof was needed, and he had been waiting for it for a whole month, getting more and more impatient as time went by. As he lay there night after night unable to sleep he did the very thing these whipper-snapper generals were always doing, the very thing he criticized them for. He kept going over all the possible ways in which Napoleon's downfall might come about, given that his downfall was now a certainty, even a *fait accompli*. He ran through them, just as the younger generation did, but with two provisos: he refused to draw any conclusions from these suppositions, and he saw the possible contingencies not in twos or threes, but in thousands. The more he thought about them, the more he saw. He imagined Napoleon's army making all sorts of movements, acting as a whole or dividing into sections, marching on Petersburg, or against him, or right round him. He also imagined the possibility (and this scared him most of all) that Napoleon might fight against him with his own weapons, that he would stay on in Moscow and wait for him to make a move. Kutuzov even imagined Napoleon's army marching back via Medyn and Yukhnova. The one thing he could not have foreseen was what actually happened, the crazy, lurching stampede of Napoleon's army during the first eleven days of its march from Moscow, a stampede that raised a possibility Kutuzov had never dared to dream of, the complete annihilation of the French. Dorokhov's report on Broussier's division, the news brought in by guerrillas about the miseries suffered by Napoleon's army, rumours of preparations being made for the evacuation of Moscow, everything confirmed the idea that the French army was beaten and getting ready to go. But it was no more than supposition, and however important it was to the youngsters, it cut no ice with Kutuzov. With sixty years' experience behind him he knew how much weight to attach to rumours, he knew that men who want something are only too ready to arrange all the evidence to suit their wishful thinking and willingly exclude anything that contradicts it. And the more Kutuzov wanted it to be true, the less he allowed himself to believe it. This question had been absorbing all his spiritual energy. And everything else was everyday routine. Everyday routine took in conversations with his staff-officers, letters written from Tarutino to Madame de Staël, reading novels, bestowing honours on people, correspondence with Petersburg, and so on. But the destruction of the French, foreseen by him alone, was the one desire of his heart.

On the night of the 11th of October he was lying there leaning on one arm, thinking about that very thing.

There was a stir in the next room, and he heard the approaching footsteps of Toll, Konovnitsyn and Bolkhovitinov.

'Who's that then? Come on in, come on in! Anything new to report?' the commander-in-chief called out.

While a footman was lighting a candle, Toll put him in the picture.

'Who brought this news?' asked Kutuzov. As the candle flared up Toll saw a face that impressed him by its cold severity.

'There's no doubt about it, your Highness.'

'Get him. Bring him in!'

Kutuzov sat there with one leg out of bed and his big belly flopping down all over the other leg that was still bent under him. He screwed up his one good eye to get a better view of the messenger, as if he was hoping to read in his features the one thing that was on his mind.

'My dear fellow, tell me the whole story,' he said to Bolkhovitinov in his weak old man's voice, pulling his shirt together where it had fallen open over his chest. 'Come on. Come a bit nearer. So what's all this news about? Eh? Napoleon's left Moscow, has he? Has he really? Eh?'

Bolkhovitinov went through every detail of what he had been told to say.

'Come on, get on with it. Don't leave me in agony,' Kutuzov interrupted him.

Bolkhovitinov told him everything and then stopped, waiting for orders. Toll was on the point of saying something, but Kutuzov checked him. He tried to say something himself, but suddenly his face wrinkled and crumpled. Waving at Toll, he turned away to the far corner of the hut, which was blackened with candle-smoke around the holy icons. 'Lord, my Creator! Thou hast heard our prayer . . .' he said in a trembling voice with his hands clasped together. 'Russia is saved. I thank Thee, O Lord.' And he burst into tears.

CHAPTER 18

From the time he received this news to the end of the campaign Kutuzov limited his activity to nothing more than using all his authority, skill and powers of persuasion to restrain his army from any useless attacks, manœuvres and encounters with the doomed enemy. Whereas Dokhturov goes marching off to Maloyaroslavets, Kutuzov is in no hurry with the main army, issuing orders for the evacuation of Kaluga, on the grounds that retreat beyond that town seems like a real possibility. Kutuzov pulls back on all sides, but the enemy, without waiting for him to withdraw, flees in the opposite direction.

Napoleon's historians describe his tactical skill at Tarutino and Maloyaroslavets, and speculate about what might have happened if Napoleon had managed to get through to the rich provinces of the south.

But, apart from the fact that there was nothing to stop Napoleon marching straight down into these southern provinces (since the Russian army had left the road open), these historians forget that

Napoleon's army was beyond salvation by now because it carried within itself the germ of inevitable ruin. How could that army – which had come across plentiful supplies in Moscow but had trampled them underfoot instead of conserving them, and went in for random looting rather than careful management of provisions when they got to Smolensk – how could this army have suddenly come to its senses in the province of Kaluga, where the inhabitants were of the same Russian stock as in Moscow, and where fire was still fire, consuming anything that is set alight?

The army could never have come to its senses. Ever since the battle of Borodino and the sacking of Moscow it had carried within itself what you might call the chemical elements of decomposition.

This relic of an army, the men and their leaders, fled with no idea where they were going. All of them from Napoleon down to the last of his soldiers had but one thing in mind: to extricate themselves as fast as they could from a hopeless situation which they all acknowledged, however dimly.

And for this reason, when the French generals met in council at Maloyaroslavets and went through the motions of exchanging opinions in serious debate, the last contribution – from an ingenuous soul, General Mouton, who put into words what they had all been thinking, that the only thing to do was to get out as fast as they could – closed every mouth, and no one, not even Napoleon, had anything to say against a truth they all acknowledged.

But though everybody knew they had to go, there was a lingering feeling of shame at having to flee. What they needed was some external impulse strong enough to overcome the shame. And in due course the impulse came. It was what the French called 'the Emperor's *Hurrah*'.

On the day after the council, early in the morning, on the pretext of reviewing the troops and the scene of a past and future battle, Napoleon rode out with a suite of marshals and an escort right in the middle of his army lines. A party of marauding Cossacks stumbled across the Emperor and very nearly took him prisoner. What prevented the Cossacks from capturing Napoleon that day was the very thing that was bringing down the French army – the question of loot, which the Cossacks dived on here, as at Tarutino, in preference to pursuing people. Ignoring Napoleon, they dashed straight at the loot, and Napoleon managed to get away.

If the children of the Don could come within an ace of capturing the Emperor himself in the middle of his army, it was clear that the only thing to do was run away as fast as they could down the nearest known road. Napoleon, with forty years on his back and a big paunch to carry around, was not the nimble adventurer of old, and he soon took the hint. The Cossacks had given him a real scare. He agreed at once with Mouton, and historians tell us he ordered the army to backtrack and go down the road through Smolensk.

The fact that Napoleon agreed with Mouton, and the army went back on its tracks, does not prove that his orders made this happen; all it shows is that certain forces acting on the army as a whole and diverting it down the Mozhaysk road were also acting at the same time on Napoleon.

CHAPTER 19

When a man finds himself moving forwards, he never fails to think of a goal to aim at. If he is to walk a thousand miles a man must believe there is something good waiting at the end of the thousand miles. You need the vision of a promised land to keep on moving. Moscow had been the promised land for the French on their way into Russia; on their way out it was home. But home was too far away. A man on a thousand-mile walk has to forget his ultimate goal and say to himself every morning, 'Today I'm going to cover twenty-five miles and then rest up and sleep.' During this first stage of the journey the resting-place eclipses any idea of the ultimate goal, and all his hopes and desires are focused on that alone. And any impulses manifested in an individual are always magnified in a crowd.

For the French army marching back down the old Smolensk road, the ultimate goal of getting back home was too far away, and the short-term goal, the focus of all their hopes and desires, greatly magnified by the crowd effect, was Smolensk. Not that they expected to find Smolensk teeming with supplies and reinforcements, or that anyone had told them so (on the contrary, the high command and Napoleon himself knew full well there was a shortage of supplies there), but this was the only thing that buoyed them up, kept them moving and enabled them to bear the ills they had. All of them, those who knew and those who didn't, pulled the wool over their own eyes and looked on Smolensk as a promised land.

Once out on the high road the French fled towards their mythical goal with amazing energy and incredible speed. Apart from the common impulse that brought hordes of Frenchmen together into a single whole and gave them a certain momentum there was something else that held them together – their huge numbers. As with the law of gravity in physics, their very mass, huge as it was, attracted the men like individual atoms. On they went in their hundreds of thousands, like an entire state, moving with their collective mass.

Every man jack of them shared a single desire: to give himself up and escape from all his present horrors and disasters. But on the one hand, the momentum set up by the general onward drive towards the goal of Smolensk was pulling every individual in the same direction. On the other hand, a whole corps couldn't possibly surrender to a division, and although the French made the most of every opportunity to separate and find the slightest decent pretext to be taken prisoner, opportunities like these didn't always arise. They were deprived of such possibilities by sheer numbers, and meanwhile the speed of their densely packed onward movement, with all its associated mass and energy, made it more than difficult for the Russians to stop the French – in fact, it was impossible. No mechanical dismembering of the body could have accelerated beyond a certain limit the process of decomposition that was underway on the inside.

A snowball cannot be melted instantaneously. There is a fixed time limit beyond which no amount of heat can thaw the snow. It works the other way round: the more heat you apply, the harder the snow that is left.

Kutuzov was alone among the Russian generals in his understanding of this principle. Once the flight of the French army had been determined – down the road to Smolensk – the very thing Konovnitsyn had anticipated on the night of the 11th of October started to happen. All the top brass of the Russian army began looking for glory by cutting them off, intercepting, taking prisoners, overrunning the French. They were all spoiling for a fight.

Kutuzov alone used all his powers (and the powers of any commander-in-chief are very limited) to avoid a fight.

He couldn't have told them what we can say now. He couldn't have asked them what purpose was served by fighting, barring their way, losing more of our men and callously finishing the poor devils off, especially when a third of that army melted away of its own accord between Moscow and Vyazma without any battle being fought. But, drawing on his store of aged wisdom and finding something they might be able to get into their heads, he told them about the golden bridge, but they mocked and maligned him, raging and rampaging over the dead beast.

Not far from Vyazma, Yermolov, Miloradovich, Platov and others happened to find themselves near to the French, and they couldn't resist the urge to isolate two French corps and launch an attack on them. As a way of announcing their intentions to Kutuzov instead of a proper message they sent him a blank piece of paper in an envelope.

And in spite of Kutuzov's best efforts to restrain the army, the army attacked the French and tried to bar their way. The infantry regiments, so we are told, marched into battle to music and rolling drums in order to slay and be slain in their thousands.

But as for cutting off the enemy's retreat – nobody was cut off or overrun. And the French army, more united than ever because of the danger, continued on its disastrous journey to Smolensk, melting away steadily as it went.

PART III

The battle of Borodino, along with the subsequent occupation of Moscow and the flight of the French without further conflict, is one of the most instructive phenomena in history.

Historians agree that the external activity of states and peoples when they are at odds with each other finds an outlet in warfare, and that the political power of states and peoples waxes or wanes in direct proportion to success or failure on the battlefield.

We may find it strange when history describes the process by which some king or emperor falls out with another king or emperor, raises an army, fights and wins a battle against the enemy, killing three, five or ten thousand men, and thus subjugates a state and a whole nation running to millions; we may find it hard to understand how the defeat of an army, a mere hundredth part of a nation's strength, somehow forces the whole people into submission, yet all the facts of history (as far as we can know history) justify the general belief that the success or failure of one nation's army against another nation's army is the cause, or at least a major indication, of the waxing or waning of a nation's power. An army wins a battle, and the winners' rights are immediately increased at the expense of the losers'. An army suffers a defeat, and the people are immediately deprived of their rights according to the magnitude of defeat, and if defeat is total, they fall into total submission. It has been like this (history would have us believe) from ancient times right up to the present day. All of Napoleon's earlier wars serve to confirm this principle. As the Austrian armies went down to defeat, Austria was more and more deprived of her rights, while the rights and power of France grew and grew. French victories at Jena and Auerstadt destroyed Prussia as an independent state.

Then suddenly, in 1812, the French gained a victory just outside Moscow. Moscow was taken, yet subsequently, with no more battles being fought, it was not Russia that ceased to exist, but the six-hundred-thousand-strong French army, and then Napoleonic France itself. Any stretching of the truth to accommodate the laws of history by claiming that it was the Russians who won the day at Borodino, or that after Moscow there were other battles that destroyed Napoleon's army, is out of the question.

After the French victory at Borodino there were no more general engagements, not even a skirmish of any significance, yet the French army ceased to exist. What is the meaning of this? If this example had come from the history of China we could have labelled it 'unhistorical' (the sort of thing historians fall back on when the facts don't fit). If it had been a small-scale event with only a few troops involved, we might have treated it as an exception. But our fathers watched it happen with their own eyes; for them and their country it was a matter of life and death. This war was on a larger scale than any that we know of.

The aftermath of the 1812 campaign, from Borodino to the final expulsion of the French, proved that the winning of battles does not necessarily lead to conquest, and may not be a reliable indication of conquest. It proved that the determining force in the destiny of nations lies not in successful military leaders, nor even armies and battles; it lies somewhere else.

French historians, describing the situation of the French troops before they marched out of Moscow, claim that everything was all right with the Great French Army except for the cavalry, artillery and transport, and a shortage of forage for the horses and cattle. This was a calamity that couldn't be helped because the peasants in the surrounding countryside were burning their hay rather than hand it over to the French.

Victory did not lead to the usual results, because your Russian peasants, Karp and Vlas, hardly the personification of heroic behaviour, came into Moscow on their carts to grab what they could once the French had gone, and countless numbers of others like them decided not to bring their hay to Moscow, but burn it instead.

Let us imagine two men fighting a duel with swords and following all the rules laid down for the art of swordsmanship. The fencing goes on for quite some time. Suddenly one of the combatants realizes he has been wounded, and the wound is serious, life-threatening, so he throws his sword away, grabs the first club that comes to hand and weighs in with it. Then let us imagine that this duellist, having been bright enough to find the best and easiest method of getting his way but also being a champion of old-fashioned chivalry, decides to cover up what really happened and now insists he won by fighting fair.

Imagine the confusion and obscurity that would arise in his description of the duel!

The duellist who fought by the rules was the French army; his opponent, who threw his sword away and grabbed a club, was the Russian army, and those who attempt to explain everything by the rule-book are the historians who have written about this event.

The burning of Smolensk was followed by a war that flouted all the old traditions of warfare. The burning of towns and villages, the retreat after every battle, the blow administered at Borodino followed by yet another retreat, the abandoning and burning of Moscow, the hunting down of looters, the interception of transport – all of this went against the rule-book.

Napoleon could sense this, and from the moment he took up the proper stance for a fencer, in Moscow, only to see a club raised against him instead of his opponent's sword he never stopped complaining to Kutuzov and Tsar Alexander that this war wasn't following the rule-book. (As if rules existed for the killing of people!)

Despite French complaints that they weren't keeping to the rules, despite misgivings among some highly placed Russians over the rather shady practice of fighting with a club instead of following the rule-book and standing there in carte or tierce, or making a skilful thrust in prime, and so on, the people's war club was raised with all its menace, majesty and might, and indiscriminately, with no thought for the niceties of proper procedure, it rose and fell with brainless simplicity but remarkable effectiveness, hammering the French until the entire invading force was finished off.

Happy the people who, unlike the French in 1813, refuse to salute the magnanimous conqueror by following the rules laid down for this form of art and offering him the sword hilt-first with elegance and courtesy. Happy the people who, when put to the test, ask no questions about other people's behaviour under similar circumstances, but pick up the first club that comes to hand in one simple, easy movement and hammer away with it until the humiliation and vengeance deep in their hearts give way to contempt and compassion.

CHAPTER 2

One of the most obvious and successful infringements of the so-called 'rules of war' is the action of scattered groups of individuals ranged against men working together in a dense mass. This type of action is always seen in war where nationality is at stake. In this kind of fighting, instead of ganging together to attack another crowd, men split up into small groups, attack in ones and twos and run away immediately they are attacked by superior forces, only to mount another attack when chance permits. This is how the guerrillas operated in Spain, the hillsmen in the Caucasus and the Russians in 1812.

This has come to be known as 'guerrilla warfare' on the assumption that to name it is to define it. But in fact, this kind of warfare, far from obeying any laws or rules, is a flagrant contradiction of a well-known law of tactics which tends to be thought of as infallible. This law states that the attacking party shall concentrate its forces in order to be stronger than the enemy when battle begins.

Guerrilla warfare (invariably successful, as history shows) is a flagrant infringement of this rule.

The infringement arises from an assumption, made by military science, that military effectiveness is commensurate with numerical strength. Military science maintains that the greater the numbers, the greater the strength. As the saying goes, God is on the side of the big battalions.

In saying this, military science is behaving like a specialist in mechanics who bases his definition of momentum on mass alone and claims that momenta are equal or unequal only in so far as their masses are equal or unequal.

But momentum (the measurement of motion) is the product of mass *and velocity*.

In warfare the strength of an army is the product of its mass multiplied by something else, an x factor.

Military science, observing in history innumerable instances of armies in which size does not correspond with strength, and in which small numbers defeat large ones, vaguely acknowledges the existence of this unknown multiplier, and tries to locate it. Could it perhaps reside in some geometrical disposition of the troops, or better weaponry, or – the most popular explanation – military genius on the part of the leaders? But none of these attempts to define the multiplier comes up with results that agree with the facts of history.

Yet all you have to do to discover the x factor is repudiate the false view (so gratifying for heroes) that acknowledges the effectiveness of steps taken by the higher authorities during a war.

This x factor is army morale, a greater or lesser willingness to fight and face danger on the part of all the men who make up the army, whether or not they are fighting under leaders of genius, with clubs or guns that fire thirty rounds a minute. Men with the greatest desire to fight always steal the advantage when it comes to fighting. Morale is the factor which, when multiplied by mass, gives you the strength of the force. The intellectual problem is to define and express the significance of this unknown factor, morale.

This problem can be solved, but only when we stop the arbitrary business of ignoring the x factor and concentrating on circumstances in which military strength shows itself (decisions taken by a general, military equipment, etc.) and fully acknowledge the role of this unknown factor, the greater or lesser willingness to fight and face danger. Only then, by expressing the known historical facts in equations and comparing the relative significance of this factor, can we hope to define it.

Imagine a situation in which *ten* men, battalions or divisions take on and defeat *fifteen* men, battalions or divisions, killing or capturing everybody while sustaining only four losses themselves; they have lost four to the other side's fifteen. The ratio, four to fifteen, may be expressed as: $4x = 15y$. In other words: $x:y = 15:4$. This equation may not give us the value of an unknown factor, but it does give the ratio between two unknowns. And by expressing a whole range of historical data (battles, campaigns, periods of war) in equations like these, we can obtain sets of figures that must contain laws, and these laws should be discoverable.

The law of tactics that tells armies to group together for attacking purposes and split up for retreat amounts to nothing more than unwitting confirmation of the truth that the strength of an army depends on the state of its morale. To lead men into action under fire calls for greater discipline (attainable only by grouping together) than is needed for self-defence under attack. But since this rule makes no allowance for troop morale, it constantly turns out to be unreliable, and comes to grief most of all in wars where nationality is at stake and there has been a strong rise or fall in army morale.

According to the laws of tactics, in 1812 the retreating French ought to have defended themselves by splitting up, but no, they huddled together in a crowd because their morale had sunk so low it was only their numbers that kept them going. Conversely, according to the laws of tactics the Russians ought to have attacked en masse, but they didn't, they broke down into small groups because their morale was so high that individual men could be relied on to attack the French without waiting for orders, and nobody needed to be forced into hardship and danger.

CHAPTER 3

The so-called 'guerrilla' war had begun the moment the enemy marched into Smolensk. Before it was officially recognized as such by our government many thousands of enemy soldiers – stragglers caught looting or foraging – had been eliminated by Cossacks and peasants, who killed these men off instinctively, like dogs rounding on a mad stray. Denis Davydov, every inch an intuitive Russian, was the first to realize the value of this terrible weapon as an instrument for annihilating the French with no questions asked about the niceties of the military art, and he must be credited with having taken the first step towards the legitimization of this method of warfare. The first guerrilla detachment, formed on the 24th of August, was Davydov's; others soon followed. As the campaign went on, more and more such detachments were formed.

The guerrillas destroyed the Great Army bit by bit. They swept up the fallen leaves that were dropping off the withered tree, and sometimes they shook the tree itself. By October, when the French were on the run, heading back to Smolensk, there were hundreds of these detachments, varying in size and each with its own character. Some retained army methods, and still had their own infantry, artillery, staff-officers and all amenities. Some consisted solely of Cossack cavalry. There were also little bands of footsoldiers and horsemen working together, peasant groups and obscure detachments got up by landowners. One band was commanded by a deacon, and they took hundreds of prisoners in a single month. There was a village elder's wife called Vasilisa who killed Frenchmen in hundreds.

Guerrilla warfare was at its height towards the end of October. The first stage of this war was long gone, the time when the guerrillas had been amazed at their own audacity, in constant fear of being surrounded and captured by the French, never unsaddling, hardly ever dismounting as they hid away in the woods, fully expecting imminent pursuit. Guerrilla activity had now assumed a definite shape; they all knew what they could, and could not do, to the French. By now only staff-officers and commanders of units operating by the rule-book some way away from the French considered anything to be impossible. The long-established smaller bands who had been keeping a close eye on the French found it possible to do things the leaders of larger companies wouldn't have dared to undertake. For the Cossacks and peasants, who stole in and out among the French, anything was possible now.

On the 22nd of October Denisov, one of these irregulars, was out with his party at a time when guerrilla blood was up. From early morning he and his men had been on the move, working their way through the woods that skirted the high road and stalking a big French convoy of cavalry baggage and Russian prisoners that had become detached from the other French troops and was heading for Smolensk – under a strong escort, if the reports from scouts and prisoners were anything to go by. Denisov and Dolokhov (who was also a leader of a small band operating in the same area) were not the only ones who knew about this convoy. Some of the generals in charge of larger units, working with staff-officers, also knew of its existence, and Denisov claimed they were all salivating at the prospect of attacking it. Two of these generals – one a Pole, the other a German – had sent word at virtually the same time, each inviting Denisov to join his detachment and mount an attack.

'Oh no, bwother, you don't catch me like that!' said Denisov as he read these missives. He wrote back to the German that in spite of a burning desire to serve under such a brilliant and famous general he had to forgo the pleasure because he was already committed to serving under the Polish general. He wrote the same thing to the Pole, informing him that he was already serving under the German.

With this settled, Denisov now intended to bypass the higher authorities and join forces with Dolokhov to attack this transport convoy and capture it with his own small band of men. On the 22nd of October the convoy was making its way from the village of Mikulino to another one called Shamshevo. There were thick woods all down the left-hand side of the road, in some places skirting the road itself and in others receding half a mile or more away. Denisov had taken a small party and spent the whole day riding up and down through these woods, plunging deep into their centre, then emerging again near the edge, and never losing sight of the moving Frenchmen. That morning, just outside Mikulino, at a place where the wood ran close to the road, the Cossacks of Denisov's party had pounced on two French baggage-wagons loaded with cavalry saddles that had got stuck in the mud, and taken the saddles off into the wood. From that time until late afternoon they had been watching the movements of the French without attacking. The plan was to avoid alerting them and let them go quietly on to Shamshevo, where Denisov could join up with Dolokhov (who was due to meet them that evening for a conference in a watchman's hut in the wood, less than a mile from Shamshevo), and wait till dawn before coming down on them like an avalanche from two sides at once, killing and capturing the lot of them in one fell swoop.

Six Cossacks had been posted in the rear just over a mile outside Mikulino, where the wood skirted the road, and they were to bring word at once if any fresh French columns turned up.

Ahead of Shamshevo Dolokhov had the same task of watching the road to find out how far away any other French troops might be. At a rough estimate the convoy had fifteen hundred men in it. Denisov had two hundred men, and Dolokhov perhaps the same. But Denisov was not interested in numerical superiority. The only thing he still needed to know was who these troops were, and in order to find out Denisov needed an informer, someone from the enemy column. The attack on the wagons in the morning had been carried out with such speed they had killed all the French soldiers in charge of the wagons, and the only person captured alive had been a little drummer-boy who had lost touch with his own regiment, and couldn't tell them anything definite about the troops that made up the column.

It was Denisov's view that another attack would be too risky – it might stir up the whole column – so he sent a peasant by the name of Tikhon Shcherbaty on to Shamshevo to see if he could manage to capture at least one French quartermaster who had been sent on ahead.

CHAPTER 4

It was a warm, rainy, autumn day. The sky and horizon were the colour of muddy water. The weather alternated between a kind of rolling mist and torrents of driving rain.

Dressed in a felt cloak and fur cap, both streaming with rain, Denisov was riding a thin thoroughbred with sunken sides. Like his horse, which had its head turned to one side and its ears laid back, he shrank away from the driving rain and peered anxiously ahead. There was a look of annoyance on his face, which was rather thinner than before and covered with a thick black stubble.

Alongside Denisov, also wearing a felt cloak and fur cap, and mounted on a strong, sleek Don horse, rode a Cossack hetman who was working with him.

Hetman Lovaysky the Third was a gangly creature, as straight as a plank, with a pale face, fair hair, light-coloured, close-set eyes and an expression of calm self-confidence in his face and his bearing. It would have been difficult to detect anything special between horse and rider, but you could tell at a glance that Denisov, looking wet through and uncomfortable, was a man sitting mounted on a horse, whereas the hetman, calm and comfortable as always, was not just a man sitting mounted on a horse, but a man who formed a unified whole with his horse and thus possessed a twofold strength.

Shortly ahead of them walked a peasant guide, also wet through, in his grey kaftan and white woollen cap.

Shortly behind, on a skinny, scraggy Kirghiz pony, with a huge tail and mane and a mouth flecked with blood, rode a young officer in a blue French greatcoat. Beside him rode a hussar, with a boy in a tattered French uniform and blue cap perched behind on the crupper of his horse. The boy's hands were red with cold as he hung on to the hussar, waggling his bare feet to try and warm them up, and his eyebrows stood up high as he gazed round in bewilderment. This was the French drummer-boy who had been taken prisoner that morning.

Further back there were some hussars riding along the narrow, muddy, churned-up forest path in threes and fours, and some Cossacks wearing an assortment of cloaks, French greatcoats and horse-cloths pulled up over their heads. All the horses, chestnut and bay, looked black with the rain streaming down them. Their necks looked curiously thin because of their soaking manes, and steam rose from them in clouds. Clothes, saddles, bridles, everything was as wet, slippery and dank as the earth and fallen leaves strewn across their path. They sat hunched up in the saddle, trying not to move, so as to keep some warmth in the water that had got through to their skin, and stop any more cold rain trickling in anywhere under their seats, behind their knees or down their necks. In the middle of a long line of Cossacks two wagons drawn by French horses and Cossack saddle-horses rumbled over tree-stumps and branches, and splashed through ruts and puddles.

Denisov's horse tried to avoid a puddle in the track, and in doing so banged his rider's knee against a tree.

'Ow, blast you!' cried Denisov angrily. Baring his teeth, he lashed his horse three times with his whip, spattering himself and his comrades with mud. Denisov was feeling low, partly from the rain and hunger (no one had eaten since first thing that morning), but mostly because there had been no word from Dolokhov, and the man sent to catch an informer hadn't come back.

'There'll never be a chance like this to attack that wagon-twain. It's too wisky to attack on our own, but if we put it off some of the big boys will gwab the spoils wight under our noses,' said Denisov to himself, constantly peering ahead in the hope of seeing the messenger he was expecting from Dolokhov.

Emerging into a clearing with a good long open view to the right, Denisov came to a halt.

'Someone coming,' he said.

The hetman looked in the direction where Denisov was pointing.

'Two of them. An officer and a Cossack. But we can't *conjuncture* it's the colonel himself,' said the hetman, a great user of unfamiliar words.

The two figures rode downhill, disappeared from sight and came back up into view a few minutes later. The first one was an officer, looking all dishevelled and dripping wet, with his trousers working their way up above his knees, and he was lashing his horse into a weary gallop. Behind him came a Cossack, standing up in the stirrups and riding at a trot. The officer, only a youngster, with a broad, rosy face and sharp, cheery eyes, galloped up to Denisov and handed him a sopping-wet packet.

'From the general,' he said. 'I'm sorry it's got a bit wet . . .'

Denisov took the envelope with a frown and broke the seal.

'They kept on saying how dangerous it was,' said the officer, turning to the hetman while Denisov was reading the letter. 'But we were ready, me and Komarov.' He nodded to the Cossack. 'We have both two pist . . . Hey, what's all this?' he asked, seeing the French drummer-boy. 'Have you got a prisoner? Have you been into battle? May I talk to him?'

'Wostov! Petya!' Denisov suddenly called out, after a quick skim through the letter. 'Why didn't you say who you are?' And Denisov turned towards him with a smile, holding his hand out. The officer was Petya Rostov.

All the way there Petya had been rehearsing how to behave with Denisov, as one adult officer to another, with no reference to their previous acquaintance. But the moment Denisov smiled at him Petya beamed, blushed with delight, forgot all his carefully rehearsed formalities and launched into an account of how he had ridden past the French, how pleased he was to have been given this job to do, and how he had seen action at Vyazma, where a certain hussar had covered himself with glory.

'Well, it's a weal pleasure to see you,' said Denisov, cutting across him, his face once more a picture of anxiety.

'Mikhail,' he said to the hetman, 'it's another note from the German. Wostov here is on his staff.' And Denisov told the hetman that the latest letter renewed the German general's request for them to join him in attacking the convoy. 'If we don't get them by tomowwow they'll gwab the lot fwom under our noses,' he concluded.

While Denisov was talking to the hetman Petya felt embarrassed by Denisov's sudden coldness, and since the only explanation seemed to be the state of his trousers, he started working them down furtively underneath his greatcoat, trying to manage it without being seen and look as warlike as he could.

'Will your Honour have any instructions for me?' he asked Denisov, raising one hand to the peak of his cap, and reverting to the game of adjutants and generals that he had worked up in advance, 'or shall I stay here with your Honour?'

'Instwuctions?' said Denisov distractedly. 'No. Can you stay till tomowwow?'

'Oh, yes . . . Please let me stay!' cried Petya.

'Well, what instwuctions did you get from your general – go stwaight back?' asked Denisov. Petya blushed.

'No, he didn't say. I think it would be all right for me to stay,' he said, though it sounded like a question.

'All wight, then,' said Denisov. And turning to his followers he directed a party of them to proceed to the hut in the wood where they had agreed to rest up and sent the officer on the Kirghiz pony (who was acting as his adjutant) to go and look for Dolokhov, find out where he was and whether he was coming that evening.

Denisov himself intended to take the hetman and Petya out to the edge of the wood near Shamshevo to assess the position of the French and work out where to attack in the morning.

'Wight, you old gweybeard,' he said to their peasant guide, 'take us to Shamshevo.' Denisov, Petya and the hetman, accompanied by one or two Cossacks and the hussar with the prisoner, turned to the left, crossed a ravine and rode out towards the edge of the wood.

CHAPTER 5

It had stopped raining, but there was still a rolling mist and drops of water dripped from the branches of the trees. Denisov, the hetman and Petya made no noise as they followed the peasant in the woollen cap, who nipped along lightly and silently in his bark-fibre shoes, with his toes turned out, stepping over roots and wet leaves as he led them to the edge of the wood.

Coming out at the top of a slope, the peasant paused, took stock and turned towards a thining screen of trees. He stopped by a big oak-tree that had not yet shed its leaves, and beckoned mysteriously.

Denisov and Petya rode over to him. From the place where the peasant was standing the French were visible. Just outside the wood a field of spring corn ran sharply downhill. To the right, on the other side of a steep ravine, they could see the shattered roofs of a little village and a manor house. In the village itself, in the house and across the top end of the garden, by the wells and the pond, and all the way up the road from the bridge to the village, not more than five hundred yards away, masses of men could be seen through the rolling mist. Foreign voices could be heard shouting at the horses as they struggled uphill with the baggage and calling across to each other.

'Get me the pwisoner,' said Denisov in a low voice, his eyes fixed on the French.

A Cossack got off his horse, lifted the boy down, and brought him over to Denisov. Denisov pointed to the French, and asked the boy who the various troops were. The boy stood there with his red-raw hands in his pockets, and raised his eyebrows in dismay as he looked at Denisov. Despite his obvious desire to tell them everything he knew he got his answers mixed up, and all he did was agree with everything Denisov asked him. Denisov scowled, turned away and spoke to the hetman, outlining his own views on the situation.

Petya's head whipped round in all directions as he looked from the drummer-boy to Denisov, then from the hetman to the French over in the village and spread out along the road, trying not to miss anything of any significance.

'With or without Dolokhov we've got to have a go at them, haven't we?' said Denisov with a merry glint in his eyes.

'It's a good spot,' said the hetman.

'We'll send the infantwy down there fwough the swampy gwound,' Denisov went on. 'Let them cweep up to the garden. You come in with your Cossacks from over there . . .' – Denisov pointed to the woods on the other side of the village – 'and I'll take my hussars in from here. Wait for a shot . . .'

'No, not through the gully. It's too soft,' said the hetman. 'The horses will get bogged down. You'll have to send them around, a bit further left . . .'

While they were talking like this in low voices suddenly a shot rang out down below in the hollow near the pond, a puff of white smoke went up, then another, and hundreds of French voices half-way up the hill rang out in one great merry chorus. The instantaneous reaction of both Denisov and the hetman was to duck down. They were so close they could only imagine they were the cause of the shot and all the shouting. But no, the shots and the shouting had nothing to do with them. A man in red was dashing through the marshes down below. Clearly, the French were firing and shouting at him.

'Hey look, it's our Tikhon,' said the hetman.

'It is, you know!'

'Stupid idiot,' said Denisov.

'He'll be all right!' said the hetman, screwing up his eyes.

The man they called Tikhon ran up to the little river, plunged in with a great splash, disappeared for an instant, then scrambled out on all fours, all black from the water, and ran on. The pursuing French came to a halt.

'He's a good boy,' said the hetman.

'He's a stupid swine!' said Denisov, with the same look of annoyance. 'What's he think he's been doing all this time?'

'Who is he?' asked Petya.

'It's our scout. I sent him to catch an informer.'

'Oh yes,' said Petya, nodding at Denisov's first word, as if he knew the situation, though he didn't understand the first thing about it.

Tikhon Shcherbaty was one of Denisov's best men. He was a peasant from the village of Pokrovskoye, near the river Gzhat. Denisov had come to Pokrovskoye early in his career as a guerrilla leader, and as usual he had sent for the village elder and asked him what he knew about the French.

The village elder gave the same defensive answer all the others had given: see no evil, hear no evil. But once Denisov had explained that all he wanted to do was to kill the French and asked whether or not any Frenchmen had strayed their way, the village elder said yes, there had been one or two 'marorderers', but the man who dealt with things like that was Tikhon Shcherbaty. Denisov sent for Tikhon and praised him for all he had done, adding a few words, in the presence of the elder, about the kind of loyalty to Tsar and country, and hatred of the French, that all sons of the fatherland ought to cherish in their hearts.

'These Frenchies, we don't do 'em no 'arm,' said Tikhon, wary now because of what Denisov had been saying. 'It's only, like, just a bit o' fun for me and the lads. Them *marorderers* now – we can't 'ave killed more'n a couple o' dozen o' them, an' apart from that we 'aven't done no 'arm . . .'

Next day, when Denisov had left Pokrovskoye, having forgotten all about this peasant, he was told that Tikhon had joined the group and was asking to stay. Denisov agreed to let him stay.

Tikhon began by doing the rough work, making fires, fetching water, skinning dead horses and so on, but he soon showed great ability and enthusiasm as a guerrilla. He would go out at night to see what he could find, and he never came back without some French clothes or weapons, and when told to do so he would bring back prisoners too. Denisov relieved Tikhon of all menial work, took him out on expeditions and began to treat him like one of the Cossacks.

Tikhon, no horseman, went everywhere on foot, yet he was never far behind the cavalry. His weapons were a musketoon, which he carried rather as a joke, a pike and an axe, which he wielded as skilfully as a wolf uses its teeth to nip fleas in its coat and crunch big bones, all with the same dexterity. Tikhon was equally adept at swinging his axe to split logs, and holding it by the head to chip off thin skewers or carve spoons. Tikhon occupied a very special position in Denisov's band. When anything really nasty or difficult had to be done, like putting a shoulder to a wagon stuck in the mud, hauling a horse out of a bog by its tail, skinning a horse, infiltrating the French or walking thirty miles in a day, everybody chuckled and looked straight at Tikhon.

'He's good for anything, that devil. Tough as old boots,' they used to say about him.

One day when he was trying to capture a Frenchman he was shot in the buttock. This wound, which Tikhon treated only by applications of vodka, internally and externally, was the subject of the funniest jokes in the whole unit, and Tikhon took them in good part.

'That's you finished, is it, old boy? Caught you bending!' laughed the Cossacks, and Tikhon would react by pulling a face, pretending to be furious, and cursing Frenchmen with swearwords that made them all laugh. The only noticeable effect this incident had on Tikhon was that afterwards he didn't bring in many prisoners.

Tikhon was the bravest and handiest man in the unit. Nobody found more ways of attacking; nobody captured or killed as many Frenchmen as he did. This made him the camp joker, acknowledged as such by Cossacks and hussars alike, and it was a role he was only too willing to take on.

On this occasion Tikhon had been sent overnight by Denisov to Shamshevo to catch an informer. But, either because he was not satisfied with catching a single French prisoner or because he had overslept, he had waited until daylight to creep through the bushes in among the French, and, as Denisov had just seen from the hill-top, he had been discovered.

CHAPTER 6

Denisov stayed on for a few minutes chatting to the hetman about tomorrow's attack, which he now seemed to have settled on once and for all, seeing how near the French were, but then he turned his horse's head and rode back.

'Wight, my boy, let's go and get ourselves dwied out,' he said to Petya.

As he was getting close to the forester's hut Denisov stopped and peered into the wood. A man in a short jacket, bark-fibre shoes and a Kazan hat, with a gun slung across his shoulder and an axe in his belt, was striding easily through the forest on his long legs with his long arms swinging at his sides. The moment he caught sight of Denisov he made a quick movement and threw something into the bushes before taking off his sopping-wet hat with its droopy brim and walking across to his commanding officer.

It was Tikhon. His wrinkled, pock-marked face with its narrow eyes was a picture of beaming self-satisfaction and cheeriness. He held his head high and fixed Denisov with a close stare, looking as if he could hardly stop himself laughing.

'Well, where did you get to?' asked Denisov.

'Where did I get to? I been after the French.' The answer was quick and assertive, delivered in a rich and throaty bass.

'Why did you cweep up in bwoad daylight? You stupid ass! And why didn't you get me one of them?'

'Oh, I did,' said Tikhon.

'Well, where is he?'

'Got one at first light, I did,' Tikhon went on, spreading his flat feet and turned-out toes in their bark-fibre shoes. 'Yes, took him in the wood, I did. Could see 'e was no good, though. So I says to meself – better go back an' get another one, bit nearer the mark.'

'I knew it. Wotten devil,' said Denisov to the hetman. 'Why didn't you bwing him to me?'

'No point in bringing 'im in!' Tikhon was angry and he cut in quickly. 'Useless 'e was. I knows what you be after.'

'Stupid swine! . . . Well, what happened?'

'I went to get another one,' Tikhon went on. 'I creeps up through the wood like this, and I lays meself down.' Suddenly, in one smooth movement, Tikhon was down on his belly, showing them how he had done it. 'One shows up, so I grabs 'im,' he went on, 'like this . . .' Tikhon skipped lightly to his feet. '"You an' me," says I, "we'm off to see the colonel." He starts yellin' 'is 'ead off, and suddenly there's four of 'em. All rushin' at me with their little swords out. Took me axe to 'em, I did, like this. "What's all this?" says I. "Jesus, I'm off,"' cried Tikhon, waving his arms in the air and squaring his chest with a fearsome scowl.

'Yes, we were up there on the hill. We saw you legging it through the puddles,' said the hetman, screwing up his glittering eyes.

Petya was finding it hard not to laugh, but he could see they were all holding it back. His eyes flew back and forth between the three faces. He couldn't make head or tail of what was going on.

'Don't you fool about with me,' said Denisov, coughing angrily. 'Why didn't you bwing me that first one?'

Tikhon started scratching his back with one hand and his head with the other, and all at once his face broadened out, beaming with an inane grin that showed why they had called him 'gap-tooth' (Shcherbaty). Denisov broke into a smile, Petya burst out laughing and Tikhon joined in.

'I tell you, 'e was no good,' said Tikhon. 'Lousy dresser too. Couldn't take 'im nowhere. Nasty piece o' work, your Honour. "Oh no," says he, "I be a gendral's son," says he, "an' I aint goin' nowhere."'

'Agh, you swine!' said Denisov. 'I needed him for questioning . . .'

'Oh, but I asked 'im some questions,' said Tikhon. 'Said 'e didn't know very much. "There's lots of us," says 'e, "but they'm a miserable bunch, an' they'm all the same. One good shout," says he, "and you'll get the lot,"' Tikhon concluded, looking Denisov straight in the eye cheerily enough but with determination.

'I've a good mind to give you a damn good thwashing. Teach you to fool about with me,' said Denisov sternly.

'No need to go on like that,' said Tikhon, 'just because I didn't see none of your Frenchies. When it gets a bit dark I'll go an' catch whatever you want. Get you three of 'em.'

'Come on, then, let's get going,' said Denisov. All the way to the forester's hut he refused to speak, and his face wore an angry scowl.

Tikhon dropped back, and Petya heard the Cossacks laughing with him and at him about a pair of boots he had thrown into the bushes.

Tikhon's words and his smiling manner had given him plenty to laugh at, but when this passed, Petya suddenly realized Tikhon had killed the man. He felt queasy. He stole a glance at the boy prisoner and felt a pang in his heart. But the queasiness was short-lived. He felt duty-bound to hold his head high, look brave and important and ask the hetman some questions about tomorrow's assignment. He just had to live up to the company he was now in.

The officer Denisov had sent to find Dolokhov came out to meet him with the news that Dolokhov would soon be with them and all was well with him.

Denisov's spirits rose, and he beckoned to Petya. 'Wight, then. Come and tell me what's been happening to you,' he said.

CHAPTER 7

When the Rostov family had still been in the process of moving out of Moscow Petya had left them to join his regiment, and was soon taken on as an orderly by a general in charge of a large guerrilla unit.

Ever since he had received his commission, and especially since joining a regiment on active service and taking part in the battle of Vyazma, Petya had been in a constant state of elation at his grown-up status, and he was burning with all-consuming anxiety not to miss any opportunity for true heroism. He was delighted with everything he had seen and experienced in the army, but he couldn't escape the impression that the really heroic things were going on right now in places where he happened not to be. So he was in a constant hurry to get to places where he wasn't.

On the 21st of October, when his general had voiced a desire to send someone over to Denisov's company, Petya had begged so piteously to be sent that the general couldn't refuse. But even as he dispatched him the general remembered Petya's foolhardy behaviour at the battle of Vyazma, when, instead of riding straight down the road to deliver a message, Petya had got within firing range of the French and loosed off a couple of pistol-shots, so with this in mind he explicitly banned Petya from taking part in any action that Denisov might be contemplating. This was why Petya had blushed and looked embarrassed when Denisov asked if it was all right for him to stay. Until the moment he got to the edge of the wood Petya had fully intended to carry out his duty to the letter and go straight back. But once he had seen the French, and Tikhon, and learnt that tonight's attack was definitely on, he suddenly decided, with the swift change of mind that youngsters are so prone to, that the general he had greatly admired until then was a miserable specimen, and only a German, whereas Denisov was a hero, and the hetman was a hero, and Tikhon was a hero, and it would be disgraceful to leave them at such a difficult time.

It was getting dark when Denisov, Petya and the hetman rode up to the forester's hut. In the semi-darkness they could see saddled horses,

Cossacks and hussars building little shelters in the clearing, and kindling a glowing fire in a gully so no smoke would be visible to the French. In the entrance of the little hut a Cossack with his sleeves rolled up was butchering a sheep. Inside, three officers of Denisov's unit were busy converting the door into a table. Petya took off his wet clothes, handed them over for drying and got straight down to helping the officers fix up a dining-table.

In ten minutes the table was ready, covered with a napkin and set out with vodka, a flask of rum, some white bread, roast mutton and salt.

Sitting at the table with the officers, with his fingers running with fat as he tore into the mutton that smelled so good, Petya was in a state of childish rapture and tender affection for the whole of mankind matched by the certainty that everybody else felt the same affection for him.

'So what do you think, Vasily Fyodorovich?' he said to Denisov. 'It will be all right for me to stay on just for a day or so, won't it?' And without waiting for an answer, he provided his own response: 'I mean, I was told to find out about things, and I am finding out about things . . . Only you must let me get right into . . . you know, the real . . . I'm not bothered about winning medals . . . But I would like to, er . . .' Petya clenched his teeth and looked round at them, raising his head even higher and waving his hands in the air.

'Get into the thick of things,' said Denisov with a smile.

'Oh, please, put me in charge of something. I do want to be in charge,' Petya went on. 'It wouldn't be much trouble to you. Would you like to borrow my knife?' he said to an officer, who was trying to cut himself a piece of mutton. And he gave him his folding pocket-knife.

The officer admired the knife.

'Oh, please keep it. I've got several like that . . .' said Petya, colouring up. 'Gosh! I nearly forgot,' he cried suddenly. 'I've got some lovely raisins. You know, the ones without stones. We have a new canteen-man, and he does get hold of some smashing things. I bought ten pounds of them. I've got a sweet tooth! Would you like some?' And Petya ran out to his Cossack in the entrance, and came back with baskets containing five pounds of raisins. 'Help yourselves, gentlemen. Do help yourselves.'

'Do you happen to need a coffee-pot?' he said to the hetman. 'I bought a beauty from our canteen-man! He has such smashing things. And he's very honest. That's the main thing. I'll make sure I send it. Or perhaps your flints have nearly had it – these things do happen. I brought some with me. Look, I've got them here . . .' – he pointed to the baskets – 'A hundred flints. I got them cheap. Please, take as many as you like. Take them all . . .' And suddenly, dismayed at the thought that he might have let his tongue run away with him, Petya stopped short and coloured up.

He began to think back, wondering whether he might have committed any other *faux pas*. And as he ran through his recollections of the day gone by, a memory of the French drummer-boy popped up in his mind.

'We're having a wonderful time, but how is he getting on? What have they done with him? Has he been fed? Have they been nasty to him?' he wondered.

But, remembering how he had gabbled on about the flints, he was too scared to ask.

'I suppose I could ask,' he thought. 'But they'd only say, "It's one young boy worrying about another." I'll show them what kind of boy I am tomorrow! Would it be too embarrassing to ask?' Petya wondered. 'Oh, well! I don't care.' And without further ado, blushing and watching the officers' faces warily for any signs of amusement, he said, 'Do you think we might call that boy in, the one who was taken prisoner, and give him something to eat . . . er, perhaps . . .'

'Yes, poor little devil,' said Denisov, who clearly saw nothing embarrassing in the suggestion. 'Bring him in. His name is Vincent Bosse. Go and fetch him.'

'I'll get him,' said Petya.

'Yes, do. Poor little devil,' repeated Denisov.

Petya was standing near the door as Denisov said this. He wriggled between the officers and went up to Denisov.

'I must embrace you, my dear fellow,' he said. 'Oh, how splendid! How marvellous!' He embraced Denisov, and ran outside.

'Bosse! Vincent!' Petya called out, standing by the door.

'Yes, sir. Who do you want?' said a voice through the darkness. Petya said they wanted the French boy who had been taken prisoner that day.

'Oh, you mean Vesenny?' said the Cossack.

His name, Vincent, had already undergone a transformation: the Cossacks called him Vesenny, and the peasants Visenya. In both new versions the touch of spring – *vesna* in Russian – went well with the figure of the young boy.

'He's having a warm by the fire. Hey, Visenya! Visenya!' Voices and laughter echoed through the darkness.

'He's a bright boy,' said a hussar standing next to Petya. 'We've just given him a meal. Was he hungry!'

Bare feet splashed through the mud in the darkness, and the drummer-boy appeared by the door.

'Oh, there you are,' said Petya. 'Do you want something to eat? Don't be afraid. Nobody's going to hurt you,' he added shyly, touching his hand warmly. 'Come in, come in.'

'Thank you, sir,' answered the drummer, in a quavering voice, almost that of a child, and he began wiping his dirty feet. There was a lot that Petya wanted to say to the drummer-boy, but he didn't dare. He stood next to him in the entry, shifting from one foot to the other. Then he took hold of his hand in the darkness and gave it a squeeze. 'Come in, come in,' he repeated, this time in a gentle whisper.

'Oh, I wish I could do something for him!' Petya said to himself as he opened the door and ushered the boy in ahead of him.

When the drummer-boy had come inside Petya sat down some way away, feeling that it would be lowering his dignity to take much notice of him. He sat there fingering the money in his pocket and wondering whether it would be too embarrassing to give some to the drummer-boy.

CHAPTER 8

Denisov had told them to give the drummer-boy some vodka and mutton and dress him in a long Russian coat so he could stay with their unit rather than being sent off with the other prisoners. Petya's attention was distracted from him by the arrival of Dolokhov. He had heard lots of army stories about Dolokhov's outstanding bravery and his callous attitude to the French, so from the moment Dolokhov set foot inside the hut Petya couldn't take his eyes off him; he looked more and more sure of himself and tossed his head back to show himself not unworthy of the company of someone like Dolokhov.

Petya was taken aback by the ordinariness of Dolokhov's appearance.

Denisov was dressed in a Cossack coat, he had grown a beard and he wore an icon of St Nikolay the Miracle-worker on his chest; there was something about his way of speaking and his overall bearing that bore witness to his special position. By contrast, Dolokhov, who had sported a Persian costume in Moscow, now looked like a well-turned-out guards officer. He was clean-shaven, and he wore the usual guardsman's padded coat with a St George ribbon in his button-hole and an ordinary forage-cap set straight on his head. Now he took his wet cloak off in the corner, walked over to Denisov without greeting anybody and got straight down to business by asking how things were going. Denisov told him all about the designs the larger units had on the French convoy, the message Petya had brought and his response to both generals. Then he went through everything he knew about the present disposition of the French.

'That's fine. But we've got to find out what kind of troops they are, and how many they've got,' said Dolokhov. 'We must go and have a look. We can't just rush in without knowing for certain how many there are. I like to do things by the book. Come on, I'm sure one of you gentlemen wouldn't mind coming with me to pay them a little call. I've got a spare uniform with me.'

'I, er . . . I'll come!' cried Petya.

'There's absolutely no need for you to go,' said Denisov to Dolokhov, 'and I wouldn't let him go for all the tea in China.'

'I like that!' cried Petya. 'Why shouldn't I go?'

'Because there's no need for it.'

'Excuse me . . . I'm sorry . . . I . . . I *am* going, and that's it. You will take me, won't you?' he cried, turning to Dolokhov.

'Don't see why not . . .' Dolokhov answered rather vaguely as he took a good look at the French drummer-boy.

'How long have you had this youngster?' he asked Denisov.

'We caught him today, but he doesn't know anything. I've kept him with us.'

'Oh yes? What do you do with the rest of them?' said Dolokhov.

'What do I do with them? I send them in and get a witten weceipt!' cried Denisov, suddenly flushing. 'I tell you stwaight – I haven't got a single man's life on my conscience. Couldn't you manage to send thirty, or even thwee hundwed, men into town under guard wather than, to put it bluntly, stain your honour as a soldier?'

'Niceties like that are all very well for this little sixteen-year-old count,' Dolokhov said with a cold sneer, 'but it's time you said good-bye to that sort of stuff.'

'Well, I'm not saying anything. All I'm saying is – I'm definitely going with you,' said Petya diffidently.

'Yes, as far as we're concerned, my friend, we need to get rid of niceties like that,' Dolokhov persisted, apparently deriving much pleasure from going on about a subject that Denisov found so irritating. 'Now, why have you kept this lad?' he said. 'I suppose you're sorry for him. Anyway, we all know what your receipts are worth. You send off a hundred men and thirty get to town. They drop dead

on the way from starvation, or they get killed. Take no prisoners –
doesn't it come down to the same thing?'

The hetman screwed up his light-coloured eyes, and gave a nod of
approval.

'Nothing to do with me. Enough said. I just don't want their lives
on my conscience. You tell me they die. That's all wight by me, as
long as it's not my fault.'

Dolokhov laughed.

'They want to get me. The order's gone out twenty times over. And
if they do, if they catch me – and you too with all your chivalry –
they'll string us up on the nearest tree.' He paused. 'Anyway, we'd
better get down to some work. Send my Cossack in with that pack.
I've got two French uniforms. Well, are you coming with me?' he
asked Petya.

'Me? Oh yes, yes, of course I am,' cried Petya, blushing almost to
tears, with a sidelong glance at Denisov.

While Dolokhov had been arguing with Denisov about the treatment of prisoners Petya had begun to feel all awkward and anxious
again, but as before he couldn't quite grasp what they were on about.
'If that's the way these famous grown-up men think, it must be good,
it must be all right,' he thought. 'Anyway the main thing is to stop
Denisov even thinking I've got to obey him, and he can order me
about. I'm definitely going to the French camp with Dolokhov. If he
can go, I can!'

Petya's response to all Denisov's attempts at persuading him not to
go was to say that he too liked doing things by the book and not just
any old how, and he never thought about danger to himself.

'It's like this. If we don't know exactly how many men there are,
you must admit it could cost hundreds of lives, and only two of us are
involved, and I really want to go, and I am going, I am, you know,
and you can't stop me,' he said. 'It'll only make things worse . . .'

CHAPTER 9

Petya and Dolokhov changed into French uniforms and shakos, rode
out to the clearing where Denisov had looked across at the French
camp, emerged from the wood and plunged down into the hollow
through the pitch darkness. When they got to the bottom Dolokhov
told the Cossacks accompanying him to wait there, and set off at a

smart trot down the road that led to the bridge. Petya rode at his side, sick with excitement.

'If we get caught, they won't take me alive. I've got my pistol,' whispered Petya.

'Don't speak Russian,' said Dolokhov in a hurried whisper, and at that moment a challenging 'Who goes there?' rang out through the darkness accompanied by the clatter of a musket.

The blood rushed to Petya's face, and he clutched at his pistol.

'Lancers of the Sixth Regiment,' said Dolokhov, neither hastening nor slackening his horse's pace.

The black figure of a sentry stood on the bridge.

'Password?'

Dolokhov reined in his horse and slowed to a walking pace.

'I want to know if Colonel Gérard is here,' he said.

'Password?' repeated the sentry, making no reply and barring their way.

'When an officer makes his round sentries don't ask for passwords!' shouted Dolokhov, suddenly losing his temper as he bore down on the sentry. 'I'll ask you again. Is the colonel here?'

And without waiting for an answer from the sentry, who stepped aside, Dolokhov rode up the slope at walking pace.

Noticing the black shadow of a man crossing the road, Dolokhov stopped him and asked where the colonel and officers were to be found. The man, a soldier carrying a sack over his shoulder, stopped, came up close to Dolokhov's horse, patted it with one hand and told them in a simple, friendly way that the colonel and the officers were just up the hill on the right-hand side, in the courtyard of the farm, as he called the little manor house.

They kept on up the road, hearing French voices from the camp-fires on both sides, and then Dolokhov turned into the yard of the manor house. When he got to the gate, he dismounted and walked over to a big, blazing fire with several men sitting round it, engaged in loud conversation. There was something boiling in a pot over to one side, and a soldier in a peaked cap and a blue coat was down on his knees in the bright glow, stirring away with his ramrod.

'He's as tough as old boots, you know,' said one of the officers, sitting in the shadows on the other side of the fire.

'He'll get them off their backsides,' said another with a laugh.

They stopped talking and peered into the darkness when they heard Petya and Dolokhov approaching with their horses.

'Good evening, gentlemen!' Dolokhov called out clearly in a loud voice.

There was a stir among the officers in the shadows beyond the fire, and one of them, a tall man with a long neck, walked round the fire and came over to Dolokhov.

'Is that you, Clément?' said he. 'Where the devil . . . ?' but he broke off when he saw his mistake, and frowned slightly, greeting Dolokhov as a stranger, and asking whether he could be of any assistance. Dolokhov told him he and his comrade were trying to catch up with their regiment, and asked the whole company whether they knew anything about the Sixth Regiment. Nobody did, and Petya thought the officers were beginning to look at him and Dolokhov with hostility and suspicion. For several seconds nobody spoke.

'If you were hoping for some supper you've come too late,' said a voice from across the fire, with a scarcely concealed laugh.

Dolokhov said they weren't hungry, and they had to push on during the night.

He gave their horses to the soldier who was stirring the pot and squatted down on his heels next to the officer with the long neck. This man couldn't take his eyes off Dolokhov, and he asked again what regiment he belonged to. Dolokhov appeared not to hear the question. Instead of answering he took out a short French pipe, lit it and asked the officers whether the road ahead was safe from Cossacks.

'The brigands are everywhere,' answered an officer from across the fire.

Dolokhov said that the Cossacks were only a danger to stragglers like him and his comrade; they wouldn't dare to attack the big units. 'Would they?' he added inquiringly. There was no answer.

'He's bound to come away now, surely,' Petya kept thinking as he stood by the fire listening to the conversation.

But Dolokhov struck up again, and proceeded to ask direct questions. How many men did they have in their battalion? How many battalions were there? How many prisoners?

Inquiring about the Russian prisoners, Dolokhov went on to say, 'Nasty business this, dragging these corpses after you. Better to shoot vermin like that,' and he broke into such a strange, loud laugh that Petya thought the French were bound to see through their disguise, and his instinctive reaction was to take a step back from the fire.

Dolokhov's comment and laughter elicited no response, and a French officer, someone they hadn't seen because he was lying there wrapped up in a greatcoat, sat up and whispered something to his neighbour. Dolokhov got to his feet and shouted to the man holding their horses.

'Are they going to let us have our horses?' Petya wondered, instinctively edging closer to Dolokhov.

They did.

'Good evening, gentlemen,' said Dolokhov.

Petya tried to say 'Good evening', but the words stuck in his throat. The officers were whispering. Dolokhov's horse wouldn't stand still and it took him a long time to mount; then at last they were going out through the gate at a gentle walking pace. Petya rode at his side, not daring to look back, though he was dying to see whether or not the French were running after them.

Once out on the road, instead of turning back towards the open country Dolokhov rode along further into the village. At one point he stopped and listened.

'Can you hear that?' he said.

Petya recognized the sound of voices speaking Russian, and he could see camp-fires with the dark shapes of Russian prisoners all round them. When they finally got back to the bridge Petya and Dolokhov rode past the sentry, who continued to pace gloomily up and down and never said a word. They came to the hollow where the Cossacks were waiting.

'Goodbye, then. Tell Denisov. Sunrise. We'll wait for the first shot,' said Dolokhov, and he was about to ride away, but Petya snatched at his arm.

'No, wait!' he cried. 'You're such a hero! Oh! How marvellous! How splendid! I like you so much!'

'That's all right, then,' answered Dolokhov, but Petya wouldn't let go, and in the darkness Dolokhov could see him leaning across so they could embrace. Dolokhov kissed him, gave a laugh, turned his horse and vanished into the darkness.

CHAPTER 10

When he got back to the hut Petya found Denisov standing at the door. He had been waiting for Petya to come back, and he was feeling restless, anxious and annoyed with himself for letting him go.

'Oh, thank God!' he cried. 'Thank God for that!' he kept on saying as he listened to Petya's breathless account. 'You damned wascal, I haven't been able to sleep for wowwying about you!' he added. 'Anyway, thank God you're back. Now go and have a west. There's just time for some shut-eye before morning.'

'Yes, all right ... Oh, no,' said Petya. 'I just don't feel sleepy. Besides, I know what I'm like. Once I drop off that's me finished. Anyway, I don't usually get much sleep before a battle.'

Petya sat there for a while in the hut, going over the juicy details of his adventure and vividly imagining what was going to happen tomorrow. Then he noticed Denisov had fallen asleep, so he got up and went outside.

It was still pitch black. It had stopped raining, but the trees were still dripping. Close by the hut he could just make out the black shapes of the Cossacks' shanties and the horses tethered together. Back behind the hut he could see the dark blur of two wagons and a few horses, and down in the hollow a red glow came from a dying fire. Not all of the Cossacks and hussars were asleep; the murmur of whispering voices mingled with the sound of raindrops dripping and horses champing.

Petya walked out, glanced round through the darkness and went over to the wagons. A snoring sound was coming from under one of them, and saddled horses stood around munching oats. In the dark Petya saw his own horse and went over to see him. He called him Karabakh, a name that suggested the Caucasus, though in fact he came from Ukraine.

'Hey, Karabakh, we've got a job to do tomorrow,' he said, nuzzling at his nostrils and giving him a kiss.

'Can't you get to sleep sir?' said a Cossack voice from under the wagon.

'Well I ... Your name's Likhachov, isn't it? ... I've only just got back. We've been over to see the French.' And Petya gave the Cossack a detailed account not only of his trip, but also his reasons for going, and why he thought it was better to put his life on the line rather than leave things to chance.

'Well, you ought to get a bit of sleep,' said the Cossack.

'No, I'm used to it,' answered Petya. 'By the way, how are the flints in your pistols? Are they worn out? I brought some with me. Do you want some? Help yourself.'

The Cossack popped out from under the wagon to take a closer look at Petya.

'I like to do things by the book, you see,' said Petya. 'Some men, you know, aren't very bothered and they don't make preparations, and they live to regret it. I don't like that.'

'No, I'm sure you're right,' said the Cossack.

'Oh, there's one other thing. My dear chap, would you mind sharpening my sabre for me? It's gone a bit bl ...' (But Petya couldn't bring himself to tell a lie.) 'Well, actually it's never been sharpened. Could you manage that?'

'Yes. Sure I can.'

Likhachov stood up, rummaged in his pack, and soon Petya was standing there listening to the warlike sound of steel on stone. He clambered up on to the wagon, and sat on the side. The Cossack went on sharpening down below.

'All the other boys are asleep, aren't they?' said Petya.

'Some are. Some are awake like us.'

'What's happened to the boy?'

'Vesenny? He's burrowed down over yonder in the hay. He's having a good sleep after his scare. He was ready for it.'

For a long time Petya sat there saying nothing, just listening to the sounds. Then footsteps came towards them through the darkness, and a dark figure emerged.

'What's that you're sharpening?' asked the man as he came over to the wagon.

'A sabre for the gentleman here.'

'Fine job,' said the man. Petya assumed he was a hussar. 'Did that cup get left over here?'

'Yes, it's there, by that wheel.'

The hussar took the cup.

'Soon be daylight,' he added, yawning as he walked away.

Petya ought to have been fully aware that he was in a wood with Denisov's guerrillas, less than a mile from the road, perched on a wagon captured from the French with horses tethered to it, that down on the ground the Cossack Likhachov was sitting sharpening his sabre for him, that the big, black blur on the right was their hut, and the bright red glow down on the left was the dying camp-fire, and the man who had come for the cup was a thirsty hussar, but he wasn't aware of any of this, and he didn't want to know. He was far away in a land of magic where nothing bore any resemblance to real life. That big black patch of shadow might well be a hut, but it could also be a cave leading down to the centre of the earth. The red patch might be a fire, but it could also be the eye of a huge monster. Maybe he really was perched on a wagon, but it was just as likely he wasn't perched on a wagon, he was on the top of a fearfully high tower, and if he fell off it would take him a whole day, a whole month to reach the ground – or maybe he would fly on and on for ever and never reach the ground. Maybe it was only the Cossack Likhachov sitting down there under the wagon, but it was just as likely to be the kindest, bravest, most wonderful and marvellous man in the world, only nobody knew about him. Maybe it had been a hussar who had come for a drink of water and gone back down the hollow, but perhaps he was a man who had vanished, disappeared from the face of the earth, never to reappear.

Whatever Petya might have seen now, it wouldn't have come as a surprise. He was in a land of pure magic, where anything was possible.

He glanced up at the sky. That too was as magical as the earth. It was beginning to clear, and the clouds scudded across the tree-tops as if they wanted to uncover the stars. For a moment it seemed as if the heavens were clearing to open up a pure black sky. Then these black patches began to look like stormclouds. Then the sky seemed to soar away higher and higher; then it was falling back, falling down, and you could almost reach out and touch it.

Petya's eyes were closing and he was beginning to nod. Raindrops dripped. Low voices murmured. The horses neighed and shook themselves. Somebody snored.

'Swish, swish!' went the sabre on the stone, and all at once Petya seemed to hear the melodious strains of a lovely orchestra playing a sweet and solemn hymn he had never heard before. Petya's musical ear was as good as Natasha's, and much more acute than Nikolay's, but he had never studied music and never even thought about music, so the melodies that suddenly flooded into his mind had a special freshness and charm. The music swelled louder and clearer. A theme developed and passed from one instrument to another. They were playing a fugue, though Petya hadn't the slightest idea what a fugue was. Each instrument took up the theme, first the violins, then the horns, except they were brighter and purer than violins and horns, but half-way through each instrument blended into another one as it took over the theme almost exactly, then came a third and a fourth, until they all blended harmoniously together, then went off on their own, and blended once again in a splendid crescendo of holy music alternating with a brilliant and triumphant song of victory.

'Oh yes, I know I'm only dreaming,' Petya said to himself as he lurched forward, nodding. 'It's just a sound in my ears. But wait – maybe this is my music. Let's hear it again. Give me my music! Yes!'

He closed his eyes. And from all sides, as if they were starting a long way away, the sounds rose from a low tremor, blending in harmony, going their own ways and then blending again, coming together in the same sweet and solemn hymn. 'Oh, what a lovely sound! All I want, and just as I want it!' Petya said to himself. He tried conducting this tremendous orchestra.

'Sh! Sh! Let it die away there!' And the sounds responded. 'Come on, give me a bit more. Make it sound happier! More joy, yes, more joy!' And from hidden depths rose a great crescendo of triumphant sound. 'Now, the voices, let me hear you!' Petya commanded. And far away he heard the men's voices followed by the women's. The voices swelled in another rhythmic, triumphant crescendo. Petya yielded to their extraordinary beauty with a mixture of awe and delight.

The singing blended with the victory march, the raindrops dripped and sabre swished on stone as the horses shook themselves again and neighed, though instead of disrupting the harmony they were drawn into it. Petya had no idea how long this lasted. He was revelling in it, wondering all the while at his own sense of pleasure and feeling sorry there was no one to share it with. He was woken up by the friendly voice of Likhachov.

'Everything's ready, sir. Time to cut them Froggies in two.'

Petya opened his eyes.

'Hey, it's getting light. It really is,' he cried. The unseen horses were now visible from head to tail, and a watery light filtered down through the leafless branches. Petya shook himself, jumped to his feet, searched his pocket for a rouble to give to Likhachov and took a few trial swipes with his sword before sheathing it. The Cossacks were untying the horses and tightening the saddle-girths.

'Here comes the commander,' said Likhachov.

Denisov came out of the hut, shouted to Petya and told him to get ready.

CHAPTER 11

Working at speed in the half-light they sorted out the horses, tightened the saddle-girths and got themselves into their various groupings. Denisov stood by the hut, giving out final instructions. Their infantry moved off down the road, a hundred feet splashing through the mud. They were soon lost among the trees in the early-morning mist. The hetman gave an order to the Cossacks. Petya held his horse by the bridle, eagerly waiting for the signal to mount. His face was glowing from a good splash with cold water, and his eyes were burning. A cold shiver ran down his back, and his whole body shook with a quick, rhythmic trembling.

'Wight. Is ev'wybody weady?' said Denisov. 'Bwing the horses.'

The horses were led forward. Denisov rounded on the Cossack for leaving the saddle-girths too loose, and he swore at him as he got on his horse. Petya put one foot in the stirrup. His horse made its usual show of nibbling him on the leg, but Petya leapt into the saddle, oblivious of his own weight, looked round at the hussars coming up behind them in the darkness and rode over to Denisov.

'Vasily Fyodorovich, you will give me a job to do, won't you? Please ... For God's sake ...' he said. Denisov seemed to have forgotten Petya's existence. He looked round at him.

'I've only one thing to ask you,' he said sternly. 'Do what I say, and don't go wushing off anywhere.'

As they rode along Denisov didn't say another word to Petya or anyone else. By the time they got to the edge of the wood it really was getting light in the open country. Denisov whispered something to the hetman, and the Cossacks began riding ahead past Petya and Denisov. When they had all gone by, Denisov urged his horse down the slope. Slipping and sinking back on their haunches, the horses slithered down into the hollow with their riders. Petya kept close to Denisov. He still had the shakes all over his body, worse than before. It was getting lighter by the minute, but distant objects were still hidden in the mist. When he got to the bottom Denisov looked back and nodded to the Cossack at his side.

'Signal,' he said.

The Cossack raised his arm, and a shot rang out. Instantly they heard sounds up ahead: horses galloping off, voices shouting on all sides, more shots.

At the first sound of galloping hooves and men calling out Petya slackened the reins, lashed his horse and leapt forward, ignoring Denisov, who was shouting at him. A great glare of noonday light seemed to flash before Petya's eyes the moment he heard the shot. He galloped to the bridge. The Cossacks were moving on ahead of him. At the bridge he brushed up against a Cossack who was lagging behind and overtook him. Just in front Petya could see some men, presumably the French, running across the road from right to left. One slipped in the mud right under his horse's legs.

Cossacks were crowding round one of the peasant houses, doing something. A terrible scream came from the middle of the crowd. Petya galloped over to this crowd, and the first thing he saw was the white face and trembling jaw of a Frenchman, who had grabbed hold of a lance aimed at his chest.

'Hurrah! ... Come on, boys ... Our boys are here!' shouted Petya. He gave rein to his excited horse and galloped on down the village street.

He could hear shots being fired up ahead. Cossacks, hussars and scruffy Russian prisoners were running up from both sides of the road, yelling and shouting without making any sense. A plucky Frenchman in a blue coat, with a scowling red face and no cap, was defending himself with a bayonet against the hussars. By the time Petya got there the Frenchman was down. 'Too late. Again!' flashed through Petya's mind, and he galloped off towards the place where he could hear the most shooting. There was a lot of gunfire coming from the manor-house yard where he had been the night before with Dolokhov. The French had gone to ground behind a wattle-fence in among the bushes of the overgrown garden, and they were firing at the Cossacks as they poured in through the gate. As he rode up to the gate, through the gunsmoke Petya caught a glimpse of Dolokhov's pale, greenish face as he shouted to the men. 'Go on round. Wait for the infantry!' he was yelling just as Petya got there.

'I'm not waiting . . . Hurrah!' shouted Petya, and without pausing for a second he galloped towards the spot where the shots had been coming from and where the gunsmoke was thickest. A volley of shots rang out. Some bullets whistled past; others thudded home. The Cossacks and Dolokhov were galloping in through the gate after Petya. In the thick, swirling smoke the French were throwing their weapons down and rushing out of the bushes towards the oncoming Cossacks, or running away downhill towards the pond. Petya was galloping through the courtyard. Instead of holding on to the reins he was cleaving the air with weird and wonderful movements of his arms and slithering sideways out of his saddle. His horse stepped on the ashes of a camp-fire still smouldering in the early-morning light and reared back. Petya fell heavily to the wet ground. The Cossacks could see his arms and legs twitching, but his head didn't move. A bullet had gone right through his head.

After some negotiations with the senior French officer, who came out of the house with a handkerchief tied to his sword and said they were ready to surrender, Dolokhov got down from his horse and went over to Petya, who was lying there motionless with his arms outstretched.

'He's had it,' he said with a scowl, and walked back to the gate to meet Denisov, who was riding in.

'Is he dead?' yelled Denisov, who could see unmistakably even at a distance that Petya's all too familiar body, in its awkward sprawl, had no life in it.

'He's had it.' Dolokhov repeated the words, apparently with relish, and then walked over to the prisoners, who were being rapidly surrounded by the scurrying Cossacks. 'We're not taking any prisoners!'

he shouted to Denisov. Denisov didn't reply. He went over to Petya, got down from his horse and with shaking hands he turned up the bloodstained face, spattered with mud and already drained of its colour.

'I've got a sweet tooth! Smashing raisins. Take the lot.' The words came back to him. And the Cossacks looked round in surprise at the sudden sound, like a dog howling, that came from Denisov as he turned away, walked over to the fence and clutched at it.

Pierre Bezukhov was one of the Russian prisoners rescued by Denisov and Dolokhov.

CHAPTER 12

The party of prisoners that Pierre belonged to was given no further instructions by the French authorities during its long trek from Moscow. But by the 22nd of October this party was no longer being escorted by the same troops and transport that had been with them when they left the city. Half the wagons carrying the dry biscuit rations that had accompanied them during the first stages of the journey had been seized by the Cossacks, and the other half had driven on ahead. Of the dismounted cavalrymen who had been marching in front of the prisoners not a man was left; every last one had disappeared. The artillery that the prisoners had seen ahead of them in the early stages had been replaced by Marshal Junot's enormous baggage-train with its escort of Westphalians. Behind the prisoners came more wagons carrying cavalry equipment.

After Vyazma the marching French, who had started out in three columns, had come together into a single mass. By now the breakdown of good order that Pierre had witnessed at the first halt outside Moscow had gone as far as it could.

The road they were marching along was strewn on both sides with the carcasses of dead horses. There was a continual succession of scruffy soldiers, stragglers from various regiments, some joining the column on the march, others dropping back. Several times there had been false alarms, and the convoy soldiers had raised their muskets, fired and rushed on headlong, trampling each other underfoot. Then they had rallied, come together again and cursed each other for their needless panic.

These three bodies travelling the road together – the cavalry wagons, the convoy of prisoners and Junot's baggage-train – still made up a complete and separate entity, though each of its parts was rapidly melting away.

One hundred and twenty cavalry wagons had set out, but only sixty were left, the others having been stolen or abandoned. A number of wagons from Junot's train had also been stolen or abandoned. Three wagons had been attacked and looted by stragglers from Davout's regiment. Listening to the Germans, Pierre had found out that this baggage-train had been more closely guarded than the prisoners, and one of their comrades, a German, had been shot by order of the marshal himself because a silver spoon belonging to him had been found among the soldier's possessions.

The convoy of prisoners was melting away faster than the other two. Three hundred and thirty men had started from Moscow, and less than a hundred were left. The prisoners were an even more irksome burden to the escorting soldiers than the cavalry equipment and Junot's baggage. They could see that saddles for the cavalry and Junot's spoons might conceivably be of some use, but why cold and starving soldiers should have to serve as sentries, guarding cold and starving Russians who were continually freezing to death or falling by the wayside, in which case they were supposed to be shot – all this was beyond them and quite disgusting. And the escorting soldiers in their miserable plight seemed to be scared of giving way to the pity they felt for the prisoners and thus worsening their own situation, so they were particularly nasty and brutal towards them.

At Dorogobuzh the escorting soldiers had gone off to loot their own stores, leaving the prisoners locked in a stable, and several prisoners had escaped by tunnelling under the wall, only to be caught by the French and shot.

The arrangement made when they were leaving Moscow, whereby any officers among the prisoners were to march apart from the men, had long since been abandoned. All who could walk marched together, and at the third stage Pierre had rejoined Karatayev and the bandy-legged, lavender-grey dog that had chosen Karatayev as her master.

On the third day after leaving Moscow Karatayev had had another bout of the fever that had kept him in the Moscow hospital, and as Karatayev became weaker and weaker Pierre had kept further and further away from him. From the time Karatayev fell ill Pierre, without knowing why, had had to force himself to go anywhere near him. And when he did go near and listened to the subdued moans coming from Karatayev as he lay down to sleep at the halting-places, and noticed the smell given off by the sick man getting worse, Pierre distanced himself and stopped thinking about him.

In his prison shed Pierre had learnt, through his whole being rather than his intellect, through the process of living itself, that man was created for happiness, and happiness lies within, in the satisfaction of natural human needs, and any unhappiness arises from excess rather than deficiency. But now, during the last three weeks of the march, he had learnt another new truth that brought great consolation – he had learnt that there is nothing in the world to be frightened of. He had learnt that just as there is no situation in the world in which a man can be happy and perfectly free, neither is there any situation in which he should be unhappy and not free. He had learnt that there is a limit to suffering and a limit to freedom, and those limits are never far away; that a man who has felt discomfort from a crumpled petal in his bed of roses has suffered just as much as he was suffering now, sleeping on the bare, damp earth, with one side freezing while the other side warmed up; that when in former days he had squeezed into a pair of tight dancing-shoes he had suffered just as much as he was suffering now, walking barefoot, his footwear having disintegrated long ago, with his feet covered with sores. He learnt that when he had married his wife by his own free will (so he had thought), he had been no freer than he was now when they locked him up in a stable for the night. Of all the things he later identified as painful, though at the time he was hardly conscious of them, the worst thing was the state of his bare feet, which were blistered and scabby. (Horse-meat had a nice taste and did you good, the flavour of saltpetre from the gun-powder used as a salt-substitute was really rather nice, the weather was never very cold, it was always warm when they were marching during the daytime, and at night they had camp-fires, and the lice that made a meal of him gave him a pleasant feeling of being kept warm.) His feet were the only things that hurt during those early days.

On the second day of the march, when he examined his blisters by the camp-fire Pierre thought he would never be able to walk on them, but when everybody was up, he limped along with the rest, and later on, when he warmed up, it didn't hurt to go on walking, though his feet looked even more terrible that evening. But he ignored them and thought about something else.

It was now that Pierre understood the full power of human vitality, and the effectiveness of our inbuilt safety device, distraction, which works like a safety-valve in steam-engines, letting off excess steam as soon as the pressure reaches a certain point.

He never saw or heard straggling prisoners being shot, though more than a hundred had died that way. He never spared a thought for Karatayev, who was fading by the day, and seemed certain to suffer the same fate very soon. Still less did Pierre think about himself. The harder his lot became and the more ghastly his immediate future seemed, the more independent of his present plight were the gladness and consolation that came to him through the pictures provided by his mind, memory and imagination.

CHAPTER 13

At midday on the 22nd Pierre was walking up a muddy, slippery road, looking down at his feet and the rough road-surface. From time to time he glanced at the familiar crowd around him, then he would look down again at his feet. The crowd and the feet had two things in common: they were his, and he knew them well. The lavender-grey, bandy-legged dog was scampering merrily at the side of the road, sometimes lifting a back paw in the air and skipping along on three legs in a display of skill and *joie de vivre*, or dropping down on all four legs to go charging across and bark at the crows as they perched on carrion. Greycoat looked sleeker and chirpier than she had done in Moscow. On every side lay the flesh of various animals – from men to horses – in various stages of decomposition, and the marching soldiers kept the wolves away, so Greycoat could gorge herself whenever she wanted.

The rain had been coming down since early morning. It looked as if it was going to stop, and the sky seemed likely to clear at any minute, but then they would take a short break and the heavens would open again worse than ever. The road was so saturated with rain it couldn't take any more, and the ruts were filling up with running streams.

Pierre plodded on, looking from side to side, counting his steps, and marking them off on his fingers in threes. In his mind he talked to the rain, chanting to himself, 'Come rain, come rain, come away rain!'

He thought his mind was a blank, but no, somewhere in the depths of his soul he was meditating on something deeply serious that carried consolation. This something was a subtle and soulful follow-on from last night's conversation with Platon Karatayev.

During the halt yesterday evening Pierre had suddenly felt frozen next to a dying fire, so he had got up and moved across to the nearest one that still had some heat in it. Platon was sitting there with a greatcoat over his head like a priest's robe. His easy, mellifluous voice, softened by his illness, murmured on as he told the soldiers a story Pierre had heard before. It was past midnight, a time when Karatayev's fever usually abated, and he really came to life. As Pierre got near to the fire and heard Platon's feeble, sickly voice and saw his pathetic face lit up by the firelight, he felt a nasty pang in his heart. He was scared of the pity he felt for this man and would have gone off somewhere else, but there was no other fire to go to, so he sat down, trying not to look at Platon.

'Well, how have you been?' he asked.

'How have I been? When you're poorly, don't cry, or God won't let you die,' said Karatayev, and he went straight back to the story he was half-way through.

'So, listen, brother . . .' he went on with a smile on his thin, pale face, and a strangely happy light in his eyes. 'So, listen, brother . . .'

Pierre knew this story well. Karatayev had told it to him half a dozen times before, always with particular pleasure. But even though it was very familiar Pierre listened now as if it was something new, and the gentle sense of rapture that Karatayev was enjoying as he told it communicated itself to Pierre as well. It was the story of an old merchant, a good man who had lived a Godfearing life with his family, and who went off one day to the fair at Makary with a friend of his, a rich merchant.

They had put up at an inn together and gone to bed, and the next morning the rich merchant was discovered with his throat cut and his things stolen. A bloodstained knife was found under the old merchant's pillow. The merchant was tried and flogged, and had his nostrils slit – all according to the law, as Karatayev said – and he was sent off to hard labour.

'So, listen, brother . . .' (It was at this point that Pierre had come in on the story.) 'After this a dozen years or more goes by. The old man is still a convict. Resigned to 'is fate, 'e is, as is only right. Never does nothin' wrong. The only thing 'e prays to God for is death . . . Right then . . . One night they be all gathered together, them convicts, just like we be 'ere, and the old man with 'em. And they starts talkin' about what they'm all in for, what they done wrong in the eyes of God. Lots of good stories. One of 'em was in for murder, another for two murders, somebody else 'ad set fire to somethin', and there was a wanderin' tramp who never done nothin' wrong. So they turns to the old man and they says, "What are you in for, Grandad?" "Me? Payin' for me sins, I be, me dear brothers," says 'e, "and everybody else's sins as well. I 'aven't murdered nobody, or pinched nothing, just given what I 'ad to the poor. Used to be a merchant, I did, me dear brothers. I 'ad lots o' money." And 'e tells 'em all. 'Ow things 'as worked out for 'im, all the details of 'is story bit by bit. "Not bothered about meself," says 'e, "I been picked out by God. Only one thing wrong," says 'e, "I do feel sorry for me old woman, and the kiddies." And 'e sheds a few tears. And it so 'appened in that company was the very man, you know, what 'ad killed the merchant. "Where did all this 'appen, Grandad?" says 'e. "When was it? What month?" Wanted to know all the details. 'Eartbroken 'e was. Goes up to the old man just like that, 'e does, an' falls down at 'is feet. "You be in 'ere, old man," says 'e, "for somethin' what I done." 'Tis God's truth. This man be innocent. 'E be sufferin' for nothing, lads," says 'e. "I done that job," says 'e, "an' put that knife under yer 'ead while you was asleep. Forgive me, Grandad. For God's sake, forgive me!" says 'e.'

Karatayev paused with a blissful smile on his face and stared into the fire, poking the logs.

'Then the old man, 'e says, "God will forgive you," says 'e, "but we'm all sinners in the eyes of God," says 'e. "I be sufferin' for me own sins." And 'e wept bitter tears. Then guess what, me old darling,' said Karatayev, with an ever-broadening beatific smile, as if to indicate that the best bit, the whole point of his story was about to come. 'Guess what, me old darling. That murderer went up to them at the top and confessed. "I seen six men off," says 'e ('e bein' a real wrong 'un), "but I'm right sorry for this little old man. 'E shouldn't 'ave to suffer 'cos o' me." Went an' confessed, 'e did. 'Twas all wrote down on paper and sent off, as is only right. Bloomin' miles away. Looked at by all the judges. Then it all gets wrote down again right and proper by them at the top. Know what I mean? Gets to the Tsar. Then an order comes down from the Tsar. Let the merchant go. Give 'im 'is compensation, like what the judges 'as said. Piece o' paper arrives. Everybody sets to, lookin' for the old man. Where's that little old man gone what was innocent and shouldn't 'ave seen all this sufferin'? 'Ere be a paper from the Tsar! Looked everywhere they did.' Karatayev's jaw trembled. 'But God 'ad forgiven 'im. 'E was dead! That's 'ow it 'appened, me old darling!' Karatayev came to the end of his story, and sat there for some time staring ahead with a smile on his face and nothing more to say.

It was not the story itself but its mysterious inner meaning, the glow of rapture that had lit up Karatayev's face as he told it, and the mysterious significance of his rapture – this was what filled Pierre's soul with a hazy feeling of joy.

CHAPTER 14

'Get fell in!' came a sudden voice, speaking in French.

There was a cheerful commotion among the prisoners and the escorting soldiers, and an air of expectancy as if some joyous and splendid occasion was at hand. Orders rang out on all sides, and then from the left a party of very smart cavalry soldiers on fine horses came trotting up, wheeling right round the prisoners. On every face was the tense expression you normally see when important people are about to arrive. The prisoners huddled together and were shoved back from the road. The convoy soldiers formed up in ranks.

'The Emperor! The Emperor! The marshal! The duke!' And the sleek cavalry had hardly got clear when a carriage and six greys rumbled past. Pierre caught a passing glimpse of a podgy white face, serene and handsome, belonging to a man in a three-cornered hat. It was one of the marshals. The marshal's eye fell on Pierre's big, imposing figure, and in the expression on his face when he frowned and looked away Pierre thought he could see compassion and the desire to conceal it.

The general in charge whipped up his skinny horse, and galloped after the carriage with panic written all over his crimson face. Several officers came together in a group, and the soldiers gathered round them. They all looked uneasy and excited.

'What did he say? What did he say?' Pierre could hear them asking.

While the marshal had been driving past the prisoners had been hustled together in a bunch, and Pierre had caught sight of Karatayev for the first time that morning. He was sitting wrapped up in his little greatcoat, leaning back against a birch-tree. His face still wore the same look of joyous emotion as yesterday, when he had been telling the story of the merchant and his innocent suffering, but now it had another expression too, a look of quiet solemnity.

Karatayev was looking across at Pierre, and his kindly, round eyes, brimming with tears, held an unmistakable appeal, as if he had something to say to him. But Pierre feared for his own skin. He pretended he hadn't seen that look and hurried away.

When the prisoners set off again Pierre looked back. Karatayev was still sitting there under the birch-tree at the side of the road, and there were two Frenchmen standing over him, talking to each other. Pierre didn't look round again. He limped on up the hill.

A shot rang out from behind, back where Karatayev had been

sitting. Pierre heard the shot distinctly, but the moment he heard it he suddenly remembered he hadn't finished calculating how many stages were left to Smolensk, the problem he had been working on before the marshal rode past. He started counting again. Two French soldiers ran past Pierre, one of them holding a musket that was still smoking. They both looked pale, and in the expression on their faces – one of them glanced timidly at Pierre – there was something similar to what he had seen in the young soldier at the execution in Moscow. Pierre looked at the soldier and remembered an occasion, only a couple of days ago, when that man had scorched his shirt while drying it in front of the fire and they had all laughed at him.

Back where Karatayev was sitting the dog started howling. 'Silly creature! What's she got to howl about?' thought Pierre.

Pierre's fellow prisoners, marching along at his side, were, like him, refusing to look back at the place where they had heard the shot come from and then the howling of the dog. But there was a grim look on every face.

CHAPTER 15

The cavalry wagons, the prisoners and Marshal Junot's baggage-train halted for the night in the village of Shamshevo. They all crowded round the camp-fires. Pierre went over to a fire, ate some roast horse-meat, lay down with his back to the fire and fell fast asleep. He slept as he had done at Mozhaysk after the battle of Borodino.

Once again real events mingled with his dreams; once again a voice, either his own or someone else's, was murmuring thoughts in his ear, some of the same thoughts he had heard in his dream at Mozhaysk.

Life is everything. Life is God. Everything is in flux and movement, and this movement is God. And while there is life there is pleasure in being conscious of the Godhead. To love life is to love God. The hardest and the most blessed thing is to love this life even in suffering, innocent suffering.

'Karatayev!' The memory flashed into Pierre's mind. And suddenly Pierre had a vision, like reality itself, of someone long forgotten, a gentle old teacher who had taught him geography in Switzerland. 'Wait a minute,' said the little old man. And he showed Pierre a globe. This globe was a living thing, a shimmering ball with no fixed dimensions. The entire surface of the ball consisted of drops closely compressed. And the drops were in constant movement and flux, sometimes dissolving from many into one, sometimes breaking down from one into many. Each drop was trying to spread out and take up as much space as possible, but all the others, wanting to do the same, squeezed it back, absorbing it or merging into it.

'This is life,' said the little old teacher.

'It's so simple and clear,' thought Pierre. 'How could I have not known that before? God is in the middle, and each drop tries to expand and reflect Him on the largest possible scale. And it grows, gets absorbed and compressed, disappears from the surface, sinks down into the depths and bubbles up again. That's what has happened to him, Karatayev: he has been absorbed and he's disappeared.'

'Now you understand, my child,' said the teacher.

'Don't you understand, damn your eyes?' shouted a voice, and Pierre woke up.

He raised his head and sat up. A French soldier was squatting by the fire, having shoved a Russian soldier to one side, and he was roasting a piece of meat on the end of a ramrod. His sleeves were rolled up, and his sinewy, hairy red hands, with their stubby fingers, were expertly rotating the ramrod. The glowing embers lit up his scowling brown face with its sullen brows.

'Makes no difference to him,' he muttered, glancing back quickly at a soldier standing behind him. 'Brigand! Get away from here!'

And the soldier, still turning the ramrod, glanced darkly at Pierre. Pierre turned away and stared into the shadows. A Russian soldier, the one who had been shoved aside, was sitting near the fire patting something. Pierre took a closer look and saw the lavender-grey dog sitting by the soldier, wagging her tail.

'She's come then . . .' said Pierre. 'Old Plat . . .' He couldn't finish what he was saying. All at once, a host of memories rose up in Pierre's mind, all of them instantly interlinked – the look that Platon had given him as he sat there under the tree, the shot they had heard from that very spot, the dog howling, the soldiers' guilty faces as they ran past, the smoking musket, Karatayev's absence when they got to the halting-place – and it was just beginning to sink in that Karatayev had been killed when another memory rose up in his mind, coming out of nowhere, a summer evening spent with a beautiful Polish lady on the verandah of his house in Kiev. And without quite managing to connect today's memories together or make anything of them, Pierre closed his eyes, and the picture of a summer evening in the country blended with the memory of going for a swim and that shimmering ball of liquid, and there he was plunging down, with the waters closing over his head.

*

Before sunrise he was woken up by loud and rapid firing and a lot of shouting. The French were rushing past.

'The Cossacks!' one of them shouted, and a minute later Pierre was surrounded by a crowd of Russians. It took some time for him to grasp what had happened to him. He could hear his comrades crying and sobbing with joy on every side.

'Brothers! Our boys! You lovely boys!' The old soldiers were shouting, weeping and hugging the Cossacks and hussars, hussars and Cossacks that crowded round the prisoners, offering them clothes, boots, bread. Pierre sat there sobbing in their midst. He couldn't get a word out. He hugged the first soldier who came near, and wept as he kissed him.

Dolokhov was standing at the gate of the dilapidated manor house, watching as crowds of disarmed Frenchmen filed past. The French, excited by all that had happened, were talking in raised voices, but as they walked past Dolokhov, who stood there lashing his boots with his riding-crop, and watching them with a cold, glassy stare that boded nothing but ill, their chatter died away. One of Dolokhov's Cossacks stood across from him, counting the prisoners, chalking them off in hundreds on the gate.

'How many's that?' asked Dolokhov.

'Getting on for two hundred,' answered the Cossack.

'Move along there,' said Dolokhov, deliberately using an expression picked up from the French, and whenever his eyes met the eyes of the passing prisoners they had a cruel glint in them.

It was with a sombre look that Denisov, hat in hand, walked behind the Cossacks as they processed towards a hole that had been dug in the garden, carrying the body of Petya Rostov.

CHAPTER 16

From the 28th of October, when the frosts set in, the flight of the French took on a more tragic character, with men freezing to death or being roasted to death by the camp-fires, while the Emperor, the kings and the dukes continued on their way in fur coats and carriages, taking their stolen treasure with them, though, in essence, the French army's process of flight and disintegration went on unchanged.

Between Moscow and Vyazma the French army of seventy-three thousand men (not including the guardsmen, who had spent the whole war doing nothing but pillage) had been reduced to a mere thirty-six thousand, even though only five thousand had been killed in battle. This is the first term in a progressive sequence; it can be used to calculate the remaining terms with mathematical exactitude.

The French army went on melting away and disappearing at the same rate from Moscow to Vyazma, Vyazma to Smolensk, Smolensk to the Berezina, from the Berezina to Vilna, regardless of variations in the degree of cold or pursuit, the extent to which they found the way blocked and any other conditions operating individually. After Vyazma the French troops went down from three columns to one great mass, and stayed like that to the end. Allowing for the fact that generals feel able to take liberties with the truth when describing the state of their army, we note that Berthier wrote as follows to the Emperor:

> I feel obliged to report to your Majesty the state of the various corps as observed by me personally on the march over the last two or three days. They are almost disbanded. Scarcely a quarter of the men still follow the flags of their regiments; the rest wander off on their own in different directions, pursuing their own interests, looking for food and hoping to evade discipline. All of them have only one thing in mind – Smolensk, where they hope to rest and recover. During the last few days many soldiers have been seen throwing away their cartridges and muskets. Given this state of affairs, whatever your long-term plans may be, the interests of your Majesty's service demand a regrouping of the army at Smolensk, which will involve getting rid of all non-combatants, such as cavalrymen without horses, as well as any superfluous baggage and some of the artillery material, which is now disproportionate to our overall troop numbers. As well as a few days' rest the soldiers, worn out by hunger and fatigue, need supplies. In recent days many have died by the roadside or in the bivouacs. This state of affairs is getting steadily worse, and there are grounds for fearing that if immediate steps are not taken there will be no possibility of controlling the troops in any engagement.
>
> 9th November. 20 miles from Smolensk.

After staggering into Smolensk, which they had seen as the promised land, the French murdered each other for food, raided their own stores and continued the flight when everything had gone.

On they went, with no idea of where they were going or why. The one who had least idea of all was the great genius, Napoleon, since there was no one to give him any orders. Nevertheless, he and his entourage still went through the motions of writing out various

commands, letters, reports and orders of the day, addressing each
other as 'Sire', 'My dear Cousin', 'Prince of Eckmühl', 'King of
Naples', and so on. But the orders and reports were just pieces of
paper; they were not followed up, because they couldn't have been
followed up. And despite the use of terms like Majesty, Highness, and
Cousin they all felt themselves to be pathetic, loathsome creatures
who had done a huge amount of harm, and now they were having to
pay the price. And despite a great show of caring for the army, each
man was thinking only of himself, and how quickly he could get away
and save his skin.

CHAPTER 17

The behaviour of the Russian and French armies during the retreat
from Moscow to the Niemen was like the Russian version of blind
man's buff, in which two players are blindfolded and one of them
rings a bell now and then to let the other one know where he is. At
first the one who is being chased rings his bell with no fear of his
opponent, but when things begin to get tricky he runs away from
his opponent as quietly as he can, though he often walks straight into
his arms when he thinks he is running away.

At first Napoleon's army announced where it was – this was in the
early stages of retreat down the Kaluga road – but afterwards, when
they were out on the Smolensk road, they ran away holding the bell
by its little clapper, though they often ran straight into the Russians
when they thought they were running away.

Given the speed of the French retreat, and of the Russians coming
on behind, and the consequent exhaustion of the horses, the best
method of estimating the enemy's position – the gathering of intelligence on horseback – was out of the question. Besides that, frequent
and rapid changes of position on the part of both armies meant that
any available intelligence was never up to date. If information came
in on the second of the month that the enemy army had been in a
certain place on the first of the month, by the time they got to the
third of the month, and something could be done about it, the army
was two days' march further on, in a totally different position.

One army fled; the other pursued. From Smolensk, the French had
the choice of many different roads. You would have thought that,
having stayed there for four days, the French might have been able to
ascertain where the enemy was, think up something effective and do

something new. But no, after a four-day halt they took to the road again in great mobs and instead of turning right or left, instead of planning and manœuvring their way forward, they plunged off down their own beaten track, their old road – the worst possible – the one through Krasnoye and Orsha.

Expecting the enemy from the rear rather than the front, the French fled in a straggling line, scattering themselves over the distance of a twenty-four-hour march. Out in front went the fleeing Emperor, closely followed by his kings and dukes. The Russian army, assuming Napoleon would turn right and cross the Dnieper, the only sensible course to take, turned right themselves and came out on the high road at Krasnoye. At which point, just as in blind man's buff, the French ran straight into our vanguard. Shocked at the sudden sight of the enemy, the French were thrown into confusion, stopped short in a sudden panic and then resumed their flight, abandoning their colleagues in their rear. For the next three days the different sections of the French army – first Murat's (the viceroy's), then Davout's, then Ney's – ran the gauntlet of the Russian army. Everybody abandoned everybody else. They abandoned the heavy baggage, the artillery and half their men, and took to their heels, circling round to the right at night-time to skirt the Russians.

The reason Ney came along last was that, in spite of their disastrous situation, or maybe because of it, he insisted on beating the floor they had hurt themselves on, and took time out to blow up the unoffending walls of Smolensk. So along came Ney, the last to come through with his corps of ten thousand men, but when he got to Orsha and caught up with Napoleon, he was left with no more than a thousand, having abandoned all the rest along with his cannons, and made his way like a thief in the night through the woods and across the Dnieper.

From Orsha they ran on down the road to Vilna, still playing blind man's buff with the pursuing army. At the Berezina there was more confusion, many were drowned and many surrendered, and those who managed to cross the river ran on.

Their commander-in-chief wrapped himself up in his fur-coat, got into his sledge and galloped off alone, deserting his colleagues. Those who could ran away too; those who couldn't surrendered or died.

CHAPTER 18

Considering the French did their utmost during this period of the campaign to bring about their own downfall, and not a step taken by that rabble, from their turning off down the Kaluga road to the flight of the commander from his army, made the slightest bit of sense, you might imagine that the historians who attribute the behaviour of the masses to the will of one man would have found it impossible to make the French retreat fit their theory.

But no. Mountains of books have been written by historians about this campaign, and everywhere we find accounts of Napoleon's judicious decision-making and careful planning, the tactical skill with which the soldiers were led and the military genius showed by the marshals.

The retreat from Maloyaroslavets at a time when there was nothing to stop Napoleon moving into a richly supplied region and he had access to the parallel road down which Kutuzov would later pursue him, the totally unnecessary retreat through devastated countryside – these eventualities are explained away by other contributing factors of great profundity. Likewise, other contributing factors of great profundity are brought forward to explain Napoleon's retreat from Smolensk to Orsha. Then we read of his heroic stance at Krasnoye, when ostensibly he was preparing to go into battle and take personal command. The story goes that he walked about holding a birch-stick and said, 'Enough of being the Emperor – I must now be the general!'

Despite which he turns tail and runs away immediately afterwards, leaving his divided army behind him to the workings of fate.

Then we read descriptions of the greatness displayed by some of the marshals, especially Ney, whose greatness consisted in sneaking away through the forest at night, crossing the Dnieper without his flags, his artillery and nine-tenths of his men, and scuttling away to Orsha.

And last of all, the final departure of the great Emperor from his heroic army is depicted by these historians as a great event performed by a genius. Even this final act of desertion, which everyday language would describe as the lowest of the low, a lesson in shame for every youngster, even this action finds justification in the language of the historians.

When the elastic of historical argument is stretched to breaking point, when an action flagrantly infringes anything humanity can agree to call by the name of goodness and justice, these historians take refuge in the concept of greatness. 'Greatness' seems to exclude all quantification of right and wrong. A great man knows no wrong. There is no atrocity that could be laid at the door of a great man.

'This is *great*!' say the historians, and at a stroke good and bad have ceased to exist; there is only 'greatness' and 'non-greatness'. 'Great' means good; 'not great' means bad. Greatness is, by their standards, a quality enjoyed by certain exceptional creatures that go by the name of 'hero'. And Napoleon, as he wraps himself up in his warm fur-coat and scurries home, leaving behind dying men who were not only his comrades, but (by his own admission) people he brought there himself, feels 'he's a great man' and his soul is at peace.

'There is only one step from the sublime to the ridiculous,' he says (and he sees something of the sublime in himself). And for fifty years the whole world has parroted the words, 'Sublime! Great! Napoleon the Great!'

'There *is* only one step from the sublime to the ridiculous.'

And it never enters anybody's head that to acknowledge greatness as something existing beyond the rule of right and wrong is to acknowledge one's own nothingness and infinite smallness.

For us, with Jesus Christ's rule of right and wrong to go by, there is nothing that cannot be measured by it. And greatness cannot exist without simplicity, goodness and truth.

CHAPTER 19

What Russian reader has not experienced a depressing feeling of annoyance, frustration and bewilderment on reading accounts of the last phase of the 1812 campaign? Who has not asked himself questions about it? How could they have failed to capture the French or finish them off, when they had all three Russian armies surrounding them in superior numbers, when the French were a disorderly rabble starving and freezing to death, and the one aim of the Russians (according to history) was to stop them in their tracks, cut them off from each other and capture them all?

How did it come about that the same Russian army that had fought the battle of Borodino with a numerical disadvantage failed to achieve its avowed aim of capturing the French when the French were surrounded on three sides? Can it be that the French are so superior that we couldn't beat them even when we had them surrounded by numerically stronger forces? How could that have happened?

History (or what passes for history) answers these questions by saying that it all came about because Kutuzov, Tormasov, Chichagov, this general and that general, failed to execute this or that manœuvre.

But *why* did they fail to execute these manœuvres? And if they really were responsible for the aim not being achieved why were they not tried and punished? But even if we admit that Kutuzov and Chichagov and the others were responsible for the Russian 'failure', it is still not clear why, given the situation of the Russian troops at Krasnoye and the Berezina (numerical superiority in both cases), the French army and marshals were not taken prisoner, when that was the ostensible aim of the Russians.

The explanation of this strange phenomenon provided by Russian military historians – that Kutuzov stopped them attacking – won't wash, because we know Kutuzov couldn't stop the troops going on the attack at Vyazma or Tarutino. Why was it that an under-strength Russian army won the battle of Borodino against a full-strength enemy, whereas they lost at Krasnoye and the Berezina when they had greater numbers and the French were an undisciplined rabble?

If the aim of the Russians was to isolate Napoleon and his marshals and take them prisoner, and if that aim was not only frustrated, but all attempts to achieve it were defeated time after time in the most shameful way, then the French are quite right to claim the last phase of the campaign as a series of victories, and Russian historians are wrong to claim it as a success story.

Russian military historians, whenever they are forced to think logically, are bound to admit the validity of this conclusion; for all their lyrical outpourings on the subject of Russian courage, loyalty and so forth, they are bound to admit that the retreat of the French from Moscow was a series of victories for Napoleon and defeats for Kutuzov.

But disregarding all questions of national self-esteem one is left with the feeling that this conclusion contains an inherent contradiction, in that the series of French victories led to nothing less than total destruction, and the series of Russian defeats led to the complete destruction of the enemy and the deliverance of their country.

This contradiction arises from the fact that historians, studying events in the light of letters penned by sovereigns and generals, memoirs, reports, projects and so on, have jumped to the wrong conclusion based on a non-existent Russian aim during that last phase of the 1812 campaign, the aim of isolating and capturing Napoleon and his marshals and his army. There never was any such aim, because it didn't make sense and it would have been impossible to achieve.

It didn't make sense because, first, Napoleon's army was in disarray and fleeing from Russia at all possible speed, in other words doing exactly what was wanted by every last Russian. What purpose would have been served by conducting all sorts of operations against the French when they were already running away as fast as they could?

Second, it would have made no sense to stand in the way of men who were putting all their energy into running away.

Third, it made no sense to risk losing men just to destroy the French army when that army was busy destroying itself without any help from outside, and at such a rate that, without any blocking of the road, all the French were able to take back across the frontier in December was a small number of men, scarcely a hundredth of the original army.

Fourth, it would have made no sense to capture the Emperor, the kings and the dukes, since their imprisonment would have made life difficult for the Russians, as was acknowledged by the more sensitive diplomats of the day (Joseph de Maistre among others). It would have made even less sense to capture the French army when half of our own strength had dwindled away before Krasnoye, and we would have needed a whole division to guard several corps of prisoners, at a time when our own soldiers were often under-provisioned, and the prisoners they did take were dying of starvation.

Any carefully considered plan to isolate Napoleon and capture him along with his army would have been like a gardener devising a plan to drive away a herd of cattle that had been trampling his beds, and then run after them, catch them at the gate and bash them over the head. The best that could be said of the gardener would be that he had lost his temper on a grand scale. But that wouldn't apply to the authors of the plan, since it wasn't their garden that had been trampled.

Anyway, the idea of isolating Napoleon along with his army not only made no sense; it was also quite impossible.

Impossible, first because we know from experience that the movement of columns over a three-mile area on a given battlefield never coincides with any planning, so the possibility of Chichagov, Kutuzov and Wittgenstein arriving together at an appointed spot was so remote as to be virtually impossible. Kutuzov knew this even as he received planning instructions from afar, and he went on record as saying that long-distance manœuvres never work out according to plan.

Second, it was impossible because the numbers of troops needed to paralyse the force of inertia propelling Napoleon's army back the way it had come would have been far greater than anything the Russians had at their disposal.

Third, it was impossible, because the military word for the isolating process – 'to cut off' – is meaningless. You can cut off a slice of bread, but not an army. To cut off an army – to block its way forward – is quite impossible, because there are always plenty of possible detours that can be made, and there is always night-time, when things go on unseen, which students of military history ought to recognize from the examples of Krasnoye and the Berezina. You can never capture anybody unless he is willing to be captured, just as you can never catch a swallow, though you might be able to if it settles on your hand. You can only capture prisoners who are willing to surrender, as the Germans did, following set rules of strategy and tactics. But the French soldiers saw this as inexpedient, and they were quite right to do so since a similar death from cold and starvation awaited them if they fled or were taken prisoner.

The fourth and main reason why it was impossible was that never since the world had begun had a war been fought under such terrible conditions as in 1812, and the Russian troops pursuing the French were at the end of their tether, incapable of doing anything more without dying in the attempt.

In the distance between Tarutino and Krasnoye the Russian army lost fifty thousand men sick or fallen by the wayside – a total equivalent to the population of a decent-sized provincial town. Half of them quit without seeing any action.

During this phase of the campaign soldiers went without boots or fur-lined coats, they were on depleted rations with no vodka, they camped out every night in the snow month after month when the temperature stood at fifteen below, there were only seven or eight hours of daylight, and the rest was night-time, when discipline goes by the board, and men went in fear of death (which again put them beyond discipline) not for a few hours, as in battle, but for months on end, struggling every moment against cold and starvation. And it is this phase of the campaign, when half the army perished in a single month, that historians refer to when they claim that Miloradovich ought to have executed a flanking manœuvre in one direction, and Tormasov in another, while Chichagov ought to have transferred his forces to such-and-such a place (knee-deep in snow, of course), and so-and-so 'destroyed the French opposition', somebody else 'cut them off', and so on and so forth.

The Russian soldiers did everything they could or should have done to achieve an aim worthy of the people, and half of them died in the attempt. It is hardly their fault if other Russians, at home in the warmth, kept coming out with proposals for them to achieve the impossible.

This curious lack of correspondence, which we now find incomprehensible, between the facts as they were and the way they have gone down in history, arises purely and simply from the tendency of historians writing about this event to describe the history of various generals, with their noble sentiments and splendid words, rather than the history of the events themselves.

They set great store by things said by Miloradovich, honours conferred on this or that general and the propositions they all put forward, but they completely ignore the question of fifty thousand men left behind in hospitals and graves, claiming that this issue is beyond the scope of their research.

Meanwhile, all we have to do is take a break from researching the reports and plans of the generals and look into the movements of those hundred thousand men who were directly involved in the events themselves, and all the apparently insoluble questions can be resolved once and for all with extraordinary ease and simplicity.

The plan of isolating Napoleon and his army never existed outside the imagination of a dozen men. It couldn't have existed because it was absurd and impracticable.

The people had only one aim: to rid their country of the invading army. This aim was in the process of being achieved quite independently, since the French were running away, and all they had to do was not get in the way of the retreat. That was the first point. Secondly, this aim was in the process of being achieved because of the action of the guerrilla forces that were gradually destroying the French, and thirdly, a big Russian army was following close behind the French, ready to resort to force if anything held up their retreat.

The Russian army had to act like a whip used against an animal in full flight. Any driver worth his salt knew it was better to keep the whip in the air and use it as a threat than to lash the running animal about the head.

PART IV

CHAPTER I

When a man sees an animal dying he is seized with horror. What he himself consists of, his own substance, is being visibly destroyed, ceasing to exist before his very eyes. But when the dying creature is a man, and a man deeply loved, there is more to it than the horror experienced at the extinction of life: it feels like a laceration, a spiritual wound, which, like a physical wound, may heal up or may prove fatal, but it always hurts and it shrinks away from any abrasive external contact.

After Prince Andrey's death Natasha and Princess Marya both felt like this. Feeling totally demoralized, they winced and shrank away from the menacing cloud of death that hovered above them, and they could not bring themselves to look life in the face. They shielded their open wounds with great care from any rough and painful contact. Everything – a carriage driving quickly down the street, a summons to dinner, a maid asking which dress to put out; worse still, any perfunctory and obviously insincere expression of sympathy – would set the wound hurting again; it would seem like an affront, an intrusion into that silence which both of them needed as they strove to listen to the harsh and terrible chorus still ringing in their minds. It would set up a barrier between them and the deep mysteries and endless vistas that had briefly opened before them.

The only time they felt safe from such outrage and pain was when they were alone together. Not that they said much. When they did speak, it was about the most trivial things. And both of them in equal measure avoided any reference to the future.

To admit the possibility of a future seemed like an affront to his memory. They were even more cautious about mentioning anything to do with the dead man. What they had gone through and felt so deeply seemed to defy expression in words. Any reference in words to the details of his life seemed to offend against the grandeur and sanctity of the mystery that had been accomplished before their eyes.

This constant holding back and studious avoidance of anything that might lead to a mention of him, this stopping short on both sides of the barrier that determined what could and couldn't be said, left both their minds with a clearer and purer sense of what they were feeling.

But complete and unalloyed sorrow is as impossible as complete and unalloyed joy. Princess Marya, conscious of her position as the independent mistress of her own fate, and her nephew's guardian and tutor, was the first to respond to the demands of everyday life and emerge from the world of mourning she had been living in throughout those first two weeks. She had received letters from relatives that needed answering, there was damp in the room where little Nikolay had been put, and he now had a cough. Alpatych came to Yaroslavl with reports on the state of their affairs and various proposals. He advised Princess Marya to move back to Moscow and take up residence in their house on Vozdvizhenka Street, which had survived intact and needed nothing more than a few minor repairs. Life had to go on; there was no stopping it. Painful as it was for Princess Marya to emerge from the world of solitary contemplation she had so far been living in, regrettable, almost shameful, as it was to have to leave Natasha to manage on her own, the duties of everyday life were calling for attention, and she had to give in to them, however reluctantly. She went through the accounts with Alpatych, consulted Dessalles about her nephew, and then got down to the arrangements and preparations for moving back to Moscow.

Natasha was now on her own, and from the moment Princess Marya became busy with the preparations for leaving she avoided even her company.

Princess Marya asked the countess to let Natasha come and stay with her in Moscow, a suggestion that met with the immediate approval of both mother and father, who had been watching their daughter's physical decline getting worse by the day and now hoped that a change of scene and some help from the doctors in Moscow might do her good.

'I'm not going anywhere,' answered Natasha, when the suggestion was put to her. 'Please, just leave me alone.' And she ran out of the room, hardly able to hold back tears that had more to do with exasperation and anger than sorrow.

Feeling abandoned by Princess Marya and alone in her grief, Natasha now spent most of the time alone in her room sitting in a corner of the sofa with her feet tucked up under her. Her narrow, nervous fingers were continually twisting or tearing at something, and she would sit there staring fixedly at the first object that met her eyes.

This solitude was wearisome, pure torture, but it was just what she needed. The moment someone came in to see her she got quickly to her feet, changed her attitude and expression, and picked up a book or some needlework, but she was obviously anxious for the intruder to go away.

She always felt herself to be on the very brink of understanding, of focusing her spiritual vision and answering questions too terrible to contemplate.

One day towards the end of December Natasha, looking thin and pale, dressed in a black woollen gown, with her hair plaited up in a hasty coil, was sitting in the corner of the sofa with her feet tucked up under her, nervously crumpling and smoothing out the ends of her sash with her fingers while she gazed at the corner of the door.

She was looking out towards the place on the other side of life where she knew he had gone to. And that other side of life, which she had never given a thought to in days gone by because it had always seemed so remote and unbelievable, was now closer, more natural to her and more understandable than this side of life, where there was nothing but emptiness and desolation or pain and humiliation.

She was looking out towards the place where she knew he had gone to, but she could only see him as he had been here on earth. She was seeing him again as he had been at Mytishchi, Troitsa and Yaroslavl.

She could see his face, hear his voice, repeat his words to her and her words to him. Sometimes she dreamt up new phrases for herself and for him, things that might have been said at that earlier time.

There he is now, lying on a low chair in his velvet, fur-lined cloak, with his head propped up on a thin, pale hand. His chest looks terribly hollow, and his shoulders are hunched. His lips are compressed, his eyes are gleaming, and on his pale forehead a line keeps coming and going. There is a rapid tremor just noticeable in one of his legs. Natasha knows he is fighting against unbearable pain. 'What kind of pain is it? What's it all about? What can he feel? Oh the agony!' Natasha is thinking.

He had become aware of her watching him, looked up and started speaking with no smile on his face.

'The only awful thing,' he had said to her, 'would be to bind yourself for ever to a suffering invalid. It would be an everlasting torment.' And he had given her the most searching look – a look she could still remember. Natasha had replied, as always, without giving herself time to think of a proper response. She had said, 'It can't go on like this. Things will be different. You're going to get better. You'll be completely well again.'

She was seeing him now as she had seen him then, and reliving all she had felt at the time. She remembered the long, sad, severe look he had levelled at her when he heard those words, and she took in all the reproach and the despair contained in his long stare.

'I agreed with him,' Natasha told herself now, 'that it would be awful if he never recovered from his suffering. I only said it because it would have been so awful for him, but he took it the wrong way. He thought it would be awful *for me*. At that time he wanted to go on living. He was afraid of dying. And I was so clumsy and stupid in the way I said it. That wasn't what I was thinking. I was thinking something quite different. If I had told him what I was thinking about I would have said, "Even if he stayed like that, dying, dying away before my eyes, I'd have been much happier than I am now." Now I have nothing . . . nobody . . . Did he know? No, he didn't, and he never will. And now it will never, never be possible to put things right.'

And there he was saying the same words again, but this time Natasha imagined herself coming out with a different answer. She stopped him, and said, 'Awful for you, but not for me. You must know that without you there is nothing left in my life, and suffering with you is the greatest possible happiness.' And now he was taking her hand and squeezing it, just as he had done on that terrible evening four days before his death. And in her imagination she was pouring out other words of tenderness and love, which might have been said at the time and were coming out now . . . 'I love you! . . . Darling . . . I do love you!' she was saying, wringing her hands convulsively, and gritting her teeth with bitter ferocity . . .

And then she was swept by a wave of bitter-sweet sorrow, and her eyes were filling with tears, but all at once she asked herself who she was talking to. Where was he, and *what* was he now?

And again her whole mind was clouded with an arid and harsh uncertainty. Again, with an anxious furrowing of her brow she stared fixedly ahead, searching for where he was. And for a moment she seemed to be on the brink of penetrating the mystery . . . But at the very instant when the unfathomable depths seemed to be clearing, she was shocked out of her reverie by a painfully loud rattling of the door-handle. Her maid, Dunyasha, rushed straight in with panic in her eyes, showing no concern for Natasha.

'Please miss, come quickly and see your father,' said Dunyasha, looking unusually agitated. 'Something terrible has happened . . . It's young Count Petya . . . a letter,' she gasped out, choking and sobbing.

CHAPTER 2

This was a time when Natasha's general feeling of alienation was at its
worst with her own family members, from whom she felt particularly
estranged. All her own family, her father and mother and Sonya, were
so close to her, so normal and ordinary, that their every word and
feeling seemed like a desecration of the world she had been living
in of late. It was worse than indifference; she looked on them with
outright hostility. She could hear what Dunyasha was saying about
little Petya, and something terrible that had happened, but she wasn't
taking it in.

'Terrible? Nothing terrible could have happened to them, surely.
It's easy for them . . . all the old routine. Everything goes on in the
same old way,' Natasha was saying to herself.

Just as she got to the drawing-room door her father came hurrying
out of the countess's room. His face was crumpled and wet with tears.
He had clearly rushed out to give vent to the sobs that were choking
him. He took one look at Natasha, waved his arms in despair, and
broke down in a bout of violent, convulsive sobbing that completely
distorted his soft, round face.

'It's Pe . . . Petya . . . Gug-gug-go on in . . . She's c-calling . . .' And
sobbing like a child, he tottered over to a chair on his feeble legs, and
all but collapsed on to it, burying his face in his hands.

This acted like a sudden electric shock running right through
Natasha's body. Her heart lurched with a terrible searing pain. She
was struck by a feeling of terrible anguish; something seemed to give
way inside her, leaving her for dead. But the pain was immediately
followed by a feeling of release from the repressive forces that had
taken over her life. One look at her father, one ghastly, raucous scream
from her mother heard through the door, and she instantly forgot
herself and her own sorrows.

She ran over to her father, but with a feeble hand he motioned her
towards her mother's door. Princess Marya came out, ashen-faced,
jaw trembling, and said something as she took Natasha by the hand.
Natasha saw nothing and heard nothing. She hurried through the
doorway, stopped for a moment as if she was fighting something down
and then ran over to her mother.

The countess was sprawling stiffly and awkwardly across a low
chair, beating her head against the wall. Sonya and some of the maids
were holding her by the arms.

'Natasha, Natasha!' the countess was screaming. 'It's not true, not true . . . it's all lies . . . Natasha!' she screamed, pushing the maids away. 'Go away, the lot of you. It's not true! Dead? . . . ha, ha, ha! . . . It's not true! . . .'

Natasha knelt down in front of the chair, bent over her mother, gave her a hug, lifted her up with a remarkable display of strength, turned her face up, and held her close.

'Mamma! . . . Sweetheart! . . . I'm here, darling Mamma . . .' she whispered on and on, without stopping.

She wouldn't let her mother go. Gently she struggled with her, asked for a cushion and a drink of water, unfastening her mother's dress and tearing it looser. 'Listen, my sweet darling . . . my dear, lovely mamma . . .' she whispered on and on, kissing her head, her hands, her face. She could feel floods of helpless tears streaming down her face, tickling her nose and cheeks.

The countess squeezed her daughter's hand, closed her eyes, and calmed down for a moment. Then suddenly she sat up in one rapid, unnatural movement, stared round blankly, caught sight of Natasha and hugged her head with all the strength she could muster. Natasha's face winced with pain as her mother turned it towards her, and gave her a long, searching look.

'Natasha, you do love me, don't you?' she said confidingly in a gentle whisper. 'Natasha, you won't let me down, will you? You'll tell me the truth?'

Natasha was looking at her with tears in her eyes, and the expression on her face was a simple plea for forgiveness and love.

'My dear lovely mamma . . .' she repeated over and over again, concentrating all the strength of her love to find some way to relieve her mother of some of the grief that was crushing her.

And once again her mother, caught up in a hopeless struggle with reality, refused to believe that she could still be alive while her beloved little boy had been killed just as he was blossoming into life, ran away from reality and took refuge in irrationality.

Natasha would never remember how she spent that day and night, and the following day and the following night. She never went to sleep or left her mother's side. Natasha's love, patient and persistent as it was, brought no explanation or consolation, but as it enfolded the countess on all sides, with every passing second it lured her back to the land of the living.

On the third night the countess calmed down a little, and Natasha closed her eyes, propping her head up on the arm of the chair. The bed creaked. Natasha opened her eyes. The countess was sitting up in bed, talking softly.

'I'm so glad you've come back. You must be tired. Would you like some tea?' Natasha went over to her. 'You're a handsome boy now, quite the young man,' the countess went on, taking her daughter's hand.

'Mamma, what are you talking about?'

'Natasha, he's gone. He's not coming back.'

And now, hugging her daughter, the countess at last gave way to tears.

CHAPTER 3

Princess Marya delayed her departure. Sonya and the count tried to take over from Natasha, but it was beyond them. They could see that she was the only person who could keep her mother from maniacal despair. For three weeks Natasha never left her mother's side. She stayed in her room and slept in a chair, saw that she ate and drank, and talked to her continually. She kept on talking because her tender, loving voice was the only thing that could soothe the countess.

The wound in her mother's heart was beyond healing. Petya's death had torn her life in two. When the news came she had been a hale and hearty woman of fifty; now, a month later, she came out of her room an old woman, more dead than alive, and with no zest for life. But the wound that had half-killed the countess was a new wound for Natasha, and it brought her back to life.

A spiritual wound, one that comes from a laceration of the spirit, is much like a physical wound; after it has healed and knitted together on the outside, strange as it may seem, a spiritual wound behaves like a physical injury in continuing the healing process on the inside under pressure from the life force pushing up from within.

And this was how Natasha's wound was healing. She had believed her life was over. But suddenly love for her mother had shown her that the essence of her life – love – was still alive within her. When love reawakened, life reawakened.

Prince Andrey's last days had created a very close bond between Natasha and Princess Marya. This new disaster brought them even closer together. Princess Marya delayed her departure, and for the last three weeks she had been taking care of Natasha as if she was a sick child. These recent weeks spent by Natasha in her mother's room had taken their toll on her physical strength.

One day Princess Marya noticed that Natasha was shivering feverishly, so she took her off to her own room, and tucked her up in her bed in the middle of the day. Natasha lay there, but when Princess Marya let the blinds down and started walking out of the room, Natasha called her back.

'I don't feel sleepy, Marie. Stay with me, please.'

'You must be tired. Try to get some sleep.'

'No, no. Why did you bring me away? She'll want to know where I am.'

'No, she's a lot better. She's been making sense today,' said Princess Marya.

Natasha lay there on the bed, looking closely at Princess Marya's face in the semi-darkness.

'Is she like him?' Natasha wondered. 'Well, she is and she isn't. But she is somebody special, different, original, mysterious. And she does love me. What is she feeling deep in her heart? Nothing but goodness. But what does she actually feel? What does she think? How does she look on me? Oh yes, she's a wonderful woman!'

'Masha,' she said, timidly pulling her hand towards her. 'Masha, please don't think badly of me. You won't, will you? Masha, darling! I do love you. Can we be good friends, always good friends?'

Natasha gave her a hug, and started kissing her on the hands and face. Princess Marya felt embarrassed, though this demonstration of emotion gave her great pleasure.

That day marked the beginning of a new friendship between Princess Marya and Natasha, one of those tender and passionate friendships that can exist only between women. They never stopped kissing each other and saying nice things to each other, and they spent most of their time together. If one of them went away the other felt restless and soon went off to join her. They had a greater sense of harmony together than they ever did when they were separated and on their own. The feeling between them turned into something stronger than friendship, a unique sensation that life was possible only when they were together.

Sometimes they didn't speak for hours on end. Sometimes they would start chatting as they lay in bed and not stop till morning. They talked mostly about the distant past. Princess Marya would talk about her childhood, her mother, her father, and her dreams. And Natasha, who had once turned away in blissful ignorance from that life of devotion and resignation, all the poetry of Christian self-sacrifice, now felt such deep affection for Princess Marya that she came to love her past life, and she now understood the side of her that had seemed so perplexing before. She had no intention of applying the same kind of resignation and self-sacrifice to her own life, because she had got used to seeking out other delights, but now she could understand in somebody else the kind of virtue that had previously been beyond her comprehension. And Princess Marya too, as she listened to Natasha telling stories about her childhood and adolescence, gained a new insight into a side of life she knew nothing about, a belief in the goodness of living and the enjoyment of life.

They still avoided *him* as a topic of conversation, because mere words were liable to detract from what they saw as an exalted feeling in their hearts. This reluctance to talk about him meant that they were gradually forgetting him, though they would never have believed it.

Natasha had grown thin and pale, and so weak physically that the state of her health was on everybody's lips, and this pleased her. Yet sometimes she had sudden feelings of dread, not just of dying but of being ill and feeble, and losing her looks. Sometimes she would catch herself examining her bare arm, marvelling at its thinness, or getting up in the morning, glancing in the mirror at her face, and finding it pitifully pinched and drawn. This was how things had to be, she felt, yet she was left with a feeling of sadness and dread.

One day she ran upstairs too quickly, and stood gasping for breath at the top. Her immediate and instinctive reaction was to invent some excuse for going back downstairs so she could run up again, watching how she did and testing her strength.

On another occasion her voice cracked as she called for Dunyasha, so she called her again, even though she could hear her coming; she used her deepest voice, the one normally reserved for singing, and listened to how it sounded.

What she did not know, and would never have believed, was that though her soul seemed to have been grown over with an impenetrable layer of mould, some delicate blades of grass, young and tender, were already pushing their way upwards, destined to take root and send out living shoots so effectively that her all-consuming grief would soon be lost and forgotten. The wound was healing from inside.

At the end of January Princess Marya left for Moscow, and at the count's insistence Natasha went with her to consult the doctors.

CHAPTER 4

After the engagement at Vyazma, where Kutuzov had not managed to contain his troops' burning desire to rout the enemy, isolate them and so on, the onward march of the fleeing French and the fast-chasing Russians continued as far as Krasnoye without any pitched battle. The pace was so fast that the pursuing Russian army couldn't catch up with the French, the horses of the cavalry and artillery kept falling by the wayside, and any intelligence concerning the movements of the French was always unreliable.

The Russian soldiers were so exhausted by more than twenty-five miles a day of constant marching that they couldn't go any faster.

To appreciate the degree of exhaustion suffered by the Russian army all we have to do is take in the full meaning of one simple fact: the Russians lost no more than five thousand dead and wounded on the long march from Tarutino, and barely a hundred were taken prisoner, yet the army that set out with a hundred thousand men had been reduced to fifty thousand by the time it got to Krasnoye.

The speed of the Russian pursuit had the same kind of devastating effect on the Russian army as the flight of the French had on theirs, the only difference being that the Russian army was moving freely, without the threat of annihilation that hung over the French, and any sick stragglers of the French fell into enemy hands, whereas Russian stragglers found themselves on home ground among their own people. The main reason for the reduction in Napoleon's army was the sheer speed of their retreat, conclusive proof of which is provided by a corresponding reduction in the Russian army.

As before at Tarutino and Vyazma, Kutuzov (unlike the Russian generals in Petersburg, and also in the army) did everything in his power to concentrate on not getting in the way of the disastrous French retreat, indeed positively encouraging it, and slowing the pace of his own army.

Apart from the increasingly apparent exhaustion of the men and the immense losses caused by the sheer speed of their movement, Kutuzov was presented with another reason for slowing down and waiting to see how things turned out. The object of the Russian army was to pursue the French. The route taken by the French was uncertain, which meant that the more closely our men followed on the heels of the French, the more miles they covered. Only by following at a fair distance could they take short cuts and iron out the ziz-zags performed by the French. All the skilful manœuvres proposed by the generals were based on moving the troops on ever-longer forced marches, whereas the only sensible aim would have been to shorten them. So this was the one aim that Kutuzov concentrated on all the way from Moscow to Vilna, not casually, not in fits and starts, but with such consistency that he never once lost sight of it.

With all his Russian heart and soul rather than by dint of reason or science Kutuzov knew and felt what every Russian soldier felt: the French were beaten, the enemy had been put to flight, and all they had to do was see them off. He was also at one with his men in appreciating all the terrible demands of that march, an unprecedented undertaking at such speed and at that time of year.

But the generals, especially the non-Russian ones, out for glory, hoping to dazzle the world by capturing the odd duke or king for some obscure reason – these generals believed that now, the very moment when any battle would have been a senseless and disgusting spectacle, was a good time to go on the attack and bring somebody down. Kutuzov responded with nothing more than a shrug when they paraded before him one after another with their plans involving new manœuvres to be executed by ill-shod, badly clothed, half-starved soldiers whose numbers had been halved in a single month without any fighting, and who, even if the chase that was under way had the best possible outcome, would have had further to go before they got to the frontier than the distance they had already covered.

This would-be dash for glory by manœuvring, routing the foe and cutting them off came to the fore whenever the Russian army happened to stumble across the French.

This is what happened at Krasnoye, where instead of finding one of the three French columns as expected, they ran into Napoleon in person accompanied by sixteen thousand troops. Despite Kutuzov's best efforts to avoid this disastrous confrontation and keep his men safe, for three solid days at Krasnoye the exhausted soldiers of the Russian army went about the systematic slaughter of the scattered mobs of French soldiers.

Toll wrote his usual disposition: 'First column to advance to this spot . . .' and all the rest. As always, nothing took place in accordance with this disposition. From the hill-top Prince Eugene of Württemberg kept up a barrage of fire on the French hordes as they scurried by, and asked for reinforcements that never came. The French used the hours of darkness to disperse and find a way round the Russians by slinking through the woods, after which anyone who could struggled on down the road.

Miloradovich, famous for telling the world he hadn't the slightest interest in the domestic arrangements of his detachment, a man who could never be found when he was wanted, the self-styled 'chevalier beyond fear and reproach' who was always ready for a parley with the French, wasted a lot of time sending messengers over with demands for surrender and carried out none of the orders received.

'Have that column with my compliments, boys,' said he, riding over to his men and pointing out the French to his cavalry. And the cavalrymen applied spur and sabre to skinny nags that could hardly move, badgered them to something like a trot, and with a huge effort managed to reach the gift-wrapped column, which is to say a mob of frozen, numb, starving Frenchmen. Whereupon all the men in the column laid down their arms and surrendered, something they had been longing to do for many a long week.

At Krasnoye twenty-six thousand prisoners were taken, along with hundreds of field-guns and a kind of stick that was promptly dubbed a 'marshal's baton', and then the arguments started, to determine who had covered himself with the greatest glory. They were well pleased, though there was some regret at the failure to capture Napoleon or some marshal of heroic standing, for which they blamed one another, and Kutuzov in particular.

These men, carried away by their passions, were nothing more than the blind executors of the saddest law of necessity; but they saw themselves as heroes, and mistook their doings for achievements of the highest virtue and honour. They kept on blaming Kutuzov, claiming that from the outset he had prevented them from conquering Napoleon, he thought of nothing but the comforts of the flesh, he had delayed leaving the Linen Mills because he was nice and comfortable there, he had stopped the advance at Krasnoye out of sheer panic when he heard Napoleon was there, you might almost think he was in league with Napoleon, he had been suborned by him (see Sir Robert Wilson's Diary),[1] and so on and so forth.

As if it was not enough for contemporaries, carried away by their passions, to have spoken along these lines, posterity and history have labelled Napoleon 'a great man', and as for Kutuzov, foreign writers have him down as a crafty debauchee and feeble old courtier; whereas Russians see him as a rather nondescript character, a kind of puppet with the sole virtue of having a good Russian name . . .

CHAPTER 5

In 1812 and 1813 Kutuzov was openly accused of bungling. The Tsar was dissatisfied with him. And a recent history* inspired by promptings from on high, presents Kutuzov as a lying, scheming man of the court, frightened by the very name of Napoleon, whose bungling at Krasnoye and the Berezina deprived the Russian army of glory through total victory over the French.

Such is the lot, not of 'great men', since that term remains unacknowledged by the Russian mind, but of those rare and always solitary men who can divine the will of Providence and submit their personal will to it. Such men are castigated by the mob with hatred and contempt for their intuition of the higher laws.

For Russian historians (strange and terrible to relate) Napoleon, the least significant instrument of history, who never once in any place, not even in exile, displayed a trace of human virtue, is an object of admiration and enthusiasm; he is one of their 'great men'.

By contrast, Kutuzov, the man who from start to finish during his period of command in 1812, from Borodino to Vilna, never once let himself down by word or deed, an unparalleled example of self-sacrifice and the ability to see today's events with tomorrow's significance, this Kutuzov is conceived of by the same historians as a rather pathetic, nondescript character, and any mention of him in relation to the year 1812 always causes a stir of embarrassment.

And yet it is difficult to think of any historical figure whose activity shows a greater determination to focus continuously on a single aim. It is difficult to imagine a more noble aim, or one more closely attuned to the will of an entire nation. And it would be even more difficult to find an example anywhere in history of a historical personage accomplishing his declared aim more completely than Kutuzov did after total commitment to it in 1812.

Kutuzov never talked about forty centuries looking down from the Pyramids, or the sacrifices he was making for his country, or what he intended to achieve or had already achieved. In fact he never talked about himself at all, he never indulged in histrionics, and he always seemed like the simplest and most ordinary man around, saying the simplest and most ordinary things. He wrote to his daughters and

---

* [Author's note] *History of the Year 1812: The Character of Kutuzov, and Reflections on the Unsatisfactory Results of the Battles at Krasnoye*, by Bogdanovich.

Madame de Staël, read novels, enjoyed the company of pretty women, liked a little banter with the generals, officers and men, and he never raised any objections when people were trying to make a point with him. When Count Rostopchin galloped up to him at the Yauza bridge to accuse him of being personally responsible for the loss of Moscow, and said, 'I thought you promised not to abandon Moscow without a battle,' Kutuzov answered, 'I'm not going to abandon Moscow without a battle,' even though Moscow had already been abandoned. When Arakcheyev came to him from the Tsar with the news that Yermolov was to be given command of the artillery, Kutuzov said, 'Yes, just what I was saying myself,' even though he had just said the exact opposite. What difference did it make to him, a man in a crowd of simpletons, the only one who understood the enormous significance of what was happening? What difference did it make to him whether Count Rostopchin attributed the disastrous fate of the capital to Kutuzov or himself? It made even less difference whether one particular man was to be given command of the artillery. And it wasn't only under circumstances like these that this old man, who had convinced himself from a lifetime of experience that thoughts and the words used to express them are never prime movers, trotted out utterly meaningless words, blurting out the first thing that came into his head – it happened all the time.

But at no stage in his war career did this man who was so casual with words ever come out with a single expression that went against the one aim he was working towards throughout all the hostilities. On a number of occasions, under a wide range of circumstances, he did spell out his real thoughts, though evidently with the greatest reluctance and a weary certainty that he was bound to be misunderstood. He first fell out with those around him by being the only person to state that *they had won the battle of Borodino*, a claim he continued to assert both verbally and in reports and dispatches till the day he died. He was the only one who claimed that *the loss of Moscow did not mean the loss of Russia*. When Lauriston sued for peace, his reply was, *There can be no peace, for this is the will of the people*. As the French retreated he was the only one to say that *all our manœuvres were pointless, everything would happen on its own better than we could desire, the enemy must be allowed to march to destruction across a 'golden bridge', the battles of Tarutino, Vyazma and Krasnoye were totally unnecessary, we must hold something back to reach the frontier with, and he wouldn't give a single Russian for ten Frenchmen*.

And beyond that he alone, this scheming man of the court, as he is commonly portrayed, capable of lying to Arakcheyev to keep the Tsar happy, he, this courtier, was the only man in Vilna willing to risk the Tsar's displeasure by telling him that *taking the war abroad would be a wrong and harmful thing to do.*

But words alone would be insufficient proof that he understood the significance of what was happening at the time. His actions, all of them without the slightest exception, were focused on a single aim, and they can be reduced to three: (1) to gather maximum strength for a confrontation with the French; (2) to defeat them; and (3) to drive them out of Russia, minimizing the suffering of the people and the soldiers.

It is he, Kutuzov the ditherer, whose motto, 'Patience and Time', never varied, this sworn enemy of precipitate action, who gives battle at Borodino, making fastidious preparations with unheard-of solemnity. It is he, Kutuzov, the man who predicted defeat before the battle of Austerlitz had even started, who now, at Borodino, stands out against the generals and the fact that for the first time in history a victorious army is having to retreat, and defies them all by alone insisting that this has been a victory, not a defeat, and goes on saying it to his dying day. He is the only man, during the long period of retreat, to insist that battle should now be avoided since it is now pointless, the Russians should not go beyond their borders, and no new war should be entered into.

Now that all the events and their consequences lie exposed to our view it is all too easy to grasp their significance, provided we resist the temptation to invest the participating masses with aims that never existed outside the minds of a dozen men.

But how did it happen that this old man, standing alone in the teeth of universal opposition, managed to gauge the popular sense of all that was happening so accurately that he never once deviated from it while he was in charge?

The source of this amazingly intuitive insight into the significance of events as they were unfolding lay in a feeling for the people that filled his heart with rare purity and strength.

It was their recognition of this feeling in him that led the people to flout the will of the Tsar and in such a strange way light upon him, an old man out of favour, as their chosen leader in the national war. And it was this feeling alone that raised him to such an exalted position among men, to heights from which he could exert all his powers as commander-in-chief not towards killing and maiming, but towards saving and sparing them.

This simple, modest, and therefore truly great figure could never fit the false mould invented by history for the European hero, the putative leader of men.

No man is great to his valet because the valet has his own special concept of greatness.

CHAPTER 6

The 5th of November was the first day of the skirmishing that has become known as the battle of Krasnoye. By late afternoon – after much arguing and blundering by generals who never arrived where they were sent, after a day when orders and counter-orders had been flying about everywhere, borne by the adjutants – it became clear that with the enemy in full flight there would not and could not be a battle, and only then did Kutuzov leave Krasnoye for Dobroye, where the new headquarters had been set up that very day.

It had been a clear, frosty day. Kutuzov was riding towards Dobroye on his tubby little white horse, with an enormous entourage of disgruntled generals murmuring behind his back. As they went along they kept coming across groups of French prisoners – seven thousand had been taken in a single day – crowding round camp-fires to get warm. Not far from Dobroye they heard the dull roar of a huge crowd of men talking, prisoners dressed in rags, bandaged and wrapped up in whatever had come to hand, standing on the road beside a long line of unharnessed French cannons. At the approach of the commander-in-chief the roar died down, and all eyes turned to Kutuzov, who was wending his way down the road, wearing his white cap with its red band, and a padded overcoat that sat awkwardly on his hunched shoulders. One of the generals was explaining where the guns and prisoners had been captured.

Kutuzov seemed too preoccupied to take in what the general was saying. He was wincing with displeasure as he stared very closely at the figures of the most wretched-looking prisoners. Most of them had cheeks and noses disfigured by frostbite, and almost all had red, swollen and festering eyes.

A group of Frenchmen standing at the roadside contained two soldiers, one with sores all over his face, who were tearing at a piece of raw meat with their bare hands. There was something brutal and horrible in the cursory glance they bestowed on the passing party, and the savage glare that the soldier with the sore face launched at Kutuzov before turning away and going on with what he was doing.

Kutuzov stared long and hard at these two soldiers. Frowning more than ever, he screwed up his eyes, and shook his head thoughtfully. Further on, he noticed a Russian soldier saying something friendly to a French prisoner, laughing and clapping him on the shoulder. Kutuzov shook his head again with the same expression on his face.

'What's that? What were you saying?' he asked the general, who was still explaining away and trying to get the commander-in-chief to look at the French colours that had been set up in front of the Preobrazhensky regiment.

'Oh yes, the flags!' said Kutuzov, who was clearly having difficulty in dragging his mind back from what it was preoccupied with. He looked about vaguely.

Thousands of eyes were on him from all sides, waiting for him to pronounce.

He came to a standstill before the Preobrazhensky regiment, gave a deep sigh, and closed his eyes. At a signal from one member of the suite the soldiers holding the flags came forward and set them up round the commander-in-chief. Kutuzov said nothing for a second or two, then, with obvious reluctance, yielding to necessity, he looked up and spoke. Crowds of officers gathered round him. He scanned the circle of officers with a close eye, recognizing some of them.

'Thank you one and all!' he said, addressing the soldiers before turning back to the officers. Silence reigned, broken only by his words, carefully enunciated so as to be distinctly audible. 'Thank you one and all for your hard and faithful service. Victory is assured, and Russia will not forget you. Your glory will live for ever!'

He paused and looked round.

'Further down. Drop it further down,' he said to a soldier holding the French eagle, who had inadvertently lowered it in front of the Preobrazhensky colours.

'A bit further. Yes, that's it. Hurrah, boys!' he said, turning back to the soldiers with a flick of his chin.

'Hurrah-ah-ah!' came the roar from thousands of voices.

While the soldiers were cheering, Kutuzov leant forward in the saddle and bowed his head, his one good eye glinting with what looked like gentle humour.

'Listen, men . . .' he said, when the cheering had died away.

And then suddenly his face and expression looked different. It was not the commander-in-chief speaking now, it was a simple man, getting on in years, who evidently had something important to say to his comrades.

'Listen, men . . . I know you're having a rough time, but it can't be helped! Please be patient. It won't last much longer. Let's see these visitors off – then we can have a rest. The Tsar won't forget your services. You're having a rough time, but you are on home ground. Look at them. See what they've been reduced to,' he said, pointing to the prisoners. 'Lower than the meanest beggars. When they were strong we didn't spare ourselves, but now we can afford to spare them. They're men like us, aren't they, boys?'

He gazed round. And in the unflinching stare of those eyes trained on him with a mixture of respect and bemusement he could read sympathy for what he had said. His face grew brighter and brighter as a gentle smile of old age wrinkled out into starlike clusters at the corners of his mouth and his eyes. He paused and looked down uncertainly.

'But when all's said and done, who told them to come? They asked for it, the fucking bastards!' he said suddenly, looking up at them. And with a flourish of his riding-whip he rode away, seen galloping for the first time in the entire campaign, with gleeful guffaws and roars of hurrah echoing through the breaking ranks of men.

Much of what Kutuzov had said went over the heads of the men. Not one of them could have summarized the field-marshal's speech, which had begun with such solemnity and ended with an old man's warmth and simplicity, but the heartfelt meaning underlying his words was something they did understand, along with a new feeling of solemn triumph in victory combined with pity for the enemy and also a sense of righteousness – a feeling conveyed even by the old man's colourful language – and this feeling, lurking deep in the heart of every soldier, had expressed itself in the huge cheer that went on for so long. A little later, when one of the generals came to the commander-in-chief and asked if he wanted his carriage, a visibly moved Kutuzov surprised them by responding with a sob.

CHAPTER 7

The 8th of November saw the last of the skirmishes at Krasnoye. Darkness had fallen by the time the soldiers got to where they were halting for the night. All day it had been still and frosty, with the occasional sprinkling of snowflakes. By evening the clouds had gone, a purplish, starry sky could be seen through the last of the snowflakes, and the frost was hardening.

A regiment of musketeers, three thousand strong when it left

Tarutino but now down to nine hundred, was among the first to reach its assigned halting-place, a village on the main road. The quarter-masters who received the regiment reported that all the cottages were full of sick and dead Frenchmen, cavalrymen and staff-officers. There was only one hut left, and that was for the colonel.

The colonel rode on to his hut. The regiment went right through the village, and the soldiers stacked their arms near the last cottages along the road.

Like some huge, many-limbed beast the regiment got down to the business of preparing food and shelters to sleep in. One party of soldiers trudged off knee-deep in the snow and disappeared into a birch copse to the right of the village, which was soon ringing with the sounds of axes and long knives, the snap and crack of breaking branches and the loud voices of happy men. Another lot got down to work in among the regimental wagons and horses, which had been drawn up altogether, getting the cooking-pots and biscuits out, and foddering the horses. A third detachment scattered about the village, getting quarters ready for the staff-officers, carrying out the bodies of any dead Frenchmen left in the huts, and walking back with bits of board, dry wood and straw from the thatched roofs to feed their fires, and lengths of wattle for their shelters.

Behind the cottages at the end of the village more than a dozen soldiers were shouting away merrily as they worked at the high wattle wall of a barn that had already lost its roof and got it rocking.

'Come on, boys, altogether – heave!' came the voices, and in the darkness a huge section of snow-dusted wattle wall began to rock with a frosty creak. The bottom stakes creaked more and more until eventually the whole wall came crashing down, along with the soldiers who had been heaving against it, to a great roar of coarse laughter.

'Pair off, boys! Give us that crowbar! That's it. Where the hell are you going?'

'No, we'll have to work together . . . Hang on, boys! . . . Get them singing!'

They all kept quiet, and a soft, velvety voice started singing. At the end of the third verse, chiming in with the last note, twenty voices blending together roared out, 'Oo-oo-oo-oo! It's coming! All together! Come on, boys, one more heave!' But despite their combined efforts the wall hardly moved, and in the silence that followed the men could be heard breathing heavily.

'Hey, you boys in the Sixth! Come on you devils! Give us a hand . . . We'll do the same for you.'

A couple of dozen men of the Sixth Company, who were on their way into the village, joined in with their struggling comrades, and soon the wattle wall, thirty-five feet long, seven feet wide and bending under its own weight, was being heaved along the village street, weighing them all down and cutting into the shoulders of the gasping soldiers.

'Go on . . . Keep at it . . . Get on with you . . . Don't stop now! . . . Hey! . . .'

The banter and the shouting and swearing went on and on.

'What's all this?' came an authoritative voice. A sergeant came running over to them as they struggled along. 'There's gentry here. The gineral's in that there 'ut. Rowdy devils! Foul-mouthed scum! I'll soon sort you lot out!' roared the sergeant, and he went straight up to the first soldier and smashed him hard in the back. 'Can't you make less noise?'

The soldiers were quiet. The man he had hit grunted and rubbed his face; it was bleeding from being bashed against the wattle.

'Packs a punch, that bastard does! Blood all over me face,' he said in a quiet whisper as the sergeant walked away. 'You know you like it!' said a bantering voice. The soldiers moved on, keeping their voices down, though once they had got through the village they went back to talking just as loud as before, with many a meaningless swearword thrown in.

All the top brass were there inside the hut that the soldiers had just gone past, enjoying a drink of tea and a lively conversation about that day's doings and the manœuvres planned for tomorrow. They had in mind a flanking movement round to the left designed to isolate Murat, the viceroy, and take him prisoner.

By the time the soldiers had struggled back with the big piece of wattle, camp-fires were blazing on all sides and they were cooking supper. The firewood crackled, the snow was melting, and the black shadows of soldiers nipped about all over the ground they had occupied and trampled down.

Axes and big knives were at work on all sides. Nobody gave any orders, but the work got done. Enough wood was brought in to last through the night, rough shanties were thrown up for the officers, pots were boiling, guns and ammunition were being checked.

The wattle wall brought in by the men of the Eighth was bent round in a north-facing semicircle and secured against musket-stands; then they built a camp-fire in front of it. There was a drum-roll, names were checked, then they had supper and settled down for the night around the fires, some repairing their foot-gear, some smoking their pipes, while others stripped naked and steamed their clothes to get rid of the lice.

CHAPTER 8

One might have expected that under the unimaginably awful conditions endured by the Russian soldiers at that time – no warm boots, no thick coats, no roof over their heads, deep snow and eighteen degrees of frost, no regular rations because supplies often lagged behind – they must have presented a thoroughly miserable and depressing spectacle.

Quite the reverse. Never, not even when their material circumstances were at their best, had the army presented a more buoyant and lively spectacle. This was due to the fact that with every day that passed anything that smacked of dejection or feebleness was being flushed out of the army. Anything physically and morally under strength had been left behind long ago, leaving only the flower of the army, strong in body and spirit.

The camp-fire of the Eighth Company, screened by their wattle fence, became most people's preferred place. Two sergeants had moved in on them, and their fire blazed brighter than any. They had had to contribute some logs for the privilege of sitting there.

'Hey, Makeyev, did you get fucking lost, or have the wolves been at you? Get some wood,' yelled a red-faced, red-haired soldier, screwing up his eyes and blinking because of the smoke, but not moving an inch away from the fire.

'You. Don't just stand there gaping. Go and get some wood,' he shouted to another soldier. The red-haired man was no sergeant, not even a corporal, but he was a tough customer, and he gave orders to anybody weaker than himself. The thin little soldier with a sharp nose who had been accused of gaping got to his feet obediently, and was about to do what he'd been told, but at that moment into the firelight stepped the slender, handsome figure of a young soldier carrying a load of wood.

'Chuck it down here. Hey, that's not a bad lot!'

They broke the wood up and piled it on the fire, blew on it and fanned it with the flaps of their greatcoats while the flames hissed and crackled. The soldiers came up closer and lit their pipes. The handsome young soldier who had brought the wood put his hands on his hips and stamped up and down on his frozen feet.

'Oh, Mother dear, the dew's cold here, but I'm all right, I'm a musketeer! . . .' he warbled, chopping off each syllable with a kind of hiccup.

'Them soles'll come off!' cried the red-haired man, noticing that the dancing man's soles were dangling loose. 'He likes his bloody dancing!'

The dancer stopped, ripped the loose piece of leather off and threw it into the fire.

'You're right there, me old pal,' said he. He sat down, took a strip of French blue cloth out of his knapsack, and started wrapping it round his foot. 'It's the steam what does it,' he added, stretching his feet out towards the fire.

'We're due for some new ones. They say when we've gone through *them*, we're all gettin' a double issue of everythin'.'

'I see that son of a bitch, Petrov, 'as dropped out, then,' said one of the sergeants.

'I've had me eye on 'im for some time,' said the other.

'Oh, well, not much of a soldier . . .'

'Aye, an' they do say the Third Company was nine short at roll-call yesterday.'

'Well, when your feet gets frozen you can't walk much further.'

'What stupid drivel!' said the sergeant.

'So, you fancy doin' the same, do you?' said an old soldier, rounding on the man who had talked about feet being frozen.

'Well, what do you expect?' burst in the sharp-nosed 'gaping' soldier in a trembling, squeaky voice, half-sitting up on the other side of the fire. 'If you 'ave a bit of fat on you, you got somethin' to lose. For us thin 'uns it's death. Just look at me. Ain't got no strength left,' he said with sudden determination, looking straight at the sergeant. 'You ought to get me in the 'ospital. 'Ad it with me rheumatics, I 'ave. I'll get left behind anyway . . .'

'Come on, son, come on,' said the sergeant calmly.

The soldier said no more, though the conversation went on.

'We've took 'undreds of them Froggies today, and not a pair of decent boots between 'em. Nothing worth talkin' about,' put in one of the soldiers, changing the subject.

'No, them Cossacks 'as 'ad the lot. We was cleanin' a hut for the colonel, and we 'ad to carry 'em out. 'Orrible sight, boys,' said the dancer. 'Kept turnin' 'em over, we did. One was still alive. You wouldn't believe it. Jabberin' away 'e was, in their lingo.'

'Keeps 'emselves real clean, they does,' the first man went on. 'They'm all white, you know – 'e were as white as a birch-tree – and there's some grand boys among 'em. Real gentlemen they be.'

'I'm not surprised. They 'as their soldiers from all classes.'

'And they don't understand a word we says,' put in the dancer, with a smile of bemusement. 'I says to 'im, "What be your kingdom?" and 'e comes out with all that foreign stuff. They're a rum lot!'

'I'll tell you one thing, boys. Bloody marvellous,' went on the man who had been so taken with their whiteness. 'Some o' them peasants down Mozhaysk way was telling me 'ow they was shiftin' dead bodies where the big battle 'ad been, an' them dead bodies – their lot – 'ad been there a good month. They was just layin' there, their lot, clean and white like pieces of paper, and there wasn't no smell comin' off 'em.'

'Oh, that'd be the cold, wouldn't it?' asked one.

'Nay, son. I'll give you cold! No, it were really 'ot. If it 'ad been cold, our boys wouldn't 'ave rotted neither. But what they said was: go anywhere near one of ours, and 'e'd be all rottin' away – maggots everywhere. 'Ad to put 'andkerchiefs over their noses an' turn their 'eads away before they could shift 'em. That's what they said. They could 'ardly stand it. But *they* was clean and white like pieces of paper, and there wasn't no smell comin' off 'em.'

Nobody spoke.

'Must be the grub,' said the sergeant. 'Fed 'em like gentry they did.'

There was no comment.

'That there peasant down near Mozhaysk, where the battle was, 'e was saying they was fetched in from ten villages round, and they was at it twenty days and they still didn't shift all the dead bodies. And all them wolves, he was sayin' . . .'

'Now, that were a right battle, that were,' said an old soldier. 'The only one worth talkin' about. After that it was all . . . well, just puttin' people through it.'

'You're right there, old boy. Day before yesterday we came across 'em. Nothing doin'. Couldn't get near 'em. Chucked their guns away just like that. Down on their knees they was, sayin', "We do beg your pardong!" And that was just one example. I've 'eard it said that Platov 'ad 'is 'ands on Boneypart – twice! Grabs 'im once, an' whoosh! – 'e's off again. Turned into a bird in 'is 'ands. Off 'e goes! No chance of killin' 'im neither.'

'You're a lying sod, Kiselyov. I can tell by the look of you.'

'God's truth, I ain't lyin'.'

'By God, if I got me 'ands on 'im, 'e'd be six foot under. Aye, an' a wooden stake through 'is 'eart. Just think 'ow many men 'e's killed!'

'Anyway, 'e's 'ad it now, an' 'e won't be comin' 'ere again,' said the old soldier, yawning.

The conversation died down. The soldiers settled down for the night.

'Look at them stars. Never seen 'em shine like that! Like a string o' washin' 'ung out by the women!' said one soldier, goggling at the Milky Way.

'Means a good 'arvest next year, boys!'

'We need a bit more wood.'

'Give your back a little warm and your belly's frozen. Funny thing that.'

'Oh my God!'

'Who d'you think you're shovin'? It's a nice fire, but there's more than you, you know. Look at 'im, sprawled out all over the place.'

Through the gathering silence came the sound of a few men snoring. The others were turning over and over to keep warm. A few words were exchanged.

From a fire a hundred paces away came a roar of merry laughter.

''Ark at that lot. It's the Fifth, 'avin' a good laugh,' said a soldier. 'Plenty of people there!'

Another soldier got to his feet and walked over to the Fifth.

'Laugh?' he said, coming back. 'Two Froggies 'as turned up. One's froze to death, but the other's a good fellow! He's started singing.'

'Oho! Worth a quick look . . .'

Several soldiers walked over to the Fifth Company.

CHAPTER 9

The Fifth Company had set up its makeshift camp at the very edge of the forest. A huge camp-fire was blazing away in the midst of the snow, casting a bright light on branches heavy with hoar-frost.

About midnight the soldiers had heard footsteps and the snapping of twigs in the woods.

'It's a bear, boys,' said one soldier.

They all looked up and strained their ears. Out of the copse and into the bright fire-light staggered two weirdly dressed human figures clinging to one another.

It was two Frenchmen who had been hiding in the forest. They came over towards the fire, speaking in hoarse voices and saying things in a language the soldiers couldn't understand. The taller of the two, a man wearing an officer's hat, seemed almost dead on his feet. As he got to the fire he tried to sit down but collapsed in a heap. The other, a stocky little soldier with a handkerchief tied round his head, was stronger. He helped his companion up, pointed to his own mouth and said something. The soldiers gathered round the Frenchmen, laid the sick man out on a greatcoat, and brought some porridge and vodka for them both. The exhausted French officer was Ramballe; the little man with the handkerchief round his head was his servant, Morel.

When Morel had drunk some vodka and finished his bowl of porridge he suddenly became deliriously happy, and started babbling
away to the soldiers, who couldn't understand a word he was saying.
Ramballe refused any food, and just lay there leaning on one elbow
by the fire, gazing at the Russian soldiers with a blank look in his red
eyes. Now and then he gave a long-drawn-out groan followed by a
relapse into silence. Morel kept pointing to his shoulders, letting the
soldiers know that this was an officer, and he needed warming up. A
Russian officer, who had come up to the fire, sent someone to ask the
colonel whether he would take in a French officer and allow him to
get warm. When the word came back that the colonel wanted them to
bring the officer over, Ramballe was told where to go. He got to his
feet and tried to walk, but staggered, and would have fallen if he
hadn't been caught by a soldier standing near by.

'So, you don't want to go, then?' said a soldier to Ramballe with a
jokey wink.

'Damn fool! Don't talk stupid. Peasant. 'E's a real peasant,' came
voices from all sides as they rounded on the joking soldier. Ramballe
was quickly surrounded, two men held him up with their hands crossed
under him and carried him off to the cottage. Ramballe put his arms
round the soldiers' necks, and as they carried him along he kept up a
plaintive chant.

'Oh, good boys! Oh you are my good, kind friends! Real men! Oh,
my brave, kind friends!' And he leant his head against the soldier's
shoulder like a child.

Meanwhile Morel was sitting in the prime position, surrounded by
the soldiers.

Morel, a stocky little Frenchman with swollen, streaming eyes, was
wearing a woman's little coat and a handkerchief tied round his forage
cap like a peasant woman's. He was obviously under the influence,
and with one arm flung round the soldier sitting next to him, he was
singing a French song in a husky, broken voice. The soldiers held their
sides as they looked at him.

'Come on then, teach me. Tell me 'ow it goes. I'll soon pick it up.
'Ow does it go?' said the soldier embraced by Morel, himself a singer
who liked a good joke.

Vive Henri Quatre!
Vive ce roi vaillant!

sang Morel with a broad wink.

Ce diable à quatre . . .[2]

'Veeva-reeká! Veef-seru-vayár! Sidyablaká!' parroted the soldier, waving his hand and catching the tune well.

'Bravo! Ha-ha-ha!' A roar of happy laughter came from all sides. Morel screwed up his face and joined in with it.

'Come on! More, more!'

> *Qui eut le triple talent*
> *De boire, de battre,*
> *Et d'être un vert gallant . . .*[3]

'Sounds good. Your turn, Zaletayev! . . .'

'Kyu . . .' began Zaletayev, struggling with the sounds. 'Kyu-yu-yu . . .' he warbled, straining manfully to purse his lips properly. 'Letrip-talá! Deboo-debá! Ee detravagalá . . .'

'That's great! Just like the Froggy! Ha-ha-ha! Hey, do you want something else to eat?'

'Give 'im some more porridge. 'E's famished. Take some time to fill 'im up.'

They handed him more porridge, and Morel gave a laugh as he launched into his third bowlful. There were happy smiles on the faces of all the young soldiers as they watched him. The old soldiers, who considered themselves above this kind of nonsense, lay there on the other side of the fire, but now and again one of them would raise himself up on one elbow and look across at Morel with a smile on his face too.

'They're men like us,' said one, snuggling down inside his coat. 'Even wormwood grows from a root.'

'God in heaven! Look at all them stars! Means a hard frost.'

And then everybody was silent.

The stars, as if they knew they could do it without being seen, danced across the black sky. Flaring up and dying down, and trembling as they did so, they seemed to be sharing some happy whispered mystery.

CHAPTER 10

The French army was melting away with the regularity of a mathematical progression. And the crossing of the Berezina, about which so much has been written, far from being the decisive episode in the campaign, was only one of the intermediate stages on the army's road to destruction. On the French side the reason so much has been written about the Berezina is that it was there, at the broken-down bridge across the river, that the disasters raining down on the French in a kind of steady progression were suddenly concentrated in a single moment – a single tragic, never-to-be-forgotten catastrophe. On the Russian side, the reason so much has been made of the Berezina was simply that far away in Petersburg a plan had been devised (by Pfuel, of course) for the capture of Napoleon in a strategic trap on the banks of the Berezina. Everyone was so sure in advance that the trap would work exactly as planned that they were all insistent: it was indeed the crossing of the Berezina that finished off the French. In point of fact, statistics show that in terms of guns and men lost the results of the Berezina were less disastrous to the French than the fighting at Krasnoye.

The sole significance of the Berezina crossing lies in the fact that it proved conclusively and beyond a shadow of doubt the wrongness of all those plans for cutting off the enemy's retreat, and the rightness of the only possible policy – the one demanded by Kutuzov and the mass of the Russian army – which was to follow on behind the enemy. The horde of French soldiers was fleeing and constantly accelerating as it did so, with all its energies directed towards the attainment of a single goal. It was fleeing unstoppably, like a wounded beast. This was demonstrated not so much by the arrangements that existed for crossing as by what happened at the bridges themselves. When the bridges were broken down, unarmed soldiers, people from Moscow, even women with children who were travelling with the French transport, were all propelled forward by the force of inertia. Instead of surrendering they made a rush for the boats, or plunged into the ice-covered water.

This impulse was a reasonable one. The situation was equally fraught for fugitives and pursuers alike. By sticking with his own kind each fleeing individual might be able to rely on help from his comrades in misfortune, and finding a definite place of his own among them. By surrendering to the Russians he would find himself in the same miserable plight, but lower down the order when it came to the satisfaction of his basic needs. The French didn't have to wait for incontrovertible evidence that half the prisoners – men that the Russians simply couldn't handle, however much they wanted to save them – were dying of cold and starvation. They sensed that it couldn't be otherwise. The most compassionate and pro-French Russian generals, even Frenchmen serving in the Russian army, could do nothing for the prisoners. The French were perishing in the same catastrophe that the Russians themselves were involved in. There could be no question of taking bread and clothing away from our starving, much-needed soldiers to give it to Frenchmen who, although they were not hated, not dangerous, and in no way to blame, were simply superfluous to requirements. Sometimes this was actually done, though it was the exception rather than the rule.

Behind the French lay certain destruction; ahead lay hope. They had burnt their boats; massed flight was their only salvation, and it was on massed flight that the French concentrated all their efforts.

The further they fled the more wretched became the plight of those who remained, especially after the Berezina, which the Russians had set great store by because of the Petersburg plan, and the more virulently the Russian generals railed against each other, and especially against Kutuzov. The assumption was that the failure of the Petersburg plan would be laid at his door, so the dissatisfaction with him, the derision and mockery he had to put up with, became more and more pronounced. Naturally enough, the mockery and derision were always couched in terms of respect, in such terms that made it impossible for Kutuzov even to ask what he stood accused of. They didn't take him seriously, they submitted their reports and asked for his decisions like men going through the motions of some sad ritual, they winked at one another behind his back, and at every step they did their best to pull the wool over his eyes.

It was generally accepted by all those men – because they had no understanding of him – that there was no point in talking to the old man. The profound significance of their plans was beyond him; he would simply come out with all his old phrases (which they took to be meaningless) about crossing a golden bridge, and the inadvisability of going abroad with a bunch of tramps, and so on and so forth. They had heard it all before. Meanwhile everything he said – they must wait for supplies, for instance, or the men had no boots – was simplicity itself, whereas everything they proposed was so complicated and so clever that the whole thing was obvious: he was a stupid old dodderer, while they were military officers of genius, lacking only in authority.

This moody vilification by men on the staff came to a climax once the brilliant admiral, the hero of Petersburg, Wittgenstein, had joined the army. Kutuzov took note of this development with nothing more than a sigh and a shrug. Just once in the aftermath of the Berezina affair he lost his temper and wrote the following note to Bennigsen, who was still reporting back to the Tsar:

On account of your bouts of ill-health your Excellency will be so good as to retire to Kaluga on receipt of this letter, there to await further instructions from His Majesty the Emperor.

But Bennigsen's dismissal was followed by the arrival on the scene of the Grand Duke Konstantin Pavlovich, who had been a participant in the early stages of the campaign, only to be removed from the army by Kutuzov. Now the grand duke on rejoining the army informed Kutuzov of the Tsar's displeasure at the poor achievements of our troops, and the slow progress that was being made. The Tsar himself intended to be with the army in a few days' time.

The old man, as well versed in court procedure as in warfare – the same Kutuzov who in the August of that year had been chosen commander-in-chief against the Tsar's will, who had removed the grand duke and heir-apparent from the army, and had acted on his own initiative in defiance of the Tsar's will by ordering the abandonment of Moscow – saw at once that his day was done, his part was played, and his purported authority was no more. And he could see this not only from the attitude shown to him by the court. On the one hand he could appreciate that the war itself – the theatre he had been acting in – was over, and he sensed quite naturally that his work was completed. On the other hand, he was becoming conscious at this very time of a physical weariness besetting his old man's body, and the need for physical rest.

On the 29th of November Kutuzov reached Vilna – his dear Vilna, as he used to call it. Twice during his military career he had been governor of Vilna.

In the wealthy town of Vilna, which had emerged unscathed, in addition to the comforts he had gone without for so long Kutuzov rediscovered old friends and old associations. At a stroke he turned his back on all military and political matters, and immersed himself in the quiet routine of everyday life, so far as the passions raging all round him would permit, as if to say that everything that was now happening, or about to happen, in the world of history was no longer any concern of his.

It was Chichagov, a 'cutter-off' and 'overthrower' if ever there was one; Chichagov, the man who at an early stage had favoured making a diversion in Greece and then in Warsaw but was never willing to go where he was ordered; Chichagov, notorious for speaking out in the presence of the Tsar; who considered Kutuzov to be under an obligation to him, because in 1811, when he had been sent to conclude peace with Turkey over Kutuzov's head, and found when he got there that peace had already been concluded, he had admitted to the Tsar that the credit for concluding that peace belonged to Kutuzov – Chichagov it was who came out first to meet Kutuzov at the castle in Vilna where the latter was to stay. In undress naval uniform with a dirk, and his cap under his arm, he handed the commander-in-chief a garrison report and the keys to the city. The peculiar mixture of respect and derision shown by youth to old age in its dotage was quite unmistakable in Chichagov's whole bearing, he being well aware of the accusations now levelled at Kutuzov.

In conversation with Chichagov Kutuzov happened to mention that his carts packed with china that had been seized by the enemy at Borisovo had been recovered intact and would soon be restored to him.

'Are you implying I have nothing to eat from? On the contrary, I can provide you with anything, even if you want to give dinner parties,' Chichagov protested, hot under the collar, intending with every word he uttered (in French) to put himself in the right, and assuming that Kutuzov was thinking along exactly the same lines. Kutuzov gave a slight shrug, smiled his usual shrewd and subtle smile, and answered, also in French, 'I mean no more than what I say.'

In defiance of the Tsar's wishes, Kutuzov kept the greater part of the troops back in Vilna. Those who were close to him kept saying how much he had declined, how much weaker he had become during his stay in Vilna. He was reluctant to deal with the army, and left everything to his generals. Meanwhile he gave himself up to the pleasures of the flesh as he waited for the Tsar to arrive.

The Tsar left Petersburg on the 7th of December with his suite – Count Tolstoy, Prince Volkonsky, Arakcheyev, and the rest – and reached Vilna on the 11th, driving straight up to the castle in his travelling sledge. There by the castle, in spite of the intense cold, stood nigh on a hundred generals and staff-officers in full dress uniform, with a guard of honour provided by the Semyonovsky regiment.

A courier galloped up to the castle ahead of the Tsar in a troika with steaming horses, and shouted, 'He's on his way!', which prompted Konovnitsyn to hurry over to the vestibule and inform Kutuzov, who was waiting in the porter's little room.

A minute later the big, bulky figure of the old man, in dress uniform and full regalia, with a scarf drawn tight beneath his belly, tottered out on to the steps. He donned his cocked hat with the peaks sideways on, picked up his gloves and sidled ponderously down the steps, clutching the report prepared for presentation to his Majesty.

After much fuss and bother and a good deal of whispering, another troika galloped past and then suddenly all eyes were on the approaching sledge, with the figures of the Tsar and Volkonsky clearly visible in it.

Fifty years of sheer habit now took their toll; all of this had a disturbing effect on the old man. He felt rapidly about his person in great anxiety, straightened his hat and just managed to pull himself together and come to attention at the very moment when the Tsar stepped down from the sledge and turned to look at him. He handed over the report, and spoke out in his measured, ingratiating voice.

Scanning Kutuzov from head to foot in one rapid glance, the Tsar frowned for a moment, but instantly regained self-control, walked over to him, opened his arms and enfolded the old general in a close embrace. Once again Kutuzov felt the effect of long years of habit combined with some deep inner feeling of his own; this embrace made its usual impact on Kutuzov, and he gave a spluttering sob.

The Tsar greeted the officers and the Semyonovsky guard of honour, shook hands again with the old man, and walked off with him back into the castle.

Alone with his commander-in-chief, the Tsar expressed his disappointment at the slow progress in pursuing the enemy, and the blunders made at Krasnoye and the Berezina, and announced his future plans for taking the campaign abroad. Kutuzov said nothing by way of comment or objection. The same expression of mindless deference that he had adopted seven years before when listening to the Tsar's injunctions on the field at Austerlitz was now fixed on his face again.

When Kutuzov had left the room, and was trudging across the reception-hall, waddling along with downcast head, a voice stopped him.

'Your Serene Highness,' it said.

He looked up and gazed into the face of Count Tolstoy, who was standing there holding a silver salver with a small object on it. Kutuzov had every appearance of not knowing what was expected of him.

Then suddenly he seemed to come to his senses, a faint smile dawned on his podgy face, and with a low, respectful bow he picked up the object lying on the salver. It was the Order of St George, First Class.

CHAPTER II

The next day the field-marshal gave a dinner and a ball which the Tsar honoured with his presence.

Kutuzov had received the Order of St George, First Class, the Tsar had bestowed the highest honours on him, but the Tsar's dissatisfaction with the commander-in-chief was known to all. The proprieties were being observed, and in this the Tsar led by example, but everyone knew the old man was both guilty and useless. When, following an old custom from the days of Catherine the Great, Kutuzov gave orders at the ball for the captured standards to be lowered at the Tsar's feet the moment he entered the ballroom, the Tsar gave a nasty frown and muttered something that included, according to some, the phrase 'old comedian'.

The Tsar's displeasure was exacerbated at Vilna, especially by Kutuzov's obvious unwillingness or inability to see the importance of the coming campaign.

When next morning the Tsar said to the officers gathered around him, 'You have saved more than Russia, you have saved Europe!' everyone could see immediately that the war was not yet over.

Kutuzov was the only one who refused to see this, telling the world candidly that no new war could improve the position of Russia, or add to her glory; it would only weaken her situation, and detract from the lofty pinnacle of glory that in his view Russia was standing on at present. He did what he could to show the Tsar the impossibility of levying fresh troops, and he talked about the desperate plight of the population, the prospect of failure, and so on . . .

With an attitude like this the field-marshal naturally looked like nothing but a hindrance and a drag on the coming campaign.

To avoid a direct confrontation with the old man the obvious solution was the one that had proved so effective at Austerlitz and with Barclay in the early stages of the war – to cut away all the real power from under the commander-in-chief's feet, without upsetting him by going into explanations, and transfer it to the Tsar.

With this aim in mind the staff underwent a modest reshuffle by means of which all the real power of Kutuzov's staff was removed and transferred to the Tsar. Toll, Konovnitsyn and Yermolov were all given new appointments. Everyone talked openly about the commander-in-chief's increasing feebleness and failing health.

It was necessary for him to be in failing health in order to make way for his successor. But as it happened his health really was failing.

By the same natural, simple and gradual process by which he had emerged from Turkey all those years ago and come to the Treasury in Petersburg to raise the militia, and take over the army at the very time when he was most needed, he now yielded his place, now that his part was played, to the new figure demanded by the times.

The war of 1812 was about to add to its national significance, dear to every Russian heart, by taking on a new, European character.

The movement of men from west to east was to be followed by a movement of men from east to west, and this new war needed a new proponent, with aims and qualities that differed from Kutuzov's, and a different kind of motivation.

Alexander I was as necessary for the movement of men from east to west and the determination of new national frontiers as Kutuzov had been necessary for the salvation and glory of Russia.

Kutuzov had no understanding of what was meant by Europe, the balance of power and Napoleon. All of this was beyond him. For this representative of the Russian people, once the enemy had been annihilated and Russia had been liberated and raised to the highest pinnacle of glory, for this true Russian there was nothing left to do. For this representative of the national war there was nothing left to do but die. And die he did.

CHAPTER 12

As so often happens on occasions like these, Pierre felt the full effects of the physical hardships and strain he had suffered as a prisoner only when the strain and hardships were over. After being rescued he made his way down to Oryol, and two days later, just as he was getting ready to set off for Kiev, he fell ill and was laid up for three months. He was suffering from what the doctors called a 'bilious fever'. Despite their treatment – with blood-letting and various medicines – he recovered.

Everything that had happened to Pierre between his rescue and his illness had left hardly any impression on his mind. His only recollections were of dull grey weather, constant rain or snow, a physical aching inside his body and pains in his legs and his side. He had a vague memory of people suffering terribly, and of being worried by the intrusiveness of interrogating officers and generals, and how difficult it had been to get a conveyance and horses, but the overriding impression was of a time when he had lost all capacity for thought and feeling.

On the day of his rescue he had seen the dead body of Petya Rostov. The same day he learnt that Prince Andrey had lived on for more than a month after the battle of Borodino, but had died quite recently at Yaroslavl in the Rostovs' house. And also on the same day Denisov, who had given Pierre this piece of news, made a passing reference to the death of Hélène, assuming that Pierre knew all about it. Pierre's only reaction was that these things seemed rather strange. He felt incapable of absorbing the significance of these events. His only thought was to get away as fast as he could from the here and now where men were slaughtering each other, and find some quiet refuge where he could relax, recover again and think over all the strange new things he had learnt during this period. But as soon as he reached Oryol he fell ill. When he came round after his illness Pierre saw two of his servants, Terenty and Vaska, who had come down from Moscow to wait on him, and the eldest of his cousins, who had got word of Pierre's rescue and illness while staying at his estate in Yelets, and had come over to look after him.

During his convalescence it took Pierre quite some time to ease himself away from the impressions left with him from the last few months, which had become a habit of mind, and get used to the idea that no one was going to get him moving tomorrow, no one would take his warm bed away, and he was quite sure of getting his dinner, tea and supper. But for a long time to come his sleep would be disturbed by dreams of his life as a prisoner. And only by the same gradual process did Pierre come to understand all the news he had heard since his escape: the death of Prince Andrey, the death of his wife and the defeat of the French.

A blissful sense of freedom – the complete and inalienable freedom inherent in man that had made itself felt only at that first halting-place outside Moscow – began to flood through Pierre's soul during his convalescence. He was surprised to find this inner freedom, which did not depend on external circumstances, now transformed into outward freedom seemingly decked out with luxury and excess. He was alone in a strange town, without acquaintances. No one made any demands on him; no one sent him anywhere. He had everything he wanted, and the worries about his wife that he had once found so agonizing had gone, because she was gone.

'Oh, that's wonderful! It's marvellous!' he said to himself, when a neatly set-out table was moved towards him with an appetizing bowl of broth, or when he climbed into his soft, clean bed at night, or when the thought struck him that his wife and the French had gone. 'Oh, it's wonderful! It's marvellous!' And from habit he would start asking himself questions. 'What comes next, then? What am I going to do?' And immediately he knew the answer: 'Nothing. I'm just going to live. Oh, it's marvellous!'

The one thing that had tormented him in earlier days, the constant search for a purpose in life, had ceased to exist. The ending of his search for a purpose was more than a chance event or a temporary development: he now sensed that it did not and could not exist. And it was the lack of any purpose that gave him the complete and joyous sense of freedom underlying his present happiness.

He could seek no purpose now, because now he had faith – not faith in principles, words or ideas, but faith in a living God of feeling and experience. In days gone by he had sought Him by setting purposes for himself. That search for a purpose had really been a seeking after God, and suddenly during his captivity he had come to know, not through words or arguments, but from direct personal experience, something that his old nurse had told him long ago: God is here, here with us now, here and everywhere. In captivity he had come to see that Karatayev's God was greater, more infinite, more unfathomable than any Architect of the Universe recognized by the masons. He felt like a man who finds what he is looking for right under his feet after straining his eyes to seek it in the distance. All his life he had been peering into the distance over the heads of those around him when all he had to do was stop straining his eyes and look down right in front of him.

In those earlier days he had been unable to see the great, the unfathomable and the infinite in anything. All he had was a sense that it must exist somewhere, and he had gone on looking for it. In anything close to and well understood he had seen nothing but limitation, workaday triviality and pointlessness. He had armed himself with a mental telescope and peered into the far distance, where that same workaday triviality, shrouded in the mists of remoteness, had seemed great and infinite, but only because it couldn't be clearly seen. This was how he had looked on European life, politics, freemasonry, philosophy and philanthropy. But even then, at times that he had mistaken for moments of weakness, his mind had penetrated the furthest distance and recognized the same workaday triviality and pointlessness.

Now he had learnt to see the great, the eternal and the infinite in everything, and naturally enough, in order to see it and revel in its contemplation, he had thrown away the telescope that he had been using to peer over men's heads and now took pleasure in observing the ever-changing, infinitely great and unfathomable life that surrounded him. And the more closely he watched, the more he felt himself to be happy and at peace. The terrible question that had destroyed all his carefully structured thinking in the bad old days – the question *Why?* – no longer existed. His soul now had a ready-made, straightforward answer to the question *Why?* – because God is, and without God not one hair of a man's head shall fall.

CHAPTER 13

Outwardly Pierre had hardly changed at all. To look at he was the same as before. He was just as absent-minded as he had always been, and he seemed to be permanently preoccupied with something that wasn't there, something that was all his own. The difference between his former state and the one he was now in was that in the old days, when he was oblivious to everything that was going on around him and what was being said to him, he would wince and furrow his brow in an apparently vain effort to see something that was a long way away. Nowadays he could still be oblivious to everything that was going on around him and what was being said, but at least he looked at what was going on around him with the ghost of a smile, however ironical, and he also listened to what was being said, though he was obviously seeing and hearing something very different. In the old days he had seemed like a nice man who was unhappy, which inevitably kept people at arm's length. Nowadays a smile of *joie de vivre* played constantly about his mouth, his eyes shone with sympathy for others, wondering whether they were as happy as he was, and people enjoyed his company.

In the old days he had had a lot to say, he got excited when he said it, and he was a poor listener. Nowadays he was no conversationalist, but he did know how to listen, and this made people only too ready to pour out their innermost secrets to him.

His cousin, the princess, who had never liked Pierre, and had been particularly ill-disposed towards him ever since the old count's death had left her feeling under an obligation to him, had come over to Oryol with every intention of making it clear that she had felt duty-bound to ignore his ingratitude and look after him, but it wasn't long before she found herself, much to her own surprise and irritation, getting rather fond of him. Pierre made no effort to try and win her round; he just watched her with close curiosity. In the old days she had felt that there was mockery and indifference in the way he looked at her, and she had shrivelled up in his presence, as she did with other people, and shown only her aggressive side. Now she felt the reverse: it was as if he was delving into the innermost recesses of her life, and, at first with some suspicion but then with gratitude, she let him see her hidden kindly side.

The craftiest manipulator could not have wormed his way more skilfully into the princess's confidence, coaxing from her recollections of her youthful heyday and warming to them. And yet Pierre's only craftiness consisted in finding pleasure in drawing out human qualities in an embittered, hardened, and, in her own way, proud princess.

'Yes, he's a very, very nice man when he's away from the influence of bad people and is influenced by people like me,' thought the princess.

The change that had taken place in Pierre was also noticed by his servants, Terenty and Vaska, each in his own way. They found him altogether more straightforward. After undressing his master and saying good night, Terenty would often linger with the boots and clothes in his hands, on the off chance that his master might exchange a few words with him. And more often than not Pierre would stop Terenty on the way out because he could see he was dying for a chat.

'Come on then, tell me . . . how did you manage to get any food?' he would ask. And Terenty would launch forth into stories about the destruction of Moscow, or the late count, and he would stand there for ages, clothes in hand, chatting away or listening to Pierre, and when he did at last withdraw into the ante-room it was with a warm feeling of closeness to his master and affection for him.

The doctor who was treating Pierre and called in every day, though he never omitted to present himself, in the manner of all doctors, as a man whose every minute counts for suffering humanity, would stay on with him for hours on end, telling his favourite stories and commenting on the funny ways of patients in general, and ladies in particular.

'Yes, it's very nice to talk to a man like that. Not what we're used to in the provinces,' he would say.

There happened to be several prisoners from the French army in Oryol, and the doctor brought one of them, a young Italian officer, to see Pierre.

This officer became a regular visitor, and the princess used to laugh at the warmth that showed in his attitude to Pierre.

It was obvious that the Italian was only happy when he could come and see Pierre, and have a chat with him, talk about his own past years, his home life and his love and pour out his bile against the French, especially Napoleon.

'If all Russians are the slightest bit like you,' he used to say to Pierre, 'it is sacrilege to wage war on a people like yours. You've suffered so much at the hands of the French, and you don't even hold it against them.'

And yet Pierre had won the Italian's undying devotion simply by drawing out the best aspects of his soul and admiring them.

Towards the end of Pierre's stay in Oryol he was visited by an old acquaintance, Count Willarski, the freemason who had introduced him to the lodge in 1807. Willarski had married a Russian heiress with huge estates in the Oryol province, and he was temporarily employed in the town's department of supplies.

As soon as Willarski heard that Bezukhov was in Oryol, even though they had never been particularly close, he called on him and displayed the kind of friendliness and intimacy normally reserved for people coming across one another in the desert. Willarski was bored with life in Oryol, and he was delighted to meet a man of his own circle who must surely share the same interests.

But Willarski was in for a surprise: he soon spotted that Pierre had opted out of real life and – as he saw it – descended into apathy and egoism.

'You're going to seed, old fellow,' he said to him.

But for all that Willarski felt much more at ease with Pierre now than he had done in the past, and he came to see him every day. Pierre, for his part, watched Willarski and listened to him, finding it strange and incredible to think that not long ago he too had been like that.

Willarski was a married man with a family, busily occupied with the management of his wife's property, the performance of his official duties and looking after his family. He regarded all these duties as an obstacle in his life; they were beneath contempt because their purpose was the welfare of himself and his family. His mind was permanently obsessed with military, administrative, political and masonic affairs. And without attempting to change this view or even criticizing it, Pierre watched the whole phenomenon – so strange and yet so familiar – with the smile of gentle, amused irony that had now become second nature to him.

There was a new aspect to Pierre's relations with Willarski, the princess, the doctor and everyone he met nowadays that won them all over. This was an acknowledgement of everybody's capacity to think and feel for himself, to see things his way; an acknowledgement of the impossibility of ever changing anybody's mind by words. This individuality rightfully enjoyed by all people, something that had bothered Pierre and irritated him in earlier days, now formed the basis of the sympathetic interest he felt in other people. The disparities, sometimes the outright contradictions that existed between people's views and the way they lived, and between one man and another, were a source of delight for Pierre, constantly bringing to his lips a gentle smile of amusement.

In practical affairs Pierre suddenly sensed that he now had a centre of gravity that had been missing before. Before, every monetary question, especially requests for money, which came his way all the time because he was a wealthy man, had always left him worried and perplexed, not knowing which way to turn. 'To give, or not to give?' he used to ask himself. 'I have money and he needs it. But somebody else needs it more. Who needs it most? Maybe they're both crooks?' And in the old days he could never see any way out of all these speculations, so he ended up giving to all as long as he had money to give. In those days he had also had the same feeling of bafflement over every question that concerned his property, with one person telling him to do one thing and another recommending something different.

Nowadays, much to his own surprise, he found he had no more doubts or misgivings over any such questions. Now there was a judge within him determining what he must do and not do according to a set of laws of which he had no understanding. He was no more concerned about money matters than he had been before, but he was no longer troubled by doubts about what to do, or not do. The first assignment of this new judge sitting within him concerned a request from a prisoner, a French colonel, who called in one day, talked endlessly about his own splendid achievements, and ended up by issuing what amounted to a demand for four thousand francs to send to his wife and children. Pierre refused him effortlessly, without a qualm, and then wondered why something as easy and simple as this could once have seemed so impossibly difficult. And even as he refused the French colonel he made up his mind that when he left Oryol he would have to invent some subterfuge in order to induce the Italian officer to accept some money, which he obviously needed. A further demonstration to Pierre of his stronger grip on practical matters came with his resolution of two other issues: the problem of his wife's debts and the question of rebuilding, or not rebuilding, his Moscow house and his out-of-town properties.

His head steward came down to Oryol to see him, and the two of them conducted a general review of his much-changed financial situation. According to the steward's estimate the fire of Moscow had cost Pierre about two million roubles. By way of consolation for these losses the steward presented a calculation to the effect that Pierre's income, instead of being allowed to fall, could actually be increased as long as he refused to pay off the countess's debts – which he couldn't be forced to honour – and didn't restore his Moscow house or the country villa, which cost him eighty thousand a year and brought nothing in.

'Yes, yes, that's true,' said Pierre, with the broadest of smiles.

'No, no, I don't need any of them. The destruction of the city has made me a much richer man.'

But in January Savelich came down and after telling him about the situation in Moscow, he presented the architect's estimate for restoring the house and villa as if the whole thing was a foregone conclusion. At the same time Pierre received letters from Prince Vasily and other acquaintances in Petersburg. These referred to his wife's debts. And Pierre decided that the steward's plan, despite its great appeal, was not the right one, and he must travel to Petersburg to wind up his wife's affairs and see to the rebuilding in Moscow. Why this was so, he couldn't have said, but he knew beyond a shadow of doubt that this was what he had to do. His income would be down by three-quarters as a result of this decision. But it had to be. He could feel it in his bones.

Willarski was going to Moscow, and they arranged to travel together. Throughout his entire convalescence in Oryol Pierre had been enjoying a new sense of freedom and *joie de vivre*, but once he found himself travelling the open road and seeing hundreds of new faces this feeling was intensified. During the journey he felt as happy as a schoolboy in the holidays. All the people he came across – his driver, the master of a posting-station, peasants out on the road or in the villages – all of them had a new significance for him. The presence of Willarski and all his comments as he constantly deplored the poverty, ignorance and backwardness of Russia compared with Europe only heightened Pierre's pleasure. Where Willarski saw deadness, Pierre saw vitality, an amazingly powerful force sustaining the life of this indivisible, special, unique people over that immense expanse of snow. Rather than objecting to anything Willarski said, he just smiled with delight as he took it all in and pretended to agree, this being the easiest way of avoiding arguments that were bound to lead nowhere.

CHAPTER 14

Just as it is difficult to explain why ants scurry about over a scattered
ant-hill, and where they are off to when some of them drag bits of
rubbish, eggs and corpses away from the ant-hill while others hurry
back inside, or what object they could possibly have as they bump
into each other, overtake and get into fights, so it would be hard to
explain the reasons that induced the Russians, after the departure of
the French, to swarm back to the place that had once been known as
Moscow. But just as when you look at the ants scattered all over a
ruined ant-heap you can see from the persistence and the energy of
this heaving multitude of busy insects that even in the face of absolute
destruction there remains something indestructible and intangible that
has given the whole colony its strength, so too the city of Moscow in
the month of October, without any government, without its churches
and holy objects, without its wealth and its houses, was still the
Moscow it had been in August. Everything had been destroyed except
something intangible that was also hugely powerful and indestructible.

The motives of the people in rushing back to Moscow from all
points of the compass once it had been cleared of the enemy were
many and varied, though they were personal and, in the first instance,
savage and brutal. Only one impulse was shared by all – they were
drawn back home, to the place that had once been known as Moscow,
in order to get their activities going again.

Within a week there were fifteen thousand inhabitants back in
Moscow, within a fortnight twenty-five thousand, and so it went on.
The total rose and rose until by the autumn of 1813 the population
exceeded that of 1812.

The first Russians to enter central Moscow were the Cossacks of
Wintzengerode's detachment, along with a few peasants from the
nearest villages and some residents who had fled from Moscow and
hidden away in the outskirts. When they entered the ruined city and
found it pillaged, the Russians went pillaging too. They carried on the
work started by the French. Trains of peasants' carts drove into
Moscow to take back to the villages everything that had been abandoned in the ruined Moscow houses and streets. The Cossacks took
what they could back to their camps. Householders picked up anything
available in other people's houses and took it home pretending it was
their own property.

But the earliest pillaging parties were soon succeeded by a second
lot, then a third, and with each passing day, as the numbers involved

increased, the business of looting became more and more difficult and took on more specific forms.

The French had found Moscow deserted but with every outward form of organically functioning town life still in place, including all the various branches of commerce and craftsmanship, high life, political government and religion. These forms had no life in them, but they were there. There were markets, stalls, shops, corn-exchanges and bazaars – for the most part still stocked with goods; there were factories and workshops; there were palaces and wealthy houses filled with luxury items; there were hospitals, prisons, government offices, churches and cathedrals. The longer the French stayed on the more these forms of town life fell away, until finally everything collapsed into a single collective scene of pillage with no life left in it.

The longer the French looting continued the more completely it consumed the wealth of Moscow and the energies of the looters. The longer the Russian looting continued, as they began the reoccupation of the city, and the more looters there were, the more rapidly were the wealth of Moscow and normal city life restored.

Apart from the looters people of every kind were drawn back, some by curiosity, some by the duties of office, some out of self-interest – householders, clergy, officials high and low, traders, artisans and peasants – and they streamed back into Moscow from every corner, like blood rushing back to the heart.

Within a week any peasants arriving with empty carts to seize goods and take them away were stopped by the authorities and made to haul dead bodies out of town. Other peasants, hearing of companions down on their luck, drove into the town with wheat, oats and hay, undercutting each other's prices until they were lower than they had been before the war. Gangs of carpenters bent on rich pickings were arriving in Moscow by the day, and on every side you could see new houses going up, or old, half-burnt ones under repair. Tradesmen did business in booths. Cook-shops and taverns were opened in half-burnt houses. The clergy started holding services again in many churches that had escaped the fire. Stolen church goods were returned as donations. Government clerks set up their baize-covered tables and filing-cabinets in little rooms. The higher authorities worked with the police to organize the distribution of any goods left behind by the French. The owners of houses that still contained lots of goods looted from other premises complained about the unfairness of having to take everything to the Faceted Palace in the Kremlin. Others claimed that the French had taken things from all over the place into individual houses, so it was unfair to let the master of the house hang on to everything found in it. The police came in for abuse and were approached with bribes. Estimates for Crown property lost in the fire were inflated by a factor of ten. Appeals were launched. And Count Rostopchin started up again with his proclamations.

CHAPTER 15

At the end of January Pierre arrived in Moscow and settled in the one wing of his house that had emerged unscathed. He called on Count Rostopchin and several acquaintances who were back in town, and got things ready to leave for Petersburg in a couple of days' time. Everyone was full of a sense of victory; the thrill of new life ran through the shattered but rapidly reviving city. Everybody greeted Pierre warmly. They all wanted to see him, and ask about what he had seen. Pierre felt very well disposed towards everyone he met, but he was instinctively a little cautious in his dealings to avoid getting cornered in some way. To all the questions that came his way, important or trivial, he replied in the vaguest terms. Where was he going to live? Was he going in for rebuilding? When was he off to Petersburg? Would he mind taking a parcel for somebody? All he would say was, 'Yes, I might well . . . I have it in mind . . .' and so on.

He heard that the Rostovs were in Kostroma, and thoughts of Natasha rarely entered his head. When they did they were limited to pleasant memories of times gone by. He felt a sense of freedom, not only from the demands of everyday life but also from that particular feeling which he seemed once to have brought upon himself.

On the third day after his arrival in Moscow he found out from the Drubetskoys that Princess Marya was back in town. Prince Andrey's death, his suffering and his final days had been at the forefront of Pierre's mind in recent times, and now they arose again with a new insistence. When he heard over dinner that Princess Marya was in Moscow, living in her own house on Vozdvizhenka, which had escaped the fire, he went round to see her the same evening.

On the way there Pierre's mind was full of Prince Andrey, their friendship, the various occasions when they had met, and especially their last encounter at Borodino.

'Can he really have died in the foul mood he was in then? Didn't he get an inkling of the meaning of life before he died?' Pierre wondered. He thought of Karatayev, and his death, and he found himself comparing these two men, so different and yet so similar in the love he had

had for them both, and in the fact that both of them had been alive
and were now dead.

Pierre was in a very serious frame of mind as he drove up to the old
prince's home. The house had survived. There were some signs of
damage to the place, but the character of the house was just the same.
The old footman who met Pierre had a stern look on his face, as if he
wanted to convey to the new arrival an impression that the absence
of the old prince made no difference to the strict running of the
household, and he informed him that the princess, having retired to
her rooms, received only on Sundays.

'Tell her I'm here. She might just see me,' said Pierre.

'Certainly, sir,' answered the footman. 'Would you please come
through into the portrait gallery?'

A few minutes later he returned with Dessalles. Dessalles brought a
message from the princess: she would be very glad to see Pierre and
invited him, if he would excuse her not standing on ceremony, to come
up to her apartment.

In a low room lit by a single candle he found the princess, and there
was someone else with her dressed in black. Pierre remembered that
the princess had always had lady companions with her, but who they
were and what they were like he didn't know and couldn't recall.
'Must be one of her companions,' he thought, glancing at the lady in
the black dress.

The princess rose quickly to meet him, and offered her hand.

'Yes,' she said, looking closely at his much-changed face after he
had kissed her hand. 'So this is how we meet again. He often talked
about you towards the end,' she said, looking away from Pierre and
at her companion with a sudden show of diffidence that took him by
surprise.

'I was so glad to hear of your salvation. It was the only piece of
good news we had had for a long time.'

Again the princess, more unsettled than ever, glanced at her companion, and she was about to say more when Pierre interrupted her.

'You can well imagine, I knew nothing about him,' he said. 'I
thought he'd been killed. Everything I knew I got from other people,
second hand. I do know now that he ended up with the Rostovs ...
Strange how things work out!'

Pierre was talking rapidly, eagerly. He glanced round once at her
companion's face, catching a glimpse of friendly, questioning eyes
watching him closely, and, as often happens in mid-conversation, he
felt a vague intimation that this lady companion in the black dress
was a splendid person, full of goodness and kindness, who would be

no embarrassment to him as he poured out his innermost feelings to
Princess Marya.

But as he uttered the last words about the Rostovs, the uneasiness
in Princess Marya's face became even more noticeable. Again her eyes
shifted from Pierre's face to the face of the lady in the black dress, and
she said, 'Surely you know who this is?'

Pierre glanced again at the pale, thin face of her companion, with
its black eyes and strange mouth. Something very dear to him, long
forgotten and more than just pleasant gazed at him out of those
carefully watching eyes.

'No. It's not possible,' he thought. 'That grim-looking face, all thin
and pale and so much older than it was. It can't be her. It's somebody
who reminds me of her . . .' But at that moment Princess Marya said,
'Natasha!' And painfully, with all the strain of a rusty door opening,
that carefully watching face smiled at him, and as the door opened
Pierre was suddenly overwhelmed by a heady sensation of happiness
long forgotten, something that couldn't have been further from his
mind at this time. His head swam as the feeling swept over him and
enveloped his whole being. That smile of hers had left him in no doubt.
It was Natasha, and he loved her.

In that first minute Pierre unwittingly revealed to them all, to her
and Princess Marya and most of all to himself, a secret that even he
had been unaware of. He blushed with delight and squirmed with
anguish. He tried to hide his excitement. But the more he tried to
hide it, the more clearly – more clearly than the sharpest words could
have done – he was telling himself, her and Princess Marya that he
loved her.

'No, it's nothing. It's the sudden shock,' Pierre thought. But the
moment he tried to go back to the conversation with Princess Marya
he glanced again at Natasha and an even deeper blush spread over his
face, and his heart was flooded with an even more violent surge
of rapture and terror. He stammered and stuttered, and stopped in
mid-sentence.

Pierre had not noticed Natasha because she was the last person he
had expected to see here, but he had failed to recognize her because
of the immense change that had taken place in her since their last
meeting. She was much thinner and paler. But it wasn't this that
made her unrecognizable. No one would have recognized her when
he entered the room because when he had first glanced at her the face
and eyes that in days gone by had always glowed with a half-
suppressed smile of sheer *joie de vivre* had held no trace of a smile.
They were anybody's eyes, kindly, brooding, quizzical and sad.

Pierre's discomfort aroused no similar discomfort in Natasha; all it prompted was a look of pleasure, barely perceptible as it lit up her whole face.

CHAPTER 16

'She's come to stay with me,' said Princess Marya. 'The count and countess will be here in a day or two. The countess is in a terrible state. But Natasha had to see a doctor. They made her come with me.'

'Oh yes. Is any family free from sorrow?' said Pierre, turning to Natasha. 'You know it happened the day we were rescued. I saw him. He was a lovely boy!'

Natasha was looking at him, and in response to his words her eyes opened even wider and grew brighter.

'What could anybody say or think that would bring any consolation?' said Pierre. 'Nothing. Why did he have to die, a fine young boy like him, so full of life?'

'Yes. It would be hard to live without faith nowadays . . .' said Princess Marya.

'You're quite right. Only too true,' Pierre put in hurriedly.

'Why is that true?' Natasha asked, looking closely into Pierre's eyes.

'Why is it true?' said Princess Marya. 'Well, you only have to think about what is in store for us . . .'

Natasha wasn't listening to Princess Marya; she gave Pierre another quizzical look.

'And also because,' Pierre went on, 'only someone who believes there is a God guiding our lives could stand a loss like hers, and . . . yours,' said Pierre.

Natasha opened her mouth as if to speak, but she stopped short.

Pierre turned away hurriedly and asked Princess Marya about the last days of his friend's life. By now Pierre's embarrassment had almost disappeared, but he felt that all his former freedom had disappeared with it. He felt that now there was a judge listening to his every word and every action, someone whose judgement mattered more than the judgement of everybody else in the world. Here he was talking, and with every word he spoke he was conscious of the impression he was making on Natasha. He didn't go out of his way to say things that might please her, but whatever he said, he was judging himself from her point of view.

With the reluctance that is normal in a situation like this Princess

Marya started telling Pierre about the state she had found her brother in. But Pierre's questions, his excitement, his eager eyes and his face trembling with emotion gradually induced her to go into details that, for her own sake, she had so far been scared to bring back to mind.

'Yes, yes. I can see that . . .' said Pierre, leaning well forward over Princess Marya, and drinking in her every word. 'Yes, yes. So he did find peace? He did soften? He always strove with all his soul for one thing – to be a good man so he wouldn't have to be afraid of dying. His faults – if he had any – came from outside himself. Anyway, he did soften, didn't he?' he said.

'It was a great joy that he met up with you again,' he said to Natasha, turning suddenly towards her, and looking into her brimming eyes.

Natasha's face quivered. She frowned, and looked down for a moment. There was a second's hesitation: should she speak or not?

'Yes, it was,' she said in a low, deep voice. 'It really was a great joy for me.' She paused. 'And he . . . he . . . he told me he was longing for me to come to him the moment I went in . . .' Natasha's voice broke. She flushed, clasped her hands tightly on her knees and then suddenly, controlling herself with an obvious effort, she looked up and started speaking very quickly.

'We knew nothing about it when we were leaving Moscow. I didn't dare ask about him. And suddenly Sonya told me he was with us. I couldn't think. I had no idea what state he was in. I just had to see him and be with him,' she said, all breathless and trembling. And brooking no interruption she went through the story she had never told before, every detail of what she had suffered in the three weeks of their journey and the time spent in Yaroslavl.

Pierre listened to her open-mouthed, and his brimming eyes never left her. As he listened, he wasn't thinking about Prince Andrey, or death, or what she was saying. He was just listening to her voice and feeling sorry for what she was going through as she told her story.

The princess sat by Natasha's side frowning in an effort to hold back her tears. This was the first time she had heard the story of her brother's last days and the love between him and Natasha.

To speak of that agonizing and joyous time was obviously something Natasha urgently needed to do.

On she went, mixing up trivial details with the innermost secrets of her heart, and it seemed as if she would never finish. Several times she said the same thing twice.

Dessalles' voice was heard at the door asking whether little Nikolay might come in to say goodnight.

'And that's it. That's all there is . . .' said Natasha. She got quickly to her feet just as little Nikolay came in, almost ran across to the door, bumped her head against it where it was hidden by the curtain, and with a cry of pain mixed with grief she rushed out of the room.

Pierre stared at the door she had gone out through and wondered why suddenly he felt alone in the big wide world.

Princess Marya roused him from his thoughts by drawing his attention to her nephew, who had just come in.

Little Nikolay's face – so like his father's – made such an impact on Pierre at this moment of emotional strain that when he had kissed the little boy he got to his feet, took out his handkerchief and walked over to the window. He wanted to take leave of Princess Marya, but she wouldn't let him go.

'No, Natasha and I often stay up till after two o'clock. Please stay a little longer. We'll have some supper. Go downstairs. We'll be down in a minute.'

Before Pierre went down, the princess said to him, 'It's the first time she's talked about him like this.'

CHAPTER 17

Pierre was shown into the large, brightly lit dining-room. After a few minutes he heard footsteps and the princess and Natasha came into the room. Natasha was calm, though the rather grim and unsmiling expression was back on her face. Princess Marya, Natasha and Pierre were all experiencing the feeling of awkwardness that usually follows when people have just finished a serious and intimate conversation. There is no going back to the earlier subject, but light-hearted chitchat seems wrong, and saying nothing is unacceptable because the urge to talk is still there, and silence would seem like an affectation. They were silent as they came to the table. The footmen drew the chairs back and pushed them in again. Pierre unfolded his cold dinner napkin. Determined to break the silence, he glanced across at Natasha and at Princess Marya. The two of them had clearly come to the same decision at the same time; their eyes shone, they seemed glad to be alive and ready to acknowledge life's happiness along with its sorrow.

'Do you drink vodka, Count?' said Princess Marya, and at those words the shadows of the past were immediately dispelled.

'Tell us how you've been getting on,' said Princess Marya. 'We've heard the most fantastic stories about you.'

'Oh yes,' answered Pierre, with the gentle smile of irony that was now second nature to him. 'I keep hearing fantastic things too – things I would never have dreamt of myself. Marya Abramovna invited me over and spent the whole time telling me what had happened to me, or was supposed to have happened. Stepan Stepanovich gave me some lessons in telling my story. I've come to the conclusion it's an easy life being an interesting person. (I am now an interesting person.) People invite me over, and they do the talking.'

Natasha smiled and was about to speak.

'We did hear,' said Princess Marya, cutting in, 'that you had lost two million in Moscow. Is that right?'

'Oh, I'm three times as rich as I was,' said Pierre. Despite the change in his affairs brought about by his wife's debts and the need to rebuild, Pierre still went about claiming that his wealth had trebled.

'The one thing I did get,' he said, 'is freedom . . .' He was off on a serious subject, but then he thought better of it and stopped, feeling he was becoming too self-centred.

'And are you going to rebuild?'

'Yes. So Savelich tells me.'

'I gather you didn't hear of the countess's death while you stayed on in Moscow?' said Princess Marya, immediately flushing crimson as she realized that by asking this question just after he had talked about getting his freedom she was putting a construction on his words that was possibly not intended.

'No,' answered Pierre, evidently unembarrassed by Princess Marya's interpretation of his reference to gaining his freedom. 'I heard about it in Oryol, and you can't imagine how shocked I was. We were hardly the ideal couple,' he said quickly, glancing at Natasha; he could see from her face that she was wondering what he would have to say about his wife. 'But I was terribly shocked by her death. When two people fall out, the blame is always on both sides. And your own guilt becomes unbearable when it has to do with someone who is no longer with us. And when all's said and done, to die like that . . . away from your friends and without consolation. I felt very, very sorry for her,' he concluded, pleased to see a look of glad approval on Natasha's face.

'So you are back on the marriage market,' said Princess Marya.

Pierre blushed to the roots of his hair, and for a long time he tried not to look at Natasha. When he did venture to glance across her face looked cold and severe – even, he fancied, disdainful.

'But did you really see Napoleon and talk to him?' asked Princess Marya. 'That's what everybody says.'

Pierre laughed.

'No, I never did. Everybody thinks that being taken prisoner is like staying with Napoleon. I never saw him. I never heard anything about him. I was in much lower company.'

Supper was nearly over, and Pierre, who had begun by refusing to talk about his time in captivity, found himself gradually drawn into telling them all about it.

'But you did stay on to kill Napoleon, didn't you?' Natasha asked him with a slight smile. 'That was my guess when we met you by the Sukharev tower. Do you remember?'

Pierre admitted it was true, and from that question he was led on by Princess Marya's questions, and still more by Natasha's, to go into a detailed account of his adventures.

He began by telling his story with that tone of gentle irony that he always adopted nowadays towards other people and especially towards himself, but as he got on to all the horrors and suffering he had seen he got carried away without realizing it and began to speak with the controlled emotion of a man reliving powerful impressions of the past in his imagination.

Princess Marya kept looking from Pierre to Natasha and back with a gentle smile. In everything he said she could see only Pierre and his goodness. Natasha, her head propped up on one hand, and her face changing constantly as the story progressed, never took her eyes off Pierre as she relived all his stories with him. Pierre could tell from her eyes and also from the exclamations and the brief questions coming from her that she was capturing the full meaning of all that he was saying. She was clearly understanding not only what he said, but also what he wanted to convey without being able to express it in words.

When he got to the episode of the child and of the woman he was arrested for defending Pierre described it like this: 'It was a terrible sight, children abandoned, some trapped in the fire . . . One child was dragged out right in front of me . . . and women were having things wrenched off their bodies, ear-rings torn off . . .'

Pierre flushed and hesitated. 'Then this patrol came up and they just took everybody who wasn't looting – all the men, that is – including me.'

'I'm sure there's something here you're not telling us. You must have done something . . .' said Natasha, and after a moment's pause, '. . . something good.'

Pierre went on with his story. When he got to the execution he was going to spare them the horrible details, but Natasha wouldn't let him leave anything out.

Pierre was on the point of telling them about Karatayev; he had risen from the table and was walking up and down, Natasha following his every step with her eyes.

'No,' he said, stopping short in his story, 'you can't possibly understand what I got from that illiterate man – that simple creature.'

'No, go on, tell us,' said Natasha. 'Where is he now?'

'They killed him almost in front of me.'

And Pierre began to describe the last days of their retreat, Karatayev's illness (his voice shook continually) and his death.

Pierre was describing his adventures as he had never done before, as he had never actually recalled them before. It was as if he could now see a new significance in everything he had been through. Now as he unburdened himself to Natasha he was experiencing that rare happiness provided for men by listening women – not *clever* women, who when they listen are either trying to memorize what they are hearing so as to broaden their minds and acquire things worth repeating, or to adapt the story to their own experience and come out with quick, clever comments nicely polished in their own little mental workshop – no, this happiness was of the kind that is provided only by real women, those with a talent for selecting and absorbing all the best things a man can show of himself. Without knowing it, Natasha was transfixed; she didn't miss a single word, a catch in the voice, a glance, a single twitch of the facial muscles, any of Pierre's gestures. She seized upon the word before it was out and took it straight to her open heart, divining the secret meanings of all Pierre's spiritual travail.

Princess Marya listened with understanding and sympathy, but she was now seeing something new that captured all her attention. She saw the possibility of love and happiness between Natasha and Pierre. And as this idea struck her now for the first time her heart was filled with gladness.

It was three o'clock in the morning. Doleful footmen wandered in and out stiffly, replacing the candles, but nobody noticed them.

Pierre got to the end of his story. Natasha was still gazing at him closely and persistently with an excited gleam in her eyes, as if she was trying to get at something extra, something perhaps left unsaid. In sheepish but happy embarrassment, Pierre glanced at her now and then, wondering what he could say to change the subject. Princess Marya said nothing. It didn't occur to any of them that it was three in the morning, and time to go to bed.

'Everybody says that adversity means suffering,' said Pierre. 'But if you asked me now, at this moment, whether I wanted to stay as I was before I was taken prisoner, or go through it all again, my God, I'd sooner be a prisoner and eat horse-meat again. We all think we only have to be knocked a little bit off course and we've lost everything, but it's only the start of something new and good. Where there is life, there is happiness. There is a huge amount yet to come. I'm saying that for your benefit,' he said, turning to Natasha.

'Yes, you're right,' she said, responding to a different idea. 'Me too. I wouldn't want to do anything but go through it all again from start to finish.'

Pierre watched her closely.

'That, and nothing more,' Natasha declared.

'No, that's not right,' cried Pierre. 'It's not my fault I'm still alive and I want to live, and the same applies to you.'

All at once Natasha let her head drop into her hands and burst into tears.

'What's wrong, Natasha?' said Princess Marya.

'Nothing, nothing.' She smiled at Pierre through her tears. 'Goodnight. It's bedtime.'

Pierre got up and took his leave.

As always, Natasha went with Princess Marya into her bedroom. They talked about what Pierre had told them. Princess Marya didn't say what she thought about Pierre, and Natasha didn't talk about him either.

'Well, goodnight, Marie,' said Natasha. 'Do you know what? I'm afraid we often avoid talking about *him*,' (Prince Andrey) 'as if we were scared of causing offence, so we forget him.'

Princess Marya gave a deep sigh, thus acknowledging the truth of what Natasha had said, but she didn't put her agreement into words.

'How could we forget?' she said.

'I felt so good telling him all about it today. It was painful and difficult, but it felt right . . . It really did,' said Natasha; 'I'm sure he really loved him. That's why I told him . . . It didn't matter, did it?' she asked suddenly, blushing.

'What, talking to Pierre? Oh, no! He's such a good man, isn't he?' said Princess Marya.

'Marie, do you know something?' said Natasha suddenly, with a mischievous smile on her face, the like of which Princess Marya hadn't seen for a very long time. 'He's different, sort of clean and smooth and fresh. It's as if he's just come out of the bath-house. Do you know what I mean? A moral bath-house. Am I right?'

'Yes, you are,' said Princess Marya. 'He's gained a lot.'

'That short jacket of his, and his short hair . . . It's as if he'd just come out of a bath-house . . . Sometimes Papa used to . . .'

'I can see why *he*' (Prince Andrey) 'loved him more than anybody else,' said Princess Marya.

'Yes, and he's so different from him. They do say men make better friends when they are quite different from each other. It must be true. He's not a bit like him, is he?'

'No, but he's a wonderful man.'

'Oh well, goodnight,' answered Natasha.

And the same smile of mischief lingered on her face as if it had been half-forgotten.

CHAPTER 18

It was a long time before Pierre could get to sleep that night. He paced his room, scowling as he plunged into a difficult train of thought, or shrugging his shoulders and wincing, or sometimes beaming blissfully.

He was thinking about Prince Andrey, Natasha and the love between them. At one moment he felt jealous of her past, the next moment he took himself to task, and then he forgave himself for feeling like that. It was six in the morning, and he was still pacing.

'What shall I do, then? What if it has to be? What else can I do? That's it – I've got to do it,' he said to himself. Then he undressed very quickly and got into bed, happy and all worked up, but free from doubt and hesitation.

'It might seem strange and impossible, happiness like that, but I've got to do all I can to make us man and wife,' he said to himself.

Several days before Pierre had settled on the following Friday as the day he would leave for Petersburg. When he woke it was Thursday morning, and Savelich came in for instructions about packing for the journey.

'Petersburg? Who's going to Petersburg? Who's in Petersburg?' was his instinctive reaction, though he kept it to himself. 'Oh, yes, ages ago, before all this happened, I did plan to go to Petersburg for some reason or other,' he recalled. 'What could it have been? Maybe I'll still go . . . Isn't he a good man, looking after me like this? He never forgets a thing,' he thought, looking at Savelich's old face. 'What a lovely smile!' he thought.

'So, you still don't want your freedom, Savelich?' asked Pierre.

'What would I want with freedom, your Excellency? I got on well with the old count – God rest his soul – and with you, sir, there hasn't been nothing unpleasant.'

'Yes, but what about your children?'

'They'll be all right, sir. We can get along with masters like you.'

'Yes, but what about my heirs?' said Pierre. 'I might go and get married . . . It could happen, you know,' he added, with an involuntary smile.

'And a good thing too, your Excellency, if I may say so.'

'He thinks it's as easy as that,' thought Pierre. 'He's no idea how awful it is, and how dangerous. Is it too late? Or is it too soon? . . . It's such an awful business!'

'What are your orders? Will you be going tomorrow, sir?' asked Savelich.

'No. I'm putting it off for a while. I'll tell you when the time comes. I'm sorry I give you so much trouble,' said Pierre, and when he saw that Savelich was still smiling he thought to himself, 'Isn't it funny? He doesn't seem to know there's no Petersburg now – I've got *that* to settle first.'

'I'm sure he does know,' he thought. 'He's just pretending. Shall I have a word with him? Ask him what he thinks? No, some other time . . .'

Over breakfast Pierre told his cousin he had been at Princess Marya's the previous evening, and had come across – guess who – Natalie Rostov!

The princess looked as if she saw nothing unusual in this. It was just as if he had come across Anna Semyonovna.

'Do you know her?' asked Pierre.

'I have seen the princess,' she answered, 'and there was talk of a match between her and young Rostov. That would have been very nice for the Rostovs. I hear they are utterly ruined.'

'No, I meant – do you know Natasha Rostov?'

'Oh, I did hear that story about her. Very sad.'

'She doesn't understand, or she's pretending not to,' thought Pierre. 'Better not say anything.'

The princess had also been busy getting provisions ready for Pierre's journey.

'They're all being so nice to me,' thought Pierre. 'Fancy them bothering about all this now, when they can't have the slightest interest in it. And they're doing it for me – that's what's so marvellous.'

The same day the chief of police called on Pierre and invited him to send someone who could be trusted down to the Faceted Palace to receive goods that were being restored to their owners later in the day.

'And this man too,' thought Pierre, looking into the face of the chief of police. 'What a splendid, handsome officer, and how nice he is!

Fancy him bothering about such trivialities *at a time like this*. And yet they call him dishonest; they say he's on the make. What nonsense! Though incidentally why shouldn't he be on the make? That's the way he was brought up. They're all doing it. He's got such a nice, good-humoured face, and he smiles when he looks at me.'

Pierre set off to dine with Princess Marya.

As he drove through the streets between the charred ruins, he revelled in the beauty of the desolation. The chimney-stacks and collapsed walls of houses stretched out one behind another all through the burnt-out quarters of the town, reminding him of the picturesque ruins of the Rhine and the Colosseum. The cabdrivers and their passengers coming towards him, the carpenters knocking up house-frames, the women hawkers and shopkeepers all beamed at Pierre with cheerful faces and seemed to be saying, 'Oh, here he is! Now we'll see what happens . . .'

When he arrived at Princess Marya's house, Pierre was assailed by sudden doubts: had he really been there the day before, and seen Natasha and talked to her? 'Maybe I invented the whole thing, and when I go in there'll be nobody there.' But he had barely set foot in the room before the sensation of losing all his freedom made his whole being aware of her presence. She was wearing the same black dress that hung in soft folds, and her hair was done in the same way, and yet she looked quite different. If she had been like this when he had come in yesterday he would certainly have recognized her in an instant.

She was exactly like the girl he had once known, newly emerged from childhood, the girl who became engaged to Prince Andrey. There was a sharp, quizzical gleam in her eyes and a friendly, curiously mischievous look on her face.

Pierre took dinner with them, and would have gladly sat there all evening, but Princess Marya was going to evening service, so he left when they did.

Next day Pierre arrived early, dined with them and stayed the whole evening. Although Princess Marya and Natasha made him very welcome, and although the whole interest of Pierre's life was now focused on that house, as the evening wore on they reached a point where they had said all they had to say, and the conversation was drifting from one trivial topic to another and often broke down altogether. But Pierre stayed on so late that evening that Princess Marya and Natasha started looking at one another, obviously wondering how long it would be before he went home. Pierre could see this, but he couldn't bring himself to go. He felt embarrassed and uncomfortable, but still he sat on because he *could not* get up and go.

Princess Marya could see no end to it all, so she was the first to get to her feet, and complaining of a sick headache she started to say goodnight.

'So you're off to Petersburg tomorrow?' she said.

'Er no, I'm not going,' said Pierre hastily, with some surprise and something bordering on resentment in his tone. 'No ... er ... Oh, Petersburg? Yes, tomorrow ... but I'm not saying goodbye. I'll call in ... You may have some little commissions for me,' he added, standing in front of Princess Marya, turning very red and not leaving.

Natasha gave him her hand and retired. By contrast, Princess Marya, instead of going away, flopped down into an armchair, and turned her luminous, profoundly intensive eyes on Pierre in a close stare. The weariness that had been unmistakable only moments before had now gone. She gave a long, deep sigh, as if to prepare herself for a lengthy conversation.

The moment Natasha had gone, all Pierre's awkwardness and embarrassment instantly vanished, to be replaced by eager excitement. He quickly moved a chair up close to Princess Marya. 'Yes, I've been wanting to tell you ...' he said, replying to her stare as if words had been spoken. 'Princess, help me, please. What am I going to do? Is there any hope for me? Princess, my dear friend, listen to me. I know all about it. I know I'm not worthy of her. I know this is something we can't even talk about just now. But I want to be a brother to her. No I don't ... I can't ...'

He paused and ran his hands over his face and eyes.

'It's like this,' he went on, obviously struggling to make sense. 'I don't know how long I've been in love with her. But she's the only one I've ever loved, in all my life, and I love her so much I can't imagine living without her. I can't bring myself to ask for her hand now; but the thought that there's just a chance that she could be my wife and I might miss the opportunity ... opportunity ... is just awful. I want to know ... is there any hope for me? Please tell me what to do. Dear Princess,' he said, touching her arm during a brief pause when there was no answer from her.

'I'm thinking about what you have just told me,' answered Princess Marya. 'This is how I see it. You're quite right that talking to her about love just now would be ...' The princess paused. She was going to say that talking to her about love just now would be impossible, but she stopped herself because during the last three days she had seen such a sudden change come over Natasha that she would clearly be far from offended if Pierre were to declare his love – in fact, this was the one thing she was longing for.

'To speak to her now . . . wouldn't do,' she said nevertheless.

'But what can I possibly do?'

'Leave it with me,' said Princess Marya. 'I know . . .'

Pierre looked into her eyes.

'Well . . . well . . .' he said.

'I know she loves you . . . I mean she will love you,' said Princess Marya, correcting herself.

The words were hardly out of her mouth when Pierre leapt to his feet with a terrified look on his face and seized Princess Marya by the hand.

'What makes you think that? Do you really think there's some hope for me? Is that what you think?'

'Yes, it is,' said Princess Marya with a smile. 'Write to her parents. And leave it with me. I shall tell her when the time is right. I want this to happen. And I've a feeling in my heart that it will happen.'

'No, it's not possible! Oh, I'm so happy! Oh, I'm so happy! But no, it's not possible!' Pierre kept repeating, kissing Princess Marya's hands.

'Now off you go to Petersburg. That's the best thing. And I shall write to you,' she said.

'Petersburg? Do I have to? All right, I'll go. But I can call in tomorrow, can't I?'

Next day Pierre came to say goodbye. Natasha was less animated than in recent days, but there were times during that day when Pierre looked into her eyes and felt as if he was melting away, that both of them had disappeared and there was nothing left but happiness. 'Is it possible? No, it isn't,' he said to himself at every glance, every gesture, every word that came from her and filled his soul with gladness.

When the time came for him to say goodbye, he took her slender little hand and unconsciously held it a little longer in his own.

'Is it possible that this hand, this face, these eyes, all these treasures of womanly charm, so far from me now, is it possible they might one day be mine for ever, and I could know them as closely as I know myself? No, it can't be possible!'

'Goodbye, Count,' she said to him in a loud voice, though she added in a whisper, 'I shall look forward so much to seeing you again.'

And those simple words, along with the look in her eyes and the expression on her face that went with them, would last Pierre for two whole months, as the source of inexhaustible memories, meanings and happy dreams. '*I shall look forward so much to seeing you again.*' 'Yes, yes, what was it she said? Yes. "*I shall look forward so much to seeing you again.*" Oh, I'm so happy! How can I be as happy as this?' Pierre kept asking himself.

CHAPTER 19

On this occasion Pierre knew none of the spiritual torment that had troubled him under similar circumstances during his courtship of Hélène.

This time he never found himself doing what he had done before – squirming with a sickening sense of shame as he went over the things he had said; he didn't keep saying to himself, 'Oh, why didn't I say that?' or 'Why, oh why did I say, "I love you"?' Quite the reverse: he found himself going over in his imagination every word Natasha had spoken and everything he had said, along with all the details of every look and smile, without wanting to add anything, or take anything away, but just wanting to hear it over and over again. This time there wasn't a shadow of doubt about the rightness or wrongness of what he had started. Only one terrible anxiety sometimes assailed his mind. Am I dreaming? Could Princess Marya be wrong? Am I being over-confident and egotistical? I believe it's true, and yet I can just see it happening – I'm sure it will – Princess Marya will tell her about me, and she'll smile back and say, 'That's funny! He's certainly got things wrong. Doesn't he realize he's just a man, nothing more than a man, and I . . . well, I'm different, I live on a higher plane?'

This was his only doubt, but it never left Pierre alone for long. Similarly, he had stopped making plans. The happiness before him seemed so incredible that all he could do was wait for it to happen; there could be nothing beyond that. Bringing things to a conclusion was all that mattered.

Pierre was seized by a sudden frenzy of sheer joy, the sort of thing he didn't think he was capable of. The whole meaning of life, for him and the whole world, seemed to be contained in his love and the possibility of being loved in return. Sometimes it seemed as if everybody was preoccupied by nothing but his future happiness. It was as if they were all rejoicing as much as he was but trying to hide it by pretending to be interested in other things. In every word and gesture he saw intimations of his own happiness. He often surprised people by looking or smiling at them in a blissful, meaningful way that seemed to express some secret empathy. But when he realized that people might be unaware of his happiness he pitied them from the bottom of his heart, and felt an urge to get them somehow to realize that the things they were interested in were all rubbish and nonsense not worth thinking about.

When people advised him to go into government service, or when there was open discussion of political developments or the war, with implications that such-and-such an outcome of such-and-such an event would determine the happiness of all men, he would listen with a gentle smile of commiseration and then shock the company by a series of strange observations. But both types of people – those seen by Pierre as understanding the real meaning of life (his feelings), and the miserable wretches who obviously didn't – all of them presented themselves to Pierre in the brilliant light of his own radiant feelings, and in everybody he came across he hadn't the slightest difficulty in seeing nothing but goodness and deserving of love.

As he went through his dead wife's papers and things, the memory of her evoked in him nothing but a feeling of regret that she had never known the happiness he knew now. Prince Vasily, who was now at the peak of his pride, having received a new post and the star that went with it, struck him as a pathetic figure, a nice old man greatly to be pitied.

In days to come Pierre would often recall this period of mindless bliss. Any judgements of people and circumstances made by him at this time remained forever true. Far from going back on his assessment of men and things, if ever he was assailed later on by doubts or contradictory feelings he would simply go back to the view he had held during his period of madness, and inevitably that view never let him down.

'All right,' he would think, 'maybe I did seem weird and ridiculous at that time, but I wasn't as crazy as I looked. Oh no, I was sharper and cleverer then than I've ever been, and I understood everything worth understanding in life, because . . . well, because I was happy.'

Pierre's madness simply meant that he didn't wait, as in days gone by, for people to show personal qualities, what he might call virtues, before loving them. With his heart overflowing with love he loved people for no reason at all, and then had no trouble discovering many a sound reason that made them worth loving.

CHAPTER 20

After Pierre's departure that first evening, when Natasha had told Princess Marya with a happy smile of mischief that he looked exactly, yes, exactly, as if he was fresh from the bath-house, with his short jacket and close-cropped hair, from that moment something secret, unrecognized though irresistible, had awakened in Natasha's soul.

Everything about her – her face, her walk, her eyes, her voice – was suddenly changed. Much to her own surprise, a new vitality and hopes of happiness had burst forth and demanded satisfaction. After that first evening Natasha seemed to have forgotten everything that had happened to her. There was no more complaining about her present situation, not a word about the past, and she was no longer too scared to make happy plans for the future. She said very little about Pierre, but when Princess Marya mentioned him a long-dead gleam returned to her eyes, and her lips curved into a strange smile.

At first the change that had come over Natasha took Princess Marya by surprise, and when she understood what it meant she was saddened by it. 'Can she have loved my brother so little that she can forget him so quickly?' Princess Marya wondered, alone with her thoughts. But when she was with Natasha she wasn't angry with her, and she didn't blame her. The new vitality that had taken hold of Natasha was clearly so irresistible and so unexpected by Natasha herself that in her presence Princess Marya felt she had no right to blame her even in her heart of hearts.

Natasha gave herself up to this new sensation with such whole-heartedness and sincerity that she made no attempt to hide the fact that grief was behind her, and now she was happy and joyful.

When Princess Marya had returned to her room that night after her long talk to Pierre, Natasha had met her at the door.

'Has he said anything? Has he? Has he said anything?' she repeated. And Natasha's face had shone with happiness, though it also had a pathetic look as if to apologize for any happiness. 'I felt like listening at the door, but I knew you'd tell me.'

Although Princess Marya could well understand that look and was moved by it, although she felt sorry for Natasha in all her anxiety, for a moment she was offended by these words. She was thinking about her brother and his love.

'But what can we do? She can't help it,' thought Princess Marya, and with a sad and rather grim face she repeated for Natasha's benefit everything Pierre had said to her. Natasha was astounded to hear he was going to Petersburg.

'Going to Petersburg!' she repeated, as if she couldn't take it in.

But when she saw the gloomy expression on Princess Marya's face she guessed what was wrong and suddenly burst into tears.

'Marie,' she said, 'tell me what to do. I'm scared of doing the wrong thing. I'll do anything you say. Just tell me.'

'You do love him, don't you?'

'Yes!' whispered Natasha.

'Well, why are you crying? I'm so pleased for you,' said Princess Marya, so moved by her tears that she completely forgave Natasha's happiness.

'It won't happen straightaway ... One day soon. But think how happy we'll be when I'm his wife and you get married to Nikolay!'

'Natasha, I asked you not to talk about that. Let's talk about you.' Neither of them said anything.

'Oh, but why does he have to go to Petersburg?' cried Natasha suddenly, only to come back with a ready answer. 'No, no, he has to go ... Doesn't he, Marie? He does have to go ...'

EPILOGUE

PART I

CHAPTER I

Seven years had passed[1] since the events of 1812. The turbulent sea of European history had settled within its shores. It seemed to have calmed down, but the mysterious forces that move humanity (mysterious because the laws that determine their activity are unknown to us) were still at work.

Although the surface of the ocean of history seemed to be without a ripple, the movement of humanity went on as smoothly as the flow of time. Men kept coming together in various groups and splitting up again, and causes were gradually building up that would determine the formation and dissolution of empires and the displacement of peoples.

The ocean of history was no longer sent surging from one shore to another; it seethed in its depths. Historical figures were no longer borne by the waves from one shore to the other; now they stayed in one place and seemed to be going round in little eddies. The historical figures that had led armies and reflected the movement of the masses by waging war, marching men about and going into battle now reflected that same seething movement in political and diplomatic stratagems, statutes and treaties.

This kind of activity on the part of historical figures is called 'reactive' by historians.

In describing such activity the historians censure the historical figures most severely, accusing them of bringing about what they call 'reaction'. They sit in judgement on all the famous people of the age, from Alexander and Napoleon to Madame de Staël, Photius, Schelling, Fichte, Chateaubriand[2] and the rest, and find them innocent or guilty of promoting 'progress' or 'reaction'.

By their account Russia was a centre of reaction at that time, and Alexander I bears most of the blame for this – the same Alexander

who, by their account too, had been mainly responsible for liberal
initiatives taken early in his reign, and for the saving of Russia.

In modern Russian letters there is no one, from schoolboy to learned
historian, who is not ready to throw his little stone at Alexander for
the bad things he did during the latter period of his reign.

'He should have done this or that. On this occasion he did well;
on that occasion he did badly. He behaved splendidly at the beginning of his reign and throughout 1812, but he performed badly when
he gave Poland a constitution,[3] set up the Holy Alliance,[4] gave authority to Arakcheyev, encouraged first Golitsyn[5] with all his mysticism,
and then Shishkov[6] and Photius. He was wrong to go out to the front
during the war, wrong to disband the Semyonovsky regiment,[7] and
so on.'

It would take a dozen pages or more to list all the charges levelled
against him by the historians, all of them working on the safe assumption that they have a unique knowledge of what is good for humanity.

What do these charges amount to?

Is it not true that the actions of Alexander I that are applauded by
historians, the liberal initiatives taken early in his reign, his struggle
against Napoleon, his intransigence in 1812, and the campaign of
1813, flow from the same sources – the blood-line, upbringing and
life experience that made Alexander's personality what it was – that
produced the actions for which he is censured by historians, such as
the Holy Alliance, the restoration of Poland, the reaction that set in
during the 1820s?

What is the essence of these charges?

Alexander I is charged as follows: he, a figure of history standing
on the highest pinnacle of human power, with all the blinding light
of history focused upon him, a man who was prey to the strongest
blandishments of intrigue, trickery, flattery and self-delusion inextri-
cably linked with power, someone who at all stages of his life felt a
sense of personal responsibility for everything that was going on all
over Europe, a living personality as opposed to a creature of fiction,
subject like everybody else to his own practices, passions and impulses
towards goodness, beauty and truth – this man is charged not with
lacking virtue fifty years ago (the historians have no complaints on
this score), but with a failure to share the same views concerning the
good of humanity as those held today by some professor who has
spent all his adult life studying, i.e. reading books, listening to lectures
and scribbling notes from these books and lectures in a note-book.

But even if we assume that Alexander I, fifty years ago,[8] was mistaken in his view of what was good for the various peoples, we

must also assume that the historian censuring Alexander will with the passage of time also prove to be wrong in his view of what constitutes the good of humanity. Such a claim seems normal and inescapable when we look at the course of history and note that with each passing year and each new writer the view of what constitutes the good of humanity tends to change, and something that seemed good ten years ago now seems bad, and vice versa. To make matters worse, we discover that in history there are sometimes contemporaries who hold opposing views about what is good and what is bad. The granting of a constitution to Poland and the Holy Alliance are seen by some people as redounding to Alexander's credit, by others to his shame.

When discussing the actions of Alexander and Napoleon we cannot claim them as good or bad, because we cannot say what makes them good or bad. If their actions happen not to appeal to someone, the lack of appeal comes from nothing more than a disparity between the activities themselves and a narrow view of what constitutes the good of humanity. Even if I take a positive view of the survival of my father's house in Moscow in 1812, or the glory of the Russian army, or the success of Petersburg University and other universities, or the independence of Poland, or the supremacy of Russia, or the balance of power in Europe, or a particular development in European enlightenment that goes by the name of progress, I am bound to admit that the activity of any historical figure was aimed at more than these things, at more generalized goals beyond my comprehension.

But let us suppose that 'science' has the power of reconciling all contradictions, and can judge historical figures and events according to a fixed standard of goodness and badness.

Let us suppose that Alexander could have done everything differently. Let us assume that he could have been guided by those who now censure him and confidently claim to know the ultimate goal of the movement of humanity, and could have followed the programme of nationalism, freedom, equality and progress (these seem to cover the ground) that today's critics would have selected for him. Let us suppose that this programme, once found to be feasible, might have been feasible and actually implemented by Alexander. Then what would have happened to everything that was done by those who opposed the policies of the government of the day and indulged in activities that were, according to the same historians, good and beneficial? There would have been no such activities, there would have been no life, there would have been nothing.

Once you allow that human life is subject to reason you extinguish any possibility of life.

CHAPTER 2

If we assume, as historians do, that great men lead humanity towards the achievement of certain goals, such as the supremacy of Russia or France, the balance of power in Europe, the dissemination of ideas stemming from the Revolution, general progress, or anything you fancy, it becomes impossible to explain the phenomena of history without having recourse to concepts like *chance* and *genius*.

If the object of the European wars at the beginning of this century had been the aggrandizement of Russia, this object could have been attained without any of the preceding wars, and without the need for invasion. If the object had been the aggrandizement of France, this object might have been attained without the need for Revolution or empire. If the object had been the dissemination of ideas, the printing of books would have attained that object much more efficiently than soldiers. If the object had been the advancement of civilization, we can safely assume there are other more expedient ways of diffusing civilized values than slaughtering men and destroying their property.

So why did things happen this way and not otherwise? Because this is how they happened. '*Chance* set up the situation; *genius* exploited it,' history tells us.

But what is *chance*? What is *genius*?

The words *chance* and *genius* denote nothing that actually exists, and therefore they cannot be defined. All they denote is a degree of attainment in the understanding of phenomena. I don't know why a certain phenomenon occurs, I believe I never can know why, so I end up not wanting to know and I talk about *chance*. I observe a force producing an effect out of all proportion to the general run of human quality; I don't understand why this happens, so I talk about *genius*.

To a flock of sheep the sheep who gets driven into a special pen by the shepherd every evening for a good feed, and becomes twice as fat as the rest, must seem like a genius. And the fact that every evening this sheep doesn't come into the common fold, but goes into a special pen where there are lots of oats, and this same sheep fattens up nicely and then gets killed for mutton must look like a curious combination of genius and a series of unusual coincidences.

But all the sheep have to do is drop the assumption that everything that happens to them comes about solely for the furtherance of their sheepish interests; once they assume that the events occurring to them might have aims beyond their comprehension they will immediately perceive a unity and coherence in what is happening to the sheep that is being fattened up. Even if they will never quite understand why it is being fattened up, at least they will know that chance played no part in anything that happened to it, and they will have no need for concepts like *chance* or *genius*.

Only by renouncing any claim to knowledge of an immediate, intelligible purpose, and acknowledging the ultimate aim to be beyond our comprehension, shall we see any coherence or expediency in the lives of historical persons. The reason behind the effect that they produce, which does not accord with the general run of human capabilities, will then be revealed to us, and we shall have no further need for words like *chance* or *genius*.

All we have to do is admit that far from knowing the purpose of the convulsions that shook the European nations we know only the facts – a series of murders committed first in France, then in Italy, then in Africa, Prussia, Austria, Spain and Russia – and also that movements from west to east and from east to west constitute the essence and the aim of those events, and we shall not need to see anything very exceptional like *genius* in the character of Napoleon or Alexander, indeed we shall be unable to conceive of these figures as being at all different from anybody else. And not only shall we be able to dispense with *chance* as an explanation of the sequence of trivial events that made those men what they were, it will be clear to us that all these trivialities were inevitable.

Once we have renounced all knowledge of an ultimate purpose, we shall clearly perceive that just as we cannot invent for any plant a more characteristic blossom or seed than the ones it produces itself, so we cannot imagine any two persons, with all their past behind them, better attuned to their calling, even down to the smallest details, than Napoleon and Alexander.

CHAPTER 3

The essential feature underlying the events that occurred in Europe at the beginning of the present century is the mass movement of European peoples for military purposes first from west to east, then from east to west. The movement that started it all was from west to east. For the peoples of the west to carry out their military advance on Moscow, which they did complete, it was necessary for them to (1) come together in a military grouping large enough to be able to survive conflict with the military group of the east, (2) give up all their long-established traditions and customs, and (3) ensure that their military incursion was headed by a man capable of justifying, in his own name and in theirs, all the duplicity, robbery and murder that ensued.

So, beginning with the French Revolution, an old group falls apart because it is not large enough, old customs and traditions are done away with, a new group comes together bit by bit with different proportions, different customs and different traditions, and a man is groomed to stand at the head of the coming movement and assume full responsibility for what has to be done.

Along comes a man with no convictions, no customs, no traditions, no name, not even a Frenchman, and he works his way – seemingly by a series of curious chances – through the ferment of party conflict in France, and ends up in a prominent position without attaching himself to any particular party.

He finds himself in charge of the army, thanks to the incompetence of his colleagues, the spinelessness of his piffling opponents and his own bare-faced duplicity, bravura and narrow-minded over-confidence. The brilliance of the Italian soldiers, the reluctance of his opponents to take up arms, together with his boyish cockiness and over-confidence, win him military glory. Everywhere he is assisted by a string of what you might call *chance contingencies*. When he falls into disfavour with the French government this soon becomes an advantage. Every effort of his to change the course of his destiny comes to nothing; he is rejected for service in Russia, and he cannot get himself posted to Turkey.[9]

During the wars in Italy he finds himself several times staring death in the face, only to be saved on every occasion by some bolt from the blue. The Russian armies, the troops really capable of shattering his prestige, keep getting delayed by diplomacy and stay out of Europe while he is still there.[10]

On his return from Italy he finds the government in Paris in such a process of disintegration that all men entering it are being steadily wiped out and destroyed. But an escape route from this dangerous situation offers itself in the form of a pointless, totally unjustified expedition to Africa. Once again he is favoured by *chance* events. Impregnable Malta surrenders without a shot being fired; his most reckless schemes are now being crowned with success. The enemy navy, which later on will never miss a single rowing-boat, now lets a whole army through. In Africa a series of atrocities is perpetrated against the virtually defenceless inhabitants. Meanwhile the men per-petrating these atrocities, and especially their leader, persuade themselves that this is wonderful, this is glory, something worthy of Julius Caesar and Alexander the Great, a good thing all round.

This ideal of *glory* and *greatness* – stemming from a belief that one's every action is beyond reproach, and every crime a proud achievement invested with a supernatural significance beyond all understanding – this ideal, which would prove to be the guiding principle of this man and those around him, is deployed on a massive scale in Africa. Whatever he does comes off. The plague doesn't touch him. The callous slaughtering of his prisoners is not held against him. His childishly impetuous, unwarranted and ignoble departure from Africa, leaving behind comrades in distress, redounds to his credit, and again the enemy navy lets him slip through their fingers – twice. Dizzy with the success of his crimes and ready for his new role, he arrives in Paris without any plan in mind just as the disintegration of the Republican government, which might have brought him down a year earlier, completes its course; his arrival there as a man untainted by party loyalty serves only to raise his standing.

He has no sort of plan, he is scared of his own shadow, but all parties grab at him and solicit his support.

He alone – with his ideal of glory and greatness developed in Italy and Egypt, with his maniacal self-adulation, outrageous criminality and bare-faced duplicity – he alone can justify what has to be done.

He is needed to fill the place that awaits him, and so it is that, almost independently of his own will, and in spite of his dithering, his failure to plan ahead and his proneness to error, he finds himself drawn into a conspiracy aimed at the seizure of power, and the conspiracy comes off.

He is dragged before the legislature. Thinking all is lost, he panics and tries to run away, pretends to faint and says the most outrageous things that ought to have spelt ruin for him. But the once proud and discerning rulers of France, now under the impression that their day is done, turn out to be more confused than he is, and they say anything but what needs to be said in order to maintain their own power and see him off.

Chance contingencies, millions of them, bring him to power, and all men now seem to collude in asserting his authority. It is *chance* that determines the personalities of those who rule France at this time, and now cringe before him; *chance* that determines the personality of Paul I in Russia, who recognizes his authority; *chance* that sets up a plot against him that enhances his power instead of bringing him down. *Chance* delivers the Duc d'Enghien into his hands and somehow impels him to kill him and thereby persuades the mob by the strongest of all arguments that because he has the power he also has the right. *Chance* determines that although he strains every fibre to launch an expedition against England, which quite clearly would have led to his downfall, he never carries out this intention; instead he falls upon Mack with the Austrians, who give in without a fight. *Chance* and *genius* bring him victory at Austerlitz, and *chance* determines that all men, not only the French but every country in Europe except England, which will have no involvement in the events about to unfold, set aside their former horror and repugnance at his criminality and now legitimize the power he has acquired, the title he has bestowed on himself and his ideal concept of greatness and glory, which appeals to everybody as something splendidly reasonable.

As if to flex their muscles and prepare for the great movement ahead of them, the forces of the west lunge eastward on several occasions – in 1805, 1806, 1807 and 1809 – building up strength and adding to their numbers. In 1811 a group of men formed in France joins forces with an enormous group from the peoples of Central Europe. The growth in numbers is matched by an increase in the force of justification on the part of the man at the head of the movement. Throughout the ten-year preparatory period preceding the great movement this man has been hobnobbing with all the crowned heads of Europe. The discredited rulers of the world have no sensible concept or rational ideal with which to challenge the mindless Napoleonic ideal of *glory* and *greatness*. They fall over each other to demonstrate their lack of substance. The King of Prussia sends his wife to suck up to the great man; the Emperor of Austria considers it a mark of esteem that this man should take a daughter of the Kaisers to his bed. The Pope, the guardian of all that the nations hold sacred, uses religion to enhance the great man's reputation. It is not a question of Napoleon preparing himself for his new part; everything around him encourages him to assume personal responsibility for what is being done and is about to be done. There is no action, no atrocity, no little bit of trickery he could indulge in without it being immediately represented on the lips of those about him as a great deed. The best tribute the Germans can dream up for him is the celebration of Jena and Auerstadt. Here, not only is he a great man, but greatness devolves also to his ancestors, brothers, stepsons and brothers-in-law. Everything conspires to deprive him of the last scintilla of reason, and prepare him for his terrible role. Once he is ready, so are his forces.

The invading army flows east and reaches its ultimate goal: Moscow. The capital is taken; the Russian army suffers heavier losses than any opposing army in previous wars from Austerlitz to Wagram. But all of a sudden, instead of the *chance contingencies* and *genius* that had ensured such a consistent, uninterrupted run of successes leading him towards his destined goal he is faced with a vast number of *chance contingencies* working in reverse, from the cold he caught at Borodino to the spark that set Moscow on fire, and instead of *genius* we see in him unparalleled stupidity and wickedness.

The invading army runs away, turns back and runs away again; by now all the chance contingencies are going against him rather than for him.

Then comes the reverse movement from east to west, astonishingly similar to the west-to-east movement that has preceded it. As in 1805, 1807 and 1809 the same tentative westward lunges precede the great eastward movement. There is the same combination into a single group of vast proportions, the same process by which the peoples of Central Europe join in with the general movement, the same half-way hesitation and the same acceleration as the goal gets nearer.

Paris, the ultimate goal, is reached. Napoleon's government and armies are in tatters. Napoleon himself is of no further consequence; all his actions are obviously mean and pathetic, but once again inexplicable chance intervenes. The allies detest Napoleon, seeing him as the cause of all their troubles. Stripped of all power and authority, exposed as a crook and a villain, he ought to have been recognized as he had been ten years earlier, and would be a year later, as a bandit and an outlaw. But by some curious contingency no one sees this. His part has not been fully played out. The man who ten years before, and one year later, was looked on as a bandit and an outlaw is now dispatched to an island two days' journey from France presented to him as his dominion, with guards and millions to spend, as if he had done something worth paying for.

CHAPTER 4

The oceanic surge of the peoples begins to settle down within its shores. Its huge waves have flooded back, leaving little eddies on a calm surface – diplomats who fondly imagine that they have been the calming influence.

Then suddenly the calm sea surges up again. The diplomats imagine that they and their bones of contention are the cause of this new upheaval, and they anticipate warfare between their sovereigns. The situation seems impossible. But although they can sense the gathering wave, it doesn't come from where they expect it. It is the same wave with the same starting point – in Paris – the last backwash of the movement from the west, a wave that will soon resolve the diplomatic difficulties that seem so intractable and put an end to the military unrest of the period.

The man who has devastated France comes back to France alone, with no secret plan and no soldiers. Any policeman could arrest him, but by a strange contingency no one does; on the contrary, everybody gives a warm welcome to the man they were cursing only yesterday and will curse again within the month.

This man is still needed to vindicate events occurring in the last act of a collective drama.

The act is over. The last part has been played. The actor is told to take off his costume and wash off his powder and paint. He won't be needed again.

And for several years to come this man, alone on his island, plays out his pathetic little comedy to himself as the only audience, scheming and lying over silly details in order to vindicate his actions when vindication is no longer required, and demonstrating for all the world to see the true nature of what had been mistaken for power when all the time he had been guided by an unseen hand.

The theatre manager has brought the drama to a close, and made the actor take off his costume. Now he shows him to us.

'Look, this is what you have believed in! Here he is! I hope you can all see now that *he* hasn't been moving you – *I* have.'

But, dazzled by the power of movement, the people take a long time to absorb this.

There is even greater consistency and inevitability in the life of Alexander I, the figure who stood at the head of the east–west counter-movement.

What qualities would be needed for a man to eclipse all others and stand at the head of an east–west counter-movement?

He would need a sense of justice, deep involvement in the affairs of Europe tempered by sufficient detachment to leave his view unobscured by petty interests. He would need moral superiority over his fellows, the other sovereigns of the day. He would need to have a gentle and appealing personality and also a personal grudge against Napoleon. And Alexander I satisfies these requirements, all of them prepared long before by an infinite number of chance contingencies arising in his earlier life, in his upbringing and early liberalism, in the advisers circulating around him, in Austerlitz, Tilsit and Erfurt.

While ever the war centres on his own country this character stands idle; he is not needed. But once the need for a pan-European war becomes inevitable this character, finding himself in the right place at the right time, brings the European peoples together and leads them towards their goal.

The goal is reached. After the last of the wars in 1815 Alexander finds himself at the very summit of human power. How does he use it?

Alexander, the peacemaker of Europe, the man who from early youth had striven for nothing but the good of his peoples, the first champion of liberal reforms in his own country, now the possessor of maximum power and therefore the opportunity of promoting the welfare of his people, behaved very differently from Napoleon in exile, who was busy concocting childish and duplicitous schemes for blessings to be showered on humanity if only he had the power. Alexander, sensing that his mission is now accomplished and God's hand is upon him, and recognizing the paltriness of this mirage of power, turns away from it, hands it on to despicable creatures, men he despises and has only this to say:

'Not unto us, not unto us, but unto Thy Name . . . !'[11] I am a man, a man like you. Let me live like a man, and think about my soul and God.'

Just as the sun and every atom of ether is both a sphere complete in itself and also only a tiny part of an inconceivably vast whole, so every personality bears within himself his own aims whilst bearing them also in the service of generalized aims that lie beyond human comprehension.

A bee has settled on a flower and stung a child. And the child is scared of bees and says that bees are there to sting people. A poet admires the bee as it imbibes inside the sepals of the flower and says that bees are there to imbibe nectar inside flowers. A beekeeper, observing that the bee collects pollen and brings it back to the hive, says that the bee is there to collect honey. Another beekeeper, one who has studied the life of the swarm more closely, says the bee collects pollen to feed the young ones and rear a queen, and the bee is there for the propagation of its species. A botanist observes the bee flying over with pollen to fertilize the pistil on a diclinous flower and sees this as the purpose of the bee. Another one, observing the tendency for plants to migrate and the bee's contribution to this process, feels able to claim this as the purpose of the bee. But the ultimate purpose of the bee is not exhausted by the first, second or third purpose discernible by the human intellect. The higher the human intellect goes in discovering more and more purposes, the more obvious it becomes that the ultimate purpose is beyond comprehension.

Human comprehension does not extend beyond observation of the interaction between the living bee and other manifestations of life. The same applies to the purposes of historical characters and nations.

CHAPTER 5

Natasha's marriage to Bezukhov in 1813 was the last happy occasion enjoyed by the old Rostov family. Count Ilya died the same year, and, as always, with the father's death the family was broken up.

The events of the previous year – the burning of Moscow and the flight from the city, the death of Prince Andrey and Natasha's despair, the death of Petya and the old countess's grief – had rained down on the old count's head in a series of blows. He seemed not to understand, and he felt unable to understand, the significance of all these events, his morale collapsed and he bowed his old head as if to invite further blows that would finish him off. His mood swung between abject fear and frenzied excitement.

Natasha's marriage kept him busy on the outside for quite some time. He organized dinners and suppers, and he was patently doing his best to look cheerful, but his good cheer, instead of infecting everybody else as it used to do, had the opposite effect, arousing sympathy in those who knew and loved him.

Once Pierre and his wife had gone away he withdrew into himself and started complaining of depression. A few days later he fell ill and took to his bed. In spite of soothing words from the doctors he knew from the first days of his illness that he would never get up again. For two solid weeks the countess sat in a chair at his bedside and never changed her clothes. Every time she gave him his medicine, he snuffled as he kissed her hand and never said a word. On the last day, racked with sobs, he asked his wife and his absent son to forgive him for squandering their property, the worst of the sins that lay on his con-science. After receiving communion and extreme unction he died peacefully, and the next day a crowd of people who had known him turned up to pay their last respects, filling the Rostovs' rented apartments. These acquaintances, who had dined and danced so often in his house, and so often enjoyed a good laugh at his expense, were all feeling the same kind of inner self-reproach mixed with deep emotion, and they kept saying the same things, as if to vindicate themselves: 'Oh yes, say what you will about him, he was a splendid man. You don't meet people like him any more. And we all have our faults, don't we? . . .'

At the very time when the old count's affairs had become so involved there was no imagining how it would all have ended if things had gone on for another year, he had suddenly died.

Nikolay was away in Paris with the Russian army when news of his father's death reached him. He applied for immediate discharge, and instead of waiting for it to come through he took leave and left for Moscow. Within a month of the old count's death his financial position became absolutely clear, astounding everyone by the vast sums owed in various petty debts, the existence of which no one had suspected. The debts came to more than double the value of the estate.

Nikolay's friends and relations advised him to refuse his inheritance. But Nikolay thought this would be a slur on his father's honoured memory, so he wouldn't hear of any such thing; he took on the inheritance including the obligation to pay off all the debts.

The creditors, who had kept quiet for so long, restraining themselves during the old count's lifetime under the vague but powerful influence of his easy-going nature, descended on Nikolay all at once. As always happens, they began to compete with each other for early payment, and people like Mitenka and others who held IOUs given to them as presents were among the most persistent of the creditors. They wouldn't give Nikolay a moment's peace, and the same people who had shown obvious pity for the old man who had been responsible for their losses (in the case of losses rather than presents) now hounded the young heir without mercy, even though he was clearly innocent as far as they were concerned and had volunteered to settle the debts.

None of the schemes devised by Nikolay paid off. The estate went under the hammer and realized only half its true value, leaving half the debts still unpaid. Nikolay accepted thirty thousand roubles offered by his brother-in-law, Bezukhov, and paid off anything he recognized as a genuine monetary obligation. Then, to avoid being thrown into prison for the remaining debts, as threatened by the creditors, he re-entered government service.

Any possibility of returning to the army, where he was next in line for promotion to colonel, was out of the question, because his mother now clung on to her son for dear life. And so despite his reluctance to stay on in Moscow, mingling with people who had known him in days gone by, and despite his hatred of the civil service, he accepted a civilian post in Moscow, discarded his dearly loved uniform and set himself up with his mother and Sonya in modest lodgings in one of the poorer districts.

Natasha and Pierre were living in Petersburg at this time, and they had no clear idea of Nikolay's situation. Having borrowed money from his brother-in-law, Nikolay did everything he could to hide his poverty-stricken situation from him. What made things worse was the need not only to keep himself, Sonya and his mother on a salary of twelve hundred roubles, but to keep his mother in such a way that she wouldn't notice how poor they had become. The countess couldn't conceive of life without the luxuries she had been used to since childhood, and, blissfully unaware of causing any problems for her son, she would insist on sending a carriage round to fetch a friend, even though they had no carriage, ordering expensive delicacies for herself, or wine for her son, and asking for money to buy surprise presents for Natasha, Sonya or Nikolay himself.

Sonya ran the house, waited on her aunt, read to her, put up with her tantrums and half-concealed enmity and conspired with Nikolay to conceal from the old countess their poverty-stricken situation. Nikolay felt irredeemably indebted to Sonya, deeply grateful for everything she did for his mother, and he also greatly admired her patience and devotion. Nevertheless, he did what he could to distance himself from her.

In his heart of hearts he seemed to resent the fact that she was too perfect, beyond all criticism. She possessed all the admirable qualities, but very little to make him love her. And he felt that the more admirable she became the less he loved her. He had taken her at her word when she had written to give him his freedom, and now he behaved towards her as if what had happened between them was ancient history, long forgotten, something that could never under any circumstances be returned to.

Nikolay's position was going from bad to worse. His idea of building up some savings out of his salary proved to be an idle dream. Far from saving anything, he was even running up small debts to satisfy his mother's demands. There seemed to be no way out of this situation. He had no time for the idea of marrying a rich woman, which his female relatives kept suggesting. The only other solution – his mother's death – never even crossed his mind. There was soon nothing he wanted, nothing to hope for, and in his heart of hearts he took a grim and gloomy satisfaction in the stoical way he put up with things. He went out of his way to avoid old acquaintances, with their expressions of sympathy and humiliating offers of assistance. He avoided every kind of frivolity and amusement; and even at home he did nothing but play patience with his mother, and pace the room silently, smoking one pipe after another. He seemed to cultivate this dark mood of his; it was the only thing that kept him going.

CHAPTER 6

At the beginning of the winter Princess Marya arrived in Moscow. From the city's rumour mill she heard about the Rostovs' situation; the word was that 'the son was sacrificing himself for his mother'. 'I would have expected nothing less of him,' Princess Marya told herself, only too delighted to find confirmation of her love for him. Bearing in mind her friendly, almost intimate relationship with the Rostovs – she was almost a member of the family – she felt duty-bound to call on them. But when she thought of her relations with Nikolay in Voronezh she was scared to do so. A few weeks after her arrival in Moscow, however, she plucked up the courage and went to see the Rostovs.

Nikolay was the first to meet her because it was impossible to get to the countess's room without walking through his. Princess Marya took one glance at him and instead of the anticipated expression of delight all she saw was a look of chilly aloofness and pride that she had never seen before. Nikolay asked after her health, led her through to his mother and stayed no more than five minutes before walking out.

When Princess Marya was leaving Nikolay met her again, and saw her through into the hall with almost exaggerated formality and stiffness. He made no comment on what she said about the countess's health. 'It's got nothing to do with you. Just leave me alone,' his eyes seemed to say.

'What does she think she's doing prowling about in here? What's she after? I can't stand these fine ladies and their nice ways!' he said out loud in Sonya's presence, obviously unable to contain his annoyance, once the princess's carriage had trundled away.

'Oh, Nicolas, how can you talk like that?' said Sonya, beside herself with delight. 'She's such a nice person, and Mamma is so fond of her.'

Nikolay said nothing in reply, and would have liked to drop the subject of Princess Marya, but from then on the old countess brought her into the conversation several times a day. She praised her to the skies, told her son he must go and see her, wanted to see more of her herself, yet she was always in a funny mood when she spoke about her.

Nikolay tried to hold back when his mother talked about Princess Marya, but his silence annoyed her.

'She's a lovely girl. I think very highly of her,' she would say, 'and you must go round and see her. At least you'd be outside meeting people. You must be bored stiff spending all your time in here with us.'

'But I've no wish to do that, Mamma.'

'Hm, you used to like meeting people. Now all you can say is, "I've no wish to do that." I really don't understand you, my dear. One minute you're bored stiff, and the next you're refusing to go out and meet people.'

'I didn't say I was bored.'

'Oh no? I distinctly heard you say you don't even want to see her. I think very highly of her, and you used to like her yourself. Now all of a sudden you're behaving oddly and you have your own funny reasons. Nobody tells me anything.'

'That's not true, Mamma.'

'It would be different if I was asking you to do something unpleasant, but as things stand I'm just asking you to go round and see her. It's the polite thing to do ... Anyway, I've said my say, and I shan't interfere any more. You can go on keeping secrets from your mother.'

'All right, I'll go round, if that's what you want.'

'I don't mind one way or the other. I'm only thinking of you.'

Nikolay gave a sigh, bit his moustache and dealt the cards in an attempt to change the subject.

The next day and the following day, and the day after that, they went through exactly the same conversation again and again.

After her visit to the Rostovs and the unexpectedly frigid reception she had been given by Nikolay, Princess Marya told herself she had been right in not wanting to call on them before they called on her.

'I got what I expected,' she said to herself, summoning pride to her aid. 'He's no concern of mine. I just wanted to see the old lady. She's always been so kind to me, and I owe her a great deal.'

But thoughts like these were not enough to put her mind at rest. She was plagued with a feeling of something not far from remorse whenever she thought of her visit. Despite her firm resolve to forget the whole thing and make sure she didn't call on the Rostovs again, she couldn't get it out of her mind that her situation was not quite so clear cut. And when she wondered exactly what it was that was plaguing her, she was forced to admit that it was her relationship with Rostov. His frigid and formal attitude had nothing to do with any feelings he might have for her (this much she knew); it was all a cover for something else. This something else had to be brought out into the open, and she knew she wouldn't be able to rest until it was.

One day in mid-winter she was sitting in the classroom, keeping an eye on her nephew as he did his school-work, when the servant announced that Rostov had called to see her. Grimly determined not to let him guess her secret, and not to show any embarrassment, she summoned Mademoiselle Bourienne, and the two of them went into the drawing-room.

One glance at Nikolay's face told her this was no more than a courtesy call, and she decided to adopt whatever tone he adopted towards her.

They spoke about the countess's health, people they had in common, the latest news of the war, and when the statutory ten minutes were up Nikolay rose to say goodbye.

With Mademoiselle Bourienne's assistance Princess Marya had kept the conversation going quite well, but at the very last moment, just as he got to his feet, she became so weary with talking about things that didn't matter to her, and so absorbed in wondering why she should be the only one to have so little joy in her life, that in a fit of absent-mindedness she sat there like a stone, staring ahead and ignoring the fact that he was getting up.

Nikolay looked down at her, pretended not to notice her absent-mindedness and said a few words to Mademoiselle Bourienne before glancing at the princess again. She was still sitting there like a stone, with a painful look on her gentle face. Suddenly he felt sorry for her, and he was vaguely aware that he might be the cause of the sadness he could read on her face. He felt an urge to help her, to say something nice, but he couldn't think of anything to say.

'Goodbye, Princess,' he said.

She started, blushed and gave a deep sigh.

'Oh, I'm so sorry,' she said, as if she had just woken up. 'Are you going already, Count. Goodbye, then. Oh, what about that cushion for the countess?'

'Wait a minute. I'll go and get it,' said Mademoiselle Bourienne, and she left the room.

Neither of them spoke. They exchanged a few glances.

'You know, Princess,' said Nikolay at last, with a lugubrious smile. 'It seems like yesterday, but a lot of water has flowed under the bridge since the first time we met at Bogucharovo. We all seemed to be in so much trouble then, but I'd give a lot to go back to that time . . . but there's no going back.'

Princess Marya's luminous eyes were watching him closely as he spoke. It seemed as if she was trying to get at some secret meaning behind his words that would make his feelings clear.

'Yes, yes,' she said, 'but there's no need for you to regret the past, Count. From what I've heard about your present life you will always look back on it with pleasure, because of the sacrifices you are making . . .'

'I can't accept your praise,' he cut in hastily. 'It's the other way round. I'm always criticizing myself . . . but this is such a gloomy and boring topic of conversation.'

And once again his eyes took on that formal, frigid look. But by this time Princess Marya had seen in him the man she had known and loved, and this was the man she was speaking to now.

'I thought you wouldn't mind my saying that,' she said. 'I've been such a close friend of yours . . . and of your family, and I didn't think you would find my sympathy intrusive. But I was wrong,' she said. There was a sudden catch in her voice. 'I don't know why,' she went on, recovering her composure. 'You weren't like this before, and . . .'

'*Why?* There are thousands of reasons.' (He stressed the word *why*.) 'Thank you so much, Princess,' he added softly. 'Sometimes . . . it's hard . . .'

'Now you know why! Now you know why!' said an inner voice speaking to Princess Marya's heart. 'No, it wasn't just that happy, kind, open look of his, not just his handsome person that I loved. I had an intuition of his nobility and strength, his spirit of self-sacrifice,' she said to herself.

'Yes, he's a poor man now, and I am rich . . . And that's all there is to it . . . Yes, if it wasn't for this . . .' By recalling his earlier tenderness and looking into his kind, sad face she had suddenly seen the reason for his frigid attitude.

'Why, Count, why?' she suddenly cried, almost shouting and moving closer to him without being aware of it. 'Please tell me why. You really must.' He said nothing. 'I don't know about your *why*, Count,' she went on. 'But it's not easy for me . . . I don't mind admitting it. For some reason you want to deprive me of our old friendship. And that hurts me.' There were tears in her eyes and her voice. 'I've had so little happiness in my life that any loss is hard to bear . . . Do forgive me. Goodbye.'

She burst into tears, and set off out of the room.

'Princess! Wait a minute, for heaven's sake,' he cried, trying to stop her. 'Princess!'

She looked round. For a few seconds they gazed into each other's eyes. Nothing was said, but suddenly what had been remote and impossible became close, possible and inevitable . . .

CHAPTER 7

In the autumn of 1814 Nikolay married Princess Marya, and went to live at Bald Hills with his wife, his mother and Sonya.

It took him three years to pay off the rest of his debts without selling any of his wife's property, and when he was left a little something by a cousin he also managed to repay the money borrowed from Pierre.

In another three years, by 1820, Nikolay had managed his finances so efficiently he was able to purchase a modest estate adjoining Bald Hills, and had started negotiations to buy back his family estate at Otradnoye, which was his pet dream.

Although he had been forced into farming to begin with, he soon became so enthusiastic that it became his favourite occupation to the exclusion of almost everything else. Nikolay was a farmer of the old school; he didn't like new-fangled ideas, especially the English ones that were coming in at that time. He laughed at theoretical studies of estate management, and had little time for factory processing, expensive production methods, or seed that cost a fortune. And he refused to specialize in anything, preferring to keep an eye on *the overall estate* rather than any of its parts. And on the estate itself what mattered most to his mind was not the nitrogen or oxygen content of the soil or air, not a new kind of plough or manure, but the vital agencies that made the hydrogen, the oxygen, the plough and the manure work effectively, and that meant the peasants who did the work. When Nikolay took up farming, and began to investigate its different branches, it was the peasant that claimed most of his attention. He saw the peasant as something more than a useful tool; he was an end in himself and a source of good judgement. He began by closely observing the peasants in an attempt to understand what they wanted, and what they considered good and bad practice. He went through the motions of making arrangements and giving out orders, but what he was really doing was learning from the peasants by following their methods, their language and their notions of what was good and bad. And it was only when he came to understand the peasants' appetites and aspirations, when he had learnt their way of speaking and the hidden meaning behind their words, when he felt a kind of kinship with them, that he began to manage them with confidence, in other words to fulfil the obligation towards them that was demanded of him. And Nikolay's management produced the most brilliant results.

The first thing Nikolay did when he took over the estate was to make three faultless appointments that came to him in a flash of inspired insight; he chose a bailiff, a village elder and a peasant representative, all of whom would have been elected by the peasants themselves if the choice had been theirs, and these leading figures were never replaced. Before researching the chemical properties of manure, or 'dabbling in debits and credits' (his description of book-keeping), he found out how many cattle the peasants possessed and tried everything he could think of to get the numbers up. He kept the peasants together in large family groupings and wouldn't allow them to split up into separate households. He was equally hard on the lazy, the dissolute and the feckless, and tried to have them ejected from the community. When it came to sowing and reaping the hay and corn, he took as much care over the peasants' fields as he did over his own. And few landowners achieved what Nikolay did in terms of early sowing and reaping, and the overall yield.

He wouldn't have anything to do with the house serfs because he saw them as scroungers, and everybody said he spoilt them by neglect. When a decision had to be taken and a house serf was involved, especially if one of them had to be punished, he could never make his mind up and consulted the entire household, but whenever it was possible to send a house serf for conscription instead of a peasant he did that with no compunction. In all his dealings with the peasants he never experienced the slightest hesitation. Every order he gave would, to his certain knowledge, be approved by a massive majority.

He never allowed himself either to dole out extra work or punishment just because he felt like it or to let people off or give them rewards out of personal preference. He couldn't have said what his standards were when judging what to do and what not to do, but standards there were, firmly fixed in his heart and mind.

Whenever anything went wrong or someone made a mess of things he would complain long and hard about 'these Russian peasants of ours', and he himself thought he couldn't stand them, but actually he loved 'these Russian peasants of ours' and their way of life with every fibre of his being, and it was only by loving them that he found and adopted the only way of doing things on the estate that was guaranteed to produce good results.

Countess Marya was jealous of her husband's passion, and sorry she couldn't share it with him, but she couldn't begin to understand the delights and disappointments that came his way in this other world to which she had no access. She couldn't understand why he seemed so excited and exuberant when he came in for a drink of tea with her after hours of sowing, mowing or harvesting, having got up at the crack of dawn to spend all morning in the fields or on the threshing-floor. She couldn't understand why he was so enthusiastic when he went on and on about Matvey Yermishin, a successful peasant farmer who had been up all night with his family carting his sheaves, and got his harvest stacked before anyone else had started reaping. She couldn't understand why he was smiling under his moustache and winking at her as he walked out through the window on to the verandah to watch a mild drizzle descending on young oats that had been wilting from the dry weather, or why, when the wind blew an ominous cloud away from them while they were mowing or harvesting, he would come in from the barn flushed, sunburnt and covered in sweat, with his hair reeking of wormwood and gentian, rub his hands together and say with such glee, 'Give me one more day and it'll all be in, mine and theirs.'

Something else she could understand even less was how on earth he, with all his goodheartedness and eternal readiness to anticipate her wishes, almost went berserk when she presented him with petitions from peasants or their women who had come to her asking to be excused from work, and how he, her good, kind Nicolas, could refuse point blank and tell her quite sharply to keep her nose out of his business. She felt as if he lived in a much-loved separate world that was governed by laws she couldn't understand.

Sometimes in an effort to understand him she would talk about all the good he was doing in looking after the welfare of his subjects, but he would round on her and say, 'Oh no, not that. I never even think about it. I wouldn't go out of my way for their benefit. It's all airy-fairy nonsense, women's talk, all this doing good to your neighbour. I don't want our children to go short. I've got to build up our fortunes in my lifetime, and that's all there is to it. And to do that you have to have discipline. You have to be hard!' he would declare, clenching his fist with great passion. 'And of course you have to be fair as well,' he would add, 'because if the peasant is naked and starving and he's down to his last scraggy horse he's no good to man or beast.'

And it was probably because Nikolay would not entertain any idea that he was doing things for other people, or being virtuous, that everything he attempted bore fruit. His wealth increased by leaps and bounds, serfs from nearby estates came and asked him to buy them in, and long after he was dead and gone his rule was reverently preserved in folk memory. 'What a master 'e was . . . Put the peasants first and 'imself second, 'e did. Didn't stand no nonsense neither. Right good master 'e was!'

CHAPTER 8

The one thing that worried Nikolay in the management of his serfs
was his quick temper along with an old habit, acquired in the hussars,
of being too ready with his fists. At first he saw nothing wrong with
this, but in the second year of his married life his views on this form
of discipline underwent a sudden change.

One day during the summer he had sent for the village elder from
Bogucharovo, the man who had taken over when Dron died and now
stood accused of various acts of fraud and negligence. Nikolay went
out to the steps to meet him, and the first answers were barely out of
the man's mouth when shouts and blows were heard in the hall. Later
on, when he came back in for lunch, Nikolay went over to his wife,
who was sitting with her head bent low over her embroidery frame,
and started telling her in the usual way about everything he had been
doing during the morning, including the business with the elder from
Bogucharovo. Countess Marya sat there in the same position, tight-
lipped, turning alternately red and pale and not responding.

'Insolent swine,' he said, flaring up at the mere recollection. 'Should
have told me he was drunk and couldn't see properly . . . Hey, what's
all this, Marie?' he asked suddenly.

Countess Marya looked up, started to say something but looked
straight down again and tightened her lips.

'What is it? What's wrong, my love?' Tears always improved Countess Marya's rather plain looks. Pain and anger never made her cry,
but sadness and pity always did. And when she cried her luminous
eyes took on an irresistible loveliness.

The moment Nikolay took her by the hand she lost control and
burst into tears.

'Nikolay, I saw you . . . He was in the wrong, but you . . . why did
you do that? Nikolay!' and she buried her face in her hands.

Nikolay said nothing. He went bright red, walked away and started
pacing up and down in silence. He knew what she was crying about,
but deep down he couldn't bring himself just like that to acknowledge
that something he had been used to since childhood, something he
considered perfectly normal, could be wrong. 'Sentimental nonsense,
women's thinking . . . Or could she be right?' he said to himself. Still
uncertain, he glanced again at her loving face that was so full of pain,
and suddenly it came to him: she was right – all this time he had been
sinning against himself.

'Marie,' he said softly, going over to her, 'it won't happen again. I promise. Ever,' he repeated in a trembling voice, like a little boy wanting to be forgiven.

The tears flowed faster from the countess's eyes. She took her husband's hand and kissed it.

'Nikolay, when did you break your cameo ring?' she said, changing the subject as she looked at the finger that wore a ring with a cameo head of Laocoön.[12]

'Today. Same thing. Oh, Marie, don't remind me!' he burst out again. 'I swear it won't happen again. And let this always be a reminder to me,' he said, pointing to the broken ring.

And from then on, whenever he was having things out with his village elders and foremen, as soon as he felt a rush of blood to his face and began to clench his fists, Nikolay would twist the broken ring around his finger and look away from the man who had made him so angry. Even then a couple of times a year he would forget himself, and then he would go straight to his wife, make a full confession and promise once again that this really was the last time.

'Marie, you must despise me,' he said to her. 'It's what I deserve.'

'You must walk away, just walk away as fast as you can if you feel yourself losing control,' his wife said despondently, trying to pacify him.

Among the gentry of the province Nikolay was respected but not well liked. The gentry's interests were not his interests. This meant that some people saw him as arrogant and others thought he was stupid. He spent the whole of the summer, from spring sowing to harvest-time, farming. When autumn came he went off hunting with the same kind of businesslike attitude he applied to farming, disappearing with his hunt for weeks on end. In winter he went round their other properties, or did a lot of reading, mainly historical works, on which he spent a little money each year. He was putting together what he called a serious library, and he made it a matter of principle to read every book he bought. He would retire to his study looking very important and sit there engaged in his reading. The occupation that he had originally taken on as a duty soon became a habit, and it now gave him a special thrill of pleasure as he revelled in the sense of doing something that mattered. Apart from the trips away on business he spent all winter ensconced at home with his family, involving himself very closely in the day-to-day relations between his children and their mother. He felt closer and closer to his wife, discovering new spiritual treasures in her with each passing day.

From the time of Nikolay's marriage Sonya had lived in his house. Before they were married Nikolay had told his wife everything that had happened between him and Sonya, blaming himself and praising her. He asked Princess Marya to be kind and affectionate to his cousin. His wife fully appreciated that he had treated Sonya badly, and she had too; she couldn't help thinking that her wealth had influenced Nikolay in his choice, she could find no fault in Sonya, and she wanted to like her. But she didn't, and to make matters worse she often found herself harbouring feelings of enmity towards her that she couldn't suppress.

One day she was talking to her friend Natasha about Sonya and her own unfair prejudice against her.

'Do you know what I think?' said Natasha. 'You're always reading the Bible, aren't you? There's a passage there that's all about Sonya.'

'Which one?' asked Countess Marya in some surprise.

' "To him that hath shall be given, and from him that hath not shall be taken away even that which he hath." You remember. She's the one that hath not. I don't know why – perhaps she's not selfish enough. I just don't know, but from her it shall certainly be taken away – in fact, it already has been. Sometimes I feel terribly sorry for her. In the old days I used to want Nikolay to marry her, but I had a kind of feeling it wasn't going to happen. She's what they call a *barren flower*. You know – you get them on strawberry plants. Sometimes I feel sorry for her, but sometimes I think she doesn't feel things the way we would have done.'

And although Countess Marya argued that these words from the Bible didn't have quite that meaning, as she watched Sonya she couldn't help agreeing with Natasha's explanation. Sonya really did seem to find her situation quite bearable; she seemed fully reconciled to her lot as a *barren flower*. She seemed to be fonder of the family as a whole than the people in it. Like a cat, she had attached herself to the house rather than the people. She waited on the old countess, petted the children and spoilt them, and never refused to do any little thing she could, but everything she did was taken for granted, without any great show of gratitude . . .

The manor house at Bald Hills had been rebuilt, but not on the same scale as under the old prince.

The building work begun in days of hardship was no more than rudimentary. The huge house on its old stone foundations was wood-built and plastered only on the inside. The great rambling house with its bare boards was furnished with plain, hard armchairs and sofas and tables knocked up by serf carpenters using local birch-timber. The house was very roomy, with quarters for the house serfs and accommodation for visitors.

Relatives – Rostovs and Bolkonskys – would sometimes descend on Bald Hills bringing the whole family, sixteen horses and dozens of servants, and stay for months at a time. And four times a year, on the name-days and birthdays of the master and mistress, up to a hundred visitors would come together for a day or two. The rest of the year consisted of the smooth routine of family life with its normal occupations, and with breakfast, lunch, dinner and supper all coming from their own produce.

CHAPTER 9

It was the eve of St Nicholas, the 5th of December 1820. That year Natasha had been staying at Bald Hills with her husband and children since the beginning of the autumn. Pierre was away in Petersburg 'on personal business', as he liked to put it. He had gone originally for three weeks, but he had already been away for six, and they expected him home any minute now.

On this 5th of December, as well as the Bezukhovs there was another visitor staying with the Rostovs – Nikolay's old friend, the now retired General Vasily Denisov.

On the 6th more guests were coming to celebrate his name-day, and Nikolay knew he would have to exchange his loose Tatar coat for a frock-coat and tight boots with pointed toes, and drive over to the new church he had built, and after that to listen to congratulations, offer refreshments to his guests and chat about the elections of the Nobility and this year's harvest. But the day before all that he felt he had a right to spend as usual. By dinner-time Nikolay had gone through the bailiff's accounts from the Ryazan estate, the property of his wife's nephew, written a couple of business letters and walked round the granaries, cattle-yard and stables. After taking certain steps to control the general drunkenness expected next day among the peasants at such a big saint's day celebration, he came in to dinner without having had a chance to talk to his wife in private all day long and sat down at a long table set for twenty, where all the family were assembled, including his mother, old Mademoiselle Belov, her companion, his wife and three children, their governess and tutor, his wife's nephew with his tutor, Sonya, Denisov, Natasha, her three children, their governess and Mikhail Ivanych, the old prince's architect, who was living on at Bald Hills in retirement.

Countess Marya was sitting at the other end of the table. The moment her husband sat down at the table she could tell from the way he snatched up his napkin and shoved back the tumbler and wine-glass set for him that he was in a bad mood, as he sometimes was just before the soup when he had come in from work and sat straight down to dinner. Countess Marya knew this mood only too well, and when she herself was in a good mood she would wait quietly until he had finished his soup, and only then open up a conversation and make him admit there was no reason to be in a bad mood, but today she quite forgot this way of dealing with him, she felt hurt that he was angry with her for no good reason, and she was miserable. She asked where he had been. He told her. She asked whether everything was all right with the estate. He scowled unpleasantly at her forced way of speaking and gave a curt response.

'I wasn't wrong, then,' thought Countess Marya, 'but why should he take things out on me?' In his manner of speaking she could read ill will towards her and a desire to cut short the conversation. She was well aware that her words did sound rather forced, but she couldn't resist asking one or two more questions.

Thanks to Denisov it wasn't long before the conversation over dinner became generalized and animated, and she said nothing more to her husband. When they got up from the table and went over to thank the old countess, Countess Marya held out her hand, kissed her husband and asked why he was angry with her.

'You always look on the black side,' he said. 'It never occurred to me that I was angry.'

But the word 'always' implied something different: 'Yes, I am angry, but I'm not saying why.'

Nikolay got on so well with his wife that even Sonya and the old countess, both of whom would have been envious enough to enjoy any discord between them, could never find anything to criticize them for, though there were occasional outbursts of hostility even between them. Sometimes – especially when they had just come through one of their happiest periods – a feeling of alienation and hostility would suddenly arise between them. It was a feeling that came upon them most frequently when Countess Marya was pregnant. And she was in this condition now.

'Well, *messieurs et mesdames*,' said Nikolay in a loud voice with a great show of bonhomie (which his wife saw as deliberately getting at her), 'I've been on my feet since six o'clock this morning. Tomorrow's my day of suffering. Today I can go and have a rest.' And without a word to his wife he went off to the little sitting-room, and lay down on the sofa.

'It's *always* like that,' thought Countess Marya. 'He talks to anybody but me. I can see it. I can see it. I'm repulsive to him, especially in this condition.' She looked down at her swollen belly and then glanced in the mirror at her pale, sallow, sunken face with its eyes that looked bigger than ever.

Everything riled her: Denisov's shouting and guffawing, Natasha's chatter and above all the quick glance from Sonya.

Sonya was always the first object for Countess Marya to rail against.

She sat on with her guests for a little while longer without taking in a word they were saying and then slipped out and went along to the nursery.

The children were perched on chairs playing at driving to Moscow, and they invited her to join in. She sat down and played with them for a while, but the thought of her husband and his uncalled-for bad mood wouldn't leave her in peace. She got to her feet and tiptoed rather awkwardly down to the little sitting-room.

'Perhaps he's not asleep. I'll have it out with him,' she said to herself. Little Andrey, her elder boy, followed behind on tiptoe, mimicking her. His mother didn't notice.

'Marie dear, I think he's asleep. He's tired out,' said Sonya, coming across her in the next room (Countess Marya seemed to come across her everywhere). 'Don't let Andrey wake him up.'

Countess Marya looked round, saw Andrey behind her and sensed that Sonya was right, which was enough in itself to make her go red in the face, and only just manage to bite back a cruel retort. She said nothing and to avoid the impression of obeying her she let him come on behind as she went up to the door, though she signalled for him to keep quiet. Sonya went out through another door. From the room where Nikolay was asleep his wife could hear his steady breathing, so familiar to her in every tone. As she listened she could see his smooth, handsome forehead, his moustache, the whole of the face she had so often stared at in the dead of the night while he was asleep. Nikolay stirred and cleared his throat. And at the same instant Andrey shouted from the doorway, 'Papa, Mamma's here!'

Countess Marya turned pale with dismay and signalled again to the little boy. He said no more, and a terrible silence ensued lasting almost a minute. She knew how Nikolay hated being woken up. Then suddenly through the door she heard him stir and clear his throat again, and in a tone of some irritation he said, 'I never get a minute's peace. Is that you Marie? Why did you bring him here?'

'I just came to have a look . . . I didn't see . . . I'm so sorry . . .'

Nikolay had a good cough and said nothing more. His wife went away, and took her son back to the nursery. Five minutes later little black-eyed three-year-old Natasha, her father's pet, heard from her brother that Papa was asleep in Mamma's little room, escaped unnoticed and ran in to see her father.

The black-eyed little girl rattled the door open with a bang, and her stumpy little legs were soon scurrying across to the sofa, where she took stock of the figure of her father asleep with his back to her, before standing on tiptoe and kissing him on the arm that was pillowing his head. Nikolay turned over with the gentlest of smiles on his face.

'Natasha, Natasha!' came the countess's dismayed whisper from the doorway. 'Papa's having a nap.'

'No, he's not, Mamma,' answered little Natasha with great certainty. 'He's laughing.'

Nikolay put his feet down on the floor, got up from the sofa and picked his little girl up in his arms.

'Come on in, Masha,' he said to his wife. She went in and sat down beside him.

'I didn't see him running up after me,' she said diffidently. 'I was just . . .'

Holding his little girl on one arm, Nikolay glanced at his wife, and when he saw the look of guilt on her face he put the other arm round her and kissed her on the hair.

'Can I kiss your mamma?' he asked Natasha.

The little girl smiled demurely.

'Again,' she said, pointing imperiously to the spot where Nikolay had kissed his wife.

'I don't know why you think I'm in a bad mood,' said Nikolay in response to the question he knew was in his wife's mind.

'You've no idea how sad and lonely I am when you go like that. I always think . . .'

'Marie, shush. You're being silly. Shame on you,' he said merrily.

'I think you don't love me any more, I'm so ugly . . . all the time . . . but especially in this condi . . .'

'Oh, you're so funny! We're not loved because we look good – we look good because we're loved. It is only the likes of Malvina who are loved for being beautiful. So the question is: do I love my wife? No, it's not love, it's . . . I don't know how to put it. When you're away, or there's a bit of trouble between us like today, I feel lost, I can't do anything. Put it another way – do I love my finger? No, I don't, but you try cutting it off . . .'

'Well I'm not like that, but I do understand. So you're not angry with me?'

'Oh yes I am – horribly!' he said with a smile. He got to his feet, smoothed back his hair and began pacing up and down the room.

'Do you know what I've been thinking, Marie?' he began. Now they had made their peace he had gone straight back to thinking aloud in her presence. He didn't stop to ask whether she was ready to listen; it made no difference. An idea had occurred to him, so it must have occurred to her, too. And he told her he was going to persuade Pierre to stay on there until next spring.

Countess Marya listened, made a few comments, and then it was her turn to start thinking aloud. Her thoughts were about the children.

'You can see the woman in her already,' she said in French, pointing to little Natasha. 'You tell us off for being illogical. You can see our women's logic in her. I tell her papa's having a nap, and she says no, he's laughing. And she's right,' said Countess Marya with a happy smile

'Yes, yes,' said Nikolay. He picked his little girl up in his strong arms, lifted her high in the air, sat her on his shoulders, holding on to her little feet, and started walking round the room with her. The same look of mindless happiness lit up the faces of father and daughter.

'But listen, I don't think you're being fair. This one's your favourite,' his wife whispered in French.

'Yes, but what can I do? . . . I try not to show it . . .'

At that moment noises from the hall and ante-room – the sound of the door-pull followed by footsteps – seemed to suggest someone had just arrived.

'Somebody's come.'

'It must be Pierre. I'll go and see,' said Countess Marya, and she went out of the room.

While she was gone Nikolay allowed himself one good gallop round the room with his little girl. Panting for breath, he quickly lowered the giggling child down from his shoulders, and hugged her to his chest. All this jigging around made him think of dancing, and as he looked at the child's happy little round face, he wondered what she would be like when he was an old man taking her out into society, and he remembered his father dancing the Daniel Cooper and the mazurka with his daughter.

'Yes, it's him, Nikolay!' said Countess Marya, returning a few minutes later. 'Our Natasha's come to life again. You should have seen how pleased she was. And didn't he get scolded for staying away too long! Come on, let's go and see him. Hurry up. Do come on! Time to split you two up,' she said, smiling as she watched the little girl cuddling up to her father. Nikolay walked out, holding his daughter by the hand.

Countess Marya stayed there in the sitting-room.

'I would never have believed it, never,' she murmured to herself, 'that anyone could be as happy as this.' Her face glowed with a happy smile, but at the same moment she gave a sigh, and a gentle sadness showed in the depths of her eyes. It was as if there was a different kind of happiness, not like the happiness she was feeling here and now, a form of happiness beyond human experience, and it had come to her in an involuntary memory just at that moment.

CHAPTER 10

Natasha was married in the early spring of 1813, and by 1820 she had three daughters and the son she had been longing for and was now nursing herself. She had put on weight and filled out; the waif-like, energetic Natasha of former days was almost unrecognizable in this sturdy young mother. Her facial features were more sharply defined, and they carried a placid expression of quiet serenity that had replaced the undying fire of excitement that had once been the most charming thing about her. Often nowadays all you saw was her face and body; her spirit was not in evidence. All you saw was a picture of lovely, buxom female fertility. It was a rare thing nowadays for the old fire to flare up again. This would only happen when her husband came back from a long trip, as now, or when a sick child recovered, or when she talked about Prince Andrey to Countess Marya (she never talked to her husband about him because she thought he might be jealous of her memories), or very occasionally when something prompted her to sing – she had not done any serious singing since she got married. And on those rare occasions when the old fire did flare up again her lovely full figure made her more attractive than ever before.

Since her marriage Natasha and her husband had lived in Moscow and Petersburg, on their estate near Moscow and at her mother's house, or rather Nikolay's. The young Countess Bezukhov was not much seen in society, and those who saw her were not greatly impressed. She was neither charming nor friendly. It wasn't that Natasha was a lover of solitude (she wasn't sure whether she liked it or not – probably not, she thought), but busy as she was with pregnancy, confinements and nursing children, as well as involving herself in every minute of her husband's life, the only way she could satisfy all these demands was by renouncing society. Everybody who had known Natasha before her marriage was astonished to see how much she had changed, as if this was something out of the ordinary. Only the old countess, whose maternal instinct had told her that Natasha's wild behaviour had sprung from the need to have a husband and children of her own – as Natasha herself had declared more than once at Otradnoye, and more in earnest than in jest – had known and the only thing that amazed her was the amazement of other people who simply didn't understand Natasha. She never stopped saying she had always known that her daughter would make an ideal wife and mother.

'But she does go to extremes with all this devotion to her husband and children,' the countess would say. 'It's getting rather absurd.'

Natasha had failed to follow the golden rule laid down by so many clever people, especially the French, that tells a newly married young girl not to neglect herself, not to drop the things she is good at, to take even more care over her appearance than when she was a maid and to make every effort to stay as attractive to her husband as she was before he came to be her husband. Natasha did the very opposite: she immediately dropped all the things that had charmed everybody else, including the one thing she was really good at – her singing. She gave it up precisely because of its charming effect on people. In the words of the popular phrase, she let herself go. Natasha didn't bother any more about nice manners or choosing her words carefully, she made no attempt to show herself off to advantage or look her best when her husband was around, and she didn't hesitate to make demands on him. She flagrantly broke every one of these rules. She felt that the seductive arts that had come to her by instinct in earlier days couldn't help but seem ridiculous now to her husband, to whom she had completely surrendered herself from the first moment – with her whole soul, that is, no corner of which was kept from him. She now felt bound to her husband not by the romantic emotions that had first attracted him to her, but by something different, something hard to define but as strong as the tie between her body and soul.

Fussing with her hair, dressing up and singing songs just to appeal to her husband would have seemed as weird as adorning herself to please herself. Adorning herself to please other people might have been quite nice – she wasn't sure – but she simply didn't have the time. The real reason why she didn't bother about singing, or grooming herself or picking her words carefully was that she simply didn't have the time for anything like that.

We all know that people are capable of absorbing themselves in one single subject, however trivial it may seem to be. We also know there is no subject so trivial that it won't go on infinitely expanding once people have become absorbed in it.

The subject that now absorbed Natasha so completely was her family: her husband, who had to be held on to very firmly to ensure he belonged exclusively to her and the family, and also the children she had to carry, give birth to, nurse and bring up.

And the more she absorbed herself in this subject, mind, body and soul, the more the subject expanded before her very eyes, and the skimpier and more inadequate her resources for coping with it seemed to be, so she ended up concentrating them totally on this one subject and still didn't manage to do all that seemed necessary.

Then as now much time was spent arguing about the rights of women, husband-and-wife relationships and freedom and rights within marriage (though these things were not called 'serious issues', as they now are), but Natasha had no interest in any such questions and no knowledge of them.

Questions like these, then as now, existed exclusively for people who see marriage only in terms of satisfaction given and received by the married couple, though this is only one principle of married life rather than its overall meaning, which lies in the family.

All the latest issues and debates, such as the problem of getting maximum pleasure out of eating your dinner, did not exist then and do not exist now for people who see dinner as a source of nourishment, and family life as the aim of marriage.

If the purpose of dinner is nourishment for the body, anybody who eats two dinners one after the other may get some extra pleasure, but this won't achieve the aim because the stomach cannot digest two dinners.

If the purpose of marriage is family life, anybody who fancies having several wives and several husbands may get a lot of pleasure out of it, but will have no chance of enjoying a family. If the purpose of dinner is nourishment and the purpose of marriage is family life there is only one solution: don't eat more than the stomach can manage and don't have more husbands or wives than you need for a family, which means one wife and one husband. Natasha had needed a husband. A husband was given to her. And her husband gave her a family. And far from sensing any need for another, better husband, she put all her spiritual energy into serving the husband and family that she had, and couldn't imagine – she had no interest in trying to imagine – how things might have worked out if it had all been different.

Natasha was no great lover of society in general, but this made her all the more appreciative when it came to the company of her relatives – Countess Marya, her brother, her mother and Sonya. She valued the company of these people she could run to straight from the nursery, still in her dressing-gown and with her hair all over the place, and delightedly show them a diaper stained yellow instead of green, and listen to their reassurances that the baby must be getting much better.

Natasha let herself go to such an extent that her clothes, her untidy hair, her thoughtless jibes and her jealousy – she was jealous of Sonya, the governess and all women, pretty or plain – were a constant source of humour amongst her friends. The general opinion was that Pierre was under her thumb, and this was true. From the earliest days of their marriage Natasha had laid down what she wanted. Pierre had been taken aback by the novel attitude adopted by his wife – that every minute of his life belonged to her and their home. He was surprised to discover what she wanted, but so flattered by it all that he gave in immediately.

Pierre was so much under the thumb that he didn't dare look at another woman let alone smile at one in conversation, didn't dare drop in at his club for a spot of dinner just to enjoy himself, didn't dare spend money on anything frivolous and didn't dare go away for long periods except on business, though his wife conceded that this included his reading and research. This was something she had no understanding of, but she did think it was very important. Pierre was compensated by having the complete run of the house and could do what he wanted with himself and all the family. In their home Natasha was happy to be a slave to her husband, and everybody in the house had to tiptoe about when the master was busy reading or writing in his study. Pierre had only to say the word and his slightest wish was fulfilled. He had only to say he wanted something and Natasha would jump to her feet and run off and get it.

The whole household was run on the basis of orders supposedly issued by the master, in other words Pierre's wishes as interpreted by Natasha. Their lifestyle and place of residence, their friends and contacts, Natasha's occupations, and the children's upbringing – everything came about in accordance with Pierre's expressed wishes, and, what is more, Natasha did her best to draw further conclusions from ideas of his expressed in conversation. She was very good at using her intuition to grasp the essence of what Pierre was after, and once she had guessed it she stuck to it, even to the extent of turning his own weapons against him if ever he felt like deviating.

In the unforgettably difficult days following the birth of their first, underweight baby, they had gone through three wet nurses one after another, and Natasha was sick with worry, when Pierre suddenly mentioned Rousseau's ideas about the unnaturalness and great harm of giving babies over to wet nurses, and said he completely agreed with them. When the next baby came along Natasha defied her own mother, the doctors and even her husband himself, all of whom thought that nursing your own baby was an outrageously dangerous practice; she got her own way, and from that day forth had nursed all the children herself.

It sometimes happened that irritation between husband and wife led to long arguments, but later on Pierre would often notice to his surprise and delight that his wife was implementing in deed as well as in word the very thing she had been arguing against. There it was, his own idea, stripped of all the inessentials that had been added to it in the heat of the argument.

After seven years of married life Pierre felt happy and secure in the knowledge that he wasn't a bad man, and he felt this because he could see himself reflected in his wife. In himself he could sense the good and bad all mixed up together, the one obscuring the other. But in his wife he could see a reflection of nothing but good; anything that fell short of that was discarded. And this reflection was not achieved by logical thought processes; it came from a different source, a mysterious realm of direct personal experience.

CHAPTER 11

Two months before this, when Pierre had already come to stay with the Rostovs, he received a letter from a certain Prince Fyodor, urging him to come to Petersburg to discuss a number of important questions that were exercising the Petersburg membership of a society which Pierre had served as one of its founding fathers.

Natasha was in the habit of reading all her husband's letters, and she read this one. Much as she hated the idea of him going away, she took the lead in persuading him to go. Anything to do with her husband's abstract, intellectual life she thought of as highly significant, though it was all beyond her, and she lived in constant fear of being an encumbrance to her husband in such matters. When Pierre gave her a timid and quizzical glance after reading the letter she responded by insisting that he go, as long as he told her exactly when he would be back. He was given four weeks' leave of absence.

He was now two weeks overdue and ever since his leave ran out Natasha had been in a constant state of alarm, despondency and irritability.

Retired General Denisov, already frustrated at the current state of public affairs, had arrived during that fortnight, and now he looked at Natasha in sad surprise – it was like looking at a badly painted portrait of someone near and dear. A sad look of bored indifference, one or two irrelevant remarks and a constant stream of nursery talk was all he saw and heard from the seductive creature of days gone by.

Natasha had spent the whole time looking miserable and irritable, especially when her mother, her brother, Sonya or Countess Marya tried to soothe her by making excuses for Pierre, and thinking up reasons for his delay in returning.

'It's nothing but childish nonsense,' Natasha would say. 'All these grand ideas that never come to anything.' And she would go on about 'all these stupid societies of his', referring to matters of the greatest importance, which she really believed in. And off she would go to the nursery to feed her only little boy, baby Petya.

No one could provide such soothing and sensible consolation as that little three-month-old creature when it lay at her breast, and she could feel its little mouth moving and its nose snuffling. That little creature would say to her, 'You're feeling angry and jealous, you'd like to get your own back, you're worried, but I'm here – and I am him. Look, I am him.' There was no answer to that. It was more than true.

Natasha had gone to her baby for comfort and fussed over him so often during those two restless weeks that she had overfed him and made him poorly. She was terrified at his illness, but it was just what she needed. She was so preoccupied with looking after him that her worries about her husband were easier to bear.

She was feeding the baby when Pierre's sledge came grinding up to the entrance, whereupon the nurse, knowing how to please her mistress, hurried in quietly with her face all aglow.

'Is that him?' asked Natasha in a quick whisper, afraid to move for fear of waking the baby, who was just dropping off.

'Yes, ma'am,' whispered the nurse.

The blood rushed to Natasha's face, and her feet moved instinctively, but she couldn't just leap up and run away. The baby opened his little eyes again, glanced at her as if to say, 'Oh, you're still here,' and gave another lazy smack of his lips.

Cautiously easing her breast away, Natasha cradled her little boy, handed him over to the nurse and then walked quickly off towards the door. But she stopped in the doorway as if she felt guilty for being so quick and happy to get rid of the baby, and she looked back. The nurse with her elbows raised, lifted the baby over the rail and into the cot.

'Yes, go along, ma'am, go along. Don't you worry. You go along,' whispered the nurse, smiling with the close familiarity that is bound to arise between nurse and mistress.

Natasha tripped down to the ante-room. Denisov was on his way out of the study into the hall with his pipe in his mouth, and for him it was like seeing Natasha again for the first time. Her face was transformed, flooded with a new radiance and joyful brightness.

'He's back!' she called across as she flew past, and Denisov felt delighted to hear that Pierre was back, even though he didn't like him very much. Running into the ante-room, Natasha caught sight of a tall figure in a fur-coat busy undoing his scarf.

'Yes, it's him. It's true. He's back,' she said to herself as she rushed at him, gave him a hug and pressed her head against his chest, before pulling back to look at her husband's ruddy, frosted face glowing with happiness. 'Yes, it's him. All happy and contented . . .'

Then suddenly she remembered all the suspense and torment she had gone through during the last two weeks. The glow of joy was wiped off her face, she scowled and a torrent of angry words and recrimination rained down on Pierre's head.

'Oh yes, it's all right for you. You've been having a good time, enjoying yourself . . . What about me? You might have thought about the children. Here I am nursing. My milk went wrong. Petya nearly died. And you've been off enjoying yourself. Enjoying yourself!'

Pierre knew it wasn't his fault; he couldn't have come any earlier. He knew this outburst on her part was unseemly, but it would be over in a couple of minutes. Most important of all, he knew that he himself was deliriously happy. He felt like smiling, but he wouldn't dare think of it. He put on a pathetic show of dismay and bowed his head to the storm.

'God's truth, I just couldn't . . . Anyway, how is Petya?'

'He is all right now. Come and see. You ought to be ashamed of yourself. If you could have seen what I'm like without you, what I've been through . . .'

'Are you well?'

'Come on. Come on,' she said, holding on to his hand. And off they went to their rooms. When Nikolay and his wife came to look for Pierre they found him in the nursery, dandling his baby son, who was now awake again, on the palm of his big right hand. There was a gleeful smile on the baby's broad face with its wide-open, toothless mouth. The storm had long blown over, and Natasha's face was flooded with brightness, happiness and sunshine as she gazed tenderly at her husband and son.

'How did your discussions with Prince Fyodor go?' Natasha was saying.

'Oh, splendidly.'

'Look, he can hold his head up,' said Natasha, pointing to the baby. 'Oh, what a scàre he gave me . . . And did you see the princess? Is it true she's in love with that . . .'

'Yes, you can well imagine . . .'

At that moment Nikolay and his wife came in. Pierre kept hold of his son as he bent down, exchanged kisses and answered their various questions. But it was obvious that in spite of all the interesting things they had to talk about, Pierre's only real interest was in the baby, with his wobbly head in its little cap.

'What a sweetie!' said Countess Marya, looking at the baby and playing with him. 'That's one thing I don't understand about you, Nikolay,' she said, turning to her husband. 'How it is you don't feel the charm of these exquisite little creatures?'

'Well, I don't and I can't,' said Nikolay, looking coldly at the baby. 'Just a lump of flesh. Come on, Pierre.'

'The main thing is, he really is a very loving father,' said Countess Marya, apologizing for her husband, 'but only after they are a year or so old . . .'

'Oh, Pierre's a splendid nurse,' said Natasha. 'He says his hand is just right for a baby's bottom. Look.'

'Yes, but not this one,' Pierre cried with a laugh as he snatched up the baby and handed him back to his nurse.

CHAPTER 12

As in any family worthy of the name, several separate worlds co-existed within the one household at Bald Hills, and while each pre-served its own individuality, they all made allowances for each other and they blended together into one harmonious whole. Every event that occurred in the house, happy or sad, was of equal importance to each of these little worlds, but each of them also had its own personal and quite independent reasons for applauding or regretting every event.

Thus Pierre's homecoming, a joyful and important event, was accepted as such in all circles.

The servants – infallible judges of their masters, because their judge-ments are based not on talk or emotion but on deeds and real life – were delighted to see him back because they knew that when Pierre was there the other count, their master, would stop doing his rounds and he would be in a much better mood, much nicer to them, and also because they knew they would all get expensive presents for the festive day.

The children and their governesses were pleased to see him back because there was no one like Pierre for bringing them into the mainstream of things in the house. He was the one person who could sit down at the clavichord and play the all-purpose *écossaise*, the only piece he knew, though he said it was good for all dances, and he had probably brought presents for them.

Young Nikolay Bolkonsky, who was by now a slim, delicate but intelligent boy of fifteen, with curly light-brown hair and beautiful eyes, was delighted because his 'Uncle Pierre' was the object of his admiration and deep affection. No one had particularly encouraged Nikolay to be so fond of Pierre, and he didn't see him very often. Countess Marya, who had brought him up, had gone out of her way to make Nikolay love her husband as much as she did, and the boy did like his uncle, but his affection was tinged with contempt. But he worshipped Pierre. He didn't want to be a dashing hussar or a Knight of St George like his Uncle Nikolay, he wanted to be a learned, clever and kindly man like Pierre. In Pierre's presence his face glowed with pleasure, and he blushed and felt short of breath when Pierre spoke to him. He never missed a word that fell from Pierre's lips, and later on, with or without Dessalles, he would go over his every phrase and think about its meaning. Pierre's past life, his unhappy career before 1812 (a vague, romantic version of which he had compiled from the few words he had heard dropped), his adventures in Moscow and his period of imprisonment, Platon Karatayev (whom he had heard about from Pierre), his love for Natasha (which the boy shared in his own special way) and, above all, his friendship with the father Nikolay couldn't remember – all of this made Pierre a hero and a saint in his eyes.

From occasional references to his father and Natasha, Pierre's inability to talk about his father without becoming emotional and Natasha's cautious, tender and reverential tone whenever she spoke about him, the boy, who was just beginning to work out the meaning of love, had formed an impression that his father had loved Natasha, and bequeathed her to his friend on his deathbed. And as for the father himself, despite having no memories to go on the boy saw him as a godlike creation beyond all imagining, and every time he brought him to mind he did so with a sinking heart and bitter-sweet tears.

So he too was happy when Pierre came back.

All the house guests welcomed Pierre back as a man who could be counted on to bring people together and raise their spirits.

The adult members of the household, including his wife, were welcoming back a friendly figure who always made life run more smoothly and peacefully.

The old ladies were pleased at the thought of the presents he must have brought, but it meant more to them that Natasha would now be a lot livelier.

Pierre could sense the different attitudes coming from the several different worlds, and lost no time in satisfying everybody's expectations.

He was the most absent-minded and forgetful of men, but he had stuck to the list supplied by his wife and bought everything, not forgetting a single commission from his mother-in-law or brother-in-law, the dress material for Madame Belov or the toys for his nephews.

In the early days of his married life it had struck him as odd that his wife should insist so strongly that he mustn't forget anything he was supposed to buy, and he had been shocked by seeing her so put out when he had come back from his first trip without remembering a thing. But eventually he got the knack of it. Knowing that Natasha never asked him to get anything for her, and only told him to get things for other people when he had already offered to do so, he now surprised himself by taking a childish pleasure in getting presents for all the household, and he never forgot anything. If he incurred Natasha's displeasure now it was only for buying too much and spending over the odds. To her other defects (as seen by other people, though Pierre saw them as positive qualities) – her slipshod manner and personal untidiness – Natasha had by now added penny-pinching.

Ever since Pierre had set up home and family on a large scale involving considerable expenditure he had noticed to his astonishment that he was living on half what he had been spending in the past, and his finances, which until recently had been all over the place largely because of the debts incurred by his first wife, were now looking up.

He was getting by on less money because his life was now coherent. The greatest luxury in his former lifestyle, the possibility of completely changing it at a moment's notice, was something Pierre no longer had and no longer wanted. He felt that his lifestyle was now settled once and for all till the day of his death; he had no power to change it, and that made it all cheaper.

Pierre had a happy smile on his face as he unpacked his purchases. 'How about that?' he said as he unfolded a length of material like a draper. Natasha was sitting opposite with her eldest daughter on her knee, and her sparkling eyes darted from her husband to the things he was putting on display.

'Is that for Madame Belov? Splendid.' She felt it for quality. 'What was it, a rouble a yard?' Pierre told her how much.

'That's a lot,' said Natasha. 'Anyway, the children will be delighted, and so will Mamma. But you shouldn't have bought me this,' she added, unable to suppress a smile as she admired one of the gold combs set with pearls that were just coming in.

'It's Adèle's fault. She kept on at me to buy it,' said Pierre.

'When shall I wear it?' Natasha stuck it in her coil of hair. 'It'll do nicely when we bring little Masha out. Maybe they'll be in fashion again. Come on then. Let's go in.'

They scooped up the presents, and set off, first for the nursery, then to see the countess.

As usual the countess was sitting playing patience with Madame Belov when Pierre and Natasha came into the drawing-room with parcels under their arms.

The countess was now in her sixties. Her hair was completely grey, and she wore a cap with a frill that went right round her face. Her face was covered in wrinkles, her top lip had sunk in, and her eyes had no sparkle.

After her son and her husband had died so suddenly one after another she had felt like a creature left behind in this world by mistake, with nothing to live for and no meaning to her existence. She ate and drank, slept and lay awake, but she didn't live. Life made no impression on her. All she wanted from life was to be left in peace, and real peace would only be found in death. But death was a long time coming and meanwhile she had to go on living, to put her time and her vital forces to some kind of use. She manifested in the highest degree something you see only in very small children and in very old people. She led an existence without any visible aim; all that could be seen in it was the need to exercise various faculties and capabilities. She had to do a little eating, sleeping, thinking, talking, weeping, working, getting angry and so on, but only because she had a stomach, brain, muscles, nerves and liver. She did all these things not from any external motivation, as people do when they are fully alive and the aim they are striving towards conceals the underlying aim of exercising their faculties. When she talked it was only because she needed physical exercise for her lungs and tongue. When she cried like a child it was because she needed to clear the airways, and so on. What would have been an aim for people who are fully alive for her was obviously nothing more than a pretext.

So, for example, in the morning, especially if she had eaten something too fatty the day before, she might feel the need to be angry with someone and she would latch on to the nearest pretext – Madame Belov's deafness.

From the far end of the room she would launch forth in a low voice.

'I fancy it's a little warmer today, my dear,' she would whisper. And when Madame Belov replied, 'No, I think they're here now,' she would mutter angrily, 'Mercy on us, she's so deaf and stupid!'

Her snuff was another pretext. It was either too dry or too damp, or perhaps too coarse. After these outbursts of irritability you could see the bile on her face. And to her maids the signs were unmistakable: they could tell when Madame Belov was going to be deaf again, when the snuff was going to be damp again, and when her face was going to turn yellow. Just as she had to give her bile something to work on, sometimes she felt the need to exercise what was left of her powers of thought, and the pretext for this was patience. When she needed to shed a few tears, the late count was the pretext. When she needed something to worry about, it would be Nikolay and the state of his health. When she wanted to come out with something spiteful, the pretext was Countess Marya. When she needed to exercise her organs of speech – usually about seven in the evening after she had had her little rest in a darkened room to let dinner digest – she would find a pretext in the retelling of old stories, always the same stories and the same listeners.

The old countess's condition was understood by the whole household, though no one ever talked about it, and they all went out of their way to satisfy her various needs. Just now and then a quick glance or a sad half-smile would pass between Nikolay, Pierre, Natasha and Countess Marya, enough to imply their shared awareness of her condition.

But these glances implied something else besides. They said that her life's work was done, that what they saw now was not her whole self, that one day we'll all be like that, and they were only too pleased to indulge her, to hold back for the sake of this pathetic creature, once so dear, once as full of life as they were. What their glances said was, 'Memento mori.'

Within the household only one or two completely heartless and stupid people and the little ones failed to understand this, and they kept away from her.

CHAPTER 13

When Pierre and his wife came into the drawing-room the countess happened to be in her usual condition of needing the intellectual exercise of a game of patience, and so – although by force of habit she trotted out the same words she always said when Pierre or her son came back from a trip: 'About time too, my dear boy. We thought you'd never come. Well, thank God you're back!' and when she got her presents she came out with more stock phrases: 'It's not the gift that counts, my dear . . . Thank you for thinking of an old woman like me . . .' – it was quite clear that Pierre's entrance at that moment was unwelcome, because it was a distraction from her half-finished round of patience. She finished her game, and only then got down to opening the presents. These consisted of a beautifully carved card-case, a bright blue Sèvres cup with a lid and shepherdesses painted on it and a gold snuff-box with the count's portrait on it, which Pierre had ordered from a miniature-painter in Petersburg. The countess had been longing for a snuff-box like this, but just now she didn't feel like weeping, so she gave the portrait nothing more than a casual glance and concentrated on the card-case.

'Thank you so much, my dear. You're a real comfort,' she said, as always. 'But best of all, you have brought yourself back. It has been like nothing on earth here. You really must speak to your wife. You wouldn't believe it – she's like a mad woman when you're not here. She can't so much as see or think,' she said, using all the old phrases. 'Look here, Anna, my dear,' she added. 'Look what a nice card-case my son has brought for us.'

Madame Belov admired the presents, and enthused about her dress material.

Pierre, Natasha, Nikolay, Countess Marya and Denisov had a lot to talk about, but it couldn't be gone into in front of the old countess, not because they hid things from her, but simply because she was so far out of touch that if you started a conversation while she was there you would have to answer all sorts of irrelevant questions and repeat things constantly, reminding her that so-and-so was dead and somebody else was married, and knowing she wouldn't remember it this time round. So they just sat there in the usual way taking tea round the samovar in the drawing-room, and Pierre answered the countess's questions, which were of no use to her and no interest to anybody, by letting her know that Prince Vasily was looking older, and Countess Marya Alexeyevna still remembered them and sent her kind regards, etc.

This kind of conversation, quite unavoidable for all its lack of interest, was kept going all through tea-time. All the adult members of the family had come to sit together at the round tea-table, with Sonya presiding by the samovar. The children with their tutors and governesses had already had their tea, and their voices rang through from the next room. At tea they all sat in their usual places. Nikolay sat at his own little table by the stove, and his tea was handed across. An old borzoi bitch with a grizzled old muzzle and black eyes more prominent than ever – Milka, daughter of the original Milka – lay on a chair beside him. Denisov, with a lot of grey in his curly hair, moustache and side-whiskers, sat next to Countess Marya with his general's tunic unbuttoned. Pierre sat between his wife and the old countess. He was talking about things he knew the old lady might be interested in and could also understand. He talked about superficial social events and referred to people who had once made up the circle of the old countess's contemporaries, and once formed a distinct and lively grouping, though they were now for the most part scattered about the world, living out their days like her and gathering up the last ears from crops sown in earlier life. But as far as the old countess was concerned these contemporaries of hers were the only real world of any significance.

Pierre was looking excited and Natasha could tell that his visit had been full of interest; he obviously had a lot to say about it, but not while the countess was still there. Not being family, Denisov couldn't understand Pierre's reluctance, and, dissatisfied as he was with the way things were going, he was very keen to hear the latest word from Petersburg. He made several challenging attempts to get Pierre talking about the recent scandal in the Semyonovsky regiment, or Arakcheyev, or the Bible Society.[13] Once or twice Pierre got carried away and was about to launch forth, only for Nikolay and Natasha to steer him back to the health of Prince Ivan and Countess Marya Antonovna.

'So what's this widiculous nonsense about Gossner and Madame Tatawinova?'[14] Denisov asked. 'Is it still going on?'

'Going on?' said Pierre. 'It's worse than ever. And the Bible Society has taken over the government.'

'What was that, my dear friend?' inquired the old countess. Having drunk her tea, she was clearly on the look-out for a pretext to vent a little ill-humour after indulging in refreshments. 'What were you saying about the government? I don't know what you mean.'

'It's like this, Mamma,' put in Nikolay, skilled as he was in translating into his mother's language. 'Prince Alexander Golitsyn has started a society. They do say he's a big man nowadays.'

'Arakcheyev and Golitsyn,' said Pierre rather rashly. 'They *are* the government now. And what a government! They see a conspiracy round every corner, and they're scared of their own shadows.'

'Now what can Prince Golitsyn possibly have done wrong? He is a pillar of society. I used to meet him in the old days at Marya Antonovna's,' said the countess, greatly aggrieved. And still more aggrieved by the ensuing silence, she went on. 'People are always finding fault nowadays. A Gospel Society? There's no harm in that!' She got to her feet (as did all the company), and grimly sailed forth to find her table in the next room.

The lugubrious silence that ensued was interrupted by the sound of children's voices and laughter coming from the next room. There was evidently some boisterous excitement afoot among the children.

'It's finished! It's finished!' Little Natasha's gleeful shriek could be heard above all the rest. Pierre's eyes were on his Natasha, but he exchanged quick glances with Countess Marya and Nikolay, and gave a happy smile.

'Music to my ears!' he said.

'Anna Makarovna has finished her stocking,' said Countess Marya.

'Oh, I'm going in to have a look,' said Pierre, jumping to his feet. 'You know something,' he said, stopping at the door. 'I really love that kind of music. I wonder why? It's the first thing that tells me everything's all right. On the way back today, the nearer I got to the house, the more worried I was. Then I heard Andryusha roaring with laughter in the hall, and I knew everything was all right . . .'

'Yes, I know that feeling,' Nikolay chimed in. 'I can't go in with you. The stockings are a present for me.'

Pierre went in to the children, and the shrieks and laughter were louder than ever. 'Now then, Anna Makarovna,' cried Pierre's voice. 'We want you here in the middle of the room. Wait for the command – one, two . . . and then I'll say three! You stand here. I'll have you in my arms. Ready? One . . . two . . .' There was complete silence. 'Three!' and a roar of excited children's voices filled the room.

'There are *two*! There are *two*!' cried the children.

And there were indeed two stockings, because, by a secret process known only to herself, Anna Makarovna could knit two on one pair of needles, and she always made a great show of bringing the children round and producing one stocking from inside the other when the pair was done.

CHAPTER 14

Soon after this the children came in to say goodnight. They did the rounds, kissing everybody; the tutors and governesses made their bows and went out. Dessalles and his pupil were the only ones left. The tutor whispered to the boy, asking him to come downstairs.

'No, Monsieur Dessalles, I'm going to ask my aunt if I can stay,' young Nikolay Bolkonsky answered, also in a whisper.

'Auntie, please may I stay?' said Nikolay, going over to Countess Marya. His face was a picture of entreaty, excitement and enthusiasm. She looked at him and turned to Pierre.

'While ever you are here he can't tear himself away . . .' she said.

'I'll bring him down soon, Monsieur Dessalles. Goodnight,' said Pierre, offering his hand to the Swiss tutor, and turning with a smile to Nikolay. 'We haven't seen much of each other. Marie, he's getting more and more like him, isn't he?' he added, turning to Countess Marya.

'Like my father?' said the boy, blushing to the roots of his hair and gazing up at Pierre with blissful, glittering eyes.

Pierre nodded, and went on with the conversation that had been interrupted by the children. Countess Marya had some canvas embroidery to work on, Natasha sat there with her eyes on her husband, and Nikolay and Denisov put question after question to Pierre while getting to their feet, asking for a pipe, having a smoke and accepting cups of tea from a gloomy Sonya, doggedly manning the samovar. The delicate curlyheaded boy sat unnoticed in a corner, his eyes gleaming and his curly head on its slender neck protruding from a turned-down collar never moved except to follow Pierre round the room. Now and then he shivered, and mumbled something under his breath, evidently thrilled by some powerful new sensation.

The conversation turned on the latest scandals at the top of the government, most people's favourite topic in the politics of their country. Denisov, who was disappointed in the government because of his own setbacks in the service, was delighted to hear about what he saw as a series of ridiculous new developments in Petersburg, and his harsh comments on Pierre's words came out in a few trenchant phrases.

'In the old days you had to be a German to be anybody – nowadays you have to dance with that Tatawinov woman and Madame Kwüdner,[15] and wead . . . Eckartshausen, and all the west of them. Huh! Might as well let good old Bonaparte loose again! He'd bang a few heads together. What on earth are they doing giving the Semyonovsky wegiment to that man Schwartz?' he shouted.

Nikolay did not have Denisov's predisposition to find fault with everything, but he did think it was right and proper to criticize the government, and he believed that the latest developments – A being appointed minister of this department, and B governor of that province, the Tsar saying one thing, and the minister saying another – were all very important. And he thought it behoved him to show an interest and ask questions. With contributors like Nikolay and Denisov interrogating Pierre the conversation never looked like straying from the usual lines of gossip about the top government people.

But Natasha was familiar with her husband's every idea and mannerism, and she could see that Pierre had long been wanting to steer the conversation in another direction and speak out passionately on his own subject, the subject that had taken him to Petersburg for consultations with his new friend, Prince Fyodor, but so far he had been unable to do so. She helped him out by asking how things had gone with Prince Fyodor.

'What was that?' asked Nikolay.

'It's the same thing again and again,' said Pierre, looking round the room. 'Everybody can see that things have come to such a pass something has to be done. All honest men have a duty to resist as far as they can.'

'Yes, but what can honest men do?' said Nikolay with a slight frown. 'What can they actually do?'

'I'll tell you what . . .'

'Let's go into the study,' said Nikolay.

Natasha, who had long been expecting a call to go and feed the baby, now heard the nurse and went off to the nursery. Countess Marya went with her. The men went to the study, and little Nikolay crept in unnoticed and sat down at a desk in the shadows near the window.

'Come on, then. What are you going to do?' said Denisov.

'Castles in the air again,' said Nikolay.

'I'll tell you,' Pierre began. Instead of sitting down he paced the room, stopping now and then, lisping as he spoke and making wild gestures. 'I'll tell you. Do you know how things stand in Petersburg? The Tsar has lost his grip. He's so absorbed in his mysticism.' (For the new Pierre mysticism was unforgivable.) 'All he asks is to be left in peace, and he can only get peace through men with no faith or conscience, people who are strangling and destroying everything – Magnitsky,[16] Arakcheyev and *tutti quanti* . . . You must admit: if you didn't look after your own property because all you wanted was peace and quiet, your bailiff would get the quickest results by being as vicious as he could,' he said, turning to Nikolay.

'Yes, but what are you getting at?' asked Nikolay.

'Well, everything's going downhill. Thieving in the law-courts. Brutality, round-the-clock drill and forced labour in the army. People are being tortured, and ideas are being suppressed. Anything youthful and honourable has had it! Everybody knows it can't go on like this. The strain is too great. Something's got to give,' exclaimed Pierre (speaking about the government as men have spoken about governments from time immemorial). 'I did tell them one thing in Petersburg.'

'Who?' asked Denisov.

'Oh, you know who,' said Pierre, with a shifty, meaningful look, 'Prince Fyodor and the rest of them. It's all right pushing education and charitable work. Of course it is. It's all very well intentioned, but as things stand we need more than that.'

Suddenly Nikolay became aware of his nephew's presence. His face darkened, and he went over to him.

'What are you doing in here?'

'Oh, leave him alone. Why not?' said Pierre, taking Nikolay by the arm. He had more to say. 'I told them it won't do. We need something else. While you're standing there waiting for something to give, while everybody's waiting for the coup that is bound to come, as many people as possible ought to get together, close ranks and join hands against the disaster that's coming to us all. All our youth and strength is being enticed away and corrupted. Some are seduced by women, some by honours, others by ambition or money – they're all going over to the other side. When it comes to independent, honest men like you and me – there's nobody left. I'll tell you what to do: broaden the scope of our Society. Let the watchword be not just loyalty, but independence and action!'

Nikolay had walked away from his nephew, and now he moved an armchair up, and irritably sat down in it. As he listened to Pierre he kept clearing his throat to show he wasn't happy, and his scowl grew darker and darker.

'Yes action, but what for?' he shouted. 'And how will you stand in relation to the government?'

'I'll tell you how. We'll be on the government's side! Maybe the Society doesn't have to be a secret one, as long as the government will allow it. We're not hostile to the government, we're a society of real conservatives. A society of *gentlemen*, in the fullest sense of the word. We're here to stop Pugachov[17] coming along tomorrow and massacring my children and yours, to stop Arakcheyev sending me to a labour camp. That's why we're joining hands – with the sole object of ensuring everybody's welfare and security.'

'Yes, but it's a secret society, so it's hostile and dangerous. It can only spawn evil.'

'Why's that, then? Did the Tugendbund[18] that saved Europe turn out to be dangerous?' (At that time no one was bold enough to think that Russia had saved Europe.) 'That's what it is, a League of Virtue. It's love and mutual help. It's what Christ preached on the cross . . .'

Natasha came in at this point, in mid-conversation, and looked at her husband with great delight. It was not what he was saying that made her happy. That didn't seem particularly interesting, because she saw it all as very straightforward, something she had known for a very long time. (She saw it this way because she knew where it all came from – the depths of Pierre's soul.) What pleased her was his eager, enthusiastic presence.

Pierre was being watched with even more solemn rapture by the forgotten boy with the slender neck protruding from its turned-down collar. Every word Pierre uttered set his heart on fire, and his fingers moved nervously as he picked up sticks of sealing-wax and quill pens that came to hand on his uncle's desk and snapped them in pieces without realizing what he was doing.

'It's not what you're thinking. What I'm proposing is a society just like the German Tugendbund.'

'Well, my fwend, it may be all wight for the kwauts, this Tugendbund, but I can't understand it. I can't even pwonounce it pwoperly,' came the loud, authoritative voice of Denisov. 'Everything's wotten and cowwupt, I give you that. But I can't understand all this *Tugendbund* wigmawole. Now give me a good old *Wussian bunt*[19] and I'm your man!'

Pierre smiled and Natasha laughed, but Nikolay scowled more darkly than ever, and began arguing with Pierre that no coup was in the offing, and the danger he was on about didn't exist outside his imagination. Pierre took the opposite line, and since his intellectual capacity was sharper and more versatile, Nikolay was soon at a loss for words. This made him angrier than ever, because deep down he felt convinced, not by reason but by something stronger than reason, that his point of view was the right one.

'Well, let me tell you this,' he said, getting to his feet, trying nervously to stand his pipe up in the corner, and then flinging it down. 'I can't prove what I'm saying. You say everything's rotten, and there's going to be a coup. I can't see it. But you also say our oath of allegiance is only provisional, and what I say is this – you're my closest friend, as you well know, but if you formed a secret society and began working against the government – any government of ours – I know it would be my duty to obey the government. And if Arakcheyev tells me today to march a squadron against you and finish you off, I shan't hesitate for a second, I shall go. So there you have it.'

An awkward silence ensued. Natasha was the first to break it by defending her husband and attacking her brother. Her defence was feeble and clumsy, but it did its job. The discussion began again, and without the unpleasant hostility engendered by Nikolay's last words.

When they all got up to go in to supper little Nikolay went over to Pierre with a pale face and a gleam in his luminous eyes.

'Uncle Pierre . . . you . . . er, no . . . If Papa had been alive . . . would he have been on your side?' he asked.

Pierre saw in an instant what an unusual, complex and powerfully moving series of thoughts and feelings must have been going through the boy's mind quite independently while they had been talking, and when he thought back to what he had been saying he felt annoyed that the boy had heard it all. But he still had to give him an answer.

'I think he probably would,' he said reluctantly, and walked out.

The boy looked down, and saw, apparently for the first time, what a mess he had made on the desk. He went beetroot red and walked over to Nikolay.

'I'm very sorry, Uncle. It was an accident,' he said, pointing to the broken bits of sealing-wax and pens.

Nikolay reacted with a face like thunder. 'All right. All right,' he said, throwing the broken pens and sealing-wax down under the table. And he turned away, all too obviously fighting down his mounting fury.

'You shouldn't have been here at all,' he said.

CHAPTER 15

Over supper no more was said about politics or societies; the conversation turned to Nikolay's favourite subject: memories of 1812. Denisov led off, and Pierre was at his genial and amusing best. The family broke up on the friendliest of terms.

Nikolay got undressed in his study, gave some instructions to his steward, who had been waiting for him, went into the bedroom in his dressing-gown and found his wife still at her desk, writing.

'What are you writing, Marie?' asked Nikolay. Countess Marya coloured up. She was afraid that what she was writing would not be understood or approved of by her husband.

She would have liked to hide what she was writing, but at the same time she was glad she had been caught, and had to tell him.

'It's my diary, Nikolay,' she said, handing him a blue note-book, filled with her bold, meticulous handwriting.

'A diary!' said Nikolay with a touch of mockery, taking the note-book. It was in French.

December 4th
Andryusha [their eldest son] refused to get dressed when he woke up this morning, so Mademoiselle Louise sent for me. He was naughty and stubborn. Tried threatening him, but he only got more bad-tempered. I said leave it to me, put him to one side, helped nurse to get the other children up, and told him I didn't love him. He was quiet for a long time – seemed surprised. Then he rushed at me still in his night-shirt, and sobbed so much it took me ages to calm him down. Clearly, what hurt him most was that he had upset me. Then when I gave him his report in the evening he cried pitifully again as he kissed me. You can do anything with him by showing affection.

'What's this about a report?' asked Nikolay.

'I've started giving the older ones little marks in the evening to let them know how well they've been behaving.'

Nikolay glanced at the luminous eyes watching him and carried on leafing through the diary and dipping in. The children's lives were documented with every detail that their mother deemed to be significant in showing the character of the children, or leading to general ideas about bringing them up. It was mostly a mass of trivial detail, but it didn't seem like that to the mother or the father, as he now read through this record of his children's lives for the very first time. An entry for the 5th of December read as follows:

Mitya was naughty at table. Papa said no pudding. He had none, but he looked so miserable and positively greedy while the others were eating. My belief – punishing them by not letting them have any sweet things only encourages greediness. Must tell Nikolay.

Nikolay put the book down and looked at his wife. The luminous eyes were staring at him in some doubt: would he, or would he not, approve? There was no doubt about it: Nikolay not only approved, he was delighted with his wife.

Perhaps it was all a bit too pedantic, perhaps it didn't need to be done at all, thought Nikolay, but he was delighted by this constant, unflagging spiritual application, aimed only at improving the children's moral well-being. If Nikolay had been able to pin down his attitude he would have found that his strong, proud and tender love for his wife was actually founded on a certain reverence for her spirituality, and the lofty world of morality that she lived in and he had virtually no access to.

He was so proud that she was clever and good, he acknowledged his own insignificance alongside her in the spiritual world and he rejoiced all the more to realize that she, with her spirit, not only belonged to him, but was part of his very self.

'I really do approve of this, darling!' he said, with a meaningful air. And after a short pause he added, 'I've behaved very badly today. You weren't there in the study. Pierre and I were having things out, and I lost my temper. I just couldn't help it. He's such a baby. I don't know what would happen to him if Natasha didn't keep him under control. Can you imagine why he went to Petersburg? . . . They've set up a . . .'

'Yes, I do know,' said Countess Marya. 'Natasha told me.'

'Oh, well, you know, then,' Nikolay went on, hot under the collar at the mere recollection of their argument. 'He wants me to believe that every honest man has a duty to go against the government, when according to your oath of allegiance and your sense of duty . . . I'm sorry you weren't there. As it was, they all came down on me, Denisov, and Natasha, too . . . Natasha is just ridiculous. We know she can twist him round her little finger, but when it comes to an argument she hasn't an idea to call her own, she just repeats what he's said,' added Nikolay, yielding to that irresistible temptation that leads us criticize our nearest and dearest. Nikolay was forgetting that what he was saying about Natasha applied word for word to him and his wife.

'Yes, I have noticed that,' said Countess Marya.

'When I told him duty and the oath of allegiance come first, he went on and on . . . God knows what he said. It's such a pity you weren't there. What would you have said?'

'Well, I think you were absolutely right. I said as much to Natasha. Pierre says there's nothing but suffering, torment and corruption, and it's our duty to help our neighbour. He's right, of course,' said Countess Marya, 'but he forgets that charity begins at home, and God Himself has shown us where our duty lies. We can run risks for ourselves, but not for our children.'

'That's just what I said,' cried Nikolay, who imagined he had. 'But he would insist. All this talk about loving your neighbour, and

Christianity, and right in front of little Nikolay. He slipped in and sat there breaking things to pieces.'

'You know, Nikolay, I often worry about little Nikolay,' said Countess Marya. 'He's a very unusual boy. And I'm afraid I neglect him for my own. We all have our children, our own ties, and he's got nobody. He's always alone with his thoughts.'

'Well, I must say you've nothing to reproach yourself for on that score. Anything the fondest mother could do for her son you've done for him, and you're still doing it. And of course I'm very pleased you do. He's a splendid boy, he really is! This evening he sat there in a kind of dream as he listened to Pierre. And just imagine, we got up to go into supper. I have a look, and lo and behold he's crumbled everything on my desk into little pieces, and he came up and told me. I've never known him tell a fib. He's a splendid boy, he really is!' repeated Nikolay, who deep down didn't much like Nikolay, though he always felt a need to keep calling him a splendid boy.

'Still, it's not like having a mother,' said Countess Marya. 'I know it's not the same, and it worries me. He's a wonderful boy, but I'm terribly afraid for him. Some company would be good for him.'

'Well, we've not long to wait. Next summer I'm taking him to Petersburg,' said Nikolay. 'Yes, Pierre's always been a dreamer and he always will be,' he went on, reverting to the argument in the study, which was obviously still on his mind. 'Why should I bother what's going on up there – Arakcheyev the villain, and all that stuff – why should I have bothered about that when we got married and I was up to my ears in debt and they were going to put me in prison, and my mother couldn't see it or understand what was going on? After that I had you, and the children, and my work. I'm at it from morning to night either in the office or out at work, and I'm not doing it for fun. No, I know I've got to work to keep mother happy, pay you back and make sure my children are not left in poverty as I was.'

Countess Marya wanted to tell him that man does not live by bread alone, and he attached too much importance to all this *work*, but she knew it didn't need saying, and it would be useless. She simply took his hand and kissed it. Taking his wife's gesture as a sign of approval and an endorsement of his line of thinking, he thought for a few moments without saying anything, and then went on expounding his ideas.

'Do you know something, Marie,' he said, 'Ilya Mitrofanych [his steward] was here today from the Tambov estate, and he tells me the forest would fetch eighty thousand.' And Nikolay's face was a picture of excitement as he began talking about the possibility of buying

Otradnoye back before long. 'All I need is another ten years of life, and I'll leave the children . . . well provided for.'

Countess Marya listened to her husband, taking it all in. She knew that when he was thinking aloud like this he would sometimes ask her what he had been saying, and he was annoyed when he found out her thoughts had been elsewhere. But she had to work hard at this because she hadn't the slightest interest in what he was saying. As she watched him it wasn't really a question of her thoughts being elsewhere – her feelings were elsewhere. She felt a submissive and tender love for this man who was never going to understand everything that she understood, and this seemed to make her love him all the more, with a love verging on passion. But apart from these feelings that absorbed her entirely and stopped her going into the details of her husband's plans, she was conscious of other ideas flashing through her mind that had nothing to do with what he was saying. She kept thinking of her nephew (what her husband had told her about his excitement listening to Pierre had made its mark on her), and recalling various aspects of his tender, sensitive personality, and when she was thinking about her nephew she thought about her own children too. She didn't compare her nephew with her own children, but she did compare her own feelings for him, and she felt, sadly, that there was something lacking in her feelings towards little Nikolay.

Sometimes it had occurred to her that the difference might have something to do with his age, but he still made her feel guilty, and she swore in the depths of her soul to put things right and achieve the impossible by loving them all in one lifetime, loving her husband, her children, little Nikolay and all her fellow creatures, as Jesus had loved all mankind. Countess Marya's spirit was always striving towards the infinite, the eternal, absolute perfection, which meant she was never at peace. Her face froze in a grim expression that came from the hidden, lofty suffering of a spirit weighed down by the flesh. Nikolay stared at her. 'My God!' he thought, 'what will become of us if she dies, as I fear she will when she looks like that?' He stood there before the icon and began to say his bedtime prayers.

CHAPTER 16

The moment they were alone together Natasha too began to converse with her husband in that manner peculiar to husbands and wives, one of those in which ideas are perceived and exchanged with extraordinary clarity and speed by some means that transcends all the rules of logic and develops its own way without any spoken assertions, deductions or conclusions. Natasha was so used to talking to her husband like this that she took any process of logical thinking on Pierre's part as an unmistakable sign that something was wrong between them. Whenever he started to lay out an argument, speaking calmly and reasonably, and she followed his example by doing the same thing, she knew they were definitely in for a quarrel.

When they were alone together and Natasha, wide-eyed and blissfully happy, crept over to him and grabbed him by the head, suddenly, swiftly, pressing it to her bosom and saying, 'Now you're all mine, mine! I'm not letting you go!' this moment marked the beginning of the conversation, and it transcended all the rules of logic not least because they talked about several different things at once. This simultaneous discussion of all sorts of everything, far from marring any clarity of perception, was the surest guarantee of their mutual understanding.

In a dream everything is uncertain, senseless and contradictory except the overall feeling that directs the dream; similarly in this form of communication, which offends against every law of reason, it is not the flow of words that is clear and coherent, but the feeling behind them.

Natasha had much to tell: the details of her brother's lifestyle, how much she had suffered without him (it was no kind of life), all about her ever-growing fondness for Marie, and the fact Marie was better than her in every way. Even as she said this Natasha was perfectly sincere in acknowledging Marie's superiority, but at the same time she expected Pierre to prefer her to Marie and all other women, and now, especially after seeing so many women in Petersburg, to remind her of that. In response to Natasha's words Pierre told her that the soirées and dinners with all those ladies in Petersburg had been absolutely intolerable.

'I can't talk to ladies any more,' he said. 'It's just boring. All the more so because I was so busy.'

Natasha gave him a close scrutiny, and went on. 'Marie is so wonderful!' she said. 'She's so good with children. She seems to see right down into their souls. Take yesterday. Mitenka was being naughty . . .'

'Just like his father, isn't he?' Pierre put in.

Natasha knew why he had made a comment about the similarity between Mitenka and Nikolay. The argument with his brother-in-law was still rankling, and he was dying to hear what she thought about it.

'It's one of Nikolay's failings that he won't agree to anything unless everybody accepts it. Whereas what you like, as I well know, are fresh fields and pastures new,' she said, repeating one of Pierre's old phrases.

'No, the thing about Nikolay,' said Pierre, 'is that for him thoughts and ideas are a diversion, just a way of passing the time. There he is, building up a library and he's made it a rule not to buy a new book until he's read the last one he bought – Sismondi, then Rousseau, then Montesquieu . . .' Pierre added with a smile. 'Of course you know how much I . . .' He was beginning to soften his criticism, but Natasha interrupted him, making it clear that he didn't need to do that.

'So you say he treats ideas like a diversion . . .'

'Yes, but with me it's the other way round. All the time I was in Petersburg it was like seeing people in a dream. When I've got an idea in my head everything else seems a frivolous waste of time.'

'Oh, I'm sorry I missed your meeting with the children,' said Natasha. 'Who was most pleased to see you? I bet it was Liza.'

'Yes, it was,' said Pierre, and he went on talking about what interested him. 'Nikolay tells us not to think. But I can't help thinking. Not to mention the fact (I can say this to you) that in Petersburg I felt the whole thing was falling apart without me. They were all pulling in different directions. I did manage to bring them together, but then my way of thinking is so clear and straightforward. I don't say we ought to oppose X and Y. We might get things wrong. But I do say this: let those who believe in goodness come together hand in hand, and let us march under the banner of virtue in action. Prince Sergey is a splendid man, and so clever.'

Natasha would never have doubted that Pierre's idea was a great idea, except for one thing that bothered her. He was her husband. 'Surely such an important man, a man of such value to society, couldn't also be *my husband*? How could it have happened?' She wanted to share this doubt with him. 'What man, what men could decide whether he really is so much cleverer than everybody else?' she wondered, and in her imagination she ran through the people Pierre admired. To judge by all the stories he had told there was no one he admired more than Platon Karatayev.

'Do you know what's just crossed my mind?' she said. 'Platon Karatayev. How would he have reacted? Would he have approved of what you're doing?'

Pierre was not at all surprised by this question. He could see his wife's train of thought.

'Platon Karatayev?' he said, and thought for a while, evidently making a genuine attempt to imagine what Karatayev's verdict would have been on this subject. 'He wouldn't have understood it, and yet – maybe he would.'

'Oh I do love you!' said Natasha all at once. 'I love you! I love you so much!'

'No, he wouldn't have approved,' said Pierre, when he had thought about it. 'But I'll tell you what he would have approved of – our family life. He looked for decency, happiness and peace in everything he saw, and I'd have been proud to shown him all of us. You talk about what it's like when we're apart, but you wouldn't believe what I feel for you when we're back together again.'

'And anyway . . .' began Natasha.

'No, listen. I never stop loving you. And I couldn't love you more than I do – it's very special. I think I . . .' His voice tailed off when their eyes met; there was nothing more to be said.

'You know it's stupid,' said Natasha suddenly, 'all this business about honeymoons, and happiness being right at the beginning. It's not right. Now is the best time. Oh, if only you wouldn't go away. Do you remember how we used to quarrel? And it was always my fault. It was, you know. What did we quarrel about? I can't even remember.'

'Always the same thing,' said Pierre smiling, 'jealou . . .'

'Don't say that word. I can't stand it!' cried Natasha, with a sudden chilly glint of nastiness in her eyes. 'Did you see her?' she added after a pause.

'No, and if I had, I wouldn't have recognized her.'

For a while neither of them spoke.

'Oh, I've got something to tell you. When you were talking in the study I was watching you,' said Natasha in a rather obvious attempt to scatter the dark cloud that was threatening them. 'And do you know, you're like two peas in a pod, you and the boy.' (That was what she called her baby son.) 'Oh dear, I suppose I ought to go to him . . . My milk . . . It's a pity I have to go now.'

They were both silent for a few seconds. Then suddenly, at exactly the same moment, they turned to each other and started to speak. Pierre's tone was complacent and passionate, Natasha began with a gentle, happy smile. They clashed, stopped, and each waited for the other to go on.

'No, what were you going to say? Go on.'

'No, you tell me. Mine was only a bit of nonsense,' said Natasha.

Pierre said what he had been going to say. It was a continuation of his rather smug reflections on his success in Petersburg. At that moment he felt he was destined to give a new direction to Russian society as a whole, and the world in general.

'I was just going to say that all ideas that have a huge impact are always simple ones. And my idea comes down to this: if all the bad people can get together and show strength in unity, honest men must do the same. You see – it's as simple as that.'

'Yes.'

'What were you going to say?'

'Oh, nothing, just a bit of nonsense.'

'No, tell me . . .'

'Oh, it's nothing. I'm just being silly,' said Natasha, though her broad smile was broader than ever. 'I was only going to tell you about Petya. Nurse came to take him from me today, and he laughed and wrinkled his little face and snuggled up close – I'm sure he thought he was hiding away. He's such a sweetie . . . That's him crying. I must be off!' and she walked away.

Meanwhile, downstairs in young Nikolay Bolkonsky's bedroom the little lamp was burning as always. (The boy was afraid of the dark and couldn't be cured of this weakness.) Dessalles was asleep, propped up high on his four pillows, and snoring steadily through his Roman nose. Nikolay had just woken up in a cold sweat, and he was sitting up in bed, wide-eyed and staring. He had been woken up by a bad dream. He had dreamt that he and Uncle Pierre were wearing helmets like the ones in his illustrated edition of Plutarch. He and Uncle Pierre were leading a huge, marching army. The army was one mass of white threads slanting through the air like those floating autumn spider-webs that Dessalles called gossamer. Ahead of them lay glory, thread-like itself though a bit more substantial. The pair of them – he and Pierre – were speeding along, getting nearer and nearer to their goal. Then suddenly the threads that worked them became droopy and tangled. It was heavy going. And suddenly there was Uncle Nikolay, grim and menacing, waiting for them.

'Did you do this?' he said, pointing to a pile of broken sealing-wax and pens. 'I used to love you, but now I'm under orders from Arak-cheyev, and I shall kill the first one of you that moves.' Nikolay looked round for Pierre, but Pierre wasn't there. Pierre had been replaced by his father – Prince Andrey – and his father had no shape or form, but he was there, and the moment he saw him Nikolay felt weak at the knees with love, he turned to jelly like a man with no skeleton. His father took pity and cuddled him. But there was Uncle Nikolay bearing down on them, getting closer and closer. Nikolay felt a great wave of horror – and woke up.

'My father!' he thought. (There were two very good portraits of

Prince Andrey in the house, but Nikolay had never thought of his father in human form.) 'My father was with me. He gave me a cuddle. He was pleased with me; he was pleased with Uncle Pierre. I'll do anything he says. Mucius Scaevola[20] put his hand in the flames. But why shouldn't that kind of thing happen to me one day? I know they want me to study. And I will. But one day I'll have finished, and then I shall go out and do things. I ask only one thing of God: let what happened to Plutarch's men happen to me, and let me do what they did. No, I'll do more. Everybody will know me and love me and admire me.' And suddenly Nikolay's chest was choked with sobs, and he burst into tears.

'Are you feeling ill?' came the voice of Dessalles.

'No,' answered Nikolay, and he sank back down on his pillow. 'He's such a nice, kind man. I do love him!' He was thinking of Dessalles. 'But Uncle Pierre! Oh, what a wonderful man he is! And then there's my father. Father! Father! Yes, I'm going to do something even *he* would have been pleased with.'

PART II

CHAPTER I

The subject matter of history is the life of peoples and humanity. To catch hold of and express in words, to describe directly, the life of a single people, let alone the whole of humanity, is beyond possibility.

Ancient historians all employed the same technique for catching the apparently uncatchable – describing the life of a people. They would describe the activities of individual rulers and accept these activities as an expression of the activity of an entire people.

Questions arose. How did these individuals compel whole nations to act in accordance with their will? And what was it that directed the actual will of these individuals? The answer to the first question was that the will of a Deity subjected a people to the will of one chosen person; and the answer to the second question was that the same Deity directed the will of the chosen person to a predetermined end.

For the ancients these questions were resolved by a belief in the direct intervention of the Deity in human affairs.

Both propositions are now unacceptable to modern historical theory.

You might have thought that modern history, having rejected the ancients' belief in man's subjection to a Deity, and the direction of peoples towards predetermined ends, would have turned away from the outward manifestations of power to look for the causes that lie behind it. But modern history has not done that. It has rejected the views of the ancients in theory, while continuing to follow them in practice.

In place of men imbued with divine authority and directly controlled by the will of God, modern history has created either heroes endowed with extraordinary, superhuman powers, or simply men of widely differing qualities, from monarchs to journalists, who have become leaders of the masses. Modern history has replaced the 'divinely ordained' aims of various peoples – the Jews, the Greeks, the Romans

– which ancient historians saw as the progressive aims of humanity as a whole, by new aims of its own – the well-being of the French people, the German or the English, or, in the most abstract terms, the single, noble aim of civilizing all of humanity, by which is usually meant the inhabitants of a small north-western corner of a large continent.

Modern history has rejected the ancient creeds without putting any new ideas in their place, and the logic of their position has forced the very historians who claim to have rejected the old beliefs in a divine right of kings or fate to come back by a devious route to the point where they started, and to two basic premises: (1) that nations are directed by individuals, and (2) that there is such a thing as a goal towards which nations and humanity in general are proceeding.

In everything written by modern historians from Gibbon to Buckle,[1] for all the ostensible differences between them and their ostensibly original approaches, everything is underpinned by these two ancient and inescapable premises.

In relation to the first of these, the historian describes the activities of certain individuals who in his opinion are leaders of humanity (one of them will limit this accolade to monarchs, military generals and ministers of state; the next will bestow it on monarchs and orators, but also on cultivated reformers, philosophers and poets). In relation to the second one, historians always know the goals towards which humanity is being conducted. For one of them this goal is the aggrandizement of Rome, Spain or France; for the next it will be freedom, equality or the imposition of some sort of civilization on that little corner of the world known as Europe.

It is 1789 and Paris is in ferment. The ferment grows, spreads and manifests itself in a movement of people from west to east. This eastward movement repeats itself several times, clashing with a counter-movement coming from east to west. In the year 1812 it reaches its furthest point, Moscow, and then, with incredible symmetry, the east–west counter-movement gets under way, drawing along behind it all the people in the middle, just as its predecessor had done in the other direction. The counter-movement returns to the starting point of the first movement, Paris, and then subsides.

Throughout this twenty-year period a vast number of fields go unploughed, houses are burnt down, trade flows in different directions, millions of men grow poor, get rich or migrate, and millions of good Christian folk who claim to love their neighbour go about murdering each other.

What does it all mean? Why did it happen? What can have induced these people to burn houses down and murder their fellow creatures?

What were the causes of these events? What force impelled men to act in this fashion? These are the simple and honest questions that leap to mind when humanity comes across memorials and traditions stemming from that bygone age of turmoil.

Commonsensical humanity turns for answers to the science of history, the object of which is the bringing of nations and of humanity to self-knowledge.

If history had clung on to the ancient creeds it would have said that the Deity, wishing to reward or punish His people, gave power to Napoleon and directed his will for the attainment of His own divine ends. A clear and complete answer. You could believe in Napoleon's divine significance or not, but for a believer the entire history of that period would have been comprehensible and beyond contradiction.

But modern history can no longer respond like that. Science now repudiates the old idea of a Deity intervening in human affairs, so other answers must be found.

In answer to these questions modern history says, 'Do you really want to know the meaning of this movement, where it came from, and what force produced these events? Listen to this.

'Louis XIV was a very proud and arrogant man; he had such and such mistresses, and such and such ministers, and he ruled France badly. Louis' successors were weak men as well, and they ruled France badly. And they had such and such favourites, and such and such mistresses. But at that time a few men started scribbling in books. At the end of the eighteenth century a couple of dozen men in Paris began to hold forth about men being equal and free. This led to murder and mayhem all over France. These men killed the King and a lot of other people. But at that time there lived in France a genius by the name of Napoleon. He conquered everybody everywhere, or at least he killed a lot of people because he was a great genius. And for reasons best known to himself he went off to Africa to kill people there, and he killed them so effectively, and he was so bright and clever, that when he got back to France he ordered everyone to obey him, and everyone did. Setting himself up as Emperor, he marched off with the intention of killing a lot more people in Italy, Austria and Prussia. And this he did. Meanwhile in Russia there was an Emperor called Alexander who declared war on Napoleon with a view to getting some order back into Europe. In '07 he made friends with him quite suddenly, but they fell out again in 1811 and started killing lots of people. Whereupon Napoleon brought six hundred thousand men into Russia and conquered Moscow, but suddenly he ran away again and Emperor Alexander, advised by Heinrich Stein et al., united all of Europe against the disturber of her peace. Every one of Napoleon's allies suddenly became his enemy, and the new force marched against fresh troops raised by Napoleon. The allies defeated Napoleon, entered Paris, forced Napoleon to abdicate and exiled him to the Isle of Elba, though without stripping him of the title of Emperor and continuing to show him the greatest respect, despite the fact that five years earlier and one year later he was universally regarded as a villain and outlaw. At which point Louis XVIII came to the throne, even though he had been until then a laughing stock to France and all her allies. Napoleon shed a few tears before the old guard, renounced the throne and went off into exile. Along came the clever statesmen and diplomats (especially Talleyrand, who was the first to grab the famous armchair, sit in it and thereby extend the frontiers of France), and they chatted for a while in Vienna, as a result of which nations emerged happy or unhappy. Suddenly the diplomats and monarchs all but fell out again and they were on the point of telling their armies to go off and kill each other again when Napoleon raised another battalion and invaded France, and the French, who had only just begun to hate him, gave in. But this infuriated the allied monarchs and they set off yet again to fight the French. And Napoleon, the genius, was defeated, proclaimed a villain at long last and shipped off to the island of St Helena. And in that rocky place the exile died a lingering death, cut off from those dear to his heart and his beloved France, and leaving all his fine deeds for the benefit of posterity. Meanwhile back on the European mainland reaction set in, and all the sovereigns turned again to playing havoc with their own people.'

You shouldn't run away with the idea that this is just a joke, a caricature of historical description. Quite the reverse, it is the mildest possible depiction of the kind of contradictory and irrelevant answers provided by *history as a whole*, from collected memoirs and histories of nation states to generalized accounts of history, and also that modern genre known as contemporary *cultural* history.

What is so weird and ridiculous about these answers is that modern history is like a deaf man answering questions no one has asked.

If the aim of history is to describe the movement of humanity and nations, the first question that needs an answer for anything else to become intelligible is this: what kind of force is it that moves nations? Modern history will respond by patiently relating that Napoleon was a great genius, that Louis XIV was too arrogant, or maybe that certain writers wrote certain books.

All of this may well be true, and humanity stands ready to acknowledge it, except that humanity is actually asking a different question. It would all be very fascinating if we still recognized a divine power, self-sustaining and immutable, guiding nations through the agency of your Napoleons, Louis and writers, but we no longer acknowledge any such power, and so, before we can start talking about Napoleons, Louis and great writers, we have to demonstrate some kind of connection between those persons and the movements of nations. If some other power is substituted for divine will, we have to explain what it consists of, since this power is the very focus of all historical interest.

History seems to assume that such power is universally acknowledged and can be taken for granted. But any reader, however willing to accept this power as universally acknowledged, once he has ploughed through the many historical works available, is bound to have doubts and wonder whether this power, which is interpreted in so many different ways by the historians themselves, really does enjoy universal acknowledgement.

CHAPTER 2

What kind of force is it that moves nations?

Historians specializing in biography and historians dealing with single nations understand this force as power vested in heroes and sovereigns. The way they put it, all events are due exclusively to the will of Napoleon, or Alexander, or the particular personality the individual historian happens to be writing about. The answers produced by this type of historian to any question concerning the force that moves events are perfectly adequate, but only so long as there is only one historian for any one event. The moment historians of different nationalities and attitudes begin to describe the same event, the answers produced lose all kind of sense, because the same force is interpreted by them not just differently, but often in exactly the opposite way. One historian claims that an event was caused by the power of Napoleon, another says no, it was caused by the power of Alexander, a third attributes it to the power of some third person. And in any case, this type of historian contradicts all the others even in the basic explanation of the very force on which the particular person's influence is founded. Thiers,[2] a Bonapartist, says that Napoleon's power rested on virtue and genius; Lanfrey,[3] a Republican, says it rested on duplicity and deception of the people. So it is that this type of historian, so keen to undermine everybody else's position, manages to undermine the very concept of a force behind events, and runs away from all the essential questions of history.

General historians, dealing as they do with all nations, appear to acknowledge that specialist historians are wrong in what they say about the forces behind events. They do not recognize any such force as a power vested in heroes and sovereigns; they regard it as the result of many different forces working in conjunction. In describing a war or the subjugation of a people, the writer of general history looks for causes not in the power of any single person, but in some kind of interaction between the many persons involved.

According to this view it would seem that, since the power that resides in historical figures is the product of many different forces, it can hardly be regarded as sufficient in itself to making things happen. Nevertheless writers of general history do in the great majority of cases retain the concept of power that is sufficient in itself to make events happen and assume a causal relationship with them. The way these historians write, at one moment a historical figure is the product of his time, and his power is nothing but the product of various forces, but at the next, his power is a special force which makes things happen. Take Gervinus and Schlosser,[4] for instance (though there are others like them): at one point they argue that Napoleon is a product of the French Revolution and the ideas of 1789, and so on, but elsewhere they state plainly that the campaign of 1812 and other events not to their liking are simply products of Napoleon's misdirected will, and the actual ideas of 1789 were stopped in their tracks by Napoleon's eccentric behaviour. So ideas associated with the Revolution and the spirit of the age – these were what produced Napoleon's power. But at the same time it was Napoleon's power that snuffed out ideas associated with the Revolution and the spirit of the age.

This curious inconsistency is no chance event. We come across the like of it at every end and turn; in fact everything written by these general historians consists of an inevitable stream of inconsistencies like this one. And it is all due to the fact that the historians have only gone half-way down the road of analysis.

For component forces to equate with a composite or resultant force, the sum of the components must equal the resultant. This condition is never observed by general writers, and this is why they can explain resultant forces only by making allowances for some deficiency in the contributory forces and also an extra, unexplained force affecting the resultant.

The specialist historian describing the campaign of 1813, or the restoration of the Bourbons, states categorically that these events were produced by the will of Alexander. But the general historian Gervinus stands this view on its head when he seeks to prove that the campaign of 1813 and the restoration of the Bourbons were not caused by Alexander on his own, they were caused also by Stein, Metternich, Madame de Staël, Talleyrand, Fichte, Chateaubriand and others. The historian has evidently broken down Alexander's power into its component forces: Talleyrand, Chateaubriand and the others, but the sum of these component forces – the interaction between Chateaubriand, Talleyrand, Madame de Staël and all the rest – is obviously not equal to the resultant effect, which was nothing less than the capitulation of millions of Frenchmen to the Bourbons. The only thing that emerges from all the words exchanged between Chateaubriand, Madame de Staël and the others is their own interrelationship, which cannot account for the capitulation of millions. So, in order to explain how the capitulation of millions came about as a direct result of their interrelationship, in other words how it was that component forces equal to a given quantity *A* somehow produced a resultant equal to a thousand times *A*, the historian has to fall back on the strength of individual power, which is something he has already denied by acknowledging it as a resultant force – he has to allow for an unexplained outside force acting on the resultant. This is precisely what the general historians do. Which is why they contradict not only the specialist historians, but also themselves.

Country folk, watching out for either rain or fair weather but lacking all knowledge of where the rain comes from, will say the wind has blown the rain up, or the wind has blown the rain away. General historians are just like that; when they are looking out for something, and it fits in with their theory, they'll say that power is the result of events, but on other occasions, when they want to prove something different, they'll say that power determines events.

There is a third group of historians, historians of *culture*, who follow the path laid down by the universalists in being prepared sometimes to acknowledge literary men and women as determining forces, though they interpret this power rather differently. For them power resides in 'culture', intellectual activity. Historians of culture are perfectly consistent in taking after their progenitors, the writers of universal history, for if historical events can be explained by certain persons dealing with one another in certain ways, why not explain them by certain persons writing certain books? From the vast array of connotations associated with every aspect of life, these historians select the single connotation of intellectual activity and call this connotation a cause. But despite their best efforts to demonstrate that the cause of events lies in intellectual activity, only by a great stretch of the imagination can one agree that there is anything in common between intellectual activity and the movements of peoples, and in no way can we allow intellectual activity to have determined the actions of men, for any idea that the savage butchery of the French Revolution stemmed from the doctrine of the equality of man, or that the bloodiest of wars and executions arose from the doctrine of love, falls short of confirming such a proposition.

But let us say for the purposes of argument that all the clever sophistries that fill these histories are right; let us accept that nations are directed by mysterious forces called *ideas* – even so, the essential question of history remains unanswered; either that, or we have to add another force to the power of monarchs and the influence of counsellors and other persons introduced by the universal historians, and this new force is *the idea*, and how the idea relates to the masses calls for some explanation. We can understand that Napoleon possessed power and because of that an event came to pass; with a little latitude we can even imagine that Napoleon, along with some other influences, might have been the actual cause of an event, but precisely how Rousseau's book *The Social Contract* could have made the French people go out and slaughter each other must be beyond comprehension unless some causal connection can be established between this new force and the event.

There clearly is a connection between all living things at any one time, and so it must be possible to establish some sort of connection between the intellectual activity of men and their historical movements, just as a connection can be established between the movements of humanity and commerce, handicrafts, horticulture and anything else you care to name. But why intellectual activity should be singled out by cultural historians as the cause or the expression of an entire historical movement is not easy to understand. Historians could arrive at such a conclusion only with the following provisos: (1) that history is written by educated people who find it natural and agreeable to believe that the activity of their social group is a source of movement for the whole of humanity, just as this kind of belief would come naturally and agreeably to tradesmen, agriculturalists and soldiers (only their beliefs don't get expressed because merchants and soldiers don't write history), and (2) that spiritual activity, enlightenment, civilization, culture and ideas are all vague and indeterminate concepts, flags of convenience under which even more opaque phrases can be used very conveniently, thus accommodating any kind of theory.

But even allowing histories of this kind a certain intrinsic value (maybe they are of use to somebody or something), histories of culture – and all general histories now show tendencies in that direction – are notorious for presenting a serious and detailed analysis of various religious, philosophical and political doctrines as causes of events, and every time they are called upon to describe an actual historical event like the campaign of 1812 they automatically describe it as resulting from the exercise of power, baldly stating that this campaign came about by Napoleon's will. By saying things like this, cultural historians automatically fall into self-contradiction, or else they demonstrate that the new force invented by them does not reflect historical events, and the sole means of explaining history is by the very power they seemed to have rejected.

CHAPTER 3

A railway engine moves along. The question is: what makes it move? A peasant says the devil is moving it. Another man says the engine is moving because its wheels are going round. A third tells you to look for the cause of the movement in the smoke wafting away on the wind.

The peasant's claim is irrefutable. To refute what he says someone would have to prove there is no such thing as the devil, or else another peasant would have to explain that it's not the devil who makes it go, it's a German. At that point their contradictory views will show them they are both wrong. But the man who says the cause is in the move-ment of the wheels refutes his own argument; once embarked on analysis, he ought to have kept going. He ought to have explained why the wheels are moving, and he has no right to stop looking for a cause until he finds the ultimate cause of the movement of the engine, which is steam under compression in the boiler. As for the man who explained the movement of the engine in terms of the smoke wafting away on the wind, all he has done is noticed that the wheel explanation doesn't produce a cause, seized on the first available indicator and proclaimed this as his cause.

The only concept capable of explaining the movement of the engine is the concept of a force that equates to the movement observed.

The only concept capable of explaining the movements of nations is the concept of a force that equates to the entire movement of the nations. Yet we see all manner of forces pressed into the service of this concept by all manner of historians, and they still do not equate to the movement observed. Some use it to identify a force arising spontaneously in heroes, just as the peasant sees the devil in the engine. Others identify a force made up of several other forces, like the movement of the wheels. A third group identifies an intellectual influence, like the smoke wafted on the wind.

While ever authors continue to write histories of individuals – your Julius Caesars, Alexanders, Luthers and Voltaires – and not histories of everybody, *absolutely everybody*, involved in an event, there is no possibility of describing the movement of humanity without falling back on the concept of a force that impels men to direct their activity to a single end. And the only concept of this kind known to historians is the concept of power.

This concept is the only way of getting a handle on history as presently expounded, and anyone who broke off this handle, as Buckle did, without finding some other technique for dealing with historical material, would only be depriving himself of the last possible way of dealing with it. The necessity for this concept of power as an explanation of historical phenomena is supremely well illustrated by the writers of universal and cultural history themselves; having ostensibly repudiated the concept of power, they keep returning to it at every step, and they are bound to do so.

So far the study of history as part of the human spirit of inquiry has been like money in circulation, notes and coins. Biographies and national histories are like paper money. They can pass and circulate, doing their job without harming anyone and fulfilling a useful function, as long as no one questions the guarantee behind them. And as long as no one questions precisely how the will of heroes is supposed to direct events, historical works by Thiers and his ilk will retain a certain interest and educational value, not to mention the odd touch of poetry. But just as doubts about the validity of banknotes can arise, either when too many go into circulation because they are so easy to make, or because of a sudden rush to covert them into gold, in the same way doubts about the real value of this type of historical work will arise either when too many of them are written, or when some naive person asks the simple question, 'Precisely what force was it that made it possible for Napoleon to do that?' – in other words, when someone wishes to change a working note for the pure gold of a valid concept.

The writers of universal and cultural history are like men who feel let down by paper money and decide to stop making notes and make hard coins instead, using a metal of lower density than gold. Their coins would certainly turn out to be 'hard', but that's all they would be. Ignorant people might be taken in by a paper note, but nobody is going to be deceived by a hard coin made of low-value metal. Just as gold remains gold only as long as it can be used for something as well as exchanged, so the universal historians will be golden only when they can answer the crucial question of history, 'What is power?' Universal historians give contradictory answers, and as for cultural historians, they evade the issue and give answers to completely different questions. Imitation gold tokens can be used, but only within a community that has agreed to accept them as gold, or in one where no one knows the properties of gold; in the same way, the universal and cultural historians who, for reasons best known to themselves, keep running away from the crucial questions of humanity, are still accepted as hard coinage in our universities and by a wide readership with a taste for what they like to call 'serious reading'.

CHAPTER 4

Having repudiated the ancient view of the people's will being subjected to a chosen person by divine inspiration, and through him subjected to the Deity, history cannot take a step without running into contradictions. It has to choose between two alternatives: either a return to the old belief in the Deity's direct intervention in human affairs, or a definitive explanation of the force called 'power' that is responsible for historical events.

Any return to the old way of thinking is out of the question, the old beliefs having been shattered, which means that an explanation must be found for the meaning of power.

Napoleon gave the order for an army to be raised and go to war. This idea is so familiar, we have grown so used to it, that the question why six hundred thousand men go off to do battle just because Napoleon has said a few words seems to have no meaning. He had the power, so his orders were carried out.

This answer is perfectly satisfactory if we believe that power was given to him by God. But the moment we decide not to accept this, it becomes necessary to define the significance of this power, the power of one man over others.

This power cannot be the straightforward power deriving from the physical superiority of a strong creature over a weak one, a superiority based on the application or threat of physical force – like the power of Hercules. Nor can it be based on the moral superiority, as several simple-minded historians seem to think, since they keep setting certain historical figures up as heroes, men imbued with a special quality of mind and spirit which goes by the name of genius. This power cannot be based on moral superiority, because, even if we forget about historical heroes like Napoleon, opinions of whose moral stature differ widely, history shows that none of your Louis XIs or Metternichs, who governed men in millions, showed any special propensity for spiritual strength; quite the reverse, in most cases they were morally weaker than every last one of the millions they governed.

If the source of power lies not in the physical or moral qualities of the possessor, it is obvious that the source of this power must be found outside the particular person – in the relationship which the possessor enjoys with the masses.

That is precisely how power is seen by the science of jurisprudence, the historical bank of exchange that undertakes to exchange historical power-tokens for pure gold.

Power is the collective will of the masses transferred to rulers selected by open or tacit consent.

In the realm of jurisprudence, which is based on arguments about how a state and power should be constructed if only they could be constructed, this is as clear as crystal, but when applied to actual history this definition of power calls for further elucidation.

Jurisprudence treats the state and power as the ancients treated fire, seeing them as absolute entities, whereas for history the state and power are merely phenomena, just as for modern physics fire is a phenomenon rather than an element.

Because of this fundamental difference in attitude between history and jurisprudence the latter can hold forth in great detail about power, how in the lawyers' opinion it should be organized, and even what it is, this absolute entity with its timeless existence, but jurisprudence has no answers to historical questions about power as it exists and develops over time itself.

If power is the transfer of collective will to rulers, was Pugachov a representative of the will of the masses? If not, why was Napoleon I considered to be one? Why was Napoleon III a criminal when he was seized at Boulogne,[5] whereas afterwards it was the people seized by him who turned out to be the criminals?

In a palace coup, which might involve only two or three people, do we observe the will of the masses being transferred to a new person? In international affairs is the will of the popular masses transferred to their conqueror? In 1808 was the will of the Conference of the Rhine transferred to Napoleon? Was the will of the mass of the Russian people transferred to Napoleon in 1809 when our army allied itself with the French and went to war with Austria?

The possible answers are threefold:

(1) The will of the masses is always transferred unconditionally to a chosen ruler or rulers, which means that every upsurge of new power, all resistance to transferred power, must be regarded as an infringement of real power; or

(2) The will of the masses is transferred to rulers on known and specific conditions, which means that every time power is curtailed, resisted or even abolished this must be due to non-observance by the rulers of the conditions on which power was transferred to them; or

(3) The will of the masses is transferred to rulers conditionally, but on conditions that are unknown and unspecific, which means that when many different authorities arise, clash and decline, this must be due to the greater or lesser extent to which the rulers have been observing the unknown conditions by which the will of the masses is transferred from one group to another.

This is the historians' threefold explanation of the relationship between the masses and their rulers.

Some historians – the specialist biographers referred to above, naive enough not to understand questions about the meaning of power – seem to accept that the collective will of the masses is transferred to historical leaders unconditionally, and therefore, when these historians come to describe any such authority, they assume it to be the only authority, absolute and real, so that any other force that opposes this real authority is no authority at all, but an infringement of authority amounting to violence.

The theory works well enough for primitive people in peace-time, but when applied to complex and turbulent periods in national life, with different authorities arising simultaneously and fighting each other, it runs into trouble: legitimist historians will argue that the National Convention, the Directory and Bonaparte amounted to nothing more than infringements of real authority, whereas Republicans and Bonapartists will argue that the Republic or perhaps the Empire was the real authority, and everything else an infringement. It soon becomes clear that the explanations offered by these historians, which cancel each other out, are good for children of tender years but nobody else.

Another type of historian, seeing the error of this view of history, will tell us that authority rests on the conditional transfer of collective will from the masses to their rulers, and that historical leaders possess power only on condition that they fulfil a certain programme which by tacit consent the will of the people has set for them. But these historians fail to tell us what this programme consists of, or if they do they constantly contradict one another.

Every historian will have his own view of what constitutes the goal of a people in movement, and will therefore imagine the conditions to be greatness, wealth, freedom or enlightenment for the citizens of France or some other country. But if we overlook the contradictions between historians concerning the nature of these conditions, and even allow for the possibility of one overall set of conditions applicable to everybody, the facts of history almost always contradict this theory.

If the conditions determining any transfer of power amount to wealth, freedom and enlightenment for the people, how is it that monarchs like Louis XIV and Ivan the Terrible lived out their reigns in peace and quiet, while monarchs like Louis XVI and Charles I were executed by their people? To this question these historians reply that the effects of things done by Louis XIV in violation of his programme were visited upon Louis XVI. But why not Louis XIV and Louis XV? Why did they have to be visited specifically on Louis XVI? And is there any time limit on this kind of visitation? To questions like these there are no answers, and there never can be. Equally inexplicable in terms of this view of history is the reason why collective popular will can remain century after century in the hands of rulers and their heirs, and then all at once during a fifty-year period transfer itself to a Convention, a Directory, a Napoleon, an Alexander, a Louis XVIII, back to another Napoleon, a Charles X, a Louis Philippe, a Republican government and then to a Napoleon III. To explain these rapid transferences of popular will from one individual to another, especially in the broader context of international affairs, conquests and alliances, these historians are forced to admit that at least some of these developments do not amount to a proper transfer of popular will, they are chance events dependent on cleverness, error, double-dealing or weakness on the part of some diplomat, monarch or party leader. So, most historical phenomena – civil wars, revolutions, conquests – are, according to these historians, not the results of popular will freely transferred but the results of misdirected will on the part of one or more persons, which means, once again, infringements of authority. So it is that even this type of historian comes to regard historical events as exceptions to his theory.

These historians are like a botanist who observes that some plants develop with a double seed-leaf and therefore insists that every growing thing grows only by dividing into two leaves, with the result that palm-trees and mushrooms and even fully grown oak-trees with a canopy of foliage nothing like the original double seed-leaf have to be regarded as exceptions to his theory. There is a third type of historian who agrees that the will of the masses is transferred to historical leaders conditionally, but without us knowing what the conditions are. He will claim that historical leaders retain power only because they are carrying out the transferred will of the masses.

But in that case, if the force that moves nations lies not in their historical leaders but in the people themselves, what is the role of the leaders?

Historical leaders are, according to these historians, living embodiments of popular will, and the activity of historical leaders represents the activity of the masses.

But that gives rise to another question: does all the activity of historical leaders represent the will of the masses, or only one particular aspect of it? If all the activities of historical leaders amount to an expression of the popular will, as some believe, then the entire biographies of people like Napoleon and Catherine the Great, with all the bits and pieces of court scandal, amount to expressions of the peoples' lives, which is obviously nonsensical, but if only one aspect of a historical leader's activity amounts to an expression of the peoples' lives, as other self-styled philosophical historians believe, then in order to determine which aspect of a leader's activity is the one that expresses the life of a people, we need to know at the outset what constitutes the life of the people.

Confronted by this difficulty, this type of historian will invent the most obscure, insubstantial and generalized abstraction that can be found to cover the greatest possible number of events, and tell us that this abstraction represents the aim of humanity in movement. The most commonly encountered abstractions, accepted by virtually all historians, are: freedom, equality, enlightenment, progress, civilization, culture. Presenting any old abstraction as the goal of human movements, the historians go on to study those people who have left behind the greatest number of memorials – kings, ministers, generals, authors, reformers, popes and journalists – arranging them in order, according to the effect these people have had (in the historians' opinion) in advancing or retarding the abstraction in question. But since there is no proof whatsoever that the goal of humanity really is freedom, equality, enlightenment or civilization, and since the connection between the masses and their rulers or educators rests on the arbitrary assumption that the collective will of the masses is always transferred to figures who attract our attention – it so happens that the activities of the millions who uproot themselves, burn their houses down, abandon the fields and go off to butcher each other never find expression in the descriptions of activities limited to a dozen personalities who don't happen to burn houses down, work the soil or kill their fellow creatures.

History shows this at every end and turn. Take the ferment among western people towards the end of the last century, and the way they went rampaging eastward – is all of this explained by the actions of Louis XIV, Louis XV and Louis XVI, or their mistresses and ministers, or by the lives of Napoleon, Rousseau, Diderot, Beaumarchais[6] and others?

The eastward movement of the Russians, to Kazan and Siberia, is that expressed in the details of the morbid character of Ivan the Terrible and his correspondence with Kurbsky?[7]

The movement of peoples at the time of the Crusades, is that explained by studying any number of Godfreys and Louis[8] and their ladies? That particular movement of people from west to east has remained incomprehensible, having had no goal, no leadership, nothing but a crowd of vagrants, followers of Peter the Hermit.[9] And even more incomprehensible is why it suddenly stopped, at a point when a rational and sacred aim for the Crusades – the liberation of Jerusalem – had been clearly established by the historical leaders.

Popes, kings and knights urged the people to liberate the Holy Land. But the people didn't go, because the unknown cause that had got them going before was no longer there. The history of the Godfreys and the Minnesingers[10] clearly cannot encompass the lives of the people. Meanwhile what has remained is the history of the Godfreys and the Minnesingers, whereas the history of the people's lives and their motivation remains for ever unknown. And the biographies of writers and reformers will tell us even less about ordinary people's lives.

Cultural history will elucidate the motivation, the lifestyle and the thoughts of a writer or a reformer. We learn from them that Luther had a quick temper and made certain speeches, we learn that Rousseau was suspicious and wrote certain books, but what we don't learn is why the nations hacked each other to pieces after the Reformation, or why men guillotined one another during the French Revolution.

If we combine these two different kinds of history, as most modern historians do, all we shall get is the history of monarchs and writers instead of a history of the lives of nations.

CHAPTER 5

The lives of nations cannot be contained within the lives of a few men, since the connection between those few men and the nations has never been discovered. The theory that this connection is based on a transfer of collective popular will from a people to its historical leaders is a hypothesis not borne out by historical experience.

The theory of the transfer of collective popular will from a people to historical personages may perhaps explain a good deal in the realm of jurisprudence, and may well be essential for its purposes. But when you apply it to history – the moment revolutions, conquests and civil strife come into the picture, the moment history begins, in fact – this theory explains nothing.

This theory has an air of infallibility, for one good reason: the act of transferring the popular will can never be verified, because it has never existed.

Whatever the turn of events, and whoever takes charge of them, this theory can always say that such and such a person took charge of events because the collective popular will had been transferred to him.

The answers to historical questions provided by this theory are like those of a man observing the movements of a flock of sheep who ignores the variable quality of the pasturage in different parts of the field and the shepherd coming up behind, and thinks that the reasons why the flock takes one direction or another depend on which animal happens to be out in front.

'The flock is moving in that direction because it is being led by the animal in front, and the collective will of all the other animals has been transferred to the leader of the flock.' This is the answer we can expect from the first category of historians, the ones who believe in the unconditional transfer of power.

'If the animals at the head of the flock change from time to time, this is due to the transfer of all the animals' collective will from one leader to another, and everything depends on whether the leader follows the direction chosen by the whole flock.' This is the answer we can expect from historians who assume that the collective popular will gets transferred to leaders on conditions which they regard as known and understood. (With this technique of observation it happens all too often that the observer, looking on things from his own chosen direction, identifies leaders who end up, when the direction of the masses changes, not in front, but off to one side and sometimes even at the back.)

'If the animals at the front are changing all the time, and the whole flock keeps changing direction all the time, this is because in order to move in a given direction the animals transfer their will to others that are particularly prominent, so if we wish to study the movements of the flock we need to observe all the prominent animals on every side of the flock.' This is the answer we can expect from the third category of historians, the ones who identify all historical personages, from monarchs down to journalists, as expressions of their age.

The theory of the transfer of popular will to historical persons is nothing but a paraphrase, a rephrasing of the question.

What is the cause of historical events? Power.

What is power? Power is the collective will of the masses transferred to a single person.

On what terms is the will of the masses transferred to a single person? On condition that he expresses the will of the whole people. In other words, power is power. Which is to say that power is a word with a meaning we cannot understand.

If the realm of human knowledge was restricted to abstract thinking, then humanity, after a critical examination of power as explained by juridical science, would come to the conclusion that power is only a word, with no existence in reality. But for a cognitive inquiry into real-life phenomena, man has another instrument besides abstract reasoning – experience – which enables him to verify the results of his reasoning. And experience tells him that power is not just a word; it is something that actually exists.

We can ignore the fact that no account of concerted action by men can get by without the concept of power; the actual existence of power is demonstrated for us not only by history, but by observation of contemporary events.

Whenever an event takes place, a man or men appear whose will is said to have determined the deed. Napoleon III says the word, and off go the French to Mexico.[11] The King of Prussia and Bismarck say the word, and off go the troops to Bohemia.[12] At the bidding of Napoleon I, his soldiers march into Russia. At the bidding of Alexander I, the French submit to the Bourbons. Experience shows that whenever an event takes place it is always connected with the will of one person, or several people, who decreed it.

Historians, steeped in the old habit of acknowledging divine intervention in human affairs, tend to look for the cause of events in the will exercised by a person invested with power, though this conclusion is never confirmed by reason or experience.

On the one hand, reason shows that a person's will – the power of his word – forms only a part of the generalized activity that finds expression in an event, say a revolution or a war, and therefore unless we fall back on some incomprehensible, supernatural force – a miracle – it is not arguable that words alone could be the direct cause of the movements of millions of men.

On the other hand, even if we argued that they could, history shows that in most cases an expression of will by historical personages leads absolutely nowhere – their orders are often ignored, and sometimes what occurs is the exact opposite of what they have ordered.

Without allowing for divine intervention in human affairs, we cannot accept power as an actual cause of events.

And when it comes to real-life experience, power is nothing more or less than the dependent relationship that exists between an expression of will and its execution by other people.

If we are to explain the conditions of that dependency, we must first of all reinstate the concept of the expression of will, but with reference to man rather than the Deity.

If we think of the Deity giving a command, expressing His will, the expression of that will, as ancient history relates, is timeless and uncaused, since the Deity has no connection with the event. But when we speak of commands as the expression of men's will, men existing in time and interacting, we must recreate two conditions if we are to clarify for ourselves the connection between command and event: (1) that of the occurrence in its entirety, the dynamic time-bound wholeness of the event itself and the person commanding it; and (2) that of the indispensable bond which links the person issuing the command with those who carry it out.

CHAPTER 6

Only the will of a timeless Deity could possibly affect a whole series of events occurring over years or centuries, and only a spontaneous Deity could by sheer will power direct the movement of humanity. Man acts within time, and is involved in events.

Reinstating the first condition – time – we perceive that no order can be carried out without an earlier order making its execution possible.

There is no such thing as a command that comes from nowhere or one that embraces a whole series of events. Every command flows from an earlier one, and never relates to a whole series of events, being always limited to a single moment within those events.

When we say, for instance, that Napoleon ordered his troops to go to war, we are bringing together under one word of command a whole series of subsequent commands, all of them interdependent. Napoleon couldn't have ordered the invasion of Russia, and he never did. All that happened was that one day he ordered certain documents to be sent to Vienna, Berlin and Petersburg, and the next day he issued one or two decrees and some instructions to the army, the fleet, the quartermaster service and so on and so forth – millions of orders coming together in a series of orders associated with a series of events which brought the French troops to Russia.

If it is true that Napoleon kept issuing orders throughout his reign for an expedition to England, and spent more time and effort on this than any other enterprise without ever carrying it out in the whole of his reign, though he did carry out an expedition against Russia (even though, as he emphasized on numerous occasions, this was a country that would make a useful ally) – all of this is due to the fact that in the first case his orders did not correspond with the course of events, and in the second case they did.

For an order to be properly carried out it is necessary for a man to issue an order that is capable of being carried out. But to know what is and what isn't capable of being carried out is impossible, not only in the case of Napoleon's campaign against Russia, involving millions, but even in the case of the simplest occurrence, since millions of obstacles can always get in the way of either of these. Every order carried out is always one of many that are not. All the impossible orders fail to engage with the course of events and don't get carried out. It is only the possible ones that do engage with the run of sub-sequent orders, do correspond with the course of events and do get carried out.

Our false impression that an order preceding an event is the cause of it is due to the fact that when an event has occurred and one or two orders out of a thousand issued have been carried out (the ones that happen to correspond with events), we forget those that were not carried out because they never could have been. Apart from that, our major source of error arises from the fact that in any historical account a whole series of innumerable, disparate and trivial events (say every single thing responsible for bringing the French soldiers over to Russia) are subsumed into the single end-result of that series of events, and the whole series of orders issued are correspondingly subsumed into a single expression of will.

We say: Napoleon chose to invade Russia and did so. In point of fact, we shall never discover in all that Napoleon ever did anything resembling such an expression of will. What we shall find is a series of commands or expressions of his will issued with maximum vagueness in a multiplicity of ways. From the incalculable series of Napoleon's orders that were never carried out, one series of orders for the campaign of 1812 was carried out, not because of any essential difference between these and the ones not carried out, but simply because this series happened to correspond with the course of events bringing the French soldiers into Russia, just as in stencil-work the eventual figure depends not on the direction or the working of the paint, but on the stencilled cut-out being filled in, in every corner.

So, when we consider the relationship between commands and events in real time, we find that no command is ever the cause of an event, though a definite dependency exists between the two. To understand the nature of this dependency it is essential to reinstate the second of the two forgotten conditions that accompany any order issued by a man rather than a Deity – that the man issuing the order is himself involved in the event.

This relationship between the person issuing an order and the person receiving it is the essence of what we call power. The relationship is made up as follows.

For the purpose of common action men always come together in certain combinations, in which, even though the goals of the common action may vary, the relationship between the participants always remains the same.

Men who come together in these combinations always form a special relationship whereby the greater number participate more directly, and the smaller number less directly, in the combined action for which they have come together. One of the best and clearest examples of such combinations of men coming together for concerted action is the army.

All armies are made up as follows: the rank and file, who always form the majority; the slightly higher ranks, corporals and non-commissioned officers, fewer in number than the common soldiers; even higher ranks, of whom there are fewer still; and so on, right up to the highest military authority, which is concentrated in a single person.

A military organization can be accurately represented by a cone, with a base of the largest diameter consisting of the rank and file, a higher section with a smaller base for soldiers of higher rank, and so on right up to the apex, the point of which will be the commander-in-chief.

The common soldiers, who are the largest number, form the lower sections of the cone and its base. It is the soldier who does all the stabbing and hacking and burning and pillaging, orders for which he receives from above, and he never gives an order himself. The non-commissioned officer (and there are fewer such people) sees less direct action than the soldier, but he does give orders. The commissioned officer sees even less action, but gives a lot more orders. The general does nothing but issue instructions to the army and hardly ever uses a weapon. The commander-in-chief is never allowed into the action; all he does is make general arrangements for the movements of the masses. This same kind of interrelationship exists in every combination of men who come together for concerted action – in agriculture, business and all administrative departments.

And so, without slicing these cones artificially from the bottom up into various sections, ranks, titles and grades in whatever department or common enterprise, a law emerges, by which men coming together for concerted action always form a relationship which guarantees that the ones most directly involved in the action give the fewest orders and exist in the greatest numbers, while the ones least directly involved in the action give most orders and exist in the smallest numbers, rising thus from the lower strata right up to one last man at the top, with the very least direct involvement in what is going on, and maximum devotion of his effort to the issuing of orders.

This is the relationship that exists between those involved in the giving and receiving of orders, and it constitutes the essence of the concept known as power. With the time condition reinstated, since all events occur within time, we have found that an order gets carried out only when it corresponds to a relevant sequence of events. And by reinstating as an essential condition the link between people giving and receiving orders, we have found that by their very nature the people giving the orders have the least involvement in any action, their energies being directed exclusively to the issuing of orders.

CHAPTER 7

When an event takes place various opinions and desires are expressed about it, and as the event evolves out of the concerted action of many men, one particular version of the opinions or desires expressed is bound to be fulfilled, if only approximately. When one of the opinions expressed is fulfilled, that opinion becomes enshrined, by association, as the order that preceded the event.

Some men are hauling a log. Each of them speaks out and says where and how it should be hauled. The log is hauled away and it ends up just as one of them had said it would. So he gave the order. This is command and power at their most primitive.

The man who did most of the manual labour must have been able to think least about what he was doing and give least consideration to the possible outcome of the collective endeavour or any issuing of orders. The man who issued most of the orders was so busy with his verbal activity that he must obviously have had less time for the manual labour. In a bigger group of people directing their efforts towards a particular goal, the category of those less involved in the actual labour because they are more involved in the issuing of orders stands out even more clearly.

When a man is acting alone he always carries in his mind a particular set of presumptions that seem to have governed his actions in the past, justify his present activity and govern his thinking about any future projects.

People in groups act in just the same way, except that they leave it to those least involved in the action to think up any presumptions, justification or future projects for their collective endeavour.

For various reasons known and unknown, the French set about butchering and destroying one another. And with the event comes a corresponding justification in the expressed will of certain men who believe it to be necessary for the good of France, or in the interests of freedom or equality. The butchery stops, and along comes a corresponding justification of this event in terms of the need to centralize power, resist Europe and so on. Men march from west to east, murdering their fellow creatures, and this event is accompanied by fine words about the glory of France, the vileness of England, and so on. History shows that these forms of justification are no less nonsensical and contradictory than, for instance, murdering somebody as a declaration of his human rights, or murdering millions in Russia in order to take England down a peg or two.

But these justifications are very necessary at the time, shifting moral responsibility away from the men who produce the events. These short-term measures operate like brushes on the front of a train clearing the rails ahead: they sweep away men's moral responsibility. Without this kind of justification there would be no answer to the simplest question that arises the moment you start to examine any historical event: why do millions of men commit crimes collectively, murdering, fighting wars and so on?

Under the present complex forms of political and social life in Europe, can you imagine any event that was not predetermined, decreed or ordered by some sovereign, minister, parliament or newspaper? Is there any form of concerted action that could not be justified in terms of political unity, patriotism, the balance of power or the advancement of civilization? No, every event that occurs inevitably coincides with some desire that has been expressed, soon acquires its own justification and comes to be regarded as the result of the will power of one or more persons.

Wherever a moving ship decides to go you will always see a stream of divided waves ahead of it. For those on board the flow of those waves will be their only sensation of movement.

Only by carefully observing the movement of that stream, from moment to moment, and comparing it with the movement of the ship, shall we learn that every surge through the flow is due to the forward movement of the ship, and it was a false impression that led us to believe we were the ones who were moving along imperceptibly.

We can see the same thing happening if we observe the movement of historical figures from moment to moment – that is, if we reinstate the inevitable condition that applies to every occurrence – the continuous flow of time – and provided we never lose sight of the inevitable link between historical figures and the masses.

As long as the ship keeps going in one direction you will always see the same divided stream ahead of it, but when it starts to weave about, the flowing stream up front will keep changing. But wherever it turns there will always be a flowing stream ahead, anticipating the ship's movement.

Whatever happens, the outcome will always seem to have been foreseen and preordained. Whichever way the ship turns, the boiling waves will surge ahead of it, neither directing the vessel nor speeding its progress, though from a distance that stream will seem to be moving on its own and even responsible for the ship's forward movement.

Historians have tended to study expressions of will by historical figures only in terms of the relationship between orders and events, and they have jumped to the conclusion that the events were dependent on the orders. But our analysis of the events themselves and the link between historical figures and the masses has shown that historical figures and the orders they give are dependent on events. We have incontrovertible proof of this in the fact that, however many orders are given, the event will not take place if there is no other cause to produce it. But the moment an event does take place, whatever it may be, among all the expressions of will by all sorts of different people there will always be some that happen to coincide in meaning and time so that events correspond to orders given.

With this conclusion in mind, we can give straight and positive answers to two of history's crucial questions: (1) What is power? (2) What is the force that determines the movement of peoples?

(1) Power is a relationship between a given person and other persons by which the less directly a person participates in a collective enterprise the more involved he is in expressing opinions and theories about it and providing justification for it.

(2) The movement of peoples is determined not as historians have supposed, by the exercise of power, or the intellect, or both together, but by the actions of *all involved*; all the people who come together in such a way that those who participate most directly in the activity assume the least responsibility for it, and vice versa.

In moral terms power is the cause of the event; in physical terms it is those who are subject to that power. But since moral activity is inconceivable without physical activity, the cause of the event is actually found in neither of them, but in a combination of the two.

To put it another way, the concept of cause does not apply to the phenomenon under review.

In the last analysis we come to the circle of infinity, the furthest limit to which the human intellect must come in every realm of thought if it is not toying with its subject matter. Electricity produces heat; heat produces electricity. Atoms attract; atoms repel.

On the subject of the relationship between heat and electricity, and atoms, we cannot say why things happen like this, so we say they do it because anything else is unimaginable, it has to be, it's a law. The same applies to historical phenomena. Why do wars or revolutions happen? We don't know. All we know is that for either of these to happen men must come together in a particular combination with everybody taking part, and we say that this is so because anything else is unimaginable, it has to be, it's a law.

CHAPTER 8

If history dealt with external phenomena all we would have to do is state this simple and obvious law and our argument would be at an end. But the law of history relates to man. A particle of matter cannot tell us that it doesn't feel bound by laws of attraction and repulsion and it thinks they are wrong. But man, the subject matter of history, makes no bones about it: 'I am free,' he says, 'and therefore not subject to any laws.'

The problem of man's free will may often remain unarticulated, but it is felt at every step in history.

All serious-minded historians are inevitably confronted with this question. All the inconsistencies and uncertainties of history, and the wrong path taken by historical studies, can be attributed to this problem and the lack of any solution to it.

If every man enjoyed free will – in other words, if every man could do what he wanted – the whole of history would be a tissue of sporadic accidents.

If one man in millions once in a thousand years had complete freedom of action, freedom to do anything he wanted, it is obvious that any act of free will performed by that man in defiance of all laws would deny the possibility of any laws at all for humanity. Conversely, if there is any one law that controls the actions of men, free will cannot exist, because men's will would have to be subject to that law.

This contradiction embodies the whole problem of free will, which has occupied the best minds from time immemorial, and from time immemorial has stood out as an issue of tremendous importance.

The problem is that, taking man as a subject for observation from any angle – theological, historical, ethical, philosophical – we find him subject to a universal law of necessity just like everything else that exists. But looking at him from within ourselves, looking at our own consciousness, we feel free.

This consciousness is a separate source of self-awareness independent of reason. Through reason man can observe himself, but he knows himself only through consciousness. Without consciousness, no observation or application of reason is conceivable.

In order to understand, observe and draw any conclusions a man must first of all be conscious of being alive. A man's sense of being alive derives from his yearning, which means being conscious of his own will. But there is only one way that man becomes conscious of his will, the very essence of his being – he conceives of it as free will.

If during self-observation a man sees that his will always operates by the same law (whether it be the need to consume food, exercise the brain, or whatever else), he can only see this unvarying direction of his will as a limitation placed upon it. It wouldn't be possible to limit something without it being free in the first place. A man's will seems limited precisely because he cannot conceive of it as anything but free.

You tell me I'm not free. But I have just raised my arm and put it down again. Everybody understands that this reply may be illogical, but it is also irrefutable evidence of freedom. It is an expression of consciousness and not subject to reason.

If consciousness of freedom was not a separate source of self-awareness independent of reason, it would be subject to reason and experience, which in fact it is not and never could be.

Every man discovers from a series of experiments and arguments that he, the object under examination, is subject to certain laws, and he submits to them; once he has been told about the law of gravity, for instance, or the law of impermeability, he will never try to overcome them. But he also discovers from the same series of experiments and reflections that the total freedom he is conscious of is an impossibility; any action depends on his organization, character and motivation. But he never submits to the conclusions offered by these experiments and arguments.

Once he knows from experience and reasoning that a stone falls in a downward direction man accepts this as beyond doubt and expects this known law to be observed in every instance. But when he knows also beyond doubt that his own will is subject to laws, he will not, and cannot, believe it.

However often a man learns from experience and reason that in the same circumstances and with the same character he will always do what he did before, the thousandth time he encounters the same circumstances with the same character and this leads to an action that always ends in the same way, he still feels beyond doubt that he is free to do whatever he wants, no less now than before the experiment. Every man, savage or sage, despite the irrefutable evidence provided by reason and experience that there is no possibility of two different courses of action emerging from exactly the same circumstances, still feels that without this nonsensical concept (the very essence of freedom) he cannot conceive of life. He feels that, however impossible it might be, it is still true; without that concept of freedom he would not only find life incomprehensible, he would be unable to live for a split second. Unable to live because all human striving, all the motivation for living, is nothing other than a striving towards greater freedom.

Wealth and poverty, fame and obscurity, authority and subjugation, strength and weakness, health and disease, culture and ignorance, labour and leisure, repletion and hunger, virtue and vice – these are all greater or lesser degrees of freedom.

To imagine a man without freedom is impossible except as a man deprived of life.

If reason sees the concept of freedom as a meaningless contradiction, like the possibility of doing two different things at exactly the same time or something occurring without a cause, this tells us one simple thing: consciousness is not subject to reason.

It is this unwavering, irrepressible consciousness of freedom, not subject to experience or reason, acknowledged by all thinking people and sensed by everybody without exception, this consciousness without which no concept of humanity is imaginable, that constitutes the other side of the question.

Man is the creation of an omnipotent, infinitely good and omniscient God. What is sin, the concept of which flows from man's consciousness of freedom? That is a question for theology.

All human actions are subject to universal and immutable laws which can be expressed in statistics. What is social responsibility, the concept of which flows from consciousness of freedom? That is a question for jurisprudence.

A man's actions flow from his innate character and motivation. What is conscience and the sense of right and wrong in relation to actions that flow from the consciousness of freedom? That is a question for ethics.

Man in connection with the life of humanity in general appears to be governed by laws determining that life. But the same man without that connection appears to be free. How are we to look on the past life of nations and humanity, as the product of activity by people who are free or not free? That is a question for history.

Only in our age of arrogance and the popularization of knowledge, thanks to that most powerful weapon of ignorance, the spread of the printed word, has the question of free will been transferred to new terrain where it cannot continue to exist as a question. In our day most of the so-called advanced people – nothing but a bunch of ignoramuses – have accepted the research of the natural scientists, which is only interested in one side of the question, as a solution to the question as a whole.

There is no soul and no free will, because the life of man is expressed in muscular movements, and muscular movements are conditioned by activity in the nervous system. There is no soul and no free will, because at some unknown period of time we descended from the apes. This is what they are saying, writing and printing, and it never even crosses their mind that thousands of years ago all religions and all thinkers were ready to acknowledge – in fact, they have never denied it – the very law of necessity which they are now trying so hard to prove by physiology and comparative zoology. They cannot see that the only thing the natural sciences can do for this question is to throw light on one side of it. For even if we can show empirically that reason and will are nothing but secretions of the brain, and man has followed a universal law of evolution by managing to develop from the lower animals at some unknown period of time, all of this will only give us a new angle on a truth which has been recognized for thousands of years by all religious and philosophic theories, that from the standpoint of reason man is subject to the laws of necessity; it does not contribute one iota to the solution of the problem, which has another side, diametrically opposite, based on the consciousness of freedom.

If men did descend from the apes at an unknown period of time, that is as intelligible as the idea that they were formed from a handful of earth at a known period of time (in the first case, X, the unknown quantity, stands for the date, in the second it stands for the method of formation), and the problem of reconciling man's consciousness of free will with the overriding law of necessity cannot be solved by comparative physiology and zoology, for one good reason: in the frog, the rabbit, and the monkey we can observe nothing but muscular and nervous activity, whereas in man we have muscular and nervous activity plus consciousness.

The natural scientists and their followers who think they are in the process of solving this problem are like plasterers commissioned to plaster one side of a church wall, who, in a rush of enthusiasm while the foreman is away, go on to plaster over the windows, the holy icons, the woodwork and the walls waiting to be buttressed, happy that from a plasterer's point of view everything has turned out so beautifully smooth and even.

CHAPTER 9

In solving the problem of free will versus necessity history has one advantage over the other branches of knowledge that have dealt with this question: for the purposes of history the problem concerns not the essential nature of man's will but the actual manifestation of that will in the past under certain specific conditions.

In attempting to solve this problem, history's position vis-à-vis the other sciences is the same as the relationship between applied and theoretical science.

History takes as its subject not the will of man, but our representation of that will.

So, the insoluble mystery of reconciling two opposites, freedom and necessity, does not exist for history as it does for theology, ethics and philosophy. History examines manifestations of human life in which these two opposites have already been reconciled.

In real life every historical event, every human action, is spelt out and understood, with no sense of contradiction, despite the fact that every event appears to be partly free, and partly determined by necessity.

To solve the problem of reconciling freedom and necessity and deciding on the essence of these two concepts, the philosophy of history can and must move in the opposite direction to that of the other sciences. Instead of first defining the actual concepts of freedom and necessity and then arranging living phenomena according to these definitions, history has to define the concepts of free will and necessity in among the vast multiplicity of relevant phenomena that are always dependent on free will and necessity.

However carefully we examine any representation of the activity of one man or several persons, we always regard it as having been produced by a combination of free will and the laws of necessity.

Whether we are discussing people migrating and vandals attacking, or decisions taken by Napoleon III, or the action taken by a man only an hour ago when he preferred one walk to all the others, we see nothing contradictory in any of this. The degree of freedom and necessity directing the actions of these men has been clearly defined for us.

It happens all too often that our concept of a greater or lesser amount of freedom varies according to our different attitudes to an event, but every human action unfailingly appears to us as a kind of compromise between free will and necessity. In every action examined we see a certain amount of freedom and a certain amount of necessity. And the same thing always happens: the more freedom we see in any action, the less necessity there is, and the greater the necessity the smaller the amount of freedom.

The proportions of freedom and necessity will rise and fall according to one's attitude to the event, but there is always an inverse ratio between them.

A drowning man who clutches at another drowning man and drags him under, or a starving mother weakened by feeding her baby who steals some food, or a man drilled and disciplined who obeys an order to kill a defenceless man in the course of duty – these people will all seem less guilty, in other words less free and more subject to the law of necessity, to anyone who knows their circumstances, and more free to anyone who did not know the man himself was drowning, the mother was starving, the soldier was on duty and so on. In the same way a man who committed a murder twenty years ago and has gone on living calmly and innocently in society ever since will seem less guilty, and what he did will seem more subject to the law of necessity, to anyone looking back on it after a lapse of twenty years than to someone looking at the same deed the day after it was done. And again, anything done by a madman, a man who was drunk or a violently excited man will seem less free and more inevitable to anyone who knows the mental state of the man who did the deed, and more free and less inevitable to someone who doesn't. In each case the concept of freedom increases or diminishes, and the concept of necessity diminishes or increases, according to the onlooker's point of view. The greater the necessity, the less freedom there is, and vice versa.

Religion, everyday common sense, the science of jurisprudence and history itself share the same understanding of this relationship between necessity and free will.

In every single case, where our concept of free will and necessity increases or diminishes there are only three basic variable entities:

1. The relationship between the man committing the act and the external world.
2. His relationship to time.
3. The relationship between him and the causes which led to the act.

The first variable (1) concerns the greater or lesser clarity with which we see the man's relation to the external world, the greater or lesser clarity of his particular situation in relation to everything existing along with him at the time. It is this point that makes it obvious that a drowning man is less free and more subject to necessity than a man standing on terra firma; it makes the actions of a man living in close contact with other people under crowded conditions, a man bound by ties of family, service or business, seem undoubtedly less free and more subject to necessity than those of a man living in solitude and seclusion.

If we study one man on his own, removed from his surroundings, all of his actions will seem to be free. But if we see the slightest relationship between him and his surroundings, if we see him in contact with anything at all, a man talking to him, a book that he is reading, a job that he is busy with, even the air he breathes or the light that falls on the objects around him, we shall soon see that every one of these circumstances has some kind of influence on him, and determines at least one aspect of his behaviour. And the more we take account of these influences, the more our perception of his freedom is reduced, and our concept of his being subject to necessity is increased.

The second variable (2) is the greater or lesser extent of a man's visible temporal relationship with the world, and the greater or lesser clarity by which we perceive the place in time occupied by his action. Because of this variable the fall of the first man, which led to the origin of the human race, stands out rather obviously as less free than the act of getting married is for a man of today. Because of this variable, the lives and actions of men who lived centuries ago and have a temporal connection with me cannot seem to me as free as the life of a contemporary, with all its consequences still unknown.

In the present case, this variability, our concept of greater or lesser freedom or necessity, will depend on the greater or lesser time-lapse between the action and our judgement of it.

If I examine something I did a moment ago in virtually the same circumstances that I am still in, there can be no doubt that my action appears to have been free. But if I start to pass judgement on something I did a month ago, now that my circumstances have changed I am bound to recognize that if that deed had not been done many of its beneficial, agreeable and even inevitable consequences would never have taken place. And if I allow memory to take me back even further to something I did ten years ago or more, the consequences of my action are even clearer but it will be difficult for me to imagine what might have happened if it had not taken place. The further back I go in memory, or, to put it another way, the longer I postpone judgement of my action, the more dubious my view of its freedom becomes.

The same variable degree of certainty about the role of free will in the general run of human affairs applies also to history. An event occurring in the present day appears beyond doubt to be the product of all the people known to have been concerned in it. But when it comes to an event more distant in time we can't help seeing its inevitable consequences, and this prevents us from imagining any other possibilities. And the further back we go in our examination of events, the less spontaneous they seem to have been.

The Austro-Prussian war appears beyond doubt to have been caused by the actions of that cunning man Bismarck, and so on.

The Napoleonic wars are a little more dubious, though they still seem to have been the consequences of heroes exercising their will. But in the Crusades we see an event with a clearly defined place in history, and without it the modern history of Europe is inconceivable, though the chroniclers of the Crusades saw those events as the direct consequences of a few persons exercising their will. And as for the migration of peoples, it never occurs to anybody nowadays that the renewal of the European world depended on an idea plucked out of the air by Attila the Hun. The further back we go with our studies of history, the more dubious is the concept of people determining events by the exercise of free will, and the more obvious the law of necessity becomes.

The third variable (3) is the greater or lesser degree to which we can apprehend that endless chain of causation demanded by our reason, in which every phenomenon, if it is to be properly understood, and therefore every human action, must have its own specific place, as a consequence of past actions and a cause of those to come.

It is this that makes our own actions and those of other people appear, on the one hand, all the freer and less subject to necessity the more we know of the physiological, psychological and historical laws deduced from observation as applicable to mankind, and the more thoroughly we have scrutinized the physiological, psychological or historical cause of an action, and, on the other hand, the simpler the action observed and the more straightforward the character and mind of the man whose action we are examining.

When we simply do not know the cause of an action – a crime, a good deed or something that has nothing to do with right and wrong – we put it down to maximum free will. In the case of a crime we particularly demand that it be punished; in the case of a good deed, we are especially appreciative of what was done. And when the action has nothing to do with right and wrong we think of it in terms of maximum individuality, originality and independence. But if a single one of the innumerable causes of the action is known to us, we allow for a certain element of necessity, we are less keen on retribution for a crime, less appreciative of merit in a good deed, less ready to acknowledge free will in relation to an action of ostensible originality. The fact that a criminal was brought up among villains mitigates his guilt. The self-sacrifice of a father, or a mother, or self-sacrifice with a view to possible reward is more comprehensible than gratuitous self-sacrifice, and therefore appears less deserving of sympathy and less the product of free will. The founder of a sect, or a party, or an inventor, appears less impressive once we understand the ins and outs of all the preparatory work that preceded his activity. If we conduct a whole series of experiments, and if our observation is constantly focused on a search for correspondence between the causes and effects of men's actions, the actions themselves will appear to be more determined by necessity and less by free will, the better we succeed in the linking of cause and effect. If the actions examined are simple ones, and we have a vast number of such actions available for study, our impression of their inevitability will be all the more completely confirmed. A dishonest deed by the son of a dishonest father, the bad behaviour of a woman who has drifted into certain company, the recidivism of a reformed drunkard, and so on – these are all actions which appear to be less freely determined the better we understand the reason behind them. And if the man whose behaviour we are studying happens to be someone at the lowest level of mental development, like a child, a madman or a simpleton, then, fully apprised of the reasons behind his actions and his simplicity of character and intelligence, we observe in all of this such a huge amount of necessity and so little free will that once we know the cause the action becomes predictable.

These three variable entities alone account for the concept of unfitness to plead, which exists in all legislative codes, and the idea of extenuating circumstances. The degree of accountability will be considered greater or lesser according to our greater or lesser knowledge of the circumstances experienced by the man under judgement, the greater or lesser time-lapse between his committing the crime and being brought to justice, and our greater or lesser understanding of the causes behind the action.

CHAPTER 10

Thus our sensation of free will and necessity gradually contracts or expands according to the greater or lesser degree of association with the external world, the greater or lesser degree of remoteness in time, and the greater or lesser degree of dependence on the causes through which we examine the phenomenon of a human life.

It follows that if we consider the situation of a man with maximum known association with the external world, a maximum time-lapse between his action and any judgement of it and maximum access to the causes behind his action, we get an impression of maximum necessity and minimal free will. Whereas if we consider a man with minimal dependence on external circumstances, whose action has been committed at the nearest possible moment to the present, and for reasons beyond our ken, then we get an impression of minimal necessity and maximum freedom of action.

But in neither case, however much we vary our standpoint, however much we clarify the man's association with the external world, however accessible we think this is, however much we lengthen or shorten the time-lapse, however understandable or opaque the reasons behind his action may appear to be, can we ever have any concept of absolute freedom of action or absolute necessity.

(1) However hard we try to imagine a man excluded from any influence of the external world, we can never achieve a concept of freedom in space. A man's every action is inevitably conditioned by what surrounds him, and his own body. I raise my arm and let it fall again. My action seems to be free, but when I start wondering whether I could have raised my arm in any direction, I notice that I moved it in the direction where the action encountered least resistance from any surrounding bodies or from my own bodily structure. If I chose one particular direction out of all those available I did so because in that direction I encountered least resistance. For my action to be completely free it would have to have encountered no resistance at all. In order to imagine a man who was completely free we would have to imagine him existing beyond space, an obvious impossibility.

(2) However much we shorten the time-lapse between action and judgement, we could never arrive at a concept of freedom within time. For if I examine an action performed only one second ago, I must still acknowledge it to be unfree, since the action is locked into the moment when it was performed. Can I lift my arm? I do lift it, but this sets me wondering: could I have decided not to lift my arm in that moment of time that has just gone by? To convince myself that I could, I do not lift my arm the next moment. But the non-lifting of my arm did not happen at that first moment when I was wondering about freedom. Time has gone by which I had no power to detain, and the hand which I lifted then and the air through which I lifted it are no longer the same as the air which now surrounds me and the hand that I now decide not to move. The moment when the first movement occurred is irrevocable, and at that moment there was only one action I could have performed, and whatever movement I made, that movement was the only one possible. The fact that the very next moment I decided not to lift my arm did not prove that I had the power not to lift it. And since there was only one possible movement for me at that one moment in time, it couldn't have been any other movement. In order to think of it as a free movement, it would have to be imagined as

existing in the present on the very edge where past and future meet, which means beyond time, and that is impossible.

(3) However much we build up the difficulty of pinning down causes we can never arrive at a concept of complete freedom, the total absence of any cause. However elusive the cause behind an active expression of free will, our own or somebody else's, the first demand of an intelligent mind is to look for an assumed cause, without which no phenomenon is conceivable. I raise my arm in order to perform an action independent of any cause, but my wish to perform an action without a cause is the cause of my action.

But even if we could imagine a man excluded from all outside influence and examine one momentary action of his, performed in the present and unprovoked by any cause, thus reducing the infinitely small amount of necessity to zero, even then we would not have achieved a concept of complete free will in a man, because a creature impervious to all outside worldly influence, existing beyond time, and with no dependence on cause, is no longer a man.

In just the same way we could never conceive of a human action lacking any element of free will and entirely subject to the law of necessity.

(1) However much we expand our knowledge of the spatial conditions in which mankind dwells, such knowledge could never become complete since the number of these conditions is infinitely great, because space itself is inifinite. And as long as it remains true that not *all* the conditions that could influence a man can be defined, there can be no such thing as total necessity and there is always a certain amount of free will.

(2) However much we extend the time-lapse between an action under examination and our judgement of it, the period itself will be finite, whereas time is infinite, so here is another sense in which there can be no such thing as absolute necessity.

(3) However accessible the chain of causation behind a given action, we can never know the whole chain, because it is infinitely long, so once again we cannot attain absolute necessity.

And beyond that, even if we reduced the minimal amount of free will to zero by acknowledging its total absence in some cases – a dying man, an unborn baby, or an idiot – in the process of doing so we should have destroyed the very concept of what it is to be human, which is what we are examining, because once there is no free will, there is no man. And therefore the idea of a human action subject only to the law of necessity and devoid of all free will is just as impossible as the idea of a completely free human action.

Thus in order to imagine a human action subject only to the law of necessity and lacking all freedom, we would have to postulate know-ledge of an *infinite* number of spatial conditions, an *infinitely* long period of time and an *infinite* line of causation.

And in order to imagine a man who was perfectly free and not subject to the law of necessity, we would have to imagine a man who existed *beyond space, beyond time, and beyond all dependence on cause.*

In the first case, if necessity was possible without free will, we would have to define the law of necessity in terms of necessity itself, which means form without content.

In the second case, if free will was possible without necessity, we would arrive at unconditional free will existing beyond space, time and cause, which by its own unconditional and limitless nature would amount to nothing but content without form.

In general terms, we would have arrived at two fundamentals under-lying the entire world view of humanity – the unknowable essence of life and the laws that determine that essence.

Reason tells us: (1) Space and all the forms that give it visibility, matter itself, is infinite, and cannot be imagined otherwise. (2) Time is endless motion without a moment of rest, and cannot be imagined otherwise. (3) The connection between cause and effect has no beginning, and can have no end.

Consciousness tells us: (1) I alone exist, and I am everything that exists; consequently I include space; (2) I measure the course of time by a fixed moment in the present, in which moment alone I am aware of being alive; consequently I am beyond time; and (3) I am beyond cause, since I feel myself to be the cause of my own life in all its manifestations.

Reason gives expression to the laws of necessity. Consciousness gives expression to the essence of free will.

Unlimited freedom is the essence of life in man's consciousness. Necessity without content is human reason in its threefold form.

Free will is what is examined; necessity does the examining. Free will is content; necessity is form.

Only by separating the two sources of cognition, which are like form versus content, do we arrive at the mutually exclusive and separately unimaginable concepts of free will and necessity.

Only by bringing them together again do we arrive at a clear concept of human life.

Beyond these two concepts, which share a mutual definition when brought together, like form and content, there is no other possible representation of life.

All that we know about human life is a certain relationship between free will and necessity, or between consciousness and the laws of reason.

All that we know about the external world of nature is a certain relationship between the forces of nature and necessity, or between the essence of life and the laws of reason.

The forces of life in nature lie beyond us and our cognitive powers, and we put names to these forces: gravity, inertia, electricity, the life force and so on. But the force of life in man is not beyond our cognitive powers, and we call it free will.

But just as the force of gravity, intrinsically unintelligible despite being sensed by everyone, is understandable only in terms of the laws of necessity to which it is subject (from our first awareness that all bodies possess weight to Newton's law), the force of free will is also intrinsically unintelligible but recognized by all and understandable only in terms of the laws of necessity to which it is subject (all the way from the fact that all men die to knowledge of the most complex laws of economics or history).

All knowledge is simply the essence of life subsumed by the laws of reason.

Man's free will differs from all other forces in being accessible to human consciousness, but in the eyes of reason it is no different from any other force.

The forces of gravity, electricity or chemical affinity differ from each other only by being differently defined by reason. Similarly, the force of man's free will is distinguished by reason from the other forces of nature only by the definition assigned to it by reason. And free will divorced from necessity, from the laws of reason by which it is defined, is no different from gravity, heat or the force of organic growth; in the eyes of reason it is only a fleeting and indefinable sensation of life.

And just as the indefinable essence of the force that moves the heavenly bodies, the indefinable essence that drives heat, electricity, chemical affinity or the life force, forms the content of astronomy, physics, chemistry, botany, zoology and so on, the essence of the force of free will forms the subject matter of history. But just as the content of all science is the manifestation of this unknown essence of life, even though the essence itself can only be the subject of metaphysics, so too the manifestation of the force of man's free will in space, in time and in dependence on cause, forms the subject of history, while free will itself remains the subject of metaphysics.

In the biological sciences, what we know, we call the laws of necessity; what we don't know, we call the life force. The life force is simply an expression for an unexplainable leftover from what we know about the essence of life.

It is the same with history: what we know, we call the laws of necessity; what we don't know, we call free will. In the eyes of history free will is simply an expression for an unexplainable leftover from what we know about the laws of human life.

CHAPTER 11

History examines manifestations of human free will in relation to the external world existing in time and dependent on cause; in other words, it defines free will by the laws of reason, which means that history can be considered a science only to the extent that free will can be defined by those laws.

In the eyes of history the acknowledgement of human free will as a force capable of influencing historical events and therefore not subject to any laws is what the acknowledgement of free will in the movements of the heavenly bodies would be to astronomy.

Such an acknowledgement negates any possibility of the existence of laws, or indeed any kind of science. If there is even one freely moving body, the laws of Kepler and Newton go out of existence, along with any representation of the movement of the heavenly bodies. If there is a single human action determined by free will, all historical laws go out of existence, along with any representation of historical events.

For history the free will of human beings consists in lines of movement with one end disappearing into the unknown and the other belonging to the present time as man's consciousness of free will moves along in space and time, fully dependent on cause.

The more this field of movement unfolds before our eyes, the clearer its laws become. The discovery and definition of these laws is the purpose of history.

From the attitude now adopted by the science of history towards its subject matter, from the way it is going at present in looking for ultimate causes in man's free will, no scientific delineation of laws is possible, since, whatever limits we place on human freedom of action, the moment we recognize it as a force not subject to law, the existence of any law becomes impossible.

Only by infinitely limiting this freedom of action, reducing it to an infinitesimal minimum, shall we come to know the absolute impossibility of finding any causes, and then, instead of looking for them, history can set itself the task of looking for laws.

The search for these laws began a long time ago, and the new thinking methods which history has to adopt are being developed today even as the old way of looking at history marches towards self-destruction, still breaking everything down into ever tinier pieces in a vain search for the causes that lie behind things.

All branches of human science have gone the same way. Confronted by infinite smallness, mathematics, the most exact of all the sciences, drops the habit of continual sub-division and enters on a new process of integration of the infinitesimal unknown. Abandoning the concept of causation, mathematics now seeks a new law, a set of properties common to all infinitely small unknown elements.

The other sciences in their different ways have taken the same route. When Newton promulgated the law of gravity, he did not say that either the sun or the earth has the property of attraction. What he said was that all bodies, large and small, seem to have the property of attracting one another; in other words, putting to one side questions about the cause of the movements of bodies, he expressed one property common to all bodies, from the infinitely large to the infinitely small. The natural sciences are doing the same thing as they abandon the question of cause and search for laws. History is beginning to go the same way. And if the subject matter of history really is the study of the movements of peoples and humanity, rather than descriptions of episodes in the lives of individual people, it too is bound to abandon the concept of cause and look for laws that apply to all the equal and inseparably interconnected, infinitesimal elements of free will.

CHAPTER 12

Once the law of Copernicus had been discovered and demonstrated all it took was acknowledgement that the earth moves round the sun rather than vice versa for the entire cosmic view of the ancients to be destroyed. It might have been possible by the refutation of this law to carry on with the old ideas of motion, but in the absence of any such refutation it would seem impossible to carry on studying Ptolemaic worlds. Nevertheless, long after the discovery of the law of Copernicus Ptolemaic worlds continued to be a subject of study.

Once the first person had said and demonstrated that the birth-rate or crime-rate is subject to mathematical laws, that certain geographical and politico-economical laws determine this or that form of government, or that a given relationship between the population and the soil causes mass migration – from that moment the foundations on which history had been built were essentially destroyed.

It might have been possible by the refutation of the new laws to carry on with the former view of history, but in the absence of any such refutation it would seem impossible to carry on studying historical events as if they were the product of man's free will. For if a certain form of government has been set up, or a certain mass movement has taken place as a result of certain geographical, ethnographic or economic conditions, free will on the part of those persons who have been described as setting up that form of government or inspiring the mass migration cannot be regarded as the cause. And yet history goes on being studied in the same old way, in the teeth of laws of statistics, geography, political economy, comparative philology and geology that totally contradict its basic premises.

In the philosophy of physics the struggle between old and new attitudes was long and hard. Theology, the guardian of the old, called the new attitude an offence against divine revelation. But when truth prevailed theology re-established itself just as firmly on new territory.

And now in just the same way a long and hard struggle is being conducted between old and new attitudes to history, and in just the same way theology, guardian of the old, calls the new attitude an offence against revelation.

In both cases and on both sides the struggle arouses deep passions and obscures the truth. On one side fear and regret battle against the demolition of an edifice that has stood for centuries; on the other, there is an intense passion for destruction.

Those who fought against the new truth that was dawning in the philosophy of physics believed that acceptance of this truth would destroy all faith in God, the creation story and the miracle of Joshua.[13] Defenders of the laws of Copernicus and Newton such as Voltaire, for instance, believed that the laws of astronomy would destroy religion, and he used the law of gravity as a weapon against religion.

In just the same way it now seems that once we accept the law of necessity we destroy all concepts of the soul, or good and evil, and all the towering political and ecclesiastical institutions founded on them.

Like Voltaire in his day, the uninvited defenders of the law of necessity use the law of necessity as a weapon against religion, though in fact – like the law of Copernicus in astronomy – the law of necessity in history, far from destroying the foundations on which political and ecclesiastical institutions are constructed, actually strengthens them.

As with astronomy in days gone by, so today in matters of history the conflict of opinion depends on the recognition or non-recognition of an absolute entity for the measurement of visible phenomena. In astronomy it was the earth's immobility; in history it is personal independence, or free will.

Just as in astronomy the problem of recognizing the earth's motion lay in the difficulty of getting away from a direct sensation of the earth's immobility and a similar sensation of the planets' motion, so in history the problem of recognizing the dependence of personality on the laws of space, time and causation lies in the difficulty of getting away from the direct sensation of one's own personal independence. But just as in astronomy the new attitude was, 'No, we cannot feel the earth's movement, but if we accept its immobility we are reduced to absurdity, whereas if we accept the movement that we cannot feel we arrive at laws,' so in history the new attitude is, 'No, we cannot feel our dependence, but if we accept free will we are reduced to absurdity, whereas if we accept dependence on the external world, time and causation we arrive at laws.'

In the first case, we had to get away from a false sensation of immobility in space and accept movement that we could not feel. In the present case it is no less essential to get away from a false sensation of freedom and accept a dependence that we cannot feel.

Notes

VOLUME I

PART I

1. *Genoa and Lucca ... Buonaparte family*: Genoa and Lucca were territories recently annexed by France. Napoleon's Corsican name was Napoleone Buonaparte; the original version (with a 'u') is used here as a deliberate insult.

2. *Novosiltsev's dispatch*: N. N. Novosiltsev was a special ambassador sent to Paris by Emperor Alexander to assist with (ultimately abortive) peace negotiations.

3. *'Oh, don't talk to me about Austria!'*: Only a few weeks earlier (in April 1805) the Third Coalition had been formed between Great Britain, Austria and Russia. Their plan was to defeat Napoleon by means of a three-pronged attack. The Russians had been let down before by the Austrians, and there were many who believed they could not be relied on now.

4. *the hydra of revolution ... murdering villain*: The French Revolution is still fresh in the memory. In its wake revolutionary stirrings were being sensed in other European countries, including Russia. Napoleon, with his common background, seems to embody the new republican spirit which threatens the stability of countries ruled by monarchs.

5. *She has refused to evacuate Malta*: Malta had been taken by Napoleon in 1798, and then captured by the British in 1800. Under the Peace of Amiens Great Britain was due to leave the island, but refused to do so. Russia's offer to mediate between the British and the French was rejected, and the two countries went to war in 1803, with Russia supporting the British against Napoleon.

6. *Wintzengerode*: Many of the characters are real people; the most important ones are identified as 'Historical Figures in *War and Peace*' in 'The Characters' (p. 1372).

7. *Lavater ... paternity bump*: J. K. Lavater (1741–1801) was a Swiss physiognomist, one of the forerunners of phrenology, a pseudo-science

based on the idea that bumps on the skull indicate various mental capacities.

8. *the Duke of Enghien*: The Duke of Enghien was shot by the French in 1804, after being wrongfully accused of plotting to assassinate Napoleon.

9. *Louis XV*: King of France from 1715 until his death in 1774.

10. *the Social Contract*: Jean-Jacques Rousseau's *Contrat Social* (1762), a treatise on government and citizenship, was regarded by some people as a cause of the violent excesses of the French Revolution of 1789.

11. *the 18th Brumaire*: The date on the French Revolutionary Calendar (9 November 1799) of a successful coup, following which Napoleon became First Consul. 'Brumaire' was the second month in the French Revolutionary Calendar, 22 October–20 November. *Brume* is French for 'fog'.

12. *all those prisoners ... killed in Africa*: A reference to Napoleon's authorization of the brutal killing of 3,000 Turkish prisoners at Jaffa in September 1799.

13. *Jacobin*: Popular name for one of the French revolutionary societies, which met in the hall of a Jacobin convent.

14. *Napoleon on the bridge at Arcola ... plague-victims*: At Arcola in 1796, leading the French against the Austrians, Napoleon had risked his life by rushing on to a bridge carrying a flag. In Jaffa in 1799 he had taken another risk by visiting a plague hospital.

15. *Caesar's Commentaries*: Julius Caesar's *Commentaries on the Gallic War*, one of the foundation stones of military history written by a highly successful general.

16. *a freemason*: Freemasons were a byword for liberal thinking, but were also regarded by the authorities as proto-revolutionaries. It isn't clear here which way Pierre is thinking.

17. *typical of Petersburg in June*: It is actually July; Tolstoy must mean it is like the best nights in June.

18. *name-day*: A saint's day celebrated by Russians who were named after that particular saint, here St Natalya's Day.

19. *Catherine's time*: Catherine the Great was Empress of Russia from 1762 to 1796.

20. *Salomoni*: An Italian opera-singer resident in Russia and appearing with a touring German company in the winter of 1805–6.

21. *Madame de Genlis*: Félicité Ducrest de Saint-Aubin (1746–1830), a French writer of popular romances with strong moral content, a byword with the children for boring grown-up repectability.

22. *Count Orlov*: Count Alexey Orlov was a popular and generous Moscow grandee, famous for his lavish hospitality and entertainment.

23. *errare humanum est*: It is human to err (Latin).

24. *his last duty*: This duty is to receive extreme unction, be anointed with consecrated oil by a priest.

25. *Mr Pitt*: William Pitt (1759–1806), one of Britain's finest prime ministers, was a bitter opponent of the French Revolution and now of Napoleon.

26. *Boulogne expedition . . . Villeneuve*: At this time Napoleon was gathering his forces at Boulogne, on the English Channel, in preparation for an invasion of England. Admiral Pierre-Charles de Villeneuve (1763–1806) was ordered to leave the Mediterranean and join them. In the event Villeneuve was blockaded, and Napoleon's navy was destroyed at the Battle of Trafalgar.

27. *a thousand roubles to get Taras*: Even by Count Rostov's extravagant standards this is a very large sum of money, which suggests that the serf, Taras, must have had special training under a French chef.

28. *boston*: A popular variation of whist.

29. *Cossack*: The Cossacks were free peasants living in southern Russia, renowned for their wild behaviour. The countess is virtually (and affectionately) calling her a little savage.

30. *Suvorov*: A. S. Suvorov (1729–1800), a Russian general who, after many successful campaigns, ended his career in ignominious retreat over the Alps from Italy into Austria (1799).

31. *'The Spring'*: A song dubiously attributed to Mozart that Tolstoy used to sing to his pupils.

32. *Nikolay's my cousin*: The Russian Orthodox Church normally prohibited marriage between first cousins, though this prohibition could sometimes be circumvented by obtaining special permission.

33. *écossaise . . . Daniel Cooper . . . anglaise*: The 'écossaise' is a lively country dance (not to be confused with the 'schottische' (German – both mean 'Scottish'), which is a round dance akin to the polka) in which the performers stand opposite each other, often in couples. 'Anglaise' is a vague term often applied in the eighteenth and nineteenth centuries to country dances of putative English character. It allowed for many variations, of which the 'Daniel Cooper' was one.

34. *'Our eagle!'*: Peasant language, and Russian folklore, often used birds – eagle, falcon, dove, etc. – as terms of endearment or pride in family members.

35. *Voltaire armchair*: A deep chair with a high back associated with the French writer and historian F. M. Arouet (Voltaire) (1694–1778).

36. *the reign of Paul*: Catherine was succeeded by her son Paul. His short reign (1796–1801) ended by his being murdered in a palace coup.

37. *'From your Héloïse?'*: An ironical reference to the heroine of Rousseau's novel, *Julie, ou La Nouvelle Héloïse*, which the prince regards as romantic nonsense. The ensuing correspondence between Princess Marya and Julie Karagin is based on 'a whole volume' of similar letters exchanged between two friends, M. A. Volkova and V. I. Lanskaya, which Tolstoy read in manuscript in 1863.

38. *a new book with uncut pages*: The book has come from the publisher

with the folded leaves untrimmed. Thus the first reader uses a page-knife to slit them open.

39. *A Key to the Mystery*: K. Eckartshausen's mystical work, *A Key to the Mysteries of Nature*, was popular in Russia at the time, and widely read by freemasons.

40. *the Great Century*: The French term 'Le Grand Siècle' meant the age of Louis XIV (1638–1715), King of France (1643–1715). Here it is loosely applied by the Russians to the age of Catherine the Great.

41. *it is easier for a camel ... kingdom of God*: Quoted from Matthew 19:24 and Mark 10:25.

42. *a Dussek sonata*: Jan Ladislav Dussek, born in Bohemia in 1760 and died near Paris in 1812, enjoyed great popularity in Europe as a first-rate pianist and composer of piano pieces.

43. *Mikhelson's army, and Tolstoy's*: The old prince refers to a plan for attacking the French from three sides at once, Generals Mikhelson and Tolstoy commanding two of the armies involved.

44. *Marlborough ... God knows when we'll see him*: A French comic song that became popular early in the eighteenth century, when the Duke of Marlborough led the English army in several campaigns against the French.

45. *Rurik*: A Scandinavian prince, who, according to legend, came down to Novgorod in the ninth century and founded the Russian state.

46. *Potyomkins*: G. A. Potyomkin (1739–91) was a famous Russian army commander of the late eighteenth century.

47. *Hofs-kriegs-wurst-schnapps-rath*: Court-war-sausage-schnapps-council (German). This is the prince's ironical version of the name bestowed on the Austrian War Council.

48. *Ochakov*: A fortress, at the mouth of the Dnieper, successfully stormed by General Suvorov during the Russo-Turkish war of 1787–91.

49. *Zubov ... false teeth*: There is an easy pun here on the Russian word *zub*, which means tooth.

PART II

1. *11th of October 1805*: Until 1918 Russia used the Julian Calendar, as opposed to the Gregorian Calendar universally accepted today. At this period Julian (or 'Old Style') dates lagged behind Gregorian (or 'New Style') dates by a difference of twelve days. The dates used throughout *War and Peace* are predominantly Old Style.

2. *Tsaritsyn Field*: Tsar's Field, soon to be renamed 'The Field of Mars', was in Petersburg.

3. *Bacchus*: The Roman god of wine.

4. *leg-bands*: Soldiers, like peasants, did not wear socks; they were issued with strips of cloth for use as foot-bindings.

5. *Got a move on then, didn't we?*: Neither the Russian nor the Austrian

army had hurried into position, believing Napoleon to be busy with preparations for the invasion of England. When the news came through that Napoleon was already at the Rhine it was essential to speed up the movement of the Russians, so they were supplied with carts, which doubled the rate of their advance.

6. *doppel-kümmel*: A strong liqueur flavoured with cumin and caraway seeds (German).

7. *shakos*: Tall, nearly cylindrical military caps with plumes.

8. *sabretache*: Flat ornamental bag slung from a cavalry officer's sword belt.

9. *Campo Formio*: The little town where the French and the Austrians signed the peace treaty (17 October 1797) which ended Napoleon's successful campaign in Italy.

10. *Demosthenes . . . golden mouth*: According to legend the Greek orator Demosthenes (383–322 BC) corrected a speech impediment by practising oratory with a pebble in his mouth.

11. *all three are Gascons*: The Gascons were renowned for their clever talk and boasting.

12. *Napoleon rose from obscurity at Toulon*: During the siege of Toulon, a royalist stronghold, in 1793, Napoleon commanded the republican artillery with distinction and gained his first significant promotion to brigadier-general, at the age of twenty-four.

13. *Chasseurs*: Cavalry.

PART III

1. *state councillor*: The Russian civil service was divided into eleven ranks, the top eight of which conferred hereditary nobility. A state councillor occupied the fifth rank and was entitled to be addressed as 'your Worship'.

2. *Emperor Alexander's visit to Potsdam*: In October 1805 Alexander I had gone to Berlin to solicit Friedrich Wilhelm III's support in opposing Napoleon. Their secret agreement signed at Potsdam was overtaken by events on the battlefield.

3. *Paris possessing his Helen*: In Greek legend Paris, the son of Priam (King of Troy), precipitated the siege of Troy by abandoning his wife, Oenone, and abducting the beautiful Helen.

4. *petizanfan, alley cooshey dormir*: Phonetic version of the French '*petits enfants, allez coucher dormir*' ('off you go to bed, little children').

VOLUME II

PART I

1. *Will you call her 'tu' or 'vous'*: Russian is like French in using the second person plural in a formal situation and the second person singular between intimates. Sonya and Nikolay are at that delicate stage when it might, or might not, be appropriate to advance their relationship from the former to the latter.

2. *Duport*: Louis Duport (1782–1853), a celebrated French ballet-master currently enjoying great popularity in Russia.

3. *the Arkharovs' ball*: The Arkharovs were a real-life Moscow family, very rich and famed for their lavish hospitality.

4. *Sing hymns . . . fight us*: These execrable verses by N. P. Nikolev were declaimed at a real-life banquet in honour of Bagration.

5. *Pavel Ivanovich Golenishchev-Kutuzov*: Golenishchev-Kutuzov was present at the real-life occasion, handing out copies of his verses, no less execrable than those of Nikolev.

6. *How the devil . . . mess like that?*: Géronte's repeated question in *Les Fourberies de Scapin* (1671), 'Mais que diable allait-il faire dans cette galère?', had become proverbial in Russia.

7. *frustik*: *Frühstück* is German for breakfast.

8. *when they had dropped . . . surface of the water*: At baptism in the Russian Orthodox Church a little of the child's hair is cut off and pressed into wax. If it floats rather than sinks in the font this is regarded as a good omen.

9. *the talk was of war with Napoleon . . . last year*: During the autumn of 1806 Napoleon, with two major victories behind him at Jena and Auerstadt, appeared to pose a direct threat to the borders of Russia. More than half a million men were conscripted into the army.

10. *piquet*: A two-handed card game played with a reduced pack of thirty-two cards.

11. *corner there*: Dolokhov and Rostov are adversaries in the game of faro (the game played by Herman in Pushkin's and Tchaikovsky's *Queen of Spades*). Bending down the corner of a card indicated a doubling of the stake.

PART II

1. *Madame de Souza*: Adelaide Filleul de Souza (1761–1836), a writer of sentimental romances set in eighteenth-century aristocratic French society.

2. *freemasonry*: Freemasonry on the Anglo-Scottish model was introduced into Russia in 1761. Although seen as subversive and frequently

suppressed, it was undergoing a period of prosperity under Alexander I.

3. *a leading freemason and Martinist since the days of Novikov*: The Martinists were a branch of Russian freemasonry founded in 1780, taking their name from L. C. de Saint Martin, a noted theosophist. N. I. Novikov (1744–1818) was a satirical journalist and freemason who had been imprisoned under Catherine the Great for his outspoken anti-government opinions.

4. *a volume of Thomas à Kempis*: This would have been *Imitation of Christ* (1426), a highly influential religious treatise commonly attributed to Thomas à Kempis (*c.* 1380–1471). Mystical in tone, it explores the inner life and the value of contemplation.

5. *Sic transit gloria mundi*: Thus the glory of the world passes away.

6. *Marat*: Jean-Paul Marat (1743–93) was a Swiss-born French politician, active in republican and revolutionary circles.

7. *Hard luck . . . George Dandin*: A well-known quotation from Molière's comedy *George Dandin* (1668).

8. *a joke he had heard in Vienna*: According to a current French idiom 'to do something for the King of Prussia' meant 'to get nothing but trouble for your pains'.

9. *Count Buxhöwden*: The Russian general left in charge of the allied forces after the battle of Austerlitz.

10. *complete liberation of his peasants from serf rule*: Pierre is an early reformer in freeing his serfs; the serf system would survive officially in Russia until 1861.

11. *this is Herder's doctrine*: J. G. Herder (1744–1803) was a German historian and philosopher who argued the merits of intuition and irrationalism.

12. *Platov's division*: General M. I. Platov (1751–1818) was a distinguished Cossack commander who had served alongside Suvorov and Kutuzov.

13. *the battle of Friedland*: This was fought in East Prussia on 14 June 1807. The French, with their superior artillery, defeated the Russians.

PART III

1. *Speransky*: Count M. M. Speransky (1772–1839) was a close adviser to Alexander I on home affairs. He was a would-be reformer, but his ideas offended the conservative aristocracy, and he was dismissed in 1812.

2. *Montesquieu*: Baron de la Brède et de Charles Louis de Secondat (1689–1755) was a French lawyer, philosopher and man of letters whose most famous work, *L'Esprit des lois* (1748), analyses the relationship between human and natural law.

3. *Illuminism*: A secret, pseudoscientific movement of the late eighteenth

century founded in Germany. Among its wide-ranging beliefs was a clear strain of republicanism, which led to its suppression.

4. *Finnish campaign*: Russia occupied Finland in February–May 1808. At home the war was unpopular.

5. '*ein Mann zu sein*': 'Being a man'.

6. *a brother killed in Turkey*: Russia had been at war with Turkey on and off since 1806 and hostilities would continue until 1812.

PART IV

1. *pas de châle*: A French shawl dance, given here as an example of Natasha's training in western formal dance routines.

2. *fetch me a cockerel ... oats*: This would be for fortune-telling based on the way the fowl pecked up the oats.

3. *The Water-Carrier*: This is a reference to Cherubini's opera *Les Deux Journées* (1804).

4. *my favourite nocturne, the one by Mr Field*: Born in Dublin in 1782, John Field settled in Russia and died in Moscow 1837. A composer of piano music, he devised the style and name of the nocturne, handing it on to its greatest exponent, Chopin.

PART V

1. *the Astraea lodge ... the 'Manna Seekers'*: Masonic lodges in Petersburg.

2. *Napoleon's seizure ... sent to every European court*: The seizure of the Duchy of Oldenburg in north-west Germany in 1810 was a breach of the Tilsit agreement. Tsar Alexander circulated a strong protest against it.

3. *Peter the Great's old cudgel*: Peter the Great, Tsar 1682–1725, oversaw Russia's emergence as a major European power. Despite introducing many reforms, Peter was an authoritarian ruler who imposed swift, often cruel, punishments on all wrongdoers.

4. *Mademoiselle George*: A French actress, whose real name was Marguerite-Joséphine Weimer (1787–1867), celebrated for her beauty and accomplished performances on stage.

5. *they all sat down*: It is still a Russian tradition to sit down for a few moments of reflection before starting out on a journey.

VOLUME III

PART I

1. *Continental System*: An embargo on trade with England announced by Napoleon in 1806 and imposed on all of Europe.

2.   *Metternich, Rumyantsev or Talleyrand*: Prince Clemens von Metternich (1773–1859) was the Austrian Foreign Minister; Count N. P. Rumyantsev (1754–1826) was a Russian diplomat; Charles Maurice de Talleyrand Périgord (1754–1838) was a French statesman and Foreign Minister (1797–1807), who opposed Napoleon's Russian campaign.

3.   *Each of the three armies*: The western army under Barclay de Tolly (1761–1818), the southern one under Bagration (1765–1812) and a reserve force being built up near the Austrian frontier.

4.   *Shishkov*: The conservative Admiral Shishkov had replaced Speransky as Foreign Secretary.

5.   *The King of Naples*: General Joachim Murat had been appointed King of Naples by Napoleon in 1808.

6.   *Bal-macheve*: This mispronunciation of Balashev's not-too-difficult name has an amusing ring, suggesting 'a ball (bullet) that finishes me off' ('balle m'achève').

7.   *Bernadotte*: Jean Baptiste Bernadotte (1763–1844) founded the Swedish royal family in 1818 as Karl XIV. In 1812 he was crown prince.

8.   *the road to Poltava chosen by Charles XII*: A century before, in 1709, Charles XII of Sweden had invaded Russia only to be roundly defeated by Peter the Great.

9.   *Thermopylae*: A narrow pass in eastern Greece, the scene of a famous defence by Leonidas during the Persian invasion of 480 BC.

10.   *champignon ... German toadstool*: *Champignon* is French for mushroom.

11.   *Tsar-Cannon*: A huge cannon (Tsar'-Pushka), which still stands in the Kremlin.

PART II

1.   *Lyubomirsky, Bronnitsky, Wlocki*: Polish adjutants-general serving in the Russian army during 1812.

2.   *Dessalles looked in amazement ... already at the Dnieper*: Vitebsk and the river Dnieper are 300 miles east of the Niemen.

3.   *Vasily Pushkin*: (1779–1837), a poetaster of average merit, is not to be confused with his nephew, Alexander Pushkin (1799–1837), Russia's greatest poet.

4.   *Charon's ferry*: In classical Greek myth Charon ferried the dead over the river Styx into Elysium, the abode of the blessed.

5.   *a huge balloon that was being built by Leppich*: Franz Leppich was the constructor of an expensive balloon intended for use against the French, which failed while being tested.

6.   *here that the whole battle ... took place*: Tolstoy drew up his own sketch map after consulting Russian and French historians, and also

visiting the actual territory at Borodino, and included it here in his text.

7.   *Marin . . . Gerakov*: S. N. Marin and G. V. Gerakov were two minor writers. Here, the former adds to the many parodies of the latter's work.

PART III

1.   *Columbus's egg*: A trick that is easy once you know how to do it. Legend has it that Columbus, riled by the charge that anyone could have discovered America, once asked the company how to make an egg stand on end. When nobody could do it he tapped one end of an egg against the table and stood it up, showing how easy things can be once a pioneer has led the way.

2.   *boyars*: The boyars had been the Tsar's right-hand men in medieval Russia. The title had been abolished almost a century before, and Napoleon's repeated use of the term is an ironic indicator of his ignorance.

3.   *attempt on Napoleon's life in Vienna in 1809*: Friedrich Staps failed in an attempt to stab Napoleon outside the Schönbrünn Palace in October 1809, and was summarily executed.

4.   *the business of the 7th of September*: That is, the battle of Borodino. Ramballe is using the New Style date.

5.   *Talma, la Duchénois, Potier, the Sorbonne*: Talma was a celebrated tragedienne, la Duchénois a popular actress and Potier a well-known comedian. The Sorbonne, the University of Paris, founded in the mid-thirteenth century, had been closed down in 1792.

VOLUME IV

PART I

1.   *the possible implications of the words, 'Natasha is nursing him'*: Under Russian Church law a man could not marry his sister-in-law; Nikolay and Princess Marya would therefore be unable to get married if Prince Andrey were to survive and marry Natasha.

2.   *Fraula and Laura*: The martyred brothers Florus and Laurus (third century AD), beatified in the Russian Orthodox Church, became the patron saints of horses for the peasants, who mispronounced their names.

PART IV

1.   *Sir Robert Wilson's Diary*: Sir Robert Wilson (1774–1849) was Britain's military commissioner in Russia during the period 1812–14.

His *Private Diary* was fresh in Tolstoy's mind, having been published in 1861.

2.   *Vive Henri Quatre . . . à quatre*: 'Long live Henry IV, that valiant king, that devil with four . . .'

3.   *Qui eut . . . vert gallant*: 'Who had a threefold talent, for drinking, fighting and being a ladies' man'.

EPILOGUE

PART I

1.   *Seven years had passed*: the story ended in 1813; it is now 1820.

2.   *Photius, Schelling, Fichte, Chateaubriand*: Photius (1792–1838), the conservative-minded head of the Novgorod monastery, castigator of freemasonry and all forms of liberalism. Friedrich Wilhelm Joseph von Schelling (1775–1854), a German philosopher who saw nature as a single organism working towards self-consciousness and art as a vital part of this process. Johann Gottlieb Fichte (1762–1814), a German Idealist philosopher and political thinker whose early enthusiasm for the French Revolution developed into strong condemnation of Napoleon. François René Vicomte de Chateaubriand (1768–1848), a French writer and statesman who spent much of his life abroad, supported the restoration of the French monarchy and refused to serve under Napoleon.

3.   *gave Poland a constitution*: Following the Congress of Vienna (1815) Poland was re-established as a country with its own constitution.

4.   *the Holy Alliance*: An alliance founded in 1815 between Austria, Prussia and Russia as a means of guaranteeing peace; it soon became an instrument of political repression.

5.   *Golitsyn*: Prince A. N. Golitsyn (1773–1844), Minister of Education and Spiritual Affairs under Alexander I, head of the Bible Society, was charged with implementing the increasingly reactionary principles of the Holy Alliance.

6.   *Shishkov*: Admiral A. S. Shishkov (1754–1841), President of the Russian Academy (1813–41), a keen Slavophile opposed to any reform of the Russian language.

7.   *Semyonovsky regiment*: This famous regiment, founded by Peter the Great in 1687, was disbanded by Alexander I in 1820 following a mutinous protest against a German commander, with cruel punishments meted out to its members.

8.   *fifty years ago: War and Peace* was completed in 1869.

9.   *posted to Turkey*: In 1795 Napoleon applied unsuccessfully for a posting in Turkey for the purpose of reorganizing the Sultan's artillery.

10.   *During the wars in Italy . . . while he is still there*: By the time General

Suvorov entered northern Italy and defeated the French in 1799 Napoleon had left for Egypt.

11. *Not unto us . . . but unto Thy Name*: At the instigation of Alexander I these, the opening words of Psalm 115, were inscribed on a victory medal of 1812.

12. *Laocoön*: In Greek mythology, a Trojan prince who offended the gods and was strangled by a sea-serpent.

13. *the Bible Society*: The Russian Bible Society had been formed in 1813 by A. N. Golitsyn, a lifelong friend of Alexander I, who was influenced by the society's reactionary views concerning the superiority of the Gospel over scientific methods of study and education. The society would be suppressed in 1826 by Tsar Nicholas I.

14. *Gossner and Madame Tatawinova*: The Munich-born pastor and mystic Johann Gossner was expelled from Bavaria in 1817 and invited to Petersburg by the Russian Bible Society, of which he became a popular director. Also in 1817, E. F. Tatarinova founded a 'spiritual union' in Petersburg which enabled its followers to achieve ecstasy and make prophecies through dervish-like dancing.

15. *Madame Kwüdner*: Baroness Barbara Juliana Krüdener (1764–1825), a popular sentimental novelist from Riga, living in Petersburg in 1821, whose mystical writings held a strong appeal for Alexander I.

16. *Magnitsky*: M. L. Magnitsky (1778–1855), Minister of Education and Spiritual Affairs in 1819, was despised by the liberals for his reactionary attitudes and oppressive measures.

17. *Pugachov*: Yemelyan Pugachov (1726–75), the Cossack leader of a revolutionary movement, ultimately ill fated, in the Volga region during the years 1773–5.

18. *Tugendbund*: A German patriotic league (founded in 1808) devoted to the overthrow of Napoleon.

19. *Wussian bunt*: A pun on the German word *bund* (union) and the Russian word *bunt* (riot).

20. *Mucius Scaevola*: The Roman Gaius Mucius Scaevola famously showed resistance to torture by thrusting his right hand into a fire and holding it there until it was consumed. 'Scaevola' means 'left-handed'.

PART II

1. *Gibbon to Buckle*: Edward Gibbon (1737–94), an English historian, best known for his six-volume *Decline and Fall of the Roman Empire* (1776–88). Thomas Henry Buckle (1821–62), a self-educated English intellectual, chess-player and cultural historian, best known for his two-volume *History of Civilization* (1857–61).

2. *Thiers*: Adolphe Thiers (1797–1877), statesman and historian, twice Prime Minister of France.

3. *Lanfrey*: Pierre Lanfrey (1828–77) began publishing a historical study highly critical of Napoleon as Tolstoy completed *War and Peace*.

4. *Gervinus and Schlosser*: G. G. Gervinus and F. C. Schlosser were contemporary German historians.

5. *seized at Boulogne*: Louis Napoleon, nephew of Napoleon, was arrested at Boulogne in 1840 after his second attempt to seize the throne.

6. *Rousseau, Diderot, Beaumarchais*: Jean Jacques Rousseau (1712–78), French philosopher and writer, author of the *Social Contract* (see volume I, Part I, note 10); Denis Diderot (1713–84), French Enlightenment philosopher and one of the authors of the *Encyclopédie*, a major work of eighteenth-century rationalist thought; Pierre Augustin Caron de Beaumarchais (1732–99), French playwright, author of *The Barber of Seville* and *The Marriage of Figaro*, which satirized the ruling classes of pre-revolutionary France.

7. *Kurbsky*: Prince Andrey Kurbsky (1528–83), one of Ivan the Great's principal boyars, left the country in order to criticize Ivan for his cruelty; Ivan responded by arguing the need for a strong autocracy.

8. *any number of Godfreys and Louis*: Godfrey of Bouillon (1061?–1100), French nobleman, soldier and leader of the First Crusade (1095–9); Louis VII (1121–80), King of France 1137–80, a participant in the Second Crusade (1145–8).

9. *Peter the Hermit*: (*c.* 1050–1115), a French preacher who led a band of Crusaders during the First Crusade, which was defeated by the Ottomon Turks in 1096. He later fought with Godfrey of Bouillon in the conquest of Jerusalem in 1099.

10. *Minnesingers*: German lyric poets and singers in the twelfth to fourteenth centuries. Godfrey was the hero of many medieval songs and epic poems.

11. *off go the French to Mexico*: The French supported F. J. Maximilian (1832–67) in his bid to become Emperor of Mexico in 1864, but when the French army withdrew at the end of the American Civil War he was betrayed and executed.

12. *The King of Prussia ... Bohemia*: The reference is to the Austro-Prussian war of 1866, which ended in defeat for the Austrians.

13. *the miracle of Joshua*: Joshua was the successor to Moses who gave his name to the sixth book of the Old Testament. His most famous exploit was commanding the sun and moon to stand still. (Joshua 10: 12–13).

The Characters

The Bezúkhovs[1]

Count Kiríll Bezúkhov

Pierre Bezúkhov, his natural son, also known as Pyotr Kirillovich (or Kirillych), which means Peter, son of Kirill

Pierre's cousins, the Mamontov sisters, **Katerina** (or **Katishe**), **Olga** and **Sofya**

The Bolkónskys

Prince Nikoláy Bolkónsky

Prince Andréy Bolkónsky, his son

Princess Márya, his daughter

Princess Líza, or Lise, Andrey's wife

Prince Nikoláy Bolkónsky, son of Andrey and Lise

The Rostóvs

Count Ilyá Rostóv

Countess Natálya, his wife

Count Nikoláy Rostóv, their elder son

Count Pyotr Rostóv, or **Pétya**, their younger son

Countess Véra, their elder daughter

Countess Natálya, or **Natásha**, their younger daughter

Sófya, or Sónya, a cousin brought up in the family

The Kurágins

Prince Vasíly Kurágin

Prince Anatole, his elder son

Prince Hippolyte, his younger son

Princess Yeléna, known throughout as **Hélène**, his daughter

The Drubetskóys

Princess Ánna, known throughout as Ánna Mikháylovna

Borís, her son

Other Prominent Characters

Akhrosímov, Márya Dmítriyevna, a formidable personality, friend of the Rostov family

Alpátych, old Prince Bolkonsky's steward

Bazdéyev, Ósip, a leading freemason, a strong influence on Pierre

Berg, Alphonse, a Russian officer

Bilíbin, a Russian diplomat

Bourienne, Mademoiselle, Princess Marya's French Companion

Denísov, Vasíly or **Váska**, a Russian officer, a close friend of Nikolay Rostov

Dólokhov, Fédya, a Russian officer and high-living man-about-town

Dron, a village elder at Bogucharovo

Ilágin, one of the Rostovs' neighbours at Otradnoye

Iógel, a dancing master

Karágin, Julie, an heiress

Karatáyev, Platón, a simple peasant whose natural goodness makes a great impact on Pierre

Karp, an insubordinate serf at Bogucharovo

Mávra, a maid with the Rostovs

Pelagéya, a pilgrim

Schérer, Ánna (Ánna Pávlovna), a leading Petersburg society hostess

Túshin, Captain, a battery captain at the battle of Schöngrabern

Historical Figures *in* War and Peace

Alexander I, Tsar of Russia, often referred to as the Emperor

Arakchéyev, Count A., minister under Alexander, a reactionary and ruthless figure

Armfeldt, Count G. M., a Swedish soldier and statesman

Bagration, Prince P., a Russian general

Barcláy de Tólly, M., a senior Russian general

Baláshev, General A., one of Alexander's most trusted aides

Bennigsen, Count I., a Hanoverian general in the Russian army

Berthier, P.-A., Marshal of France, Chief of Staff to Napoleon

Bessières, Jean-Baptiste, a distinguished soldier, Marshal of France

Caulaincourt, General A. de, French Ambassador to Russia

Chichagóv, Admiral P., commander of the Army of Moldavia

Clausewitz, Karl Marie von, a Prussian soldier serving as a Russian staff-officer, later to become famous for his treatise *On War* (1833)

Davout, L., Prince of Eckmühl, Marshal of France

Dokhtúrov, D., a Russian general

Kutúzov, Field-Marshal M., Russian commander-in-chief at Borodino

Milorádovich, M., a Russian general

Murat, Joachim, King of Naples, commander of Napoleon's cavalry in 1812

Napoleon I, Emperor of the French

Pfuel, Ernst von, Colonel, then General, a Prussian soldier in Russian service

Rostopchín, Count F., governor-general of Moscow
Speránsky, M., the minister who inspired Alexander's first reforms
Stein, Baron H. K. von, a Prussian statesman noted for his liberal views
Toll, Karl von, Quartermaster-general of the Russian army
Wintzengerode, Count F., General, a Würtemberger in Russian service
Wittgenstein, General Ludwig, a Westphalian in Russian service
Wolzogen, General Ludwig von, a Prussian soldier in Russian service

NOTE

1. Word stress is important in Russian and the correct stresses are marked in the names listed here. Two names that are pronounced differently from what you may expect are Vasily (Vass-ee-ly) and Boris (Ba-**rees**), both stressed on the second syllable.

1. The 1805 Campaign

2. Austerlitz

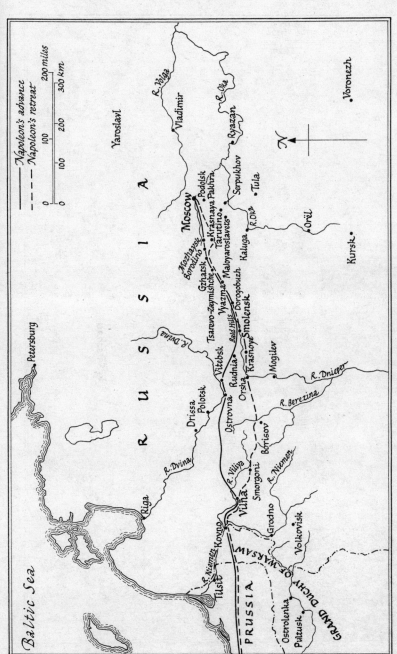

3. The 1812 Campaign

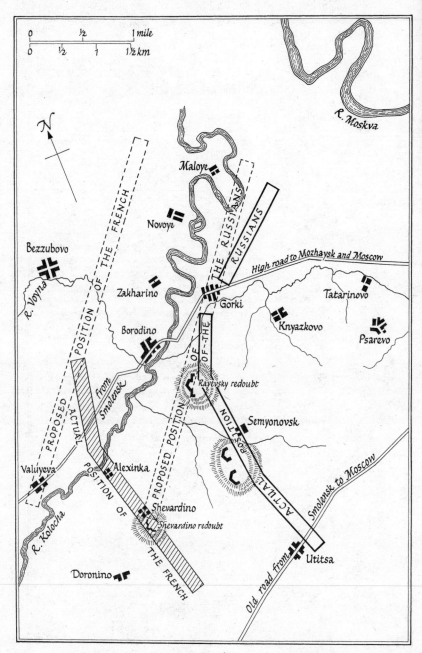

4. Borodino

Summary of Chapters

VOLUME I

Part I (July–August 1805)

20. The count does not recognize anyone. Pierre's discomfort.
21. Death of the count.
22. Bald Hills. Old Prince Nikolay Bolkonsky and his daughter, Princess Marya.
23. Prince Andrey arrives with Lise.
24. The old prince discusses Napoleon's merits with his son.
25. Andrey leaves for the army. Lise is unhappy and frightened about giving birth.

Part II (October–November 1805)

1. The Russian army prepares for an inspection at Braunau.
2. The inspection takes place. Zherkov and Dolokhov.
3. Kutuzov and an Austrian general. The 'unfortunate General Mack'.
4. The Pavolgrad hussars. Nikolay Rostov, Telyanin and the stolen purse.
5. Nikolay is encouraged to apologize to his commanding officer.
6. Crossing the Enns.
7. Incidents on the crowded bridge.
8. The burning of the bridge. Nikolay's undistinguished baptism of fire.
9. Andrey is sent with dispatches to the Austrian court. The war minister.
10. Andrey stays with Bilibin.
11. Bilibin's guests, 'our people', including Hippolyte Kuragin.
12. Andrey meets the Emperor Francis. Bilibin's story of the Tabor bridge.
13. Andrey returns to Kutuzov.
14. Bagration is sent to Hollabrünn. Napoleon writes to Murat.
15. Andrey reports to Bagration. Captain Tushin. Soldiers at the front.
16. Andrey surveys the position. The first shot.
17. The battle of Schöngrabern. Captain Tushin sets fire to the village.
18. Battle scenes. Bagration in the thick of things.
19. Two Russian commanders at loggerheads. Nikolay is injured.

20. Panic. Dolokhov's moment of glory. Relief for the battling Tushin.

21. Retreat. Nikolay cadges a lift. Andrey defends Tushin.

Part III (November 1805)

1. Prince Vasily and Pierre. Pierre is manoeuvered close to Hélène.

2. Pierre is trapped into a fashionable but loveless marriage.

3. Prince Vasily takes Anatole to Bald Hills – a match for Princess Marya?

4. Anatole impresses the ladies, but not the old prince.

5. The old prince's opposition. Marya catches Anatole kissing Mlle Bourienne.

6. A letter from Nikolay. Sonya and Natasha.

7. Nikolay visits Boris and Berg, and meets Prince Andrey.

8. Nikolay is inspired by a close view of the Emperor inspecting the troops.

9. Boris visits Andrey at Olmütz. Prince Dolgorukov.

10. Nikolay remains ecstatically inspired by the Emperor.

11. Dolgorukov tells of his meeting with Napoleon. Kutuzov is pessimistic.

12. Kutuzov sleeps through a council of war. Andrey thinks things over.

13. Nikolay at the front. Visit of Bagration and Dolgorukov.

14. The battle of Austerlitz begins. The Russians' tactical ineptitude.

15. Kutuzov at loggerheads with the Emperor.

16. Andrey halts the Russian retreat, but is then badly wounded.

17. Nikolay meets the wounded Boris. He cannot believe how bad things are.

18. Nikolay misses a chance to assist the Emperor. Disaster on a frozen dam.

19. Andrey, despite medical treatment, seems likely to die, and is left behind.

VOLUME II

Part I (1805–6)

1. Nikolay brings Denisov home on leave.
2. Count Ilya Rostov prepares a grand dinner in honour of Bagration.
3. The dinner at the English Club, Count Rostov's finest hour.
4. Insulted by Dolokhov, Pierre challenges him to a duel.
5. Pierre wounds Dolokhov and emerges unscathed.
6. Pierre and Hélène have a furious argument. He sends her away.
7. At Bald Hills Andrey is presumed dead, but the news is kept from Lise.
8. Lise is about to give birth. Andrey returns.
9. A baby son is born, but Lise dies in childbirth.
10. Denisov and Dolokhov at the Rostovs'. Love is in the air.
11. Dolokhov proposes to Sonya and is turned down.
12. Iogel's ball. Denisov's impressive mazurka.
13. Dolokhov goads Nikolay into gambling, and losing.
14. Nikolay ends up owing 43,000 roubles.
15. Nikolay returns home. Natasha enchants the company with her singing.
16. Nikolay tells his father about his losses. Denisov proposes to Natasha.

Part II (1807)

1. Pierre meets Osip Bazdeyev, a celebrated freemason.
2. Bazdeyev talks about supreme wisdom and Pierre's unhappy life.
3. Pierre becomes a freemason.
4. At the conclusion of the ceremony Pierre feels like a new man.
5. Prince Vasily, seeking a reconciliation between Pierre and Hélène, is violently rejected.
6. At another of Anna Scherer's soirées Hélène invites Boris to visit her.
7. Boris goes to her soirée and Hélène urgently invites him to dinner next day.

8. Old Prince Bolkonsky gives Andrey his own estate at Bogu-charovo.

9. Bilibin writes caustically about the campaign. The sick baby recovers.

10. Pierre visits his southern estates bent on reform, but he is easily duped.

11. Pierre visits Andrey at Bogucharovo. They argue about methods of reform.

12. A philosophical discussion on the ferry.

13. The 'Servants of God' at Bald Hills.

14. The old prince takes to Pierre.

15. Nikolay rejoins his regiment. Food shortages.

16. Denisov illegally seizes supplies from his own army and is wounded.

17. Nikolay visits Denisov, waiting in a vile hospital for his court martial.

18. Denisov reluctantly agrees to petition the Emperor for a pardon.

19. Nikolay's inopportune visit to Boris at Tilsit.

20. Nikolay manages to get the petition to the Emperor, but it is rejected.

21. Alexander and Napoleon meet. Nikolay is depressed and gets drunk.

Part III (1808–10)

1. Andrey empathizes with a moribund oak-tree that refuses to welcome spring.

2. Visiting Otradnoye, Andrey overhears Natasha in a late-night conversation.

3. Andrey revisits the old oak-tree, which is now bursting with new life.

4. Arakcheyev rejects Andrey's memorandum on reform of the military code.

5. Andrey is more impressed by Speransky, admiring his self-assurance.

6. Andrey agrees to work on a committee for the reform of the Legal Code.

7. Pierre, dissatisfied with freemasonry, seeks reassurance from Bazdeyev.

8. Pierre, wanting to do good, agrees to a reconciliation with Hélène.

9. Hélène, a successful society hostess, now receives Boris regularly.

10. Pierre's diaries and dreams show how disturbed he is.

11. Berg demands a dowry for marrying Count Rostov's eldest daughter, Vera.

12. Natasha and Boris are mutually attracted. Sonya seems to love him too.

13. Following a late-night talk with Natasha, the countess sends Boris away.

14. Natasha is involved in fastidious preparations for her first grand ball.

15. Natasha makes a good impression. Pierre is seen talking to Andrey.

16. Pierre asks Andrey to dance with Natasha. They captivate the company.

17. Andrey decides he must marry Natasha. Pierre feels humiliated by his wife.

18. Andrey visits Speransky and is disillusioned by his vacuous character.

19. Andrey visits the Rostovs and is once more enchanted by Natasha.

20. Berg and Vera, assiduous social-climbers, invite Pierre to dinner.

21. The evening is exactly like all the others – just what the Bergs aspire to.

22. Natasha's head is turned. Pierre tells Andrey to go ahead with the match.

23. The old prince insists on a year's delay for the wedding. Natasha is shocked.

24. The engagement is kept secret. Andrey leaves for western Europe.

25. The old prince's attitude to Marya becomes increasingly cruel.

26. He threatens to marry Mlle Bourienne. Marya would like to run away.

Part IV (1810–11)

1. Nikolay returns home, and has doubts about Natasha's marriage.
2. Nikolay gives Mitenka some rough treatment.
3. Nikolay decides to go hunting.
4. The wolf-hunt begins.
5. A wolf is caught.
6. Ilagin's courtesy. Triumph of 'Uncle's' dog, Rugay.
7. An evening at 'Uncle's'. Balalaika playing. Natasha's Russian dancing.
8. Countess Rostov wants Nikolay to marry Julie Karagin. She nags Sonya.
9. Chistmas at Otradnoye. Natasha is bored and depressed.
10. The Rostov children reminisce. Mummers. A troika ride to the Melyukovs'.
11. At Melyukovka. Sonya tries her fortune outside, at the barn.
12. Nikolay and Sonya in love. Natasha and Sonya try their fate with mirrors.
13. Nikolay's marriage to Sonya is opposed. Nikolay rejoins the regiment.

Part V (1811–12)

1. Moscow. Pierre ruminates over what to do with himself.
2. Marya teaches little Nikolay. Prince Bolkonsky and Mlle Bourienne.
3. Prince Bolkonsky treats Dr Métivier as a spy. Congenial conversation.
4. Pierre and Marya discuss Boris Drubetskoy and Natasha.
5. Boris empathizes with Julie in her 'melancholy'. His proposal is accepted.
6. Count Ilya, Sonya and Natasha stay with Marya Dmitriyevna in Moscow.
7. The Rostovs call on the Bolkonskys. Disastrous relationships.
8. The Rostovs at the opera. Hélène is in the next box.
9. The opera. Anatole and Pierre. Natasha meets Hélène. Dancing of Duport.

10. Natasha meets the seductive Anatole and falls under his spell.
11. Anatole and Dolokhov in Moscow.
12. Hélène tells Natasha Anatole is in love with her.
13. Mme Georges' recitation at Hélène's. Natasha is bemused by Anatole's persistent wooing.
14. Marya's letter to Natasha. Anatole writes a letter to Natasha.
15. Natasha renounces Andrey. A note from Anatole. Sonya is suspicious.
16. Anatole rejects Dolokhov's dissuasion as he prepares to abduct Natasha.
17. The abduction begins but is frustrated by a footman.
18. Marya Dmitriyevna is furious with Natasha. Count Ilya is not told.
19. Pierre sees Natasha and confirms that Anatole is already married.
20. Pierre sees Anatole, and vents his fury on him. Anatole leaves town.
21. Natasha takes poison. Andrey is now back. Pierre goes to see him.
22. Pierre assures Natasha of his devotion. The great comet of 1812.

VOLUME III

Part I (May–July 1812)

1. For all their illusion of self-will 'great leaders' are directed by history.
2. Napoleon crosses the Niemen. Polish uhlans are drowned in the Viliya.
3. Alexander at Vilna. Boris eavesdrops. Alexander writes to Napoleon.
4. Balashev is sent to Napoleon, and meets Murat, 'King of Naples'.
5. Balashev, treated badly by Davout, is finally brought to Napoleon.
6. Balashev's meeting with Napoleon.
7. Balashev dines with Napoleon.
8. Kutuzov sends Andrey to Barclay's army. He calls in at Bald Hills.
9. Andrey at Drïssa. His ideas on the three armies and eight parties.

10. Andrey meets Pfuel, a conceited theorist and military 'expert'.

11. An informal council-of-war. Pfuel's ludicrous dogmatism.

12. Nikolay writes to Sonya. He and Ilyin get caught in a storm.

13. Marya Genrikhovna. The officers and the doctor.

14. Nikolay controls his fear as he goes into action at Ostrovna.

15. Nikolay, with his huntsman's eye, excels in battle.

16. Natasha's illness. The absurd and expensive ministrations of doctors.

17. Natasha and Pierre. She takes Communion. A slight improvement.

18. At Mass Natasha hears the special prayer for victory.

19. Pierre, haunted by the number 666, sees that he must destroy Napoleon.

20. Petya is keen on the army. Pierre decides to stop visiting Natasha.

21. Petya is crushed at the Kremlin, but overwhelmed by seeing the Emperor.

22. Assembly of nobility, including Pierre, and merchants at Sloboda palace.

23. The Emperor speaks. Pierre offers to fund a thousand men.

Part II (August 1812)

1. The events of 1812, despite the 'planning', were unforeseen and fortuitous.

2. Prince Bolkonsky's mind is going. Julie writes to Marya.

3. Alpatych is sent to Smolensk.

4. Smolensk is under fire. Alpatych meets Andrey, who tells them to leave.

5. Prince Andrey visits Bald Hills. The bathing soldiers – cannon-fodder.

6. Matter v. form. Anna Pavlovna's and Hélène's competing salons.

7. Napoleon orders the advance on Moscow. An encounter with Lavrushka.

8. Prince Bolkonsky has a stroke, and then dies, nursed by Princess Marya.

9. The truculent peasantry. Alpatych speaks to Dron.

10. Princess Marya speaks to Dron.

11. She addresses the suspicious peasants, who refuse to leave Bogu-
    charovo.

12. Princess Marya recalls her father's death.

13. Nikolay and Ilyin arrive at Bogucharovo, willing to help Marya.

14. Nikolay brings the peasants into line. Marya falls in love with
    him.

15. Andrey meets Denisov, who wants to develop guerrilla resistance.

16. Andrey trusts Kutuzov and his motto: 'Patience and Time'.

17. Moscow. Rostopchin's broadsheets. Pierre hears of Marya's
    arrival.

18. A public flogging. Pierre leaves for the front.

19. Borodino – a senseless struggle wrongly interpreted by historians.

20. Pierre arrives in the theatre of war and seeks out the army's
    position.

21. The Icon of Smolensk is deeply revered by the soldiers and
    Kutuzov.

22. Kutuzov notices Pierre. Dolokhov wants Pierre to be reconciled.

23. Bennigsen explains the army position; it is all beyond Pierre.

24. Andrey reflects on life and death. Pierre visits him.

25. The spirit of the army. What is war? Andrey thinks of Natasha.

26. De Beausset brings Napoleon his son's portrait. Napoleon's pro-
    clamation.

27. Napoleon's dispositions, and how they failed to materialize.

28. Napoleon's cold. The reasons behind the battle.

29. Napoleon talks to De Beausset and Rapp. The game begins.

30. Pierre watches the battlefield from a mound at Gorki.

31. Pierre sees violent action in and around the Rayevsky redoubt.

32. The redoubt is taken and retaken. Pierre tackles a French officer.

33. The battle proceeds in its own way despite the many orders issued.

34. Expected successes are not achieved. Massive, useless slaughter.

35. Kutuzov. An order to renew the attack tomorrow. The spirit of
    the army.

36. Andrey is hit by a bursting shell. The dressing-station.

37. Andrey undergoes an operation on his thigh. Anatole's leg is amputated.

38. Napoleon's dark mood, though he believes few Frenchmen fell in Russia.

39. Moral victory for the Russians, but everyone doubts the value of it all.

Part III (September 1812)

1. Continuity of motion. Achilles and the tortoise. Image of the locomotive.

2. The campaign before Borodino. Kutuzov's subsequent movements.

3. Kutuzov and his generals. To defend or not to defend Moscow?

4. The war council at Fili. With a heavy heart Kutuzov opts for retreat.

5. The abandonment of Moscow. Rostopchin's inconsistent behaviour.

6. In Petersburg Hélène converts to Catholicism and plans remarriage.

7. Hélène writes to Pierre asking for his co-operation over the divorce.

8. Pierre walks back to Mozhaysk, where he meets his own groom.

9. Pierre's vivid dreams. He travels on to Moscow.

10. Pierre goes to see Rostopchin. The 'traitor' Vereshchagin.

11. Rostopchin warns Pierre that he must leave. He goes away in secrecy.

12. The Rostovs prepare to leave. Petya is in the army, but still with them.

13. Natasha invites wounded men to occupy their house.

14. Natasha rearranges the packing. Unknown to her, Andrey is brought in.

15. Natasha defeats her mother; they take wounded men instead of luggage.

16. Berg wants to borrow a cart. More and more wounded men fill their carts.

17. They trundle off in heavy traffic, with Andrey. An encounter with Pierre.

18. Pierre lives at Bazdeyev's. Gerasim gets him peasant clothing and a gun.

19. Napoleon surveys Moscow, awaiting a deputation of boyars.

20. Moscow is empty, like a dead beehive. Napoleon's grand *coup de théâtre* has failed.

21. Incoming soldiers block the bridge. There is looting.

22. A young relative arrives at the Rostovs'. Mavra gives him money.

23. Abandoned workmen drink and brawl.

24. Rostopchin, feeling sidelined, needs a victim. Vereshchagin is available.

25. The killing of Vereshchagin. Lunatics on the loose. Kutuzov at the bridge.

26. The French enter Moscow. Much looting. The fire begins.

27. Pierre stays on to do his deed. The drunken Makar Bazdeyev has a pistol.

28. Pierre saves the occupying Captain Ramballe's life. They dine together.

29. They talk confidingly of women and love. A small fire is visible.

30. The Rostovs' staff see the fire at Mytishchi.

31. The count is informed. Natasha gets through to see Andrey.

32. Andrey is in and out of consciousness. Natasha now stays at his side.

33. Pierre sets out. He saves a child from the fire.

34. He defends an Armenian woman, and is then arrested as an arsonist.

VOLUME IV

Part I (August 1812)

1. Anna Scherer's soirée. News that Hélène is seriously ill.

2. A victory at Borodino is reported. Death of Hélène.

3. Michaud reports the loss of Moscow to the Tsar.

4. Nikolay is sent to Voronezh. He stands out in provincial society.

5. He flirts. The governor's wife advises him against marrying Sonya.

6. He visits Princess Marya, loves her but cannot imagine her as his wife.

7. A letter from Sonya sets Nikolay free. He still thinks fondly of Marya.

8. She had written under pressure from the countess.

9. Pierre under interrogation. Fourteen men await their verdict.

10. Pierre is sentenced to death as a spy.

11. Five prisoners are brutally executed. Pierre and the others are spared.

12. Pierre meets Platon Karatayev in prison.

13. Pierre sees Karatayev as the embodiment of simplicity and truth.

14. Princess Marya joins the Rostovs in Yaroslavl. Andrey is in a bad way.

15. Little Prince Nikolay is taken to see his dying father.

16. Andrey experiences joy and a lightness of being just before he dies.

Part II (October 1812)

1. The flanking manoeuvre leading to Tarutino was natural and inevitable.

2. Correspondence between Napoleon and Kutuzov. Changes in strength.

3. Alexander, and others, urge attack. Kutuzov sees no need to risk lives.

4. Battle dispositions are made, but Yermolov is slow to follow them up.

5. Kutuzov prepares reluctantly for battle but finds it has been postponed.

6. The Cossacks then attack, find Murat but fail to follow up their success.

7. A small victory, with some (useless) losses. Naopleon is on his way out.

8. Napoleon, the 'genius', made all the wrong decisions in Moscow.

9. He took charge, issuing proclamations and orders. Nothing worked.

10. He failed in militarism, diplomacy, justice, religion and everything else.

11. Pierre spends four weeks in prison. Karatayev and the French soldier.

12. Pierre wants freedom, but he is full of *joie de vivre* and energy.

13. Departure of the French. Pierre's group is marched away.

14. Pierre laughs at the idea of them locking up his real self and immortal soul.

15. The Russians at Fominsk and Maloyaroslavets. Dokhturov the real hero.

16. Konovnitsyn, who brought news of the retreat, is another unsung hero.

17. Kutuzov, awakened at night, thanks God for the salvation of Russia.

18. The French run away in panic, and Napoleon comes near to being caught.

19. The French army melts away. Kutuzov wants to let them go, unharassed.

Part III (October–November 1812)

1. Russia behaved like a duellist who dropped his rapier and seized a cudgel.

2. Russia did not play by the book. The success of guerrilla warfare.

3. Denisov and Dolokhov plan to join forces and attack the fleeing French.

4. Young Petya Rostov turns up with a message.

5. From afar Denisov and Petya observe Tikhon Shcherbaty at work.

6. Sent to catch a Frenchman, Shcherbaty returns empty-handed.

7. Petya feels sympathy for a captured French drummer-boy.

8. Dolokhov and Denisov plan their attack. Petya insists on going with them.

9. Dolokhov and Petya infiltrate the French camp to get information.

10. Night. Petya is in a magic kingdom, dreaming. He is ready for anything.

11. In his impetuosity Petya is soon killed. Pierre is among the men rescued.

12. Pierre struggles on with the other prisoners. Karatayev is ill.

13. Pierre still derives great joy from Karatayev's solemn happiness.

14. Karatayev lags behind and is shot. His dog is left howling.

15. They are rescued by Dolokhov. Pierre sees Petya's dead body.

16. The French army, at half strength, is a ragged shambles.

17. Russian and French manoeuvres are like a game of blind man's buff.

18. Even in retreat the absurd Napoleon is described as a 'great man'.

19. Four good reasons why the Russians did not cut off the French.

Part IV (November–December 1812)

1. The Rostovs. Natasha's grief is interrupted by bad news.

2. At first the countess cannot accept the news of Petya's death.

3. Marya stays on with Natasha, then they leave for Moscow.

4. The Russian generals want more glory, hence the battle of Krasnoye.

5. Kutuzov's natural good sense and total consistency.

6. Kutuzov's speech of simplicity and sincerity moves the men.

7. A wattle wall is brought in to shield the fire.

8. Soldiers talk round the camp-fire under the night sky.

9. Two Frenchmen emerge from the woods, Ramballe and his orderly.

10. Crossing of the Berezina. Kutuzov receives the Order of St George.

11. Kutuzov, his job done, declines and dies.

12. Pierre gets used to freedom and reviews his life.

13. Pierre is happy now, full of good will and liked by everyone.

14. The people return to Moscow and the city begins to recover.

15. Pierre meets Natasha again, much changed. She is pleased to see him.

16. Natasha unburdens herself, telling the whole story of Andrey's death.

17. Pierre spends long hours in the company of Marya and Natasha.

18. Pierre wants to marry Natasha. He leaves things to Marya.

19. Pierre is in a frenzy of joy. He loves everybody he meets.

20. Pierre has to go briefly to Petersburg, but the marriage is on.

EPILOGUE

Part I (1813–20)

1. The forces at work in history act beyond human reason.

2. The popular concepts of chance and genius are entirely superfluous.

3. An infinity of chance contingencies caused these events, not Napoleon.

4. Alexander renounces power. Why do bees exist? For no single reason.

5. Death of Count Ilya Rostov. Nikolay resigns. His position worsens.

6. Marya comes to Moscow. The match with Nikolay becomes possible.

7. They live at Bald Hills, raising a family. The debts are paid off.

8. Nikolay eschews violence. Sonya, the 'sterile flower', lives with them.

9. The happiness and imperfections of family life.

10. Natasha monopolizes Pierre, but gives him total freedom round the house.

11. Pierre returns, in trouble for staying away too long in Petersburg.

12. The separate microcosms at Bald Hills. Little Nikolay idolizes Pierre.

13. Pierre is worried about growing repression in the capital.

14. Pierre attacks the government, Nikolay defends, and little Nikolay listens.

15. The mutual, though different, love that exists between Marya and Nikolay.

16. Natasha's jealous love. Little Nikolay's desire to be worthy of his father.

Part II

1. The different faults of ancient and modern historians.

2. Historians, inconsistent and contradictory, stop short of real analysis.

3. The force of history is power, but how is it used to direct events?

4. The transfer of popular will to heroic leaders is a fallacy.

5. Will is only part of an event. Events often defy the will behind them.

6. No result stems from a given order. Orders come from the uninvolved.

7. Causation is complex. Retrospective explanations are too convenient.

8. We are not free, but consciousness creates in us an illusion of free will.

9. Actions are partly free, partly the products of necessity.

10. Freedom and necessity are interdependent. Neither is absolute.

11. Free will is an illusion. There are laws, and history must find them.

12. Free will must go. Personality depends on space, time and causality.

Afterword

by Orlando Figes

In 1951, after reading *War and Peace* for the twelfth time, the Russian writer Mikhail Prishvin (1873–1954) noted in his diary that he felt, at last, that he understood his life. Like all great works of art, Tolstoy's masterpiece has the capacity, on each successive reading, to transform our understanding of the world.

On any first reading, *War and Peace* is bound to dazzle with its immense panorama of humanity. The whole of life appears to be contained in its pages. Tolstoy presents us with a cast of several hundred characters. Yet to each one he brings such profound understanding of the human condition, with all its frailties and contradictions, that we recognize and love these characters as reflections of our own identity.

Tolstoy has an extraordinary clarity of expression – a quality which Anthony Briggs has happily maintained in this superb translation. Tolstoy might write longer novels than anybody else, but no other writer can recreate emotion and experience with such precision and economy. There are scenes in *War and Peace* – the unforgettable depiction of the Battle of Austerlitz, for example, or the ball where Natasha Rostov meets Prince Andrey – in which Tolstoy manages in a few words to sketch the mental images which allow us to picture ourselves at the scene and seemingly to feel the emotions of the protagonists. There are passages, like the death-scene of Prince Andrey, in which Tolstoy may give to his readers the extraordinary sensation that they too have felt the experience of death; and moments, like the wonderful description of the hunt, when Tolstoy lets them imagine what it is like to be a dog.

Tolstoy once said famously that *War and Peace* was not meant to be a novel at all. Like all great works of art, it certainly defies all conventions. Set against the historical events of the Napoleonic Wars, its complex narrative development is a long way from the tidy plot structure of the European novel in its nineteenth-century form. Tolstoy's novel does not even have a clear beginning, middle and end, though it does, in one sense, turn on a moment of epiphany, the year of 1812, when Russia's liberation from Napoleon is made to coincide with the personal liberation of the novel's central characters.

While clearly still a novel, *War and Peace* can be understood, at another level, as a novelist's attempt to engage with the truth of history. Tolstoy's interest in history developed long before his career as a novelist. But history-writing disappointed him. It seemed to reduce the richness of real life. For whereas the 'real' history of lived experience was made up of an infinite number of factors and contingencies, historians selected just a few (for example, the political or the economic) to develop their theories and expla-nations. Tolstoy concluded that the histories of his day represented 'perhaps only 0.001 per cent of the elements which actually constitute the real history of peoples'.[1] He was particularly frustrated by the failure of historians to illuminate the 'inner' life of a society – the private thoughts and relationships that make up the most real and immediate experience of human beings. Hence he turned to literature.

During the 1850s Tolstoy was obsessed with the idea of writing a historical novel which would contrast the real texture of historical experience, as lived by individuals and communities, with the distorted image of the past presented by historians. This is what he set out to achieve in *War and Peace*.

Through the novel's central characters Tolstoy juxtaposes the immediate human experience of historical events with the historical memory of them. For example, when Pierre Bezukhov wanders as a spectator on to the battle-field of Borodino he expects to find the sort of neatly arranged battle scene that he has seen in paintings and read about in history books. Instead, he finds himself in the chaos of an actual battlefield:

> Everything Pierre saw on either hand looked so indistinct that, glancing left or right over the landscape, he could find nothing that quite lived up to his expec-tations. Nowhere was there a field of battle as such, the kind of thing he had expected; there was nothing but ordinary fields, clearings, troops, woods, smoking camp-fires, villages, mounds and little streams. Here was a living landscape, and try as he might he could not make out any military positioning. He could not even tell our troops from theirs. (Vol. III, Book II, ch. 21)

Having served as an officer in the Crimean War (1854–6), Tolstoy drew from his own experience to recreate the human truth of this celebrated battle, and to examine how its public memory could become distorted by the medium of written history. As Tolstoy shows, in the confusion of the battle nobody can understand or control what occurs. In such a situation, chance events, individual acts of bravery or calm thinking by the officers can influence the morale of the troops en masse and thus change the course of the battle; and this in turn creates the illusion that what is happening is somehow the result of human agency. So when the military dispatches are later written up, they invariably ascribe the outcome of the battle to the commanders, although in reality they had less influence than the random actions of the rank and file. By using these dispatches, historians are able to impose a rational pattern and 'historical meaning' on the battle, although neither was apparent at the time of fighting.

As a novelist, Tolstoy was interested most of all in the inner life of Russian society during the Napoleonic Wars. In *War and Peace* he presents this period of history as a crucial watershed in the culture of the Russian aristocracy. The war of 1812 is portrayed as a national liberation from the cultural domination of the French – a moment when Russian noblemen like the Rostovs and Bolkonskys struggled to break free from the foreign conventions of their society and began new lives on Russian principles. Tolstoy plots this transformation in a series of motifs. In Tolstoy's text the novel opens, for example, in the French language of the Petersburg salon – a language that Tolstoy gradually reveals to be false and artificial (the novel's most idealized characters, such as Princess Marya and the peasant Karatayev, speak exclusively in Russian, or, like Natasha, speak French only with mistakes). Tolstoy shows the aristocracy renouncing *haute cuisine* for Spartan lunches of rye bread and cabbage soup, adopting national dress, settling as farmers on the land and rediscovering their country's native culture, as in the immortal scene when Natasha, a French-educated young countess, dances to a folk song in the Russian style.

On this reading, *War and Peace* appears as a national epic – the revelation of a 'Russian consciousness' in the inner life of its characters. In narrating this drama, however, Tolstoy steps out of historical time and enters the time-space of cultural myth. He allows himself considerable artistic licence. For example, the aristocracy's return to native forms of dress and recreations actually took place over several decades in the early nineteenth century, whereas Tolstoy has it happen almost overnight in 1812. But the literary creation of this mythical time-space was central to the role which *War and Peace* was set to play in the formation of the national consciousness.

When the first part of the novel appeared, in 1865–6, educated Russia was engaged in a profound cultural and political quest to define the country's national identity. The emancipation of the serfs, in 1861, had forced society to confront the humble peasant as a fellow-citizen and to seek new answers to the old accursed questions about Russia's destiny in what one poet (Nikolay Nekrasov) called the 'rural depths where eternal silence reigns'.[2] The liberal reforms of Tsar Alexander II (Emperor of Russia 1855–81), which included the introduction of jury trials and elected institutions of local government, gave rise to hopes that Russia, as a nation, would emerge and join the family of modern European states. Writing from this perspective, Tolstoy saw a parallel between the Russia of the 1860s and the Russia that had arisen in the wars against Napoleon.

War and Peace was originally conceived and drafted as a novel about the Decembrists, a group of liberal army officers who rose up in a failed attempt to impose a constitution on the Tsar in December 1825. In this original version of the novel the Decembrist hero returns after thirty years of exile in Siberia to the intellectual ferment of the early years of Alexander II's reign. But the more Tolstoy researched into the Decembrists, the more he realized that their intellectual roots were to be found in the war of 1812.

This was when these officers had first become acquainted with the patriotic virtues of the peasant soldiers in their ranks; when they had come to realize the potential of Russia's democratic nationhood. Through this literary genesis, *War and Peace* acquired several overlapping spheres of historical consciousness: the real-time of 1805–20 (the fictional setting of the novel); the living memory of this period (from which Tolstoy drew in the form of personal memoirs and historical accounts); and its reflection in the political consciousness of 1855–65. Thus the novel can and should be read, not just as an intimate portrait of Russian society in the age of the Napoleonic Wars, but as a broader statement about Russia, its people and its history as a whole. That is why the Russians will always turn to *War and Peace*, as Mikhail Prishvin did, to find in it the keys to their identity.

English readers will learn more about the Russians by reading *War and Peace* than they will by reading perhaps any other book. But they will also find in it the inspiration to make them think about the world and their own place in it. For *War and Peace* is a universal work and, like all the great artistic prose works of the Russian tradition, it functions as a huge poetic structure for the contemplation of the fundamental questions of our existence.

Above all, *War and Peace* will move readers by virtue of its beauty as a work of art. It is a triumphant affirmation of human life in all its richness and complexity. That is why one can return to it and always find new meanings and new truths in it.

NOTES

1. Cited in Isaiah Berlin, *Russian Thinkers*, edited by Henry Hardy and Aileen Kelly (Harmondsworth, Penguin, 1994), pp. 32–3.
2. From 'Silence' (1857) in N. A. Nekrasov, *Sochineniia* (3 vols., Moscow, 1959), Vol. I, p. 201.